THE ENDYMION
OMNIBUS

◆

Endymion

AND

The Rise of Endymion

◆

DAN SIMMONS

VICTOR GOLLANCZ

LONDON

First published in Great Britain in 1996 by Headline Publishing

This edition published in 2005 by
Gollancz
An imprint of the Orion Publishing Group
Orion House, 5 Upper St Martin's Lane, London WC2H 9EA

1 3 5 7 9 10 8 6 4 2

A CIP catalogue record for this book is available
from the British Library

ISBN 0 575 07634 8

Typeset at The Spartan Press Ltd,
Lymington, Hants

Printed in Great Britain by
Clays Ltd, St Ives plc

www.orionbooks.co.uk

ENDYMION

We must not forget that the human soul,
however independently created
our philosophy represents it as being,
is inseparable
in its birth and in its growth
from the universe into which it is born.
— Teilhard de Chardin

Give us gods. Oh give them us!
Give us gods.
We are so tired of men
And motor-power.   — D.H. Lawrence

ONE

You are reading this for the wrong reason.

If you are reading this to learn what it was like to make love to a messiah – *our* messiah – then you should not read on, because you are little more than a voyeur.

If you are reading this because you are a fan of the Old Poet's *Cantos* and are obsessed with curiosity about what happened next in the lives of the Hyperion pilgrims, you will be disappointed. I do not know what happened to most of them. They lived and died almost three centuries before I was born.

If you are reading this because you seek more insight into the message from the One Who Teaches, you may also be disappointed. I confess that I was more interested in her as a woman than as a teacher or messiah.

Finally, if you are reading this to discover *her* fate or even *my* fate, you are reading the wrong document. Although both our fates seem as certain as anyone's could be, I was not with her when hers was played out, and my own awaits the final act even as I write these words.

If you are reading this at all, I would be amazed. But this would not be the first time that events have amazed me. The past few years have been one improbability after another, each more marvelous and seemingly inevitable than the last. To share these memories is the reason that I am writing. Perhaps the motivation is not even to share – knowing that the document I am creating almost certainly will never be found – but just to put down the series of events so that I can structure them in my own mind.

'How do I know what I think until I see what I say?' wrote some pre-Hegira writer. Precisely. I must *see* these things in order to know what to think of them. I must see the events turned to ink and the emotions in print to believe that they actually occurred and touched me.

If you are reading this for the same reason that I am writing it – to bring some pattern out of the chaos of the last years, to impose some order on the essentially random series of events that have ruled our lives for the past standard decades – then you may be reading this for the right reason, after all.

Where to start? With a death sentence, perhaps. But whose – my death sentence or hers? And if mine, which of mine? There are several from which to choose. Perhaps this final one is appropriate. Begin at the beginning.

I am writing this in a Schrödinger cat box in high orbit around the

5

quarantined world of Armaghast. The cat box is not much of a box, more of a smooth-hulled ovoid a mere six meters by three meters. It will be my entire world until the end of my life. Most of the interior of my world is a spartan cell consisting of a black-box air-and-waste recycler, my bunk, the food-synthesizer unit, a narrow counter that serves as both my dining table and writing desk, and finally the toilet, sink, and shower, which are set behind a fiberplastic partition for reasons of propriety that escape me. No one will ever visit me here. Privacy seems a hollow joke.

I have a text slate and stylus. When I finish each page, I transfer it to hard copy on microvellum produced by the recycler. The low accretion of wafer-thin pages is the only visible change in my environment from day to day.

The vial of poison gas is not visible. It is set in the static-dynamic shell of the cat box, linked to the air-filtration unit in such a way that to attempt to fiddle with it would trigger the cyanide, as would any attempt to breach the shell itself. The radiation detector, its timer, and the isotope element are also fused into the frozen energy of the shell. I never know when the random timer activates the detector. I never know when the same random timing element opens the lead shielding to the tiny isotope. I never know when the isotope yields a particle.

But I will know when the detector is activated at the instant the isotope yields a particle. There should be the scent of bitter almonds in that second or two before the gas kills me.

I hope that it will be only a second or two.

Technically, according to the ancient enigma of quantum physics, I am now neither dead nor alive. I am in the suspended state of overlapping probability waves once reserved for the cat in Schrödinger's thought experiment. Because the hull of the cat box is little more than position-fused energy ready to explode at the slightest intrusion, no one will ever look inside to see if I am dead or alive. Theoretically, no one is directly responsible for my execution, since the immutable laws of quantum theory pardon or condemn me from each microsecond to the next. There are no observers.

But *I* am an observer. *I* am waiting for this particular collapse of probability waves with something more than detached interest. In the instant after the hissing of cyanide gas begins, but before it reaches my lungs and heart and brain, *I* will know which way the universe has chosen to sort itself out.

At least, I will know so far as I am concerned. Which, when it comes right down to it, is the only aspect of the universe's resolution with which most of us are concerned.

And in the meantime, I eat and sleep and void waste and breathe and go through the full daily ritual of the ultimately forgettable. Which is ironic, since right now I live – if 'live' is the correct word – only to remember. And to write about what I remember.

If you are reading this, you are almost certainly reading it for the wrong reason. But as with so many things in our lives, the reason for doing something is not the important thing. It is the fact of *doing* that remains.

Only the immutable facts that I have written this and you are reading it remain important in the end.

Where to begin? With her? She is the one you want to read about and the one person in my life whom I wish to remember above everything and everyone else. But perhaps I should begin with the events that led me to her and then to here by way of much of this galaxy and beyond.

I believe that I shall begin with the beginning – with my first death sentence.

TWO

My name is Raul Endymion. My first name rhymes with Paul. I was born on the world of Hyperion in the year 693 ADC on our local calendar, or AD 3099 pre-Hegira reckoning, or, as most of us figure time in the era of the Pax, two hundred and forty-seven years after the Fall.

It was said about me when I traveled with the One Who Teaches that I had been a shepherd, and this was true. Almost. My family had made its living as itinerant shepherds in the moors and meadows of the most remote regions on the continent of Aquila, where I was raised, and I sometimes tended sheep as a child. I remember those calm nights under the starry skies of Hyperion as a pleasant time. When I was sixteen (by Hyperion's calendar) I ran away from home and enlisted as a soldier of the Pax-controlled Home Guard. Most of those three years I remember only as a dull routine of boredom with the unpleasant exception of the four months when I was sent to the Claw Iceshelf to fight indigenies during the Ursus uprising. After being mustered out of the Home Guard, I worked as a bouncer and black-jack dealer in one of the rougher Nine Tails casinos, served as a bargemaster on the upper reaches of the Kans for two rainy seasons, and then trained as a gardener on some of the Beak estates under the landscape artist Avrol Hume. But 'shepherd' must have sounded better to the chroniclers of the One Who Teaches when it came time to list the former occupation of her closest disciple. 'Shepherd' has a nice biblical ring to it.

I do not object to the title of shepherd. But in this tale I will be seen as a shepherd whose flock consisted of one infinitely important sheep. And I lost her more than found her.

At the time my life changed forever and this story really begins, I was twenty-seven years old, tall for a Hyperion-born, notable for little except for the thickness of calluses on my hands and my love of quirky ideas, and was then working as a hunter's guide in the fens above Toschahi Bay a hundred kilometers north of Port Romance. By that time in my life I had learned a little bit about sex and much about weapons, had discovered firsthand the power greed has in the affairs of men and women, had learned how to use my fists and modest wits in order to survive, was curious about a great many things, and felt secure only in the knowledge that the remainder of my life would almost certainly hold no great surprises.

I was an idiot.

Most of what I was that autumn of my twenty-seventh year might be described in negatives. I had never been off Hyperion and never considered that I might travel offworld. I had been in Church cathedrals, of course; even in the remote regions where my family had fled after the sacking of the city of Endymion a century earlier, the Pax had extended its civilizing influence – but I had accepted neither the catechism nor the cross. I had been with women, but I had never been in love. Except for my grand-mother's tutelage, my education had been self-directed and acquired through books. I read voraciously. At age twenty-seven, I thought that I knew everything.

I knew nothing.

So it was that in the early autumn of my twenty-seventh year, content in my ignorance and stolid in my conviction that nothing of importance would ever change, I committed the act that would earn me a death sentence and begin my real life.

The fens above Toschahi Bay are dangerous and unhealthy, unchanged since long before the Fall, but hundreds of wealthy hunters – many from offworld – come there every year for the ducks. Most of the protomallards died off quickly after their regeneration and release from the seedship seven centuries earlier, either unable to adapt to Hyperion's climate or stalked by its indigenie predators, but a few ducks survived in the fens of north-central Aquila. And the hunters came. And I guided them.

Four of us worked out of an abandoned fiberplastic plantation set on a narrow thumb of shale and mud between the fens and a tributary to the Kans River. The other three guides concentrated on fishing and big-game hunting, but I had the plantation and most of the fens to myself during duck season. The fens were a semitropical marsh area consisting mostly of thick chalma growth, weirwood forest, and more temperate stands of giant prometheus in the rocky areas above the floodplain, but during the crisp, dry cold snap of early autumn, the mallards paused there on their migration from the southern islands to their lakes in the remotest regions of the Pinion Plateau.

I woke the four 'hunters' an hour and a half before dawn. I had fixed a breakfast of jambon, toast, and coffee, but the four overweight businessmen grumbled and cursed as they wolfed it down. I had to remind them to check and clean their weapons: three carried shotguns, and the fourth was foolish enough to bring an antique energy rifle. As they grumbled and ate, I went out behind the shack and sat with Izzy, the Labrador retriever I'd had since she was a pup. Izzy knew that we were going hunting, and I had to stroke her head and neck to calm her down.

First light was coming up just as we left the overgrown plantation grounds and poled off in a flat-bottomed skiff. Radiant gossamers were visible flitting through dark tunnels of branches and above the trees. The hunters – M. Rolman, M. Herrig, M. Rushomin, and M. Poneascu – sat forward on the thwarts while I poled. Izzy and I were separated from them by the heap of floatblinds stacked between us, the curved bottoms of the disks still showing the rough malting of the fiberplastic husk. Rolman and Herrig were wearing expensive chameleon-cloth ponchos, although they did not activate the polymer until we were deep in the swamp. I asked them to quit talking so loudly as we approached the freshwater fens where the mallards would be setting in. All four men glared at me, but they lowered their voices and soon fell silent.

The light was almost strong enough to read by when I stopped the skiff just outside the shooting fen and floated their blinds. I hitched up my well-patched waterproofs and slid into the chest-deep water. Izzy leaned over the side of the skiff, eyes bright, but I flashed a hand signal to restrain her from jumping in. She quivered but sat back.

'Give me your gun, please,' I said to M. Poneascu, the first man. These once-a-year hunters had enough trouble just keeping their balance while getting into the small floatblinds; I did not trust them to hang on to their shotguns. I had asked them to keep the chamber empty and the safety on, but when Poneascu handed his weapon over, the chamber indicator glowed red for loaded and the safety was off. I ejected the shell, clicked the safety on, set the gun in the waterproof carrier strapped across my shoulders, and steadied the floatblind while the heavyset man stepped from the skiff.

'I'll be right back,' I said softly to the other three, and began wading through chalma fronds, pulling the blind along by the harness strap. I could have had the hunters pole their floatblinds to a place of their own choosing, but the fen was riddled with quickmud cysts that would pull down both pole and poler, populated by dracula ticks the size of blood-filled balloons that liked to drop on moving objects from overhead branches, decorated with hanging ribbon snakes, which looked precisely like chalma fronds to the unwary, and rife with fighting gar that could bite through a finger. There were other surprises for first-time visitors. Besides, I'd learned from experience that most of these weekend hunters would position their floats so that they would be shooting at each other as soon as the first flight of mallards appeared. It was my job to keep that from happening.

I parked Poneascu in a concealing curl of fronds with a good view from the south mudbank of the largest body of open water, showed him where I was going to place the other floatblinds, told him to watch from within the slit of the floatblind canvas and not to begin shooting until everyone was placed, and then went back for the other three. I placed Rushomin about twenty meters to the first man's right, found a good place closer to the inlet for Rolman, and then went back for the man with the idiot energy weapon, M. Herrig.

The sun would be up in another ten minutes.

'About crossdamned time you fucking remembered me,' snapped the fat man as I waded back to him. He'd already got onto his float; his chameleon-cloth trousers were wet. Methane bubbles between the skiff and the mouth of the inlet indicated a large mudcyst, so I had to work my way close to the mudflat each time I came or went.

'We're not paying you to waste your crossdamn time like this,' he growled from around a thick cigar.

I nodded, reached up, plucked the lighted cigar from between his teeth, and tossed it away from the cyst. We were lucky that the bubbles had not ignited. 'Ducks can smell the smoke,' I said, ignoring his gaping mouth and reddening face.

I slipped into the harness and pulled his float into the open fen, my chest cutting a path through the red-and-orange algae that had covered the surface again since my last trip.

M. Herrig fondled his expensive and useless energy rifle and glared at me. 'Boy, you watch your crossdamn mouth or I'll crossdamn watch it for you,' he said. His poncho and chameleon-cloth hunting blouse were unsealed enough for me to see the gleam of a gold Pax double cross hanging around his neck and the red welt of the actual cruciform on his upper chest. M. Herrig was a born-again Christian.

I said nothing until I had his float positioned properly to the left of the inlet. All four of these experts could fire out toward the pond now without fear of hitting one another. 'Pull your canvas around and watch from the slit,' I said, untying the line from my harness and securing it around a chalma root.

M. Herrig made a noise but left the camouflage canvas still furled on the dome wands.

'Wait until I've got the decoys out before shooting,' I said. I pointed out the other shooting positions. 'And don't fire toward the inlet. I'll be there in the skiff.'

M. Herrig did not answer.

I shrugged and waded back to the skiff. Izzy was sitting where I had commanded her to stay, but I could see from her straining muscles and gleaming eyes that in spirit she was bounding back and forth like a puppy. Without climbing into the skiff, I rubbed her neck. 'Just a few minutes now, girl,' I whispered. Released from her stay command, she ran to the bow as I began dragging the skiff toward the inlet.

The radiant gossamers had disappeared, and the sky-streaks of meteor showers were fading as the predawn light solidified into a milky glow. The symphony of insect sounds and the croak of amphisbands along the mudflats were giving way to morning birdcalls and the occasional gronk of a gar inflating its challenge sac. The sky was deepening to its daytime lapis in the east.

I pulled the skiff under fronds, gestured for Izzy to stay in the bow, and pulled four of the decoys out from under the thwarts. There was the slight-est film of ice along the shoreline here, but the center of the fen was clear, and I began positioning the decoys, activating each one as I left it. The water was never deeper than my chest.

I had just returned to the skiff and lay down next to Izzy under the concealing fronds when the ducks arrived. Izzy heard them first. Her entire body went rigid, and her nose came up as if she could sniff them on the wind. A second later there came the whisper of wings. I leaned forward and peered through the brittle foliage.

In the center of the pond the decoys were swimming and preening. One of them arched its neck and called just as the real mallards became visible above the tree line to the south. A flight of three ducks swept out of their

11

pattern, extended wings to brake, and came sliding down invisible rails toward the fen.

I felt the usual thrill I always encounter at such moments: my throat tightens and my heart pounds, seems to stop for a moment, and then palpably aches. I had spent most of my life in remote regions, observing nature, but confrontation with such beauty always touched something so deep in me that I had no words for it. Beside me, Izzy was as still and rigid as an ebony statue.

The gunfire started then. The three with shotguns opened up at once and kept firing as quickly as they could eject shells. The energy rifle sliced its beam across the fen, the narrow shaft of violet light clearly visible in the morning mists.

The first duck must have been hit by two or three patterns at once: it flew apart in an explosion of feathers and viscera. The second one's wings folded and it dropped, all grace and beauty blasted out of it. The third mallard slipped to its right, recovered just above the water, and beat its wings for altitude. The energy beam slashed after it, slicing through leaves and branches like a silent scythe. Shotguns roared again, but the mallard seemed to anticipate their aim. The bird dived toward the lake, banked hard right, and flew straight toward the inlet.

Straight toward Izzy and me.

The bird was no more than two meters above the water. Its wings were beating strongly, its entire form was bent to the purpose of escape, and I realized that it was going to fly under the trees right through the inlet opening. Despite the fact that the bird's unusual flight pattern had taken it between several shooting positions, all four men were still firing.

I used my right leg to push the skiff out of the concealing branches. 'Cease fire!' I shouted in a command-voice that I'd acquired during my brief career as a sergeant in the Home Guard. Two of the men did. One shotgun and the energy rifle continued firing. The mallard never wavered as it passed the skiff a meter to our left.

Izzy's body quivered and her mouth seemed to drop farther open in surprise as the duck flapped low past us. The shotgun did not fire again, but I could see the violet beam panning toward us through the rising mists. I shouted and pulled Izzy down between the thwarts.

The mallard escaped the tunnel of chalma branches behind us and beat its wings for altitude. Suddenly the air smelled of ozone, and a perfectly straight line of flame slashed across the stern of the boat. I threw myself flat against the bottom of the skiff, grabbing Izzy's collar and tugging her closer as I did so.

The violet beam missed my curled finger and Izzy's collar by a millimeter. I saw the briefest glimmer of a quizzical look in Izzy's excited eyes, and then she tried to lower her head to my chest the way she had as a puppy when she acted penitent. At the movement, her head and the section of neck above her collar separated from her body and went over the side with a soft splash. I still held the collar and her weight was still on me, her forepaws still quivering against my chest. Then blood geysered out over me from arteries in the cleanly severed neck, and I rolled aside, pushing the spasming, headless body of my dog away from me. Her blood was warm and it tasted of copper.

The energy beam slashed back again, cut a heavy chalma branch from its trunk a meter away from the skiff, and then switched off as if it had never existed.

I sat up and looked across the pond at M. Herrig. The fat man was lighting a cigar; the energy rifle lay across his knees. The smoke from his cigar mingled with the tendrils of mist still rising from the fen.

I slipped over the side of the skiff into the chest-deep water. Izzy's blood still swirled around me as I began wading toward M. Herrig.

He lifted his energy rifle and held it across his chest in port arms as I approached. When he spoke, it was around the cigar clenched between his teeth. 'Well, are you going out there to retrieve the ducks I got, or are you just going to let them float out there until they ro—'

As soon as I was within arm's length I grabbed the fat man's chameleon poncho with my left hand and jerked him forward. He tried to raise the energy rifle, but I seized it with my right hand and flung it far out into the fen. M. Herrig shouted something then, his cigar tumbled into the floatblind, and I pulled him off his stool and into the water. He came up spluttering and spitting algae and I hit him once, very hard, squarely in the mouth. I felt the skin on my knuckles tear as several of his teeth snapped, and then he was sprawling backward. His head hit the frame of the floatblind with a hollow bang, and he went under again.

I waited for his fat face to rise to the surface again like the belly of some dead fish, and when it did I held it down, watching the bubbles rise while his arms flailed and his pudgy hands batted uselessly at my wrists. The other three hunters began shouting from their shooting positions across the fen. I ignored them.

When M. Herrig's hands had dropped away and the stream of bubbles had thinned to a weak trickle, I released him and stepped back. For a moment I did not think that he was going to come up, but then the fat man exploded to the surface and hung on the edge of the float. He vomited water and algae. I turned my back on him and waded across to the others.

'That's all for today,' I said. 'Give me your guns. We're going in.'

Each man opened his mouth as if to protest; each man took a look at my eyes and blood-spattered face and handed me his shotgun.

'Retrieve your friend,' I said to the last man, Poneascu. I carried the weapons back to the skiff, unloaded them, sealed the shotguns in the watertight compartment under the bow, and carried the boxes of shells to the stern. Izzy's headless corpse had already begun to stiffen as I eased it over the side. The bottom of the skiff was awash with her blood. I went back to the stern, stowed the shells, and stood leaning on the pole.

The three hunters returned eventually, awkwardly paddling their own floats while pulling the one in which M. Herrig was sprawled. The fat man was still hanging over the side, his face pale. They climbed into the skiff and began trying to pull the floats aboard.

'Leave them,' I said. 'Tie them to that chalma root. I'll come back for them later.'

They tied off the floats and pulled M. Herrig aboard like some obese fish. The only sounds were the birds and insects of the fen coming alive and M. Herrig's continued retching. When he was aboard, the other three hunters seated and muttering, I poled us back to the plantation as the sun burned through the last of the morning vapors rising from the dark waters.

And that should have been the end of it. Except, of course, it was not.

I was making lunch in the primitive kitchen when M. Herrig came out of the sleeping barracks with a stubby military flechette gun. Such weapons were illegal on Hyperion; the Pax allowed no one except the Home Guard to carry them. I could see the white, shocked faces of the other three hunters peering from the barracks door as M. Herrig staggered into the kitchen amid a fog of whiskey fumes.

The fat man could not resist the impulse to give a short, melodramatic speech before killing me. 'You crossdamned heathen son of a bitch . . .' he began, but I did not stand around to listen to the rest. I threw myself down and forward even as he fired from the hip.

Six thousand steel flechettes blew apart the stove, the pan of stew I had been cooking on the stove, the sink, the window above the sink, and the shelves and crockery on the shelves. Food, plastic, porcelain, and glass showered over my legs as I crawled under the open counter and reached for M. Herrig's legs even as he leaned over the counter to spray me with a second burst of flechettes.

I grabbed the big man's ankles and jerked. He went down on his back with a crash that sent a decade's worth of dust rising from the floorboards. I clambered up over his legs, kneeing him in the groin as I climbed, and grabbed his wrist with the intention of forcing the gun out of his hands. He had a firm grip on the stock; his finger was still on the trigger. The magazine whined softly as another flechette cartridge clicked into place. I could smell M. Herrig's whiskey-and-cigar breath on my face as he grimaced triumphantly and forced the weapon's muzzle toward me. In one movement I slammed my forearm against his wrist and the heavy gun, squeezing it tight under M. Herrig's fleshy chins. Our eyes met for the instant before his struggles made him complete his squeeze of the trigger.

I told one of the other hunters how to use the radio in the common room, and a Pax security skimmer was setting down on the grassy lawn within the hour. There were only a dozen or so working skimmers on the continent, so the sight of the black Pax vehicle was sobering, to say the least.

They banded my wrists, slapped a cortical come-along to my temple, and hurried me into the holding box in the rear of the vehicle. I sat there, dripping sweat in the hot stillness of the box, while Pax-trained forensic specialists used needle-nosed pliers to try to retrieve every shard of M. Herrig's skull and scattered brain tissue from the perforated floor and wall. Then, when they had interrogated the other hunters and had found as much of M. Herrig as they were going to find, I watched through the scarred Perspex window as they loaded his body-bagged corpse aboard the skimmer. Lift blades whined, the ventilators allowed me a bit of cooler air just as I thought I could no longer breathe, and the skimmer rose, circled the plantation once, and flew south toward Port Romance.

My trial was held six days later. Ms. Rolman, Rushomin, and Poneascu testified that I had insulted M. Herrig on the trip to the fen and then assaulted him there. They pointed out that the hunting dog had been killed in the melee that I had begun. They testified that once back at the plantation, I had brandished the illegal flechette gun and threatened to kill all of them. M. Herrig had tried to take the weapon away from me. I had shot him at point-blank range, literally blowing his head off in the process.

M. Herrig was the last to testify. Still shaken and pale from his three-day resurrection, dressed in a somber business suit and cape, his voice shook as he confirmed the other men's testimony and described my brutal assault on him. My court-appointed attorney did not cross-examine him. As born-again Christians in good standing with the Pax, none of the four could be forced to testify under the influence of Truthtell or any other chemical or electronic form of verification. I volunteered to undergo Truthtell or full-scan, but the prosecuting attorney protested that such gimmickry was irrelevant, and the Pax-approved judge agreed. My counselor did not file a protest.

There was no jury. The judge took less than twenty minutes to reach a verdict. I was guilty and sentenced to execution by deathwand.

I stood and asked that the sentence be delayed until I could get word to my aunt and cousins in north Aquila so that they could visit me one last time. My request was denied. The time of execution was set for sunrise on the following day.

THREE

A priest from the Pax monastery in Port Romance came to visit me that evening. He was a small, somewhat nervous man with thinning blond hair and a slight stutter. Once in the windowless visiting room, he introduced himself as Father Tse and waved the guards away.

'My son,' he began, and I felt the urge to smile, since the priest looked to be about my age, 'my son . . . are you prepared for tomorrow?'

Any urge to smile fled. I shrugged.

Father Tse chewed his lip. 'You have not accepted Our Lord . . .' he said, voice tense with emotion.

I had the urge to shrug again but spoke instead. 'I haven't accepted the cruciform, Father. It might not be the same thing.'

His brown eyes were insistent, almost pleading. 'It *is* the same thing, my son. Our Lord has revealed this.'

I said nothing.

Father Tse set down his missal and touched my bound wrist. 'You know that if you repent this night and accept Jesus Christ as your personal Savior, that three days after . . . tomorrow . . . you will rise to live again in the grace of Our Lord's forgiveness.' His brown eyes did not blink. 'You do know this, do you not, my son?'

I returned his gaze. Some prisoner in the adjoining cell block had screamed most of the last three nights. I felt very tired. 'Yes, Father,' I said. 'I know how the cruciform works.'

Father Tse vigorously shook his head. 'Not the cruciform, my son. The grace of Our Lord.'

I nodded. 'Have you gone through resurrection, Father?'

The priest glanced down. 'Not yet, my son. But I have no fear of that day.' He looked up at me again. 'Nor must you.'

I closed my eyes for a moment. I had been thinking about this for almost every minute of the past six days and nights. 'Look, Father,' I said, 'I don't mean to hurt your feelings, but I made the decision some years ago not to go under the cruciform, and I don't think that this is the right time to change my mind.'

Father Tse leaned forward, eyes bright, 'Any time is the right time to accept Our Lord, my son. After sunrise tomorrow there will be no more time. Your dead body will be taken out from this place and disposed of at sea, mere food for the carrion fish beyond the bay—'

This was not a new image for me. 'Yes,' I said, 'I know the penalty for a murderer executed without converting. But I have this—' I tapped the cortical come-along now permanently attached to my temple. 'I don't need a cruciform symbiote embedded in me to put me in a deeper slavery.'

Father Tse pulled back as if I had slapped him. 'One mere lifetime of commitment to Our Lord is not slavery,' he said, his stutter banished by cold anger. 'Millions have offered this *before* the tangible blessing of immediate resurrection in this life was offered. Billions gratefully accept it now.' He stood up. 'You have the choice, my son. Eternal light, with the gift of almost unlimited life in this world in which to serve Christ, or eternal darkness.'

I shrugged and looked away.

Father Tse blessed me, said good-bye in tones commingled with sadness and contempt, turned, called the guards, and was gone. A minute later pain stabbed at my skull as the guards tickled my come-along and led me back to my cell.

I won't bore you with a long litany of the thoughts that chased through my mind that endless autumn night. I was twenty-seven years old. I loved life with a passion that sometimes led me into trouble . . . although never anything as serious as this before. For the first few hours of that final night, I pondered escape the way a caged animal must claw at steel bars. The prison was set high on the sheer cliff overlooking the reef called the Mandible, far out on Toschahi Bay. Everything was unbreakable Perspex, unbendable steel, or seamless plastic. The guards carried deathwands, and I sensed no reluctance in them to use them. Even if I should escape, a touch of a button on the come-along remote would curl me up with the universe's worst migraine until they followed the beacon to my hiding place.

My last hours were spent pondering the folly of my short, useless life. I regretted nothing but also had little to show for Raul Endymion's twenty-seven years on Hyperion. The dominant theme of my life seemed to be the same perverse stubbornness that had led me to reject resurrection.

So you owe the Church a lifetime of service, whispered a frenzied voice in the back of my skull, *at least you get a lifetime that way! And more lifetimes beyond that! How can you turn down a deal like that? Anything's better than real death . . . your rotting corpse being fed to the ampreys, coelacanths, and skarkworms. Think about this!* I closed my eyes and pretended to sleep just to flee from the shouts echoing in my own mind.

The night lasted an eternity, but sunrise still seemed to come early. Four guards walked me to the death chamber, strapped me into a wooden chair, and then sealed the steel door. If I looked over my left shoulder, I could see faces peering through the Perspex. Somehow I had expected a priest – maybe not Father Tse again, but a priest, some representative of the Pax – to offer me one final chance at immortality. There was none. Only part of me was glad. I cannot say now whether I would have changed my mind at the last moment.

The method of execution was simple and mechanical – not as ingenious as a Schrödinger cat box, perhaps, but clever nonetheless. A short-range deathwand was set on the wall and aimed at the chair where I sat. I saw the red light click on the small comlog unit attached to the weapon. Prisoners in adjoining cells had gleefully whispered the mechanics of my death to me even before the sentence had been passed. The comlog computer had a random-number generator. When the number generated was a prime smaller than seventeen, the deathwand beam would be activated. Every synapse in the gray lump that was the personality and memory of Raul Endymion would be fused. Destroyed. Melted down to the neuronic equivalent of radioactive slag. Autonomic functions would cease mere milliseconds later. My heart and breathing would stop almost as soon as my mind was destroyed. Experts said that death by deathwand was as painless a way to die as had ever been invented. Those resurrected after deathwand execution usually did not want to talk about the sensation, but the word in the cells was that it hurt like hell – as if every circuit in your brain were exploding.

I looked at the red light of the comlog and the business end of the short deathwand. Some wag had rigged an LED display so that I could see the numerals being generated. They flicked by like floor numbers on an elevator to hell: 26-74-109-19-37 . . . they had programmed the comlog to generate no numbers larger than 150 . . . 77-42-12-60-84-129-108-14—

I lost it then, I balled my fists, strained at the unyielding plastic straps, and screamed obscenities at the walls, at the pale faces distorted through the Perspex windows, at the fucking Church and its fucking Pax, at the fucking coward who'd killed my dog, at the goddamned fucking cowards who . . .

I did not see the low prime number appear on the display. I did not hear the deathwand hum softly as its beam was activated. I *did* feel something, a sort of hemlock coldness starting at the back of my skull and widening to every part of my body with the speed of nerve conduction, and I felt surprise at feeling something. *The experts are wrong and the cons are right*, I thought wildly. *You can feel your own death by deathwand.* I would have giggled then if the numbness had not flowed over me like a wave.

Like a black wave.

A black wave that carried me away with it.

FOUR

I was not surprised to wake up alive. I suppose one is surprised only when one awakens dead. At any rate, I awoke with no more discomfort than a vague tingling in my extremities and lay there watching sunlight crawl across a rough plaster ceiling for a minute or more until an urgent thought shook me full awake.

Wait a minute, wasn't I . . . didn't they . . . ??

I sat up and looked around. If there was any lingering sense that my execution had been a dream, the prosaic quality of my surroundings dispelled it immediately. The room was pie-shaped with a curved and white-washed outer stone wall and thick plaster ceilings. The bed was the only piece of furniture, and the heavy off-white linen on it complemented the texture of plaster and stone. There was a massive wooden door – closed – and an arched window open to the elements. One glance at the lapis sky beyond the window told me that I was still on Hyperion. There was no chance that I was still in the Port Romance prison; the stone here was too old, the details of the door too ornamental, the quality of linen too good.

I rose, found myself naked, and walked to the window. The autumn breeze was brisk, but the sun was warm on my skin. I was in a stone tower. Yellow chalma and the thick tangle of low weirwood wove a solid canopy of treetops up hills to the horizon. Everblues grew on granite rock faces. I could see other walls, ramparts, and the curve of another tower stretching away along the ridgeline upon which this tower stood. The walls seemed *old*. The quality of their construction and the organic feel of their architecture was from an era of skill and taste long predating the Fall.

I guessed at once where I must be: the chalma and weirwood suggested that I was still on the southern continent of Aquila; the elegant ruins spoke of the abandoned city of Endymion.

I had never been to the town from which my family took its surname, but I had heard many descriptions of it from Grandam, our clan storyteller. Endymion had been one of the first Hyperion cities settled after the drop-ship crash almost seven hundred years earlier. Until the Fall it had been famous for its fine university, a huge, castlelike structure that towered over the old town in the valley. Grandam's great-grandfather's grandfather had been a professor at the university until the Pax troops commandeered the entire region of central Aquila and literally sent thousands of people packing.

19

And now I had returned.

A bald man with blue skin and cobalt-blue eyes came through the door, set underwear and a simple daysuit of what looked like homespun cotton on the bed, and said, 'Please get dressed.'

I admit that I stared silently as the man turned and went out the door. Blue skin. Bright-blue eyes. No hair. He . . . it . . . had to be the first android that I had ever seen. If asked, I would have said that there were no androids left on Hyperion. They had been illegal to biofacture since before the Fall, and although they had been imported by the legendary Sad King Billy to build most of the cities in the north centuries ago, I had never heard of one still existing on our world. I shook my head and got dressed. The daysuit fit nicely, despite my rather unusually large shoulders and long legs.

I was back at the window when the android returned. He stood by the open door and gestured with an open hand. 'This way please, M. Endymion.'

I resisted the impulse to ask questions and followed him up the tower stairs. The room at the top took up the entire floor. Late-afternoon sunlight streamed in through yellow-and-red stained-glass windows. At least one window was open, and I could hear the rustle of the leaf canopy far below as a wind came up from the valley.

This room was as white and bare as my cell had been, except for a cluster of medical equipment and communication consoles in the center of the circle. The android left, closing the heavy door behind him, and it took me a second to realize that there was a human being in the locus of all that equipment.

At least I thought it was a human being.

The man was lying on a flowfoam hoverchair bed that had been adjusted to a sitting position. Tubes, IV drips, monitor filaments, and organic-looking umbilicals ran from the equipment to the wizened figure in the chair. I say 'wizened', but in truth the man's body looked almost mummified, the skin wrinkled like the folds of an old leather jacket, the skull mottled and almost perfectly bald, the arms and legs emaciated to the point of being vestigial appendages. Everything about the old man's posture made me think of a wrinkled and featherless baby bird that had fallen out of the nest. His parchment skin had a blue cast to it that made me think *android* for a moment, but then I saw the different shade of blue, the faint glow of the palms, ribs, and forehead, and realized that I was looking at a real human who had enjoyed – or suffered – centuries of Poulsen treatments.

No one receives Poulsen treatments anymore. The technology was lost in the Fall, as were the raw materials from worlds lost in time and space. Or so I thought. But here was a creature at least many centuries old who must have received Poulsen treatments as recently as decades ago.

The old man opened his eyes.

I have since seen eyes with as much power as his, but nothing in my life to that point had prepared me for the intensity of such a gaze. I think I took a step back.

'Come closer, Raul Endymion.' The voice was like the scraping of a dull blade on parchment. The old man's mouth moved like a turtle's beak.

I stepped closer, stopping only when a com console stood between me and the mummified form. The old man blinked and lifted a bony hand that still seemed too heavy for the twig of a wrist. 'Do you know who I am?' The scratch of a voice was as soft as a whisper.

I shook my head.

'Do you know where you are?'

I took a breath. 'Endymion. The abandoned university, I think.'

The wrinkles folded back in a toothless smile. 'Very good. The namesake recognizes the heaps of stone which named his family. But you do not know who I might be?'

'No.'

'And you have no questions about how you survived your execution?'

I stood at parade rest and waited.

The old man smiled again. 'Very good, indeed. All things come to he who waits. And the details are not that enlightening . . . bribes in high places, a stunner substituted for the deathwand, more bribes to those who certify the death and dispose of the body. It is not "how" we are interested in, is it, Raul Endymion?'

'No,' I said at last. 'Why.'

The turtle's beak twitched, the massive head nodded. I noticed now that even through the damage of centuries, the face was still sharp and angular – a satyr's countenance.

'Precisely,' he said. 'Why? Why go to the trouble of faking your execution and transporting your fucking carcass across half a fucking continent? Why indeed?'

The obscenities did not seem especially harsh from the old man's mouth. It was as if he had sprinkled his speech with them for so long that they deserved no special emphasis. I waited.

'I want you to run an errand for me, Raul Endymion.' The old man's breath wheezed. Pale fluid flowed through the intravenous tubes.

'Do I have a choice?'

The face smiled again, but the eyes were as unchanging as the stone in the walls. 'We always have choices, dear boy. In this case you can ignore any debt you might owe me for saving your life and simply leave here . . . walk away. My servants will not stop you. With luck you will get out of this restricted area, find your way back to more civilized regions, and avoid Pax patrols where your identity and lack of papers might be . . . ah . . . embarrassing.'

I nodded. My clothes, chronometer, work papers, and Pax ID were probably in Toschahi Bay by now. Working as a hunting guide in the fens made me forget how often the authorities checked IDs in the cities. I would soon be reminded if I wandered back to any of the coastal cities or inland towns. And even rural jobs such as shepherd and guide required Pax ID for tax and tithe forms. Which left hiding in the interior for the rest of my life, living off the land and avoiding people.

'Or,' said the old man, 'you can run an errand for me and become rich.'
He paused, his dark eyes inspecting me the way I had seen professional
hunters inspect pups that might or might not prove to be good hunting
dogs.

'Tell me,' I said.

The old man closed his eyes and rattled in a deep breath. He did not
bother to open his eyes when he spoke. 'Can you read, Raul Endymion?'

'Yes.'

'Have you read the poem known as the *Cantos*?

'No.'

'But you have heard some of it? Surely, being born into one of the
nomadic shepherd clans of the north, the storyteller has touched on the
Cantos?' There was a strange tone in the cracked voice. Modesty, perhaps.

I shrugged. 'I've heard bits of it. My clan preferred the *Garden Epic* or the
Glennon-Height Saga.'

The satyr features creased into a smile. 'The *Garden Epic*. Yes. Raul was a
centaur-hero in that, was he not?'

I said nothing. Grandam had loved the character of the centaur named
Raul. My mother and I both had grown up listening to tales of him.

'Do you believe the stories?' snapped the old man. 'The *Cantos* tales, I
mean.'

'*Believe* them?' I said. 'That they actually happened that way? The
pilgrims and the Shrike and all that?' I paused a minute. There were those
who believed all the tall tales told in the *Cantos*. And there were those who
believed none of it, that it was all myth and maundering thrown together to
add mystery to the ugly war and confusion that was the fall. 'I never really
thought about it,' I said truthfully. 'Does it matter?'

The old man seemed to be choking, but then I realized that the dry,
rattling sounds were chuckles. 'Not really,' he said at last. 'Now, listen. I will
tell you the outline of the . . . errand. It takes energy for me to speak, so
save your questions for when I am finished.' He blinked and gestured with
his mottled claw toward the chair covered with a white sheet. 'Do you wish
to sit?'

I shook my head and remained at parade rest.

'All right,' said the old man. 'My story begins almost two hundred and
forty-some years ago during the Fall. One of the pilgrims in the *Cantos* was a
friend of mine. Her name was Brawne Lamia. She was real. After the Fall . . .
after the death of the Hegemony and the opening of the Time Tombs . . .
Brawne Lamia gave birth to a daughter. The child's name was Diana, but the
little girl was headstrong and changed her name almost as soon as she was
old enough to talk. For a while she was known as Cynthia, then Cate . . .
short for Hecate . . . and then, when she turned twelve, she insisted that her
friends and family call her Temis. When I last saw her, she was called
Aenea . . .' I heard the name as Ah-nee-a.

The old man stopped and squinted at me. 'You think this is not important, but names *are* important. If you had not been named after this city,
which was in turn named after an ancient poem, then you would not have

22

come to my attention and you could not be here today. You would be dead. Feeding the skarkworms in the Great South Sea. Do you understand, Raul Endymion?'

'No,' I said.

He shook his head. 'It does not matter. Where was I?'

'The last time you saw the child, she called herself Aenea.'

'Yes.' The old man closed his eyes again. 'She was not an especially attractive child, but she was . . . unique. Everyone who knew her felt that she was different. Special. Not spoiled, despite all the nonsense with the name changes. Just . . . different.' He smiled, showing pink gums. 'Have you ever met someone who is profoundly different, Raul Endymion?'

I hesitated only a second. 'No,' I said. It was not quite true. This old man was different. But I knew he was not asking that.

'Cate . . . Aenea . . . was different,' he said, eyes closed again. 'Her mother knew it. Of course, Brawne knew that the child was special before she was born . . .' He stopped and opened his eyes enough to squint at me. 'You've heard this part of the *Cantos*?'

'Yes,' I said. 'It was foretold by a cybrid entity that the woman named Lamia was to give birth to a child known as the One Who Teaches.'

I thought that the old man was going to spit. 'A stupid tale. No one called Aenea that during the time I knew her. She was simply a child, brilliant and headstrong, but a child. Everything that was unique was unique only in potential. But then . . .'

His voice trailed off and his eyes seemed to film over. It was as if he had lost track of the conversation. I waited.

'But then Brawne Lamia died,' he said several minutes later, voice stronger, as if there had been no gap in the monologue, 'and Aenea disappeared. She was thirteen. Technically, I was her guardian, but she did not ask my permission to disappear. One day she left and I never heard from her again.' Here the story paused again, as if the old man were a machine that ran down occasionally and required some internal rewinding.

'Where was I?' he said at last.

'You never heard from her again.'

'Yes. I never heard *from* her, but I know where she went and when she will reappear. The Time Tombs are off-limits now, guarded from public view by the Pax troops stationed there, but do you remember the names and functions of the tombs, Raul Endymion?'

I grunted. Grandam used to grill me on aspects of the oral tales in much this way. I used to think that Grandam was old. Next to this ancient, wizened thing, Grandam had been an infant. 'I think I remember the tombs,' I said. 'There was the one called the Sphinx, the Jade Tomb, the Obelisk, the Crystal Monolith, where the soldier was buried . . .'

'Colonel Fedmahn Kassad,' muttered the old man. Then his gaze returned to me. 'Go on.'

'The three Cave Tombs . . .'

'Only the Third Cave Tomb led anywhere,' interrupted the old man again. 'To labyrinths on other worlds. The Pax sealed it. Go on.'

'That's all I can remember . . . oh, the Shrike Palace.'

The old man showed a turtle's sharp smile. 'One mustn't forget the Shrike Palace or our old friend the Shrike, must one? Is that all of them?'

'I think so,' I said. 'Yes.'

The mummified figure nodded. 'Brawne Lamia's daughter disappeared through one of these tombs. Can you guess which one?'

'No.' I did not know but I suspected.

'Seven days after Brawne died, the girl left a note, went to the Sphinx in the dead of night, and disappeared. Do you remember where the Sphinx led, boy?'

'According to the *Cantos*,' I said, 'Sol Weintraub and his daughter traveled to the distant future through the Sphinx.'

'Yes,' whispered the ancient thing in the hoverbed. 'Sol and Rachel and a precious few others disappeared into the Sphinx before the Pax sealed it and closed off the Valley of the Time Tombs. Many tried in those early days – tried to find a shortcut to the future – but the Sphinx seemed to choose who might travel its tunnel through time.'

'And it accepted the girl,' I said.

The old man merely grunted at this statement of the obvious. 'Raul Endymion,' he rasped at last, 'do you know what I am going to ask of you?'

'No,' I said, although once again I had a strong suspicion.

'I want you to go after my Aenea,' said the old man. 'I want you to find her, to protect her from the Pax, to flee with her, and – when she has grown up and become what she must become – give her a message. I want you to tell her that her uncle Martin is dying and that if she wishes to speak to him again, she must come home.'

I tried not to sigh. I'd guessed that this ancient thing had once been the poet Martin Silenus. Everyone knew the *Cantos* and its author. How he had escaped the Pax purges and been allowed to live in this restricted place was a mystery, but one I did not choose to explore. 'You want me to go north to the continent of Equus, fight my way past several thousand Pax troops, somehow get into the Valley of the Time Tombs, get into the Sphinx, hope it . . . accepts me . . . then chase this child into the distant future, hang around with her for a few decades, and then tell her to go back in time to visit you?'

For a moment there was a silence broken only by the soft sounds of Martin Silenus's life-support equipment. The machines were breathing. 'Not exactly,' he said at last.

I waited.

'She has not traveled to some distant future,' said the old man. 'At least not distant from us, now. When she stepped through the entrance of the Sphinx two hundred and forty-seven years ago, it was for a short trip through time . . . two hundred and forty-seven Hyperion years, to be exact.'

'How do you know this?' I asked. From everything I had read, no one – not even the Pax scientists who had had two centuries to study the sealed tombs – had been able to predict how far into the future the Sphinx would send someone.

'I *know* it,' said the ancient poet. 'Do you doubt me?'

Instead of responding to that, I said, 'So the child . . . Aenea . . . will step out of the Sphinx sometime this year.'

'She will step out of the Sphinx in forty-two hours, sixteen minutes,' said the old satyr.

I admit that I blinked.

'And the Pax will be waiting for her,' he continued. 'They also know to the minute when she will emerge . . .'

I did not ask how they came by the information.

'. . . and capturing Aenea is the single most important thing on the Pax's agenda,' rasped the old poet. 'They know that the future of the universe depends upon this.'

I knew now that the old poet was senile. The future of the universe depended upon no single event . . . that I knew. I held my silence.

'There are – at this moment – more than thirty thousand Pax troops in and around the Valley of the Time Tombs. At least five thousand of them are Vatican Swiss Guard.'

I whistled at this. The Vatican Swiss Guard was the elite of the elite, the best-trained, best-equipped military force in the far-flung expanse of the Pax. A dozen Vatican Guard troops in full regalia could have beaten the entire ten thousand troops of Hyperion's Home Guard. 'So,' I said, 'I have forty-two hours to get to Equus, cross the Sea of Grass and the mountains, somehow get past twenty or thirty thousand of the Pax's best troops, and rescue the girl?'

'Yes,' said the ancient figure in the bed.

I managed not to roll my eyes. 'What then?' I said. 'There is nowhere we can hide. The Pax controls all of Hyperion, all spacecraft, the spacelanes, and every world of what used to be the Hegemony. If she is as important as you say, they will turn Hyperion upside down until they find her. Even if we could somehow get offplanet, which we can't, there would be no way we could escape.'

'There is a way for you to get offplanet,' the poet said in a tired voice. 'There is a ship.'

I swallowed hard. *There is a ship.* The idea of traveling between the stars for months while decades or years passed back home took my breath away. I had joined the Home Guard with the childish notion of someday belonging to the Pax military and flying between the stars. A foolish notion for a youngster who had already decided not to accept the cruciform.

'Still,' I said, not truly believing that there was a ship. No member of the Pax Mercantilus would transport fugitives. 'Even if we make it to another world, they would have us. Unless you see us fleeing by ship for centuries of time-debt.'

'No,' said the old man. 'Not centuries. Not decades. You will escape by ship to one of the nearest worlds of the old Hegemony. Then you will go a secret way. You will see the old worlds. You will travel the River Tethys.'

I knew now that the old man had lost his reason. When the farcasters fell and the AI TechnoCore abandoned humankind, the WorldWeb and

Hegemony had died that same day. The tyranny of interstellar distances had been reimposed upon humanity. Now only the Pax forces, their puppet Mercantilus, and the hated Ousters braved the darkness between the stars.

'Come,' rasped the old man. His fingers would not uncurl as he gestured me closer. I leaned over the low com console. I could smell him . . . a vague combination of medicine, age, and something like leather.

I did not need the memories of Grandam's campfire tales to explain the River Tethys and to know why I now knew that the old man was far gone into senility. Everyone knew about the River Tethys; it and the so-called Grand Concourse had been two constant farcaster avenues between the Hegemony worlds. The Concourse had been a street connecting a hundred-some worlds under a hundred-some suns, its broad avenue open to every-one and stitched together by farcaster portals that never closed. The River Tethys had been a less-traveled route, but still important for bulk commerce and the countless pleasure boats that had floated effortlessly from world to world on the single highway of water.

The Concourse had been sliced into a thousand separate segments by the Fall of the WorldWeb farcaster network; the Tethys had simply ceased to exist, the connecting portals useless, the single river on a hundred worlds reverted to a hundred smaller rivers that would never be con-nected again. Even the old poet seated before me had described the river's death. I remembered the words from Grandam's recitation of the *Cantos*:

> And the river that had flowed on
> For two centuries or more
> Linked through space and time
> By the tricks of TechnoCore
> Ceased flowing now
> On Fuji and on Barnard's World
> On Acteon and Deneb Drei
> On Esperance and Nevermore.
> Everywhere the Tethys ran,
> Like ribbons through
> The worlds of man,
> There the portals worked no more,
> There the riverbeds ran dry,
> There the currents ceased to swirl.
> Lost were the tricks of TechnoCore,
> Lost were the travelers forevermore
> Locked the portal, locked the door,
> Flowed the Tethys nevermore.

'Come closer,' whispered the old poet, still beckoning me with his yellowed finger. I leaned closer. The ancient creature's breath was like a dry wind out of an unsealed tomb – free of odor, but ancient, somehow redolent of forgotten centuries – as he whispered to me:

'A thing of beauty is a joy for ever:
Its loveliness increases; it will never
Pass into nothingness . . .'

I pulled my head back and nodded as if the old man had said something sensible. It was clear that he was mad.

As if reading my mind, the old poet chuckled. 'I have often been called insane by those who underestimate the power of poetry. Do not decide now, Raul Endymion. We will meet later for dinner and I will finish describing your challenge. Decide then. For now . . . rest! Your death and resurrection must have tired you.' The old man hunched over, and there came the dry rattling that I now understood as laughter.

The android showed me back to my room. I caught glimpses of courtyards and outbuildings through the tower windows. Once I saw another android – also male – walking past clerestory windows across the courtyard.

My guide opened the door and stepped back. I realized that I would not be locked in, that I was not a prisoner.

'Evening clothes have been set out for you, sir,' said the blue-skinned man. 'You are, of course, free to go or wander the old university grounds as you wish. I should warn you, M. Endymion, that there are dangerous animals in the forest and mountains in this vicinity.'

I nodded and smiled. Dangerous animals would not keep me from leaving if I wished to leave. At the moment I did not.

The android turned to leave then, and on impulse I stepped forward and did something that would change the course of my life forever.

'Wait,' I said. I extended a hand. 'We haven't been introduced. I'm Raul Endymion.'

For a long moment the android only looked at my extended hand, and I was sure that I had committed some breach of protocol. Androids had been, after all, considered something less than human centuries ago when they had been biofactured for use during the Hegira expansion. Then the artificial man grasped my hand in his and shook firmly. 'I am A. Bettik,' he said softly. 'It is a pleasure to make your acquaintance.'

A. Bettik. The name had some resonance for me that I could not place. I said, 'I would like to talk to you, A. Bettik. Learn more about . . . about you and this place and the old poet.'

The android's blue eyes lifted, and I thought I glimpsed something like amusement there. 'Yes, sir,' he said. 'I would be happy to speak with you. I fear that it must be later, since there are many duties I have to oversee at this moment.'

'Later, then,' I said, and stepped back. 'I look forward to it.'

A. Bettik nodded and descended the tower stairs.

I walked into my room. Except for the bed being made and a suit of elegant evening clothes laid out there, the space was just as it had been. I went to the window and looked out over the ruins of Endymion University. Tall everblues rustled in the cool breeze. Violet leaves tumbled from the weirwood stand near the tower and scraped across the flagstone pavement twenty meters below. Chalma leaves scented the air with their distinctive cinnamon. I had grown up only several hundred kilometers northeast on the Aquila moors between these mountains and the rugged area known as the Beak, but the chill freshness of the mountain air here was new to me. The sky seemed a deeper lapis than any I had seen from the moors or lowlands. I breathed in the autumn air and grinned: whatever strangeness lay ahead, I was damned glad to be alive.

Leaving the window, I headed for the tower stairs and a look around the university and city after which my family had taken its name. However crazy the old man was, dinner conversation should be interesting.

Suddenly, when I was almost at the base of the tower stairs, I stopped in my tracks.

A. Bettik. The name was from Grandam's telling of the Cantos. *A. Bettik was the android who piloted the pilgrims' levitation barge* Benares *northeast from the city of Keats on the continent of Equus, up the Hoolie River past Naiad River Station, the Karla Locks, and Doukhobor's Copse to where the navigable river ended in Edge. From Edge the pilgrims had gone on alone across the Sea of Grass.* I remembered listening as a child, wondering why A. Bettik was the only android named, and wondering what had happened to him when the pilgrims left him behind at Edge. The name had been lost for me for more than two decades.

Shaking my head slightly, wondering whether it was the old poet or I who was mad, I went out into the late-afternoon light to explore Endymion.

FIVE

At the same moment that I am taking my leave of A. Bettik, six thousand light-years away, in a star system known only by NGC numbers and navigation coordinates, a Pax task force of three fast-attack torchships led by Father Captain Federico de Soya is destroying an orbital forest. The Ouster trees have no defenses against the Pax warships, and the encounter might be described more accurately as slaughter than battle.

I must explain something here. I am not speculating about these events: they occurred precisely as I describe them. Nor am I extrapolating or guessing in the scenes I am about to share when I tell you what Father Captain de Soya or the other principals did when there were no witnesses present. Or what they thought. Or what emotions they felt. These things are literal truth. Later, I will explain how I came to know these things . . . to know them without hint of distortion . . . but for now I ask that you accept them for what they are – the truth.

The three Pax torchships drop from relativistic velocities under more than six hundred gravities of deceleration – what spacefarers for centuries have called 'raspberry jam delta-v' – meaning, of course, that if the internal containment fields were to fail for a microsecond, the crews would be a little more than a layer of raspberry jam on the deckplates.

The containment fields do not fail. At one AU, Father Captain de Soya brings up the orbital forest in the viewsphere. Everyone in the Combat Control Center pauses to glance at the display: several thousand of the Ouster-tailored trees, each at least half a kilometer long, move in an elaborate choreography along the plane of the ecliptic – gravity-clustered copses, braided strands, and subtly shifting patterns of trees, always moving, their leaves always turned toward the G-type sun, their long branches shifting to find the perfect alignment, their thirsty roots deep in the vaporous fog of moisture and nutrients provided by the shepherd comets moving among the forest clusters like giant dirty snowballs. Flitting between the branches of these trees and between the trees themselves, Ouster variants are visible – humanoid shapes with silver-reflective skin and micron-thin butterfly wings extending hundreds of meters. These wings catch the sunlight from moment to moment as they open and blink like brilliant Christmas lights within the green foliage of the orbital forest.

'Fire!' says Father Captain Federico de Soya.

At two-thirds AU, the three torchships of Pax Task Force MAGI open up with their long-distance weapons. At that distance even energy beams would seem to crawl toward their targets like lightning bugs on a black bedsheet, but the Pax ships carry hypervelocity and hyperkinetic weapons: essentially small Hawking-drive starships in their own right, some carrying plasma warheads, which are spun up to relativistic velocities in micro-seconds to detonate within the forest, others designed simply to drop back into real space, their mass enlarged, and to plow through the trees like cannonballs fired through wet cardboard at point-blank range. Minutes later the three torchships are within energy-beam distance, and the CPBs lance out in a thousand directions simultaneously, their beams visible because of the riot of colloidal particles now filling space like dust in an old attic.

The forest burns. Tailored bark, oh-two pods and self-sealing leaves burst from violent decompression or are sawed through by beams and shaped plasma blast-tendrils, and the escaping globules of oxygen fuel the fires amid the vacuum until the air freezes or burns away. And the forest burns. Tens of millions of leaves fly away from the exploding forest, each leaf or cluster of leaves its own blazing pyre, while trunks and branches burn against the black background of space. The shepherd comets are struck and they volatilize in an instant, blasting the braided strands of forest apart in expanding shock waves of steam and molten rock fragments. Space-tailored Ousters – 'Lucifer's angels' as the Pax forces have contemptuously called them for centuries – are caught in the explosions like translucent moths in a flame. Some are simply blown apart by the plasma explosions or comet bursts. Others are caught in the path of CPBs and become hyperkinetic objects themselves before their delicate wings and organs are flung apart. Some attempt to flee, expanding their solar wings to the maximum in a vain attempt to outrun the carnage.

None survive.

The encounter takes less than five minutes. When it is done, the MAGI task force decelerates through the forest at a diminished thirty gravities, the fusion-flame tails of the torchships igniting any tree fragments that have escaped the initial attack. Where the forest had floated in space five minutes before – green leaves catching the sunlight, roots drinking the spheres of comet-water, Ouster angels floating like radiant gossamers among the branches – now there is only a torus of smoke and expanding debris filling the plane of the ecliptic along this arc of space.

'Any survivors?' asks Father Captain de Soya, standing along the edge of the C^3 central display, his hands clasped behind his back, balancing easily with only the balls of his feet touching the sticktight strip around the display rim. Despite the fact that the torchship is still decelerating under thirty gravities, the Combat Control Center is held at a constant one-fiftieth standard-g microgravity. The dozen officers in the room sit and stand with their heads toward the center of the sphere. De Soya is a short man in his mid-thirties, standard. His face is round, the skin dark, and friends have noticed over the years that his eyes reflected priestly compassion more frequently than military ruthlessness. They are troubled now.

'No survivors,' says Mother Commander Stone, de Soya's executive officer and another Jesuit. She turns from the tactical display to shunt into a blinking com unit.

De Soya knows that none of his officers in the C^3 are pleased by this engagement. Destroying Ouster orbital forests is part of their mission – the seemingly innocuous trees serve as refueling and refitting centers for combat Swarms – but few Pax warriors take pleasure in wanton destruction. They were trained as knights of the Church, defenders of the Pax, not as destroyers of beauty or murderers of unarmed life-forms, even if those life-forms were tailored Ousters who had surrendered their souls.

'Lay in the usual search pattern,' de Soya orders. 'Tell the crew to stand down from battle stations.' On a modern torchship the crew consists of only these dozen officers and half a dozen others spread throughout the ship.

Suddenly Mother Commander Stone interrupts. 'Sir, a Hawking-drive distortion reading up-angle seventy-two, coordinates two-twenty-nine, forty-three, one-oh-five. C-plus exit point at seven-oh-oh-point-five-thousand klicks. Probability of single vehicle, ninety-six percent. Relative velocity unknown.'

'Full battle stations,' says de Soya. He smiles slightly without being aware of doing so. Perhaps the Ousters are rushing to the rescue of their forest. Or perhaps there *was* a single defender and it has just launched a standoff weapon from somewhere beyond the system's Oort cloud. Or perhaps it is the vanguard of an entire Swarm of Ouster fighting units and his task force is doomed. Whatever the threat, Father Captain de Soya prefers a fight to this . . . this vandalism.

'Vehicle is translating,' reports the acquisition officer from his perch above de Soya's head.

'Very good,' says Father Captain de Soya. He watches displays flicker before his eyes, resets his shunt, and opens several virtual-optic channels. Now the C^3 fades away and he stands in space, a giant five million klicks tall, seeing his own ships like specks with flaming tails, the curved column of smoke that is the destroyed forest bending past at belt height, and now this intruder flicking into existence seven hundred thousand klicks and an armreach above the plane of the ecliptic. Red spheres around his ships show external fields at combat strength. Other colors fill space, displaying sensor readings, acquisition pulses, and targeting preparation. Working on the millisecond tactical level, de Soya can launch weapons or unleash energies by pointing and snapping his fingers.

'Transponder beacon,' reports the com officer. 'Current codes check. It is a Pax courier. Archangel class.'

De Soya frowns. What can be so important that the Pax Command is sending the Vatican's fastest vehicle – a craft so swift that it is also the Pax's greatest secret weapon? De Soya can see the Pax codes surrounding the tiny ship in tactical space. Its fusion flame reaches scores of kilometers. The ship is using almost no energy on internal containment fields, and the gravities involved are beyond raspberry-jam levels.

'Uncrewed?' queries de Soya. He desperately hopes so. Archangel-class ships can travel anywhere in known space within days – real-time days! – rather than the weeks of shiptime and years of real time demanded by all other craft – but no one survives archangel voyages.

Mother Commander Stone steps into the tactical environment with him. Her black tunic is almost invisible against space so that her pale face seems to float above the ecliptic, sunlight from the virtual star illuminating her sharp cheekbones. 'No, sir,' she says softly. Her voice can be heard only by de Soya in this mode. 'Beacon indicates two members of the crew in fugue.'

'Dear Jesus,' whispers de Soya. It is more prayer than curse. Even in high-g fugue tanks, these two people, already killed during C-plus travel, will now be more a microthin layer of protein paste than healthy raspberry jam. 'Prepare the resurrection creches,' he says on the common band.

Mother Commander Stone touches the shunt behind her ear and frowns. 'Message embedded in code. Human couriers are to be resurrected priority alpha. Dispensation level Omega.'

Father Captain de Soya's head snaps around and he stares at his executive officer for a silent moment. The smoke from the burning orbital forest swirls around their waists. Priority resurrection defies the doctrine of the Church and the rules of Pax Command; it is also dangerous – the chances for incomplete reintegration go from near zero at the usual three-day rate, to almost fifty percent at the three-hour level. And priority level Omega means His Holiness on Pacem.

De Soya sees the knowledge in his exec's eyes. This courier ship is from the Vatican. Either someone there or someone in Pax Command, or both, considered this message important enough to send an irreplaceable arch-angel courier ship, to kill two high-ranking Pax officers – since no one else would be trusted with an archangel – and to risk incomplete reintegration of those same two officers.

In tactical space de Soya raises his eyebrows in response to his exec's questioning look. On the command band he says, 'Very well, Commander. Instruct all three ships to match velocities. Prepare a boarding party. I want the fugue tanks transferred and the resurrections completed by oh-six-thirty hours. Please give my compliments to Captain Hearn on the *Melchior* and Mother Captain Boulez on the *Gaspar*, and ask them to join me on the *Balthasar* for a meeting with the couriers at oh-seven-hundred.'

Father Captain de Soya steps from tactical space into the reality of the C^3. Stone and the others are still looking at him.

'Quickly,' says de Soya, and kicks off from the display rim, flying across the space to his private door and pulling himself through the circular hatch. 'Wake me when the couriers are resurrected,' he says to the white faces watching him in the seconds before the door irises shut.

SIX

I walked the streets of Endymion and tried to come to grips with my life, my death, and my life again.

I should say here that I was not as cool about these things – my trial, my 'execution,' my strange meeting with the mythic old poet – as this narrative would suggest. Part of me was shaken to its core. They had tried to *kill* me! I wanted to blame the Pax, but the courts were not agents of the Pax – not directly. Hyperion had its own Home Rule Council, and the Port Romance courts were set up according to our own local politics. Capital punishment was not an inevitable Pax punishment, especially on those worlds where the Church governed via theocracy, but was a holdover from Hyperion's old colonial days. My quick trial, its inevitable outcome, and my summary execution were, if anything, more expressions of Hyperion's and Port Romance's business leaders' terror of frightening away Pax offworld tourists than anything else. I was a peasant, a hunting guide who had killed the rich tourist assigned to my care, and an example had been made of me. Nothing more. I should not take it personally.

I took it very personally. Pausing outside the tower, feeling the sun's heat bounced from the broad paving stones of the courtyard, I slowly raised my hands. They were shaking. Too much had happened too soon, and my enforced calm during the trial and the brief period before my execution had demanded too much from me.

I shook my head and walked through the university ruins. The city of Endymion had been built high on a brow of a hill, and the university had sat even higher along this ridge during colonial days, so the view to the south and east was beautiful. Chalma forests in the valley below glowed bright yellow. The lapis sky was free of contrails or airship traffic. I knew that the Pax cared nothing about Endymion, and that it was the Pinion Plateau region to the northeast that their troops still guarded and their robots still mined for the unique cruciform symbiotes, but this entire section of the continent had been off-limits for so many decades that it had a fresh, wilderness feel to it.

Within ten minutes of idle walking, I realized that only the tower where I had awakened and its surrounding buildings seemed occupied. The rest of the university was in absolute ruins – its great halls open to the elements, its physical plant ransacked centuries before, its playing fields overgrown, its observatory dome shattered – and the city farther down the hillside looked

33

even more abandoned. I saw entire city blocks there reclaimed by weirwood tangle and kudzu.

I could see that the university had been beautiful in its day: post-Hegira, neo-Gothic buildings were constructed of the sandstone blocks quarried not far from here in the foothills of the Pinion Plateau. Three years earlier, when I had worked as an assistant to the famous landscape artist Avrol Hume, doing much of the heavy work as he redesigned the First Family estates along the fashionable coast of the Beak, much of the demand then had been for 'follies' – ersatz ruins set near ponds or forest or hilltop. I had become somewhat of an expert in setting old stones in artful states of decomposition to simulate ruins – most of them absurdly older than humankind's history on this Outback world – but none of Hume's follies had been as attractive as these real ruins. I wandered through the bones of a once-great university, admired the architecture, and thought of my family.

Adding the name of a local city to its own had been the tradition of most indigenie families – for my family was indeed indigenie, descended from those first seedship pioneers almost seven centuries earlier, third-class citizens on our own world: third now after the Pax offworlders and the Hegira colonists who came centuries after my ancestors. For centuries, then, my people had lived and worked in these valleys and mountains. Mostly, I was sure, my indigenie relatives had labored at menial jobs – much as my father had before his early death when I was eight, much as my mother had continued to until her death five years later, much as I had until this week. My grandmother had been born the decade after everyone had been removed from these regions by the Pax, but Grandam was old enough actually to remember the days when our clan families roamed as far as the Pinion Plateau and worked on the fiberplastic plantations to the south of here.

I had no sense of homecoming. The cold moors of the area northeast of here were my home. The fens north of Port Romance had been my chosen place to live and work. This university and town had never been part of my life and held no more relevance to me than did the wild stories of the old poet's *Cantos*.

At the base of another tower, I paused to catch my breath and consider this last thought. If the poet's offer was real, the 'wild stories' of the *Cantos* would hold every relevance for me. I thought of Grandam's recitation of that epic poem – remembered the nights watching the sheep in the north hills, our battery-driven caravans pulled in a protective circle for the night, the low cooking fires doing little to dim the glory of the constellations of meteor showers above, remembered Grandam's slow, measured tones until she finished each stanza and waited for me to recite the lines back to her, remembered my own impatience at the process – I would much rather have been sitting by lantern reading a book – and smiled to think that this evening I would be dining with the author of those lines. More, the old poet was one of the seven pilgrims whom the poem sang about.

I shook my head again. Too much. Too soon.

There was something odd about this tower. Larger and broader than the one in which I had awakened, this structure had only one window – an open archway thirty meters up the tower. More interestingly, the original doorway had been bricked up. With an eye educated by my seasons as bricklayer and mason under Avrol Hume, I guessed that the door had been closed up before the area had been abandoned a century ago – but not that long before.

To this day I do not know what drew my curiosity to that building when there were so many ruins to explore that afternoon – but curious I was. I remember looking up the steep hillside beyond the tower and noticing the riot of leafy chalma that had wound its way out and around the tower like thick-barked ivy. *If one scrambled up the hillside and penetrated the chalma grove just . . . there . . . one could crawl out along that vining branch and just barely reach the sill of that lone window . . .*

I shook my head again. This was nonsense. At the least, such a childish expedition would result in torn clothes and skinned hands. At the most, one could easily fall the thirty meters to the flagstones there. And why risk it? What could be in this old bricked-up tower other than spiders and cobwebs?

Ten minutes later I was far out on the curled chalma branch, inching my way along and trying to hang on by finding chinks in the stones or thick-enough branches on the vines above me. Because the branch grew against the stone wall, I could not straggle it. Rather, I had to shuffle along on my knees – the overhanging chalma vine was too low to allow me to stand – and the sense of exposure and of being pushed outward toward the drop was terrifying. Every time the autumn wind came up and shook the leaves and branches, I would stop moving and cling for all I was worth.

Finally, I reached the window and began cursing softly. My calculations – so easily made from the pavement thirty meters below – had been off a bit. The chalma branch here was almost three meters below the sill of the open window. There were no usable toeholds or fingerholds in this expanse of stone. If I was to reach the sill, I would have to jump and hope that my fingers found a grasp there. That would be insane. There was nothing in this tower that could justify such a risk.

I waited for the wind to die down, crouched, and leaped. For a sickening second my curved fingers scrabbled backward on crumbling stone and dust, tearing my nails and finding no hold, but then they encountered the rotted remnants of the old windowsill and sank in. I pulled myself up, panting and ripping the shirt fabric over my elbows. The soft shoes A. Bettik had laid out for me scrambled against stone to find leverage.

And then I was up and curling myself onto the window ledge, wondering how in the hell I would get back down to the chalma branch. My concerns in that area were amplified a second later as I squinted into the darkened interior of the tower.

'Holy shit,' I whispered to no one in particular. There was an old wooden landing just below the window ledge on which I clung, but the tower was essentially empty. The sunlight streaming through the window illuminated bits of a rotting stairway above and below the landing, spiraling around the inside of the tower much as the chalma vines wrapped around the exterior, but the center of the tower was thick with darkness. I glanced up and saw speckles of sunlight through what may have been a temporary wooden roof some thirty meters higher and realized that this tower was little more than a glorified grain silo – a giant stone cylinder sixty meters tall. No wonder it had needed only one window. No wonder the door had been bricked up even before the evacuation of Endymion.

Still maintaining my balance on the windowsill, not trusting the rotted landing inside, I shook my head a final time. My curiosity would get me killed someday.

Then, still squinting into the darkness so different from the rich after-noon sunlight outside, I realized that the interior was *too* dark. I could not see the wall or spiral staircase across the interior. I realized that scattered sunlight illuminated the stone interior here, I could see a bit of rotted stairway there, and the full cylinder of the inside was visible meters above me – but here, on my level, the majority of the interior was just . . . gone.

'Christ,' I whispered. Something was filling the bulk of this dark tower.

Slowly, careful to hold most of my weight on my arms still balanced on the sill, I lowered myself to the interior landing. The wood creaked but seemed solid enough. Hands still clutching the window frame, I let some of my weight on my feet and turned to look.

It still took me the better part of a minute to realize what I was looking at. A spaceship filled the inside of the tower like a bullet set into the chamber of an old-fashioned revolver.

Setting all my weight on the landing now, almost not caring if it held me, I stepped forward to see better.

The ship was not tall by spacecraft standards – perhaps fifty meters – and it was slender. The metal of the hull – if metal it was – looked matte black and seemed to absorb the light. There was no sheen or reflection that I could see. I made out the ship's outline mostly by looking at the stone wall behind it and seeing where the stones and reflected light from them ended.

I did not doubt for an instant that this was a spaceship. It was almost too much a spaceship. I once read that small children on hundreds of worlds still draw houses by sketching a box with a pyramid on top, smoke spiraling from a rectangular chimney – even if the kids in question reside in organ-ically grown living pods high in RNAd residential trees. Similarly, they still draw mountains as Matterhorn-like pyramids, even if their own nearby mountains more resemble the rounded hills here at the base of the Pinion Plateau. I don't know what the article said the reason was – racial memory, perhaps, or the brain being hardwired for certain symbols.

The thing I was looking at, peering at, seeing mostly as negative space, was not so much spaceship as SPACESHIP.

I have seen images of the oldest Old Earth rockets – pre-Pax, pre-Fall, pre-Hegemony, pre-Hegira . . . hell, pre-Everything almost – and they looked like this curved blackness. Tall, thin, graduated on both ends, pointed on top, finned on the bottom – I was looking at the hardwired, racial-memoried, symbolically perfect image of SPACESHIP.

36

There were no private or misplaced spaceships on Hyperion. Of this I was sure. Spacecraft, even of the simple interplanetary variety, were simply too expensive and too rare to leave lying around in old stone towers. At one time, centuries ago before the Fall, when the resources of the WorldWeb seemed unlimited, there may have been a plethora of spacecraft – FORCE military, Hegemony diplomatic, planetary government, corporate, foundation, exploratory, even a few private ships belonging to hyper-billionaires – but even in those days only a planetary economy could afford to build a starship. In my lifetime – and the lifetime of my mother and grandmother and *her* mothers and grandmothers – only the Pax – that consortium of Church and crude interstellar government – could afford spaceships of any sort. And no individual in the known universe – not even His Holiness on Pacem – could afford a private starship.

And this was a starship. I knew it. Don't ask me how I knew it, but I knew it.

Paying no attention to the terrible condition of the steps, I began descending and ascending the spiral steps. The hull was four meters from me. The unfathomable blackness of it made me dizzy. Halfway around the interior of the tower and fifteen meters below me, just visible before the curve of blackness blocked it off, a landing extended almost to the hull itself.

I ran down to it. One rotted step actually broke under me, but I was moving so fast that I ignored it.

The landing had no railings here and extended out like a diving board. A fall from it would almost certainly break bones and leave me lying in the blackness of a sealed tower. I gave it no thought at all as I stepped out and set my palm against the hull of the ship.

The hull was warm. It did not feel like metal – more like the smooth skin of some sleeping creature. To add to that illusion, there was the softest movement and vibration from the hull – as if the ship were breathing, as if I could detect a heartbeat beneath my palm.

Suddenly there was true motion beneath my hand, and the hull simply fell and folded away – not irising mechanically like some portals I had seen, and certainly not swinging on hinges – simply *folding* into itself and out of the way, like lips pulling back.

Lights turned on. An interior corridor – its ceiling and walls as organic as a glimpse of some mechanical cervix – glowed softly.

I paused about three nanoseconds. For years my life had been as calm and predictable as most people's. This week I had accidentally killed a man, been condemned and executed, and had awakened in Grandam's favourite myth. Why stop there?

I stepped into the spaceship, and the doors folded shut behind me like a hungry mouth closing on a morsel.

The corridor into the ship was not as I would have imagined it. I had always thought of spacecraft interiors as being like the hold of the seagoing troop-ships that transported our Home Guard regiment to Ursus: all gray metal, rivets, dogged hatches, and hissing steam pipes. None of that was evident here. The corridor was smooth, curved, and almost featureless, the interior bulkheads covered with a rich wood as warm and organic as flesh. If there was an air lock, I hadn't seen it. Hidden lights came on ahead of me as I advanced and then extinguished themselves as I passed, leaving me in a small pool of light with darkness ahead and behind. I knew that the ship couldn't be more than ten meters across, but the slight curve of this corridor made it seem larger on the inside than it had appeared on the outside.

The corridor ended at what must have been the center of the ship: an open well with a central metal staircase spiraling upward and downward into darkness. I set my foot on the first step and lights came on somewhere above. Guessing that the more interesting parts of the ship lay above, I began to climb.

The next deck above filled the entire circle of the ship and held an antique holopit of the kind I had seen in old books, a scattering of chairs and tables in a style I could not identify, and a grand piano. I should say here that probably not one person out of ten thousand born on Hyperion could have identified that object as a piano – especially not as a grand piano. My mother and Grandam both had held a passionate interest in music, and a piano had filled much of the space in one of our electric caravans. Many had been the time I had heard my uncles or grandfather complaining about the bulk and weight of that instrument – about all of the jules of energy used to trundle that heavy pre-Hegira apparatus across the moors of Aquila, and about the commonsense efficiency of having a pocket synthesizer that could create the music of any piano . . . or any other instrument. But mother and Grandam were insistent – nothing could equal the sound of a true piano, no matter how many times it had to be tuned after transport. And neither grandfather nor uncles complained when Grandam played Rachmaninoff or Bach or Mozart around the camp-fire at night. I learned about the great pianos of history from that old woman – the pre-Hegira grand pianos included. And now I was looking at one.

Ignoring the holopit and furniture, ignoring the curved window wall that showed only the dark stone of the interior of the tower, I walked to the grand piano. The gold lettering above the keyboard read STEINWAY. I whistled softly and let my fingers caress the keys, not yet daring to depress one. According to Grandam, this company had ceased making pianos before the Big Mistake of '08, and none had been produced since the Hegira. I was touching an instrument at least a thousand years old. Stein-ways and Stradivariuses were myths among those of us who loved music. How could this be? I wondered, my fingers still trailing over keys that felt like the legendary ivory – tusks of an extinct creature called an elephant. Human beings like the old poet in the tower might possibly survive from pre-Hegira days – Poulsen treatments and cryogenic storage could theoret-ically account for that – but artifacts of wood and wire and ivory had little chance of making that long voyage through time and space.

My fingers played a chord: C-E-G-B-flat. And then a C-major chord. The tone was flawless, the acoustics of the spaceship perfect. Our old upright piano had needed tuning by Grandam after every trip of a few miles across the moors, but this instrument seemed perfectly tuned after countless light-years and centuries of travel.

I pulled the bench out, sat, and began playing *Für Elise*. It was a corny, simple piece, but one that seemed to fit the silence and solitude of this dark place. Indeed, the lights seemed to dim around me as the notes filled the circular room and seemed to echo up and down the dark staircase well. As I played, I thought of Mother and Grandam and how they would never have guessed that my early piano lessons would lead to this solo in a hidden spaceship. The sadness of that thought seemed to fill the music I was playing.

When I was finished, I pulled my fingers back from the keyboard quickly, almost guiltily, struck with the presumption of my poor playing of such a simple piece on this fine piano, this gift from the past. I sat in silence for a moment, wondering about the ship, about the old poet, and about my own place in this mad scheme of things.

'Very nice,' said a soft voice behind me.

I admit that I jumped. I had heard no one climb or descend the stairs, sensed no one entering the room. My head jerked around.

There was no one in the room.

'I have not heard that particular piece played in some time,' came the voice again. It seemed to emanate from the center of the empty room. 'My previous passenger preferred Rachmaninoff.'

I set my hand on the edge of the bench to steady myself and thought of all the stupid questions I could avoid asking.

'Are you the ship?' I asked, not knowing if this was a stupid question but wanting the answer.

'Of course,' came the reply. The voice was soft but vaguely masculine. I had, of course, heard talking machines before – such things had been around forever – but never one that might actually be intelligent. The Church and Pax had banned all true AIs more than two centuries before, and after seeing how the TechnoCore had helped the Ousters destroy the Hegemony, most of the trillions of people on a thousand devastated worlds had agreed wholeheartedly. I realized that my own programming in that regard had been effective: the thought that I was talking to a truly sentient device made my palms moist and my throat tight.

'Who was your . . . ah . . . previous passenger?' I said.

There was the hint of a pause. 'The gentleman was generally known as the Consul,' said the ship at last. 'He had been a diplomat for the Hegemony for much of his life.'

It was my turn to hesitate before speaking. It occurred to me that perhaps the 'execution' in Port Romance had only scrambled my neurons to the point where I thought I was living in one of Grandam's epic poems.

'What happened to the Consul?' I asked.

'He died,' said the ship. There may have been the slightest undertone of regret in the voice.

'How?' I said. At the end of the old poet's *Cantos*, after the Fall of the WorldWeb, the Hegemony Consul had taken a ship back to the Web. *This* ship? 'Where did he die?' I added. According to the *Cantos*, the ship the Hegemony Consul had left Hyperion in had been infused with the persona of the second John Keats cybrid.

'I can't remember where the Consul died,' said the ship. 'I only remember that he died, and that I returned here. I presume there was some programming of that directive in my command banks at the time.'

'Do you have a name?' I asked, mildly curious as to whether I was speaking to the AI persona of John Keats.

'No,' said the ship. 'Only *Ship*.' Again there came something more pause than simple silence. 'Although I do seem to recall that I had a name at one point.'

'Was it John?' I asked. 'Or Johnny?'

'It may have been,' said the ship. 'The details are cloudy.'

'Why is that?' I said. 'Is your memory malfunctioning?'

'No, not at all,' said the ship. 'As far as I can deduce, there was some traumatic event about two hundred standard years ago which deleted certain memories, but since then my memory and other faculties have been flawless.'

'But you don't remember the event? The trauma?'

'No,' said the ship, cheerily enough. 'I believe that it occurred at about the same time that the Consul died and I returned to Hyperion, but I am not certain.'

'And since then?' I said. 'Since your return you've been hidden away here in this tower?'

'Yes,' said the ship. 'I was in the Poet's City for a time, but for most of the past two local centuries, I have been here.'

'Who brought you here?'

'Martin Silenus,' said the ship. 'The poet. You met him earlier today.'

'You're aware of that?' I said.

'Oh, yes,' said the ship. 'I was the one who gave M. Silenus the data about your trial and execution. I helped to arrange the bribe to the officials and the transport of your sleeping body here.'

'How did you do that?' I asked, the image of this massive, archaic ship on the telephone too absurd to deal with.

'Hyperion has no true datasphere,' said the ship, 'but I monitor all free microwave and satellite communications, as well as certain "secure" fiber-optic and maser bands which I have tapped into.'

'So you're a spy for the old poet,' I said.

'Yes,' said the ship.

'And what do you know about the old poet's plans for me?' I asked, turning toward the keyboard again and beginning Bach's *Air on a G-string*.

'M. Endymion,' said a different voice behind me.

I quit playing and turned to see A. Bettik, the android, standing at the head of the circular staircase.

'My master had become worried that you were lost,' said A. Bettik. 'I came to show you the way back to the tower. You just have time to dress for dinner.'

I shrugged and walked to the stairwell. Before following the blue-skinned man down the stairs, I turned and said to the darkening room, 'It was nice talking to you, Ship.'

'It was a pleasure meeting you, M. Endymion,' said the ship. 'I will see you again soon.'

SEVEN

The torchships *Balthasar, Melchior,* and *Gaspar* are a full AU beyond the burning orbital forests and still decelerating around the unnamed sun when Mother Commander Stone buzzes at Father Captain de Soya's compartment portal to inform him that the couriers have been resurrected.

'Actually, only one was successfully resurrected,' she amends, floating at the open iris-door.

Father Captain de Soya winces. 'Has the . . . unsuccessful one . . . been returned to the resurrection creche?' he asks.

'Not yet,' says Stone. 'Father Sapieha is with the survivor?'

De Soya nods. 'Pax?' he asks, hoping that this will be the case. Vatican couriers bring more problems than military ones.

Mother Commander Stone shakes her head. 'Both are Vatican. Father Gawronski and Father Vandrisse. Both are Legionaries of Christ.'

De Soya avoids a sigh only by an effort of will. Legionaries of Christ had all but replaced the more liberal Jesuits over the centuries – their power had been growing in the Church a century before the Big Mistake – and it was no secret that the Pope used them as shock troops for difficult missions within the Church hierarchy. 'Which one survived?' he asks.

'Father Vandrisse.' Stone glances at her comlog. 'He should be revived by now, sir.'

'Very well,' says de Soya. 'Adjust the internal field to one-g at oh-six-forty-five. Pipe Captains Hearn and Boulez aboard and give them my compliments. Please escort them to the forward meeting room. I'll be in with Vandrisse until we convene.'

'Aye, aye,' says Mother Commander Stone, and kicks off.

The revival room outside the resurrection creche is more chapel than infirmary. Father Captain de Soya genuflects toward the altar and then joins Father Sapieha by the gurney, where the courier is sitting up. Sapieha is older than most Pax crew – at least seventy standard – and the soft halogen beams reflect from his bald scalp. De Soya has always found the ship's chaplain short-tempered and not very bright, much like several of the parish priests he had known as a boy.

'Captain,' acknowledges the chaplain.

De Soya nods and steps closer to the man on the gurney. Father Vandrisse is young – perhaps in his late twenties standard – and his dark hair is long and curled in the current Vatican fashion. Or at least in the fashion that

42

had been coming in when de Soya had last seen Pacem and the Vatican: a time-debt of three years had already accrued in the two months they had been on this mission.

'Father Vandrisse,' says de Soya, 'can you hear me?'

The young man on the cot nods and grunts. Language is hard for the first few minutes after resurrection. Or so de Soya has heard.

'Well,' says the chaplain, 'I'd better get the other's body back in the creche.' He frowns at de Soya as though the captain had personally brought about the unsuccessful resurrection. 'It is a waste, Father Captain. It will be weeks – perhaps months – before Father Gawronski can be successfully revived. It will be very painful for him.'

De Soya nods.

'Would you like to see him, Father Captain?' persists the chaplain. 'The body is . . . well . . . barely recognizable as human. The internal organs are quite visible and quite . . .'

'Go about your duties, Father,' de Soya says quietly. 'Dismissed.'

Father Sapieha frowns again as if he is going to reply, but at that moment the gravity klaxon sounds, and both men have to orient themselves so that their feet touch the floor as the internal containment field realigns itself. Then the gravity slowly climbs to one-g as Father Vandrisse sinks back into the gurney's cushions and the chaplain shuffles out the door. Even after only a day of zero-g, the return of gravity seems an imposition.

'Father Vandrisse,' de Soya says softly. 'Can you hear me?'

The young man nods. His eyes show the pain he is in. The man's skin glistens as if he has just received grafts – or as if he is newborn. The flesh looks pink and raw to de Soya, almost burned, and the cruciform on the courier's chest is livid and twice normal size.

'Do you know where you are?' whispers de Soya. *Or who you are?* he mentally adds. Post-resurrection confusion can last for hours or days. De Soya knows that couriers are trained to overcome that confusion, but how can anyone be trained for death and revival? An instructor of de Soya's at the seminary had once put it plainly – 'The cells remember dying, being dead, even if the mind does not.'

'I remember,' whispers Father Vandrisse, and his voice sounds as raw as his skin looks. 'You are Captain de Soya?'

'Father Captain de Soya. Yes.'

Vandrisse tries to lever himself up on his elbow and fails. 'Closer,' he whispers, too weak to lift his head from the pillow.

De Soya leans closer. The other priest smells faintly of formaldehyde. Only certain members of the priesthood are trained in the actual mysteries of resurrection, and de Soya had chosen not to be one of these. He could officiate at a baptism and administer Communion or Extreme Unction – as a starship captain he has had more opportunities for the latter than the former – but he had never been present at the Sacrament of Resurrection. He has no idea of the processes involved, beyond the miracle of the cruciform, in returning this man's destroyed and compressed body, his decaying neurons and scattered brain mass, to the human form he now sees before him.

Vandrisse begins whispering and de Soya has to lean even closer, the resurrected priest's lips almost brushing de Soya's ear.

'Must . . . talk . . .' Vandrisse manages with great effort.

De Soya nods. 'I've scheduled a briefing in fifteen minutes. My other two ship captains will be there. We'll provide a hoverchair for you . . .'

Vandrisse is shaking his head. 'No . . . meeting. Message for . . . you . . . only.'

De Soya shows no expression. 'All right. Do you want to wait until you are . . .'

Again the agonized shake of his head. The skin of the priest's face is slick and striated, as if the muscle were showing through. 'Now . . .' he whispers.

De Soya leans close and waits.

'You are . . . to . . . take the . . . archangel courier . . . ship . . . im-mediately . . .' gasps Vandrisse. 'It is programmed for its destination.'

De Soya remains expressionless, but he is thinking, *So it is to be a painful death by acceleration. Dear Jesus, could you not let this cup pass from me?*

'What do I tell the others?' he asks.

Father Vandrisse shakes his head. 'Tell them nothing. Put your execu-tive officer in command of the . . . *Balthasar.* Transfer task force command to Mother Captain Boulez. Task Force MAGI will . . . have . . . other orders.'

'Will I be informed of these orders?' asks de Soya. His jaw hurts with the tension of sounding calm. Until thirty seconds ago the survival and success of this ship, this task force, had been the central reason for his existence.

'No,' says Vandrisse. 'These . . . orders . . . do . . . not . . . concern you.'

The resurrected priest is pale with pain and exhaustion. De Soya realizes that he is taking some satisfaction in that fact and immediately says a short prayer for forgiveness.

'I am to leave immediately,' repeats de Soya. 'Can I take my few personal possessions?' He is thinking of the small porcelain sculpture that his sister had given him shortly before her death on Renaissance Vector. That fragile piece, locked in a stasis cube during high-g maneuvers, has been with him for all of his years of spacefaring.

'No,' says Father Vandrisse. 'Go . . . immediately. Take nothing.'

'This is upon order of . . .' queries de Soya.

Vandrisse frowns through his grimace of pain. 'This is upon direct command of His Holiness, Pope Julius XIV,' says the courier. 'It is . . . Omega Priority . . . superseding all orders of Pax Military Command or SpaComC-Fleet. Do . . . you . . . understand . . . Father . . . Captain . . . de . . . Soya?'

'I understand,' says the Jesuit, and bows his head in compliance.

*

The archangel-class courier ship has no name. De Soya has never considered torchships beautiful – gourd-shaped, the command and weapons mod dwarfed by the huge Hawking drive and in-system fusion-thrust sphere – but the archangel is actively ugly in comparison. The courier ship is a mass of asymmetrical spheres, dodecahedrons, lash-ons, structural cables, and Hawking-drive mounts, with the passenger cabin the merest of afterthoughts in the center of all that junk.

De Soya has met briefly with Hearn, Boulez, and Stone, explained only that he has been called away, and transferred command to the new – and amazed – task force and *Balthasar* captains, then taken a one-person transfer pod to the archangel. De Soya tries not to look back at his beloved *Balthasar*, but at the last moment before attaching to the courier, he turns and looks longingly at the torchship, sunlight painting its curved flank into a crescentlike sunrise over some lovely world, then turns resolutely away.

He sees upon entering that the archangel has no virtual tactical command, no manual controls, and no bridge. The interior is not much larger than de Soya's crowded cubby on the *Balthasar*, although this space is crowded with cables, fiber-optic leads, tech diskeys, and two acceleration couches.

No, de Soya sees at once, these are not standard acceleration couches. These are unpadded steel trays in human form, more like autopsy slabs than couches. The trays have a lip – to keep fluid from sloshing under high-g, he is sure – and he realizes that the only compensating containment field in the ship would be around these couches – to keep the pulverized flesh, bone, and brain matter from floating away in the zero-g intervals after final deceleration. De Soya can see the nozzles where water or some cleansing solution has been injected at high speed to clean the steel. It has not been totally successful.

'Acceleration in two minutes,' says a metallic voice. 'Strap in now.'

No niceties, thinks de Soya. *Not even a 'please'*.

'Ship?' he says. He knows that no true AIs are allowed on Pax ships – indeed, no AIs are allowed anywhere in Pax-controlled human space – but he thinks that the Vatican might have made an exception on one of its archangel-class courier ships.

'One minute thirty seconds until initial acceleration,' comes the metallic voice, and de Soya realizes that he is talking to an idiot machine. He hurries to strap himself in. The bands are broad, thick, and almost surely for show. The containment field will hold him – or his remains – in place.

'Thirty seconds,' said the idiot voice. 'Be advised that the C-plus translation will be lethal.'

'Thanks,' says Father Captain Federico de Soya. His heart is pounding so fiercely that he can hear it in his ears. Lights flicker in the various instruments. Nothing here is meant for human monitoring, so de Soya ignores them.

'Fifteen seconds,' says the ship. 'You might wish to pray now.'

'Fuck you,' says de Soya. He has been praying since he left the courier's recovery room. Now he adds a final prayer for forgiveness for the obscenity.

'Five seconds,' comes the voice. 'There will be no further communications. May God bless you and speed your resurrection, in Christ's name.'

'Amen,' says Father Captain de Soya. He closes his eyes as acceleration commences.

EIGHT

Evening came early in the ruined city of Endymion. I watched the last of the autumn light dim and die from my vantage point in the tower where I had awakened earlier on this endless day. A. Bettik had led me back, shown me to my room, where stylish but simple evening clothes – tan cotton trousers tightening just below the knees, white flax blouse with a hint of ruffled sleeves, black leather vest, black stockings, soft black leather boots, and a gold wristband – were still laid out on the bed. The android also showed me to the toilet and bathing facilities a floor below and told me that the thick cotton robe hanging on the door was for my use. I thanked him, bathed, dried my hair, dressed in everything that had been laid out except for the gold band, and waited at the window while the light grew more golden and horizontal and shadows crept down from the hills above the university. When the light had died to the point where shadows had fled and the brightest stars in the Swan were visible above the mountains to the east, A. Bettik returned.

'Is it time?' I asked.

'Not quite, sir,' replied the android. 'Earlier you requested that I return so that we might talk.'

'Ahh, yes,' I said, and gestured toward the bed, the only piece of furniture in the room. 'Have a seat.'

The blue-skinned man stood where he was by the door. 'I am comfortable standing, sir.'

I folded my arms and leaned against the windowsill. The air coming in the open window was cool and smelled of chalma. 'You don't have to call me sir,' I said. 'Raul would do.' I hesitated. 'Unless you're programmed to talk to . . . ah . . .' I was about to say 'humans,' but did not want to make it seem as if I thought A. Bettik was *not* human. '. . . to talk to people that way,' I finished lamely.

A. Bettik smiled. 'No, sir. I am not programmed at all . . . not like a machine. Except for several synthetic prostheses – to augment strength, for instance, or to provide resistance to radiation – I have no artificial parts. I was merely taught deference to fulfil my role. I could call you M. Endymion, if that would be preferable.'

I shrugged. 'It doesn't matter. I'm sorry I'm so ignorant about androids.'

A. Bettik's thin-lipped smile returned. 'There is no need to apologize, M. Endymion. Very few human beings now alive have seen one of my race.'

My race. Interesting. 'Tell me about your race,' I said. 'Wasn't the biofacture of androids illegal in the Hegemony?'

'Yes, sir,' he said. I noticed that he stood at parade rest, and wondered idly if he had ever served in a military capacity. 'Biofacture of androids was illegal on Old Earth and many of the Hegemony homeworlds even before the Hegira, but the All Thing allowed biofacture of a certain number of androids for use in the Outback. Hyperion was part of the Outback in those days.'

'It still is,' I said.

'Yes, sir.'

'When were you biofactured? Which worlds did you live on? What were your duties?' I asked. 'If you don't mind my asking.'

'Not at all, M. Endymion,' he said softly. The android's voice had the hint of a dialect that was new to me. Offworld. Ancient. 'I was created on the world of Asquith, in the year 26 ADC by your calendar.'

'In the twenty-fifth century AD,' I said. 'Six hundred and ninety-four years ago.'

A. Bettik nodded and said nothing.

'So you were born . . . biofactured . . . after Old Earth was destroyed,' I said, more to myself than to the android.

'Yes, sir.'

'And was Hyperion your first . . . ah . . . work destination?'

'No, sir,' said A. Bettik. 'For the first half century of my existence, I remained on Asquith in the service of His Royal Highness, King Arthur the Eighth, sovereign lord of the Kingdom of Windsor-in-Exile, and also in the service of his cousin, Prince Rupert of Monaco-in-Exile. When King Arthur died, he willed me to his son, His Royal Highness King William the Twenty-third.'

'Sad King Billy,' I said.

'Yes, sir.'

'And did you come to Hyperion when Sad King Billy fled Horace Glennon-Height's rebellion?'

'Yes,' said A. Bettik. 'Actually, my android brothers and I were sent ahead to Hyperion some thirty-two years before His Highness and the other colonists joined us. We were dispatched here after General Glennon-Height won the Battle of Fomalhaut. His Highness thought it wise if an alternate site for the kingdoms-in-exile were prepared.'

'And that's when you met M. Silenus,' I prompted, pointing toward the ceiling, imagining the old poet up there within his web of life-support umbilicals.

'No,' said the android. 'My duties did not bring me into contact with M. Silenus during the years when the Poet's City was occupied. I had the pleasure of meeting M. Silenus later, during his pilgrimage to the Valley of the Time Tombs two and a half centuries after the death of His Highness.'

'And you've been on Hyperion since,' I said. 'More than five hundred years on this world.'

'Yes, M. Endymion.'

'Are you immortal?' I asked, knowing the question was impertinent but wanting the answer.

A. Bettik showed his slight smile. 'Not at all, sir. I will die from accident or injury that is too serious for me to be repaired. It is just that when I was biofactured, my cells and systems were nanoteched with an ongoing form of Poulssen's treatments so that I am essentially resistant to aging and disease.'

'Is that why androids are blue?' I asked.

'No, sir,' said A. Bettik. 'We are blue because no known race of human-kind was blue at the time of my biofacture, and my designers felt it imperative to keep us visually separate from humans.'

'You do not consider yourself human?' I asked.

'No, sir,' said A. Bettik. 'I consider myself android.'

I smiled at my own naïveté. 'You still act in a service capacity,' I said. 'Yet use of slave android labor was outlawed throughout the Hegemony centuries ago.'

A. Bettik waited.

'Don't you wish to be free?' I said at last. 'To be an independent person in your own right?'

A. Bettik walked to the bed. I thought that he was going to sit down, but he only folded and stacked the shirt and trousers I had been wearing earlier. 'M. Endymion,' he said, 'I should point out that although the laws of the Hegemony died with the Hegemony, I have considered myself a free and independent person for some centuries now.'

'Yet you and the others work for M. Silenus here, in hiding,' I persisted.

'Yes, sir, but I have done so from my own free choice. I was designed to serve humanity. I do it well. I take pleasure in my work.'

'So you've stayed here from your own free will,' I perseverated.

A. Bettik nodded and smiled briefly. 'Yes, for as much as any of us have a free will, sir.'

I sighed and pushed myself away from the window. It was full dark out now. I presumed that I would be summoned to the old poet's dinner party before long. 'And you will continue staying here and caring for the old man until he finally dies,' I said.

'No, sir,' said A. Bettik. 'Not if I am consulted on the matter.'

I paused, my eyebrows lifting. 'Really?' I said. 'And where will you go if you are consulted on the matter?'

'If you choose to accept this mission which M. Silenus has offered you, sir,' said the blue-skinned man, 'I would choose to go with you.'

When I was led upstairs, I discovered that the top floor was no longer a sickroom; it had been transformed into a dining room. The flowfoam hoverchair was gone, the medical monitors were gone, the communication consoles were absent, and the ceiling was open to the sky. I glanced up and located the constellations of the Swan and the Twin Sisters with the trained eye of a former shepherd. Braziers on tall tripods sat in front of each of the stained-glass windows, their flames adding both warmth and light to the room. In the center of the room, the com consoles had been replaced with a three-meter-long dining table. China, silver and crystal glimmered in the light of candles flickering from two ornate candelabras. A place had been set at each end of the table. At the far end, Martin Silenus awaited, already seated in a tall chair.

The old poet was hardly recognizable. He seemed to have shed centuries in the hours since I had last seen him. From being a mummy with parchment skin and sunken eyes, he had transformed into just another old man at a dining table – a *hungry* old man from the look in his eyes. As I approached the table, I noticed the subtle IV drips and monitor filaments snaking under the table, but otherwise the illusion of someone restored to life from the dead was almost perfect.

Silenus chuckled at my expression. 'You caught me at my worst this afternoon, Raul Endymion,' he rasped. The voice was still harsh with age, but much more forceful than before. 'I was still recovering from my cold sleep.' He gestured me to my place at the other end of the table.

'Cryogenic fugue?' I said stupidly, unfurling the linen napkin and dropping it to my lap. It had been years since I had eaten at a table this fancy – the day that I had demobilized from the Home Guard, I had gone straight to the best restaurant in the port city of Gran Chaco on South Talon Peninsula and ordered the finest meal on the menu, blowing my last month's pay in the process. It had been worth it.

'Of course cryogenic fucking fugue,' said the old poet. 'How else do you think I pass these decades?' He chuckled again. 'It merely takes me a few days to get up to speed again after defrosting. I'm not as young as I used to be.'

I took a breath. 'If you don't mind my asking, sir,' I said, 'how old are you?'

The poet ignored me and beckoned to the waiting android – not A. Bettik – who nodded toward the stairwell. Other androids began carrying up the food in silence. My water glass was filled. I watched as A. Bettik showed a bottle of wine to the poet, waited for the old man's nod, and then went through the ritual, offering him the cork and a sample to taste. Martin Silenus sloshed the vintage wine around in his mouth, swallowed, and grunted. A. Bettik took this for assent and poured the wine for each of us.

The appetizers arrived, two for each of us. I recognized the charbroiled chicken *yakitori* and the tender Mane-raised beef carpaccio arugula. In addition, Silenus helped himself to the sautéed *foie gras* wrapped in mandrake leaves that had been set near his end of the table. I lifted the ornamented skewer and tried the *yakitori*. It was excellent.

Martin Silenus might be eight or nine hundred years old, perhaps the oldest human alive, but the codger had an appetite. I saw the gleam of his perfect white teeth as he attacked the beef carpaccio, and I wondered if these were dentures or Arnied substitutes. Probably the latter.

I realized that I was ravenous. Evidently either my pseudo-resurrection or the exercise involved in climbing to the ship had instilled an appetite in me. For several minutes there was no conversation, only the soft sound of the serving androids' footsteps on stones, the crackle of flames in the braziers, an occasional hint of night breeze overhead, and the sounds of our chewing.

As the androids removed our appetizer plates and brought in bowls of steaming black mussel bisque, the poet said, 'I understand that you met our ship today.'

'Yes,' I said. 'It was the Consul's private ship?'

'Of course.' Silenus gestured to an android, and bread was brought still hot from the oven. The smell of it mingled with the rising vapors from the bisque and the hint of autumn foliage on the breeze.

'And this is the ship you expect me to use to rescue the girl?' I said. I expected the poet to ask for my decision then.

Instead, he said, 'What do you think of the Pax, M. Endymion?'

I blinked, the spoon of bisque halfway to my mouth. 'The Pax?'

Silenus waited.

I set the spoon back and shrugged. 'I don't think much of it, I guess.'

'Not even after one of its courts sentenced you to death?'

Instead of sharing what I had been thinking earlier – how it had not been the Pax influence that sentenced me, but Hyperion's brand of frontier justice – I said, 'No. The Pax has been mostly irrelevant to my life.'

The old poet nodded and sipped his bisque. 'And the Church?'

'What about it, sir?'

'Has it been largely irrelevant to your life?'

'I guess so.' I realized that I was sounding like a tongue-tied adolescent, but these questions seemed less important than the question he was supposed to ask me, and the decision I was supposed to give him.

'I remember the first time we heard of the Pax,' he said. 'It was only a few months after Aenea disappeared. Church ships arrived in orbit, and troops seized Keats, Port Romance, Endymion, the university, all of the spaceports and important cities. Then they lifted off in combat skimmers, and we realized that they were after the cruciforms on the Pinion Plateau.'

I nodded. None of this was new information. The occupation of the Pinion Plateau and search for cruciforms had been the last great gamble of a dying Church, and the beginning of the Pax. It had been almost a century and a half before *real* Pax troops had arrived to occupy all of Hyperion and to order the evacuation of Endymion and other towns near the Plateau.

'But the ships which put in here during the expansion of the Pax,' continued the poet, 'what tales they brought! The Church's expansion from Pacem through the old Web worlds, then the Outback colonies . . .'

The androids removed the bisque bowls and returned with plates of carved fowl with pommery mustard sauce and a gratin of Kans River manta with caviar mousseline.

'Duck?' I said.

The poet showed his reconstituted teeth. 'It seemed appropriate after your . . . ah . . . trouble of the last week.'

I sighed and touched the slice of fowl with my fork. Moist vapors rose to my cheek and eyes. I thought of Izzy's eagerness as the ducks approached the open water. It seemed a lifetime ago. I looked at Martin Silenus and tried to imagine having centuries of memories to contend with. How could anyone stay sane with entire lifetimes stored in one human mind? The old poet was grinning at me in that wild way of his, and once again I wondered if he *was* sane.

'So we heard about the Pax and wondered what it would be like when it truly arrived,' he continued, chewing while he spoke. 'A theocracy . . . unthinkable during the centuries of the Hegemony. Religion then was, of course, purely personal choice – I belonged to a dozen religions and started more than one of my own during my days as a literary celebrity.' He looked at me with bright eyes. 'But of course you know that, Raul Endymion. You know the *Cantos*.'

I tasted the manta and said nothing.

'Most people I knew were Zen Christians,' he continued. 'More Zen than Christian, of course, but not too much of either, actually. Personal pilgrimages were fun. Places of power, finding one's baedecker point, all of that crap . . .' He chuckled. 'The Hegemony would never have dreamed of getting involved with religion, of course. The very thought of mixing government and religious opinion was barbaric . . . something one found on Qom-Riyadh or somesuch Outback desert world. And then came the Pax, with its glove of velvet and its cruciform of hope . . .'

'The Pax doesn't rule,' I said. 'It advises.'

'Precisely,' agreed the old man, pointing his fork at me while A. Bettik refilled his wineglass. 'The Pax advises. It does not rule. On hundreds of worlds the Church administers to the faithful and the Pax advises. But, of course, if you are a Christian who wishes to be born again, you will not ignore the advice of the Pax or the whispers of the Church, will you?'

I shrugged again. The influence of the Church had been a constant of life as long as I had been alive. There was nothing strange about it to me.

'But you are not a Christian who wishes to be born again, are you, M. Endymion?'

I looked at the old poet then, and a terrible suspicion formed in the back of my mind. *He somehow finessed my fake execution and transported me here when I should have been buried at sea by the authorities. He has clout with the Port Romance authorities. Could he have dictated my conviction and sentencing? Was all this some sort of test?*

'The question is,' he continued, ignoring my basilisk stare, '*why* are you not a Christian? Why do you not wish to be born again? Don't you enjoy life, Raul Endymion?'

'I enjoy life,' I said tersely.

'But you have not accepted the cross,' he continued. 'You have not accepted the gift of extended life.'

I put down my fork. An android servant interpreted that as a sign that I was finished and removed the plate of untouched duckling. 'I have not accepted the *cruciform*,' I snapped. How to explain the suspicion bred into my nomadic clan through generations of being the expatriates, the outsiders, the unsettled indigenies? How to explain the fierce independence of people like Grandam and my mother? How to explain the legacy of philosophical rigor and inbred skepticism passed on to me by my education and upbringing? I did not try.

Martin Silenus nodded as if I had explained. 'And you see the cruciform as something other than a miracle offered the faithful through the miraculous intercession of the Catholic Church?'

'I see the cruciform as a parasite,' I said, surprising myself by the vehemence in my voice.

'Perhaps you are afraid of losing . . . ah . . . your masculinity,' rasped the poet.

The androids brought in two swans sculpted of mocha chocolate and filled with highland branch-truffles and set them at our places. I ignored mine. In the *Cantos* the priest pilgrim – Paul Duré – tells his tale of discovering the lost tribe, the Bikura, and learning how they had survived centuries by a cruciform symbiote offered to them by the legendary Shrike. The cruciform resurrected them much as it did today in the era of the Pax, only in the priest's tale the side effects included irreversible brain damage after several resurrections and the disappearance of all sexual organs and impulses. The Bikura were retarded eunuchs – all of them.

'No,' I said. 'I know that the Church has somehow solved that problem.'

Silenus smiled. He looked like a mummified satyr when he did that. '*If* one has taken Communion and *if* one is resurrected under the auspices of the Church,' he rasped. 'Otherwise, even if one has somehow stolen a cruciform, his fate remains that of the Bikura.'

I nodded. Generations had attempted to steal immortality. Before the Pax sealed off the Plateau, adventurers smuggled out cruciforms. Other symbiotes had been stolen from the Church itself. The result had always been the same – idiocy and sexlessness. Only the Church held the secret of successful resurrection.

'So?' I said.

'So why has allegiance to the Church and a tithing of every tenth year of service to the Church been too high a price for you, my boy? Billions have opted for life.'

I sat in silence for a moment. Finally I said, 'Billions can do what they want. My life is important to me. I want to keep it . . . *mine.*'

This made no sense even to me, but the poet once again nodded as if I had explained matters to his satisfaction. He ate his chocolate swan while I watched. The androids removed our plates and filled our cups with coffee.

'All right,' the poet said, 'have you thought about my proposition?'

The question was so absurd that I had to stifle the urge to laugh. 'Yes,' I said at last. 'I've thought about it.'

'And?'

'And I have a few questions.'

Martin Silenus waited.

'What is in this for me?' I asked. 'You talk about the difficulty of my going back to a life here on Hyperion – lack of papers and all that – but you know I'm comfortable in the wilderness. It would be a hell of a lot easier for me to take off for the fens and avoid the Pax authorities than it would be to chase across space with your kid-friend in tow. Besides, to the Pax, I'm dead. I could go home to the moors and stay with my clan with no problem.'

Martin Silenus nodded.

After another moment of silence I said, 'So why should I even consider this nonsense?'

The old man smiled. 'You want to be a hero, Raul Endymion.'

I blew out my breath in derision and set my hands on the tablecloth. My fingers looked blunt and clumsy there, out of place against the fine linen.

'You want to be a hero,' he repeated. 'You want to be one of those rare human beings who make history, rather than merely watch it flow around them like water around a rock.'

'I don't know what you're talking about.' I did, of course, but there was no way he could know me that well.

'I *do* know you that well,' said Martin Silenus, seemingly responding to my thought rather than my last statement.

I should say here that I did not think for a second that the old man was telepathic. First of all, I do not believe in telepathy – or, rather, I did not at that time and secondly, I was more intrigued by the potential of a human being who had lived almost a thousand standard years. *Why, even if he were insane*, I thought, *it was possible that he had learned to read facial expressions and physical nuance to the point where the effect would be almost indistinguishable from telepathy!*

Or perhaps it was just a lucky guess.

'I don't want to be a hero,' I said flatly. 'I saw what happens to heroes when my brigade was sent to fight the rebels on the southern continent.'

'Ahh, Ursus,' he muttered. 'The south polar bear. Hyperion's most useless mass of ice and mud. I remember some rumors of a disturbance there.'

The war there had lasted eight Hyperion years and killed thousands of us local boys who were stupid enough to enlist in the Home Guard to fight there. Perhaps the old poet wasn't as astute as I was making him out to be.

'I don't mean hero as in the fools who throw themselves on plasma grenades,' he continued, licking his thin lips with a lizard's flick of tongue. 'I mean hero as in he whose prowess and beneficence is so legendary that he comes to be honored as a divinity. I mean hero in the literary sense, as in central protagonist given to forceful action. I mean hero as in he whose tragic flaws will be his undoing.' The poet paused and looked expectantly at me, but I stared back in silence.

'No tragic flaws?' he said at last. 'Or not given to forceful action?'

'I don't want to be a hero,' I said again.

The old man hunched over his coffee. When he looked up, his eyes held a mischievous glint. 'Where do you get your hair cut, boy?'

'Pardon me?'

He licked his lips again. 'You heard me. Your hair is long, but not wild. Where do you get it cut?'

I sighed and said, 'Sometimes, when I was in the fens for a long period, I'd cut it myself, but when I'm in Port Romance, I go to a little shop on Datoo Street.'

'Ahhhh,' said Silenus, settling back in his tall-backed chair. 'I know Datoo Street. It's in the Night District. More of an alley than a street. The open market there used to sell ferrets in gilded cages. There were street barbers, but the best barber*shop* there belonged to an old man named Palani Woo. He had six sons, and as each came of age, he would add another chair to the shop.' The old eyes raised to look at me, and once again I was struck by the power of personality there. 'That was a century ago,' he said.

'I get my hair cut at Woo's,' I said. 'Palani Woo's great-grandson, Kalakaua, owns the shop now. There are still six chairs.'

'Yes,' said the poet, nodding to himself. 'Not too much changes on our dear Hyperion, does it, Raul Endymion?'

'Is that your point?'

'Point?' he said, opening his hands as if showing that he had nothing so sinister as a point to hide. 'No point. Conversation, my boy. It amuses me to think of World Historical Figures, much less heroes of future myths, paying to get their hair cut. I thought of this centuries ago, by the way . . . this strange disconnection between the stuff of myth and the stuff of life. Do you know what "Datoo" means?'

I blinked at this sudden change of direction. 'No.'

'A wind out of Gibraltar. It carried a beautiful fragrance. Some of the artists and poets who founded Port Romance must have thought that the chalma and weirwood forests which covered the hills above the bog there smelled nice. Do you know what Gibraltar is, boy?'

'No.'

'A big rock on Earth,' rasped the old man. He showed his teeth again. 'Notice that I didn't say Old Earth.'

I had noticed.

'Earth is Earth, boy. I lived there before it disappeared, so I should know.'

The thought still made me dizzy.

'I want you to find it,' said the poet, his eyes gleaming.

'Find . . . it?' I repeated. 'Old Earth? I thought you wanted me to travel with the girl . . . Aenea.'

His bony hands waved away my sentence. 'You go with her and you'll find Earth, Raul Endymion.'

I nodded, all the while pondering the wisdom of explaining to him that Old Earth had been swallowed by the black hole dropped into its guts during the Big Mistake of '08. But, then, this ancient creature had fled from that shattered world. It made little sense to contradict his delusions. His *Cantos* had mentioned some plot by the warring AI TechnoCore to steal Old Earth – to spirit it away to the Magellanic Clouds – but that was fantasy. This was a separate *galaxy* . . . more than 160,000 light-years from the Milky Way, if I remembered correctly . . . and no ship, neither Pax nor Hegemony, had ever been sent farther than our small sphere in one spinal arm of *our* galaxy – and even with the Hawking-drive exclusion to Einsteinian realities, a trip to the Large Magellanic Cloud would take many centuries of shiptime and tens of thousands of years time-debt. Even the Ousters who savored the dark places between the stars would not undertake a voyage like that.

Besides, planets are not kidnapped.

'I want you to find Earth and bring it back,' continued the old poet. 'I want to see it again before I die. Will you do that for me, Raul Endymion?'

I looked the old man in the eye. 'Sure,' I said. 'Save this child from the Swiss Guard and the Pax, keep her safe until she becomes the One Who Teaches, find Old Earth and bring it back so you can see it again. Easy. Anything else?'

'Yes,' said Martin Silenus with the tone of absolute solemnity that comes with dementia, 'I want you to find out what the fuck the TechnoCore is up to and stop it.'

I nodded again. 'Find the missing TechnoCore and stop the combined power of thousands of godlike AIs from doing whatever they're planning to do,' I said, sarcasm dripping from my tongue. 'Check. Will do. Anything else?'

'Yes. You are to talk with the Ousters and see if they can offer me immortality . . . *true* immortality, not this born-again Christian bullshit.'

I pretended to write this on an invisible notepad. 'Ousters . . . immortality . . . not Christian bullshit. Can do. Check. Anything else?'

'Yes, Raul Endymion. I want the Pax destroyed and the Church's power toppled.'

I nodded. Two or three hundred known worlds had willingly joined the Pax. Trillions of humans had willingly been baptized in the Church. The Pax military was stronger than anything Hegemony Force had ever dreamed of at the height of its power. 'OK,' I said. 'I'll take care of that. Anything else?'

'Yes. I want you to stop the Shrike from hurting Aenea or wiping out humanity.'

I hesitated at this. According to the old man's own epic poem, the Shrike had been destroyed by the soldier Fedmahn Kassad in some future era. Knowing the futility of projecting logic into a demented conversation, I still mentioned this.

'Yes!' snapped the old poet. 'But that is *then*. Millennia from now. I want you to stop the Shrike *now*.'

'All right,' I said. Why argue?

Martin Silenus slumped back in his chair, his energy seemingly dissipated, I glimpsed the animated mummy again in the folds of skin, the sunken eyes, the bony fingers. But those eyes still blazed with intensity. I tried to imagine the force of this man's personality when he'd been in his prime: I could not.

Silenus nodded and A. Bettik brought two glasses and poured champagne.

'Then you accept, Raul Endymion?' asked the poet, his voice strong and formal. 'You accept this mission to save Aenea, travel with her, and accomplish these other things?'

'With one condition,' I said.

Silenus frowned and waited.

'I want to take A. Bettik with me,' I said. The android still stood by the table. The champagne bottle was in his hand. His gaze was aimed straight forward, and he did not turn to look at either of us or register any emotion.

The poet showed surprise. 'My android? Are you serious?'

'I am serious.'

'A. Bettik has been with me since before your great-great-grandmother had tits,' rasped the poet. His bony hand slammed down on the table hard enough to make me worry about brittle bones. 'A. Bettik,' he snapped. 'You wish to go?'

The blue-skinned man nodded without turning his head.

'Fuck it,' said the poet. 'Take him. Do you want anything else, Raul Endymion? My hoverchair, perhaps? My respirator? My teeth?'

'Nothing else,' I said.

'And so, Raul Endymion,' said the poet, his voice formal once again, 'do you accept this mission? Will you save, serve, and protect the child Aenea until her destiny is fulfilled . . . or die trying?'

'I accept,' I said.

Martin Silenus lifted his wineglass and I matched the motion. Too late, I thought that the android should be drinking with us, but by then the old poet was giving his toast.

'To folly,' he said. 'To divine madness. To insane quests and messiahs crying from the desert. To the death of tyrants. To confusion to our enemies.'

I started to raise the glass to my lips, but the old man was not done.

'To heroes,' he said. 'To heroes who get their hair cut.' He drank the champagne in one gulp.

And so did I.

NINE

Born again, seeing – literally – with the wondering eyes of a child, Father Captain Federico de Soya crosses the Piazza San Pietro between the elegant arcs of Bernini's colonnade and approaches St Peter's basilica. The day is beautiful with cold sunlight, pale-blue skies, and a chill in the air – Pacem's single inhabitable continent is high, fifteen hundred meters above standard sea level, and the air is thin but absurdly rich in oxygen – and everything de Soya sees is bathed in rich afternoon light that creates an aura around the stately columns, around the heads of the hurrying people; light that bathes the marble statues in white and brings out the brilliance of the red robes of bishops and the blue, red, and orange stripes of the Swiss Guard troopers standing at parade rest; light that paints the tall obelisk in the center of the plaza, the fluted pilasters of the basilica's facade, and ignites into brilliance the great dome itself, rising more than a hundred meters above the level of the plaza. Pigeons take wing and catch this rich, horizontal light as they wheel above the plaza, their wings now white against the sky, now dark against the glowing dome of St Peter's. Throngs move by on either side, simple clerics in black cassocks with pink buttons, the bishops in white with red trimming, cardinals in blood-scarlet and deep magenta, citizens of the Vatican in their ink-black doublets, hose, and white ruffs, nuns in rustling habits and soaring white gull wings, male and female priests in simple black, Pax officers in dress uniforms of scarlet and black such as de Soya himself wears this day, and a scattering of lucky tourists or civilian guests – privileged to attend a papal Mass – dressed in their finest clothes, most in black, but all of a richness in cloth that makes even the blackest fiber gleam and shimmer in the light. The multitudes move toward the soaring basilica of St Peter's, their conversation muted, their demeanor excited but somber. A papal Mass is a serious event.

With Father Captain de Soya this day – only four days after his fatal leave-taking from Task Force MAGI and three days after his resurrection – are Father Baggio, Captain Marget Wu, and Monsignor Lucas Oddi. Baggio, plump and pleasant, is de Soya's resurrection chaplain; Wu, lean and silent, is aide-de-camp to Pax Fleet Admiral Marusyn; and Oddi, eighty-seven standard years old but still healthy and alert, is the factotum and Undersecretary to the powerful Vatican Secretary of State, Simon Augustino Cardinal Lourdusamy. It is said that Cardinal Lourdusamy is the second most powerful human being in the Pax, the only member of the Roman Curia to have the ear of His Holiness, and a person of frightening brilliance.

The Cardinal's power is reflected in the fact that he also acts as Prefect for the *Sacra Congregatio pro Gentium Evangelizatione se de Propaganda Fide* – the legendary Congregation for the Evangelization of Peoples, or *De Propaganda Fide*.

To Father Captain de Soya, the presence of these two powerful people is no more surprising or astounding than the sunlight on the facade above him as the four climb the broad steps to the basilica. The crowd, already quiet, stills to silence as they file through into the vast space, walk past more Swiss Guard in both ornamental and battle dress, and move into the nave. Here even the silence echoes, and de Soya is moved to tears at the beauty of the great space and of the timeless works of art they pass on the way to the pews: Michelangelo's *Pietà* visible in the first chapel to the right; Arnolfo di Cambio's ancient bronze of St Peter, its right foot polished to the point of being worn away by centuries of kisses, and – lit brilliantly from beneath – the striking figure of Guiliana Falconieri Santa Vergine, sculpted by Pietro Campi in the sixteenth century, more than fifteen hundred years earlier.

Father Captain de Soya is weeping openly by the time he crosses himself with holy water and follows Father Baggio into their reserved pew. The three male priests and the female Pax officer kneel in prayer as the last scuffling and coughing dies in the vast space. The basilica is in near darkness now, with only pinpoint halogen spots illuminating the art and architectural treasures glowing like gold. Through his tears de Soya looks at the fluted pilasters and the dark bronze baroque columns of Bernini's *Baldacchino* – the gilded and ornate canopy over the central altar where only the Pope can say Mass – and contemplates the wonder of the last twenty-four hours since his resurrection. There has been pain, yes, and confusion – as if he were recovering from a particularly disorientating blow to the head – and the pain was more general and terrible than any headache, as if every cell in his body remembered the indignity of death and even now rebelled against it – but there has been wonder as well. Wonder and awe at the smallest things: the taste of the broth Father Baggio had fed him, the first sight of Pacem's pale-blue sky through the rectory windows, the overwhelming humanness of the faces he had seen that day, the voices he had heard. Father Captain de Soya, although a sensitive man, has not wept since he was a child of five or six standard years, but he weeps this day . . . weeps openly and unashamedly. Jesus Christ has given him the gift of life for the second time, the Lord God has shared the Sacrament of Resurrection with him – this faithful, honorable man from a poor family on a backwater world – and de Soya's individual cells now seem to remember the sacrament of rebirth as well as the pain of death; he is suffused with joy.

The Mass begins in an explosion of glory – trumpet notes cutting through the expectant silence like golden blades, choral voices raised in triumphant song, ascending organ notes reverberating in the great space, and then a series of brilliant lights switching on to illuminate the Pope and his retinue as they emerge to celebrate Mass.

59

De Soya's first impression is of how young the Holy Father is: Pope Julius XIV is, of course, a young man in his thirties, despite the fact that he has been Pope almost continuously for more than two hundred and fifty years, his reign broken only by his own death and rebirth for eight coronations, first as Julius VI – following the eight-year reign of the antipope, Teilhard I – and again as Julius in each succeeding incarnation. As de Soya watches the vital young man celebrate Mass, the Pax captain thinks of the story of Julius's ascendancy – learned through both official Church history and the banned poem the *Cantos*, which every literate teenager reads at the risk of his soul, but reads nonetheless.

In both versions Pope Julius had been, prior to his first resurrection, a young man named Lenar Hoyt, who had come to the priesthood in the shadow of Paul Duré, a charismatic Jesuit archaeologist and theologian. Duré had been a proponent of St Teilhard's teachings that humankind had the potential to evolve toward the Godhead – indeed, according to Duré when he ascended to the Throne of St Peter after the Fall, humans could evolve *to* the Godhead. It was precisely this heresy which Father Lenar Hoyt, after becoming Pope Julius VI, had worked to wipe out after his first resurrection.

Both accounts – Church history and the forbidden *Cantos* – agreed that it had been Father Duré, during his exile on the Outback world of Hyperion, who had discovered the symbiote called the cruciform. There the histories diverged beyond reconciliation. According to the poem, Duré had received the cruciform from the alien creature called the Shrike. According to the Church's teachings, the Shrike – a representation of Satan if ever there was one – had nothing to do with the discovery of the cruciform, but had later tempted both Father Duré and Father Hoyt. The Church's history reported that only Duré had succumbed to the creature's treachery. The *Cantos* told, in their confused mix of pagan mythology and garbled history, of how Duré had crucified himself in the flame forests of Hyperion's Pinion Plateau rather than return the cruciform to the Church. According to the pagan poet, Martin Silenus, this was to save the Church from reliance on a parasite in the place of faith. According to the Church history, which de Soya believed, Duré had crucified himself to end the pain the symbiote caused him and, in alliance with the Shrike demon, to prevent the Church – which Duré considered his enemy after having excommunicated him for falsifying archaeological records – from regaining its vitality through the discovery of the Sacrament of Resurrection.

According to both stories, Father Lenar Hoyt had traveled to Hyperion in search of his friend and former mentor. According to the blasphemous *Cantos*, Hoyt had accepted Duré's cruciform as well as his own, but had later returned to Hyperion in the last days before the Fall to beg the evil Shrike to relieve him of his burden. The Church pointed out the falseness of that, explaining how Father Hoyt had courageously returned to face down the demon in its own lair. Whatever the interpretation, facts recorded that Hoyt had died during that last pilgrimage to Hyperion. Duré had been resurrected carrying Father Hoyt's cruciform as well as his own, and had then returned during the chaos of the Fall to become the first antipope in modern history. Duré/Teilhard I's nine standard years of heresy had been a low point for the Church, but after the false pope's death by accident, Lenar Hoyt's resurrection from the shared body had led to the glory of Julius VI, the discovery of the sacramental nature of what Duré had called a parasite, Julius's revelation from God – still understood only by the innermost sancta of the Church – of how the resurrections could be guided to success, and the subsequent growth of the Church from a minor sect to the official faith of humanity.

Father Captain Federico de Soya watches the Pope – seemingly a man younger than himself – lift the Eucharist high above the altar, and the Pax commander shivers in the chill of sheer wonder.

Father Baggio had explained that the overwhelming sense of newness and wonder that was the after effect of Holy Resurrection would wear off to some extent in the days and weeks to come, but that the essential feeling of well-being would always linger, growing stronger with each rebirth in Christ. De Soya could see why the Church held suicide as one of its most mortal sins – punishable by immediate excommunication – since the glow of nearness to God was so much stronger after tasting the ashes of death. Resurrection could easily become addictive if the punishment for suicide were not so terrible.

Still aching from the pain of death and rebirth, his mind and senses literally lurching from vertigo, Father Captain de Soya watches the papal Mass approach the climax of Communion, St Peter's basilica filling now with the same burst of sound and glory with which the service began, and – knowing that in a moment he will taste the Body and Blood of Christ as transubstantiated by the Holy Father himself – the warrior weeps like a little child.

After the Mass, in the cool of the evening, with the sky above St Peter's the color of pale porcelain, Father Captain de Soya walks with his new friends in the shadows of the Vatican Gardens.

'Federico,' Father Baggio is saying, 'the meeting we are about to have is very important. Very, very important. Is your mind clear enough to understand the important things that will be said?'

'Yes,' says de Soya. 'My mind is very clear.'

Monsignor Lucas Oddi touches the young Pax officer's shoulder. 'Federico, my son, you are certain of this? We can wait another day if we must.'

De Soya shakes his head. His mind is reeling with the beauty and solemnity of the Mass he has just witnessed, his tongue still tastes the perfection of the Eucharist and the wine, he feels that Christ is whispering to him at this very moment, but his thoughts are clear. 'I am ready,' he says. Captain Wu is a silent shadow behind Oddi.

'Very good,' says the Monsignor, and nods to Father Baggio. 'We will need your services no longer, Father. Thank you.'

Baggio nods, bows slightly, and leaves without another word. In his perfect clarity, de Soya realizes that he will never see his kindly resurrection chaplain again, and a surge of pure love brings more tears to his eyes. He is grateful to the darkness that hides these tears; he knows he must be in control for the meeting. He wonders where this important conference will be held – in the fabled Borgia Apartment? In the Sistine Chapel? In the Vatican Offices of the Holy See? Perhaps in the Pax Liaison offices in what had once been called the Borgia Tower.

Monsignor Lucas Oddi stops at the far end of the gardens, waves the others to a stone bench near where another man waits, and Father de Soya realizes that the seated man is Cardinal Lourdusamy and that the conference is happening here, in the scented gardens. The priest goes to his knee on the gravel in front of the Monsignor and kisses the ring on the extended hand.

'Rise,' says Cardinal Lourdusamy. He is a large man with a round face and heavy jowls, and his deep voice sounds like the voice of God to de Soya. 'Be seated,' says the Cardinal.

De Soya sits on the stone bench as the others remain standing. To the Cardinal's left, another man sits in the shadows. De Soya can make out a Pax uniform in the dim light but not the insignia. He is vaguely aware of other people – at least one seated and several standing – within the deeper shadows of a bower to their left.

'Father de Soya,' begins Simon Augustino Cardinal Lourdusamy, nodding toward the seated man on his left, 'may I present Fleet Admiral William Lee Marusyn.'

De Soya is on his feet in an instant, saluting, holding himself at rigid attention. 'My apologies, Admiral,' he manages through clenched jaws. 'I did not recognize you, sir.'

'At ease,' says Marusyn. 'Be seated, Captain.'

De Soya takes his seat again, but gingerly now, awareness of the company he is in burning through the joyous fog of resurrection like hot sunlight.

'We are well pleased with you, Captain,' says Admiral Marusyn.

'Thank you, sir,' mumbles de Soya, glancing around the shadows again. There are definitely others watching from the bower.

'As are we,' rumbles Cardinal Lourdusamy. 'That is why we have chosen you for this mission.'

'Mission, Your Excellency?' says de Soya. He feels dizzy with tension and confusion.

'As always, you will be serving both the Pax and the Church,' says the Admiral, leaning closer in the dim light. The world of Pacem has no moon, but the starlight here is very bright as de Soya's eyes adapt to the dim light. Somewhere a small bell rings monks to Vespers. Lights from the Vatican buildings bathe the dome of St Peter's in a soft glow.

'As always,' continues the Cardinal, 'you will report to both the Church and the military authorities.' The huge man pauses and glances at the Admiral.

'What is my mission, Your Excellency? Admiral?' asks de Soya, not knowing which man to address. Marusyn is his ultimate superior, but Pax officers usually defer to high officials of the Church.

Neither man answers, but Marusyn nods toward Captain Marget Wu, who stands several meters away near a hedge. The Pax officer steps forward quickly and hands de Soya a holocube.

'Activate it,' says Admiral Marusyn.

De Soya touches the underside of the small ceramic block. The image of a female child mists into existence above the cube. De Soya rotates the image, noticing the girl's dark hair, large eyes, and intense gaze. The child's dis-embodied head and neck are the brightest things in the darkness of the Vatican Gardens. Father de Soya looks up and sees the glow from the holo in the eyes of the Cardinal and the Admiral.

'Her name . . . well, we are not sure of her name,' says Cardinal Lourdusamy. 'How old does she look to you, Father?'

De Soya looks back at the image, considers her age, and converts the years to standard. 'Perhaps twelve?' he guesses. He has spent little time around children since he was one. 'Eleven? Standard.'

Cardinal Lourdusamy nods. 'She was eleven, standard, on Hyperion, when she disappeared more than two hundred and sixty-seven standard years ago, Father.'

De Soya looks back at the holo. So the child is probably dead – he could not remember if the Pax had brought the Sacrament of Resurrection to Hyperion two hundred and sixty years ago – or certainly grown and reborn. He wonders why they are showing him a holo of this person as a child from centuries ago. He waits.

'This child is the daughter of a woman named Brawne Lamia,' says Admiral Marusyn. 'Does the name mean anything to you, Father?'

It does, but for a moment de Soya cannot think why. Then the verses of the *Cantos* come to mind, and he remembers the female pilgrim in that story.

'Yes,' he says. 'I remember the name. She was one of the pilgrims with His Holiness during that final pilgrimage before the Fall.'

Cardinal Lourdusamy leans closer and folds pudgy hands together on his knee. His robe is bright red where the light from the holo touches it. 'Brawne Lamia had sexual intercourse with an abomination,' rumbles the Cardinal. 'A cybrid. A cloned human construct whose mind was an artificial intelligence residing in the TechnoCore. Do you remember the history and the banned poem?'

Father de Soya blinks. Is it possible that they have brought him here to the Vatican to punish him for reading the *Cantos* when he was a child? He confessed the sin twenty years ago, did penance, and never reread the forbidden work. He blushes.

Cardinal Lourdusamy chuckles. 'It is all right, my son. Everyone in the Church has committed this particular sin . . . Curiosity is too great, the appeal of the forbidden too strong . . . We have all read the banned poem. Do you remember that the woman Lamia had carnal relations with the cybrid of John Keats?'

'Vaguely,' says de Soya, then hurriedly adds, 'Your Excellency.'

'And do you know who John Keats was, my son?'

'No, Your Excellency.'

'He was a pre-Hegira poet,' says the Cardinal in his rumble of a voice. High overhead, the blue-plasma braking tails of three Pax dropships cut across the starfield. Father Captain de Soya does not even have to glance at them to recognize the make and armament of the ships. He is not surprised that he had not remembered the details of the poet's name from the forbidden *Cantos*: even as a boy, Federico de Soya had been more interested in reading about machines and great space battles than anything pre-Hegira, especially poetry.

'The woman in the blasphemous poem – Brawne Lamia – not only had intercourse with the cybrid abomination,' continued the Cardinal, 'but she bore the creature's child.'

De Soya raises his eyebrows. 'I did not know that cybrids . . . I mean . . . I thought that they were . . . well . . .'

Cardinal Lourdusamy chuckles. 'Were sterile?' he says. 'Like androids? No . . . the AI obscenities had cloned the man. And the man impregnated this daughter of Eve.'

De Soya nods, although all this talk of cybrids and androids might as well be about griffins and unicorns for all he is concerned. These things existed once. To his knowledge, none could exist today. Father Captain de Soya's mind races as he tries to imagine just what in God's universe all this talk of dead poets and pregnant women might have to do with him.

As if answering de Soya's mental query, Admiral Marusyn says, 'The girl whose image floats in front of you is that child, Captain. After the cybrid abomination was destroyed, this child was born to Brawne Lamia on the world of Hyperion.'

'She was not fully . . . human,' whispers Cardinal Lourdusamy. 'Although the body of her . . . father . . . the Keats cybrid . . . was destroyed, his AI persona was stored in a Schrön Loop shunt.'

Admiral Marusyn also leans closer, as if this information is for just the three of them. 'We believe that this child communicated with the Keats persona trapped in that Schrön Loop even before she was born,' he says softly. 'We are almost certain that this . . . fetus . . . was in touch with the TechnoCore via that cybrid persona.'

De Soya feels and ignores an impulse to cross himself. His reading, instruction, and faith have taught him that the TechnoCore had been evil incarnate, simply the most active manifestation of the Evil One in modern human history. The destruction of the TechnoCore had been the salvation of not only the beleaguered Church, but of humanity itself. De Soya tries to imagine what an unborn human soul would learn from direct contact with those disembodied, soulless intelligences.

'The child is dangerous,' whispers Cardinal Lourdusamy. 'Even though the TechnoCore was banished by the Fall of the farcasters, even though the Church no longer allows soulless machines to have true intelligence, this child has been programmed as an agent of those fallen AIs . . . an agent of the Evil One.'

De Soya rubs his cheek. He is suddenly very tired. 'You speak as though she is still alive,' he says softly. 'And still a child.'

Cardinal Lourdusamy's silken robes rustle as he shifts position. His voice is an ominous baritone. 'She lives,' he says. 'She is still a child.'

De Soya looks back at the young girl's holo as it floats between them. He touches the cube and the image fades. 'Cryogenic storage?' he says.

'On Hyperion there are Time Tombs,' rumbles Lourdusamy. 'One of them – a thing called the Sphinx, which you may remember from the poem or Church history – has been used as a portal across time. No one knows how it works. For most people, it does not work at all.' The Cardinal glances at the Admiral and then back to the priest-captain before him. 'This child disappeared in the Sphinx some two hundred and sixty-three standard years ago. We knew at the time that she was dangerous to the Pax, but we arrived days late. We have reliable information that she will emerge from that tomb in less than a standard month . . . still a child. Still lethally dangerous to the Pax.'

'Dangerous to the Pax . . .' repeats de Soya. He does not understand.

'His Holiness has foreseen this danger,' rumbles Cardinal Lourdusamy. 'Almost three centuries ago Our Lord saw fit to reveal to His Holiness the threat this poor child represents, and the Holy Father has now moved to deal with this danger.'

'I don't understand,' confesses Father Captain de Soya. The holo is off, but he can still see the innocent face of the child in his mind. 'How can this little girl be a danger . . . then or now?'

Cardinal Lourdusamy squeezes de Soya's forearm. 'As an agent of the TechnoCore, she will be a virus introduced into the Body of Christ. It has been revealed to His Holiness that the girl will have powers . . . powers that are not human. One of these powers is the power to persuade the faithful to leave the light of God's teachings, to abandon salvation for service to the Evil One.'

De Soya nods, although he does not understand. His forearm aches from the pressure of Lourdusamy's powerful hand. 'What do you wish of me, Your Excellency?'

Admiral Marusyn answers in a loud voice that shocks de Soya after all of the soft tones and whispering. 'As of this moment,' snaps Marusyn, 'you are detached from your Fleet assignment, Father Captain de Soya. As of this moment, you are assigned to find and return this child . . . this girl . . . to the Vatican.'

The Cardinal seems to catch a glint of anxiety in de Soya's eyes. 'My son,' he says, his deep voice soothing now, 'are you afraid the child might be harmed?'

'Yes, Your Excellency.' De Soya wonders if this admission will disqualify him from service.

Lourdusamy's touch lightens, becomes a friendlier grip. 'Be assured, my son, that no one in the Holy See . . . no one in the Pax . . . has any intention of harming this little girl. Indeed, the Holy Father has instructed us . . .

has instructed you . . . to make it your second-highest priority that no harm shall come to her.'

'Your first priority,' says the Admiral, 'is to return her here . . . to Pacem. To Pax Command here in the Vatican.'

De Soya nods and swallows. The question foremost in his mind is *Why me?* Aloud, he says, 'Yes, sir. I understand.'

'You will receive a papal-authority diskey,' continues the Admiral. 'You may requisition any materials, help, liaison or personnel it is in the power of local Pax authorities to provide. Do you have any questions about that?'

'No, sir.' De Soya's voice is firm, but his mind is reeling. A papal-authority diskey would give him more power than that bestowed on Pax planetary governors.

'You will translate to Hyperion system this very day,' continues Admiral Marusyn in the same brisk, no-nonsense voice of command. 'Captain Wu?'

The Pax military aide steps forward and hands de Soya a red action portfolio disk. The father-captain nods, but his mind is screaming, *To Hyperion system this day . . . The archangel courier ship! To die again. The pain. No, sweet Jesus, dear Lord. Let this cup pass from me!*

'You will have command of our newest and most advanced courier ship, Captain,' Marusyn is saying. 'It is similar to the one which brought you to Pacem system, except that it can hold six passengers, it is armed to the level of your former torchship, and it has an automated resurrection system.'

'Yes, sir,' says de Soya. *An automated resurrection system?* he thinks. *Is the sacrament to be administered by a machine?*

Cardinal Lourdusamy pats his arm again. 'The robot system is regrettable, my son. But the ship may carry you to places where the Pax and the Church do not exist. We cannot deny you resurrection simply because you are beyond the reach of God's servants. Be assured, my son, that the Holy Father himself has blessed this resurrection equipment and ordained it with the same sacramental imperative a true Resurrection Mass would offer.'

'Thank you, Your Excellency,' de Soya mumbles. 'But I do not under-stand . . . places beyond the Church . . . Did you not say that I was to travel to Hyperion? I have never been there, but I thought that this world was a member of . . .'

'It belongs to the Pax,' interrupts the Admiral. 'But if you are unsuccessful in capturing . . .' He pauses. 'In *rescuing* this child . . . if for some unfore-seen reason you must follow her to other worlds, other systems . . . we thought it best that the ship have an automated resurrection creche for you.'

De Soya bows his head in obedience and confusion.

'But we expect you to find the child on Hyperion,' continues Admiral Marusyn. 'When you arrive on that world, you will introduce yourself and show your papal diskey to Groundforce Commander Barnes-Avne. The Commander is in charge of the Swiss Guard Brigade that has been pre-positioned on Hyperion, and upon your arrival you will be in effective command of those troops.'

De Soya blinks. *Command of a Swiss Guard Brigade? I am a Fleet torchship captain! I wouldn't know a groundforce maneuver from a cavalry charge!*

Admiral Marusyn chuckles. 'We understand that this is a bit out of your regular line of duty, Father Captain de Soya, but be assured that your command status is necessary. Commander Barnes-Avne will continue day-to-day command of groundforces, but it is imperative that all resources be bent to the rescue of this child.'

De Soya clears his throat. 'What will happen to . . . You say that we do not know her name? The child, I mean.'

'Before she disappeared,' rumbles Cardinal Lourdusamy, 'she called herself Aenea. And as for what will happen to her . . . again, I reassure you, my son, our intentions are to prevent her from infecting the Body of Christ in the Pax from her virus, but we will do so without harming her. Indeed, our mission . . . *your* mission . . . is to save the child's immortal soul. The Holy Father himself will see to that.'

Something in the Cardinal's voice makes de Soya realize that the conference is over. The father-captain stands, sensing the resurrection displacement shifting inside him like a vertigo. *I must die again within the day!* Still joyous, he nonetheless feels like weeping.

Admiral Marusyn is also standing. 'Father Captain de Soya, your reassignment to this mission is effective until the child is delivered unto me, here at the Vatican military liaison office.'

'Within weeks, we are sure,' rumbles Cardinal Lourdusamy, still seated.

'This is a great and terrible responsibility,' says the Admiral. 'You must use every ounce of your faith and your abilities to carry out His Holiness's expressed wish to bring this child safely to the Vatican – *before* the destructive virus of her programmed treachery is spread among our Brothers and Sisters in Christ. We know that you will not let us down, Father Captain de Soya.'

'Thank you, sir,' says de Soya, and thinks again, *Why me?* He kneels to kiss the Cardinal's ring and rises to find that the Admiral has stepped back in the darkness of the bower where the other shadowy figures have not stirred.

Monsignor Lucas Oddi and Pax Captain Marget Wu move to either side of de Soya and act as escorts as they turn to leave the garden. It is then, his mind still lurching in confusion and shock, his heart pounding with eagerness and terror at the important service set before him, that Father Captain de Soya glances back just as a rising dropship's plasma tail lights the dome of St Peter's, the rooftops of the Vatican and the garden with its pulse of blue flame. For an instant the figures within the arched shadow of the bower are clearly visible, illuminated by the strobe of blue plasma light. Admiral Marusyn is there, already turned away from de Soya, as are two standing Swiss Guard officers in combat armor, their flechette weapons raised at port arms. But it is the seated figure illuminated for that instant who will haunt de Soya's dreams and thoughts for years to come.

Seated there on the garden bench, his sad eyes locked firmly on de Soya's retreating form, his high brow and mournful countenance painted briefly but indelibly in blue plasma glow, is His Holiness Pope Julius XIV, the Holy Father to more than six hundred billion faithful Catholics, the de facto ruler of four hundred billion more scattered souls in the far-flung Pax, and the man who has just launched Federico de Soya on his fateful voyage.

TEN

It was the morning after our banquet, and we were in the spaceship again. That is, the android A. Bettik and I were in the ship, having walked there the convenient way through the tunnel connecting the two towers; Martin Silenus was present as a hologram. It was a strange holographic image, since the old poet chose to have the transmitter or the ship's computer represent him as a younger version of himself – an ancient satyr, still, but one who stood on his own legs and had hair on his sharp-eared head. I looked at the poet with his maroon cape, full-sleeved blouse, balloon trousers, and floppy beret, and realized what a dandy he must have been when those clothes had been in fashion. I was looking at Martin Silenus as he must have appeared when he had returned to Hyperion as a pilgrim three centuries earlier.

'Do you just want to stare at me like some fucking yokel,' said the holographic image, 'or do you want to finish the fucking tour so we can get on with business?' The old man was either hungover from the previous night's wine or had regained enough health to be in an even more vicious mood than usual.

'Lead on,' I said.

From our tunnel we had taken the ship's lift up to the lowest air lock. A. Bettik and the poet's holo led me through the ascending levels: the engine room with its indecipherable instruments and webs of pipes and cables; then the cold-sleep level – four cryogenic-fugue couches in their supercooled cubbies (one couch missing, I discovered, since Martin Silenus had removed it for his own purposes); then the central air-lock corridor I had entered by the day before – the 'wood' walls concealing a multitude of storage lockers holding such things as spacesuits, all-terrain vehicles, sky-bikes, and even some archaic weapons; then the living area with its Stein-way and holopit; then up the spiral staircase again to what A. Bettik called the 'navigation room' – there was indeed a cubby with some electronic navigation instruments visible – but which I saw as the library with shelf after shelf of books – real books, print books – and several couches and daybeds next to windows in the ship's hull; and finally up the stairs to the apex of the ship, which was simply a round bedroom with a single bed in the center of it.

'The Consul used to enjoy watching the weather from here while listening to music,' said Martin Silenus. 'Ship?'

The arching bulkhead around the circular room went transparent, as did the bow of the ship above us. There were only the dark stones of the tower interior around us, but from above there fell a filtered light through the rotting roof of the silo. Soft music suddenly filled the room. It was a piano, unaccompanied, and the melody was ancient and haunting.

'Czerchyvik?' I guessed.

The old poet snorted. 'Rachmaninoff.' The satyrish features seemed suddenly mellow in the dim light. 'Can you guess who's playing?'

I listened. The pianist was very good. I had no idea who it was.

'The Consul,' said A. Bettik. The android's voice was very soft.

Martin Silenus grunted. 'Ship . . . opaque.' The walls solidified. The old poet's holo disappeared from its place by the bulkhead and flashed into existence near the spiral stairs. He kept doing that, and the effect was disconcerting. 'Well, if we're finished with the fucking tour, let's go down to the living room and figure out how to outsmart the Pax.'

The maps were the old kind – ink on paper – and they were spread out across the top of the gleaming grand piano. The continent of Aquila spread its wings above the keyboard, and the horse head of Equus curled as a separate map above. Martin Silenus's holo strode on powerful legs to the piano and stabbed a finger down about where the horse's eye should be. 'Here,' he said. 'And here.' The massless finger made no noise against the paper. 'The Pope's got his fucking troops all the way from Chronos Keep here' – the weightless finger jabbed at a point where the Bridle Range of mountains came to their easternmost point behind the eye – 'all the way down the snout. They have aircraft here, at Sad King Billy's cursed city' – the finger pounded silently at a point only a few kilometers northwest of the Valley of the Time Tombs – 'and have massed the Swiss Guard in the Valley itself.'

I looked at the map. Except for the abandoned Poet's City and the Valley, the eastern fourth of Equus had been empty desert and out of bounds for anyone except Pax troops for more than two centuries. 'How do you know the Swiss Guard troops are there?' I asked.

The satyr's brows arched. 'I have my sources,' he said.

'Do your sources tell you the units and armament?'

The holo made a noise that sounded as if the old man were going to spit on the carpet. 'You don't need to know the units,' he snapped. 'Suffice it to say that there are thirty thousand soldiers between you and the Sphinx where Aenea will step out tomorrow. Three thousand of those troops are Swiss Guard. Now, how are you going to get through them?'

I felt like laughing aloud. I doubted if the entire Home Guard of Hyperion, with air and space support, could 'get through' half a dozen Swiss Guard. Their weapons, training, and defensive systems were that good. Instead of laughing, I studied the map again.

'You say that aircraft are staging out of the Poet's City . . . Do you know the type of planes?'

The poet shrugged. 'Fighters. EMVs don't work worth shit here, of course, so they've brought in thrust-reaction planes. Jets, I think.'

'Scram, ram, pulse, or air breathing?' I said. I was trying to sound as if I knew what I was talking about, but my military knowledge gleaned in the Home Guard had been centered on fieldstripping my weapon, cleaning my weapon, firing my weapon, marching through nasty weather without getting my weapon wet, trying to get a few hours' sleep when I wasn't marching, cleaning, or fieldstripping, trying not to freeze to death when I was asleep, and – upon occasion – keeping my head down so that I wouldn't get killed by Ursus snipers.

'What the fuck does it matter what kind of planes?' growled Martin Silenus. Losing three centuries in appearance certainly had not mellowed him. 'They're fighters. We've clocked them at . . . Ship? What the fuck was the speed we clocked those last blips at?'

'Mach three,' said the ship.

'Mach three,' repeated the poet. 'Fast enough to fly down here, firebomb this place to ashes, and be back to the north continent before their beers get warm.'

I looked up from the map. 'I've been meaning to ask,' I said. 'Why don't they?'

The poet's head turned my way. 'Why don't they what?'

'Fly down here, firebomb you to ashes, and be home before their beer is warm,' I said. 'You're a threat to them. Why do they tolerate you?'

Martin Silenus grunted. 'I'm dead. They think I'm dead. How could a dead man be a threat to anyone?'

I sighed and looked back at the map. 'There has to be a troopship in orbit, but I don't suppose you know what kind of craft escorted it here?'

Surprisingly, it was the ship who replied. 'The troopship is a three-hundred-thousand-ton *Akira*-class spinship,' came the soft voice. 'It was escorted by two standard Pax-class torchships – the *Saint Anthony* and the *Saint Bonaventure*. There is also a C^3 ship in high orbit.'

'What the fuck is a C^3 ship?' grumbled the poet's holo.

I glanced at him. How could anyone live for a thousand years and not learn such a basic thing? Poets were strange. 'Command, communications, control,' I said.

'So the Pax SOB who's in charge is up there?' asks Silenus.

I rubbed my cheek and stared at the map. 'Not necessarily,' I said. 'The commander of the space task force will be there, but the head of operations may be on the ground. The Pax trains its commanders for combined operations. With so many of the Swiss Guard here, someone important is in command on the ground.'

'All right,' said the poet. 'How are you going to get through them and get my little friend out?'

'Excuse me,' said the ship, 'but there is an additional spacecraft in orbit. It arrived about three weeks ago, standard, and sent a dropship to the Valley of the Time Tombs.'

'What kind of ship?' I asked.

There was the briefest hesitation. 'I do not know,' said the ship. 'The configuration is strange to me. Small . . . perhaps courier-sized . . . but the propulsion profile is . . . strange.'

'It probably is a courier,' I said to Silenus. 'Poor bugger's been stuck in cryogenic fugue for months, paying years of time-debt, just to deliver some message Pax Central forgot to give the commander before he or she left.'

The poet's holographic hand brushed at the map again. 'Stick to the subject. How do you get Aenea away from these motherhumpers?'

I stepped away from the piano. My voice held anger when I spoke. 'How the hell should I know? You're the one who's had two and a half centuries to plan this stupid escape.' I waved my hand, indicating the ship. 'I presume this thing is our ticket to outrunning the torchships.' I paused. 'Ship? *Can* you outrun a Pax torchship to C-plus translation?' All Hawking drives provided the same pseudo-velocity above light-speed, of course, so our escape and survival, or capture and destruction, depended upon the race to that quantum point.

'Oh, yes,' said the ship immediately. 'Parts of my memory are missing, but I am aware that the Consul had me modified during a visit to an Ouster colony.'

'An Ouster colony?' I repeated stupidly. My skin prickled, despite logic. I had grown up fearing another Ouster invasion. Ousters were the ultimate bogeymen.

'Yes,' said the ship with something like pride audible in its voice. 'We will be able to spin up to C-plus velocities almost twenty-three percent faster than a Pax torchship of the line.'

'They can lance you at half an AU,' I said, not convinced.

'Yes,' agreed the ship. 'Nothing to worry about . . . if we have fifteen minutes' head start.'

I turned back to the frowning holo and silent android. 'That's all great,' I said. 'If it's true. But it doesn't help me figure out how to get the girl to the ship or the ship away from Hyperion with that fifteen-minute head start. The torchships will be in what's called a COP – a combat orbiting patrol. One or more of them will be over Equus every second, covering every square meter of space from a hundred light-minutes out to the upper atmosphere. At about thirty kilometers, the combat air patrol – probably Scorpion-class pulse fighters, able to scram into low orbit if need be – will take over. Neither the space nor atmospheric patrol would allow the ship fifteen seconds on their screens, much less fifteen minutes.' I look at the old man's younger face. 'Unless there's something you're not telling me. Ship? Did the Ousters fit you with some sort of magical stealth technology? An invisibility shield or something?'

'Not that I'm aware of,' said the ship. After a second it added, 'That wouldn't be possible, would it?'

I ignored the ship. 'Look,' I said to Martin Silenus, 'I'd like to help you get the girl—'

'Aenea,' said the old man.

'I'd like to get Aenea away from these guys, but if she's as important as you say she is to the Pax . . . I mean, three thousand Swiss Guard, good Christ . . . there's no way we can get within five hundred kilometers of the Valley of the Time Tombs, even with this nifty-keen spaceship.'

I saw the doubt in Silenus's eyes, even through holographic distortion, so I continued. 'I'm serious,' I said. 'Even if there were no space or air cover, no torchships or fighters or airborne radar, there's the Swiss Guard. I mean' – I found that I was clenching my hands into fists as I spoke – 'these guys are *deadly*. They're trained to work in squads of five, and any one of those squads could bring down a spaceship like this.'

The satyr's brows arched in surprise or doubt.

'Listen,' I said again. 'Ship?'

'Yes, M. Endymion?'

'Do you have defensive shields?'

'No, M. Endymion. I do have Ouster-enhanced containment fields, but they are only for civilian use.'

I didn't know what 'Ouster-enhanced containment fields' were, but I went on. 'Could they stop a standard torchship CPB or lance?'

'No,' said the ship.

'Could you defeat C-plus or conventional kinetic torpedoes?'

'No.'

'Could you outrun them?'

'No.'

'Could you prevent a boarding party from entering?'

'No.'

'Do you have any offensive or defensive abilities that could deal with Pax warships?'

'Unless one counts being able to run like hell, M. Endymion the answer is no,' said the ship.

I looked back at Martin Silenus. 'We're screwed,' I said softly. 'Even if I could get to the girl, they'd just capture me as well as her.'

Martin Silenus smiled. 'Perhaps not,' he said. He nodded to A. Bettik, and the android went up the spiral stairway to the upper level and returned in less than a minute. He was carrying a rolled cylinder of something.

'If this is the secret weapon,' I said, 'it had better be good.'

'It is,' said the poet's smirking hologram. He nodded again and A. Bettik unrolled the cylinder.

It was a rug, a bit less than two meters long and a bit more than a meter wide. The cloth was frayed and faded, but I could see intricate designs and patterns. A complex weave of gold threads was still as bright as . . .

'My God,' I said, the realization hitting me like a fist to the solar plexus. 'A hawking mat.'

The holo of Martin Silenus cleared his throat as if preparing to spit. 'Not *a* hawking mat,' he grumbled. '*The* hawking mat.'

I took a step back. This was the stuff of pure legend, and I was almost standing on it.

There had been only a few hundred hawking mats in existence, ever, and this was the *first* one – created by the Old Earth lepidopterist and legendary

EM-systems inventor Vladimir Sholokov shortly after the destruction of Old Earth. Sholokov – already in his seventies, standard, had fallen madly in love with his teenage niece, Alotila, and had created this flying carpet to win her love in return. After a passionate interlude, the teenager had spurned the old man. Sholokov had killed himself on New Earth only weeks after perfecting the current Hawking spindrive, and the carpet had been lost for centuries . . . until Mike Osho bought it in Carvnel marketplace and took it to Maui-Covenant, using it with his fellow shipman Merin Aspic in what would become another love affair that would enter legend – the love of Merin and Siri. This second legend, of course, had become part of Martin Silenus's epic *Cantos* and if his tale was to be believed, Siri had been the Consul's grandmother. In the *Cantos* the Hegemony Consul had used this very same hawking mat ('hawking' here with a small *h* because it referred to the Old Earth bird, not the pre-Hegira scientist whose work had led to Sholokov's C-plus breakthrough with the improved Hawking drive) to cross Hyperion in one final legend – this being the Consul's epic flight toward the city of Keats from the Valley of the Time Tombs to free this very ship and fly it back to the tombs.

I went to one knee and reverently touched the artifact.

'Jesus H. Christ,' said Silenus, 'it's only a fucking rug. And an ugly one at that. I wouldn't have it in my house – it clashes with everything.'

I looked up.

'Yes,' said A. Bettik, 'this is the same hawking mat.'

'Does it still fly?' I asked.

A. Bettik dropped to one knee next to me and extended his blue-fingered hand, tapping at the curled and complicated design. The hawking mat grew as rigid as a board and hovered ten centimeters above the floor.

I shook my head. 'I never understood . . . EM systems don't work on Hyperion because of the weird magnetic field here . . .'

'Big EM systems don't,' snapped Martin Silenus. 'EMVs. Levitation barges. Big stuff. The carpet does. And it's been improved.'

I raised an eyebrow. 'Improved?'

'The Ousters again,' came the ship's voice. 'I don't remember it well, but they tinkered with a lot of things when we visited them two and a half centuries ago.'

'Evidently,' I said. I stood and nudged the legendary mat with my foot. It bounced as if on firm springs but remained hovering where it was. 'Okay,' I said, 'we have Merin and Siri's hawking mat, which . . . if I remember the story . . . could fly along at about twenty klicks per hour . . .'

'Twenty-six kilometers per hour was its top speed,' said A. Bettik.

I nodded and nudged the hovering carpet again. 'Twenty-six klicks per hour with a good tailwind,' I said. 'And the Valley of the Time Tombs is how far from here?'

'One thousand six hundred eighty-nine kilometers,' said the ship.

'And how much time do we have before Aenea steps out of the Sphinx there?' I said.

'Twenty hours,' said Martin Silenus. He must have tired of his younger image, because the holo projection was now of the old man as I had seen him the night before, hoverchair and all.

I glanced at my wrist chronometer. 'I'm late,' I said. 'I should have started flying a couple of days ago.' I walked back to the grand piano. 'And what if I had? *This* is our secret weapon? Does *it* have some sort of super defense field to protect me . . . and the girl . . . from Swiss Guard lances and bullets?'

'No,' said A. Bettik. 'It has no defensive capabilities whatsoever, except for a containment field to deflect the wind and to keep its occupants in place.'

I shrugged. 'So what do I do . . . carry the rug to the Valley and offer the Pax a trade – one old hawking mat for the kid?'

A. Bettik remained kneeling by the hovering carpet. His blue fingers continued to caress the faded fabric. 'The Ousters modified it to hold a charge longer – up to a thousand hours.'

I nodded. Impressive superconductor technology, but totally irrelevant.

'And it now flies at speeds in excess of three hundred kilometers per hour,' continued the android.

I chewed my lip. So I *could* get there by tomorrow. If I wanted to sit on a flying rug for five and a half hours. And then what . . . ?

'I thought we had to pluck her away in this ship,' I said. 'Get her out of the Hyperion system and all that . . .'

'Yes,' said Martin Silenus, his voice suddenly as tired as his aged image, 'but first you have to get her *to* the ship.'

I walked away from the piano, stopping at the spiral staircase to whirl back toward the android, the holo, and the hovering carpet. 'You two just don't understand, do you?' I said, my voice louder and sharper than I had intended. 'These are *Swiss Guard*! If you think that damned rug can get me in under their radar, motion detectors, and other sensors, you're crazy. I'd just be a sitting duck flapping along at three hundred klicks per hour. Believe me, the Swiss Guard grunts – much less the pulse jets in combat air patrol – much less the orbiting torchships – would lance this thing in a nanosecond.'

I paused and squinted at them. 'Unless . . . there's something else you're not telling me . . .'

'Of course there is,' said Martin Silenus, and managed a satyr's tired smile. 'Of course there is.'

'Let's take the hawking mat out to the tower window,' said A. Bettik. 'You have to learn how to handle it.'

'Now?' I said, my voice suddenly small. I felt my heart begin to hammer.

'Now,' said Martin Silenus. 'You have to be proficient at flying it by the time you leave at oh-three-hundred hours tomorrow.'

'I do?' I said, staring at the hovering, legendary rug with a growing sense of THIS IS REAL . . . I MAY DIE TOMORROW.

'You do,' said Martin Silenus.

A. Bettik deactivated the hawking mat and rolled it into a cylinder. I followed him down the metal stairs and out the corridor to the tower staircase. The sunlight was bright through the open tower window. *My God*, I thought as the android spread the carpet on the stone ledge and activated it again. It was still a long drop to the stones below. *My God*, I thought again, my pulse pounding in my ears. There was no sign of the old poet's holo.

A. Bettik gestured me onto the hovering hawking mat. 'I'll go with you on the first flight,' the android said softly. A breeze rustled the leaves atop the nearby chalma tree.

My God, I thought a final time, and climbed onto the sill and then onto the hawking mat.

ELEVEN

Precisely two hours before the child is scheduled to emerge from the Sphinx, an alarm sounds in Father Captain de Soya's command skimmer.

'Airborne contact, bearing one-seven-two, northbound, speed two-seven-four-klicks, altitude four meters,' comes the voice of the COP defense-perimeter controller from the C^3 ship six hundred kilometers above. 'Distance to intruder, five hundred and seventy klicks.'

'Four meters?' says de Soya, looking at Commander Barnes-Avne where she sits across from him at the CIC console amidships in the skimmer.

'Trying to come in low and slow under detection,' says the Commander. She is a small woman with pale skin and red hair, but very little of either skin or hair is visible under the combat headgear she wears. In the three weeks de Soya has known the Commander, he has not seen her smile. 'Tactical visor,' she says. Her own visor is in place. De Soya lowers his.

The blip is near the southern tip of Equus, moving north from the coast. 'Why didn't we see it before?' he asks.

'Could have just launched,' says Barnes-Avne. She is checking combat assets within her tactical display. After the first difficult hour in which de Soya had to present the papal diskey to convince her that command of the Pax's most elite brigades was to be handed over to a mere ship's captain, Barnes-Avne has shown total cooperation. Of course, de Soya has left the minute-to-minute operation to her. Many of the Swiss Guard Brigade leaders believe de Soya to be a mere papal liaison. De Soya does not care. The child is his concern, the girl, and as long as the groundforce is being well commanded, the details are of little concern.

'No visual,' says the Commander. 'Dust storm down there. It'll be here before S-hour.'

'S-hour' is what the troops have been calling the opening of the Sphinx for months now. Only a few officers among them know that a child has been the focus of all this firepower. Swiss Guards do not grumble, but few could appreciate such a provincial posting, so far from the action, in such sandy and uncomfortable surroundings.

'Contact remains northbound, one-seven-two, velocity now two-five-nine klicks, altitude three meters,' says the C^3 controller. 'Distance five hundred and seventy kilometers.'

'Time to bring it down,' says Commander Barnes-Avne on the command channel limited to her and de Soya. 'Recommendations?'

De Soya glances up. The skimmer is banking to the south. Outside the mantis-eye blisters, the horizon tilts and the bizarre Time Tombs of Hyperion pass a thousand meters beneath them. The sky to the south is a dull brown-and-yellow band. 'Lance it from orbit?' he says.

Barnes-Avne nods but says, 'You're familiar with the torchships' work. Let's put a squad on it.' With her god-glove she touches red pips at the southern tip of the defensive perimeter. 'Sergeant Gregorius?' She has switched to the tactical-channel tightbeam.

'Commander?' The sergeant's voice is deep and graveled.

'You're monitoring the bogey?'

'Affirmative, Commander.'

'Intercept it, identify it, and destroy it, Sergeant.'

'Affirmative, Commander.'

De Soya watches as the C^3 cameras zoom toward the southern desert. Five human forms suddenly appear rising from the dunes, their chameleon polymer fading as they rise above dust cloud. On a normal world they would be flying by EM repulsors; on Hyperion they wear the bulkier reaction paks. The five fan out so that several hundred meters separate them and hurtle southward into the dust cloud.

'IR,' says Barnes-Avne, and the visual shifts to the infrared to follow them through the thickening cloud. 'Illuminate target,' she says. The image shifts south, but the target is only a heat blur.

'Small,' says the Commander.

'Plane?' Father Captain de Soya is used to spaceborne tactical displays.

'Too small, unless it's some sort of motorized paraglider,' says Barnes-Avne. There is absolutely no stress in her voice.

De Soya looks down as the skimmer passes over the south end of the Valley of the Time Tombs and accelerates. The dust storm is a gold-brown band along the horizon ahead of them.

'Distance to intercept one hundred eighty klicks,' comes Sergeant Gregorius's laconic voice. De Soya's visor is slaved to the Commander's, and they are seeing what the Swiss Guard sergeant sees – nothing. The squad of troops is flying on instruments through blowing sand so thick that the air is as dark as night around them.

'Reaction paks are heating up,' comes another calm voice. De Soya checks the readout. It is Corporal Kee. 'Sand's foulin' up the intakes,' continues the corporal.

De Soya looks through his visor at Commander Barnes-Avne. He knows she has a tough choice to make – another minute in that dust cloud could send one or more of her troops falling to their deaths; failure to identify the bogey could lead to trouble later.

'Sergeant Gregorius,' she says, her voice still rock calm, 'take out the intruder now.'

There is the briefest of pauses on the comline. 'Commander, we can hang in here a few more . . .' begins the sergeant. De Soya can hear the howl of the dust storm over the man's voice.

'Take it out now, Sergeant,' says Barnes-Avne.

'Affirmative.'

De Soya switches to the wide-range tactical and looks up to see the Commander watching him. 'You think this might be a feint?' she says. 'A distraction to pull us away so that the real intruder can infiltrate elsewhere?'

'Could be,' says de Soya. He sees from the display that the Commander has raised the alert all along the perimeter to Level Five. A Level Six alert is combat.

'Let's see,' she says, just as Gregorius's troops fire.

The dust storm is a rolling cauldron of sand and electricity. At a hundred and seventy-five kilometers, their energy weapons are reliable. Gregorius chooses a steel rain dart and launches it himself. The dart accelerates to Mach six. The bogey does not divert from its path.

'No sensors, I think,' says Barnes-Avne. 'It's flying blind. Programmed.'

The dart passes over the heat target and detonates at a distance of thirty meters, the shaped charge propelling the twenty thousand flechettes directly downward into the intruder's path.

'Contact down,' says the C^3 controller at the same second that Sergeant Gregorius reports, 'Got him.'

'Find and identify,' says the Commander. Their skimmer has banked back toward the Valley.

De Soya glances through the visor display. She has taken the kill at a distance but is not removing the troops from the storm.

'Affirmative,' says the sergeant, and the storm is wild enough to add static to a tightbeam.

The skimmer flies low over the valley, and de Soya identifies the tombs for the thousandth time: here, in reverse order from the usual pilgrims' approach – although there have been no pilgrims for more than three centuries – comes first the Shrike Palace, farther south than the others, its barbed and serrated buttresses reminiscent of the creature that has not been seen here since the days of the pilgrims; then the more subtle Cave Tombs – three in all – their entrances carved out of the pink stone of the canyon wall; then the huge centrally placed Crystal Monolith; then the Obelisk; then the Jade Tomb; and finally the intricately carved Sphinx with sealed door and outflung wings.

De Soya glances at his chronometer.

'One hour and fifty-six minutes,' says Commander Barnes-Avne.

Father Captain de Soya chews his lip. The cordon of Swiss Guard troops is in place around the Sphinx – has been in place for months. Farther out, more troops are placed in a broader perimeter. Each tomb has its detail of waiting soldiers, just in case the prophecy might have been mistaken. Beyond the Valley, more troops. Above them, the torchships and command ship keep watch. At the entrance to the Valley, de Soya's private dropship awaits, its engines already powered up, ready for immediate liftoff as soon as the sedated child is aboard. Two thousand klicks above, the archangel-class courier ship *Raphael* waits with its child-sized acceleration couch.

First, though, de Soya knows, the girl whose name might be Aenea must receive the sacrament of the cruciform. This will happen at the chapel in the torchship *Saint Bonaventure* in orbit, moments before the sleeping child is transferred to the courier ship. Three days after that, she will be resurrected on Pacem and delivered to the Pax authorities.

Father Captain de Soya licks his dry lips. He is as worried that an innocent child will be hurt as he is that something will go wrong in the detention. He cannot imagine how a child – even a child from the past, one who has communicated with the TechnoCore – can be a threat to the far-flung Pax or the Holy Church.

Father Captain de Soya throttles back his thoughts; it is not his place to imagine. It is his place to carry out orders and serve his superiors, and through them, to serve the Church and Jesus Christ.

'Here's your bogey,' comes Sergeant Gregorius's rasp. The visual is hazy, the dust storm is still very wild, but all five troops have made it to the crash site.

De Soya raises the resolution on his visor display and sees the shattered wood and paper, the riddled, twisted metal that might have been a simple solar battery-pulse reaction outboard.

'Drone,' says Corporal Kee.

De Soya flips up his visor and smiles at Commander Barnes-Avne. 'Another drill from you,' he says. 'That's five today.'

The Commander does not return the smile. 'Next time it may be the real thing,' she says. To her tactical mike she says, 'Level Five continues. At S-minus sixty, we go to Level Six.'

Confirmations ring on all bands.

'I still don't understand who might want to interfere,' says Father Captain de Soya. 'Or how they could do it.'

Commander Barnes-Avne shrugs. 'The Ousters could be spinning down from C-plus even as we speak.'

'Then they'd better bring a full Swarm,' says the father-captain. 'Anything less and we'll handle them easily.'

'Nothing in life is easy,' says Commander Barnes-Avne.

The skimmer touches down. The lock cycles and the ramp lowers. The pilot turns in his seat, slides his visor up, and says, 'Commander, captain, you wanted to land at the Sphinx at S-minus one hour and fifty minutes. We're a minute early.'

De Soya disconnects himself from the skimmer console. 'I'm going to stretch my legs before the storm arrives,' he says to the Commander. 'Care to join me?'

'No.' Barnes-Avne lowers her visor and begins whispering commands.

Outside the skimmer, the air is thin and charged with electricity. Overhead, the sky is still the peculiar deep lapis of Hyperion, but already the southern rim of the canyon has a haze hanging over it as the storm approaches.

De Soya glances at his chronometer. One hour and fifty minutes. He takes a deep breath, vows not to look again at the timepiece for at least ten minutes, and walks into the looming shadow of the Sphinx.

TWELVE

After hours of talk I was sent to bed to sleep until three AM. Of course, I did not; I always have had trouble sleeping the night before a trip, and this night I did not sleep at all.

The city after which I was named was quiet after midnight; the autumn breeze had dropped and the stars were very bright. For an hour or two I stayed in my sleep shirt, but by one AM I rose, dressed in the sturdy clothes they had given me the night before, and went through the contents of my pack for the fifth or sixth time.

There was not much for so daunting an adventure: a change of clothes and underwear, socks, a flashlight laser, two water bottles, a knife – I had specified the type – in a belt scabbard, a heavy canvas jacket with thermal lining, an ultralight blanket to use as a bedroll, an inertial guidance compass, an old sweater, night-vision glasses, and a pair of leather gloves. 'What else would you need to explore the universe?' I muttered.

I had also specified the type of clothing I would wear on this day – a comfortable canvas shirt and an overvest with numerous pockets, tough whipcord trousers of the sort I'd worn while duck hunting in the fens, soft high boots – what I thought of as 'buccaneer boots' from the description in Grandam's stories – that were only a bit too tight, and a soft tricorn cap that would fold away in a vest pocket when I did not need it.

I clasped the knife to my belt, set the compass in my vest pocket, and stood at the window watching the stars wheel over the mountaintops until A. Bettik came to wake me at two forty-five.

The old poet was awake and in his hoverchair at the end of the table on the highest level of the tower. The canvas roof had been pulled back and the stars burned coldly overhead. Flames sputtered in the braziers along the wall, and actual torches were set higher on the stone wall. There was breakfast laid out – fried meats, fruits, meal patties with syrup, fresh bread – but I took only a cup of coffee.

'You'd better eat,' grumbled the old man. 'You don't know when your next meal will come.'

I stood looking at him. Steam from the coffee rose to warm my face. The air was chill. 'If things go according to plan, I'll be in the spaceship in less than six hours. I'll eat then.'

Martin Silenus made a rough noise. 'When do things ever go according to plan, Raul Endymion?'

81

I sipped coffee. 'Speaking of plans, you were going to tell me about the sort of miracle that's going to distract the Swiss Guard while I whisk your young friend away.'

The ancient poet peered at me for a silent moment. 'Just trust me on that, will you?'

I sighed. I had been afraid he would say that. 'That's a lot to take on trust, old man.'

He nodded but remained silent.

'All right,' I said at last. 'We'll see what happens.' I turned to where A. Bettik was standing near the stairway. 'Just don't forget to be there with the ship when we need you.'

'I will not forget, sir,' said the android.

I walked to where the hawking mat was laid out on the floor. A. Bettik had set my pack on it. 'Any last instructions?' I asked, not knowing which person I was speaking to.

The old man floated closer on his hoverchair. He looked ancient in the torchlight: more wizened and mummified than ever. His fingers were like yellowed bones. 'Just this,' he rasped. 'Listen—

'In the wide sea there lives a forlorn wretch,
Doomed with enfeebled carcass to outstretch
His loathed existence through ten centuries,
And then to die alone. Who can devise
A total opposition? No one. So
A million times ocean must ebb and flow,
And he oppressed. Yet he shall not die,
These things accomplished. If he shall not die,
Scans all depths of magic, and expounds
The meanings of all motions, shapes and sounds;
If he explores all forms and substances
Straight homeward to their symbol-essences;
He shall not die. Moreover, and in chief,
He must pursue this task of joy and grief
Most piously – all lovers tempest-tossed,
And in the savage overwhelming lost,
He shall deposit side by side, until
Time's creeping shall the dreary space fulfil:
Which done, and all these labours ripened,
A youth, by heavenly power loved and led,
Shall stand before him, whom he shall direct
How to consummate all. The youth elect
Must do the thing, or both will be destroyed.'

'What?' I said. 'I don't . . .'

'Fuck it,' rasped the poet. 'Just get Aenea, take her to the Ousters, and get her back alive. It's not too complicated. Even a shepherd should be able to do it.'

'Don't forget landscape apprentice, bartender, and duck hunter,' I said, and set my cup of coffee down.

'It's almost three,' said Silenus. 'You need to get going.'

I took a breath. 'Just one minute,' I said. I clattered down the stairs, went into the lavatory, relieved myself, and leaned against the cool stone wall for a moment. *Are you mad, Raul Endymion?* It was my thought, but I heard it in Grandam's soft voice. *Yes,* I answered.

I walked back up the stairs, amazed at how shaky my legs were and how rapidly my heart was beating.

'All set,' I said. 'Mother always said to take care of these things before leaving home.'

The thousand-year-old poet grunted and hovered his chair near the hawking mat. I sat on the rug, activated the flight threads, and hovered a meter and a half above the stone floor.

'Remember, once you're in the Cleft and find the entrance, it's programmed,' said Silenus.

'I know, you told me all about . . .'

'Shut up and listen,' he rasped. Ancient parchment fingers pointed to the proper thread designs. 'You remember how to fly it. Once in, tap in the sequence there . . . there . . . there . . . and the program will take over. You can interrupt the sequence to fly manually by touching the interrupt design here . . .' His fingers caressed air above the ancient threads. 'But don't try to fly it yourself down there. You'll never find your way out.'

I nodded and licked dry lips. 'You didn't tell me who programmed it. Who did this flight before?'

The satyr showed new teeth. 'I did, my boy. It took me months, but I did. Almost two centuries ago.'

'Two centuries!' I almost stepped off the mat. 'What if there have been cave-ins? Shiftings due to earthquakes? What if something's got in the way since then?'

Martin Silenus shrugged. 'You'll be going over two hundred klicks per hour, boy,' he said. 'I guess you'll die.' He slapped me on the back. 'Get going. Give my love to Aenea. Tell her that Uncle Martin is waiting to see Old Earth before he dies. Tell her that the old fart is eager to hear her expound the meanings of all motions, shapes, and sounds.'

I raised the hawking mat another half meter.

A. Bettik stepped forward and extended a blue hand. I shook it. 'Good luck, M. Endymion.'

I nodded, found nothing else to say, and flew the hawking mat up and out of the tower in rising spirals.

To fly directly from the city of Endymion in the middle of the continent of Aquila to the Valley of the Time Tombs on the continent of Equus, I should have headed almost due north. I headed east.

My test-flying the day before – it was the same day to my tired mind – had shown how easy it was to handle the hawking mat, but that was at speeds of a few klicks per hour. When I was a hundred meters above the tower, I set the direction – the penlight clamped in my teeth illuminating the inertial compass, lining up the mat along that invisible line, checking it against the topographic map the old poet had given me – and held the palm of my hand on the acceleration pattern. The mat continued to speed up until the gentle containment field activated to shield me from the wind blast. Too late, I glanced back to catch a last glimpse of the tower – perhaps to see the old poet watching from a window – but already the ruined university town was lost to sight in the mountain darkness.

There was no speed indicator, so I had to assume the mat was flying at its top speed as it soared toward the high peaks to the east. Starlight reflected on snowfields higher than my own altitude, so to be cautious, I stowed the penlight, pulled on the night-vision glasses, and continued to check my position against the topo map. As the land rose, so did I, holding the hawking mat at a hundred meters above the boulders, waterfalls, avalanche chutes, and icefalls all glowing green in the enhanced starlight from the night-vision goggles. The mat was perfectly silent in its flight – even the wind noise was hushed by the deflective containment field – and several times I saw large animals leap to hiding, surprised by the sudden appearance of this wingless bird above them. I crossed the continental divide half an hour after leaving the tower, keeping the mat in the center of the five-thousand-meter pass. It was cold there, and though the containment field held some of my own body heat in the traveling bubble of still air, I had long since pulled on my thermal jacket and gloves.

Beyond the mountains, descending quickly to stay close to the rugged terrain, I watched the tundra give way to fenfields, the fenfields to low lines of dwarf everblues and triaspen, and then saw these high-mountain trees trail off and disappear as the glow of the tesla flame forests began to light the east like a false dawn.

I stowed the night-vision glasses in my pack. The sight ahead was beautiful and somewhat frightening – the entire eastern horizon snapping and crackling with electricity, ball lightning leaping between the hundred-meter-tall tesla trees, chain lightning rippling through the air between tesla and exploding prometheus, phoenix shrubs and random ground fires burning in a thousand places. Both Martin Silenus and A. Bettik had warned me about this, and I took the hawking mat high, accepting the risk of detection at this altitude as preferable to being caught in that electric maelstrom below.

Another hour and there was a hint of sunrise to the east, beyond the flame-forest glow, but just as the sky paled and then deepened into daylight, the flame forests fell behind me and the Cleft came into sight.

I had been aware that I had been climbing for the past forty minutes as I checked my route above the Pinion Plateau on the creased topo map, but now I felt the altitude as the depth of that great crevice in this part of Aquila became visible ahead. In its own way, the Cleft was as frightening as the flame forests – narrow, vertical, dropping three thousand meters in a straight fall from the flatlands above. I crossed the southern edge of the great split in the continent and dived toward the river three kilometers below. The Cleft continued east, the river beneath me roaring along at nearly the same speed as the mat as I slowed. Within moments the morning sky darkened above me and the stars reappeared; it was as if I had fallen into a deep well. The river at the base of these terrifying cliffs of fall was wild, clogged with bergs of its own ice, leaping over boulders the size of the spaceship I had left behind. I stayed five meters above the spray and slowed even further. I must be close.

I checked my chronometer and then the map. It should be somewhere ahead in the next two klicks . . . there!

It was larger than they had described – at least thirty meters to a side – and perfectly square. The entrance to the planetary labyrinth had been carved in the form of a temple entrance, or a giant door. I slowed the hawking mat further and then banked left, pausing at the entrance. According to my chronometer, it had taken just under ninety minutes to reach the Cleft. The Valley of the Time Tombs were still a thousand klicks north of here. Four hours of flying at high cruising speed. I looked again at my chronometer – four hours and twenty minutes until the time the child was scheduled to step out of the Sphinx.

I edged the hawking mat forward, into the cavern. Trying to remember the details of the 'Priest's Tale' in the old man's *Cantos*. I could remember only that it was here – just within the labyrinth entrance – that Father Duré and the Bikura had encountered the Shrike and the cruciforms.

There was no Shrike. I was not surprised – the creature had not been sighted since the Fall of the WorldWeb two hundred and seventy-seven years ago. There were no cruciforms. Again, I was not surprised – the Pax had harvested them long ago from these cavern walls.

I knew what everyone knew about the Labyrinth. There had been nine known labyrinthine worlds in the old Hegemony. All of those worlds had been Earth-like – seven-point-nine on the ancient Solmev Scale – except that they were tectonically dead, more Mars-like than Earth-like in that respect. The labyrinth tunnels honeycombed those nine worlds – Hyperion included – and served no known purpose. They had been tunneled tens of thousands of years before humankind had left Old Earth, although no clue to the tunnelers had ever been found. The labyrinths fueled numerous myths – including the *Cantos* – but their mystery remained. The Labyrinth of Hyperion had never been mapped – except for the part I was ready to travel at two hundred and seventy klicks per hour. It had been mapped by a mad poet. Or so I hoped.

I slipped the night-vision glasses back on as the sunlight faded behind me. I felt the skin on the back of my neck prickle as the darkness closed around. Soon the glasses would be useless, as there would be no light to enhance. Taking tape from my pack, I secured the flashlight laser to the front of the hawking mat and set the beam to its widest dispersal. The light would be faint, but the goggles would amplify it. Already I could see branchings ahead – the cavern remained a great, hollow, rectangular prism, thirty meters on a side, with only the smallest signs of cracks of collapse – and ahead, tunnels branched to the right, then left, then downward.

I took a breath and tapped in the programmed sequence. The hawking mat leaped ahead, accelerating to its preset speed, the sudden lurch making me lean far backward despite the compensating effect of the containment field.

That field would not protect me if the carpet took a wrong turn and smashed into a wall at this speed. Rocks flashed past. The hawking mat banked sharply to make a right turn, leveled itself in the center of the long cavern, then dived to follow a descending branch.

It was terrifying to watch. I took the night-vision glasses off, secured them in my coat pocket, gripped the edge of the leaping, lurching mat, and closed my eyes. I need not have bothered. The darkness was now absolute.

THIRTEEN

With fifteen minutes until the opening of the Sphinx, Father Captain de Soya paces the valley floor. The storm has long since arrived, and sand fills the air in a rasping blizzard. Hundreds of Swiss Guard are deployed here along the Valley floor, but their armored CTVs, their gun emplacements, their missile batteries, their observation posts – all are invisible due to the dust storm. But de Soya knows that they would be invisible at any rate, concealed behind camouflage fields and chameleon polymer. The father-captain has to rely on his infrared to see anything in this howling storm. And even then, with his visor down and sealed, fine particles of sand make their way down his combat suit collar and up into his mouth. This day tastes of grit. His sweat leaves tiny trails of red mud, like blood from some holy stigmata, on his brow and cheeks.

'Attention,' he says over the all-call channels. 'This is Father Captain de Soya, commanding this mission under papal imperative. Commander Barnes-Avne will repeat these orders in a moment, but right now I want to specify that there will be no actions taken, no shots fired, no defensive acts initiated that will in any way endanger the life of the child who will be stepping from one of these tombs in . . . thirteen and a half minutes. I want this understood by every Pax officer and trooper, every torchship captain and space-navy sailor, every pilot and airborne flight officer . . . *this child must be captured but unharmed*. Failure to heed this warning will result in court-martial and summary execution. May we all serve our Lord and our Church this day . . . In the name of Jesus, Mary, and Joseph, I ask that our efforts be successful. Father Captain de Soya, Acting Commander Hyperion expedition, out.'

He continues walking as the chorus of amens comes in over tactical channels. Suddenly he pauses. 'Commander?'

'Yes, Father Captain.' Barnes-Avne's voice is calm in his earphones.

'Would it screw up your perimeter if I asked for Sergeant Gregorius's squad to join me here at the Sphinx?'

There is the briefest pause, which tells him how little the ground Commander thinks of such last-minute changes in plans. The 'reception committee' – a squad of specially chosen Swiss Guard, the doctor with the sedative ready to be administered, and a medic with the living cruciform in its stasis container – are even now waiting at the foot of the Sphinx's stairs.

'Gregorius and his troops will be there in three minutes,' says the Commander. De Soya can hear the commands going out over the tactical tightbeam and the confirmations coming in. Once again he has asked these five men and women to fly in dangerous conditions.

The squad touches down in two minutes forty-five seconds. De Soya can see them only on infrared; their reaction paks are glowing white-hot.

'Shed the flying paks,' he says. 'Just stay near me no matter what happens. Watch my back.'

'Yes, sir,' comes Sergeant Gregorius's rumble through the wind howl. The huge noncom steps closer, his visor and combat suit looming in de Soya's IR vision. Obviously the sergeant wants a visual confirmation on whose back he is watching.

'S-minus ten minutes,' says Commander Barnes-Avne. 'Sensors indicate unusual activity in the antientropic fields around the tombs.'

'I feel it,' says de Soya. Indeed, he can. The shifting of the time fields in the Valley creates a sense of vertigo in him not too dissimilar from nausea. Both this and the raging sandstorm make the father-captain feel unattached to the ground, light-headed, almost drunk. Planting his feet carefully, de Soya walks back to the Sphinx. Gregorius and his troopers follow in a tight V.

The 'welcoming committee' is standing on the steps of the Sphinx. De Soya approaches, flashes his infrared and radio ID, talks briefly with the doctor carrying the sedative ampoule – warns the woman not to harm the child – and then waits. There are thirteen forms on the steps now, counting Gregorius's team. De Soya realizes that the combat squads do not look especially welcoming with their raised heavy weapons. 'Step back a few paces,' he says to the two squad sergeants. 'Keep the squads ready, but out of sight in the storm.'

'Affirmative.' The ten troopers take a dozen steps back and are totally invisible in the blowing sand. De Soya knows that nothing living could break through the perimeter they have established.

To the doctor and his medic aide carrying the cruciform, de Soya says, 'Let's get closer to the door.' The suited figures nod and the three slowly climb the stairs. The antientropic fields are intense now. De Soya remembers once, as a young boy, he had stood up to his chest in a vicious surf, the tide and undertow trying to pull him out into an unfriendly ocean on his homeworld. This is a bit like that.

'S-minus seven minutes,' says Barnes-Avne on the common channel. Then, on the tightbeam to de Soya, 'Father Captain, would you like the skimmer to land and get you? There's a better overview up here.'

'No, thank you,' says de Soya. 'I'll stay with the contact team.' He sees on his display that the skimmer is climbing for altitude, finally pausing at ten thousand meters, above the worst of the dust storm. Like any good commander, Barnes-Avne wants to control the action while not being caught up in it.

De Soya keys the private channel to his dropship pilot. 'Hiroshe?'

'Yes, sir?'

'Be ready to lift off in ten minutes or less.'

'Ready, sir.'

'The storm won't be a problem?' As with all deep-space combat captains, de Soya is more distrustful of atmosphere than of almost anything else.

'No problem, sir.'

'Good.'

'S-minus five minutes,' comes Commander Barnes-Avne's steady voice. 'Orbital detectors show no space activity for thirty AUs. Northern hemispheric airwatch shows no vehicles airborne. Ground detection shows no unauthorized movement from the Bridle Range to the coast.'

'COP screens clear,' comes the C^3 controller's voice.

'CAP clear,' says the lead Scorpion pilot. 'It's still a beautiful day up here.'

'Radio and tightbeam silence from this point on until Level Six goes to standdown,' says Barnes-Avne. 'S-minus four minutes and sensors show maximum antientropic activity throughout the Valley. Contact team, report in.'

'I'm at the door,' says Dr Chatkra.

'Ready,' says the medic, a very young trooper named Caf. The trooper's voice is shaky. De Soya realizes that he does not know if Caf is male or female.

'All set here,' reports de Soya. He glances over his shoulder through the clear visor. Even the bottom of the stone stairway is invisible in the howling sand. Electrical discharges crackle and pop. De Soya switches to IR and sees the ten Swiss Guards standing there, weapons literally hot.

Even in the midst of storm noise, a terrible quiet suddenly descends. De Soya can hear his own breathing within the helmet of his combat suit. The unused com channels hiss and pop with static. More static lashes his tactical and IR visors, and de Soya slides them up in exasperation. The sealed portal of the Sphinx is less than three meters in front of him, but the sand now conceals it, now reveals it, like a shifting curtain. De Soya takes two steps closer, and Dr Chatkra and her medic follow.

'Two minutes,' says Barnes-Avne. 'All weapons to full hot. High-speed recorders to automatic. Medical dustoff teams stand by.'

De Soya closes his eyes to fight the vertigo of the time tides. *The universe,* he thinks, *is truly wondrous.* He is sorry that he has to sedate the child within seconds of meeting her. Those are his orders – she would sleep through the attachment of the cruciform and the fatal flight back to Pacem – and he knows that he will, in all probability, never hear the girl's voice. He is sorry. He would like to talk to her, ask her questions about the past, about herself.

'One minute. Perimeter fire control on full auto.'

'Commander!' De Soya has to slide the tactical visor down to identify the voice as belonging to a science lieutenant on the interior perimeter. 'The fields are building to max along *all* the tombs! Doors opening on the caves, the Monolith, the Shrike Palace, the Jade Tomb . . .'

'Silence on all channels,' snaps Barnes-Avne. 'We're monitoring it here. Thirty seconds.'

De Soya realizes that the child is going to step into this new era only to be confronted with three helmeted, visored figures in combat armour, and slides all of his visors up. He may never get to talk to the girl, but she will see his human face before she sleeps.

'Fifteen seconds.' For the first time de Soya hears tension in the Commander's voice.

Blowing sand claws at Father Captain de Soya's exposed eyes. He raises a gloved hand, rubs, and blinks through tears. He and Dr Chatkra take another step closer. The doors of the Sphinx are opening inward. The interior is dark. De Soya wishes he could see in IR, but he does not flip the visor down. He is determined that this child will see his eyes.

A shadow moves within darkness. The doctor begins to step toward the form, but de Soya touches her arm. 'Wait.'

The shadow becomes a figure; the figure becomes a form; the form is a child. She is smaller than de Soya expected. Her shoulder-length hair blows in the wind.

'Aenea,' says de Soya. He had not planned on speaking to her, or calling her by her name.

The girl looks up at him. He sees the dark eyes, but senses no fear there – just . . . anxiety? Sadness?

'Aenea, don't worry . . .' he begins, but the doctor moves forward quickly at that moment, injector raised, and the girl takes a quick step back.

It is then that Father Captain de Soya sees the second figure in the gloom. And it is then that the screaming begins.

FOURTEEN

I hadn't known that I was claustrophobic until this trip. The flying at high speeds through pitch-black catacombs, the encircling containment field blocking even the wind of my passage, the sense of stone and darkness all around – twenty minutes into the wild flight I disengaged the autopilot program, landed the hawking mat on the labyrinth floor, collapsed the containment field, stepped away from the mat, and screamed.

I grabbed the flashlight laser and played it on the walls. A square corridor of stone. Here, outside the containment field, the heat struck me. The tunnel must be very deep. There were no stalactites, no stalagmites, no bats, no living things . . . only this square-hewn cavern stretching on to infinity. I played the light over the hawking mat. It seemed dead, totally inert. In my haste I might have exited the program incorrectly, wiped it. If so, I was dead. We had jinxed and banked on a score of branchings so far; there was no way I would ever find my own way out.

I screamed again, although it was a bit more of a deliberate, tension-breaking shout than a scream this time. I fought the sense of walls and darkness closing in. I willed away the nausea.

Three and a half hours left. Three and a half hours of this claustrophobic nightmare, barreling along through blackness, hanging on to a leaping flying carpet . . . and then what?

I wished then that I had brought a weapon. It seemed absurd at the time; no handgun would have given me a chance against even a single Swiss Guard trooper – not even against a Home Guard irregular – but now I wished I had something. I removed the small hunting knife from its leather scabbard on my belt, saw the steel gleam in the flashlight beam, and started laughing.

This was absurd.

I set the knife back, dropped onto the mat, and tapped in the 'resume' code. The hawking mat stiffened, rose, and lurched into violent motion. I was going somewhere fast.

Father Captain de Soya sees the huge shape for an instant before it is gone, and the screaming begins. Dr Chatkra steps toward the retreating child, blocking de Soya's view, there is a rush of air tangible even within the wind roar all around, and the doctor's helmeted head is rolling and bouncing past de Soya's boots.

'Mother of God,' he whispers into his open microphone. Dr Chatkra's body still stands. The girl – Aenea – screams then, the sound almost lost under the howling sandstorm, and as if the force of the scream has acted upon Chatkra's body, the corpse falls to the stone. The medic, Caf, shouts something unintelligible and lunges for the girl. Again the dark blur, more sensed than seen, and Caf's arm is separated from the medic's body. Aenea runs toward the stairway. De Soya lunges at the child but collides with some sort of huge, metallic statue made of barbs and razor wire. Spikes puncture his combat armor – impossible! – but he feels the blood pouring from half a dozen minor wounds.

'No!' screams the girl again. 'Stop! I command you!'

The three-meter metal statue turns in slow motion. De Soya has a confused impression of blazing red eyes staring down at the girl, and then the metal sculpture is gone. The father-captain takes a step toward the child, still wanting to reassure her as well as capture her, but his left leg goes out from under him, and he goes to his right knee on the broad stone step.

The girl comes to him, touches his shoulder, and whispers – somehow audibly above the wind howl and the worse howling of people in pain coming over his earphones – 'It will be all right.'

Father Captain de Soya's body is suffused with well-being, his mind is filled with joy. He weeps.

The girl is gone. A huge figure looms over him, and de Soya clenches his fists, tries to rise, knowing that it is futile – that the creature has returned to kill him.

'Easy!' shouts Sergeant Gregorius. The big man helps de Soya to his feet. The father-captain cannot stand – his left leg is bleeding and useless – so Gregorius holds him in one giant arm while he sweeps the area with his energy lance.

'Don't shoot!' shouts de Soya. 'The girl . . .'

'Gone,' says Sergeant Gregorius. He fires. A spike of pure energy lashes into the crackling swirl of sand. 'Damn!' Gregorius lifts the father-captain over his armored shoulder. The screams on the net are growing wilder.

My chronometer and compass tell me that I am almost there. Nothing else suggests that. I am still flying blind, still hanging on to the lurching hawking mat as it selects which branch of the endless labyrinth to hurtle down. I have had little sense of the tunnels climbing toward the surface, but, then, I have had little sense of anything except vertigo and claustrophobia.

For the last two hours I have worn my night-vision glasses and illuminated our flight path with the flashlight laser at its widest setting. At three hundred klicks per hour, the rock walls rush by with alarming rapidity. But rather that than darkness.

I am still wearing the goggles when the first light appears and blinds me. I sweep off the glasses, stow them in a vest pocket, and blink away afterimages. The hawking mat is hurtling me toward a rectangle of pure light.

I remember the old poet saying that the Third Cave Tomb had been closed for more than two and a half centuries. All of the Time Tombs on Hyperion had their portals sealed after the Fall, but the Third Cave Tomb actually had a wall of rock sealing it off from the labyrinth *behind* the closed portal. For hours now I had half expected to barrel into that wall of rock at almost three hundred klicks per hour.

The square of light grows rapidly. I realize that the tunnel has been climbing for some time, rising to the surface here. I lie full-length on the hawking mat, feeling it slow as it reaches the end of its programmed flight plan. 'Good work, old man,' I say aloud, hearing my voice for the first time since the shouting interlude three and a half hours ago.

I set my hand over the acceleration threads, afraid to let the mat slow to a walking pace here where I am bound to be a sitting duck. I had said that it would take a miracle to keep from being shot by the Swiss Guard; the poet had promised me one. It is time.

Sand swirls in the tomb opening, covering the doorway like a dry waterfall. *Is this the miracle?* I hope not. Troopers can see through a sandstorm easily enough. I brake the mat to a stop just within the doorway, pull a bandanna and sunglasses from my pack, tie the scarf over my nose and mouth, lie full-length on my belly again, set my fingers over the flight designs, and punch the acceleration threads.

The hawking mat flies through the doorway and into open air.

I jink hard right, rising and dropping the mat in a wild evasive pattern, knowing even as I do so that such efforts are useless against autotargeting. It does not matter – my urge to stay alive overrides my logic.

I cannot see. The storm is so wild that everything two meters beyond the leading edge of the mat is obscured. This is insane . . . the old poet and I never discussed the possibility of a sandstorm here. I can't even tell my altitude.

Suddenly a razor-sharp flying buttress passes less than a meter beneath the hurtling carpet, immediately I fly *under* another barbed metal strut, and I realize that I have almost just collided with the Shrike Palace. I am headed precisely the wrong direction – south – when I need to be at the north end of the Valley. I look at my compass, confirm my folly, and swing the hawking mat around. From the glimpse I had of the Shrike Palace, the mat is about twenty meters above ground level. Stopping the carpet, feeling it rocked and buffeted by the wind, I lower it like an elevator until it touches windswept stone. Then I raise it three meters, lock in that altitude, and move due north at little more than a walking pace.

Where are the soldiers?

As if to answer my unspoken question, dark forms in battle armor hurtle by. I flinch as they fire their baroque energy lances and stubby flechette guns, but they are not firing at me. They are shooting over their shoulders. *They are Swiss Guard and they are running.* I had never heard of such a thing.

Suddenly I realize that beneath the wind howl, the Valley is alive with human screams. I don't see how this is possible – troopers would keep their helmets fastened and visors down in such a storm. But the screams are there. I can hear them.

A jet or skimmer suddenly roars overhead, no more than ten meters above me, its autoguns firing to either side – I survive because I am directly beneath the thing – and I have to brake suddenly as the storm ahead of me is illuminated by a terrible blast of light and heat. The skimmer, jet, whatever, has flown directly into one of the tombs ahead of me. I guess that it is the Crystal Monolith or the Jade Tomb.

More firing to my left. I fly right, then northwest again, trying to bypass the tombs. Suddenly there are screams to my right and directly ahead. Bolts of lancefire slash through the storm. This time someone *is* shooting at me. *Shooting and missing? How can this be?*

Not waiting for an answer, I drop the hawking mat like an express elevator. Slamming into the ground, I roll aside, bolts of energy ionizing the air not twenty centimeters above my head. The inertial compass, still on a lanyard around my neck, punches me in the face as I roll. There are no boulders to hide behind, no rocks; the sand is flat here. I try to dig a ditch with my fingers as the blue bolts crisscross the air over my head. Flechette clouds flash overhead with that characteristic ripping sound they have. If I had been airborne now, the hawking mat and I would be in small tatters.

Something huge is standing not three meters from me in the whipping sand. Its legs are planted wide. It looks like a giant in barbed combat armour – a giant with too many arms. A plasma bolt strikes it, outlining the spiked form for an instant. The thing does not melt or fall or fly apart.

Impossible. Fucking impossible. Part of my mind coolly notes that I am thinking in obscenities the way I always have in combat.

The huge shape is gone. There are more screams to my left, explosions straight ahead. *How the hell am I supposed to find the kid in all this carnage? And if I did, how could I find my way to the Third Cave Tomb? The idea – the Plan – had been for me to swoop Aenea up in the miracle distraction the old poet had promised, make a dash for the Third Cave again, and then punch in the final bit of autopilot for the thirty-klick run for Chronos Keep on the edge of the Bridle Range, where A. Bettik and the spaceship would be waiting for me in . . . three minutes.*

Even in all this confusion, whatever the hell it is, there is no way that the orbital torchships or ground-based AA batteries can miss something as big as the ship if it hangs around for more than the thirty seconds we'd allotted for it to be on the ground. This whole rescue mission is screwed.

The earth shakes and a boom fills the Valley. Either something huge has blown up – an ammo dump, at least – or something much larger than a skimmer has crashed. A wild red glow illuminates the entire northern part of the Valley, blossoms of flame visible even through the sandstorm. Against that glow I can see scores of armored figures running, firing, flying, falling. One form is smaller than the rest and is unarmored. The barbed giant is standing next to it. The smaller form, still silhouetted against the fiery glow of pure destruction, is attacking the giant, pounding small fists against barbs and spikes.

'Shit!' I crawl toward the hawking mat, cannot find it in the storm, rub sand out of my eyes, crawl in a circle, and feel cloth under my right palm. In the seconds I have been off the mat, it has become almost buried beneath the sand. Digging like a frenzied dog, I unearth the flight designs, activate the mat, and fly toward the fading glow. The two figures are no longer visible, but I have kept the presence of mind to take a compass reading. Two lance bolts scorch the air – one centimeters above my prone body, one millimeters under the mat.

'Shit! Goddamn!' I shout to no one in particular.

Father Captain de Soya is only semiconscious as he bounces along on Sergeant Gregorius's armored shoulder. De Soya half senses other dark shapes running through the storm with them, occasionally firing plasma bolts at unseen targets, and he wonders if this is the rest of Gregorius's squad. Fading in and out of awareness, he desperately wishes he could see the girl again, talk to her.

Gregorius almost runs into something, stops, orders his squad to close up. A scarab armored fighting vehicle has dropped its camouflage shield and is sitting askew on a boulder. The left track is missing, and the barrels of the rear miniguns have been twisted like jail-cell bars in a cartoon. The right eye blister is shattered and gaping.

'Here,' pants Gregorius, and carefully lowers Father Captain de Soya through the blister. A second later the sergeant pulls himself through, illuminating the interior of the scarab with the torch beam on his energy lance. The driver's seat looks as if someone has spray-painted it red. The rear bulkheads seem to have been spattered with random colors, rather like some absurd pre-Hegira 'abstract art' Father Captain de Soya once saw in a museum. Only this metal canvas has been daubed with human parts.

Sergeant Gregorius pulls him deeper into the tilted scarab and leans the torchship captain against the lower bulkhead. Two other suited figures squeeze through the shattered blister.

De Soya rubs blood and sand out of his eyes and says, 'I'm all right.' He has meant to say it in a command tone, but his voice is weak, almost childlike.

'Yessir,' growls Gregorius. The sergeant is pulling his medkit from his beltpak.

'I don't need that,' de Soya says weakly. 'The suit . . .' All combat suits have their own sealant and semiintelligent doc liners. De Soya is sure that for such minor slash or puncture wounds, the suit has already dealt with it. But now he looks down.

His left leg has been all but severed. The impact-proof, energy-resistant, omnipolymer combat armor is hanging in shreds, like tattered rubber on a cheap tire. He can see the white of his femur. The suit has tightened into a crude tourniquet around his upper thigh, saving his life, but there are half a dozen serious puncture wounds in his chest armor, and the medlights on his chest display are blinking red.

'Ah, Jesus,' whispers Father Captain de Soya. It is a prayer.

'It's all right,' says Sergeant Gregorius, tightening his own tourniquet around the thigh. 'We'll be getting you to a medic and then liftin' you to the ship's hospital in no time, sir.' He looks to the two suited figures crouched in exhaustion behind the front seats. 'Kee? Rettig?'

'Yes, Sergeant?' The smaller of the two figures looks up.

'Mellick and Ott?'

'Dead, Sergeant. The thing got them at the Sphinx.'

'Stay on the net,' says Sergeant Gregorius, and turns back to de Soya. The noncom removes his gauntlet and touches huge fingers to one of the larger puncture wounds. 'Does that hurt, sir?'

De Soya shakes his head. He cannot even feel the touch.

'All right,' says the sergeant, but he looks displeased. He begins calling on the tactical net.

'The girl,' says Father Captain de Soya. 'We have to find the girl.'

'Yes, sir,' says Gregorius, but continues calling on different channels. De Soya listens now and can hear the babble.

'Look out! Christ! It's coming back . . .'

'*Saint Bonaventure! Saint Bonaventure!* You are venting into space! Say again, you are venting into . . .'

'Scorpion one-niner to any controller . . . Jesus . . . Scorpion one-niner, left engine out, any controller . . . can't see the Valley . . . will divert . . .'

'Jamie! Jamie! Oh, God . . .'

'Get off the net! Goddammit, maintain com discipline! Get off the fucking net!'

'Our Father, who art in heaven, hallowed be Thy name . . .'

'Watch the fucking . . . oh, shit . . . the fucking thing took a hit but . . . shit . . .'

'Multiple bogeys . . . say again . . . multiple bogeys . . . disregard fire control . . . there are multiple—' This is interrupted by screams.

'Command One, come in. Command One, come in.'

Feeling consciousness draining from him like the blood pooling under his ruined leg, de Soya flips down his visors. The tactical display is garbage. He keys the tightbeam com channel to Barnes-Avne's command skimmer. 'Commander, this is Father Captain de Soya. Commander?'

The line is no longer operative.

'The Commander is dead, sir,' says Gregorius, pressing an adrenaline ampoule against de Soya's bare arm. The father-captain has no memory of his gauntlet and combat armor being removed. 'I saw her skimmer go in on tactical before it all went to hell,' continues the sergeant, wiring de Soya's dangling leg to his upper thighbone like someone tying down loose cargo. 'She's dead, sir. Colonel Brideson's not responding. Captain Ranier's not answering from the torchship. The C^3 ain't answerin'.'

De Soya fights to stay conscious. 'What's happening, Sergeant?'

Gregorius leans closer. His visors are up, and de Soya sees for the first time that the giant is a black man. 'We had a phrase for this in the Marines before I joined Swiss Guard, sir.'

'Charlie Fox,' says Father Captain de Soya, trying to smile.

'That's what you polite navy types call it,' agrees Gregorius. He gestures the other two troopers toward the broken blister. They crawl out. Gregorius lifts de Soya and carries him out like a baby. 'In the Marines, sir,' continues the sergeant, not even breathing heavily, 'we called it a cluster fuck.'

De Soya feels himself fading. The sergeant sets him down on the sand.

'You stay with me, Captain! Goddammit, you hear me? You stay with me!' Gregorius is shouting.

'Watch your language, Sergeant,' says de Soya, feeling himself sliding into unconsciousness but unable and unwilling to do anything about it. 'I'm a priest, remember . . . Taking the name of God in vain is a mortal sin.' The blackness is closing in, and Father Captain de Soya does not know if he has said the last sentence aloud or not.

FIFTEEN

Since I was a boy on the moors, standing apart to watch smoke from the peat fires rise from within the protective ring of circled caravans, waiting for the stars to appear, then seeing them cold and indifferent in the deepening lapis sky and wondering about my future while waiting for the call that would bring me in to warmth and dinner, I have had a sense of the irony of things. So many important things pass quickly without being understood at the time. So many powerful moments are buried beneath the absurd. I saw this as a child. I have seen it throughout my life since then.

Flying toward the fading orange light of the explosion, I suddenly came across the child. Aenea. My first glimpse had been of two figures, the small one attacking the huge one, but when I arrived a moment later, sand howling and rasping around the bobbing hawking mat, there was only the girl.

This is the way we looked to each other at that moment: the girl with an expression of shock and anger, eyes red and narrowed against the sand or from her fury at something, her small fists clenched, her shirt and loose sweater flapping like wild banners in the wind, her shoulder-length hair – brown but with blonde streaks that I would notice later – matted and blowing, her cheeks streaked with the muddy path of tears and snot, her rubber-soled, canvas kid's shoes totally inappropriate to the adventure upon which she'd embarked, and her cheap backpack hanging from one shoulder; I must have been a wilder, less sane sight – a bulky, muscled, not-very-bright-looking twenty-seven-year-old lying flat on my belly on a flying carpet, my face largely obscured by the bandanna and dark glasses, my short hair filthy and spiked in the wind, my pack also lashed over one shoulder, my vest and trousers filthy with sand and grime.

The girl's eyes widened in recognition, but it took only a second for me to realize that she was recognizing the hawking mat, not me.

'Get on!' I shouted. Armored forms ran by, firing as they went. Other shadows loomed in the storm.

The girl ignored me, turning away as if to find the shape she had been attacking. I noticed then that her fists were bleeding. 'Goddamn him,' she was shouting, almost weeping. 'God*damn* him.'

These were the first words I heard our messiah utter.

'Get on!' I shouted again, and began to dismount from the hawking mat to seize her.

Aenea turned, looked at me for the first time, and – somehow clearly over the rasping sandstorm – said, 'Take that mask off.'

I remembered the bandanna. Lowering it, I spit sand as red mud.

As if satisfied, the girl stepped closer and jumped onto the mat. Now we were both sitting on the hovering, bobbing carpet – the girl behind me, our backpacks squeezed between us. I tugged the bandanna back up and shouted, 'Hang on to me!'

She ignored me and gripped the edges of the mat.

I hesitated a moment, tugging my sleeve back to study my wrist chronometer. Less than two minutes remained before the ship was scheduled to perform its touch-and-go at Chronos Keep. I couldn't even find the entrance to the Third Cave Tomb in that time – perhaps I could never find it in this carnage. As if to underline that point, a tracked scarab suddenly plowed over a dune, almost grinding us under its treads before it wheeled left, guns firing at something out of sight to the east.

'Hang on!' I shouted again, and keyed the mat to full acceleration, gaining altitude as I went, watching my compass and trying to keep flying north until we left the Valley. This was no time to crash into a cliff wall.

A great stone wing passed under us. 'Sphinx!' I shouted back to the girl huddling behind me. I realized in an instant how stupid this comment was – she had just come from that tomb.

Guessing our altitude to be several hundred meters, I leveled off and increased our speed. The deflection shield came on, but sand still whirled around us within the nacelle of trapped air. 'We shouldn't hit anything at this altitu—' I began, shouting over my shoulder again, but was interrupted by the looming shape of a skimmer flying directly at us in the storm cloud. I did not have time to react, but somehow I did, diving the mat so quickly that only the containment field held us in place, the shape of the skimmer passing over us with less than a meter to spare. The little hawking mat tumbled and twisted in the monster machine's lift-wake.

'Heck and spit,' said Aenea behind me. 'Hell and shit.'

It was the second utterance I heard from our messiah-to-be.

Leveling off again, I peered over the edge of the mat, trying to make out anything on the ground. It was folly to be flying so high – certainly every tactical sensor, detector, radar, and targeting imager in the area was tracking us. Except for the taste of chaos we had left behind, I had no idea why they hadn't fired at us yet. Unless . . . I looked over my shoulder again. The girl was leaning close to my back, shielding her face from the stinging sand.

'Are you all right?' I called.

She nodded, her forehead touching my back. I had the sense that she was crying, but I could not be sure.

'I'm Raul Endymion,' I shouted.

'Endymion,' she said, pulling her head back. Her eyes were red, but dry. 'Yes.'

'You're Aenea . . .' I stopped. I could not think of anything intelligent to say. Checking the compass, I adjusted our direction of flight and hoped that our altitude was sufficient to clear the dunes here beyond the Valley.

Without much hope, I looked up, wondering if the plasma trail of the ship would be visible through the storm. I saw nothing.

'Uncle Martin sent you,' said the girl. It was not a question.

'Yes,' I shouted back. 'We're going . . . well, the ship . . . I'd arranged for it to meet us at Chronos Keep, but we're late . . .'

A bolt of lightning ripped the clouds not thirty meters to our right. Both the child and I flinched and ducked. To this day I do not know if it was a lightning discharge or someone shooting at us. For the hundredth time on this endless day, I cursed the crudeness of this ancient flying device – no speed indicators, no altimeter. The wind roar beyond the deflection field suggested that we were traveling at full speed, but with no guidepoints except the shifting curtains of cloud, it was impossible to tell. It was as bad as hurtling through the labyrinth, but at least there the autopilot program had been dependable. Here, even with the entire Swiss Guard after us, I would have to decelerate soon: the Bridle Range of mountains with their vertical cliffs lay somewhere dead ahead. At almost three hundred klicks per hour, we should reach the mountains and the Keep within six minutes. I had checked my chronometer when we accelerated, now I glanced at it again. Four and a half minutes. According to maps I had studied, the desert ended abruptly at the Bridle Cliffs. I would give it another minute . . .

Things happened simultaneously then.

Suddenly we were out of the dust storm; it did not taper off, we just flew out of it the way one would emerge from under a blanket. At that second I saw that we were pitched slightly down – or the ground here was rising – and that we were going to strike some huge boulders within seconds.

Aenea shouted. I ignored her, tweaked the control designs with both hands, we lifted over the boulders with enough g-force to press us heavily against the hawking mat, and at that instant both the child and I saw that we were twenty meters from the cliff face and flying into it. There was no time to stop.

Theoretically, I knew, Sholokov's design for the hawking mat allowed it to fly vertically, the incipient containment field keeping the pas-senger – theoretically, his beloved niece – from tumbling off backward. Theoretically.

It was time to test the theory.

Aenea's arms came around my midsection as we accelerated into a ninety-degree climb. The mat took all of the twenty meters of free space to initiate the climb, and by the time we were vertical, the granite of the rock face was centimeters 'beneath' us. Instinctively, I leaned full forward and grabbed the rigid front of the carpet, trying not to lean on the flight-control designs as I did so. Equally instinctively, Aenea leaned forward and increased her bear hug on my midsection. The effect was that I could not breathe for the minute or so it took the carpet to clear the top of the cliffs. I tried not to look back over my shoulder during the duration of the climb. A thousand or more meters of open space directly beneath me might have been more than my overworked nerves could stand.

We reached the top of the cliffs – suddenly there were stairs carved there, stone terraces, gargoyles – and I leveled the carpet.

The Swiss Guard had set up observation posts, detector stations, and antiaircraft batteries here along the terraces and balconies on the east side of Chronos Keep. The castle itself – carved out of the stone of the mountain – loomed more than a hundred meters above us, its overhanging turrets and higher balconies directly above us. There were more Swiss Guard on these flat areas.

All of them were dead. Their bodies, still clad in impermeable impact armor, were sprawled in the unmistakable attitudes of death. Some were grouped together, their lacerated forms looking as if a plasma bomb had exploded in their midst.

But Pax body armor could withstand a plasma grenade at that distance. These corpses had been shredded.

'Don't look,' I called over my shoulder, slowing the mat as we banked around the south end of the Keep. It was too late. Aenea stared with wide eyes.

'Damn him!' she cried again.

'Damn who?' I asked, but at that moment we flew out over the garden area on the south end of the Keep and saw what there was there. Burning scarabs and an overturned skimmer littered the landscape. More bodies lay thrown like toys scattered by a vicious child. A CPB lancet, its beams capable of reaching to low orbit, lay shattered and burning by an ornamental hedge.

The Consul's ship hovered on a tail of blue plasma sixty meters above the central fountain. Steam billowed up and around it. A. Bettik stood at the open air-lock door and beckoned us on.

I flew us directly into the air lock, so quickly that the android had to leap aside and we actually skittered down the polished corridor.

'Go!' I shouted, but either A. Bettik had already given the command or the ship did not require it. Inertial compensators kept us from being smashed to jelly as the ship accelerated, but we could hear the fusion reaction-drive roar, hear the scream of atmosphere from beyond the hull, as the Consul's spaceship climbed away from Hyperion and entered space again for the first time in two centuries.

SIXTEEN

'How long have I been unconscious?' Father Captain de Soya is gripping the tunic of the medic.

'Uh . . . thirty, forty minutes, sir,' said the medic, attempting to pull his shirt free. He does not succeed.

'Where am I?' De Soya feels the pain now. It is very intense – centered in his leg but radiating everywhere – but bearable. He ignores it.

'Aboard the *Saint Thomas Akira*, Father sir.'

'The troopship . . .' De Soya feels light-headed, unconnected. He looks down at his leg, now freed from its tourniquet. The lower leg is attached to the upper only by fragments of muscle and tissue. He realizes that Gregorius must have given him a painkiller – insufficient to block such a torrent of agony, but enough to give him this narcotic high. 'Damn.'

'I'm afraid that the surgeons are going to amputate,' says the medic. 'The surgeries are working overtime. You're next, though, sir. We've been carrying out *triage* and . . .'

De Soya realizes that he is still gripping the young medic's tunic. He releases it. 'No.'

'Excuse me, Father sir?'

'You heard me. There'll be no surgery until I've met with the captain of the *Saint Thomas Akira*.'

'But sir . . . Father sir . . . you'll die if you don't . . .'

'I've died before, son.' De Soya fights off a wave of giddiness. 'Did a sergeant bring me to the ship?'

'Yessir.'

'Is he still here?'

'Yes, Father sir, the sergeant was receiving stitches for wounds that . . .'

'Send him in here immediately.'

'But, Father sir, your wounds require . . .'

De Soya looks at the young medic's rank. 'Ensign?'

'Yessir?'

'You saw the papal diskey?' De Soya had checked; the platinum template still hangs from the unbreakable chain around his neck.

'Yes, Father sir, that's what led us to prioritize your . . .'

'Upon pain of execution . . . and worse . . . upon pain of excommunication, shut up and send the sergeant in immediately, Ensign.'

Gregorius is out of his battle armor, but is still huge. The father-captain looks at the bandages and temporary doc paks on the big man's body and realizes that the sergeant had been badly wounded even as he was carrying de Soya out of danger. He makes a note to respond to that sometime – not now. 'Sergeant!'

Gregorius snaps to attention.

'Bring the captain of this ship here immediately. Quickly, before I black out again.'

The captain of the *Saint Thomas Akira* is a middle-aged Lusian, as short and powerful looking as all Lusians. He is perfectly bald but sports a neatly trimmed gray beard.

'Father Captain de Soya, I am Captain Lempriere. Things are very hectic now, sir. The surgeons assure me that you require immediate attention. How can I be of help?'

'Tell me the situation, Captain.' De Soya has not met the captain before, but they have spoken on tightbeam. He hears the deference in the troop-ship captain's voice. Out of the corner of his eye, de Soya sees Sergeant Gregorius excusing himself from the room. 'Stay, Sergeant. Captain? The situation?'

Lempriere clears his throat. 'Commander Barnes-Avne is dead. As far as we can tell, about half of the Swiss Guard in the Valley of the Time Tombs are also dead. Thousands of other casualties are pouring in. We have medics on the ground setting up mobile surgical centers, and we are ferrying the most severely wounded here for urgent care. The dead are being recovered and tagged for resurrection upon return to Renaissance Vector.'

'Renaissance Vector?' De Soya feels as if he is floating within the confined space of the surgical prep room. He *is* floating – within the confines of the gurney restraints. 'What the hell happened to the gravity, Captain?'

Lempriere smiles wanly. 'The containment field was damaged during the battle, sir. As for Renaissance Vector . . . well, it was our staging area, sir. Standing orders call for us to return there after the mission is completed.'

De Soya laughs, stopping only when he hears himself. It is not a totally sane laugh. 'Who says our mission is completed, Captain? What battle are we talking about?'

Captain Lempriere glances at Sergeant Gregorius. The Swiss Guard does not break his fixed, at-attention stare at the bulkhead. 'The support and covering craft in orbit were also decimated, sir.'

'Decimated?' The pain is making de Soya angry. 'That means one in ten, Captain. Are ten percent of ship's personnel on the casualty list?'

'No, sir,' says Lempriere, 'more like sixty percent. Captain Ramirez of the *Saint Bonaventure* is dead, as is his executive officer. My own first is dead. Half the crew of the *Saint Anthony* have not answered roll.'

'Are the ships damaged?' demands Father Captain de Soya. He knows that he has only a minute or two of consciousness . . . and perhaps life . . . left.

'There was an explosion on the *Saint Bonaventure*. At least half the compartments aft of the CIC vented to space. The drive is intact . . .'

De Soya closes his eyes. As a torchship captain himself, he knows that opening the craft to space is the penultimate nightmare. The ultimate

103

nightmare was the implosion of the Hawking core itself, but at least that indignity would be instantaneous. Having a hull breached across so many of the ship's areas was – like this shattered leg – a slow, painful path to death.

'The *Saint Anthony*?'

'Damaged, but operable, sir. Captain Sati is alive and . . .'

'The girl?' demands de Soya. 'Where is she?' Black spots dance in the periphery of his vision, and the cloud of them grows.

'Girl?' says Lempriere. Sergeant Gregorius says something to the captain that de Soya does not hear. There is a loud buzzing in his ears.

'Oh, yes,' says Lempriere, 'the acquisition objective. Evidently a ship retrieved her from the surface and is accelerating toward C-plus translation . . .'

'A ship!' De Soya fights away unconscious with a sheer effort of will. 'Where the hell did a ship come from?'

Gregorius speaks without breaking his staring match with the bulkhead. 'From the planet, sir. From Hyperion. During the . . . during the Charlie Fox event, the ship skipped through the atmosphere, set down at the castle . . . Chronos Keep, sir . . . and plucked the kid and whoever was flying her—'

'Flying her?' interrupts de Soya. It is hard to hear through the growing buzz.

'Some sort of one-person EMV,' says the sergeant. 'Although why it works, the tech boffins don't know. Anyway, this ship got 'em, got past the COP during the carnage, and is spinning up to translation.'

'Carnage,' repeats de Soya stupidly. He realizes that he is drooling. He wipes his chin with the back of his hand, trying not to look down at the remnants of his leg as he does so. 'Carnage. What caused it? Who were we fighting?'

'We don't know, sir,' answers Lempriere. 'It was like the old days . . . Hegemony Force days when the jumptroops came in by farcaster portal, sir. I mean, thousands of armored . . . things . . . appeared . . . everywhere, at the same second, sir. I mean, the battle only lasted five minutes. There were thousands of them. And then they were gone.'

De Soya is straining to hear this through the gathering darkness and the roaring in his ears, but the words make no sense. 'Thousands? Of what? Gone where?'

Gregorius steps forward and looks down at the father-captain. 'Not thousands, sir. Just one. The Shrike.'

'That's a legend . . .' begins Lempriere.

'Just the Shrike,' continues the huge black man, ignoring the troopship captain. 'It killed most of the Swiss Guard and half the regular Pax troops on Equus, downed all of the Scorpion fighters, took two torchships of the line out of business, killed everyone aboard the C^3 ship, left his calling card here, and was gone in under thirty seconds. Total. All the rest was our guys shooting each other in panic. The Shrike.'

'Nonsense!' shouts Lempriere, his bare scalp growing red with agitation.

'That's a fantasy, a tall tale, and a heresy at that! Whatever struck us today was no . . .'

'Shut up,' says de Soya. He feels as if he is looking and talking down a long, dark tunnel. Whatever he has to say, he must say quickly. 'Listen . . . Captain Lempriere . . . on my authority, on papal authority, authorize Captain Sati to take the survivors of the *Saint Bonaventure* aboard the *Saint Anthony* to round out the crew. Order Sati to follow the girl . . . the spacecraft bearing the girl . . . follow it to spinup, to fix its translation coordinates, and to follow . . .'

'But, Father Captain . . .' begins Lempriere.

'Listen,' shouts de Soya over the waterfall noise in his ears. He can no longer see anything but dancing spots. 'Listen . . . order Captain Sati to follow that ship anywhere . . . even if it takes a lifetime . . . and to capture the girl. That is his prime and total directive. Capture the girl and return her to Pacem. Gregorius?'

'Yes, sir.'

'Don't let them operate on me, Sergeant. Is my courier ship still intact?'

'The *Raphael*? Yes, sir. It was empty during the battle, the Shrike didn't touch it.'

'Is Hiroshe . . . my dropship pilot . . . still around?'

'No, sir. He was killed.'

De Soya can barely hear the sergeant's booming voice over the louder booming. 'Requisition a pilot and shuttle, Sergeant. Get me, you, and the rest of your squad—'

'Just two men now, sir.'

'Listen. Get the four of us to the *Raphael*. The ship will know what to do. Tell it that we're going to follow the girl . . . the ship . . . and the *Saint Anthony*. Wherever those ships go, we go. Sergeant?'

'Yes, Father Captain!'

'You and your men are born again, aren't you?'

'Yes, Father Captain!'

'Well, prepare to be born again for real, Sergeant.'

'But your leg . . .' says Captain Lempriere from very, very far away. His voice doppler-shifts as it recedes.

'I'll be reunited with it when I'm resurrected,' mutters Father Captain de Soya. He wants to close his eyes to say a prayer now, but he does not have to close his eyes to shut out the light – the darkness around him is absolute. Into that roaring and buzzing, not knowing if anyone can hear him or if he is really speaking, he says, 'Quickly, Sergeant. Now!'

SEVENTEEN

Now, writing this so many years later, I had thought it would be difficult to remember Aenea as a child. It is not. My memories are so full of later years, later images – rich sunlight on the woman's body as we floated among the branches of the orbital forest, the first time we made love in zero-gravity, strolling with her along the hangway walkways of Hsuan-k'ung Ssu with the rose-red cliffs of Hua Shan catching the rich light above us – that I had worried that those earlier memories would be too insubstantial. They are not. Nor have I given in to the impulse to leap ahead to the later years, despite my fear that this narrative will be interrupted at any second with the quantum-mechanical hiss of Schrödinger's poison gas. I will write what I can write. Fate will determine the ending point of this narrative.

A. Bettik led the way up the spiral staircase to the room with the piano as we roared up into space. The containment field kept the gravity constant, despite the wild acceleration, but still there was a wild sense of exhilaration in me – although perhaps it was just the aftermath of so much adrenaline in so little time. The child was dirty, disheveled, and still upset.

'I want to see where we are,' she said. 'Please.'

The ship complied by turning the wall beyond the holopit into a window. The continent of Equus receded below, the face of the horse obscured by red dust cloud. To the north, where clouds covered the pole, the limb of Hyperion arced into a distinct curve. Within a minute the entire world was a globe, two of the three continents visible beneath scattered cloud, the Great South Sea a breathtaking blue while the Nine Tails archipelago was surrounded by the green of shallows, and then the world shrank, became a blue-and-red-and-white sphere, and fell behind. We were leaving in a hurry.

'Where are the torchships?' I asked the android. 'They should have challenged us by now. Or blown us to bits.'

'The ship and I were monitoring their wideband channels,' said A. Bettik. 'They were . . . preoccupied.'

'I don't understand,' I said, pacing the rim of the holopit, too agitated to sit in the deep cushions. 'That battle . . . who . . .'

'The Shrike,' said Aenea, and really looked at me for the first time. 'Mother and I hoped it would not happen like that, but it did. I am so sorry. So terribly sorry.'

The girl's eyes were bright. Despite the mud and grit on her cheek, I could see the fairness of her complexion. 'So you're Endymion, like the poem,' she said.

'Poem?' I said. 'I don't know about a poem. It's Endymion like the old city.'

She smiled. 'I only know the poem because my father wrote it. How fitting of Uncle Martin to choose a hero with such a name.'

I squirmed at hearing the word 'hero'. This whole endeavor was turning out to be absurd enough without that.

The girl held out her small hand. 'Aenea,' she said. 'But I guess you know that.'

Her fingers were cool in my palm. 'The old poet said that you had changed your name a few times.'

Her smile lingered. 'And will again, I wager.' She withdrew her hand and then offered it to the android. 'Aenea. Orphan of time.'

A. Bettik shook her hand more gracefully than I had, bowed deeply, and introduced himself. 'I am at your service, M. Lamia,' he said.

She shook her head. 'My mother is . . . was . . . M. Lamia. I'm just Aenea.' She noticed my change in expression. 'You know of my mother?'

'She is famous,' I said, blushing slightly for some reason. 'All of the Hyperion pilgrims are. Legendary, actually. There is this poem, epic oral tale, actually . . .'

Aenea laughed. 'Oh, God, Uncle Martin finished his damn *Cantos*.'

I admit that I was shocked. My face must have shown it. I'm glad I was not playing poker this particular morning.

'Sorry,' said Aenea. 'Obviously the old fart's scribblings have become some sort of priceless cultural heritage. He's still alive? Uncle Martin, I mean.'

'Yes, M . . . yes, M. Aenea,' said A. Bettik. 'I have had the privilege of serving your uncle for over a century.'

The girl made a face. 'You must be a saint, M. Bettik.'

'A. Bettik, M. Aenea,' he said. 'And no, I am no saint. Merely an admirer and long acquaintance of your uncle.'

Aenea nodded. 'I met a few androids when we would fly up from Jacktown to visit Uncle Martin in the Poet's City, but not you. More than a century, you say. What year is it?'

I told her.

'Well, we got that part right, at least,' she said, and fell silent, staring at the hole of the receding world. Hyperion was only a spark now.

'You've really come from the past?' I said. It was a stupid question, but I wasn't feeling especially bright that morning.

Aenea nodded. 'Uncle Martin must have told you.'

'Yes. You're fleeing the Pax.'

She looked up. Her eyes were bright with unshed tears. 'The Pax? Is that what they call it?'

I blinked at that. The thought of someone being unfamiliar with the concept of the Pax shook me. This was real. 'Yes,' I said.

'So the Church does run everything now?'

'Well, in a way,' I said. I explained the role of the Church in the complex entity that was the Pax.

'They run everything,' concluded Aenea. 'We thought it might go that way. My dreams got that right, too.'

'Your dreams?'

'Never mind,' said Aenea. She stood, looked around the room, and walked to the Steinway. Her fingers picked out a few notes on the keyboard. 'And this is the Consul's ship.'

'Yes,' said the ship, 'although I have only vague memories of the gentleman. Did you know him?'

Aenea smiled, her fingers still trailing across the keys. 'No. My mother did. She gave him a present of that—' She pointed to the sand-covered hawking mat where it lay near the staircase. 'When he left Hyperion after the Fall. He was going back to the Web. He didn't return during my time.'

'He never did,' said the ship. 'As I say, my memories have been damaged, but I am sure that he died somewhere there.' The ship's soft voice changed, became more businesslike. 'We were hailed upon leaving the atmosphere, but have not been challenged or pursued since then. We have cleared cislunar space and will be out of Hyperion's critical gravity well within ten minutes. I need to set the course for spinup. Instructions, please.'

I looked at the girl. 'The Ousters? That's where the old poet said you'd want to go.'

'I changed my mind,' said Aenea. 'What's the nearest inhabited world, Ship?'

'Parvati. One-point-two-eight parsecs. Six and a half days' shiptime transit. Three months' time-debt.'

'Was Parvati part of the Web?' asked the girl.

A. Bettik answered. 'No. Not at the time of the Fall.'

'What's the nearest old Web world, traveling from Parvati?' said Aenea.

'Renaissance Vector,' said the ship immediately. 'It is an additional ten days' shiptime, five months' time-debt.'

I was frowning. 'I don't know,' I said. 'The hunters . . . I mean, off-worlders I used to work for usually came from Renaissance Vector. It's a big Pax world. Busy. Lots of ships and troops there, I think.'

'But it's the closest Web world?' said Aenea. 'It used to have farcasters.'

'Yes,' said the ship and A. Bettik at the same moment.

'Set course for Renaissance Vector by way of Parvati System,' said Aenea.

'It would be a shiptime day and two weeks of time-debt quicker to jump directly to Renaissance Vector, if that is our destination,' advised the ship.

'I know,' said Aenea, 'but I want to go by way of Parvati System.' She must have seen the question in my eyes, for she said, 'They'll be following us, and I don't want them to know the real destination when we spin up out of this system.'

'They are not in pursuit now,' said A. Bettik.

'I know,' said Aenea. 'But they will be in a few hours. Then and for the rest of my life.' She looked back at the holopit as if the ship's persona resided there. 'Carry out the command, please.'

The stars shifted on the holodisplay as the ship obeyed. 'Twenty-seven minutes to translation point for Parvati System,' it said. 'Still no challenge or pursuit, although the torchship *Saint Anthony* is underway, as is the troopship.'

'What about the other torchship?' I said. 'The . . . what was it? The *Saint Bonaventure*.'

'Common band communications traffic and sensors show that it is open to space and emitting distress signals,' said the ship. 'The *Saint Anthony* is responding.'

'My God,' I whispered. 'What was it, an Ouster attack?'

The girl shook her head and walked away from the piano. 'Just the Shrike. My father warned me . . .' She fell silent.

'The Shrike?' It was the android who spoke. 'To my knowledge, in legend and the old records, the creature called the Shrike never left Hyperion – usually staying in the area within a few hundred kilometers around the Time Tombs.'

Aenea dropped back into the cushions. Her eyes were still red and she looked tired. 'Yeah, well, he's wandering farther afield now, I'm afraid. And if Father is right, it's just the beginning.'

'The Shrike hasn't been seen or heard from for almost three hundred years,' I said.

The girl nodded, distracted. 'I know. Not since the tombs opened right before the Fall.' She looked up at the android. 'Gosh, I'm starved. And filthy.'

'I will help the ship prepare lunch,' said A. Bettik. 'There are showers upstairs in the master bedroom and on the fugue deck below us,' he said. 'Also a bath in the master bedroom.'

'That's where I'm headed,' said the girl. 'I'll be down before we make the quantum jump. See you in twenty minutes.' On her way to the stairs she stopped and took my hand again. 'Raul Endymion, I'm sorry if I seem ungrateful. Thank you for risking your life for me. Thank you for coming with me on this trip. Thank you for getting into something so big and complicated that neither one of us can imagine where we're going to end up.'

'You're welcome,' I said stupidly.

The child grinned at me. 'You need a shower, too, friend. Someday we'll take it together, but right now I think you should use the one on the fugue deck.'

Blinking, not knowing what to think, I watched her bounce up the stairs.

EIGHTEEN

Father Captain de Soya awakens in a resurrection crechage aboard the *Raphael*. He had been allowed to name the archangel-class ship. Raphael is the archangel in charge of finding lost loves.

He has been reborn only twice before, but each time he has been greeted formally and given the ceremonial sip of sacramental wine from the cup and then the customary glass of orange juice. There have been resurrection experts there to talk to him, explain things to him, until his befuddled mind begins to work again.

This time there are only the claustrophobic, curved walls of the resurrection creche. Telltales blink and readouts share lines of print and symbols. De Soya cannot read yet. He feels lucky to be thinking at all. He sits up and dangles his legs over the edge of the resurrection bed.

My legs. I have two of them. He is naked, of course, his skin pink and gleaming in the strange, parboiled wetness of the resurrection tank, and now he feels his ribs, his abdomen, his left leg – all the places slashed and ruined by the demon. He is perfect. There is no sign of the terrible wound that had separated his leg from his body.

'*Raphael?*'

'Yes, Father Captain?' The voice is angelic, which is to say, totally devoid of sexual identity. De Soya finds it soothing.

'Where are we?'

'Parvati System, Father Captain.'

'The others?' De Soya has only the foggiest memory of Sergeant Gregorius and his two surviving squad members. No memory of boarding the courier ship with them.

'Being awakened as we speak, Father Captain.'

'How much time has passed?'

'Just a bit less than four days since the sergeant brought you aboard, Father Captain. The enhanced jump was carried out within the hour of your installation in the resurrection creche. We have been station-keeping ten AUs from the world of Parvati, as per your instructions via Sergeant Gregorius, for the three days of your resurrection.'

De Soya nods his understanding. Even that slight motion is painful. Every cell in his body aches from resurrection. But the pain is a healthy ache, unlike the terrible pain of his wounds. 'Have you contacted the Pax authorities on Parvati?'

'No, Father Captain.'

'Good.' Parvati had been a remote colony world during the days of the Hegemony; now it is a remote Pax colony. It holds no interstellar spacecraft – Pax military or Mercantilus – and only a small military contingent and a few crude interplanetary ships. If the girl was going to be captured in this system, the *Raphael* would have to do the capturing.

'Update on the girl's ship?' he says.

'The unidentified spacecraft spun up two hours and eighteen minutes before we did,' said *Raphael*. 'The translation coordinates were undoubtedly for Parvati System. Arrival time for the unidentified ship is approximately two months, three weeks, two days, and seventeen hours.'

'Thank you,' says de Soya. 'When Gregorius and the others are revived and dressed, have them meet me in the situation room.'

'Yes, Father Captain.'

'Thank you,' he says again. He thinks, *Two months, three weeks, two days . . . Mother of Mercy, what am I going to do for almost three months in this backwater system?* Perhaps he had not thought through this clearly. Certainly he had been distracted by trauma, pain, and drugs. But the next nearest Pax system was Renaissance Vector, which was ten days' shiptime travel from Parvati, five months' time-debt – three and a half days and two months after the girl's ship would arrive from Hyperion System. No, he might not have been thinking clearly – he is not now, he realizes – but he had made the right decision. Better to come here and think things over.

I could jump to Pacem. Ask for instructions directly from Pax Command . . . from the Pope, even. Recuperate for two and a half months and jump back here with time to spare.

De Soya shakes his head, grimaces from the discomfort of doing so. He has his instructions. Capture the girl and return her to Pacem. Returning to the Vatican would be only an admission of failure. Perhaps they would send someone else. During the preflight briefing, Captain Marget Wu had made it clear that the *Raphael* was unique – the only armed, six-person archangel-class courier ship in existence – and although another might have come on-line in the months of time-debt that have elapsed since he left Pacem, there is little sense in returning now. If *Raphael* was still the only armed arch-angel, all de Soya could do would be add two more troopers to the ship's roster.

Death and resurrection are not to be taken lightly. That precept had been driven home time and again in de Soya's catechism when he was growing up. Just because the sacrament exists and is offered to the faithful, does not mean it should be exercised without great solemnity and restraint.

No, I'll talk to Gregorius and the others and figure things out here. We can make our plans, then use the cryogenic-fugue cubbies to wait the last couple of months. When the girl's ship arrives, the Saint Anthony *will be in hot pursuit. Between the torchship and* Raphael, *we should be able to interdict the ship, board her, and retrieve the girl without problem.*

Logically, this all makes sense to de Soya's aching brain, but another part of his mind is whispering, *Without problem . . . this is what you thought about the Hyperion mission.*

Father Captain de Soya groans, lifts himself down from the resurrection couch, and pads off in search of a shower, hot coffee, and some clothes.

NINETEEN

I knew little about the principles of the Hawking drive when I first experienced it years ago; I know little more about it now. The fact that it was essentially (if accidentally) the brainchild of someone who lived in the twentieth century, Christian Era, boggled my mind then as it does now, but not nearly as much as the experience itself.

We met in the library – formally known as the navigation level, the ship informed us – a few minutes before translation to C-plus speeds. I was dressed in my spare set of clothes and my hair was wet, as was Aenea's. The child wore only a thick robe, which she must have found in the Consul's closet, because the garment was far too large for her. She looked even younger than her twelve years, swallowed as she was in all those yards of terry cloth.

'Shouldn't we be getting to the cryogenic-fugue couches?' I asked.

'Why?' said Aenea. 'Don't you want to see the fun?'

I frowned. All the offworld hunters and military instructors I had spoken to had spent their C-plus time in fugue. That's the way humans had always spent their time between the stars. Something about the effect of the Hawking field on the body and mind. I had images of hallucinations, waking nightmares, and unspeakable pain. I said as much while trying to sound calm about it.

'Mother and Uncle Martin told me that C-plus can be endured,' said the girl. 'Even enjoyed. It just takes some getting used to.'

'And this ship was modified by the Ousters to make it easier,' said A. Bettik. Aenea and I were sitting at the low glass table in the middle of the library area; the android stood to one side. Try as I might to treat him as an equal, A. Bettik insisted on acting like a servant. I resolved to quit being an egalitarian horse's ass about it and to let him act any way he wanted.

'Indeed,' said the ship, 'the modifications included an enhanced containment-field capability, which makes the side effects of C-plus travel much less disagreeable.'

'What exactly *are* the side effects?' I asked, not willing to show the full extent of my naïveté, but also not willing to suffer if I didn't have to.

The android, the girl, and I looked at each other. 'I have traveled between the stars in centuries past,' A. Bettik said at last, 'but I was always in fugue. In storage, actually. We androids were shipped in cargo holds, stacked like frozen sides of beef, I am told.'

Now the girl and I looked at each other, embarrassed to meet the blue-skinned man's gaze.

The ship made a noise that sounded remarkably like someone clearing his throat. 'Actually,' it said, 'from my observations of human passengers – which, I must say, is suspect because . . .'

'Because your memory is hazy,' the girl and I said in unison. We looked at each other again and laughed. 'Sorry, Ship,' said Aenea. 'Go on.'

'I was just going to say that from my observations, the primary effect of the C-plus environment on humans is some visual confusion, mental depression brought about by the field, and simple boredom. I believe that cryogenic fugue was developed for the long voyages, and is used as a convenience for shorter trips such as this.'

'And your . . . ah . . . Ouster modifications ameliorate these side effects?' I said.

'They are designed to,' replied the ship. 'All except boredom, of course. That is a peculiarly human phenomenon, and I do not believe that a cure has been found.' There was a moment of silence, and then the ship said, 'We will reach the translation point in two minutes ten seconds. All systems are functioning optimally. Still no pursuit, although the *Saint Anthony* is tracking us on its long-range detectors.'

Aenea stood up. 'Let's go down and watch the shift to C-plus.'

'Go down and watch?' I said. 'Where? The holopit?'

'No,' called the girl from the stairway. 'From outside.'

The spaceship had a balcony. I hadn't known that. One could stand outside on it even while the ship was hurtling through space, preparing to translate to C-plus pseudo-velocities. I hadn't known that – and if I had, I would not have believed it.

'Extend the balcony, please,' the girl had said to the ship, and the ship had extended the balcony – the Steinway moving out with it – and we'd walked through the open archway into space. Well, not really into space, of course; even I, the provincial shepherd, knew that our eardrums would have exploded, our eyes burst, and our blood boiled in our bodies if we had stepped into hard vacuum. But it *looked* as if we were walking out into hard vacuum.

'Is this safe?' I asked, leaning against the railing. Hyperion was a star-sized speck behind us, Hyperion's star a blazing sun to port, but the plasma tail of our fusion drive – tens of klicks long – gave the impression that we were perched precariously on a tall blue pillar. The effect was a definite inducement to acrophobia, as the illusion of standing unprotected in space created something akin to agoraphobia. I had not known until that instant that I was susceptible to any phobia.

'If the containment field fails for a second,' said A. Bettik, 'under this g-load and velocity, we will die immediately. It matters little if we are inside or outside the ship.'

'Radiation?' I said.

'The field deflects cosmic and harmful solar radiation, of course,' said the android, 'and opaques the view of Hyperion's sun so that we do not go blind when we stare at it. Other than that, it allows the visible spectrum through quite nicely.'

'Yes,' I said, not convinced. I stepped back from the railing.

'Thirty seconds to translation,' said the ship. Even out here, its voice seemed to emanate from midair.

Aenea sat at the piano bench and began playing. I did not recognize the tune, but it sounded classical . . . something from the twenty-sixth century, perhaps.

I guess that I had expected the ship to speak again prior to the actual moment of translation – intone a final countdown or something – but there was no announcement. Suddenly the Hawking drive took over from the fusion drive; there was a momentary hum, which seemed to come from my bones; a terrible vertigo flooded over me and through me – it felt as if I were being turned inside out, painlessly but relentlessly; and then the sensation was gone before I could really comprehend it.

Space was also gone. By space, I mean the scene that I had been viewing less than a second earlier – Hyperion's brilliant sun, the receding disk of the planet itself, the bright glare along the hull of the ship, the few bright stars visible through that glare, even the pillar of blue flame upon which we had been perched – all gone. In its place was . . . It is hard to describe.

The ship was still there, looming 'above and below' us – the balcony upon which we stood still seemed substantial – but there seemed to be no light striking any part of it. I realize how absurd that sounds even as I write the words – there must be reflected light for anything to be seen – but the effect was truly as if part of my eyes had ceased working, and while they registered the *shape* and *mass* of the ship, light seemed to be missing.

Beyond the ship, the universe had contracted into a blue sphere near the bow and a red sphere behind the fins at the stern. I knew enough basic science to have expected a Doppler effect, but this was a false effect, since we had not been anywhere near the speed of light until translation to C-plus and were now far beyond it within the Hawking fold. Nonetheless, the blue and red circles of light – I could make out stars clustered in both spheres if I stared hard enough – now migrated farther to the bow and stern, shrinking to tiny dots of color. In between, filling the vast field of vision, there was . . . nothing. By that, I do not mean blackness or darkness. I mean void. I mean the sense of sickening nonsight one has when trying to look into a blind spot. I mean a nothing so intense that the vertigo it induced almost immediately changed to nausea within me, wracking my system as violently as the transitory sense of being pulled inside out had seconds before.

'My God!' I managed to say, gripping the rail tightly and squeezing my eyes shut. It did not help. The void was there as well. I understood at that second why interstellar voyagers always opted for cryogenic fugue.

Incredibly, unbelievably, Aenea continued playing the piano. The notes were clear, crystalline, as if unmodified by any connecting medium. Even with my eyes closed I could see A. Bettik standing by the door, blue face raised to the void. No, I realized, he was no longer blue . . . colors did not exist here. Nor did black, white, or gray. I wondered if humans who had been blind since birth dreamed of light and colors in this mad way.

'Compensating,' said the ship, and its voice had the same crystalline quality as Aenea's piano notes.

Suddenly the void collapsed in on itself, vision returned, and the spheres of red and blue returned fore and aft. Within seconds the blue sphere from the stern migrated along the ship like a doughnut passing over a writing stylus. It merged with the red sphere at the bow, and without warning colored geometries burst from the forward sphere like flying creatures emerging from an egg. I say 'colored geometries,' but this does nothing to share the complex reality: fractal-generated shapes pulsed and coiled and twisted through what had been the void. Spiral forms, spiked with their own subgeometries, curled in on themselves, spitting smaller forms of the same cobalt and blood-red brilliance. Yellow ovoids became pulsar-precise explosions of light. Mauve and indigo helixes, looking like the universe's DNA, spiraled past us. I could *hear* these colors like distant thunder, like the pounding of surf just beyond the horizon.

I realized that my jaw was hanging slack. I turned away from the railing and tried to concentrate on the girl and android. The colors of the fractal universe played across them. Aenea still played softly, her fingers moving across keys even as she looked up at me and at the fractal heavens beyond me.

'Maybe we should go inside,' I said, hearing each word in my own voice hanging separately in the air like icicles along a branch.

'Fascinating,' said A. Bettik, arms still folded, his gaze on the tunnel of forms surrounding us. His skin was blue again.

Aenea stopped playing. Perhaps sensing my vertigo and terror for the first time, she rose, took my hand, and led me inside the ship. The balcony followed us in. The hull re-formed. I was able to breathe again.

'We have six days,' the girl said. We were sitting in the holopit because the cushions were comfortable there. We had eaten, and A. Bettik had fetched us cold fruit drinks from the refrigerator drawers. My hand shook only slightly as we sat and talked.

'Six days, nine hours, and twenty-seven minutes,' said the ship.

Aenea looked up at the bulkhead. 'Ship, you can stay quiet for a while unless there's something vital you have to say or we have a question for you.'

'Yes, M . . . Aenea,' said the ship.

'Six days,' repeated the girl. 'We have to get ready.'

I sipped my drink. 'Ready for what?'

'I think they'll be there waiting for us. We have to come up with a way to get through Parvati System and on to Renaissance Vector without their stopping us.'

I considered the child. She looked tired. Her hair was still straggly from the shower. With all of the *Cantos* talk of the One Who Teaches, I had expected someone extraordinary – a young messiah in toga, a prodigy delivering cryptic utterances – but the only thing extraordinary about this young person was the powerful clarity of her dark eyes. 'How could they be waiting for us?' I said. 'The fatline hasn't worked for centuries. The Pax ships behind us can't call ahead as they could in your time.'

Aenea shook her head. 'No, the fatline had fallen before I was born. Remember, my mother was pregnant with me during the Fall.' She looked at A. Bettik. The android was drinking juice, but he had not chosen to sit down. 'I'm sorry I don't remember you. As I said, I used to visit the Poet's City and thought I knew all of the androids.'

He bowed his head slightly. 'No reason for you to remember me, M. Aenea. I had left the Poet's City even before your mother's pilgrimage. My siblings and I were working along the Hoolie River and on the Sea of Grass then. After the Fall, we . . . left service . . . and lived alone in different places.'

'I see,' she said. 'There was a lot of craziness after the Fall. I remember. Androids would have been in danger west of the Bridle Range.'

I caught her gaze. 'No, seriously, how could someone be waiting for us at Parvati? They can't outrun us – we got to quantum velocity first – so the best they can do is translate into Parvati space an hour or two after us.'

'I know,' said Aenea, 'but I still think that, somehow, they'll be waiting. We have to come up with a way this unarmed ship can outrun or out-maneuver a warship.'

We talked for several more minutes, but none of us – not even the ship when queried – had a clever idea. All the time we were talking, I was observing the girl – the way her lips turned up slightly in a smile when she was thinking, the slight furrow in her brow when she spoke earnestly, how soft her voice was. I understood why Martin Silenus wanted her protected from harm.

'I wonder why the old poet didn't call us before we left the system?' I mused aloud. 'He must have wanted to talk to you.'

Aenea ran her fingers through her hair like a comb. 'Uncle Martin would never greet me via tightbeam or holo. We were agreed that we would speak after this trip was over.'

I looked at her. 'So you two planned the whole thing? I mean – your getaway, the hawking mat – everything?'

She smiled again at the thought. 'My mother and I planned the essential details. After she died, Uncle Martin and I discussed the plan. He saw me off to the Sphinx this morning . . .'

'This morning?' I said, confused. Then I understood.

'It's been a long day for me,' the girl said ruefully. 'I took a few steps this morning and covered half the time that humans have been on Hyperion. Everyone I knew – except Uncle Martin – must be dead.'

'Not necessarily,' I said. 'The Pax arrived not long after you disappeared, so many of your friends and family could have accepted the cross. They would still be here.'

'"Accepted the cross,"' repeated the girl, and shivered slightly. 'I don't have any family – my mother was my only real family – and I sort of doubt that many of my friends or my mother's friends would have . . . accepted the cross.'

We stared at each other in silence for a moment, and I realized how exotic this young creature was; most of the historical events on Hyperion I was familiar with had not yet occurred when this girl had taken her step into the Sphinx 'this morning'.

'So, anyway,' she said, 'we didn't plan things down to the detail of the hawking mat – we didn't know if the Consul's ship would return with it, of course – but Mother and I did plan to use the Labyrinth if the Valley of the Tombs was off-limits. That worked out all right. And we hoped that the Consul's ship would be here to get me offplanet.'

'Tell me about your time,' I said.

Aenea shook her head. 'I will,' she said, 'but not now. You know about my era. It's history and legend to you. I don't know anything about your time – except for my dreams – so tell me about the present. How wide is it? How deep is it? How much is mine to keep?'

I did not recognize the allusion of the last questions, but I began telling her about the Pax – about the great cathedral in Saint Joseph and the . . .

'Saint Joseph?' she said. 'Where's that?'

'You used to call it Keats,' I said. 'The capital. It was also called Jacktown.'

'Ah,' she said, settling back in the cushions, the glass of fruit juice balanced in her slender fingers, 'they changed the heathen name. Well, my father wouldn't mind.'

It was the second time she had mentioned her father – I assumed she was speaking of the Keats cybrid – but I did not stop to ask her about that.

'Yes,' I said, 'many of the old cities and landmarks were renamed when Hyperion joined the Pax two centuries ago. There was talk of renaming the world itself, but the old name stuck. Anyway, the Pax does not govern directly but the military brought order to . . .' I went on for some time, filling her in on details of technology, culture, language, and government. I described what I had heard, read, and watched of life on more advanced Pax worlds, including the glories of Pacem.

'Gee,' she said when I paused, 'things really haven't changed that much. It sounds as if technology is sort of stuck . . . still not caught up to Hegemony days.'

'Well,' I said, 'the Pax is partly responsible for that. The Church prohibits thinking machines – true AIs – and its emphasis is on human and spiritual development rather than technological advancement.'

Aenea nodded. 'Sure, but you'd think that they would have caught up to WorldWeb levels in two and a half centuries. I mean, it's like a Dark Ages or something.'

I smiled as I realized that I was taking offense – being annoyed at criticism of the Pax society I had chosen not to join. 'Not really,' I said. 'Remember, the largest change has been the granting of virtual immortality. Because of that, the population growth is regulated carefully and there is less incentive to change exterior things. Most born-again Christians consider themselves to be in this life for the long haul – many centuries, at least, and millennia with luck – so they aren't in a hurry to change things.'

Aenea regarded me carefully. 'So the cruciform resurrection stuff really works?'

'Oh, yes.'

'Then why haven't you . . . accepted the cross?'

For the third time in recent days, I was at a loss to explain. I shrugged. 'Perversity, I guess. I'm stubborn. Also, a lot of people like me stay away from it when we're young – we all plan to live forever, right – and then convert when age starts setting in.'

'Will you?' Her dark eyes were piercing.

I stopped myself from shrugging again, but the gesture of my hand was the equivalent. 'I don't know,' I said. I had not told her yet about my 'execution' and subsequent resurrection with Martin Silenus. 'I don't know,' I said again.

A. Bettik stepped into the holopit circle. 'I thought that I might mention that we have stocked the ship with an ample supply of ice cream. In several flavors. Could I interest either of you in some?'

I formed a phrase reminding the android that he was not a servant on this voyage, but before I could speak, Aenea cried, 'Yes! Chocolate!'

A. Bettik nodded, smiled, and turned in my direction. 'M. Endymion?'

It had been a long day: hawking-mat voyages through the Labyrinth, dust storms, carnage – she said it was the Shrike! – and my first offworld trip. Quite a day.

'Chocolate,' I said. 'Yes. Definitely chocolate.'

TWENTY

The surviving members of Sergeant Gregorius's squad are Corporal Bassin Kee and Lancer Ahranwhal Gaspa K. T. Rettig. Kee is a small man, compact and quick in both reflexes and intelligence, while Rettig is tall – almost as tall as the giant Gregorius – but as thin as the sergeant is massive. Rettig is from the Lambert Ring Territories and has the radiation scars, skeletal frame, and independent bent so stereotypical of 'stroiders. De Soya has learned that the man had never set foot on a full-sized, full-g world until he was twenty-three standard years old. RNA medication and serious Pax military exercise has toughened and strengthened the trooper until he can fight on any world. Reserved to the point of muteness, A.G.K.T. Rettig listens well, follows orders well, and – as the battle on Hyperion showed – survives well.

Corporal Kee is as voluble as Rettig is silent. During their first day of discussion, Kee's questions and comments show insight and clarity, despite the brain-fogging effects of resurrection.

All four of the men are shaken by the experience of death. De Soya tries to convince them that it gets easier with experience, but his own shaken body and wits put the lie to these reassurances. Here, without counseling and therapy and the welcoming resurrection chaplains, each of the Pax soldiers is dealing with the trauma as best they can. Their conferences on the first day in Parvati space are interrupted frequently as fatigue or sheer emotion overcome them. Only Sergeant Gregorius is outwardly unshaken by the experience.

On the third day they meet in *Raphael*'s tiny wardroom cubby to plot their final course of action.

'In two months and three weeks, that ship is going to translate into this system less than a thousand klicks from where we're station-holding,' says Father Captain de Soya, 'and we have to be certain we can intercept it and detain the girl.'

None of the Swiss Guard soldiers has asked why the girl's detention is required. None will discuss the issue until their commanding officer – de Soya – raises it first. Each will die, if necessary, to carry out the cryptic order.

'We don't know who else is on board the ship, right?' says Corporal Kee. They have discussed these items, but memories are faulty for the first few days of their new lives.

'No,' says de Soya.

'We don't know the armament of the ship,' says Kee, as if checking off a mental list.

'Correct.'

'We don't know if Parvati is the ship's destination.'

'Correct.'

'It could be,' says Corporal Kee, 'that the ship is scheduled to rendezvous with another ship here . . . or perhaps the girl means to meet someone on the planet.'

De Soya nods. 'The *Raphael* doesn't have the sensors of my old torchship, but we're sweeping everything between the Oort cloud and Parvati itself. If another ship translates before the girl's, we'll know at once.'

'Ouster?' says Sergeant Gregorius.

De Soya raises his hands. 'Everything's speculation. I can tell you that the child is considered a threat to the Pax, so it's reasonable to conclude that the Ousters – if they know of her existence – might want to grab her. We're ready if they try.'

Kee rubs his smooth cheek. 'I still can't quite believe we could hop home in a day if we wanted to. Or go for help.' Home for Corporal Kee is the Jamnu Republic on Deneb Drei. They have discussed why it would be useless to ask for help – the closest Pax warship is the *Saint Anthony*, which should be, if de Soya's orders were obeyed, in hot pursuit of the girl's ship.

'I've tightbeamed the commander of the Pax garrison on Parvati,' says de Soya. 'As our computer inventory showed, they have just their orbital patrol craft and a couple of rock jumpers. I've ordered him to put every spacecraft they have into cislunar defensive positions, to alert all the outposts on the planet, and to await further orders. If the girl was to get past us and land there, the Pax would find her.'

'What kind of world is Parvati?' asks Gregorius. The man's bass rumble of a voice always gets de Soya's attention.

'It was settled by Reformed Hindus not long after the Hegira,' says de Soya, who has accessed all this on the ship's computer. 'Desert world. Not enough oxygen to support humans – mostly CO_2 atmosphere – and it was never enough of a success to terraform, so either the environments are tailored or the people are. Population was never large – a few dozen million before the Fall. Fewer than half a million now, and most of them live in the one big city of Gandhiji.'

'Christians?' asks Kee. De Soya guesses that the question is more than idle curiosity; Kee asks few random questions.

'A few thousand in Gandhiji have converted,' says de Soya. 'There is a new cathedral there – St Malachy's – and most of the born-again are prominent businesspeople who favor joining the Pax. They talked the planetary government – a sort of elective oligarchy – into inviting the Pax garrison here about fifty standard years ago. They're close enough to the Outback to worry about the Ousters.'

Kee nods. 'I just wondered if the garrison could count on the populace reporting it when the girl's ship lands.'

'Doubtful,' says de Soya. 'Ninety-nine percent of the world is empty –

never settled, or gone back to sand dunes and lichen fields – with most of the people huddled around the big boxite mines near Gandhiji. But the orbital patrols would track her.'

'If she gets that far,' says Gregorius.

'Which she will not,' says Father Captain de Soya. He touches a tabletop monitor, which brings up the graphic he has prepared. 'Here's the intercept plan. We snooze until T-minus three days. Don't worry – remember, fugue doesn't have the hangover time of resurrection. Half an hour to shake the cobwebs out. Okay . . . so T-minus three days, the alarm goes off. *Raphael's* been looping out to here—' He taps the diagram at a point two-thirds the way around the ellipsoid trajectory. 'We know their ship's C-plus entry velocity, which means we know their exit velocity . . . it will be about point-zero-three C, so if they're decelerating toward Parvati at the same rate they left Hyperion . . .' The trajectory and timeline diagrams fill the screen. 'This is hypothetical, but their translation point is not . . . it will be *here*.' He touches a stylus to a red point ten AUs from the planet. Their own trajectory ellipsoid blinks its way to that point. 'And *here* is where we intercept them, less than a minute from their translation point.'

Gregorius leans over his monitor. 'We'll all be going like a fucking bat out of hell, pardon the language, Father.'

De Soya smiles. 'You are absolved, my son. Yes, velocities will be high, as will be our combined delta-v's if their ship commences deceleration toward Parvati, but relative velocities for the two ships will be almost nil.'

'How close will we be, Captain?' says Kee. The man's black hair glistens in the overhead spots.

'When they translate, we'll be bearing down on them at a distance of six hundred klicks. Within three minutes we'll be able to throw a rock at them.'

Kee frowns. 'But what will they throw at us?'

'Unknown,' says de Soya. 'But the *Raphael* is tough. I'm betting that her shields can take anything this unidentified ship throws at us.'

Lancer Rettig grunts. 'Bad bet to lose.'

De Soya swivels his chair to look at the trooper. He had almost forgotten Rettig was there. 'Yes,' he says, 'but we have the advantage of being close. Whatever they throw at us, they'll have a limited time to throw.'

'And what do we throw at them?' rumbled Gregorius.

De Soya pauses. 'I've gone over *Raphael's* armament with you,' he says at last. 'If this were an Ouster warship, we could fry, bake, ram, or burn it. Or we could just make its crew die quietly.' *Raphael* carries deathbeam weaponry. At five hundred klicks, there would be no doubt of its effectiveness.

'But we're not going to use any of that . . .' continues the father-captain. 'Unless we absolutely have to . . . to disable the ship.'

'Can you do that without danger of hurting the girl?' asks Kee.

'Not with a hundred percent assurance of not hurting her . . . and whoever else is aboard,' says de Soya. He pauses again, takes a breath, and continues. 'That's why you're going to board her.'

Gregorius grins. His teeth are very large and very white. 'We grabbed space armor for all of us before leaving the *Saint Thomas Akira*,' rumbles the giant happily. 'But it'd be better if we practiced in it before the actual boarding.'

De Soya nods. 'Three days enough?'

Gregorius is still grinning. 'I'd rather have a week.'

'All right,' says the father-captain. 'We'll wake up a week before intercept. Here's a schematic of the unidentified ship.'

'I thought it was . . . unidentified,' says Kee, looking at the ship's plans now filling the monitors. The spacecraft is a needle with fins at one end – a child's caricature of a spaceship.

'We don't know its specific identity or registration,' says de Soya, 'but the *Saint Anthony* tightbeamed video that it and the *Bonaventure* took of the ship before we translated. It's not Ouster.'

'Not Ouster, not Pax, not Mercantilus, not a spinship or torchship . . .' says Kee. 'What the hell is it?'

De Soya advances the images to ship cross-sections. 'Private spacecraft, Hegemony era,' he says softly. 'Only thirty or so ever made. At least four hundred years old, probably older.'

Corporal Kee whistles softly. Gregorius rubs his huge jaw. Even Rettig looks impressed behind his impassive mask. 'I didn't know there ever were private spacecraft,' says the corporal. 'C-plus, I mean.'

'The Hegemony used to reward high-mucka-mucks with them,' says de Soya. 'Prime Minister Gladstone used to have one. So did General Horace Glennon-Height . . .'

'The Hegemony didn't reward *him* with one,' says Kee with a chuckle. Glennon-Height was the most infamous and legendary opponent the early Hegemony ever had – the Outback's Hannibal to the WorldWeb's Rome.

'No,' agrees Father Captain de Soya, 'the general stole his from the planetary Governor of Sol Draconi Septem. Anyway, the computer says that all of these private ships were accounted for before the Fall – destroyed or reconfigured for FORCE use and then decommissioned – but the computer appears to be wrong.'

'Not the first time,' grumbles Gregorius. 'Do these long-range images show any armament or defensive systems?'

'No, the original ships were civilian – no weapons – and the *Saint Bonaventure*'s sensors didn't pick up any acquisition radars or pulse readings before the Shrike killed the imaging team,' says de Soya, 'but this ship's been around for centuries, so we have to assume that it has been modified. But even if it has modern Ouster standoff weaponry, *Raphael* should be able to get in close, fast, while we hold off their lances. Once we're alongside, they can't use kinetic weapons. By the time we grapple, the energy weapons will be useless.'

'Hand to hand,' says Gregorius to himself. The sergeant is studying the schematic. 'They'd be waiting at the air lock, so we'll blow a new door here . . . and here . . .'

De Soya feels a prickling of alarm. 'We can't let the atmosphere out . . . the girl . . .'

Gregorius shows a shark's grin. 'Not to worry, sir. It takes less than a minute to rig a big catchbag on the hull . . . I brought several with the armor . . . and then we blow the hull section inward, scoot in . . .' He keys a closer image. 'I'll rig this for stimsim, so we can rehearse in three-D for a few days. I'd like another week for sim.' The black face turns toward de Soya. 'We may not get any fugue beauty sleep after all, sir.'

Kee is tapping his lip with a finger. 'Question, Captain.'

De Soya looks at him.

'I understand that under no circumstances can we harm the girl, but what about others that get in the way?'

De Soya sighs. He has been waiting for the question. I'd prefer that no one else dies on this mission, Corporal.'

'Yes, sir,' says Kee, his eyes alert, 'but what if they try to stop us?'

Father Captain de Soya blanks the monitor. The crowded cubby smells of oil and sweat and ozone. 'My orders were that the child is not to be harmed,' he says slowly, carefully. 'Nothing was said about anyone else. If there's someone . . . or something . . . else on the ship and they try to get in the way, consider them expendable. Defend yourselves, even if you have to shoot before you're certain you're in danger.'

'Kill them all,' mutters Gregorius, 'except the kid . . . and let God sort them out.'

De Soya has always hated that ancient mercenary joke.

'Do whatever you have to do without endangering the girl's life or health,' he says.

'What if there's only one other on board standing between us and the girl?' says Rettig. The other three men look at the 'stroider. 'But it's the Shrike thing?' he finishes.

The cubby is silent except for the omnipresent ship sounds – expanding and contracting metal from the hull, the whisper of ventilators, the hum of equipment, the occasional burp of a thruster.

'If it's the Shrike . . .' begins Father Captain de Soya. He pauses.

'If it's the wee Shrike,' says Sergeant Gregorius, 'I think we can bring a few surprises for it. This round may not go so easy for that spiked son of a bitch, pardon my language, Father.'

'As your priest,' says de Soya, 'I will warn you again about the use of profanity. As your commanding officer, I order you to come up with as many surprises as you can to kill that spiked son of a bitch.'

They adjourn to eat their evening meal and plan their respective strategies.

TWENTY-ONE

Have you ever noticed how on a trip – even a very long one – it is often the first week or so that stands out most clearly in your memory? Perhaps it is the enhanced perception that voyages bring, or perhaps it is an effect of orientation response on the senses, or perhaps it is simply that even the charm of newness soon wears off, but it has been my experience that the first days in a new place, or seeing new people, often set the tone for the rest of the trip. Or in this case, the rest of my life.

We spent the first day of our magnificent adventure sleeping. The child was exhausted and – I had to admit after waking from sixteen hours of uninterrupted sleep – so was I. I can't vouch for what A. Bettik did during this first somnambulant day of the voyage – at that point I had not learned that androids do sleep, but require only a fraction of the time we humans spend comatose – but he had set his small backpack of possessions in the engine room, rigging a hammock to sleep in, and he spent much of his time down there. I had planned to give the girl the 'master bedroom' at the apex of the ship, she had showered there in the adjoining bathroom cubby that first morning, but she staked out one of the sleep couches on the fugue deck and that soon became her space. I enjoyed the size and softness of the large bed in the center of the circular top room, and – after a while – even overcame my agoraphobia and allowed the hull to go translucent to watch the fractal light show in Hawking space outside. I never kept the hull transparent for long, however, for the pulsing geometries continued to disturb me in ways I could not describe.

The library level and the holopit level were, by unspoken agreement, common ground. The kitchen – A. Bettik called it the 'galley' – was set into the wall on the holopit level, and we usually ate at the low table in the holopit or occasionally carried the food up to the round table near the navigation cubby. I admit that immediately after awakening and having 'breakfast' (shiptime said that it was afternoon on Hyperion, but why abide by Hyperion time when I might never see that world again?), I headed for the library: the books were ancient, all published during the time of the Hegemony or earlier, and I was surprised to find a copy of an epic poem by Martin Silenus – *The Dying Earth* – as well as tomes by a dozen classical authors whom I had read as a boy, and often reread during my long days and nights at the fen cabin or while working on the river.

A. Bettik joined me that first day as I browsed, and pulled a small green volume from the shelves. 'This might be of interest,' he said. The title was *A*

Traveler's Guide to the WorldWeb: with Special Sections on the Grand Concourse and River Tethys.

'It might be of great interest,' I said, opening the book with shaking fingers. The shaking, I believe, came from the reality that we were *going there* – actually *traveling to the former Web worlds!*

'These books are doubly interesting as artifacts,' said the android, 'since they came from an age when all information was instantly available to anyone.'

I nodded. As a child, listening to Grandam's tales of the old days, I had tried to imagine a world where everyone wore implants and could access the datasphere whenever they wanted. Of course, even then, Hyperion had no datasphere – and had never been part of the Web – but for most of the billions of members of the Hegemony, life must have been like an endless stimsim of visual, auditory, and printed information. No wonder a majority of humans had never learned to read during the old days. Literacy had been one of the first goals of the Church and its Pax administrators after interstellar society was stitched together long after the Fall.

That day, standing in the carpeted ship's library, the polished teak and cherrywood walls gleaming in the light, I remember taking half a dozen books from the shelves and carrying them to the table to read.

Aenea raided the library that afternoon as well – immediately pulling *The Dying Earth* from the shelves. 'There were no copies in Jacktown, and Uncle Martin refused to let me read it when I visited him,' she said. 'He did say that it was the only thing he'd ever written – other than the *Cantos* that he never finished – that was worth reading.'

'What's it about?' I asked, not looking up from the Delmore Deland novel I was looking at. Both the girl and I were munching on apples as we read and talked. A. Bettik had gone back down the spiral stairs.

'The last days of Old Earth,' said Aenea. 'It's really about Martin's pampered childhood on his family's big estate on the North American Preserve.'

I set my book down. 'What do you think happened to Old Earth?'

The girl stopped munching. 'In my day everyone thought that the Big Mistake of aught-eight black hole had eaten it. That it was gone. Kaput.'

I chewed and nodded. 'Most people still believe that, but the old poet's *Cantos* insists that the TechnoCore stole Old Earth and sent it somewhere . . .'

'The Magellanic Clouds,' said the girl, and took another bite of apple. 'My mother discovered that when she and my father were investigating his murder.'

I leaned forward. 'Do you mind talking about your father?'

Aenea smiled slightly. 'No, why should I? I suppose I'm somewhat of a half-breed, the child of a Lusian woman and a cloned cybrid male, but that's never bothered me.'

'You don't look very Lusian,' I said. Residents of that high-g world were invariably short and very strong. Most were pale of skin and dark-haired; this child was small but of a height normal to one-g worlds, her brown hair was streaked with blonde, and she was slender. Only her luminous brown eyes reminded me of the *Cantos'* description of Brawne Lamia.

Aenea laughed. It was a pleasant sound. 'I take after my dad,' she said. 'John Keats was short, blond, and skinny.'

I hesitated a moment before saying, 'You said that you spoke to your father . . .'

Aenea glanced at me from the corners of her eyes. 'Yes, and you know that the Core killed his body before I was born. But did you also know that my mother carried his persona for months in a Schrön Loop embedded behind her ear?'

I nodded. It was in the *Cantos*.

The girl shrugged. 'I remember talking to him.'

'But you weren't . . .'

'Born,' said Aenea. 'Right. What kind of conversation could a poet's persona have with a fetus? But we talked. His persona was still connected to the TechnoCore. He showed me . . . well, it's complicated, Raul. Believe me.'

'I believe you,' I said. I looked around the library. 'Did you know that the *Cantos* says that when your father's persona left the Schrön Loop, it resided in this ship's AI for a while?'

'Yeah,' said Aenea. She grinned. 'Yesterday, before I went to sleep, I spent an hour or so talking to the ship. My dad was here, all right. The persona coexisted with the ship's mind when the Consul flew back to check out what had happened to the Web after the Fall, But he's not here now, and the ship can't remember much about his residence here, and it doesn't remember anything about what happened to him – whether he left after the Consul died, or what – so I don't know if he still exists.'

'Well,' I said, trying to choose diplomatic words, 'the Core doesn't exist any longer, so I don't quite see how a cybrid persona could either.'

'Who says the Core doesn't exist?'

I admit that I was shocked by that statement. 'The last act of Meina Gladstone and the Hegemony was to destroy the farcaster links, the dataspheres, the fatline, and the entire dimension that the Core existed in,' I said at last. 'Even the *Cantos* agrees with that fact.'

The child was still smiling. 'Oh, they blew the space-based farcasters to bits, and the others quit working, all right. And the dataspheres were gone in my time, too. But who says the Core is dead? That's like saying that you swept away a couple of spiderwebs, so the spider has to be dead.'

I admit that I looked over my shoulder. 'So you think the TechnoCore still exists? That those AIs are still plotting against us?'

'I don't know about the plotting,' said Aenea, 'but I know that the Core exists.'

'How?'

She held up a small finger. 'First of all, my father's cybrid persona still existed after the Fall, right? The basis for that persona was a Core AI they had fashioned. That shows that the Core was still . . . somewhere.'

I thought about that. As I mentioned earlier, cybrids – like androids –

were essentially a mythical species to me. We might as well have been discussing the physical characteristics of leprechauns.

'Secondly,' she said, lifting a second finger to join the first, 'I've communicated with the Core.'

I blinked at that statement. 'Before you were born?' I said.

'Yes,' said Aenea. 'And when I lived with Mother in Jacktown. And after Mother died.' She lifted her books and stood. 'And this morning.'

I could only stare.

'I'm hungry, Raul,' she said from the head of the stairs. 'Want to go down and see what this old ship's galley can whomp up for lunch?'

We soon settled into a schedule on the ship, adopting Hyperion's day and night schedules roughly as waking and sleeping times. I began to see why the old Hegemony habit of keeping the twenty-four-hour Old Earth system as standard had been so important in the Web days: I'd read somewhere that almost ninety percent of the Earth-like or terraformed worlds of the Web had held days that fell within three hours of the Old Earth standard day.

Aenea still liked to extend the balcony and play the Steinway out under the Hawking-space sky, and I would sometimes stay out there and listen for a few minutes, but I preferred the sense of being surrounded that the interior of the ship gave me. None of us complained about the effects of the C-plus environment, although we felt it – the occasional lurching of emotion and balance, a constant sense that someone was watching us, and very strange dreams. My own dreams awakened me with the pounding heart, dry mouth, and sweat-soaked sheets that only the worst nightmares could cause. But I never remembered the dreams. I wanted to ask the others about their dreams, but A. Bettik never mentioned his – I did not know if androids *could* dream – and although Aenea acknowledged the strangeness of her dreams and said that she did remember them, she never discussed them.

On the second day, while we were sitting in the library, Aenea suggested that we 'experience' space travel. When I asked her how we could experience it more than we were – I had the Hawking fractals in mind when I said that – she only laughed and asked the ship to cancel the internal containment field. Immediately, we were weightless.

As a boy, I had dreamed of zero-g. Swimming in the salty South Sea as a young soldier, I had closed my eyes, floated effortlessly, and wondered if this was what space travel in the olden days had been like.

I can tell you it is not.

Zero-g, especially sudden zero-g such as the ship granted upon Aenea's request, is terrifying. It is, quite simply, falling.

Or so it first seems.

I gripped the chair, but the chair was also falling. It was precisely as if we had been sitting in one of the huge Bridle Range cable cars for the past two days, when suddenly the cable broke. My middle ear protested, trying to find a horizon line that was honest. None were.

A. Bettik kicked up from wherever he had been below and said calmly, 'Is there a problem?'

'No,' laughed Aenea, 'we're just going to experience space for a while.'

A. Bettik nodded and then pulled himself headfirst down the stairway pit to get back to whatever he was working on.

Aenea followed him to the stairwell, kicking over to the central opening. 'See?' she said. 'This stairwell becomes a central dropshaft when the ship is zero-g. Just like in the old spinships.'

'Isn't this dangerous?' I asked, switching my grip from the back of a chair to a bookshelf. For the first time I noticed the elastic cords that held the books in place. Everything else that was not attached – the book I had set on the table, the chairs around the table, a sweater I'd left thrown over the back of another chair, pieces of the orange I had been eating – was floating.

'Not dangerous,' said Aenea. 'Messy. Next time we get everything ship-shape before we cancel the internal field.'

'But isn't the field . . . important?'

Aenea was floating upside down from my perspective. My inner ear liked this even less than the rest of the experience. 'The field keeps us from being squashed and thrown around when we're moving in normal space,' she said, pulling herself to the center of the twenty-meter drop by grabbing the stairway railing, 'but we can't speed up or slow down in C-plus space, so . . . here goes!' She grabbed a handhold along the rod that ran the length of the ship in the center of what had been the open stairwell and catapulted herself out of sight, headfirst.

'Jesus,' I whispered, pushed away from the bookcase, bouncing off the opposite bulkhead, and followed her down the central dropshaft.

For the next hour we played in zero-g: zero-g tag, zero-g hide-and-seek (finding that one could hide in the oddest places when gravity was not a restraint), zero-g soccer using one of the plastic space helmets from a locker on the storage/corridor deck, and even zero-g wrestling, which was im-mensely harder than I would have imagined. My first attempt to grab the child sent both of us tumbling and crashing through the length, breadth, and height of fugue deck.

In the end, exhausted and sweaty (the perspiration hung in the air until one moved or a trickle of air from the ventilators moved it, I discovered), Aenea ordered the balcony opened again – I shouted in fear when she did so, but the ship quietly reminded me that the exterior field was quite intact – and we floated out above the bolted-down Steinway, floated to the railing and beyond, into that no-man's-land between the ship and the field, floated ten meters out and looked back at the ship itself, surrounded by exploding fractals, glowing in the cold fireworks glory of it as Hawking space folded and contracted around us several billion times a second.

Finally we kicked and swam our way back in (a difficult and awkward feat, I discovered, when there was nothing to push against), warned A. Bettik over the intercom to find a floor, and brought back the one-g internal field. Both the child and I giggled as sweaters, sandwiches, chairs, books, and several spheres of water from a glass that had been left out came crashing down to the carpet.

It was that same day, night rather, for the ship had dimmed the lights for sleep period, that I padded down the spiral stairs to the holopit level to fix a midnight snack and heard soft sounds from the opening to the fugue deck below.

'Aenea?' I said, speaking softly. There was no answer. I went to the head of the stairs, looking at the dark drop in the center of the stairwell and smiling as I remembered our midair antics there a few hours before. 'Aenea?'

There still came no answer, but the soft sounds continued. Wishing I had a flashlight, I padded down the metal stairs in my sock feet.

There was a soft glow from the fugue-sleep monitors above the couches tucked in their cubbies. The soft sound was coming from Aenea's cubby. She had her back to me. The blanket was pulled to her shoulders, but I could see the collar of the Consul's old shirt that she had appropriated for use as a nightshirt. I walked over, my sock feet making no noise on the soft floor, and knelt by the couch. 'Aenea?' The girl was crying, obviously trying to muffle her sobs.

I touched her shoulder and she finally turned. Even in the dim instrument glow I could see that she had been weeping for some time; her eyes were red and puffy, her cheeks streaked with tears.

'What's wrong, kiddo?' I whispered. We were two decks above where A. Bettik slept in his hammock in the engine room, but the stairwell was open.

For a moment Aenea did not respond, but eventually the sobs slowed, then stopped. 'I'm sorry,' she said at last.

'It's all right. Tell me what's wrong.'

'Give me a tissue and I will,' said the girl.

I rummaged in the pockets of the old robe the Consul had left. I had no tissue, but I had been using a napkin with the cake I'd been eating upstairs. I handed her the linen.

'Thanks.' She blew her nose. 'I'm glad we're not still in zero-g,' she said through the cloth. 'There'd be snot floating everywhere.'

I smiled and squeezed her shoulder. 'What's wrong, Aenea?'

She made a soft noise that I realized was an attempt at a laugh. 'Everything,' she said. 'Everything's wrong. I'm scared. Everything I know about the future scares the shit out of me. I don't know how we're going to get past the Pax guys that I know will be waiting for us in a few days. I'm homesick. I can never go back, and everybody I knew except Martin is gone forever. Mostly, though, I guess I just miss my mother.'

I squeezed her shoulder. Brawne Lamia, her mother, was the stuff of legend – a woman who had lived and died two and a half long centuries ago. A few of her bones had already turned to dust, wherever they were buried. For this child, her mother's death was only two weeks in the past.

'I'm sorry,' I whispered, and squeezed her shoulder again, feeling the texture of the Consul's old shift. 'It'll be all right.'

Aenea nodded and took my hand. Hers was still moist. I noticed how tiny her palm and fingers were against my huge paw.

'Want to come up to the galley and have some chalmaroot cake and milk with me?' I whispered. 'It's good.'

She shook her head. 'I think I'll sleep now. Thanks, Raul.' She squeezed my hand again before relinquishing it, and in that second I realized the great truth: the One Who Teaches, the new messiah, whatever Brawne Lamia's daughter would turn out to be, she was also a child – one who giggled in zero-gravity antics and who wept in the night.

I went softly up the stairs, stopping to look back at her before my head rose above the level of the next deck. She was huddled under her blanket, her face turned away again, her hair catching only a bit of the console glow from above her cubby. 'Good night, Aenea,' I whispered, knowing that she would not hear me. 'It will be all right.'

TWENTY-TWO

Sergeant Gregorius and his two troopers are waiting in the open sally-port air lock of the *Raphael* as the archangel-class starship closes on the unidentified spacecraft that has just translated from C-plus. Their spacesuit armor is cumbersome and – with their reactionless rifles and energy weapons slung – the three men fill the air lock. Parvati's sun gleams on their gold visors as they lean out into space.

'I've got it locked,' comes Father Captain de Soya's voice in their earphones. 'Distance, one hundred meters and closing.' The needle-shaped craft with fins on the stern fills their vision as the two ships close. Between the spacecraft, defensive containment fields blur and flash, dissipating high-energy CPB and lance attacks faster than the eye can follow. Gregorius's visor opaques, clears, and then opaques as the close-in battle flares.

'All right, inside their minimum lance range,' says de Soya from his perch on the Combat Control Center couch. 'Go!'

Gregorius gives a hand signal and his men kick off at the precise instant he does. Needle thrusters in their suits' reaction paks spurt tiny blue flames as they correct their arc.

'Disrupting fields . . . now!' cries de Soya.

The clashing containment fields cancel each other for only a few seconds, but it is enough: Gregorius, Kee, and Rettig are in the other ship's defensive egg now.

'Kee,' says Gregorius over the tightbeam, and the smaller figure tweaks thrusters and hurtles toward the bow of the decelerating ship. 'Rettig.' The other suit of combat armor accelerates toward the lower third of the ship. Gregorius himself waits until the last second to kill his forward velocity, does a complete forward roll at the last instant, applies full thruster, and feels his heavy soles touch hullplate with hardly a tap. He activates the electromagnets in his boots, feels the connection, widens his stance, and then crouches on the hull with only one boot in contact.

'On,' comes Corporal Kee's voice on tightbeam.

'On,' says Rettig a second later.

Sergeant Gregorius pulls the line of boarding collar from around his waist, sets it against the hull, activates the sticktight, and continues kneeling in it. He is within a black hoop a little more than a meter and a half in diameter.

'On the count from three,' he says into his mike. 'Three . . . two . . . one . . . deploy.' He touches his wrist-controller and blinks as a microthin canopy of molecular polymer spins up from the hoop, closes over his head, and continues to bulge above him. Within ten seconds he is within a twenty-meter transparent bag, like a combat-armored shape crouching within a giant condom.

'Ready,' says Kee. Rettig echoes the word.

'Set,' says Gregorius, slapping a charge against the hull and setting his gauntleted finger back against his wristplate. 'From five . . .' The ship is rotating under them now, firing thrusters and its main engines almost at random, but the *Raphael* has it locked in a containment-field death grip, and the men on its hull are not thrown free. 'Five . . . four . . . three . . . two . . . one . . . now!'

The detonation is soundless, of course, but is also without flash or recoil. A hundred-and-twenty-centimeter circle of hull flies inward. Gregorius can see only the gossamer hint of Kee's polymer bag around the curve of the hull, sees the sunlight strike it as it inflates. Gregorius's bag also inflates like a giant balloon as atmosphere rushes out of the hull-breach and fills the space around him. He hears a hurricane screech through his external pickups for five seconds, then silence as the space around him – now filled with oxygen and nitrogen according to his helmet sensors – fills with dust and detritus blown out during the brief pressure differential.

'Going in . . . now!' cries Gregorius, unslinging his reactionless plasma rifle as he kicks his way into the interior.

There is no gravity. That is a surprise to the sergeant – he is ready to hit the decks rolling – but he adapts within seconds and twists in a circle, peering around.

Some sort of common area. Gregorius sees seat cushions, some sort of ancient vid screen, bookshelves with real books—

A man floats up the central dropshaft.

'Halt!' cries Gregorius, using common radio bands and his helmet loud-speaker. The figure – little more than a silhouette – does not halt. The man has something in his hand.

Gregorius fires from the hip. The plasma slug bores a hole ten centimeters wide through the man. Blood and viscera explode outward from the tumbling figure, some of the globules spattering on Gregorius's visor and armored chestplate. The object falls from the dead man's hand, and Gregorius glances at it as he kicks by to the stairwell. It is a book. 'Shit,' mutters the sergeant. He has killed an unarmed man. He will lose points for this.

'In, top level, no one here,' radios Kee. 'Coming down.'

'Engine room,' says Rettig. 'One man here. Tried to run and I had to burn him. No sign of the child. Coming up.'

'She must be on the middle level or the air-lock level,' snaps the sergeant into his mike. 'Proceed with care.' The lights go out, and Gregorius's helmet searchlight and the penlight on his plasma rifle come on automatically, beams quite visible through air filled with dust, blood spheres, and tumbling artifacts. He stops at the top of the stairwell.

Someone or something is drifting up toward him. He shifts his helmet, but the light on the plasma rifle illuminates the shape first.

It is not the girl. Gregorius gets a confused impression of great size, razor wire, spikes, too many arms, and blazing red eyes. He must decide in a second or less: if he fires plasma bolts down the open dropshaft, he might hit the child. If he does nothing, he dies – razor talons reach for him even as he hesitates.

Gregorius has lashed the deathwand to his plasma rifle before making the ship-to-ship jump. Now he kicks aside, finds an angle, and triggers the wand.

The razor wire shape floats past him, four arms limp, the red eyes fading. Gregorius thinks, *The goddamn thing isn't invulnerable to deathwands. It has synapses.* He catches a glimpse of someone above him, swings the rifle, identifies Kee, and the two men kick down the dropshaft headfirst. *Embarrassing if someone turns the internal field back on now and gravity comes on,* thinks Gregorius. *Make a note of that.*

'I've got her,' calls Rettig. 'She was hiding in one of the fugue cubbies.'

Gregorius and Kee float down past the common level and kick out into the fugue level. A massive figure in combat armor is holding the child. Gregorius notes the brown-blonde hair, the dark eyes, and the small fists flailing uselessly against Rettig's chest armor.

'That's her,' he says. He keys the tightbeam to the ship. 'Cleared the ship. We have the girl. Only two defenders and the creature this time.'

'Affirmative,' comes de Soya's voice. 'Two minutes fifteen seconds. Impressive. Come on out.'

Gregorius nods, takes a final glance at the captive child – no longer struggling – and keys his suit controls.

He blinks and sees the other two lying next to him, their suits connected umbilically to VR tactical. De Soya has actually turned off the internal fields in the *Raphael*, better to maintain the illusion. Gregorius removes his helmet, sees the other two sweaty faces as they do the same, and begins to help Kee remove his clumsy armor.

The three meet de Soya in the wardroom cubby. They could meet as easily in the stimsim of tactical space, but they prefer physical reality for their debriefings.

'It was smooth,' says de Soya as they take their places around the small table.

'Too smooth,' says the sergeant. 'I don't believe that deathwands are going to kill the Shrike thing. And I screwed up with the guy on the navigation deck . . . He just had a book.'

De Soya nods. 'You did the right thing, though. Better to take him out than to take chances.'

'Two unarmed men?' says Corporal Kee. 'I doubt it. This is about as unrealistic as the dozen armed guys on the third run-through. We should play more of the Ouster encounters . . . Marine-level lethality, at least.'

'I don't know,' mutters Rettig.

They look at him and wait.

'We keep getting the girl without any harm coming to her,' says the man at last.

'That fifth sim . . .' begins Kee.

'Yeah, yeah,' says Rettig. 'I know we accidentally killed her then. But the whole ship was wired to blow in that one. I doubt if that will happen . . . Whoever heard of a hundred-million-mark spacecraft being rigged to self-destruct?'

The other three look at one another and shrug.

'It is a silly idea,' says Father Captain de Soya, 'but I programmed the tacticals for wide parameters of . . .'

'Yeah,' interrupts Lancer Rettig, his thin face as sharp and menacing as a knife blade, 'I just mean that if it does come to a firefight, the chances of the girl getting burned are a lot greater than our sims suggest. That's all.'

This is the most the other three have heard Rettig say in weeks of living and rehearsing on the small ship.

'You're right,' says de Soya. 'For our next sim, I'll raise the danger level for the child.'

Gregorius shakes his head. 'Captain, sir, I suggest we knock off the sims and go back to the physical rehearsals. I mean . . .' He glances at his wrist chronometer. The memory of the bulky combat suit slows his movements. 'I mean, we've just got eight hours until this is for real.'

'Yeah,' says Corporal Kee. 'I agree. I'd rather be outside doing it for real, even if we can't sim the other ship that way.'

Rettig grunts his assent.

'I agree,' says de Soya. 'But first we eat – double rations . . . It's just been tactical, but you three have each lost twenty pounds the last week.'

Sergeant Gregorius leans over the table. 'Could we see the plot, sir?'

De Soya keys the monitor. *Raphael*'s long, ellipsoid trajectory and the escape ship's translation point are almost intersecting. The intersect point blinks red.

'One more real-space run-through,' says de Soya, 'and then I want all of us to sleep at least two hours, go over our equipment, and take it easy.' He looks at his own chronometer, even though the monitor is displaying ship and intercept time. 'Barring accidents or the unexpected,' he says, 'the girl should be in our custody in seven hours and forty minutes . . . and we'll be getting ready to translate to Pacem.'

'Sir?' says Sergeant Gregorius.

'Yes, Sergeant?'

'Meaning no disrespect, sir,' says the other man, 'but there's no way in the Good Lord's fucking universe that anyone can bar accidents or the unexpected.'

TWENTY-THREE

'So,' I said, 'what's your plan?'

Aenea looked up from the book she was reading. 'Who says that I have a plan?'

I straddled a chair. 'It's less than an hour until we pop out in the Parvati System,' I said. 'A week ago you said that we needed a plan in case they know we're coming . . . so what's the plan?'

Aenea sighed and closed the book. A. Bettik had come up the stairway to the library, and now he joined us at the table – actually sitting with us, which was unusual for him.

'I'm not sure I have a plan,' said the girl.

I'd been afraid of this. The week had passed pleasantly enough; the three of us had read a lot, talked a lot, played a lot – Aenea was excellent at chess, good at Go, and terrible at Monopoly – and the days had passed without incident. Many times I had tried to press her on her plans – Where did she plan to go? Why choose Renaissance Vector? Was finding Ousters part of her quest? – but her answers, while polite, were always vague. What Aenea showed great talent for was getting me talking. I hadn't known many children – even when I was a child myself, there were few others in our caravan group, and I rarely enjoyed their company, since Grandam was infinitely more interesting to me – but the children and teenagers I'd encountered over the years had never shown this much curiosity or ability to listen. Aenea got me describing my years as a shepherd; she showed special interest in my apprenticeship as a landscape architect; she asked a thousand questions about my river-barge days and hunting-guide days – in truth, it was only my soldiering days that she did not show much interest in. What she had seemed especially interested in was my dog, although even discussing Izzy – about raising her, training her as a bird dog, about her death – upset me quite a bit.

I noticed that she could even get A. Bettik talking about his centuries of servitude, and here I often joined in the patient listening: the android had seen and experienced amazing things – different worlds, the settling of Hyperion with Sad King Billy, the Shrike's early rampages across Equus, the final pilgrimage that the old poet had made famous, even the decades with Martin Silenus turned out to be fascinating.

But the girl said very little. On our fourth evening out from Hyperion, she admitted that she had come through the Sphinx into her future not just to escape the Pax troops hunting for her then, but to seek out her own destiny.

'As a messiah?' I said, intrigued.

Aenea laughed. 'No,' she said, 'as an architect.'

I was surprised. Neither the *Cantos* nor the old poet himself had said anything about the so-called One Who Teaches earning a living as an architect.

Aenea had shrugged. 'It's what I want to do. In my dream the one who could teach me lives in this era. So here I came.'

'The one who could teach you?' I said. 'I thought that you were the One Who Teaches.'

Aenea had flopped back onto the holopit cushions and cocked her leg over the back of the couch. 'Raul, how could I possibly teach anyone anything? I'm eleven-and-a-half standard years old and I've never been off Hyperion before this . . . Hell, I never left the continent of Equus until this week. What do I have to teach?'

I had no answer to that.

'I want to be an architect,' she said, 'and in my dream the architect who can train me is somewhere out there . . .' She waggled her fingers at the outer hull, but I understood her to mean the old Hegemony Web where we were heading.

'Who is he?'

'He's a she,' said Aenea, 'and I don't know her name.'

'What world is she on?' I asked.

'I don't know.'

'Are you sure this is the right century?' I asked, trying to keep the irritation out of my voice.

'Yeah. Maybe. I think so.' Aenea rarely acted petulant during the days I spent with her that week, but her voice seemed perilously close to that now.

'And you just dreamed about this person?'

She sat up in the cushions. 'Not *just* dreamed,' she said then. 'My dreams are important to me. They're sort of more than dreams . . .' She broke off. 'You'll see.'

I tried not to sigh aloud. 'What happens after you become an architect?'

She chewed on a fingernail. It was a bad habit I planned on breaking her of. 'What do you mean?'

'I mean, the old poet's expecting big things of you . . . Being the messiah's just one part – when does that kick in?'

'Raul,' she said, rising to go down to her fugue cubby, 'no offense, but why don't you just fuck off and leave me alone?'

She had apologized for that crudity later, but as we sat at the table an hour from translation into a strange star system, I was curious if my question about her plan would elicit the same response.

It did not. She started to chew a nail, caught herself, and said, 'Okay, you're right, we need a plan.' She looked at A. Bettik. 'Do you have one?'

The android shook his head. 'Master Silenus and I discussed this many times, M. Aenea, but our conclusion was that if the Pax somehow arrived first at our destination, then all was lost. It seems an improbability, though, since the torchship pursuing us cannot travel more quickly through Hawking space than we can.'

'I don't know,' I said. 'Some of the hunters I've guided the past few years talked about rumors that the Pax . . . or the Church . . . had these superfast ships.'

A. Bettik nodded. 'We have heard similar rumors, M. Endymion, but logic suggests that if the Pax had developed such craft – a breakthrough which the Hegemony never achieved, by the way – then there seems little reason that they would not have outfitted their warships and Mercantilus vessels with such a drive . . .'

Aenea tapped the table. 'It doesn't really matter *how* they get there first,' she said. 'I've *dreamed* that they will. I've been considering plans, but . . .'

'What about the Shrike?' I said.

Aenea glanced sideways at me. 'What about it?'

'Well,' I said, 'it provided a pretty convenient *deus ex machina* for us on Hyperion, so I just thought that if it could . . .'

'Damn it, Raul!' cried the girl. 'I didn't *ask* that creature to kill those people on Hyperion. I wish to God it hadn't.'

'I know, I know,' I said, touching her sleeve to calm her. A. Bettik had cut down several of the Consul's old shirts for her, but her wardrobe was still meager.

I knew that she had been upset about the carnage during our escape. She later admitted that it had been part of the reason for her sobbing that second night out.

'I'm sorry,' I said sincerely. 'I didn't mean to be flippant about the . . . thing. I just thought that if someone tried to stop us again, maybe . . .'

'No,' said Aenea. 'I've dreamed that someone tries to stop us from getting to Renaissance Vector. But I haven't dreamed that the Shrike helps us. We have to come up with our own plan.'

'What about the Core?' I said tentatively. It was the first time I'd mentioned the TechnoCore since she had brought it up that first day.

Aenea seemed lost in thought; or at least she ignored my question. 'If we're going to get ourselves out of whatever trouble might be waiting for us, it will have to be our doing. Or maybe . . .' She turned her head. 'Ship?'

'Yes, M. Aenea.'

'Have you been listening to this conversation?'

'Of course, M. Aenea.'

'Do you have any ideas that could help us?'

'Help you to avoid capture if Pax ships are waiting for you?'

'Yeah,' said Aenea, her voice irritable. She frequently lost patience with the ship.

'Not any original ideas,' said the ship. 'I have been trying to remember how the Consul avoided the local authorities when we were just passing through a system . . .'

'And?' said Aenea.

'Well, as I have mentioned, my memory is not as complete as it should be . . .'

'Yes, yes,' said Aenea, 'but do you remember any clever ways you avoided local authorities?'

'Well, primarily by outrunning them,' said the ship. 'As we have discussed previously, the Ouster modifications were to the containment field and the fusion drive. The latter changes allow me to reach C-plus translation velocities much more quickly than standard spinships . . . or so it was when I last traveled between the stars.'

A. Bettik folded his hands and spoke to the same bulkhead area that Aenea had been watching. 'You are saying that if the authorities . . . in this case the Pax ships . . . left from the planet Parvati, or near it, you would be able to make the translation to Renaissance Vector before they could intercept us.'

'Most assuredly,' said the ship.

'How long will the turnaround take?' I asked.

'Turnaround?'

'The time in-system before we can spin up to the quantum jump to Renaissance Vector's system,' I said.

'Thirty-seven minutes,' said the ship. 'Which includes reorientation, navigation checks, and system checks.'

'What if a Pax ship is waiting right there when we spin down?' ask Aenea. 'Do you have any Ouster modifications that could help us?'

'Not that I can think of,' said the ship. 'You know of the enhanced containment fields, but they are still no match for a warship's weapons.'

The girl sighed and leaned on the table. 'I've been over this and over this, but I don't see how it can help.'

A. Bettik looked thoughtful, but then again, he always looked thoughtful. 'During the time we were concealing and caring for the ship,' he said, 'one other Ouster modification became apparent.'

'What's that?' I said.

A. Bettik gestured downward, toward the holopit level below us. 'They enhanced the ship's morphing ability. The way it can extrude the balcony is one example. Its ability to extend wings during atmospheric flight. It is able to open each separate living level to atmosphere, thus bypassing the old airlock entrance if necessary.'

'Neat,' said Aenea, 'but I don't see how that would help, unless the ship can morph to the point of passing itself off as a Pax torchship or something. Can you do that, Ship?'

'No, M. Aenea,' said the soft male voice. 'The Ousters carried out some fascinating piezodynamic engineering on me, but there is still the conservation of mass to reckon with.' After a second of silence, 'I am sorry, M. Aenea.'

'Just a silly idea,' said Aenea, then she sat straight up. It was so obvious that something had occurred to her that neither A. Bettik nor I interrupted her train of thought for two minutes. Finally she said, 'Ship?'

'Yes, M. Aenea?'

'You're able to morph an air lock . . . or a simple opening . . . anywhere on your hull?'

'Almost anywhere, M. Aenea. There are communications pods and certain drive-related areas in which I could not—'

'But on the living decks?' interrupted the girl. 'You could just open them the way you let the upper hull go transparent?'

'Yes, M. Aenea.'

'Would the air rush out if you did that?'

The ship's voice sounded mildly shocked as it answered. 'I would not allow that to happen, M. Aenea. As with the piano balcony, I would preserve the integrity of all external fields so that—'

'But you *could* open each deck, not just the air lock, and depressurize it?' The girl's persistence was new to me then. It is familiar now.

'Yes, M. Aenea.'

A. Bettik and I listened without comment. I could not speak for the android, but I had no idea where the kid was headed with all this. I leaned toward her. 'Is this part of a plan?' I said.

Aenea smiled crookedly. It was what I would later think of as her mischievous smile. 'It's too primitive to be a plan,' she said, 'and if my assumptions about why the Pax wants me are wrong . . . well, it won't work.' The mischievous smile took on a wry twist. 'It probably wouldn't work anyway.'

I glanced at my wrist. 'We have forty-five minutes until we spin down and find out if someone's waiting,' I said. 'Do you want to share your plan that wouldn't work?'

The girl began speaking. She did not talk long. When she was finished, the android and I looked at each other. 'You're right,' I said to her, 'it's not much of a plan and it wouldn't work.'

Aenea's smile did not falter. She took my hand and turned my wrist so that my chronometer was face up. 'We have forty-one minutes,' she said. 'Come up with a better one.'

TWENTY-FOUR

The *Raphael* is on the final part of her return ellipsoid, rushing in-system toward Parvati's sun at .03 of light-speed. The archangel-class courier/warship is ungainly – massive drive bays, cobbled-together compods, spin-arms, weapons' platforms and antennae array protruding, its tiny environmental sphere and attached dropship shuttle tucked into the mess almost as an afterthought – but it becomes a serious warship now as it rotates one hundred and eighty degrees so that it hurtles stern-first toward the projected translation point of the ship it pursues.

'One minute to spindown,' de Soya says over the tactical band. The three troopers in the open sally-port air lock do not need to acknowledge the transmission. They also know that even after the other ship appears in real space, it will not be visible to them – even with visor magnifiers – for another two minutes.

Strapped in his acceleration couch with the control panels arrayed around him, his gauntleted hand on the omnicontroller, his tactical shunt in place so that he and the ship are effectively one, Father Captain de Soya listens to the breathing of the three troopers over the com channel while he watches and senses the other ship's approach. 'Picking up Hawking-drive, distortion reading down angle thirty-nine, coordinates zero-zero-zero, thirty-nine, one-nine-niner,' he says into his mike. 'Exit point at zero-zero-zero, nine hundred klicks. Single vehicle probability, ninety-nine percent. Relative velocity nineteen kps.'

Suddenly the other ship becomes visible on radar, t-dirac, and all passive sensors. 'Got it,' Father Captain de Soya says to the waiting troopers. 'On time, on schedule . . . damn.'

'What?' says Sergeant Gregorius. He and his men have checked their weapons, charges, and boarding collars. They are ready to jump in less than three minutes.

'The ship's begun accelerating, not decelerating as we'd guessed in most of the sims,' says de Soya. On the tactical channel he enables the ship to carry out preprogrammed alternatives. 'Hang on!' he says to the troopers, but the thrusters have already fired, *Raphael* is already rotating. 'No problem,' he says as the main drive kicks on, boosting them to a hundred and forty-seven gravities. 'Just stay within the field during the jump. It'll take just an extra minute to match velocities.'

Gregorius, Kee, and Rettig do not respond. De Soya can hear their breathing.

Two minutes later de Soya says, 'I have a visual.'

Sergeant Gregorius and his two troopers lean out of the open air lock. Gregorius can see the other ship as a ball of fusion flame. He keys the mag-lenses so he can see beyond that, raises the filters, and sees the ship itself. 'Pretty much like the tacticals,' says Kee.

'Don't think that way,' snaps the sergeant. 'The real thing's never like the tacticals.' He knows that both these men realize that; they have been in combat. But Sergeant Gregorius was an instructor at Pax Command on Armaghast for three years, and the instinct is hard to break.

'This thing's *fast*,' says de Soya. 'If we didn't have the bounce on them, I don't think we'd catch them. As it is, we'll just be able to match velocities for five or six minutes.'

'We only need three,' says Gregorius. 'Just get us alongside, Captain.'

'Coming alongside now,' says de Soya. 'She's painting us.' The *Raphael* was not designed with stealth capabilities, and now every instrument records the other ship's sensors on her. 'One klick,' he reports, 'still no weapons activity. Fields on full. Delta-v dropping. Eight hundred meters.'

Gregorius, Kee, and Rettig unsling their plasma rifles and crouch.

'Three hundred meters . . . two hundred meters . . .' says de Soya. The other ship is passive, its acceleration high but constant. In most of the sims de Soya had factored in a wild chase before matching speeds and disrupting the other ship's fields. This is too easy. The father-captain feels concern for the first time. 'Inside minimum lance range,' he reports. 'Go!'

The three Swiss Guard troopers explode out of the air lock, their reaction paks spurting blue flame.

'Disrupting . . . now!' cries de Soya. The other ship's fields refuse to drop for an eternity – almost three seconds, a time never simulated in the tactical exercises – but eventually they drop. 'Fields down!' calls de Soya, but the troopers already know that – they are tumbling, decelerating, and dropping onto the enemy-hull at their prearranged entry points – Kee near the bow, Gregorius on what had been the navigation level on the old schematics, Rettig above the engine room.

'On,' comes Gregorius's voice. The other two confirm landing a second later.

'Boarding collars set,' pants the sergeant.

'Set,' confirms Kee.

'Set,' says Rettig.

'Deploy from three,' snaps the sergeant. 'Three, two, one . . . deploy.'

His polymer bag gossamers into sunlight.

On the command couch de Soya is watching the delta-v. The acceleration has risen to more than two hundred and thirty gravities. If the fields fail now . . . He shoves the thought aside. *Raphael* is straining to her utmost to keep velocities matched. Another four or five minutes, and he will have to fall away or risk overtaxing all the ship's fusion-drive systems. *Hurry*, he thinks toward the combat-armored shapes he sees in tactical space and video screens.

'Ready,' reports Kee.

'Ready,' comes Rettig's voice from near the stern fins on the absurd ship.

'Set charges,' orders Gregorius, and slaps his onto the hull. 'From five . . . five, four, three . . .'

'Father Captain de Soya,' says a girl's voice.

'Wait!' orders de Soya. The girl's image has appeared on all the com bands. She is sitting at a piano. It is the same child he saw at the Sphinx on Hyperion three months before.

'Stop!' echoes Gregorius, his finger above the detonate button on his wristplate. The other troopers obey. All are watching the vid broadcast on their visor inserts.

'How do you know my name?' asks Father Captain de Soya. Instantly he knows how stupid the question is: it does not matter, his men need to enter the ship within three minutes or the *Raphael* will fall behind, leaving them alone on the other ship. They had simulated that possibility – the troopers taking command of the ship after capturing the girl, slowing to wait for de Soya to catch up – but it is not a preferable scenario. He touches a presspoint that sends his vid image to the girl's ship.

'Hello, Father Captain de Soya,' says the girl, her voice in no hurry, her appearance showing little or no stress, 'if your men try to enter the ship, I will depressurize my own ship and die.'

De Soya blinks. 'Suicide is a mortal sin,' he says.

On the screen the girl nods seriously. 'Yes,' she says, 'but I am not a Christian. Also, I'd rather go to hell than go with you.' De Soya looks intently at the image – her fingers are not near any controls.

'Captain,' comes Gregorius's voice on the secure tightbeam channel, 'if she opens the air lock, I can get to her and get a transfer bag around her before complete decompression.'

On the screen the girl is watching, de Soya's lips are still as he sub-vocalizes on the tightbeam channel. 'She is not of the cross,' he says. 'If she dies, there's no guarantee that we can revive her.'

'The odds are good the ship's surgery can bring her back and repair her from simple decompression,' says Gregorius. 'It'll take thirty seconds or more for her level to lose all of its air. I can get to her. Give the word.'

'I mean it,' says the child on the screen. Instantly a circular section of hull opens under and around Corporal Kee, and atmosphere blasts into vacuum, filling Kee's boarding collar bag like a balloon and tumbling him into it as both crash into the external field and slide toward the stern of the ship. Kee's reaction pak fires madly, and he stabilizes himself before being blown into the fusion tail of the ship.

Gregorius sets his finger on the shaped-charge detonator. 'Captain!' he cries.

'Wait,' subvocalizes de Soya. It is the sight of the girl in her shirtsleeves that freezes his heart with anxiety. Space between the two ships is now filled with colloidal particles and ice crystals.

'I'm sealed away from the top room,' says the girl, 'but if you don't call your men back, I'll open all the levels.'

In less than a second the air lock blasts open, and a two-meter circle opens in the hull where Gregorius had been standing. The sergeant had burned his way through the collar bag and jetted to another location as soon as the girl spoke. Now he tumbles away from the blast of atmosphere and small debris jetting from the opening, fires his thrusters, and plants his boots on a section of hull five meters farther down the ship. In his mind he can see the schematic, knows that the girl is just inside – a few meters from his grasp. If she was to blow this section, he would catch her, bag her, and have her in the *Raphael*'s surgery within two minutes. He checks his tactical display: Rettig had jumped into space seconds before a section of hull opened under him. Now the other was station-keeping three meters from the hull. 'Captain!' Gregorius calls on the tightbeam.

'Wait,' orders de Soya. To the girl, he says, 'We mean you no harm—'

'Then call them off,' snaps the girl. 'Now! Or I open this last level.'

Federico de Soya feels time slow down as he weighs his options. He knows that he has less than a minute before he has to throttle back – alarms and telltales are flashing throughout his tactical connections to the ship and across the boards. He does not want to leave his men behind, but the most important factor is the child. His orders are specific and absolute – *Bring the child back alive.*

De Soya's entire tactical virtual environment begins to pulse red, a warning that the ship must decelerate in one minute or automatic overrides will kick in. His control boards tell the same story. He keys the audible mike channels, broadcasts on common bands as well as tightbeam.

'Gregorius, Rettig, Kee . . . return to the *Raphael*. Now!'

Sergeant Gregorius feels the fury and frustration surge through him like a blast of cosmic radiation, but he is a member of the Swiss Guard. 'Returning now, sir!' he snaps, peels off his shaped charge, and kicks off toward the archangel. The other two rise from the hull with blue pinpricks of reaction thrusters. The merged fields flicker just long enough to allow the three armored men to pass through. Gregorius reaches the *Raphael*'s hull first, grabs a hold on, and literally flings his men into the sally-port lock as they float by. He pulls himself in, confirms that the others are clinging to web restraints, and keys his mike. 'In and tight, sir.'

'Breaking off,' says de Soya, broadcasting in the clear so that the girl can also hear. He switches from tactical space to real time and tweaks the omnicontroller.

Raphael cuts back from its one hundred and ten percent thrust, separates its field from the target's, and begins to fall behind. De Soya widens the distance from the girl's ship, keeping *Raphael* as far away from the other craft's fusion tail as he can: all indications are that the other ship is unarmed, but that term is relative when the thing's fusion drive can reach a hundred kilometers through space. *Raphael*'s external fields are on full defensive, the ship's countermeasures on full automatic, ready to react in a millionth of a second.

The girl's ship continues accelerating off the plane of the ecliptic. Parvati is not the child's destination.

A rendezvous with the Ousters? wonders de Soya. His ship's sensors still show no activity beyond Parvati's orbital patrols, but entire Ouster Swarms could be waiting beyond the heliosphere.

Twenty minutes later, the child's ship already hundreds of thousands of klicks ahead of *Raphael*, the question is answered.

'We've got Hawking-space distortion here,' Father Captain de Soya reports to the three men still clinging to restraints in the sally-port lock. 'Her ship is preparing to spin up.'

'To where?' asks Gregorius. The huge sergeant's voice reveals none of his fury at the near miss.

De Soya pauses and rechecks his readings before answering. 'Renaissance Vector space,' he says. 'Very close to the planet.'

Gregorius and the other two Swiss Guard troopers are silent. De Soya can guess their unspoken questions. *Why Renaissance Vector? It's a Pax stronghold . . . two billion Christians, tens of thousands of troops, scores of Pax warships. Why there?*

'Perhaps she doesn't know what's there,' he muses aloud over the inter-com. He switches to tactical space and hovers above the plane of the ecliptic, watching the red dot spin up to C-plus and disappear from the solar system. The *Raphael* still follows its stern-chase course, fifty minutes from translation vector. De Soya leaves tactical, checks all systems, and says, 'You can come up from the lock now. Secure all boarding gear.'

He does not ask their opinion. There is no discussion of whether he will translate the archangel to Renaissance Vector space – the course has already been set in and the ship is climbing toward quantum leap – and he does not ask them again if they are prepared to die again. This jump will be as fatal as the last, of course, but it will put them into Pax-occupied space five months ahead of the girl's ship. The only question in de Soya's mind is whether or not to wait for the *Saint Anthony* to spin down into Parvati space so he can explain the situation to the captain.

He decides not to wait. It makes little sense – a few hours' difference in a five-month head start – but he does not have the patience to wait. De Soya orders *Raphael* to prepare a transponder buoy, and he records the orders for Captain Sati on the *Anthony*: immediate translation to Renaissance Vector – a ten-day trip for the torchship with the same five-month time-debt that the girl will pay – with readiness for combat immediately upon spinning down to RV space.

When he has launched the buoy and tightbeamed stand-down orders to the Parvati command, de Soya turns his acceleration couch to face the other three men. 'I know how disappointing that was to you,' he begins.

Sergeant Gregorius says nothing, and his dark face is as impassive as stone, but Father Captain de Soya can read the message behind the silence: *Another thirty seconds and I would have had her.*

De Soya does not care. He has commanded men and women for over a decade – has sent braver, more loyal underlings than this to their deaths without allowing remorse or the need for explanation to overwhelm him – so he does not blink now in front of the giant trooper. 'I think the child would have carried out her threat,' he says, his tone of voice conveying the message that this was not open to discussion or argument, now or later, 'but that's a moot point now. We know where she's going. It may be the one system in this sector of Pax space where no one – not even an Ouster Swarm – could get in or out unseen and uninterdicted. We're going to have five months to prepare for the ship's arrival, and this time we won't be operating alone.' De Soya pauses to take a breath. 'You three have worked hard, and this failure in Parvati System is not yours. I'll see to it that you are returned to your unit immediately upon arrival in Renaissance Vector space.'

Gregorius does not even have to glance at his two men before speaking for them. 'Begging the father-captain's pardon, but if we have a say in it, sir, we'd choose to stay with you and *Raphael* until this young 'un's safely in the net and on her way to Pacem, sir.'

De Soya tries not to show his surprise. 'Hmmm . . . well, we'll see what happens, Sergeant. Renaissance Vector is Fleet Headquarters for the navy, and a lot of our bosses will be there. We'll see what happens. Let's get everything tied down . . . We translate in twenty-five minutes.'

'Sir?'

'Yes, Corporal Kee?'

'Will you be hearing confessions before we die this time?'

De Soya works again to keep his expression neutral. 'Yes, Corporal. I'll finish the checklist here and be in the wardroom cubby for confession in ten minutes.'

'Thank you, sir,' says Kee with a smile.

'Thank you,' says Rettig.

'Thank 'ee, Father,' rumbles Gregorius.

De Soya watches the three jump to tie-down activities, shedding their massive combat armor as they go. In that instant he catches an intuitive glimpse of the future and feels the weight of it on his shoulders. *Lord, give me strength to carry out Thy will . . . in Jesus' name I ask . . . Amen.*

Swiveling his heavy couch back to the command panels, de Soya begins the final checklist before translation and death.

TWENTY-FIVE

Once, while guiding some duck hunters born on Hyperion into the fens, I asked one of them, an airship pilot who commanded the weekly dirigible run down the Nine Tails from Equus to Aquila, what his job was like. 'Piloting an airship?' he'd said. 'As the ancient line goes – long hours of boredom broken by minutes of sheer panic.'

This trip was a bit like that. I don't mean to say that I was bored – just the interior of the spaceship with its books and old holos and grand piano was interesting enough to keep me from being bored for the next ten days, not to mention getting to know my traveling companions – but already we had experienced these long, slow, pleasantly idle periods punctuated by interludes of wild adrenaline rush.

I admit that it had been disturbing in Parvati System to sit out of sight of the vid pickup and watch this child threaten to kill herself – and us! – if the Pax ship did not back off. I'd spent ten months dealing blackjack on Felix, one of the Nine Tails, and had watched a lot of gamblers; this eleven-year-old would be one hell of a poker player. Later, when I asked her if she would have carried through on the threat and opened our last pressurized level to space, she only smiled that mischievous smile and made a vague gesture with her right hand, a sort of flicking away, as if she were brushing the thought out of the air. I grew used to that gesture in later months and years.

'Well, how *did* you know that Pax captain's name?' I asked.

I expected to hear some revelation about the powers of a protomessiah, but Aenea only said, 'He was waiting at the Sphinx when I stepped out a week ago. I guess I heard someone call his name.'

I doubted that. If the father-captain had been at the Sphinx, Pax-army standard procedure would have had him buttoned into combat armor and communicating on secure channels. But why would the child lie?

Why am I seeking logic or sanity here? I'd asked myself at the moment. *There hasn't been any so far.*

When Aenea had gone below decks to take a shower after our dramatic departure from Parvati System, the ship had tried to reassure A. Bettik and me. 'Do not worry, gentlemen. I would not have allowed you to die from decompression.'

The android and I had exchanged a look. I think that both of us were wondering whether the ship knew what it would have done, or whether the child had some special control over it.

As the days of the second leg of the voyage passed, I found myself brooding about the situation and my reaction to it. The main problem, I realized, had been my passivity – almost irrelevancy – during this whole trip. I was twenty-seven years old, an ex-soldier, man of the world – even if the world was only backwater Hyperion – and here I had let a child deal with the one real emergency we'd faced. I understood why A. Bettik had been so passive in the situation; he was, after all, conditioned by bio-programming and centuries of habit to defer to human decisions. But why had I been such a stump? Martin Silenus had saved my life and sent me on this insane quest to protect the girl, to keep her alive and help her get wherever she had to go. So far, all I had done was fly a carpet and hide behind a piano while the kid dealt with a Pax warship.

The four of us, including the ship, talked about that Pax warship during those first few days out from Parvati space. If Aenea was right, if Father Captain de Soya had been on Hyperion during the opening of the tomb, then the Pax had found some way to take a shortcut through Hawking space. The implications of that reality were more than sobering; they scared the shit out of me.

Aenea did not seem overly worried. The days passed and we fell into the comfortable, if a bit claustrophobic, shipboard routine – Aenea playing the piano after dinner, all of us grazing in the library, checking the ship's holos and navigation logs for any clue as to where it had taken the Consul (there were many clues, none definitive), playing cards in the evening (she *was* a formidable poker player), and occasionally exercising, which I did by asking the ship to set the containment field to one-point-three-g just in the stairwell, and then running up and down the six stories worth of spiral steps for forty-five minutes. I'm not sure what it did for the rest of my body, but my calves, thighs, and ankles soon looked like they belonged to some Jovian-world elephantoid.

When Aenea realized that the field could be tailored to small regions of the ship, there was no stopping her. She began sleeping in a bubble of zero-g on the fugue deck. She found that the table on the library deck could be morphed into a billiard table, and she insisted on at least two games a day – each time under different g-loads. One night I heard a noise while reading on the navigation level, went down the stairs to the holopit level, and found the hull irised open, the balcony extended without the piano there, and a giant sphere of water – perhaps eight or ten meters across – floating between the balcony and the outer containment field.

'What the hell?'

'It's fun!' came a voice from within the pulsing blob of shifting water. A head with wet hair broke the surface, hanging upside down two meters above the floor of the balcony. 'Come on in!' cried the girl. 'The water's warm.'

I leaned away from the apparition, putting my weight on the railing and trying not to think of what would happen if that localized bubble of the field failed for a second.

'Has A. Bettik seen this?' I said.

The pale shoulders shrugged. The fractal fireworks were pulsing and folding out beyond the balcony, casting incredible colors and reflections on the sphere of water. The sphere itself was a great blue blob with lighter patches on the surface and interior where bubbles of air shifted. Actually, it reminded me of photos of Old Earth I had seen.

Aenea ducked her head under, was a pale form kicking through the water for a moment, and reemerged five meters up the curved surface. Smaller globules splashed free and curved back to the surface of the larger sphere – herded there by the field differential, I assumed – splashing and sending complex concentric circles rippling across the surface of the water globe.

'Come on in,' she said again. 'I mean it!'

'I don't have a suit.'

Aenea floated a second, kicked over onto her stomach, and dived again. When she emerged, head completely upside down from my perspective this time, she said, 'Who has a suit? You don't need one!'

I knew she was not joking because during her dive I had seen the pale vertebrae pressing against the skin of her back, her ribs, and her still-boylike butt reflecting the fractal light like two small white mushrooms poking up from a pond. All in all, the sight of our eleven-year-old messiah-to-be naked was about as sexually arousing as seeing holoslides of Aunt Merth's new grandkiddies in the tub.

'Come on in, Raul!' she called again, and dived for the opposite side of the sphere.

I hesitated only a second before kicking off my robe and outer clothes. I kept on not only my undershorts, but the long undershirt I often wore as pajamas.

For a moment I stood on the balcony, not having the slightest clue as to how to get into the sphere several meters above me. Then I heard, 'Jump, dummy!' from somewhere on the upper arc of the blob, and I jumped.

The transition to zero-g began about a meter and a half up. The water was damned cold.

I pivoted, shouted from the cold, felt everything contractable on my body contract in short order, and began splashing around, trying to keep my head above the curved surface. I was not surprised when A. Bettik came out on the balcony to see what the shouting was all about. He folded his arms and leaned against the railing, crossing his legs at the ankles.

'The water's warm!' I lied through chattering teeth. 'C'mon in!'

The android smiled and shook his head like a patient parent. I shrugged and pivoted and dived.

It took me a second or two to realize that swimming is much like moving in zero-g anyway; that floating in water in zero-g is much like ordinary swimming. Either way, the resistance of the water made the experience more swim-like than zero-g-like, although there was the added run of coming across an air bubble somewhere inside the sphere and pausing there to catch one's breath before paddling around underwater again.

After a moment of cartwheeling disorientation, I came to a bubble, stopped myself before tumbling out into the sphere, and looked directly above me to see Aenea's head and shoulders emerging there. She looked down at me and waved. The skin on her bare chest was goose-bumpy from either the cool water or cooler air.

'Some fun, huh?' she said, spluttering water out of her face and brushing back her hair with both hands. Her blonde-brown hair looked almost black when wet. I looked at the girl and tried to see her mother in her, the dark-haired Lusian detective. It was no use – I had never seen an image of Brawne Lamia, only heard descriptions from the *Cantos*.

'The hard part's keeping yourself from flying out of the water when you get to the edge,' said Aenea as our bubble shifted and contracted, the wall of water curving around and above us. 'Race you to the outside!'

She pivoted and kicked, and I tried to follow but made the mistake of flailing across the air bubble – my God, I hope that neither A. Bettik nor the child saw that pathetic spasm of arms and legs – and ended up at the edge of the sphere half a minute behind her. We trod water there; the ship and balcony were out of sight beneath us, the surface of the water curved away to the left and right, dropping out of sight like waterfalls on all sides of us, while above us the crimson fractals expanded, exploded, contracted, and expanded again.

'I wish we could see the stars,' I said, and was surprised that I had spoken aloud.

'Me too,' said Aenea. Her face was raised to the disturbing light show, and I thought I saw a shadow of sadness flicker across her features. 'I'm cold,' she said at last. I could see her clenched jaws now, sense her effort to keep her teeth from chattering. 'Next time I tell the ship to build the pool, I'll remind it not to use cold water.'

'You'd better get out,' I said. We swam down and around the curve of the sphere. The balcony seemed to be a wall rising to greet us, its only anomaly the form of A. Bettik standing sideways from it, holding out a large towel for Aenea.

'Close your eyes,' she said. I did and felt the heavy zero-g globules of splash water strike my face as she flailed her way right through the surface tension of the sphere and floated beyond it. A second later I heard the slap of her bare feet as she landed on the balcony.

I waited a few more seconds and opened my eyes. A. Bettik had set the voluminous towel around her and she was huddled in it, teeth chattering now despite her efforts to stop them. 'B-b-be care-f-ful,' she said. 'Ro-ro-tate as s-s-soon as you get out of the w-w-w-water, or you'll f-f-fall on your h-head and b-b-break your neck.'

'Thanks,' I said, having no intention of leaving the sphere before she and A. Bettik left the balcony. They did so a moment later and I paddled out, kicked arms and legs in a wild attempt to turn one hundred and eighty degrees before gravity reasserted itself, pivoted too far, overcompensated, and landed heavily on my rear end.

I pulled down the extra towel that A. Bettik had thoughtfully left on the railing for me, mopped my face, and said, 'Ship, you can collapse the zero-g microfield now.'

I realized my mistake an instant later, but before I could countermand the order, several hundreds of gallons of water collapsed onto the balcony – a massive waterfall of bone-chilling weight crashing down from a great height. If I had been directly under it, it might well have killed me – a mildly ironic end to a great adventure – but since I was sitting a couple of meters from the edge of the deluge, it merely smashed me against the balcony, caught me up in its vortex as it spilled up and over the railing, and threatened to fling me out into space and down past the stern of the ship fifteen meters below, down to the bottom of the ellipsoid bubble of containment field, where I would end up like a drowned insect in an ovoid beaker.

I grabbed at the railing and held on while the torrent roared by.

'Sorry,' said the ship, realizing its own error and reshaping the field around us to contain and collect the deluge. I noticed that none of it had washed through the open doorway into the holopit level.

When the microfield had lifted the water away in sloshing spheres, I found my sodden towel and walked through the doorway into the ship. As the hull irised shut behind me, the water presumably being returned to its holding tanks before being purified again for our use or as a reaction mass, I stopped cold.

'Ship!' I demanded.

'Yes, M. Endymion?'

'That wasn't your idea of a practical joke, was it?'

'Do you mean obeying your order to collapse the zero-g microfield, M. Endymion?'

'Yeah.'

'I assure you, the consequences were the result of a minor oversight only, M. Endymion. I do not commit practical jokes. Be assured, I do not suffer from a sense of humor.'

'Hmmm,' I said, not totally convinced. Carrying my wet shoes and clothing with me, I squished upstairs to dry off and get dressed.

I visited A. Bettik down in what he called the 'engine room' the next day. The place did have somewhat the sense of an engine room in an oceangoing ship – warm pipes, obscure but massive dynamo-shaped objects, catwalks and metal platforms – but A. Bettik showed me how the primary purpose of the space was to interface with the ship's drives and field generators via various simstimlike connectors. I admit that I've never enjoyed computer-generated realities, and after sampling a few of the virtual views of the ship, I disconnected and sat by A. Bettik's hammock while we talked. He told me about helping to service and rent this ship over the long decades, and how he had begun to believe it would never fly again. I sensed a relief that the voyage was under way.

'Had you always planned to go on the trip with whomever the old poet chose to go with the girl?' I asked.

The android looked steadily at me. 'For the past century I have harbored the thought, M. Endymion. But I rarely considered it a potential reality. I thank you for making it so.'

His gratitude was so sincere that it embarrassed me for a moment. 'You'd better not thank me until we escape the Pax,' I said to change the subject. 'I suppose they'll be waiting for us in Renaissance Vector space.'

'It seems likely.' The blue-skinned man did not seem especially concerned by the prospect.

'Do you think Aenea's threat of opening the ship to space will work a second time?' I said.

A. Bettik shook his head. 'They wish to capture the girl alive, but they will not be taken in by that bluff again.'

I raised my eyebrows. 'Do you really think she was bluffing? I had the impression that she was ready to open our level to vacuum.'

'I think not,' said A. Bettik. 'I do not know this young person well, of course, but I had the pleasure of spending some days with her mother and the other pilgrims during their crossing of Hyperion. M. Lamia was a woman who loved life and respected the lives of others. I believe that M. Aenea might have carried out the threat if she had been alone, but I do not think that she is capable of choosing to hurt you or me.'

I had nothing to say to that, so we spoke of other things – the ship, our destination, how strange the Web worlds must be after all this time since the Fall.

'If we land on Renaissance Vector,' I said, 'do you plan to leave us there?'

'Leave you?' said A. Bettik, showing surprise for the first time. 'Why would I leave you there?'

I made a lame gesture with my hand. 'Well . . . I guess . . . I mean, I always thought you wanted your freedom and would find it on the first civilized world we landed on . . .' I stopped before I made more of an idiot of myself.

'My freedom is found by being allowed to come along on this voyage,' the android said softly. He smiled. 'And, besides, M. Endymion, I could hardly blend in with the populace if I did want to stay on Renaissance Vector.'

This raised an issue I'd been thinking about. 'You could change your skin color,' I said. 'The ship's autosurgeon could do that . . .' I stopped again, seeing something subtle in his expression that I did not understand.

'As you know, M. Endymion,' began A. Bettik, 'we androids are not programmed like machines . . . not even set with basic parameters and asimotivators like the early DNA AIs which evolved into the Core intelligences . . . but certain inhibitions were . . . ah . . . strongly urged on us when our instincts were being designed. One, of course, is to obey humans whenever reasonable and to keep them from coming to harm. This asimotivator is older than robotics or bioengineering, I am told. But another . . . instinct . . . is not to change my skin color.'

'You're not capable of it?' I asked. 'You couldn't do it if our lives depended upon your concealing your blue skin?'

'Oh, yes,' said A. Bettik, 'I am a creature of free will. I could do so, especially if the action was consistent with high-priority asimotivations, such as keeping you and M. Aenea safe from harm, but my choice would make me . . . uncomfortable. Very uncomfortable.'

I nodded but did not really understand. We spoke of other things.

This was the same day that I inventoried the contents of the weapons and EVA lockers on the main air-lock level. There was more there than I'd thought upon first inspection, and some of the objects were so archaic that I had to ask the ship their purpose. Most of the things in the EVA locker were obvious enough – spacesuits and hazardous-atmosphere suits, four flybikes cleverly folded into their storage niches under the spacesuit closet, heavy-duty handlamps, camping gear, osmosis masks and scuba gear with nippers and spear-guns, one EM-flying belt, three boxes of tools, two well-equipped medkits, six sets of night-vision and IR goggles, an equal number of lightweight headsets with mike-bead communicators and vid cameras, and comlogs. These last items caused me to query the ship: on a world without a datasphere, I had grown up with little use for the things. The comlogs ranged from antiquated – the thin silver band of jewelry type that was popular several decades ago – to absolutely ancient: massive things the size of a small book. All were capable of being used as communicators, of storing massive amounts of data, of tapping into the local datasphere, and – especially with the older ones – of actually hooking into planetary fatline relays via remote so that the megasphere could be accessed.

I held one of the bracelet pieces in my palm. It weighed much less than a gram. Useless. I understood from listening to offworld hunters that there were a few worlds with primitive dataspheres once again – Renaissance Vector was one of them, I thought – but the fatline relays had been useless for almost three centuries. The fatline – that common band of FTL communication upon which the Hegemony had depended – had been silent since the Fall. I started to put the comlog back in its velvet-lined case.

'You might find it useful to take with you if you leave me for any period of time,' said the ship.

I glanced over my shoulder. 'Why?'

'Information,' said the ship. 'I would be happy to download the bulk of my basic datalogs into one or more of those. You could access it at will.'

I chewed my lip, trying to imagine any value in having the ship's confused mass of data on my wrist. Then I heard Grandam's voice from my childhood – *Information is always to be treasured, Raul. It is behind only love and honesty in a person's attempt to understand the universe.*

'Good idea,' I said, snapping the thin silver thread around my wrist. 'When can you download the data banks?'

'I just did,' said the ship.

I had gone through the weapons locker carefully before we had reached Parvati space; there had been nothing there which could have slowed a Swiss Guardsman for a second. Now I studied the contents of the locker with different purposes in mind.

It is odd how old things look old. The spacesuits and flybikes and handlamps – almost everything aboard the ship – seemed antiquated, out of style. There were no skinsuits, for instance, and the bulk, design, and color of everything seemed like a holo from a history text. But the weapons were a slightly different story. They were old, yes, but very familiar to my eye and hand.

The Consul had obviously been a hunter. There were half a dozen shotguns on the rack: well oiled and stored properly. I could have taken any one of them and headed for the fens to bag ducks. They ranged from a petite .310 over-and-under to a massive 28-gauge double barrel. I chose an ancient but perfectly preserved 16-gauge pump with actual cartridges and set it in the corridor.

The rifles and energy weapons were beautiful. The Consul must have been a collector, because these specimens were works of art as well as killing devices – scrollwork on the stocks, blue steel, hand-fitted elements, perfect balance. In the millennium and more since the twentieth century, when personal weapons were mass-produced to be incredibly deadly, cheap, and ugly as metal doorstops, some of us – the Consul and I among the few – had learned to treasure beautiful handmade or limited-production guns. On the rack here were high-caliber hunting rifles, plasma rifles (not a misnomer, I had learned while in Home Guard basic training – the plasma cartridges were bolts of sheer energy, of course, when they emerged from the barrel, but the cartridges did benefit from the barrel's rifling before they volatized), two elaborately carved laser-based energy rifles (this *was* a misnomer, an artifact of language rather than design) not that different from the one M. Herrig had killed Izzy with not so many days earlier, a matte-black FORCE assault rifle that probably resembled the one Colonel Fedmahn Kassad had brought to Hyperion three centuries ago, a huge-bore plasma weapon that the Consul must have used for shooting dinosaurs on some world, and three handguns. There were no deathwands. I was glad; I hated the damned things.

I removed one of the plasma rifles, the FORCE assault weapon, and the handguns for further inspection.

The FORCE weapon was ugly, an exception to the Consul's collecting scheme, but I saw why it had been useful. The thing was multipurpose – an 18-mm plasma rifle, a variable-beam coherent-energy weapon, grenade launcher, a bhee-keeper (beams of high-energy electrons), flechette launcher, a wideband blinder, heat-seeking dart flinger – hell, a FORCE assault weapon could do everything but cook the trooper's meals. (And, when in the field, the variable-beam, set to low, could usually do that as well.)

Before entering Parvati System, I had toyed with greeting any Swiss Guard boarders with the FORCE weapon, but modern combat suits would have shrugged off everything it could dole out, and – to be honest – I had been afraid it would make the Pax troopers mad.

Now I studied it more carefully; something this flexible might be useful if we wandered too far from the ship and I had to take on a more primitive foe – say, a caveman, or a jet fighter, or some poor slob equipped as we had been in Hyperion's Home Guard. In the end, I rejected taking it – it was prohibitively heavy if one weren't in an old FORCE exopowered combat suit, the thing had no ammunition for the flechette, grenade, or bhee settings, 18-mm pulse cartridges were impossible to find anymore, and to use the energy-weapon options, I would have to be near the ship or some other serious power source. I set the assault gun back in place, realizing as I did so that it might well have been the legendary Colonel Kassad's personal weapon. It did not fit the profile of the Kassad – perhaps he had kept the thing for sentimental reasons.

I asked the ship, but the ship did not remember. 'Surprise, surprise,' I muttered.

The handguns were more ancient than the assault gun, but much more promising. Each was a collector's item, but they used cartridge magazines that could still be purchased – at least on Hyperion. I couldn't vouch for the worlds we would visit. The biggest weapon was a .60-caliber Steiner-Ginn full-auto Penetrator. It was a serious weapon, but heavy: the cartridge templates weighed almost as much as the handgun, and it was designed to use ammunition at a prodigious rate. I set it back. The other two were more promising: a small, light, eminently portable flechette pistol that might have been the great-granddaddy of the weapon M. Herrig had tried to kill me with. It came with several hundred shiny little needle-eggs – the grip magazine held five at a time – and each of the eggs held several thousand of the flechettes. It was a good weapon for someone who was not necessarily a good shot.

The final handgun amazed me. It was in its own oiled leather holster. I removed the weapon with fingers that were slightly shaking. I knew it only from old books – a .45-caliber semiautomatic handgun, actual cartridges – the kind that came in brass casings, not a magazine template that created them as the gun was fired – patterned grip, metal sights, blue steel. I turned the weapon over in my hands. This thing could date back more than a thousand years.

I looked in the case in which I had found it: five boxes of .45 cartridges, several hundred rounds. I thought that they must be ancient as well, but I found the manufacturer's tag: Lusus. About three centuries ago.

Hadn't Brawne Lamia carried an ancient .45 according to the Cantos? Later, when I asked Aenea, the child said that she had never seen her mother with a handgun.

Still, it and the flechette pistol seemed like weapons we should have with us. I did not know if the .45 cartridges would still fire, so I carried one out on the balcony, warned the ship that the external field should stop the slug from ricocheting, and squeezed the trigger. Nothing. Then I remembered that these things had a manual safety. I found it, clicked it off, and tried again. My God, it was loud. But the shells still worked. I set the weapon in its holster and clipped the holster to my utility belt. It felt right there. Of course, when the last .45 cartridge had been fired, that would be it forever unless I could find an antique gun club that manufactured them.

I don't plan to have to fire several hundred bullets at anything, I thought wryly at the time. If only I had known.

Meeting with the girl and android later, I showed them the shotgun and plasma hunting rifle I'd chosen, the flechette pistol, and the .45. 'If we go wandering through strange places – uninhabited strange places – we should go armed,' I said. I offered the flechette pistol to both of them, but they both refused. Aenea wanted no weapon; the android pointed out that he could not use one against a human being, and he trusted me to be around if a fierce animal was chasing him.

I grunted but set the rifle, shotgun, and flechette pistol aside. 'I'll wear this,' I said, touching the .45.

'It matches your outfit,' Aenea said with a slight smile.

There was no last-minute desperate discussion of a plan this time. None of us believed that Aenea's threat of self-destruction would work again if the Pax was waiting. Our most serious discussion of coming events came two days before we spun down into the Renaissance System. We had eaten well – A. Bettik had prepared a filet of river manta with a light sauce, and we had raided the ship's wine cellar for a fine wine from the Beak's vineyards – and after an hour of music with Aenea on the piano and the android playing a flute he had brought with him, talk turned to the future.

'Ship, what can you tell us about Renaissance Vector?' asked the girl.

There was that brief pause that I had come to associate with the ship being embarrassed. 'I am sorry, M. Aenea, but other than navigational information and orbital approach maps which are centuries out of date, I am afraid I have no information about the world.'

'I have been there,' said A. Bettik. 'Also centuries ago, but we have been monitoring radio and television traffic that refers to the planet.'

'I've heard some of my offworld hunters talk,' I said. 'Some of the richest are from Renaissance V.' I gestured to the android. 'Why don't you start?'

He nodded and folded his arms. 'Renaissance Vector was one of the most important worlds of the Hegemony. Extremely Earth-like on the Solmev Scale, it was settled by early seedships and was completely urbanized by the time of the Fall. It was famous for its universities, its medical centers – most Poulssen treatments were administered there for the Web citizens who could afford it – its baroque architecture – especially beautiful in its mountain fortress, Keep Enable – and its industrial output. Most of the FORCE spacecraft were manufactured there. In fact, *this* spacecraft must have been built there – it was a product of the Mitsubishi-Havcek complex.'

'Really?' said the ship's voice. 'If I knew that, the data must have been lost. How interesting.'

Aenea and I exchanged worried glances for the dozenth time on this voyage. A ship that couldn't remember its past or point of origin did not inspire confidence during the complexities of interstellar flight. *Oh, well,* I thought for the dozenth time, *it got us in and out of Parvati System all right.*

'DaVinci is the capital of Renaissance Vector,' continued A. Bettik, 'although the entire landmass and much of the single large sea are urbanized, so there is little distinction between one urban center and the other.'

'It's a busy Pax world,' I added. 'One of the earliest to join the Pax after the Fall. The military is there in spades . . . both Renaissance V. and

Renaissance M. have orbital and lunar garrisons, as well as bases all over each planet.'

'What's Renaissance M.?' asked Aenea.

'Renaissance Minor,' said A. Bettik. 'The second world from the sun . . . Renaissance V. is the third. Minor is also inhabited, but much less so. It is a largely agricultural world – huge automated farms covering much of the planet – and it feeds Vector. After the Fall of the farcasters, both worlds benefited from this arrangement; before regularly scheduled interstellar commerce was reinstated by the Pax, the Renaissance System was fairly self-contained. Renaissance Vector manufactured goods; Renaissance Minor provided the food for the five billion people on Renaissance Vector.'

'What's the population on Renaissance V. now?' I asked.

'I believe it is about the same – five billion people, give or take a few hundred million,' said A. Bettik. 'As I said, the Pax arrived early and offered both the cruciform and the birth-control regime that goes with it.'

'You said you'd been there,' I said to the android. 'What's the world like?'

'Ahh,' said A. Bettik with a rueful smile, 'I was at the Renaissance Vector spaceport for less than thirty-six hours while being shipped from Asquith in preparation for our colonizing King William's new land on Hyperion. They did rouse us from cryogenic sleep but did not allow us to leave the ship. My personal recollections of the world are not extensive.'

'Are they mostly born-again Christians there?' asked Aenea. The girl seemed thoughtful and somewhat withdrawn. I noticed that she had been chewing her nails again.

'Oh, yes,' said A. Bettik. 'Almost all five billion of them, I'm afraid.'

'And he wasn't kidding about the heavy Pax military presence,' I said. 'The Pax troopers who trained us in the Hyperion Home Guard staged out of Renaissance V. It's a major garrison world and transshipment point for the whole war against the Ousters.'

Aenea nodded but still seemed distracted.

I decided not to beat around the bush. 'Why are we going there?' I asked.

She looked up at me. Her dark eyes were beautiful but remote that moment. 'I told you, Raul. I want to see the River Tethys.'

I shook my head. 'The River Tethys was a farcaster construct, you know. It didn't exist outside the Web. Or, rather, it existed as a thousand small sections of other rivers.'

'I know,' she said. 'But I want to see a river that was *part* of Tethys during the Web days. My mother told me about it. How it was like the Grand Concourse, only more leisurely. How one could ride a barge from world to world for weeks – months.'

I resisted the impulse to get angry. 'You know there's almost no chance we can get past their defences to Renaissance Vector,' I said. 'And if we get there, the River Tethys won't be there . . . just whatever portion used to be there. What's so important about seeing that?'

The girl started to shrug, then caught herself. 'Remember how I said that there's an architect I need to . . . want to . . . study with?'

'Yes,' I said. 'A woman. But you don't know her name or what world she's on. So why come to Renaissance Vector to start your search? Couldn't we look on Renaissance Minor, at least? Or just skip this system and go somewhere empty, like Armaghast?'

Aenea shook her head. I noticed that she had brushed her hair especially well; the blonde highlights were very visible. 'In my dreams,' she said, 'the architect lives on a former Web world, near the River Tethys.'

'There are hundreds of other old Web worlds,' I said, leaning closer to her so she could see that I was very serious. 'Not all of them will get us caught or killed by the Pax. Do we have to start in Renaissance System?'

'I think so,' she said softly.

I dropped my large hands to my knees. Martin Silenus had not said that this trip would be easy or make sense – he had just said that it would make me a hero. 'All right,' I said again, hearing the weariness in my own voice, 'what's our plan this time, kiddo?'

'No plan,' said Aenea. 'If they're waiting for us, I'm just going to tell them the truth – that we're going to land the ship on Renaissance Vector. I think they'll let us land.'

'And if they do?' I said, trying to imagine the ship surrounded by thousands of Pax troopers.

'We'll take it from there, I guess,' said the girl. She smiled at me. 'Want to play one-sixth-g billiards, you two? For money this time?'

I started to say something sharp, then changed my tone. 'You don't have any money,' I said.

Aenea's grin grew wider. 'Then I can't lose, can I?'

TWENTY-SIX

During the one hundred and forty-two days that Father Captain de Soya waits for the girl to enter Renaissance System, he dreams about her every night. He sees her clearly as she was when first encountered at the Sphinx on Hyperion – willow thin, eyes alert but not terrified despite the sandstorm and threatening figures before her, her small hands partially raised as if ready to cover her face or rush forward to hug him. Often in his dreams she is his daughter and they are walking the crowded canal-streets of Renaissance Vector, discussing de Soya's older sister, Maria, who has been sent to the St Jude Medical Center in DaVinci. In his dreams de Soya and the child walk hand in hand through the familiar canal-streets near the huge medical complex while he explains to her how he plans to save his sister's life this time, how he will not allow Maria to die the way she had the first time.

In reality, Federico de Soya had been six standard years old when he and his family came to Renaissance Vector from their isolated region of Llano Estacado on their provincial world of MadredeDios. Almost everyone on the sparsely populated stone-and-desert world was Catholic, but not Pax born-again Catholic. The de Soya family had been part of the break-away Mariaist movement and had left Nuevo Madrid more than a century earlier when that world had voted to join the Pax and have all of its Christian churches submit to the Vatican. The Mariaists venerated the Holy Mother of Christ more than Vatican orthodoxy allowed, so young Federico had grown up on a marginal desert world with its devout colony of sixty thousand heretical Catholics who would not accept the cruciform as a form of protest.

Then twelve-year-old Maria had become sick with an offworld retrovirus that swept like a scythe through the colony ranching region. Most sufferers of the Red Death either died within thirty-two hours or recovered, but Maria had lingered, her once-beautiful features all but obscured by the terrible crimson stigmata. The family had taken her to the hospital in Ciudad del Madre on the windswept southern reach of Llano Estacado, but Mariaist medics there could do nothing but pray. There was a new Pax born-again Christian mission in Ciudad del Madre, discriminated against but tolerated by the locals, and the priest there – a kindly man named Father Maher – begged Federico's father to allow their dying child to accept the cruciform. Federico was too young to remember the details of his parents' agonized discussions, but he did remember the entire family – his mother and father, his other two sisters and younger brother – all on their knees in the Mariaist church there, begging for the Holy Mother's guidance and intercession.

It was the other ranchers of the Llano Estacado Cooperative who raised the money to send the entire family offworld to one of the famous medical centers on Renaissance Vector. While his brother and other sisters were left behind with a neighboring ranch family, for some reason six-year-old Federico was chosen to accompany his parents and dying sister on the long voyage. It was everyone's first experience with actual coldsleep – more dangerous but cheaper than cryogenic fugue – and de Soya later remembered the chill in his bones that seemed to last through their weeks on Renaissance Vector.

At first the Pax medics in DaVinci seemed to arrest the spread of the Red Death through Maria's system, even banishing some of the bleeding stigmata, but then, after three local weeks, the retrovirus again gained the upper hand. Once again a Pax priest – in this case, several who were on the staff of the hospital – beseeched de Soya's parents to bend their Mariaist principles and allow the dying child to accept the cruciform before it was too late. Later, as he entered adulthood, de Soya could better imagine the agonies of such a decision – the death of one's deepest beliefs, or the death of one's child.

In his dream, where Aenea is his daughter and they are walking the canal-streets near the medical center, he describes to her how Maria had given him her most prized possession – a tiny porcelain sculpture of a unicorn – just hours before she had slipped into a coma. In his dream, he walks with the eleven-year-old Hyperion girl's small hand in his, and tells her how his father – a strong man in both body and belief – had finally surrendered and asked for the Pax priests to administer the sacrament of the cross to his daughter. The priests at the hospital agreed, but insisted that de Soya's parents and Federico formally convert to universal Catholicism before Maria could receive her cruciform.

De Soya explains to his daughter, Aenea, how he remembers the brief re-baptism ceremony at the local cathedral – St John the Divine – where he and his parents renounced the ascendancy of the Holy Mother, and accepted the sole dominion of Jesus Christ as well as the power of the Vatican over their religious lives. He remembers receiving both First Communion and the cruciform that same evening. Maria's Sacrament of the Cross was scheduled for ten PM. She died suddenly at eight forty-five PM. By the rules of the Church and the laws of the Pax, someone who suffered braindeath before receiving the cross could not be revived artificially to receive it.

Instead of being furious or feeling betrayed by his new Church, Federico's father took the tragedy as a sign that God – not the God he had grown up praying to, the gentle Son infused with the universal female principles of the Holy Mother, but the fiercer New and Old Testament God of the Universal Church – had punished him, his family, and the entire Mariaist world of Llano Estacado. Upon the return to their homeworld with their child's body dressed in white for burial, the elder de Soya had become an unrelenting apostle for the Pax version of Catholicism. It came at a fertile time, as the ranching communities were being swept with the Red Death. Federico was sent to the Pax school in Ciudad del Madre at age seven, and his sisters were sent away to the convent in northern Llano. Within his father's lifetime – indeed, before Federico was sent to New Madrid with Father Maher to attend St Thomas's Seminary there – the surviving Mariaists on MadredeDios had all converted to Pax Catholicism. Maria's terrible death had led to a world being born again.

In his dreams Father Captain de Soya explains little of this to the child walking with him through the nightmare-familiar streets of DaVinci on Renaissance Vector. The girl, Aenea, seems to know all this.

In his dreams, repeated almost every night for one hundred and forty-two nights before the girl's ship arrives, de Soya is explaining to the child how he has discovered the secret to curing the Red Death and saving his sister. The first morning that de Soya awakens, heart pounding and sheets soaked with sweat, he assumes that the secret to Maria's rescue is the cruciform, but the next night's dream proves him wrong.

The secret, it seems, is the return of Maria's unicorn figure. All he has to do, he explains to his daughter, Aenea, is find the hospital through this maze of streets, and he knows that the return of the unicorn will save his sister. But he cannot find the hospital. The maze defeats him.

Almost five months later, on the eve of the arrival of the ship from Parvati System, in a variation on the same dream, de Soya *does* find the St Jude Medical Center where his sister is sleeping, but he realizes with growing horror that he has now lost the figurine.

In this dream Aenea speaks for the first time. Drawing the small porcelain statuette from the pocket of her blouse, the child says, 'You see, we've had it with us the entire time.'

The reality of de Soya's months in Renaissance System is literally and figuratively light-years away from the Parvati experience.

Unknown to de Soya, Gregorius, Kee, and Rettig – each a mangled corpse in the heart of *Raphael*'s resurrection creches – the ship is challenged within an hour of translating in-system. Two Pax ramscouts and a torchship come alongside after exchanging transponder codes and data with *Raphael*'s computer. It is decided to transfer the four bodies to a Pax resurrection center on Renaissance V.

Unlike their solitary awakening in Parvati System, de Soya and his Swiss Guard troopers return to consciousness with the proper ceremony and care. Indeed, the resurrection is a difficult one for the father-captain and Corporal Kee, and the two are returned to their creche for an additional three days. Later, de Soya can only speculate whether the ship's automated resurrection facilities would have been up to the task.

As it is, the four are reunited after a week in-system, each man with his own chaplain/counselor. Sergeant Gregorius finds this unnecessary; he is eager and impatient to return to duty, but de Soya and the other two welcome their extra days of rest and recuperation from death.

The *Saint Anthony* translates only hours after *Raphael,* and eventually de Soya is reunited with Captain Sati of the torchship and Captain Lempriere of the troopship *Saint Thomas Akira,* which has returned to the Pax base in Renaissance System with more than eighteen hundred dead in cold storage, and twenty-three hundred wounded men and women from the carnage in Hyperion System. The hospitals and cathedrals on Renaissance V. and in orbital Pax bases begin the surgeries and resurrections at once.

De Soya is present at her bedside when Commander Barnes-Avne regains life and consciousness. The small red-haired woman seems another person, diminished to the point that it makes de Soya's heart ache with pity, with her head shaved, her skin red and slick with rebirth, and dressed only in a hospital gown. But her aggressiveness and demeanor have not been diminished. Almost at once she demands, 'What the hell happened?'

De Soya tells her about the Shrike carnage. He fills her in on the seven months he has spent chasing the girl during the four months Barnes-Avne has spent in cold storage and transit from Hyperion.

'You've really screwed the pooch, haven't you?' says the Commander.

De Soya smiles. So far, the Groundforce Commander is the only one to speak honestly to him. He is all too aware that he has screwed the proverbial pooch: twice he has been in charge of a major Pax operation with a single objective – take a child into custody – and twice he has failed miserably. De Soya expects, at the very least, to be relieved of duty; more likely to be court-martialed. To that end, when an archangel courier arrives in-system two months before the girl's arrival, de Soya orders the couriers to return at once to Pacem, to report his failure, and to return with instructions from Pax Command. In the meantime, Father Captain de Soya concludes his courier message, he will continue arranging the details of preparation for the girl's capture in Renaissance System until he is relieved.

The resources available to him this time are impressive. Besides more than two hundred thousand ground troops, including several thousand elite Pax Marines and the surviving Swiss Guard Brigades from Hyperion, de Soya finds extensive sea and space naval forces. Present in Renaissance System and subject to his papal diskey command, are twenty-seven torchships – eight of them omega class – as well as a hundred and eight nesting ram-scouts to probe ahead of the torchships, C^3 fleet command-and-control ships with their escort cloud of thirty-six fast-attack ALRs, the attack carrier *Saint Malo* with more than two hundred space/air Scorpion fighters and seven thousand crew aboard, the antiquated cruiser *Pride of Bressia,* now renamed the *Jacob,* two additional troop transports in addition to the *Saint Thomas Akira,* an even score of Benediction-class destroyers, fifty-eight perimeter defense pickets – any three of which would be capable of defending an entire world (or a mobile task force) from attack – and more than a hundred lesser ships, including in-system frigates that carried a lethal punch for close-in fighting, minesweepers, in-system couriers, drones, and the *Raphael.*

Three days after he has dispatched the second archangel courier to Pacem and seven weeks before Aenea's arrival, the MAGI Task Force arrives – the

Melchior, the *Gaspar*, and Father Captain de Soya's old ship, the *Balthasar*. At first de Soya is excited to see his old companions, but then he realizes that they will be present during his humiliation. Nonetheless, he goes out in *Raphael* to greet them while they are still six AUs from Renaissance V., and the first thing Mother Commander Stone does upon his stepping into the *Balthasar* is to hand him his duffel of personal possessions that he had been forced to leave behind. On top of his neady folded clothes, carefully wrapped in foam, is his sister Maria's gift of the porcelain unicorn.

De Soya is honest with Captain Hearn, Mother Captain Boulez, and Mother Commander Stone – he outlines the preparations he has made but tells them that a new commander will almost certainly be arriving before the girl's ship arrives. Two days later he is proved a liar. The archangel-class courier translates in-system with two aboard: Captain Marget Wu, aide to Fleet Admiral Marusyn, and the Jesuit Father Brown, special adviser to Monsignor Lucas Oddi, Undersecretary of Vatican State and confidant of Secretary of State Simon Augustino Cardinal Lourdusamy.

Captain Wu's sealed orders for de Soya come with instructions to be opened even before her resurrection. He opens them immediately. The instructions are simple – he is to continue on his mission to capture the child, he will never be relieved of this duty, and Captain Wu, Father Brown, and any other dignitaries to arrive in-system are there only to observe and to underline – if any underlining is necessary – Father Captain de Soya's total authority over all Pax officials in the pursuit of this goal.

This authority has been grudgingly accepted in the past weeks and months – there are three Pax Fleet admirals and eleven Pax groundforce commanders in Renaissance System, and none are used to taking orders from a mere father-captain. But the papal diskey has been heard and obeyed. Now, in the final weeks, de Soya reviews his plans and meets with Commanders and civilian leaders of all levels, down to the mayors of DaVinci and Benedetto, Toscanelli and Fioravante, Botticelli and Mosaccio.

In the final weeks, with all plans made and forces assigned, Father Captain de Soya actually finds time for personal reflection and activities. Alone now, away from the controlled chaos of staff meetings and tactical simulations – away even from Gregorius, Kee, and Rettig, who accepted assignments as his personal bodyguards – de Soya walks the streets of DaVinci, visits the St Jude Medical Center, and remembers his sister Maria. Somehow, he discovers, the nightly dreams are more compelling than seeing the real places.

De Soya has discovered that his old patron, Father Maher, has been serving for many years as rector in the Ascension Benedictine Monastery in the city-region of Florence on the opposite side of Renaissance V. from Da-Vinci, and he flies there to spend a long afternoon talking to the old man. Father Maher, now in his late eighties and 'looking forward to my first new life in Christ,' is as optimistic, patient, and kind as de Soya remembers from almost three decades ago. Maher, it seems, has returned to MadredeDios more recently than de Soya. 'The Llano Estacado has been abandoned,' says the old priest. 'The ranches are empty now. Ciudad del Madre has a few dozen inhabitants, but only Pax researchers – seeing if the world is truly worth terraforming.'

'Yes,' says de Soya, 'my family emigrated back to Nuevo Madrid more than twenty standard years ago. My sisters serve the Church – Loretta as a nun on Nevermore, Melinda as a priest on Nuevo Madrid.'

'And your brother Estaban?' asks Father Maher with a warm smile.

De Soya takes a breath. 'Killed by the Ousters in a space battle last year,' he says. 'His ship was vaporized. No bodies were recovered.'

Father Maher blinks as if he has been slapped. 'I had not heard.'

'No,' says de Soya, 'you wouldn't have. It was far away – beyond the old Outback. Word has not officially reached even my family yet. I know only because my duties took me to the vicinity and I met a returning captain who told me the news.'

Father Maher shakes his bald and mottled head. 'Estaban has found the only resurrection which Our Lord promised,' he says softly, tears in his eyes. 'Eternal resurrection in Our Saviour Jesus Christ.'

'Yes,' says de Soya. A moment later he says, 'Do you still drink Scotch, Father Maher?'

The old man's rheumy eyes lift to meet the other's gaze. 'Yes, but only for medicinal purposes, Father Captain de Soya.'

De Soya's dark brows rise a bit. 'I am still recovering from my last resurrection, Father Maher.'

The older priest nods seriously. 'And I am preparing for my first one, Father Captain de Soya. I shall find the dusty bottle.'

On the following Sunday, de Soya celebrates Mass at the Cathedral of St John the Divine where he had accepted the cross so long ago. More than eight hundred of the faithful are in attendance, including Father Maher and Father Brown, the intelligent and insightful aide to Monsignor Oddi. Sergeant Gregorius, Corporal Kee, and Lancer Rettig also attend, taking Communion from de Soya's hand.

That night de Soya again dreams of Aenea. 'How is it that you are my daughter?' he asks this night. 'I have always honored my vows of celibacy.'

The child smiles and takes his hand.

One hundred hours before the girl's ship is to translate, de Soya orders his fleet into position. The translation point is perilously close to the gravity well of Renaissance Vector, and many of the experts are concerned that the old ship will break up, either under the gravity torque of such an unadvisable close exit from C-plus or from the horrendous deceleration needed if the ship is to land on the planet. Their concerns remain largely unspoken, as is their frustration at being kept in Renaissance System: many of the Fleet units had assignments along the frontier or deep in Ouster space. This waste of time has most of the officers on edge.

It is largely because of this undercurrent of tension that Father Captain de Soya calls a meeting of all line officers ten hours before the translation. Such conferences are usually handled over tightbeam linkups, but de Soya has the men and women physically transfer to the carrier *Saint Malo*. The huge ship's main briefing room is large enough to handle the scores of attending officers.

De Soya begins by reviewing the scenarios they have practiced for weeks or months now. If the child once again threatens self-destruction, three torchships – de Soya's old MAGI Task Force – will close rapidly, wrap class-ten fields around the ship, stun whoever is aboard into unconsciousness, and hold the ship in stasis until the *Jacob* can take it in tow with its massive field generators.

If the ship tries to leave the system the way it ran from Parvati, ramscouts and fast-attack fighters will harass it while the torchships maneuver to disable it.

De Soya pauses in the briefing. 'Questions?' Among the familiar faces he can see in the row upon row of briefing chairs are Captains Lempriere, San, Wu, and Hearn, Father Brown, Mother Captain Boulez, Mother Commander Stone, and Commander Barnes-Avne. Sergeant Gregorius, Kee, and Rettig stand at parade rest near the back of the briefing room, allowed in this august company only because of their status as personal bodyguards.

Captain Marget Wu says, 'And if the ship attempts to land on Renaissance Vector, Renaissance Minor, or one of the moons?'

De Soya steps away from the low podium. 'As we discussed at our last meeting, should the ship attempt to land, we will make the judgement at the time.'

'Based on what factors, Father Captain?' asks Fleet Admiral Serra from the C^3 ship *Saint Thomas Aquinas*.

De Soya hesitates only a second. 'Several factors, Admiral. Where the ship is headed . . . whether it would be safer – for the girl – to allow it to land or to attempt to disable it en route . . . whether there is any chance for the ship to escape.'

'Is there any chance?' asks Commander Barnes-Avne. The woman is hale and formidable again in her space-black uniform.

'I will not say that there is no chance,' says Father Captain de Soya. 'Not after Hyperion. But we will minimize any chance.'

'If the Shrike creature appears . . .' begins Captain Lempriere.

'We have rehearsed the scenario,' says de Soya, 'and I see no reason to vary from our plans. This time we will rely upon computerized fire control to a greater extent. On Hyperion the creature remained in one spot for less than two seconds. This was too fast for human reactions and confused the programming in automated fire-control systems. We have reprogrammed those systems – including individual troopers' suit fire-control systems.'

'So the Marines will board the ship?' asks a ramscout captain in the last row.

'Only if all else fails,' says de Soya. 'Or after the girl and any companions have been locked in the stasis fields and stunned into unconsciousness.'

'And deathwands will be used against the creature?' asks a destroyer captain.

'Yes,' says de Soya, 'as long as doing so does not put the child in danger. Any other questions?'

The room is silent.

'Father Maher from Ascension Monastery will close with the blessing,' says Father Captain de Soya. 'Godspeed to you all.'

TWENTY-SEVEN

I am not sure what made us all go up to the Consul's bedroom at the apex of the ship to watch the translation to normal space. His large bed – the one I had been sleeping in for the past couple of weeks – was in the center of the room, but it folded to a sort of couch, and I did that now. Behind his bed were two opaque cubes – the wardrobe cubby and the shower-lavatory cube – but when the hull was allowed to go transparent, these cubes were just dark blocks against the starfield all around and overhead. As the ship spun down from Hawking velocities, we asked that the hull be made transparent.

Our first glimpse, before the ship started its rotation to line up for deceleration, was of the world of Renaissance Vector, close enough to be a blue-and-white disk rather than a starry speck, with two of its three moons visible. The Renaissance sun was brilliant to the left of the illuminated planet and moons. There were scores of stars visible, which was unusual, since the glare of the sun usually darkened the sky so that only a few of the brightest stars could be seen. Aenea commented on this.

'Those are not stars,' said the ship as it completed its slow rotation. The fusion drive roared into existence as we began decelerating toward the planet. Normally we never would have exited from C-plus this close to a planet and moons – their gravity wells made spindown velocities very dangerous – but the ship had assured us that its augmented fields would handle any problems. But not this problem.

'Those are not stars,' repeated the ship. 'There are more than fifty ships under drive within a one-hundred-thousand-kilometer radius of us. There are dozens more in orbital defense positions. Three of those ships – torch-ships, from their fusion signature – are within two hundred kilometers of us and are closing.'

None of us said a word. The ship had not had to tell us this final bit of information – the three fusion-drive streaks seemed to be directly overhead, burning down at the top of our decelerating ship like blowtorch flames coming at our faces.

'We are being hailed,' said the ship.

'Visual?' said Aenea.

'Audio only.' The ship's voice sounded more terse and businesslike than usual. Was it possible for an AI to feel tension?

'Let's hear it,' said the girl.

'. . . the ship which has just entered Renaissance System,' the voice was saying. It was a familiar voice. We had heard it in Parvati System. Father

Captain de Soya. 'Attention, the ship which has just entered Renaissance System,' he said again.

'Which ship is the call coming from?' asked A. Bettik as he watched the three torchships close on us. His blue face was bathed in blue light from the plasma drives overhead.

'Unknown,' said the ship. 'It is a tightbeam transmission and I have not located the source. It might be coming from any of the seventy-nine ships I am currently tracking.'

I felt as if I should make some comment, say something intelligent. 'Yoicks,' I said. Aenea glanced at me and then looked back at the closing torchship drives.

'Time to Renaissance V.?' she asked softly.

'Fourteen minutes at constant delta-v,' said the ship. 'But this level of deceleration would be illegal within four planetary distances.'

'Continue this level,' Aenea said.

'Attention, the ship which has just entered Renaissance System,' the de Soya voice was saying. 'Prepare to be boarded. Any resistance will result in your being rendered unconscious. I repeat . . . attention, the ship which has just entered . . .'

Aenea looked up at me and grinned. 'I guess I can't use the depressurization ploy, huh, Raul?'

I could not think of anything clever to say beyond my 'yoicks' commentary. I lifted my hands, palms up.

'Attention, the ship which has just entered the system. We are coming alongside. Do not resist as we merge external containment fields.'

For some reason, at that moment, as Aenea and A. Bettik raised their faces to watch the three fusion drives separate as the torchships actually became visible less than a kilometer away, one on each point of an equilateral triangle around us, I watched the girl's face. Her features were tense, perhaps – a slight tension at the corners of her mouth – but all in all, she seemed perfectly composed and raptly interested. Her dark eyes were large and luminous.

'Attention, the ship,' said the Pax captain's voice again. 'We will be merging fields in thirty seconds.'

Aenea walked to the edge of the room, reaching out to touch the invisible hull. From my vantage point, it was as if we were standing on a circular summit of a very tall mountain, with stars and blue comet tails on every side, and Aenea was perched on the edge of the precipice.

'Ship, please give me widebeam audio so all the Pax ships can hear me.'

Father Captain de Soya is watching the proceedings in tactical reality as well as real space. In tactical, he stands above the plane of the ecliptic and sees his ships arrayed around the decelerating target ship like points of light set along the spokes and rim of a wheel. Near the hub, so close to the girl's ship as to be almost indistinguishable, are the *Melchior*, the *Gaspar*, and the *Balthasar*. Farther out, but decelerating in perfect synchronicity with the four ships at the hub, are more than a dozen other torchships under the close command of Captain Sati on the *Saint Anthony*. Ten thousand klicks beyond them, set around a slowly rotating perimeter hub, also decelerating into cislunar Renaissance V. space, are the Benediction-class destroyers, three of the six C^3 ships, and the attack carrier *Saint Malo*, upon which de Soya watches the events from the ship's Combat Control center. He had, of course, wanted to be with the MAGI Task Force, closing on the girl's ship, but he realized it would be inappropriate to be in such close command. It would have been especially galling to Mother Captain Stone – promoted only last week by Admiral Serra – to have her first full command undermined in such a way.

So de Soya watches from the *Saint Malo* his archangel *Raphael* in parking orbit around Renaissance V. with the defense pickets and protective ALRs. Switching quickly from the crowded red-lit reality of *Saint Malo*'s CCC to the fusion-flame view of tactical space, he sees the sparks above this rotating wheel of ships, the dozens of ships set in a giant sphere to stop the girl's ship from fleeing in any direction. Moving awareness back to the crowded CCC, he notes the blood-red faces of observers Wu and Brown, as well as Commander Barnes-Avne, who is in tightbeam contact with the fifty Marines aboard the MAGI ships. In the corners of the crowded Combat Control Center, de Soya can see Gregorius and his two troopers. All three of them had been bitterly disappointed not to be in the boarding parties, but de Soya is holding them back as personal bodyguards for the trip back to Pacem with the child.

He keys the tightbeam channel to the girl's ship again. 'Attention, the ship,' he says, feeling the pounding of his heart almost as background noise, 'we will be merging fields in thirty seconds.' He realizes that he is terrified for the girl's safety. If something is to go wrong, it will be in the next few minutes. Simulations have honed the process so that there is only a six percent projected chance of the girl's being harmed . . . but six percent is too large for de Soya. He has dreamed of her every night for one hundred and forty-two nights.

Suddenly the common band rasps and the girl's voice comes over the Combat Control Center's speakers. 'Father Captain de Soya,' she says. There is no visual. 'Please do not attempt to merge fields or board this ship. Any attempt to do so will be disastrous.'

De Soya glances at the readout. Fifteen seconds to fields merging. They have gone over this . . . no threats of suicide will prevent their boarding this time. Less than a hundredth of a second after the fields merge, all three of the MAGI torchships will spray the target ship with stunbeams.

'Think, Father Captain,' comes the girl's soft voice. 'Our ship is controlled by a Hegemony-era AI. If you stun us . . .'

'Stop fields merge!' snaps de Soya with less than two seconds until that is to happen automatically. Acknowledgment lights flick on from the *Melchior, Gaspar*, and *Balthasar*.

'You've been thinking silicon,' continues the girl, 'but our ship's AI core is completely organic – the old DNA type of processor banks – if you stun us into unconsciousness, you stun it.'

'Damn, damn, damn,' de Soya hears. At first he thinks it is himself whispering, but he turns to see Captain Wu cursing under her breath.

'We are decelerating at . . . eighty-seven gravities,' continues Aenea. 'If you knock our AI out . . . well, it controls all internal fields, the drives . . .'

De Soya switches to the engineering bands on the *Saint Malo* and the MAGI ships. 'Is this true? Will this knock out their AI?'

There is an unbearable pause of at least ten seconds. Finally Captain Hearn, whose Academy degree had been in engineering, comes on the tightbeam. 'We don't know, Federico. Most of the details of true AI bio-technology have been lost or suppressed by the Church. It is a mortal sin to . . .'

'Yes, yes,' snaps de Soya, 'but is she telling the truth? Somebody here has to know. Will a DNA-based AI be at risk if we spray the ship with stunners?'

Bramly, the chief engineer of the *Saint Malo*, keys in. 'Sir, I would think that the designers would have protected the brain from such a possibil-ity . . .'

'Do you *know*?' demands de Soya.

'No, sir,' says Bramly after a moment.

'But that AI is totally organic?' persists de Soya.

'Yes,' comes Captain Hearn's voice on tightbeam. 'Except for the elec-tronic and bubble-memory interfaces, a ship's AI of that era would have been cross-helix-structured DNA held in suspension with . . .'

'All right,' says de Soya on multiple tightbeams to all ships. 'Hold your positions. Do not . . . repeat . . . do not let the girl's ship change course or attempt spinup to C-plus. If it attempts this, merge and stun.'

Acknowledgement lights flicker from MAGI and the outer ships.

'. . . so please don't create this disaster,' comes the end of Aenea's broad-cast. 'We are only trying to land on Renaissance Vector.'

Father Captain de Soya opens his tightbeam to her ship. 'Aenea,' he says, his voice gentle, 'let us board and we'll take you to the planet.'

'I guess I'd rather land there myself,' says the girl. De Soya thinks that he can hear a hint of amusement in her voice.

'Renaissance Vector is a big world,' says de Soya, watching the tactical readout as he speaks. They are ten minutes from entering atmosphere. 'Where do you want to land?'

Silence for a full minute. Then Aenea's voice. 'The Leonardo Spaceport in DaVinci would be all right.'

'That spaceport has been closed for more than two hundred years,' says de Soya. 'Aren't your ship's memory banks more recent than that?'

Only silence on the com channels.

'There is a Pax Mercantilus spaceport at the western quadrant of DaVinci,' he says. 'Will that do?'

'Yes,' says Aenea.

'You will have to change direction, enter orbit, and land under space traffic control,' tightbeams de Soya. 'I will download the delta-v changes now.'

'No!' says the girl. 'My ship will land us.'

De Soya sighs and looks at Captain Wu and Father Brown. Commander Barnes-Avne says, 'My Marines can board within two minutes.'

'Her ship will be entering atmosphere in . . . seven minutes,' de Soya says. 'At her velocity, even the slightest miscalculation will be fatal.' He keys the tightbeam. 'Aenea, there is too much space and aircraft traffic over DaVinci for you to try a landing like this. Please instruct your ship to obey the orbital insertion parameters I've just transmitted and—'

'I'm sorry, Father Captain,' says the girl, 'but we're going to land now. If you want the spaceport traffic control to send up approach data, that would help. If I talk to you again, it'll be when we're all on the ground. This is . . . me . . . out.'

'Damn!' says de Soya. He keys Pax Mercantilus Traffic Control. 'Did you copy that, Control?'

'Sending approach data . . . now,' comes the controller's voice.

'Hearn, Stone, Boulez,' snaps de Soya. 'You copy?'

'Acknowledged,' says Mother Captain Stone. 'We're going to have to break off in . . . three minutes ten seconds.'

De Soya flicks into tactical long enough to see the hub and wheel breaking up as the torchships initiate their delta-v's to achieve braking orbits. The ships were never designed for atmosphere. The *Saint Malo* has been in orbit around the planet and now lies almost in the path of the girl's ship as it brakes wildly before entering atmosphere. 'Prepare my dropship,' commands de Soya. 'CAP?' he says over the planetary com channel.

'Here, sir,' comes Flight Commander Klaus's acknowledgment. She and forty-six other Scorpions are waiting in combat air patrol high above DaVinci.

'Are you tracking?'

'Good plots, sir,' says Klaus.

'I remind you that no shots will be fired except under my direct command, Flight Commander.'

'Yes, sir.'

'The *Saint Malo* will be launching . . . ah . . . seventeen fighters, which will follow the target ship down,' says de Soya. 'My dropship will make the number eighteen. Our transponders will be set to oh-five-nine.'

'Affirmative,' says Klaus. 'Beacons to oh-five-niner. Target ship and eighteen friendlies.'

'De Soya out,' he says, and unplugs his umbilicals to the Combat Control Center panels. Tactical space disappears. Captain Wu, Father Brown, Commander Barnes-Avne, Sergeant Gregorius, Kee, and Rettig follow him to the dropship. The dropship pilot, a lieutenant named Karyn Norris Cook, is waiting with all systems ready. It takes less than a minute for them to buckle in and launch from the *Saint Malo*'s flight tube. They have rehearsed this many times.

De Soya is getting tactical feed through the dropship net as they enter atmosphere.

'The girl's ship has wings,' says the pilot, using the ancient phrase. For millennia, 'feet dry' has meant an aircraft crossing over land, 'feet wet' signifies crossing over water, and 'has wings' means translation from space to atmospheric travel.

A visual of the ship shows that this is not literally true. While data on the old ship suggests that it has some morphing capability, it has not actually grown wings in this case. Cameras from the defense pickets clearly show the girl's ship entering the atmosphere stern-first, balancing on a tail of fusion flame.

Captain Wu leans close to de Soya. 'Cardinal Lourdusamy said that this child is a threat to the Pax,' she whispers so that the others cannot hear.

Father Captain de Soya nods tersely.

'What if he meant that she could be a threat to millions of people on Renaissance V.?' Wu whispers. 'That fusion drive alone is a terrible weapon. A thermonuclear explosion above the city . . .'

De Soya feels his insides clamping with the chill of those words, but he has thought this out. 'No,' he whispers back. 'If she turns the fusion trail on anything, we stun the ship, shoot out its engines, and let it fall.'

'The girl . . .' begins Captain Wu.

'We can only hope she'll survive the crash,' says de Soya. 'We won't let thousands . . . or millions . . . of Pax citizens die.' He leans back in his acceleration couch and keys the spaceport, knowing that the tightbeam has to punch through the layer of ionization around the screeching dropship. Glancing at the external video, he sees that they are crossing the terminator: it will be dark at the spaceport.

'Spaceport Control,' acknowledges the Pax traffic director. 'The target ship is decelerating on our directed flight path. Delta-v is high . . . illegal . . . but acceptable. All aircraft traffic cleared for a thousand-kilometer radius. Time to landing . . . four minutes thirty-five seconds.'

'Spaceport secured,' chimes in Commander Barnes-Avne on the same net.

De Soya knows there are several thousand Pax troops in and around the spaceport. Once the girl's ship is down, it will never be allowed to take off again. He looks at the live video: the lights of DaVinci gleam from horizon to horizon. The girl's ship has its navigation lights on, red and green beacons flashing. The powerful landing lights flick on and stab downward through cloud.

'On path,' comes the traffic controller's calm voice. 'Deceleration nominal.'

'We have a visual!' cries CAP Commander Klaus over the net.

'Keep your distance,' tightbeams de Soya. The Scorpions can sting from several hundred klicks out. He does not want them crowding the descending ship.

'Affirmative.'

'On path, ILS reports nominal descent, three minutes to touchdown,' the controller calls up to the girl's ship. 'Unidentified ship, you are cleared to land.'

Silence from Aenea.

De Soya blinks in tactical. The girl's ship is a red ember now, almost hovering ten thousand meters above the Pax spaceport. De Soya's dropship and the fighters are a klick higher, circling like angry insects. *Or vultures*, thinks the father-captain. The Llano Estacado had vultures, although why the seedship colonists had imported them, no one knew. The staked plains – the stakes being the atmosphere generators set in a grid every thirty klicks – had been dry and windy enough to reduce any corpse to a mummy within hours.

De Soya shakes his head to clear it.

'One minute to landing,' reports the controller. 'Unidentified ship, you are approaching zero descent rate. Please modify delta-v to continue descent along designated flight path. Unidentified ship, please acknowledge . . .'

'Damn,' whispers Captain Wu.

'Sirs,' says Pilot Karyn Cook, 'the ship has stopped descending. It's hanging there about two thousand meters above the spaceport.'

'We see it, Lieutenant,' says de Soya. The ship's red and green lights are flashing. The landing lights on the rear fins are bright enough to illuminate the spaceport tarmac more than a mile and a half below them. Other spacecraft at the port are dark; most have been pulled into hangars or onto secondary taxiways. The circling aircraft, including his own dropship, show no lights. On the multiple tightbeam he says, 'All ships and aircraft, keep your distance, hold your fire.'

'Unidentified ship,' says the Pax controller, 'you are drifting off path. Please resume nominal descent rate at once. Unidentified ship, you are leaving controlled airspace. Please resume controlled descent at once . . .'

'Shit,' whispers Barnes-Avne. Her troopers wait in concentric circles around the spaceport, but the girl's ship is no longer above the spaceport – drifts over the center of DaVinci. The ship's landing lights wink off.

'The ship's fusion drive shows no signs of coming on,' de Soya says to Captain Wu. 'Note that it's on repulsors alone.'

Wu nods but is obviously not satisfied. A fusion-drive ship hovering above an urban center is like a guillotine blade over an exposed neck.

'CAP,' calls de Soya, 'I'm moving within five hundred meters. Please close with me.' He nods to the pilot, who brings the dropship down and around in a predatory swoop. In their rear couches Gregorius and the other two troopers sit stiffly in full combat armor.

'What the hell is she up to?' whispers Commander Barnes-Avne. On his tactical band de Soya can see that the commander has authorized a hundred or so troopers to rise on reaction paks to follow the drifting ship. To the external cameras the troopers are invisible.

De Soya remembers the small aircraft or flying pak that had plucked the girl from the Valley of the Time Tombs. He keys ground control and the orbital pickets. 'Sensors? Are you watching for small objects leaving the target ship?'

The acknowledgment is from the primary picket ship. 'Yessir . . . don't worry, sir, nothin' bigger'n a microbe's gonna get out of that ship without us trackin' it, sir.'

'Very good,' says de Soya. *What have I forgotten?* Aenea's ship continues floating slowly over DaVinci, heading north-northwest at about twenty-five klicks per hour – a slow, vertical dirigible drifting on the wind. Above the ship swirl the fighters that have entered atmosphere with de Soya's drop-ship. Around the ship, like the rotating walls of a hurricane around the eye, are the CAP Scorpions. Beneath, flitting just above city buildings and bridges, tracking proceedings on their own suit-visor infrared sensors and tracking feeds, fly the spaceport Marines and troopers.

The girl's ship floats on silent EM repulsors over the skyscrapers and industrial areas of DaVinci on Renaissance Vector. The city is ablaze with highway lights, building lights, the green swaths of playing fields, and the brightly lit rectangles of parking areas. Tens of thousands of groundcars creep along ribbons of elevated highways, their headlights adding to the city light show.

'It's rotating, sirs,' reports the pilot. 'Still on repulsors.'

On video as well as tactical, de Soya can see Aenea's ship slowly turning from the vertical to the horizontal. No wings appear. This attitude would be strange for the passengers, but makes no practical difference – the internal fields must still be controlling 'up' and 'down.' The ship, looking more than ever like a silver dirigible drifting with the soft breezes, floats over the river and railyards of northwest DaVinci. Traffic control demands a response, but the com channels remain silent.

What have I forgotten? wonders Father Captain de Soya.

When Aenea asked the ship to rotate to the horizontal, I admit that I almost lost my composure for a moment.

The sense of losing one's balance was all but overwhelming. All three of us had been standing near the edge of the circular room, looking down through the clear hull as if peering over a cliff's edge. Now we tipped over toward those lights a thousand meters below. A. Bettik and I took several involuntary steps back toward the center of the room – I actually flailed my arms to keep my balance – but Aenea remained at the edge of the room, watching the ground tip up and become a wall of city buildings and lights.

I almost sat down on the couch, but I managed to remain standing and control my vertigo by seeing the ground as a giant wall we were flying past. Streets and the rectangular grid of city blocks moved past as we drifted forward. I turned in a complete circle, seeing the few brightest stars through the city glare behind me. The clouds reflected back the orange lights of the city.

'What are we looking for now?' I asked. At intervals the ship reported the presence of the circling aircraft and the number of sensors probing us. We had ordered the ship to shut off the insistent demands of spaceport traffic control.

Aenea had wanted to see the river, but now we were over the river. It was a dark serpentine ribbon through the city lights. We drifted over it toward the northwest. Occasionally a barge or pleasure boat passed underneath – although from this perspective, the lights seemed to crawl up or down the 'wall' of the city we were drifting by.

Instead of answering me directly, Aenea said, 'Ship, you're sure that this used to be part of the Tethys?'

'According to my charts,' said the ship. 'Of course, my memory is not . . .'

'There!' cried A. Bettik, pointing directly ahead down the line of dark river.

I could see nothing, but evidently Aenea did. 'Get us lower,' she ordered the ship. 'Quickly.'

'The safety margins have already been violated,' said the ship. 'If we drop below this altitude, we may . . .'

'Do it!' shouted the girl. 'Override. Code "Prelude – C-Sharp". Do it!'

The ship lurched down and forward.

'Head for that arch,' said Aenea, pointing directly overhead along the wall of city and dark river.

'Arch?' I said. Then I saw it – a black chord, an arc of darkness against the city lights.

A. Bettik looked at the girl. 'I had half expected it to be gone . . . torn down.'

Aenea showed her teeth. 'They can't tear it down. It would take atomic explosives . . . and even those might not work. The TechnoCore directed the construction of those things . . . they're built to last.'

The ship was hurtling forward now on repulsors. I could clearly see the arch of the farcaster portal like a giant hoop over the river. An industrial park had grown up around the ancient artifact, and the railyards and storage yards were empty except for cracked concrete, weeds, rusting wire, and the hulks of abandoned machines. The portal was still a kilometer away. I could see the lights of the city through it . . . no, now it seemed to shimmer a bit, as if a curtain of water were falling from the metal arch.

'We're going to make it!' I said. No sooner were the words out than a violent explosion rattled the ship and we began plunging toward the river.

'The old farcaster portal!' cries de Soya. He had seen the arch a minute earlier but had thought it another bridge. Now it sinks in. 'They're headed for the farcaster portal. This used to be part of the River Tethys!' He brings up tactical. Sure enough – the girl's ship is accelerating toward the arch.

'Relax,' says Commander Barnes-Avne. 'The portals are dead. They haven't worked since the Fall. It can't—'

'Get us closer!' de Soya shouts at the pilot. The dropship accelerates, throwing them all deep into their couch cushions. There is no internal containment field in a dropship. 'Get us close! Close the gap!' de Soya shouts at the lieutenant. On the wideband command channels, he says, 'All aircraft, close on the target.'

'They're going to beat us to it,' says Pilot Cook through the three-g force pressing her back into the command chair.

'CAP leader!' calls de Soya, his voice strained by the high-g load. 'Fire at the target. Fire to disable engines and repulsors. Now!'

Energy beams lance through the night. The girl's ship seems to stumble in midair, like a gutshot beast, and then falls into the river several hundred meters short of the farcaster portal. An explosion of steam mushrooms up into the night.

The dropship banks around the pillar of steam at an altitude of a thousand meters. The air is filled with circling aircraft and flying troopers. The com channels are suddenly alive with excited chatter.

'Shut up!' orders de Soya over the widebands. 'CAP leader, can you see the ship?'

'Negative,' comes Klaus's voice. 'Too much steam and debris from the explosion . . .'

'Was there an explosion?' demands de Soya. Then, on tightbeam to the defense pickets a thousand klicks above, 'Radar? Sensors?'

'The target ship is down,' comes the reply.

'I know that, you idiot,' says de Soya. 'Can you scan it under the river surface?'

'Negative,' answers the picket. 'Too much airborne and ground clutter. Deep radar can't discriminate between—'

'Damn,' says de Soya. 'Mother Captain Stone?'

'Yes,' comes his former exec's voice from her torchship in orbit.

'Slag it,' orders de Soya. 'The portal. The river beneath it. Slag it for a full minute. Slag it until it melts. Wait . . . slag it in thirty seconds.' He switches to airborne tactical bands. 'Every aircraft and trooper in the vicinity . . . you have thirty seconds before a CPB lances this entire area. Scatter!'

Pilot Cook takes the advice and banks the dropship sharply, accelerating back toward the spaceport at Mach one point five. 'Whoa! Whoa!' shouts de Soya through the g-load. 'Just a klick out. I need to watch.'

Both visual and tactical are a visual demonstration of chaos theory as hundreds of aircraft and airborne troopers fly away from the portal as if flung outward by an explosion. The area is barely empty on radar before the violet beam burns down from space. Ten meters wide and too bright to look at directly, the CPB strikes the ancient farcaster portal perfectly on target. Concrete, steel, and ferroplast melt into lakes and rivers of lava on either bank of the real river. The river itself turns to steam in an instant, sending the shock wave and steam cloud billowing out over the city for kilometers in every direction. This time the mushroom cloud reaches toward the stratosphere.

Captain Wu, Father Brown, and all the others are staring at Father Captain de Soya. He can almost hear their thoughts: *the girl was to be captured alive.*

He ignores their stares and says to the pilot, 'I'm not familiar with this model of dropship. Can it hover?'

'For a few minutes,' responds the pilot. Her face is slick with sweat under her helmet.

'Get us down there and hover over the portal arch,' commands de Soya. 'Fifty meters would be fine.'

'Sir,' says the pilot, 'the thermals and shock waves from the steam explosions—'

'Do it, Lieutenant.' The father-captain's voice is level, but there will be no arguing with it.

They hover. Steam and a violent drizzle fill the air, but their searchlight beams and high-profile radar stab downward. The farcaster arch is glowing white-hot, but it still stands.

'Amazing,' whispers Commander Barnes-Avne.

Mother Captain Stone comes over tactical. 'Father Captain, the target was hit, but it's still there. Do you want me to lance it again?'

'No,' says de Soya. Beneath the arch the river has cauterized itself, water flowing back into the superheated scar. New steam billows upward as the riverbanks of melted steel and concrete flow into water. The hissing is audible through the external pickups. The river is wild with eddies and whirlpools. It is filled with swirling debris.

De Soya looks up from tactical and his monitors and sees the others looking at him again. *The orders were to take the child alive and return her to Pacem.*

'Commander Barnes-Avne,' he says formally. 'Would you please order your troopers to land and begin an immediate search of the river and adjoining areas?'

'Certainly,' says Barnes-Avne, keying her command net and issuing orders. Her gaze never leaves Father Captain de Soya's face.

TWENTY-EIGHT

In the days that follow the dragging of the river and the discovery of no spaceship, no bodies, and only a hint of debris of what may have been the girl's ship, Father Captain de Soya fully expects a court-martial and perhaps an excommunication. The archangel courier is dispatched to Pacem with the news, and within twenty hours the same ship, with different human couriers, returns with the verdict: there will be a Board of Review. De Soya nods when he hears the news, believing it to be a precursor to his return to Pacem for court-martial and worse.

Surprisingly, it is the pleasant Father Brown who heads the Board of Review, as personal representative of Secretary of State Simon Augustino Cardinal Lourdusamy, with Captain Wu standing in for Admiral Marusyn of Pax Fleet. Other members of the board include two of the admirals present during the debacle and Commander Barnes-Avne. De Soya is offered counsel, but he refuses.

The father-captain is not under arrest during the five days of the board hearing – not even under house arrest – but it is understood that he will remain on the Pax military base outside of DaVinci until the hearing is concluded. During those five days, Father Captain de Soya walks along the river path within the base confines, watches news on local television and direct-access channels, and occasionally looks skyward, imagining that he can guess where *Raphael* still swings in parking orbit, uncrewed and silent except for its automated systems. De Soya hopes that the ship's next captain brings it more honor.

Many of his friends visit him: Gregorius, Kee, and Rettig are nominally still his bodyguards, although they no longer carry weapons and – like de Soya – remain on the Pax base in virtual arrest. Mother Captain Boulez, Captain Hearn, and Mother Captain Stone all stop by after giving their testimony and before shipping out for the frontier. That evening de Soya watches the blue tails of their dropships rising toward the night sky and envies them. Captain Sati of the *Saint Anthony* has a glass of wine with de Soya before returning to his torchship and active duty in another system. Even Captain Lempriere comes by after testifying, and it is that bald man's halting sympathy that finally angers de Soya.

On the fifth day de Soya goes before the board. The situation is odd – de Soya still holds the papal diskey and thus is technically beyond reproach or indictment – but it is understood that Pope Julius through Cardinal Lourdusamy has willed this Board of Review, and de Soya, shaped to obedience through both his military and Benedictine training, complies with humility. He does not expect exoneration. In the tradition of ship captains since the Middle Ages on Old Earth, de Soya knows well that the coin of a captain's prerogatives has two sides – almost godlike power over everyone and everything aboard one's ship, balanced by the requirement to take total responsibility for any damage to the ship or failure of one's mission.

De Soya has not damaged his ship – neither his former task force, nor his new ship, the *Raphael* – but he is acutely aware that his failure has been total. With immense resources of the Pax available to him both on Hyperion and in Renaissance space, he has failed to capture an eleven-year-old child. He can see no excuse for this, and so he testifies during his part of the hearing.

'And why did you order the lancing of the farcaster portal on Renaissance Vector?' asks Father Admiral Coombs after de Soya's statement.

De Soya raises a hand, then drops it. 'I realized at that moment that the reason for the girl's trip to this world was to reach the portal,' he says. 'Our only hope for detaining her was to destroy the portal arch.'

'But it was not destroyed?' queries Father Brown.

'No,' says de Soya.

'In your experience, Father Captain de Soya,' says Captain Wu, 'has there been any target that one minute of fully applied CPB fire would not destroy?'

De Soya thinks for a moment. 'There are targets such as orbital forest or Ouster Swarm asteroids that would not be fully destroyed by even a full minute of lancefire,' he says. 'But they would have been severely damaged.'

'And the farcaster portal was not damaged?' persists Father Brown.

'Not to my knowledge,' says de Soya.

Captain Wu turns to the other board members. 'We have an affidavit from Chief of Planetary Engineers Rexton Hamn that the alloy of the farcaster portal – although radiating heat for more than forty-eight hours – was not damaged by the attack.'

The panel members converse among themselves for several minutes.

'Father Captain de Soya,' begins Admiral Serra when the questioning resumes, 'were you aware that your attempt to destroy the portal might have destroyed the girl's ship?'

'Yes, Admiral.'

'And in so doing,' continues Serra, 'killed the child?'

'Yes, Admiral.'

'And your orders were – specifically – to bring the child to Pacem . . . unharmed. Am I correct?'

'Yes, Admiral. Those were my precise orders.'

'But you were willing to defy those orders?'

De Soya takes a breath. 'In this case, Admiral, I felt it was a calculated risk. My instructions were that it was of paramount importance to bring the child to Pacem within the shortest time possible. In those few seconds when I realized that she might be able to travel by farcaster portal and escape apprehension, I felt that destroying the portal – not the child's ship – was our best hope. To be honest, I felt that the ship had either already traversed the portal or had not yet reached it. All indications were that the ship had been struck and fallen into the river. I did not know whether the ship had the capacity to travel underwater through the portal – or, for that matter, whether the portal could farcast an object underwater.'

Captain Wu folds her hands. 'And to your knowledge, Father Captain, has the farcaster portal shown any signs of activity since that night?'

'Not to my knowledge, Captain.'

'To your knowledge, Father Captain,' she continues, 'had any farcaster portal – on any world of the former Web or any spaceborne portal, for that matter – had any farcaster shown any sign of renewed activity since the Fall of the farcasters more than two hundred and seventy standard years ago?'

'To my knowledge,' says de Soya, 'they have not.'

Father Brown leans forward. 'Then, Father Captain, perhaps you can tell this board why you thought that the girl had the capacity to open one of these portals and was attempting to escape through this particular one.'

De Soya does open his hands this time. 'Father, I . . . I don't know. I guess that I had the distinct feeling that she was not willing to be captured, and her flight along the river . . . I don't know, Father. The use of the portal is the only thing that made sense that night.'

Captain Wu looks at her fellow panelists. 'Any more questions?' After a silence the captain says, 'That will be all, Father Captain de Soya. This board will apprise you of its findings by tomorrow morning.'

De Soya nods and leaves.

That night, walking the base path along the river, de Soya tries to imagine what he will do if he is court-martialed and stripped of his priesthood but not imprisoned. The thought of freedom after such failure is more painful than the thought of prison. Excommunication has not been mentioned by the board – no punishment has – but de Soya clearly sees his conviction, his return to Pacem for higher court proceedings, and his ultimate banishment from the Church. Only a terrible failure or heresy could bring about such punishment, but de Soya sees – unblinkingly – what a terrible failure his efforts have been.

In the morning he is called into the low building where the board has met all night. He stands at attention in front of the dozen men and women behind the long table.

'Father Captain de Soya,' begins Captain Wu, speaking for the others, 'this Board of Review was convened to answer queries from Pax Command and the Vatican as to the disposition and outcome of recent events – specifically, in this command and this commander's failure to apprehend the child known as Aenea. After five days of deliberation and after many hundreds of hours of testimony and depositions, it is the finding of this board that all possible efforts and preparations were made to carry out this mission. The fact that the child known as Aenea – or someone or something traveling with her – was able to escape via a farcaster that has not worked for almost three standard centuries could not have been anticipated by you or by any other officer working with you or under your command. The fact that the farcasters could resume operation at all, is, of course, of grave concern to the Pax Command and to the Church. The implications of this will be explored by the highest echelons of Pax Command and the Vatican hierarchy.

'As for your role in this, Father Captain de Soya, with the exception of possible concern we have for your risking the life of the child you are charged with taking into custody, we find your actions responsible, correct, in keeping with your mission priorities, and legal. This board while official only in the capacity of review – recommends that you continue your mission with the archangel-class ship designated the *Raphael*, that your use of the papal-authority diskey continue, and that you requisition those materials and personnel you consider necessary for the continuance of this mission.'

De Soya, still at rigid attention, blinks rapidly several times before saying, 'Captain?'

'Yes, Father Captain?' says Wu.

'Does this mean that I can keep Sergeant Gregorius and his troopers as my personal guard?'

Captain Wu – whose authority strangely overwhelms that of the admirals and planetary ground commanders at the table – smiles. 'Father Captain,' she says, 'you could order the members of this board to go along as your personal guard if you wish. The authority of your papal diskey remains absolute.'

De Soya does not smile. 'Thank you, Captain . . . sirs. Sergeant Gregorius and his two men will suffice. I will leave this morning.'

'Leave for where, Federico?' asks Father Brown. 'As you know, exhaustive searches of the records have not given us a clue as to where the farcaster might have sent that ship. The River Tethys had changeable connections, and any data about the next world on the line has evidently been lost to us.'

'Yes, Father,' says de Soya, 'but there are only two-hundred-some worlds that used to be connected by that farcaster river. The girl's ship has to be on one of them. My archangel ship can reach all of them – given time for resurrection after translation – in less than two years. I will begin immediately.'

At this, the men and women at the table can only stare. The man in front of them is facing several hundred deaths and difficult resurrections. As far as they know, no one since the beginning of the Sacrament of Resurrection has ever submitted to such a cycle of pain and rebirth.

Father Brown stands and lifts his hand in benediction. '*In Nomine Patris, et Filii, et Spiritus Sancti*,' he intones. 'Go with God, Father Captain de Soya. Our prayers go with you.'

TWENTY-NINE

When they shot us down several hundred meters short of the farcaster portal, I was sure we were dead this time. The internal containment field failed the second the generators were struck, the wall of the planet we were looking *up* at suddenly and inarguably became *down*, and the ship fell like an elevator with its cables cut.

The sensations that followed are hard for me to describe. I know now that the internal fields switched to what was known as a 'crash field' – no misnomer, I can assure you – and for the next few minutes it felt precisely as if we were caught up in a giant vat of gelatin. In a sense, we were. The crash field expanded in a nanosecond to fill every square millimeter of the ship, cushioning us and keeping us absolutely immobile as the spacecraft plunged into the river, bounced off the bottom mud, fired its fusion engine – creating a giant plume of steam – and plowed ahead relentlessly through mud, steam, water, and debris from the imploding riverbanks until the ship fulfilled the last command given to it – pass through the farcaster portal. The fact that we did so three meters beneath the broiling river surface did not keep the portal from working. The ship later told us that while its stern was passing through the farcaster, the water above and behind it suddenly became superheated steam – as if one of the Pax ships or aircraft were lancing it with a CPB. Ironically, it was the steam that deflected the beam for the milliseconds necessary for the ship to complete its transition.

Meanwhile, knowing none of these details, I stared. My eyes were open – I could not close them against the cloying force of the crash field – and I was watching the external video monitors set along the foot of the bed as well as looking out through the still-transparent hull apex as the farcaster portal flickered to life amid the steam and sunlight poured over the river's surface, until suddenly we were through the steam cloud and once again smashing against rock and river bottom, then hitting a beach beneath blue sky and sun.

Then the monitors went off and the hull went dull. For several minutes we were trapped in this cave blackness – I was floating in midair, or would have been had it not been for the gelatinous crash field – my arms were thrown wide, my right leg was half-bent in a running posture behind me, my mouth was open in a silent scream, and I could not blink. At first the fear of suffocation was very strong – the crash field was *in* my open mouth – but I soon realized that my nose and throat were receiving oxygen. The crash field, it turns out, worked much like the expensive osmosis masks used for deep-sea diving during the Hegemony days: air leached through the field mass pressing against one's face and throat. It was not a pleasant experience – I've always detested the thought of choking – but my anxiety was manageable. More disturbing was the blackness and claustrophobic sense of being caught in a giant, sticky web. During those long minutes in the darkness, I had thoughts of the ship being stuck there forever, disabled, with no way to relax the crash fields, and the three of us starving to death in our undignified postures, until someday the ship's energy banks would be depleted, the crash field would collapse, and our whitened skeletons would drop and rattle around the interior hull of the ship like so many bones being cast by an invisible fortune-teller.

As it was, the field slowly folded away less than five minutes later. The lights came on, flickered, and were replaced by red emergency lighting even as we were gently lowered to what had been the wall a short while before. The outer hull became transparent once again, but very little light filtered in through the mud and debris.

I had not been able to see A. Bettik and Aenea while stuck in place – they had been just out of my frozen field of sight – but now I saw them as the field lowered them to the hull with me. I was amazed to hear a scream issue from my throat and realized that it was the shout that had welled up in me the instant of the crash.

For a moment the three of us just sat on a curved hull wall, rubbing and testing our own arms, legs, and head to make sure we weren't injured. Then Aenea spoke for us all. 'Holy shit,' she said, and stood up on the curving floor of the hull. Her legs were shaky.

'Ship!' called the android.

'Yes, A. Bettik.' The voice was as calm as always.

'Are you damaged?'

'Yes, A. Bettik,' said the ship. 'I have just completed a full damage assessment. Field coils, repulsors, and Hawking translators have suffered extensive damage, as have sections of the aft hull and two of the four landing fins.'

'Ship,' I said, struggling to my feet and looking out through the transparent nose of the hull. There was sunlight coming through the curved wall above us, but most of the exterior hull was opaque with mud, sand, and other debris. The dark river came two-thirds the way up the sides and was sloshing against us. It looked as if we had run aground on a sandy bank, but not before plowing through many meters of river bottom. 'Ship,' I tried again, 'are your sensors working?'

'Only radar and visual,' it replied.

'Is there any pursuit?' I said. 'Did any Pax ships come through the farcaster with us?'

'Negative,' said the ship. 'There are no inorganic ground or air targets within my radar range.'

Aenea walked to the vertical wall that had been the carpeted floor. 'No troopers even?' she asked.

'No,' said the ship.

'Is the farcaster still operational?' asked A. Bettik.

'Negative,' said the ship. 'The portal ceased functioning eighteen nanoseconds after we transited it.'

I relaxed a bit then and looked at the girl, trying to make sure just by staring that she hadn't been injured. Except for wildly disarrayed hair and the excitement in her eyes, she looked normal enough. She grinned at me. 'So how do we get out of here, Raul?'

I looked up and saw what she meant. The central stairwell was about three meters above our heads. 'Ship?' I said. 'Can you turn the internal fields back on long enough for us to get out of the ship?'

'I'm sorry,' said the ship. 'The fields are down and will not be repaired for some time.'

'Can you morph an opening in the hull above us?' I said. The feeling of claustrophobia was coming back.

'I am afraid not,' said the ship. 'I am functioning on battery power at the moment, and morphing would demand far more energy than I have available. The main air lock is functional. If you can get to that, I will open it.'

The three of us exchanged glances. 'Great,' I said at last. 'We get to crawl thirty meters back through the ship while everything's cattywampus.'

Aenea was still looking up at the stairwell opening. 'The gravity's different here – feel it?'

I realized that I did. There was a lightness to everything. I must have been noticing it but putting it down to a variation in the internal field – but there was no more internal field. This was a different world, with different gravity! I found myself grinning back at the child.

'So are you saying we can fly up there?' I said, pointing to the bed hanging on the wall above us and the stairwell next to it.

'No,' said Aenea, 'but the gravity here seems a little less than Hyperion's. You two boost me up there and I'll drop something down to you and we'll crawl back to the air lock.'

And that is precisely what we did. We made a stirrup with our hands and boosted Aenea to the bottom lip of the stairwell opening, where she balanced, reached out and plucked the loosely hanging blanket from the bed, tied it around the balustrade and dropped the other end down to us, and then, after A. Bettik and I pulled our way up, all three of us walked precariously on the central dropshaft post, hanging on to the circular stairs to the side and above to keep our balance, and gradually made our way through the red-lit mess of a ship – through the library where books and cushions had fallen to the lower hull despite the cord restraints on the shelves, through the holopit area where the Steinway was still in place because of its restraining locks, but where our loose personal belongings had tumbled to the bottom of the ship. Here we made a stop while I lowered myself to the cluttered hull bottom and retrieved the pack and weapons I had left on the couch. Strapping the pistol on my belt, tossing up the rope I had stored in the pack, I felt more prepared for the next eventuality than I had a moment before.

When we got to the corridor, we could see that whatever had damaged the drive area below had also played havoc with the storage lockers: parts of the corridor were blackened and buckled outward, the contents of the lockers were scattered along the torn walls. The inner air lock was open but was now several meters directly above us. I had to free-climb the last vertical expanse of corridor and toss the rope down to the others while I crouched just within the inner lock. Jumping up onto the outer hull and pulling myself out into the bright sunlight, I reached into the red-lit air lock, found Aenea's wrist, and pulled her out. A second later I did the same for A. Bettik. Then we all took time to look around.

A strange new world! I will never be able to explain the thrill that jolted through me at that moment despite our crash, despite our predicament, despite everything – *I was looking at a new world!* The effect on me was more profound than I had expected in all my anticipation of interworld travel. This planet was very Hyperion-like: breathable air, blue sky – although a much lighter blue than Hyperion's lapis – wisps of clouds overhead, the river behind us – wider than the river had been on Renaissance Vector – and jungle on both banks, stretching as far away as I could see to the right, and back beyond the overgrown farcaster portal to our left. Ahead of us, the bow of the ship had indeed plowed up the river bottom and beached itself on a sandy spit, and then the jungle began again, hanging over everything like a tattered green curtain above a narrow stage.

But as familiar as this sounds, it was all strange: the scents in the air were alien, the gravity felt odd, the sunlight was a bit too bright, the 'trees' in the jungle were unlike anything I had ever seen – feathery green gymnosperms was how I would have described them then – and overhead, flights of frail white birds of a sort I had never seen flapped away from the sound of our clumsy entrance to this world.

We walked up the hull toward the beach. Soft breezes ruffled Aenea's hair and tugged at my shirt. The air smelled of subtle spices – traces of cinnamon and thyme, perhaps – although softer and richer than these. The bow of the ship was not transparent from the outside, although I did not know at the time whether the ship had opaqued its skin again or whether it never looked transparent from the outside. Even lying on its side, the hull would have been too high and too steep to slide from it if it had not plowed such a deep furrow in the beach sand, but as it was, I used my rope again to lower A. Bettik to the sand, then we lowered the girl, and finally I shouldered my pack – the plasma rifle folded and strapped atop it – and slid down on my own, rolling as I hit the tightly packed soil.

My first footstep on an alien world, and it was no footstep at all – just a mouthful of sand.

The girl and the android helped me to my feet. Aenea was squinting up at the hull. 'How do we get back up?' she said.

'We can build a ladder, drag a fallen tree over, or' – I tapped my pack – 'I brought the hawking mat.'

We turned our attention to the beach and jungle. The former was narrow – only a few meters across from the bow to the forest, the sand gleaming more red than sand-colored in the bright sunlight – and the latter was dense and dark. The breeze was cool here on the beach, but the heat was palpable under the thickly packed trees. Twenty meters above, the gymnosperm fronds rustled and quaked like the antennae of some great insects.

'Wait here a minute,' I said, and stepped under the cover of the trees. The underbrush was thick, a type of clinging fern for the most part, and the soil was made up of so much humus that it was more sponge than dirt. The jungle smelled of dampness and decay, but of a whole different sort than the fens and swamps of Hyperion. I thought of the dracula ticks and biting gar in my own little tame bit of wilderness, and watched where I stepped. Vines spiraled down from the gymnosperm trunks and created a ropy latticework ahead of me in the gloom. I realized that I should have added a machete to my list of basic gear.

I had not penetrated the woods ten meters when suddenly a tall shrub holding heavy red leaves a meter in front of my face exploded into motion and the 'leaves' flapped away beneath the jungle canopy, the creatures' leathery wings sounding much like the large fruit bats our Hyperion ancestors had brought on their seedships.

'Damn,' I whispered, and shoved and battered my way out of the dank tangle. My shirt was torn when I staggered onto the beach sand. Aenea and A. Bettik looked expectantly at me.

'It's a jungle in there,' I said.

We walked to the water's edge, sat on a partially submerged stump there, and looked at our spaceship. The poor thing looked like a great beached whale from some Old Earth wildlife holo.

'I wonder if it will ever fly again,' I mused, breaking a chocolate bar into pieces and handing one to the child and the other to the blue-skinned man.

'Oh, I think I will,' said a voice on my wrist.

I admit that I levitated a dozen or so centimeters. I'd forgotten about the comlog bracelet.

'Ship?' I said, raising my wrist and speaking directly into the bracelet the way I would have used a portable radio in the Home Guard.

'You don't have to do that,' said the ship's voice. 'I can hear everything quite clearly, thank you. Your question was – would I ever fly again? The answer is – almost certainly. I had more complicated repairs to carry out upon my arrival in the city of Endymion after my return to Hyperion.'

'Good,' I said. 'I'm glad you can . . . ah . . . repair yourself. Will you need raw materials? Replacement parts?'

'No, thank you, M. Endymion,' said the ship. 'It is mostly a matter of reallocating existing materials and redesigning certain damaged units. The repairs should not take long.'

'How long is not long?' asked Aenea. She finished her chocolate and licked her fingers.

'Six standard months,' said the snip. 'Unless I run into unforeseen difficulties.'

The three of us exchanged glances. I looked back at the jungle. The sun seemed lower now, its horizontal rays illuminating the tops of the gymnosperms and casting the shadows beneath into deeper gloom. 'Six months?' I said.

'Unless I run into unforeseen difficulties,' repeated the ship.

'Ideas?' I said to my two comrades.

Aenea rinsed her fingers in the river's edge, tossed some water onto her face, and brushed back her wet hair. 'We're on the River Tethys,' she said. 'We'll just go downstream until we find the next farcaster portal.'

'You can do that trick again?' I said.

She brushed water from her face and said, 'What trick?'

I made a dismissive gesture with my hand. 'Oh, nothing . . . making a machine work that's been dead for three centuries. That trick.'

Her dark eyes were earnest. 'I wasn't sure that I could do that, Raul.' She looked at A. Bettik, who was watching us impassively. 'Honest.'

'What would have happened if you hadn't been able to do it?' I asked softly.

'They would have caught us,' said Aenea. 'I think they would have let you two go. They would have brought me back to Pacem. That would have been the last you or anyone else would have heard of me.'

Something about the flat, emotionless way she said that gave me chills. 'All right,' I said, 'it worked. But *how* did you do it?'

She made that slight-movement-of-her-hand gesture with which I was becoming familiar. 'I'm not . . . certain,' she said. 'I knew from the dreams that the portal would probably let me through . . .'

'*Let* you through?' I said.

'Yes. I thought it would . . . recognize me . . . and it did.'

I set my hands on my knees and straightened my legs, the heels of my boots digging into the red sand. 'You talk about the farcaster as if it's an intelligent, living organism,' I said.

Aenea looked back at the arch half a klick behind us. 'In a way it is,' she said. 'It's hard to explain.'

'But you're sure that the Pax troops can't follow us through?'

'Oh, yes. The portal will not activate for anyone else.'

My eyebrows raised a bit. 'Then how did A. Bettik and I . . . and the ship . . . get through?'

Aenea smiled. 'You were with me.'

I stood up. 'All right, we'll hash this out later. First, I think we need a plan. Do we reconnoiter now, or get our stuff out of the ship first?'

Aenea looked down at the dark water of the river. 'And then Robinson Crusoe stripped naked, swam out to his ship, filled his pockets with biscuits, and swam back to shore . . .'

'What?' I said, hefting my pack and frowning at the child.

'Nothing,' she said, getting to her feet. 'Just an old pre-Hegira book that Uncle Martin used to read to me. He used to say that proofreaders have always been incompetent assholes – even fourteen hundred years ago.'

I looked at the android. 'Do you understand her, A. Bettik?'

He showed that slight twitch of his thin lips that I was learning to take as a smile. 'It is not my role to understand M. Aenea, M. Endymion.'

I sighed. 'All right, back to the subject . . . Do we reconnoiter before it gets dark, or dig the stuff out of the ship?'

'I vote that we look around,' said Aenea. She looked at the darkening jungle. 'But not through that stuff.'

'Uh-uh,' I agreed, pulling the hawking mat from its place atop my pack and unrolling it on the sand. 'We'll see if this works on this world.' I paused, raised the comlog closer. 'What world is this, anyway? Ship?'

There was a second's hesitation, as if the ship was busy mulling over its own problems. 'I'm sorry, I can't identify it given the state of my memory banks. My navigation systems could tell us, of course, but I will need a star sighting. I can tell you that there are no unnatural electromagnetic or microwave transmissions currently broadcasting on this area of the planet. Nor are there relay satellites or other man-made objects in synchronous orbit overhead.'

'All right,' I said, 'but where *are* we?' I looked at the girl.

'How should I know?' said Aenea.

'You brought us here,' I said. I realized that I was being short-tempered with her, but I *felt* short-tempered right then.

Aenea shook her head. 'I just activated the farcaster, Raul. My big plan was to get away from Father Captain Whatshisname and all those ships. That was it.'

'And find your architect,' I said.

'Yes,' said Aenea.

I looked around the jungle and river. 'It doesn't look like a promising place to find an architect. I guess you're right . . . we'll just have to keep moving down the river to the next world.' The vine-shrouded arch of the farcaster we'd passed through caught my eye. I saw now why we'd plowed ashore: the river took a bend to the right here, about half a kilometer from the portal. The ship had come through and just kept going straight, right up through the shallows and onto the beach.

'Wait,' I said, 'couldn't we just reprogram that portal and use it to go somewhere else? Why do we have to find another one?'

A. Bettik stepped away from the ship so he could get a better look at the farcaster arch. 'The River Tethys portals did not work like the millions of personal farcasters,' he said softly. 'Nor was it designed to function like the Grand Concourse portals, or the large spaceborne farcasters.' He reached into his pocket and removed a small book. I saw the title – *A Traveler's Guide to the WorldWeb*. 'It seems that the Tethys was designed primarily for wandering and relaxation,' he said. 'The distance between the portals varied from a few kilometers to many hundreds of kilometers . . .'

'Hundreds of kilometers!' I said. I had been expecting to find the next portal just around the next bend in the river.

'Yes,' continued A. Bettik. 'The concept, as I understand it, was to offer the traveler a wide variety of worlds, views, and experiences. To that end only the downstream portals would activate, and they programmed themselves randomly . . . that is, the sections of river on different worlds were shuffled constantly, like so many cards in a deck.'

I shook my head. 'In the old poet's *Cantos* it says that the rivers were sliced up after the Fall . . . that they dried up like water holes in the desert.'

Aenea made a noise. 'Uncle Martin's full of shit sometimes, Raul. He never saw what happened to the Tethys after the Fall . . . He was on Hyperion, remember? He's never been back to the Web. He made stuff up.'

It was no way to talk about the greatest work of literature in the past three hundred years – or of the legendary old poet who had composed it – but I started laughing then and found it hard to stop. By the time I did, Aenea was looking at me strangely. 'Are you all right, Raul?'

'Yep,' I said. 'Just happy.' I turned and made a motion that encompassed the jungle, the river, the farcaster portal – even our beached whale of a ship. 'For some reason, I'm just happy,' I said.

Aenea nodded as if she understood perfectly.

To the android I said, 'Does the book say what world this is? Jungle, blue sky . . . it must be about a nine-point-five on the Solmev Scale. That must be fairly rare. Does it list this world?'

A. Bettik flipped through the pages. 'I don't remember a jungle world like this mentioned in the sections I read, M. Endymion. I will read more carefully later.'

'Well, I think we need to look around,' said Aenea, obviously impatient to explore.

'But we should salvage some important things from the ship first,' I said. 'I made a list . . .'

'That could take hours,' said Aenea. 'The sun could set before we're finished.'

'Still,' I said, ready to argue, 'we need to get organized here . . .'

'If I may suggest a course of action,' A. Bettik interrupted softly, 'perhaps you and M. Aenea could . . . ah . . . reconnoiter, while I begin removing the necessary items you mentioned. Unless you think it wiser to sleep in the ship tonight.'

We all looked at the poor ship. The river swirled around it, and just above the water level I could see the bent and blackened stumps which had been the proud rear fins. I thought of sleeping in that tumble of stuff, in the red-lit emergency light or the absolute darkness of the central levels, and said, 'Well, it would be safer in there, but let's get the stuff out that we'll need to move downriver, and then we'll decide.'

The android and I discussed it for several minutes. I had the plasma rifle with me, as well as the .45 in its holster on my belt, but I wanted the 16-gauge shotgun I'd set aside, as well as camping gear I'd seen in the EVA locker closet. I wasn't sure how we'd get downriver – the hawking mat would probably hold the three of us, but I couldn't see it transporting us *and* our gear, so we decided to unpack three of the four flybikes from their niches under the spacesuit closet. There was also a flying belt in there that I thought might be handy, as well as some camping accessories such as a heating cube, sleeping bags, foam mats, flashlight lasers for each of us, and the headset communicators I'd noticed. 'Oh, and a machete if you see one,' I added. 'There were several boxes of knives and multiuse blades in the small EVA closet. I don't remember a machete, but if there is one . . . let's get it out.'

A. Bettik and I walked to the end of the narrow beach, found a fallen tree at the river's edge, and dragged it – with me sweating and cursing – back to the side of the ship to act as a de facto ladder so that we could crawl back up on the curved hull. 'Oh, yeah, see if there's a rope ladder in that mess,' I said. 'And an inflatable raft of some sort.'

'Anything else?' A. Bettik asked wryly.

'No . . . well, maybe a sauna if you find one. And a well-stocked bar. And maybe a twelve-piece band to play some music while we unpack.'

'I'll do my best, sir,' said the android, and began climbing the tree ladder back to the top of the hull.

I felt guilty leaving A. Bettik to do all the heavy lifting, but it seemed wise to know how far it was to the next farcaster portal, and I had no intention of allowing the girl to fly off on a scouting mission of her own. She sat behind me as I tapped the activator thread designs and the carpet stiffened and rose several centimeters from the wet sand.

'Wick,' she said.

'What?'

'It stands for "wicked",' said the girl. 'Uncle Martin said that it was kid slang when he was a brat on Old Earth.'

I sighed again and tapped the flight threads. We spiraled up and around, soon rising above the treetop level. The sun was definitely lower now in the direction I assumed was west. 'Ship?' I said to my comlog bracelet.

'Yes?' The ship's tone always made me feel that I was interrupting it at some important task.

'Am I talking to you, or to the data bank you downloaded?'

'As long as you are within communicator range, M. Endymion,' it answered, 'you are talking to me.'

'What's the communicator range?' We leveled off thirty meters above the river. A. Bettik waved from where he stood next to the open air lock.

'Twenty thousand kilometers or the curve of the planet,' said the ship. 'Whichever comes first. As I mentioned earlier, there are no relay satellites around this world that I can locate.'

I tapped the forward design and we began flying upriver, toward the overgrown arch there. 'Can you talk to me through a farcaster portal?' I asked.

'An activated portal?' said the ship. 'How could I do that, M. Endymion? You would be light-years away.'

This ship had a way of making me feel stupid and provincial. I usually enjoyed its company, but I admit that I wouldn't mind too much when we left it behind.

Aenea leaned against my back and spoke directly into my ear so as to be heard over the wind noise as we accelerated. 'The old portals used to have fiber-optic lines running through them. 'That worked . . . although not as well as the fatline.'

'So if we wanted to keep talking to the ship when we go downriver,' I said back over my shoulder, 'we could string telephone wire?'

Out of the corner of my eye, I could see her grinning. The silliness did give me a thought, however; 'If we can't go back upriver through the portals,' I said, 'how do we find our way back to the ship?'

Aenea put her hand on my shoulder. The portal was approaching quickly now. 'We just keep going down the line until we come back around,' she said over the wind noise. 'The River Tethys was a big circle.'

I turned so that I could see her. 'Are you serious, kiddo? There were – what? – a couple of hundred worlds connected by the Tethys.'

'At least a couple of hundred,' said Aenea. 'That we know of.'

I did not understand that, but sighed again as we slowed near the portal. 'If each section of the river ran for a hundred klicks . . . that's twenty thousand kilometers of travel just to get back here.'

Aenea said nothing.

I hovered us near the portal, realizing for the first time just how massive these things were. The arch appeared to be made of metal with many designs, compartments, indentations – perhaps even cryptic writing – but the jungle had sent tendrils of vines and lichens up the top and sides of the thing. What I had first taken as rust on the complicated arch turned out to be more of the red 'bat-wing leaves' hanging in clusters from the main tangle of vines. I gave them a wide berth.

'What if it activates?' I said as we hovered a meter or two short of the underside of the arch.

'Try it,' said the girl.

I sent the hawking mat forward slowly, almost stopping as the front of the carpet reached the invisible line directly under the arch.

Nothing happened. We flew through, I turned the mat around, and we came back from the south. The farcaster portal was just an ornate metal bridge arching high over the river.

'It's dead,' I said. 'As dead as Kelsey's nuts.' It had been one of Grandam's favorite phrases, used only when we kids weren't supposed to be able to hear, but I realized that there *was* a kid in earshot. 'Sorry,' I said over my shoulder, my face red. Perhaps I'd spent too many years in the army or working with river bargemen, or as a bouncer in the casinos. I'd turned into a jerk.

Aenea actually threw her head back, she was laughing so hard. 'Raul,' she said, 'I grew up visiting Uncle Martin, remember?'

We flew back over the ship and waved at A. Bettik as the android was lowering pallets of gear to the beach. He waved a blue hand in response.

'Shall we go on downriver to see how far it'll be to the next portal?' I said.

'Absolutely,' said Aenea.

We flew downriver, seeing very few other beaches or breaks in the jungle: trees and vines came all the way to the river's edge. It bothered me not to know which direction we were heading, so I removed the inertial guidance compass from my pack and activated it. The compass had been my guide on Hyperion, where the magnetic field was too treacherous to trust, but it was useless here. As with the ship's guidance system, the compass would work perfectly if it knew its starting point, but that luxury had been lost the instant we transited the farcaster.

'Ship,' I said to the bracelet comlog, 'can you get a magnetic compass reading on us?'

'Yes,' came the instant reply, 'but without knowing precisely where magnetic north is on this world, the actual direction of travel would be a rough estimate.'

'Give me the rough estimate, please.' I banked the mat slightly as we rounded a wide bend. The river had broadened out again – it must have been almost a kilometer wide at this point. The current looked swift, but not especially treacherous. My barge, work on the Kans had taught me to read the river for eddies, snags, sandbars, and the like. This river seemed easy enough to navigate.

'You are headed approximately east-southeast,' said the comlog. 'Airspeed is sixty-eight kilometers per hour. Sensors indicate that your hawking-mat deflection field is at eight percent. Altitude is . . .'

'All right, all right,' I said. 'East-southeast.' The sun was lowering behind us. This world revolved like Old Earth and Hyperion.

The river straightened out and I accelerated the mat a bit. In the labyrinths on Hyperion, I'd been scooting along at almost three hundred klicks per hour, but I wasn't eager to fly that fast here unless I had to. The flight threads in this old mat held a charge for quite a while, but there was no need to run it out quicker than necessary. I made a mental note to recharge the threads from the ship's leads before we left, even if we took the skybikes as transportation.

'Look,' said Aenea, pointing to our left.

Far to the north, illuminated by the now visibly setting sun, something like a mesa top or some very large man-made thing broke through the jungle canopy. 'Can we go look?' she said.

I knew better. We had an objective, we had a time limit – the setting sun, for one – and we had a thousand reasons not to take chances by swooping around strange artifacts. For all we knew, this mesa or tower-thing was the Central Pax Headquarters for the planet.

'Sure,' I said, mentally kicking myself for being an idiot, and banked the hawking mat to the north.

The thing was farther north than it seemed. I kicked the mat up to two hundred klicks per hour, and we still spent a good ten minutes flying to it.

'Excuse me, M. Endymion,' came the ship's voice on my wrist, 'but you appear to have gone off course and are now headed north-northeast, approximately one hundred and three degrees from your former heading.'

'We're investigating a tower or butte or something poking up from the jungle almost due north of us,' I said. 'Do you have it on your radar?'

'Negative,' said the ship, and I thought I heard a hint of dryness in its tone again. 'My vantage point here stuck in the mud is not optimum. Anything below a twenty-eight-degree inclination from the horizon is lost in clutter. You are just within my angle of detection. Another twenty kilometers north, and I will lose you.'

'That's all right,' I said. 'We're just going to check this out and get right back to the river.'

'Why?' said the ship. 'Why investigate something which has nothing to do with your plans to travel downriver?'

Aenea leaned over and lifted my wrist. 'We're human,' she said.

The ship did not reply.

The thing, when we finally reached it, rose a sheer hundred meters above the jungle canopy. Its lower levels were surrounded so tightly by the giant gymnosperms that the tower looked like a weathered crag rising from a green sea.

It appeared to be both natural and man-made – or at least modified by some intelligence. The tower was about seventy meters across and appeared to be made of red rock, perhaps some type of sandstone. The setting sun – only ten degrees or so above the jungle-canopy horizon now – bathed the crag in a rich red light. Here and there along the east and west faces of the crag were openings that both Aenea and I first thought were natural – wind – or water-hewn – but we soon realized had been carved. Also on the east side were niches carved – niches about the right distance from one another to be steps and handholds for human feet and hands. But they were shallow, narrow niches, and the thought of free-climbing that hundred-plus-meter crag with nothing but such shallow toe and fingerholds made my insides clench.

'Can we go closer?' asked Aenea.

I had been keeping the hawking mat about fifty meters out as we circled. 'I don't think we should,' I said. 'We're already within firearms range. I don't want to tempt anyone or anything with a spear or a bow and arrows.'

'A bow could pick us off at this range,' she said, but did not insist on flying closer.

For a second I thought I saw a glimmer of something moving within one of the oval openings carved in the red rock, but an instant later I decided it was a trick of the evening light.

'Had enough?' I said.

'Not really,' said Aenea. Her small hands were holding on to my shoulders as we banked. The breeze ruffled my short hair, and when I looked back, I could see the girl's hair streaming behind her.

'We need to get back to business, though,' I said, aiming the hawking mat south toward the river and accelerating again. The gymnosperm canopy looked soft, feathery, and deceptively continuous forty meters beneath us, as if we could land on it if we had to. A pang of tension filled me as I thought of the consequences if we had to. *But A. Bettik has the flying belt and flybikes*, I thought. *He can come fetch us if he has to.*

We intercepted the river again a klick or so southeast of where we had left it, and we could see the thirty klicks or so to the horizon. No farcaster portal. 'Which way?' I said.

'Let's go a bit farther.'

I nodded and banked left, staying out over the river. We had seen no signs of animal life other than the occasional white bird and the red bat-plant things. I was thinking of the footsteps in the side of the red monolith when Aenea tugged at my sleeve and pointed almost straight downward.

Something very large was moving just under the surface of the river. The low sunlight reflecting from the water hid most of the details from us, but I could make out leathery skin, something that might have been a barbed tail, and fins or cilia on the side. The creature must have been eight to ten meters long. It dived and we were past before I could see any more detail.

'That was sort of like a river manta,' called Aenea over my shoulder. We were moving quickly again, and the sound of the wind against the rising deflection field made some noise.

'Bigger,' I said. I had harnessed and worked with river mantas, and I'd never seen one that long or broad. Suddenly the hawking mat seemed very frail and insubstantial. I brought us thirty meters lower – we were flying almost at tree level now – so that a fall would not necessarily be fatal if the ancient flying carpet decided to quit on us without warning.

We banked south around another bend, noticed the river narrowing rapidly, and soon were greeted with a roar and a wall of rising spray.

The waterfall was not overly spectacular – it fell only ten to fifteen meters – but a huge volume of water was dropping over it, the klick-wide river pressed between rock cliffs to a width of only a hundred meters or so, and the force expended there was impressive. Below, there was another rapids over the rocks of the tumbled falls, then a wide pool, and then the river grew wide and relatively placid again. For a second I wondered stupidly if the river critter we'd seen was prepared for this sudden drop.

'I don't think we're going to find the portal in time to get back before dark,' I said over my shoulder to the girl. 'If there's a portal downriver at all.'

'It's there,' said Aenea.

'We've come at least a hundred klicks,' I said.

'A. Bettik said that the Tethys sections *averaged* that. This one might be two or three hundred kilometers between portals. Besides . . . there were numerous portals along the various rivers. The sections of the river varied in length even on the same world.'

'Who told you that?' I asked, twisting to look at her.

'My mother. She was a detective, you know. She once had a divorce case where she followed a married guy and his girlfriend for three weeks on the River Tethys.'

'What's a divorce case?' I asked.

'Never mind.' Aenea scooted around so that she was facing backward, her legs still crossed. Her hair whipped around her face. 'You're right, let's get back to A. Bettik and the ship. We'll come this way tomorrow.'

I banked us around and accelerated toward the west. We crossed over the falls and laughed as the spray wet our faces and hands.

'M. Endymion?' said the comlog. It was not the ship's voice, but A. Bettik's.

'Yes,' I said. 'We're heading back. We're about twenty-five, thirty minutes out.'

'I know,' came the android's calm voice. 'I was watching the tower, the waterfall, and all the rest in the holopit.'

Aenea and I looked at each other with what must have been comical expressions. 'You mean this comlog thing sends back pictures?'

'Of course,' came the ship's voice. 'Holo or video. We have been monitoring on holo.'

'Although the viewing is a bit odd,' said A. Bettik, 'since the holopit is now an indentation in the wall. But I was not calling to check your progress.'

'What, then?' I said.

'We appear to have a visitor,' said A. Bettik.

'A big river thing?' called Aenea. 'Sort of like a manta, only bigger?'

'Not exactly,' came A. Bettik's calm voice. 'It is the Shrike.'

THIRTY

Our hawking mat must have looked like a blur during our wild rush back to the ship. I asked if the ship could send us a real-time holo of the Shrike, but it said that most of its hull sensors were covered with mud and it had no clear view of the beach.

'It's on the beach?' I said.

'It was a moment ago, when I went up to carry another load out,' came A. Bettik's voice.

'Then it was in the Hawking-drive accumulator ring,' said the ship.

'What?' I said. 'There's no entrance to that part of the ship—' I stopped before I made a total idiot of myself. 'Where is it now?' I said.

'We are not sure,' said A. Bettik. 'I am going out onto the hull now and will be taking one of the radios. The ship will relay my voice to you.'

'Wait . . .' I began.

'M. Endymion,' interrupted the android, 'rather than urging you to rush back here, I called to suggest that you and M. Aenea . . . ah . . . extend your sight-seeing for a bit until the ship and I receive an indication of our . . . ah . . . visitor's intentions.'

This made sense to me. Here I was charged with protecting this girl, and when what might well be the deadliest killing machine in the galaxy appears, what do I do but rush her toward the danger? I was being a bit of an asshole this long day. I reached for the flight threads to slow us and bank back to the east.

Aenea's small hand intercepted mine. 'No,' she said. 'We'll go back.'

I was shaking my head. 'That thing is . . .'

'That thing can go anywhere it pleases,' said the girl. Her eyes and tone were deadly serious. 'If it wanted me . . . or you . . . it would appear right here on the mat with us.'

The thought made me look around.

'Let's go back,' said Aenea.

I sighed and turned back upriver, slowing the mat just a bit as I did so. Pulling the plasma rifle from my pack and swinging the stock out to lock it, I said, 'I don't get it. Is there any record of that monster ever leaving Hyperion?'

'I don't think so,' said the girl. She was leaning so that her face was against my back to stay out of the windblast as the deflection field lessened.

'So . . . what's happening? Is it following you?'

'That seems logical.' Her voice was muffled as she spoke into the cotton of my shirt.

'Why?' I said.

Aenea pushed away so strongly that I began to reach for her instinctively to keep her from tumbling off the back of the mat. She shrugged away from my hand. 'Raul, I don't really know the answers to these questions yet, all right? I didn't know if the thing would leave Hyperion. I certainly didn't want it to. Believe me.'

'I do,' I said. I lowered my hand to the mat, noticing how large it was next to her small hand, small knee, tiny foot.

She set her hand on mine. 'Let's get back.'

'Right.' I loaded the rifle with a plasma-cartridge magazine. The shell casings were not separate but were molded into the magazine until each fired. One magazine held fifty plasma bolts. When the last was fired, the magazine was gone. I slammed the magazine up and in with a slap of my hand as I'd been taught in the Guard, set the selector to single-shot, and made sure the safety was on. I laid the weapon across my knees as we flew.

Aenea touched my shoulders with her hands and said in my ear, 'Do you think that thing will do any good against the Shrike?'

I swiveled my head to look at her. 'No,' I said.

We flew into the setting sun.

A. Bettik was alone on the narrow beach when we arrived. He waved to reassure us that everything was all right, but I still circled once above the treetops before landing. The sun was a red globe balancing on the jungle canopy to the west.

I set the mat down next to the pile of crates and equipment on the beach, in the shadow of the great ship's hull, and jumped to my feet, the plasma rifle's safety set to off.

'It's still gone,' said A. Bettik. He had radioed this fact to us upon his leaving the ship, but I was still tense with expectation. The android led us over to a clear place on the beach where there was a single pair of footprints – if one could call them footprints. It looked as if someone had pressed a very heavy piece of bladed farm equipment into the sand in two places.

I crouched next to the prints like the experienced tracker I was, then realized the silliness of that exercise. 'He just appeared here, again in the ship, and then disappeared?'

'Yes,' said A. Bettik.

'Ship, did you ever get the thing on radar or visual?'

'Negative,' came the reply from the bracelet. 'There are no video recorders in the Hawking-drive accumulator . . .'

'How did you know it was there?' I asked.

'I have a mass sensor in every compartment,' said the ship. 'For flight purposes I must know precisely how much mass is displaced in every section of the ship.'

'How much mass did it displace?' I said.

'One-point-oh-six-three metric tons,' said the ship.

197

I froze in the act of straightening up. 'What? Over a thousand kilos? That's ridiculous.' I looked at the two footprints again. 'No way.'

'Way,' said the ship. 'During the creature's stay in the Hawking-drive accumulator ring, I measured a precise displacement of one-point-oh-six-three-thousand kilos and . . .'

'Jesus wept,' I said, turning to A. Bettik. 'I wonder if anyone's ever weighed this bastard before.'

'The Shrike is almost three meters tall,' said the android. 'And it may be very dense. It may also vary its mass as required.'

'Required for what?' I muttered, looking at the line of trees. It was very dark under there as the sun set. The gymnosperm feather fronds high above us caught the last of the light and faded. Clouds had rolled in during the last minutes of our flight back, and now they also glowed red and then grew dull as the sunset faded.

'You ready to get a star fix?' I said to the comlog.

'Quite ready,' said the ship, 'although this cloud cover will have to clear. In the meantime, I have made one or two other calculations.'

'Such as?' said Aenea.

'Such as – based upon the movement of this world's sun during the past few hours – this planet's day is eighteen hours, six minutes, fifty-one seconds long. Units in Old Hegemony Standard, of course.'

'Of course,' I said. To A. Bettik, 'Any of those River Tethys vacation worlds in your book show an eighteen-hour day?'

'None that I have come across, M. Endymion.'

'All right,' I said. 'Let's decide about tonight. Do we camp out here, stay in the ship, or load this stuff on the flybikes and get downriver to the next portal as soon as possible? We can haul the inflatable raft with us. I vote we do that. I'm not real keen on staying on this world if the Shrike is around here.'

A. Bettik raised one finger like a child in a classroom. 'I should have radioed you earlier . . .' he said as if embarrassed. 'The EVA locker, as you know, suffered some damage from the attack. There was no sign of an inflatable raft, although the ship remembers one in the inventory, and three of the four bikes are inoperable.'

I frowned. 'Totally?'

'Yes, sir,' said the android. 'Quite. The fourth is repairable, the ship thinks, but it will take several days.'

'Shit,' I said to no one in particular.

'How much charge do those bikes have?' asked Aenea.

'One hundred hours under normal use,' piped up my comlog.

The girl made a dismissive gesture. 'I don't think they'd be that useful, anyway. One bike isn't going to make that much difference, and we might never find a recharge source.'

I rubbed my cheek, feeling the stubble there. In the day's excitement I had forgotten to shave. 'I thought of that,' I said, 'but if we take any gear at all, the hawking mat's not big enough to haul the three of us *plus* weapons, *plus* what we need to take.'

I thought that the child would argue with us about needing the gear, but instead she said, 'Let's take it all, but let's not fly.'

'Not fly?' I said. The idea of hacking our way through that jungle made me queasy. 'Without an inflatable raft, it's either fly or walk . . .'

'We can still have a raft,' said Aenea. 'We could build a wooden raft and float it downstream . . . not only on this section of the river, but all of them.'

I rubbed my cheek again. 'The waterfall . . .'

'We can ferry our stuff down there on the hawking mat in the morning,' she said. 'Build the raft below the falls. Unless you don't think we can construct a raft . . .'

I looked at the gymnosperms: tall, thin, tough, just about the right thickness. 'We can build a raft,' I said. 'We used to cobble them together on the Kans to haul extra junk downstream with the barges.'

'Good,' said Aenea. 'We'll camp here tonight . . . it shouldn't be too long a night if the day is only eighteen standard hours. Then get moving at first light.'

I hesitated a moment. I didn't want to get into the habit of letting an eleven-year-old kid make decisions for us all, but the idea seemed sensible.

'It's too bad the ship's kaput,' I said. 'We could just go downriver on repulsors . . .'

Aenea laughed out loud. 'I'd never considered going on the River Tethys in this ship,' she said, rubbing her nose. 'It'd be just what we need – inconspicuous as a giant dachshund squeezing under croquet hoops.'

'What's a dachshund?' I said.

'What's a croquet hoop?' asked A. Bettik.

'Never mind,' said Aenea. 'Do you guys agree about staying here tonight and building a raft tomorrow?'

I looked at the android. 'It seems eminently sensible to me,' he said, 'although a subset of an equally eminent nonsensical voyage.'

'I'll take that as a yes vote,' said the girl. 'Raul?'

'All right,' I said, 'but where do we sleep tonight? Here on the beach, or in the ship, where it will be safer?'

The ship spoke. 'I will endeavor to make my interior as safe and hospitable as possible tonight, given the circumstances. Two of the couches on the fugue deck will still serve as beds, and there are hammocks which might be strung . . .'

'I vote we camp on the beach,' said Aenea. 'The ship's no safer from the Shrike than out here.'

I looked at the darkening forest. 'There might be other things we don't want to meet in the dark,' I said. 'The ship seems safer.'

A. Bettik touched a small crate. 'I found some small perimeter alarms,' he said. 'We could set those around our camp. I would be happy to stand watch through the night. I confess to some interest in sleeping outside after so many days aboard the ship.'

I sighed and surrendered. 'We'll trade off watches,' I said. 'Let's get this junk set up before it gets too dark.'

The 'junk' included the camping gear I'd asked the android to dig out: a tent of microthin polymer, thin as the shadow of a spiderweb, but tough, rainproof, and light enough to carry in one's pocket; the superconductor heating cube, cool on five sides and able to heat any meal on the sixth; the perimeter alarms A. Bettik had mentioned – actually a hunter's version of old military motion detectors, three-centimeter disks that could be spiked into the ground in any-sized perimeter up to two klicks; sleeping bags, infinitely compressible foam pads, night goggles, the com units, mess kits, and utensils.

We set the alarms in place first, spiking them down in a half circle from just within the forest's edge to the edge of the river.

'What if that big thing crawls out of the river and eats us?' said Aenea as we finished setting the perimeter. It was getting dark in earnest now, but the clouds hid any stars. Breezes rustled the fronds above with a more sinister sound than earlier.

'If that or anything else crawls out of the river and eats us,' I said, 'you're going to wish we'd stayed one more night in the ship.' I set the last detectors at the river's edge.

We pitched the tent in the center of the beach, not far from the bow of the crippled ship. The microfabric did not need tent poles or stakes – all you had to do was double-crease the lines of the fabric you wanted rigid, and those folds would stay taut in a hurricane, but setting a microtent up was a bit of an art, and the other two watched while I expanded the fabric, creased the edges into A-line with a dome center tall enough to stand in, and folded the suddenly rigid edges into the sand to stake it. I had left an expanse of microfabric as the floor of the tent, and by stretching it just so, we had mesh for the entrance. A. Bettik nodded his appreciation for the trick, and Aenea set the sleeping bags in place while I set a pan on the heating cube and opened a can of beef stew. At the last moment I remembered that Aenea was a vegetarian – she had eaten mostly salads during the two weeks aboard ship.

'That's all right,' she said, poking her head out of the tent. 'I'll have some of the bread that A. Bettik's heating up, and perhaps some of the cheese.'

A. Bettik was carrying fallen wood over and setting stones into a fire ring.

'We don't need that,' I said, indicating the heating cube and the bubbling pot of stew.

'Yes,' said the android, 'but I thought a fire might be pleasant. And the light welcome.'

The light, it turned out, was very welcome. We sat under the awning vestibule of my elaborately folded tent and watched the flames spit sparks toward the sky as a storm moved in. It was a strange storm, with bands of shifting lights in lieu of lightning. The pale bands of shimmering color danced from the bottoms of the hurrying clouds to points just meters above the gymnosperm fronds gyrating wildly in the rising wind. There was no thunder with the phenomenon, but a sort of subsonic rumble set my nerves on edge. Within the jungle itself, pale globes of red and yellow phosphorescence jiggled and danced – not gracefully like the radiant gossamers in

Hyperion's forests, but nervously, almost malevolently. Behind us, the river lapped at the beach with increasingly active waves. Sitting by the fire, my headset in place and turned to the perimeter detectors' frequency, the plasma rifle across my lap, the night goggles on my forehead ready to be flipped down at a second's notice, I must have been a comical sight. It did not seem funny at the time: images of the Shrike's footprints in the sand kept coming to mind.

'Did it act threatening?' I'd asked A. Bettik a few minutes earlier. I had been trying to get him to hold the 16-gauge shotgun – no weapon is easier for a non-weapon-user to use than a shotgun – but all he would do was keep it by him as he sat by the fire.

'It did not act anything at all,' he had replied, 'It simply stood there on the beach – tall, spiked, dark but gleaming. Its eyes were very red.'

'Was it looking at you?'

'It was looking east, down the river,' A. Bettik had replied.

As if waiting for Aenea and me to return, I had thought.

So I sat by the flickering fire, watched the aurora dance and shimmer over the wind-tossed jungle, tracked the will-o'-the-wisps as they jiggled in the jungle darkness, listened to the subsonic thunder rumbling like some great, hungry beast, and passed the time wondering how the hell I'd got myself here. For all I knew, there were velociraptors and packs of carrion-breed kalidergas slinking through the jungle toward us even as we sat fat and stupid by the fire. Or perhaps the river would rise – a wall of water could be rushing downstream toward us at that very moment. Camping on a sand spit was not terribly bright. We should have slept in the ship with the air lock sealed tight.

Aenea lay on her stomach looking into the fire. 'Do you know any stories?' she said.

'Stories!' I cried. A. Bettik looked up from where he sat hugging his knees beyond the fire.

'Yes,' said the girl. 'Like ghost stories.'

I made a noise.

Aenea propped her chin on her palms. The fire painted her face in warm tones. 'I just thought it might be fun,' she said. 'I like ghost stories.'

I thought of four or five responses and held them back. 'You'd better get to sleep,' I said at last. 'If the ship's right about the short day, we don't have too much night . . .' *Please, God, let that be true*, I was thinking. Aloud, I said, 'You'd better get some sleep while you can.'

'All right,' said Aenea, and took one last look across the fire at the wind-tossed jungle, the aurora, and the St Elmo's fire in the forest, rolled into her sleeping bag and went to sleep.

A. Bettik and I sat in silence for a while. Occasionally I would converse with my bracelet comlog, asking the ship to inform me immediately if the river started rising, or if it detected some mass displacement, or if . . .

'I would be happy to take the first watch, M. Endymion,' said the android.

'No, go ahead and sleep,' I said, forgetting that the blue-skinned man required very little sleep.

'We will watch together, then,' he said softly. 'But do feel free to doze when you need to, M. Endymion.'

Perhaps I did doze off sometime before the tropical dawn about six hours later. It was cloudy and stormy all night; the ship never got its star fix while we were there. No velociraptors or kalidergas ate us. The river did not rise. The storm aurora did not harm us, and the balls of swamp gas never came out of the swamp to burn us.

What I remember most about that night, besides my galloping paranoia and terrible tiredness, was the sight of Aenea sleeping with her brown-blonde hair spilled out over the edge of her red sleeping bag, her fist raised to her cheek like an infant preparing to suck its thumb. I realized that night the import and the terrible difficulty in the task ahead of me – of keeping this child safe from the sharp edges of a strange and indifferent universe.

I think that it was on this alien and storm-tossed night that I first understood what it might be like to be a parent.

We got moving at first light, and I remember that morning mixture of bone-tiredness, gritty eyes, stubbled cheeks, aching back, and sheer joy that I usually felt after my first night on a camping trip. Aenea went down to the river to wash up, and I have to admit that she looked fresher and cleaner than she should have, given the circumstances.

A. Bettik had heated coffee over the cube, and he and I drank some while we watched the morning fog curl up from the quickly moving river. Aenea sipped from a water bottle she'd brought from the ship, and we all munched on dry cereal from a ration pak.

By the time the sun was shining over the jungle canopy, burning away the mists that rose from the river and forest, we were ferrying the gear downriver on the hawking mat. Since Aenea and I had done the fun part the previous evening, I let A. Bettik fly the gear while I dragged more stuff out of the ship and made sure we had what we needed.

Clothing was a problem. I had packed everything I thought I might need, but the girl had only the clothes she'd been wearing on Hyperion and carrying in her pack, and a few shirts we'd cut down from the Consul's wardrobe. With more than two hundred and fifty years to think about rescuing the child, one would think that the old poet would have thought to pack some clothes for her. Aenea seemed happy enough with what she had brought, but I was worried that it would not be enough if we ran into cold or rainy weather.

The EVA locker was a help there. There were several suit liners fitted out for the spacesuits, and the smallest of these came dose to fitting the girl. I knew that the micropore material would keep her warm and dry in any but the most arctic conditions. I also appropriated a liner for the android and myself; it seemed absurd to be packing for winter in the rising tropical heat of that day, but one never knew. There was also an old outdoors vest of the Consul's in the locker: long but fitted with more than a dozen pockets, clips, tie-on rings, secret zippered compartments. Aenea let out a squeal when I dug it out of the tumbled mess of the locker, put it on, and wore it almost constantly from then on.

We also found two EVA geology specimen bags with shoulder straps, which made excellent packs, Aenea hoisted one to her shoulder and loaded the extra clothes and bric-a-brac we were finding.

I still was convinced that there had to be a raft there, but no amount of digging and opening locker compartments could bring one up.

'M. Endymion,' said the ship when I mentioned to the child what I was rooting around for, 'I have a vague memory . . .'

Aenea and I stopped what we were doing and listened. There was something strange, almost pained, about the ship's voice.

'I have a vague memory of the Consul taking the inflatable raft . . . of him waving good-bye to me from it.'

'Where was that?' I asked. 'Which world?'

'I do not know,' said the ship in that same bemused, almost pained tone. 'It may not have been a world at all . . . I remember stars shining *below* the river.'

'Below the river?' I said. I was worried about the ship's mental integrity after the crash.

'The memory is fragmented,' said the ship in brisker tone. 'But I do remember the Consul departing in the raft. It was a large raft, quite comfortable for eight or ten people.'

'Great,' I said, slamming a compartment door. Aenea and I carried out the last load – we had rigged a metal folding ladder to hang down from the air lock, so climbing in and out was not the struggle it had been earlier.

A. Bettik swooped back after ferrying the camping gear and food cartons down to the waterfall, and now I looked at what remained: my backpack filled with my personal gear, Aenea's backpack and shoulder bag, the extra com units and goggles, some of the food packs, and – lashed under the top of my pack – the folded plasma rifle and the machete A. Bettik had found yesterday. The long knife was awkward to carry, even in its leather sheath, but my few minutes in the jungle the day before had convinced me that we might need it, I had also dug out an ax and an even more compact tool – a folding shovel, actually, although for millennia we idiots who had joined the infantry had been trained to call it 'an entrenching tool'. All of our cutlery was beginning to take up space.

I would have been happy to have skipped the ax and brought along a cutting laser to fell the trees for the raft – even an old chain saw would have been preferable – but my flashlight laser wasn't up to that sort of work, and the weapons locker had been strangely devoid of cutting tools. For one long self-indulgent moment I considered bringing the old FORCE assault rifle and just blasting and burning those trees down, splitting them with pulse bolts if need be, but then I rejected the idea. It would be too loud, too messy, and too imprecise. I would just have to use the ax and sweat a bit. I did bring one of the tool kits with hammer, nails, screwdrivers, screws, pivot bolts – all the things I might need for raft building – as well as some rolls of waterproof plastalum that I thought might make crude but adequate flooring for the raft. On top of the tool kit were several hundred meters of nylon-sheathed climbing rope in three separate coils. In a red waterproof pouch, I'd found some flares and simple *plastique*, the kind that had been used for blasting stumps and rocks out of fields for countless centuries, as well as a dozen detonators. I included those, although they would be of doubtful use in felling trees for a raft. Also included in this pile for the next trip east were two medkits and a bottle-sized water purifier.

I had carried the EM-flying belt out, but the thing was bulky with its harness and power pak. I propped it against my pack anyway, thinking that we might need it. Also propped against my pack was the 16-gauge shotgun, which the android had not bothered taking with him during his flight east. Next to it were three boxes of shells. I had also insisted on bringing the flechette pistol, although neither A. Bettik nor Aenea would carry the thing.

On my belt was the holster holding the loaded .45, a pocket for an old-fashioned magnetic compass we'd found in the locker, my folded pair of night goggles and daytime binoculars, a water bottle, and two extra clips for the plasma rifle. 'Bring on the velociraptors!' I muttered while taking inventory.

'What?' said Aenea, looking up from her packing.

'Nothing.'

Aenea had her things packed neatly in her new bag by the time A. Bettik touched down on the sand. She had also packed the android's few personal items in the second shoulder bag.

I have always enjoyed breaking camp, even more than setting it up. I think it's the neatness of packing everything away that I enjoy.

'What are we forgetting?' I said to the other two as we stood there on the narrow beach, looking at the packs and weapons.

'Me,' said the ship through the comlog on my wrist. The spacecraft's voice did sound a bit plaintive.

Aenea walked across the sand to touch the curved metal of the beached ship. 'How are you doing?'

'I have begun repairs, M. Aenea,' it said. 'Thank you for inquiring.'

'Do you still project six months for repairs?' I asked. The last of the clouds were dissipating overhead, and the sky was that pale blue again. The green and white fronds moved against it.

'Approximately six standard months,' said the ship. 'That is for my internal and external condition, of course. I do not have the macromanipulators to repair such things as your broken flybikes.'

'That's all right,' said Aenea. 'We're leaving them all behind. We'll fix them when we see you again.'

'When will that be?' said the ship. Its voice seemed smaller than usual coming from the comlog.

The child looked at A. Bettik and me. None of us spoke. Finally Aenea said, 'We *will* need your services again, Ship. Can you conceal yourself here for months . . . or years . . . while you repair yourself and wait?'

'Yes,' said the ship. 'Would the river bottom do?'

I looked out at the great gray mass of the snip rising from the water. The river was wide here, and probably deep, but the thought of the wounded ship backing itself into it seemed strange. 'Won't you . . . leak?' I said.

'M. Endymion,' said the ship in that tone which made me think it was acting haughty, 'I am an interstellar spacecraft capable of penetrating nebulae and existing quite comfortably within the outer shell of a red giant star. I shall hardly – as you put it – *leak* because of being immersed in H_2O for a brief period of years.'

'Sorry,' I said, and then – refusing to have the ship's rebuke as the last word – 'Don't forget to close your air lock when you go under.'

The ship did not comment.

'When we come back for you,' said the girl, 'will we be able to call you?'

'Use the comlog bands or ninety-point-one on the general radio band,' said the ship. 'I will keep a buggy-whip antenna above waterline to receive your call.'

'Buggy-whip antenna,' mused A. Bettik. 'What a lovely phrase.'

'I am sorry that I do not recall the derivation of that term,' said the ship. 'My memory is not what it used to be.'

'That's all right,' said Aenea, patting the hull. 'You've served us well. Now you *get* well . . . We want you in top shape when we return.'

'Yes, M. Aenea. I will be in contact and monitoring your progress until you transit the next farcaster portal.'

A. Bettik and Aenea sat on the hawking mat with their packs and our last boxes of gear taking up the rest of the space. I strapped the bulky flying belt on. It meant that I had to carry my own pack against my chest with a strap looped over my shoulder, the rifle in my free hand, but it worked all right. I knew how to operate the thing only from books – EM belts were useless on Hyperion – but the controls were simple and intuitive. The power indicator showed full charge, so I did not anticipate being dropped into the river for this short hop.

The mat was hovering about ten meters above the river when I squeezed the handheld controller, lurched into the air, almost clipped a gymnosperm, found my balance, and flew out to hover next to them. Hanging from this padded body harness was not as comfortable as sitting on a flying carpet, but the exhilaration of flying was even stronger. With the controller still held in my fist, I gave them the thumbs-up, and we flew east along the river, toward the rising sun.

There weren't many other sand pits or beaches between the ship and the waterfall, but there was a good spot just below the waterfall, along the south side of the river where it widened into a lazy pool just beyond the rapids, and it was here that A. Bettik unloaded our camping gear and the first load of material. The noise from the falls was loud as we stacked the last of the small crates. I unlimbered the ax and looked at the nearest gymnosperms.

'I was thinking,' A. Bettik said so softly that I could hardly hear him over the noise of the waterfall.

I paused with the ax on my shoulder. The sunlight was very hot, and my shirt was already sticking to me.

'The River Tethys was meant to be a pleasure cruise,' he continued. 'I wonder how the pleasure cruisers dealt with that.' He pointed a blue finger at the roaring falls.

'I know,' said Aenea. 'I was thinking the same thing. They had levitation barges then, but not everyone going down the Tethys would have been in one. It would have been embarrassing to go for a romantic boat ride and find yourself and your sweetheart going over those.'

I stood looking at the rainbow-dappled spray of the falls and found myself wondering if I was as intelligent as I often assumed. This had not occurred to me. 'The Tethys has been unused for almost three standard centuries,' I said. 'Maybe the falls are new.'

'Perhaps,' said A. Bettik, 'but I doubt it. These falls appear to have been formed by tectonic shelving that runs for many miles north and south through the jungle – do you see the difference in elevation there? And they have been eroding for a very long time. Note the size of the boulders in the rapids? I would think this has been here for as long as the river has run.'

'And it's not in your Tethys guidebook?' I said.

'No,' said the android, holding the book out. Aenea took it.

'Maybe we're not on the Tethys,' I said. Both of the others stared at me. 'The ship didn't get a starsighting,' I went on, 'but what if this is some world not on the original Tethys tour?'

Aenea nodded. 'I thought of that. The portals are the same as the ones along the remnants of the Tethys today, but who is to say that the Techno-Core did not have other portals . . . other farcaster-connected rivers?'

I set the head of the ax down and leaned on the shaft. 'In which case, we're in trouble,' I said. 'You'll never find your architect, and we'll never find our way back to the ship and home.'

Aenea smiled. 'It's too early to worry about that. It *has* been three centuries. Maybe the river here just cut a new channel since the Tethys days. Or maybe there's a canal and locks we missed because the jungle grew over it. We don't have to worry about this now. We just have to get downriver to see if there's another portal.'

I held up one finger. 'Another thought,' I said, feeling a bit smarter than I had a moment before. 'What if we go to all this trouble of building a raft here and find another waterfall between us and the portal? Or ten more? We didn't spot the farcaster arch last night, so we don't know how far it is.'

'I thought of that,' said Aenea.

I tapped my fingers on the ax handle. If that kid said that phrase one more time, I would seriously consider using the implement on her.

'M. Aenea asked me to reconnoiter,' said the android. 'I did so during my last shuttle here.'

I was frowning. 'Reconnoiter? You didn't have time to fly that mat a hundred klicks or more downriver.'

'No,' agreed the android, 'but I flew the mat very high and used the extra set of binoculars to search our path. The river appears to run straight and true for almost two hundred kilometers. It was difficult to be sure, but I saw what may be the arch approximately a hundred and thirty kilometers downriver. There appeared to be no waterfalls or other major obstacles between us and it.'

My frown must have deepened. 'You saw all that?' I said. 'How high *were* you?'

'The mat has no altimeter,' said A. Bettik, 'but judging from the visible curvature of the planet and the darkening of the sky, I think I was about one hundred kilometers up.'

'Did you have one of the spacesuits on?' I asked. At that altitude a human being's blood would boil in his veins and his lungs would burst from explosive decompression. 'A respirator?' I looked around, but nothing like that was lying in our modest piles of goods.

'No,' said the android, turning to lift a crate, 'I just held my breath.'

Shaking my head, I went off to cut some trees down. I figured that the exercise and solitude would do me good.

It was evening before the raft was finished, and I would have been working all night if A. Bettik had not taken turns with me on the tree cutting. The finished product was not beautiful, but it floated. Our little raft was about six meters long and four wide, with a long steering pole carved into a crude rudder set onto a forked support at the rear, a raised area just in front of the steering pole where Aenea molded the tent into a lean-to with openings front and rear, and crude oarlocks on each side with long oar-poles that would lie along the sides of the ship unless they were needed for rowing in dead water or emergency steering in rapids. I had been worried that the fern trees might soak up too much water and sink too low to be useful as a raft, but with only two layers of them wrapped together into a honeycomb with our climbing rope and bolted in strategic places, the logs rode very nicely and kept the top of the raft about fifteen centimeters above the water.

Aenea had shown a fascination with the microtent, and I had to admit that her sculpting of it was more skillful and efficient than anything I had shaped in all my years of using the things. Our lean-to could be ducked into from the steering position at the rudder, had a nice overhang in front to shield us from sun or rain while keeping the view intact, and had nice vestibules on either side to keep the extra crates of gear dry. She had already spread our foam pads and sleeping bags in various corners of the tent; the high sitting area in the center where we had the best view forward now boasted a meter-wide river stone, which she had set there as a hearth with the mess gear and heating cube on it; one of the handlamps was opened to lantern mode and was hanging from a centerloop – and, I had to admit, the overall effect was cosy.

The girl did not just spend her afternoon making cozy tents, however. I guess that I had expected her to stand by and watch while the two men sweated through the heavy work – I had stripped to the waist an hour into the heat of the day – but Aenea joined in almost immediately, dragging downed logs to the assembly point, lashing them, driving nails, setting bolts and pivot joints in place, and generally helping in the design. She pointed out why the standard way I'd been taught to jerry-rig a rudder was inefficient, and by moving the base of the support tripod lower and farther apart, I was able to move the long pole easier and to better effect. Twice she showed me different ways to tie the cross supports on the underside of the raft so that they would be tighter and sturdier. When we needed a log shaped, it was Aenea who set to with the machete, and all A. Bettik and I could do was stand back or be hit by flying chips.

Still, even with the three of us working hard, it was almost sundown before the raft was finished and our gear loaded.

'We could camp here tonight, get onto the river early in the morning,' I said. Even as I said it, I knew that I did not want to do that. Neither did the other two. We climbed aboard, and I pushed us away from the shore with the long pole I'd chosen as our main source of locomotion when the current failed. A. Bettik steered, and Aenea stood near the front of the raft, looking for shoals or hidden rocks.

For the first hour or so, the voyage seemed almost magical. After the sultry jungle heat and the tremendous exertion all day, it seemed like paradise to stand on the slowly moving raft, push against the river mud occasionally, and watch the darkening walls of jungle slip past. The sun set almost directly behind us, and for a few minutes the river was as red as molten lava, the undersides of the gymnosperms on either side aflame with reflected light. Then the grayness turned to darkness, and before we caught more than a glimpse of the night sky, the clouds moved in from the east just as they had the previous night.

'I wonder if the ship got a fix,' said Aenea.

'Let's call and ask,' I said.

The ship had not been able to fix its position. 'I was able to ascertain that we are not on Hyperion or Renaissance Vector,' said the small voice from my wrist comlog.

'Well, that's a relief,' I said. 'Any other news?'

'I have fixed my position on the river bottom,' said the ship. 'It is quite comfortable, and I am preparing to . . .'

Suddenly the colored lightning rippled across the northern and western horizons, the wind whipped across the river so strongly that each of us had to rush to keep things from being blown away, the raft began moving toward the south shore with the whitecaps, and the comlog spit static. I thumbed the bracelet off and concentrated on poling while A. Bettik steered again. For several minutes I was afraid that the raft would come apart in the high waves and roaring wind; the bow was chopping, lifting, and dropping, and our only illumination came from the explosions of magenta and crimson lightning. The thunder was audible this night – great, pealing waves of sound, as if someone were rolling giant steel drums down stone stairs at us – and the aurora lightning tore at the sky rather than danced as it had the night before. Each of us froze for a second as one of those magenta bolts struck a gymnosperm on the north bank of the river, instantly causing the tree to explode in flame and colored sparks. As an ex-bargeman, I cursed my stupidity for letting us out here in the middle of such a wide river – the Tethys had opened up to the better part of a klick wide again – without lightning rod or rubber mats. We hunkered down and grimaced when the colored bolts struck either shore or lit the eastern horizon in front of us.

Suddenly it was raining and the worst of the lightning was over. We ran for the tent Aenea and A. Bettik crouched near the front opening, still hunting for sandbanks or floating logs, me standing at the rear where the girl had rigged the tent to provide the person at the rudder shelter even while steering.

It had rained hard and often on the Kans River when I was a bargeman – I remember huddling in the leaky old barge fo'c'sle and wondering if the damned boat was going to go down just because of the weight of the rain on it – but I do not remember any rain like this one.

For a moment I thought that we had come up against another waterfall, a much larger one this time, and had unwittingly poled under the full force of it – but we were still moving downriver, and it was no waterfall descending on us, just the terrible force of the worst rainstorm I had ever experienced.

The wise course would have been to make for the riverbank and hold up until the deluge passed, but we could see nothing except colored lightning exploding behind this vertical wall of water, and I had no idea how far the banks were, or whether they held any chance of our landing and tying up. So I lashed the rudder in its highest position so that it would do little but keep our stern to the rear, abandoned my post, and huddled with the child and android as the heavens opened and dropped rivers, lakes, *oceans* of water on us.

It says something about the girl's ability or luck in shaping and securing the tent that not once did it begin to fold or come loose from its cinchings to the raft. I say that I huddled with them, but in truth all three of us were busy holding down crates that had already been lashed in place as that raft pitched, tossed, swung around, and then brought its nose back around yet again. We had no idea which direction we were headed, whether the raft was safe in the middle of the river or was bearing down on boulders in a rapids, or was tearing hell-bent for cliffs as the river turned and we did not. Not one of us cared at that point: our goal was to keep our gear together, not be washed overboard, and to keep track of the other two as best we could.

At one point – with one arm around our stack of backpacks and my other hand clenched on the girl's collar as she leaned out to retrieve some cookware headed out of the tent at high speed – I looked out from under our vestibule awning toward the front of the raft and realized that every part of the raft except for our little raised platform where the tent sat was under water. The wind whipped whitecaps that glowed red or bright yellow depending upon the color of the curtain of the lightning aurora raging at that moment. I remembered something I had forgotten to search for in the ship: life vests – personal notation devices.

Pulling Aenea back under the flapping cover of the tent, I screamed against the storm, 'Can you swim when it's not zero-g?'

'What?' I could see her lips form the word, but I could not actually hear it. 'Can . . . you . . . swim!?'

A. Bettik looked up from his position among the pitching crates. Water blew from his bald head and long nose. His blue eyes looked violet when the aurora crashed.

Aenea shook her head, although I was unsure whether she was answering my question in the negative or signifying she could not hear. I pulled her closer; her many-pocketed vest was soaked through and flapping like a wet sheet in a windstorm. 'CAN . . . YOU . . . SWIM??' I was screaming literally at the top of my lungs. The effort took my breath away. I made frenzied swimming motions with both hands cupped in front of me. The raft pitched us apart, then tossed us back into close proximity.

I saw understanding light her dark eyes. The rain or spray whipped from the long strands of her hair. She smiled, the spray making her teeth look wet, and leaned closer to shout back into my ear.

'THANKS! I'D . . . LIKE TO . . . TAKE A . . . SWIM. BUT . . . MAYBE . . . LATER.'

We must have hit an eddy then, or perhaps the rising wind just caught the tent and used it as a sail to spin the raft on its axis, but that was when the raft went all the way around, seemed to hesitate, and then continued its spin. The three of us gave up trying to hold on to anything other than our lives and each other and just huddled together in the center of the raft platform. I realized that Aenea was shouting – a sort of happy 'Yee-HAW' – and before I could scream at her to shut up, I echoed the cry. It felt good to scream against that spinning and the storm and the deluge, unable to be heard, but feeling your own shouts echoing in your skull and bones even as the thunder rumble echoed there as well. I looked to my right as a crimson bolt illuminated the entire river, saw a boulder sticking up at least five meters above the water and the raft twisting around and past it like a dreidel spinning by a cinder, and was more amazed by the sight of A. Bettik on his knees, his head thrown back, 'Yee-HAWing' with us at the top of his android lungs.

The storm lasted all night. Toward dawn the rain let up until it was a mere downpour. The aurora lightning and sonic boom thunder must have ended about then, but I cannot be certain of that – I was, as were both my young friend and my android friend, fast asleep and snoring.

We awoke to find the sun already high, no sign of clouds, the river wide and smooth and slow, the jungle moving by on either side like a seamless tapestry being unwound past us, and the sky gentle and blue.

For a while we could only sit in the sunlight, our elbows on our knees, our clothes still wet and dripping. We said nothing, I think the maelstrom of the night was still in our eyes, the blasts of color still popping in our retinas.

After a while Aenea stood up on wobbly legs. The surface of the raft was wet, but still above water. One log on the starboard side had broken free: there were a few tattered cords where knots should be; but all in all, our vessel was still seaworthy . . . riverworthy. Whatever. We checked fittings and took inventory for a while. The handlamp we had hung as a lantern was gone, as was one of the smaller cartons of rations, but everything else seemed in place.

'Well, you two can stand around,' said Aenea. 'I'm going to make some breakfast.'

She turned the heating cube to maximum, had water boiling in a kettle within a minute, poured water for her tea and set it in the coffeepot for our coffee, and then shifted that aside to set a skillet frying with breakfast strips of jambon with tiny slices of potato she was cutting up.

I looked at the ham sizzling and said, 'I thought you were a vegetarian.'

'I am,' said the girl. 'I'm having wheat chips and some of that terrible reconstituted milk from the ship, but for this one and only time, I'm chef and you fellows are eating well.'

We ate well, sitting on the front edge of the tent platform where the sun could bathe our skins and dry our clothes. I pulled the crushed tricorn cap from one pocket of my wet vest, squeezed water out of it, and set it on my head for some shade. This started Aenea laughing again. I glanced over at A. Bettik, but the android was as observant and impassive as ever – as if his hour of 'Yee-HAWing' with us had never occurred.

A. Bettik pulled a pole upright on the front of the raft – I had rigged it to swivel so we might hang a lantern there at night – but he pulled off his tattered white shirt and hung it there to dry instead. The sun glinted on his perfect blue skin.

'A flag!' cried Aenea. 'It's what this expedition has been needing.'

I laughed. 'Not a white flag, though. That stands for . . .' I stopped in midsentence.

We had moved slowly with the current around a wide bend in the river. Now we each saw the huge and ancient farcaster portal arching for hundreds of meters above and to either side of us. Entire trees had grown on its wide back; vines fell many meters from its designs and indentations.

Each of us moved to our stations: me at the rudder this time, A. Bettik standing at the long pole as if ready to ward off rocks or boarders, and Aenea crouching at the front.

For a long minute I knew that this farcaster was a dud, that it would not work. I could see the familiar jungle and blue sky under it, watch the river go on beyond it. The view was normal right up to the point we reached the shadow of the giant arch. I could see a fish jump from the water ten meters in front of us. The wind ruffled Aenea's hair and teased waves from the river. Above us, tons of ancient metal hung there like a child's effort at drawing a bridge.

'Nothing happened—' I began.

The air filled with electricity in a manner more sudden and more terrifying than last night's storm. It was as if a giant curtain had fallen from the arch directly onto our heads. I fell to one knee, feeling the weight and then the weightlessness of it. For an instant too short to measure, I felt as I had when the crash field had exploded around us in the tumbling spacecraft like a fetus struggling against a clinging amniotic sac.

Then we were through. The sun was gone. The daylight was gone. The riverbanks and jungle were no longer there. Water stretched to the horizon on all sides. Stars in number and magnitude I had never imagined, much less observed, filled a sky that seemed too large.

Directly ahead of us, silhouetting Aenea like orange searchlights, rose three moons, each one the size of a full-fledged planet.

THIRTY-ONE

'Fascinating,' said A. Bettik.

It would not have been my choice of words, but it sufficed for the time being. My first reaction was to begin cataloging our situation in negatives: we were not on the jungle world any longer; we were not on a river – the ocean stretched to the night sky in each direction; we were no longer in daylight; we were not sinking.

The raft rode quite differently in these gentle but serious ocean swells, but my bargeman's eye noted that while the waves tended to lap over the edges a bit more, the gymnosperm wood seemed even more buoyant here. I went to one knee near the rudder and gingerly lifted a palmful of sea to my mouth. I spat it out quickly and rinsed my mouth with fresh water from the canteen on my belt. This seawater was far more saline than even Hyperion's undrinkable oceans.

'Wow,' Aenea said softly to herself. I guessed that she was talking about the rising moons. All three were huge and orange, but the center one was so large that even half of its diameter as it rose seemed to fill what I still thought of as the eastern sky. Aenea rose to her feet, and her standing silhouette still came less than halfway up the giant orange hemisphere. I lashed the rudder in place and joined the other two at the front of the raft. Because of the rocking as the gentle ocean swells rolled under us, all three of us were holding on to the upright post there, which still held A. Bettik's shirt flapping in the night wind. The shirt glowed whitely in the moonlight and starlight.

I quit being a bargeman for a moment and scanned the sky with a shepherd's eyes. The constellations that had been my favorites as a child – the Swan, the Geezer, the Twin Sisters, Seedships, and Home Plate – were not there or were so distorted that I could not recognize them. But the Milky Way was there: the meandering highway of our galaxy was visible from the wave-chopped horizon behind us until it faded in the glow around the rising moons. Normally, stars were much fainter with even an Old Earth-standard moon in the sky, much less these giants. I guessed that a dustless sky, no competing light sources of any sort, and thinner air offered this incredible show. I had trouble imagining the stars here on a moonless night.

Where is 'here'? I wondered. I had a hunch. 'Ship?' I said to my comlog. 'Are you still there?'

I was surprised when the bracelet answered. 'The downloaded sections are still here, M. Endymion. May I help you?'

The other two tore their gazes away from the rising moon giant and looked at the comlog. 'You're not the ship?' I said. 'I mean . . .'

'If you mean are you in direct communication with the ship, no,' said the comlog. 'The com bands were severed when you transited the last farcaster portal. This abbreviated version of the ship is, however, receiving video feed.'

I had forgotten that the comlog had light-sensitive pickups. 'Can you tell us where we are?' I said.

'One minute, please,' said the comlog. 'If you will hold the comlog up a bit – thank you – I will do a sky search and match it to navigational coordinates.'

While the comlog was searching, A. Bettik said, 'I think I know where we are, M. Endymion.'

I thought I did as well, but I let the android speak. 'This seems to fit the description of Mare Infinitus,' he said. 'One of the old worlds in the Web and now part of the Pax.'

Aenea said nothing. She was still watching the rising moon, and her expression was rapt. I looked up at the orange sphere dominating the sky and realized that I could see rust-colored clouds moving above the dusty surface. Looking again, I realized that surface features were visible: brown blemishes that might be volcano flows, a long scar of a valley with tributaries, the hint of icefields at the north pole, and indefinable radiation lines connecting what might be mountain ranges. It looked a bit like holos I'd seen of Mars – before it had been terraformed – in Old Earth's system.

'Mare Infinitus appears to have three moons,' A. Bettik was saying, 'although in reality it is Mare Infinitus which is the satellite of a near Jovian-sized rocky world.'

I gestured toward the dusty moon. 'Like that?'

'Precisely like that,' said the android. 'I have seen pictures . . . It is uninhabited, but was heavily mined by robots during the Hegemony.'

'I think it's Mare Infinitus as well,' I said. 'I've heard some of my offworld Pax hunters talk about it. Great deep-sea fishing. They say that there's some sort of antennaed cephalochordate thing in the ocean on Mare Infinitus that grows to be more than a hundred meters long . . . it swallows fishing ships whole unless it's caught first.'

I shut up then. All three of us peered down into the wine-dark waters. Into the silence suddenly chirped my comlog, 'I've got it! The starfields match perfectly with my navigational data banks. You are on a satellite surrounding a sub-Jovian world orbiting star Seventy Ophiuchi A, twenty-seven-point-nine light-years from Hyperion, sixteen-point-four-oh-eight-two light-years from Old Earth System. The system is a binary, with Seventy Ophiuchi A your primary star at point-six-four AU, and Seventy Ophiuchi B your secondary at eight-nine AU. Since you appear to have atmosphere and water there, it would be safe to say that you are on the second moon from sub-Jovian DB Seventy Ophiuchi A-prime, known in Hegemony days as Mare Infinitus.'

'Thanks,' I said to the comlog.

'I have more astral navigational data . . .' chirped the bracelet.

'Later,' I said, and tapped the comlog off.

A. Bettik removed his shirt from the makeshift mast and pulled it on. The ocean breeze was strong, the air thin and chilly. I pulled my insulated over-vest from my pack, and the other two retrieved jackets from their own packs. The incredible moon continued rising into the unbelievable starry sky.

The Mare Infinitus segment of the river is a pleasant, if brief, interlude between more recreation-oriented river passages, read the *Travelers' Guide to the Web*. The three of us crouched by the stone hearth to read the page by the light of our last handlamp-lantern. The lamp was redundant, actually, since the moonlight was almost as bright as a cloudy day on Hyperion. *The violet articulated seas are caused by a form of phytoplankton in the water and are not a result of the atmospheric scattering which grants the traveler such lovely sunsets. While the Mare Infinitus interlude is very short – five kilometers of such ocean travel is enough for most of the River's wanderers – it does include the Web-famous Gus's Oceanic Aquarium and Grill. Be sure to order the grilled sea giant, the hectapus soup, and the excellent yelloweed wine. Dine on one of the many terraces on Gus's Oceanic platform so that you can enjoy one of Mare Infinitus's exquisite sunsets and even more exquisite moonrises. While this world is noted for its empty ocean expanses (it has no continents or islands) and aggressive sea life (the 'Lantern-Mouth Leviathan' for example), please be assured that your Tethys Traveler's ship will stay safely within the Mid-littoral Stream from portal to portal, and be escorted by several Mare Protectorate outrider ships – all so that your brief aquatic interval, set off by a fine dinner at Gus's Oceanic Grill, will leave only pleasant memories. (NOTE: The Mare Infinitus segment of the Tethys will be omitted from the tour if inclement weather or dangerous sea-life conditions prevail. Be prepared to catch this world on a later tour!)*

That was all. I gave the book back to A. Bettik, turned the lamp off, went to the front of the raft, and scanned the horizon with night-vision ampli-fiers. The goggles were not necessary in the brilliant light from the three moons. 'The book lies,' I said. 'We can see at least twenty-five klicks to the horizon. There's no other portal.'

'Perhaps it moved,' said A. Bettik.

'Or sank,' said Aenea.

'Ha ha,' I said, tossing the goggles into my pack and sitting with the others near the glowing heating cube. The air was cold.

'It is possible,' said the android, 'that – as with the other river segments – there is a longer and shorter version of this section.'

'Why do we always get the longer versions?' I said. We were cooking breakfast, each of us starved after the long night's storm on the river, although the toast, cereal, and coffee seemed more like a midnight snack on the moonlit sea.

We soon got used to the pitching and rolling of the raft on the large swells and none of us showed any signs of seasickness. After my second cup of coffee, I felt better about it all. Something about the guidebook entry had piqued my sense of the absurd. I had to admit, though, that I didn't like the 'Lantern-Mouth Leviathan' bit.

'You're enjoying this, aren't you?' Aenea said to me as we sat in front of the tent. A. Bettik was behind us, at the steering rudder.

'Yeah,' I said, 'I guess I am.'

'Why?' said the girl.

I raised my hands. 'It's an adventure,' I said. 'But no one's got hurt . . .'

'I think we came close in that storm,' said Aenea.

'Yes, well . . .'

'Why else do you like it?' There was real curiosity in the child's voice.

'I've always liked the outdoors,' I said truthfully. 'Camping. Being away from things. Something about nature makes me feel . . . I don't know . . . connected to something larger.' I stopped before I began sounding like an Orthodox Zen Gnostic.

The girl leaned closer. 'My father wrote a poem about that idea,' she said. 'Actually, it was the ancient pre-Hegira poet my father's cybrid was cloned from, of course, but my father's sensibilities were in the poem.' Before I could ask a question, she continued, 'He wasn't a philosopher. He was young, younger than you, even, and his philosophical vocabulary was fairly primitive, but in this poem he tried to articulate the stages by which we approach fusion with the universe. In a letter he called these stages "a kind of Pleasure Thermometer".'

I admit that I was surprised and a little taken back by this short speech. I hadn't heard Aenea talk this seriously about anything yet, or use such large words, and the 'Pleasure Thermometer' part sounded vaguely dirty to me. But I listened as she went on:

'Father thought that the first stage of human happiness was a "fellowship with essence",' she said softly. I could see that A. Bettik was listening from his place at the steering pole. 'By that,' she said, 'Father meant an imaginative and sensuous response to nature . . . just the sort of feeling you were describing earlier.'

I rubbed my cheek, feeling the longer bristles there. A few more days without shaving and I would have a beard. I sipped my coffee.

'Father included poetry and music and art as part of that response to nature,' she said. 'It's a fallible but human way of resonating to the universe – nature creates that energy of creation in us. For Father imagination and truth were the same thing. He once wrote, "the Imagination may be compared to Adam's dream – he awoke and found it truth."'

'I'm not quite sure I get that,' I said. 'Does that mean that fiction is truer than . . . truth?'

Aenea shook her head. 'No, I think he meant . . . well, in the same poem he has a hymn to Pan—

'Dread opener of the mysterious doors
Leading to universal knowledge.'

Aenea blew on her cup of hot tea to cool it. 'To Father, Pan became a sort of symbol of imagination . . . especially romantic imagination.' She sipped her tea. 'Did you know, Raul, that Pan was the allegorical precursor to Christ?'

I blinked. This was the same child who had been asking for ghost stories two nights ago. 'Christ?' I said. I was enough a product of my time to flinch at any hint of blasphemy.

Aenea drank her tea and looked at the moons. Her left arm was wrapped around her raised knees as she sat. 'Father thought that some people – not all – were moved by their response to nature to be stirred by that elemental, Pan-like imagination.

> 'Be still the unimaginable lodge
> For solitary thinkings; such as dodge
> Conception to the very bourne of heaven,
> Then leave the naked brain: be still the leaven
> That spreading in this dull and clodded earth
> Gives it a touch ethereal – a new birth;
> Be still a symbol of immensity;
> A firmament rejected in a sea;
> An element filling the space between;
> An unknown . . .'

We were all silent a moment after this recitation. I had grown up listening to poetry – shepherds' rough epics, the old poet's *Cantos*, the *Garden Epic*, of young Tycho and Glee and the centaur Raul – so I was used to rhymes under starry skies. Most of the poems I had heard and learned and loved were simpler to understand than this, however.

After a moment broken only by the lapping of waves against the raft and the wind against our tent, I said, 'So this was your father's idea of happiness?'

Aenea tossed her head back so that her hair moved in the wind. 'Oh, no,' she said. 'Just the first stage of happiness on his Pleasure Thermometer. There were two higher stages.'

'What were they?' said A. Bettik. The android's soft voice almost made me jump; I had forgotten he was on the raft with us.

Aenea closed her eyes and spoke again, her voice soft, musical, and free from the singsong cant of those who ruin poetry.

> 'But there are
> Richer entanglements far
> More self-destroying, leading, by degrees,
> More self-destroying, leading, by degrees,
> Is made of love and friendship, and sits high
> Upon the forehead of humanity.'

I looked up at the dust storms and volcanic flashes on the giant moon. Sepia clouds moved across the orange-and-amber landscape up there. 'So those are his other levels?' I said, a bit disappointed. 'First nature, then love and friendship?'

'Not exactly,' said the girl. 'Father thought that true friendship between humans was on an even higher level than our response to nature, but that the highest level attainable was love.'

I nodded. 'Like the Church teaches,' I said. 'The love of Christ . . . the love of our fellow humans.'

'Uh-uh,' said Aenea, sipping the last of her tea. 'Father meant erotic love. Sex.' She closed her eyes again . . .

'Now I have tasted her sweet soul to the core
All other depths are shallow: essences,
Once spiritual, are like muddy lees,
Meant but to fertilize my earthly root,
And make my branches lift a golden fruit
Into the bloom of heaven.'

I admit that I did not know what to say to that. I shook the last of the coffee out of my cup, cleared my throat, studied the hurtling moons and still-visible Milky Way for a moment, and said, 'So? Do you think he was onto something?' As soon as I said it, I wanted to kick myself. This was a child I was talking to. She might spout old poetry, or old pornography for that matter, but there was no way she could understand it.

Aenea looked at me. The moonlight made her large eyes luminous. 'I think there are more levels on heaven and earth, Horatio, than are dreamt of in my father's philosophy.'

'I see,' I said, thinking, *Who the hell is Horatio?*

'My father was very young when he wrote that,' said Aenea. 'It was his first poem and it was a flop. What he wanted – what he wanted his shepherd hero to learn – was how exalted these things could be – poetry, nature, wisdom, the voices of friends, brave deeds, the glory of strange places, the charm of the opposite sex. But he stopped before he got to the real essence.'

'What real essence?' I asked. Our raft rose and fell on the sea's breathing.

'The meanings of all motions, shapes, and sounds,' whispered the girl. *'. . . all forms and substances/Straight homeward to their symbol-essences.'*

Why were those words so familiar? It took me a while to remember.

Our raft sailed on through the night and sea of Mare Infinitus.

We slept again before the suns rose, and after another breakfast I rose to sight in the weapons. Philosophical poetry by moonlight was all right, but guns that shot straight and true were a necessity.

I hadn't had time to test the firearms aboard ship or after our crash on the jungle world, and carrying around unfired, unsighted weapons made me nervous. In my short time in the Home Guard and longer years as a hunting guide, I'd long since discovered that familiarity with a weapon was easily as important as – and probably more important than – having a fancy rifle.

The largest of the moons was still in the sky as the suns rose – first the smaller of the binaries, a brilliant mote in the morning sky, palling the Milky Way to invisibility and dulling the details on the large moon, and then the primary, smaller than Hyperion's Sol-like sun, but very bright. The sky deepened to an ultramarine and then deepened further to a cobalt-blue, with the two stars blazing and the orange moon filling the sky behind us. Sunlight made the moon's atmosphere a hazy disk and banished the surface features from our sight. Meanwhile, the day grew warm, then hot, then blazing.

The sea came up a bit, easy swells turning into regular two-meter waves that jostled the raft some but were far enough apart to let us ride them without undue discomfort. As the guidebook had promised, the sea was a disturbing violet, serrated by wave-top crests of a blue so dark as to be almost black, and occasionally broken by yellowkelp beds or foam of an even darker violet. The raft continued toward the horizon where the moons and suns had risen – we thought of it as east – and we could only hope that the strong current was carrying us somewhere. When we doubted that the current was moving us at all, we trailed a line or tossed some bit of debris overboard and watched the difference between wind and current tug at it. The waves were moving from what we perceived as south to north. We continued east.

I fired the .45 first, checking the magazine to make sure that the slugs were securely in place. I was afraid that the archaic quality of having ammunition separate from the structure of the magazine itself would make me forgetful of reloading at an awkward time. We did not have much to toss overboard for target practice, but I kept a few used ration containers at my feet, tossed one, and waited until it had floated about fifteen meters away before firing.

The automatic made an indecent roar when it went off. I knew that slug-throwers were loud – I had fired some in basic training, since the Ice Claw rebels often used them – but this blast almost made me drop the pistol into the violet sea. It scared Aenea, who had been staring off to the south and musing over something, right to her feet, and even made the unflappable android jump.

'Sorry,' I said, and braced the heavy weapon with both hands and fired again.

After using two clips' worth of the precious ammunition, I was assured that I could hit something at fifteen meters. Beyond that – well, I hoped that whatever I was shooting at had ears and would be spooked by the noise the .45 made.

As I broke the weapon down after firing, I mentioned again that this ancient piece could have been Brawne Lamia's.

Aenea looked at it. 'As I said, I never saw Mother with a handgun.'

'She could have lent it to the Consul when he went back to the Web in the ship,' I said, cleaning the opened pistol.

'No,' said A. Bettik.

I turned to look at him as he leaned against the steering oar. 'No?' I said.

'I saw M. Lamia's weapon when she was on the *Benares*,' said the android. 'It was an antiquated pistol – her father's, I believe – but it had a pearl handle, a laser sight, and was adapted to hold flechette cartridges.'

'Oh,' I said. Well, the idea had been appealing. 'At least this thing's been well preserved and rebuilt,' I said. It must have been kept in some sort of stasis-box; a thousand-year-old handgun would not have worked otherwise. Or perhaps it was some sort of clever reproduction that the Consul had picked up on his travels. It did not matter, of course, but I had always been struck by the . . . sense of history, I guess you would call it . . . that old firearms seemed to emanate.

I fired the flechette pistol next. It took only one burst to see that it worked quite nicely, thank you. The floating ration pak was blown into a thousand flowfoam shards from thirty meters away. The entire wave top jumped and shimmered as if a steel rain were pelting it. Flechette weapons were messy, hard to miss with, and eminently unfair to the target, which is why I had chosen this. I set the safety on and put it back in my pack.

The plasma rifle was harder to sight in. The click-up optical sight allowed me to zero in on anything from the floating ration pak thirty meters away to the horizon twenty-five klicks or so away, but while I sank the ration pak in the first shot, it was hard to tell the effectiveness of the longer shots. There was nothing out there to shoot at. Theoretically, a pulse rifle could hit anything one could see – there was no allowance necessary for windage or ballistic arc – and I watched through the scope as the bolt kicked a hole in waves twenty klicks out, but it did not create the same confidence that firing at a distant target would have. I raised the rifle to the giant moon now setting behind us. Through the scope I could just make out a white-topped mountain there – probably frozen CO_2 rather than snow, I knew – and, just for the hell of it, squeezed off a round. The plasma rifle was essentially silent compared to the semiautomatic slug-thrower pistol: only the usual cat's-cough when it fired. The scope was not powerful enough to show a hit, and at those distances, rotation of the two worlds *would* be a problem, but I would be surprised if I had not hit the mountain. Home Guard barracks were full of stories of Swiss Guard riflemen who had knocked down Ouster commandos after firing from thousands of klicks away on a neighbouring asteroid or somesuch. The trick, as it had been for millennia, was *seeing* the enemy first.

Thinking of that after firing the shotgun once, cleaning it, and setting away all the weapons, I said, 'We need to do some scouting today.'

'Do you doubt that the other portal will be there?' asked Aenea.

I shrugged. 'The guide said five klicks between portals. We must have floated at least a hundred since last night. Probably more.'

'Are we going to take the hawking mat out?' asked the girl. The suns were burning her fair skin.

'I thought I'd use the flying belt,' I said. *Less radar profile if anyone's watching*, I thought but did not say aloud. 'And you're not going, kiddo,' I did say aloud. 'Just me.'

I pulled the belt from its place under the tent, cinched the harness tightly, pulled my plasma rifle out, and activated the hand controller. 'Well, shit,' I said. The belt did not even try to lift me. For a second I was sure that we were on a Hyperion-like world with lousy EM fields, but then I looked at the charge indicator. Red. Empty. Flat out. 'Shit,' I said again. I unbuckled the harness, and the three of us gathered around the useless thing as I checked the leads, the battery pak, and the flight unit.

'It was charged right before we left the ship,' I said. 'The same time we charged the hawking mat.'

A. Bettik tried running a diagnostic program, but with zero-power, even that would not run. 'Your comlog should have the same subprogram,' said the android.

'It does?' I said stupidly.

'May I?' said A. Bettik, gesturing toward the comlog. I removed the bracelet and handed it to him.

A. Bettik opened a tiny compartment I had not even noticed on the trinket, removed a bead-sized lead on a microfilament, and plugged into the belt. Lights blinked. 'The flying belt is broken,' announced the comlog in the ship's voice. 'The battery pak is depleted approximately twenty-seven hours prematurely. I believe it is a fault in the storage cells.'

'Great,' I said. 'Can it be fixed? Will it hold a charge if we find one?'

'Not this battery unit,' said the comlog. 'But there are three replacements in the ship's EVA locker.'

'Great,' I said again. I lifted the belt with its bulky battery and harness and tossed it over the side of the raft. It sank beneath the violet waves without a trace.

'All set here,' said Aenea. She was sitting cross-legged on the hawking mat, which was floating twenty centimeters above the raft. 'Want to look around with me?'

I did not argue, but sat behind her on the mat, folded my legs, and watched her tap the flight threads.

About five hundred meters up, gasping for air and leaning out over the edge of our little carpet, things seemed a lot scarier than they had on the raft. The violet sea was very big, very empty, and our raft only a speck below, a tiny black rectangle on the reticulated violet-and-black sea. From this altitude, the waves that had seemed so serious on the raft were invisible.

'I think I've found another level of that "fellowship with essence" response to nature that your father wrote about,' I said.

'What's that?' Aenea was shivering in the cold air of the jet stream. She had worn just the undershirt and vest she had been wearing on the raft.

'Scared shitless,' I said.

Aenea laughed. I have to say here that I loved Aenea's laugh then, and I warm at the thought of it now. It was a soft laugh, but full and unself-conscious and melodic to the extreme. I miss it.

'We should have let A. Bettik come up to scout instead of us,' I said.

'Why?'

'From what he said about his high-altitude scouting before,' I said, 'evidently he doesn't need to breathe air, and he's impervious to little things like depressurization.'

Aenea leaned back against me. 'He's not impervious to anything,' she said softly. 'They just designed his skin to be a little tougher than ours – it can act like a pressure suit for short periods, even in hard vacuum – and he can hold his breath a bit longer, that's all.'

I looked at her. 'Do you know a lot about androids?'

'No,' said Aenea, 'I just asked him.' She scooted forward a bit and laid her hands on the control threads. We flew 'east'.

I admit that I was terrified of the thought of losing contact with the raft, of flying around this ocean-planet until these flight threads lost their charge and we plummeted to the sea, probably to be eaten by a Lantern-Mouth Leviathan. I'd programmed my inertial compass with the raft as a starting point, so unless I dropped the compass – which was unlikely because I now kept it on a lanyard around my neck – we would find our way back, all right. But still I worried.

'Let's not go too far,' I said.

'All right.' Aenea was keeping the speed down, about sixty or seventy klicks, I guessed, and had swooped back down to where we could breathe more easily and the air was not so cold. Below us, the violet sea stayed empty in a great circle to the horizon.

'Your farcasters seem to be playing tricks on us,' I said.

'Why do you call them my farcasters, Raul?'

'Well, you're the one they . . . recognize.'

She did not answer.

'Seriously,' I said, 'do you think there's some rhyme or reason to the worlds they're sending us to?'

Aenea glanced over her shoulder at me. 'Yes,' she said, 'I do.'

I waited. The deflection fields were minimal at this speed, so the wind tossed the girl's hair back toward my face.

'Do you know much about the Web?' she asked. 'About farcasters?'

I shrugged, realized that she was not looking back at me now, and said aloud, 'They were run by the AIs of the TechnoCore. According to both the Church and your Uncle Martin's *Cantos*, the farcasters were some sort of plot by the AIs to use human brains – neurons – as a sort of giant DNA computer thingy. They were parasites on us each time a human transited the farcasters, right?'

'Right,' said Aenea.

'So every time we go through one of these portals, the AIs . . . wherever they are . . . are hanging on our brains like big, blood-filled ticks, right?' I said.

'Wrong,' said the girl. She swiveled toward me again.' Not all of the farcasters were built or put in place or maintained by the same elements of the Core,' she said. 'Does Uncle Martin's finished *Cantos* tell about the civil war in the Core that my father discovered?'

'Yeah,' I said. I closed my eyes in an effort to remember the actual stanzas of the oral tale I'd learned. It was my turn to recite: 'In the *Cantos*, it's some sort of AI persona that the Keats cybrid talks to in the Core megasphere of dataspace,' I say.

'Ummon,' says the girl. 'That was the AI's name. My mother traveled there once with Father, but it was my . . . my uncle, the second Keats cybrid, who had the final showdown with Ummon. Go on.'

'Why?' I said. 'You must know the thing better than I do.'

'No,' she said. 'Uncle Martin hadn't gone back to work on the *Cantos*, when I knew him . . . He said he didn't want to finish it. Tell me how he described what Ummon said about the civil war in the Core.'

I closed my eyes again.

'Two centuries we brooded thus
and then the groups went
their separate ways:
Stables wishing to preserve the symbiosis,
Volatiles wishing to end humankind,
Ultimates deferring all choice until the next
level of awareness is born.
Conflict raged then;
true war wages now.'

'That was two hundred and seventy-some standard years ago for you,' said Aenea. 'That was right before the Fall.'

'Yeah,' I said, opening my eyes and searching the sea for anything other than violet waves.

'Did Uncle Martin's poem explain the motivations of the Stables, Volatiles, and Ultimates?'

'More or less,' I said. 'It's hard to follow – the poem has Ummon and the other Core AIs speaking in Zen koans.'

Aenea nodded. 'That's about right.'

'According to the *Cantos*,' I said, 'the group of Core AIs known as the Stables wanted to keep being parasites on our human brains when we used the Web. The Volatiles wanted to wipe us out. And I guess the Ultimates didn't give much of a damn as long as they could keep working on the evolution of their own machine god . . . what'd they call it?'

'The UI,' said Aenea, slowing the carpet and swooping lower. 'The Ultimate Intelligence.'

'Yes,' I said. 'Pretty esoteric stuff. How does it relate to our going through these farcaster portals . . . if we ever find another portal?' At that moment I doubted that we would: the world was too big, the ocean too large. Even if the current was bearing our little raft in the right direction, the odds that we would float within that hundred-meter-or-so hoop of the next portal seemed too small to consider.

'Not all of the farcaster portals were built or maintained by the Stables to be . . . how did you put it? . . . like big ticks on our brains.'

'All right,' I said. 'Who else built the farcasters?'

'The River Tethys farcasters were designed by the Ultimates,' said Aenea. 'They were an . . . experiment, I guess you'd say . . . with the Void Which Binds. That's the Core phrase . . . did Martin use it in his *Cantos*?'

'Yeah,' I said. We were lower now, just a thousand or so meters above the waves, but there was no sight of the raft or anything else. 'Let's head back,' I said.

'All right.' We consulted the compass and set our course home . . . if a leaky raft can be called home.

'I never understood what the hell the Void Which Binds was supposed to be,' I said. 'Some sort of hyperspace stuff that the farcasters used and where the Core was hiding while it preyed on us. I got that part. I thought it was destroyed when Meina Gladstone ordered bombs dropped into the farcasters.'

'You can't destroy the Void Which Binds,' said Aenea, her voice remote, as if she were thinking about something else. 'How did Martin describe it?'

'Planck time and Planck length,' I said. 'I don't remember exactly – something about combining the three fundamental constants of physics – gravity, Planck's constant, and the speed of light. I remember it gave some tiny little units of length and time.'

'About 10^{35th} of a meter for the length,' said the girl, accelerating the carpet a bit. 'And 10^{43rd} second for time.'

'That doesn't tell me much,' I said. 'It's just fucking small and short . . . pardon the language.'

'You're absolved,' said the girl. We were gently gaining altitude. 'But it wasn't the time or length that was important, it was how they were woven into . . . the Void Which Binds. My father tried to explain it to me before I was born . . .'

I blinked at that phrase but continued listening.

'. . . you know about the planetary dataspheres.'

'Yes,' I said, and tapped the comlog. 'This trinket says that Mare Infinitus doesn't have one.'

'Right,' said Aenea. 'But most of the Web worlds used to. And from the dataspheres, there was the megasphere.'

'The farcaster medium . . . the Void thing . . . linked dataspheres, right?' I said. 'FORCE and the Hegemony electronic government, the All Thing, they used the megasphere as well as the fatline to stay connected.'

'Yep,' said Aenea. 'The megasphere actually existed on a subplane of the fatline.'

'I didn't know that,' I said. The FTL medium had not existed in my lifetime.

'Do you remember what the last message on the fatline was before it went down during the Fall?' asked the child.

'Yes,' I said, closing my eyes. The lines of the poem did not come to me this time. The ending of the *Cantos* had always been too vague to interest me enough to memorize all those stanzas, despite Grandam's drilling. 'Some cryptic message from the Core,' I said. 'Something about – get off the line and quit tying it up.'

'The message,' said Aenea, 'was THERE WILL BE NO FURTHER MISUSE OF THIS CHANNEL. YOU ARE DISTURBING OTHERS WHO ARE USING IT TO SERIOUS PURPOSE. ACCESS WILL BE RESTORED WHEN YOU UNDERSTAND WHAT IT IS FOR.'

'Right,' I said. 'That's in the *Cantos*, I think. And then the hyperstring medium just quit working. The Core sent that message and shut down the fatline.'

'The Core did not send that message,' said Aenea.

I remember the slow chill that spread through me then, despite the heat of the two suns. 'It didn't?' I said stupidly. 'Who did?'

'Good question,' said the child. 'When my father talked about the meta-sphere – the wider datumplane that was somehow connected to or by the Void Which Binds – he always used to say it was filled with lions and tigers and bears.'

'Lions and tigers and bears,' I repeated. Those were Old Earth animals. I don't think that any of them made the Hegira. I don't think any of them were still around to make the trip – not even their stored DNA – when Old Earth crumbled into its black hole after the Big Mistake of '08.

'Hmm-hmm,' said Aenea. 'I'd like to meet them someday. There we are.'

I looked over her shoulder. We were about a thousand meters above the sea now, and the raft looked tiny but clearly visible. A. Bettik was standing – shirtless once again in the midday heat – at the steering oar. He waved a bare blue arm. We both waved back.

'I hope there's something good for lunch,' said Aenea.

'If not,' I said, 'we'll just have to stop at Gus's Oceanic Aquarium and Grill.'

Aenea laughed and set up our glide path to home.

It was just after dark and the moons had not risen when we saw the lights blinking on the eastern horizon. We rushed to the front of the raft and tried to make out what was out there – Aenea using the binoculars, A. Bettik the night goggles on full amplification, and me with the rifle's scope.

'It's not the arch,' said Aenea. 'It's a platform in the ocean – big – on stilts of some sort.'

'I do see the arch, however,' said the android, who was looking several degrees north of the blinking light. The girl and I looked in that direction.

The arch was just visible, a chord of negative space cutting into the Milky Way just above the horizon. The platform, with its blinking navigation beacons for aircraft and lamplit windows just becoming visible, was several klicks closer. And between us and the farcaster.

'Damn,' I said. 'I wonder what it is?'

'Gus's?' said Aenea.

I sighed. 'Well, if it is, I think it's under new ownership. There's been a dearth of River Tethys tourists the last couple of centuries.' I studied the large platform through the rifle scope. 'It has a lot of levels,' I muttered. 'There are several ships tied up . . . fishing boats is my bet. And a pad for skimmers and other aircraft. I think I see a couple of thopters tied down there.'

'What's a thopter?' asked the girl, lowering the binoculars.

A. Bettik answered. 'A form of aircraft utilizing movable wings, much like an insect, M. Aenea. They were quite popular during the Hegemony, although unseen on Hyperion. I believe they were also called dragon-flies.'

'They're still called that,' I said. 'The Pax had a few on Hyperion. I saw one down on the Ursus iceshelf.' Raising the scope again, I could see the eye-like blisters on the front of the dragonfly, illuminated by a lighted window. 'They're thopters,' I said.

'It seems that we will have some trouble passing that platform to get to the arch undetected,' said A. Bettik.

'Quick,' I said, turning away from the blinking lights, 'let's get the tent and mast down.'

We had rerigged the tent to provide a sort of shelter/wall on the starboard side of the raft near the back – for purposes of privacy and sanitation that I won't go into here – but now we tumbled the microfiber down and folded it away into a packet the size of my palm. A. Bettik lowered the pole at the front. 'The steering oar?' he said.

I looked at it a second. 'Leave it. It doesn't have much of a radar cross section, and it's no higher than we are.'

Aenea was studying the platform again through the binoculars. 'I don't think they can see us now,' she said. 'We're between these swells most of the time. But when we get closer . . .'

'And when the moons rise,' I added.

A. Bettik sat near the hearth. 'If we could just go around in a large arc to get to the portal . . .'

I scratched my cheek, hearing the stubble there. 'Yeah. I thought of using the flying belt to tow us, but . . .'

'We have the mat,' said the girl, joining us near the heating cube. The low platform seemed empty without the tent above it.

'How do we connect a tow line?' I said. 'Burn a hole in the hawking mat?'

'If we had a harness . . .' began the android.

'We *had* a nice harness on the flying belt,' I said. 'I fed it to the Lantern-Mouth Leviathan.'

'We could rig another harness,' continued A. Bettik, 'and run the line to the person *on* the hawking mat.'

'Sure,' I said, 'but as soon as we're airborne, the mat offers a stronger radar return. If they land skimmers and thopters there, they almost certainly have some sort of traffic control, no matter how primitive.'

'We could stay low,' said Aenea. 'Keep the mat just above the waves . . . no higher than we are.'

I scratched at my chin. 'We can do that,' I said, 'but if we make a big enough detour to stay out of the platform's sight, it'll be long after moon-rise before we get to the portal. Hell . . . it will be if we head straight for it on this current. They're bound to see us in that light. Besides, the portal's only a klick or so from the platform. They're high enough that they'd see us as soon as we get that close.'

'We don't know that they're looking for us,' said the girl.

I nodded. The image of that priest-captain who had been waiting for us in Parvati System and Renaissance never left my mind for long: his Roman collar on that black Pax Fleet uniform. Part of me expected him to be on that platform, waiting with Pax troops.

'It doesn't matter too much if they're looking for us,' I said. 'Even if they just come out to rescue us, do we have a cover story that makes sense?'

Aenea smiled. 'We went out for a moonlit cruise and got lost? You're right, Raul. They'd "rescue" us and we'd spend the next year trying to explain who we are to the Pax authorities. They may not be looking for us, but you say they're on this world . . .'

'Yes,' said A. Bettik. 'The Pax has extensive interests on Mare Infinitus. From what we gleaned while hiding in the university city, it was clear that the Pax stepped in long ago to restore order here, to create sea-farming conglomerates, and to convert the survivors of the Fall to born-again Christianity. Mare Infinitus had been a protectorate of the Hegemony; now it is a wholly owned subsidiary of the Church.'

'Bad news,' said Aenea. She looked from the android to me. 'Any ideas?'

'I think so,' I said, rising. We had been whispering all during the conversation, even though we were still at least fifteen klicks from the platform. 'Instead of guessing about who's out there or what they're up to, why don't I go take a look? Maybe it's just Gus's descendants and a few sleeping fishermen.'

Aenea made a rueful sound. 'When we first saw the light, do you know what I thought it might be?'

'What?' I said.

'Uncle Martin's toilet.'

'I beg your pardon?' said the android.

Aenea tapped her knees with her palms. 'Really. Mother said that back when Martin Silenus was a big-name hack writer during the Web days, he had a multiworld house.'

I frowned. 'Grandam told me about those. Farcasters instead of doors between the rooms. One house with rooms on more than one world.'

'Dozens of worlds for Uncle Martin's house, if Mother was to be believed,' said Aenea. 'And he had a bathroom on Mare Infinitus. Nothing else . . . just a floating dock with a toilet. Not even any walls or ceiling.'

I looked out at the ocean swells. 'So much for oneness with nature,' I said. I slapped my leg. 'All right, I'm going before I lose my nerve.'

No one argued with me or offered to take my place. I might have been persuaded if they had.

I changed into darker trousers and my darkest sweater, pulling my drab hunting vest over the sweater, feeling a little melodramatic as I did so. *Commando Boy goes to war*, muttered the cynical part of my brain. I told it to shut up. I kept on the belt with the pistol, added three detonators and a wad of plastic explosive from the flare pak to my belt pouch, slipped the night goggles over my head so they could hang unobtrusively within my vest collar when I wasn't wearing them, and set one of the com-unit hearphones in my ear with the pickup mike pressed to my throat for subvocals. We tested the unit, Aenea wearing the other headset. I took the comlog off and handed it to A. Bettik. 'This thing catches the starlight too easily,' I said. 'And the ship's voice might start squawking stellar navigation trivia at a bad time.'

The android nodded and set the bracelet in his shirt pocket. 'Do you have a plan, M. Endymion?'

'I'll make one up when I get there,' I said, raising the hawking mat just above the level of the raft. I touched Aenea's shoulder – the contact suddenly feeling like an electric jolt. I had noticed that effect before when our hands touched: not a sexual thing, of course, but electrical nonetheless. 'You stay low, kiddo,' I whispered to her. 'I'll holler if I need help.'

Her eyes were serious in the brilliant starlight. 'It won't help, Raul. We can't get to you.'

'I know, I was just kidding.'

'Don't kid,' she whispered. 'Remember, if you're not with me on the raft when it goes through the portal, you'll be left behind here.'

I nodded, but the thought sobered me more than the thought of getting shot had. 'I'll be back,' I whispered. 'It looks to me like this current will take us by the platform in . . . what do you think, A. Bettik?'

'About an hour, M. Endymion.'

'Yeah, that's what I think, too. The damn moon should be coming up about then. I'll . . . think of something to distract them.' Patting Aenea's shoulder again, nodding to A. Bettik, I took the mat out over the water.

Even with the incredible starlight and the night-vision goggles, it was difficult piloting the hawking mat for those few klicks to the platform. I had to keep between the ocean swells whenever possible, which meant that I was trying to fly *lower* than the wave tops. It was delicate work. I had no idea what would happen if I cut off the tops of one of those long, slow swells – perhaps nothing, perhaps the hawking mat's flight threads would short out – but I also had no intention of finding out.

The platform seemed huge as I approached. After seeing nothing but the raft for two days on this sea, the platform *was* huge – some steel but mostly dark wood, from the looks of it, a score of pylons holding it fifteen meters or so above the waves . . . that gave me an idea of what the storms must be like on this sea, and made me feel all the luckier that we hadn't encountered one – and the platform itself was multi-tiered: decks and docks lower down where at least five long fishing boats bobbed, stairways, lighted compartments beneath what looked like the main deck level, two towers that I could see – one of them with a small radar dish – and three aircraft landing pads, two of which had been invisible from the raft. There were at least half a dozen thopters that I could see now, their dragonfly wings tied down, and two larger skimmers on the circular pad near the radar tower.

I had figured out a perfect plan while flying the mat over here: create a diversion – the reason I had brought the detonators and *plastique*, small explosives but capable of starting a fire at least – steal one of the dragonflies, and either fly through the portal with it if we were being pursued, or just use it to drag the raft through at high speed.

It was a good plan except for one flaw: I had no idea how to fly a thopter. That never happened in the holodramas I'd watched in Port Romance theaters or in the Home Guard rec rooms. The heroes in those things could fly anything they could steal – skimmers, EMVs, thopters, copters, rigid airships, spaceships. Evidently I had missed Hero Basic Training; if I managed to get into one of those things, I'd probably still be chewing my thumbnail and staring at the controls when the Pax guards grabbed me. It must have been easier being a Hero back during Hegemony days – the machines were smarter then, which made up for hero stupidity. As it was – although I would hate to admit it to my traveling companions – there weren't many vehicles that I could drive. A barge. A basic groundcar, if it was one of the truck models the Hyperion Home Guard had used. As for piloting something myself . . . well, I had been glad when the spaceship hadn't had a control room.

I shook myself out of this reverie on my heroic shortcomings and concentrated on closing the last few hundred meters to the platform. I could see the lights quite clearly now: aircraft beacons on the towers near the landing decks, a flashing green light on each of the ship docks, and lighted windows. Lots of windows. I decided to try to land on the darkest part of the platform, directly under the radar tower on the east side, and took the mat around in a long, slow, wave-hugging arc to approach from that direction. Looking back over my shoulder, I half expected to see the raft closing on me, but it was still invisible out toward the horizon.

I hope it's invisible to these guys. I could hear voices and laughter now: men's voices, deep laughter. It sounded like a lot of the offworld hunters I'd guided, filled with booze and bonhomie. But it also sounded like the dolts I'd served with in the Guard. I concentrated on keeping the mat low and dry and sneaking up on the platform.

'I'm about there,' I subvocalized on the comlink.

'Okay,' was Aenea's whispered reply in my ear. We had agreed that she would only reply to my calls unless there were an emergency on their end.

Hovering, I saw a maze of beams, girders, subdecks, and catwalks under the main platform on this side. Unlike the well-lighted stairs on the north and west side, these were dark – inspection catwalks, maybe – and I chose the lowest and darkest of them to land the carpet on. I killed the flight threads, rolled the little rug up, and lashed it in place where two beams met, cutting the cord I'd brought with a sweep of my knife. Setting the blade back in its sheath and tugging my vest over it, I had the sudden image of having to stab someone with that knife. The thought made me shudder. Except for the accident when M. Herrig attacked me, I had never killed anyone in hand-to-hand combat. I prayed to God that I would never have to again.

The stairs made noises under my soft boots, but I hoped that the occasional squeak wouldn't be heard over the sound of the waves against the pylons and the laughter from above. I crept up two flights of stairs, found a ladder, and followed it up to a trapdoor. It was not locked. I slowly raised it, half expecting to tumble an armed guard on his ass.

Raising my head slowly, I saw that this was part of the flight deck on the seaward side of the tower. Ten meters above, I could see the turning radar antenna slicing darkness out of the brilliant Milky Way with each revolution.

I pulled myself to the deck, defeated the urge to tiptoe, and walked to the corner of the tower. Two huge skimmers were tied down to the flight deck here, but they looked dark and empty. On the lower flight decks I could see starlight on the multiple insect-wings of the thopters. The light from our galaxy gleamed in their dark observation blisters. The flesh between my shoulder blades was crawling with the sense of being observed as I walked out on the upper deck, applied plastic explosive to the belly of the closest skimmer, set a detonator in place, which I could trigger with the appropriate frequency code from my com unit, went down the ladder to the closest thopter deck, and did the same there. I was sure that I was being observed from one of the lighted windows or ports on this side, but no outcry went up. As casually as I could, I went soundlessly up the catwalk from the lower thopter deck and peered around the corner of the tower.

Another stairway led down from the tower module to one of the main levels. The windows were very bright there and covered only with screens now, their storm shields up. I could hear more laughter, some singing, and the sound of pots and pans.

Taking a breath, I moved down the stairs and across the catwalk, following another catwalk to keep me away from the doorway. Ducking under lighted windows, I tried to catch my breath and slow my pounding heart. If someone came out of that first doorway now, they would be between me and the way back to the hawking mat. I touched the grip of the .45 under my vest and the flap of the holster and tried to think brave thoughts. Mostly I was thinking about wanting to be back on the raft. I had planted the diversion explosives . . . what else did I want? I realized that I was more than curious: if these were not Pax troops, I did not want to set off the *plastique*. The rebels I had signed up to fight on the Ice Claw Shelf had used bombs as their weapon of choice – bombs in the villages, bombs in Home Guard barracks, masses of explosives in snowmobiles and small ships targeted against civilians as well as Guard troops – and I had always considered this cowardly and detestable. Bombs were totally nondiscriminating weapons, killing the innocent as surely as the enemy soldier. It was silly to moralize this way, I knew, but even though I hoped that the small charges would do no more than set empty aircraft ablaze here, I was not going to detonate those charges unless I absolutely had to. These men – and women, probably, and perhaps children – had done nothing to us.

Slowly, excruciatingly slowly, absurdly slowly, I raised my head and peered in the closest window. One glimpse and I ducked down out of sight. The pots and pans noises were coming from a well-lighted kitchen area – galley, I corrected myself, since this was a ship, sort of. At any rate, there had been half-a-dozen people there, all men, all of military age but not in uniform except for undershirts and aprons, cleaning, stacking, and washing dishes. Obviously I'd come too late for dinner.

Staying next to the wall, I duck-walked the length of this catwalk, slid down another stairway, and stopped at a longer bank of windows. Here, in the shadows of a corner where two modules came together, I could see in some of the windows along this west-facing wall without lifting my face to one. It was a mess hall – or a dining room of some sort. About thirty men – all men! – were sitting over cups of coffee. Some were smoking recom-cigarettes. At least one man appeared to be drinking whiskey: or at least amber fluid from a bottle. I would not have minded some of whatever it was.

Many of the men were in khaki, but I couldn't tell if this was some sort of local uniform, or just the traditional garb of sports fishermen. I didn't see any Pax uniforms, which was definitely good. Perhaps this was just a fishing platform now, a hotel for rich offworld jerks who didn't mind paying years of time-debt – or having their friends and families back home pay it, actually – for the thrill of killing something big or exotic. Hell, I might know some of those guys: fishermen now, duck hunters when they visited Hyperion. I did not want to go in to find out.

Feeling more confident now, I moved down the long walkway, the light from the windows falling on me. There did not seem to be any guards. No sentries. Maybe we would not need a diversion – just sail the raft right past these guys, moonlight or no moonlight. They'd be sleeping, or drinking and laughing, and we'd just follow the current right into the farcaster portal that I could see less than two klicks to the northeast now, the faintest of dark arches against the starry sky. When we got to the portal, I would send a prearranged frequency shift that would not detonate the *plastique* I'd hidden but would disarm the detonators.

I was looking at the portal when I moved around the corner and literally bumped into a man leaning against the wall there. There were two others standing at the railing. One of them was holding night-vision binoculars and looking off to the north. Both of the men at the railing had weapons.

'Hey!' yelled the man I'd bumped into.

'Sorry,' I said. I definitely had never seen this scene in a holodrama.

The two men at the railing were carrying flechette miniguns on slings and were resting their forearms on them with that casual arrogance that military types had practiced for countless centuries. Now one of these two shifted the gun so that its barrel was aimed in my direction. The man I bumped into had been in the process of lighting a cigarette. Now he shook out the match flame, removed the lighted cigarette from his mouth, and glared at me.

'What are you doing out here?' he demanded. The man was younger than I – perhaps early twenties, standard – and I could see now that he was wearing a variation on the Pax Groundforces uniform with the lieutenant's bar I'd learned to salute on Hyperion. His dialect was pronounced, but I couldn't place it.

'Getting some air,' I said lamely. Part of me was thinking that a real Hero would have had his pistol out, blazing away. The smarter part of me did not even consider it.

The other Pax trooper also shifted the sling of his flechette auto. I heard the click of a safety. 'You are with the Klingman group?' he asked in the same thick dialect. 'Or the Otters?' I heard *Oor dey autors?* I didn't know if he was saying 'others' or 'otters' or, perhaps, 'authors'. Maybe this was a seaborne concentration camp for bad writers. Maybe I was trying too hard to be mentally flippant when my heart was pounding so fiercely that I was afraid I was going to have a heart attack right in front of these two.

'Klingman,' I said, trying to be as terse as possible. Whatever dialect I should have, I was sure I did not.

The Pax lieutenant jerked a thumb toward the doorway beyond him. 'You know the rules. Curfew after dark.' *Yewe knaw dey rues. Cufue affa dok.*

I nodded, trying to look contrite. My overvest was hanging down over the top of the holster on my hip. Perhaps they hadn't seen the pistol.

'Come,' said the lieutenant, jerking his thumb again but turning to lead the way. *Comb!* The two enlisted types still had their hands on the flechette guns. At that distance, if they fired, there wouldn't be enough of me left intact to bury in a boot.

I followed the lieutenant down the catwalk, through the door, and into the brightest and most crowded room I had ever entered.

THIRTY-TWO

They grow weary of death. After eight star systems in sixty-three days, eight terrible deaths and eight painful resurrections for each of the four men, Father Captain de Soya, Sergeant Gregorius, Corporal Kee, and Lancer Rettig are weary of death and rebirth.

Each time now upon his resurrection, de Soya stands naked in front of a mirror, seeing his skin raw and glistening like someone who has been flayed alive, gingerly touching the now-livid, now-crimson cruciform under the flesh of his chest. In the days following each resurrection, de Soya is distracted, his hands shaking a bit more each time. Voices come to him from afar, he cannot seem to concentrate totally, whether his interlocutor is a Pax admiral or a planetary governor or a parish priest.

De Soya begins dressing like a parish priest, trading his trim Pax priest-captain uniform for the cassock and collar. He has a rosary on his belt-thong and says it almost constantly, working it like Arabic worry beads: prayer calms him, brings his thoughts to order. Father Captain de Soya no longer dreams of Aenea as his daughter; he no longer dreams of Renaissance Vector and his sister Maria. He dreams of Armageddon – terrible dreams of burning orbital forests, of worlds aflame, of deathbeams walking over fertile farming valleys and leaving only corpses.

He knows after their first River Tethys world that he has miscalculated. Two standard years to cover two hundred worlds, he had said in Renaissance System, figuring three days resurrection in each system, a warning, and then translation to the next. It does not work that way.

His first world is Tau Ceti Center, former administrative capital of the far-flung Hegemony WorldWeb. Home to tens of billions during the days of the Web, surrounded by an actual ring of orbital cities and habitats, served by space elevators, farcasters, the River Tethys, the Grand Concourse, the fatline, and more – center to the Hegemonic datumplane megasphere and home of Government House, site of Meina Gladstone's death by infuriated mobs after the destruction of the Web farcasters by FORCE ships on her command, TC^2 was hard hit by the Fall. Floating buildings crashed as the power grid went down. Other urban spires, some many hundreds of stories tall, were served only by farcasters and lacked stairs or elevators. Tens of thousands starved or perished from falls before they could be lifted out by skimmer. The world had no agriculture of its own, bringing in its food from a thousand worlds via planet-based farcasters and great orbital spaceborne portals. The Starvation Riots lasted fifty local years on TC^2, over thirty standard, and when they were finished, billions had died from human hands, to add to the total of billions dead from hunger.

Tau Ceti Center had been a sophisticated, wanton world during the days of the Web. Few religions had taken hold there except the most self-indulgent or violent ones – the Church of the Final Atonement, the Shrike Cult, had been popular among the bored sophisticates. But during the centuries of Hegemony expansion, the only true object of worship on TC^2 had been power: the pursuit of power, the proximity to power, the preservation of power. Power had been the god of billions, and when that god failed – and pulled down billions of its worshipers in its failure – the survivors cursed the memories of power amid their urban ruins, scratching out a peasant's living in the shadows of the rotting skyscrapers, pulling their own plows through weeded lots between the abandoned highways and flyways and the skeletons of old Grand Concourse malls, fishing for carp where the River Tethys had carried thousands of elaborate yachts and pleasure-barges each day.

Tau Ceti Center had been ripe for born-again Christianity, for the New Catholicism, and when the Church missionaries and Pax police had arrived sixty standard years after the Fall, conversion of the planet's few billion survivors was sincere and universal. The tall, ruined, but still-white spires of business and government during the Web were finally torn down, their stone and smart glass and plasteel recycled into massive cathedrals, raised by the hands of the new Tau Ceti born-again, filled each day of the week by the thankful and faithful.

The archbishop of Tau Ceti became one of the most important and – yes – powerful humans in the reemerging human domain now known as Pax Space, rivaling His Holiness on Pacem in influence. This power grew, found boundaries that could not be overstepped without incurring papal wrath – the excommunication of His Excellency Klaus Cardinal Kronenberg in the Year of Our Lord 2978, or 126 After the Fall, helped settle those boundaries – and it continued to grow within those bounds.

So Father Captain de Soya discovers on his first jump from Renaissance space. Two years, he had anticipated, approximately six hundred days and two hundred self-imposed deaths to cover all of the former River Tethys worlds.

He and his Swiss Guard troopers are on Tau Ceti Center for eight days. The *Raphael* enters the system with its automatic beacon pulsing in code. Pax ships respond and rendezvous within fourteen hours. It takes another eight hours to decelerate into TC^2 orbital traffic, and another four to transfer the bodies to a formal resurrection creche in the planetary capital of St Paul. One full day is thus lost.

After three days of formal resurrection and another day of enforced rest, de Soya meets with the Archbishop of TC^2, Her Excellency Achilla Silvaski, and must endure another full day of formalities. De Soya carries the papal diskey, an almost unheard-of delegation of power, and the court of the Archbishop must sniff out the reason and projected results of that power like hunting dogs on a scent. Within hours de Soya gets the slightest hint of the layers of intrigue and complexity within this struggle for provincial power: Archbishop Silvaski can not aspire to become Cardinal, for after the Kronenberg excommunication, no spiritual leader of TC^2 can rise to a rank higher than Archbishop without transfer to Pacem and the Vatican, but her current power in this sector of the Pax far outweighs that of most cardinals and the temporal subset of that power puts Pax Fleet admirals in their place. She must understand this delegation of papal authority that de Soya carries, and render it harmless to her ends.

Father Captain de Soya does not give a damn about Archbishop Silvaski's paranoia or the Church politics on TC^2. He cares only about stopping up the escape route of the farcaster portals there. On the fifth day since his translation to Tau Ceti space, he makes the five hundred meters from St Paul's Cathedral and the Archbishop's palace to the river – just part of a minor tributary channeled into a canal flowing through the city, but once part of the Tethys.

The huge farcaster portals, still extant because any attempt to dismantle them had promised a thermonuclear explosion according to engineers, have long since been draped over by Church banners, but they are close together here – the Tethys had meandered only two kilometers from portal to portal, past the busy Government House and the formal Deer Park gardens. Now Father Captain de Soya, his three troopers, and the scores of watchful Pax troops loyal to Archbishop Silvaski who accompany them, can stand at the first portal and look down the grassy banks at a thirty-meter-long tapestry – showing the martyrdom of St Paul – hanging from the second portal clearly visible beyond the blooming peach trees of the bishopric palace gardens.

Because this section of the former Tethys is now within Her Excellency's private gardens, guards are posted along the length of the canal and on all bridges crossing it. While there is no special attention to the ancient artifacts that were once farcaster portals, the officers of the palace guard assure de Soya that no vessels or unauthorized individuals have passed through those portals, nor been seen along the banks of the canal.

De Soya insists that a permanent guard be placed upon the portals. He wants cameras erected for twenty-nine-hour-a-day surveillance there. He wants sensors, alarms, and trip wires. The local Pax troops confer with their Archbishop and grudgingly comply with this perceived slight to their sovereignty. De Soya all but despairs at this useless politics.

On their sixth day Corporal Kee falls ill to a mysterious fever and is hospitalized. De Soya believes it is a result of their resurrection: each of them has privately suffered the shakes, emotional swings, and minor ailments. On the seventh day Kee is able to walk and implores de Soya to get him out of the infirmary and off this world, but now the Archbishop insists that de Soya help celebrate a High Mass that evening in honor of His Holiness, Pope Julius. De Soya can hardly refuse, so that night – amid scepters and pink-buttoned *monsignore*, beneath the giant insignia of His Holiness's Triple Crown and Crossed Keys (which also appears on the papal diskey that de Soya now wears around his neck), amid the smoke of incense, white miters and the tinkle of bells, under the solemn singing of a six-hundred-member children's choir, the simple priest-warrior from Madrede-Dios and the elegant Archbishop celebrate the mystery of Christ's crucifixion and resurrection. Sergeant Gregorius takes Communion that evening from de Soya's hand – which he does every day of their quest – as do a few dozen others also chosen to receive the Host, secret to the success of their cruciform immortality in this life, while three thousand of the faithful pray and watch in the dim cathedral light.

On the eighth day they leave the system, and for the first time Father Captain de Soya welcomes the coming death as a means of escape.

They are resurrected in a creche on Heaven's Gate, a once-miserable world terraformed to shade trees and comfort in the days of the Web, now largely fallen back to boiling mud, pestilent swamps, unbreathable atmosphere, and the blazing radiation source of Vega Prime in the sky. *Raphael*'s idiot computer has chosen this series of old River Tethys worlds, finding the most efficient order to visit them in since there were no clues on Renaissance V. to show where the portal there might have led, but de Soya is interested that they are coming closer and closer to Old Earth System – less than twelve light-years from TC^2, just a little more than eight from Heaven's Gate. De Soya realizes that he would like to visit Old Earth System – even without Old Earth – despite the fact that Mars and the other inhabited worlds, moons, and asteroids there have become provincial backwaters, of no more interest to the Pax than MadredeDios had been.

But the Tethys never flowed through Old Earth System, so de Soya must swallow his curiosity and be satisfied that the next few worlds will be even close to Old Earth's former home.

Heaven's Gate takes eight days as well, but not because of intra-Church politics. There is a small Pax garrison in orbit around the planet, but they rarely go down to the ruined world. Heaven's Gate's population of four hundred million residents had been reduced to eight or ten crazy prospectors wandering its mudflat surface in the two hundred and seventy-four standard years since the Fall: the Ouster Swarms had swept by this Vegan world even before Gladstone had ordered the farcasters destroyed – destroying the orbital containment sphere, lancing the capital of Mudflat City with its lovely Promenade gardens, plasma-bombing the atmosphere-generating stations it had taken centuries to build – and generally plowing the world under before the loss of farcaster connections salted the earth so that nothing would grow there again.

So now the Pax garrison guards the broiling planet for its rumored raw materials, but has little reason to go down there. De Soya must convince the garrison commander – Pax Major Leem – that an expedition has to be mounted. On the fifth day after *Raphael*'s entry into Vega System, de Soya, Gregorius, Kee, Rettig, a Lieutenant Bristol, and a dozen Pax garrison troops fitted out in environmental hazard suits, take a dropship to the mud-flats where the River Tethys had once flowed. The farcaster portals are not there.

'I thought it was impossible to destroy them,' says de Soya. 'The Techno-

Core built them to last and booby-trapped them so that destruction is impossible.'

'They're not here,' says Lieutenant Bristol, and gives the order to return to orbit.

De Soya stops him. Using his papal diskey as authority, de Soya insists that a full-sensor search be made. The farcasters are found – sixteen klicks apart and buried under almost a hundred meters of mud.

'That solves your mystery,' says Major Leem on tightbeam. 'Either the Ouster attack or later mudslides buried the portals and what had been the river. This world has literally gone to hell.'

'Perhaps,' says de Soya, 'but I want the farcasters excavated, temporary environmental bubbles erected around them so that someone coming through would survive, and a permanent guard mounted at each portal.'

'Are you out of your goddamned mind!' Major Leem explodes, and then – remembering the papal diskey – he adds, 'Sir.'

'Not yet,' says de Soya, glowering into the camera. 'I want this done within seventy-two hours, Major, or you will be serving the next three standard years on the planetary detail down here.'

It takes seventy hours to excavate, construct the domes, and post the guard. Someone traveling the River Tethys will find no river here, of course, only the boiling mud, noxious unbreathable atmosphere, and wailing troopers in full battle armor. De Soya goes to his knees on the *Raphael* that last night in orbit around Heaven's Gate and prays that Aenea has not already come this way. Her bones were not found in the excavated mud and sulfur, but the Pax engineer in charge of the excavation tells de Soya that the soil is so toxic here in its natural form that the child's bones could already have been eaten away by acid.

De Soya does not believe this to be the case. On the ninth day he translates out of system with a warning to Major Leem to keep the guards vigilant, the domes livable, and his mouth more civil to future visitors.

No one waits to resurrect them in the third system *Raphael* brings them to. The archangel ship enters System NGC^{es} 2629 with its cargo of dead men and its beacons flashing Pax Fleet code. There is no response. There are eight planets in NGC^{es} 2629, but only one of them, known by the prosaic name of NGC^{es} 2629-4BIV, can support life. From the records still available to the *Raphael* it seems likely that the Hegemony and TechnoCore had gone to the effort and expense of extending the River Tethys here as a form of self-indulgence, an aesthetic statement. The planet has never been seriously colonized or terraformed except for random RNA seeding during the early days of the Hegira, and appears to have been part of the River Tethys tour strictly for scenic and animal-viewing purposes.

That is not to say that there are not human beings on the world now, as the *Raphael* sniffs them out in parking orbit during the last days of its passengers' automated resurrections. As best the limited resources of the *Raphael*'s near-AI computers can reconstruct and understand, NGC^{es} 2629-4BIV's minimum population of visiting biologists, zoologists, tourists, and support teams had been stranded after the Fall and had gone native. Despite prodigious breeding over almost three centuries, however, only a few thousand human beings still populated the jungles and highlands of the primitive world: the RNA-seeded beasties there were capable of eating human beings, and they did so with gusto.

Raphael runs to the edge of its limits in the simple task of finding the farcaster portals. Available Web records in its memory say simply that the portals are set at varying intervals along a six-thousand-kilometer river in the northern hemisphere. *Raphael* modifies its orbit to a roughly synchronous point above the massive continent which dominates that hemisphere and begins photographing and radar-mapping the river. Unfortunately, there are three massive rivers on that continent, two flowing to the east, one to the west, and *Raphael* is unable to prioritize probabilities. It decides to map all three – a task of analysing more than twenty thousand kilometers of data.

When the four men's hearts begin to beat at the end of the third day of the resurrection cycle, *Raphael* feels some silicon equivalent of relief.

Listening to the computer's description of the task ahead while he stands naked in front of the mirror in his tiny cubby, Federico de Soya feels no relief. In truth, he feels like weeping. He thinks of Mother Captain Stone, Mother Captain Boulez, and Captain Hearn, on the Great Wall frontier by now and quite possibly engaging the Ouster enemy in fierce combat. De Soya envies them the simplicity and honesty of their task.

After conferring with Sergeant Gregorius and his two men, de Soya reviews the data, immediately rejects the western-flowing river as too unscenic for the River Tethys, since it flows primarily through deep canyons, away from the life-infested jungles and marshes; the second river he rejects because of the obvious number of waterfalls and rapids – too rough for River Tethys traffic – and so he begins a simple, fast radar-mapping of the longest river with its long, gentle stretches. The map will show up dozens, perhaps hundreds, of natural obstacles resembling farcaster portals – rocky waterfalls, natural bridges, boulder fields in rapids – but these can be scanned by the human eye in a few hours.

On their fifth day the portals are located – improbably far apart, but inarguably artificial. De Soya personally flies the dropship, leaving Corporal Kee in the *Raphael* as backup in case of emergency.

This is the scenario de Soya has dreaded – no way to tell if the girl has come this way, with or without her ship. The stretch between the inert farcasters is the longest yet – almost two hundred kilometers – and although they fly the dropship back and forth over the jungle and river's edge, there is no telling if anyone has passed this way, no witness to interview, no Pax troops to leave on guard here.

They land on an island not far from the upper farcaster, and de Soya, Gregorius, and Rettig discuss their options.

'It's been three standard weeks since the ship passed through the farcaster on Renaissance V.,' says Gregorius. The interior of their dropship is cramped and utilitarian: they discuss things from their flight chairs. Gregorius's and Rettig's combat armor hang in the EVA closet like metal second skins.

'If they came through to a world like this,' says Rettig, 'they probably just took off in the ship. There's no reason they have to keep going down the river.'

'True,' says de Soya. 'But there is a good chance the ship was damaged.'

'Aye,' says the sergeant, 'but how badly? Could it have flown? Patched itself as it went? Perhaps made it to an Ouster repair base? We're not that far from the Outback here.'

'Or the girl could have sent the ship off and gone on through the next farcaster,' says Rettig.

'Assuming any of the other portals work,' says de Soya tiredly. 'That the one on Renaissance V. was not just a fluke.'

Gregorius sets his huge hands on his knees. 'Aye, sir, this is ridiculous. Finding a needle in a haystack, as they used to say . . . that would be child's play compared to this.'

Father Captain de Soya looks out through the dropship windows. The high ferns here are blowing in a silent wind. 'I have a feeling she's going down the old river. I think she'll use the farcasters. I don't know how – the flying machine that someone used to get her out of the Valley of the Time Tombs, maybe, an inflatable raft, a stolen boat – I just think she's using the Tethys.'

'What can we do here?' asks Rettig. 'If she's already come through, we've missed her. If she's not yet arrived . . . well, we could wait forever. If we had a hundred archangel ships so that we could bring troops to each of these worlds . . .'

De Soya nods. In his hours of prayer his mind often slips away to the thought of how much simpler this task would be if the archangel couriers were simple robotic craft, translating into Pax systems, broadcasting the papal-diskey authority and ordering the search, then jumping out of system without even decelerating. As far as he knows, the Pax is building no robot ships – the Church's hatred of AIs and dependence upon human contact all but forbids it. And as far as he knows, there are only three archangel-class courier ships in existence – the *Michael*, the *Gabriel* that had first brought him the message, and his own *Raphael*. In Renaissance System, he had wanted to send the other courier ship out in search, but the *Michael* had pressing Vatican duties. Intellectually, de Soya understood why this search was his and his alone. But here they have spent almost three weeks and searched two worlds. A robot archangel could leap into two hundred systems and broadcast the alert in less than ten standard days . . . at this rate, it will take de Soya and the *Raphael* four or five standard years. The exhausted father-captain has the urge to laugh.

'There's still her ship,' he says briskly. 'If they go on without it, they have two options – send the ship somewhere else, or leave it behind on one of the Tethys worlds.'

'You say "they", sir,' Gregorius says softly. 'Are you sure there are others?'

'Someone lifted her from our trap on Hyperion,' says de Soya. 'There are others.'

'It could be an entire Ouster crew,' says Rettig. 'They could be halfway back to their Swarm by now . . . after leaving the girl on any of these worlds. Or they could be taking her with them.'

De Soya lifts a hand to shut off conversation. They have been around and around this before. 'I think the ship was hit and damaged,' he says. 'We look for it and it may lead us to the girl.'

Gregorius points to the jungle. It is raining there. 'We've flown this entire stretch of river between the portals. No sign of a ship. When we get to the next Pax system, we can send back garrison troops to watch these portals.'

'Yes,' says Father Captain de Soya, 'but they'll have a time-debt of eight or nine months.' He looks at the rain streaking the windshield and side ports. 'We'll search the river.'

'What?' says Lancer Rettig.

'If you had a damaged ship and had to leave it behind, wouldn't you hide it?' asks de Soya.

The two Swiss Guard troopers stare at their commander. De Soya sees that the men's fingers are trembling. Resurrection is affecting them as well.

'We'll deep-radar the river and as much of the jungle as we can,' says the father-captain.

'It'll take another day, at least,' begins Rettig.

De Soya nods. 'We'll have Corporal Kee instruct *Raphael* to deep-radar the jungle on a two-hundred-klick swatch on either side of the river. We'll use the dropship to search the river . . . We have a cruder system on board, but less to cover.'

The exhausted troopers can only nod their obedience.

They find something on the second sweep of the river. The object is metal, large, and in a deep pool only a few kilometers downriver from the first portal. The dropship hovers while de Soya tightbeams the *Raphael*. 'Corporal, we're going to investigate. I want the ship ready to lance this thing within three seconds of my command . . . *but only on my command.*'

'I understand, sir,' tightbeams Kee.

De Soya holds the dropship in hover while Gregorius and Rettig suit up, prepare the proper tools, and stand in the open air lock. 'Go,' says de Soya.

Sergeant Gregorius drops out of the lock, the suit's EM system kicking in just before the armored man strikes water. Both sergeant and lancer swoop above the surface, weapons ready.

'We have the deep-radar lock on tactical,' Gregorius acknowledges on tightbeam.

'Your video feeds are nominal,' says de Soya from his command chair. 'Commence dive.'

Both men drop, strike the surface, and disappear beneath it. De Soya banks the dropship so he can see out the port blister: the river is a dark green, but two bright headlamps can be seen gleaming through the water. 'About eight meters beneath the surface,' he begins.

'Got it,' says the sergeant.

De Soya looks up at the monitor. He sees swirling silt, a many-gilled fish hurrying out of the light, a curved metal hull.

'There's a hatch or air lock open,' reports Gregorius. 'Most of the thing's buried in the mud here, but I can see enough of the hull to say it's about the right size. Rettig will stay out here. I'm going in.'

De Soya has the urge to say 'Good luck', but keeps his silence. The men have been together long enough to know what is appropriate with each other. He trims the dropship, readying the crude plasma gun that is the tiny ship's only armament.

The video feed stops as soon as Gregorius enters the open hatch. A minute passes. Then two. Two minutes beyond that, and de Soya is all but squirming in the command chair. He half expects to see the spaceship leap out of the water, clawing for space in a desperate attempt to escape.

'Lancer?' he says.

'Yes, sir,' comes Rettig's voice.

'No word or video from the sergeant?'

'No, sir. I think the hull's blocking tightbeam. I'll wait another five minutes and . . . Hold it, sir. I see something.'

De Soya sees it too, the feed from the lancer's video murky in the thick water, but clear enough to show Sergeant Gregorius's armored helmet, shoulders, and arms rising from the open air-lock hatch. The sergeant's headlamp illuminates silt and riverweed, the light swinging to blind Rettig's camera for an instant.

'Father Captain de Soya,' comes Gregorius's bass rumble, only slightly out of breath, 'this ain't it, sir. I think it's one of those old go-anywhere yachts that rich folks had back in the Web days, sir. You know, sir, the kind that was submersible – could even fly a bit, I think.'

De Soya lets out his breath. 'What happened to it, Sergeant?'

The suited figure on the video gives a thumbs-up to Rettig, and the two men rise toward the surface. 'I think they scuttled it, sir,' says Gregorius. 'There are at least ten skeletons on board . . . maybe a dozen. Two of 'em are kids. As I say, sir, this thing was rigged to float on any ocean – go under it if they wanted – so there's no way all the hatches open by accident, sir.'

De Soya watches out the window as the two figures in combat armor break the surface of the river and hover five meters above it, water pouring from their suits.

'I think they must've been stranded here after the Fall, sir,' Gregorius is saying, 'and just decided to end it all there, sir. It's only a guess, Father Captain, but I have a hunch . . .'

'I have a hunch you're right, Sergeant,' says de Soya. 'Come on back.' He opens the dropship hatch as the suited figures fly toward it.

Before they arrive, while he is still alone, de Soya raises his hand and mouths a blessing of the river, the sunken craft, and those entombed there. The Church does not sanctify suicides, but the Church knows that little is certain in life or death. Or, at least, de Soya knows this, even if the Church does not.

*

They leave motion detectors sending beams across each of the portals – they will not catch the girl and her allies, but they will tell the troops de Soya will send back whether anyone has passed that way in the interim – and then they lift the dropship from NGC^{es} 2629-4BIV, tuck the stubby dropship into the ugly mass of *Raphael* above the gleaming limb of the cloud-swirled planet, and accelerate out of the world's gravity well so that they can translate to their next stop, Barnard's World.

This is as close as de Soya's pursuit itinerary will come to Old Earth System – a mere six light-years – and since this was one of the earliest interstellar colonies of the pre-Hegira era, the priest-captain likes to think that he will be getting a glimpse back in time of Old Earth itself. Upon resurrection in the Pax base some six AUs from Barnard's World, however, de Soya immediately notes the differences. Barnard's Star is a red dwarf, only about one-fifth the mass of Old Earth's G-type star, and less than 1/2500 the luminosity. Only the proximity of Barnard's World, 0.126 AU, and the centuries spent terraforming the planet have produced a world high on the adaptive Solmev Scale. But, as de Soya and his men discover upon being ferried to the planet by their Pax escort, the terraforming has been very successful indeed.

Barnard's World had suffered very much from the Ouster Swarm invasion preceding the Fall, and very little – relatively speaking – from the Fall itself. The world had been a pleasant contradiction in terms in Web days: overwhelmingly agricultural, growing mostly Old Earth imports such as corn, wheat, soybeans, and the like, but also profoundly intellectual – boasting hundreds of the finest small colleges in the Web. The combination of agricultural backwater – life on Barnard's World tended to imitate small-town life in North America, circa 1900 – and intellectual hot spot had brought some of the Hegemony's finest scholars, writers, and thinkers there.

After the Fall, Barnard's World relied more upon its agricultural heritage than its intellectual prowess. When the Pax arrived in force some five decades after the Fall, its brand of born-again Christianity and Pacem-based government was resisted for some years. Barnard's World had been self-sufficient and wished to remain that way. It was not formally accepted into the Pax until the Year of Our Lord 3061, some two hundred and twelve years after the Fall, and then only after bloody civil war between the Catholics and partisan bands loosely grouped under the name The Free Believers.

Now, as de Soya learns during his brief tour with Archbishop Herbert Stern, the many colleges lie empty or have been converted to seminaries for the young men and women of Barnard's World. The partisans have all but disappeared, although there is still some resistance in the wild forest-and-canyon areas along the river known as Turkey Run.

Turkey Run had been part of the River Tethys, and it is precisely there that de Soya and his men wish to go. On their fifth day in-system, they travel there with a protective guard of sixty Pax troopers and some of the Archbishop's own elite guard.

They meet no partisans. This bit of the Tethys runs through broad valleys, under high shale cliffs, through deciduous forests of Old Earth transplanted trees, and emerges into what has long since become tilled land – mostly cornfields sprinkled with the occasional white farmhouse and outbuildings. It does not look like a place of violence to de Soya, and he encounters none there.

The Pax skimmers search the forest well for any sign of the girl's ship, but they find none. The river of Turkey Run is too shallow to hide a ship – Major Andy Ford, the Pax officer in charge of their search, calls it 'the sweetest canoeing river this side of Sugar Creek' – and the section of River Tethys had been only a few klicks long here. Barnard's World has modern atmosphere and orbital traffic control, and no ship could have left the area without being tracked. Interviews with farmers in the Turkey Run area produce no talk of strangers. In the end, Pax military, the Archbishop's diocesan council, and local civil authorities pledge constant surveillance of the area, despite any threat of Free Believer harassment.

On their eighth day de Soya and his men take leave of scores of people who can only be referred to as newfound friends, rise to orbit, transfer to a Pax torchship, and are escorted back to the deep-orbit Barnard's Star garrison and their archangel ship. The last sight de Soya glimpses of the bucolic world is the twin spires of the giant cathedral rising in the capital of St Thomas, formerly known as Bussard City.

Swinging away from the direction of Old Earth System now, de Soya, Gregorius, Kee, and Rettig awaken in System Lacaille 9352, about as far from Old Earth as Tau Ceti had been to the early seedships. Here the delay is neither bureaucratic nor military, but environmental. The Web world here, known as Sibiatu's Bitterness then and renamed Inevitable Grace by its current population of a few thousand Pax colonists, had been environment-ally marginal then and is far below that now. The River Tethys had run under twelve kilometers of Perspex tunnel, holding in breathable air and pressure. Those runnels had fallen into decay more than two centuries ago, the water boiling away into the low pressure, the thin methane-ammonia atmosphere of the planet rushing in to fill the empty riverbanks and shattered Perspex tubes.

De Soya has no idea why the Web would have included this rock in its River Tethys. There is no Pax military garrison here, nor serious Church presence other than chaplains living with the highly religious colonists eking out a living with their boxite mines and sulfur pits, but de Soya and his men convince some of these colonists to take them to the former river.

'If she came this way, she died,' says Gregorius as he inspects the huge portals hanging over a straight line of ruined Perspex and dry riverbeds. The methane wind blows, and grains of ever-shifting dust try to find their way through the men's atmosphere suits.

'Not if she stayed in the ship,' says de Soya, turning ponderously in his suit to look up at the orange-yellow sky. 'The colonists wouldn't have noticed the ship leaving . . . it's too far from the colony.'

The grizzled man with them, a bent figure even in his worn and sand-blasted suit, grunts behind his visor. 'Zat bey true, Fadder. We-en denna gay outsed a star-gazen' too offen, bey true.'

De Soya and his men discuss the futility of ordering Pax troops to this sort of world to watch for the girl in the months and years to come.

'It's a fact that it'll be god-awful, miserable, ass-end-of-nowhere duty, sir,' says Gregorius. 'Pardon the language, Father.'

De Soya nods distractedly. They have left the last of the motion-sensor beacons there: five worlds explored out of two hundred, and he is running out of material. The thought of sending troops back here depresses him as well, but he can see little alternative. Besides the resurrection ache and emotional confusion coursing through him constantly now, there is growing depression and doubt. He feels like an ancient, blind cat sent to catch a mouse, but unable to watch and guard two hundred mouseholes simultaneously. Not for the first time does he wish he were in the Outback, fighting Ousters.

As if reading the father-captain's thoughts, Gregorius says, 'Sir, have ye really looked at the itinerary *Raphael*'s set for us?'

'Yes, Sergeant. Why?'

'Some o' the places we're headed ain't ours anymore, Captain. It's not till the later part of the trip . . . worlds way in the Outback . . . but the ship wants to take us to planets that've been overrun by the Ousters long ago, sir.'

De Soya nods tiredly. 'I know, Sergeant. I didn't specify battle areas or the Great Wall defensive zones when I told the ship's computer to plan the trip.'

'There's eighteen worlds that would be a bit dicey to visit,' says Gregorius with the hint of a grin. 'Seeing as how the Ousters own 'em now.'

De Soya nods again but says nothing.

It is Corporal Kee who says softly, 'If you want to go look there, sir, we'll be more than happy to go with you.'

The priest-captain looks up at the faces of the three men. He has taken their loyalty and presence too much for granted, he thinks. 'Thank you,' he says simply. 'We'll decide when we get to that part of the . . . tour.'

'Which may be about a hundred standard years from now at this rate,' says Rettig.

'It may indeed,' says de Soya. 'Let's strap in and get the hell out of here.'

They translate out of the system.

Still in the Old Neighborhood, hardly out of Old Earth's pre-Hegira back-yard, they jump to two heavily terraformed worlds spinning through their complicated choreography in the half-light-year space between Epsilon Eridani and Epsilon Indi.

The $Omicron_2Epsilon_3$ Eurasian Habitation Experiment had been a bold pre-Hegira Utopian effort to achieve against-all-odds terraforming and political perfection – primarily neo-Marxist – on hostile worlds while fleeing from hostile forces. It had failed miserably. The Hegemony had replaced the Utopians with FORCE space bases and automated refueling stations, but the press of Outback-bound seedships and then spinships passing through the Old Neighborhood region during the Hegira had led to successful terraforming of these two dark worlds spinning between the dim Epsilon Eridani sun and the dimmer Epsilon Indi star. Then the famous defeat of Glennon-Height's fleet there had sealed the twin-system's fame and military importance. The Pax has rebuilt the abandoned FORCE bases, regenerated the failing terraform systems.

De Soya's searching of these two river sections is dry and businesslike in a military way. Each of the Tethys segments is so deep in a military reservation area that it soon becomes obvious there is no chance that the girl – much less the ship – could have passed through in the past two months without being detected and run to ground. De Soya had surmised this from knowing about the Epsilon System – he has passed through there several times himself on his travels to the Great Wall and beyond – but had decided that he needed to see the portals for himself.

It is good that they encounter this garrison system at this time in their travels, however, for both Kee and Rettig are hospitalized. Engineers and Church resurrection specialists examine *Raphael* in dry dock and determine that there are minute but serious errors in the automated resurrection creche. Three standard days are spent in making repairs.

When they translate out of system this time, with only one more stop in the Old Neighborhood before moving into the post-Hegira reaches of the old Web, it is with the earnest hope that their health, depression, and emotional instability will be improved if they have to undergo automated resurrection again.

'Where are you headed now?' asks Father Dimitrius, the resurrection specialist who has helped them over the past days.

De Soya hesitates only a second before answering. It cannot compromise his mission if he tells the elderly priest this one fact.

'Mare Infinitus,' he says. 'It's a water world some three parsecs outward bound and two light-years above the plane of—'

'Ah, yes,' says the old priest. 'I had a mission there decades ago, weaning the indigenie fisherfolk from their paganism and bringing them into Christ's light.' The white-haired priest raises his hand in a benediction. 'Whatever you seek, Father Captain de Soya, it is my sincere prayer that you find it there.'

De Soya almost leaves Mare Infinitus before sheer chance brings him the clue he has been seeking.

It is their sixty-third day of seeking, only the second day since resurrection in their creches aboard the orbital Pax station, and the first of what should be the last three days on the planet.

A talkative young man named Lieutenant Baryn Alan Sproul is de Soya's liaison from Pax Seventy Ophiuchi A Fleet Command, and like tour guides throughout history, the youngster gives de Soya and his troopers more background than they want to hear. But he is a good thopter pilot, and on this ocean world in a flying machine that is relatively unfamiliar to him, de Soya is pleased to be passenger rather than pilot, and he relaxes some while Sproul takes them south, away from the extensive floating city of St Thérèse, and into the empty fishing areas where the farcasters still float.

'Why are the portals so far apart here?' asks Gregorius.

'Ah, well,' says Lieutenant Sproul, 'there's a story to that.'

De Soya catches his sergeant's eye. Gregorius almost never smiles unless combat is imminent, but de Soya has grown familiar with a certain glint in the big man's eye that is the sergeant's equivalent of riotous laughter.

'. . . so the Hegemony wanted to build its River Tethys portals out here in addition to the orbital sphere they had and all the little farcasters they set up everywhere . . . sort of a silly idea, isn't it, sir? Putting part of a river through the ocean here? . . . anyway, they wanted it out in the Midlittoral Current, which makes some sense because it's where the leviathans and some of the more interesting 'canths are, if the Web tourists wanted to see fish, that is . . . but the problem is, well, it's pretty obvious . . .'

De Soya looks over to where Corporal Kee is dozing in the warm sunlight coming through his thopter blister.

'It's pretty obvious that there's nothing permanent to build something big like those portals on . . . and you'll see 'em in a minute, sir, they're *big*. Well, I mean, there are the coral rings – but they're not secured to anything, they float, and the yellowkelp islands, but they're not . . . I mean, you put a foot on them, it goes right through, if you know what I mean, sir . . . There, to the starboard side, sir. That's yellowkelp. Don't get too much of it this far south. Anyway, what the old Hegemony engineers did is, they rigged the portals sort of like we've been doing with the platforms and cities for the last five hundred years, sir. That is, they run these foundation bases a couple of hundred fathoms – big, heavy things they've got to be, sir – and then run big, bladed drag anchors out on cables beneath that. But the bottom of the ocean here is sort of a problematic thing . . . usually ten thousand fathoms, at least . . . that's where the big granddaddies of our surface 'canths like Lantern-Mouth live, sir . . . monsters down that deep, sir . . . klicks long . . .'

'Lieutenant,' says de Soya, 'what does this have to do with why the portals are so far apart?' The high, almost ultrasonic hum of the thopter's dragonfly wings are threatening to put the priest-captain to sleep. Kee is now snoring, and Rettig has his feet up and his eyes closed. It has been a long flight.

Sproul grins. 'Getting to that, sir. You see, with those keelweights and twenty klicks of cable trailing to rock, our cities and platforms don't go very far, even in the Big Tide season, no, sir. But these portals . . . well, we have lots of submarine volcanic activity on Mare-Eye, sir. Whole different 'cology down there, believe me. Some of them tube worms'd give those gigacanths a battle, honestly, sir. Anyway, the old Webdays' engineers fixed those portals so that if their keelweights and cables sensed volcanic activity under them, they'd just . . . well, migrate, sir, is the best word I can think of.'

'So,' says de Soya, 'the distance between the River Tethys portals has widened because of volcanic activity on the ocean floor?'

'Yes, *sir*,' says Lieutenant Sproul with a wide grin that seems to suggest both pleasure and amazement that a Fleet officer can comprehend such a thing. 'And there's one of them now, sir,' says the liaison officer with a flourish, banking the thopter into a descending spiral. He brings the machine into a hover just a few meters above the ancient arch. Twenty meters below that, the violet sea churns and splashes against the rusted metal at the portal's base.

De Soya rubs his face. None of them can throw off the fatigue any longer. Perhaps if they had a few more days between resurrection and death.

'Can we see the other portal now, please?' he says.

'Yes, *sir*!' The thopter buzzes just meters above the waves as it covers the two hundred klicks to the next arch. De Soya does doze, and when he wakes to the lieutenant's gentle nudging, the second portal arch is visible against the sea. It is late afternoon, and the low sun throws a long shadow on the violet sea.

'Very good,' says de Soya. 'And the deep-radar searches are still being carried out?'

'Yes, sir,' says the young pilot. 'They're widening the search radius, but so far they haven't seen anything but some hellacious big Lantern-Mouths. That gets the sports-fishing guys worked up, I can tell you.'

'That's a major industry here, I take it, sir,' rumbles Gregorius from his place on the jump seat behind the pilot.

'Yes, Sergeant,' says Sproul, craning his long neck around to look at the bigger man. 'With kelp harvesting way down, it's our biggest offworld source of income.'

De Soya points to a platform only a few kilometers away. 'Another fishing and refueling platform?' The priest-captain has spent a day with the Pax commanders, going over reports from small outposts like this all over the world. None have reported any contact with a ship, or sight of a child. During this long flight south to the portals, they have passed dozens of similar platforms.

'Yes, sir,' says Sproul. 'Shall I hover for a while, or have you seen enough?'

De Soya looks at the portal – arching high above them now as the thopter hovers meters above the sea – and says, 'We can get back, Lieutenant. We have a formal dinner with Bishop Melandriano tonight.'

Sproul's eyebrows rise toward his crew cut. 'Yes, sir,' he says, bringing the thopter up and around in a final circle before heading back north.

'That platform looks as if it's been damaged recently,' says de Soya, leaning farther to his right to look down from the blister port.

'Yes, sir,' agrees the lieutenant. 'I have a friend who just rotated in from that plat . . . Station Three-twenty-six Mid-littoral, it's called sir . . . and he told me about it. They had a poacher try to blow the place up a few tides ago.'

'Sabotage?' says de Soya, watching the platform recede.

'Guerrilla war,' says the lieutenant. 'The poachers are the indigenies from back before the Pax got here, sir. That's why we've got troopers on each of the plats, and regular patrol ships during the height of the fishing season. We have to keep the fishing ships sort of herded there, sir, so the poachers don't attack them. You saw those boats tied up, sir . . . well, it's almost time for them to go fishing. Our Pax ships will escort them out. The Lantern-Mouth, well, sir, he rises up just when the moons are just so . . . you see the big one rising there, sir. So the legal fishing ships . . . they have these bright lights they shine when the moons are down, luring the big 'canths up. But the poachers do that too, sir.'

De Soya looks out at the empty expanse of ocean between the thopter and the northern horizon. 'Doesn't seem like too many places for rebels to hide,' he says.

'No, sir,' says the lieutenant. 'I mean, yes, sir. Actually, they've got fishing boats camouflaged to look like yellowkelp isles, submersibles, even one big submarine harvester that was rigged up like a Lantern-Mouth, believe it or not, sir.'

'And that platform was damaged by a poacher attack?' says de Soya, speaking to stay awake now. The drone of the thopter wings is deadly.

'Right, sir,' says Lieutenant Sproul. 'About eight Big Tides ago. One man . . . which is unusual, the poachers generally come in groups. He blew up some skimmers and thopters – common tactics, although they usually go for the boats.'

'Excuse me, Lieutenant,' says de Soya, 'you say this was eight Big Tides ago. Could you translate that into standard?'

Sproul chews his lip. 'Ah, yes, sir. Sorry, sir. I grew up on Mare-Eye, and . . . well, eight Big Tides is about two standard months ago, sir.'

'Was the poacher apprehended?'

'Yes, sir,' says Sproul with his youthful grin. 'Well, actually there's a story there, sir . . .' The lieutenant glances at the priest-captain to see if he should go on. 'Well, to make it short, sir, this poacher got apprehended first, then he blew his charges and tried to get away, and then he was shot and killed by the guards.'

De Soya nods and closes his eyes. In the last day he has reviewed over a hundred reports on 'poacher incidents' spread over the past two standard months. Blowing up platforms and killing poachers seems to be the second most popular sport – after fishing – on Mare Infinitus.

'The funny thing about this guy,' says the lieutenant, finishing his story, 'is how he tried to get away. Some sort of old flying carpet from the Hegemony days.'

De Soya snaps awake. He glances at the sergeant and his men. All three are sitting up, staring at him.

'Turn around,' snaps Father Captain de Soya. 'Take us back to that platform.'

'And then what happened?' says de Soya for the fifth time. He and his Swiss

Guard are in the platform director's office on the highest point of the platform, just beneath the radar dish. Outside the long window, three unbelievable moons are rising.

The director – a Pax captain in the Ocean Command named C. Dobbs Powl – is overweight, florid, and sweating heavily. 'When it became apparent that this man was not in either of the fishing groups we had on board that night, Lieutenant Belius took him aside for further questioning. Standard procedure, Father Captain.'

De Soya stares at the man. 'And then?'

The director licks his lips. 'And then the man managed to escape temporarily, Father Captain. There was a struggle on the upper walkway. He pushed Lieutenant Belius into the sea.'

'Was the lieutenant recovered?'

'No, Father Captain. He almost certainly drowned, although there was quite a bit of rainbow shark activity that night—'

'Describe the man you had in custody before you lost him,' interrupts de Soya, emphasizing the word 'lost'.

'Young, Father Captain, maybe twenty-five or so standard. And tall, sir. Real big young guy.'

'You saw him yourself?'

'Oh, yes, Father Captain. I was out on the walkway with Lieutenant Belius and Sea Lancer Ament when the fellow started the fight and pushed Belius through the railing.'

'And then got away from you and the lance private,' says de Soya flatly. 'With both of you armed and this man . . . Did you say he was handcuffed?'

'Yes, Father Captain.' Captain Powl mops his forehead with a moist handkerchief.

'Did you notice anything unusual about this young man? Anything else that did not make it into your . . . ah . . . extremely brief action report to Command Headquarters?'

The director puts the handkerchief away, then pulls it out again to mop his neck. 'No, Father Captain . . . I mean, well, during the struggle, the man's sweater was torn a bit in front. Enough for me to notice that he wasn't like you and me, Father Captain . . .'

De Soya raises an eyebrow.

'I mean he wasn't of the cross,' Powl hurries on. 'No cruciform 'Course, I didn't think much of that at the time. Most of these indigenie poachers've never been baptized. Wouldn't be poachers if they had, now, would they?'

De Soya ignores the question. Pacing closer to the seated, sweating captain, he says, 'So the man swung down under the main catwalk and escaped that way?'

'Didn't escape, sir,' says Powl. 'Just got to this flying dingus that he must've hidden there. I'd set off the alarm, of course. The whole garrison turned out, just like they was drilled to do.'

'But this man got the . . . dingus . . . flying? And off the platform?'

'Yes,' say the platform director, mopping his brow again and obviously thinking of his future or lack of it. 'But just for a minute. We saw him on radar and then we saw him with our night goggles. That . . . rug . . . could fly, all right, but when we opened up on it, it come swinging back around toward the platform—'

'How high was it then, Captain Powl?'

'High?' The director furrows his sweaty brow. 'I guess about twenty-five, thirty meters above the water then. About level with our main deck. He was comin' right at us, Father Captain. Like he was going to bomb the platform from a flyin' rug. Of course, in a way, he did . . . I mean the charges he'd planted went off right then. Scared the shit out of me . . . excuse me, Father.'

'Go on,' says de Soya. He looks at Gregorius where the big man is standing at parade rest behind the director. From the expression on the sergeant's face, he would be happy to garrot the sweating captain in a second.

'Well, it was quite an explosion, sir. Fire-control teams started running toward the blast, but Sea Lancer Ament and some of the other sentries and I stayed at our post there at the north catwalk . . .'

'Very commendable,' mutters de Soya, the irony audible in his voice. 'Go on.'

'Well, Father Captain, there's not much more,' the sweating man says lamely.

'You gave the order to fire at the flying man?'

'Yes . . . yes, sir.'

'And all of the sentries fired at once . . . upon your order?'

'Yeah,' says the director, his eyes glazed with the effort to remember. 'I think they all fired. There were six of them there besides Ament 'n' me.'

'And you also fired?' pressed de Soya.

'Well, yeah . . . the station was under attack. The flight deck was a burning mess. And this terrorist was flyin' at us, carrying God knows what.'

De Soya nods as if unconvinced. 'Did you see anything or anyone on the flying mat other than the one man?'

'Well, no,' says Powl. 'But it was dark.'

De Soya looks out the window at the rising moons. Brilliant orange light floods through the panes. 'Were the moons up that night, Captain?'

Powl licks his lips again as if tempted to lie. He knows that de Soya and his men have interviewed Sea Lancer Ament and the others, and de Soya knows he knows. 'They'd just risen,' he mumbles.

'So the amount of light was comparable to this?' says de Soya.

'Yeah.'

'Did you see anyone or anything else on that flying device, Captain? A package? A backpack? Anything that might be construed to be a bomb?'

'No,' says Powl, anger moving under the surface of his fear now, 'but it only took a handful of *plastique* to blow up two of our patrol skimmers and three thopters, Father Captain.'

'Very true,' says de Soya. Pacing to the brilliantly lit window, he says, 'Your seven sentries, Sea Lancer Ament included – were they all carrying flechette guns, Captain?'

'Yes.'

'And you yourself carried a flechette pistol. Is that right?'

'Yes.'

'And did all of these flechette charges strike the suspect?'

Powl hesitates, then shrugs. 'I think most of them did.'

'And did you see the result?' de Soya asks softly.

'It shredded the bastard . . . sir,' says Powl, anger winning over fear for the time being. 'I saw bits of him fly apart like gull shit hitting a fan . . . sir. Then he dropped . . . naw, he flew backward off that stupid carpet like someone being yanked by a cable. Fell into the sea right next to pylon L-3. Rainbow sharks, they came up and started feeding within ten seconds.'

'So you did not recover the body?' says de Soya.

Powl looks up with defiance in his eyes. 'Oh, no . . . we recovered it, Father Captain. I had Ament and Kilmer sweep up what was left with boat hooks, gaffes, and a hand net. That was after we'd put the fire out and I'd made sure there was no further danger to the platform.' Captain Powl was beginning to sound confident of his own correctness.

De Soya nods. 'And where is that body now, Captain?'

The director steeples his pudgy fingers. They are shaking only slightly. 'We buried it. At sea . . . of course. Off the south dock that next morning. Brought up a whole school of rainbow sharks, and we shot some for dinner.'

'But you are satisfied that the body was that of the suspect you had put under arrest earlier?'

Powl's tiny eyes become even smaller as he squints at de Soya. 'Yeah . . . what was left of him. Just a poacher. This kind of shit happens all the time out here on the big violet, Father Captain.'

'And do poachers fly ancient EM-flying carpets out here all the time on the big violet, Captain Powl?'

The director's face freezes. 'Is that what that dingus was?'

'You did not mention the carpet in your report, Captain.'

Powl shrugs. 'It didn't seem important.'

De Soya nods. 'And you say now that the . . . dingus . . . just kept going? That it overflew the deck and catwalk and disappeared out at sea? Empty?'

'Yes,' says Captain Powl, pulling himself erect in the chair and straightening his wilted uniform.

De Soya whirls around. 'Sea Lancer Ament says otherwise, Captain. Lancer Ament says that the carpet was recovered, that it was deactivated, and that it was last seen in your custody. Is this true?'

'No,' says the director, looking from de Soya to Gregorius to Sproul to Kee to Rettig and then back to de Soya. 'No, I never saw it after it flew past us. Ament's a fucking liar.'

De Soya nods to Sergeant Gregorius. To Powl he says, 'Such an ancient artifact, in working order, would be worth quite a bit of money, even on Mare Infinitus, would it not, Captain?'

'I don't know,' managed Powl, who is watching Gregorius. The sergeant has walked over to the director's private cabinet. It is made of heavy steel and it is locked. 'I don't even know what the damned thing was,' adds Powl.

De Soya is standing at the window now. The largest moon fills the entire eastern sky. The farcaster arch is quite visible, silhouetted against the moon. 'It is called a hawking mat,' he says softly, almost in a whisper. 'In a place called the Valley of the Time Tombs, it would have made just the right sort of radar signature.' He nods at Sergeant Gregorius.

The Swiss Guard noncom smashes open the steel cabinet with one blow of his gauntleted hand. Reaching in, he brushes aside boxes, papers, stacks of currency, and comes out with a rug, carefully folded. He carries it over to the director's desk.

'Arrest this man and get him out of my sight,' Father Captain de Soya says softly. Lieutenant Sproul and Corporal Kee lead the protesting director from the office.

De Soya and Gregorius unroll the hawking mat on the long desktop. The carpet's ancient flight threads still glow gold in the moonlight. De Soya touches the forward edge of the artifact, feeling the cuts and torn places there where flechettes have ripped the fabric. There is blood everywhere, obscuring the ornate designs, dulling the glow of the threads of super-conducting monofilament. Shreds of what might be human flesh are caught in the short tassels in the back of the carpet.

De Soya looks up at Gregorius. 'Have you ever read the long poem called the *Cantos*, Sergeant?'

'The *Cantos*, sir? No . . . I'm not much for reading. Besides, ain't that on the list of forbidden books, sir?'

'I believe it is, Sergeant,' says Father Captain de Soya. He moves away from the bloodied hawking mat and looks out at the rising moons and the silhouetted arch. *This is a piece of the puzzle*, he is thinking. *And when the puzzle is complete, I will have you, child.*

'I believe it is on the forbidden list, Sergeant,' he says again. He turns quickly and heads for the door, gesturing for Rettig to roll the hawking mat and bring it along. 'Come,' he says, putting more energy in his voice than he has had for weeks. 'We have work to do.'

THIRTY-THREE

My memory of the twenty minutes or so I spent in that large, bright mess hall is very much like those bad dreams we all have sooner or later: you know the ones I mean, where we find ourselves in some place out of our past but cannot remember our reason for being there or the names of the people around us. When the lieutenant and his two troopers walked me into the mess hall, everything in the room was tinged with that nightmare displacement of the formerly familiar. I say familiar because I had spent a good part of my twenty-seven years in hunting camps and military mess halls, casino bars and the galleys of old barges. I was familiar with the company of men: too familiar, I might have said then, for the elements I sensed in this room – bluster, braggadocio, and the sweat-scented ointment of city-nervous men in the throes of adventure-bound male bonding – had long since grown tiresome to me. But now that familiarity was offset by the strangeness – the smattering of dialect-laden speech I could hear, the subtle differences in clothing, the smell of cigarettes actually being used, and the knowledge that I would give myself away almost immediately if there was any need to deal with their currency, culture, or conversation.

There was a tall coffee urn on the farthest table – I had never been in a mess hall without one – and I ambled over there, trying to look casual as I did so, found a cup that was relatively clean, and poured myself some coffee. All the while I was watching the lieutenant and his two men watch me. When they seemed comfortable that I belonged there, they turned and went out. I sipped terrible coffee, noted idly that my hand holding the cup was not shaking despite the hurricane of emotions inside me, and tried to decide what to do next.

Amazingly, I still had my weapons – sheath knife and pistol – and my radio. With the radio I could detonate the *plastique* at any time and make a run for the hawking mat during the confusion. Now that I had seen the Pax sentinels, I knew that there would have to be some sort of diversion if the raft was going to get by this platform without being seen. I walked to the window; it looked the direction we had been thinking of as north, but I could see the 'eastern' sky aglow with imminent moonrise. The farcaster arch was visible to the naked eye. I tried the window, but it was either locked in some form I could not see or nailed in place. There was a corrugated steel roof of another module just a meter or so below the window level, but there seemed no way I could get to it from here.

'Who you with, son?'

I turned quickly. Five men had come over from the nearest group, and it was the shortest and fattest who was speaking to me. The man wore outdoor garb: checked flannel shirt, canvas trousers, canvas vest not too dissimilar from mine, and a fish-scaling knife on his belt. I realized then that the Pax troopers might have seen the tip of my holster poking out from under my vest but assumed it to be one of these knife sheaths.

This man had also spoken in dialect, but one quite different from the Pax guards outside. The fishermen, I remembered, were probably offworlders, so my strange accent should not be overly suspicious.

'Klingman,' I said, taking another sip of the sludge-tasting coffee. The one word had worked on the Pax troopers.

It did not work on these men. They looked at each other a moment, and then the fat one spoke again. 'We came in with the Klingman party, boy. All the way from St Thérése. You weren't on the hydrofoil. What's your game?'

I grinned. 'No game,' I said. 'I was supposed to be with the group – missed it in St Thérése – came on down with the Otters.'

I still hadn't got it right. The five men spoke among themselves. I heard the word 'poachers' several times. Two of the men left and went out the door. The fat man poked a fat finger at me. 'I was sittin' over there with the Otter guide. He never seen you before either. You stay right there, son.'

That was the one thing I was *not* going to do. Setting my cup on the table, I said, 'No, *you* wait here. I'm going to go get the lieutenant and have a few things straightened out. Don't move.'

This seemed to befuddle the fat man, and he stayed in his place as I crossed the now-silent mess hall, opened the door, and stepped out onto the catwalk.

There was nowhere to go. To my right, the two Pax troopers with flechette guns had snapped to attention at the railing. On my left, the thin lieutenant I'd bumped into earlier was hurrying down the walkway with the two civilians and what looked to be a pudgy Pax captain in tow.

'Damn,' I said aloud. Subvocalizing, I said, 'Kiddo, I'm in trouble here. They may have me. I'll leave the external mike open so you can hear. Head straight for the portal. Don't answer!' The last thing I needed during this conversation was a tiny voice chirping out of my hearplug.

'Hey!' I said, stepping forward toward the captain and raising my hands as if I was going to shake his. 'You're just the man I was looking for.'

'That's him,' cried one of the two fishermen. 'He didn't come in with us or the Otter group. It's one of them cross-damned poachers you been tellin' us about!'

'Cuff him,' said the captain to the lieutenant, and before I could do anything clever, the troopers had grabbed me from behind and the thin officer had slapped handcuffs on me. They were the old-fashioned metal kind, but they worked quite well – locking my wrists almost together and all but cutting off circulation.

I realized at that instant that I would never make it as a spy. Everything about my foray to the platform had been a disaster. The Pax troops were being sloppy – they were still crowding against me when they should have kept their distance and held their weapons on me while they searched me, and *then* cuffed me when I was disarmed – but the search would come in a few seconds.

I decided not to give them those few seconds. Bringing my cuffed hands up quickly, I grabbed the soft, almost chubby little captain by the front of his shirt and threw him back into the two civilians. There was a moment of shouting and pushing during which I turned quickly, kicked the first gun-carrying trooper in the balls as hard as I could, and grabbed the second one by the weapon still slung over his shoulder. The trooper shouted and seized the weapon with both hands, just as I grabbed the sling and pulled down and to the right on it with all of my strength. The trooper went with the weapon, hit the wall with his bare head, and sat down very quickly. The first trooper, the one I'd kicked and who was still kneeling and holding his groin with one hand, reached up with his free hand and ripped my sweater all the way down the front, ripping my night goggles off my neck as he did so. I kicked him in the throat and he went all the way down.

The lieutenant had removed his flechette pistol by this time, realized that he could not shoot me without killing the two troopers behind me, and struck me on the head with the butt of the thing.

Flechette pistols are not that heavy or substantial. This one made me see sparks behind my eyes for a moment and opened my scalp. It also made me angry.

I turned around and hit the lieutenant in the face with my fists. He went back over the waist-high railing, arms flailing, and kept on going. Everyone froze for a second as the man screamed all the way down to the water, twenty-five meters below.

I should say that everyone but I froze, for as the lieutenant's boot soles were still visible going over the railing, I had turned, leaped over the trooper on the floor, slammed open the screen door, and run into the mess hall. Men were milling around, most of them making toward the door and windows on this side to see what the commotion was, but they made way for me as I dodged through them like a deep brooder on a fifty-three-man squamish team herding the goat in for the goal.

Behind me, I heard the door slamming open again and the captain or one of the troopers shouting, 'Down! Out of the way! Lookout!'

I could feel my shoulder blades hunching again at the thought of those thousands of flechette darts flying my way, but I did not slow as I leaped to a tabletop, covered my face with my still-handcuffed wrists, and hit the window flying, my right shoulder taking the brunt of the impact.

Even while leaping, it crossed my mind that all it would take was for the window to be Perspex or smart glass and my misadventure would end in perfect farce – me bouncing back into the mess hall to be shot or captured at the troopers' leisure. It would make sense for a platform way out here to use unbreakable material instead of glass. But it had *felt* like glass when I had set my fingers against it a few minutes earlier.

It was glass.

I hit the corrugated steel of the roof and just kept rolling downhill, shards of glass flying around me and crunching beneath me. I'd brought part of the window's muntin with me – broken wood and glass was stuck in my vest and tattered sweater – but I didn't slow to disentangle myself. At the end of the roof I had a choice: instinct made me want to keep rolling over the edge, get out of sight before those gunmen opened up behind me, and hope that there was another catwalk below; logic made me want to stop and check it out before rolling over; memory suggested that there were no catwalks along this north edge of the platform.

I compromised by rolling off the edge of the roof but grabbing the overhang as I did so, peering down between my swinging boots as my fingers slipped. There was no deck or platform down there, just twenty meters of air between my boots and the violet waves. The moons were rising and the sea was coming alive with light.

I levered myself up far enough to look back at the window I'd broken through, saw the gunmen milling there, and dropped my head out of sight just as one of them fired. The flechette cloud went slightly high, missing my straining fingers by two or three centimeters, and I flinched as I listened to the angry-bee hum of thousands of steel needles flying past. There was no deck below me, but I could see a pipe running horizontally along the side of the module. It was six or eight centimeters across. There was the narrowest of gaps between the inside of the pipe and the wall of the module, perhaps wide enough for my fingers to find a grip – if the pipe did not break under my weight, if the shock did not dislocate my shoulders, if my handcuffed hands did not fail, if . . . I did not think: I dropped. My forearms and the steel of my handcuffs slammed into the pipe, almost flipping me backward, but my fingers were ready to grip and they did so, sliding upward along the inside of the pipe but then holding my weight.

The second burst of flechette fire above me blew the roof overhang to shreds and perforated the outer wall in a hundred places. Splinters and steel shards tumbled past in the moonlight as the men shouted and cursed up there. I heard footsteps on the roof.

I was shuffling and swinging to my left as quickly as I could. There was a deck protruding below the corner of the module down there, at least three meters below me and four or five meters to the east. The progress was maddeningly slow. My shoulders were shrieking with discomfort, my fingers were becoming numb from lack of circulation, I could feel glass shards in my hair and scalp, and blood was running in my eyes. The men above me were going to get to the edge of the roof before I could get to a point above the platform.

Suddenly there was cursing and shouting, and a section of the roof caved in right where I had been hanging. Evidently their flechette fire had undermined that section of roofing, and now their weight was adding to the problem. I could hear them shoving back, cursing, and finding alternate routes to the edge.

This delay only gave me an extra eight to ten seconds, but it was enough to allow me to shuffle my hands to the end of the pipe, swing my body once, twice, release on the third swing, and fall heavily to the platform below, rolling up against the east railing hard enough to knock the wind out of me.

I knew that I could not lie there and get my wind back. I moved quickly, rolling toward the darker section of deck under the module. At least two flechette guns fired – one missing and roiling the waters fifteen meters below, the other pounding the end of the deck like a hundred nail guns firing at once. I rolled to my feet and ran, ducking low beams and trying to see amid the maze of shadows down there. Footsteps pounded somewhere above me. They had the advantage of knowing the layout of these decks and stairways; but only I knew where I was headed.

I was headed to the easternmost and lowest deck, where I had left the mat, but this maintenance deck had opened onto a long catwalk that ran north and south. When I had cut far enough under the main platform that I thought I would be even with the east deck, I swung up onto a support beam – it was about six centimeters wide – and, handcuffed arms flailing left and then right for balance, crossed an open section to the next vertical post. I did this again, shifting north and south when the beams ended, but always finding another beam running east.

Trapdoors were flying open and footsteps pounded on the main catwalks beneath the main deck, but I reached the eastern deck first. I jumped to it, found the mat where I had lashed it to the post, unrolled it, tapped the flight threads, and was up and flying over the railing just as the trapdoor opened above the long flight of stairs coming down to the deck. I was lying prone on the carpet, trying to make the least silhouette I could against moons or glowing waves, tapping flight threads clumsily because of the handcuffs.

My instinct was to fly due north, but I realized that this would be a mistake. The flechette guns would be accurate only to sixty or seventy meters out, but someone up there must have a plasma rifle or the equivalent. All the attention had rushed to the east end of the platform now. My best chance was to head west, perhaps even south.

I banked left, swooped beneath the support beams there, and skipped just above the waves, heading west under the protective edge of the platform. Only the one deck protruded out this far – the one I'd dropped onto – and I could see that it was empty at the north end. No, not empty, I realized, just shot to bits from the flechette fire and probably too dangerous to stand on. I flew under it and headed west. There were boot sounds on the upper catwalks, but anyone catching a glimpse of me would have a hell of a rough time lining up a shot because of the dozens of pylons and cross girders here.

I swooped out from under the platform into the shadow of it – the moons were higher now – and stayed just millimeters above the wave tops, staying low, trying to keep the long ocean swell between me and the western end of the platform. I was fifty or sixty meters out and almost ready to breathe a sigh of relief when I heard the splashing and coughing a few meters to my right, just beyond the next swell.

I knew instantly what it was, *who* it was – the lieutenant I had slugged and sent sprawling over the railing. My impulse was to keep on flying. The platform behind me was a mass of confusion at this point – men shouting, others shooting off the north side, more men screaming at the east end where I had slipped away – but no one had seen me out here. This man had struck me in the head with his flechette pistol and would happily have killed me if his pals hadn't been in the way. The fact that the current had pulled him out here away from the platform was his bad luck; there was nothing I could do about it.

I can drop him off at the base of the platform – perhaps on one of the support beams. I got away once this way; I can do it again. The man was doing his job. He does not deserve to die for it.

It is fair to say that I hated my conscience at moments like that – not that I had had many moments like that.

I stopped the hawking mat just above the waves. I was still lying on my belly, my head and shoulders hunched low so that the shouting men on the platform would not spot me. Now I leaned out and to the right to see if I could spot the source of the coughing and splashing.

I saw the fish first. They had dorsals like holos I'd seen of Old Earth sharks, or the cannibal saberbacks of Hyperion's South Sea, but two shining dorsal fins rather than one. I could see the fish clearly in the moonlight: they seemed to glitter a dozen bright colors, from the twin dorsal fins to their long bellies. They were about three meters long, they moved like predators with powerful surges of their tails, and their teeth were very white.

Following one of these killers over the swell toward the coughing sounds, I saw the lieutenant. He was splashing and struggling to keep his head above water, all the while pivoting, trying to keep the multicolored killer fish at bay. One of the twin-dorsaled things would lunge toward him through the violet water, and the lieutenant would kick at it, trying to strike its head or fin with his boot. The fish would snap and then wheel away. Others were circling closer. The Pax officer was obviously exhausted.

'Damn,' I whispered. There was no way I could leave him there.

The first thing I did was tap the code that killed the deflection field – that low-scale containment field designed to keep the wind out at high speeds and the hawking-mat occupants, especially children, from tumbling off at any speed. If I was going to be pulling this waterlogged man aboard, I did not want to have to struggle against the EM-field. Then I slid the mat down the long swell toward him, bringing it to a halt right where he had been.

He was no longer there. The man had slipped under. I considered diving for him, then saw the pale forms of his arms struggling just under the waves. The shark-things were circling closer, but not attacking at the moment. Perhaps the shadow of the hawking mat disconcerted them.

I reached down with both manacled arms, found his right wrist, and pulled him up. His weight almost tumbled me off the mat, but I leaned back, found my balance, and tugged him up far enough that I could grab the back of his pants and haul him – dripping, coughing water – onto the hawking mat.

The lieutenant was pale and cold, shaking all over, but after an initial bout of retching up seawater, he seemed to be breathing all right. I was glad for that: I was not sure my generosity would go so far as administering mouth-to-mouth resuscitation. Making sure that he was sprawled on the mat far enough that one of the passing dorsal-fish wouldn't leap up and take one of his legs off, I turned my attention back to the controls. I set a course back to the platform, rising slightly as we went. Fumbling in my vest, I found the com unit and keyed in the code needed to detonate the *plastique* I had planted on the skimmer and thopter decks. We would approach the platform from the south, where I could make sure those decks were clear of people; I would then transmit the detonate code with a simple push of the button and, in the ensuing confusion, swing back around and come in from the west, dropping the lieutenant off at the first dry place I could find under there.

I turned to see if the man was still breathing and had an instant's glimpse of the Pax officer on one knee, something gleaming in his hand . . .

. . . he stabbed me in the heart.

Or it would have been directly through my heart, if I had not twisted in the split second it took for the knife to cut through my vest, sweater, and flesh. As it was, the short blade ripped into my side and grated against a rib. I did not feel pain at the moment so much as a shock – a literal electric shock. I gasped and grabbed for his wrist. The blade came in fast, higher this time, and my hands slippery with seawater and my own blood – slipped back along his wrist. The best I could do was pull downward, using the band of metal connecting the manacles on my wrists to pull his arm down as he stabbed me again, a downward thrust this time that would have come in over the same rib and punctured my heart had it not been for my pull on his arm slowing the movement and the com unit in my vest pocket deflecting the blade. Even so, I felt the blade rip at the flesh of my side again and I staggered back, trying to get my footing on the rising hawking mat.

I was dimly aware of the explosions at my back: the knife blade must have struck the transmit button. I did not turn to look as I found my balance, feet apart. The mat continued to rise – we were eight or ten meters above the ocean now and still climbing.

The lieutenant had also leaped to his feet, falling into the natural crouch of a born knife fighter. I have always hated edged weapons. I have skinned animals and gutted innumerable fish. Even when I was in the Guard, I could not understand how humans could do that to humans at close range. I had a knife on my belt somewhere, but I knew that I was no match for this man. My only hope was to get the automatic out of its holster, but it was a difficult movement – the pistol was on my left hip, turned backward so that I could draw across my body, but now I had to use both hands, fumble aside the hanging vest, pull up the flap over the weapon, pull it out, aim it . . .

He slashed across my body, left to right. I jumped back to the very front of the hawking mat, but too late – the sharp little blade cut through flesh and muscle along the back of my right arm as I was reaching across my body for the pistol. I felt the pain of this cut and cried out. The lieutenant smiled, his teeth slick with seawater. Still crouching, knowing that I had nowhere to go, he took a half step forward and swung the knife upward in an eviscerating arc that had to end in my belly.

I had been turning to my right when he slashed me before, now I kept the motion going and pushed off from the climbing hawking mat in a clean dive, my manacled hands directly in front of me as I broke the water ten meters below. The ocean was salty and dark. I had not taken much of a breath before hitting the water, and for a terrible moment I literally did not know which way was up. Then I saw the glow of the three moons and kicked in that direction. My head cleared the surface in time to see the lieutenant still standing aboard the rising mat, now thirty meters closer to the platform and perhaps twenty-five meters high and rising. He was crouched and looking in my direction as if waiting for me to return so that he could finish the fight.

I would not be returning, but I did want to finish the fight. Fumbling underwater for the automatic, I unsnapped the holster, pulled the heavy weapon out, and tried to float on my back so that I could aim the damned thing. My target was climbing and disappearing, but he was still silhouetted against the impossible moon as I thumbed back the hammer and steadied my arms.

The lieutenant had just given up on me and turned toward the commotion on the platform when the men there fired. They beat me to it by a second or two. I doubt if I would have hit him at that distance. There was no way they could have missed.

At least three flechette clusters struck him at once, knocking him back off the hawking mat like a load of laundry someone had tossed through the air. I literally saw moonlight through his riddled body as it tumbled down to the wave tops. A second later one of the colored shark-things cruised past me, actually bashing my shoulder aside in its eagerness to get to the mass of bleeding bait that had been the Pax lieutenant.

I floated there a second, watching the hawking mat until someone on the platform grabbed it. I had childishly hoped that the carpet would swoop around and come back to me, lift me out of the sea, and carry me back to the raft a klick or two north of here now. I had grown fond of the hawking mat – fond of being part of the myth and legend it represented – and watching it fly away from me forever like that made me sick to my stomach.

I was sick to my stomach. Between the wounds and the salt water I'd ingested – not to mention the effect of salt water in the wounds – the nausea was real. I kept floating there in the salty sea, kicking to keep my head and shoulders above water, the heavy automatic held in my two hands.

If I was going to swim, I had to shoot the handcuffs apart. But how could I do that? The steel band between the manacles was only a little longer than the thickness of my wrist; no matter how I contorted, I could not get the muzzle of the weapon around where I could sever the band with a bullet.

Meanwhile, the dorsal fins were circling away from their feeding on the lieutenant. I knew that I was bleeding badly. I could feel the heavier wetness at my side and on the back of my arm, where the salty blood was spilling into the salty sea. If those things were anything like the saberbacks or sharks, they could sense blood for kilometers. My only hope was to kick toward the platform, use the pistol on the first fins to come near me, and hope I could reach one of the pylons and pull myself out or yell for help. That was my only hope.

I leaned back, kicked, rolled onto my stomach, and started swimming north, toward the open ocean. I had been on the platform once this long day. That was enough.

THIRTY-FOUR

I had never before tried swimming with my hands tied in front of me. It is my earnest hope that I never have to try it again. Only the strong salinity of this world's ocean kept me afloat as I kicked, floated, flailed, and thrashed my way north. I had no real hope of reaching the raft; the current began running strongest at least a klick north of the platform, and our plan had been to keep the raft as far away from the structure as we could without losing the river within the sea.

It was only a few minutes before the colored sharks began circling again. Their shimmering, electric colors were visible beneath the waves, and when one moved in for the attack, I stopped trying to swim, floated, and kicked at its head in precisely the same way as I had seen the late lieutenant hold the things at bay. It seemed to work. The fish were undoubtedly deadly, but they were stupid – they attacked one at a time, as if there were some unseen pecking order among them – and I kicked them in the snout one at a time. But the process was exhausting. I had started to remove my boots just before the first color-shark attack – the heavy leather was dragging me down – but the thought of kicking bare feet at those fanged, bullet-shaped heads made me keep the boots on as long as I could. I also soon decided that I could not swim with the pistol in my hands. The saberback things were diving during their actual lunges at me, coming up from beneath seemed to be their preferred mode of attack, and I doubted whether a bullet from the old slug-thrower would do any good through a meter or two of water. Eventually I tucked the pistol back into its holster, although I soon wished I had dropped it altogether. Floating, swiveling to keep twin dorsal fins in view, I finally pulled off my boots and let them slip away into the depths. When the next shark attacked, I kicked harder, feeling the sandpaper roughness of the skin above its tiny brain. It snapped at my bare feet but moved away and began circling again.

This is the way I swam north, pausing, floating, kicking, cursing, swimming a few meters, pausing again to twist in circles waiting for the next attack. If it had not been for the combination of the brilliant moons and the saberback things' glowing skin, one of them would have pulled me down long before. As it was, I soon reached the point where I was too exhausted to try to swim any longer – all I could do was float on my back, gasp for air, and get my feet between those white teeth and my legs every time I saw the colors flashing my way.

Both the knife wounds were beginning to hurt in earnest now. I could feel the deeper slash along my ribs as a terrible burning combined with a stickiness down the length of my side. I was sure that I was bleeding into the water, and once, when the dorsal fins were circling far enough out that I could ignore them for a moment, I lowered my hands to my side and pulled them out of the water. They were red – much redder than the violet sea glowing in the light of the great moon that had now cleared the horizon. I felt the weakness growing in me and realized that I was bleeding to death. The water was becoming warmer, as if my blood were heating it to a comfortable temperature, and the temptation to close my eyes and move deeper into that warmth grew stronger from moment to moment.

I admit that each time the ocean swell bore me up, I kept looking over my shoulder for some sign of the raft – for some miracle from the north. I saw nothing there. Part of me was pleased at this – the raft had probably transited the farcaster portal by now. It had not been intercepted. I had seen no skimmers, no thopters, and the platform was only a diminishing blaze to the south. I realized that my best hope was to be picked up by a searching thopter now that the raft was safely gone, but even the thought of such rescue did not cheer me. I had been to the platform once this day.

Floating on my back, twisting my head and neck to keep the colored dorsals in view, I kicked my way north, rising with each great movement of the violet sea, dropping into wide troughs as the ocean seemed to breathe in. I rotated to my stomach and tried kicking more strongly, my handcuffed fists straight ahead of me, but I was too exhausted to keep my head above water that way. My right arm seemed to be bleeding more fiercely now and seemed three times as heavy as the left. I guessed that the lieutenant's blade had severed tendons there.

Finally I had to give up swimming and concentrate on floating, my feet kicking to keep me up, my head and shoulders above water, my fists clenched in front of my face. The saberback things seemed to sense my weakness; they took turns swimming at me, their great mouths open to feed. Each time I pulled my legs up and kicked straight out, trying to strike their snouts or brainpans with my heels without having my feet bitten off. Their rough skin had abraded the flesh of my heels and soles to the point that I was adding more blood to the sphere that must surround me. It made the dorsal-things wilder. Their attacks came closer together as I grew too tired to pull my legs up each time. One of the long fish ripped my right pant leg off from the knee to ankle, pulling a layer of skin with it as it moved away with a triumphant stroke of its tail.

Part of my tired mind had been pondering theology during all this – not praying, but wondering about a Cosmic God who allowed Its creatures to torture each other like this. How many hominids, mammals, and trillions of other creatures had spent their last minutes in mortal fear such as this, their hearts pounding, their adrenaline coursing through them and exhausting them more quickly, their small minds racing in the hopeless quest of escape? How could any God describe Him or Herself as a God of Mercy and fill the universe with fanged things such as this? I remembered Grandam telling me about an early Old Earth scientist, one Charles Darwin, who had come up with one of the early theories of evolution or gravitation or somesuch, and how – although raised a devout Christian even before the reward of the cruciform – he had become an atheist while studying a terrestrial wasp that paralysed some large species of spider, planted its embryo, and let the spider recover and go about its business until it was time for the hatched wasp larva to burrow its way out of the living spider's abdomen.

I shook water out of my eyes and kicked at two of the dorsal fins rushing at me. I missed the head but struck one of the sensitive fins. Only by pulling my legs up into a ball did I avoid that snapping maw. Losing my buoyancy for a moment, I went a meter or more under the next wave, swallowed salt water, and came up gasping and blind. More fins circled closer. Swallowing water again, I struggled with my numb hands underwater and came up with the pistol, almost dropping it before propping it against my chin. I realized that it would be easier just to leave the muzzle under my chin and pull the trigger than to try to use it against these sea killers. Well, there were quite a few slugs left in the thing – I had not used it during all of the excitement of the last couple of hours – so it would remain an option.

Swiveling, watching the closest dorsal move even closer, I remembered a story Grandam had read me when I was a boy. It was also an ancient classic – a thing by Stephen Crane called 'The Open Boat' – and it was about several men who had survived the sinking of their ship and days at sea without water only to be stuck a few hundred meters from land by surf too high to cross without capsizing. One of the men in the boat – I could not remember which character – had moved through all of the circles of theological supposition: praying, believing that God was a merciful Deity who sat up nights worrying about him, then believing that God was a cruel bastard, and finally deciding that no one was listening. I realized now that I had not understood that story, despite Grandam's Socratic questions and careful guidance. I thought that I remembered the weight of epiphany that had fallen on that character as he realized they would have to swim for it and that not all of them could survive. He had wanted Nature – for this is how he now thought of the universe – to be a huge glass building, just so that he could cast stones at it. But even that, he realized, would be useless.

The universe is indifferent to our fates. This was the crushing burden that the character took with him as he struggled through the surf toward survival or extinction. The universe just does not give a shit.

I realized that I was laughing and weeping at the same time, shouting curses and invitations to the saberback things that were only two or three meters out. I leveled the pistol and fired at the closest fin. Amazingly, the soaked slug-thrower fired, the noise that had been so loud on the raft now seemingly swallowed by the waves and immensity of the sea. The fish dived out of sight. Two more lunged at me. I shot at one, kicked at the other, just as something struck me hard on the neck from behind.

I was not so lost in theology and philosophizing that I was ready to die. I swiveled quickly, not knowing how badly I had been bitten but determined to shoot the goddamn thing in the mouth if I had to. I had the heavy pistol cocked and aimed before I saw the girl's face there half a meter from my own. Her hair was plastered to her skull and her dark eyes were bright in the moonlight.

'Raul!' She must have been calling my name before, but I had not heard over the gunshot and the rushing in my ears.

I blinked salt water away. This could not be real. Oh, Jesus, why should she be out here, away from the raft?

'Raul!' Aenea called again. 'Float on your back. Use the gun to keep those things away. I'll pull you in.'

I shook my head. I did not understand. Why would she leave the powerful android on the raft and come after me by herself? How could . . .

A. Bettik's blue scalp became visible over the next large swell. The android was swimming strongly with both arms, the long machete clamped in his white teeth. I confess that I laughed through my tears. He looked like a cheap holo's version of a pirate.

'Float on your back!' shouted the girl again.

I turned on my back, too tired to kick as a shark-thing lunged at my legs. I shot between my feet at it, striking it square between its black, lifeless eyes. The two fins disappeared beneath the wave.

Aenea set one arm around my neck, her left hand under my right arm so she was not choking me, and began swimming strongly up the next huge swell. A. Bettik swam alongside, paddling with one arm now as he wielded the sharp machete with the other. I saw him slice into the water and watched two dorsal fins shudder and swerve to the right.

'What are you . . .' I began, choking and coughing.

'Save your breath,' gasped the girl, pulling me down into the next trough and up the violet wall ahead of us. 'We have a long way to go.'

'The pistol,' I said, trying to hand it to her. I felt the darkness closing on my vision like a narrowing tunnel and did not want to lose the weapon. Too late – I felt it drop away into the sea. 'Sorry,' I managed before the tunnel closed completely.

My last conscious thought was an inventory of what I had lost on my first solo expedition: the treasured hawking mat, my night goggles, the antique automatic pistol, my boots, probably the com unit, and quite possibly my life and the lives of my friends. Total darkness cut off the end of this cynical speculation.

I was vaguely aware of their lifting me onto the raft. The girl was breathing into my mouth, then pumping water out of my lungs with pressure against my chest. A. Bettik knelt next to us, pulling strongly on a heavy line.

After retching water for several minutes, I said, 'The raft . . . how? . . . it should have been to the portal by now . . . I don't . . .'

Aenea pushed my head back against a pack and cut away rags of my shirt and right trouser leg with a short knife. 'A. Bettik rigged a sort of sea anchor using the microtent and the climbing rope,' she said. 'It's dragging behind, slowing us down but keeping us on course. It gave us time to find you.'

'How . . .' I began, then started coughing salt water again.

'Hush,' said the girl, ripping the last of my shirt away. 'I want to see how badly you're hurt.'

I winced as her strong hands touched the great gash on my side. Her fingers found the deep cut on my upper arm, ran down my side to where the fish had taken the skin down my thigh and calf. 'Ah, Raul,' she said sadly. 'I let you out of my sight for an hour or two and look what you do to yourself.'

The weakness was overwhelming me again, the darkness returning. I knew that I had lost too much blood. I was very bold. 'I'm sorry,' I whispered.

'Quiet.' She tore open the larger of our medpaks with a loud ripping noise. 'Hush.'

'No,' I insisted. 'I screwed up. I was supposed to be your protector . . . guard *you*. Sorry—' I cried out as she poured antiseptic sulfa solution directly into the wound on my side. I had seen men weep at this on the battlefield. Now I was one of them.

If it had been my modern medpak that the girl had opened, I am sure I would have died minutes if not seconds later. But it was the larger pak – the ancient FORCE-issue medpak we'd taken from the ship. My first thought was that all of the medicines and instruments would be useless after so long a time, but then I saw the blinking lights on the surface of the pak she had laid on my chest. Some were green, more were yellow, a few were red. I knew that this was not good.

'Lie back,' whispered Aenea, and tore open a sterile suture pak. She laid the clear bag against my side and the millipede suture within came to life and crawled to my wound. The sensation was not pleasant as the tailored life-form crawled *into* the ragged walls of my wound, secreted its antibiotic and cleansing secretions, then drew its sharp millipede legs together in a tight suture. I cried out again . . . then again a moment later as she applied another millipede suture to my arm.

'We need more plasma cartridges,' she said to A. Bettik as she fed two of the small cylinders into the pak injection system. I felt the burn on my thigh as the plasma entered my system.

'Those four are all that we have,' said the android. He was busy working on me now, setting an osmosis mask in place over my face. Pure oxygen began to flow into my lungs.

'Damn,' said the girl, injecting the last of the plasma cartridges. 'He's lost too much blood. He's going into deep shock.'

I wanted to argue with them, explain – that my shaking and shivering was just a result of the cold air, that I felt much better, but the osmosis mask pressed everywhere against my mouth, eyes, nose, and did not allow me to speak. For a moment I hallucinated that we were back in the ship and the crash field was holding me secure again. I think that all the salt water on my face at that moment was not from the sea.

Then I saw the ultramorph injector in the girl's hands and I began to struggle. I did not want to be knocked out: if I was going to die, I wanted to be awake when it happened.

Aenea pushed me back against the backpack. She understood what I was trying to say. 'I *want* you out, Raul,' she said softly. 'You're going into shock. We need to get your vital signs stabilized . . . it'll be easier if you're out.' The injector hissed.

I thrashed for another few seconds, weeping tears of frustration now. After all that effort, to slip away while unconscious. Goddamm it, it wasn't fair . . . it wasn't right . . .

I awoke to bright sunlight and terrible heat. For a moment I was sure that we were still on the sea of Mare Infinitus, but when I worked up enough energy to lift my head, I could see that the sun was different – larger, hotter – and the sky was a much paler shade of blue. The raft seemed to be moving along some sort of concrete canal with only a meter or two to spare on either side. I could see concrete, sun, and blue sky – nothing else.

'Lie back,' said Aenea, pushing my head and shoulders back on the pack and adjusting the microtent fabric so that my face was in shade again. Obviously they had retrieved their 'sea anchor'.

I tried to speak, failed, licked dry lips that seemed stitched together, and finally managed, 'How long have I been out?'

Aenea gave me a sip of water from my own canteen before replying. 'About thirty hours.'

'Thirty hours!' Even trying to shout, I could do little more than squeak.

A. Bettik came around the side of the tent and crouched in the shade with us. 'Welcome back, M. Endymion.'

'Where are we?'

Aenea answered. 'Judging from the desert, sun, and the stars last night, it's almost certain that we're on Hebron. We seem to be traveling along some aqueduct. Right now . . . well, you should see this.' She supported my shoulders so I could see over the concrete lip of the canal. Nothing but air and distant hills. 'We're about fifty meters up on this section of aqueduct,' she said, lowering my head to the pack again. 'It's been like this for the last five or six klicks. If there's been a breach in the aqueduct . . .' She smiled ruefully. 'We haven't seen anyone or anything . . . not even a vulture. We're waiting until we come into a city.'

I frowned, feeling the stiffness in my side and arm as I shifted position ever so slightly. 'Hebron? I thought it was . . .'

'Captured by the Ousters,' finished A. Bettik. 'Yes, that was our information as well. It does not matter, sir. We will seek medical care for you with the Ousters as happily . . . more happily . . . than we would with the Pax.'

I looked down at the medpak now lying next to me. Filaments ran to my chest, arm, and legs. Most of the lights on the pak were blinking amber. This was not good.

'Your wounds are sealed and cleaned,' said Aenea. 'We gave you all the plasma the old pak had. But you need more . . . and there seems to be some sort of infection that the multispectrum antibiotics can't handle.'

That explained the terrible feverish quality I felt beneath my skin.

'Perhaps some micro-organism in the sea on Mare Infinitus,' said A. Bettik. 'The medpak cannot quite diagnose it. We will know when we get to a hospital. It is our guess that this section of the Tethys will lead to Hebron's one large city . . .'

'New Jerusalem,' I whispered.

'Yes,' said the android. 'Even after the Fall, it was famous for its Sinai Medical Center.'

I started to shake my head but stopped when the pain and dizziness struck. 'But the Ousters . . .'

Aenea moved a damp cloth across my brow. 'We're going to get help for you,' she said. 'Ousters or no Ousters.'

A thought was trying to burrow up out of my befuddled brain. I waited until it arrived. 'Hebron . . . didn't have . . . I don't think it had . . .'

'You are right, sir,' said A. Bettik. He tapped the small book in his hand. 'According to the guide, Hebron was not part of the River Tethys and allowed only a single farcaster terminex in New Jerusalem, even during the height of the Web. Offworld visitors were not allowed to leave the capital. They treasured privacy and independence here.'

I looked out at the passing aqueduct walls. Suddenly we were off the high trestle and moving between high dunes and sun-baked rocks. The heat was terrible.

'But the book must have been wrong,' said Aenea, mopping my brow again. 'The farcaster portal was there . . . and we're here.'

'You're sure . . . it's . . . Hebron?' I whispered.

Aenea nodded. A. Bettik held up the comlog bracelet. I had forgotten about it. 'Our mechanical friend here got a reliable star sighting,' he said. 'We are on Hebron and . . . I would guess . . . only hours away from New Jerusalem.'

Pain tore through me then, and no matter how I tried to hide it, I must have writhed. Aenea brought the ultramorph injector out.

'No,' I said through cracked lips.

'This is the last one for a while,' she whispered. I heard the hiss and felt the blessed numbness spreading. *If there is a God*, I thought, *it's a painkiller*.

When I awoke again, the shadows were long and we were in the shade of a low building. A. Bettik was carrying me from the raft. Each step sent pain wracking through me. I made no sound.

Aenea was walking ahead. The street was wide and dusty, the buildings low – none over three stories – and made of an adobelike material. No one was in sight.

'Hello!' called the child, cupping her hands to her mouth. The two syllables echoed down the empty street.

I felt foolish being carried like a child, but A. Bettik did not seem to mind, and I knew that I could not stand if my life depended upon it.

Aenea walked back to us, saw my open eyes, and said, 'This is New Jerusalem. There's no doubt. According to the guidebook, three million people lived here during the Web days, and A. Bettik says that there were at least a million still here the last he heard.'

'Ousters . . .' I managed.

Aenea nodded tersely. 'The shops and buildings near the canal were empty, but they looked like they'd been lived in until a few weeks or months ago.'

A. Bettik said, 'According to the transmissions we monitored on Hyperion, this world was supposed to have fallen to the Ousters approximately three standard years ago. But there are signs of habitation here much more recent than that.'

'The power grid's still on,' said Aenea. 'Food that was left out has all spoiled, but the fridge compartments are still cold. Tables are set in some of the houses, holopits humming with static, radios hissing. But no people.'

'But also no signs of violence,' said the android, laying me carefully in the back of a groundcar with a flat metal bed behind the cab. Aenea had set out a blanket to keep my skin away from the hot metal. The pain in my side sent spots dancing in front of my eyes.

Aenea rubbed her arms. There were goose bumps there despite the blazing heat of the evening. 'But *something* terrible happened here,' she said. 'I can feel it.'

I admit that I felt nothing but pain and fever. My thoughts were like mercury – always shifting away before I could grab them or form them into a cohesive shape.

Aènea jumped up onto the flatbed of the groundcar and crouched next to me while A. Bettik opened the door to the cab and crawled in. Amazingly, the vehicle started with a touch of the ignition plate. 'I can drive this,' said the android, putting the vehicle in gear.

So can I, I thought at them. *I drove one like it in Ursus. It's one of the few things in the universe I know how to drive. It may be one of the few things I can do right.*

We bumped down the main street. The pain made me cry out a few times, despite my best efforts to stay quiet. I clamped my jaws tight.

Aenea was holding my hand. Her fingers felt so cool that they almost made me shiver. I realized that my own skin was on fire.

'. . . it's that damned infection,' she was saying. 'Otherwise you'd be recovering now. Something in that ocean.'

'Or on his knife,' I whispered. I closed my eyes and saw the lieutenant flying to pieces as the flechette clouds tore into him. I opened my eyes to escape the image. The buildings were taller here, ten stories at least, and they cast a deeper shade. But the heat was terrible.

'. . . a friend of my mother's on the last Hyperion pilgrimage lived here for a while,' she was saying. Her voice seemed to move in and out of hearing range, like a poorly tuned radio station.

'Sol Weintraub,' I croaked. 'The scholar in the old poet's *Cantos*.'

Aenea patted my hand. 'I forget that everything Mother lived has become grist for Uncle Martin's legend mill.'

We bounced over a bump. I ground my back teeth together to keep from screaming.

Aenea's grip on my hand intensified. 'Yes,' she said. 'I wish I had met the old scholar and his daughter.'

'They went ahead . . . in the . . . Sphinx,' I managed. 'Like . . . you . . . did.'

Aenea leaned close, moistened my lips from the canteen, and nodded. 'Yes. But I remember Mother's stories about Hebron and the kibbutzim here.'

'Jews,' I whispered, and then quit talking. It took too much energy that I needed to fight the pain.

'They fled the Second Holocaust,' she said, looking ahead now as the groundcar rounded a corner. 'They called their Hegira the Diaspora.'

I closed my eyes. The lieutenant flew apart, his clothing and flesh mangled to long streamers that spiraled slowly down to the violet sea . . .

Suddenly A. Bettik was lifting me. We were entering a building larger and more sinuous than the others – all soaring plasteel and tempered glass. 'The medical center,' the android said. The automatic door whispered open ahead of us. 'It has power . . . now if only the medical machinery is intact.'

I must have dozed briefly, for when I opened my eyes again, terrified because the twin dorsal fins were circling closer and closer, I was on a gurney-trolley being slid into a long cylinder of some sort of diagnostic autosurgeon.

'See you later,' Aenea was saying, releasing my hand. 'See you on the other side.'

We were on Hebron for thirteen of its local days – each day being some twenty-nine standard hours. For the first three days the autosurgeon had its way with me: no fewer than eight invasive surgeries and an even dozen therapy treatments according to the digitized record at the end.

It was, indeed, some micro-organism from that miserable ocean on Mare Infinitus that had decided to kill me, although when I saw the magnetic resonance and deep bioradar scans, I realized that the organism had not been so micro after all. Whatever it was – the autodiagnostic equipment was ambivalent – had taken hold along the inside of my scraped rib and grown like fen fungus until it had begun to branch out to my internal organs. Another standard day without surgery, the autosurgeon reported later, and they would have made the initial incision to find only lichen and lique-faction.

After opening me up, cleaning me out, and then repeating the process twice more when infinitesimal traces of the oceanborne organism started colonizing again, the autosurgeon pronounced the fungus kaput and began working on my lesser life-threatening wounds. The knife cut in the side had opened me up enough that I should have bled to death – especially with all of my kicking and high pulse rate brought on by my dorsaled friends in the sea. Evidently the plasma cartridges in the old medpak and several days of being kept near comatose by Aenea's liberal doses of ultramorph had kept me alive until the surgeon could transfuse eight more units of plasma into me.

The deep wound in my arm had not – as I had feared – severed tendons, but enough important muscles and nerves had been slashed that the auto-surgeon had worked on that arm during operations two and three. Because the hospital still had power when we arrived, the surgeon had taken it upon its own silicon initiative to have the organ tanks in the basement grow the replacement nerves I needed. On the eighth day, when Aenea sat at my bedside and told me how the autosurgeon repeatedly kept asking for advice and authorization from its human overseers, I was even able to laugh when she talked of how 'Dr Bettik' authorized each critical operation, transplant, and therapy.

The leg the color-shark had tried to bite off turned out to be the most painful part of the ordeal. After the infinitus-fungus had been cleaned out of the area laid bare by the shark's teeth, new skin and muscle tissue had been transplanted layer by layer. It hurt. And after it quit hurting, it itched. During my second week of confinement in that hospital, I was undergoing ultramorph withdrawal and would seriously have considered holding my pistol on the girl or the android and demanding morph if I had actually believed they could be intimidated into bringing me relief from withdrawal symptoms and that hellish itching. But the pistol was gone – sunk in the bottomless violet sea.

It was on about the eighth day, when I could sit up in bed and actually eat food – although just bland, vat-replicated hospital food – that I talked to Aenea about my short stint as Hero. 'On my last night on Hyperion, I got drunk with the old poet and promised him I'd accomplish certain things on this trip,' I said.

'What things?' said the girl, her spoon in my dish of green gelatin.

'Nothing much,' I said. 'Protect you, get you home, find Old Earth and bring it back so he could see it again before he died . . .'

Aenea paused in her gelatin eating. Her dark eyebrows were very high on her forehead. 'He told you to bring Old Earth back? Interesting.'

'That's not all,' I said. 'Along the way I was supposed to talk to the Ousters, destroy the Pax, overthrow the Church, and – I quote – "find out what the fuck the Techno Core is up to and stop it."'

Aenea set her spoon down and dabbed at her lips with my napkin. 'Is that all?'

'Not quite,' I said, leaning back into the pillows. 'He also wanted me to keep the Shrike from hurting you or destroying humanity.'

She nodded. 'Is that it?'

I rubbed my sweaty forehead with my good left hand. 'I think so. At least that's all I remember. I was drunk, as I said.' I looked at the child. 'How am I doing with the list?'

Aenea made that casting-away gesture with her slender hands. 'Not bad.

You have to remember that we've only been at this a few standard months . . . less than three, actually.'

'Yeah,' I said, looking out the window at the low shafts of sunlight striking the tall adobe building across from the hospital. Beyond the city, I could see the rocky hills burning red with evening light. 'Yeah,' I said again, all of the energy and amusement drained from my voice, 'I'm doing great.' I sighed and pushed the dinner tray farther away. 'One thing I don't understand – even in all that confusion, I don't know why their radar didn't track the raft when we were so close.'

'A. Bettik shot it out,' said the girl, working on the green gelatin again.

'Say what?'

'A. Bettik shot it out. The radar dish. With your plasma rifle.' She finished the green goop and set the spoon in place. During the last week she had been nurse, doctor, chef, and bottle washer.

'I thought he said he could not shoot at humans,' I said.

'He can't,' said Aenea, clearing the tray and setting it on a nearby dresser. 'I asked him. But he said that there was no prohibition against his shooting as many radar dishes as he wanted. So he did. Before we fixed your position and dived in to save you.'

'That was a three- or four-klick shot,' I said, 'from a pitching raft. How many pulse bolts did he use?'

'One,' said Aenea. She was looking at the monitor readouts above my head.

I whistled softly. 'I hope he never gets mad at me. Even from a distance.'

'I think you'd have to be a radar dish before you'd have to worry,' she said, tucking in the clean sheets.

'Where is he?'

Aenea walked to the window and pointed east. 'He found an EMV that had a full charge and was checking out the kibbutzim way out toward the Great Salt Sea.'

'All the others have been empty?'

'Every one. Not even a dog, cat, horse, or pet chipmunk left behind.'

I knew that she was not kidding. We had talked about it – when communities are evacuated in a hurry, or when disaster strikes, pets are often left behind. Packs of wild dogs had been a problem during the South Talon uprising on Aquila. The Home Guard had to shoot former pets on sight.

'That means they had time to take their pets with them,' I said.

Aenea turned toward me and crossed her thin arms. 'And leave their clothes behind? And their computers, comlogs, private diaries, family holes . . . all their personal junk?'

'And none of those tell you what happened? No final diary entries? No surveillance cameras or frenzied last-minute comlog entries?'

'Nope,' said the girl. 'At first I was reluctant to intrude into their private comlogs and such. But by now I've played back dozens of them. During the last week there was the usual news of the fighting nearby. The Great Wall was less than a light-year away and the Pax ships were filling the system. They didn't come down to the planet much, but it was obvious that Hebron would have to join the Pax Protectorate after it was all over. Then there were some final newscasts about the Ousters breaking through the lines . . . then nothing. Our guess is that the Pax evacuated the entire population and then the Ousters moved on, but there's no notice of evacuation in the news holos, or in the computer entries, or anywhere. It's like the people just disappeared.' She rubbed her arms. 'I have some of the holocast disks if you want to see them.'

'Maybe later,' I said. I was very tired.

'A. Bettik will be back in the morning,' she said, pulling the thin blanket up to my chin. Beyond the window, the sun had set but the hills literally glowed from stored-up light. It was a twilight effect of the stones on this world that I thought I would never tire of watching. But right then, I could not keep my eyes open.

'Do you have the shotgun?' I mumbled. 'The plasma rifle? Bettik gone . . . all alone here . . .'

'They're on the raft,' said Aenea. 'Now, go to sleep.'

On the first day I was fully conscious, I tried to thank both of them for saving my life. They resisted.

'How did you find me?' I asked.

'It wasn't hard,' said the girl. 'You left the mike open right up to the time the Pax officer stabbed it and broke it. We could hear everything. And we could see you through the binoculars.'

'You shouldn't have both left the raft,' I said. 'It was too dangerous.'

'Not really, M. Endymion,' said A. Bettik. 'Besides rigging the sea anchor, which slowed the raft's progress considerably, M. Aenea had the idea of tying one of the climbing ropes to a small log for flotation and allowing the line to trail behind the raft for almost a hundred meters. If we could not catch up to the raft, we felt certain we could get you back to the trailing line before it moved out of reach. And, as events showed, we did.'

I shook my head. 'It was still stupid.'

'You're welcome,' said the girl.

On the tenth day I tried standing. It was a short-lived victory, but a victory nonetheless. On the twelfth day I walked the length of the corridor to the toilet there. That was a major victory. On the thirteenth day, the power failed all over the city.

Emergency generators in the hospital basement kicked in, but we knew our time there was limited.

'I wish we could take the autosurgeon with us,' I said as we sat on the ninth-floor terrace that last evening, looking down on the shadowed avenues.

'It would fit on the raft,' said A. Bettik, 'but the extension cord would be a problem.'

'Seriously,' I said, trying not to sound like the paranoid, victimized, demoralized patient that I was then, 'we need to check the pharmacies here for stuff we need.'

'Done,' said Aenea. 'Three new and improved medpaks. One whole pouch of plasma ampules. A portable diagnosticator. Ultramorph . . . but don't ask, you aren't getting any today.'

I held out my left hand. 'See this? It just stopped shaking this afternoon. I won't be asking for any again soon.'

Aenea nodded. Overhead, feathery clouds glowed with the last evening light.

'How long do you think these generators will hold out?' I said to the android. The hospital was one of only a handful of city buildings still lighted.

'A few weeks, perhaps,' said A. Bettik. 'The power grid has been repairing and running itself for months, but the planet is harsh – you've noticed the dust storms that sweep in from the desert each morning – and even though the technology is quite advanced for a non-Pax world, the place needs humans to maintain it.'

'Entropy is a bitch,' I said.

'Now, now,' said Aenea from where she was leaning on the terrace wall. 'Entropy can be our friend.'

'When?' I said.

She turned around so that she was leaning back on her elbows. The building behind her was a dark rectangle, serving to highlight the glow of her sunburned skin. 'It wears down empires,' she said. 'And does in despotisms.'

'That's a hard phrase to say quickly,' I said. 'What despotisms are we talking about here?'

Aenea made that casting-away gesture, and for a minute I thought she was not going to speak, but then she said, 'The Huns, the Scythians, the Visigoths, the Ostrogoths, the Egyptians, Macedonians, Romans, and Assyrians.'

'Yeah,' I said, 'but . . .'

'The Avars and Northern Wei,' she continued, 'and the Juan-Juans, the Mamelukes, the Persians, Arabs, Abbasids, and Seljuks.'

'Okay,' I said, 'but I don't see . . .'

'The Kurds and Ghaznavids,' she continued, smiling now. 'Not to mention the Mongols, Sui, Tang, Buminids, Crusaders, Cossacks, Prussians, Nazis, Soviets, Japanese, Javanese, North Ammers, Greater Chinese, Colum-Peros, and Antarctic Nationalists.'

I held up a hand. She stopped. Looking at A. Bettik, I said, 'I don't even know these planets, do you?'

The android's expression was neutral. 'I believe they all relate to Old Earth, M. Endymion.'

'No shit,' I said.

'No shit is, I believe, correct in this context,' A. Bettik said in a flat tone.

I looked back at the girl. 'So this is our plan to topple the Pax for the old poet? Hide out somewhere and wait for entropy to take its toll?'

She crossed her arms again. 'Uh-uh,' she said. 'Normally that would have been a good plan – just hunker down for a few millennia and let time take its course – but these damn cruciforms complicate the equation.'

'How do you mean?' I said, my voice serious.

'Even if we wanted to topple the Pax,' she said, 'which – by the way – I don't. That's your job. But even if we wanted to, entropy's not on our side anymore with that parasite that can make people almost immortal.'

'Almost immortal,' I murmured. 'When I was dying, I must admit that I thought of the cruciform. It would have been a lot easier . . . not to mention less painful than all the surgery and recovery . . . just to die and let the thing resurrect me.'

Aenea was looking at me. Finally she said, 'That's why this planet had the best medical care in or out of the Pax.'

'Why?' I said. My head was still thick with drugs and fatigue.

'They were . . . are . . . Jews,' the girl said softly. 'Very few accepted the cross. They only had one chance at life.'

We sat for some time without speaking that evening, as the shadows filled the city canyons of New Jerusalem and the hospital hummed with electric life while it still could.

The next morning I walked as far as the old groundcar that had hauled me to the hospital thirteen days earlier, but – sitting in the back where they had made a mattress bed for me – I gave orders to find a gun shop.

After an hour of driving around, it became obvious that there were no gun shops in New Jerusalem. 'All right,' I said. 'A police headquarters.'

There were several of these. As I hobbled into the first one we encountered, waving away offers from both girl and android to act as a crutch, I soon discovered how underarmed a peaceful society could be. There were no weapons racks there, not even riot guns or stunners. 'I don't suppose Hebron had an army or Home Guard?' I said.

'I believe not,' replied A. Bettik. 'Until the Ouster incursion three standard years ago, there were no human enemies or dangerous animals on the planet.'

I grunted and kept looking. Finally, after breaking open a triple-locked drawer in the bottom of some police chief's desk, I found something.

'A Steiner-Ginn, I believe,' said the android. 'A pistol firing reduced-charge plasma bolts.'

'I know what it is,' I said. There were two magazines in the drawer. That should be about sixty bolts. I went outside, aimed the weapon at a distant hillside, and squeezed the trigger ring. The pistol couched and the hillside showed a tiny flash. 'Good,' I said, fitting the old weapon in my empty holster. I was afraid that it would be a signature weapon – capable of being fired only by its owner. Those weapons went in and out of vogue over the centuries.

'We have the flechette pistol on the raft,' began A. Bettik.

I shook my head. I wanted nothing to do with those things for a good while.

A. Bettik and Aenea had stocked up on water and food while I had been recuperating, and by the time I hobbled to the landing at the canal and looked at our refitted and refurbished raft, I could see the extra boxes. 'Question,' I said. 'Why are we going on with this floating woodpile when there are comfortable little runabout boats tied up over there? Or we could take an EMV and travel in air-conditioned comfort.'

The girl and the blue-skinned man exchanged glances. 'We voted while you were recovering,' she said. 'We go on with the raft.'

'Don't I get a vote?' I snapped. I had meant to feign anger, but when it came, it was real enough.

'Sure,' said the girl, standing on the dock with her feet planted, legs apart, and her hands on her hips. 'Vote.'

'I vote we get an EMV and travel in comfort,' I said, hearing the petulant tone in my voice and hating it even while continuing it. 'Or even one of these boats. I vote we leave these logs behind.'

'Vote recorded,' said the girl. 'A. Bettik and I voted to keep the raft. It's not going to run out of power, and it can float. One of these boats would have shown up on the radar on Mare Infinitus, and an EMV couldn't have made the trip on some worlds. Two for keeping the raft, one against. We keep it.'

'Who made this a democracy?' I demanded. I admit that I had images of spanking this kid.

'Who made it anything else?' said the girl.

All through this A. Bettik stood by the edge of the dock, fiddling with a rope, his face a study in that embarrassed expression that most people get when around members of another family squabbling. He was wearing a loose tunic and baggy shorts made of yellow linen. There was a wide-brimmed yellow hat on his head.

Aenea stepped onto the raft and loosened the stern line. 'You want a boat or an EMV . . . or a floating couch, for that matter . . . you take it, Raul. A. Bettik and I are going on in this.'

I started hobbling toward a nice little dinghy tied up along the dock. 'Wait,' I said, pivoting on my stronger leg to look at her again. 'The farcaster won't work if I try to go through alone.'

'Right,' said the girl. A. Bettik had stepped aboard the raft, and now she cast off the forward line. The canal was much wider here than it had been in the concrete trough of the aqueduct: about thirty meters across as it ran through New Jerusalem.

A. Bettik stood at the steering oar and looked at me as the girl picked up one of the longer poles and pushed the raft away from the dock.

'Wait!' I said. 'Goddammit, wait!' I hobbled down the pier, jumped the meter or so to the raft, landed on my recuperating leg, and had to catch myself with my good arm before I rolled into the microtent.

Aenea offered me her hand, but I ignored it as I got to my feet. 'God, you're a stubborn brat,' I said.

'Look who's talking,' said the girl, and went forward to sit at the front of the raft as we moved into the center current.

Out of the shade of the buildings, Hebron's sun was even fiercer. I pulled on my old tricorn cap for a bit of shade as I stood by the steering oar with A. Bettik.

'I imagine you're on her side,' I said at last as we moved into the open desert and the river narrowed to a canal once again.

'I am quite neutral, M. Endymion,' said the blue-skinned man.

'Hah!' I said. 'You voted to stay with the raft.'

'It has served us well so far, sir,' said the android, stepping back as I hobbled closer and took the steering oar in my hands.

I looked at the new crates of provisions stacked neatly in the shade of the tent, at the stone hearth with its hearing cube and pots and pans, at the shotgun and plasma rifle – freshly oiled and laid under canvas covers – and at our packs, sleeping bags, medkits, and other stuff. The forward 'mast' had been raised while I was gone, and now one of A. Bettik's extra white shirts flew from it like a flapping pennant.

'Well,' I said at last, 'screw it.'

'Precisely, sir,' said the android.

The next portal was only five klicks out of town. I squinted up at Hebron's blazing sun as we passed through the arch's thin shadow, then into the line of the portal itself. With the other farcaster portals, there had been a moment when the air within shimmered and changed, giving us a glance at what lay ahead.

Here there was only absolute blackness. And the blackness did not change as we continued on. The temperature dropped at least seventy degrees centigrade. At the same instant, the gravity changed – it suddenly felt as if I were carrying someone my own mass on my back.

'The lamps!' I called, still holding the steering oar against a suddenly strong current. I was struggling to stay on my feet against the terrible drag of increased gravity there. The combination of chilling cold, absolute blackness, and oppressive weight was terrifying.

The two had loaded lanterns they had found in New Jerusalem, but it was the old handlamp that Aenea flicked on first. Its beam cut through icy vapor, across black water, and lifted to illuminate a roof of solid ice some fifteen meters above us. Stalactites of patterned ice hung down almost to the water. Daggers of ice protruded from the black current on either side and ahead of us. Far ahead, about where the beam began to dim at a hundred meters or so, there seemed to be a solid wall of icy blocks running right down to the water's surface. We were in an ice cave . . . and one with no visible way out. The cold burned at my exposed hands, arms, and face. The gravity lay on my neck like so many iron collars.

'Damn,' I said. I locked the steering oar in place and hobbled toward the packs. It was hard to stay upright with a bad leg and eighty kilos on my back. A. Bettik and the girl were already there, digging for our insulated clothing.

Suddenly there was a loud crack. I looked up, expecting to see a stalactite falling on us, or the roof caving in under this terrible weight, but it was only our mast snapping where it had struck a low-hanging shelf of ice. The mast fell much faster than it would have in Hyperion gravity – rushing to the raft as if someone had fast-forwarded a holo. Wood chips flew as it hit. A. Bettik's shirt struck with an audible crash. It was frozen solid and covered with a thin coat of hoar frost.

'Damn,' I said again, my teeth chattering, and dug for my woollen undies.

THIRTY-FIVE

Father Captain de Soya uses the power of the papal diskey in ways he has never before attempted.

Mare Infinitus Station Three-twenty-six Mid-littoral, where the hawking mat was discovered, is declared a crime zone and put under martial law. De Soya brings in Pax troops and ships from the floating city of St Thérése and places all of the former Pax garrison and the fishing guests under house arrest. When St Thérése's governing prelate, Bishop Melandriano, protests this high-handedness and argues the limits of the papal diskey, de Soya goes to the planetary Governor, Archbishop Jane Kelley. The archbishop bows to the papal diskey and silences Melandriano under threat of excommunication.

Appointing young Lieutenant Sproul as his adjutant and liaison during the investigation, de Soya brings in Pax forensic experts and top investigators from St Thérése and the other large city platforms to carry out the crime-scene studies. Truthtell and other drugs are administered to Captain C. Dobbs Powl – who is being held under arrest in the station's brig – the other members of the former Pax garrison there, and to all the fishermen who had been present.

Within a few days it becomes obvious that Captain Powl, the late Lieutenant Belius, and many of the other officers and men of this remote platform had been conspiring with area poachers to allow illegal catches of local game fish, to steal Pax equipment – including one submersible that had been reported as sunk by rebel fire – and to extort money from fishing guests. None of this interests Father Captain de Soya. He wants to know precisely what happened on that evening two standard months earlier.

Forensic evidence mounts. The blood and tissue on the hawking mat are DNA-tested and transmitted back to the Pax records section in St Thérése and at the orbital Pax base. Two distinct strains of blood are found: the majority is positively identified as the DNA pattern of Lieutenant Belius; the second is unidentified in Mare Infinitus Pax records, despite the fact that every Pax citizen on the sea world has been typed and recorded.

'So how did Belius's blood end up on the flying carpet?' asks Sergeant Gregorius. 'According to everyone's testimony under Truthtell, Belius was knocked in the drink long before the fellow they captured tried to escape on the mat.'

De Soya nods and steeples his fingers. He has turned the former director's office into his command center, and the platform is very crowded with three times its former population now aboard. Three large Pax Sea Navy frigates are at sea anchor off the platform, and two of them are combat submersibles. The former skimmer deck is full of Pax aircraft, and engineers have been brought in to repair and extend the thopter deck. Just this morning de Soya has ordered another three ships to the area. Bishop Melandriano transmits his written protests at the mounting costs at least twice a day; Father Captain de Soya ignores them.

'I think our unknown stopped to pull the lieutenant out of the . . . how did you call it, Sergeant? . . . out of the drink. They struggled. The unknown was injured or killed. Belius tried to make it back to the station. Powl and the others killed him by mistake.'

'Aye,' says Gregorius, 'that's the best scenario I've heard.' In the hours since the DNA results were transmitted back from St Therése, they had woven many others – plots with poachers, conspiracies between the unknown and Lieutenant Belius, Captain Powl murdering former conspirators. This theory is the simplest.

'It means that our unknown is one of those traveling with the girl,' says de Soya. 'And he has a merciful – if stupid – side to him.'

'Or he could have been a poacher,' says Gregorius. 'We'll never know.'

De Soya taps his fingertips together and looks up. 'Why not, Sergeant?'

'Well, Captain, the evidence is all down there, ain't it, sir?' he says, jerking a thumb toward the surging violet sea outside the windows. 'The navy boys here say it's ten thousand fathoms deep or more – that's almost twenty thousand meters of water, sir. Any bodies there have been eaten by the fishes, sir. And if he was a poacher who got away . . . well, we'll never know. And if he was an offworlder . . . well, there aren't any central Pax DNA records . . . We'd have to search the files on several hundred worlds. We'll never find him.'

Father Captain de Soya drops his hands and smiles thinly. 'This is one of those rare times where you are wrong, Sergeant. Watch.'

In the next week de Soya has every poacher within a thousand-kilometer radius rounded up and – questioned under Truthtell. The rounding up involves two dozen sea-naval ships and over eight thousand Pax personnel. The cost is enormous. Bishop Melandriano becomes apoplectic and flies to Station Three-twenty-six Mid-littoral to stop the madness. Father Captain de Soya places the cleric under arrest and has him flown to a remote monastery nine thousand kilometers away near the polar ice caps.

De Soya also decides to search the ocean bottom.

'You won't find anything, sir,' says Lieutenant Sproul. 'There are so many predators down there that nothing organic makes it a hundred fathoms deep, much less to the bottom . . . and according to our soundings this week, that's twelve thousand fathoms. Besides, there are only two submersibles on Mare Infinitus that can operate at that depth.'

'I know,' says de Soya. 'I've ordered them here. They will arrive tomorrow with the frigate *Passion of Christ*.'

For once Lieutenant Sproul is speechless.

De Soya smiles. 'You're aware, aren't you, son, that Lieutenant Belius was a born-again Christian? And his cruciform was not recovered?'

Sproul's mouth hangs open for a moment. 'Yessir . . . I mean . . . yes, but . . . sir, to be resurrected, I mean . . . don't they need to find the body intact, sir?'

'Not at all, Lieutenant,' says Father Captain de Soya. 'Merely a good-sized segment of the cross we all bear. Many a good Catholic has been resurrected from a few centimeters of intact cruciform and a bit of flesh that can be DNA-typed and grown to order.'

Sproul shakes his head. 'But, sir . . . it's been over nine Big Tides, sir. There's not a square millimeter of Lieutenant Belius or his cruciform left, sir. That's a giant feeding tank out there, sir.'

De Soya walks to the window. 'Perhaps, Lieutenant. Perhaps. But we owe it to our fellow Christian to make every attempt, do we not? Besides, if Lieutenant Belius *were* to be granted the miracle of resurrection, he has to stand charges for theft, treason, and attempted murder, doesn't he?'

Using the most advanced techniques available to them, the local forensic experts are available to lift unidentified fingerprints from a mess-hall coffee cup in spite of the many washings the cup has undergone over the past two months. Of the thousands of latent prints, all are laboriously identified as belonging to garrison troops or visiting fisherman except for this one reconstructed print. It is set aside with unidentified DNA evidence.

'During the Web days,' says Dr Holmer Ryum, the chief forensic officer, 'the megadatasphere would have put us in touch with central Hegemony files within seconds via the fatline. We could get a match almost instantly.'

'If we had some cheese, we could have a ham-and-cheese sandwich,' replies Father Captain de Soya, 'if we had some ham.'

'What?' says Dr Ryum.

'Never mind,' says de Soya. 'I expect to have a match within days.'

Dr Ryum is puzzled. 'How, Father Captain? We've checked the planetary data banks. Run checks against every poacher you've captured . . . and I have to say, there's never been a mass arrest like this on Mare Infinitus before. You're upsetting a delicate balance of corruption that has existed here for centuries.'

De Soya rubs the bridge of his nose. He has not slept much in the past weeks. 'I am not interested in delicate balances of corruption, Doctor.'

'I understand,' says Ryum. 'But I fail to understand how you can expect a match within days. Neither the Church nor Pax Central has files of all the citizens on various Pax worlds, much less of the Outback and Ouster areas . . .'

'All Pax worlds keep their own records,' de Soya says quietly. 'Of baptisms and cross sacraments. Of marriages and deaths. Military and police records.'

Dr Ryum opens his hands in helplessness. 'But where would you start?'

'Where the odds are the best in finding him,' answers Father Captain de Soya.

*

Meanwhile, nothing is found of the hapless Lieutenant Belius within the six-hundred-fathom depths to which the two deep-sea submersibles agree to descend. Hundreds of rainbow sharks are stunned to the surface and the contents of their stomachs analysed. Still no Belius, neither remnants of him nor of his cruciform. Thousands of other sea scavengers are harvested within a two-hundred-klick radius, and bits of two poachers are identified in gullets, but no sign of Belius or the stranger. A funeral mass is held on Station Three-twenty-six Mid-littoral for the lieutenant, who is said to have died the true death and found true immortality.

De Soya orders the deep-sea submersible captains to go deeper, looking for artifacts. The captains refuse.

'Why?' demands the priest-captain. 'I brought you here because your machines can go to the bottom. Why won't you?'

'The Lantern-Mouths,' says the senior of the two captains. 'To search, we'll have to use lights. To six hundred fathoms, our sonar and deep radar can detect them rising and we could beat them to the surface. Below that, and we wouldn't have a chance. We won't go deeper.'

'You will go deeper,' says Father Captain de Soya, the papal diskey glowing against the black of his cassock.

The senior captain takes a step closer. 'You can arrest me, shoot me, excommunicate me . . . I won't take my men and machine down to certain death. You haven't *seen* a Lantern-Mouth, Father.'

De Soya sets a friendly hand on the captain's shoulder. 'I will not arrest, shoot, or excommunicate you, Captain. And I will see a Lantern-Mouth soon. Perhaps more than one.'

The captain does not understand.

'I've ordered in three more of the Ocean Fleet's attack submarines,' says de Soya. 'We are going to find, flush, and kill every Lantern-Mouth and any other threatening 'canth within five hundred klicks. When you dive, the area will be completely safe.'

The senior captain looks at the other deep-sea submersible captain and then back to de Soya. Both of the captains appear to be in shock. 'Father . . . Captain . . . sir . . . do you know how much a Lantern-Mouth is *worth*? To the offworld sport fishermen and the big factories at Therése . . . sir.'

'About fifteen thousand Mare-Eye seidons,' says de Soya. 'That's about thirty-five thousand Pax florins. Almost fifty thousand Mercantilus marks. Each.' De Soya smiles. 'And since you two will receive thirty percent finders' fees for locating the Mouths for the navy, I wish you good hunting.'

The two deep-submersible captains hurry out the door.

For the first time de Soya sends someone else off in the *Raphael* to run his errands. Sergeant Gregorius travels alone in the archangel, carrying the DNA and fingerprint information, as well as threads from the hawking mat.

'Remember,' says de Soya over tightbeam from the platform a few minutes before *Raphael* spins up to total quantum state, 'there's still a heavy Pax presence on Hyperion and at least two torchships in-system at all times. They will bring you to the capital of St Joseph's for a proper resurrection.'

Lashed into his acceleration couch, Sergeant Gregorius only grunts. His face looks relaxed and calm on camera, despite his imminent death.

'Three days there, of course,' continues de Soya, 'and – I would think – no more than one day to go through the files. And then you return.'

'Got it, Captain,' says Gregorius. 'I won't waste any time in any Jacktown bars.'

'Jacktown?' says de Soya. 'Oh, yes . . . the old nickname for the capital. Well, Sergeant, if you want to spend your one real evening on Hyperion in a bar, be my guest. It's been a dry few months with me.'

Gregorius grins. The clock says thirty seconds before quantum leap and his painful extinction. 'I ain't complainin', Captain.'

'Very good,' says de Soya. 'Have a good trip. Oh . . . and Sergeant?'

'Yessir?' Ten seconds.

'Thank you, Sergeant.'

There is no response. Suddenly there is nothing on the other end of the coherent tachyon tightbeam. *Raphael* has made its quantum leap.

Five Lantern-Mouths are tracked and killed by the navy. De Soya flies to each carcass in his command thopter.

'Good Lord, they're larger than I could have imagined,' he said to Lieutenant Sproul when they arrive above the spot where the first one floats.

The grub-white beast is easily three times the size of the station platform; a mass of eyestalks, gaping maws, fibrillating gill slits each the size of the thopter, pulsating tendrils extending hundreds of meters, dangling antennae each carrying a cold-light 'lantern' of great brilliance – even out here in the daylight – and mouths, many mouths, each large enough to swallow a fleet submarine. As de Soya watches, the harvesting crews are already flocking over the pressure-exploded carcass, sawing off tendrils and eyestalks and cutting the white meat to portable cubes before the hot sun spoils it all.

Satisfied that the area is cleared of Mouths and other deadly 'canths, the two deep-dive captains take their submersibles twelve thousand fathoms down. There, amid forests of tube worms the size of Old Earth redwood trees, they find an amazing array of old wrecks – poacher submersibles crushed to the size of small suitcases by the pressure, one naval frigate that has been missing for more than a century. They also find boots – dozens of boots.

'It's the tanning process,' says Lieutenant Sproul to de Soya as the two watch the monitors. 'It's an oddity, but it was true on Old Earth as well. Some of the oldest deep-sea salvage operations – a surface ship called the *Titanic*, for instance – never turned up bodies, the sea's too hungry for that, but lots of boots. Something in the tanning process of leather discourages sea critters there . . . and here.'

'Bring them up,' commands de Soya over the umbilical link.

'The boots?' comes back the submersible captain's voice. 'All of them?'

'All of them,' says de Soya.

The monitors show a profusion of junk on the seabed: things lost by the platform station crew over almost two centuries of carelessness, personal belongings of the drowned poachers and sailors, metal and plastic garbage tossed by the fishermen and others. Most items are corroded and misshapen by deep-sea crustaceans and unimaginable pressure, but a few are new enough and tough enough to be identified.

'Bag those and send them up,' says de Soya as they encounter shiny objects that might be a knife, a fork, a belt buckle, a . . .

'What's that?' demands de Soya.

'What?' says the captain of the deepest submersible. He is watching the remote handlers rather than his monitors.

'That shiny thing . . . It looks like a handgun.'

The monitor shifts its view as the submersible turns. The powerful search-lights track, return, and illuminate the object as the camera zooms in. 'It is a handgun,' comes the captain's voice. 'Still clean. Damaged some by pressure, but basically intact.' De Soya can hear the click of the single-frame imager capturing this from the monitor. 'I'll collect it,' says the captain.

De Soya has the urge to add – 'carefully' – but does not speak. His years as torchship captain have taught him to let his people do their jobs. He watches as the grapple arm appears on the monitor and the remote handler gently lifts the shiny object.

'It could be Lieutenant Belius's flechette pistol,' says Sproul. 'It went over with him and hasn't been recovered yet.'

'This is quite a bit farther out,' muses de Soya, watching the image shift and change on the monitor.

'The currents here are powerful, weird,' says the young officer. 'But I have to admit that it didn't look like a flechette pistol. Too . . . I don't know . . . squarish.'

'Yes,' says de Soya. The underwater searchlights are flickering over the encrusted hull of a submersible that has been buried down there for decades. De Soya is thinking of his years in space and how empty that different unknown is from any ocean on the world, teeming with life and history. The priest-captain is thinking about the Ousters and their strange attempt to adapt themselves to space the way these tube worms and 'canths and bottom-hugging species have adapted themselves to eternal darkness and terrible pressures. Perhaps, he is thinking, the Ousters under-stand something about humanity's future that we in the Pax have only denied.

Heresy. De Soya shakes away the thoughts and looks at his young liaison officer. 'We'll know what it is soon enough,' he says. 'They're bringing this load up within the hour.'

Gregorius returns four days after his departure. He is dead. *Raphael* sends out its sad beacon, a torchship rendezvouses with it twenty light-minutes out, and the sergeant's body is removed and brought to the resurrection chapel at St Therése. De Soya does not wait for the man's revival. He orders the courier pouch brought to him at once.

Pax records on Hyperion have positively identified the DNA taken from the hawking mat, and have also matched the partial fingerprint on the cup. Both belong to the same man: Raul Endymion, born AD 3099 on planet Hyperion, not baptized; enlisted in the Hyperion Home Guard in Thomasmonth of the year AD 3115, fought with the twenty-third Mechanized Infantry Regiment during Ursus Uprising – three commendations for bravery, including one for rescuing a squadmate while under fire – stationed at Fort Benjing in the South Talon region of the continent of Aquila for eight standard months, served out the remainder of his time at Kans River Station 9 on Aquila, patrolling the jungle there, guarding against rebel terrorist activity near the fiberplastic plantations. Mustered out (honorable discharge) on Lentmonth 15, AD 3119, whereabouts unknown until less than ten standard months ago, Ascensionmonth 23, AD 3126, when he was arrested, tried, and convicted in Port Romance (continent of Aquila) for the murder of one M. Dabil Herrig, a born-again Christian. Records showed that Raul Endymion refused offers to accept the cross and was executed by deathwand one week after the arrest, on the 30th of Ascensionmonth, AD 3126. His body was disposed of at sea. The death certificate and autopsy reports were notarized by the local Pax Inspector General.

The next day latent prints on the crushed, ancient .45-caliber automatic pistol brought up from the ocean floor are matched: Raul Endymion.

Bits of thread from the hawking mat are not so easily identified by Hyperion Pax records, but the human clerk doing the search included a handwritten note that such a mat figures prominently in the legendary *Cantos* composed by a poet who had lived on Hyperion until a century or so ago.

When Sergeant Gregorius is resurrected, rests a few hours, and flies to Station Three-twenty-six Mid-littoral to report, de Soya tells him the various findings. He also informs the sergeant that the two dozen Pax engineers who have been swarming over the farcaster portal for three weeks report only that there is no sign that the ancient arch had been activated, despite sightings of a bright flash by several fishermen on the platform that night. The engineers also report that there is no way to get inside the ancient Coreconstructed arch, nor to tell where – if anywhere – someone might have been transported through it.

'Same as Renaissance V.,' says Gregorius. 'But at least you have some idea of who helped the girl escape.'

'Possibly,' says de Soya.

'He came a long way to die here,' says the sergeant.

Father Captain de Soya leans back in his chair. '*Did* he die here, Sergeant?' Gregorius has no answer.

Finally de Soya says, 'I think we're finished on Mare Infinitus. Or will be in a day or two.'

The sergeant nods. Through the long bank of windows here in the director's office, he can see the bright glow that precedes the moonrise. 'Where to next, Captain? Back on the old search pattern?'

De Soya is also watching the east, waiting for the giant orange disk to appear above the darkened horizon. 'I'm not sure, Sergeant. Let's get things tidied up here, Captain Powl handed over to Pax Justice in Orbit Seven, and soothe Bishop Melandriano's feathers . . .'

'If we can,' says Sergeant Gregorius.

'If we can,' agrees de Soya. 'Then we'll pay our respects to Archbishop Kelley, get back to *Raphael*, and decide where to jump next. It may be time for us to come up with some theories on where this child is headed and try to get there first, not just follow *Raphael*'s shortest-line pattern.'

'Yes, sir,' says Gregorius. He salutes, goes to the door, and hesitates there a moment. 'And *do* you have a theory, sir? Based on just the few things we've found here?'

De Soya is watching the three moons rise. He does not turn his chair around to face his sergeant as he says, 'Perhaps. Just perhaps.'

THIRTY-SIX

We leaned on our poles and stopped the raft's forward motion before it crashed into the ice wall. We had all of our lanterns lit now, the electric lamps throwing their beams into the frigid darkness of this ice cavern. Mist rose from the black waters and hung beneath the jagged roof of the cavern like ominous spirits of the drowned. Crystal facets distorted and then threw back the beams of puny light, making the surrounding darkness all the more profound.

'Why is the river still liquid?' asked Aenea, hugging her hands under her arms and stamping her feet. She had on every layer she had brought, but it was not enough. The cold was terrible.

I went to one knee at the edge of the raft, lifted a palmful of river water to my lips, and tasted. 'Salinity,' I said. 'This is as salty as Mare Infinitus's sea.'

A. Bettik played his handlamp on the ice wall ten meters ahead of us. 'It comes down to the water's edge,' he said. 'And extends somewhat beneath it. But the current still flows.'

For an instant I had a surge of hope. 'Shut down the lanterns,' I said, hearing my voice echo in the vaporous hollow of the place. 'Turn off the handlamps.'

When this was accomplished, I had hoped to see a glimmer of light through or under the ice wall – a hint of salvation, an indication that this ice cavern was finite and that only the exit had collapsed.

The darkness was absolute. No amount of waiting gave us night vision. I cursed and wished for the night goggles I had lost on Mare Infinitus: if they worked here, it would have meant that light was seeping in from somewhere. We waited another moment in the blindness. I could hear Aenea's shaking, actually feel the vapor from all of our breaths.

'Turn the lights on,' I said at last. There had been no glimmer of hope.

We played the beams on the walls, roof, and river again. Mist continued to rise and condense near the ceiling. Icicles fell constantly into the steaming water.

'Where . . . are . . . we?' asked Aenea, trying without total success to stop the chattering of her teeth.

I dug in my pack, found the thermal blanket I had packed at Martin Silenus's tower so long ago, and wrapped it around her. 'That will hold the heat in. No . . . keep it on,'

'We can share,' said the girl.

I crouched near the heating cube, turning its conductive power to maximum. Five of the six ceramic faces began to glow. 'We'll share it when we have to,' I said. Playing the light over the ice wall that blocked our way, I said, 'To answer your question, my guess is Sol Draconi Septem. Some of my richer . . . and tougher . . . fen clients hunted arctic wraiths there.'

'I concur,' said A. Bettik. His blue skin made him look even colder than I felt as he huddled near the glowing lantern and heating cube. The micro-tent had become frost-laden and as brittle as thin metal. 'That world has a one-point-seven-g gravity field,' he said. 'And since the Fall and destruction of the Hegemony terraforming project there, most of it is said to have returned to its state of hyperglaciation.'

'Hyperglaciation?' repeated Aenea. 'What does that mean?' Some color was returning to her cheeks as the thermal blanket captured her warmth.

'It means that most of the atmosphere of Sol Draconi Septem is a solid,' said the android. 'Frozen.'

Aenea looked around. 'I think that I remember my mother talking about this place. She chased someone through here once on a case. She was Lusian, you know, so she was used to one-point-five standard gravities, but even she remembered that this world was uncomfortable. I'm surprised that the River Tethys ran through here.'

A. Bettik stood to shine his light around again, then crouched close to the glowing cube. Even his strong back was hunched against the massive gravity.

'What does the guidebook say?' I asked him.

He removed the small volume. 'Very terse entries, sir. The Tethys had extended to Sol Draconi Septem for only a brief period before the book was published. It is in the northern hemisphere, just beyond the area the Hegemony was attempting to terraform. The main attraction of this section of the river appears to have been the possibility of seeing an arctic wraith.'

'That's the thing your hunter friends were after?' Aenea said to me.

I nodded. 'White. Lives on the surface. Very fast. Very deadly. Almost extinct during the Web days, but they've made a comeback since the Fall according to the hunters I listened to. Evidently their diet consists of the human residents of Sol Draconi Septem . . . what's left of them. Only the indigenies – the Hegira colonists who had gone native centuries ago – survived the Fall. They're supposed to be primitive. The hunters said that the only animal the indigenies can hunt here is the wraith. And the indig-enies hate the Pax. Word was that they kill missionaries . . . use their sinews for bowstring, just as they would a wraith's.'

'This world was never very amenable to having the Hegemony authorities here,' said the android. 'Legend has it that the locals were quite pleased by the Fall of the farcasters. Until the plague, of course.'

'Plague?' said Aenea.

'A retrovirus,' I said. 'It trimmed the Hegemony human population from several hundred million to fewer than a million. Most of those were killed by the few thousand indigenies here. The rest were evacuated during the early days of the Pax.' I paused and looked at the girl. She looked like a sketch for a young Madonna with the thermal blanket draped around her like that, her skin glowing in the lantern and cube light. 'Times were rough around the old Web after the Fall.'

'So I gather,' she said dryly. 'They weren't so bad when I was growing up on Hyperion.' She looked around at the black water lapping at the raft, up at the stalactites of ice. 'I wonder why they went to all that trouble just to have a few kilometers of ice cavern on the tour.'

'That's the strange part,' I said, nodding toward the little guidebook. 'It says that the main attraction is the chance of sighting an arctic wraith. But the wraiths . . . at least from what I heard the offworld hunters say . . . don't burrow down in the ice. They live on the surface.'

Aenea's dark eyes were fixed on me as she absorbed the meaning of that. 'So this wasn't a cavern then . . .'

'I think not,' said A. Bettik. He pointed to the icy ceiling fifteen meters above us. 'The terraform attempt in those days concentrated on creating enough temperature and surface pressure in certain low areas to allow sublimation of the largely carbon-dioxide-and-oxygen atmosphere from frozen to gaseous form.'

'Did it work?' asked the girl.

'In limited areas,' replied the android. He made a gesture toward the surrounding darkness. 'My guess would be that this was quite open during the days when River Tethys tourists transited this short section. Or I should say, open except for containment fields that helped to hold in the atmosphere and hold back the more inclement weather. Those fields, I daresay, are gone.'

'And we're locked under a mass of what the tourists used to breathe,' I said. Looking toward the ceiling and then down at the plasma rifle still in its case, I muttered, 'I wonder how thick . . .'

'Most probably several hundred meters, at least,' said A. Bettik. 'Perhaps a vertical kilometer of ice. This was, I understand, the thickness of the atmospheric glaciation to the immediate north of the terraformed areas.'

'You know a lot about this place,' I said.

'On the contrary, sir,' he said. 'We have now exhausted the totality of my knowledge on the ecology, geology, and history of Sol Draconi Septem.'

'We could ask the comlog,' I said, nodding toward my pack, where I now kept the bangle.

The three of us exchanged looks. 'Nahh,' said Aenea.

'I concur,' said A. Bettik.

'Maybe later,' I said, although I admit that even while I spoke, I was thinking of some of the things I should have insisted upon bringing from the EVA locker: hazardous environment suits with powerful heaters, scuba gear, even a spacesuit would be much preferable to the inadequate cold-weather gear in which we now shivered.

'I was thinking of shooting at the roof, trying to break through to daylight,' I said, 'but the risk of collapsing it on us seems much greater than any chance of escape that way.'

A. Bettik nodded. He had pulled on a strange woollen cap with long earflaps. The usually thin-looking android now appeared downright roly-poly in all of his layers of clothing. 'You have some *plastique* left in the flare pouch, M. Endymion.'

'Yes. I was just thinking about that. There's enough left for half a dozen more moderate-sized charges . . . but I only have four detonators left, so we could try blasting our way up, or sideways, or through that ice wall that's blocking us. But only four blasts' worth.'

The shivering little Madonna figure looked at me. 'Where did you learn about explosives, Raul? In Hyperion's Home Guard?'

'Initially,' I said. 'But I really learned how to use old-fashioned *plastique* clearing stumps and boulders for Avrol Hume when we were landscaping the Beak estates . . .' I stood up, realizing that it was too cold to stay still for so long. The numbness in my fingers and toes sent that signal. 'We could try going back upriver,' I said, stamping my feet and flexing fingers.

Aenea frowned. 'The next operating farcasters are always downriver . . .'

'True,' I said, 'but maybe there's a way out *up*river. We find some warmth, a way out of this cave, a place to hole up for a while, and *then* we worry about getting through the next portal.'

Aenea nodded.

'Good idea, sir,' said the android, moving to the starboard push-pole.

Before pushing off, I reset the forward mast – cutting a meter or more off so it would clear the lowest stalactites – and hung a lantern there. Another lamp at each corner of the raft, and we pushed off upstream, our lights making thin yellow halos in the freezing mist.

The river was quite shallow – not quite three meters deep – and the poles found good traction against the bottom. But the current was very strong, and A. Bettik and I had to use all our strength to move the heavy raft upstream. Aenea pulled an extra pole from the back of the raft and joined me on my side, pushing and straining to move the vessel. Behind us, quickly flowing black water swelled and swirled over the stern boards.

For a few minutes this terrible exertion kept us warm – I was even pouring sweat, which froze against my clothing – but thirty minutes of poling and resting, resting and poling found us freezing again and just a hundred meters upstream from where we had started.

'Look,' said Aenea, setting her pole down and fetching the most powerful handlamp.

A. Bettik and I leaned against our staffs, holding the raft in place while we stared. One end of a massive farcaster portal was just visible, protruding from the massive blocks of ice like a small arc of some old groundcar's wheel rim locked in a bank of ice. Beyond the tiny bit of portal still exposed, the river channel narrowed and then narrowed again until it became a fissure only a meter or so wide, until finally it disappeared beneath another ice wall.

'The River must have been five or six times the width it is now at its widest,' said A. Bettik, 'if the portal arch extended from bank to bank.'

'Yeah,' I said, exhausted and dispirited. 'Let's go back to the other end.'

We raised our poles and quickly floated the length of our ice gallery, covering in two minutes what it had taken us thirty minutes to pole upstream. All three of us had to use our poles to slow the raft and fend off the ice wall at the end.

'Well,' said Aenea, 'here we are again.' She shone her headlamp on the vertical ice cliffs on either side. 'We could go ashore if there was a bank of some sort. But there isn't.'

'We could blow one with *plastique*,' I said. 'Make a sort of ice cave.'

'Would that be any warmer?' asked the girl. Out of the thermal blanket now, she was shivering badly again. I realized that she had so little body fat that heat just poured out of her.

'No,' I said honestly. For the twentieth time I walked over to our tent and gear to find something that would be our salvation. Flares. *Plastique*. The weapons – their cases now covered with the hoarfrost that was settling on everything. One thermal blanket. Food. The heating cube was still glowing, and now the girl and blue-skinned man were crouching by it again. At that setting it would last for a hundred hours or so before losing its charge. If we had some good insulating material, we could make an ice cave cosy enough to keep us alive for three or four times that long at a lower setting . . .

We did not have the insulating material. The microtent fabric was good stuff, but it had poor insulating qualities. And the thought of huddling in an ice tomb as our handlamps and lanterns failed – which they would do quickly, in this cold – just watching the heating cube cool and waiting to die . . . well, it made my belly hurt.

I walked to the front of the raft, ran the handlamp beam over the milky ice and black water for the final time, and said, 'All right, here's what we'll do.'

Aenea and A. Bettik stared at me from the small circle of light by the heating cube. All of us were shivering.

'I'm going to take some *plastique*, the detonators, all the fuse cord we have, the rope, a com unit, my flashlight laser, and' – I took a breath – 'and dive under this goddamned wall, let the current carry me downstream, and hope to hell it's just a cave-in and that the river opens up down there. If it does, I'll surface and set the charges where they'll do the most good. Maybe we can blow an opening for the raft. If not, we'll leave the raft behind and all swim down there—'

'You'll die,' the girl said flatly. 'You'll be hypothermic in ten seconds. And how will you swim upstream against this current?'

'That's why I'm bringing the rope. If there's a place to get out of the way of the blast there, I'll stay at the other end while we blow the opening, but if not, I tug a code on the rope and you two haul me back. When I get on the raft, I'll strip and wrap myself in the thermal blanket,' I said. 'It's a hundred percent insulative. If I have any body heat left, I'll survive.'

'What if we all have to swim for it?' said Aenea in the same doubting tone. 'The thermal blanket's not big enough for the three of us.'

'We bring the heating cube,' I said. 'Use the blanket like a tent until we warm up.'

'What are we warming up *on*?' asked the girl, her voice small. 'There's no riverbank here . . . why should there be one there?'

I made a gesture. 'That's why we try to blow an opening for the raft,' I said patiently. 'If we can't, I'll use the *plastique* to knock some of the ice wall down. We'll float on our own chunk of ice. Anything to get down to the next farcaster portal.'

'What if we use all the *plastique* to get another twenty meters and there's another ice wall?' said the girl. 'What if the farcaster's fifty klicks away through ice?'

I started to make another gesture with my hands, but they were shaking too much – from the cold, I hope. I set them in my armpits. 'Then we die on the other side of this wall,' I said, the vapor from my breath hanging in front of me. 'It's better than dying here.'

After a moment of silence, A. Bettik said, 'The plan seems our best chance, M. Endymion, but – you must see the logic of this – it should be I who swims. You are recuperating, weakened by your recent wounds. I was biofactured for resistance to extreme temperatures.'

'Not this extreme,' I said. 'I can see you shivering. Also, you won't know where to place the charges.'

'You can instruct me, M. Endymion. Using the com unit.'

'We don't know if they'll work through this ice,' I said. 'Besides, it will be a difficult call. It'll be like trying to cut a diamond – the charges will have to be set in just the right places.'

'Still,' said the android, 'it only makes sense that I—'

'It may make sense,' I interrupted, 'but that's not the way it's going to be. This is my job. If I . . . fail, you try. Besides, I'll need someone very strong to pull me back through the current, win or lose.' I walked over and put my hand on the blue man's shoulder. 'I'm pulling rank on you this time, A. Bettik.'

Aenea cast off the thermal blanket despite her shivering. 'What rank?' she demanded.

I pulled myself to my full height and struck a mock-heroic pose. 'I'll have you know that I was a Lancer specialist first class in the Hyperion Home Guard.' The delivery was marred only a bit by the chattering of my teeth.

'A private,' said the child.

'First class,' I said.

The girl put her arms around me. The hug surprised me and I lowered my arms to pat her awkwardly.

'First class is right,' she said softly. Stepping back, stamping her feet, and blowing into her hands, she said, 'All right . . . what do we do?'

'I'll get the things I need. Why don't you get that hundred-meter section of line you used as a sea anchor on Mare Infinitus? That should be enough. A. Bettik, if you would please let the raft move up against the ice wall in a way that the entire stern won't be awash with current. Perhaps by tucking the front in under that low shelf of ice there . . .'

All three of us were busy for a moment. When we reassembled at the front of the raft again, under the abbreviated mast with its fading lantern glow, I said to Aenea, 'Do you still think that someone or something is sending us to these specific River Tethys worlds for a reason?'

The girl looked around at the darkness for a few seconds. Somewhere behind us another stalactite of ice fell into the river with a hollow splash. 'Yes,' she said.

'And what's the reason for this dead end?'

Aenea shrugged, which – under different circumstances – would have looked a bit comical, she was so swathed in layers. 'A temptation,' she said.

I did not understand. 'Temptation for what?'

'I hate the cold and dark,' said the girl. 'I always have. Perhaps someone is tempting me to use certain . . . abilities . . . which I have not properly explored yet. Certain powers which I haven't *earned*.'

I looked down at the swirling black waters in which I would be swimming in less than a minute. 'Well, kiddo, if you have powers or abilities that would get us the hell out of here, I suggest you explore them and use them whether you've earned them or not.'

Her hand touched my arm. She was wearing an extra pair of my wool socks as mittens. 'I'm guessing,' she said, the vapor of her breath freezing on the brim of the floppy cap she had pulled low. 'But nothing I will ever learn could get all three of us out of here now. I know that's true. Perhaps the temptation is . . . It doesn't matter, Raul. Let's just see if we can get through this icefall.'

I nodded, took a breath, and stripped out of everything but my underwear. The shock of cold air was terrible. Completing the knot that held the line around my chest, noticing that my fingers were already growing stiff and useless from the cold, I took the shoulder bag holding the *plastique* from A. Bettik and said, 'The river water may be cold enough to stop my heart. If I don't tug once, hard, within the first thirty seconds, pull me back.'

The android nodded. We had gone over the other rope signals I would use.

'Oh, if you pull me back and I am in a coma or dead,' I said, trying to keep my tone matter-of-fact, 'don't forget I might be revived even after several minutes of having my heart stopped. This cold water should retard brain death.'

A. Bettik nodded again. He was standing with the rope over one shoulder and curled around his waist to the other hand in a classic climber's belay.

'Okay,' I said, realizing that I was delaying and losing body heat. 'See you guys in a few minutes.' I slipped over the side into the black water.

I believe that my heart did stop for a minute, but then it began pounding almost painfully. The current was stronger than I had bargained for. It almost swept me down and under the ice wall before I was ready to go. As it was, it swirled me several meters to the port of the raft and banged me up sharply against the jagged ice, cutting my forehead and slamming my forearms brutally. I clung to a jagged crystal with all of my strength, feeling my legs and lower body being pulled into that subterranean vortex and struggling to keep my face out of the water. The stalactite that had fallen behind us crashed against the ice wall just half a meter to my left. If it had struck me, I would have been unconscious and drowned without knowing what had happened.

'This . . . might . . . not . . . be . . . such a . . . good idea,' I gasped, teeth chattering, before I lost my grip and was pulled under the jagged icefall.

THIRTY-SEVEN

De Soya's idea is to abandon *Raphael*'s plodding search pattern and jump directly to the first of the Ouster-captured systems.

'What good will that do, sir?' asks Corporal Kee.

'Perhaps none,' admits Father Captain de Soya. 'But if there is an Ouster connection, we might get a hint of it there.'

Sergeant Gregorius rubs his jaw. 'Aye,' he says, 'and we may get captured by a Swarm. This ship isn't the best armed in His Holiness's fleet, if you don't mind me sayin' so, sir.'

De Soya nods. 'But it's fast. We could probably outrun most Swarm ships. And they may have abandoned the system by now . . . they tend to do that, hit, run, push back the Pax Great Wall, then leave the system with only a token perimeter defense after wreaking as much damage as they can on the world and populace . . .' De Soya stops. He has seen only one Ouster-pillaged world firsthand – Svoboda – but he hopes never to have to see another. 'Anyway,' he says, 'it's the same to us on this ship. Normally the quantum leap to beyond the Great Wall would be eight or nine months' shiptime, eleven or more years' time-debt. For us it will be the usual instantaneous jump and three days' resurrection.'

Lancer Rettig raised his hand, as he often did in these discussions. 'There's that to consider, sir.'

'What's that?'

'The Ousters have never captured an archangel courier, sir. I doubt if they know this sort of ship exists. Heck, sir, most of the Pax Fleet has no idea archangel technology exists.'

De Soya sees his point immediately, but Rettig continues. 'So we'd be running quite a risk, sir. Not just for ourselves, but for the Pax.'

There is a long silence. Finally de Soya speaks. 'That's a good point, Lancer. I've given it quite a bit of thought. But Pax Command built this ship with its automated resurrection creche just so we could go beyond Pax space. I think it's understood that we might have to follow leads into the Outback . . . into Ouster-held territory if need be.' The priest-captain takes a breath. 'I've been there, gentlemen. I've burned their orbital forests and fought my way out of Swarms. The Ousters are . . . strange. Their attempts to adapt to odd environments . . . to space even . . . are . . . blasphemous. They may no longer be human. But their ships are not fast. *Raphael* should be able to get in and translate back to quantum velocities if there is a threat to her capture. And we can program her to self-destruct before being captured.'

None of the three Swiss Guard troopers says a word. Each appears to be thinking about the death within death that would entail – the destruction without warning of destruction. They would go to sleep on their acceleration couches/resurrection creches as always and simply never awaken . . . at least not in this life. The cruciform sacrament is truly miraculous – it can bring shattered and blasted bodies back to life, return the shape and souls of born-again Christians who have been shot, burned, starved, drowned, asphyxiated, stabbed, crushed, or ravaged by disease – but it has its limits: too much time of decomposition defeats it, as would a thermonuclear explosion of a ship's in-system drive.

'I guess we're with you,' Sergeant Gregorius says at last, knowing that Father Captain de Soya has asked for this discussion because he hates simply ordering his men into such a risk of true death.

Kee and Rettig merely nod.

'Good,' says de Soya. 'I will program *Raphael* accordingly . . . that if there is no chance for her to escape before we can be resurrected, she'll trigger her fusion engines. And I'll be very careful setting the parameters for her on what "no escape" means. But I don't think there's much chance of that happening. We will awaken in . . . My God, I haven't even checked to see which system is the first Ouster-occupied Tethys world. Is it Tai Zhin?'

'Negative, sir,' says Gregorius, leaning over the hard-copy star chart of the search plot *Raphael* has prepared. His massive finger strikes down on a circled region beyond the Pax. 'It's Hebron. The Jew world.'

'All right, then,' says the priest-captain. 'Let's get to our couches and head for the translation point. Next year in New Jerusalem!'

'Next year, sir?' says Lancer Rettig, floating above the plot-table before kicking off to his own couch.

De Soya smiles. 'It's a saying I've heard from some of my Jewish friends. I don't know what it means.'

'I didn't know that there were any Jews around anymore,' says Corporal Kee, floating above his own couch. 'I thought they all stuck to themselves in the Outback.'

De Soya shakes his head. 'There were a few converted Jews at the university when I was taking courses outside of seminary,' he says. 'Never mind. You'll meet some soon enough on Hebron. Strap in, gentlemen.'

The priest-captain knows immediately upon awakening that something has, indeed, gone wrong. A few times during his wilder days as a young man, Federico de Soya has got drunk with his fellow seminarians, and on one of these outings he had awakened in a strange bed – alone, thank God – but in a strange bed in a strange part of the city, with no memory of whose bed it was or how he got there. This awakening is like that.

Rather than opening his eyes to see the enclosed and automated creche couches on *Raphael*, smelling the ozone and recycled-sweat scents of the ship, feeling the awakening-to-falling terror of zero-gravity, de Soya finds himself in a comfortable bed in a lovely room in a reasonably normal gravity field. There are religious icons on the wall – the Virgin Mary, a large crucifix with the heavenly raised eyes of a suffering Christ, a painting of the martyrdom of St Paul. Weak sunlight comes through lace curtains.

All this is vaguely familiar to the stupefied de Soya, as is the kindly face of the plump little priest who brings him broth and idle conversation. Finally Father Captain de Soya's reengaging synapses make the connection: Father Baggio, the resurrection chaplain he had last seen in the Vatican Gardens and had been sure he would never see again. Sipping broth, de Soya looks out the rectory window at the pale-blue sky and thinks, *Pacem*. He struggles to recall the events that have brought him there, but the last thing he can remember is the conversation with Gregorius and his men, the long climb up out of the gravity well of Mare Infinitus and Seventy Ophiuchi A, then the jolt of translation.

'How?' he mumbles, grasping the kindly priest's sleeve, 'Why? . . . How?'

'Now, now,' says Father Baggio, 'just rest, my son. There will be time to discuss everything later. Time for everything.'

Lulled by the soft voice, the rich light, and the oxygen-rich air, de Soya closes his eyes and sleeps. His dreams are ominous.

By the noon meal – more broth – it becomes obvious to de Soya that kindly, plump Father Baggio is not going to answer any of his questions: not answer how he got to Pacem, not answer where and how his men are, and not answer why he will not answer. 'Father Farrell is coming soon,' says the resurrection chaplain as if that explains everything. De Soya gathers his strength, bathes and dresses, tries to gather his wits, and waits for Father Farrell.

Father Farrell arrives in midafternoon. He is a tall, thin, ascetic priest – a commander in the Legionaries of Christ, de Soya learns quickly and with little surprise – and his voice, although soft, is clipped and businesslike. Farrell's eyes are a cold gray.

'You are understandably curious,' says Father Farrell. 'And undoubtedly still somewhat confused. It is normal for the newly born-again.'

'I am familiar with the side effects,' says de Soya with a slightly ironic smile. 'But I am curious. How is it that I awake on Pacem? What occurred in Hebron System? And how are my men?'

Farrell's gray eyes do not blink as he speaks. 'The last question first, Father Captain. Your Sergeant Gregorius and Corporal Kee are well . . . recovering from resurrection in the Swiss Guard resurrection chapel even as we speak.'

'Lancer Rettig?' asks de Soya. The sense of foreboding that has been hanging above him since his awakening now stirs its dark wings.

'Dead, I fear,' says Farrell. 'The true death. Last Rites have been administered, and his body has been consigned to the depths of space.'

'How did he die . . . the true death, I mean?' manages de Soya. He feels like weeping, but resists because he is not sure if it is simple sorrow or the effects of resurrection.

'I do not know the details,' says the tall man. The two are in the rectory's small sitting room, used for meetings and important discussions. They are alone except for the eyes of saints, martyrs, Christ, and His mother. 'It seems there was a problem with the automated resurrection creche upon *Raphael*'s return from Hebron System,' continues Farrell.

'*Return* from Hebron?' says de Soya. 'I'm afraid I do not understand, Father. I had programmed the ship to stay unless pursued by Ouster forces. Was that the case?'

'Evidently,' replied the Legionary. 'As I say, I am not acquainted with the technical details . . . nor am I competent in technical matters . . . but as I understand it, you had programmed your archangel courier to penetrate Ouster-controlled space—'

'We needed to pursue our mission to Hebron,' interrupts Father Captain de Soya.

Farrell does not protest the interruption, nor does his neutral expression change, but de Soya looks into those cold gray eyes and does not interrupt again.

'As I was saying, Father Captain, according to my understanding, you programmed your ship to enter Ouster space and – if unchallenged – go into orbit around the planet Hebron.'

De Soya gives his silence as confirmation. His dark eyes return the gray stare – with no animosity as of yet, but ready to defend against any accusation.

'It is my understanding that the . . . I believe your courier ship is named the *Raphael*?'

De Soya nods. He realizes now that the careful phrasing, the questions posed when answers are known – all this is the hallmark of a lawyer. The Church has many legal consultants. And inquisitors.

'The *Raphael* appears to have carried out your programming, found no immediate opposition during deceleration, and gone into orbit around Hebron,' continues Farrell.

'Is that when the resurrection failure occurred?' asks de Soya.

'It is my understanding that this is not the case,' says Farrell. The Legionary's gray gaze leaves de Soya for an instant, flicks around the room as if assessing the value of the furniture and art objects there, apparently finds nothing of interest, and returns to the priest-captain. 'It is my understanding,' he says, 'that all four of you on board were close to full resurrection when the ship had to flee the system. Translation shock was, of course, fatal. Secondary resurrection after incomplete resurrection is – as I am sure you are aware – much more difficult than primary resurrection. It is here that the sacrament was circumvented by mechanical failure.'

When Farrell stops speaking, there is a silence. Lost in thought, de Soya is only vaguely aware of the sound of groundcar traffic on the narrow street outside, the rumble of a transport lifting from the nearby spaceport. Finally he says, 'The creches were inspected and repaired while we were in orbit around Renaissance Vector, Father Farrell.'

The other priest nods almost imperceptibly. 'We have the records. I believe that it was the same sort of calibration error in Lancer Rettig's automated creche. The investigation continues in Renaissance System garrison. We have also expanded the investigation to Mare Infinitus

System, Epsilon Eridani and Epsilon Indi, the world of Inevitable Grace in System Lacaille 9352, Barnard's World, NGC^{es} 2629-4BIV, Vega System, and Tau Ceti.'

De Soya can only blink. 'You are being very thorough,' he says at last. He is thinking, *They must be using both of the other archangel couriers to carry out such an investigation. Why?*

'Yes,' says Father Farrell.

Father Captain de Soya sighs and slumps a bit in the soft cushions of the rectory chair. 'So they found us in Svoboda System and could not resuscitate Lancer Rettig . . .'

There is the slightest downward twitch of Farrell's thin lips. 'Svoboda System, Father Captain? No. It is my understanding that your courier ship was discovered in System Seventy Ophiuchi A, while decelerating toward the ocean world of Mare Infinitus.'

De Soya sits up. 'I don't understand. I'd programmed *Raphael* to translate to the next Pax system on her original search pattern if she had to leave Hebron System prematurely. The next world should have been Svoboda.'

'Perhaps the form of its pursuit by hostile craft in the Hebron System precluded such a translation alignment,' says Farrell without emphasis. 'The ship's computer could have then decided to return to its starting point.'

'Perhaps,' says de Soya, trying to read the other's expression. It is useless. 'You say "could have decided", Father Farrell. Don't you know by now? Haven't you examined the ship's log?'

Farrell's silence could communicate affirmation or nothing at all.

'And if we returned to Mare Infinitus,' continues de Soya, 'why are we waking up here on Pacem? What happened in Seventy Ophiuchi A?'

Now Farrell does smile. It is the narrowest extension of those thin lips. 'By coincidence, Father Captain, the archangel courier *Michael* was in the Mare Infinitus garrison space when you translated. Captain Wu was aboard the *Michael*—'

'Marget Wu?' asks de Soya, not caring if he irritates the other man by interrupting.

'Precisely so.' Farrell removes an imaginary bit of lint from his starched and creased black trousers. 'Considering the . . . ah . . . consternation that your previous visit had caused on Mare Infinitus—'

'Meaning my removal of Bishop Melandriano to a monastery to get him out of my way,' says de Soya. 'And the arrest of several treasonous and corrupt Pax officers who were almost certainly carrying out their theft and conspiracy under Melandriano's supervision—'

Farrell holds up one hand to stop de Soya. 'These events are not under my wing of the investigation, Father Captain. I was simply answering your question. If I may continue?'

De Soya stares, feeling the anger mix with his sorrow at Rettig's death, all swirling amid the narcotic high of resurrection.

'Captain Wu, who had already heard the protests of Bishop Melandriano and other Mare Infinitus administrators, decided that it would be most felicitous if you were returned to Pacem for resurrection.'

'So our resurrection was interrupted a second time?' asks de Soya.

'No.' There is no irritation in Farrell's voice. 'The resurrection process had not been initiated in System Seventy Ophiuchi A when the decision was made to return you to Pax Command and the Vatican.'

De Soya looks at his own fingers. They are trembling. In his mind's eye he can see the *Raphael* with its cargo of corpses, his included. First a death tour of Hebron System, then decelerating toward Mare Infinitus, then the spinup to Pacem. He looks up quickly. 'How long have we been dead, Father?'

'Thirty-two days,' says Farrell.

De Soya almost pulls himself up out of the chair. Finally he settles back and says in his most controlled voice, 'If Captain Wu decided to route the ship back here *before* resurrection was begun in Mare Infinitus space, Father, and if no resurrection was achieved in Hebron space, we should have been dead less than seventy-two hours at that point. Assuming three days here . . . where were the other twenty-six days spent, Father?'

Farrell runs his fingers along his trouser crease. 'There were delays in Mare Infinitus space,' he says coolly. 'The initial investigation was begun there. Protests were filed. Lancer Rettig was buried in space with full honors. Other . . . duties . . . were carried out. The *Raphael* returned with the *Michael*.'

Farrell stands abruptly and de Soya gets to his feet as well. 'Father Captain,' Farrell announces formally, 'I am here to extend Cardinal Secretary Lourdusamy's compliments to you, sir, his wish for your full recovery in health and life in the arms of Christ, and to request your presence, tomorrow morning at oh-seven-hundred hours, at the Vatican offices of the Sacred Congregation for the Doctrine of the Faith, to meet with Monsignor Lucas Oddi and other appointed officials of the Sacred Congregation.'

De Soya is stunned. He can only click his heels and bow his head in compliance. He is a Jesuit and an officer in the Pax Fleet. He has been trained to discipline.

'Very good,' says Father Farrell, and takes his leave.

Father Captain de Soya stands in the rectory foyer for several minutes after the Legionary of Christ has left. As a mere priest and a line officer, de Soya has been spared most Church politics and infighting, but even a provincial priest or preoccupied Pax warrior knows the basic structure of the Vatican and its purpose.

Beneath the Pope, there are two major administrative categories – the Roman Curia and the so-called Sacred Congregations. De Soya knows that the Curia is an awkward and labyrinthine administrative structure – its 'modern' form was set down by Sixtus V in AD 1588. The Curia includes the Secretariat of State, Cardinal Lourdusamy's power base, where he serves as a sort of prime minister with the misleading title of Cardinal Secretary of State. This Secretariat is a central part of what is often referred to as the 'Old Curia', used by popes since the sixteenth century. In addition, there is the 'New Curia', begun as sixteen lesser bodies created by the Second Vatican Council – still popularly known as Vatican II – which concluded in AD 1965.

Those sixteen bodies have grown to thirty-one intertwining entities under Pope Julius's two hundred and sixty-year reign.

But it is not the Curia to which de Soya has been summoned, but to one of its separate and sometimes countervailing clusters of authority, the Sacred Congregations. Specifically, he has been ordered to appear before the so-called Sacred Congregation for the Doctrine of the Faith, an organization that has gained – or, to be more precise, *regained* – enormous power in the past two centuries. Under Pope Julius, the Sacred Congregation for the Doctrine of the Faith again welcomed the Pope as its Prefect – a change in structure that revitalized the office. For the twelve centuries prior to Pope Julius's election, this Sacred Congregation – known as the Holy Office from AD 1908 to AD 1964 – had been deemphasized to the point it had become almost a vestigial organ. But now, under Julius, the Holy Office's power is felt across five hundred light-years of space and back through three thousand years of history.

De Soya returns to the sitting room and leans against the chair he had been sitting in. His mind is swirling. He knows now that he will not be allowed to see Gregorius or Kee before his meeting in the Holy Office the next morning. He may never see them again. De Soya tries to unravel the thread that has pulled him to this meeting, but it becomes lost in the snarl of Church politics, offended clerics, Pax power struggles, and the swirl of his own befuddled, born-again brain.

He knows this: the Sacred Congregation for the Doctrine of the Faith, previously known as the Sacred Congregation of the Holy Office, had – for many centuries prior to that – been known as the Sacred Congregation of Universal Inquisition.

And it is under Pope Julius XIV that the Inquisition has once again begun living up to its original name and sense of terror. And, without preparation, counsel, or knowledge of what accusations may be levied against him, de Soya must appear before them at oh-seven-hundred hours the next morning.

Father Baggio bustles in, a smile on the chubby priest's cherubic features. 'Did you have a nice conversation with Father Farrell, my son?'

'Yes,' says de Soya distractedly. 'Very nice.'

'Good, good,' says Father Baggio. 'But I think it's time for a bit of broth, a bit of prayer – the Angelus, I think – and then an early beddie-bye. We must be fresh for whatever tomorrow brings, mustn't we?'

THIRTY-EIGHT

When I was a child listening to Grandam's endless parade of verses, one short piece I demanded to hear over and over started: 'Some say the world will end in fire/Some say in ice.' Grandam did not know the name of the poet – she thought it might be by a pre-Hegira poet named Frost, but even at my young age I thought that was too cute to be true for a poem about fire and ice – but the *idea* of the world ending in either fire or ice had long stayed with me, as enduring as the singsong rhythm of the simple verse.

My world seemed to be ending in ice.

It was dark beneath the ice wall, and too cold for me to find adequate words to describe. I had been burned before – once a gas stove had exploded on a barge going upriver on the Kans and given me slight but painful burns over my arms and chest – so I knew the intensity of fire. This cold seemed that intense, sort of slow-motion flames cutting my flesh to shreds.

The rope was secured under my arms, and the powerful current soon whirled me around so I was being dragged feet-first down the black chute, my hands raised to keep my face from bashing against inverted ridges of rock-hard ice, my chest and underarms constrained by the tight rope as A. Bettik acted as brake by staying on belay. My knees were soon torn by razor-sharp ice as the current kept throwing my body higher, striking the uneven ceiling of passing ice like someone being dragged across rocky ground.

I had worn socks with the ice more in mind than the cold, but they did little to protect my feet as I banged into the ice ridges. I was also wearing undershorts and undershirt, but they provided no buffer against the needles of cold. Around my neck was the band of the com unit, the mike-patches pressed against my throat for voice or subvocal transmission, the hearplug in place. Over my shoulder and tightly secured with tape was the water-proof bag with the *plastique*, detonators, cord, and two flares I had put in at the last moment. Taped to my wrist was my little flashlight laser, its narrow beam cutting through the black water and bouncing office, but illuminating little. I had used the laser sparingly since the labyrinth on Hyperion: the handlamps were more useful in widebeam and required less charge. The laser was largely useless as a cutting weapon, but should serve to bore holes in ice for the *plastique*.

If I lived long enough to bore holes.

The only method behind my madness of allowing myself to be swept away down this subterranean river had been a bit of knowledge from my

Home Guard training, on the Iceshelf of the continent Ursus. There, on the Bearpaw Glacial Sea, where the ice froze and refroze almost daily through the brief antarctic summer, the risk of breaking through the thin surface ice had been very high. We had been trained that even if we were swept away beneath the thickest ice, there was always a thin layer of air between the sea and icy ceiling. We were to rise to that brief layer, set our snouts into it even if it meant that the rest of our faces had to stay submerged, and move along the ice until we came to a break or thin-enough patch that we could smash our way out.

That had been the theory. My only actual test of it had been as a member of a search party fanning out to hunt for a scarab driver who had stepped out of his vehicle, broken through not two meters from where the ice supported the weight of his four-ton machine, and disappeared. I was the one who found him, almost six hundred meters from the scarab and safe ice. He had used the breathing technique. His nose was still pressed tight against the too-thick ice when I found him – but his mouth was open underwater, his face was as white as the snow that blew across the glacier, and his eyes were frozen as solid as steel bearings. I tried not to think of this as I fought my way to the surface against the current, tugged on the rope to signal A. Bettik to stop me, and scraped my face against shards of ice to find air.

There were several centimeters of space between water and ice – more where fissures ran up into the glacier of frozen atmosphere like inverted crevasses. I gasped the cold air into my lungs, shone the flashlight laser into the crevasses, and then moved the red beam back and forward along the narrow tunnel of ice. 'Going to rest a minute,' I gasped. 'I'm okay. How far have I come?'

'About eight meters,' whispered A. Bettik's voice in my ear.

'Shit,' I muttered, forgetting that the com would send the subvocal. It had seemed like twenty or thirty meters, at least. 'All right,' I said aloud. 'I'm going to set the first charge here.'

My fingers were still flexible enough to trigger the flashlight laser to high intensity and burn out a small niche into the side of the fissure. I had premolded the *plastique*, and now I worked it, shaped it, and vectored it. The material was a shaped explosive – that is, the blast would discharge itself in precisely the directions I wanted, provided that my preparations were correct. In this case I had done most of the work ahead of time, knowing that I wanted the blast directed upward and back toward the ice wall behind me. Now I aimed precise tendrils of that explosive force: the same technology that allowed a plasma bolt to cut through steel plate like hot bolts dropped into butter would send these plasma tendrils lancing back through the incredible mass of the ice behind me. It should cut the eight-meter section of ice wall into chunks and drop them into the river very nicely. We were counting on the fact that the atmosphere generators through the years of terraforming had added enough nitrogen and CO_2 to the atmosphere to keep the explosion from turning into one massive blast of burning oxygen.

Because I knew exactly where I wanted to aim the force of the blast, the shaping of the charges took less than forty-five seconds and required little dexterity. Still, I was shaking and almost numb by the time the tiny detonator squibs were set in place. Since I knew the com units had no trouble penetrating this amount of ice, I set the detonators to the preset code and ignored the wire in my bag.

'Okay,' I gasped, settling lower in the water, 'let out the slack.'

The wild ride began again, the current pulling me lower into blackness and then battering me against the crystal ceiling, then the wild search for air, the gasped commands, the struggle to see and work while the last warmth drained from me.

The ice continued for another thirty meters – right at the outer limits of what I thought the *plastique* could handle. I set the charges in two more places, another fissure and the last bundle in a narrow tube I burned into solid ceiling ice. My hands were totally numb during the last placement – it was as if I were wearing thick gloves of ice – but I directed the charges up and downstream in roughly the proper vectors. If there were not an end to this ice wall soon, all this would be in vain. A. Bettik and I had anticipated chopping away at some ice with the ax, but we could not hack our way through many meters of the stuff.

At forty-one meters I burst up and out into air again. At first I was afraid it was merely another crevasse, but when I aimed the flashlight laser, the red beam flicked through a chamber longer and wider than the one where I had left the raft. We had discussed it and decided that we would not blow the explosives if I could see the end of any second chamber, but when I lowered the beam down the length of the black river here, illuminating the same mist and stalactites, I could see that the river – about thirty meters wide at that point – curved out of sight several hundred meters downstream. There were no more riverbanks or visible tunnels here than there had been in our earlier stretch of river, but at least the river appeared to keep running.

I wanted to see what the river did once it rounded the turn, but I had neither the rope nor body heat I needed to float that far, report, and get back alive. 'Pull me back!' I gasped.

For the next two minutes I hung on – or tried to hang on, my hands no longer worked – as the android hauled me back against that terrible current, stopping occasionally as I floated on my back and gasped in the frigid air of the crevasses. Then the black ride would begin again.

If A. Bettik had been in the water and I had been pulling – or even if it had been the child – I could not have pulled either of them back through that heavy current in four times the time it took A. Bettik. I knew that he was strong, but no superman – no miraculous android strength – but he showed superhuman strength that day. I could only guess at the reservoirs of energy he used to pull me back to the raft so quickly. I helped as best I could, slashing my hands by pulling myself along the icy ceiling and fending off sharper crystals, kicking weakly against the current.

When my head broke the surface again, seeing the haloed lantern light and the shapes of my two companions leaning toward me, I did not have the strength to lift my arms or to help pull myself onto the raft. A. Bettik seized me under the arms and lifted me gently out. Aenea grabbed my dripping legs, and they carried me toward the stern of the raft. I admit that my dulled brain was reminded of the Catholic Church we stopped by occasionally in the north-moor village of Latmos, the little town where we picked up our food and simple shepherd supplies, and of one of the large religious paintings on the south wall of that church: Christ being taken off the cross, one of his disciple's arms under his limp arms, his bare and mutilated feet being held by the Virgin.

Don't flatter yourself, came the unbidden thought through my mental fog. It spoke in Aenea's voice.

They carried me to the frost-laden tent where the thermal blanket was ready on a pile of two sleeping bags and a thin mat. The heating cube glowed next to this nest. A. Bettik stripped me of my sodden undershirt, flare bag and com unit. He untaped the flashlight laser, set it carefully in my pack, laid me firmly within the top sleeping bag with the thermal blanket around me, and opened a medpak. Setting sticky biomonitor contacts against my chest, the inside of my thigh, my left wrist, and temple, he looked at the readouts a moment and then injected me with one ampule of adrenonitrotaline, as we had planned.

You must be getting tired of pulling me out of the water, I wanted to say, but my jaws and tongue and vocal apparatus would not oblige. I was so cold that I was not even shivering. Consciousness was a slender thread connecting me to the light, and it wavered in the cold wind that blew through me.

A. Bettik leaned closer. 'M. Endymion, the charges are set?'

I managed a nod. It was all I could do, and it seemed that I was operating a clumsy marionette to do that.

Aenea dropped to her knees next to me. To A. Bettik she said, 'I'll watch him. You get us out of here.'

The android left the tent to push us away from the ice wall and to pole us upstream, using the push-pole from that end of the raft. After the expenditure of energy it had taken to drag me back against the current, I could not believe he could find the strength to move the entire raft the necessary distance upriver.

We began moving. I could see the lantern glow on the mist and distant ceiling through the triangular opening at the end of the tent. The fog and icy stalactites moved slowly across the tiny reference triangle, as though I were peering through an isoscelean hole in reality at the Ninth Circle of Dante's hell.

Aenea was watching the simple medpak monitors. 'Raul, Raul . . .' she whispered.

The thermal blanket held in all the heat I was producing, but I felt as if I were not producing any body heat. My bones ached with the chill, but my frozen nerve ends did not convey the pain. I was very, very sleepy.

Aenea shook me awake. 'You stay with me, dammit!'

I'll try, I thought at her. I knew I was lying. All I wanted to do was sleep.

'A. Bettik!' cried the child, and I was vaguely aware of the android entering the tent and consulting the medpak. Their words were a distant humming that no longer made sense to me.

I was far, far away when I dimly sensed a body next to me. A. Bettik had gone away to pole our ice-laden raft upstream against bitter current. The child Aenea had crawled under the thermal blanket and edge of the sleeping bag with me. At first the heat of her skinny body did not penetrate the layers of permafrost that now lay in me, but I was aware of her breathing, of the angular intrusion of her elbows and knees in the tented space with me.

No, no, I thought in her direction. *I'm the protector here . . . the strong one hired to save you.* The cold sleepiness did not allow me to speak aloud.

I do not remember if she put her arms around me. I know that I was no more responsive than a frozen log, no more receptive to company than one of the icy stalactites that moved across my triangular field of vision, its underside lighted by the lantern's glow, its top lost in darkness and mist much as was my mind.

Eventually I began to feel some of the warmth her small body poured out. The heat was dimly perceived, but my skin began to prickle with needles of pain where the warmth flowed from her skin to mine. I wished I could speak just to tell her to move away so that I could doze in nerveless peace.

Sometime later – it might have been fifteen minutes or two hours – A. Bettik returned to the tent. I was conscious enough to realize that he must have followed our plan: 'anchoring' the raft with lodged push-poles and steering oar somewhere in the narrowing upper part of the ice cave under the visible segment of farcaster portal. Our theory had been that the metal arch might protect us from avalanche and icefall when the charges went off.

Blow the charges, I wanted to say to him. Instead of keying the com band, however, the android stripped to his tropical yellow short pants and shirt, then crawled under the thermal blanket with the girl and me.

This should have been comical – it may sound comical to you as you read this – but nothing in my life had moved me as deeply as this act, this sharing of warmth by my two traveling companions. Not even their brave and foolhardy rescue of me in the violet sea had touched me so deeply. The three of us lay there – Aenea on my left, her left arm around me, A. Bettik on my right, his body curled against the cold that crept in under the corner of the thermal blanket. In a few minutes I would be weeping from the pain that came from returning circulation, from the agony of thawing flesh, but at this moment I wept at the intimate gift of their warmth as life's heat flowed from both child and blue-skinned man, flowed from their blood and flesh to mine.

I weep now in the telling of it.

How long we stayed that way, I cannot say. I never asked the two of them and they never spoke of it. It must have been at least an hour. It felt like a lifetime of warmth and pain and the overpowering joy of life's return.

Eventually I began trembling, then shaking slightly, and then shaking violently, as if possessed by seizures. My friends held me then, not allowing me to escape from the warmth. I believe that Aenea was also weeping by that point, although I have never asked, and in later days she never spoke of it.

Finally, after the pain and palsy had largely passed, A. Bettik slipped out from under our common cover, consulted the medpak, and spoke to the child in a language I could once again comprehend. 'All within the green,' he said softly. 'No permanent frostbite. No permanent damage.'

Shortly after that, Aenea slipped out of the blanket and helped me sit up, putting two of the hoar-frosted packs behind my back and head. She set water to boiling over the glowing cube, made mugs of steaming tea, and held one to my lips. I could move my hands by then, even flex my fingers, but the pain there was too great to grasp anything successfully.

'M. Endymion,' said A. Bettik, crouching just outside the tent, 'I am prepared to transmit the detonation code.'

I nodded.

'There may be falling debris, sir,' he added.

I nodded again. We had discussed the risk of that. The shaped charges should shatter just the ice walls ahead of us, but the resulting seismic vibrations through the ice might well bring the entire glacier of frozen atmosphere down around us, driving the raft to the shallow bottom and entombing us there. We had judged it worth the risk. Now I glanced up at the frost-rimmed interior of the microtent and smiled at the thought that this would give us any shelter. I nodded a third time, urging him to go ahead.

The sound of the blast was more subdued than I expected, much less noisy than the concomitant tumble of ice blocks and stalactites and the wild surging of the river itself. For a second I thought that we were going to be lifted and crushed against the cave ceiling as wave after wave of pressure-propelled and ice-displaced river water surged under the raft, We huddled on our little stone hearth, trying to stay out of the frigid water, and riding the bucking logs like passengers on a storm-tossed life dinghy.

Eventually the surging and rumbling calmed itself. The violent maneuvers had snapped our steering oar, flung one of the push-poles away, dislodged us from our safe haven, and floated us downstream to the ice wall.

To where the ice wall used to be.

The charges had done their job much as we had planned: the cavern they had created was low and jagged, but as probing it with the flashlight laser showed, it appeared to go through to the open channel beyond. Aenea cheered. A. Bettik patted me on the back. I am ashamed to admit that I may have wept again.

It was not so easy a victory as it first seemed. Fallen ice blocks and surviving columns of ice still blocked parts of the passage, and even after the initial rush of ice into the breach slowed a bit, it meant heavy going with the surviving push-pole and frequent pauses as A. Bettik hacked away at icy obstacles with the ax.

Half an hour into this effort I staggered to the front of our battered raft and gestured that it was my turn with the ax.

'Are you sure, M. Endymion?' asked the blue-skinned man.

'Quite . . . sure . . .' I said carefully, forcing my cold tongue and jaw to enunciate properly.

The work with the ax soon warmed me to the point that the last of the shaking stopped. I could feel the terrible bruises and scrapes where the ice ceiling had battered me, but I would deal with those pains later.

Finally we hacked our way through the last bars of ice to float into the open current. The three of us pounded sock-mittens together for a moment, but then retreated to huddle near the heating cube and to play the handlamps on either side as new scenery floated by.

The new scenery was identical to the old: vertical walls of ice on either side, stalactites threatening to drop on us at any moment, the rushing black water.

'Maybe it will stay open all the way to the next arch,' said Aenea, and the fog of her breath remained in the air like a promise.

We all stood up as the raft swept around the bend in the ice-buried river. For a moment it was confusion as A. Bettik used the pole and I used the shattered stub of the steering oar to fend us off the port-side ice wall. Then we were in the central current again and picking up speed.

'Oh . . .' said the girl from where she stood at the front of the raft. Her tone told us everything.

The river went another sixty meters or so, narrowed, and ended at a second ice wall.

It was Aenea's idea to send the comlog bracelet ahead as a scout. 'It has the video microbead,' she said.

'But we have no monitor,' I pointed out. 'And it can't send the video feed to the ship . . .'

Aenea was shaking her head. 'No, but the comlog itself can *see*. It can *tell* us what it sees.'

'Yes,' I said, finally understanding, 'but is it smart enough without the ship AI behind it to understand what it sees?'

'Shall we ask it?' said A. Bettik, who had retrieved the bracelet from my pack.

We reactivated the thing and asked it. It assured us, in that almost-arrogant ship's voice, that it was quite capable of processing its visual data and relaying its analysis to us via the com band. It also assured us that although it could not float and had not learned to swim, it was completely waterproof.

Aenea used the flashlight laser to cut off the end of one of the logs, pounded nails and pivot-bolt rings to hold the bracelet in place around it, and added a hook ring for the climbing rope. She used a double half hitch to secure the line.

'We should have used this for the first ice wall,' I said.

She smiled. Her cap was rimmed with frost. Actual icicles hung on the short brim. 'The bracelet might have had some trouble setting the charges,' she said. I realized as she spoke that the child was very weary.

'Good luck,' I said idiotically as we tossed the braceleted log into the river. The comlog had the good grace not to respond. It was swept under the ice wall almost immediately.

We brought the heating cube forward and crouched near it as A. Bettik let out the line. I turned up the volume of the com unit's speakers, and none of us said a word as the line snaked out and the tinny voice of the comlog reported back.

'Ten meters. Crevasses above, but none wider than six centimeters. No end to the ice.'

'Twenty meters. Ice continues.'

'Fifty meters. Ice.'

'Seventy-five meters. No end in sight.'

'One hundred meters. Ice.' The comlog was at the end of its tether. We spliced on our last length of climbing rope.

'One hundred and fifty meters. Ice.'

'One hundred and eighty meters. Ice.'

'Two hundred meters. Ice.'

We were out of rope and out of hope. I began hauling in the comlog. Even though my hands were sensate and awkwardly functional now, it was difficult for me to haul the essentially weightless bracelet back upstream, so vicious was the current and heavy the ice-laden rope. Once again I had difficulty imagining the effort A. Bettik had put forth in saving me.

The line was almost too stiff to curl. We had to chip away the ice from around the comlog when it was finally hauled aboard. 'Although the cold depletes my power unit and the ice covers my visual pickups,' chirped the bracelet, 'I am willing and able to continue the exploration.'

'No, thank you,' A. Bettik said politely, turning off the device and returning it to me. The metal was too cold to handle, even with my sock-mittens on. I dropped the bangle into the frosted backpack.

'We wouldn't have had enough *plastique* for fifty meters of ice,' I said. My voice was absolutely calm – even the shivering had stopped – and I realized that it was because of the absolute unblinking clarity of the death sentence that had just descended upon us.

There was – I realize now – another reason for that oasis of calm amid the desert of pain and hopelessness there. It was the warmth. The remembered warmth. The flow of life from those two people to me, my acceptance of it, the sacred communion-sense of it. Now, in the lanterned darkness, we went ahead with the urgent business of attempting to stay alive, discussing impossible options such as using the plasma rifle to blast a way through, discarding impossible options, and discussing more of the same. But all the while in that cold, dark pit of confusion and rising hopelessness, the core of warmth that had been breathed back into me from these two . . . friends . . . kept me calm, even as their human proximity had kept me alive. In the difficult times to come – and even now, as I write this, even while expecting death's stealthy arrival by cyanide on every breath I take –

that memory of shared warmth, that first total sharing of vitality, keeps me calm and steady through the storm of human fears.

We decided to pole the raft back the length of the new channel, seeking some overlooked crevasse or niche or airshaft. It seemed hopeless, but perhaps a shade less hopeless than leaving the raft pressed up against this terminal icefall.

We found it right below where the river had made its dogleg to the right. Evidently we had all been too busy fending off the ice walls and regaining the center current to notice the narrow rift in the jagged ice along what had been our starboard side. Although we were searching diligently, we would not have discovered the narrow opening without the tightbeam of the flashlight laser: our lantern light, twisted by crystal facet and hanging ice, passed right over it. Common sense told us that this was just another folding in the ice, a horizontal equivalent of the vertical crevasses I had found in the ice ceiling: a breathing space leading nowhere. Our need for hope prayed that common sense was wrong.

The opening – fold – whatever, was less than a meter wide and opened onto air almost two meters above the river's surface. Poling closer, we could see by laser light that either the opening ended or its narrowing corridor bent out of sight less than three meters in. Common sense told us that it was the end of the icy cul-de-sac. Once again we ignored common sense.

While Aenea leaned into the long pole, straining to hold the raft in place against the churning water, A. Bettik boosted me up. I used the claw end of our hammer as a climbing tool, chipping it deep into the ice floor of the narrow defile and pulling myself up by speed and desperation. Once up there on my hands and knees, panting and weak, I caught my breath, stood, and waved down to the others. They would wait for my report.

The narrow ice tunnel bent sharply to the right. I aimed the flashlight laser down this second corridor with rising hope. Another ice wall reflected back the red beam, but this time there did not seem to be a bend in the tunnel. No, wait . . . As I moved down the second corridor, stooping low as the ice ceiling lowered, I realized that the tunnel rose steeply just beyond this point. The light had been shining on the floor of the icy ramp. Depth perception did not exist here.

Squeezing through the tight space, I crawled on all fours for a dozen meters, boots scrabbling on the jagged ice. I thought of the shop in echoing, empty New Jerusalem where I had 'bought' those boots – leaving my hospital slippers behind and a handful of Hyperion script on the counter – and tried to remember if there had been any ice crampons for sale in the camping section there. Too late now.

At one point I had to slither on my belly, once again sure that the corridor was going to end within a meter, but this time it turned sharply to the left and ran straight and level – deep into the ice – for twenty more meters or so before angling right and climbing again. Panting, shaking with excitement, I jogged, slid, and claw-hammered my way back downhill to the opening. The laser beam cast back countless reflections of my excited expression from the clear ice.

Aenea and A. Bettik had begun packing necessary equipment as soon as I had disappeared from sight. The girl had already been boosted to the ice niche and was setting aside gear as A. Bettik tossed it up. We shouted instructions and suggestions to one another. Everything seemed necessary – sleeping bags, thermal blanket, the folded tent – which could be compressed to only a third of its former tiny size, due to the ice and frost on it – heating cube, food, inertial compass, weapons, handlamps.

In the end, we had most of the raft's gear on the landing. We argued some more – the exercise and hot air of it keeping us warm for a minute – then chose just what was necessary and what could fit in our packs and shoulder bags. I carried the pistol on my belt and lashed the plasma rifle on my pack. A. Bettik agreed to carry the shotgun, its ammunition topping off his already bulging pack. Luckily the packs were empty of clothes – we were wearing everything we owned – so we loaded up on food paks and gear. Aenea and the android kept the com units; I slid the still-icy comlog onto my bulky wrist. Despite the precaution, we had no intention of losing sight of one another.

I was worried about the raft drifting away – the lodged push-pole and shattered steering oar would not hold it for long – but A. Bettik solved that in a moment by rigging bow and stern lines, melting niches in the ice wall with the flashlight laser, and tying the lines around solid ice cleats.

Before we started up the narrow ice corridor, I took a final look at our faithful raft, doubtful that we would ever see it again. It was a pathetic sight: the stone hearth was still in place, but the steering oar was in splinters, our lantern mast in the bow had been broken and splinted, the leading edges had been bashed about and the logs on both sides were all but splintered, the stern was awash, and the entire vessel was filmed with ice and half-hidden by the icy vapors that swirled around us. I nodded my gratitude and farewell to the sad wreck, turned, and led the way to the right and up – pushing the heavy pack and bulging shoulder bag ahead of me during the lowest and narrowest bit.

I had feared that the corridor would run to an end a few meters beyond where I had explored, but thirty minutes of climbing, crawling, sliding, and outright scrambling led to more tunnels, more turns, and always climbing. Even though the exertion kept us alive, if not actually warm, each of us could feel the invasive cold making gains on us. Sooner or later exhaustion would claim us and we would have to stop, set our rolled mats and sleeping bags out, and see if we would awaken after sleeping in such cold. But not yet.

Passing chocolate bars back, pausing to thaw the ice in one of our canteens by passing the laser beam across it at its widest setting, I said, 'Not much farther now.'

'Not much farther to *what?*' asked Aenea from beneath her crest of frost and ice. 'We can't be near the surface yet . . . we haven't climbed that far.'

'Not much farther to something interesting,' I said. As soon as I spoke, the vapor from my breath froze to the front of my jacket and the stubble on my chin. I knew that my eyebrows were dripping ice.

'Interesting,' repeated the girl, sounding dubious. I understood. So far, 'interesting' had done its best to get us killed.

An hour later we had paused to heat some food over the cube – which had to be rigged carefully so it would not melt its way through the ice floor while heating our pot of stew – and I was consulting in my inertial compass to get some idea of how far we had come and how high we'd climbed, when A. Bettik said, 'Quiet!'

All three of us seemed to be holding our breath for minutes. Finally Aenea whispered, 'What? I don't hear anything.'

It was a miracle that we could hear each other when we shouted, our heads were so wrapped about with makeshift scarves and balaclavas.

A. Bettik frowned and held his finger to his lips for silence. After a moment he whispered, 'Footsteps. And they're coming this way.'

THIRTY-NINE

On Pacem the main interrogation center for the Holy Roman Office of the Universal Inquisition is not in the Vatican proper, but in the great heap of stone called Castel Sant'Angelo, a massive, circular fort begun as Hadrian's tomb in AD 135, connected to the Aurelian wall in AD 271 to become the most important fortress in Rome, and one of the few buildings of Rome to be moved with the Vatican when the Church evacuated its offices from Old Earth in the last days before the planet's collapse into the core-gobbling black hole. The castle – actually a conical monolith of moat-surrounded stones – became important to the Church during the Plague Year of AD 587 when Gregory the Great, while leading a prayer procession beseeching God to end the plague, had a vision of Michael the Archangel atop the tomb. Later, Castel Sant'Angelo sheltered popes from angry mobs, offered its dank cells and torture chambers to such perceived enemies of the Church as Benvenuto Cellini, and, in its nearly three thousand years of existence, had proved itself impervious to both barbarian invasion and nuclear explosion. It now sits like a low gray mountain in the center of the only open land remaining within the busy triangle of highways, buildings, and administrative centers running between the Vatican, the Pax administrative city, and the spaceport.

Father Captain de Soya presents himself twenty minutes before his oh-seven-thirty appointment and is given a badge that will guide him through the sweating, windowless vaults and corridors of the castle. The frescoes, beautiful furnishings, and airy loggias set there by popes of the Middle Ages have long since faded and fallen into disrepair. Castel Sant'Angelo has once again taken on the character of a tomb and fortress. De Soya knows that a fortified passage from the Vatican to the castle had been brought along from Old Earth, and that one of the purposes of the Holy Office in the past two centuries has been to supply Castel Sant'Angelo with modern weapons and defenses so that it might still offer quick refuge to the Pope should interstellar war come to Pacem.

The walk takes the full twenty minutes, and he must pass through frequent checkpoints and security doors, each guarded not by the brightly garbed Swiss Guard police of the Vatican, but by the black-and-silver uniformed security forces of the Holy Office.

The interrogation cell itself is infinitely less dreary than the ancient corridors and stairs that lead to it; two of the three interior stone walls are brightened by smart-glass panels that glow a soft yellow; two sunbundles spread sunlight from their collector on the roof thirty meters above; the spartan room is furnished by a modern conference table – de Soya's chair sits opposite that of his five Inquisitors, but is identical to theirs in design and comfort – a standard office work center with keyboards, datascreens, diskey plate, and virtual inputs, and a sideboard with a coffee urn and breakfast rolls.

De Soya has to wait only a minute before the Inquisitors arrive. The cardinals – one Jesuit, one Dominican, and three Legionaries of Christ – introduce themselves and shake hands. De Soya has worn his black Pax Fleet dress uniform with its Roman collar, and it stands in contrast to the crimson Holy Office tunics with their black-labelled collars. There are a few niceties – a moment's conversation about de Soya's health and successful resurrection, offers of food and coffee – de Soya accepts the coffee – and then they take their seats.

In the tradition of the early days of the Holy Office and as has been the custom in the Renewed Church when priests are the subject of investigation, the discussion is held in Latin. Only one of the five cardinals on the panel actually speaks. The questions are polite, formal, and invariably phrased in the third person. At the end of the interview, transcripts in Latin and Web English are given to the interview subject.

Inquisitor: Has Father Captain de Soya reported success in finding and detaining the child known as Aenea?

F.C. de Soya: I have had contact with the child. I have not succeeded in detaining her.

Inquisitor: Let him say what the meaning of 'contact' is within this context.

F.C. de Soya: I have twice intercepted the ship which carried the child away from Hyperion. Once in Parvati System, a second time near and on Renaissance Vector.

Inquisitor: These unsuccessful attempts at taking the child into custody have been recorded and are duly entered into the record. Is it his contention that the child would have died by her own hand in Parvati System before the specially trained Swiss Guard troops aboard his ship could have forced entry and taken the child into protective custody?

F.C. de Soya: It was my belief at the time. I felt the risk was too great.

Inquisitor: And to his knowledge, did the ranking Swiss Guard Commander in charge of the actual boarding operation – one Sergeant Gregorius – agree with the Father Captain that the operation should be called off?

F.C. de Soya: I am not sure of Sergeant Gregorius's opinion after the boarding operation was canceled. At the time he argued to go.

Inquisitor: And does he know the opinion of the other two troopers involved in the boarding operation?

F.C. de Soya: At the time they wanted to go. They had trained hard and were ready. It was my opinion at the time, however, that the risk of the girl harming herself was too great.

Inquisitor: And was this the same reason he did not intercept the runaway ship prior to its entering the atmosphere of the world known as Renaissance Vector?

F.C. de Soya: No. In that instance the girl said that she was landing on the planet. It seemed safer for everyone concerned to allow her to do so before taking her into custody.

Inquisitor: And yet, when the aforementioned ship approached the dormant farcaster portal on Renaissance Vector, the priest-captain ordered various ships in the Fleet and air forces to fire on the child's ship . . . Is this correct?

F.C. de Soya: Yes.

Inquisitor: Is it his contention, then, that this command held no danger of harming the girl?

F.C. de Soya: No. I knew that there was a risk. However, when I realized that the girl's ship was headed for the farcaster portal, it was my firm belief that we would lose her if we did not attempt to disable her spacecraft.

Inquisitor: Did he have some knowledge that the farcaster portal along the river would activate itself after almost three centuries of dormancy?

F.C. de Soya: No knowledge. A sudden intuition. A hunch.

Inquisitor: Is he in the habit of risking the success or failure of a mission – a mission labeled the highest priority by the Holy Father himself – on a hunch?

F.C. de Soya: I am not in the habit of being sent on a mission of highest priority by the Holy Father. In certain instances where my ships have been in combat, I have made command decisions based upon insights which would not have seemed totally logical outside the context of my experience and training.

Inquisitor: Is he saying that knowledge of a farcaster's renewed activity some two hundred and seventy-four years after the Fall of the Web which sustained them is within the context of his experience and training?

F.C. de Soya: No. It was . . . a hunch.

Inquisitor: Is he aware of the expense of the combined Fleet operation in Renaissance System?

F.C. de Soya: I know it was considerable.

Inquisitor: Is he aware that several ships of the line were delayed in carrying out their orders from Pax Fleet Command – orders which were sending them to vital trouble spots along the so-called Great Wall of our defensive perimeter against the invading Ousters?

F.C. de Soya: I was aware that ships were delayed in Renaissance System upon my order. Yes.

Inquisitor: On the world of Mare Infinitus, the father-captain saw fit to arrest several Pax officers.

F.C. de Soya: Yes.

Inquisitor: And to administer Truthtell and other restricted psychotropic drugs to these officers without due process or the advice of the Pax and Church authorities on Mare Infinitus?

F.C. de Soya: Yes.

Inquisitor: Is it his contention that the papal diskey conferred upon him to carry out his mission of finding the child also authorized him to arrest Pax officers and carry out such interrogation without the due process of military courts or provided counsel?

F.C. de Soya: Yes. It was and is my understanding that the papal diskey gives me . . . gave me . . . full authorization in the field for whatever command decision I deemed necessary in the completion of this mission.

Inquisitor: Is it his contention, then, that the arrest of these Pax officers will lead to the successful detention of the child named Aenea?

F.C. de Soya: My investigation was necessary to determine the truth of the events surrounding the probable passage of that child from farcaster to farcaster on Mare Infinitus. During the course of that investigation, it became apparent that the director of the platform on which the events occurred had been lying to his superiors, covering up elements of the incident involving the girl's traveling companion, and also had been involved in treasonable deals with the poachers in those waters. At the conclusion of our investigation, I turned over the officers and men who had been involved to the Pax garrison for due process handling within the Fleet Code of Military Justice.

Inquisitor: And did he feel that his treatment of Bishop Melandriano was also justified under the requirements of the . . . investigation?

F.C. de Soya: Despite explanations of the need for swift action, Bishop Melandriano objected to our investigation on Platform Station Three-twenty-six Mid-littoral. He tried to stop the investigation from a distance – despite direct orders to cooperate from his superior, Archbishop Jane Kelley.

Inquisitor: Is it the father-captain's contention that Archbishop Kelley offered her help in soliciting the cooperation of Bishop Melandriano?

F.C. de Soya: No. I sought her help.

Inquisitor: In truth, did the father-captain not invoke the authority of the papal diskey in compelling Archbishop Kelley to intervene on the behalf of the investigation?

F.C. de Soya: Yes.

Inquisitor: Can he state the events which occurred after Bishop Melandriano came in person to Platform Station Three-twenty-six Mid-littoral?

F.C. de Soya: Bishop Melandriano was in a rage. He ordered the Pax troops guarding my prisoners—

Inquisitor: When the Father Captain refers to 'my prisoners', he means the former director and Pax officers of the platform?

F.C. de Soya: Yes.

Inquisitor: He may continue.

F.C. de Soya: Bishop Melandriano ordered the Pax troops I had brought in to release Captain Powl and the others. I countermanded the order. Bishop Melandriano refused to recognize my authority as delegated by the papal diskey. I had the Bishop put under temporary arrest and transported to the Jesuit monastery on a platform six hundred kilometers from the planet's south pole. Storms and other contingencies prevented the Bishop from leaving for several days. By the time he did, my investigation was complete.

Inquisitor: And what did the investigation purport to show?

F.C. de Soya: Among other things, it showed that Bishop Melandriano had been receiving large payments of cash from the poachers within the jurisdiction of Platform Station Three-twenty-six Mid-littoral. It also showed that Director Powl of the platform had been under the direction of Bishop Melandriano in carrying out illegal activities with the poachers and in extorting money from the offworld fishermen.

Inquisitor: Did the father-captain confront Bishop Melandriano with these allegations?

F.C. de Soya: No.

Inquisitor: Did he bring them to the attention of Archbishop Kelley?

F.C. de Soya: No.

Inquisitor: Did he bring them to the attention of the ranking Pax garrison commander?

F.C. de Soya: No.

Inquisitor: Can he explain these omissions of action as required by the Pax Fleet Code of Conduct and the rules of the Church and Society of Jesus?

F.C. de Soya: The Bishop's involvement in these crimes was not the focus of my investigation. I turned Captain Powl and the others over to the garrison Commander because I knew their cases would be dealt with quickly and fairly under the Fleet Code of Military Justice. I also knew that any complaints against Bishop Melandriano, whether filed under Pax civil-suit or Church judicial procedures, would require my presence on Mare Infinitus for weeks and months. The mission could not wait for that. I judged the Bishop's corruption less important than pursuing the girl.

Inquisitor: He understands the seriousness of these unsubstantiated and undocumented charges against a Bishop of the Roman Catholic Church?

F.C. de Soya: Yes.

Inquisitor: And what led him to abandon his former search pattern and take the archangel courier *Raphael* to the Ouster-controlled Hebron System?

F.C. de Soya: Again, a hunch.

Inquisitor: He shall elaborate.

F.C. de Soya: I did not know where the girl had farcast after Renaissance Vector. Logic dictates that the ship had been left behind somewhere and they had continued on the River Tethys by other means . . . the hawking mat, perhaps, more likely by boat or raft. Certain evidence gathered in the investigation of the girl's flight prior to and during the Mare Infinitus crossing suggested a connection with the Ousters.

Inquisitor: He shall elaborate.

F.C. de Soya: First, the spacecraft . . . it was of Hegemony design . . . a private interstellar spacecraft, if such a thing can be believed. Only a few were given out during the history of the Hegemony. The one most closely resembling the ship we encountered was presented to a certain Hegemony Consul some decades before the Fall. This Consul was later immortalized in the epic poem, the *Cantos*, composed by the former Hyperion pilgrim Martin Silenus. In the *Cantos* the Consul tells a tale of betraying the Hegemony by spying for the Ousters.

Inquisitor: He shall continue.

F.C. de Soya: There were other connections. Sergeant Gregorius was sent to the world of Hyperion with certain forensic evidence which identified the man believed to have been traveling with the child. It is one Raul Endymion, a native of Hyperion and former member of the Hyperion Home Guard. There are certain connections of the name Endymion to works by the girl's . . . father – the Keats cybrid abomination. Once again we come to the *Cantos*.

Inquisitor: He will continue.

F.C. de Soya: Well, there was another connection. The flying device captured after the escape and possible shooting of Raul Endymion on Mare Infinitus—

Inquisitor: Why does he say the 'possible shooting'? Reports from all eyewitnesses on the platform say the suspect was shot and fell into the sea.

F.C. de Soya: Lieutenant Belius had fallen into the ocean earlier, yet his blood and tissue fragments were found on the hawking mat. Only a small portion of blood identified as having the DNA pattern of Raul Endymion was found on the flying mat. It is my theory that Endymion either tried to rescue Lieutenant Belius from the sea or was surprised by him somehow, that the two fought on the mat, that the real suspect – Raul Endymion – was wounded and fell from the mat before the guards fired. I believe it was Lieutenant Belius who died from flechette fire.

Inquisitor: Does he have any proof – other than blood and tissue samples – which might just as easily have come from Raul Endymion pausing long enough in his escape flight to murder Lieutenant Belius?

F.C. de Soya: No.

Inquisitor: He shall continue.

F.C. de Soya: The other reason I suspected an Ouster connection was the hawking mat. Forensic studies show it to be very old – perhaps old enough to be the famous mat used by Shipman Merin Aspic and Siri on the world of Maui-Covenant. Once again there is a connection to the Hyperion pilgrimage and stories related in the Silenus *Cantos*.

Inquisitor: He shall continue.

F.C. de Soya: That's all. I thought that we could get to Hebron without encountering an Ouster Swarm. They often abandon the systems they win in combat. Obviously, my hunch was wrong this time. It cost Lancer Rettig his life. For that I am deeply and truly sorry.

Inquisitor: So his contention is that the upshot of the investigation he carried out at such expense and such pain and embarrassment to Bishop Melandriano was successful because several items seemed to connect to the poem called the *Cantos*, which in turn had a slight connection to the Ousters?

F.C. de Soya: Essentially . . . yes.

Inquisitor: Is the father-captain aware that the poem called the *Cantos* is on the Index of Prohibited Books and has been so for more than a century and a half?

F.C. de Soya: Yes.

Inquisitor: Does he admit to having read this book?

F.C. de Soya: Yes.

Inquisitor: Does he remember the punishment within the Society of Jesus for willfully violating the Index of Prohibited Books?

F.C. de Soya: Yes. It is banishment from the Society.

Inquisitor: And does he recall the maximum punishment listed under the Church Canon of Peace and Justice set upon those in the Body of Christ for willful violations of restrictions offered through the Index of Prohibited Books?

F.C. de Soya: Excommunication.

Inquisitor: The father-captain is released to his quarters at the Vatican Rectory of the Legionaries of Christ and is requested to remain there until recalled for further testimony before this panel or as otherwise directed. We do so abjure, swear, promise, and bind our Brother in Christ: through the power of the Holy, Catholic, and the Apostolic Roman Church do we so compel and abjure thee; in Jesus' name we speak.

F.C. de Soya: Thank you, Most Eminent and Reverend Lord Cardinal, Inquisitors. I shall await word.

FORTY

We spent three weeks with the Chitchatuk on the frozen world of Sol Draconi Septem, and in that time we rested, recovered, wandered the frozen tunnels of their frozen atmosphere with them, learned a few words and phrases of their difficult language, visited Father Glaucus in the embedded city, stalked and were stalked by arctic wraiths, and made that final, terrible trek downriver.

But I am getting ahead of myself. It is easy to do, to rush the tale, especially with the probability increasing of inhaling cyanide on the next breath I take. But enough: this story will end abruptly when I do, not before, and it matters little if it is here or there or in-between. I will tell it as if I shall be allowed to tell it all.

Our first glimpse of the Chitchatuk almost ended in tragedy for both sides. We had doused our handlamps and were crouching in the weighted darkness of that ice corridor, my plasma rifle charged and ready, when the dimmest of lights appeared at the next bend in the tunnel and large, inhuman shapes ambled around the corner. I flicked on my handlamp and its cold-dulled beam illuminated a terrifying sight: three or four broad beasts – white fur, black claws the length of my hand, white teeth that were even longer, reddish-glowing eyes. The creatures moved in a fog of their own breath. I raised the plasma rifle to my shoulder and clicked the select to rapid fire.

'Don't shoot!' cried Aenea, grabbing my arm. 'They're human!'

Her cry stayed not only my hand, but that of the Chitchatuk. Long bone spears had appeared from the folds of white fur, and our lamp beams illuminated sharpened points and pale arms pulled back to hurl them. But Aenea's voice seemed to freeze the tableau with both sides a muscle's twitch away from violence.

I then saw the pale faces beneath the visors of wraith teeth – broad faces, blunt-nosed, wrinkled, pale to the point of albinoism, but all too human, as were the dark eyes that gleamed back at us. I lowered the light so that it was not in their eyes.

The Chitchatuk were broad and muscular – well adapted to Sol Draconi Septem's punishing 1.7-gs – and they looked even wider and more powerful with the layers of wraith furs wrapped around them so. We were soon to learn that they each wore the forward half of the animal's hide, including its head, so the black wraith-claws hung below their hands, the wraith-teeth covering their faces like a dagger-sharp portcullis. We also learned that the wraith's black eye lenses – even without the complicated optics and nerves that allowed the monsters to see in almost total darkness – still worked like simple night-vision goggles. Everything the Chitchatuk wore and were carrying had come from the wraiths: bone spears, rawhide thongs made from wraith-gut and tendon, their water bags formed from tied-off wraith-intestines, their sleeping robes and pallets, even the two artifacts they carried with them – the miter-shaped brazier fashioned from wraith-bone, carried on rawhide thongs, which held the glowing embers that lighted their way, and the more complicated bone bowl and funnel, which melted the ice to water over the brazier. We did not know until later that their already ample bodies looked broader and lumpier because of the water bags they carried under their robe, using their body heat to keep the water liquid.

The standoff must have held for a full minute-and-a-half before Aenea stepped forward on our side and the Chitchatuk we later knew as Cuchiat stepped forward toward us. Cuchiat spoke first, a torrent of harsh noises sounding like nothing so much as great icicles crashing to a hard surface.

'I'm sorry,' said Aenea. 'I don't understand.' She looked back at us.

I looked at A. Bettik. 'Do you recognize this dialect?' Web English had been the standard for so many centuries that it was almost shocking to hear words that bore no meaning. Even three centuries after the Fall, according to the offworlders who had come through Hyperion, most planetary and regional dialects were still understandable.

'No, I do not,' said A. Bettik. 'M. Endymion, if I might suggest . . . the comlog?'

I nodded and retrieved the bracelet from my pack. The Chitchatuk watched warily, still speaking among themselves, eyes alert for a weapon. Their spear arms relaxed as I raised the bangle to eye level and pressed it on.

'I am activated and awaiting your question or command,' chirped the ice-frosted bracelet.

'Listen,' I said as Cuchiat began speaking again. 'Tell me if you can translate this.'

The wraith-garbed warrior made a short, crashing speech.

'Well?' I said to the comlog.

'This language or dialect is not familiar,' chimed the ship's voice from the comlog. 'I am familiar with several Old Earth languages, including pre-Web English, German, French, Dutch, Japanese . . .'

'Never mind,' I said. The Chitchatuk were staring at the babbling comlog, but there was no fear or superstition visible in those large dark eyes that peered from between wraith-teeth – only curiosity.

'I would suggest,' continued the comlog, 'that you keep me activated for some weeks or months while this language is being spoken. I could then collect a data base from which a simple lexicon could be constructed. It might also be preferable to—'

'Thanks anyway,' I said, and pressed it off.

Aenea took a step closer to Cuchiat and pantomimed our being cold and tired. She made gestures for food, pulling a blanket over us, and sleep.

Cuchiat grunted and conferred with the others. There were seven of the

Chitchatuk crowding the ice tunnel now, and we were to learn that their hunting parties always travelled in prime numbers, as did their larger bands. Finally, after speaking separately to each of his men, Cuchiat spoke to us briefly, turned back up the ascending corridor, and gestured for us to follow.

Shivering, bent under the weight of the world's gravity, straining to see by their dim ember light after we had switched off our handlamps to conserve the batteries, making sure that my inertial compass was working, leaving its digital trail of crumbs behind as we walked, we followed Cuchiat and his men toward the Chitchatuk camp.

They were a generous people. They gave us each a wraith-robe to wear, more hind-robes to sleep in and on, wraith-broth heated over their little brazier, water from their body-heated bags, and their trust. The Chitchatuk, we soon learned, did not war among themselves. The thought of killing another human was alien to them. Essentially, the Chitchatuk – indigenies who had been adapting to the ice for almost a thousand years – were the only survivors of the Fall, the viral plagues, and the wraiths. The Chitchatuk took everything they needed from the monstrous wraiths, and – from what we could glean – the wraiths depended solely upon the Chitchatuk for their own food. All other life-forms – always marginal – had fallen below the survival threshold after the Fall and the failure of terraforming.

Our first couple of days with them were spent sleeping, eating, and trying to communicate. The Chitchatuk had no permanent villages in the ice: they would sleep for a few hours, fold their robes, and move on through the warren of tunnels. When heating ice to water – their only use of fire, since the embers were not enough to warm them and they ate their meat raw – they suspended the miter-brazier from the ice ceiling with three wraith-tendon thongs so that it would leave a telltale melted point in the ice.

There were twenty-three of them in the tribe, band, clan – whatever you could call them – and at first it was not possible to tell if there were any females among them. The Chitchatuk seemed to wear their robes at all times, just lifting them enough to avoid soiling them while urinating or defecating in one of the ice fissures. It was not until we saw the woman named Chatchia mating with Cuchiat in our third sleep period that we were sure that females were in the band.

Slowly, as we walked and talked with them through the never-changing dimness of tunnels over the next two days, we began to learn their faces and names. Cuchiat, the leader, was – despite the avalanche of his voice – a gentle man, given to smiling with both his thin lips and his black eyes. Chiaku, his second in command, was the tallest of the band and wore a wraith-robe with a streak of blood on it, which we later realized was a mark of honor. Aichacut was the angry one, often scowling at us and always keeping his distance. I think that if Aichacut had been leader of the hunting band when we'd encountered them, there would have been dead bodies in the ice that day.

Cuchtu was, we thought, a sort of medicine man, and it was his job to circle the ice niche or tunnel where we slept, muttering incantations and removing his wraith-leather gloves to press his bare palms against the ice. It was my guess that he was driving away bad spirits. Aenea suggested wryly that he might just be doing what we were – trying to find a way out of this ice maze.

Chichticu was the fire carrier and obviously proud of having attained that honor. The embers were a mystery to us: they continued to glow and give off heat and light for days – weeks – yet were never stoked or renewed. It was not until we met Father Glaucus that this puzzle was cleared up.

There were no children with the band, and it was hard to tell the ages of the Chitchatuk we got to know. Cuchiat was obviously older than most – his face was a web of wrinkles radiating from the bridge of that wide blade of a nose – but we never succeeded in discussing ages with any of them. They recognized Aenea as a child – or at least a young adult – and treated her accordingly. The women, we noticed after identifying three of them as such, carried out the role of hunter and sentry in equal rotation with the men. Although they were to honor A. Bettik and me with the job of standing guard while the band slept – three people with weapons were always left awake – they never asked Aenea to perform that chore. But they obviously enjoyed her and enjoyed talking with her, everyone using the combination of simple words and elaborate signs that have served to bridge the gap between peoples since the Paleolithic.

On the third day Aenea succeeded in asking them to return to the river with us. At first they were puzzled, but her signs and the few words she had picked up soon communicated the concept – the river, the raft floating, the arch of the farcaster frozen in ice (they exclaimed at this), then the ice wall and our walking up the ice tunnel before meeting our friends the Chitchatuk.

When Aenea suggested that we return to the river together, the band gathered up the sleeping robes, stuffed them into the wraith-hide packs, and were marching with us within moments. For once I led the way, the glowing dial of the inertial compass unraveling the many twists, turns, ascents, and descents we had taken in our three days of wandering.

I should say here that if it had not been for our chronometers, time would have disappeared in the ice tunnels of Sol Draconi Septem. The unchanging dim glow from the bone brazier, the glint of ice walls, the darkness ahead of us and behind, the in-pressing cold, the short sleep periods and endless hours of laboring up icy corridors with the weight of the planet on our backs – everything combined to destroy our sense of time. But according to the chronometer, it was late on the third day since abandoning the raft that we descended the last bit of narrow corridor and returned to the river.

It was a sad sight: the splintered foremast and battered logs, the stern of the craft almost submerged from a buildup of ice, the lanterns we had left behind coated white with frost, and the entire vessel looking empty and forlorn without our tent and gear. The Chitchatuk were fascinated, showing the most animation we had seen from them since our initial encounter. Using lines of braided wraith-hide, Cuchiat and several of the others lowered themselves to the raft and examined every detail carefully – the stone of our abandoned hearth, the metal of the lanterns, the nylon line used to lash the logs. Their excitement was tangible, and I realized that in a society where the only source of building material, weaponry, and clothing came from a single animal – a skilful predator, at that – the raft must represent a treasure trove of raw material.

They could have attempted to kill or abandon us then and taken that wealth, but the Chitchatuk were a generous people, and not even greed could alter their view that all humans were allies, just as all wraiths were enemies and prey. We had not seen a wraith at that time ~ except, of course, for the skins we wore over our tropical clothing, since the robes were so incredibly warm, rivaling the thermal blanket for insulative efficiency, that we were able to pack away most of the outer layers we had bundled on. But if we were innocent of the wraith's power and hunger then, we would not stay so innocent for long.

Once again Aenea communicated the idea of our floating downriver through the arch. She pantomimed the ice wall – pointed to it – and then showed them our continued trip downriver to the second arch.

This got Cuchiat and his band even more animated, and they tried to talk to us without sign language, their harsh words and sentences falling on us like a load of gravel dumped at our ears. When that failed, they turned and talked excitedly to one another. Finally Cuchiat stepped forward and spoke a short sentence to the three of us. We heard the word 'glaucus' repeated – we had heard it before in their speeches, the word standing out as alien to their language – and when Cuchiat gestured upward and repeated the sign for all of us walking up toward the surface, we eagerly agreed.

And thus it was, each of us swathed in robes of wraith-fur, our backs hunched against the weight of our packs in the exhausting gravity, our feet scrabbling on rock-hard ice, that we set out toward the ice-buried city to meet the priest.

FORTY-ONE

When the summons finally comes to release father Captain de Soya from virtual house arrest in the Legionaries of Christ rectory, it arrives not from the Holy Office of the Inquisition, as has been expected, but in the person of Monsignor Lucas Oddi, undersecretary to the Vatican Secretariat of State, His Excellency Simon Augustino Cardinal Lourdusamy.

The walk into Vatican City and through the Vatican Gardens is all but overwhelming to de Soya. Everything he sees and hears – the pale-blue skies of Pacem, the flittering of finches in the pear orchards, the soft stroke of Vespers bells – makes emotion surge within him to the point that he has to work to hold back tears. Monsignor Oddi chats while they walk, mixing Vatican gossip with mild pleasantries in a way that makes de Soya's ears buzz long after they have passed the section of garden where bees hum between the floral displays.

De Soya focuses on the tall, elderly man who is leading him with such a brisk pace. Oddi is very tall and he seems to glide forward, his legs making little noise within the long cassock. The Monsignor's face is thin and crafty, lines and wrinkles molded by many decades of amusement, the long beak of a nose seeming to sniff the Vatican air for humor and rumor. De Soya has heard the jokes about Monsignor Oddi and Cardinal Lourdusamy, the tall, funny man and the huge, crafty man – how together they might look almost comical if it were not for the truly terrifying power they wield.

De Soya is momentarily surprised when they come out of the garden and step into one of the outside elevators that rise to the loggias of the Vatican Palace. Swiss Guard troopers, resplendent in their ancient uniforms of red, blue and orange stripes, snap to attention as they step into and then out of the wire-mesh elevator cages. The troopers here carry long pikes, but de Soya remembers that these can be used as pulse rifles.

'You remember that His Holiness, during his first resurrection, decided to reoccupy this level because of his fondness for his namesake, Julius the Second,' says Monsignor Oddi, gesturing down the long corridor with an easy sweep of his hand.

'Yes,' says de Soya. His heart is pounding wildly. Pope Julius II – the famous warrior-pope who had commissioned the Sistine ceiling during his reign from AD 1503 to 1513 had been the first to live in these rooms. Now Pope Julius – in all of his incarnations from Julius VI to Julius XIV – has lived and ruled here almost twenty-seven times as long as the decade of that first warrior-pope. Certainly he could not be meeting the Holy Father! De

Soya manages an outward calm as they start down the great corridor, but his palms are moist and his breathing is rapid.

'We are going to see the Secretariat, of course,' says Oddi, smiling, 'but if you have not seen the papal apartments, this is a pleasant walk. His Holiness is meeting with the Interstellar Synod of Bishops in the smaller hall of the Nervi building all this day.'

De Soya nods attentively, but, in truth, his attention is focused on the Raphael Stanze he is glimpsing through open doors of the papal apartments as they pass. He knows the outlines of the history: Pope Julius II had grown tired of the 'old-fashioned' frescoes by such minor geniuses as Piero della Francesca and Andrea del Castagno, so in the fall of 1508 he had brought a twenty-six-year-old genius from Urbino, Raffaello Sanzio – also known as Raphael. De Soya can see the Stanza della Segnatura, with its overwhelming fresco representing the Triumph of Religious Truth contrasted with the Triumph of Philosophical and Scientific Truth.

'Ahhh,' says Monsignor Oddi, pausing so that de Soya can stand and stare a moment. 'You like it, eh? You see Plato there among the philosophers?'

'Yes,' says de Soya.

'Do you know to whom the likeness actually belonged? Who the model was?'

'No,' says de Soya.

'Leonardo da Vinci,' says the monsignor with a hint of a smile. 'And Heraclitus – see him there? Do you know whom Raphael depicted from life?'

De Soya can only shake his head. He is remembering the tiny adobe Mariaist chapel on his homeworld, with the sand always blowing in under the doors and pooling under the simple statue of the Virgin.

'Heraclitus was Michelangelo,' says Monsignor Oddi. 'And Euclid there . . . you see him . . . that was Bramante. Come in, come closer.'

De Soya can hardly bear to set foot on the rich tapestry of carpet. The frescoes, statuary, gilded molding, and tall windows of the room seem to whirl around him.

'You see these letters on Bramante's collar here? Come, lean closer. Can you read them, my son?'

'R-U-S-M,' reads de Soya.

'Yes, yes,' chuckles Monsignor Lucas Oddi. '*Raphael Urbinus Sua Manu.* Come, come, my son . . . translate for an old man. You have had your review lesson in Latin for this week, I believe.'

'Raphael of Urbino,' translates de Soya, muttering more to himself than the taller man, 'by his hand.'

'Yes. Come along. We shall take the papal lift down to the apartments. We must not keep the Secretary waiting.'

The Borgia Apartment takes up much of the ground floor of this wing of the palace. They enter through the tiny Chapel of Nicholas V, and Father Captain de Soya thinks that he has never seen any work of man lovelier than this small room. The frescoes here were painted by Fra Angelico between AD 1447 and 1449 and are the essence of simplicity, the avatar of purity.

Beyond the chapel, the rooms of the Borgia Apartment become darker and more ominous, much as the ensuing history of the Church had grown darker under the Borgia popes. But by Room IV – Pope Alexander's study, dedicated to the sciences and the liberal arts – de Soya begins to appreciate the power of the rich color, the extravagant applications of gold leaf, and the sumptuous uses of stucco. Room V explores the lives of the saints through fresco and statuary, yet has a stylized, inhuman feel to it, which de Soya associates with old pictures he has seen of Old Earth Egyptian art. Room VI, the Pope's dining room according to the Monsignor, explores the mysteries of the faith in an explosion of color and figures that literally takes de Soya's breath away.

Monsignor Oddi pauses by a huge fresco of the Resurrection and points two fingers toward a secondary figure whose intense piety can be felt through the centuries and faded oils. 'Pope Alexander the Sixth,' Oddi says softly. 'The second of the Borgia popes.' He flicks his hand almost negligently toward two men standing nearby in the thickly populated fresco. Both have the lighting and expressions reserved for saints. 'Cesare Borgia,' says Oddi, 'Pope Alexander's bastard son. The man next to him is Cesare's brother . . . whom he murdered. The Pope's daughter, Lucrezia, was in Room V . . . you may have missed her . . . the virgin Saint Catherine of Alexandria.'

De Soya can only stare. He looks up at the ceiling and sees the design that has appeared in each of these rooms – the brilliant bull and crown that were the Borgia emblems.

'Pinturicchio painted all this,' says Monsignor Oddi, on the move again now. 'His real name was Bernardino di Betto, and he was quite mad. Possibly a servant of darkness.' The Monsignor pauses to look back into the room as Swiss Guards snap to attention. 'And most certainly a genius,' he says softly. 'Come. It is time for your appointment.'

Cardinal Lourdusamy awaits behind a long, low desk in Room VI, the *Sala dei Pontifici* – the so-called 'Room of the Popes'. The huge man does not rise but shifts sideways in his chair as Father Captain de Soya is announced and allowed to approach. De Soya goes to one knee and kisses the Cardinal's ring. Lourdusamy pats the priest-captain on the head and waves away any further formality. 'Take that chair, my son. Get comfortable. I assure you, that little chair is more comfortable than this straight-backed throne they found for me.'

De Soya has almost forgotten the power of the Cardinal's voice: it is a great bass rumbling that seems to come up out of the earth as much as from the large man's body. Lourdusamy is huge, a great mass of red silk, white linen, and crimson velvet, a geological massif of a man culminating in the large head atop layers of jowls, the small mouth, tiny, lively eyes, and almost hairless skull set off by the crimson skullcap.

'Federico,' rumbles the Cardinal, 'I am so pleased and delighted that you have come through so many deaths and troubles without harm. You look well, my son. Tired, but well.'

'Thank you, Your Excellency,' says de Soya. Monsignor Oddi has taken a chair to the priest-captain's left, a bit farther away from the Cardinal's desk.

'And I understand you went before the tribunal of the Holy Office yesterday,' rumbles Cardinal Lourdusamy, his eyes piercing into de Soya.

'Yes, Your Excellency.'

'No thumbscrews, I hope? No iron maidens or hot irons. Or did they have you on the rack?' The Cardinal's chuckle seems to echo in the man's huge chest.

'No, Your Excellency.' De Soya manages a smile.

'Good, good,' says the Cardinal, the light from a fixture ten meters overhead gleaming on his ring. He leans closer and smiles. 'When His Holiness ordered the Holy Office to take back its old title – the Inquisition – a few of the nonbelievers thought that the days of madness and terror within the Church had returned. But now they know better, Federico. The Holy Office's only power is in its role of giving advice to the Orders of the Church, its only punishment is to recommend excommunication.'

De Soya licks his lips. 'But that is a terrible punishment, Your Excellency.'

'Yes,' agrees Cardinal Lourdusamy, and the banter is gone from his voice. 'Terrible. But not one you have to worry about, my son. This incident is over. Your name and reputation have been fully exonerated. The report the tribunal shall send to His Holiness clears you of any blemish larger than . . . shall we say . . . a certain insensitivity to the feelings of a certain provincial Bishop with enough friends in the Curia to demand this hearing,'

De Soya does not let out his breath yet. 'Bishop Melandriano is a thief, Your Excellency.'

Lourdusamy's lively eyes flick toward Monsignor Oddi and then return to the priest-captain's face. 'Yes, yes, Federico. We know that. We have known that for some time. The good Bishop on his remote floating city on that watery world shall have his time before the lord cardinals of the Holy Office, be assured. And you also may be assured that the recommendations in his case will not be so lenient.' The Cardinal settled back into his high-backed chair. Ancient wood creaked. 'But we must talk of other things, my son. Are you ready to resume your mission?'

'Yes, Your Excellency.' De Soya is surprised by the immediacy and sincerity of his answer. Until that second he had thought it best that this part of his life and service was over.

Cardinal Lourdusamy's expression grows more serious. The great jowls seem to become firmer. 'Excellent. Now, I understand that one of your troopers died during your expedition to Hebron.'

'An accident during resurrection, Your Excellency,' says de Soya.

Lourdusamy is shaking his head. 'Terrible. Terrible.'

'Lancer Rettig,' adds Father Captain de Soya, feeling that the man's name needs to be spoken. 'He was a good soldier.'

The Cardinal's small eyes glint, as if from tears. He looks directly at de Soya as he says, 'His parents and sister will be taken care of. Lancer Rettig had a brother who rose to the rank of priest-commander on Bressia. Did you know that, my son?'

'No, Your Excellency,' says de Soya.

Lourdusamy nods. 'A great loss.' The Cardinal sighs and sets a plump hand on the empty desktop. De Soya sees the dimples in the back of the hand and looks at it as if it is its own entity, some boneless creature from the sea.

'Federico,' rumbles Lourdusamy, 'we have a suggestion for someone to fill the vacancy on your ship left by Lancer Rettig's death. But first we must discuss the reason for this mission. Do you know *why* we must find and detain this young female?'

De Soya sits straight up. 'Your Excellency explained that the girl was the child of a cybrid abomination,' he says. 'That she poses a threat to the Church itself. That she may well be an agent of the AI TechnoCore.'

Lourdusamy is nodding. 'All true, Federico. All true. But we did not tell you precisely *how* she is a threat . . . not only to the Church and the Pax, but to all humanity. If we are to send you back out there on this mission, my son, you have the right to know.'

Outside, their volume muffled but still audible through the palace windows and walls, come two sudden and disparate sounds. In the same instant the midday cannon is fired from the Janiculum Hill along the river toward Tratevere, and the clocks of St Peter's begin to strike the noon hour.

Lourdusamy pauses, removes an ancient watch from the folds of his crimson robe, nods as if satisfied, winds it, and returns it to its place.

De Soya waits.

329

FORTY-TWO

It took us a little more than a day to walk the ice tunnels to Father Glaucus and the buried city, but there were three short sleep periods during that time, and the voyage itself – darkness, cold, narrow passages through the ice – would have been quite forgettable if the wraith had not taken one of our party.

As with all real acts of violence, it happened too quickly to observe. One second we were trudging along, Aenea, the android, and I near the back of the single-file line of Chitchatuk, and suddenly there was an explosion of ice and movement – I froze, thinking that an explosive mine had been set off – and the robed figure two forms in front of Aenea disappeared without a cry.

I was still frozen, the plasma rifle in my mittened hands, but useless, its safety still on, when the nearest Chitchatuk began ululating in rage and helplessness, the closest hunters throwing themselves down the new corridor that opened where none had been a second before.

Aenea was already shining her handlamp down the nearly vertical shaft when I pushed next to her, my weapon raised. Two of the Chitchatuk had hurled themselves down that shaft, braking their fall with their boots and their short bone knives throwing ice splinters above them, and I was about to squeeze in when Cuchiat grabbed my shoulder. 'Ktchey!' he said. 'Ku tcheta chi!'

By this fourth day I knew that he was ordering me not to go. I obeyed, but brought out the flashlight laser to illuminate the way for the shouting hunters already twenty meters below us and out of sight where the new tunnel curved away to the horizontal. At first I thought it was an effect of the red laser beam, but then I saw that the shaft was coated – almost totally painted – in bright blood.

The ululation among the Chitchatuk continued even after the hunters returned empty-handed. I understood that there had been no sight of the wraith, and no sight of its victim except for blood, shredded robe, and the little finger from her right hand. Cuchtu, the one we thought of as the medicine man, knelt, kissed the severed digit, brought a bone knife across his forearm until his own blood dripped on the bloody finger, and then carefully, almost reverently, set the finger in his hide bag. The ululation stopped immediately. Chiaku – the tall man with the bloodstained robe that was twice bloodstained now, since he had been one of the hunters who had thrown himself down the shaft – turned to us and spoke earnestly for a long moment while the others shouldered their packs, set their spears away, and resumed the trek.

As we continued up the ice tunnel, I could not help but glance back and see the wraith's jagged entrance hole fade into the blackness that seemed to follow us. Knowing that the animals lived on the surface and came below mostly to hunt, I had not been nervous. But now the very ice of the floor seemed treacherous, the ice facets and ridges of the walls and ceilings mere hunting blinds for the next wraith. I found that I was trying to walk lightly, as if that would keep me from falling through to where the killer waited. It was not easy to walk lightly on Sol Draconi Septem.

'M. Aenea,' said the robed figure of A. Bettik, 'I could not understand what M. Chaiku was saying. Something about numbers?'

Aenea's face was all but lost under the wraith-teeth of her robe. I had known that all these robes were taken from wraith cubs – infants – but the one glimpse of white arms the thickness of my torso coming through the ice wall, black talons the length of my forearm, made me realize how large these things must be. Sometimes, I realized, the safety off on my plasma rifle, trying to walk lightly in the grinding weight of Sol Draconi Septem, the shortest route to courage is absolute ignorance.

'. . . so I think he was talking about the fact that the band no longer comprises a prime number,' Aenea was saying to A. Bettik. 'Until she . . . was taken . . . we had twenty-six, which was all right, but now they have to do something soon or . . . I don't know . . . more bad luck.'

As far as I could tell, they solved the prime-number jinx by sending Chiaku ahead as a scout. Or perhaps he just volunteered to be apart from the group until they could drop us off in the frozen city – twenty-five, as an odd number, could be tolerated briefly, but without us their band would be back to twenty-two, still an unacceptable number.

I left behind all thoughts of the Chitchatuk's preoccupation with primes when we arrived at the city.

First, we saw the light. After just a few days, our eyes had grown so accustomed to the ember-glow of the 'chuchkituk' – the miter-shaped bone brazier – that even the occasional flash of our handlamps seemed blinding. The light from the frozen city was actually painful.

At one time, the building had been steel or plasteel and smart glass, perhaps seventy stories tall, and must have looked out at a pleasant green terraformed valley – perhaps looking south to where the river flowed half a kilometer away. Now our ice tunnel opened on to a hole in the glass somewhere around the fifty-eighth floor, and tongues of the atmospheric glacier had bent the steel frame of the building and found inroads on various levels.

But the skyscraper still stood, perhaps with its upper stories protruding into the black near vacuum of the surface above the glacier. And it still blazed with light.

The Chitchatuk paused at the entrance, shielding their eyes from the glare and ululating in a different tone from that of their earlier mourning wail in the tunnel when the woman had been taken. This was a beckoning. While we stood and waited, I stared at the open steel-and-glass skeleton of this place, at the dozens upon dozens of burning lamps hung everywhere here, floor after floor, so that we could stare down beneath our feet through the clear ice and see the building dropping away beneath us, windows brightly lit.

Then Father Glaucus ambled toward us across the space that was half ice cavern, half office-building room. He wore the long black cassock and crucifix that I associated with the Jesuits at their monastery near Port Romance. It was obvious that the old man was blind – his eyes were milky with cataracts and as unseeing as stones – but that was not the first thing that struck me about Father Glaucus: he was old, ancient, hoary, bearded like a patriarch, and when Cuchiat called to him, his features came alive and he awoke as if from a trance, his snow-white brows arching up, plowing wrinkles into his large forehead. Chapped and weathered lips curled up in a smile. This may sound grotesque, but nothing about Father Glaucus was bizarre in any way – not his blindness, not the blindingly white beard, not the weathered, mottled old man's skin or withered lips. He was so much . . . himself . . . that comparisons fail.

I had many reservations about meeting this 'glaucus' – afraid that he would have some association with the Pax we were fleeing – and now, having seen that he was a priest, I should have grabbed the girl and A. Bettik and left with the Chitchatuk. But none of the three of us had that impulse at all. This old man was not the Pax . . . he was only Father Glaucus. This we learned only minutes after our first encounter.

But first, before any of us spoke, the blind priest seemed to sense our presence. After speaking to Cuchiat and Chichticu in their own tongue, he suddenly swiveled our way, holding one hand high as if his palm could sense our heat – Aenea's, A. Bettik's, and mine. Then he crossed the small space to where we stood at the boundary between encroaching ice cavern and encroached-upon room.

Father Glaucus walked directly up to me, set his bony hand on my shoulder, and said, loudly and clearly in Web English, 'Thou art the man!'

It took me a while – years – to put that comment in the proper perspective. At the time I simply thought the old priest was mad as well as blind.

The arrangement was for us to stay a few days with Father Glaucus in his subglacial high-rise while the Chitchatuk went off to do important Chitchatuk things – Aenea and I guessed that settling the prime-number problem was their highest priority – and then the band would check back on us. Aenea and I had succeeded in communicating via signs that we wanted to take the raft apart and carry it downriver to the next farcaster portal. The Chitchatuk seemed to understand – or at least they had nodded and used their word for assent – 'chia' – when we pantomimed the second arch and the raft passing through it. If I had understood their signed and verbal response, the trip to the second farcaster would require traveling across the surface, would take several days, and would pass through an area of many arctic wraiths. I was sure that they said we would discuss it again after they acted on their immediate need of going off to 'seek insoluble balance' – which we guessed meant finding another member for the band – or losing three. The last thought gave one pause.

At any rate, we were to stay with Father Glaucus until Cuchiat's band returned. The blind priest chatted animatedly with the hunters for several minutes and then stood at the opening of the ice cave, obviously listening, until the glow of their bone-brazier had long since disappeared.

Then Father Glaucus greeted us again by passing his hands across our faces, shoulders, arms, and hands. I confess that I had never experienced an introduction quite like it. When he cupped Aenea's face in his bony hands, the old man said, 'A human child. I had never expected to see a human child's face again.'

I did not understand. 'What about the Chitchatuk?' I said. 'They're human. They must have children.'

Father Glaucus had led us deeper into the skyscraper and up a flight of stairs to a warmer room before our 'introductions'. This was obviously a living area for him – lanterns and braziers burned brightly with the same glowing pellets that the Chitchatuk used, only there were hundreds more here, comfortable furniture was set around, there was an ancient music-disc player, and the inner walls were lined with books – which I found incongruous in the home of a blind man.

'The Chitchatuk have children,' said the old priest, 'but they do not allow them to stay with the bands that roam this far north.'

'Why?' I said.

'The wraiths,' said Father Glaucus. 'There are so many wraiths north of the old terraforming line.'

'I thought the Chitchatuk depended upon the wraiths for everything,' I said.

The old man nodded and stroked his beard. It was full, white, and long enough to hide his Roman collar. His cassock was carefully patched and darned, but still frayed and threadbare. 'My friends the Chitchatuk depend upon wraith *cubs* for everything,' he said. 'The metabolism of the adults makes their hides and bones worthless for the bands' purposes . . .'

I did not understand this, but I let him continue without interruption.

'. . . the wraiths, on the other hand, love nothing more than Chitchatuk children,' he said. 'It is why Chitchatuk and the others are so puzzled by our young friend's presence this far north.'

'Where are their children?' asked Aenea.

'Many hundreds of kilometers south,' said the priest. 'With the child-rearing bands. It is . . . tropical there. The ice is only thirty or forty meters thick and the atmosphere is almost breathable.'

'Why don't the wraiths hunt the children there?' I asked.

'It is poor country for the wraiths . . . far too warm.'

'Then why don't all the Chitchatuk play it safe and move south . . .' I began, and stopped. The heavy g-load and cold must have been making me more stupid than I usually was.

'Exactly,' said Father Glaucus, hearing comprehension in my silence. 'The Chitchatuk totally depend upon the wraiths. The hunting bands – like our friend Cuchiat's – risk terrible odds to provide the child-rearing bands with meat, hides, and tools. The child-rearing bands run a chance of starving before the food is provided. The Chitchatuk have few children, but those few are precious to them. Or, as they would say – 'Utchai tuk aichit chacutkuchit.'

'More . . . sacred, I think the word is . . . than warmth,' translated Aenea.

'Precisely,' said the old priest. 'But I am forgetting my manners. I shall show you all to your quarters – I keep several rooms furnished and heated, although you are my first non-Chitchatuk guests for . . . ah . . . five standard decades, I believe. While you settle in, I shall start warming our dinners.'

FORTY-THREE

In the middle of his explanation of the real reason for de Soya's mission, Cardinal Lourdusamy leans back in his throne and waves his plump hand toward the distant ceiling. 'What do you think of this room, Federico?'

Father Captain de Soya, poised to hear something vitally important, can only blink and lift his face. This great hall is as ornate as the others in the Borgia Apartment – more ornate, he realizes, for the colors are livelier, more vibrant – and then he sees the difference: these tapestries and frescoes are more current, depicting Pope Julius VI receiving the cruciform from an angel of the Lord, another showing God reaching down – in an echo of Michelangelo's ceiling of the Sistine Chapel – to confer the Sacrament of Resurrection on Julius. He sees the evil antipope, Teilhard I, being banished by an archangel with a flaming sword. Other ceiling images and wall tapestries proclaim the glory of the first great century of the Church's own resurrection and Pax expansion.

'The original ceiling in here collapsed in AD 1500,' rumbles Cardinal Lourdusamy, 'almost killing Pope Alexander. Most of the original decoration was destroyed. Leo the Tenth had it replaced after the death of Julius the Second, but the work was inferior to the original. His Holiness commissioned the new work one hundred and thirty standard years ago. Notice the central fresco – it is by Halaman Ghena of Renaissance Vector. The Pax Ascending tapestry – there – is by Shiroku. The architectural restoration was by the cream of Pacem's own artisans, including Peter Baines Cort-Bilgruth.'

De Soya nods politely, having no clue as to how this relates to what they were discussing. Perhaps the Cardinal, as is true of many men and women of power, has become used to digressing at will because his underlings never protest the loss of focus.

As if reading the priest-captain's mind, Lourdusamy chuckles and sets his soft hand on the leather surface of the table. 'I mention this for a reason, Federico. Would you agree that the Church and Pax have brought an era of unprecedented peace and prosperity to humanity?'

De Soya pauses. He has read history but is not sure if this era has been unprecedented. And as for 'peace' . . . memories of burning orbital forests and ravaged worlds still haunt his dreams. 'The Church and its Pax allies have certainly improved the situation for most of the former Web worlds I have visited, Your Excellency,' he says. 'And no one can deny the unprecedented gift of resurrection.'

Lourdusamy's throat rumbles with amusement. 'The saints save us . . . a diplomat!' The Cardinal rubs his thin upper lip. 'Yes, yes, you are perfectly correct, Federico. Every age has its shortcomings, and ours includes a constant struggle against the Ousters and an even more urgent struggle to establish the Reign of Our Lord and Savior in the hearts of all men and women. But, as you see' – his hand gestures once again toward the frescoes and tapestries – 'we are in the midst of a Renaissance every bit as real as that imbued with the spirit of the early Renaissance, which gave us the Chapel of Nicholas the Fifth and the other wonders you saw on the way in. And this Renaissance is truly one of the spirit, Federico . . .'

De Soya waits.

'This . . . abomination . . . will destroy all that,' says Lourdusamy, his voice deadly serious now. 'As I said to you one year ago, this is not a child we seek, it is a virus. And we know now whence that virus comes.'

De Soya listens.

'Our Holiness has had one of his visions,' the Cardinal says in a voice so soft it is just above a whisper. 'You are aware, Federico, that the Holy Father is often visited by dreams granted by God?'

'I have heard rumors, Your Excellency.' This magical aspect of the Church has always had the least appeal to de Soya. He waits.

Lourdusamy waves his hand as if brushing away the sillier rumors. 'It is true that His Holiness has received vital revelations after much prayer, much fasting, and exhibiting the utmost humility. Such a revelation was the source of our knowledge on when and where the child would appear on Hyperion. His Holiness was correct to the moment, was he not?'

De Soya bows his head.

'And it was one of these sacred revelations which prompted the Holy Father to ask for you in this service, Federico. He saw that your fate and the salvation of our Church and society were inextricably entwined.'

Father Captain de Soya can only stare without blinking.

'And now,' rumbles Cardinal Lourdusamy, 'the threat to the future of humankind has been revealed in much greater detail.' The Cardinal rises to his feet, but when de Soya and Monsignor Oddi hurry to stand, the huge man waves them back to their chairs. De Soya sits and watches the giant mass of red and white move through the pools of light in the dark room, the flesh of the Cardinal's cheeks gleaming, his small eyes lost in shadows from the overhead spots.

'This is, indeed, the AI TechnoCore's great attempt at our destruction, Federico. The same mechanical evil which destroyed Old Earth, which preyed upon humanity's minds and souls through their parasitic farcasters, and which prompted the Ouster attack that presaged the Fall . . . the same Evil is at work here. The cybrid offspring, this . . . Aenea . . . is their instrument. That is why the farcasters have worked for her when they admit no one else. That is why the Shrike demon slayed thousands of our people and soon may slay millions – perhaps billions. Unless stopped, this . . . *succubus* . . . will succeed in returning us to the Rule of the Machine.'

De Soya watches the great red form of the Cardinal move from light to dark. None of this is new.

Lourdusamy stops his pacing. 'But His Holiness now knows that this cybrid spawn is not only the agent of the Core, Federico . . . she is the instrument of the Machine God.'

De Soya understands. When the Inquisition had queried him about the *Cantos*, his insides had turned to jelly at the thought of punishment for having read the banned poem. But even this book on the Index admitted that the elements of the AI Core had been working for centuries to produce an Ultimate Intelligence – a cybernetic deity that would spread its power back through time to dominate the universe. Indeed, both the *Cantos* and official Church history acknowledged the battle across time between this false god and Our Lord. The Keats cybrid – cybrids, actually, since there had been a replacement after one sect of the Core destroyed the first one in the megasphere – had been falsely represented as a candidate for the messiah of the 'human UI' – that blasphemous Teilhardian concept of an evolved human god – in the prohibited *Cantos*. That poem had talked about *empathy* being the key to human spiritual evolution. The Church had corrected that, pointing out that obeying God's Will was the source of revelation and salvation.

'Through revelation,' Lourdusamy says, 'His Holiness knows where the cybrid spawn and her dupes are at this very moment.'

De Soya sits forward. 'Where, Your Excellency?'

'On the abandoned ice world of Sol Draconi Septem,' rumbles the Cardinal. 'His Holiness is quite clear on that. And he is quite clear on the consequences if she is not stopped.' Lourdusamy walks around the long desk and stands next to the priest-captain. De Soya looks up to see gleaming red, brilliant white, the tiny eyes boring into him. 'She runs now to find allies,' comes the Cardinal's sincere growl. 'Allies to help in the destruction of the Pax and the desecration of the Church. To this moment she has been like a deadly virus in an empty region – a potential danger, but containable. Soon, if she escapes us now, she shall grow to maturity and full power . . . the full power of the Evil One.'

Above the Cardinal's gleaming shoulder, de Soya can see the writhing figures of the ceiling fresco.

'Every one of the old farcaster portals will open simultaneously,' rumbles the red form. 'The Shrike demon . . . in a million iterations . . . will step through to slaughter Christians. The Ousters will be empowered by Techno-Core weapons and terrible AI technologies. Already they have used subcellular machinery to make themselves something more and less than human. Already they have traded their immortal souls for the machinery to adapt to space, to eat sunlight, to exist like . . . like plants in darkness. Their war-making abilities will be augmented a thousandfold by the Core's secret engines. That hideous strength will not be denied, even by the Church. Billions will die the true death, their cruciforms torn from them, their souls ripped out of their bodies like beating hearts from living chests. Tens of billions will die. The Ousters will burn their way across the Pax, laying waste like the Vandals and Visigoths, destroying Pacem, the Vatican, and everything we know. They will kill peace. They will deny life and desecrate our principle of the dignity of the individual.'

De Soya sits and waits.

'This does not have to happen,' says Secretariat Cardinal Lourdusamy. 'His Holiness prays every day that it will *not* happen. But these are perilous times, Federico . . . for the Church, for the Pax, for the future of the race of man. He has seen what *may* be and has dedicated all our lives and sacred honors as Princes of the Church to preventing the birth of such a terrible reality.'

De Soya looks up as the Cardinal leans closer.

'I must reveal something to you at this moment, Federico, which billions of the Faithful will not learn for months . . . Today, this hour, at the Interstellar Synod of Bishops . . . His Holiness is announcing a Crusade.'

'A Crusade?' repeats de Soya. Even the unflappable Monsignor Oddi makes a low noise in his throat.

'A Crusade against the Ouster menace,' rumbles Cardinal Lourdusamy. 'For centuries we have defended ourselves – the Great Wall is a defensive strategem, putting Christian bodies and ships and lives in the way of the Ouster aggression – but as of this day, by the grace of God, the Church and Pax will go on the offensive.'

'How?' says de Soya. He knows that the battles already rage in the no-man's-land of gray space between the Pax and Ouster regions, filling thousands of parsecs with fleet lunge and parry, thrust and retreat. But with the time-debt – the maximum voyage from Pacem to the farthest reaches of the Great Wall is two years of shiptime, more than twenty years of time-debt – there can be little or no coordination of either offense or defense.

Lourdusamy smiles grimly and answers. 'Even as we speak, every world in the Pax and Protectorate is being asked . . . commanded . . . to devote planetary resources to build one great ship . . . one ship for each world.'

'We have thousands of ships . . .' begins the priest-captain and stops.

'Yes,' purrs the Cardinal. 'These ships will use the new archangel technology. But they will not be like your *Raphael* – a lightly armed courier – but the deadliest battle cruisers this spiral arm has ever seen. Capable of translating anywhere in the galaxy in less time than it takes a dropship to rise to orbit. Each ship named after its homeworld, each staffed by devoted Pax officers such as yourself – men and women willing to suffer death and receive resurrection – and each capable of destroying entire Swarms.'

De Soya nods. 'Is this the Holy Father's answer to his revelation of the child's threat, Your Excellency?'

Lourdusamy moves back around the desk and settles into his high-backed throne as if exhausted. 'In part, Federico. In part. These new craft will begin to be built within the next standard decade. The technology is difficult . . . *very* difficult. Meanwhile, the cybrid *succubus* continues to circulate disease like a spreading virus. That part depends upon you – you and your enhanced crew of virus seekers.'

'Enhanced?' repeats de Soya. 'May Sergeant Gregorius and Corporal Kee still travel with me?'

'Yes,' rumbles the Cardinal. 'They have already been assigned.'

'Where does the enhancement come in?' asks de Soya, dreading the possibility that a Cardinal from the Holy Office will be assigned to his mission.

Cardinal Lourdusamy opens his fat fingers as if lifting the lid of a treasure box. 'Just one addition to your crew, Federico.'

'An officer of the Church?' asks the priest-captain, wondering if the papal diskey is to be passed to a different commander.

Lourdusamy shakes his head. His great jowls flow with the movement. 'A simple warrior, Father Captain de Soya. A new breed of warrior, bred for the renewed Army of Christ.'

De Soya does not understand. It sounds as if the Church is answering Ouster nanotechnology with biomodifications of its own. That would defy all of the Church doctrine de Soya has been taught.

Once again, the Cardinal seems to read the priest-captain's thoughts. 'Nothing like that, Federico. Some . . . augmentations . . . and much unique training from a new branch of the Pax military, but still totally human . . . and Christian.'

'One trooper?' says de Soya, mystified.

'One warrior,' said Lourdusamy. 'Not within the Pax Fleet chain of command. The first member of the elite Legions which shall spearhead the Crusade that His Holiness will announce today.'

De Soya rubs his chin. 'And will he be under my direct command, as Gregorius and Kee have been?'

'Of course, of course,' rumbles Lourdusamy, sitting back and folding his hands on his ample stomach. 'There will be just one change, as was deemed necessary by His Holiness in council with the Holy Office. She will have her own papal diskey, for separate authority on military decisions and those actions deemed necessary for the preservation of the Church.'

'She,' repeats de Soya, trying hard to understand this. If both he and this mystery 'warrior' have equal papal authority, how can they make decisions at all? Every aspect of their quest for the child so far has had military facets and implications. Every decision he has made has been dedicated to the preservation of the Church. It would be better if he were simply dismissed and replaced than this false sharing of power.

Before he can articulate this, Cardinal Lourdusamy leans forward and speaks as softly as the bass rumble will allow. 'Federico, His Holiness still sees you involved in this . . . and primarily responsible. But Our Lord has revealed a terrible necessity which the Holy Father seeks to take from your hands, knowing you as the ultimate man of conscience you are.'

'Terrible necessity?' says de Soya, knowing with an immediate and total sinking feeling exactly what it is.

Lourdusamy's features are all bright light and deep shadow as he leans across the desk. 'The cybrid-spawned *succubus* must be terminated. Destroyed. The virus eradicated from the Body of Christ as the first step toward the corrective surgery which is to come.'

De Soya counts to eight before speaking. 'I find the child,' he says. 'This . . . warrior . . . kills her.'

'Yes,' says Lourdusamy. There is no discussion of whether Father Captain de Soya will accept this modified mission. Born-again Christians, priests, Jesuits in particular, and Pax Fleet officers do not quibble when the Holy Father and the Holy Mother Church assign them duties.

'When do I meet this warrior, Your Excellency?' asks de Soya.

'The *Raphael* will translate to Sol Draconi System this very afternoon,' pipes up Monsignor Oddi from his place behind and to the left of de Soya. 'Your new crew member is already aboard.'

'May I ask her name and rank?' says de Soya, turning to look at the tall Monsignor.

Secretary Cardinal Simon Augustino Lourdusamy answers. 'She has no formal rank as of yet, Father Captain de Soya. Eventually she will be an officer in the newly formed Legions of the Crusade. As of now, you and your troopers may refer to her by her name.'

De Soya waits.

'Which is Nemes,' rumbles the Cardinal. 'Rhadamnth Nemes.' His small eyes flick to Lucas Oddi. The Monsignor stands. De Soya hurries to his feet. The audience is obviously at an end.

Lourdusamy's pudgy hand rises in a three-fingered benediction. De Soya bows his head.

'May Our Lord and Savior, Jesus Christ, keep you and preserve you and give you success on this most important of voyages. In the name of Jesus we ask this.'

'Amen,' murmurs Monsignor Lucas Oddi.

'Amen,' says de Soya.

FORTY-FOUR

It was not just a single building frozen in the ice. An entire city was buried here in Sol Draconi Septem's resublimated atmosphere, a small bit of the old Hegemony's hubris frozen in place like an ancient insect locked in amber.

Father Glaucus was a gentle, humorous, generous man. We soon learned that he had been exiled to Sol Draconi Septem as a punishment for belonging to one of the last Teilhardian orders in the Church. While his order had rejected the basic tenets of Teilhard after Julius VI had published a bull proclaiming the antipope's philosophy as blasphemy, the order was dissolved and its members either excommunicated or sent to the ass-ends of the Pax's dominion. Father Glaucus did not refer to his fifty-seven standard years in this icy tomb as exile – he called it his mission.

While admitting that none of the Chitchatuk had shown the slightest interest in converting, Father Glaucus confessed that he had little interest in converting them. He admired their courage, respected their honesty, and was fascinated with their hard-earned culture. Before he had become blind – snowblindness, he called it, not simple cataracts . . . a combination of cold, vacuum, and hard radiation found on the surface – Father Glaucus had traveled with numerous Chitchatuk bands. 'There were more then,' said the old priest as we sat in his brightly lit study. 'Attrition has taken its toll. Where there were tens of thousands of the Chitchatuk in this region fifty years ago, only a few hundred survive today.'

In the first day or two, while Aenea, A. Bettik, and the blind priest spoke, I spent much of my time exploring the frozen city.

Father Glaucus illuminated four floors of one tall building with the fuel-pellet lanterns. 'To keep away the wraiths,' he said. 'They hate the light.' I found a stairway and descended into the darkness with a handlamp and my rifle ready. Twenty-some stories lower and a warren of ice tunnels led to the other buildings in the city. Decades earlier, Father Glaucus had marked the entrances to these buried structures with a light pen – WAREHOUSE, COURTHOUSE, COMMUNICATIONS CENTER, HEGEMONY DOME, HOTEL, and so forth. I explored some of these, seeing signs of the priest's more recent visits here. On my third exploration I found the deep vaults where the high-energy fuel pellets were stored. These were the source of both heat and light for the old priest, and they were also his principal bargaining chip to bring the Chitchatuk in to visit.

'The wraiths give them everything except combustible material,' he had said. 'The pellets give them light and a wee bit of heat. We enjoy the barter – they give me wraith-meat and hides, I give them light and heat and garrulous conversation. I think they first began talking to me because my band consisted of the most elegant prime number . . . one! In the early days I used to hide the location of the cache. Now I know that the Chitchatuk would never steal from me. Even if their lives depended on it. Even if the lives of their *children* depended on it.'

There was little else to see in the buried city. The darkness was absolute down there, and my handlamp did little to dispel the gloom. If I had harbored hopes of finding some easy way to get us downriver to the second arch – a giant blowtorch perhaps, or a fusion borer – those hopes were soon dashed. The city was, with the exception of Father Glaucus's four floors of furniture, books, light, food, warmth, and conversation, as cold and dead as the ninth circle of hell.

On our third or fourth day there, just prior to our mealtime, I joined them in the old priest's study as they chatted. I had already gone over the books on the shelf: volumes of philosophy and theology, mysteries, astronomy texts, ethnology studies, newanthro tomes, adventure novels, carpentry guides, medical texts, zoology books . . .

'The greatest sadness of my blindness thirty years ago,' Father Glaucus had said, that first day he proudly showed us his library, 'was that I could no longer read my dear books. I am Prospero denied. You can't imagine the time it took me to drag these three thousand volumes up from the library fifty stories down!'

In the afternoons, while I explored and A. Bettik went off to read by himself, Aenea would read aloud to the old priest. Once when I entered the room without knocking, I saw tears on the ancient missionary's cheeks.

This day when I joined them, Father Glaucus was explaining Teilhard – the original Jesuit, not the antipope whom Julius VI had supplanted.

'He was a stretcher bearer in World War One,' Father Glaucus was saying. 'He could have been a chaplain and stayed out of the line of fire, but he chose to be a stretcher bearer. They awarded him medals for his courage, including one called the Legion of Honor.'

A. Bettik cleared his throat politely. 'Excuse me, Father,' he said softly. 'Am I correct in assuming that the First World War was a pre-Hegira conflict limited to Old Earth?'

The bearded priest smiled. 'Precisely, precisely, my dear friend. Early twentieth century. Terrible conflict. Terrible. And Teilhard was in the thick of it. His hatred of war lasted the rest of his life.'

Father Glaucus had long ago built his own rocking chair, and now he rocked back and forth in front of the fuel-pellet fire set in a crudely fashioned fireplace. The golden embers threw long shadows and more warmth than we had enjoyed since coming through the farcaster portal. 'Teilhard was a geologist and paleontologist. It was in China – a nation-state on Old Earth, my friends – in the nineteen-thirties that he devised his theories that evolution was an uncompleted process, yet one with a design.

He saw the universe as God's design to bring together the Christ of Evolution, the Personal, and the Universal into a single conscious entity. Teilhard de Chardin saw every step of evolution as a hopeful sign – even mass extinctions as a cause for joy – with cosmogenesis, his word, occurring when humanity became central to the universe, noogenesis as the continued evolution of man's mind, and hominization and ultra-hominization as the stages of *Homo sapiens* evolving to true humanity.'

'Excuse me, Father,' I heard myself saying, only slightly aware of the incongruity of this abstract discussion amid the frozen city, beneath the frozen atmosphere, surrounded by wraith-killers and cold, 'but wasn't Teilhard's heresy that humankind could evolve into God?'

The blind priest shook his head, his expression still pleasant. 'During his lifetime, my son, Teilhard was never sanctioned for heresy. In 1962 the Holy Office – it was quite a different Holy Office then, I assure you – issued a monitum—'

'A what?' said Aenea, who sat on the carpet near the fire.

'A monitum is a warning against uncritical acceptance of his ideas,' said Father Glaucus. 'And Teilhard did not say that human beings would *become* God . . . he said that the entire conscious universe was part of a process of evolving toward the day – he called it the Omega Point – where all of creation, humanity included, would become one with the Godhead.'

'Would Teilhard have included the TechnoCore in that evolution?' Aenea asked softly. She was hugging her knees.

The blind priest stopped rocking and combed his fingers through his beard. 'Teilhardian scholars have wrestled with that for centuries, my dear. I am no scholar, but I am certain that he would have included the Core in his optimism.'

'But they are descended from machines,' said A. Bettik. 'And their concept of an Ultimate Intelligence is quite different from Christianity's – a cold, dispassionate mind, a predictive power able to absorb all variables.'

Father Glaucus was nodding. 'But they think, my son. Their earliest self-conscious progenitors were designed from living DNA—'

'Designed from DNA to *compute*,' I said, appalled at the thought of Core machines being given the benefit of the doubt when it came to souls.

'And what was *our* DNA designed to do for the first few hundred million years, my son? Eat? Kill? Procreate? Were we any less ignoble in our beginnings than the pre-Hegira silicon and DNA-based AIs? As Teilhard would have it, it is *consciousness* which God has created to accelerate the universe's self-awareness as a means to understanding His will.'

'The TechnoCore wanted to use humanity as part of its UI project,' I said, 'and then to destroy us.'

'But it did not,' said Father Glaucus.

'No thanks to the Core,' I said.

'Humanity has evolved – as far as it *has* evolved,' continued the old priest, 'with no thanks to its predecessors or itself. Evolution brings human beings. Human beings, through a long and painful process, bring humanity.'

'Empathy,' Aenea said softly.

Father Glaucus turned his blind eyes in her direction. 'Precisely, my dear. But we are not the only avatars of humanity. Once our computing machines achieved self-consciousness, they became part of this design. They may resist it. They may try to undo it for their own complex purposes. But the universe continues to weave its own design.'

'You make the universe and its processes sound like a machine,' I said. 'Programmed, unstoppable, inevitable.'

The old man shook his head slowly. 'No, no . . . never a machine. And never inevitable. If Christ's coming taught us anything, it is that nothing is inevitable. The outcome is always in doubt. Decisions for light or dark are always ours to make – ours and every conscious entity's.'

'But Teilhard thought that consciousness and empathy would win?' said Aenea.

Father Glaucus waved a bony hand at the bookcase behind her. 'There should be a book there . . . on the third shelf . . . it had a blue bookmark in it when last I looked, thirty-some years ago. Do you see it?'

'*The Journals, Notebooks, and Correspondences of Teilhard de Chardin?*' said Aenea.

'Yes, yes. Open it to where the blue bookmark is. Do you see the passage I have annotated? It is one of the last things these old eyes saw before the darkness closed . . .'

'The entry marked twelfth December, 1919?' said Aenea.

'Yes. Read it, please.'

Aenea held the book closer to the light of the fire.

' "Note this well," ' she read. ' "I attribute no definitive and absolute value to the various constructions of man. I believe that they will disappear, recast in a new whole that we cannot yet conceive. At the same time I admit that they have an essential provisional role – that they are necessary, inevitable phases which we (we or the race) must pass through in the course of our metamorphosis. What I love in them is not their particular form, but their function, which is to build up, in some mysterious way, first something divinizable – and then, through the grace of Christ alighting on our effort, something divine." '

There was a moment of silence broken only by the soft hiss of the fuel-pellet fire and the creak and groan of the tens of millions of tons of ice above and around us. Finally Father Glaucus said, 'That hope was Teilhard's heresy in the eyes of the current Pope. Belief in that hope was my great sin. This' – he gestured to the outer wall where ice and darkness pressed against the glass – 'this is my punishment.'

None of us spoke for another moment.

Father Glaucus laughed and set bony hands on his knees. 'But my mother taught me there is no punishment or pain where there are friends and food and conversation. And we have all of these. M. Bettik! I say "M. Bettik" because your honorific does you no honor, sir. It sets you apart from humanity by falsely inventing false categories. M. Bettik!'

'Sir?'

'Would you do this old man the favor of going into the kitchen to retrieve

344

the coffee that should be ready? I will see to the stew and the bread that is heating. M. Endymion?'

'Yes, Father?'

'Would you like to descend to the wine cellars to select the finest vintage available?'

I smiled, knowing that the old priest could not see me. 'And how many floors must I descend before finding the cellar, Father? Not fifty-nine, I hope?'

The old man's teeth showed through his beard. 'I have wine with every meal, my son, so I would be in far better physical shape if that were the case. No, lazy old thing that I am, I keep the wine in the closet one flight below. Near the stairwell.'

'I'll find it,' I said.

'I'll set the table,' said Aenea. 'And tomorrow night I cook.'

We all scattered to our duties.

FORTY-FIVE

The *Raphael* spins down into Sol Draconi System. Contrary to the explanations received by Father Captain de Soya and others who travel by archangel craft, its drive mechanism is not a modification of the ancient Hawking drive that has defied the light-speed barrier since before the Hegira. *Raphael*'s drive is a largely hoax: when it reaches near-quantum velocities, it keys a signal on a medium once referred to as the Void Which Binds. An energy source from elsewhere triggers a distant device that ruptures a subplane of that medium, tearing through the fabric of space and time itself. That rupture is instantly fatal to the human crew, who die in agony – cells rupturing, bones being ground to powder, synapses misfiring, bowels releasing, organs liquefying. They are never to know the details: all memory of the final microseconds of horror and death are erased during cruciform reconstruction and resurrection.

Now *Raphael* begins its braking trajectory toward Sol Draconi Septem, its very-real fusion drive slowing the ship under two hundred gravities of strain. In their acceleration couches/resurrection creches, Father Captain de Soya, Sergeant Gregorius, and Corporal Kee lie dead, their shredded bodies being pulverized a second time because the ship automatically conserves energy by not initializing internal fields until resurrection is well under way. Besides the three dead humans on board, there is one other pair of eyes. Rhadamnth Nemes has opened the lid of her resurrection creche and now lies on the exposed couch, her compact body buffeted but not damaged by the terrible deceleration. As per standard programming, the life support in the general cabin is off: there is no oxygen, atmospheric pressure is too low to allow a human to survive without a spacesuit, and the temperature is minus-thirty degrees centigrade. Nemes is indifferent. In her crimson jumpsuit, she lies on the couch and watches the monitors, occasionally querying the ship and receiving a reply on a fiberthread datalink.

Six hours later, before the internal fields switch on and the bodies begin to be repaired in their complex sarcophagi, even while the cabin is still in virtual vacuum, Nemes stands, shoulders two hundred gravities with no expression, and walks to the conference cubby and the plotting table. She calls up a map of Sol Draconi Septem and quickly finds the former route of River Tethys. Ordering the ship to overlay its long-range visuals, she runs her fingers across the holoed image of ice rills, sestrugi dunes, and glacial, crevasses. The top of one building rises from the atmospheric glacier. Nemes double-checks the plot: it is within thirty kilometers of the buried river.

After eleven hours of braking, *Raphael* swings into orbit around the gleaming white snowball of Sol Draconi Septem. The internal fields have long since switched on, the life-support systems are fully functional, but Rhadamnth Nemes takes no more note of this than she had of the weight and vacuum. Before leaving the ship, she checks the resurrection-creche monitors. She has more than two days before de Soya and his troopers will begin to stir in their creches.

Settling into the dropship, Nemes runs a fiber-optic link from her wrist to the console, commands separation, and guides the ship across the terminator into atmosphere without consulting instruments or controls. Eighteen minutes later the dropship sets down on the surface within two hundred meters of the stubby, ice-limned tower.

The sunlight is brilliant on the terraced glacier, but the sky is flat black. No stars are visible. Although the atmosphere here is negligible, the planet's massive thermal systems flowing from pole to pole drive incessant 'winds' accelerating ice crystals to four hundred kilometers per hour. Ignoring the spacesuits and hazardous-atmosphere suits hanging in the air lock, Rhadamnth Nemes cycles the doors open. Not waiting for the ladder to deploy, she jumps the three meters to the surface, landing upright in the one-point-seven-g field. Ice needles strike her at flechette-gun velocities.

Nemes triggers an internal source that activates a biomorphic field within point-eight millimeters of her body. To an outside observer the compact woman with short black hair and flat black eyes suddenly becomes a reflective quicksilver sculpture in human form. The form jogs across the jagged ice at thirty klicks an hour, stops at the building, finds no entrance, and shatters a panel of plasteel with her fist. Stepping through the gash, she walks easily across glare ice to the top of an elevator shaft. She rips open the sagging doors. The elevators have long since dropped to the basement eighty-some stories below.

Rhadamnth Nemes steps into the open shaft and drops into it, plummeting one hundred and eight point eight feet per second into the darkness. When she sees the light flashing past, she grabs a steel girder to stop herself. She has already reached her terminal velocity of more than five hundred klicks per hour and decelerates to zero in less than three-hundredths of a second.

Nemes strides from room to room, taking note of the furniture, the lanterns, the bookcases. The old man is in the kitchen. His head comes up when he hears the rapid footsteps. 'Raul?' he says. 'Aenea?'

'Exactly,' says Rhadamnth Nemes, inserting two fingers under the old priest's collarbone and lifting him off the ground. 'Where is the girl Aenea?' she asks softly. 'Where are all of them?'

Amazingly, the blind priest does not cry out in pain. His worn teeth are clenched and his blind eyes stare at the ceiling, but he says only, 'I do not know.'

Nemes nods and drops the priest to the floor. Straddling his chest, she sets her forefinger to his eye and fires a seeker microfilament into his brain, the seeker probe finding its way to a precise region of his cerebral cortex.

'Now, Father,' she says, 'let us try again. Where is the girl? Who is with her? Where are they?'

The answers begin flowing through the microfilament as coded bursts of dying neural energy.

FORTY-SIX

Our days with Father Glaucus were memorable for their comfort, their slowed pace after so many weeks of hurrying to and fro, and their conversations. Mostly, I think, I remember the conversations.

It was shortly before the Chitchatuk returned that I learned one of the reasons for A. Bettik's having taken this voyage with me.

'Do you have siblings, M. Bettik?' Father Glaucus asked, still refusing to use the android honorific.

To my amazement A. Bettik said, 'Yes.' How could this be? Androids were designed and biofactured, assembled out of component genetic elements and grown in vats . . . like organs grown for transplants, I had always thought.

'During our biofacture,' A. Bettik went on after the old priest prompted, 'androids were traditionally cloned in growth colonies of five – usually four males and one female.'

'Quintuplets,' said Father Glaucus from his rocking chair. 'You have three brothers and a sister.'

'Yes,' said the blue-skinned man.

'But surely you weren't . . .' I began, and stopped. I rubbed my chin. I had shaved there at Father Glaucus's strange home – it had seemed the civilized thing to do – and the feel of smooth skin almost startled me. 'But surely you didn't grow up together,' I said. 'I mean, weren't androids . . .'

'Biofactured as adults?' said A. Bettik with the same slight smile. 'No. Our growth process was accelerated – we reached maturity at approximately eight standard years – but there was a period of infancy and childhood. This delay was one of the reasons that android biofacture was almost prohibitively expensive.'

'What are your brothers' and sister's names?' asked Father Glaucus.

A. Bettik closed the book he had been leafing through. 'The tradition was to name each member of the quint group in alphabetic order,' he said. 'My siblings included A. Anttibe, A. Corresson, A. Darria, and A. Evvik.'

'Which was your sister?' asked Aenea. 'Darria?'

'Yes.'

'What was your childhood like?' said the girl.

'Primarily one of being educated, trained for duties, and having service parameters defined,' said A. Bettik.

Aenea was lying on the carpet, cupping her chin in her hands. 'Did you go to school? Did you play?'

349

'We were tutored at the factory, although the bulk of our knowledge came through RNA transfer.' The bald man looked at Aenea. 'And if by "play" you mean to find time to relax with my siblings, the answer is yes.'

'What happened to your siblings?' asked Aenea.

A. Bettik slowly shook his head. 'We were initially transferred to service together, but we were separated shortly thereafter. I was purchased by the Kingdom of Monaco-in-Exile and shipped to Asquith. It was my understanding at the time that each of us would render service in different parts of the Web or Outback.'

'And you never heard from any of them again?' I said.

'No,' said A. Bettik. 'Although there were a large number of android laborers imported for the construction of the Poet's City during the transfer of King William the Twenty-third's colony to that world, most had been in service on Asquith before my time, and none had encountered one of my siblings during their transshipment periods.'

'During the Web days,' I said, 'it should have been easy to search the other worlds by farcaster and datasphere.'

'Yes,' said A. Bettik, 'except for the fact that androids were forbidden by law and RNA inhibitors to travel by farcasters or access the datasphere directly. And, of course, it became illegal to biofacture or own androids within the Hegemony shortly after my own creation.'

'So you were used in the Outback,' I said. 'On distant worlds like Hyperion.'

'Precisely, M. Endymion.'

I took a breath. 'And is that why you wished to make this trip? To find one of your siblings . . . one of your brothers or your sister?'

A. Bettik smiled. 'The odds against running across one of my clone siblings would be truly astronomical, M. Endymion. Not only would the coincidence be unlikely, but the chance that any of them would have survived the wholesale destruction of androids following the Fall would be very slight. But—' A. Bettik stopped and opened his hands as if explaining foolishness.

It was that last evening before the band returned that I heard Aenea discuss her theory of love for the first time. It began with her questioning us about Martin Silenus's *Cantos*.

'All right,' she said, 'I understand that it was placed on the Index of Prohibited Books as soon as the Pax took over anywhere, but what about those worlds not yet swallowed by the Pax when it came out? Did he receive the critical acclaim he had been hungry for?'

'I remember arguing the *Cantos* in seminary,' chuckled Father Glaucus. 'We knew it was prohibited, but that just made the allure all the greater. We resisted reading Virgil, but waited our turn to read that dog-eared copy of doggerel that was the *Cantos*.'

'Was it doggerel?' asked Aenea. 'I always thought of Uncle Martin as a great poet, but that's only because he told me he was. My mother always told me that he was a pain in the ass.'

'Poets can be both,' said Father Glaucus. He chuckled again. 'In fact, it seems they often are both. As I remember it, most of the critics dismissed the *Cantos* in what few literary circles existed before the Church absorbed them. Some took him seriously . . . as a poet, not as a chronicler of what actually happened on Hyperion just before the Fall. But most made fun of his apotheosis of love toward the end of his second volume . . .'

'I remember that,' I said. 'The character of Sol – the old scholar whose daughter has been aging backward – discovers that love was the answer to what he had called the Abraham Dilemma.'

'I remember one nasty critic who reviewed the poem in our capital city,' chuckled Father Glaucus, 'who quoted some graffiti found on a wall of an excavated Old Earth city before the Hegira – "If love is the answer, what was the question?" '

Aenea looked at me for an explanation.

'In the *Cantos*,' I said, 'the scholar character seems to discover that the thing the AI Core had called the Void Which Binds is love. That love is a basic force of the universe, like gravity and electromagnetism, like strong and weak nuclear force. In the poem Sol sees that the Core Ultimate Intelligence will never be capable of understanding that empathy is inseparable from that source . . . from love. The old poet described love as *"the sub-quantum impossibility that carried information/from photon to photon . . ."* '

'Teilhard would not have disagreed,' said Father Glaucus, 'although he would have phrased it differently.'

'Anyway,' I said, 'the almost universal reaction to the poem – according to Grandam – was that it was weakened by this sentimentality.'

Aenea was shaking her head. 'Uncle Martin was right,' she said. 'Love *is* one of the basic forces of the universe. I know that Sol Weintraub really believed he had discovered that. He said as much to Mother before he and his daughter disappeared in the Sphinx, riding it to the child's future.'

The blind priest quit rocking and leaned forward, his elbows propped on his bony knees. His padded cassock would have looked comical on a less dignified man. 'Is this more complicated than saying that God is love?' he said.

'Yes!' said Aenea, standing in front of the fire now. She seemed older to me at that moment, as if she had grown and matured during our months together. 'The Greeks saw gravity at work, but explained it as one of the four elements – earth – "rushing back to its family". What Sol Weintraub glimpsed was a bit of the *physics* of love . . . where it resides, how it works, how one can understand and harness it. The difference between "God is love" and what Sol Weintraub saw – and what Uncle Martin tried to explain – is the difference between the Greek explanation of gravity and Isaac Newton's equations. One is a clever phrase. The other sees the *thing itself*.'

Father Glaucus shook his head. 'You make it sound quantifiable and mechanical, my dear.'

'No,' said Aenea, and her voice was about as strong as I had ever heard it. 'Just as you explained how Teilhard knew that the universe evolving toward greater consciousness could never be purely mechanical . . . that the forces were not dispassionate, as science had always assumed, but derived from the absolute passion of divinity . . . well, so an understanding of love's part of the Void Which Binds can never be mechanical. In a sense, it's the essence of humanity.'

I stifled the urge the laugh. 'So you're saying that there needs to be another Isaac Newton to explain the physics of love?' I said. 'To give us its laws of thermodynamics, its rules of entropy? To show us the calculus of love?'

'Yes!' said the girl, her dark eyes very bright.

Father Glaucus was still leaning forward, his hands now gripping his knees very tightly. 'Are you that person, young Aenea from Hyperion?'

Aenea turned away quickly, walking almost out of the light toward the darkness and ice beyond the smart glass before turning and slowly stepping back into the circle of warmth. Her face was downcast. Her lashes were wet with tears. When she spoke, her voice was soft, almost tremulous. 'Yes,' she said. 'I am afraid I am. I do not want to be. But I am. Or could be . . . if I survive.'

This sent chills down my back. I was sorry we had started this conversation.

'Will you tell us now?' said Father Glaucus. His voice held the simple entreaty of a child.

Aenea raised her face and then slowly shook her head. 'I cannot. I am not ready. I'm sorry, Father.'

The blind priest sat back in his chair and suddenly looked very old. 'It is all right, my child. I have met you. That is something.'

Aenea went over to the old man in his rocking chair and hugged him for a long minute.

Cuchiat and his band returned before we had awakened and got out of our beds and sleeping robes the next morning. During our days with the Chitchatuk, we had almost become accustomed to sleeping a few hours at a time and then resuming the march in the eternal ice gloom, but here with Father Glaucus we followed his system – dimming the lights a bit in the innermost rooms for a full eight hours of 'night'. It was my observation that one was always weary in a one-point-seven-g environment.

The Chitchatuk disliked coming very far into the building, so they stood in the open window, which was more ice tunnel than interior, and made a variation of their soft ululation until we hurriedly dressed and came running.

The band was back up to the healthy prime of twenty-three, although where they had found their new member – a woman – Father Glaucus did not ask and the rest of us were never to learn. When I came into the room, the image struck me then and it has stayed with me ever since – the powerful, wraith-robed Chitchatuk squatting in their most typical posture, Father Glaucus squatting and chatting with Cuchiat, the old priest's quilted and heavily patched cassock spreading out on the ice like a black flower, the glow of the fuel-pellet lanterns prisming light from the crystals at the entrance to the ice cave, and – beyond the smart glass – that terrible sense of ice and weight and darkness pressing . . . pressing.

We had long since asked Father Glaucus to be our interpreter in making – remaking, actually – our request of help to the indigenies, and now the old man broached the subject, asking the white-robed figures if they would indeed like to help us get our raft downriver. The Chitchatuk responded in turn, each waiting to address Father Glaucus and the rest of us individually, and each saying essentially the same thing – they were ready to make the voyage.

It was not to be a simple voyage. Cuchiat confirmed that there were tunnels descending all the way to the river at the second arch, almost two hundred meters lower than where we now sat, and that there was a stretch of open water where the river passed beneath this second farcaster, but . . .

There were no connecting tunnels between here and the second arch some twenty-eight kilometers to the north.

'I've been meaning to ask,' said Aenea. 'Where do these tunnels come from, anyway? They're too round and regular to be crevasses or fissures. Did the Chitchatuk make them at some time in the past?'

Father Glaucus looked at the child with an expression of bearded incredulity. 'You mean you don't know?' he said. He turned his head and rattled syllables at the Chitchatuk. Their reaction was almost explosive – excited chatter, the near barking that we associated with laughter.

'I hope I didn't offend you, my dear,' said the old priest. He was smiling, his blind eyes turned in Aenea's direction. 'It is just such a given of our existence here, that it struck me – and the Indivisible People – as strangely humorous that someone could move through the ice and not know.'

'The Indivisible People?' said A. Bettik.

'Chitchatuk,' said Father Glaucus. 'It means "indivisible" – or perhaps closer to the actual shading of the word – "incapable of being made more perfect".'

Aenea was smiling. 'I'm not offended. I'd just like in on the joke. What *did* make the tunnels?'

'The wraiths,' I guessed before the priest could speak.

His smile turned in my direction. 'Precisely, my friend, Raul. Precisely.'

Aenea frowned. 'Their claws are formidable, but even the adults couldn't carve tunnels that extensive through such solid ice . . . could they?'

I shook my head. 'I don't think we've really seen the adult form.'

'Precisely, precisely.' The old man was nodding deeply as he tended to do. 'Raul is correct, my dear. The Chitchatuk hunt the youngest cubs when possible. The older cubs hunt the Chitchatuk when possible. But the wraith cub-form you see is the larval stage of the creature. It feeds and moves about the surface during that stage, but within three of Sol Draconi Septem's orbits—'

'That would be twenty-nine years, standard,' murmured A. Bettik.

'Precisely, precisely,' nodded the priest. 'Within three local years, twenty-nine standard, the immature wraith – the "cub", although that word is usually used with mammals – passes through metamorphosis and becomes the true wraith, which bores through the ice at approximately twenty kilometers per hour. It is approximately fifteen meters long and . . . well, you may well encounter one on your trip north.'

I cleared my throat. 'I believe Cuchiat and Chiaku were explaining that there were no tunnels connecting this area to the farcaster tunnels some twenty-eight klicks north . . .'

'Ah, yes,' said Father Glaucus, and resumed his conversation in the clattering Chitchatuk language. When Cuchiat had responded, the blind man said, 'Approximately twenty-five kilometers across the surface, which is more than the Indivisible People like to do at one spell. And Aichacut kindly points out that this area is thick with wraiths – both cub and adult – that the Indivisible People who lived there for centuries have all been turned into skull necklaces for the wraiths. He points out that the summer storms are battering the surface this month. But for you, my friends, they are willing to make the voyage.'

I shook my head. 'I don't understand. The surface is essentially airless, isn't it? I mean . . .'

'They have all the materials you will need for the trip, Raul, my son,' said Father Glaucus.

Aichacut snarled something. Cuchiat added something in a more tempered tone.

'They are ready to depart when you are, my friends. Cuchiat says that it will take two sleeps and three marches to return to your raft. And then they will head north until the burrows run out . . .' The old priest paused and turned his face away for a moment.

'What is it?' asked Aenea, concern in her voice.

Father Glaucus turned back. His smile was forced. He ran bony fingers through his beard. 'I will miss you. It has been a long time since . . . hah! I am getting senile. Come, we will help you pack, have a fast breakfast, and see if we can round out your provisions with a few things from the store-room.'

The leave-taking was painful. The thought of the old man alone there in the ice once again, fending off wraiths and the planetary glacier with nothing more than a few lighted lamps . . . it made my chest hurt to think of it. Aenea wept. When A. Bettik went to shake the old priest's hand, Father Glaucus fiercely hugged the startled android. 'Your day is yet to come, my friend M. Bettik. I feel this. I feel this strongly.'

A. Bettik did not respond, but later, as we followed the Chitchatuk into the deep glacier, I saw the blue man glancing back toward the tall silhouette against the light before we rounded another corner in the tunnel and lost sight of the building, the light, and the old priest.

It did take us three marches and two sleeps before we slid and scraped our way down the final steep incline of ice, twisted right through a narrow break in the ice, and came out where the raft was tied up. I saw no way that the logs could be transported around the bends and turns of these endless tunnels, but this time the Chitchatuk wasted not a minute admiring the ice-laden craft, but immediately went to work unlashing it and separating log from log.

The entire band had marveled most visibly at our ax during the first visit, and now I was able to show them how it worked as I chopped each log into shorter segments, each segment only a meter-and-a-half in length. Using my fading flashlight laser, A. Bettik and Aenea were doing the same thing on our impromptu assembly line – the Chitchatuk scraping ice off the almost-sinking craft, cutting or untying knots, and handing the long segments up to where we cut and stacked. When we were done, the stone hearth, extra lanterns, and ice were on the iceshelf and the wood was piled up the long tunnel like next year's firewood.

The thought amused me at first, but then I realized how welcome a store of combustible material such as this might have been to the Chitchatuk – heat, light to drive the wraiths away. I looked at our dismantled raft in a different way. Well, if we failed to get through the second portal . . .

Using Aenea as our translator now, we communicated to Cuchiat that we would like to leave the ax, the hearth, and the other odds and ends with them. It is fair to say that the faces behind the wraith-teeth visors looked stunned. The Chitchatuk milled around, hugging and patting us on the back with enough strength to knock the wind out of each of us. Even angry Aichacut patted and shoved us with something like rough affection.

Each member of the band lashed three or four of the log segments to his or her back; A. Bettik, Aenea, and I did the same – they were as heavy as concrete in this g-field – and we began the long trek uphill toward the surface, vacuum, storm, and wraiths.

FORTY-SEVEN

It takes less than a minute for Rhadamnth Nemes's neural tap to finish its probe of Father Glaucus's brain. In a combination of visual images, language, and raw synaptic chemical data, Nemes has as full a picture of Aenea's visit to the frozen city as she will get without a complete neurological disassembly. She withdraws the microfilament and allows herself a few seconds to ponder the data.

Aenea, her human companion, Raul, and the android left three and a half standard days earlier, but at least one of those days will have been taken up with cutting their raft apart. The second farcaster is almost thirty klicks to the north, and the Chitchatuk will lead them over the surface, which is dangerous and slow traveling. Nemes knows that there is a good chance that Aenea has not survived the surface trek – Nemes has seen in the old priest's mind the crude means by which the Indivisible People try to cope with the surface conditions.

Rhadamnth Nemes smiles thinly. She will not leave such things to chance.

Father Glaucus moans feebly.

Nemes pauses with her knee on the old priest's chest. The neural probe has done little harm: a sophisticated medkit could heal the filament bore between the old man's eye and brain. And he was already blind when she arrived.

Nemes considers the situation. Encountering a Pax priest on this world had not been part of the equation. As Father Glaucus begins to stir, his bony hands lifting toward his face, Nemes weighs the balance: leaving the priest alive will pose very little risk – a forgotten missionary, in exile, destined to die in this place anyway. On the other hand, Nemes knows, not leaving him alive poses no risk whatsoever. It is a simple equation.

'Who . . . are you?' moans the priest as Nemes easily lifts him and carries him from the kitchen through the dining area, from the dining area through the book-lined library with its warm fuel-pellet fire, from the library to the hallway to the building's central core. Even here lanterns burn to discourage wraiths.

'Who *are* you?' says the blind priest again, struggling in her grip like a two-year-old in the arms of a strong adult. 'Why are you doing this?' says the old man as Nemes reaches the elevator shaft, kicks the plasteel doors open, and holds the priest a final moment.

There is a blast of cold air rushing down from the surface to the glacial depths two hundred meters below. The noise sounds as if the frozen planet is screaming. At the last second Father Glaucus realizes precisely what is happening. 'Ah, dear Jesus, Lord,' he whispers, his chapped lips quivering. 'Ah, St Teilhard . . . dear Jesus . . .'

Nemes drops the old man into the shaft and turns away, only mildly surprised that no scream echoes behind her. She takes the frozen stairway to the surface, leaping four or five steps at a time in the weighted g-field. At the top, she must punch her way up the icy waterfall where the frozen atmosphere has dribbled down five or six flights of stairs. Standing on the roof of the building, the sky black with vacuum and the Coriolis storm whipping ice crystals at her face, she activates the phase-shift field and jogs across the ice to the dropship.

There are three immature wraiths investigating the ship. In a second Nemes takes note of the creatures – nonmammalian, the white 'fur' actually tubuled scales capable of holding gaseous atmosphere, which acts to hold in body heat, eyes working on the deep infrared, redundant lung capacity which allows them to go twelve hours or more without oxygen, each animal more than five meters long, forearms powerful, rear legs designed for digging and disemboweling, each beast very fast.

They turn toward her as she jogs closer. Seen against the black background, the wraiths look more like immense white weasels or iguanas than anything else. Their elongated bodies move with blinding speed.

Nemes considers bypassing them, but if they attack the ship it could cause complications during takeoff. She shifts into fast time. The wraiths freeze in midmotion. The blowing ice crystals hang suspended against the black sky.

Working efficiently, using only her right hand and the diamond-hard blade of her phase-shifted forearm, she butchers the three animals. During the work two things mildly surprise her: each wraith has two huge five-chambered hearts, and the beasts seem capable of fighting on with only one intact; each wears a necklace of small human skulls. When she is finished and has shifted back to slow time, after the three wraiths have dropped like giant bags of organic offal onto the ice, Nemes takes a moment to inspect the necklaces. Human skulls. Probably from human children. Interesting.

Nemes activates the dropship and flies north – keeping it on reaction thrusters since the stubby wings can find no lift in this near vacuum. Deep radar probes the ice until the river becomes visible. Above the level of the river are many hundreds of kilometers of tunnels. The wraiths have been very busy in this area. On the deep-radar display, the metal arch of the farcaster portal stands out like a bright light in dark fog. The instrument is less successful in finding living, moving things under the ice. Various echoes show the clear track of adult wraiths tunneling their way through the atmosphere glacier, but these soundings are klicks to the north and east.

She lands the dropship directly above the farcaster portal and searches the sestrugi-patterned surface for a cave entrance. Finding one, she moves into the glacier at a jog, dropping her biomorphic shield when the pressure moves about three psi and the temperature rises within thirty degrees of freezing.

The tunnel maze is daunting, but she keeps her bearings relative to the great mass of portal metal a third of a kilometer beneath her, and within an hour she is nearing the level of the river. It is too near absolute darkness down there to see by light amplification or infrared, and she has not brought a flashlight, but she opens her mouth, and a brilliant beam of yellow light illuminates the tunnel and ice fog ahead of her.

She hears their approach long before the dim ember-lanterns come into view down the long, descending corridor. Killing the light, Rhadamnth Nemes stands in the tunnel and waits. When they first round the corner, it looks more like a herd of diminutive wraiths than a band of human beings, but she recognizes them from Father Glaucus's memory: Cuchiat's band of Chitchatuk. They stop in surprise at the sight of a lone female without robes or outer insulation standing in the glacier tunnel.

Cuchiat steps forward and speaks rapidly. 'The Indivisible People greet the warrior/hunter/seeker who chooses to travel in the glow of the next-to-perfect indivisibility. If you need warmth, food, weapons, or friends, speak, for our band loves all those who walk on two feet and respect the path of the prime.'

In the Chitchatuk language she has taken from the old priest, Rhadamnth Nemes says, 'I seek my friends – Aenea, Raul, and the blue man. Have they passed through the metal arch yet?'

The twenty-three Chitchatuk talk among themselves of the strange woman's command of their language. They reason that she must be a friend or kin of the glaucus, for this person speaks with precisely the same dialect as the blind man in black who shares his warmth with visitors. Still, Cuchiat speaks with something like suspicion. 'They have passed under the ice and out of sight through the arch. They wished us well and gave us gifts. We wish you well and offer you gifts. Is the next-to-perfect indivisibility wishing to travel the magical riverway with your friends?'

'In a moment,' says Rhadamnth Nemes with her thin smile. This encounter offers the same equation as the quandary of what to do with the old priest. She takes a step forward. The twenty-three Chitchatuk exclaim with almost childish delight as she phase-shifts into featureless quicksilver. She knows that their ember light reflecting from a thousand ice facets must be mirrored now on her surface. Shifting into fast time, she kills the twenty-three men and women without wasting motion or effort.

Dropping out of fast time, she chooses the nearest corpse and fires a neural probe through the corner of the man's eye. The brain's neural network is collapsing from lack of blood and oxygen, creating the usual burst of hallucinations and wild creativity common to the death of such networks – human or AI – but in the middle of the life-to-death synaptic replay of birth images . . . emerging from long tunnels into bright light and warmth . . . she catches the fading images of the child, the tall man, and the android pushing off the crudely rebuilt raft, ducking their heads as they pass under the low ice beneath the frozen-in-place arch.

'Damn,' breathes Nemes.

Leaving the bodies piled where they fell in the darkening tunnel, she jogs the last kilometer or so to the level of the river.

There is little open water here, and the farcaster portal is only a brief metal chord in the jagged ice above. Icy fog and mist roil around her as she stands on the low, broad shelf of ice where heat imprints show the Chitchatuk had gathered to bid farewell to their friends.

Nemes wants to interrogate the farcaster, but to reach the arch she has either to bore through many meters of ice or climb the overhanging ceiling to the exposed section twenty-some meters above. She phase-shifts just her hands and feet and climbs, digging steps and handholds deep into the ice.

Hanging upside down from the exposed curve of the arch, Nemes sets her hand on a panel and waits until the frosted metal folds back on itself like skin being pulled back from a wound. Extending both microfilaments and a fiber-optic probe, she contacts the interface module that puts her in touch with the actual farcaster. Whispers impinging directly upon her auditory nerve tell her that the Three Sectors of Consciousness are monitoring her and discussing events.

All during the centuries of the Hegemony of Man, everyone knew that there were hundreds of thousands, perhaps millions, of TechnoCore-created farcaster portals – from the smallest doorway to the larger River Tethys arches to the huge spaceborne portals. Everyone was wrong. There is only one farcaster portal. But it is everywhere.

Using the interface module, Rhadamnth Nemes queries the pulsing, living warmth of the true farcaster within its camouflage disguise of metal, electronics, and fusion shield. For centuries, humans jumping by farcaster within the Web – at its height, one human analyst suggested that there were more than one billion jumps a second taking place – had served the Ultimates, those elements of the TechnoCore who existed to create a more advanced AI . . . the Ultimate Intelligence whose consciousness would absorb the galaxy, perhaps the universe. Every time a human had accessed the fatline-connected dataspheres or farcast during those Webdays, that human being's synapses and DNA had added to the computing power of the Web-wide neural net the Core had built. The Core had cared nothing for humankind's visceral urge to move about, to travel without energy expenditure or time lapse, but the farcaster Web had been the perfect bait to weave the very fabric of those teeming hundreds of billions of primitive, organic brains into something useful.

Now, its hiding place in the interstices of space/time ferreted out by Meina Gladstone and her damned Hyperion pilgrims, its web-within-the-Web home attacked by the deathwand device the Core had helped human-ity to build, its fatline connections severed by powers from somewhere beyond the known circle of the megasphere, all facets of the single, omnipresent farcaster portal are dead and useless.

Except this one. It has just been used. The interface module reports to Nemes what she and all the Sectors already know – the facet has been activated by Something Else. From Somewhere Else.

The portal still registers its connection points in real space/time in its bubble memory of modulated neutrinos. Nemes accesses this memory.

Aenea and the others have farcast to Qom-Riyadh. Nemes must ponder another puzzle. She can lift the dropship to the archangel *Raphael* and be in Qom-Riyadh System within a few minutes. But she will have to interrupt de Soya's and the others' resurrection cycle to do so, as well as come up with a plausible explanation as to the reason for the shift. In addition, Qom-Riyadh is a Pax-quarantined system: officially listed as having been overrun by the Ousters, it is one of the early Justice and Peace projects. As had been the case with Hebron, neither the Pax nor its advisers can allow de Soya and his men to see the truth the planet represents. Finally, Nemes knows that the River Tethys runs for only a few kilometers, crossing through the red-rock desert of the southern hemisphere and passing the Grand Mosque in Mashhad. If she allows *Raphael*'s resurrection cycle to run its course, de Soya and the others will not be active for three standard days, allowing Aenea and her raft of misfits time to pass the length of the section of Tethys. Once again the equation seems to demand that Nemes finish de Soya and the others and press on alone. But her instructions have been to avoid that possibility unless absolutely necessary. De Soya's involvement with the final capture of the One Who Teaches, the Aenea Threat, has been registered in too many full simulations, recorded in too many Full-Sector Looks Forward, to be ignored without hazard. The fabric of space/time is much like one of the elaborate Vatican tapestries, thinks Nemes, and she who begins pulling on loose threads does so at the peril of watching the whole tapestry ravel.

Nemes takes several seconds to consider this. Finally she extends a neural network filament deeper into the interface module's synapses. All of the farcaster's activation route is there – past and present. The memory pattern of Aenea and her accomplices is a fleeting bubble memory, but Nemes can easily see the recent past and future openings. There are only two more downriver possibilities in the foreseeable future. After Qom-Riyadh the Something Else has structured the portals to open only on to God's Grove, and then . . .

Nemes gasps and withdraws the microfilament before the full import of the last activation can sear her. That last is obviously Aenea's goal or more precisely, the goal of the Something Else who opens the way for her – and it is inaccessible to both the Church Pax and the Three Sectors.

But the timing will be about right. Nemes can keep de Soya and his men alive while still jumping ahead to the God's Grove System. She has already thought of a plausible explanation. Assuming two days to transit Qom-Riyadh and another full day on the river system on God's Grove, she will still be able to intercept the raft and do what she has to do before de Soya's resurrection. She will even have an hour or two to tidy up, so that when she drops to God's Grove with the priest-captain and Swiss Guard commandos, there will be nothing visible except signs that the child and her friends have passed that way and farcast on.

Nemes withdraws her probe, jogs to the surface, takes the dropship to *Raphael*, erases any record in the ship's computer that she has awakened or used the dropship, plants a false message in the ship's computer, and crawls into her resurrection creche to sleep. While in Pacem System, she had removed the creche from the resurrection system and rewired the telltales to simulate activity, and now she lies back in the humming coffin and closes her eyes. The jumps to fast time and the use of the phase-shift skin in such quantities tires her. She welcomes the rest before de Soya and the others arise from death.

Remembering that detail with a smile, Rhadamnth Nemes activates a phase-shift glove and touches her chest between her breasts, reddening and rearranging the skin there into the simulation of a cruciform. She carries no such parasite, of course, but the men in the ship may glimpse her naked, and she has no intention of revealing anything through a stupid lapse of attention to detail.

The *Raphael* continues to orbit the glaring ice world of Sol Draconi Septem while three of its crew lie in their creche coffins, the monitoring lights and telltales recording their slow climb up from death. Their other passenger sleeps. She does not dream.

FORTY-EIGHT

As we floated through the desert world, blinking in the harsh light of the G2 sun and drinking water from the air/water wraith-gut pouches we had brought with us, our final couple of days on Sol Draconi Septem seemed like a quickly fading dream to me.

Cuchiat and his band had paused fifty-some meters beneath the surface – we had noticed the air getting noticeably thinner in the tunnels – and there, in the jagged ice corridor, we had prepared for our expedition. To our amazement, the Chitchatuk stripped naked. Even while glancing away in embarrassment, we noticed how muscular and solid their bodies were – the women as well as the men – as if a body builder on a one-g world had been flattened and compressed into a more compact specimen. Cuchiat and the female warrior Chatchia came over to supervise our own undressing and preparation for the surface, while Chiaku and the others pulled items from their hide packs.

We watched the Chitchatuk and followed their lead in dressing, with help from Cuchiat and Chatchia. For the few seconds that we were actually naked – standing on the wraith-robes we had been wearing so that our feet would not freeze – the cold burned at us. Then we pulled on a thin membrane material – an inner skin of the wraith, we later learned – that had been tailored for arms and legs and head. But obviously for *smaller* arms and legs and head. As it was, the membrane was tighter than skintight: the translucent skin hugged me so firmly that I must have looked like so many cannonballs stuffed into a sausage skin. A. Bettik looked no better. I realized after a moment that these must be the Chitchatuk equivalent of pressure suits – perhaps even of the sophisticated skinsuits the Hegemony military once used in space. The membranes passed sweat and provided much of their own heating and cooling while serving well to keep the lungs from exploding in vacuum, the skin bruising, or the blood boiling. The membranes pulled low over our foreheads and up to our chins like a cowl, leaving our eyes, noses, and mouths uncovered.

Cuchiat and Chatchia removed membrane masks from the pack. The other Chitchatuk had already donned theirs. These were obviously created-things – the mask itself was made of the same inner skin as the pressure suit, with wraith-hide padding sewn in here and there. The eyepieces were made from the outer lenses of the wraith-eyes, offering the same limited access to the infrared as our outer-robe eyes. From the snout of the mask ran a length of coiled wraith-intestine, the end of which Cuchiat carefully sewed into one of their water bags.

Not just a water bag, I realized as the Chitchatuk began breathing through their masks: the fuel-pellet brazier melted the glacier ice into both water and atmosphere gas. They had somehow filtered this atmosphere mix until they had adequate quantities of breathable air. I tried breathing through the mask – my eyes watered from the other compounds there, definitely a hint of methane and perhaps even of ammonia, but breathable. I guessed that there must be only a couple of hours of air in the bag.

With our g-suit skins on, we donned the outer layer of wraith-robes. Cuchiat pulled the heads of the robes lower than we had ever worn them before, locking the teeth shut so we were peering through the lenses, the head acting as a crude helmet above our pressure suit. We then donned an outer pair of wraith-hide bootees, which laced up our calves almost to the knee. The outer robe was then quickly stitched shut with a few bold strokes from Chiaku's bone needle. The water bag and air bag hung from straps beneath our robes, near a flap that could be unstitched and opened quickly when the bags needed to be refilled. Chichticu, our fuel-pellet fire carrier, was constantly busy melting atmosphere into water and air, even as we hiked, and he handed the replacement skin bags out in precise order, from Cuchiat first to me last. At least I now understood the band's pecking order. I also understood why – when danger threatened on the surface – the band moved into a protective circle with Chichticu, the fire carrier, in the center. It was not just that he held religious and symbolic importance. His constant vigilance and labors kept us alive.

There was one final addition to our wardrobe as we emerged from the cave onto the whirling wind and surface ice. From a cache near the entrance, Chiaku and the others retrieved a store of long black skate blades, sharp as razors on the bottom, flat and broad on top where our booteed feet fit quite nicely. Once again wraith-hide thongs were used to lash us to the blades. The things were an effective combination of skates and cross-country skis, and I awkwardly skated ten meters across the patterned ice of the glacier before I realized that we were skiing on wraith-claws.

I admit that I had a great fear of falling in one-point-seven-g since every tumble felt like the equivalent of seven-tenths of another Raul Endymion falling on top of me, but we soon got the hang of movement on the things and we were well padded for falls. I ended up using one of the cut-up logs from the raft as a plump ski pole when the surface got too rough, poling myself along as if I were a one-man raft.

I'll confess here that I wish I had a holo-image or photograph of our party on that outing. With our wraith-hides, inner-skin g-suits, wraith-gut air bags, lower-intestine air hoses, bone spears, my plasma rifle, packs, and claw-skis, we must have looked like some Old Earth Paleolithic astronauts.

It all worked. We moved more quickly across the ice and ice-crystal sestrugi than we had in the ice tunnels. When the wind blew from the south, which it did during only a short part of our surface trek, we could spread our wraith-robed arms and be propelled across flat sections of the ice like sailing ships.

Walking the surface of Sol Draconi Septem's frozen atmosphere had a harsh but memorable beauty to it. The sky was vacuum and moon-surface black when the sun was up, but an instant after sunset many thousands of stars seemed to explode into existence. Our robes and inner suits handled the near-space high and low temperatures well during the day, but it was obvious that even the Chitchatuk could not survive the cold at night. Luckily we moved quickly enough across the surface that we had only one six-hour darkness period to shelter from, and the Chitchatuk had planned our departure so that we got the benefit of a full day's sunlight before that nightfall.

There were no mountains or other surface features larger than ice ridges or rills, except for our first few hours on the ice when the rising sun struck an icy object far to the south of us. This, I realized, was the tip of Father Glaucus's skyscraper protruding from the ice many kilometers away. The surface was so featureless that I wondered for a minute how the Chitchatuk were managing to navigate, but then I saw Cuchiat glancing at the sun and then at his own shadow. We continued skating north during the brief day.

The Chitchatuk moved in a tight defensive pattern as they skated/skied, with the fire carrier and medicine man, who tended the fire and air/water bags in the center, warriors with ready spears on the wings, Cuchiat in the lead, and Chiaku – obviously second in command, we realized now – bringing up the rear and skating almost backward in his vigilance. Each Chitchatuk had a length of wraith-rope wrapped around his or her robe – they had wound some around the three of us when we were dressed – and I better understood the purpose of all that line after Cuchiat stopped abruptly and skated to the east to avoid several crevasses that had been invisible to my eye. I looked down one of these – the rift seemed to drop into eternal darkness – and tried to imagine what that fall would be like. It was late the same afternoon that one of the outriders disappeared in a sudden, silent burst of ice crystals – only to reappear a moment later as Chiaku and Cuchiat were readying rescue ropes. The warrior had arrested his own fall and then pulled off his black claw-skates, and was now using them as climbing tools, hacking his way up the sheer wall of the crevasse like a technical climber on an icefall. I was learning not to underestimate the Chitchatuk.

We saw no wraiths that first day. As the sun set, we realized – through our exhaustion – that Cuchiat and the others had ceased skating north and were circling, peering down into the ice as if looking for something. All this while the thin winds lashed ice crystals against us. If we had been on the surface in spacesuits, I am convinced that the visor would have been scratched and marred. The wraith-robes and eye lenses showed no damage.

Finally Aichacut waved his arms from where he had skated far to our west – there was no verbal communication through masks and vacuum – and we all skated in that direction, eventually stopping at a place that looked no different from all the rest of the pressure-rippled surface. Cuchiat waved us back, untied our gift of the ax from where he had lashed it onto his back, and began chopping at the ice. When the surface layer broke away, we could see that this was not another crevasse or rill, but the narrow entrance to an ice cave. Four of the warriors readied their spears, Chichticu joined them with his ember-lamp, and – with Cuchiat leading – the group crawled into the hole while the rest of us waited in a defensive circle.

A moment later Cuchiat's robed head emerged and he waved us in. He still held the ax, and I could imagine him grinning broadly behind his wraith-teeth visor and membrane mask. The ax had been an important gift.

We spent the night in the wraith-den. I helped Chiaku caulk the entrance with snow and ice, we packed another meter of the entrance tunnel with loose ice crystal and larger fragments, and then we went in to watch Chichticu heat blocks of snow-ice until the ice den was filled with enough atmosphere to breathe. We slept bundled together, the twenty-three Indivisible People and the three Indivisible Travelers, still wearing our robes and pressure membranes but masks removed, breathing the welcome scent of each other's sweat. Our huddled warmth kept us alive through the terrible night outside as the Coriolis storms blasted ice crystals at nearly the speed of sound . . . had there been any sound in that near vacuum.

I remember one other detail about our last night with the Chitchatuk. The wraith-den was lined, completely lined, with human skulls and bones, each set into the circular ice wall of the den with what seemed to be an artist's care.

We saw no wraiths – cubs or ice-boring adults – during our next day's travel, and shortly before sunset we doffed and cached our skates, then entered the ice tunnels above the second farcaster. When we were deep enough to be in captured atmosphere again, we removed the masks and pressure-suit membranes, handing them back to Chatchia with something like reluctance. It was as if we were surrendering our membership badges to the Indivisible People.

Cuchiat spoke briefly. I could not follow the quick syllables, but Aenea translated – 'We were lucky . . . something and something about how unusual it is not to have to fight wraiths when crossing the surface . . . but, he says, luck on one day almost always leads to bad luck the next.'

'Tell him that I hope he's wrong,' I said.

The open river with its floating mist and ice ceiling was almost a shock to see. Even though everyone was exhausted, we set to work at once. Assembling the shortened raft was difficult with wraith-mittens on, but the Chitchatuk worked quickly to help, and within two hours we had a cut-down, awkward version of our earlier vessel – minus the foremast, tent, and hearthstone. But the steering oar was in place, and although the push-poles were shorter and clumsy looking when lashed together, we thought they should work on this shallow stretch of the Tethys.

The leave-taking was sadder than I would have imagined. Everyone hugged everyone else at least twice. There was ice on Aenea's long lashes, and I had to admit a strain of powerful emotion in my own throat.

Then we were shoving off into the current – it felt strange to be traveling while standing still, I still had the push-and-glide motion of the claw-skates echoing in my muscles and mind – the farcaster portal and ice wall approached, we ducked under the ever-lower ledge of ice, and suddenly we were . . . elsewhere.

We poled into sunrise. The river was wide and unruffled here, the current slow but steady. The riverbanks were of red rock, striated like wide, gradual steps climbing up from the water; the desert was red rock with small yellow shrubs; the distant slabs of hill and arch were also of smooth red stone. All this redness was ignited by the huge red sun rising to our left. The temperature was already a hundred degrees above what it had been in the ice cave. We shielded our eyes and pulled off our wraith-robes, setting them like thick white rugs near the stern of the shortened raft. Layers of ice on the logs first glistened and then melted in the morning sun.

We decided that we were on Qom-Riyadh even before consulting the comlog or Tethys guidebook. It was the red-rock desert that cued us – bridges of the bright-red sandstone, fluted columns of red rock rising against the pink sky, delicate red arches dwarfing the receding farcaster portal. The river ran through canyons overarched by these red-stone parabolas, then curved into a wider valley where the hot wind blew the yellow sage and raised a red grit that caught in the long, tubular 'hairs' of the wraith-robes and lodged in our mouths and eyes. By midday we were moving through a more fertile valley. Irrigation canals ran at right angles from our river, and short yellow palms and magenta bottlebrushes lined the waterways. Soon small buildings came into sight, and shortly after, an entire village of pink and ocher homes, but no people.

'It's like Hebron,' whispered Aenea.

'We don't know that,' I said. 'Maybe they're just working out of sight somewhere.'

But midday heated to midafternoon – Qom-Riyadh had a twenty-two-hour day, according to the guidebook – and although the canals proliferated, plants multiplied, and villages became more common, there was no hint of humans or their domestic animals. We poled the raft ashore twice – once to draw water from an artesian well and again to explore a small village from which sounds of hammering could be heard on the river. It was a broken awning banging in the desert wind.

Suddenly Aenea doubled over with a cry of pain. I dropped to one knee and swept the empty street with the plasma pistol as A. Bettik ran to her side. There was no one on the street. The windows were empty of movement.

'It's all right,' the girl gasped as the android held her. 'A sudden pain . . .'

I jogged to her, feeling foolish for having drawn the weapon. Setting it in my belt holster, I went to one knee and held her hand. 'What's the matter, kiddo?' She was sobbing.

'I . . . don't . . . know,' she managed between sobs. 'Something . . . terrible has . . . I don't know.'

We carried her back to the raft. 'Please,' whispered Aenea, her teeth chattering despite the heat, 'let's go. Let's get out of here.'

A. Bettik set up the microtent, even though it now took up most of our abbreviated raft. We pulled the wraith-robes into the shade, laid the girl on them, and gave her water from one of the water bags.

'Is it this village?' I said. 'Did something about it—'

'No,' said Aenea between dry sobs. I could see her fighting the waves of emotion that were crashing over her. 'No . . . something awful . . . this world, but also . . . behind us.'

'Behind us?' I looked out the door of the tent and upriver, but there was nothing but the valley, the wide canal of a river, and the receding village with its wind-tossed yellow palms.

'Behind us on the ice world?' A. Bettik asked softly.

'Yes,' managed Aenea before doubling up with pain. 'It . . . hurts.'

I laid my palm on her forehead and bare stomach. Her skin was hotter than it should have been, even accounting for the heat of the valley and the day's sunburn on her face and arms. We pulled one of the medkits from my backpack and I set a diagnostic patch in place. It showed a high fever, pain in the six-point-three range of the dolorometer, muscle cramps, and an uneven EEG. It recommended water, ibuprofen, and contacting a doctor.

'There's a city,' said the android as the river rounded a bluff.

I stepped out of the tent to see. The rose-red towers, domes, and minarets were still far away – perhaps fifteen kilometers across the widening valley floor – and the current on this river was in no hurry. 'You stay with her,' I said, and moved to starboard side to pole. Our shortened raft was considerably lighter than the old one, and we moved quickly with the current.

A. Bettik and I consulted the water-warped guidebook and decided that the city was Mashhad, the capital of the southern continent and home of the Grand Mosque, whose minarets we could see clearly now as the river moved through thickening villages, suburbs, industrial areas, and into the city proper. Aenea was sleeping fitfully. Her temperature had risen, and the medkit diagnostic was blinking red lights to suggest a doctor's intervention.

Mashhad was as eerily empty as New Jerusalem had been.

'I seem to remember rumor that the Qom-Riyadh System had fallen to the Ousters about the same time they took the Coal Sack,' I said. A. Bettik agreed, saying that they had monitored Pax radio traffic to that effect from the university city.

We tied the raft up at a low pier, and I carried the girl into the shade of the city streets. This was a replay of Hebron, only this time I was the healthy one and the girl unconscious. I made a mental note to avoid desert worlds from now on if I could help it.

The streets were less tidy than New Jerusalem had been: groundcars parked at odd angles and left abandoned on the sidewalks, detritus blowing in the streets, windows and doors open to the red sand, and strange little carpets lying on sidewalks, streets, and dying lawns. I paused at the first cluster of rugs we encountered, thinking that they might be hawking mats. They were only rugs. And they were all oriented in the same direction.

'Prayer mats,' said A. Bettik as we moved back into the shade of the city street. Even the tallest buildings were not overly tall here – none as high as the minarets, which looked out from a park area with tropical trees. 'The population of Qom-Riyadh was almost one hundred percent Islamic,' he continued. 'The Pax was said to have found no inroads here, even with the promise of resurrection. The people wanted nothing to do with the Protectorate.'

I turned the corner, still hunting for a hospital or any sign that might lead us to one. Aenea's hot forehead was against my neck. Her breathing was rapid and shallow. 'I think this place was in the *Cantos*,' I said. The child seemed to weigh nothing.

A. Bettik nodded. 'M. Silenus wrote of Colonel Kassad's victory over the so-called New Prophet here some three hundred years ago.'

'The Shi'ites took power again once the Web fell, didn't they?' I said. We looked down another side street. I was looking for a red crescent rather than the universal red-cross sign of medical help.

'Yes,' said A. Bettik, 'and they have been violently opposed to the Pax. The supposition was that they had welcomed the Ousters when the Pax Fleet retreated from this sector.'

I looked at the empty streets. 'Well, it looks like the Ousters didn't appreciate the welcome. This is like Hebron. Where do you think they've all gone? Could they have taken an entire planetary population hostage and—'

'Look, a caduceus,' interrupted A. Bettik.

The age-old symbol of a winged staff wrapped with two entwined serpents was on the window of a tall building. The interior was littered and tossed about, but it seemed more a standard office building than any sort of hospital I had been in. A. Bettik walked to a digital sign that was scrolling lines of text in Arabic. It was also muttering in a machine voice.

'Do you read Arabic?' I said.

'I do,' said the android. 'I also understand some of the spoken language, which is Farsi. There is a private clinic on the tenth floor. I would think that it would have a full diagnostic center and perhaps an autosurgeon.'

I headed for the stairway with Aenea in my arms, but A. Bettik tried the elevator. The empty glass shaft hummed, and a levitation car floated to a stop at our level.

'Uncanny that the power's still on,' I said.

We rode the lift to the tenth floor. Aenea was awakening and moaning as we walked down the tiled hallway, across an open terrace-garden where yellow and green palms rustled in the wind, and into an airy, glassed-in room with banks of autosurgeon beds and centralized diagnostic equipment. We chose the bed closest to the window, stripped the child to her underwear, and laid her between clean sheets. Replacing the medkit diagnostic patches with patch filaments, we waited for the diagnostic panels.

The synthesized voice was in Arabic and Farsi, as was part of the display readout, but there was a Web English band and we switched to it.

The autosurgeon diagnosed exhaustion, dehydration, and an unusual EEG pattern, which might have resulted from a serious blow to the head. A. Bettik and I looked at each other. Aenea had received no blow to the head.

We authorized treatment for the exhaustion and dehydration and stepped back as flowfoam restrainers extruded from the bed panels, pseudo-fingers felt for Aenea's vein, and an IV was started with a sedative and saline solution.

Within minutes the child was sleeping easily. The diagnostic panel spoke in Arabic, and A. Bettik translated before I could walk over to read the monitor. 'It says that the patient should have a good night's sleep and be better in the morning.'

I shifted the plasma rifle from where I had been carrying it on my back. Our dusty packs sat on one of the visiting chairs. Moving to the window, I said, 'I'll check out the city before it gets dark. Make sure we're alone.'

A. Bettik folded his arms and watched the great red sun touch the tops of the buildings across the street. 'I think that we are very much alone,' he said. 'It took a little longer here, is all.'

'What took longer?'

'Whatever it was that stole the people. On Hebron there was no sign of panic or struggle. Here people had time to abandon their vehicles. But the prayer rugs are the surest sign.' I noticed for the first time that there were fine wrinkles in the blue skin of the android's forehead and around his eyes and mouth.

'Surest sign of what?' I said.

'They knew that something was happening to them,' said A. Bettik, 'and they spent their last minutes in prayer.'

I set the plasma rifle next to the visitor's chair and unclipped the flap over my holster. 'I'm still going to take a look,' I said. 'You watch her in case she wakes, okay?' I pulled the two com units out of my pack, tossed one to the android, and clipped the other onto my collar with the bead mike in place. 'Leave the common frequency open. I'll check in. Call me if there's a problem.'

A. Bettik was standing by her bedside. His large hand gently touched the sleeping girl's forehead. 'I will be here when she wakes, M. Endymion.'

It is odd that I remember that evening's walk through the abandoned city so clearly. A digital sign on a bank said that it was forty degrees centigrade – one hundred and four fahrenheit – but the dry wind from the red-rock desert quickly carried away any perspiration, and the pink-and-red sunset had a calming effect on me. Perhaps I remember that evening because it was the last night of our voyage before things changed forever.

Mashhad was a strange mixture of modern city and bazaar from *A Thousand and One Arabian Nights*, a wonderful series of stories Grandam used to tell me as we sat under Hyperion's starry sky. This place had a musky hint of romance about it. On the corner there would be a news kiosk and automatic banking machine, and as soon as one turned the corner, there would be stalls in the middle of the street with brightly striped awnings and heaps of fruit rotting in bins. I could imagine the din and movement here – camels or horses or some other pre-Hegira beasts milling and stamping, dogs barking, sellers shouting and buyers haggling, women in black *chadors* and lacy *burqas*, or veils, gliding by, and on either side the baroque and inefficient groundcars growling and spewing out filthy carbon monoxide or ketones or whatever dirty stuff the old internal-combustion engines used to pour into the atmosphere . . .

I was shocked out of my reverie by a man's voice calling musically, the words echoing down the stone-and-steel canyons of the city. It seemed to be coming from the park only a block or two to my left, and I ran in that direction, holding my hand on the grip of my pistol in the unbuttoned holster as I went.

'You hear this?' I said into the bead mike as I ran.

'Yes,' came A. Bettik's voice in my hearplug. 'I have the door to the terrace open and the sound is quite clear here.'

'It sounds Arabic. Can you translate?' I was panting only slightly as I finished the two-block sprint and came out into the open park area where the mosque dominated the entire block. A few minutes before, I had looked down one of the connecting streets and glimpsed the last of the red sunset painting the side of one of the minarets, but now the stone tower was a dull gray and only the highest wisps of cirrus caught the light.

'Yes,' said A. Bettik. 'It is a *muezzin* call to evening prayer.'

I pulled the binoculars from my belt pouch and scanned the minarets. The man's voice was coming from loudspeakers on a balcony encircling each tower. There was no sign of movement there. Suddenly the rhythmic cry ended and birds chattered within the branches of the forested square.

'It is most probably a recording,' said A. Bettik.

'I'll check it out.' Setting away the binoculars, I followed a crushed-stone path through the extensive lawns and yellowish palm trees to the mosque's entrance. I passed through a courtyard and paused at the entrance to the mosque proper. I could see the interior – it was filled with hundreds of the prayer mats. Elaborate arches of striped stone were supported by elegant pillars, and on the far wall a beautiful arch opened on a semicircular niche. To the right of this niche there was a flight of steps guarded by a lovingly carved stone railing, and a stone-canopied platform at the top. Not yet entering the large space, I described it to A. Bettik.

'The niche is the *mihrab*,' he responded. 'It's reserved for the prayer leader, the *imam*. The balcony to the right of it is the *minbar*, the pulpit. Is there anyone in either place?'

'No.' I could see the red dust on the prayer rugs and stone steps.

'Then there is no doubt that the call to prayer was a timed recording,' said A. Bettik.

I had the urge to enter the great stone space, but the urge was canceled by my reluctance to profane anyone's sacred house. I had felt this as a child in the Catholic cathedral at Beak's End, and as an adult when a friend in the Home Guard wanted to take me to one of the last Zen Gnostic temples on Hyperion. I had realized when I was a boy that I would always be an outsider when it came to holy places . . . never having one of my own, never feeling comfortable in another's. I did not enter.

Walking back through the cooling and darkening streets, I found a palm-lined boulevard through an attractive section of town. Pushcarts held food and toys for sale. I paused by a cart selling fried dough and sniffed one of the bracelet-sized dough rings. It had gone bad days, not weeks or months, ago.

The boulevard came out by the river, and I turned to my left, taking the riverside esplanade back to the street that would lead me once again to the clinic. Occasionally I checked in with A. Bettik. Aenea was still sleeping soundly.

The stars were dimmed by dust in the atmosphere as night settled on the city. Only a few of the downtown buildings had lights on – whatever had stolen the populace must have happened in the daytime – but stately old streetlamps ran the length of the esplanade and they were glowing with gas light. If it had not been for one of the lamps at the street end of the pier where we had tied the raft, I probably would have turned back toward the clinic without seeing it. As it was, the lamplight allowed me to spot it from more than a hundred meters away.

Someone was standing on our raft. The figure was motionless, very tall, and seemed to be wearing a silver suit. Lamplight gleamed from the figure's surface as if it were wearing a chrome spacesuit.

Whispering to A. Bettik to guard the girl, that there was an intruder on the raft, I pulled my pistol from my holster and the binoculars from my belt. The second I focused the glasses, the gleaming silver shape turned its head in my direction.

FORTY-NINE

Father Captain de Soya awakens in the familiar warmth of *Raphael*'s creche. After the first few moments of inevitable confusion and disorientation, he pulls himself from the enclosed couch and drifts, naked, to the command console.

Things are as they should be: in orbit around Sol Draconi Septem – the world a blinding white sphere just beyond the command console's windows, the braking burn optimum, the other three creches close to reawakening their valuable human cargo, the internal field set to zero-g until they all reacquire strength, internal temperature and atmosphere optimum for reawakening, the ship in proper geosynchronous orbit. The priest-captain gives his first command of this new life – he orders the ship to begin brewing coffee for all of them in the wardroom cubby. Usually his first thought upon resurrection is of his coffee bulb, tucked in the plotting table/wardroom table niche, filling with the hot black drink.

Then de Soya notices the ship's computer flashing a priority-message light. No message had arrived while he was conscious in Pacem System, and it seems unlikely that one has found them here in this remote ex-colony system. There is no Pax presence in Sol Draconi System – at most, transiting torchships use the three gas giants in the system for refueling their hydrogen tanks – and a brief query of the ship's computer confirms that no other ship was contacted during the three days of braking and orbit insertion. The same query brings forth the fact that there is no Church mission on the planet below them, the last missionary contact lost more than fifty standard years ago.

De Soya plays the message. Papal authority routed through Pax Fleet. According to the display codes, the message arrived mere hundredths of a second before *Raphael* had gone quantum in Pacem space. It is a text-only message and brief – HIS HOLINESS COUNTERMANDS MISSION TO SOL DRACONI SEPTEM. NEW AREA OF ACQUISITION: GOD'S GROVE. PROCEED THERE IMMEDIATELY. AUTHORIZATION LOURDUSAMY AND MARUSYN. MESSAGE ENDS.

De Soya sighs. This trip, these deaths and resurrections, have been for nothing. For a moment the priest-captain does not move but sits naked in the command couch, pondering the glaring white limb of the ice planet that fills the curved window above him. Then he sighs again and moves off to shower, stopping by the wardroom cubby to take his first sip of coffee. He reaches out automatically for the bulb while he taps commands into the shower-cubby console – needle spray, as hot as he can stand it. He makes a note to find some bathrobes somewhere. This is no longer an all-male locker room.

Suddenly de Soya freezes in irritation. His questing hand has not closed on the handle of his coffee bulb. Someone has shifted the bulb in its niche.

Their new recruit, Corporal Rhadamnth Nemes, is the last to leave her creche. All three of the men avert their eyes as she leaves her creche and kicks off for the shower/wardrobe cubby, but there are enough reflective surfaces in *Raphael*'s crowded command bubble for each of them to catch a glimpse of the small woman's firm body, her pale skin, and the livid cruciform between her small breasts.

Corporal Nemes joins them in taking Communion and seems disoriented and vulnerable as they sip their coffee and allow the internal fields to build to one-sixth-g.

'Your first resurrection?' de Soya asks gently.

The corporal nods. Her hair is very black and cut short, the bangs hanging limply on the pale forehead.

'I'd like to say that you get used to it,' says the priest-captain, 'but the truth is, every awakening is like the first one . . . difficult and exhilarating.'

Nemes sips her coffee bulb. She seems tentative in the microgravity. Her crimson-and-black uniform makes her skin seem all the more pale in contrast.

'Shouldn't we be leaving immediately for the God's Grove System?' she says tentatively.

'Soon enough,' says Father Captain de Soya. 'I've instructed *Raphael* to break orbit here in fifteen minutes. We'll accelerate out to the closest translation point at two-gs so we can recover for a few hours before we have to go back to the couches and the creches.'

Corporal Nemes appears to shudder a bit at the thought of another resurrection. As if eager to change the subject, she glances at the blinding limb of the planet filling the windows and viewscreen. 'How can anyone be traveling a river on all that ice?'

'Under it, I'd think,' says Sergeant Gregorius. The giant trooper has been watching Nemes carefully. ''Tis the atmosphere that's frozen there again since the Fall. The Tethys must flow beneath it.'

Corporal Nemes raises a dark eyebrow in surprise. 'And what is God's Grove like?'

'Ye don't know it?' asks Gregorius. 'I thought everyone in the Pax'd heard of God's Grove.'

Nemes shakes her head. 'I grew up on Esperance. It's a farming and fishing world, mostly. People there don't pay too much interest in other places. Not other worlds of the Pax . . . not old stories of the Web. Most of us are too busy scraping a living from the land or sea.'

'God's Grove is the old Templar world,' says Father Captain de Soya, setting his coffee bulb in its niche in the plotting table. 'It was burned pretty badly during the Ouster invasion preceding the Fall. In its time it was beautiful.'

'Aye,' nods Sergeant Gregorius, 'the Templar Brotherhood of the Muir was a sort of nature-worship cult. They turned God's Grove into a world forest – trees taller and more beautiful than the redwoods and sequoias of Old Earth. The Templars lived there, all twenty-some million of 'em – in cities and platforms in those lovely trees. But they chose the wrong side in the war . . .'

Corporal Nemes looks up from sipping her coffee. 'You mean they were on the Ousters' side?' She sounds shocked at the idea.

'That they were, lass,' says Gregorius. 'Perhaps it was because they had spacegoing trees in those days . . .'

Nemes laughs. It is a short, brittle sound.

'He's serious,' says Corporal Kee. 'The Templars used ergs – energy-binders from Aldebaran – to encapsulate the trees in a Class-nine containment field and provide a reaction-drive in-system. They even had regular Hawking drives installed for interstellar flight.'

'Flying trees,' says Corporal Nemes, and laughs harshly again.

'Some o' them flew off in such trees when the Ousters paid back their allegiance with a Swarm attack on God's Grove,' continues Gregorius, 'but most of them burned . . . just as most of the planet burned. For a century, they say, most of the world was ash. The clouds o' smoke created a nuclear winter effect.'

'Nuclear winter?' says Nemes.

De Soya is watching the young woman carefully, wondering why one so naïve has been chosen to carry the papal diskey under certain circumstances. Was the ingenuousness part of her strength as a killer, should the need arise?

'Corporal,' he says, speaking to the woman, 'you say you grew up on Esperance . . . Did you join the Home Guard there?'

She shakes her head. 'I went directly into the Pax army, Father Captain. There was a potato famine . . . the recruiters offered offworld travel . . . and, well . . .'

'Where did ye serve?' asks Gregorius.

'Just training on Freeholm,' says Nemes.

Gregorius leans on his elbows. The one-sixth-g makes sitting easier. 'Which brigade?'

'The Twenty-third,' says the woman. 'Sixth Regiment.'

'The Screaming Eagles,' says Corporal Kee. 'I had a female buddy who transferred there. Was Commander Coleman your CO?'

Nemes shakes her head again. 'Commander Deering was in charge while I was there. I just spent ten local months . . . ah . . . about eight-and-a-half standard, I guess. I was trained as a general combat specialist. Then they asked for volunteers for the First Legion . . .' She trails off as if this is classified material.

Gregorius scratches his chin. 'It's odd I haven't heard of this outfit in the building. Nothing stays secret very long in the military. How long did ye say ye were training with this . . . legion?'

Nemes gives the big man a direct stare. 'Two standard years, Sergeant.

And it *has* been secret . . . until now. Most of our training was on Lee Three and the Lambert Ring Territories.'

'Lambert,' muses the big sergeant. 'So ye've had your share of low-g and zero-g training.'

'More than my share,' agrees Corporal Rhadamnth Nemes with a thin smile. 'While in the Lambert Ring, we trained in the Peregrine Trojan Cluster for five months.'

Father Captain de Soya feels the conversation turning into an interrogation. He does not want their new crewmate to feel assaulted by their questions, but he is as curious as Kee and Gregorius. Besides that, he feels something . . . not right. 'So the Legions' job will be pretty much like the Marines?' he says. 'Ship-to-ship fighting?'

Nemes shakes her head. 'Uh-uh . . . Captain. Not just zero-g combat tactics for ship to ship. The Legions are being formed to take the war to the enemy.'

'What does that mean, Corporal?' asks the priest-captain softly. 'In all my years in the Fleet, ninety percent of our battles were in Ouster territory.'

'Yes,' says Nemes, her small smile returning, 'but we hit and run . . . Fleet actions. The Legions will *occupy*.'

'But most of the Ouster holdings are in vacuum!' says Kee. 'Asteroids, orbital forests, deep space itself . . .'

'Exactly,' says Nemes, her smile remaining. 'The Legions will fight them on their own ground . . . or vacuum, as the case may be.'

Gregorius catches de Soya's glance saying, *No more questions*, but the sergeant shakes his head and says, 'Well, I don't see what these vaunted Legions are learning that the Swiss Guard hasn't done – and done well – for sixteen centuries.'

De Soya floats to his feet. 'Acceleration in two minutes. Let's get to our couches. We'll talk more about God's Grove and the mission there during our drive to the translation point.'

It had taken *Raphael* almost eleven hours of braking deceleration at two hundred gravities to kill its near light-speed upon entry into the system, but the computer has located an adequate translation point to God's Grove only thirty-five million klicks out from Sol Draconi Septem. The ship could accelerate at a leisurely one-g and reach that point in around twenty-five hours, but de Soya has ordered it to lift out of the planet's gravity well at a constant two-gs for six hours before using more energy to bring on the internal fields during the last hour's dash at one-hundred-gs.

When the fields finally come up, the team goes through their final checklist for God's Grove – three days to resurrect, then immediate dropship deployment with Sergeant Gregorius in charge of the ground party, surveillance of the fifty-eight-klick River Tethys segment between portals, and then final preparation for the capture of Aenea and her party.

'After all this, why does His Holiness start directing us in the search?' asks Corporal Kee as they move to their creches.

'Revelation,' says Father Captain de Soya. 'Okay . . . everyone tuck in. I'll watch the boards.'

For the last few minutes before translation, it has been their custom to close their creches. Only the captain stays on watch.

In the few minutes he has alone at the command board, de Soya quickly calls up the records of their abortive entry and escape from Hebron System. He had viewed these before their departure from Pacem System, but now he fast-forwards through the visual and data records again. It's all there and it all seems correct: the shots from orbit around Hebron while he and his two troopers were still in creche – the burning cities, cratered landscape, and shattered villages of Hebron lifting smoke into the desert atmosphere, New Jerusalem in radioactive ruins – and then the radar acquisition by three Swarm cruisers. *Raphael* had aborted the resurrection cycles and made a run for it, lifting out of the system at the two hundred and eighty gravities her enhanced fusion drive could provide with her cargo of dead men. The Ousters, on the other hand, had to divert energy to their internal fields or die – no resurrection for heathens – and could never muster more than eighty-gs during the stern chase.

The visuals were there, though – the long green tails of the Ouster fusion drives, their attempts to lance *Raphael* at a distance of almost a full AU, the ship's record of the defense fields easily handling the lance energy at that distance, the final translation to Mare Infinitus System since that was the closest jump point . . .

It all made sense. The visuals were compelling. De Soya did not believe a bit of it.

The father-captain was not sure why he was so skeptical. The visual records meant nothing, of course; for more than a thousand years, since the beginning of the Digital Age, even the most compelling visual images could be faked by a child at a home computer. But ship's records would require a gigantic effort – a technical conspiracy – to falsify. Why should he not trust *Raphael*'s memory now?

With only a few minutes before translation, de Soya calls up the records of their recent descent into Sol Draconi Septem's system. He glances over his shoulder from the command couch – all three creche couches are sealed and silent, their telltales green. Gregorius, Kee, and Nemes are still awake, waiting for translation and death. De Soya knows that the sergeant prays during these last minutes. Kee usually reads a book from his creche monitor. De Soya has no idea what the woman is doing within her comfortable coffin.

He knows he is being paranoid. *My coffee bulb was moved out of place. The handle was shifted sideways.* During his hours awake de Soya has tried to remember whether someone might have been in the wardrobe cubby and jarred the bulb in Pacem System. No – they had not used the wardrobe cubby during the climb out of Pacem's gravity wall. The woman, Nemes, had been aboard before the others, but de Soya had used the coffee bulb and returned it to its place after she had gone to her couch/creche. He was sure of that. He had been the last to turn in, just as he always was. Acceleration or deceleration might smash bulbs not designed for terrible gravities, but the deceleration vector *Raphael* had been following was linear along the courier ship's line of travel and would not have moved things laterally. The coffee-bulb niche was designed to hold things in place.

Father Captain de Soya is part of a millennia-long line of sailors, sea, and space who become fanatic about a place for everything and everything in its place. He is a spacer. Almost two decades of serving in frigates, destroyers, and torchships have shown him that anything he leaves out of place will literally be in his face as soon as the ship goes to zero-g. More important, he has the age-old sailor's need to be able to reach out and find anything without looking, in darkness or storm. Granted, he thinks, the alignment of the handle of his coffee bulb is not a major issue . . . except it is. Each man has learned to use one of the chair niches at the five-person plotting table that doubles for the mess table in the crowded command pod. When they are using the table to plot courses or view planetary maps, each of the men – Rettig included when he was alive – had sat or stood or floated at their usual places at the table. It was human nature. It was second nature to spacers to keep their habits neat and predictable.

Someone had tapped his coffee-bulb handle out of alignment – perhaps with a knee nestled there in zero-g to hold him . . . *her* . . . in place. Paranoid. Definitely.

In addition, there had been the troubling news whispered to him by Sergeant Gregorius in the minutes between that man's emergence from the resurrection creche and Corporal Nemes's awakening.

'A friend of mine in the Swiss Guard in the Vatican, Captain. Had a drink with him the night before we left. He knew us all – Kee and Rettig – and he swore he saw Lancer Rettig bein' carried unconscious on a litter to an ambulance outside the Vatican infirmary.'

'Impossible,' de Soya had said. 'Lancer Rettig died of resurrection complications and was buried in space while in Mare Infinitus space.'

'Aye,' Gregorius had growled, 'but my friend was sure . . . almost sure . . . that it was Rettig in the ambulance. Unconscious, life-support paks attached, oxygen mask an' all, but Rettig.'

'That makes no sense,' de Soya had said. He had always been suspicious of conspiracy theories, knowing from personal experience that secrets shared by more than two people rarely stayed secrets for long. 'Why would Pax Fleet and the Church lie to us about Rettig? And where is he if he was alive on Pacem?'

Gregorius had shrugged. 'Maybe it wasn't him, Captain. That's what I've been telling myself. But the ambulance—'

'What about it?' de Soya had snapped, more sharply than he had intended.

'It was headed for Castel Sant'Angelo, sir,' said Gregorius. 'Headquarters for the Holy Office.'

Paranoia.

The records of the eleven hours of deceleration are normal – high-g braking, the usual three-day resurrection cycle ensuring the maximum chance for their safe recovery. De Soya glances at the orbital-insertion figures and runs the video of Sol Draconi Septem's slow rotation. He always wonders at those lost days – *Raphael* carrying out her simple tasks while the creches revive him and the others – he wonders at the eery silence that must fill the ship.

'Three minutes until translation,' comes *Raphael*'s crude synthesized voice. 'All personnel should be in creche couches.'

De Soya ignores the warning and calls up data files on the two and a half days the ship spent in orbit around Sol Draconi Septem before he and the others regained life. He is not sure what he is looking for . . . no record of dropship deployment . . . no sign of early life-support activation . . . all creche monitors reporting the regular cycle, the first quickenings of life in the last hours of the third day . . . all orbital ship records normal . . . *wait*!

'Two minutes until translation,' says the ship's flat voice.

There on the first day, shortly after attaining standard geosynchronous orbit . . . and there again about four hours later. Everything normal except the dry details of four small reactor-thruster firings. To attain and hold a perfect geosynchronous orbit, a ship like *Raphael* will fire dozens of little thruster tweaks such as these. But most such fine-tunings, de Soya knows, involve the large reaction-thruster pods on the stern near the fusion drive, and on the command-pod boom at the bow of the awkwardly configured courier ship. These thruster burps were similar – first a double firing to stabilize the ship during a roll so the command pod was facing away from the planet – normal during rotisserie mode to spread the solar heating uniformly along the ship's surface without using field coolant – but only eight minutes here – and here! And after the roll, those paired reaction tweaks. Two and two. Then the final paired burps, which might accompany the larger thruster firings that would roll the ship back with the command-pod cameras aimed down at the planet. Then, four hours and eight minutes later, the entire sequence again. There are thirty-eight other station-keeping thruster sequences on the record, and none of the major thruster firings that would signify a roll of the entire ship stack, but these twin four-burp interludes stand out to de Soya's trained eye.

'One minute until translation,' warns *Raphael*.

De Soya can hear the huge field generators beginning to whine in preparation for the shift to the modified Hawking system that will kill him in fifty-six seconds. He ignores it. His command chair will carry his dead body to the creche after translation if he does not move now. The ship is designed that way – messy, but necessary.

Father Captain Federico de Soya has been a torchship captain for many years. He has made more than a dozen archangel-courier jumps. He knows that double-burp, roll, double-burp signature on a reaction-thruster record. Even with the actual roll event deleted from the ship's records, the fingerprint for the maneuver is there in outline. The roll is to orient the dropship, which is tied down on the opposite side of the command-pod cluster, to the planet's atmosphere. The second double burp – the one still on record here – is to counteract the propellant squids separating the dropship from the center of *Raphael*'s mass. The final double firing is to stabilize the stack once the ship has returned to normal altitude, command-pod cameras trained on the planet below once again.

None of this is as obvious as it sounds, since the entire stack is slowly rotating in rotisserie mode during the entire time, occasional tweaks aligning the stack for better heating or cooling purposes. But to de Soya the signature is unmistakable. He taps directions to bring up the other records again. Negative sign of dropship deployment. Negative record of dropship deployment roll maneuver. Positive indicators of constant dropship attachment. Negative sign of life-support activation prior to everyone's resurrection a few hours before. Negative images of the dropship moving toward atmosphere on video records. Constant image-record of dropship attached and empty.

The only anomaly is two eight-minute thruster-tweak sequences four hours apart. Eight minutes of roll away from the planet would allow a dropship to disappear into atmosphere without main-camera visual record. Or to reappear and rendezvous. Boom cameras and radar would have recorded the event unless commanded to ignore it prior to dropship separation. That would have required less tampering with the record after the fact.

If someone had ordered the ship's computer to delete all records of dropship deployment, *Raphael*'s limited AI might have altered the record in just such a way, not realizing that the small-thruster firings during rotisserie mode would leave any footprint. And for anyone less experienced than a twelve-year torchship captain, it would not have. If de Soya had an hour or so to call up all the hydrogen fuel data, cross-check against dropship refueling needs and system-entry requirements, then double-check with the Bussard hydrogen collector input during deceleration, he would have a better idea if the main stack-roll maneuvers and dropship deployment had occurred. If he had an hour or so to himself.

'Thirty seconds until translation.'

De Soya does not have time to reach his creche couch. He does have time to call up a special command sequence for ship operations, tap in his override code, confirm it, change monitor parameters, and do it twice more. He has just heard the confirmation acknowledgment on the third override when the quantum leap to archangel C-plus occurs.

The translation literally tears de Soya apart within the confines of his couch. He dies grinning fiercely.

FIFTY

'Raul!'

It was at least an hour before Qom-Riyadh's sunrise. Both A. Bettik and I were sitting in chairs in the room where Aenea slept. I had been dozing. A. Bettik was awake – as he always seemed to be – but I reached the girl's bedside first. The light from the biomonitor readouts over the bed was the only illumination. Outside, the dust storm had been howling for hours.

'Raul . . .' The readouts said that her fever was down, pain was gone, that only the erratic EEGs remained.

'Right here, kiddo.' I took her right hand in mine. Her fingers no longer felt feverish.

'You saw the Shrike?'

This caught me by surprise, but I realized in a moment that it did not have to be prescience or telepathy at work here. I had radioed A. Bettik about the sighting. He must have had the com unit's speakers on and Aenea had been awake enough to register it.

'Yeah,' I said, 'but it's okay. It's not here.'

'But you saw it.'

'Yes.'

She gripped my hand with both of hers and sat up in bed. I could see her dark eyes gleaming in the faint light. 'Where, Raul? Where did you see it?'

'On the raft.' I used my free hand to push her back onto the pillows. The pillowcase and her undershirt were soaked with sweat. 'It's all right, kiddo. It didn't do anything. It was there when I left.'

'Did it turn its head, Raul? Did it look at you?'

'Well, yes, but . . .' I stopped. She was moaning softly, her head thrashing back and forth on the pillow. 'Kiddo . . . Aenea . . . it's all right . . .'

'No, it's not,' said the girl. 'Ah, God, Raul. I asked him to come with me. That last night. Did you know that I asked him to come along? He said no—'

'Who said no?' I asked. 'The Shrike?' A. Bettik came up behind me. Outside, the red sand chafed at the windows and sliding door.

'No, no, no,' said Aenea. Her cheeks were moist, although whether it was from tears or her fever breaking, I did not know. 'Father Glaucus,' she said, her voice almost lost under the wind noise. 'That last night . . . I asked Father Glaucus to come with us. I shouldn't have asked him, Raul . . . it was not part of my . . . my dreams . . . but I did ask, and if I asked, I should have insisted . . .'

'It's all right,' I said, pushing a damp tendril of hair off her brow. 'Father Glaucus is all right.'

'No, he's not,' said the girl, and moaned softly. 'He's dead. The thing that's chasing us killed him. Him and all the Chitchatuk.'

I looked at the monitor board again. It still showed improvement from the fever, despite her ravings. I looked at A. Bettik, but the android was staring intently at the child.

'You mean the Shrike killed them?' I said.

'No, not the Shrike,' she said softly, and laid her wrist against her lips. 'At least I don't think so. No, it wasn't the Shrike.' Suddenly she gripped my hand in both of hers. 'Raul, do you love me?'

I could only stare a moment. Then, not withdrawing my hand, I said, 'Sure, kiddo. I mean . . .'

Aenea seemed to really look at me then for the first time since she had come awake and called my name. 'No, stop,' she said. She laughed softly. 'I'm sorry. I came unglued in time for a minute. Of course you don't love me. I forgot when we were . . . who we were to each other now.'

'No, it's all right,' I said, not understanding. I patted her hand. 'I do care for you, kiddo. So does A. Bettik, and we're going to—'

'Hush,' said Aenea. She freed her hand and set one finger against my lips. 'Hush. I was lost for a moment. I thought we were . . . us. The way we're going to . . .' She lay back deeper in the pillows and sighed. 'My God, it's the night before God's Grove. Our last night traveling . . .'

I was not sure if she was making sense yet. I waited.

A. Bettik said, 'M. Aenea, is God's Grove our next destination on the river?'

'I guess so,' said the girl, sounding more like the child I knew. 'Yes. I don't know. It all fades . . .' She sat up again. 'It's not the Shrike chasing us, you know. Nor the Pax.'

'Of course it's the Pax,' I said, trying to get her to make contact with reality. 'They've been after us since . . .'

Aenea was shaking her head adamantly. Her hair hung in damp tendrils. 'No,' she said softly but very firmly. 'The Pax is after us because the Core tells it we're dangerous to them.'

'The Core?' I said. 'But it's . . . ever since the Fall it's been . . .'

'Alive and dangerous,' said Aenea. 'After Gladstone and the others destroyed the farcaster system that provided the Core with its neural net, it retreated . . . but it never went far, Raul. Can't you see that?'

'No,' I said. 'I can't. Where has it been if it didn't go far?'

'The Pax,' the girl said simply. 'My father – his persona in Mother's Schrön Loop – explained it to me before I was born. The Core waited until the Church began being revitalized under Paul Duré . . . Pope Teilhard I. Duré was a good man, Raul. My mother and Uncle Martin knew him. He carried two cruciforms . . . his own and Father Lenar Hoyt's. But Hoyt was . . . weak.'

I patted her wrist. 'But what does this have to do with—'

'Listen!' said the girl, pulling her arm back. 'Anything can happen tomorrow on God's Grove. I can die. We can all die. The future is never written . . . only penciled in. If I die but you survive, I want you to explain to Uncle Martin . . . to whoever will listen . . .'

'You're not going to die, Aenea—'

'Just *listen!*' pleaded the girl. There were tears in her eyes again.

I nodded and listened. Even the wind howl seemed to abate.

'Teilhard was murdered in his ninth year. My father predicted it. I don't know if it was by TechnoCore agents . . . they use cybrids . . . or just Vatican politics, but when Lenar Hoyt was resurrected from their shared cruciforms, the Core acted. It was the *Core* that provided the technology of allowing the cruciform to revive humans without the sexlessness or idiocy visited on the Bikura tribe on Hyperion . . .'

'But how?' I said. 'How could the TechnoCore AIs know how to tame the cruciform symbiote?' I saw the answer even before she spoke.

'They *created* the cruciforms,' said Aenea. 'Not the current Core, but the UI they create in the future. It sent the things back in time on Hyperion just as it did the Time Tombs. Tested the parasites on the lost tribe . . . the Bikura . . . saw the problems . . .'

'Little problems,' I said, 'like resurrection destroying reproductive organs and intelligence.'

'Yes,' said Aenea. She took my hand again. 'The Core was able to correct those problems with their technology. Technology they gave the Church under its new Pope . . . Lenar Hoyt. Julius VI.'

I began to understand. 'A Faustian bargain . . .' I said.

'*The* Faustian bargain,' said the girl. 'All the Church had to do to gain the universe was sell its soul.'

'And thus the Pax Protectorate was born,' A. Bettik said softly. 'Political power through the barrel of a parasite . . .'

'It's the *Core* that's after us . . . after me,' continued the child. 'I'm a threat to them, not just to the Church.'

I shook my head slowly. 'How are you a threat to the Core? You're one child . . .'

'One child who was in touch with a renegade cybrid persona before I was born,' she whispered. 'My father was loose, Raul. Not just in the datasphere or the megasphere . . . but in the metasphere. Loose in the wider psycho-cerbernet that even the Core was terrified of . . .'

'Lions and tigers and bears,' muttered A. Bettik.

'Exactly,' said Aenea. 'When my father's persona penetrated the Core megasphere, he asked the AI, Ummon, what the Core was afraid of. They said that they didn't range farther in the metasphere because it was full of lions and tigers and bears.'

'I don't get it, kiddo,' I said. 'I'm lost.'

She leaned forward and squeezed my hand. Her breath on my cheek was warm and sweet. 'Raul, you know Uncle Martin's *Cantos*. What happened to the Earth?'

'Old Earth?' I said stupidly. 'In the *Cantos* the AI Ummon said that the three elements of the TechnoCore were at war . . . We talked about this.'

'Tell me again.'

'Ummon told the Keats persona . . . your father . . . that the Volatiles wanted to destroy humanity. The Stables . . . his group . . . wanted to save it. They faked the black-hole destruction of Old Earth and spirited it away to the Magellanic Clouds. The Ultimates . . . the third group . . . didn't give a damn what happened to Old Earth or humanity as long as their Ultimate Intelligence project came to fruition.'

Aenea waited.

'And the Church agrees with what everyone else believes,' I continued somewhat lamely. 'That Old Earth was swallowed by the black hole and died when it was supposed to have died.'

'Which version do you believe, Raul?'

I took a breath. 'I don't know,' I said. 'I'd like Old Earth to still exist, I guess, but somehow it doesn't seem that important.'

'What if there was a third possibility?' said Aenea.

The glass doors suddenly rattled and shook. I put my hand on the plasma pistol, half-expecting the Shrike to be scratching at the glass. Only the desert wind howled there. 'A third possibility?' I said.

'Ummon lied,' said Aenea. 'The AI lied to my father. No element of the Core moved the Earth . . . not the Stables, not the Volatiles, not the Ultimates.'

'So it *was* destroyed,' I said.

'No,' said Aenea. 'My father did not understand then. He did later. Old Earth was moved to the Magellanic Clouds, all right, but not by any element of the Core. They didn't have the technology or the energy resources or that level of control of the Void Which Binds. The Core can't even *travel* to the Magellanic Cloud. It's too far . . . unimaginably distant.'

'Who, then?' I said. 'Who stole Old Earth?'

Aenea laid back on the pillows. 'I don't know. I don't think the Core knows, either. But they don't want to know – and they're terrified that we'll find out.'

A. Bettik stepped closer. 'So it is not the Core that is activating the farcasters on our voyage?'

'No,' said Aenea.

'Will we find out who is?' I said.

'If we live,' said Aenea. 'If we live.' Her eyes looked tired now, not feverish. 'They'll be waiting for us tomorrow, Raul. And I don't mean that priest-captain and his men. Someone . . . some*thing* from the Core will be waiting for us.'

'The thing that you think killed Father Glaucus, Cuchiat, and the others?' I said.

'Yes.'

'Is this some sort of vision?' I said. 'To know about Father Glaucus, I mean.'

'Not a vision,' said the girl in an empty voice. 'Just a memory from the future. A certain memory.'

I looked out at the diminishing storm. 'We can stay here,' I said. 'We can get a skimmer or EMV that works, fly to the northern hemisphere, and hide in Ali or one of the bigger cities that the guidebook talks about. We don't have to play their game and go through that farcaster portal tomorrow.'

'Yes,' said Aenea, 'we do.'

I started to protest and then remained silent. After a while I said, 'And where does the Shrike come in?'

'I don't know,' said the girl. 'It depends upon who sent it this time. Or it could be acting on its own. I don't know.'

'On its own?' I said. 'I thought it was just a machine.'

'Oh, no,' said Aenea. 'Not just a machine.'

I rubbed my cheek. 'I don't understand. It could be a friend?'

'Never a friend,' said the girl. She sat up and put her hand on my cheek where I had rubbed it a second before. 'I'm sorry, Raul, I don't mean to talk in circles. It's just that I don't *know*. Nothing's written. Everything's fluid. And when I do get a glimpse of things shifting, it's like watching a beautiful sand painting in the second before the wind gets it . . .'

The last of the desert storm rattled the windows as if to demonstrate her simile. She smiled at me. 'I'm sorry I got unstuck in time a while ago . . .'

'Unstuck?' I said.

'That bit about your loving me,' she said with a rueful smile. 'I forget where and when we are.'

After a moment I said, 'It doesn't matter, kiddo. I *do* love you. And I'll die before I let anyone hurt you tomorrow – not the Church, not the Core, not anyone.'

'And I also will strive to prevent such an eventuality, M. Aenea,' said A. Bettik.

The girl smiled and touched both our hands. 'The Tin Woodsman and the Scarecrow,' she said. 'I don't deserve such friends.'

It was my turn to smile. Grandam had told me that old story. 'Where's the Cowardly Lion?' I said.

Aenea's smile went away. 'That's me,' she said very quietly. 'I'm the cowardly one.'

None of us slept any more that night. We loaded up and went down to the raft when the first hint of dawn touched the red hills beyond the city.

FIFTY-ONE

Because of *Raphael*'s relatively low velocity at the translation point in Sol Draconi System, she has less speed to kill while spinning down into God's Grove space. The deceleration is mild – never more than twenty-five-gs – and lasts only three hours. Rhadamnth Nemes lies in her padded resurrection creche and waits.

When the ship slides into its orbit around the planet, Nemes opens her coffin door and kicks off to the wardrobe cubby to suit up. Before leaving the command pod for the dropship tube, she checks the creche monitors and makes a direct connection to ship's operations. The other three creches are functioning normally, programmed for the nominal three-day revival period. By the time de Soya and his men are awake, Nemes knows, this issue will have been settled. Using the microfilament connection to the ship's main computer, she sets the same programming directives and recording overrides she had used in Sol Draconi System. The ship acknowledges the coming dropship roll program and prepares to forget it.

Before kicking up the tube to the dropship air lock, Nemes taps the combination for her private locker. Besides a few changes of clothes and some false personal items – holos of 'family' and some forged letters from her fictional brother – the only thing in the locker is an extra belt with the usual pouches. Someone examining those pouches would find only a playing-card computer of the kind available at any convenience store for eight or ten florins, a spool of thread, three vials of pills, and a packet of tampons. She slides the belt around her waist and heads for the dropship.

Even from orbit at thirty thousand kilometers, God's Grove – where it is visible at all through the heavy cloud layers – reveals itself as the damaged world it is. Rather than being divided into discrete continents and oceans, the planet has tectonically evolved as a single landmass with thousands of long salty-sea 'lochs' raking across the landscape like claw marks on a green baize billiard table. Besides the sea-lochs and countless fingerlakes following the fault lines through the verdant landmasses, there are now thousands of brown slash marks where the Ouster invasion – what the humans still think of as the Ouster invasion – had lanced and relanced the peaceful land almost three hundred years ago.

As the dropship hurtles through atmosphere entry and ionization, ripping into solid atmosphere with a triple sonic boom, Nemes looks down at the landscape coming into sight from beneath the extensive cloud masses. Most of the two-hundred-meter-tall recombinant redwood and sequoia forests that had originally attracted the Brotherhood of the Muir to this world are gone, burned away in the planetwide forest fire that had brought on the nuclear winter. Large segments of the northern and southern hemispheres still glare white from the snowfall and glaciation, which only now is beginning to abate as the cloud cover recedes from a thousand-klick band on either side of the equator. It is precisely this recovering equatorial region that is Nemes's destination.

Taking over manual control of the lifting-body dropship, Nemes clips in her filament jack. She rifles through the planetary maps she has downloaded from *Raphael*'s main library: there it is . . . the River Tethys had once run some hundred and sixty klicks, primarily west to east, around the roots of God's Grove Worldtree and past the Muir Museum. Nemes sees that most of the Tethys Tour had been in a giant semicircular arc as the river winds around a small bite of the northern circumference of Worldtree. The Templars had fancied themselves the ecological conscience of the Hegemony – always inserting their unsolicited opinion into any terraforming effort in the Web or Outback – and the Worldtree had been the symbol of their arrogance. Indeed, the tree had been unique in the known universe: with a trunk diameter of more than eighty kilometers and a branch diameter of more than five hundred klicks, equal to the base of Mars's legendary Olympus Mons, the single living organism had thrust its upper branches into the fringes of space.

It is gone now, of course, shattered and burned by the Ouster fleet that slagged the entire planet just before the Fall. Instead of the glorious, living Tree, there is now only the Worldstump, a heap of ash and carbon looking like the eroded remains of an ancient shield volcano. With the Templars gone – killed or fled in their erg-powered treeships on the day of the attack – God's Grove has lain fallow for more than two and a half centuries. Nemes knows that the Pax would have recolonized the world long ago if the Core had not ordered them to desist: the AIs have their own long-term plan for God's Grove, and it does not involve missionaries and human colonies.

Nemes finds the upriver farcaster portal – looking tiny compared to the ashy slopes of the Worldstump to the south – and hovers above it. Secondary growth has come up along the river and on the eroded ash slopes there, looking like mere weeds compared to the old forests but still boasting trees twenty meters and more in height, and Nemes can see the occasional tangle of thick undergrowth where the sunlight strikes the gullies. Not a good place for an ambush. Nemes lands the dropship on the north bank of the river and walks to the farcaster arch.

Discarding an access panel, she finds an interface module and peels off the human flesh on her right hand and wrist. Carefully storing the skin for her return to *Raphael*, she jacks directly into the module and reviews the data. This portal has not been activated since the Fall. Aenea's group has not yet passed this way.

Nemes returns to the dropship and flies downriver, trying to find the perfect spot. It should be a place where they cannot escape by land – enough forest growth to conceal her and her traps, but not so much as to give Aenea and her companions cover – and, finally, a place where Nemes can clean up the mess after it is all over. She would prefer a rocky surface: something easy to hose down before returning to *Raphael*.

She finds the perfect spot only fifteen klicks downriver. The Tethys enters a rocky gorge at this point, a series of rapids created by the Ouster slagging and subsequent avalanches. New trees have grown up along the ash slopes by the entrance to this stretch of rapids and along the narrow ravines feeding into it. The narrow canyon itself is bordered by tumbled boulders and by great slabs of black lava that had flowed downhill during the Ouster slagging and formed into terraces as they cooled. The rough terrain makes a portage impossible, and anyone piloting a raft toward these rapids will be intent upon guiding their craft into white water and will have little time to watch the rocks or riverbanks.

She lands the dropship a klick to the south, pulls a vacuum-locked specimen bag from the EVA locker, tucks it into her belt, conceals the dropship under branches, and jogs quickly back to the river.

Nemes removes the spool of thread from her kit, tosses away the thread, and extrudes several hundred meters of invisible monofilament. She runs this back and forth across the river above the rapids like an unseen spider's web, spreading clear, saplike polycarbon goo on the landward side of objects where she loops the wire, both to give her a visual reference and to prevent the monofilament from slicing through trees and boulders wherever it touches them. Even if someone were hiking the boulders and lava fields here, the goo would show up only as a faint line of sap or as lichen on the rocks. The monofilament web would slice through *Raphael* in a dozen places if someone tried to drive the spacecraft through here now.

When she has woven the monofilament trap, Nemes moves upriver along the only flat shelf of land, opens her pill case, and spreads several hundred miniclaymores on the ground and in the trees there. The chameleon-polymered microexplosives immediately blend in colour and texture with the surface on which they have fallen. Each claymore will leap toward the walking or running target before it explodes, and its blast is shaped to burrow inward. The claymores are triggered by the proximity of pulse, carbon-dioxide exhalations, and body heat, as well as by the pressure of a footstep within ten meters.

Nemes assesses the terrain. This flat area is the only section of riverbank near the rapids where a person on foot can retreat, and with the claymores scattered there, nothing on foot will survive. Nemes jogs back to the boulder field and activates the claymores' sensors with a coded pulse.

To prevent someone from swimming back upriver, she breaks open the tampon casings and seeds the river bottom with ceramic-encased earwig eggs. These lie on the river bottom looking exactly like the water-worn pebbles around them. If someone then tries to return upriver, the gnat-sized earwigs will burst through their ceramic eggs and scream through water or air to bore into their target's skull, exploding into a mass of wiry filaments only after making contact with brain tissue.

Waiting on a boulder ten meters above the rapids, Rhadamnth Nemes lies back to wait. The two items left in her belt are the playing-card computer and the specimen bag.

The 'computer' is the most advanced item she has brought on this hunting trip. Called the 'sphinx trap' by those entities that created it for her, named after the Sphinx Tomb on Hyperion, which had been designed by the same species of AIs, the card is capable of creating its own five-meter bubble of antientropic or hyperentropic tides. The energy needed to create this bubble could power a crowded planet such as Renaissance Vector for a decade, but Nemes needs only three minutes of temporal displacement. Fingering the flat card, Nemes thinks that it should be called the Shrike trap.

The short woman with the skinless hand looks upriver. Any time now. Even though the portal is fifteen klicks away, she will have some warning: Nemes is sensitive to the farcaster distortion. She expects the Shrike to be with them and anticipates that it will treat her as an adversary. Indeed, she would be disappointed if the Shrike were not there and adversarial.

Rhadamnth Nemes fingers the last item on her belt. The specimen bag is just what it appears to be – a vacuum-locked EVA specimen bag. In it she will transport the girl's head back to the *Raphael*, where she will store it in the secret locker behind the fusion-drive access panel. Her masters want proof.

Smiling slightly, Nemes lies back on the black lava, shifts her position so the afternoon sun warms her face, covers her eyes with her wrist, and allows herself to take a brief nap. Everything is ready.

FIFTY-TWO

I admit that I expected the Shrike to be gone when we reached the river-front street of Mashhad on Qom-Riyadh just before dawn of that last, fateful day. It was not gone.

We all stopped in our tracks at the sight of the three-meter-tall chrome-and-blade sculpture on our little raft. The thing was standing just as I had last seen it the night before. I had backed away warily then, rifle raised, and now I took another wary step closer, rifle raised.

'Easy,' said Aenea, her hand on my forearm.

'What the hell does it want?' I said, slipping off the safety on the rifle. I levered the first plasma cartridge into the firing chamber.

'I don't know,' said Aenea. 'But your weapon won't hurt it.'

I licked my lips and looked down at the child. I wanted to tell her that a plasma bolt would hurt *anything* not wrapped in twenty centimeters of Web-era impact armor. Aenea looked pale and drawn. There were dark circles under her eyes. I said nothing.

'Well,' I said, lowering the rifle a bit, 'we can't get on the raft while that thing's there.'

Aenea squeezed my arm and released it. 'We have to.' She started walking toward the concrete pier.

I looked at A. Bettik, who seemed no happier at this idea than I was; then we both jogged to keep up with the girl.

Close up, the Shrike was even more terrifying than when seen from a distance. I used the word 'sculpture' earlier, and there was something sculpted about the creature – if one can imagine a sculpture done in chromed spikes, razor wire, blades, thorns, and smooth metal carapace. It was *large* – more than a meter taller than I was, and I am not short. The actual form of the thing was complicated – solid legs with joints sheathed in thorn-studded bands; a flat foot with curved blades where the toes should be and a long spoon-shaped blade at the heel, which might be a perfect utensil for disemboweling; a complicated upper carapace of smooth chromed shell interspersed with bands of razor wire; arms that were too long, too jointed, and too many – there was an extra pair tucked under the longer, upper set of arms; and four huge bladed hands hanging limply by the thing's side.

The skull was mostly smooth and strangely elongated, with a steam-shovel jaw set in with row upon row of metal teeth. There was a curved blade on the creature's forehead and another high up on the armored skull. The eyes were large, deep-set, and dull red.

'You want to get on the raft with that . . . *thing*?' I whispered to Aenea as we stood four meters away on the pier. The Shrike had not turned its head to watch us as we approached, and its eyes seemed as dead as glass reflectors, but the urge to back away from the thing and then turn and run was very strong.

'We have to get on the raft,' the girl whispered back. 'We have to get out of here today. Today is the last day.'

Without really taking my eye off the monster, I glanced at the sky and buildings behind us. With the night's wild dust storm, one would have expected the sky to be pinker with more sand in the air, but the storm seemed to have cleared the air a bit. While reddish clouds still stirred on the last desert breeze, the sky above was bluer than it had been the day before. Sunlight was just touching the tops of the taller buildings now.

'Maybe we could find a working EMV and travel in style,' I whispered, the rifle raised. 'Something without this type of hood ornament.' The joke sounded lame even to my ear, but it took most of the bravado I had that morning to attempt any joke at all.

'Come on,' whispered Aenea, and went down the iron ladder off the pier and onto the battered raft. I hurried to keep up with her, one hand keeping the rifle trained on the chrome nightmare, the other grasping the old ladder. A. Bettik followed us without a word.

I had not paid attention to how battered and flimsy the raft seemed. The abbreviated logs were torn and splintered in places, water came over the forward third and lapped around the Shrike's huge feet, and the tent was filled with red sand from the night's storm. The steering-oar assembly looked as if it would give way any second, and the gear we had left aboard had an abandoned look to it. We dropped our packs into the tent and stood indecisively, watching the back of the Shrike and waiting for movement – three mice who had crawled onto the sleeping cat's carpet.

The Shrike did not turn. Its back was no more reassuring than its front, with the exception that its dull-red eyes no longer were watching us.

Aenea sighed and walked up to the thing. She raised one small hand but did not actually touch that spiked and razor-wired shoulder. Turning back to us, she said, 'It's all right. Let's go.'

'How can it be all right?' I whispered fiercely at her. I don't know why I was whispering . . . but for some reason it was next to impossible to speak normally around that thing.

'If it was going to kill us today, we would be dead already,' the girl said flatly. She walked to the port side, her face still pale and shoulders drooping, and picked up one of the poles. 'Cast off the lines, please,' she said to A. Bettik. 'We have to go.'

The android did not flinch as he walked within monster-arm's length of the Shrike to untie the forward line and curl it into a loop. I untied our stern line with one hand while holding the rifle with the other.

The raft rode lower with the mass of the creature on the front end, and water lapped across the boards almost back to the tent. Several of the front and port-side logs were hanging loose.

'We need to work on the raft,' I said, taking the steering oar in hand and laying the rifle at my feet.

'Not on this world,' said Aenea, still straining against the pole to move us out into the center current. 'After we go through the portal.'

'Do you know where we're headed?' I said.

She shook her head. Her hair seemed dull this morning. 'I just know that this is the last day.'

She had said that a few minutes earlier, and I had felt the same stab of alarm then as I did now. 'Are you sure, kiddo?'

'Yes.'

'But you don't know where we're going?'

'No. Not exactly.'

'What do you know? I mean . . .'

She smiled wanly. 'I know what you mean, Raul. I know that if we survive the next few hours, we hunt for the building I've seen in my dreams.'

'What does it look like?'

Aenea opened her mouth to speak but then just rested against the pole a moment. We were moving quickly now in the center of the river. The tall downtown buildings gave way to small parks and walkways on either bank. 'I'll know the building when I see it.' She laid the pole down and walked closer, pulling at my sleeve. I bent to hear her whisper. 'Raul, if I don't . . . make it . . . and you do . . . please get home to tell Uncle Martin about what I said. About the lions and tigers and bears . . . and what the Core is up to.'

I grabbed her by her thin shoulder. 'Don't talk like that. We're all going to make it. *You* tell Martin when we see him.'

Aenea nodded without conviction and went back to the pole. The Shrike continued to stare ahead, water lapping at its feet and the morning light beginning to glint on its thorns and razor surfaces.

I had expected us to move into open desert beyond the city of Mashhad, but once again my expectations were mistaken. The riverside parks and walkways grew more luxuriant with trees – everblues, deciduous Old Earth varieties, and a proliferation of yellow and green palms. Soon the city buildings were behind us and the wide, straight river was passing through a rich forest. It was still early morning, but the heat of the rising sun was very powerful.

The steering oar was not really needed in the central current. I lashed it in place, took off my shirt, folded it on top of my pack, and took the port push-pole from the obviously exhausted girl. She looked at me with dark eyes but did not complain.

A. Bettik had collapsed the microtent and shaken out most of the accumulated sand. Now he sat near me as the current moved us around a wide bend and into an even deeper tropical rain forest. He was wearing the loose shirt and ragged shorts of yellow linen I had seen him in on

Hebron and Mare InfInitus. The broad-brimmed straw hat was at his feet. Surprisingly, Aenea moved to the front of the raft to sit near the motionless Shrike as we drifted deeper into the heavy jungle.

'This can't be native,' I said, straightening the raft as the current tried to swing it sideways. 'There can't be enough rainfall in this desert to support all this.'

'I believe it was an extensive garden area planted by the Shi'a religious pilgrims, M. Endymion,' said A. Bettik. 'Listen.'

I listened. The rainforest was alive with the rustle of birds and wind. Beneath these sounds I could hear the hiss and rattle of sprinkler systems. 'Incredible,' I said. 'That they'd use precious water to maintain this ecosystem. It must stretch for kilometers.'

'Paradise,' said Aenea.

'What, kiddo?' I poled us back into the center current.

'The Muslims were primarily desert people on Old Earth,' she said softly. 'Water and greenery was their idea of paradise. Mashhad was a religious center. Maybe this was to give the faithful a glimpse of what was to come if the teachings of Allah in the Qur'an were obeyed.'

'Expensive sneak preview,' I said, dragging the pole a bit as we turned again to the left as the river widened. 'I wonder what happened to the people?'

'The Pax,' said Aenea.

'What?' I did not understand. 'These worlds . . . Hebron, Qom-Riyadh . . . were under Ouster control when the population disappeared.'

'According to the Pax,' said Aenea.

I thought about this.

'What do the two worlds have in common, Raul?' she said.

It took no time to answer that. 'They were both adamantly non-Christian,' I said. 'They refused to accept the cross. Jew and Muslim.'

Aenea said nothing.

'That's a terrible thought,' I said. My stomach hurt. 'The Church may be misguided . . . the Pax can be arrogant with its power . . . but . . .' I wiped sweat out of my eyes. 'My God . . .' I said, struggling to say the one word. 'Genocide?'

Aenea shifted to look at me. Just behind her the Shrike's bladed legs caught the light. 'We don't know that,' she said very quietly. 'But there are elements of the Church and of the Pax that would do it, Raul. Remember, the Vatican depends almost totally on the Core to maintain its control of resurrection – and through that, its control of all the people on all the worlds.'

I was shaking my head. 'But . . . genocide? I can't believe it.' That concept belonged with the legends of Horace Glennon-Height and Adolf Hitler, not with people and institutions I had seen in my lifetime.

'Something terrible is going on,' said Aenea. 'That has to be why we were routed this way . . . through Hebron and Qom-Riyadh.'

'You said that before,' I said, pushing hard on the pole. 'Routed. But not by the Core. Then by whom?' I looked at the back of the Shrike. I was pouring sweat in the heat of the day. The looming creature was all cool blades and thorns.

'I don't know,' said Aenea. She swiveled back around and rested her forearms on her knees. 'There's the farcaster.'

The portal rose, vine-shrouded and rusted, from the overgrown jungle. If this was still Qom-Riyadh's paradise park, it had grown out of control. Above the green canopy, the blue sky carried a hint of red dust clouds on the wind.

Steering for the center of the river, I laid the pole along the port side and went back to pick up my rifle. My stomach was still tight with the thought of genocide. Now it tightened further with the image of ice caves, waterfalls, ocean worlds, and of the Shrike coming to life as we passed into whatever waited.

'Hang on,' I said needlessly as we passed under the metal arch.

The view ahead of us faded and shifted as if a curtain of heat haze had begun to shimmer ahead of us and around us. Suddenly the light changed, the gravity changed, and our world changed.

FIFTY-THREE

Father Captain de Soya awakes to screaming. It is several minutes before he realizes it is his voice doing the screaming.

Thumbing open the coffin-lid catch, he pulls himself to a sitting position within the creche. Lights are blinking red and amber on the monitor panel, although all of the essential guidelines are green. Moaning in pain and confusion, de Soya starts to pull himself out. His body floats above the open creche, his flailing hands can get no grip. He notices that his hands and arms are glistening red and pink, as if all his skin has been burned off.

'Dear Mother of Mary . . . where am I?' He is weeping. The tears hang in front of his eyes in tumbling beads. 'Zero-g . . . where am I? The *Balthasar*? What's . . . happened? Space battle? Burns?'

No. He is aboard the *Raphael*. Slowly the outraged dendrites in his brain begin to work. He is floating in instrument-lighted darkness. The *Raphael*. It should be in orbit around God's Grove. He had set the creche cycles for Gregorius, Kee, and him for a dangerous six hours rather than the usual three days. *Playing God with the troopers' lives*, he remembers thinking. The chances for unsuccessful resurrection are very high at this hurried pace. De Soya remembers the second courier who had brought orders to him on the *Balthasar*, Father Gawronski – it seems like decades ago to him – he had not achieved successful resurrection . . . the resurrection chaplain on *Balthasar* . . . what was that old bastard's name? Father Sapieha . . . had said that it would take weeks or months for Father Gawronski to be resurrected after that initial failure . . . a slow, painful process, the resurrection chaplain had said accusingly . . .

Father Captain de Soya's mind is clearing as he floats above the creche. Still in freefall as he had programmed. He remembers thinking that he might not be in shape to walk in one-g. He is not.

Kicking off to the wardrobe cubby, de Soya checks himself in the mirror there – his body glistens redly, he does look like a burn victim, and the cruciform is a livid welt in all that pink, raw flesh.

De Soya closes his eyes and pulls on his underclothes and cassock. The cotton hurts his raw skin, but he ignores the pain. The coffee has percolated as programmed. He lifts his bulb from the plotting table and kicks back into the common room.

Corporal Kee's creche glows green in the last seconds of revival. Gregorius's creche has flashing warning lights. De Soya curses softly and pulls himself down to the sergeant's creche panel. The resurrection cycle has been aborted. The hurried revival has failed.

'Goddammit,' whispers de Soya, and then offers an Act of Contrition for taking the Lord's name in vain. He had needed Gregorius.

Kee revives safely, however, although the corporal is confused and in pain. De Soya lifts him out, kicks off with him to the wardroom cubby to sponge-bath the other man's burning skin and to offer him a drink of orange juice. Within minutes Kee can understand.

'Something was wrong,' de Soya explains. 'I had to take this risk to see what Corporal Nemes was up to.'

Kee nods his understanding. Even though dressed with the cabin temperature set high, the corporal is shivering violently.

De Soya leads the way back to the command core. Sergeant Gregorius's creche is all amber lights now as the cycle surrenders the big man to death again. Corporal Rhadamnth Nemes's creche shows green lights for the normal three-day resurrection. Monitor displays show that she is inside, lifeless, and receiving the secret sacramental ministrations of resurrection. De Soya taps the release code.

Warning lights blink. 'Creche release not allowed during resurrection cycle,' comes *Raphael*'s emotionless voice. 'Any attempt to open the creche now could result in true death.'

De Soya ignores the lights and warning buzzers and tugs at the lid. It stays locked. 'Give me that pry bar,' he says to Kee.

The corporal tosses the iron bar across the weightless space. De Soya finds a niche for the head of the bar, says a silent prayer that he is not wrong and paranoid, and pries up the lid. Alarm bells fill the ship.

The creche is empty.

'Where is Corporal Nemes?' de Soya asks the ship.

'All instruments and sensors show her in her creche,' says the ship's computer.

'Yeah,' says de Soya, tossing the bar aside. It tumbles into a corner in zero-g slow motion. 'Come on,' he says to the corporal, and the two kick back to the wardroom cubby. The shower stall is empty. There is no place to hide in the common area. De Soya kicks forward to his command chair while Kee heads for the connecting tube.

Status lights show geosynchronous orbit at thirty thousand kilometers. De Soya looks out the window and sees a world of swirling cloud banks except for a wide band at the equator, where slash marks cut across green and brown terrain. Instruments show the dropship attached and powered down. Voice queries have the ship confirm that the dropship is where it should be, its air lock undisturbed since translation. 'Corporal Kee?' de Soya says on the intercom. He must concentrate to keep his teeth from chattering. The pain is very real; it is as if his skin is on fire. He has a tremendous urge to close his eyes and sleep. 'Report,' commands de Soya.

'The dropship's gone, Captain,' says Kee from the access tunnel. 'All the connector lights are green, but if I cycled the air lock, I'd be breathing vacuum. I can see out the port here that the dropship's gone.'

'*Merde,*' whispers de Soya. 'All right, come on back here.' He studies the other instruments while he waits. The telltale double burps are there on the thruster record . . . about three hours ago. Calling up the map of the equatorial region of God's Grove, de Soya keys in a telescope and deep-radar search of the stretch of river around the stump of the Worldtree. 'Find the first farcaster portal and show me every stretch of the river in between. Report on location of dropship transponder.'

'Instruments show dropship attached to the command-core boom,' says the ship. 'Transponder confirms this.'

'Okay,' says de Soya, imagining himself ripping out silicon chips like teeth, 'ignore the dropship beacon. Just begin telescope and deep-radar searches of this region. Report any life-forms or artifacts. All data on main screens.'

'Affirmative,' says the computer. De Soya sees the screen lurch forward as telescopic magnification begins. He is looking down on a farcaster portal now from only a few hundred meters above it. 'Pan downriver,' he says.

'Affirmative.'

Corporal Kee slides into the copilot's seat and straps himself in. 'With the dropship gone,' he says, 'there's no way we can get down there.'

'Combat suits,' says de Soya through the ripples of pain that shake him. 'They have an ablative shield . . . hundreds of microlayers of colored ablative in case of a coherent light firefight, right?'

'Correct,' says Corporal Kee, 'but—'

'My plan was for you and Sergeant Gregorius to use the ablative for reentry,' continues de Soya. 'I could get *Raphael* in as low an orbit as possible. You use an auxiliary reaction pak for retro thrust. The suits should survive reentry, shouldn't they?'

'Possibly,' says Kee, 'but—'

'Then you go to EM repulsors and find this . . . woman,' says de Soya. 'Find her and stop her. Afterward, you use the dropship to get back.'

Corporal Kee rubs his eyes. 'Yes, sir. But I checked the suits. All of them have integrity breaches . . .'

'Integrity . . .' repeats de Soya stupidly.

'Someone slashed the ablative armor,' says Kee. 'Not noticeable to the eye, but I ran a class-three integrity diagnostic. We'd be dead before ionization blackout.'

'All the suits?' says de Soya weakly.

'All of them, sir.'

The priest-captain overcomes the urge to curse again. 'I'm going to bring the ship lower anyway, Corporal.'

'Why, sir?' says Kee. 'Anything that happens down there is still going to be several hundred klicks away, and we can't do a damn thing about it.'

De Soya nods but taps in the parameters he wants to the guidance core. His befuddled brain makes several mistakes at least one of which would burn them up in the atmosphere of God's Grove – but the ship catches them. De Soya resets the parameters.

'I advise against such a low orbit,' says the sexless ship's voice. 'God's

Grove has a volatile upper atmosphere, and three hundred kilometers does not satisfy safety-margin requirements as listed in the—'

'Shut up and do it,' says Father Captain de Soya.

He closes his eyes as the main thrusters fire. The return of weight makes the pain in his flesh and body all the more fierce. De Soya hears Kee groan in the copilot's couch.

'Internal containment-field activation will alleviate the discomfort of four-g deceleration,' says the ship.

'No,' says de Soya. He is going to save power.

The noise, vibration, and pain continue. The limb of God's Grove grows in the windscreen until it fills the view.

What if that . . . traitor . . . has programmed the ship to drive us into atmosphere if we awake and try any maneuver? de Soya suddenly thinks. He grins despite the punishing g-pull. *Then she doesn't go home either.*

The punishment continues.

FIFTY-FOUR

The Shrike was gone when we came through the other side of the portal.

After a moment I lowered my rifle and looked around. The river was broad and shallow here. The sky was a deep blue, darker than Hyperion's lapis lazuli, and towering stratocumulus was visible far to the north. The cloud columns seemed to be catching evening light, and a glance behind us showed a large sun low in the sky. My feeling was that it was near sunset rather than just after sunrise.

The riverbanks showed rocks, weeds, and ashy soil. The very air smelled of ash, as if we were moving through an area destroyed by forest fire. The low growth supported that impression. To our right, many kilometers away, from the look of it, rose a blackened shield volcano.

'God's Grove, I think,' said A. Bettik. 'That is the remnant of the World-tree.'

I looked again at the black volcanic cone. No tree could ever have grown that large.

'Where's the Shrike?' I said.

Aenea stood and walked to the place where the creature had stood a moment before. She passed her hand through the air as if the monster had become invisible.

'Hang on!' I said again. The raft was coming up on a modest set of rapids. I returned to the steering oar and unlashed it while the android and girl took up poles on either side. We bounced, splashed, and tried to turn end to end, but were soon past the white ripples.

'That was fun!' said Aenea. It was the most animated I had heard her in some time.

'Yeah,' I said, 'fun. But the raft's coming apart.' This was a slight exaggeration, but not total hyperbole. The loose logs at the front were coming untethered. Our gear was rattling around loose on the collapsed microtent fabric.

'There is a flat space to put in,' said A. Bettik, pointing to a grassy area along the right riverbank. 'The hills look more formidable ahead.'

I pulled the binoculars out and studied those black ridges. 'You're right,' I said. 'There may be real rapids ahead, and few places to put in. Let's tie up loose ends here.'

The girl and android poled us to the right bank. I jumped out and pulled the raft higher onto the muddy bank. Damage was not serious to the front and starboard sides, just loose wraith-hide thongs and a few splintered boards. I glanced upriver. The sun was lower, although it looked as if we had another hour or so of light.

'Do we camp tonight?' I said, thinking that this might be the last good place. 'Or keep on moving?'

'Keep moving,' Aenea said adamantly.

I understood the impulse. It was still morning, Qom-Riyadh time. 'I don't want to be caught on white water after dark,' I said.

Aenea squinted at the low sun. 'And I don't want to be sitting here after dark,' she said. 'Let's get as far as we can.' She borrowed the binoculars and studied the black ridges to our right, the dark hills to the left of the river. 'They wouldn't have put the Tethys section on a river with dangerous rapids, would they?'

A. Bettik cleared his throat. 'It would be my guess,' he said, 'that much of that lava flow was created during the Ouster attack on this world. Very severe rapids may have resulted from the seismic disruption such a lancing would cause.'

'It wasn't the Ousters,' Aenea said softly.

'What was that, kiddo?'

'It wasn't the Ousters,' she said more firmly. 'It was the TechnoCore that built ships to attack the Web . . . they were simulating an Ouster invasion.'

'Okay,' I said. I had forgotten that Martin Silenus had said as much toward the end of his *Cantos*. That part had not made much sense to me when I was learning the poem. It was all irrelevant now. 'But the slagged hills are still there, and some nasty white water may be as well. White water or actual waterfalls. It could be that we can't get the raft through it.'

Aenea nodded and set the binoculars back in my pack. 'If we can't, we can't. We'll walk it and swim through the next portal. But let's fix the raft quickly and get as far as we can. If we see bad rapids, we'll pole for the closest bank.'

'It may be more cliff than riverbank,' I said. 'That lava looks mean.'

Aenea shrugged. 'Then we'll climb and keep hiking.'

I admit that I admired that child that evening. I knew that she was tired, sick, overwhelmed by some emotion I could not understand, and scared half to death. But I had never seen her ready to quit.

'Well,' I said, 'at least the Shrike's gone. That's a good sign.'

Aenea only looked at me. But she tried to smile.

The repairs took only twenty minutes. We relashed the bindings, shifted some of the center supports to the front, and laid the microtent fabric down as a sort of liner to keep our feet dry.

'If we're going to travel in the dark,' said Aenea, 'we should rig our lantern mast again.'

'Yeah,' I said. I had kept a tall pole free for just that purpose and now set it in its socket and lashed its base in place. I used my knife to cut a niche for the lantern handle. 'Shall I light it?' I said.

'Not yet,' said Aenea, glancing at the setting sun behind us.

'Okay,' I said, 'if we're going to be bouncing through any white water, we should keep gear in our packs and load the most important things in the waterproof shoulder bags.' We set to work doing just that. In my shoulder bag I put an extra shirt, an extra coil of rope, the folded plasma rifle, a hand-lamp, and the flashlight laser. At the last minute I changed my mind about the laser and clipped it onto my belt. I started to toss the useless comlog into my regular backpack, thought, *It's useless, but it doesn't weigh much*, and clipped it around my wrist instead. We had fully charged the comlog, laser, and handlamp batteries at the Qom-Riyadh clinic.

'All set?' I asked, ready to pole us out into the current again. Our raft *looked* better with its new floor and mast, packs loaded and tied down for white water, lantern ready to be lit at the bow.

'Ready,' said Aenea.

A. Bettik nodded and leaned on his pole. We moved out onto the river.

The current was fast – at least twenty or twenty-five klicks per hour – and the sun was still above the horizon when we moved into the black lava country. Riverbanks changed to bluffs on either side, and we bounced through a few ripples of white water, coming out high and dry each time, and I began to search the banks for places to set in if we heard the roar of a waterfall or wild rapids ahead. There were places – gullies and flat areas – but the land was visibly rougher ahead. I noticed that there was more growth here in the ravines – everblues and stunted redwoods – and the low sun painted the higher branches in rich light. I was beginning to think about getting our lunch . . . dinner . . . whatever, out of the packs and fixing something hot when A. Bettik called, 'Rapids ahead.'

I leaned on the steering oar and looked. Rocks in the river, white water, some spray. My years as a bargeman on the Kans helped assess this stretch of rapids. 'It'll be all right,' I said. 'Keep your legs braced, move a bit toward the center if it gets too wild. Push hard when I say push. The trick will be to keep the front headed where we want it, but we can do it. If you go over, swim for the raft. I've got a line ready.' I had one booted foot on the coiled rope.

I did not like the black lava cliffs and boulders on the right side of the river ahead, but the river looked wider and milder beyond this stretch of rough water. If this was all we faced, we could probably continue on into the night, using the lantern and widebeam laser to light our way.

All three of us were concentrating on lining the raft up properly to enter the rapids, trying to miss several boulders rising from the frothing water, when it all began. If it had not been for an eddy there that spun us around twice, it would have been over before I'd known what was happening. As it was, it almost happened that way.

Aenea was shouting in glee. I was grinning. Even A. Bettik had a smile. Mild white water does that, I knew from experience. Class V rapids usually just freeze a rictus of terror on people's faces, but harmless bumps like this were fun. We shouted directions at one another – Push! Hard right! Avoid that rock! – Aenea was a few steps to my right, A. Bettik a few steps farther to my left, and we had just been grabbed by the swirling eddy downstream from the large rock we had avoided, when I looked up to see the mast at the front and the hanging lantern suddenly sliced into pieces.

'What the hell?' I had time to say, and then the old memories hit, and with them the reflexes I would have guessed had atrophied years before.

We were spinning to my left. I screamed 'Down!' at the top of my lungs, abandoned the steering oar, and tackled Aenea headfirst. Both of us rolled off the raft into white water.

A. Bettik had reacted almost instantly, throwing himself down and toward the stern of the raft, and the monofilaments that had sliced the mast and lantern like soft butter must have missed him by millimeters. I came up out of the water with my boots scraping against rocks and my forearm around Aenea's chest in time to see the underwater monofilament slice the raft in two sections, then reslice it as the eddy swirled the logs around. The filaments were invisible, of course, but that kind of cutting power meant only one thing. I had seen this trick used on buddies of mine in the brigade on Ursus; the rebels had strung monofilament across the road, sliced through a bus hauling thirty guys back from the cinema in town, and decapitated all of them.

I tried to shout at A. Bettik, but the water was roaring and it filled my mouth. I grabbed at a boulder, missed it, scrabbled my feet against the bottom, and caught the next rock. My scrotum tightened as I thought of those goddamn wires underwater, in front of my face . . .

The android saw the raft being sliced a third time and dived into the shallow water. The current flipped him over, his left arm rising instinctively as his head was forced under. There was a brief mist of blood as the arm was sliced off just below his elbow. His head came above the water, but he did not cry out as he grabbed a sharp rock with his right hand and hung on. His left arm and still-spasming hand were swept out of sight downriver.

'Oh, Jesus!' I yelled. 'Damn . . . damn!'

Aenea pulled her face out of the water and looked at me with wild eyes. But there was no panic there.

'Are you all right?' I shouted over the rapids. A monofilament slices so cleanly that you could be missing a leg and not know it for half a minute.

She nodded.

'Hang on to my neck!' I yelled. I had to get my left arm free. She clung to me, her skin already cold from the freezing water.

'Damn, damn, damn,' I said as a mantra while I fumbled in my shoulder bag with my left hand. My pistol was in its holster, pinned under my right hip against the river bottom. It was shallow here . . . less than a meter in places . . . barely enough water to dive for cover when the sniper started shooting. But that was irrelevant – any attempt to dive would sweep us downriver, into the monofilaments.

I could see A. Bettik hanging on for his life eight meters or so downriver. He lifted his left arm from the water. Blood spurted from the stump. I could see him grimace and almost lose his grip on the rock as the pain began to pour through shock. *Do androids die like humans?* I shook the thought away. His blood was very red.

I scanned the lava flows and boulder fields for a glint of dying sunlight on metal. Next would come the sniper's bullet or bolt. We would not hear it. It was a beautiful ambush – straight out of the book. And I had literally steered us into it.

I found the flashlight laser in the bag, resealed the bag, and clamped the laser cylinder in my teeth. Fumbling underwater with my left hand, I undid my belt and tugged it out of the water. I nodded wildly for Aenea to grab the pistol with her free hand.

Still clinging to my neck with her left arm, she unsnapped the cover and pulled the pistol out. I knew that she would never use it, but that did not matter right now. I needed the belt. I fumbled, setting the laser under my chin and holding it in place while my left hand straightened the belt.

'Bettik!' I screamed.

The android looked up at us. His eyes held agony. 'Catch!' I screamed, pulling my arm back over my head and throwing the leather belt at him. I almost lost the flashlight laser with the maneuver, but grabbed it as it hit the water and gripped it in my left hand.

The android could not release his right hand from the rock. His left hand was gone. But he used the bleeding stump of his arm and his chest to stop the hurtling belt. The throw had been perfect . . . but, then, I had had only one chance.

'Medkit!' I shouted, leaning my head toward the bag rising and falling next to me. 'Tourniquet now!'

I don't think that he heard me, but he did not have to. Pulling himself up against the rock, trying to lodge himself on the upstream side of it, he pulled the leather belt around his left arm below the elbow and pulled tight on the strap with his teeth. There was no notch that low on the belt, but he pulled it tight with a jerk of his head, wrapped it again, and pulled it tight again.

By this time I had triggered on the flashlight laser, set the beam to widest dispersal, and played it above the river.

The wire was monofilament but not superconducting monofilament. That would not have glowed. This did. There was a web of heated wire, glowing red like crisscrossed laser beams, streaking back and forth above and into the river. A. Bettik had floated down beneath some of the glowing wires. Others disappeared into the water to the left and right of him. The first filaments began about a meter in front of Aenea's feet.

I moved the widebeam, playing it above us and to our left and right. Nothing glowed there. The wires above A. Bettik glowed for a few seconds as they dissipated heat, and then disappeared as if they had never existed. I fanned the widebeam across them again, bringing them back into existence, then dialed a tighter beam. The filament I had targeted glowed white but did not melt. It wasn't a superconductor, but it wasn't going to go away with the low energies I could pour into it with a flashlight laser.

Where is the sniper? Maybe it was just a passive trap. Years old. Nobody waiting in ambush.

I did not believe it for a second. I could see A. Bettik's grip on the rock slip as the current threatened to pull him under.

'Shit,' I said. Setting the laser into the waistband of my pants, I grabbed Aenea with my left arm. 'Hang on.'

With my right arm I pulled myself higher onto the slippery boulder. It was triangular in shape and very slick. Wedging my body on the upstream side, I pulled Aenea there. The current was like someone battering me with body blows. 'Can you hold on?' I shouted.

'Yeah!' Her face was white. Her hair was plastered to her skull. I could see scratches on her cheek and temple and a rising bruise near her chin, but no other sign of injury.

I patted her on the shoulder, made sure her arms were secure on the rock, and let go. Downstream, I could see the raft – now sliced into half a dozen segments – tumbling into the curve of white water by the lava cliffs.

Bouncing and scraping along the bottom, trying to stand but being swept and battered by the current, I managed to hit A. Bettik's small rock without knocking him off or myself out. I grabbed him and hung on, noticing that his shirt had been almost ripped off him by the sharp rocks and current. Blood oozed from a dozen scratches in his blue skin, but it was his left arm I wanted to see. He moaned when I lifted the arm from the water.

The tourniquet was helping to staunch the bleeding, but not enough. Red swirled in the sunlit waters. I thought of the rainbow sharks on Mare Infinitus and shivered.

'Come on,' I said, half lifting him, prying his cold hand from the rock. 'We're leaving.'

The water was only to my waist when I stood, but it had the force of several fire hoses. Somehow, despite shock and serious loss of blood, A. Bettik helped. Our boots scrabbled at the sharp rocks on the river bottom.

Where is the sniper's bolt? My shoulder blades ached from the tension.

The closest riverbank was to our right – a flat, grassy shelf that was the last easy spot to reach as far as I could see downriver. It was inviting. Far too inviting.

Besides, Aenea was still clinging to the rock eight meters upstream.

With A. Bettik's good arm over my shoulder, we staggered, lurched, half-swam, and half-crawled our way upstream, the water battering us and splashing in our faces. I was half-blind by the time we reached Aenea's rock. Her fingers were white with cold and strain.

'The bank!' she shouted as I helped her to her feet. Our first step took us into a hole, and the current battered against her chest and neck, covering her face with white spray.

I shook my head. 'Upriver!' I shouted, and the three of us began leaning into the current, water pounding and spraying to both sides. Only my maniacal strength at that moment kept us upright and moving. Every time the current threatened to throw us down, to pull us under, I imagined myself as solid as the Worldtree that had once stood to the south, roots running deep into the bedrock. I had my eye on a fallen log perhaps twenty meters up on the right bank. If we could shelter behind that . . . I knew that

I had to get the medkit tourniquet on A. Bettik's arm within minutes, or he would be dead. If we tried to stop here in the river to do it, the medkit, shoulder bag, and everything else ran the risk of being whirled down-river. But I did not want to lie exposed on that inviting shelf of grassy riverbank.

Monofilaments. I tugged the flashlight laser from my waistband and played its wideband in the air over the river upstream. No wires. *But they could be under the water, waiting to slice us off at the ankles.*

Trying to shut down my imagination, I pulled the three of us upstream against the force of the river. The flashlight laser was slippery in my hand. A. Bettik's grip was growing weaker around my shoulder. Aenea clung to my left arm as if it was her only lifeline. It *was* her only lifeline.

We had struggled less than ten meters upstream when the water ahead of us exploded. I almost tumbled backward. Aenea's head went under and I pulled her up, gripping her soaked shirt with frenzied fingers. A. Bettik seemed to slump against me.

The Shrike exploded out of the river directly upstream from us, red eyes blazing, arms lifting.

'Holy shit!' I don't know which one of us shouted. Perhaps all three.

We turned, all of us looking over our shoulders, as the bladed fingers sliced through the air centimeters behind us.

A. Bettik went down. I grabbed him under the arm and pulled him out. The temptation to surrender to that current and ride it downriver was very powerful. Aenea tripped, pulled herself up, and pointed to the right river-bank. I nodded and we struggled in that direction.

Behind us, the Shrike stood in the middle of the river, each of its metallic arms raised and bobbing like a metal scorpion's tail. When I looked back again, it was gone.

We each fell half-a-dozen times before my feet felt mud rather than rocks under foot. I shoved Aenea up on the bank, then turned and rolled A. Bettik onto the grass. The river still roared to my waist. I did not bother crawling out myself, but tossed the shoulder bag onto the grass, away from the water. 'Medkit,' I gasped, trying to pull myself out. My arms were almost useless. My lower torso was numb from the freezing water.

Aenea's fingers were also cold – they fumbled at the medpak stickstrips and the tourniquet sleeve – but she managed. A. Bettik was unconscious as she attached the diagnostic patches, pulled off my leather belt, and tight-ened the sleeve around his amputated lower arm. The sleeve hissed and tightened, then hissed again as it injected painkiller or stimulant. Monitor lights blinked urgently.

I tried again, succeeded in getting my upper body on the bank, and pulled myself out of the river. My teeth were chattering as I said to Aenea, 'Where's . . . the . . . pistol?'

She shook her head. Her teeth were also chattering. 'I lost it . . . when we . . . the . . . Shrike . . . came . . . up . . .'

I had just enough energy to nod. The river was empty. 'Maybe he went away,' I said, jaws clenching between words. Where was the thermal blanket? Swept away downriver in the pack. Everything not in my shoulder bag was gone.

Lifting my head, I looked downriver. The last sunlight of the day lighted the treetops, but the canyon was already in gloom. A woman was walking down the lava rocks toward us.

I lifted the flashlight laser and thumbed the select to tightbeam.

'You wouldn't use that on me, would you?' asked the woman in amused tones.

Aenea looked up from the medkit diagnostics and stared at the figure. The woman was wearing a black-and-crimson uniform that I was not familiar with. She was not a large person. Her hair was short and dark, her face was pale in the fading light. Her right hand to above the wrist seemed to have been flayed and embedded with carbon-fiber bones.

Aenea began shaking, not in fear but out of some deeper emotion. Her eyes narrowed, and I would have described the girl's expression at that moment as something between feral and fearless. Her cold hand made a fist.

The woman laughed. 'Somehow I expected something more interesting,' she said, and stepped down off the rock and onto the grass.

FIFTY-FIVE

It had been a long, boring afternoon for Nemes. She had napped away a few hours, awakening when she felt the displacement disruption as the farcaster portal was activated some fifteen klicks upriver. She had moved up the rock a few meters, hiding herself behind deadfall, and waited for the next act.

The next act, she thought, had been a farce. She had watched the flailing around in the river, the awkward rescue of the artificial man – artificial man minus one artificial arm, she amended – and then, with some interest, the odd appearance of the Shrike. She had known the Shrike was around, of course, since the displacement tremors of its movement through the continuum were not that different from the portal's opening. She had even shifted to fast time to watch it wade into the river and play bogeyman for the humans. It bemused her: what was the obsolete creature doing? Keeping the humans out of her earwig trap or just herding them back toward her, like a good little sheepdog? Nemes knew that the answer depended upon which powers had sent the bladed monstrosity on this mission in the first place.

It was largely irrelevant. It was thought in the Core that the Shrike had been created and sent back in time by an early iteration of the UI. It was known that the Shrike had failed and that it would be defeated again in the far-future struggles between the fledgling human UI and the maturing Machine God. Whichever the case, the Shrike was a failure and a footnote to this journey. Nemes's only interest in the thing was her fading hope that it might provide a moment's excitement as an adversary.

Now, watching the exhausted humans and comatose android sprawl on the grass, she grows bored of being passive. Tucking the specimen bag more firmly in her belt and slipping the Sphinx-trap card into the sticktight band at her wrist, she walks down the rock and onto the grassy shelf.

The young man, Raul, is on one knee adjusting a low-power laser. Nemes cannot help but smile. 'You wouldn't use that on me, would you?' she says.

The man does not answer. He lifts the laser. Nemes thinks that if he uses it on her, in an attempt to blind her, no doubt, she will phase-shift and ram it all the way up past his colon into his lower intestine – without turning the beam off.

Aenea looks at her for the first time. Nemes can see why the Core is nervous about the young human's potential – access elements of the Void

Which Binds shimmer around the girl like static electricity – but Nemes also sees that the girl is years away from using any potential she has in that area. All this *Sturm und Drang* and galloping urgency has been for nothing. The human girl is not just immature in her powers, she is innocent of their true meaning.

Nemes realizes that she has harbored some small anxiety that the child herself would pose a problem in the final seconds, somehow tapping into a Void interface and creating difficulties. Nemes realizes that she was mistaken to have worried. Oddly enough, it is a disappointment. 'Somehow I expected something more interesting,' she says aloud, and takes another step closer.

'What do you want?' demands young Raul, struggling to his feet. Nemes sees that the man has become exhausted just pulling his friends from the river.

'I want nothing from you,' she says easily. 'Nor from your dying blue friend. From Aenea, I need just a few seconds of conversation.' Nemes nods toward the nearby trees where the claymores are seeded. 'Why don't you take your golem into the trees and wait for the girl to join you? We'll just have a word in private, and then she's yours.' She takes another step closer.

'Stay back,' says Raul, and lifts the little flashlight laser.

Nemes holds up her hands as if frightened. 'Hey, don't shoot, pardner,' she says. If the laser carried ten thousand times the amperage it did, Nemes would not be worried.

'Just back away,' says Raul. His thumb is on the trigger button. The toy laser is aimed at Nemes's eyes.

'All right, all right,' says Nemes. She takes a step back. And phase-shifts into a gleaming chrome figure only sketchily human.

'Raul!' cries Aenea.

Nemes is bored. She shifts into fast time. The tableau in front of her is frozen. Aenea's mouth is open, still speaking, but the vibrations in the air do not move. The rushing river is frozen, as if in a photograph with an impossibly high shutter speed. Droplets of spray hang in the air. Another droplet of water hangs suspended a millimeter beneath Raul's dripping chin.

Nemes strides over and takes the flashlight laser from Raul's hand. She is tempted to act on her earlier impulse right now and then drop to slow time to watch everyone's reaction, but she sees Aenea out of the corner of her eye – the girl's little hand is still molded into a fist – and Nemes realizes that she has work to do before having fun.

She drops her phase-shifted morphic layer long enough to retrieve the specimen bag from her belt and then shifts again. She walks over to the crouching girl, holds the open bag like a waiting basket beneath the child's chin with her left hand, and rigidifies the edge of her phase-shifted right hand and all of her forearm into a cutting blade not much duller than the monofilament wire still hanging over the river.

Nemes smiles behind her chrome mask. 'So long . . . kiddo,' she says. She had eavesdropped on their conversation when the trio had been kilometers upriver.

She brings her blade-sharp forearm down in a killing arc.

'What the hell's going on?' shouts Corporal Kee. 'I can't see.'

'Quiet,' orders de Soya. Both men are in their command chairs, leaning over the telescope monitors.

'Nemes turned . . . I don't know . . . metallic,' says Kee, playing the video again in an insert box while watching the milling tableau below, 'and then she disappeared.'

'Radar doesn't show her,' says de Soya, keying through different sensor modes. 'No IR . . . although the ambient temperature's risen almost ten degrees centigrade in the immediate region. Heavy ionization.'

'Local storm cell?' says Kee, bewildered. Before de Soya can answer, Kee points to the monitor. 'Now what? The girl's down. Something's happening with the guy . . .'

'Raul Endymion,' says de Soya, trying to improve the image quality on the monitor. The rising heat and atmospheric turbulence make the image ripple and blur in spite of the computer's best efforts to stabilize it. *Raphael* is holding its place only two hundred and eighty klicks above hypothetical sea level on God's Grove, far too low for an easy geosynchronous orbit and low enough that the ship is paranoid about expansion of the atmosphere adding to the already molecular heating the ship is encountering.

Father Captain de Soya has seen enough to make a decision. 'Divert all power from ship functions and drop life support to minimal levels,' his voice orders. 'Bring the fusion core to one hundred and fifteen percent and kill forward deflection shields. Shift power for tactical use.'

'That would not be advisable—' begins the ship's voice.

'Override all voice response and safety protocols,' snaps de Soya. 'Priority code delta-nine-nine-two-zero. Papal diskey override . . . now. Readout confirmation.'

The monitors fill with data columns superimposed over the shifting image on the ground. Kee is watching wide-eyed. 'Dear sweet Jesus,' whispers the corporal. 'My God.'

'Yes,' whispers de Soya, watching the power to all systems except visual monitoring and tactical fade to below red lines.

The explosions on the surface begin then.

At this point I had precisely enough time to have a retinal echo of the woman becoming a silver blur, I blinked, and the flashlight laser was gone from my fingers. The air was becoming superheated. On either side of Aenea the air suddenly misted and seemed filled with a struggling chrome figure – six arms, four legs, flailing blades – and then I was leaping at the girl, knowing that nothing I could do would be in time, but – amazingly – reaching her in time to pull her down and roll aside from the blast of hot air and blurred motion.

The medkit warning alarm went off like fingers on slate – a sound impossible to ignore. We were losing A. Bettik. I covered Aenea with my body and pulled her toward A. Bettik's body. Then the explosions began in the woods behind us.

Nemes swings her arm, expecting to feel nothing as the edge slices through muscle and vertebrae, and is shocked by the violent contact.

She looks down. The sharpened edge of her phase-shifted hand is in the grip of two sets of fingerblades. Her forearm is gripped by two other scalpel-sharp hands. The bulk of the Shrike presses close, the blades on the lower body almost in the frozen girl's face. The creature's eyes are bright red.

Nemes is momentarily startled and seriously irritated, but not alarmed. She rips her hand away and jumps back.

The tableau is exactly as it had been a second before – river in freeze time, Raul Endymion's empty hand outstretched as if pressing the firing stud on the little laser, the android dying on the ground with medpak lights frozen in midblink – only the girl is now overshadowed by the huge bulk of the Shrike.

Nemes smiles beneath her chrome mask. She had been concentrating on the girl's neck and not noticed the clumsy thing coming up on her in fast time. That is a mistake she will not make again.

'You want her?' says Nemes. 'Have you also been sent to kill her? Be my guest . . . as long as I get the head.'

The Shrike pulls its arms back and steps around the child, its thorns and knee blades missing her eyes by less than a centimeter. Legs apart, the Shrike stands between Nemes and Aenea.

'Oh,' says Nemes, 'you don't want her? Then I'll have to take her back.' Nemes moves faster than fast time, feinting left, circling right, and swinging down. If the space around her had not been warped by displacement, sonic booms would have shattered everything within kilometers.

The Shrike blocks the blow. Sparks leap from chrome, and lightning discharges into the ground. The creature slashes the air where Nemes had been a nanosecond before. She comes around from the rear, kicking at the child's back with a blow that will drive the girl's spine and heart out through her chest.

The Shrike deflects the kick and sends Nemes flying. The chromed woman-shape is hurled thirty meters into the trees, smashing branches and trunks, which hang in midair after she has passed. The Shrike hurtles through fast time after her.

Nemes strikes a boulder and is embedded five centimeters in solid rock. She senses the Shrike shifting down to slow time as it flies toward her, and she follows the displacement back into noise and motion. The trees snap, break, and burst into flame. The miniclaymores sense no heartbeat or respiration, but they feel the pressure and leap toward it, hundreds exploding in a chain reaction of shaped charges that drive Aenea and the Shrike together like halves of an old imploding uranium bomb.

The Shrike has a long curved blade on its chest. Nemes has heard all the stories about the victims the creature has impaled and dragged off to stick on the longer thorns of its Tree of Pain. She is not impressed. As the two are driven together by the shaped charges exploding all around them, Nemes's displacement field bends the Shrike's chest thorn back on itself. The creature opens steam-shovel jaws and roars in the ultrasonic. Nemes swings a bladed forearm into its neck and sends it fifteen meters into the river.

She ignores the Shrike and turns toward Aenea and the others. Raul has thrown himself across the girl. *How touching*, thinks Nemes, and shifts up into fast time, freezing even the billowing clouds of orange flame that spread from where she stands in the heart of the explosion's flowering.

She jogs out through the semisolid wall of the shock wave and breaks into a run toward the girl and her friend. She will sever both their heads, keeping the man's as a memento after delivering the girl's.

Nemes is within a meter of the brat when the Shrike emerges from the cloud of steam that had been the river and blindsides her from the left. Her swinging arm misses the two human heads by centimeters as she and the Shrike roll away from the river, slicing up turf to bedrock and snapping off trees until they slam into another rock wall. The Shrike's carapace throws sparks as the huge jaws open, teeth closing on Nemes's throat.

'You've . . . got . . . to be . . . fucking . . . kidding,' she gasps behind the displacement mask. Being chewed to death by an obsolete time-shifter is not on her itinerary for today. Nemes makes a blade of her hand and drives it deep into the Shrike's thorax as the rows of teeth throw sparks and lightning from her shielded throat. Nemes grins as she feels the four fingers of her hand penetrate armor and carapace. She grabs a fistful of innards and jerks them out, hoping to remove whatever foul organs keep the beast alive but coming away with only a handful of razor-wire tendons and shards of carapace. But the Shrike staggers backward, four arms swinging like scythes. Its massive jaws are still working as if the creature cannot believe it is not chewing bits of its victim.

'Come on!' says Nemes, stepping toward the thing. 'Come on!' She wants to destroy it – her blood is up, as the humans used to say – but she is still calm enough to know that this is not her purpose. She has only to distract it or disable it to the point that she can decapitate the human child. Then the Shrike will be irrelevant forever. Perhaps Nemes and her kind will keep it in a zoo to hunt it when they are bored. 'Come on,' she taunts, taking another step forward.

The creature is hurt enough to drop out of fast time without dropping the displacement fields around it. Nemes could have destroyed it at her leisure except for the displacement field; if she walks around it now, it can shift up to fast time behind her. She follows it down to slow time, pleased to conserve energy.

'Jesus!' I cried, looking up from where I had thrown myself across Aenea. She was watching from the protective circle of my arm.

It was all happening at once. A. Bettik's medkit alarm was screeching, the air was as hot as a breath from a blastfurnace, the forest behind us exploded in flame and noise, splinters from trees exploded by superheated steam filled the air above us, the river erupted in a geyser of steam, and suddenly the Shrike and a chromed human shape were feinting and slashing not three meters from us.

Aenea ignored the carnage and crawled out from the shelter of my body, scrabbling across the muddy ground to get to A. Bettik. I slid along behind her, watching the chrome blurs surging and smashing into each other behind us. Static electricity whipped from the two forms and leaped to the rocks and savaged ground.

'CPR!' cried the girl, and began administering to A. Bettik. I jumped to the other side and read the medkit telltales. He was not breathing. His heart had stopped half a minute before. Too much blood loss.

Something silver and sharp hurtled toward Aenea's back. I moved to pull her down, but before I could reach her, another metallic shape intercepted the first one and the air exploded with the sound of metal striking metal. 'Let me!' I shouted, pulling her around the android's body, trying to keep her behind me while picking up the rhythm of resuscitation. The medkit lights showed that blood was being pumped to his brain by our efforts. His lungs were receiving and expelling air, although not without our help. I continued the motion, watching over my shoulder as two figures crashed, rolled, and collided with near-supersonic speed. The air stank of ozone. Embers from the burning forest drifted around us and steam clouds billowed and hissed.

'Next . . . year . . .' shouted Aenea above the din, her teeth chattering despite the sweat-dripping heat, 'we . . . take . . . our vacation . . . somewhere else.'

I lifted my head to stare, thinking that she had gone insane. Her eyes were bright but not totally crazy. That was my diagnosis. The medkit chirped alarm, and I continued my ministrations.

Behind us there was a sudden implosion, quite audible over the crackling of flames, hissing of steam, and clashing of metal surfaces. I turned to look over my shoulder, never ceasing the CPR motions on A. Bettik.

The air shimmered, and a single chrome figure stood where the two forms had been warring. Then the metallic surface rippled and disappeared. The woman from the rock was standing there. Her hair was not mussed and she showed no signs of exertion.

'Now,' said the woman, 'where were we?' She came forward at an easy walk.

In those last seconds of the battle, it was not easy getting the Sphinx trap in place. Nemes is using all her energy fighting off the Shrike's whirring blades. It is like fighting several whirring propellers at once, she thinks. She has been on worlds with propeller-driven aircraft. Two centuries earlier she had killed the Hegemony Consul on such a world.

Now she bats away whirling arms, never removing her gaze from the glaring red eyes. *Your time has passed*, she thinks at the Shrike as their displacement-shrouded arms and legs slash and counterslash like invisible

411

blades. Reaching through the thing's less-focused field, she seizes a joint on its upper arm and rips thorns and blades away. That arm falls away, but five scalpels on the lower hand dig at her abdomen, trying to disembowel her through the field.

'Uh-uh,' she says, kicking the thing's right leg out from under it for a split second. 'Not so fast.'

The Shrike staggers, and in that instant of vulnerability she slips the Sphinx card from her wristband, slides it through a five-nanosecond gap in her displacement field squarely into the palm of her hand, and slaps it onto a spike rising from the Shrike's banded neck.

'That's all,' cries Nemes as she jumps back, shifts to fast time to bat away the Shrike's attempt to remove the card, and activates it by thinking of a red circle.

She leaps back farther as the hyperentropic field hums into existence, propelling the flailing monster five minutes into the future. It has no way back while the field exists.

Rhadamnth Nemes shifts down from fast time and drops the field. The breeze – superheated and ember laden as it is – feels delightfully cool to her. 'Now,' she says, enjoying the look in the two pairs of human eyes, 'where were we?'

'Do it!' shouts Corporal Kee.

'I can't,' says de Soya at the controls. His finger is in the tactical omnigrip. 'Groundwater. Steam explosion. It would kill them all.' *Raphael*'s boards show every erg of energy diverted, but it does no good.

Kee flips down his microphone bead, throws the switch to all channels, and begins broadcasting on tightbeam, making sure that the reticule is on the man and girl, not on the advancing woman.

'That won't do any good,' says de Soya. He has never been so frustrated in his life.

'Rocks,' Kee is shouting into his bead mike. 'Rocks!'

I was standing, pushing Aenea behind and wishing that I had the pistol, the flashlight laser, anything, as the woman approached. The plasma rifle was still in the watertight shoulder bag near the riverbank just two meters away. All I had to do was jump, unseal the bag, lever off the safety, snap open the folding stock, aim, and fire. I did not think that the smiling woman would give me the time. Nor did I believe that Aenea would be alive when I turned to fire.

At that moment the idiot comlog bracelet on my wrist started vibrating its inner lining against my skin like one of those antique soundless alarm watches. I ignored it. The comlog began pricking tiny needles into my wrist. I raised the stupid thing to my ear. It whispered at me, 'Get to the rocks. Take the girl and get to the lava rocks.'

Nothing made sense. I looked down at A. Bettik, the telltales shifting from green through amber as I watched, and began backing away from the smiling woman, keeping my body between her and Aenea as we stumbled backward.

'Now, now,' said the woman. 'That's not very nice. Aenea, if you come here, your boyfriend can live. Your phony blue man can live also, if your boyfriend can keep him alive.'

I glanced down to see Aenea's face, afraid that she would accept the offer. She clung to my arm. Her eyes showed a terrible intensity, but still no fear. 'It'll be all right, kiddo,' I whispered, still moving to our left. Behind us was the river. Five meters to our left and the lava rocks began.

The woman moved right, blocking our movement. 'This is taking too long,' she said softly. 'I only have another four minutes. Oodles and oodles of time. An eternity of time.'

'Come on.' I grabbed Aenea's wrist and ran for the rocks. I had no plan. I had only the nonsensical words whispered in a voice that was not the comlog's.

We never reached the lava rocks. There was a blast of heated air and the chrome shape of the woman was ahead of us, standing three meters above us on the black rock face. 'Bye, bye, Raul Endymion,' the chrome mask said. The shimmering metal arm rose.

The blast of heat burned off my eyebrows, set fire to my shirt, and threw the girl and me backward through the air. We hit hard and rolled away from the unspeakable heat. Aenea's hair was smoldering, and I batted my fore-arms against her, trying to keep her hair from bursting into flame. A. Bettik's medkit was screeching again, but the avalanche roar of superheated air behind us drowned the noise. I saw that my shirtsleeve was smoking, and I ripped it away before it ignited. Aenea and I turned our backs to the heat and crawled and scrabbled away as quickly as we could. It was like being on the lip of a volcano.

We grabbed A. Bettik's body and pulled him to the riverbank, not hesitat-ing a second before sliding into the steaming current. I struggled to keep the unconscious android's head above water while Aenea fought to keep both of us from sliding away on the current. Just above the surface of the water, where our faces were pressed against the wet mud of the riverbank, the air was almost cool enough to breathe.

Feeling the blisters forming on my forehead, not yet knowing that my eyebrows and swaths of hair were missing, I raised my head to the edge of the riverbank and peered over.

The chromed figure stood in the center of a three-meter circle of orange light that stretched up to the heavens and disappeared only when it narrowed to an infinite point hundreds of kilometers above. The air rippled and roiled where the beam of almost solid energy ripped through the atmosphere.

The metallic woman-shape tried to move toward us, but the high-energy lance seemed to exert too much pressure. Still she stood, the chrome field around her turning red, then green, then a blinding white. But still she stood, her fist raised and shaking at the sky. Beneath her feet the lava rock boiled, turned red and ran downhill in great molten rivers. Some ran into the river not ten meters downstream from us, and the steam clouds billowed up with a loud hissing. At that moment I admit that I considered becoming religious for the first time in my life.

The chrome shape seemed to see the danger seconds before it was too late. It disappeared, reappeared as a blur – fist shaking toward the sky – disappeared again, reappeared a final time, and then sank into the lava under its feet where solid rock had been an instant earlier.

The beam stayed on for another full minute. I could not look directly at it any longer, and the heat was burning away the skin of my cheeks. I pressed my face against the cool mud again and held A. Bettik and the girl against the bank even as the current tried to pull us downstream into the steam and lava.

I looked up one final time, saw the chromed fist sinking beneath the surface of the lava, and then the field seemed to shift down in colors for a moment before it winked off. The lava began to cool at once. By the time I had pulled Aenea and A. Bettik out of the water and we had begun CPR again, the rock was solidifying with only rivulets and pseudo-pods of lava still flowing. Bits of cooling rock flaked off and rose in the heated air, joining the embers from the forest fire still raging behind us. There was no sign of the chrome woman.

Amazingly, the medkit was still functioning. Lights went from red to amber as we kept blood moving to A. Bettik's brain and limbs and breathed life back into him. The tourniquet sleeve was tight. When he seemed to be holding his own, I looked up at the girl crouched across from me. 'What next?' I said.

There was a soft implosion of air behind us, and I turned in time to see the Shrike flash into existence.

'Jesus wept,' I said softly.

Aenea was shaking her head. I could see the heat blisters on her lips and forehead. Strands of her hair had burned away, and her shirt was a sooty mess. Other than that, she seemed all right. 'No,' she said. 'It's all right.'

I had stood up and was fumbling in the shoulder bag for the plasma rifle. No use. It had been too close to the beam of energy. The trigger guard was half-melted and plastic elements in the folded stock had fused with the metal barrel. It was a miracle that the plasma cartridges had not gone off and blasted us to vapor. I dropped the bag and faced the Shrike with my fists balled. Let it come through me, goddammit.

'It's all right,' Aenea said again, pulling me back. 'It won't do anything. It's all right.'

We crouched next to A. Bettik. The android's eyelashes were fluttering. 'Did I miss anything?' he whispered hoarsely.

We did not laugh. Aenea touched the blue man's cheek and looked at me. The Shrike stayed where it had first appeared, burning embers drifting by its red eyes and soot settling on its carapace.

A. Bettik closed his eyes and the telltales began to blink again. 'We need to get him serious help,' I whispered to Aenea, 'or we're going to lose him.'

She nodded. I thought she had whispered something back, but it was not her voice speaking.

I lifted my left arm, ignoring the tattered shirt and rising red welts there. All the hair had been burned off my forearm.

We both listened. The comlog was speaking in a familiar man's voice.

FIFTY-SIX

Father de Soya is surprised when they finally respond on the common band. He had not thought their archaic comlog capable of transmitting on the tightbeam the ship was holding on them. There is even a visual display – the fuzzy holographic image of two burned and sooty faces float above the main monitor.

Corporal Kee looks at de Soya. 'Well I'll be damned, Father.'

'Me too,' says de Soya. To the waiting faces he says, 'I am Father Captain de Soya on the Pax ship *Raphael*'s . . .'

'I remember you,' says the girl. De Soya realizes that the ship is transmitting holo images and that they can see him – no doubt a miniature ghostly face above a Roman collar, all floating above the comlog on the man's wrist.

'I remember you, too,' is all de Soya can think to say. It has been a long search. He looks at the dark eyes and pale skin beneath the soot and superficial burns. So close . . .

The image of Raul Endymion speaks. 'Who was that? *What* was that?'

Father Captain de Soya shakes his head. 'I don't know. Her name was Rhadamnth Nemes. She was assigned to us just a few days ago. She said that she was part of a new Legion they are training—' He stops. All of this is classified. He is speaking to the enemy. De Soya looks at Corporal Kee. In the other man's slight smile, he sees their situation. They are condemned men anyway. 'She said she was part of a new Legion of Pax warriors,' he continues, 'but I don't think that was the truth. I don't think she was human.'

'Amen,' says the image of Raul Endymion. The face looks away from the comlog for a minute and then returns. 'Our friend is dying, Father Captain de Soya. Can you do anything to help?'

The priest-captain shakes his head. 'We can't get to you. The Nemes creature took our dropship and overrode the remote autopilot. We can't even get the beacon to respond. But if you can get to it, it has an auto-surgeon.'

'Where is it?' says the girl.

Corporal Kee leans into the imaging field. 'Our radar shows it to be about a klick and a half southeast of you,' he says. 'In the hills. It has some camouflage crap on it, but you'll be able to find it. We'll lead you there.'

Raul Endymion says, 'It was *your* voice on the comlog. Telling us to get to the rocks.'

'Well, yeah,' says Kee. 'We had everything diverted into the ship's tactical fire-control system – that was about eighty gigawatts that we could deliver through atmosphere – but the groundwater would have turned to steam and killed all of you. The rocks seemed the best bet.'

'She beat us there,' says Raul with a crooked smile.

'That was the idea,' responds Corporal Kee.

'Thank you,' says Aenea.

Kee nods, embarrassed, and ducks out of the imaging field. 'As the good corporal said,' continues Father Captain de Soya, 'we will help guide you to the dropship.'

'Why?' says the blurred image of Raul. 'And why did you kill your own creature?'

De Soya shakes his head. 'She was not my creature.'

'The Church's, then,' insists Raul. 'Why?'

'I hope she was not the Church's creature,' de Soya says quietly. 'If she was, then my Church has become the monster.'

There is a silence broken only by the hiss of the tightbeam. 'You'd better get moving,' de Soya says at last. 'It is getting dark.'

Both faces in the holo look around them almost comically, as if they have forgotten their surroundings. 'Yeah,' says Raul, 'and your lance or CPB or whatever it was melted my handlamp to slag.'

'I could light your way,' says de Soya without smiling, 'but it would mean activating the main weapons system again.'

'Never mind,' says Raul. 'We'll manage. I'm shutting down the imager, but I'll keep the audio channel open until we get to the dropship.'

FIFTY-SEVEN

It took us more than two hours to go the kilometer and a half. The lava hills were *very* rough. It would have been easy to break an ankle on those rills and fissures without the added weight of A. Bettik on my back. It was very dark – clouds had moved in to occlude the stars – and I don't think we would have made it at all that night if Aenea hadn't found the flashlight laser lying in the grass when we were packing up to move out.

'How the hell did that get there?' I said. The last I remembered of the little laser, I had been ready to trigger it at the hell-woman's eyes. Then it had been gone. *Well*, I thought, *to hell with it*. It had been a day for mysteries. We left with one last mystery behind us – the silent form of the Shrike, still frozen where it had reappeared. It did not attempt to follow us.

With Aenea leading the way with the flashlight set at widebeam, we struggled and scrabbled our way across the black rock and shifting ash back into the hills. We would have made it in half the time if A. Bettik had not required constant treatment.

The medkit had used up its modest share of antibiotics, stimulants, painkillers, plasma, and IV drip. A. Bettik was alive because of the kit's work, but it was still a close thing. He had simply lost too much blood in the river; the tourniquet had made a difference, but the belt had not been tight enough to staunch all the bleeding. We administered CPR when we had to, just to keep the blood flowing to his brain if nothing else, and stopped when the medkit alarms started squawking. The comlog kept us on track in the Pax corporal's voice, and I decided that even if this was all a trick to capture Aenea, we owed those two men up there a hell of a debt of gratitude. And all the time we were scrambling through the darkness, Aenea's flashlight beam playing over black lava and the skeletons of dead trees, I expected that hell-woman's chromed hand to slash up through the rock and grab me by the ankle.

We found the dropship right where they said it would be. Aenea started up the metal ladder, but I grabbed her tattered pant leg and made her come down.

'I don't want you in the ship, kiddo,' I said. 'We only have their word that they can't fly it by remote. If you get in and they can fly it from up there, they've got you.'

She sagged against the ladder. I had never seen her look so exhausted. 'I trust them,' she said. 'They said—'

418

'Yeah, but they can't grab you if you're not in there. You stay here while I carry A. Bettik up and see if there's an autosurgeon.'

As I went up the ladder, I had a stomach-twisting thought. What if the metal door above me was locked and the keys were in the hell-woman's jumper pocket?

There was a lighted diskey pad. 'Six-nine-nine-two,' said Corporal Kee's voice from the comlog.

I tapped it in and the outer air-lock door slid open. The autosurgeon was in there and it came alive with a touch. I gently lowered my blue friend into the cushioned enclosure – taking great pains not to hit the raw stump of his arm – made sure that the diagnostic patches and pressure cuffs were placing themselves properly, and then closed the lid. It felt too much like closing a coffin.

The readouts were not promising, but the surgeon went to work. I watched the monitor for a moment until I realized that my eyes were blurring and that I was dozing on my feet. Rubbing my cheeks, I went back to the open air lock.

'You can stand on the ladder, kiddo. If the snip starts to take off, jump.'

Aenea stepped up onto the ladder and winked off the flashlight laser. Our light came from the glowing autosurgeon and from some of the console lights. 'Then what?' said Aenea. 'I jump off and the ship takes off with you and A. Bettik. Then what do I do?'

'Head for the next farcaster portal,' I said.

The comlog said, 'We don't blame you for being suspicious.' It spoke in Father Captain de Soya's voice.

Sitting in the open hatch, listening to the breeze rustle the broken branches tossed atop the aircraft-sized lifting body, I said, 'Why this change of heart and program, Father Captain? You came to get Aenea. Why the turnabout?' I remembered the chase through Parvati System, his order to fire on us at Renaissance Vector.

Instead of answering, the priest-captain's voice said, 'I have your hawking mat, Raul Endymion.'

'Yeah?' I said tiredly. I tried to remember where I had seen it last. Flying toward the platform station on Mare Infinitus. 'Small universe,' I said as if it did not matter. Inwardly, I would have given anything to have that little flying carpet right now. Aenea clung to the ladder and listened. From time to time, we both glanced over to make sure the autosurgeon had not given up.

'Yes,' said the voice of Father Captain de Soya, 'and I have begun to understand a little of how you think, my friends. Perhaps someday you will understand how I think.'

'Perhaps,' I said. I did not know it then, but that would be literally true someday.

His voice became businesslike, almost brusque. 'We believe that Corporal Nemes defeated the remote autopilot with some program override, but we won't try to convince you of that. Feel free to use the dropship to continue your voyage without fear of our trying to capture Aenea.'

'How do we do that?' I said. The burns were beginning to hurt. In a minute I would find the energy to go through the bins above the auto-surgeon and find out if the ship had its own medkit. I was sure it would.

'We will leave the system,' said Father Captain de Soya.

I perked up. 'How can we be sure of that?'

The comlog chuckled. 'A ship climbing out of a planet's gravity well on fusion power is rather obvious,' he said. 'Our telescope shows that you have only scattered clouds above you at the moment. You will see us.'

'See you leaving near orbit,' I said. 'How can we know you've translated out of system?'

Aenea pulled my wrist down and spoke into the comlog. 'Father? Where are you going?'

There was a hiss of silence. 'Back to Pacem,' de Soya said eventually. 'We have one of the three fastest ships in the universe, and my corporal friend and I have each silently considered heading . . . elsewhere . . . but when it comes down to it, we are both soldiers. In the Pax Fleet and in the Army of Christ. We will return to Pacem and answer questions . . . face whatever we must face.'

Even on Hyperion the Holy Office of the Inquisition had cast its cold shadow. I shivered, and it was not just the cold wind from the ash heap of the Worldtree that made me cold.

'Besides,' continued de Soya, 'we have a third comrade here who did not come through resurrection successfully. We must return to Pacem for medical care.'

I looked at the humming autosurgeon and – for the first time that endless day – believed that the priest above us was not an enemy.

'Father de Soya,' said Aenea, still holding my hand so that the comlog was near her, 'what will they do to you? To all of you?'

Again came the sound of a chuckle above the static. 'If we're lucky, they will execute us and then excommunicate us. If unlucky, they will reverse the order of those two events.'

I could see that Aenea was not amused. 'Father Captain de Soya . . . Corporal Kee . . . come down and join us. Send the ship back with your friend, and join us to go through the next portal.'

This time the silence stretched long enough that I feared the tightbeam connection had broken. Then came de Soya's soft voice. 'I am tempted, my young friend. Both of us are tempted. I would love to travel by farcaster someday, and even more, I would love to get to know you. But we are faithful servants of the Church, my dear, and our duties are clear. It is my hope that this . . . aberration . . . that was Corporal Nemes was a mistake. We must return if we are ever to know.'

Suddenly there was a burst of light. I leaned out of the air lock, and we both watched the blue-white fusion tail cross between the scattered clouds.

'Besides that,' came de Soya's voice, strained now as if under a g-load, 'we really do not have any way down to you without the dropship. The Nemes person slashed the troopers' combat suits, so even that desperate attempt is not an option.'

Aenea and I were both sitting on the edge of the open air lock now, watching the fusion tail grow longer and brighter. It seemed a lifetime since we had flown in our own ship. A thought struck me like a blow to the stomach, and I lifted the comlog. 'Father Captain, is this . . . Nemes . . . dead? I mean, we saw her buried in molten lava . . . but could she be burrowing out even as we speak?'

'We have no idea,' said Father Captain de Soya over the tightbeam hiss. 'My recommendation would be to get out of there as soon as possible. The dropship is our parting gift to you. Wear it in good health.'

I looked out at the black lava landscape for a minute. Every time the wind rustled dead branches or scraped ash on ash, I was sure it was the hell-woman gliding toward us.

'Aenea,' came the priest-captain's voice.

'Yes, Father Captain?'

'We're going to shut off the tightbeam in a second . . . we'll be passing out of line-of-sight anyway . . . but I have to tell you one thing.'

'What's that, Father?'

'My child, if they order me back to find you . . . not to hurt you, but to find you . . . well, I am an obedient servant of the Church and a Pax Fleet officer . . .'

'I understand, Father,' said Aenea. Her eyes were still on the sky where the fusion tail was fading near the eastern horizon. 'Good-bye, father. Good-bye, Corporal Kee. Thank you.'

'Good-bye, my daughter,' said Father Captain de Soya. 'God bless you.' We could both hear the sound of a benediction. Then the tightbeam snapped off and there was only silence.

'Come on in,' I said to Aenea. 'We're leaving. Now.'

Closing the inner and outer air-lock doors was a simple enough task. We checked on the autosurgeon a final time – all of the lights were amber but steady – and then strapped ourselves into the heavy acceleration couches. There were shields to cover the windscreen, but they were raised, and we could see across the dark lava fields. A few stars were visible in the east.

'Okay,' I said, looking at the myriad switches, diskeys, touchplates, holopads, monitors, flatscreens, buttons, and gewgaws. There was a low console between us and two omnicontrollers there, each with finger insets and more diskey patterns. I could see half a dozen places where one could jack in directly. 'Okay,' I said again, looking at the pale girl dwarfed by her padded chair, 'any ideas?'

'Get out and walk?' she said.

I sighed. 'That might be the best plan except for—' I jerked my thumb back toward the humming autosurgeon.

'I know,' said Aenea. She sagged in the heavy straps. 'I was joking.'

I touched her hand on the console. As always, there was a jolt of electricity there – a sort of physical *déjà vu*. Pulling my hand away, I said, 'Goddammit, the more advanced a technology is supposed to be, the simpler it's supposed to be. This looks like something out of an eighteenth-century Old Earth fighter-plane cockpit.'

'It's built for professionals to fly,' said Aenea. 'We just need a professional pilot.'

'You have one,' chirped the comlog. It was speaking in its own voice.

'You know how to fly a ship?' I said suspiciously.

'In essence, I *am* a ship,' the comlog said primly. The clasp panel clicked open. 'Please connect the red filament jack to any red interface port.'

I connected it to the console. Immediately the panel came alive, monitors glowed, instruments checked in, the dropship's ventilators hummed, and the omnicontroller twitched. A flatscreen monitor in the center of the dash glowed yellow, and the comlog's voice said, 'Where do you wish to go, M. Endymion? M. Aenea?'

The girl spoke first. 'The next farcaster,' she said softly. 'The last farcaster.'

FIFTY-EIGHT

It was daylight on the other side. We hovered above the stream and moved forward slowly. The comlog had shown us how to use the controllers while it ran all the rest of the ship's systems and kept us from making stupid mistakes. Aenea and I glanced at each other and inched the dropship over the treetops. Unless the hell-woman could transit a farcaster portal, we were safe.

It felt strange making our last farcaster shift without the raft, but the raft would not have worked here anyway. The River Tethys had become little more than a trickling stream between deep banks – the creek could not have been more than eight or ten centimeters deep and only three or four meters wide. It meandered through heavily wooded countryside. The trees were strange, but familiar at the same time . . . mostly deciduous like champa or weirwood, but broadleafed and expansive like halfoak. The leaves were bright yellow and brilliant red, and carpets of them lined the banks of the streambed.

The sky was a pleasant blue – not as deep blue as Hyperion's, but deeper than most earthlike worlds we had seen on this trip. The sun was large and bright but not overpowering. Sunlight came through the windshield and fell across our laps.

'I wonder what it's like out there,' I said.

The comlog . . . ship . . . whatever it was now, must have thought I was talking to it. The central monitor pulsed and data began to flow down it.

Atmosphere: 0.77 N_2
0.21 O_2
0.009 Ar
0.0003 CO_2
variable H_2O (– 0.01)
Surface pressure: 0.986 bar
Magnetic field: 0.318 gauss
Mass: 5.976 x 10^{24} kg
Escape velocity: 11.2 km/s
Surface gravity: 980 km/s
Tilt angle of magnetic axis: 11.5^0
Dipole moment: 7.9 x 10^{25} gauss/cm^3

'That's strange,' said the ship. 'An improbable coincidence.'

'What?' I said, already knowing.

'These planetary data match almost perfectly with my database for Old Earth,' said the ship, 'It is very unusual for any world to match so closely with—'

'Stop!' screamed Aenea, pointing out the windscreen. 'Land! Please, now.'

I would have smashed into trees on the way down, but the ship took over, found us a flat, rocky spot within twenty meters of the tree-lined streambed, and set us down without a bump. Aenea was punching the air-lock combination while I was still staring out the windscreen at the flat roof of the house beyond the trees.

She was down the ladder before I could talk to her. I paused to check the autosurgeon, was pleased to see several of the lights switched to green, and said to the ship, 'Watch over him. Keep everything ready for a quick getaway.'

'I shall, M. Endymion.'

We came at the house from downstream and across the stream from it. The building is hard to describe, but I will try.

The house itself was built out over a modest waterfall that spilled only three or four meters to a small natural pool beneath. Yellow leaves floated in the pool before being whisked away downstream on the quickening current. The most noticeable features of the house were the thin roofs and rectangular terraces that seemed to hang out over the stream and waterfall as if defying gravity. The house appeared to be built of stone and glass, concrete and some steel. To the left of the slabs of terrace, a stone wall rose three floors with a glass-cornered window rising in it almost the entire height. The metal framework around those windows was painted a gentle orange.

'Cantilevered,' said Aenea.

'What?'

'That's what the architect calls those overhanging terraces,' she said. 'Cantilevered. They echo the limestone ledges that have been here for millions of years.'

I paused in our walk to look at her. The dropship was out of sight beyond the trees behind us. 'This is your house,' I said. 'The one you dreamed of before you were born.'

'Yes.' Her lips were trembling slightly. 'I even know its name now, Raul. Fallingwater.'

I nodded and sniffed the air. The scent was rich with decaying leaves, living plants, rich soil, water, and a certain tang to the air. It was very different from Hyperion's air, but it somehow smelled like home. 'Old Earth,' I whispered. 'Can it be?'

'Just . . . Earth,' said Aenea. She touched my hand. 'Let's go in.'

We crossed the stream on a small bridge upstream from the house, crunched our way up a gravel drive, and entered through a loggia and narrow entranceway. It was like coming into a comfortable cave.

Pausing in the large living room, we called, but no one answered. Aenea walked across the open space as if in a trance, running her fingers over wood and stone surfaces, exclaiming at small discoveries.

The floor was carpeted in places, bare stone in others. Books filled low shelves in at least one alcove, but I did not take time to check the titles. Metal shelves ran under the low ceiling, but these were empty – perhaps just a design element. The far wall was taken up by a huge fireplace. The hearth was of rough stone – perhaps the top of the boulder upon which the house seemed to balance – and ran out two meters or so from the fireplace.

A large fire was crackling in the fireplace, despite the warmth of the sunny autumn day. I called again, but the silence was heavy. 'They were expecting us,' I said, making a weak joke. The only weapon I had now was the flashlight laser in my pocket.

'Yes, they were,' said Aenea. She went over to the left of the fireplace and set her small hands on a metal sphere that was set into its own hemispherical niche in the stone wall. The sphere was a meter and a half or so in diameter and was painted a rich, rusty red.

'The architect meant this as a kettle to heat wine in,' Aenea said softly. 'It was only used once . . . and the wine was heated in the kitchen and brought here. It's too big. And the paint is probably toxic.'

'This is the architect you're looking for?' I said. 'The one you plan to study with?'

'Yes.'

'I thought he was a genius. Why would he make a wine kettle too big and too toxic to use?'

Aenea turned and smiled. No – she grinned. 'Geniuses screw up, Raul. Look at our trip if you need proof. Come on, let's look around.'

The terraces were lovely, the view from above the little waterfall pleasant. Inside, the ceilings and overhangs were low, but that just gave one more of a sense of peering out of a cave into the green world of the forest through all that glass. In the living room again, a glass-and-metal hatchway folded back to steps – supported by bars from the floor above – which led down only to a larger cement platform over a pool in the stream above the waterfall.

'The plunge,' said Aenea, as if coming home to something very familiar.

'What's it for?' I said, peering around.

'Nothing practical,' said Aenea. 'But the architect considered it – and I quote – "absolutely necessary from every standpoint".'

I touched her shoulder. She turned and smiled at me, not mechanically or dreamily, but with an almost radiant vitality.

'Where are we, Aenea?'

'Fallingwater,' she said. 'Bear Run. In western Pennsylvania.'

'Is that a nation?' I said.

'Province,' said Aenea. 'State, I mean. In the former United States of America. North American continent. Planet Earth.'

'Earth,' I repeated. I looked around. 'Where is everybody? Where's your architect?'

The girl shook her head. 'I don't know. We should know soon.'

'How long are we going to stay here, kiddo?' I had thoughts of laying in food, weapons, and other equipment while A. Bettik recovered and before we headed off again.

'A few years,' said Aenea. 'No more than six or seven, I think.'

'*Years?*' I had stopped on the upper terrace where we had stepped out at the head of the flight of stairs. 'Years?'

'I have to study under this man, Raul. I have to learn something.'

'About architecture?'

'Yes, and about myself.'

'And what will I be doing while you're . . . learning about yourself?'

Instead of making a joke, Aenea nodded seriously. 'I know. It doesn't seem fair. But there will be a few things for you to do while I'm . . . growing up.'

I waited.

'The Earth needs to be explored,' she said. 'My mother and father visited here. It was Mother's idea that the . . . lions and tigers and bears – the forces that stole the Earth away before the TechnoCore could destroy it – it was Mother's idea that they were running experiments here.'

'Experiments?' I said. 'What kind of experiments?'

'Experiments in genius, mostly,' said Aenea. 'Although perhaps experiments in humanity would be a better phrase.'

'Explain.'

Aenea gestured toward the house around us. 'This place was completed in 1937.'

'AD,' I said.

'Yes. I'm sure it was destroyed in the twenty-first century North American class riots, if not before. Whoever brought the Earth here rebuilt it somehow. Just as they rebuilt nineteenth-century Rome for my father.'

'Rome?' I felt that I was standing around with my thumb in my ear repeating everything the child said. It was one of those days.

'The Rome where John Keats spent his last days,' said Aenea. 'But that's another story.'

'Yeah,' I said, 'I read it in your Uncle Martin's *Cantos*. And I didn't understand it then, either.'

Aenea made the gesture with her hands that I was growing used to. 'I don't understand it, Raul. But whoever brought the Earth here brings back people as well as old cities and buildings. They create . . . *dynamics*.'

'Through resurrection?' My voice was doubtful.

'No . . . more like . . . well, my father was a cybrid. His persona resided in an AI matrix, his body was human.'

'But you're not a cybrid.'

Aenea shook her head. 'You know I'm not.' She led me farther out on the terrace. Below us, the stream rushed over the little waterfall. 'There will be other things for you to do while I'm . . . in school.'

'Such as?'

'Besides exploring all of the Earth and figuring out just what these . . . entities . . . are up to here, you'll need to leave before I do and go back to fetch our ship.'

'Our ship?' I resolved to pull my metaphorical thumb out of my ear. 'You mean travel by farcaster to get the Consul's ship.'

'Yep.'

'And bring it here?'

She shook her head. 'That would take a few centuries. We'll agree to meet somewhere in the former Web.'

I rubbed my cheek, feeling the whiskers scratch. 'Anything else? Any other little ten-year odysseys to keep me occupied?'

'Just the trip to the Outback to see the Ousters,' she said. 'But I'll be going with you on that trip.'

'Good,' I said. 'I hope that's all the adventures that we'll have waiting for us. I'm not as young as I used to be, you know.'

I was trying to be light about all this, but Aenea's eyes were deep and serious. She put her fingers in my palm. 'No, Raul,' she said. 'That's just the beginning.'

The comlog beeped and tapped. 'What?' I said with a spasm of concern about A. Bettik.

'I've just received coordinates on the common band,' came the comlog/ship's voice. It sounded puzzled.

'Any voice or visual transmissions?' I said.

'No, just travel coordinates and optimum cruise altitudes. It's a flight plan.'

'To where?' I said.

'A point on this continent some three thousand kilometers to the southwest of our current position,' said the ship.

I looked at Aenea. She shook her head.

'No idea?' I said.

'An idea,' she said. 'Not a certainty. Let's go be surprised.'

Her small hand was still in mine. I did not release it as we walked back through the yellow leaves and morning sunlight to the waiting dropship.

FIFTY-NINE

I once said to you that you were reading this for the wrong reason. What I should have said was that I was writing this for the wrong reason.

I have filled these seamless days and nights and smooth pages of microvellum with memories of Aenea, of Aenea as a child, with not one word of her life as the messiah whom you must know and perhaps whom you mistakenly worship. But I have not written these pages for you, I discover, nor have I written them for myself. I have brought Aenea the child alive in my writing because I want Aenea the woman to be alive – despite logic, despite fact, despite all loss of hope.

Each morning – each self-programmed brightening of the lights, I should say – I awaken in this three-by-six-meter Schrödinger cat box and find myself amazed to be alive. There has been no scent of bitter almonds in the night.

Each morning I fight despair and terror by writing these memories on my test slate, stacking the microvellum pages as they accumulate. But the recycler in this little world is limited; it can produce only a dozen or so pages at a time. So as I finish each dozen or so pages of memory, I feed the oldest pages into the recycler to have them come out fresh and empty so as to have new pages upon which to write. It is the snake swallowing its own tail. It is insanity. Or the absolute essence of sanity.

It is possible that the chip in the text slate has the full memory of what I have written here . . . what I shall write in the coming days if fate grants me those days . . . but the truth is, I do not really care. Only the dozen pages of microvellum are of interest to me each day – pristine, empty pages in the morning, crowded, ink-splashed pages filled with my small and spidery script each evening.

Aenea comes alive for me then.

But last night – when the lights in my Schrödinger cat box were off and nothing separated me from the universe but the static-dynamic shell of frozen energy around me with its little vial of cyanide, its ticking timer, and its foolproof radiation detector – last night I heard Aenea calling my name. I sat up in the absolute blackness, too startled and hopeful even to command the lights on, certain that I was still dreaming, when I felt her fingers touch my cheek. They were her fingers. I knew them when she was a child. I kissed them when she was a woman. I touched them with my lips when they took her away for the final time.

Her fingers touched my cheek. Her breath was warm and sweet against my face. Her lips were warm against the corner of my mouth.

'We're leaving here, Raul, my darling,' she whispered in the darkness last night. 'Not soon, but as soon as you finish our tale. As soon as you remember it all and understand it all.'

I reached for her then, but her warmth was receding. When the lights came on, my egg-shaped world was empty.

I admit that I paced back and forth until the normal waking time arrived. My greatest fear these days or months has not been death – Aenea had taught me how to put death in perspective – but insanity. Madness would rob me of clarity, of memory . . . of Aenea.

Then I saw something that stopped me. The text slate was activated. The stylus was lying not in its usual place, but tucked behind the slate cover, much as Aenea had kept her pen folded away in her journal during our voyages after leaving Earth. My fingers shaking, I recycled yesterday's writings and activated the printer port.

Only one page emerged crowded with handwritten lines. It was Aenea's writing; I know it well.

This is a turning point for me. Either I am truly insane and none of this matters, or I am saved and everything matters very much.

I read this, as you do, with hope for my sanity and hope for salvation, not of my soul, but salvation of self in the renewed certainty of reunion – real reunion, physical reunion – with the one whom I remember and love above all others.

And this is the best reason to read.

SIXTY

Raul, consider this a postscript to the memories you wrote about today, and which I read tonight. Years ago, years ago . . . those last three hours of our first journey together, when you, my darling Raul, and dear sleeping A. Bettik and I flew the dropship southwest toward Taliesin West and my long apprenticeship there, I longed to tell you everything that day – the dreams that showed us being lovers of whom the poets would sing, visions of the great dangers that lay ahead, dreams of the discovery of friends, dreams of the deaths of friends, certainty of unspeakable sorrow to be borne, certainty of unimaginable triumphs still unborn.

I said nothing.

Do you remember? We dozed during our flight. How strange life is that way . . . our last few hours alone together, this ending to one of the most intimate periods of our life together, the end of my childhood and the beginning of our time as equals, and we spent most of our last minutes sleeping. In separate couches. Life is brutal that way . . . the loss of irrecoverable moments amid trivia and distraction.

But we were tired. It had been a rough few days.

As the dropship was beginning to descend over the southwestern desert toward Taliesin West and my new life, I took a page from my soiled journal – it had survived the water and flames when most of my clothing had not – and wrote a hasty note to you. You were sleeping. Your face was against the vinyl of the acceleration chair and you were drooling slightly. Your eyelashes were burned away, as was a patch of hair at the crown of your head, and the effect was to make you look comical – a clown surprised in the act of sleeping. (We later talked of clowns, remember, Raul? During our Ouster odyssey. You had seen clowns at a circus in Port Romance as a teenager; I had seen clowns in Jacktown during the annual First Settlers Fair.)

The burns and burn ointment we had liberally applied to your cheeks and temples, eyes and upper lip, looked for all the world like clown makeup – red and white. You were beautiful. I loved you then. I loved you backward and forward in time. I loved you beyond boundaries of time and space.

I wrote my note hurriedly, tucked it in what was left of the pocket on your ruined shirt, and kissed you ever so softly on the corner of your mouth, in the one spot that was not burned or salved. You stirred but did not wake. You did not mention the note the next day – nor ever again – and I always wondered if you found it, or if it fell out of the pocket, or was tossed away unread when you threw away the shirt at Taliesin.

The words were my father's. He wrote them centuries ago. Then he died, was reborn – after a fashion – as a cybrid persona, and died again as a man. But still he lived in essence, his persona roving through metaspace, and eventually leaving Hyperion with the Consul, in the DNA coils of the ship's AI. His final spoken words to my mother will never be known, despite Uncle Martin's creative license in the *Cantos*. But these words were discovered in my mother's text stylus when she awoke that morning after he left forever, and she kept the original printout for the rest of her life. I know . . . I used to sneak into her room in Jacktown on Hyperion and read the hurried handwriting on that yellowed slip of vellum, at least once a week from the time I was two.

These were the words that I gave to you with a sleeping kiss that last hour of our last day of our first voyage, my darling Raul. These are the words I leave tonight with a waking kiss. These are the words I will claim from you when I return next, when the tale is complete and our final voyage begins.

A thing of beauty is a joy for ever:
Its loveliness increases; it will never
Pass into nothingness; but still will keep
A bower quiet for us, and a sleep
Full of sweet dreams, and health, and quiet breathing.

And so, Raul Endymion, until we meet again on your pages, in wild ecstasy, I bid you *adieu*—

Thou foster-child of silence and slow time,
Sylvan historian, who canst thus express
A flowery tale more sweetly than our rhyme:
What leaf-fringed legend haunts about thy shape
Of deities or mortals, or of both,
In Tempe or the tales of Arcady?
What men or gods are these? What maidens loth?
What mad pursuit? What struggle to escape?
What pipes and timbrels? What wild ecstasy?

For now, my love, I wish you sweet dreams, and health, and quiet breathing.

THE RISE
OF
ENDYMION

This book is for **Jack Vance**, our finest creator of worlds.

It is also dedicated to the memory of **Dr Carl Sagan**, scientist, author, and teacher, who articulated the noblest dreams of humankind.

ACKNOWLEDGMENTS

The author would like to thank the following people: Kevin Kelly for his account of the evolution of a-life from 80-byte critters in his book *Out of Control*; Jean-Daniel Breque and Monique Labailly for their personal guided tour through the catacombs of Paris; Jeff Orr, cybercowboy *extraordinaire*, for boldly going into cyberspace to retrieve the forty-some pages of this tale kidnapped by the TechnoCore, and my editor, Tom Dupree, for his patience, enthusiasm, and shared good taste for loving *Mystery Science Theater 3000*.

We are not stuff that abides, but patterns that perpetuate themselves.
— Norbert Wiener,
*Cybernetics, or Control and
Communication in the Animal
and the Machine*

The universal nature out of the universal substance, as if it were wax, now moulds the figure of a horse, and when it has broken this up, it uses the material for a tree, next for a man, next for something else; and each of these things subsists for a very short time. But it is no hardship for the vessel to be broken up, just as there was none in its being fastened together.
— Marcus Aurelius,
Meditations

But here is the finger of God, a flash of the will that can,
    Existent behind all laws, that made them and, lo, they are!
And I know not if, save in this, such gift be allowed to man,
    That out of three sounds he frame, not a fourth sound, but a star.
— Robert Browning,
Abt Vogler

If what I have said should not be plain enough, as I fear it may not be, I will but [sic] you in the place where I began in this series of thoughts – I mean, I began by seeing how man was formed by circumstances – and what are circumstances? – but touchstones of his heart—? and what are touchstones? – but proovings [sic] of his hearrt [sic]? – and what are the proovings [sic] of his heart but fortifiers or alterers of his nature? and what is his altered nature but his soul? – and what was his soul before it came into the world and had These provings and alterations and perfectionings? – An intelligences [sic] – without Identity – and how is this Identity to be made? Through the medium of the Heart? And how is the heart to become this Medium but in a world of Circumstances? – There now I think what with Poetry and Theology you may thank your Stars that my pen is not very long-winded—

— John Keats,
In a letter to his brother

PART ONE

ONE

'The Pope is dead! Long live the Pope!' The cry reverberated in and around the Vatican courtyard of San Damaso where the body of Pope Julius XIV had just been discovered in his papal apartments. The Holy Father had died in his sleep. Within minutes the word spread through the mismatched cluster of buildings still referred to as the Vatican Palace, and then moved out through the Vatican State with the speed of a circuit fire in a pure-oxygen environment. The rumor of the Pope's death burned through the Vatican's office complex, leaped through the crowded St Anne's Gate to the Apostolic Palace and the adjacent Government Palace, found waiting ears among the faithful in the sacristy of St Peter's Basilica to the point that the archbishop saying Mass actually turned to look over his shoulder at the unprecedented hiss and whispering of the congregation, and then moved out of the Basilica with the departing worshipers into the larger crowds of St Peter's Square where eighty to a hundred thousand tourists and visiting Pax functionaries received the rumor like a critical mass of plutonium being slammed inward to full fission.

Once out through the main vehicle gate of the Arch of Bells, the news accelerated to the speed of electrons, then leaped to the speed of light, and finally hurtled out and away from the planet Pacem at Hawking-drive velocities thousands of times faster than light. Closer, just beyond the ancient walls of the Vatican, phones and comlogs chimed throughout the hulking, sweating Castel Sant'Angelo where the offices of the Holy Office of the Inquisition were buried deep in the mountain of stone originally built to be Hadrian's mausoleum. All that morning there was the rattle of beads and rustle of starched cassocks as Vatican functionaries rushed back to their offices to monitor their encrypted net lines and to wait for memos from above. Personal communicators rang, chimed, and vibrated in the uniforms and implants of thousands of Pax administrators, military commanders, politicians, and Mercantilus officials. Within thirty minutes of the discovery of the Pope's lifeless body, news organizations around the world of Pacem were cued to the story: they readied their robotic holocams, brought their full panoply of in-system relay sats on-line, sent their best human reporters to the Vatican press office, and waited. In an interstellar society where the Church ruled all but absolutely, news awaited not only independent confirmation but official permission to exist.

Two hours and ten minutes after the discovery of Pope Julius XIV's body, the Church confirmed his death via an announcement through the office of the Vatican Secretary of State, Cardinal Lourdusamy. Within seconds, the recorded announcement was tightcast to every radio and holovision on the teeming world of Pacem. With its population of one and a half billion souls, all born-again Christians carrying the cruciform, most employed by the Vatican or the huge civilian, military, or mercantile bureaucracy of the Pax state, the planet Pacem paused to listen with some interest. Even before the formal announcement, a dozen of the new archangel-class starships had left their orbital bases and translated across the small human sphere of the galaxy arm, their near-instantaneous drives instantly killing their crews but carrying their message of the Pope's death secure in computers and coded transponders for the sixty-some most important archdiocese worlds and star systems. These archangel courier ships would carry a few of the voting cardinals back to Pacem in time for the election, but most of the electors would choose to remain on their homeworlds – forgoing death even with its sure promise of resurrection – sending instead their encrypted, interactive holo wafers with their *eligo* for the next Supreme Pontiff.

Another eighty-five Hawking-class Pax ships, mostly high-acceleration torchships, made ready to spin up to relativistic velocities and then into jump configurations, their voyage time to be measured in days to months, their relative time-debt ranging from weeks to years. These ships would wait in Pacem space the fifteen to twenty standard days until the election of the new Pope and then bring the word to the one-hundred-and-thirty-some less critical Pax systems where archbishops tended to billions more of the faithful. Those archdiocese worlds, in turn, would be charged with sending the word of the Pope's death, resurrection, and reelection on to lesser systems, distant worlds, and to the myriad colonies in the Outback. A final fleet of more than two hundred unmanned courier drones was taken out of storage at the huge Pax asteroid base in Pacem System, their message chips waiting only for the official announcement of Pope Julius's rebirth and reelection before being accelerated into Hawking space to carry the news to elements of the Pax Fleet engaged in patrol or combat with the Ousters along the so-called Great Wall defensive sphere far beyond the boundaries of Pax space.

Pope Julius had died eight times before. The Pontiff's heart was weak, and he would allow no repair of it – either by surgery or nanoplasty. It was his contention that a pope should live his natural life span and – upon his death – that a new pope should be elected. The fact that this same Pope had been reelected eight times did not dissuade him from his opinion. Even now, as Pope Julius's body was being readied for a formal evening of lying in state before being carried to the private resurrection chapel behind St Peter's, cardinals and their surrogates were making preparations for the election.

The Sistine Chapel was closed to tourists and made ready for the voting that would occur in less than three weeks. Ancient, canopied stalls were brought in for the eighty-three cardinals who would be present in the flesh while holographic projectors and interactive datumplane connections were set in place for the cardinals who would vote by proxy. The table for the Scrutineers was set in front of the Chapel's high altar. Small cards, needles, thread, a receptacle, a plate, linen cloths, and other objects were carefully placed on the table of the Scrutineers and then covered with a larger linen cloth. The table for the Infirmarii and the Revisors was set to one side of the altar. The main doors of the Sistine Chapel were closed, bolted, and sealed. Swiss Guard commandos in full battle armor and state-of-the-art energy weapons took their place outside the Chapel doors and at the blastproof portals of St Peter's papal resurrection annex.

Following ancient protocol, the election was scheduled to occur in no fewer than fifteen days and no more than twenty. Those cardinals who made their permanent home on Pacem or within three weeks' time-debt travel canceled their regular agendas and prepared for the enclave. Everything else was in readiness.

Some fat men carry their weight like a weakness, a sign of self-indulgence and sloth. Other fat men absorb mass regally, an outward sign of their growing power. Simon Augustino Cardinal Lourdusamy was of the latter category. A huge man, a veritable mountain of scarlet in his formal cardinal robes, Lourdusamy looked to be in his late fifties, standard, and had appeared thus for more than two centuries of active life and successful resurrection. Jowled, quite bald, and given to speaking in a soft bass rumble that could rise to a God-roar capable of filling St Peter's Basilica without the use of a speaker system, Lourdusamy remained the epitome of health and vitality in the Vatican. Many in the inner circles of the Church's hierarchy credited Lourdusamy – then a young, minor functionary in the Vatican diplomatic machine – with guiding the anguished and pain-ridden ex-Hyperion pilgrim, Father Lenar Hoyt, to finding the secret that tamed the cruciform to an instrument of resurrection. They credited him as much as the newly deceased Pope with bringing the Church back from the brink of extinction.

Whatever the truth of that legend, Lourdusamy was in fine form this first day after the Holy Father's ninth death in office and five days before His Holiness's resurrection. As Cardinal-Secretary of State, president of the committee overseeing the twelve Sacred Congregations, and prefect of the most feared and misunderstood of those agencies – the Sacred Congregation for the Doctrine of the Faith, now officially known once again after more than a thousand-year interregnum as the Holy Office of the Universal Inquisition – Lourdusamy was the most powerful human being in the Curia. At that moment, with His Holiness, Pope Julius XIV, lying in state in St Peter's Basilica, the body awaiting removal to the resurrection annex as soon as night should fall, Simon Augustino Cardinal Lourdusamy was arguably the most powerful human being in the galaxy.

The fact was not lost on the Cardinal that morning.

'Are they here yet, Lucas?' he rumbled at the man who had been his aide and factotum for more than two hundred busy years. Monsignor Lucas Oddi was as thin, bony, aged-looking, and urgent in his movements as Cardinal Lourdusamy was huge, fleshy, ageless, and languid. Oddi's full title as undersecretary of state for the Vatican was Substitute and Secretary of the Cypher, but he was usually known as the Substitute. 'Cypher' might have been an equally apt nickname for the tall, angular Benedictine administrator, for in the twenty-two decades of smooth service he had given his master, no one – not even Lourdusamy himself – knew the man's private opinions or emotions. Father Lucas Oddi had been Lourdusamy's strong right arm for so long that the Secretary-Cardinal had long since ceased to think of him as anything but an extension of his own will.

'They have just been seated in the innermost waiting room,' answered Monsignor Oddi.

Cardinal Lourdusamy nodded. For more than a thousand years – since long before the Hegira that had sent humankind fleeing the dying Earth and colonizing the stars – it had been a custom of the Vatican to hold important meetings in the waiting rooms of important officials rather than in their private offices. Secretary of State Cardinal Lourdusamy's innermost waiting room was small – no more than five meters square – and unadorned except for a round marble table with no inset com units, a single window that, if it had not been polarized to opaqueness, would have looked out on to a marvelously frescoed external loggia, and two paintings by the thirtieth-century genius Karo-tan – one showing Christ's agony in Gethsemane, the other showing Pope Julius (in his pre-papal identity of Father Lenar Hoyt) receiving the first cruciform from a powerful but androgynous-looking archangel while Satan (in the form of the Shrike) looked on powerlessly.

The four people in the waiting room – three men and a woman – represented the Executive Council of the Pancapitalist League of Independent Catholic Transstellar Trade Organizations, more commonly known as the Pax Mercantilus. Two of the men might have been father and son – M. Helvig Aron and M. Kennet Hay-Modhino – alike even to their subtle, expensive capesuits, expensive, conservative haircuts, subtly bio-sculpted Old Earth Northeuro features, and to the even-more-subtle red pins showing their membership in the Sovereign Military Order of the Hospital of St John of Jerusalem, of Rhodes, and of Malta – the ancient society popularly known as the Knights of Malta. The third man was of Asian descent and wore a simple cotton robe. His name was Kenzo Isozaki and he was this day – after Simon Augustino Cardinal Lourdusamy – arguably the second most powerful human in the Pax. The final Pax Mercantilus representative, a woman in her fifties, standard, with carelessly cropped dark hair and a pinched face, wearing an inexpensive work suit of combed fiberplastic, was M. Anna Pelli Cognani, reputedly Isozaki's heir apparent and rumored for years to be the lover of the female Archbishop of Renaissance Vector.

The four rose and bowed slightly as Cardinal Lourdusamy entered and took his place at the table. Monsignor Lucas Oddi was the only bystander and he stood away from the table, his bony hands clasped in front of his cassock, the tortured eyes of Karo-tan's Christ in Gethsemane peering over his black-frocked shoulder at the small assembly.

M.s Aron and Hay-Modhino moved forward to genuflect and kiss the Cardinal's beveled sapphire ring, but Lourdusamy waved away further

446

protocol before Kenzo Isozaki or the woman could approach. When the four Pax Mercantilus representatives were seated once again, the Cardinal said, 'We are all old friends. You know that while I represent the Holy See in this discussion during the Holy Father's temporary absence, any and all things discussed this day shall remain within these walls.' Lourdusamy smiled. 'And these walls, my friends, are the most secure and bugproof in the Pax.'

Aron and Hay-Modhino smiled tightly. M. Isozaki's pleasant expression did not change. M. Anna Pelli Cognani's frown deepened. 'Your Eminence,' she said. 'May I speak freely?'

Lourdusamy extended a pudgy palm. He had always distrusted people who asked to speak freely or who vowed to speak candidly or who used the expression 'frankly'. He said, 'Of course, my dear friend. I regret that the pressing circumstances of the day allow us so little time.'

Anna Pelli Cognani nodded tersely. She had understood the command to be precise. 'Your Eminence,' she said, 'we asked for this conference so that we could speak to you not only as loyal members of His Holiness's Pancapitalist League, but as friends of the Holy See and of yourself.'

Lourdusamy nodded affably. His thin lips between the jowls were curled in a slight smile. 'Of course.'

M. Helvig Aron cleared his throat. 'Your Eminence, the Mercantilus has an understandable interest in the coming papal election.'

The Cardinal waited.

'Our goal today,' continued M. Hay-Modhino, 'is to reassure Your Eminence – both as Secretary of State and as a potential candidate for the papacy – that the League will continue to carry out the Vatican's policy with the utmost loyalty after the coming election.'

Cardinal Lourdusamy nodded ever so slightly. He understood perfectly. Somehow the Pax Mercantilus – Isozaki's intelligence network – had sniffed out a possible insurrection in the Vatican hierarchy. Somehow they had overheard the most silent of whispers in whisperproof rooms such as this: that it had come time to replace Pope Julius with a new pontiff. And Isozaki knew that Simon Augustino Lourdusamy would be that man.

'In this sad interregnum,' M. Cognani was continuing, 'we felt it our duty to offer private as well as public assurances that the League will continue serving the interests of the Holy See and the Holy Mother Church, just as it has for more than two standard centuries.'

Cardinal Lourdusamy nodded again and waited, but nothing else was forthcoming from the four Mercantilus leaders. For a moment, he allowed himself to speculate on why Isozaki had come in person. *To see my reaction rather than trust the reports of his subordinates*, he thought. *The old man trusts his senses and insights over anyone and anything else.* Lourdusamy smiled. *Good policy.* He let another minute of silence stretch before speaking. 'My friends,' he rumbled at last, 'you cannot know how it warms my heart to have four such busy and important people visit this poor priest in our time of shared sorrow.'

Isozaki and Cognani remained expressionless, as inert as argon, but the

Cardinal could see the poorly hidden glint of anticipation in the eyes of the other two Mercantilus men. If Lourdusamy welcomed their support at this juncture, however subtly, it put the Mercantilus on an even level with the Vatican conspirators – made the Mercantilus a welcomed conspirator and de facto co-equal to the next Pope.

Lourdusamy leaned closer to the table. The Cardinal noticed that M. Kenzo Isozaki had not blinked during the entire exchange. 'My friends,' he continued, 'as good born-again Christians' – he nodded toward M.s Aron and Hay-Modhino – 'as Knights Hospitaller, you undoubtedly know the procedure for the election of our next Pope. But let me refresh your memory. Once the cardinals and their interactive counterparts are gathered and sealed in the Sistine Chapel, there are three ways in which we can elect a pope – by acclamation, by delegation, or by scrutiny. Through acclamation, all of the cardinal electors are moved by the Holy Spirit to proclaim one person as Supreme Pontiff. We each cry *eligo* – "I elect" – and the name of the person we unanimously select. Through delegation, we choose a few of those among us – say a dozen cardinals – to make the choice for all. Through scrutiny, the cardinal electors vote secretly until a candidate receives two-thirds majority plus one. Then the new pope is elected and the waiting billions see the *sfumata* – the puffs of white smoke which means that the family of the Church once again has a Holy Father.'

The four representatives of the Pax Mercantilus sat in silence. Each of them was intimately aware of the procedure for electing a pope – not only of the antiquated mechanisms, of course, but of the politicking, pressuring, deal-making, bluffing, and outright blackmail that had often accompanied the process over the centuries. And they began to understand why Cardinal Lourdusamy was emphasizing the obvious now.

'For the last nine elections,' continued the huge Cardinal, his voice a heavy rumble, 'the Pope has been elected by acclamation . . . by the direct intercession of the Holy Spirit.' Lourdusamy paused for a long, thick moment. Behind him, Monsignor Oddi stood watching, as motionless as the painted Christ behind him, as unblinking as Kenzo Isozaki.

'I have no reason to believe,' continued Lourdusamy at last, 'that this election will be any different.'

The Pax Mercantilus executives did not move. Finally M. Isozaki bowed his head ever so slightly. The message had been heard and understood. There would be no insurrection within the Vatican walls. Or if there were, Lourdusamy had it well in hand and did not need the support of the Pax Mercantilus. If the former were the case and Cardinal Lourdusamy's time had not yet come, Pope Julius would once again oversee the Church and Pax. Isozaki's group had taken a terrible risk because of the incalculable rewards and power that would be theirs if they had succeeded in allying themselves with the future Pontiff. Now they faced only the consequences of the terrible risk. A century earlier, Pope Julius had excommunicated Kenzo Isozaki's predecessor for a lesser miscalculation, revoking the sacrament of the cruciform and condemning the Mercantilus leader to a life of separation from the Catholic community – which, of course, was every

man, woman, and child on Pacem and on a majority of the Pax worlds –
followed by the true death.

'Now, I regret that pressing duties must take me from your kind
company,' rumbled the Cardinal.

Before he could rise and contrary to standard protocol for leaving the
presence of a prince of the Church, M. Isozaki came forward quickly,
genuflected, and kissed the Cardinal's ring. 'Eminence,' murmured the old
Pax Mercantilus billionaire.

This time, Lourdusamy did not rise or leave until each of the powerful
CEOs had come forward to show his or her respect.

An archangel-class starship translated into God's Grove space the day after
Pope Julius's death. This was the only archangel not assigned to courier
duty; it was smaller than the new ships and it was called the *Raphael*.

Minutes after the archangel established orbit around the ash-colored
world, a dropship separated and screamed into atmosphere. Two men and
a woman were aboard. The three looked like siblings, united by their lean
forms, pale complexions, dark, limp, short-cropped hair, hooded gazes, and
thin lips. They wore unadorned shipsuits of red and black with elaborate
wristband comlogs. Their presence in the dropship was a curiosity – the
archangel-class starships invariably killed human beings during their violent translation through Planck space and the onboard resurrection creches
usually took three days to revive the human crew.

These three were not human.

Morphing wings and smoothing all surfaces into an aerodynamic shell,
the dropship crossed the terminator into daylight at Mach 3. Beneath it
turned the former Templar world of God's Grove – a mass of burn scars, ash
fields, mudflows, retreating glaciers, and green sequoias struggling to reseed
themselves in the shattered landscape. Slowing now to subsonic speeds,
the dropship flew above the narrow band of temperate climate and viable
vegetation near the planet's equator and followed a river to the stump of
the former Worldtree. Eighty-three kilometers across, still a kilometer high
even in its devastated form, the stump rose above the southern horizon like
a black mesa. The dropship avoided the Worldstump and continued to
follow the river west, continuing to descend until it landed on a boulder
near the point where the river entered a narrow gorge. The two men and the
woman came down the extruded stairs and reviewed the scene. It was
midmorning on this part of God's Grove, the river made a rushing noise as
it entered the rapids, birds and unseen arboreals chittered in the thick trees
farther downriver. The air smelled of pine needles, unclassifiable alien
scents, wet soil, and ash. More than two and a half centuries earlier, this
world had been smashed and slashed from orbit. Those two-hundred-meter-
high Templar trees that did not flee to space had burned in a conflagration
that continued to rage for the better part of a century, extinguished at last
only by a nuclear winter.

'Careful,' said one of the men as the three walked downhill to the river.
'The monofilaments she webbed here should still be in place.'

The thin woman nodded and removed a laser weapon from the flowfoam pak she carried. Setting the beam to widest dispersal, she fanned it over the river. Invisible filaments glowed like a spider's web in morning dew, crisscrossing the river and wrapping around boulders, submerging and reemerging from the white-frothed river.

'None where we have to work,' said the woman as she shut off the laser. The three crossed a low area by the river and climbed a rocky slope. Here the granite had been melted and flowed downhill like lava during the slagging of God's Grove, but on one of the terraced rockfaces there were even more recent signs of catastrophe. Near the top of a boulder ten meters above the river, a crater had been burned into solid rock. Perfectly circular, indented half a meter below the level of the boulder, the crater was five meters across. On the southeast side, where a waterfall of molten rock had run and splattered and fountained to the river below, a natural staircase of black stone had formed. The rock filling the circular cavity on top of the boulder was darker and smoother than the rest of the stone, looking like polished onyx set in a granite crucible.

One of the men stepped into the concavity, lay full length on the smooth stone, and set his ear to the rock. A second later he rose and nodded to the other two.

'Stand back,' said the woman. She touched her wristband comlog.

The three had taken five steps back when the lance of pure energy burned from space. Birds and arboreals fled in loud panic through the screening trees. The air ionized and became superheated in seconds, rolling a shock wave in all directions. Branches and leaves burst into flame fifty meters from the beam's point of contact. The cone of pure brilliance exactly matched the diameter of the circular depression in the boulder, turning the smooth stone to a lake of molten fire.

The two men and the woman did not flinch. Their shipsuits smoldered in the open hearth-furnace heat, but the special fabric did not burn. Neither did their flesh.

'Time,' said the woman over the roar of the energy beam and widening firestorm. The golden beam ceased to exist. Hot air rushed in at gale-force winds to fill the vacuum. The depression in the rock was a circle of bubbling lava.

One of the men went to one knee and seemed to be listening. Then he nodded to the others and phase-shifted. One second he was flesh and bone and blood and skin and hair, the next he was a chrome-silver sculpture in the form of a man. The blue sky, burning forest, and lake of molten fire reflected perfectly on his shifting silver skin. He plunged one arm into the molten pool, crouched lower, reached deeper, and then pulled back. The silver form of his hand looked as if it had melted onto the surface of another silver human form – this one a woman. The male chrome sculpture pulled the female chrome sculpture out of the hissing, spitting cauldron of lava and carried it fifty meters to a point where the grass was not burning and the stone was cool enough to hold their weight. The other man and woman followed.

The man shifted out of his chrome-silver form and a second later the female he had carried did the same. The woman who emerged from the quicksilver looked like a twin of the short-haired woman in the shipsuit.

'Where is the bitch child?' asked the rescued female. She had once been known as Rhadamanth Nemes.

'Gone,' said the man who rescued her. He and his male sibling could be her brothers or male clones. 'They made the final farcaster.'

Rhadamanth Nemes grimaced slightly. She was flexing her fingers and moving her arms as if recovering from cramps in her limbs. 'At least I killed the damned android.'

'No,' said the other woman, her twin. She had no name. 'They left in the *Raphael*'s dropship. The android lost an arm, but the autosurgeon kept him alive.'

Nemes nodded and looked back at the rocky hillside where lava still ran. The glow from the fire showed the glistening web of the monofilament over the river. Behind them, the forest burned. 'That was not . . . pleasant . . . in there. I couldn't move with the full force of the ship's lance burning down on me, and then I could not phase-shift with the rock around me. It took immense concentration to power down and still maintain an active phase-shift interface. How long was I buried there?'

'Four Earth years,' said the man who had not spoken until now.

Rhadamanth Nemes raised a thin eyebrow, more in question than surprise. 'Yet the Core knew where I was . . .'

'The Core knew where you were,' said the other woman. Her voice and facial expressions were identical to those of the rescued woman. 'And the Core knew that you had failed.'

Nemes smiled very thinly. 'So the four years were a punishment.'

'A reminder,' said the man who had pulled her from the rock.

Rhadamanth Nemes took two steps, as if testing her balance. Her voice was flat. 'So why have you come for me now?'

'The girl,' said the other woman. 'She is coming back. We are to resume your mission.'

Nemes nodded.

The man who rescued her set his hand on her thin shoulder. 'And please consider,' he said, 'that four years entombed in fire and stone will be nothing to what you may expect if you fail again.'

Nemes stared at him for a long moment without answering. Then, turning away from the lava and flames in a precisely choreographed motion, matching stride for stride, all four of them moved in perfect unison toward the dropship.

On the desert world of MadredeDios, on the high plateau called the Llano Estacado because of the atmosphere-generator pylons crisscrossing the desert in neat ten-kilometer grid intervals, Father Federico de Soya prepared for early-morning Mass.

The little desert town of Nuevo Atlan held fewer than three hundred residents – mostly Pax boxite miners waiting to die before traveling home, mixed with a few of the converted Mariaists who scratched out livings as corgor herders in the toxic wastelands – and Father de Soya knew precisely how many would be in chapel for early Mass: four – old M. Sanchez, the ancient widow who was rumored to have murdered her husband in a dust storm sixty-two years before, the Perell twins who – for unknown reasons – preferred the old run-down church to the spotless and air-conditioned company chapel on the mining reservation, and the mysterious old man with the radiation-scarred face who knelt in the rearmost pew and never took Communion.

There was a dust storm blowing – there was always a dust storm blowing – and Father de Soya had to run the last thirty meters from his adobe parish house to the church sacristy, a transparent fiberplastic hood over his head and shoulders to protect his cassock and biretta, his breviary tucked deep in his cassock pocket to keep it clean. It did not work. Every evening when he removed his cassock or hung his biretta on a hook, the sand fell out in a red cascade, like dried blood from a broken hourglass. And every morning when he opened his breviary, sand gritted between the pages and soiled his fingers.

'Good morning, Father,' said Pablo as the priest hurried into the sacristy and slid the cracked weather seals around the door frame.

'Good morning, Pablo, my most faithful altar boy,' said Father de Soya. Actually, the priest silently corrected himself, Pablo was his *only* altar boy. A simple child – simple in the ancient sense of the word as mentally slow as well as in the sense of being honest, sincere, loyal, and friendly – Pablo was there to help de Soya serve Mass every weekday morning at oh-six-thirty hours and twice on Sunday – although only the same four people came to the early-morning Sunday Mass and half a dozen of the boxite miners to the later Mass.

The boy nodded his head and grinned again, the smile disappearing for a moment as he pulled on his clean, starched surplice over his altar-boy robes.

Father de Soya walked past the child, ruffling his dark hair as he did so, and opened the tall vestment chest. The morning had grown as dark as the high-desert night as the dust storm swallowed the sunrise, and the only illumination in the cold, bare room was from the fluttering sacristy lamp. De Soya genuflected, prayed earnestly for a moment, and began donning the vestments of his profession.

For two decades, as Father Captain de Soya of the Pax Fleet, commander of torchships such as the *Balthasar*, Federico de Soya had dressed himself in uniforms where the cross and collar were the only signs of his priesthood. He had worn plaskev battle armor, spacesuits, tactical com implants, datumplane goggles, godgloves – all of the paraphernalia of a torchship captain – but none of those items touched him and moved him as much as these simple vestments of a parish priest. In the four years since Father Captain de Soya had been stripped of his rank of captain and removed from Fleet service, he had rediscovered his original vocation.

De Soya pulled on the amice that slipped over his head like a gown and fell to his ankles. The amice was white linen and immaculate despite the incessant dust storms, as was the alb that slid on next. He set the cincture around his waist, whispering a prayer as he did so. Then he raised the white stole from the vestment chest, held it reverently a moment in both hands, and then placed it around his neck, crossing the two strips of silk. Behind him, Pablo was bustling around the little room, putting away his filthy outside boots and pulling on the cheap fiberplastic running shoes his mother had told him to keep here just for Mass.

Father de Soya set his tunicle in place, the outer garment showing a T-cross in front. It was white with a subtle purple piping: he would be saying a Mass of Benediction this morning while quietly administering the sacrament of penance for the presumed widow and murderer in the front pew and the radiation-scarred cypher in the last pew.

Pablo bustled up to him. The boy was grinning and out of breath. Father de Soya set his hand on the boy's head, trying to flatten the thatch of flyaway hair while also calming and reassuring the lad. De Soya lifted the chalice, removed his right hand from the boy's head to hold it over the veiled cup, and said softly, 'All right.' Pablo's grin disappeared as the gravity of the moment swept over him, and then the boy led the procession of two out of the sacristy door toward the altar.

De Soya noticed at once that there were five figures in the chapel, not four. The usual worshipers were there – all kneeling and standing and then kneeling again in their usual places – but there was someone else, someone tall and silent standing in the deepest shadows where the little foyer entered the nave.

All during the Renewed Mass, the presence of the stranger pulled at Father de Soya's consciousness, try as he might to block out all but the sacred mystery of which he was part.

'Dominus vobiscum,' said Father de Soya. For more than three thousand years, he believed, the Lord *had* been with them . . . with all of them.

'Et cum spiritu tuo,' said Father de Soya, and as Pablo echoed the words, the priest turned his head slightly to see if the light had illuminated the tall, thin form in the dark recess at the front of the nave. It had not.

During the Canon, Father de Soya forgot the mysterious figure and succeeded in focusing all of his attention on the Host that he raised in his blunt fingers. 'Hoc est enim corpus meum,' the Jesuit pronounced distinctly, feeling the power of those words and praying for the ten-thousandth time that his sins of violence while a Fleet captain might be washed away by the blood and mercy of this Savior.

At the Communion rail, only the Perell twins came forward. As always. De Soya said the words and offered the Host to the young men. He resisted the urge to glance up at the figure in the shadows at the back of the church.

The Mass ended almost in darkness. The howl of wind drowned out the last prayers and responses. This little church had no electricity – it never had – and the ten flickering candles on the wall did little to pierce the gloom. Father de Soya gave the final benediction and then carried the chalice into the dark sacristy, setting it on the smaller altar there. Pablo hurried to shrug out of his surplice and pull on his storm anorak.

'See you tomorrow, Father!'

'Yes, thank you, Pablo. Don't forget . . .' Too late. The boy was out the door and running for the spice mill where he worked with his father and uncles. Red dust filled the air around the faulty weather-stripped door.

Normally, Father de Soya would have been pulling off his vestments now, setting them back in the vestment chest. Later in the day, he would take them to the parish house to clean them. But this morning he stayed in the tunicle and stole, the alb and cincture and amice. For some reason he felt he needed them, much as he had needed the plaskev battle armor during boarding operations in the Coal Sack campaign.

The tall figure, still in shadows, stood in the sacristy doorway. Father de Soya waited and watched, resisting the urge to cross himself or to hold the remaining Communion wafer up as if to shield against vampires or the Devil. Outside, the wind went from a howl to a banshee scream.

The figure took a step into the ruby light cast by the sacristy lamp. De Soya recognized Captain Marget Wu, personal aide and liaison for Admiral Marusyn, commanding officer of Pax Fleet. For the second time that morning, de Soya corrected himself – it was Admiral Marget Wu now, the pips on her collar just visible in the red light.

'Father Captain de Soya?' said the Admiral.

The Jesuit slowly shook his head. It was only oh-seven-thirty hours on this twenty-three-hour world, but already he felt tired. 'Just *Father* de Soya,' he said.

'Father Captain de Soya,' repeated Admiral Wu, and this time there was no question in her voice. 'You are hereby recalled to active service. You will take ten minutes to gather your belongings and then come with me. The recall is effective now.'

Federico de Soya sighed and closed his eyes. He felt like crying. *Please, dear Lord, let this cup pass from me.* When he opened his eyes, the chalice was still on the altar and Admiral Marget Wu was still waiting.

'Yes,' he said softly, and slowly, carefully, he began removing his sacred vestments.

On the third day after the death and entombment of Pope Julius XIV, there was movement in his resurrection creche. The slender umbilicals and subtle machine probes slid back and out of sight. The corpse on the slab at first lay inanimate, except for the rise and fall of a bare chest, then visibly twitched, then moaned, and – after many long minutes – raised itself to one elbow, and eventually sat up, the richly embroidered silk and linen shroud sliding around the naked man's waist.

For several minutes the man sat on the edge of the marble slab, his head in his shaking hands. Then he looked up as a secret panel in the resurrection-chapel wall slid back with less than a hiss. A cardinal in formal red moved across the dimly lit space with a rustle of silk and a rattle of beads. Next to him walked a tall, handsome man with gray hair and gray eyes. This man was dressed in a simple but elegant one-piece suit of gray flannel. Three steps behind the Cardinal and the man in gray came two Swiss Guard troopers in medieval orange and black. They carried no weapons.

The naked man on the slab blinked as if his eyes were unaccustomed to even the muted light in the dim chapel. Finally the eyes focused. 'Lourdusamy,' said the resurrected man.

'Father Duré,' said Cardinal Lourdusamy. He was carrying an oversized silver chalice.

The naked man moved his mouth and tongue as if he had awakened with a vile taste in his mouth. He was an older man with a thin, ascetic face, sad eyes, and old scars across his newly resurrected body. On his chest, two cruciforms glowed red and tumescent. 'What year is it?' he asked at last.

'The Year of Our Lord 3131,' said the Cardinal, still standing next to the seated man.

Father Paul Duré closed his eyes. 'Fifty-seven years after my last resurrection. Two hundred and seventy-nine years since the Fall of the Farcasters.' He opened his eyes and looked at the Cardinal. 'Two hundred and seventy years since you poisoned me, killing Pope Teilhard the First.'

Cardinal Lourdusamy rumbled a laugh. 'You recover quickly from resurrection disorientation if you can do your arithmetic so well.'

Father Duré moved his gaze from the Cardinal to the tall man in gray. 'Albedo. You come to witness? Or do you have to give courage to your tame Judas?'

The tall man said nothing. Cardinal Lourdusamy's already thin lips tightened to the point of disappearance between florid jowls. 'Do you have anything else to say before you return to hell, Antipope?'

'Not to you,' murmured Father Duré and closed his eyes in prayer.

The two Swiss Guard troopers seized Father Duré's thin arms. The Jesuit did not resist. One of the troopers grabbed the resurrected man by the brow and pulled his head back, stretching the thin neck in a bow.

Cardinal Lourdusamy took a graceful half step closer. From the folds of his silken sleeve snicked a knife blade with a horn handle. While the troopers held the still passive Duré, whose Adam's apple seemed to grow more prominent as his head was forced back, Lourdusamy swept his arm up and around in a fluid, casting-away gesture. Blood spurted from Duré's severed carotid artery.

Stepping back to avoid staining his robes, Lourdusamy slid the blade back into his sleeve, raised the broad-mouthed chalice, and caught the pulsing stream of blood. When the chalice was almost filled and the blood had ceased spurting, he nodded to the Swiss Guard trooper, who immediately released Father Duré's head.

The resurrected man was a corpse once again, head lolling, eyes still shut, mouth open, the slashed throat gaping like painted lips on a terrible, ragged grin. The two Swiss Guard troopers arranged the body on the slab and lifted the shroud away. The naked dead man looked pale and vulnerable – torn throat, scarred chest, long, white fingers, pale belly, flaccid genitals, scrawny legs. Death – even in an age of resurrection – leaves little or no dignity even to those who have lived lives of sustained self-control.

While the troopers held the beautiful shroud out of harm's way, Cardinal Lourdusamy poured the heavy chalice's blood onto the dead man's eyes, into his gaping mouth, into the raw knife wound, and down the chest, belly, and groin of the corpse, the spreading scarlet matching and surpassing the intensity of color in the Cardinal's robes.

'*Sie aber seid nicht fleischlich, sondern geistlich,*' said Cardinal Lourdusamy. 'You are not made of flesh, but of spirit.'

The tall man raised an eyebrow. 'Bach, isn't it?'

'Of course,' said the Cardinal, setting the now-empty chalice next to the corpse. He nodded to the Swiss Guard troopers and they covered the body with the two-layered shroud. Blood immediately soaked the beautiful fabrics. '*Jesu meine Freude,*' added Lourdusamy.

'I thought so,' said the taller man. He gave the Cardinal a questioning look.

'Yes,' agreed Cardinal Lourdusamy. 'Now.'

The man in gray walked around the bier and stood behind the two troopers, who were completing their tucking-in of the blood-soaked shroud. When the troopers straightened and stepped back from the marble slab, the man in gray lifted his large hands to the back of each man's neck. The troopers' eyes and mouths opened wide, but they had no time to cry out: within a second their open eyes and mouths blazed with an incandescent light, their skin became translucent to the orange flame within their bodies, and then they were gone – volatilized, scattered to particles finer than ash.

The man in gray brushed his hands together to rid them of the thin layer of micro-ash.

'A pity, Councillor Albedo,' murmured Cardinal Lourdusamy in his thick rumble of a voice.

The man in gray looked at the suggestion of airborne dust settling in the dim light and then back at the Cardinal. His eyebrow rose once again in query.

'No, no, no,' rumbled Lourdusamy, 'I mean the shroud. The stains will never come out. We have to weave a new one after every resurrection.' He turned and started toward the secret panel, his robes rustling. 'Come, Albedo. We need to talk and I still have a Mass of Thanksgiving to say before noon.'

After the panel slid shut behind the two, the resurrection chamber lay silent and empty except for the shrouded corpse and the slightest hint of gray fog in the dim light, a shifting, fading mist suggestive of the departing souls of the more recent dead.

TWO

On the week that Pope Julius died for the ninth time and Father Duré was murdered for the fifth time, Aenea and I were one hundred and sixty thousand light-years away on the kidnapped planet Earth – Old Earth, the *real* Earth – circling a G-type star that was not the sun in the Lesser Magellanic Cloud, a galaxy that was not the Earth's home galaxy.

It had been a strange week for us. We did not know that the Pope had died, of course, since there was no contact between this relocated Earth and Pax space except for the dormant farcaster portals. Actually, I know now, Aenea *was* aware of the Pope's demise through means we did not suspect then, but she did not mention events in Pax space to us and no one thought to ask her. Our lives on Earth during those years of exile were simple and peaceful and profound in ways that are now hard to fathom and almost painful to recall. At any rate, that particular week had been profound but not simple or peaceful for us: the Old Architect with whom Aenea had been studying for the last four years had died on Monday, and his funeral had been a sad and hasty affair out on the desert that wintry Tuesday evening. On Wednesday, Aenea had turned sixteen, but the event was overshadowed by the pall of grief and confusion at the Taliesin Fellowship and only A. Bettik and I had tried to celebrate the day with her.

The android had baked a chocolate cake, Aenea's favorite, and I had worked for days to whittle an elaborately carved walking stick out of a sturdy branch we had found during one of the Old Architect's compulsory picnic expeditions to the nearby mountains. That evening we ate the cake and drank some champagne in Aenea's beautiful little apprentice shelter in the desert, but she was subdued and distracted by the old man's death and the Fellowship's panic. I realize now that much of her distraction must have come from her awareness of the Pope's death, of the violent events that were gathering on the future's horizon, and of the end of what would be the most peaceful four years we would ever know together.

I remember the conversation that evening of Aenea's sixteenth birthday. It had grown dark early and the air was chill. Outside the comfortable stone-and-canvas home she had built four years earlier for her apprenticeship challenge, the dust was blowing and the sagebrush and yucca plants rasped and contorted in the wind's grip. We sat by the hissing lantern, traded our champagne glasses for mugs of warm tea, and talked softly beneath the hiss of sand on canvas.

'It's strange,' I said. 'We knew he was old and ill, but no one seemed to believe that he would die.' I was speaking of the Old Architect, of course, not of the distant Pope who meant so little to us. And, like all of us on the exiled Earth, Aenea's mentor had not carried the cruciform. His death was final in the way the Pope's could not be.

'He seemed to know,' Aenea said softly. 'He's been calling in each of his apprentices for the past month. Imparting some last bit of wisdom.'

'What last bit of wisdom did he share with you?' I asked. 'I mean, if it's not a secret or too personal.'

Aenea smiled over the steaming mug of tea. 'He reminded me that the patron will always agree to pay twice what the bid was if you send along the extra expenses bit by bit once construction has started and the structure is taking shape. He said that was beyond the point of no return, so the client was hooked like a trout on a six-pound line.'

Both A. Bettik and I laughed. It was not a disrespectful laugh – the Old Architect had been one of those rare creatures, a true genius combined with an overpowering personality – but even when thinking of him with sadness and affection, we could recognize the selfishness and deviousness that had also been part of his personality. And I don't mean to be coy here by referring to him only as the Old Architect: the cybrid's personality template had been reconstructed from a pre-Hegira human named Frank Lloyd Wright who had worked in the nineteenth and twentieth centuries, AD. But while everyone at the Taliesin Fellowship had referred to him respectfully as Mr Wright, including even those older apprentices who were his age, I had always thought of him as the Old Architect because of things Aenea had said about her future mentor before we came here to Old Earth.

As if thinking along these same lines, A. Bettik said, 'It's odd, isn't it?'

'What's that?' said Aenea.

The android smiled and rubbed his left arm where it ended at a smooth stump just below the elbow. It is a habit he had developed over the past few years. The autosurgeon on the dropship that had carried us through the farcaster from God's Grove had kept the android alive, but his chemistry had been sufficiently different to prevent the ship from growing him a new arm. 'I mean,' he said, 'that despite the ascendancy of the Church in the affairs of humankind, the question of whether human beings have a soul which leaves the body after death has yet to be definitely answered. Yet in Mr Wright's case, we know that his cybrid personality still exists separate from his body – or at least did for some time after the moment of his death.'

'Do we know that for sure?' I said. The tea was warm and good. Aenea and I bought it – traded for it actually – at the Indian market located in the desert where the city of Scottsdale should have been.

It was Aenea who answered my question. 'Yes. My father's cybrid personality survived the destruction of his body and was stored in the Schrön Loop in Mother's skull. Even after that, we know that it had a separate existence in the megasphere and then resided in the Consul's ship for a time. A cybrid's personality survives as a sort of holistic wave front propagated along the matrices of the datumplane or megasphere until it returns to the AI source in the Core.'

I had known this but never understood it. 'Okay,' I said, 'but where did Mr Wright's AI-based personality wave front go? There can't be any connections to the Core out here in the Magellanic Cloud. There are no dataspheres here.'

Aenea set down her empty mug. 'There has to be a connection, or Mr Wright and the other reconstructed cybrid personalities assembled here on Earth couldn't have existed. Remember, the TechnoCore used the Planck space between the farcaster portals as their medium and hiding place before the dying Hegemony destroyed the farcaster openings to it.'

'The Void Which Binds,' I said, repeating the phrase from the old poet's *Cantos*.

'Yeah,' said Aenea. 'Although I always thought that was a dumb name.'

'Whatever it's called,' I said, 'I don't understand how it can reach *here* . . . a different galaxy.'

'The medium the Core used for farcasters reaches everywhere,' said Aenea. 'It permeates space and time.' My young friend frowned. 'No, that's not right, space and time are bound up in *it* . . . the Void Which Binds transcends space and time.'

I looked around. The lantern light was enough to fill the little tent structure, but outside it was dark and the wind howled. 'Then the Core *can* reach here?'

Aenea shook her head. We had held this discussion before. I had not understood the concept then. I did not understand it now.

'These cybrids are connected to AIs which aren't really part of the Core,' she said. 'Mr Wright's persona wasn't. My father . . . the second Keats cybrid . . . wasn't.'

This was the part I had never understood. 'The *Cantos* said that the Keats cybrids – including your father – were created by Ummon, a Core AI. Ummon told your father that the cybrids were a Core experiment.'

Aenea stood and walked to the opening of her apprentice shelter. The canvas on either side rippled with the wind, but kept its shape and held the sand outside. She had built it well. 'Uncle Martin wrote the *Cantos*,' she said. 'He told the truth as best he could. But there were elements he did not understand.'

'Me too,' I said and dropped the matter. I walked over and put my arm around Aenea, feeling the subtle changes in her back and shoulder and arm since the first time I had hugged her four years earlier. 'Happy birthday, kiddo.'

She glanced up at me and then laid her head against my chest. 'Thank you, Raul.'

There had been other changes in my youthful friend since first we met when she was just turning twelve, standard. I could say that she had grown to womanhood in the intervening years, but despite the rounding of her hips and obvious breasts beneath the old sweatshirt she wore, I still did not see her as a woman. No longer a child, of course, but not yet a woman. She was . . . Aenea. The luminous dark eyes were the same – intelligent, questioning, a bit sad with some secret knowledge – and the effect of being physically touched when she turned the attention of her gaze on you was as strong as ever. Her brown hair had grown somewhat darker in the past few years. She had cut it the previous spring – now it was shorter than mine had been when I was in the Home Guard military on Hyperion a dozen years earlier; when I set my hand on her head the hair was barely long enough to rise between my fingers – but I could see some glints of the old blonde streaks there, brought out by the long days she spent working in the Arizona sunlight.

As we stood there listening to the blowing dust scraping canvas, A. Bettik a silent shadow behind us, Aenea took my hand in both of hers. She might have been sixteen that day, a young woman rather than a girl, but her hands were still tiny in my huge palm. 'Raul?' she said.

I looked at her and waited.

'Will you do something for me?' she said softly, very softly.

'Yes.' I did not hesitate.

She squeezed my hand and looked directly *into* me then. 'Will you do something for me tomorrow?'

'Yes.'

Neither her gaze nor the pressure on my hand let up. 'Will you do *anything* for me?'

This time I did hesitate. I knew what such a vow might entail, even though this strange and wonderful child had never asked me to do anything for her – had not asked that I come with her on this mad odyssey. That had been a promise I had made to the old poet, Martin Silenus, before I had even met Aenea. I knew that there were things that I could not – in good conscience or bad – bring myself to do. But foremost among those things I was incapable of doing was denying Aenea.

'Yes,' I said, 'I will do anything you ask.' At that moment I knew that I was lost – and resurrected.

Aenea did not speak then, but only nodded, squeezed my hand a final time, and turned back to the light, the cake, and our waiting android friend. On the next day I was to learn what her request truly meant, and how difficult it would be to honor my vow.

I will stop for a moment. I realize that you might not know about me unless you have read the first few hundred pages of my tale, which, because I had to recycle the microvellum upon which I wrote them, no longer exist except in the memory of the 'scriber. I told the truth in those lost pages. Or at least the truth as I knew it then. Or at least I *tried* to tell the truth. Mostly.

After having recycled the microvellum pages of that first attempt to tell the story of Aenea, and because the 'scriber has never been out of my sight, I have to assume that no one has read them. The fact that they were written in a Schrödinger cat box execution egg in exile orbit around the barren world of Armaghast – the cat box being little more than a fixed-position energy shell holding my atmosphere, air, and food-recycling equipment, bed, table, 'scriber, and a vial of cyanide gas waiting to be released by a random isotope emission – would seem to have insured that you have not read those pages.

But I am not sure.

Strange things were happening then. Strange things have happened since. I will reserve judgment on whether those pages – and these – could ever have been, or ever will be, read.

In the meantime, I will reintroduce myself. My name is Raul Endymion, my first name rhyming with tall – which I am – and my last name deriving from the 'abandoned' university city of Endymion on the backwater world of Hyperion. I qualify the word 'abandoned' because that quarantined city is where I met the old poet – Martin Silenus, the ancient author of the banned epic poem the *Cantos* – and that is where my adventure began. I use the word 'adventure' with some irony, and perhaps in the sense that all of life is an adventure. For it is true that while the voyage began as an adventure – an attempt to rescue twelve-year-old Aenea from the Pax and to escort her safely to the distant Old Earth – it has since become a full lifetime of love, loss, and wonder.

Anyway, at the time of this telling, during the week of the Pope's death, the Old Architect's death, and Aenea's inauspicious sixteenth birthday in exile, I was thirty-two years old, still tall, still strong, still trained mostly in hunting, brawling, and watching others lead, still callow, and just teetering on the precipice of falling forever in love with the girl-child I had protected like a little sister and who – overnight, it seemed – had become a girl-woman whom I knew now as a friend.

I should also say that the other things I write of here – the events in Pax space, the murder of Paul Duré, the retrieval of the female-thing named Rhadamanth Nemes, the thoughts of Father Federico de Soya – are not surmised or extrapolated or made up in the way that the old fiction novels were in Martin Silenus's day. I *know* these things, down to the level of Father de Soya's thoughts and Councillor Albedo's apparel that day, not because I am omniscient, but because of later events and revelations that gave access to such omniscience.

It will make sense later. At least I hope it will.

I apologize for this awkward reintroduction. The template for Aenea's cybrid father – a poet named John Keats – said in his last letter of farewell to his friends, 'I have always made an awkward bow.' In truth, so have I – whether in departure or greeting or, as is perhaps the case here, in improbable reunion.

So I will return to my memories and ask your indulgence if they do not make perfect sense at my first attempt to share and shape them.

The wind howled and the dust blew for three days and three nights after Aenea's sixteenth birthday. The girl was gone for all that time. Over the past four years I had grown used to her 'time-outs', as she called them, and I usually did not fret the way I had the first few times she had disappeared for days on end. This time, however, I was more concerned than usual: the death of the Old Architect had left the twenty-seven apprentices and the sixty-some support people at the desert camp – which is what the Old Architect called Taliesin West – anxious and uneasy. The dust storm added to that anxiety, as dust storms always do. Most of the families and support staff lived close by, in one of the desert-masonry dormitories Mr Wright had his interns build south of the main buildings, and the camp complex itself was almost fortlike with its walls and courtyards and covered walkways – good for scuttling between buildings during a dust storm – but each successive day without either sunlight or Aenea made me increasingly nervous.

Several times each day I went to her apprentice shelter: it was the farthest from the main compound, almost a quarter of a mile north toward the mountains. She was never there – she had left the door untethered and a note telling me not to worry, that it was just one of her excursions and that she was taking plenty of water – but every time I visited I appreciated her shelter more.

Four years earlier, when she and I had first arrived with a dropship stolen from a Pax warship, both of us exhausted, battered, and burned, not to mention with an android healing in the ship's autosurgeon, the Old Architect and the other apprentices had greeted us with warmth and acceptance. Mr Wright had not seemed surprised that a twelve-year-old child had come across world after world via farcaster to find him and to ask to be his apprentice. I remember that first day when the Old Architect had asked her what she knew of architecture – 'Nothing,' Aenea had replied quietly, 'except that you are the one I should learn from.'

Evidently this had been the correct response. Mr Wright had told her that all of the apprentices who had arrived before her – all twenty-six others, as it turned out – had been asked to design and build their own shelters in the desert as a sort of entry exam. The Old Architect had offered some crude materials from the compound – canvas, stone, cement, a bit of cast-off lumber – but the design and effort were up to the girl.

Before she set to work (not being an apprentice, I made do with a tent close to the main compound), Aenea and I toured the other apprentice shelters. Most were variations on tent-shacks. They were serviceable and some showed style – one particularly exhibited a nice design flair but, as Aenea pointed out to me, would not keep the sand or rain out with the slightest wind – but none was particularly memorable.

Aenea worked eleven days on her shelter. I helped her do some of the heavy lifting and a bit of the excavating (A. Bettik was still recovering at that time – first in the autosurgeon, then in the compound's infirmary), but the girl did all of the planning and most of the work. The result was this wonderful shelter that I visited four times a day during this, her last hiatus in the desert. Aenea had excavated the main sections of the shelter so that most of it was below ground level. Then she had set flagstones in place, making sure that they fit tightly, to create a smooth floor. Over the stones she set colorful rugs and blankets she traded for at the Indian Market fifteen miles away. Around the excavated core of the home she set walls that were about a meter high, but with the sunken main room, they seemed taller.

They were constructed of the same rough 'desert masonry' that Mr Wright had used in building the walls and superstructure of the main compound buildings and Aenea used the same technique, although she had never heard him describe it.

First, she gathered stones from the desert and the many arroyos and washes around the hilltop compound. The rocks were of every size and color – purple, black, rusty reds, and deep umbers – and some held petroglyphs or fossils. After gathering the stones, Aenea built wooden forms and set the larger rocks in with their flat sides against the inside face of the form. She then spent days in the broiling sun, shoveling sand from the washes and carting it back to her building site in wheelbarrows, mixing it there with cement to form the concrete that held the stones in place as the mixture hardened. It was a rough concrete/stone concoction – desert masonry, Mr Wright called it – but it was strangely beautiful, the colorful rocks showing through the surface of the concrete, fissures, and textures everywhere. Once in place, the walls were about a meter high and thick enough to hold out the desert heat in the daytime and hold in the inner heat at night.

Her shelter was more complex than it first appeared to the eye – it was months before I appreciated the subtle tricks she had pulled in its design. One ducked to enter the vestibule, a stone-and-canvas porte cochère with three broad steps leading one down and around to the wood and masonry portal that served as the entrance to the main room. This twisting, descending vestibule acted as a sort of air lock, sealing out the desert sand and harshness, and the way she had rigged the canvas – almost like overlapping jib sails – improved the air-lock effect. The 'main room' was only three meters across and five long, but it seemed much larger. Aenea had used built-in benches around a raised stone table to create a dining and sitting area, and then placed more niches and stone seats near a hearth she had fashioned in the north wall of the shelter. There was an actual stone chimney built into the wall, and it did not touch the canvas or wood at any point. Between the stone walls and the canvas – at about eye height when seated – she had rigged screened windows that ran the length of the north and south sides of the shelter. These panoramic viewslits could be battened down by both canvas and sliding wood shutters, operated from the inside. Overhead, she had used old fiberglass rods found in the compound junk heap to shape the canvas in smooth arches, sudden peaks, cathedral vaults, and odd, folded niches.

She had actually fashioned a bedroom for herself, again removed from the main room by two steps twisted at sixty-degree angles, the entire niche built into the gently rising slope and set back against a huge boulder she had found on the site. There was no water or plumbing out here – we all shared the communal showers and toilets in the compound annex – but Aenea had built a lovely little rock basin and bath next to her bed (a plywood platform with mattress and blankets), and several times a week she would heat water in the main kitchen and carry it to her shelter, bucket by bucket, for a hot bath.

The light through the canvas ceilings and walls was warm at sunrise, buttery at midday, and orange in the evening. In addition, Aenea had deliberately placed the shelter in careful relation to saguaros, prickly pear bushes, and staghorn cactus so that different shadows would fall on different planes of canvas at different times of day. It was a comfortable, pleasant place. And empty beyond description when my young friend was absent.

I mentioned that the apprentices and support staff were anxious after the Old Architect's death. Distraught might be a better word. I spent most of those three days of Aenea's absence listening to the concerned babble of almost ninety people – never together, since even the dinner shifts in the dining hall were spaced apart because Mr Wright had not liked huge crowds at dinner – and the level of panic seemed to grow as the days and dust storms went by. Aenea's absence was a big part of the hysteria: she was the youngest apprentice at Taliesin – the youngest person, actually – but the others had grown used to asking advice of her and to listening when she spoke. In one week, they had lost both their mentor and their guide.

On the fourth morning after her birthday, the dust storms ended and Aenea returned. I happened to be out jogging just after sunrise and saw her coming across the desert from the direction of the McDowell Mountains: she was silhouetted in the morning light, a thin figure with short hair against the corona brilliance, and in that second I thought of the first time I had seen her in the Valley of the Time Tombs on Hyperion.

She grinned when she saw me. 'Hey, Boo,' she called. It was an old joke based on some book she had read as a very young child.

'Hey, Scout,' I called back, answering in the same in-joke language.

We stopped when we were five paces apart. My impulse was to hug her and hold her close and beg her not to disappear again. I did not do that. The rich, low light of morning threw long shadows behind the cholla cacti, greasebushes, and sage, and bathed our already-sunburned skin in an orange glow.

'How're the troops doing?' asked Aenea. I could see that despite her promises to the contrary, she had been fasting during the past three days. She had always been thin, but now her ribs almost showed through her thin cotton shirt. Her lips were dry and cracked. 'They upset?' she said.

'They're shitting bricks,' I said. For years I'd avoided using my Home Guard vocabulary around the kid, but she was sixteen now. Besides, she had always used a saltier vocabulary than I knew.

Aenea grinned. The brilliant light illuminated the sandy streaks in her short hair. 'That'd be good for a bunch of architects, I guess.'

I rubbed my chin, feeling the rough stubble there. 'Seriously, kiddo. They're pretty upset.'

Aenea nodded. 'Yeah. They don't know what to do or where to go now that Mr Wright's gone.' She squinted toward the Fellowship compound, which showed up as little more than asymmetrical bits of stone and canvas just visible above the cacti and scrub brush. Sunlight glinted off unseen windows and one of the fountains. 'Let's get everybody in the music pavilion and talk,' said Aenea, and began striding toward Taliesin.

And thus began our last full day together on Earth.

I am going to interrupt myself here. I hear my own voice on the 'scriber and remember the pause in the telling at this point. What I *wanted* to do here was tell all about the four years of exile on Old Earth – all about the apprentices and other people at the Taliesin Fellowship, all about the Old Architect and his whims and petty cruelties, as well as about his brilliance and childlike enthusiasms. I wanted to describe the many conversations with Aenea over those forty-eight local months (which – as I never got tired of being amazed by – corresponded perfectly to Hegemony/Pax *standard* months!) and my slow growth of understanding of her incredible insights and abilities. Finally, I wanted to tell of all my excursions during that time – my trip around the Earth in the dropship, the long driving adventures in North America, my fleeting contact with the other islands of humanity huddled around cybrid figures from the human past (the gathering in Israel and New Palestine around the cybrid Jesus of Nazareth was a memorable group to visit), but primarily, when I hear the brief silence on the 'scriber that took the place of these tales, I remember the reason for my omission.

As I said before, I 'scribed these words in the Schrödinger cat box orbiting Armaghast, while awaiting the simultaneous emission of an isotopic particle and the activation of the particle detector. When these two events coincided, the cyanide gas built into the static-energy field around the recycling equipment would be released. Death would not be instantaneous, but near enough. While protesting earlier that I would take my time in telling our story – Aenea's and mine – I realize now that there was some editing, some attempt to get to the important elements before the particle decayed and the gas flowed.

I will not double-guess that decision now, except to say that the four years on Earth would be worth telling about at some other point in time: the ninety people of the Fellowship were decent, complex, devious, and interesting in the way of all intelligent human beings, and their tales should be told. Similarly, my explorations across Earth, both in the dropship and in the 1948 'Woody' station wagon that the Old Architect loaned me, might support an epic poem of their own.

But I am not a poet. But I was a tracker in my hunting-guide days, and my job here is to follow the path of Aenea's growth to womanhood and messiahship without wandering down too many sidetracks. And so I shall.

The Old Architect always referred to the Fellowship compound as 'desert camp'. Most of the apprentices referred to it as 'Taliesin' – which means 'Shining Brow' in Welsh. (Mr Wright was of Welsh extraction. I spent weeks trying to remember a Pax or Outback world named Welsh, before I remembered that the Old Architect had lived and died before spaceflight.) Aenea often referred to the place as 'Taliesin West', which suggested to even someone as dull as me that there had to be a Taliesin East.

When I asked her three years earlier, Aenea had explained that the original Mr Wright had built his first Taliesin Fellowship compound in the early 1930s in Spring Green, Wisconsin – Wisconsin being one of the political and geographical sub-units of the ancient North American nation-state called the United States of America. When I asked Aenea if the first Taliesin was like this one, she had said, 'Not really. There were a series of Wisconsin Taliesins – both homes and fellowship compounds – and most were destroyed by fire. That's one of the reasons Mr Wright installed so many pools and fountains here at this compound – sources of water to fight the inevitable fires.'

'And his first Taliesin was built in the 1930s?' I said.

Aenea shook her head. 'He opened his first Taliesin Fellowship in 1932,' she said. 'But that was mostly a way to get slave labor from his apprentices – both for building his dream and raising food for him – during the Depression.'

'What was the Depression?'

'Bad economic times in their pure capitalist nation-state,' Aenea said. 'Remember, the economy wasn't really global then, and it depended upon private money institutions called banks, gold reserves, and the value of physical money – actual coins and pieces of paper that were supposed to be worth something. It was all a consensual hallucination, of course, and in the 1930s, the hallucination turned nightmare.'

'Jesus,' I said.

'Precisely,' said Aenea. 'Anyway, long before that, in 1909 AD, the middle-aged Mr Wright abandoned his wife and six children and ran away to Europe with a married woman.'

I admit that I blinked at this news. The thought of the Old Architect – a man in his mid-eighties when we had met him four years ago – with a sex life, and a scandalous one at that, took some getting used to. I also wondered what all this had to do with my question about Taliesin East.

Aenea was getting to that. 'When he returned with the other woman,' she said, smiling at my rapt attention, 'he began building the first Taliesin – his home in Wisconsin – for Mamah . . .'

'His mother?' I said, totally confused.

'Mamah Borthwick,' said Aenea, spelling the first name for me. 'Mrs Cheney. The Other Woman.'

'Oh.'

The smile fading, she continued. 'The scandal had destroyed his architectural practice and made him a branded man in the United States. But he built Taliesin and forged ahead, trying to find new patrons. His first wife, Catherine, would not give him a divorce. The newspapers – those were databanks printed on paper and distributed regularly – thrived on such gossip and fanned the flames of the scandal, not letting it die.'

We had been walking in the courtyard when I asked Aenea the simple question about Taliesin, and I remember pausing by the fountain during this part of her answer. I was always amazed at what this child knew.

'Then,' she said, 'on August 15, 1914, a worker at Taliesin went crazy, killed Mamah Borthwick and her son John and daughter Martha with a hatchet, burned their bodies, set fire to the compound, and then killed four of Mr Wright's friends and apprentices before swallowing acid himself. The entire place burned down.'

'My God,' I whispered, looking toward the dining hall where the cybrid Old Architect was having lunch with a few of his oldest apprentices even as we spoke.

'He never gave up,' said Aenea. 'A few days later, on August 18, Mr Wright was touring an artificial lake on the Taliesin property when the dam he was standing on gave way and he was swept into a rain-swollen creek. Against all odds, he swam out of the torrent. A few weeks later, he started to rebuild.'

I thought that I understood then what she was telling me about the Old Architect. 'Why aren't we at *that* Taliesin?' I asked as we strolled away from the bubbling fountain in the desert courtyard.

Aenea shook her head. 'Good question. I doubt if it even exists in this rebuilt version of Earth. It was important to Mr Wright, though. He died here . . . near Taliesin West . . . on April 9, 1959, but he was buried back near the Wisconsin Taliesin.'

I stopped walking then. The thought of the Old Architect dying was a new and disturbing thought. Everything about our exile had been steady-state, calm and self-renewing, but now Aenea had reminded me that everything and everyone ends. Or had, before the Pax introduced the cruciform and physical resurrection to humanity. But no one at the Fellowship – perhaps no one on this kidnapped Earth – had submitted to a cruciform.

That conversation had been three years earlier. This morning, the week after the cybrid Old Architect's death and incongruous burial in the small mausoleum he had built out in the desert, we were ready to face the consequences of death without resurrection and the end of things.

While Aenea went off to the bath and laundry pavilion to wash up, I found A. Bettik and the two of us got busy with spreading the word of the meeting in the music pavilion. The blue-skinned android did not act surprised that Aenea, the youngest of us, was calling and leading the meeting. Both A. Bettik and I had watched silently over the past few years as the girl became the locus of the Fellowship.

I jogged from the fields to the dormitories, from the dormitories to the kitchen – where I rang the large bell set in the fanciful bell tower above the stairway to the guest deck. Those apprentices or workers whom I did not contact personally should hear the bell and come to investigate.

From the kitchen, where I left cooks and some of the apprentices taking their aprons off and wiping their hands, I announced the meeting to people having coffee in the large Fellowship dining room (the view from this beautiful room looked north toward the McDowell peaks, so some had watched Aenea and me return and knew that something was up), and then I poked my head in Mr Wright's smaller, private dining room – empty – and then jogged over to the drafting room. This was probably the most attract-ive room in the compound with its long rows of drafting tables and filing cabinets set under the sloping canvas roof, the morning light flooding in through the two rows of offset windows. The sun was high enough now to fall on the roof and the smell of heated canvas was as pleasant as the butter-rich light. Aenea had once told me that it was this sense of camping out – of working within the confines of light and canvas and stone – that had been the real reason for Mr Wright coming west to the second Taliesin.

There were ten or twelve of the apprentices in the drafting room, all standing around – none working now that the Old Architect was no longer around to suggest projects – and I told them that Aenea would like us to gather in the music pavilion. None protested. None grumbled or made any comment about a sixteen-year-old telling ninety of her elders to come together in the middle of a workday. If anything, the apprentices looked relieved to hear that she was back and taking charge.

From the drafting room I went to the library where I had spent so many happy hours and then checked the conference room, lit only by four glowing panels in the floor, and announced the meeting to the people I found in both places. Then I jogged down the concrete path under the covered walkway of desert masonry and peered in the cabaret theater where the Old Architect had loved to show movies on Saturday nights. This place had always tickled me – its thick stone walls and roof, the long descending space with plywood benches covered with red cushions, the well-worn red carpet on the floor, and the many hundreds of white Christmas lights running back and forth on the ceiling. When we first arrived, Aenea and I were amazed to find that the Old Architect demanded that his apprentices and their families 'dress for dinner' on Saturday – ancient tuxedoes and black ties, of the sort one sees in the oldest history holos. The women wore strange dresses out of antiquity. Mr Wright provided the formal clothes for those who failed to bring them in their flight to Earth through Time Tombs or farcaster.

That first Saturday, Aenea had shown up dressed in a tuxedo, shirt, and black tie rather than one of the dresses provided. When I first saw the Old Architect's shocked expression, I was sure that he was going to throw us out of the Fellowship and make us eke out a living in the desert, but then the old face creased into a smile and within seconds he was laughing. He never asked Aenea to dress in anything else.

After the formal Saturday dinners, we would either have a group musical event or assemble in the cabaret theater for a movie – one of the ancient, celluloid kinds that had to be projected by a machine. It was rather like learning to enjoy cave art. Both Aenea and I loved the films he chose – ancient twentieth-century flat things, many in black and white – and for some reason that he never explained, Mr Wright preferred to watch them with the 'sound track', optical jiggles and wiggles, visible on the screen. Actually, we'd watched films there for a year before one of the other apprentices told us that they had been made to be watched *without* the sound track visible.

Today the cabaret theater was empty, the Christmas lights dark. I jogged on, moving from room to room, building to building, rounding up apprentices, workers, and family members until I met A. Bettik by the fountain and we joined the others in the large music pavilion.

The pavilion was a large space, with a broad stage and six rows of eighteen upholstered seats in each row. The walls were of redwood painted Cherokee Red (the Old Architect's favorite color) and the usual thick desert masonry. A grand piano and a few potted plants were the only things on the red-carpeted stage. Overhead, stretched tight above a gridwork of wood and steel ribs, was the usual white canvas. Aenea had once told me that after the death of the first Mr Wright, plastic had taken the place of canvas to relieve the necessity of replacing canvas every couple of years. But upon *this* Mr Wright's return, the plastic was ripped out – as was the glass above the main drafting room – so that pure light through white canvas would be the rule once again.

A. Bettik and I stood near the rear of the music pavilion as the murmuring apprentices and other workers took their seats, some of the construction workers standing on the aisle steps or at the back with the android and me, as if worried about tracking mud and dust onto the rich carpet and upholstery. When Aenea entered through the side curtains and jumped to the stage, all the conversation stopped.

The acoustics were good in Mr Wright's music pavilion, but Aenea had always been able to project her voice without seeming to raise it. She spoke softly. 'Thank you for gathering. I thought we should talk.'

Jaev Peters, one of the older apprentices, immediately stood up in the fifth row. 'You were gone, Aenea. In the desert again.'

The girl on the stage nodded.

'Did you talk to the Lions and Tigers and Bears?'

No one in the audience tittered or giggled. The question was asked in deadly seriousness and the answer was awaited by ninety people just as seriously. I should explain.

It all began in the *Cantos* Martin Silenus wrote more than two centuries ago. That tale of the Hyperion pilgrims, the Shrike, and the battle between humanity and the TechnoCore explained how the early cyberspace webs had evolved into planetary dataspheres. By the time of the Hegemony, the AI TechnoCore had used their secret farcaster and fatline technologies to weave hundreds of dataspheres into a single, secret, interstellar information medium called the megasphere. But, according to the *Cantos*, Aenea's father – the cybrid John Keats – had traveled in disembodied datapersona form to the megasphere's Core and discovered that there was a larger datumplane medium, perhaps larger than our galaxy, which even the Core AIs were afraid to explore because it was full of 'lions and tigers and bears' – those were Ummon the AI's words. These were the beings – or intelligences – or gods, for all we knew – who had kidnapped the Earth and brought it here before the Core could destroy it a millennium ago. These Lions and Tigers and Bears were the bugaboo guardians of our world. No one in the Fellow-ship had ever seen any of these entities, or spoken to them, or had any solid evidence of their existence. No one except Aenea.

'No,' said the girl on the stage, 'I didn't talk to them.' She looked down as if embarrassed. She was always reticent to talk about this. 'But I think I heard them.'

'They spoke to you?' said Jaev Peters. The pavilion was hushed.

'No,' said Aenea. 'I didn't say that. I just . . . heard them. A bit like when you overhear someone else's conversation through a dormitory wall.'

There was a rustle of amusement at this. For all the thick stone walls on the Fellowship property, the dorm partitions were notably thin.

'All right,' said Bets Kimbal from the first row. Bets was the chief cook and a large, sensible woman. 'Tell us what they said.'

Aenea stepped up to the edge of the red-carpeted stage and looked out at her elders and colleagues. 'I can tell you this,' she said softly. 'There'll be no more food and supplies from the Indian Market. That's gone.'

It was as if she had set off a grenade in the music pavilion. When the babble began to subside, one of the biggest of the construction workers, a man named Hussan, shouted over the noise. 'What do you mean it's gone? Where do we get our food?'

There was good reason for the panic. In Mr Wright's day, way back in the twentieth century, his Fellowship desert camp had been about fifty kilometers from a large town called Phoenix. Unlike the Depression-era Wisconsin Taliesin, where apprentices raised crops in the rich soil even while they worked on Mr Wright's construction plans, this desert camp had never been able to grow its own food. So they drove to Phoenix and bartered or paid out their primitive coins and paper money for basic supplies. The Old Architect had always depended upon the largesse of patrons – large loans never to be paid back – for such month-to-month survival.

Here in our reassembled desert camp, there were no towns. The only road – two gravel ruts – led west into hundreds of miles of emptiness. I knew this because I had flown over the area in the dropship and driven it in the Old Architect's groundcar. But about thirty klicks from the compound there was a weekly Indian market where we had bartered craft items for food and basic materials. It had been there for years before Aenea's and my arrival; everyone had obviously expected it to be there forever.

'What do you mean it's gone?' repeated Hussan in a hoarse shout. 'Where'd the Indians go? Were they just cybrid illusions, like Mr Wright?'

Aenea made a gesture with her hands that I had grown accustomed to over the years – a graceful setting-aside motion that I had come to see as a physical analog of the Zen expression 'mu', which, in the right context, can mean 'unask the question'.

'The market's gone because we won't need it anymore,' said Aenea. 'The Indians are real enough – Navajo, Apache, Hopi, and Zuni – but they have their own lives to live, their own experiments to conduct. Their trading with us has been . . . a favor.'

The crowd became angry at that, but eventually they settled down again. Bets Kimbal stood. 'What do we do, child?'

Aenea sat on the edge of the stage as if trying to become one with the waiting, expectant audience. 'The Fellowship is over,' she said. 'That part of our lives has to end.'

One of the younger apprentices was shouting from the back of the pavilion. 'No it doesn't! Mr Wright could still return! He was a cybrid, remember . . . a construct! The Core . . . or the Lions and Tigers and Bears . . . whoever shaped him can send him back to us . . .'

Aenea shook her head, sadly but firmly. 'No. Mr Wright is gone. The Fellowship is over. Without the food and materials the Indians brought from so far away, this desert camp can't last a month. We have to go.'

It was a young female apprentice named Peret who spoke quietly into the silence. 'Where, Aenea?'

Perhaps it was at this moment that I first realized how this entire group had given themselves over to the young woman I had known as a child. When the Old Architect was around, giving lectures, holding forth in seminars and drafting-room bull sessions, leading his flock on picnics and swimming outings in the mountains, demanding solicitude and the best food, the reality of Aenea's leadership had been somewhat masked. But now it was evident.

'Yes,' someone else called from the center of the rising rows of seats, 'where, Aenea?'

My friend opened her hands in another gesture I had learned. Rather than *Unask the question*, this one said, *You must answer your own question*. Aloud, she said, 'There are two choices. Each of you traveled here either by farcaster or through the Time Tombs. You can go back by way of farcaster . . .'

'No!'

'How can we?'

'Never . . . I'd rather die!'

'No! The Pax will find us and kill us!'

The cries were immediate and from the heart. It was the sound of terror made verbal. I smelled fear in the room the way I used to smell it on animals caught in leg traps on the moors of Hyperion.

Aenea lifted a hand and the outcries faded, 'You can return to Pax space by farcaster, or you can stay on Earth and try to fend for yourself.'

There were murmurs and I could hear relief at the option of not returning. I understood that feeling – the Pax had come to be a bogeyman to me, as well. The thought of returning there sent me gasping up out of sleep at least once a week.

'But if you stay here,' continued the girl seated on the edge of Mr Wright's music stage, 'you will be outcasts. All of the groups of human beings here are involved in their own projects, their own experiments. You will not fit in there.'

People shouted questions about that, demanding answers to mysteries not understood during their long stay here. But Aenea continued with what she was saying. 'If you stay here, you will waste what Mr Wright has taught you and what you came to learn about yourself. The Earth does not need architects and builders. Not now. We have to go back.'

Jaev Peters spoke again. His voice was brittle, but not angry. 'And does the Pax need builders and architects? To build its cross-damned churches?'

'Yes,' said Aenea.

Jaev pounded the back of the seat in front of him with his large fist.

'But they'll capture or kill us if they learn who we are . . . where we've been!'

'Yes,' said Aenea.

Bets Kimbal said, 'Are you going back, child?'

'Yes,' said Aenea and pushed herself away from the stage.

Everyone was standing now, shouting or talking to the people next to them. It was Jaev Peters who spoke the thoughts of the ninety Fellowship orphans. 'Can we go with you, Aenea?'

The girl sighed. Her face, as sunburned and alert as it looked this morning, also looked tired. 'No,' she said. 'I think that leaving here is like dying or being born. We each have to do it alone.' She smiled. 'Or in very small groups.'

The room fell silent then. When Aenea spoke, it was as if a single instrument were picking up where the orchestra had stopped. 'Raul will leave first,' she said. 'Tonight. One by one, each of you will find the right farcaster portal. I will help you. I will be the last to leave Earth. But leave I will, and within a few weeks. We all must go.'

People pushed forward then, still silent, but moving closer to the girl with the short-cropped hair. 'But some of us will meet again,' said Aenea. 'I feel certain that some of us will meet again.'

I heard the flip side of that reassuring prediction: some of us would not survive to meet again.

'Well,' boomed Bets Kimbal, standing with one broad arm around Aenea, 'we have enough food in the kitchen for one last feast. Lunch today will be a meal you'll remember for years! If you have to travel, as my mum used to say, never travel on an empty stomach. Who's to help me in the kitchen, then?'

The groups broke up then, families and friends in clusters, loners standing as if stunned, everyone moving closer to Aenea as we began filing out of the music pavilion. I wanted to grab her at that moment, shake her until her wisdom teeth fell out, and demand, *What the hell do you mean – 'Raul will leave first . . . tonight.' Who the hell are you to tell me to leave you behind? And how do you think you can make me?* But she was too far away and too many people were pressing around her. The best I could do was stride along behind the crowd as it moved toward the kitchen and dining area, anger written in my face, fists, muscles, and walk.

Once I saw Aenea glance back, straining to find me over the heads of the crowd around her, and her eyes pleaded, *Let me explain.*

I stared back stonily, giving her nothing.

It was almost dusk when she joined me in the large garage Mr Wright had ordered built half a klick east of the compound. The structure was open on the sides except for canvas curtains, but it had thick stone columns supporting a permanent redwood roof; it had been built to shelter the dropship in which Aenea, A. Bettik, and I had arrived.

I had pulled back the main canvas door and was standing in the open hatch of the dropship when I saw Aenea crossing the desert toward me. On my wrist was the comlog bracelet that I had not worn in more than a year: the thing held much of the memory of our former spaceship – the Consul's ship from centuries ago – and it had been my liaison and tutor when I had learned to fly the dropship. I did not need it now – the comlog memory had been downloaded into the dropship and I had become rather good at piloting the dropship on my own – but it made me feel more secure. The comlog was also running a systems check on the ship: chatting with itself, you might say.

Aenea stood just within the folded canvas. The sunset threw long shadows behind her and painted the canvas red. 'How's the dropship?' she said.

I glanced at the comlog readings. 'All right,' I grunted, not looking her way.

'Does it have enough fuel and charge for one more flight?'

Still not looking up, fiddling with touchplates on the arm of the pilot's chair inside the hatch, I said, 'Depends on where it's flying to.'

Aenea walked to the dropship stairway and touched my leg. 'Raul?'

This time I had to look at her.

'Don't be angry,' she said. 'We have to do these things.'

I pulled my leg away. 'Goddammit, don't keep telling me and everyone else what we have to do. You're just a kid. Maybe there are things some of us *don't* have to do. Maybe going off on my own and leaving you behind is one of those.' I stepped off the ladder and tapped the comlog. The stairs morphed back into the dropship hull. I left the garage and began walking toward my tent. On the horizon, the sun was a perfect red sphere. In the last low rays of light, the stones and canvas of the main compound looked as if they had caught fire – the Old Architect's greatest fear.

'Raul, wait!' Aenea hurried to catch up to me. One glance in her direction told me how exhausted she was. All afternoon she had been meeting with people, talking to people, explaining to people, reassuring people, hugging people. I had come to think of the Fellowship as a nest of emotional vampires and Aenea as their only source of energy.

'You said that you would . . .' she began.

'Yeah, yeah,' I interrupted. I suddenly had the sense that she was the adult and that I was the petulant child. To hide my confusion, I turned away again and watched the last of the sunset. For a moment or two we were both silent, watching the light fade and the sky darken. I had decided that Earth sunsets were slower and more lovely than the Hyperion sunsets I had known as a child, and that desert sunsets were particularly fine. How many sunsets had this child and I shared in the past four years? How many lazy evenings of dinner and conversation under the brilliant desert stars? Could this really be the last sunset we would watch together? The idea made me sick and furious.

'Raul,' she said again when the shadows had grown together and the air was cooling, 'will you come with me?'

I did not say yes, but I followed her across the rocky field, avoiding the bayonet spikes of yucca and the spines of low cacti in the gloom, until we came into the lighted area of the compound. *How long*, I wondered, *until the fuel oil for the generators runs out?* This answer I knew – it was part of my job to keep the generators maintained and fueled. We had six days' supply in the main tanks and another ten days' in the reserve tanks that were never to be touched except in emergency. With the Indian Market gone, there would be no resupply. Almost three weeks of electric lights and refrigeration and power equipment and then . . . what? Darkness, decay, and an end to the incessant construction, tearing down, and rebuilding that had been the background noise at Taliesin for the last four years.

I thought perhaps that we were going to the dining hall, but we walked past those lighted windows – groups of people still sitting at the tables, talking earnestly, glancing up with eyes only for Aenea as we passed – I was invisible to them in their hour of panic – and then we approached Mr Wright's private drafting studio and his office, but we did not stop there. Nor did we stop in the beautiful little conference room where a small group sat to watch a final movie – three weeks until the movie projectors did not run – nor did we turn into the main drafting room.

Our destination was a stone-and-canvas workshop set far down the driveway on the south side, a useful outbuilding for working with toxic chemicals or noisy equipment. I had worked here often in the first couple of years at the Fellowship, but not in recent months.

A. Bettik was waiting at the door. The android had a slight smile on his bland, blue face, rather like the one he had worn when carrying the birthday cake to Aenea's surprise party.

'What?' I said, still irritated, looking from the girl's tired face to the android's smug expression.

Aenea stepped into the workshop and turned on the light.

On the worktable in the center of the little room sat a small boat, not much more than two meters in length. It was shaped rather like a seed sharpened on both ends, enclosed except for a single round cockpit opening with a nylon skirt that could obviously be tightened around the occupant's waist. A two-bladed paddle lay on the table next to the boat. I stepped closer and ran my hand over the hull: a polished fiberglass compound with internal aluminum braces and fittings. Only one other person at the Fellowship could do such careful work. I looked at A. Bettik almost accusingly. He nodded.

'It's called a kayak,' said Aenea, running her own hand over the polished hull. 'It's an old Earth design.'

'I've seen variations on it,' I said, refusing to be impressed. 'The Ice Claw Ursus rebels used small boats like this.'

Aenea was still stroking the hull, all of her attention there. It was as if I had not spoken. 'I asked A. Bettik to make it for you,' she said. 'He's worked for weeks here.'

'For me,' I said dully. My stomach tightened at the realization of what was coming.

Aenea moved closer. She was standing directly under the hanging light, and the shadows under her eyes and cheekbones made her look much older than sixteen. 'We don't have the raft anymore, Raul.'

I knew the raft she meant. The one that had carried us across so many worlds until it was chopped up in the ambush that almost killed us on God's Grove. The raft that had carried us down the river under the ice on Sol Draconi Septem and through the deserts of Hebron and Qom-Riyadh and across the world ocean of Mare Infinitus. I knew the raft she meant. And I knew what this boat meant.

'So I'm to take this back the way we came?' I raised a hand as if to touch the thing, but then did not.

'Not the way we came,' said Aenea. 'But down the River Tethys. Across different worlds. Across as many worlds as it takes to find the ship.'

'The ship?' I said. We had left the Consul's spaceship hiding under a river, repairing itself from damage sustained in our flight from the Pax, on a world whose name and location we did not know.

My young friend nodded and the shadows fled, then regrouped around her tired eyes. 'We'll need the ship, Raul. If you would, I'd like you to take this kayak down the River Tethys until you find the ship, then fly back with it to a world where A. Bettik and I will be waiting.'

'A world in Pax space?' I said, my stomach tightening another notch at the danger present in that simple sentence.

'Yes.'

'Why me?' I said, looking significantly at A. Bettik. I was ashamed at my thought then: *Why send a human being . . . your best friend . . . when the android can go?* I lowered my gaze.

'It will be a dangerous trip,' said Aenea. 'I believe that you can do it, Raul. I trust you to find the ship and then find us.'

I felt my shoulders slump. 'All right,' I said. 'Do we head back to where we came through the farcaster before?' We had come through from God's Grove on a small stream near the Old Architect's masterpiece building, Fallingwater. It was two-thirds of a continent away.

'No,' said Aenea. 'Closer. On the Mississippi River.'

'All right,' I said again. I had flown over the Mississippi. It was almost two thousand klicks east of here. 'When do I go? Tomorrow?'

Aenea touched my wrist. 'No,' she said, tiredly but firmly. 'Tonight. Right now.'

I did not protest. I did not argue. Without speaking, I took the bow of the kayak, A. Bettik took the stern, Aenea held the center steady, and we carried the damned thing back to the dropship in the deepening desert night.

THREE

The Grand Inquisitor was late.

Vatican Air/Space Traffic Control routed the Inquisitor's EMV across normally closed airspace near the spaceport, shut down all airborne traffic on the east side of the Vatican, and held a thirty-thousand-ton robot freighter in orbital final approach until after the GI's car had flown across the southeast corner of the landing grid.

Inside the specially armored EMV, the Grand Inquisitor – His Eminence John Domenico Cardinal Mustafa – did not glance out the window or at the video monitors at the lovely sight of the approaching Vatican, its walls rosy in the morning light, or at the busy, twenty-lane highway called the Ponte Vittorio Emanuele beneath them, glimmering like a sunlit river because of sunlight on windshields and bubbletops. The Grand Inquisitor's attention was focused solely on the intelligence update scrolling by on his comlog template.

When the last paragraph had scrolled past and was committed to memory and deleted to oblivion, the Grand Inquisitor said to his aide, Father Farrell, 'And there have been no more meetings with the Mercantilus?'

Father Farrell, a thin man with flat gray eyes, never smiled, but a twitch of his cheek muscle conveyed the simulation of humor to the Cardinal. 'None.'

'You're certain?'

'Absolutely.'

The Grand Inquisitor sat back in the EMV's cushions and allowed himself a brief smile. The Mercantilus had made only that one early, disastrous approach to any of the papal candidates – the sounding out of Lourdusamy – and the Inquisitor had heard the complete recording of that meeting. The Cardinal allowed himself another few seconds of smile: Lourdusamy had been right to think that his conference room was bugproof – absolutely resistant to taps, bugs, wires, and squirts. Any recording device in the room – even implanted in one of the participants – would have been detected and homed in on. Any attempt to tightbeam out would have been detected and blocked. It had been one of the Grand Inquisitor's finest moments, getting the complete visual and auditory recording of that meeting.

Monsignor Lucas Oddi had gone into the Vatican Hospital for a routine eyes, ears, and heart replacement two local years ago. The surgeon had been approached by Father Farrell and the full weight of the Holy Office had been shown ready to descend upon the poor medico's neck if he did not

476

implant certain state-of-the-art devices in the Monsignor's body. The surgeon did so and died the true death – no resurrection possible – in a car accident far out over the Big North Shallow shortly after that.

Monsignor Lucas Oddi had no electronic or mechanical bugs in his system, but connected to his optic nerve were seven fully biological nanorecorders. Four auditory nanorecorders were tapped into his auditory nerve system. These biorecorders did not transmit inside the body, but stored the data in chemical form and physically carried it through the bloodstream to the squirt transmitter – also fully organic – set into Monsignor Oddi's left ventricle. Ten minutes after Oddi had left the secured area of Cardinal Lourdusamy's office, the transmitter had squirted a compressed record of the meeting to one of the Grand Inquisitor's nearby relay transponders. It was not real-time eavesdropping from Lourdusamy's bugproof rooms – a fact that still worried Cardinal Mustafa – but it was as close to it as current technology and stealth could get.

'Isozaki is frightened,' said Father Farrell. 'He thinks . . .'

The Grand Inquisitor raised one finger. Farrell stopped in mid-sentence. 'You do not know that he is frightened,' said the Cardinal. 'You do not know what he thinks. You can only know what he says and does and infer his thoughts and reactions from that. *Never* make unsupportable assumptions about your enemies, Martin. It can be a fatal self-indulgence.'

Father Farrell bowed his head in agreement and submission.

The EMV touched down on the landing pad atop Castel Sant'Angelo. The Grand Inquisitor was out the hatch and down the ramp so quickly that Farrell had to trot to catch up to his master. Security commandos, dressed in Holy Office red armorcloth, fell into escort step ahead and behind, but the Grand Inquisitor waved them away. He wanted to finish his conversation with Father Farrell. He touched his aide's left arm – not out of affection, but to close the bone-conduction circuits so that he could subvocalize – and said, 'Isozaki and the Mercantilus leaders are not frightened. If Lourdusamy wanted them purged, they would be dead by now. Isozaki had to get his message of support to the Cardinal and he did. It's the Pax military who are frightened.'

Farrell frowned and subvocalized on the bone circuit. 'The military? But they haven't played their card yet. They have done nothing disloyal.'

'Precisely,' said the Grand Inquisitor. 'The Mercantilus has made its move and knows that Lourdusamy will turn to them when the time comes. Pax Fleet and the rest have been terrified for years that they'll make the wrong choice. Now they're terrified that they've waited too long.'

Farrell nodded. They had taken a dropshaft deep into the stone bowels of Castel Sant'Angelo, and now they moved past armed guards and through lethal forcefields down a dark corridor. At an unmarked door, two red-garbed commandos stood at attention, energy rifles raised.

'Leave us,' said the Grand Inquisitor and palmed the door's ideyplate. The steel panel slid up and out of sight.

The corridor had been stone and shadows. Inside the room, everything was bright light, instruments, and sterile surfaces. Technicians looked up as the Grand Inquisitor and Farrell entered. One wall of the room was taken up by square doors, looking like nothing so much as the multitiered human file drawers of an ancient morgue. One of those doors was open and a naked man lay on a gurney that had been pulled from the cold storage drawer there.

The Grand Inquisitor and Farrell stopped on either side of the gurney.

'He is reviving well,' said the technician who stood at the console. 'We're holding him just beneath the surface. We can bring him up in seconds.'

Father Farrell said, 'How long was his last cold sleep?'

'Sixteen local months,' said the technician. 'Thirteen and a half standard.'

'Bring him up,' said the Grand Inquisitor.

The man's eyelids began to flutter within seconds. He was a small man, muscular but compact, and there were no marks or bruises on his body. His wrists and ankles were bound by sticktite. A cortical shunt had been implanted just behind his left ear and an almost invisible bundle of microfibers ran from it to the console.

The man on the gurney moaned.

'Corporal Bassin Kee,' said the Grand Inquisitor. 'Can you hear me?'

Corporal Kee made an unintelligible sound.

The Grand Inquisitor nodded as if satisfied. 'Corporal Kee,' he said pleasantly, conversationally, 'shall we pick up where we left off?'

'How long . . .' mumbled Kee between dry, stiff lips. 'How long have I been . . .'

Father Farrell had moved to the technician's console. Now he nodded to the Grand Inquisitor.

Ignoring the corporal's question, John Domenico Cardinal Mustafa said softly, 'Why did you and Father Captain de Soya let the girl go?'

Corporal Kee had opened his eyes, blinking as if the light pained him, but now he closed them again. He did not speak.

The Grand Inquisitor nodded to his aide. Father Farrell's hand passed over icons on the console diskey, but did not yet activate any of them.

'Once again,' said the Grand Inquisitor. 'Why did you and de Soya allow the girl and her criminal allies to escape on God's Grove? Who were you working for? What was your motivation?'

Corporal Kee lay on his back, his fists clenched and his eyes shut fast. He did not answer.

The Grand Inquisitor tilted his head ever so slightly to the left and Father Farrell waved two fingers over one of the console icons. The icons were as abstract as hieroglyphics to the untutored eye, but Farrell knew them well. The one he had chosen would have translated as *crushed testicles*.

On the gurney, Corporal Kee gasped and opened his mouth to scream, but the neural inhibitors blocked that reaction. The short man's jaws opened as wide as they could and Father Farrell could hear the muscles and tendons stretching.

The Grand Inquisitor nodded and Farrell removed his fingers from the activation zone above the icon. Corporal Kee's entire body convulsed on the gurney, his stomach muscles rippling in tension.

'It is only virtual pain, Corporal Kee,' whispered the Grand Inquisitor. 'A neural illusion. Your body is not marked.'

On the slab, Kee was straining to raise his head to look down at his body, but the sticktite band held his head in place.

'Or perhaps not,' continued the Cardinal. 'Perhaps this time we have resorted to older, less refined methods.' He took a step closer to the gurney so that the man could see his face. 'Again . . . why did you and Father Captain de Soya let the girl go on God's Grove? Why did you attack your crewmate, Rhadamanth Nemes?'

Corporal Kee's mouth worked until his back teeth became visible. 'F . . . f . . . fuck you,' he managed, his jaws tight against the shaking that was racking him.

'Of course,' said the Grand Inquisitor and nodded to Father Farrell.

This time the icon Farrell activated could be translated as *hot wire behind the right eye.*

Corporal Kee opened his mouth in a silent scream.

'Again,' said the Grand Inquisitor softly. 'Tell us.'

'Excuse me, Your Eminence,' said Father Farrell, glancing at his comlog, 'but the Conclave Mass begins in forty-five minutes.'

The Grand Inquisitor waved his fingers. 'We have time, Martin. We have time.' He touched Corporal Kee's upper arm. 'Tell us these few facts, Corporal, and you will be bathed, dressed, and released. You have sinned against your Church and your Lord by this betrayal, but the essence of the Church is forgiveness. Explain your betrayal, and all will be forgiven.'

Amazingly, muscles still rippling with shock, Corporal Kee laughed. 'Fuck you,' he said. 'You've already made me tell you everything I know under Truthtell. You know why we killed that bitch thing and let the child go. And you'll never let me go. Fuck you.'

The Grand Inquisitor shrugged and stepped back. Glancing at his own gold comlog, he said softly, 'We have time. Much time.' He nodded to Father Farrell.

The icon that looked like a double parenthesis on the virtual pain console stood for *broad and heated blade down esophagus.* With a graceful motion of his fingers, Father Farrell activated it.

Father Captain Federico de Soya was returned to life on Pacem and had spent two weeks as a de facto prisoner in the Vatican Rectory of the Legionaries of Christ. The rectory was comfortable and tranquil. The plump little resurrection chaplain who attended to his needs – Father Baggio – was as kindly and solicitous as ever. De Soya hated the place and the priest.

No one told Father Captain de Soya that he could not leave the Legionaries rectory, but he was made to understand that he should stay there until called. After a week of gaining strength and orientation after his resurrection, he was called to Pax Fleet headquarters, where he met with Admiral Wu and her boss, Admiral Marusyn.

Father Captain de Soya did little during the meeting except salute, stand at ease, and listen. Admiral Marusyn explained that a review of Father Captain de Soya's court martial of four years earlier had shown several irregularities and inconsistencies in the prosecution's case. Further review of the situation had warranted a reversal of the court-martial board's decision: Father Captain de Soya was to be reinstated immediately at his former rank of captain in Pax Fleet. Arrangements were being made to find him a ship for combat duty.

'Your old torchship the *Balthasar* is in drydock for a year,' said Admiral Marusyn. 'A complete refitting – being brought up to archangel-escort standards. Your replacement, Mother Captain Stone, did an excellent job as skipper.'

'Yes, sir,' said de Soya. 'Stone was an excellent exec. I'm sure she's been a good boss.'

Admiral Marusyn nodded absently as he thumbed through vellum sheets in his notebook. 'Yes, yes,' he said. 'So good, in fact, that we've recommended her as skipper for one of the new planet-class archangels. We have an archangel in mind for you as well, Father Captain.'

De Soya blinked and tried not to react. 'The *Raphael*, sir?'

The Admiral looked up, his tanned and creased face set in a slight smile. 'Yes, the *Raphael*, but not the one you skippered before. We've retired that prototype to courier duty and renamed her. The new archangel *Raphael* is . . . well, you've heard about the planet-class archangels, Father Captain?'

'No, sir. Not really.' He had heard rumors on his desert world when boxite miners had talked loudly in the one cantina in town.

'Four standard years,' muttered the Admiral, shaking his head. His white hair was combed back behind his ears. 'Bring Federico up to speed here, Admiral.'

Marget Wu nodded and touched the diskey on a standard tactical console set into Admiral Marusyn's wall. A holo of a starship came into existence between her and de Soya. The father-captain could see at once that this ship was larger, sleeker, more refined, and deadlier than his old *Raphael*.

'His Holiness has asked each industrial world in the Pax to build – or at least to bankroll – one of these planet-class archangel battlecruisers, Father Captain,' said Admiral Wu in her briefing voice. 'In the past four years, twenty-one of them have been completed and have entered active service. Another sixty are nearing completion.' The holo began to rotate and enlarge until suddenly the main deck was shown in cutaway. It was as if a laser lance had sliced the ship in half.

'As you see,' continued Wu, 'the living areas, command decks, and C-three tactical centers are much roomier than on the earlier *Raphael* . . . roomier even than your old torchship. The drives – both the classified C-plus instantaneous Gideon drive and the in-system fusion plant – have been reduced in size by one-third while gaining in efficiency and ease of maintenance. The new *Raphael* carries three atmospheric dropships and a high-speed scout. There are automated resurrection creches aboard to serve a crew of twenty-eight and up to twenty-two Marines or passengers.'

'Defenses?' asked Father Captain de Soya, still standing at ease, his hands clasped behind him.

'Class-ten containment fields,' said Wu crisply. 'The newest stealth technology. Omega-class ECM and jamming ability. As well as the usual assortment of close-in hyperkinetic and energy defenses.'

'Attack capabilities?' said de Soya. He could tell from the apertures and arrays visible on the holo, but he wanted to hear it.

Admiral Marusyn answered with a tone of pride, as if showing off a new grandchild. 'The whole nine meters,' he said. 'CPBs, of course, but feeding off the C-plus drive core rather than the fusion drive. Slag anything within half an AU. New Hawking hyperkinetic missiles – miniaturized – about half the mass and size of the ones you carried on *Balthasar*. Plasma needles with almost twice the yield of the warheads of five years ago. Deathbeams . . .'

Father Captain de Soya tried not to react. Deathbeams had been prohibited in Pax Fleet.

Marusyn saw something in the other man's face. 'Things have changed, Federico. This fight is to the finish. The Ousters are breeding like fruit flies out there in the dark, and unless we stop them, they'll be slagging Pacem in a year or two.'

Father Captain de Soya nodded. 'Do you mind if I ask which world paid for the building of this new *Raphael*, sir?'

Marusyn smiled and gestured toward the holo. The hull of the ship seemed to hurtle toward de Soya as the magnification increased. The view cut through the hull and closed on the tactical bridge, moving to the edge of the tactical center holopit until the father-captain could make out a small bronze plaque with the name – HHS RAPHAEL – and beneath that, in smaller script: BUILT AND COMMISSIONED BY THE PEOPLE OF HEAVEN'S GATE FOR THE DEFENSE OF ALL HUMANITY.

'Why are you smiling, Father Captain?' asked Admiral Marusyn.

'Well, sir, it's just . . . well, I've been to the world of Heaven's Gate, sir. It was, of course, more than four standard years ago, but the planet was empty except for a dozen or so prospectors and a Pax garrison in orbit. There's been no real population there since the Ouster invasion three hundred years ago, sir. I just couldn't imagine that world financing one of these ships. It seems to me that it would take a planetary GNP of a society like Renaissance Vector's to pay for a single archangel.'

Marusyn's smile had not faltered. 'Precisely, Father Captain. Heaven's Gate is a hellhole – poison atmosphere, acid rain, endless mud, and sulfur flats. It's never recovered from the Ouster attack. But His Holiness thought that the Pax's stewardship of that world might be better transferred to private enterprise. The planet still holds a fortune in heavy metals and chemicals. So we have sold it.'

This time de Soya blinked. 'Sold it, sir? An entire world?'

While Marusyn openly grinned, Admiral Wu said, 'To the *Opus Dei*, Father Captain.'

De Soya did not speak, but neither did he show comprehension.

' "The Work of God" used to be a minor religious organization,' said Wu.

'It's . . . ah, I believe . . . about twelve hundred years old. Founded in AD 1920. In the past few years, it has become not only a great ally of the Holy See, but a worthy competitor of the Pax Mercantilus.'

'Ah, yes,' said Father Captain de Soya. He could imagine the Mercantilus buying up entire worlds, but he could not imagine the trading group allowing a rival to gain such power in the few years he had been out of Pax news. It did not matter. He turned to Admiral Marusyn. 'One last question, sir.'

The Admiral glanced at his comlog chronometer and nodded curtly.

'I have been out of Fleet service for four years,' de Soya said softly. 'I have not worn a uniform or received a tech update in all that time. The world where I served as a priest was so far out of the mainstream that I might as well have been in cryogenic fugue the whole time. How could I possibly take command of a new-generation archangel-class starship, sir?'

Marusyn frowned. 'We'll bring you up to speed, Father Captain. Pax Fleet knows what it's doing. Are you saying no to this commission?'

Father Captain de Soya hesitated a visible second. 'No, sir,' he said. 'I appreciate the confidence in me that you and Pax Fleet are showing. I'll do my best, Admiral.' De Soya had been trained to discipline twice – once as a priest and Jesuit, again as an officer in His Holiness's fleet.

Marusyn's stone face softened. 'Of course you will, Federico. We're pleased to have you back. We'd like you to stay at the Legionaries rectory here on Pacem until we're ready to send you to your ship, if that would be all right.'

Dammit, thought de Soya. *Still a prisoner with those damned Legionaries*. He said, 'Of course, sir. It's a pleasant place.'

Marusyn glanced at his comlog again. The interview was obviously at an end. 'Any requests before the assignment becomes official, Father Captain?'

De Soya hesitated again. He knew that making a request would be bad form. He spoke anyway. 'Yes, sir . . . one. There were three men who served with me on the old *Raphael*. Swiss Guard commandos whom I brought from Hyperion. . . Lancer Rettig, well, he died, sir . . . but Sergeant Gregorius and Corporal Kee were with me until the end, and I wondered . . .'

Marusyn nodded impatiently. 'You want them on new *Raphael* with you. It sounds reasonable. I used to have a cook that I dragged from ship to ship . . . poor bugger was killed during the Second Coal Sack engagement. I don't know about these men . . .' The Admiral looked at Marget Wu.

'By great coincidence,' said Admiral Wu, 'I ran across their files while reviewing your reinstatement papers, Father Captain. Sergeant Gregorius is currently serving in the Ring Territories. I am sure that a transfer can be arranged. Corporal Kee, I am afraid . . .'

De Soya's stomach muscles tightened. Kee had been with him around God's Grove – Gregorius had been returned to the creche after an unsuccessful resurrection – and the last he had seen of the lively little corporal had been after their return to Pacem space, when the MPs had taken them away to separate holding cells after their arrest. De Soya had shaken the corporal's hand and assured him that they would see each other again.

'I am afraid that Corporal Kee died two standard years ago,' finished Wu. 'He was killed during an Ouster attack on the Sagittarius Salient. I understand that he received the Silver Star of St Michael . . . posthumously, of course.'

De Soya nodded tersely. 'Thank you,' he said.

Admiral Marusyn gave his paternal politician's smile and extended his hand across the desk to de Soya. 'Good luck, Federico. Give them hell from the *Raphael*.'

The headquarters for the Pax Mercantilus was not on Pacem proper, but was located – fittingly – on the L_5 Trojan point trailing behind the planet by some sixty orbital degrees. Between the Vatican world and the huge, hollow Torus Mercantilus – a carbon-carbon doughnut two hundred and seventy meters thick, a full klick wide, and twenty-six kilometers in diameter, its interior webbed with spidery drydocks, com antennae, and loading bays – floated half of Pax Fleet's total orbital-based firepower. Kenzo Isozaki once calculated that a coup attempt launched from Torus Mercantilus would last twelve-point-oh-six nanoseconds before being vaporized.

Isozaki's office was in a clear bulb on a whiskered-carbon flower stem raised some four hundred meters above the outer rim of the torus. The bulb's curved hullskin could be opaqued or left transparent according to the whim of the CEO inside it. Today it was transparent except for the section polarized to dim the glare of Pacem's yellow sun. Space seemed black at the moment, but as the torus rotated, the bulb would come into the ring's shadow and Isozaki could glance up to see stars instantly appear as if a heavy black curtain had been pulled aside to reveal thousands of brilliant, unflickering candles. *Or the myriad campfires of my enemies*, thought Isozaki as the darkness fell for the twentieth time on this working day.

With the walls absolutely transparent, his oval office with its modest desk, chairs, and soft lamps seemed to become a carpeted platform standing alone in the immensity of space, individual stars blazing and the long swath of the Milky Way lighting the interior. But it was not this familiar spectacle that made the Mercantilus CEO look up: set amid the starfield, three fusion tails of incoming freighters could be picked out, looking like smudges on an astronomical holo. Isozaki was so adept at gauging distances and delta-vs from fusion tails that he could tell at a glance how long it would be before these freighters docked . . . and even which ships they were. The PM *Moldahar Effectuator* had refueled by skimming a gas giant in the Epsilon Eridani System and was burning redder than usual. The HHMS *Emma Constant*'s skipper was in her usual rush to get her cargo of Pegasus 51 reaction metals to the torus and was decelerating inbound a good fifteen percent above Mercantilus recommendations. Finally, the smallest smudge could only be the HHMS *Elemosineria Apostolica* just passing spindown from its C-plus translation point from Renaissance System: Isozaki knew this from a glance, just as he knew the three hundred-some other optimal translation points visible in his part of the Pacem System sky.

The lift tube rose from the floor and became a transparent cylinder, its passenger lit by starlight. Isozaki knew that the cylinder was transparent only from the outside: in it, the occupants stood in a mirrored interior, seeing nothing of the CEO's office, staring at their own reflection until Isozaki keyed their door open.

Anna Pelli Cognani was the only person in the tube. Isozaki nodded and his personal AI rotated the cube door open. His fellow CEO and protégée did not even glance up at the moving starfield as she crossed the carpet toward him. 'Good afternoon, Kenzo-san.'

'Good afternoon, Anna.' He waved her toward the most comfortable chair, but Cognani shook her head and remained standing. She never took a seat in Isozaki's office. Isozaki never ceased offering her one.

'The Conclave Mass is almost over,' said Cognani.

Isozaki nodded. At that second his office AI darkened the bubble walls and projected the Vatican's tightbeam broadcast.

St Peter's Basilica was awash in scarlet and purple and black and white this morning as the eighty-three cardinals soon to be sealed in the Conclave bowed, prayed, genuflected, knelt, stood, and sang. Behind this *terna*, or herd of theoretically possible candidates for the papacy, were the hundreds of bishops and archbishops, deacons and members of the Curia, Pax military officials and Pax civil administrators, Pax planetary governors and high elected officials who happened to be on Pacem at the time of the Pope's death or who were within three weeks' time-debt, delegates from the Dominicans, the Jesuits, the Benedictines, the Legionaries of Christ, the Mariaists, the Salesians, and a single delegate standing for the few remaining Franciscans. There were the 'valued guests' in the back rows – honorary delegates from the Pax Mercantilus, the *Opus Dei*, the *Istituto per Opere di Religione* – also known as the Vatican Bank, delegates from the Vatican administrative wings of the *Prefettura*, the *Servizio Assistenziale del Santo Padre* – the Holy Father's Welfare Service, from the APSA – the Administration of the Patrimony of the Holy See, as well as from Cardinal Camerlengo's own Apostolic Chamber. Also in the rear pews were honored guests from the Pontifical Academy of Sciences, the Papal Commission on Interstellar Peace and Justice, many papal academies such as the Pontifical Ecclesiastical Academy, and other quasi-theological organizations necessary to the running of the vast Pax state. Finally, there were the bright uniforms of the Corps Helvetica – the Swiss Guard – as well as commanders of the Palatine Guard reconstituted by Pope Julius, and the first appearance of the commander of the hitherto secret Noble Guard – a pale, dark-haired man in a solid red uniform.

Isozaki and Cognani watched this pageant with knowledgeable eyes. Each of them had been invited to the Mass, but it had become a tradition in recent centuries for the Pax Mercantilus CEOs to honor major Church-ceremonies by their absence – sending only their official Vatican delegates. Both watched Cardinal Couesnongle celebrate this Mass of the Holy Spirit and saw Cardinal Camerlengo as the powerless figurehead he was; their eyes were on Cardinal Lourdusamy, Cardinal Mustafa, and half a dozen other power brokers in the front pews.

With the final benediction, the Mass ended and the voting cardinals filed out in solemn procession to the Sistine Chapel, where the holocams lingered while the doors were sealed, the entrance to the Conclave was closed and that door bolted on the inside and padlocked on the outside, and the sealing of the Conclave pronounced official by the Commandant of the Swiss Guards and the Prefect of the Pontifical Household. The Vatican coverage then shifted to commentary and speculation while the image remained of the sealed door.

'Enough,' said Kenzo Isozaki. The broadcast flashed off, the bubble grew transparent, and sunlight flooded the room under a black sky.

Anna Pelli Cognani smiled thinly. 'The voting shouldn't take too long.'

Isozaki had returned to his chair. Now he steepled his fingers and tapped his lower lip. 'Anna,' he said, 'do you think that we – all of us in the chairmanship of the Mercantilus – have any real power?'

Cognani's neutral expression showed her surprise. She said, 'During the last fiscal year, Kenzo-san, my division showed a profit of thirty-six billion marks.'

Isozaki held his steepled fingers still. 'M. Cognani,' he said, 'would you be so kind as to remove your jacket and shirt?'

His protégée did not blink. In the twenty-eight standard years they had been colleagues – subordinate and master, actually – M. Isozaki had never done, said, or implied anything that might have been interpreted as a sexual overture. She hesitated only a second, then unsealed her jacket, slipped it off, set it on the chair she never sat in, and unsealed her shirt. She folded it atop her jacket on the back of the chair.

Isozaki rose and came around his desk, standing only a meter from her. 'Your underthings as well,' he said, slipping off his own jacket and un-buttoning his own old-fashioned shirt. His chest was healthy, muscled, but hairless.

Cognani slipped off her chemise. Her breasts were small but perfectly formed, rosy at the tips.

Kenzo Isozaki lifted one hand as if he were going to touch her, pointed, and then returned the hand to his own chest and touched the double-barred cruciform that ran from his sternum to just above his navel. 'This,' he said, 'is power.' He turned away and began dressing. After a moment, Anna Pelli Cognani hugged her shoulders and then also began dressing.

When they were both dressed, Isozaki sat behind his desk again and gestured toward the other chair. To his quiet astonishment, M. Anna Pelli Cognani sat in it.

'What you are saying,' began Cognani, 'is that no matter how successful we are in making ourselves indispensable to the new Pope – if there ever is a new pope – the Church will always have the ultimate leverage of resurrection.'

'Not quite,' said Isozaki, steepling his fingers again as if the previous interlude had not happened. 'I am saying that the power controlling the cruciform controls the human universe.'

'The Church . . .' began Cognani and stopped. 'Of course, the cruciform is just part of the power equation. The TechnoCore provides the Church with the secret of successful resurrection. But they've been in league with the Church for two hundred and eighty years . . .'

'For their own purposes,' said Isozaki softly. 'What are those purposes, Anna?'

The office rotated into night. Stars exploded into existence. Cognani raised her face to the Milky Way to gain a moment to think. 'No one knows,' she said at last. 'Ohm's Law.'

Isozaki smiled. 'Very good. Following the path of least resistance here may not lead us through the Church, but via the Core.'

'But Councillor Albedo meets with no one except His Holiness and Lourdusamy.'

'No one that we know of,' amended Isozaki. 'But that is a matter of the Core coming to the human universe.'

Cognani nodded. She understood the implicit suggestion: the illicit, Core-class AIs that the Mercantilus was developing could find the datum-plane avenue and follow it to the Core. For almost three hundred years, the prime commandment enforced by the Church and Pax had been: *Thou shalt not build a thinking machine equal or superior to humankind.* 'AIs' in use within the Pax were more 'All-purpose Instruments' than 'Artificial Intelligences' of the kind that had evolved away from humanity almost a millennium earlier: idiot thinking machines like Isozaki's office AI or the cretinous ship computer on de Soya's old ship, the *Raphael.* But in the past dozen years, secret research departments of the Pax Mercantilus had recreated the autonomous AIs equal to or surpassing those in common use during the days of the Hegemony. The risk and benefits of this project were almost beyond measure – absolute domination of Pax trade and a breaking of the old balance-of-power stand-off between Pax Fleet and Pax Mercantilus if successful; excommunication, torture in the dungeons of the Holy Office, and execution if discovered by the Church. And now this prospect.

Anna Pelli Cognani stood. 'My God,' she said softly, 'that would be the ultimate end run.'

Isozaki nodded and smiled again. 'Do you know where that term originated, Anna?'

'End run? No . . . some sport, I imagine.'

'A very ancient warfare-surrogate sport called football,' said Isozaki.

Cognani knew that this irrelevancy was anything but irrelevant. Sooner or later her master would explain why this datum was important. She waited.

'The Church had something that the Core wanted . . . needed,' said Isozaki. 'The taming of the cruciform was their part of the deal. The Church had to barter something of equal worth.'

Cognani thought, *Equal in worth to the immortality of a trillion human beings?* She said, 'I had always assumed that when Lenar Hoyt and Lourdusamy contacted the surviving Core elements more than two centuries ago, the Church's bartering point was in secretly reestablishing the TechnoCore in human space.'

Isozaki opened his hands. 'To what ends, Anna? Where is the benefit to the Core?'

'When the Core was an integral part of the Hegemony,' she said, 'running the WorldWeb and the fatline, they were using the neurons in the billions of human brains transiting the farcasters as a sort of neural net, part of their Ultimate Intelligence project.'

'Ah, yes,' said her mentor. 'But there are no farcasters now. If they are using human beings . . . how? And where?'

Without meaning to, Anna Pelli Cognani raised one hand to her breast-bone.

Isozaki smiled. 'Irritating, isn't it? Like a word that is on the tip of one's tongue but will not come to mind. A puzzle with a missing piece. But there is one piece that was missing which has just been found.'

Cognani raised an eyebrow. 'The girl?'

'Back in Pax space,' said the older CEO. 'Our agents close to Lourdusamy have confirmed that the Core has revealed this. It happened after the death of His Holiness . . . only the Secretary of State, the Grand Inquisitor, and the top people in Pax Fleet know.'

'Where is she?'

Isozaki shook his head. 'If the Core knows, they haven't revealed it to the Church or any other human agency. But Pax Fleet has called up that ship's captain – de Soya – because of the news.'

'The Core had predicted that he would be involved in the girl's capture,' said Cognani. The beginnings of a smile were working at the corners of her mouth.

'Yes?' said Isozaki, proud of his student.

'Ohm's Law,' said Cognani.

'Precisely.'

The woman stood and again touched her chest without being aware of doing so. 'If we find the girl first, we have the leverage to open discussions with the Core. *And* the means – with the new abilities we will have on-line.' None of the CEOs who knew of the secret AI project ever said the words or phrases aloud, despite their bugproof offices.

'If we have the girl and the means of negotiating,' continued Cognani, 'we may have the leverage we need to supplant the Church in the Core's arrangement with humanity.'

'*If* we can discover what the Core is getting from the Church in return for control of the cruciform,' murmured Isozaki. 'And offer the same or better.'

Cognani nodded in a distracted manner. She was seeing how all of this related to her goals and efforts as CEO of *Opus Dei*. *In every way*, she realized at once. 'In the meantime, we have to find the girl before the others do . . . Pax Fleet must be utilizing resources they would never reveal to the Vatican.'

'And vice versa,' said Isozaki. This kind of contest pleased him very much.

'And we will have to do the same,' said Cognani, turning toward the lift tube. 'Every resource.' She smiled at her mentor. 'It's the ultimate three-way, zero-sum game, isn't it, Kenzo-san?'

'Just so,' said Isozaki. 'Everything to the winner – power, immortality, and wealth beyond human imagining. To the loser – destruction, the true death, and eternal slavery for one's descendants.' He held up one finger. 'But not a three-way game, Anna. Six.'

Cognani paused by the lift door. 'I see the fourth,' she said. 'The Core has its own imperative to find the girl first. But . . .'

Isozaki lowered his hand. 'We must presume that the child has her own goals in this game, mustn't we? And whoever or whatever has introduced her as a playing piece . . . well, that must be our sixth player.'

'Or one of the other five,' said Cognani, smiling. She also enjoyed a high-stakes game.

Isozaki nodded and turned his chair to watch the next sunrise above the curving-away band of the Torus Mercantilus. He did not turn back when the lift door closed and Anna Pelli Cognani departed.

Above the altar, Jesus Christ, his face stern and unrelenting, divided men into camps of the good and the bad – the rewarded and the damned. There was no third group.

Cardinal Lourdusamy sat in his canopied stall inside the Sistine Chapel and looked at Michelangelo's fresco of the *Last Judgment*. Lourdusamy had always thought that this Christ was a bullying, authoritarian, merciless figure – perhaps an icon perfectly suited to oversee this choice of a new Vicar of Christ.

The little chapel was crowded with the eighty-three canopied stalls seating the eighty-three cardinals present in the flesh. An empty space allowed for activation of the holos representing the missing thirty-seven cardinals – one holo of a canopied stall at a time.

This was the first morning after the cardinals had been 'nailed up' in the Vatican Palace. Lourdusamy had slept and eaten well – his bedroom a cot in his Vatican office, his repast a simple meal cooked by the nuns of the Vatican guest house: simple food and a cheap white wine served in the glorious Borgia Apartments. Now all were gathered in the Sistine Chapel, their stall-thrones in place, their canopies raised. Lourdusamy knew that this splendid sight had been missing from the Conclave for many centuries – ever since the number of cardinals had grown too large to accommodate the stalls in the small chapel, sometime pre-Hegira, the nineteenth or twentieth century AD, he thought – but the Church had grown so small by the end of the Fall of the Farcasters that the forty-some cardinals could once again easily fit. Pope Julius had kept the number small – never more than a hundred and twenty cardinals, despite the growth of the Pax. And with almost forty of them unable to travel in time to the Conclave, the Sistine Chapel could hold the stalls of those cardinals permanently based on Pacem.

The moment had come. All of the cardinal-electors in the chapel stood as one. In the empty space near the Scrutineers' table near the altar, the holos of the thirty-seven absent cardinal-electors shimmered into existence. Because the space was small, the holos were small – little more than doll-sized human figures in doll-sized wooden stalls – all of them floating in midair like ghosts of Conclave-electors past. Lourdusamy smiled, as he always did, at how appropriate the reduced size of these absent electors seemed.

Pope Julius had always been elected by acclamation. One of the three cardinals acting as Scrutineers raised his hand: the Holy Spirit may have been prepared to move these men and women, but some coordination was required. When the Scrutineer's hand dropped, the eighty-three cardinals and thirty-seven holos were to speak as one.

'*Eligo* Father Lenar Hoyt!' cried Cardinal Lourdusamy and saw Cardinal Mustafa shouting the same words from beneath the canopy of his stall.

The Scrutineer in front of the altar paused. The acclamation had been loud and clear, but obviously not unanimous. This was a new wrinkle. For two hundred and seventy years, the acclamation had been immediate.

Lourdusamy was careful not to smile or look around. He knew which of the newer cardinals had not cried out Pope Julius's name for reelection. He knew the wealth it had taken to bribe these men and women. He knew the terrible risk they were running and would almost certainly suffer for. Lourdusamy knew all this because he had helped to orchestrate it.

After a moment of consultation among the Scrutineers, the one who had called for acclamation now said, 'We shall proceed by scrutiny.'

There was excited talk among the cardinals as the ballots were prepared and handed out. This had never happened before in the lifetime of most of these princes of the Church. Immediately the acclamation holos of the missing cardinal-electors had become irrelevant. Although a few of the absent cardinals had prepared their interactive chips for scrutiny, most had not bothered.

The Masters of Ceremonies moved among the stalls, distributing voting cards – three to each cardinal-elector. The Scrutineers moved among the forest of stalls to make sure that each of the cardinals had a pen. When all was in readiness, the Cardinal Deacon among the Scrutineers raised his hand again, this time to signify the moment of voting.

Lourdusamy looked at his ballot. On the upper left, the words '*Eligo in Summum Pontificem*' appeared in print. There was room for one name beneath it. Simon Augustino Cardinal Lourdusamy wrote in *Lenar Hoyt* and folded the card and held it up so that it could be seen. Within a minute, all eighty-three of the cardinals were holding a card aloft, as were half a dozen of the interactive holos.

The Scrutineer began calling the cardinals forward in order of precedence. Cardinal Lourdusamy went first, leaving his stall and walking to the Scrutineers' table next to the altar beneath the gaze of the terrible Christ of the fresco. Genuflecting and then kneeling at the altar, Lourdusamy bowed his head in silent prayer. Rising, he said aloud, 'I call to witness Christ the Lord who will be my judge, that my vote is given to the one who before God I consider should be elected.' Lourdusamy solemnly set his folded card on the silver plate that sat atop the vote receptacle. Lifting the plate, he dropped his vote into the receptacle. The Cardinal Deacon among the Scrutineers nodded; Lourdusamy bowed toward the altar and returned to his stall.

Cardinal Mustafa, the Grand Inquisitor, moved majestically toward the altar to cast the second vote.

It was more than an hour later that the votes were tallied. The first Scrutineer shook the receptacle to mix the votes. The second Scrutineer counted them – including the six votes copied from the interactive holos – depositing each in a second receptacle. The count equaled the number of voting cardinals in the Conclave. The Scrutiny proceeded.

The first Scrutineer unfolded a card, wrote down the name on it, and passed the card to the second Scrutineer, who made a note and passed it to the third and final Scrutineer. This man – Cardinal Couesnongle as it turned out – said the name aloud before making a note of it.

In each of the stalls, a cardinal jotted the name on a 'scriber pad provided by the Scrutineers. At the end of the Conclave, the 'scribers would be scrambled, their files deleted so that no record of the voting would remain.

And so the voting proceeded. For Lourdusamy as for the rest of the living cardinals present, the only suspense was whether the dissident cardinal-electors from the acclamation would actually put someone else's name into play.

As each card was read, the last Scrutineer ran a threaded needle through the word '*Eligo*' and slid the card down the thread. When all of the ballots had been read aloud, knots were tied in each end of the thread.

The winning candidate was admitted to the Chapel. Standing before the altar in a simple black cassock, the man looked humble and a bit over-whelmed.

Standing before him, the senior Deacon Cardinal said, 'Do you accept your canonical election as Supreme Pontiff?'

'I do so accept it,' said the priest.

At this point, a stall was brought out and set behind the priest. The Cardinal Deacon raised his hands and intoned, 'Thus accepting your canon-ical election, this gathering does – in the sight of God Almighty – acknow-ledge you as Bishop of the Church of Rome, true Pope, and Head of the College of Bishops. May God advise you well as He grants you full and absolute power over the Church of Jesus Christ.'

'Amen,' said Cardinal Lourdusamy and pulled the cord that lowered the canopy over his stall. All eighty-three physical canopies and thirty-seven holographic ones lowered at the same time, until only the new Pope's remained raised. The priest – now Pontiff – sat back in the seat beneath the papal canopy.

'What name do you choose as Supreme Pontiff?' asked the Deacon Cardinal.

'I choose the name Urban the Sixteenth,' said the seated priest.

There was a murmuring and hum from the cardinals' stalls. The Cardinal Deacon held out his hand and he and the other Scrutineers led the priest from the Chapel. The murmuring and whispering rose in volume.

Cardinal Mustafa leaned out of his stall and said to Lourdusamy, 'He must be thinking of Urban the Second. Urban the Fifteenth was a sniveling little coward in the twenty-ninth century who did little but read detective novels and write love letters to his former mistress.'

'Urban the Second,' mused Lourdusamy. 'Yes, of course.'

After several minutes, the Scrutineers returned with the priest – now the Pope dressed in pure white – a white-caped cassock, a white *zuchetto* or skullcap, a pectoral cross, and a white fascia sash. Cardinal Lourdusamy went to his knees on the stone floor of the Chapel, as did all the other cardinals, real and holographic, as the new Pontiff gave his first benediction.

Then the Scrutineers and the attending cardinals went to the stove to burn the votes now tethered on black thread, adding enough *bianco* chemical to make sure that the *sfumata* would indeed be white smoke.

The cardinals filed out of the Sistine Chapel and walked the ancient paths and corridors to St Peter's, where the senior Cardinal Deacon went alone onto the balcony to announce the name of the new Pontiff to the waiting multitudes.

Among the five hundred thousand waiting individuals in the multitude squeezed into, out of, and around St Peter's Square that morning was Father Captain Federico de Soya. He had been released from his de facto imprisonment at the Legionaries rectory only hours before. He was to report to Pax Fleet's spaceport later that afternoon for shuttle to his new command. Walking through the Vatican, de Soya had followed the crowds – then had been engulfed by them – as men, women, and children had flowed like a great river toward the Square.

A great cheer had gone up when the puffs of white smoke first became visible from the stovepipe. The impossibly thick throng beneath the balcony of St Peter's somehow became thicker as tens of thousands more flowed around the colonnades and past the statuary. Hundreds of Swiss Guard troopers held the crowd back from the entrance to the Basilica and away from private areas.

When the Senior Deacon emerged and announced that the new Pope was to be called His Holiness Urban XVI, a great gasp went up from the crowd. De Soya found himself gaping in surprise and shock. Everyone had expected Julius XV. The thought of anyone else as Pope was . . . well, unthinkable.

Then the new Pontiff stepped onto the balcony and the gasps turned to cheers that went on and on and on.

It was Pope Julius – the familiar face, the high forehead, the sad eyes. Father Lenar Hoyt, the savior of the Church, had once again been elected. His Holiness raised his hand in the familiar benediction and waited for the crowd to stop cheering so that he could speak, but the crowd would not stop cheering. The roar rose from half a million throats and went on and on.

Why Urban XVI? wondered Father Captain de Soya. He had read and studied enough history of the Church in his years as a Jesuit. Quickly he thumbed back through his mental notes on the Urban popes. . . most were forgettable or worse. Why . . .

'Damn,' Father Captain de Soya said aloud, the soft curse lost under the continuing roar of the faithful filling St Peter's Square. 'Damn,' he said again.

Even before the crowd quieted enough for the new-old Pontiff to speak, to explain his choice of name, to announce what de Soya knew had to be announced, the father-captain understood. And his heart sank with that understanding.

Urban II had served from AD 1088 to 1099. At the synod the Pope had called in Clermont in . . . November, in the year 1095, de Soya thought . . . Urban II had made his call for holy war against the Muslims in the Near East, for the rescue of Byzantium, and for the liberation of all eastern Christian holy places from Muslim domination. That call had led to the First Crusade . . . the first of many bloody campaigns.

The crowd finally quieted. Pope Urban XVI began to speak, the familiar but newly energized voice rising and falling over the heads of the half-million faithful listening in person and the billions listening via live broadcast.

Father Captain de Soya turned away even before the new Pope began to speak. He pushed and elbowed his way back through the unmoving crowd, trying to escape the suddenly claustrophobic confines of St Peter's Square.

It was no use. The crowd was rapt and joyous and de Soya was trapped in the mob. The words from the new Pontiff were also joyous and impassioned. Father Captain de Soya stood, unable to escape, and bowed his head. As the crowd began cheering and crying *'Deus le volt!'* – God wills it – de Soya began to weep.

Crusade. Glory. A final resolution of the Ouster Problem. Death beyond imagining. Destruction beyond imagining. Father Captain de Soya squeezed his eyes shut as tightly as he could, but the vision of charged particle beams flaring against the blackness of space, of entire worlds burning, of oceans turning to steam and continents into molten rivers of lava, visions of orbital forests exploding into smoke, of charred bodies tumbling in zero-g, of fragile, winged creatures flaring and charring and expanding into ash . . .

De Soya wept while billions cheered.

FOUR

It has been my experience that late-night departures and farewells are the hardest on the spirit.

The military was especially good at beginning major voyages in the middle of the night. During my time in the Hyperion Home Guard, it seemed that all important troop movements began in the wee hours. I began to associate that odd blend of fear and excitement, dread and anticipation, with predawn darkness and the smell of *lateness*. Aenea had said that I would be leaving that night of her announcement to the Fellowship, but it took time to load the kayak, for me to pack my gear and decide what to leave behind forever, and to close up my tent and work area in the compound, so we weren't airborne in the dropship until after two AM and it was almost sunrise before we reached our destination.

I admit that I felt rushed and ordered about by the girl's preemptive announcement. Many people had come to look to Aenea for leadership and advice during the four years we spent at Taliesin West, but I wasn't one of those people. I was thirty-two years old. Aenea was sixteen. It was my job to watch out for her, to protect her, and – if it came to that – to tell *her* what to do and when to do it. I didn't like this turn of events one bit.

I'd assumed that A. Bettik would be flying with us to wherever I was supposed to shove off, but Aenea said that the android would be staying behind at the compound, so I wasted another twenty minutes tracking him down and saying good-bye.

'M. Aenea says that we will meet up again in due course,' said the blue man, 'so I am confident that we shall, M. Endymion.'

'Raul,' I said for the five hundredth time. 'Call me Raul.'

'Of course,' said A. Bettik with that slight smile that suggested insubordination.

'Fuck it,' I said eloquently and stuck out my hand. A. Bettik shook it. I had the urge then to hug our old traveling companion, but I knew that it would embarrass him. Androids were not literally *programmed* to be stiff and subservient – they were, after all, living, organic beings, not machines – but between RNA-training and long practice, they were hopelessly formal creatures. At least this one was.

And then we were away, Aenea and I, taxiing the dropship out of its hangar into the desert night and lifting off with as little noise as possible. I had said good-bye to as many of the other Fellowship apprentices and workers as I had found, but the hour was late and the people were scattered to their dorm cubbies, tents, and apprentice shelters. I hoped that I would run into some of them again – especially some of the construction crewmen and women with whom I'd worked for four years – but I had little real belief that I would.

The dropship could have flown itself to our destination – just a series of coordinates Aenea had given it – but I left the controls on semimanual so I could pretend I had something to do during the flight. I knew from the coordinates that we would be traveling about fifteen hundred klicks. Somewhere along the Mississippi River, Aenea had said. The dropship could have done that distance in ten suborbital minutes, but we had been conserving its dwindling energy and fuel reserves, so once we had extended the wings to maximum, we kept our velocity subsonic, our altitude set at a comfortable ten thousand meters, and avoided morphing the ship again until landing. We ordered the Consul's starship's persona – which I'd long ago loaded from my comlog into the dropship's AI core – to keep quiet unless it had something important to tell us, and then we settled back in the red instrument glow to talk and watch the dark continent pass beneath us.

'Kiddo,' I said, 'why this galloping hurry?'

Aenea made the self-conscious, throwing-away gesture I had first seen her use almost five years earlier. 'It seemed important to get things going.' Her voice was soft, almost lifeless, drained of the vitality and energy that had moved the entire Fellowship to her will. Perhaps I was the only living person who could identify the tone, but she sounded close to tears.

'It can't be that important,' I said. 'To make me leave in the middle of the night . . .'

Aenea shook her head and looked out the dark windscreen for a moment. I realized that she was crying. When she finally turned back, the glow from the instruments made her eyes look very moist and red. 'If you don't leave tonight, I'll lose my nerve and ask you not to go. If you don't go, I'll lose my nerve again and stay on Earth . . . never go back.'

I had the urge to take her hand then, but I kept my big paw on the omnicontroller instead. 'Hey,' I said, 'we can go back together. This doesn't make any sense for me to go off one way and you another.'

'Yes it does,' said Aenea so quietly that I had to lean to my right to hear her.

'A. Bettik could go fetch the ship,' I said. 'You and I can stay on Earth until we're ready to return . . .'

Aenea shook her head. 'I'll *never* be ready to go back, Raul. The thought scares me to death.'

I thought of the wild chase that had sent us fleeing through Pax space from Hyperion, barely eluding Pax starships, torchships, fighter aircraft, Marines, Swiss Guard, and God knows what else – including that bitch-thing from hell that had almost killed us on God's Grove – and I said, 'I feel the same way, kiddo. Maybe we *should* stay on Earth. They can't reach us here.'

Aenea looked at me and I recognized the expression: it was not mere stubbornness, it was a closing of all discussion on a matter that was settled.

'All right,' I said, 'but I still haven't heard why A. Bettik couldn't take this kayak and go get the ship while I farcast back with you.'

'Yes, you have,' said Aenea. 'You weren't listening.' She shifted sideways in the big seat. 'Raul, if you leave and we agree to meet at a certain time in a certain place in Pax space, I *have* to go through the farcaster and do what I have to do. And what I have to do next, I have to do on my own.'

'Aenea,' I said.

'Yes?'

'That's really stupid. Do you know that?'

The sixteen-year-old said nothing. Below and to the left, somewhere in western Kansas, a circle of campfires became visible. I looked out at the lights amid all that darkness. 'Any idea what experiment your alien friends are doing down there?' I said.

'No,' said Aenea. 'And they aren't my alien friends.'

'Which aren't they?' I said. 'Aliens? Or friends?'

'Neither,' said Aenea. I realized that this was the most specific she had ever been about the godlike intelligences that had kidnapped Old Earth – and us, it seemed to me at times, as if we had been harried and driven through the farcasters like cattle.

'Care to tell me anything else about these nonalien nonfriends?' I said. 'After all, something could go wrong . . . I might not make it to our rendez-vous. I'd like to know the secret of our hosts before I go.'

I regretted saying that as soon as the words were out. Aenea pulled back as if I had slapped her.

'Sorry, kiddo,' I said. This time I did put my hand on hers. 'I didn't mean that. I'm just angry.'

Aenea nodded and I could see the tears in her eyes again.

Still mentally kicking myself, I said, 'Everyone in the Fellowship was sure that the aliens were benevolent, godlike creatures. People said "Lions and Tigers and Bears" but what they were thinking was "Jesus and Yahweh and E.T." from that old flat film that Mr W. showed us. Everyone was sure that when it came time to fold up the Fellowship, the aliens would appear and lead us back to the Pax in a big mothership. No danger. No muss. No fuss.'

Aenea smiled but her eyes still glistened. 'Humans have been waiting for Jesus and Yahweh and E.T. to save their asses since before they covered those asses with bearskins and came out of the cave,' she said. 'They'll have to keep waiting. This is our business . . . our fight . . . and we have to take care of it ourselves.'

'Ourselves being you and me and A. Bettik against eight hundred billion or so of the born-again faithful?' I said softly.

Aenea made the graceful gesture with her hand again. 'Yeah,' she said. 'For now.'

When we arrived it was not only still dark, but raining hard – a cold, sleety, end-of-autumn rain. The Mississippi was a big river – one of Old Earth's largest – and the dropship circled over it once before landing in a small town on the west bank. I saw all this on the viewscreen under image enhancement: the view out the actual windscreen was blackness and rain.

We came in over a high hill covered with bare trees, crossed an empty highway that spanned the Mississippi on a narrow bridge, and landed in an open, paved area about fifty meters from the river. The town ran back from the river here in a valley between wooded hills and on the viewscreen I could make out small, wooden buildings, larger brick warehouses, and a few taller structures near the river that might have been grain silos. Those kinds of structures had been common in the nineteenth, twentieth, and twenty-first centuries in this part of Old Earth: I had no idea why this city had been spared the earthquakes and fires of the Tribulations, or why the Lions and Tigers and Bears had rebuilt it, if they had. There had been no sign of people in the narrow streets, nor of heat signatures on the infrared bands – neither living creatures nor groundcars with their overheated, internal-combustion drive systems – but then again, it was almost four-thirty in the morning on a cold, rainy night. No one with an ounce of sense would be out in that lousy, stinking weather.

We both pulled on ponchos, I hefted my small backpack and said, 'So long, Ship. Don't do anything I wouldn't do,' and we were down the morphed stairs and into the rain.

Aenea helped me tug the kayak out of the storage area in the belly of the dropship and we headed down the slick street toward the river. On our previous river adventure, I had carried night-vision goggles, an assortment of weapons, and a raft full of fancy gadgets. This night I had the flashlight laser that was our only memento of the trip out to Earth – set to its weakest, most energy-conserving setting, it illuminated about two meters of rainslick street – a Navajo hunting knife in my backpack, and some sandwiches and dried fruit packed away. I was ready to take on the Pax.

'What is this place?' I said.

'Hannibal,' said Aenea, struggling to hold the slick kayak as we stumbled down the street.

By this point I had to shift the slim flashlight laser in my teeth, keeping both hands on the bow of the stupid little boat. When we reached the point where the street became a loading ramp, running into the black torrent of the Mississippi, I set the kayak down, removed the flashlight, and said, 'St Petersburg.' I had spent hundreds and hundreds of hours reading in the Fellowship compound's rich library of print books.

I saw Aenea's hooded figure nod in the reflected glow of the flashlight beam.

'This is crazy,' I said, swinging the flashlight beam around the empty street, against the wall of the brick warehouses, out to the dark river. The rush of dark water was frightening. Any thought of setting off on that was insane.

'Yes,' said Aenea. 'Crazy.' The cold rain beat on the hood of her poncho.

I went around the kayak and took her by the arm. 'You see the future,' I said. 'When are we going to see each other again?'

Her head was bowed. I could make out only the barest gleam of her pale cheek in the reflected beam. The arm I gripped through the sleeve of the poncho might as well have been the branch of a dead tree for all the life I felt there. She said something too softly for me to make it out over the sound of the rain and the river.

'What?' I said.

'I said I don't *see* the future,' she said. 'I remember parts of it.'

'What's the difference?'

Aenea sighed and stepped closer. It was cold enough that our breaths actually mingled in the air. I felt the adrenaline rush from anxiety, fear, and anticipation.

'The difference is,' she said, 'that seeing is a form of clarity, remembering is . . . something else.'

I shook my head. Rain dripped in my eyes. 'I don't understand.'

'Raul, do you remember Bets Kimbal's birthday party? When Jaev played the piano and Kikki got falling-down drunk?'

'Yeah,' I said, irritated at this discussion in the middle of the night, in the middle of the storm, in the middle of our departure.

'When was it?'

'What?'

'When was it?' she repeated. Behind us, the Mississippi flowed out of the darkness and back into darkness with the speed of a maglev train.

'April,' I said. 'Early May. I don't know.'

The hooded figure before me nodded. 'And what did Mr Wright wear that night?'

I had never had the impulse to hit or spank or scream at Aenea. Not until this minute. 'How should I know? Why should I remember that?'

'Try to.'

I let out my breath and looked away at the dark hills in the black night. 'Shit, I don't know . . . his gray wool suit. Yeah, I remember him standing by the piano in it. That gray suit with the big buttons.'

Aenea nodded again. 'Bets's birthday party was in mid-March,' she said over the patter of rain on our hoods. 'Mr Wright didn't come because he had a cold.'

'So?' I said, knowing very well what point she had just made.

'So I *remember* bits of the future,' she said again, her voice sounding close to tears. 'I'm afraid to trust those memories. If I say when we will see each other again, it may be like Mr Wright's gray suit.'

For a long minute I said nothing. Rain pounded like tiny fists on closed coffins. Finally I said, 'Yeah.'

Aenea took two steps and put her arms around me. Our ponchos crinkled against each other. I could feel the tightness of her back and the new softness of her chest as we hugged clumsily.

She stepped back. 'Can I have the flashlight a moment?'

I handed it to her. She pulled back the nylon apron in the tiny cockpit of the kayak and shined the light on the narrow strip of polished wood there beneath the fiberglass. A single red button, under its clear, protective panel, gleamed in the rain. 'See that?'

'Yeah.'

'Don't touch it, whatever you do.'

I admit that I barked a laugh at that. Among the things I had read in the Taliesin library were plays of the absurd like *Waiting for Godot*. I had the feeling that we had flown into some latitude of the absurd and surreal here.

'I'm serious,' said Aenea.

'Why put a button in if it's not to be touched?' I said, wiping the dripping moisture out of my face.

The hooded figure shook its head. 'I mean, don't touch it until you absolutely have to.'

'How will I know when I absolutely have to, kiddo?'

'You'll know,' she said and gave me another hug. 'We'd better get this into the river.'

I bent to kiss her forehead then. I had done this dozens of times over the past few years – wishing her well before one of her retreats, tucking her in, kissing her clammy forehead when she was sick with fever or half-dead from fatigue. But as I bent to kiss her, Aenea raised her face, and for the first time since we had met in the midst of dust and confusion in the Valley of the Time Tombs, I kissed her on the lips.

I believe that I have mentioned before how Aenea's gaze is more powerful and intimate than most people's physical touches . . . how her touch is like a jolt of electricity. This kiss was . . . beyond all that. I was thirty-two years old that night in Hannibal, on the west bank of the river known as the Mississippi, on the world once known as Earth, lost now somewhere in the Lesser Magellanic Cloud, in the dark and rain, and I had never experienced a jolt of sensation like that first kiss.

I pulled back in shock. The flashlight laser had tilted up between us and I could see the glint of her dark eyes . . . looking mischievous, perhaps, relieved, perhaps, as if a long wait had ended, and . . . something else.

'Good-bye, Raul,' she said, and lifted her end of the kayak.

My mind reeling, I placed the bow in the dark water at the bottom of the ramp and leveraged myself down and into the cockpit. A. Bettik had fashioned it for me like a well-tailored suit of clothes. I made sure not to depress the red button in my flailing around. Aenea shoved and the kayak was floating in twenty centimeters of water. She handed me the double-bladed paddle, then my backpack, and then the flashlight laser.

I aimed the beam at the darkwater between us. 'Where's the farcaster portal?' I said. I heard the words from a distance, as if some third party had spoken. My mind and emotions were still dealing with the kiss. I was thirty-two years old. This child had just turned sixteen. My job was to protect her and to keep her alive until we could return to Hyperion and the old poet someday. This was madness.

'You'll see it,' she said. 'Sometime after daylight.'

Hours away then. This was theater of the absurd. 'And what do I do after I find the ship?' I said. 'Where do we meet?'

'There is a world named T'ien Shan,' said Aenea. 'It means "Mountains of Heaven". The ship will know how to find it.'

'It's in the Pax?' I said.

'Just barely,' she said, her breath hanging in the cold air. 'It was in the Hegemony Outback. The Pax has incorporated it into the Protectorate and promised to send missionaries, but it hasn't been tamed yet.'

'T'ien Shan,' I repeated. 'All right. How do I find you? Planets are big things.'

I could see her dark eyes in the bouncing flashlight beam. They were moist with rain or tears, or both. 'Find a mountain called Heng Shan . . . the Sacred Mountain of the North. Near it there will be a place called Hsuan-k'ung Ssu,' she said. 'It means "Temple Hanging in Air". I should be there.'

I made a rude gesture with my fist. 'Great, so all I have to do is stop at a local Pax garrison and ask directions to the Temple Hanging in Air, and you'll be hanging there waiting for me.'

'There are only a few thousand mountains on T'ien Shan,' she said, her voice flat and unhappy. 'And only a few . . . cities. The ship can find Heng Shan and Hsuan-k'ung Ssu from orbit. You won't be able to land there, but you'll be able to disembark.'

'Why won't I be able to land there?' I said, irritated by all of these puzzles within enigmas within codes.

'You'll see, Raul,' she said, her voice as filled with tears as her eyes had been. 'Please, go.'

The current was trying to carry me away, but I paddled the buoyant little kayak back into place. Aenea walked along the river's edge to keep pace with me. The sky seemed to be lightening a bit in the east.

'Are you certain we'll see each other there?' I shouted through the thinning rain.

'I'm not certain of anything, Raul.'

'Not even that we'll survive this?' I'm not sure what I meant by 'this'. I'm not even sure what I meant when I said 'survive'.

'Especially not of that,' said the girl, and I saw the old smile, full of mischief and anticipation and something like sadness mixed with involuntary wisdom.

The current was pulling me away. 'How long will it take me to get to the ship?'

'I think only a few days,' she called. We were several meters apart now, and the current was pulling me out into the Mississippi.

'And when I find the ship, how long to get to . . . T'ien Shan?' I called.

Aenea shouted back the answer but it was lost in the lapping of waves against the hull of my little kayak.

'What?' I yelled. 'I couldn't hear you.'

'I love you,' called Aenea, and her voice was clear and bright across the dark water.

The river pulled me out into it. I could not speak. My arms did not work when I thought to paddle against the powerful current. 'Aenea?' I aimed the flashlight toward the shore, caught a glimpse of her poncho gleaming in the light, the pale oval of her face in the shadow of the hood. 'Aenea!'

She shouted something, waved. I waved back.

The current was very strong for a moment. I paddled violently to avoid being pulled into an entire tree that had snagged on a sandbar, and then I was out in the central current and hurtling south. I looked back but walls of the last buildings in Hannibal hid my dear girl from view.

A minute later I heard a hum like the dropship's EM repulsors, but when I looked up I saw only shadow. It could have been her circling. It could have been a low cloud in the night.

The river pulled me south.

FIVE

Father Captain de Soya deadheaded from Pacem System on the HHS *Raguel*, an archangel-class cruiser similar to the ship he had been ordered to command. Killed by the terrible vortex of the classified instantaneous drive, known to Pax Fleet now as the Gideon drive, de Soya was resurrected in two days rather than the usual three – the resurrection chaplains taking the added risk of unsuccessful resurrection because of the urgency of the father-captain's orders – and found himself at the Omicron^2-Epsilon^3 Pax Fleet Strategic Positioning Station orbiting a lifeless, rocky world spinning in the darkness beyond Epsilon Eridani in the Old Neighborhood, only a handful of light-years from where Old Earth had once existed.

De Soya was given one day to recover his faculties and was then shuttled to the Omicron^2-Epsilon^3 fleet staging area, a hundred thousand klicks out from the military base. The midshipman piloting the waspshuttle went out of his way to give Father Captain de Soya a good look at his new command, and – despite himself – de Soya was thrilled with what he saw.

The HHS *Raphael* was obviously state-of-the-art technology, no longer derivative – as all of the previous Pax ships de Soya had seen had been – of rediscovered Hegemony designs from before the Fall. The overall design seemed too lean for practical vacuum work and too complicated for atmosphere, but the overall effect was one of streamlined lethality. The hull was a composite of morphable alloys and areas of pure fixed energy, allowing rapid shape and function changes that would have been impossible a few years before. As the shuttle passed the *Raphael* in a long, slow ballistic arc, de Soya watched the exterior of the long ship go from chrome silver to a stealth matte black, essentially disappearing from view. At the same time, several of the instrument booms and living cubbies were swallowed by the smooth central hull, until only weapons' blisters and containment-field probes remained. Either the ship was preparing for out-system translation checks, or the officers aboard knew very well that the passing wasp carried their new commander and they were showing off a bit.

De Soya knew that both assumptions were almost certainly true.

Before the cruiser blacked into oblivion, de Soya noticed how the fusion-drive spheres had been clustered like pearls around the central ship's axis rather than concentrated in a single swelling such as on his old torchship, the *Balthasar*. He also noticed how much smaller the hexagonal Gideon-drive array was on this ship than on the prototype *Raphael*. His last glimpse before the ship became invisible was of the lights glowing from the retracted, translucent living cubbies and the clear dome of the command deck. During combat, de Soya knew from his reading on Pacem and the RNA-instructional injections he had received at Pax Fleet headquarters that these clear areas would morph thicker armored epidermises, but de Soya had always enjoyed a view and would appreciate the window into space.

'Coming up on the *Uriel*, sir,' said the midshipman pilot.

De Soya nodded. The HHS *Uriel* seemed a near-clone of the new *Raphael*, but as the waspshuttle decelerated closer, the father-captain could pick out the extra omega-knife generators, the added, glowing conference cubbies, and the more elaborate com antennae that made this vessel the flagship of the task force.

'Docking warning, sir,' said the midshipman.

De Soya nodded and took his seat on the number-two acceleration couch. The mating was smooth enough that he felt no jolt whatsoever as the connection clamps closed and the ship's skin and umbilicals morphed around the shuttle. De Soya was tempted to praise the young midshipman, but old habits of command reasserted themselves.

'Next time,' he said, 'try the final approach without the last-second flare. It's showing off and the brass on a flagship frown on it.'

The young pilot's face fell.

De Soya set his hand on her shoulder. 'Other than that, good job. I'd have you aboard my ship as a dropship pilot anyday.'

The crestfallen midshipman brightened. 'I could only wish, sir. This station duty . . .' She stopped, realizing that she had gone too far.

'I know,' said de Soya, standing by the cycling lock. 'I know. But for now, be glad that you're not part of this Crusade.'

The lock cycled open and an honor guard whistled him aboard the HHS *Uriel* – the archangel, if Father Captain de Soya remembered correctly, that the Old Testament had described as the leader of the heavenly hosts of angels.

Ninety light-years away, in a star system only three light-years from Pacem, the original *Raphael* translated into real space with a violence that would have spat marrow from human bones, sliced through human cells like a hot blade through radiant gossamers, and scrambled human neurons like loose marbles on a steep hillside. Rhadamanth Nemes and her clone-siblings did not enjoy the sensation, but neither did they cry out or grimace.

'Where is this place?' said Nemes, watching a brown planet grow in the viewscreen. *Raphael* was decelerating under two hundred and thirty gravities. Nemes did not sit in the acceleration couch, but she did hang on to a stanchion with the casual ease of a commuter on her way to work in a crowded groundbus.

'Svoboda,' said one of her two male siblings.

Nemes nodded. None of the four spoke again until the archangel was in orbit and the dropship detached and howling through thin air.

'He'll be here?' asked Nemes. Microfilaments ran from her temples directly into the dropship console.

'Oh, yes,' said Nemes's twin sister.

A few humans lived on Svoboda, but since the Fall they had huddled in forcefield domes in the twilight zone and did not have the technology to track the archangel or its dropship. There were no Pax bases in this system. Meanwhile, the sunward side of the rocky world boiled until lead ran like water, and on the dark side the thin atmosphere hovered on the edge of freezing. Beneath the useless planet, however, ran more than eight hundred thousand kilometers of tunnels, each corridor a perfect thirty meters square. Svoboda was one of nine Labyrinthine worlds discovered in the early days of the Hegira and explored during the Hegemony. Hyperion had been another of the nine worlds. No human – alive or dead – knew the secret of the Labyrinths or their creators.

Nemes piloted the dropship through a pelting ammonia storm on the dark side, hovered an instant before an ice cliff visible only on infrared and amplification screens, and then folded the ship's wings in and guided it forward into the square opening of the Labyrinth entrance. This tunnel turned once and then stretched straight on for kilometers. Deep radar showed a honeycomb of other passages beneath it. Nemes flew forward three klicks, turned left at the first junction of tunnels, dropped half a kilometer from the surface while traveling five klicks south, and then landed the ship.

Here the infrared showed only trace heat from lava vents and the amplifiers showed nothing on the viewscreen. Frowning at the return on the radar displays, Nemes flipped on the dropship's exterior lights.

For as far as she could see down the infinitely straight corridor, the walls of the tunnel had been carved into a row of horizontal stone slabs. On each slab was a naked human body. The slabs and bodies continued on and on into darkness. Nemes glanced at the deep-radar display: the lower levels were also striated with slabs and bodies.

'Outside,' said the male sibling who had pulled Nemes from the lava on God's Grove.

Nemes did not bother with the air lock. Atmosphere rushed out of the dropship with a dying roar. There was a hint of pressure in the cavern – enough that she would not have to phase-shift to survive – but the air was thinner than Mars's had been before it was terraformed. Nemes's personal sensors indicated that the temperature was steady at minus one hundred and sixty-two degrees centigrade.

A human figure was outside waiting in the dropship's floodlights.

'Good evening,' said Councillor Albedo. The tall man was impeccably dressed in a gray suit tailored to Pacem tastes. He communicated directly on the seventy-five-megahertz band. Albedo's mouth did not move, but his perfect teeth were visible in a smile.

Nemes and her siblings waited. She knew that there would be no further reprimands or punishment. The Three Sectors wanted her alive and functioning.

'The girl, Aenea, has returned to Pax space,' said Albedo.

'Where?' said Nemes's female sibling. There was something like eagerness between the flat tones of her voice.

Councillor Albedo opened his hands.

'The portal . . .' began Nemes.

'Tells us nothing this time,' said Councillor Albedo. His smile had not wavered.

Nemes frowned at this. During all the centuries of the Hegemony's WorldWeb, the Three Sectors of Consciousness of the Core had not found a way to use the Void portal – that instantaneous interface that humans had known as farcasters – without leaving a record of modulated neutrinos in the fold matrix. 'The Something Else . . .' she said.

'Of course,' said Albedo. He flicked his hand as if discarding the useless segment of this conversation. 'But we can still register the connection. We feel sure that the girl is among those returning from Old Earth via the old farcaster network.'

'There are others?' said one of the males.

Albedo nodded. 'A few at first. More now. At least fifty activations at last count.'

Nemes folded her arms. 'Do you think the Something Else is terminating the Old Earth experiment?'

'No,' said Albedo. He walked over to the nearest slab and looked down at the naked human body on it. It had been a young woman, no more than seventeen or eighteen standard years old. She had red hair. White frost lay on her pale skin and open eyes. 'No,' he said again. 'The Sectors agree that it is just Aenea's group returning.'

'How do we find her?' said Nemes's female sibling, obviously musing aloud on the seventy-five-megahertz band. 'We can translate to every world that had a farcaster during the Hegemony and interrogate the far-caster portals in person.'

Albedo nodded. 'The Something Else can conceal the farcast destinations,' he said, 'but the Core is almost certain that it cannot hide the fact of the matrix fold itself.'

Almost certain. Nemes noted that unusual modifier of TechnoCore perceptions.

'We want you . . .' began Albedo, pointing at the female sibling. 'The Stable Sector did not give you a name, did it?'

'No,' said Nemes's twin. Limp, dark bangs fell over the pale forehead. No smile touched the thin lips.

Albedo chuckled on the seventy-five-megahertz band. 'Rhadamanth Nemes needed a name to pass as a human crewmate on the *Raphael*. I think that the rest of you should be named, if just for my convenience.' He pointed at the female. 'Scylla.' Stabbing his finger at each of the males in turn, he said, 'Gyges. Briareus.'

None of the three responded to their christenings, but Nemes folded her arms and said, 'Does this amuse you, Councillor?'

'Yes,' said Albedo.

Around them, the atmosphere vented from the dropship curled and broiled like a wicked fog. The male now named Briareus said, 'We'll keep this archangel for transport and begin searching all the old Web worlds, beginning, I assume, with the River Tethys planets.'

'Yes,' said Albedo.

Scylla tapped her nails on the frozen fabric of her jumpsuit. 'Four ships, the search would go four times as fast.'

'Obviously,' said Albedo. 'There are several reasons we have decided against that – the first being that the Pax has few of these archangel ships free to loan.'

Nemes raised an eyebrow, 'And when has the Core *asked* the Pax for loans?'

'Since we need their money and their factories and their human resources to build the ships,' said Albedo without emphasis. 'The second – and final – reason is that we want the four of you together in case you encounter someone or something impossible for one of you to handle.'

Nemes's eyebrow stayed up. She expected some reference to her failure on God's Grove, but it was Gyges who spoke. 'What in the Pax could we not handle, Councillor?'

Again the man in gray opened his hands. Behind him, the curling vapors of fog first obscured and then revealed the pale bodies on slabs. 'The Shrike,' he said.

Nemes made a rude noise on the seventy-five-megahertz band. 'I beat the thing single-handedly,' she said.

Albedo shook his head. The maddening smile stayed fixed. 'No,' he said. 'You did not. You used the hyperentropic device with which we supplied you to send it five minutes into the future. That is not the same as beating it.'

Briareus said, 'The Shrike is no longer under the control of the UI?'

Albedo opened his hands a final time. 'The gods of the future no longer whisper to us, my expensive friend. They war among themselves and the clamor of their battle echoes back through time. If our god's work is to be done in our time, we must do it ourselves.' He looked at the four clone-siblings. 'Are we clear on instructions?'

'Find the girl,' said Scylla.

'And?' said the Councillor.

'Kill her at once,' said Gyges. 'No hesitation.'

'And if her disciples intervene?' said Albedo, smiling more broadly now, his voice the caricature of a human schoolteacher's.

'Kill them,' said Briareus.

'And if the Shrike appears?' he said, the smile suddenly fading.

'Destroy it,' said Nemes.

Albedo nodded. 'Any final questions before we go our separate ways?'

Scylla said, 'How many humans are here?' She gestured toward the slabs and bodies.

Councillor Albedo touched his chin. 'A few tens of millions on this Labyrinthine world, in this section of tunnels. But there are many more tunnels here.' He smiled again. 'And eight more Labyrinth worlds.'

Nemes slowly turned her head, viewing the swirling fog and receding line of stone slabs on various levels of the spectrum. None of the bodies showed any sign of heat above the ambient temperature of the tunnel. 'And this is the Pax's work,' she said.

Albedo chuckled on the seventy-five-megahertz band. 'Of course,' he said. 'Why would the Three Sectors of Consciousness or our future UI want to stockpile human bodies?' He walked over to the body of the young woman and tapped her frozen breast. The air in the cavern was far too thin to carry sound, but Nemes imagined the noise of cold marble being tapped by fingernails.

'Any more questions?' said Albedo. 'I have an important meeting.'

Without a word on the seventy-five-megahertz band – or any other band – the four siblings turned and reentered the dropship.

Gathered on the circular tactical conference-center blister of the HHS *Uriel* were twenty Pax Fleet officers, including all of the captains and executive officers of Task Force GIDEON. Among those executive officers was Commander Hoagan 'Hoag' Liebler. Thirty-six standard years old, born-again since his baptism on Renaissance Minor, the scion of the once-great Liebler Freehold family whose estate covered some two million hectares – and whose current debt ran to almost five marks per hectare – Liebler had dedicated his private life to serving the Church and given his professional life to Pax Fleet. He was also a spy and a potential assassin.

Liebler had looked up with interest as his new commanding officer was piped aboard the *Uriel*. Everyone in the task force – almost everyone in Pax Fleet – had heard of Father Captain de Soya. The former torchship CO had been granted a papal diskey – meaning almost unlimited authority – for some secret project five standard years earlier, and then had failed at his mission. No one was sure what that mission had been, but de Soya's use of that diskey had made enemies among Fleet officers across the Pax. The father-captain's subsequent failure and disappearance had been cause for more rumor in the wardrooms and Fleet staff rooms: the most accepted theory was that de Soya had been turned over to the Holy Office, had been quietly excommunicated, and probably executed.

But now here he was, given command of one of the most treasured assets in Pax Fleet's arsenal: one of the twenty-one operational archangel cruisers.

Liebler was surprised at de Soya's appearance: the father-captain was short, dark-haired, with large, sad eyes more appropriate to the icon of a martyred saint than to the skipper of a battlecruiser. Introductions were made quickly by Admiral Aldikacti, the stocky Lusian in charge of both this meeting and the task force.

'Father Captain de Soya,' said Aldikacti as de Soya took his place at the gray, circular table within the gray, circular room, 'I believe you know some of these officers.' The Admiral was famous for her lack of tact as well as for her ferocity in battle.

'Mother Captain Stone is an old friend,' said de Soya, nodding toward his former executive officer. 'Captain Hearn was a member of my last task force, and I have met Captain Sati and Captain Lempriere. I have also had the privilege of working with Commanders Uchikawa and Barnes-Avne.'

Admiral Aldikacti grunted. 'Commander Barnes-Avne is here representing the Marine and Swiss Guard presence on Task Force GIDEON,' she said. 'Have you met your exec, Father Captain de Soya?'

The priest-captain shook his head and Aldikacti introduced Liebler. The commander was surprised at the firmness in the diminutive father-captain's grip and the authority in the other man's gaze. *Eyes of a martyr or no,* thought Hoag Liebler, *this man is used to command.*

'All right,' growled Admiral Aldikacti, 'let's get started. Captain Sati will present the briefing.'

For the next twenty minutes, the conference blister was fogged with holos and trajectory overlays. Comlogs and 'scribers filled with data and scribbled notes. Sati's soft voice was the only sound except for the rare question or request for clarification.

Liebler jotted his own notes, surprised at the scope of Task Force GIDEON's mission, and busy at the work of any executive officer – getting down all the salient facts and details that the captain might want to review later.

GIDEON was the first task force made up completely of archangel-class cruisers. Seven of the archangels had been tasked to this mission. Conventional Hawking-class torchships had been dispatched months earlier to rendezvous with them at their first sally point in the Outback some twenty light-years beyond the Great Wall defensive sphere so as to participate in a mock battle, but after that first jump, the task force of seven ships would be operating independently.

'A good metaphor would be General Sherman's march through Georgia in the pre-Hegira North American Civil War in the nineteenth century,' said Captain Sati, sending half the officers at the table tapping at their comlog diskeys to bring up that arcane bit of military history.

'Previously,' continued Sati, 'our battles with the Ousters have either been in the Great Wall no-man's-land, or on the fringes of either Pax or Ouster space. There have been very few deep-penetration raids into Ouster territory.' Sati paused in his briefing. 'Father Captain de Soya's Task Force MAGI some five standard years ago was one of the deepest of those raids.'

'Any comments about it, Father Captain?' said Admiral Aldikacti.

De Soya hesitated a moment. 'We burned an orbital forest ring,' he said at last. 'There was no resistance.'

Hoag Liebler thought that the father-captain's voice sounded vaguely ashamed.

Sati nodded as if satisfied. 'That's what we hope will be the case for this entire mission. Our intelligence suggests that the Ousters have deployed the vast bulk of their defensive forces along the sphere of the Great Wall, leaving very little in the way of armed resistance through the heart of their colonized areas beyond the Pax. For almost three centuries they have positioned their forces, their bases, and their home systems with the limitations of Hawking-drive technology as the primary determining factor.'

Tactical holos filled the conference blister.

'The grand cliché,' continued Sati, 'is that the Pax has had the advantage of interior lines of transport and communication, while the Ousters have had the defensive strength of concealment and distance. Penetration deep into Ouster space has been all but impossible due to the vulnerability of our supply lines and their willingness to cut and run before our superior strength, attacking later – often with devastating effect – when our task forces venture too far from the Great Wall.'

Sati paused and looked at the officers around the table. 'Gentlemen and ladies, those days are over.' More holos misted into solidity, the red line of Task Force GIDEON's trajectory out from and back to the Pax sphere slicing between suns like a laser knife.

'Our mission is to destroy every in-system Ouster supply base and deep-space colony we encounter,' said Sati, his soft voice taking on strength. 'Comet farms, can cities, boondoggles, torus bases, L-point clusters, orbital forest rings, birthing asteroids, bubble hives . . . everything.'

'Including civilian angels?' asked Father Captain de Soya.

Hoag Liebler blinked at his CO's question. Pax Fleet informally referred to the space-tailored DNA-altered mutants as 'Lucifer's angels', usually short-ened to 'angels' in an irony bordering on blasphemy, but the phrase was rarely used before the high brass.

Admiral Aldikacti answered. '*Especially* angels, Father Captain. His Holi-ness, Pope Urban, has declared this a Crusade against the inhuman traves-ties the Ousters are breeding out there in the darkness. His Holiness has stated in his Crusade Encyclical that these unholy mutations are to be eliminated from God's universe. *There are no civilian Ousters.* Do you have a problem understanding this directive, Father Captain de Soya?'

Officers around the table seemed to hold their breaths until de Soya finally answered. 'No, Admiral Aldikacti. I understand His Holiness's encycl-ical.'

The briefing continued. 'These archangel-class cruisers will be involved,' said Sati. 'His Holiness's Ship *Uriel* as flagship, the *Raphael*, the *Michael*, the *Gabriel*, the *Raguel*, the *Remiel*, and the *Sariel*. In each case, the ships will use their Gideon drives to make the instantaneous jump to the next system, and will take two days or more to decelerate in-system, thus allowing time for crew resurrection. His Holiness has granted us dispensation to use the new two-day resurrection-cycle creches . . . which offer a ninety-two percent probability of resurrection. After regrouping the attack force, we will do maximum damage to all Ouster forces and installations before translating to the next system. Any Pax ship damaged beyond repair will be abandoned, the crew transferred to other ships in the task force, and the cruiser destroyed. No chances will be taken with the Ousters capturing Gideon-drive technology, even though it would be useless to them without the Sacrament of Resurrection. The mission should extend some three standard months. Any questions?'

Father Captain de Soya raised his hand. 'I have to apologize,' he said, 'I've been out of touch for several standard years, but I notice that this task force is made up of archangel-class ships named after archangels referred to by name in the Old Testament.'

'Yes, Father Captain?' prompted Admiral Aldikacti. 'Your question?'

'Just this, Admiral. I seem to remember that there were only seven archangels referred to by name in the Bible. What about the rest of the archangel-class ships that have come on-line?'

There was chuckling around the circular table and de Soya could see that he had cut the tension much as he had planned.

Smiling, Admiral Aldikacti said, 'We welcome our prodigal captain back and inform him that the Vatican theologians have searched the Book of Enoch and the rest of the pseudepigrapha to find these other angels which might be promoted to "honorary archangel", and the Holy Office itself has authorized dispensation in Pax Fleet's use of their names. We found it . . . ah . . . appropriate . . . that the first seven planet-class archangels built be named after those listed in the Bible and should carry their sacred fire to the enemy.'

The chuckling turned to sounds of approval and finally to soft applause among the commanders and their execs.

There were no other questions. Admiral Aldikacti said, 'Oh, one other detail, if you see this ship . . .' A holo of a strange-looking starship floated above the center of the table. The thing was small by Pax Fleet standards, was streamlined as if built to enter atmosphere, and had fins near the fusion ports.

'What is it?' said Mother Captain Stone, still smiling from the good feeling in the room. 'Some Ouster joke?'

'No,' said Father Captain de Soya in a soft monotone, 'it's Web-era technology. A private starship . . . owned by an individual.'

A few executive officers chuckled again.

Admiral Aldikacti stopped the laughter by waving her thick hand through the holo. 'The father-captain is correct,' rumbled the Lusian admiral. 'It's an old Web-era ship, once owned by a diplomat of the Hegemony.' She shook her head. 'They had the wealth to make such gestures then. Anyway, it has a Hawking drive modified by Ouster technicians, may well be armed, and must be considered as dangerous.'

'What do we do if we encounter it?' asked Mother Captain Stone. 'Take it as a prize?'

'No,' said Admiral Aldikacti. 'Destroy it on sight. Slag it to vapor. Any questions?'

There were none. The officers dispersed to their ships to prepare for the initial translation. On the waspshuttle ride back to the *Raphael*, XO Hoag Liebler chatted pleasantly with his new captain about the ship's readiness and crew's high morale, all the while thinking, *I hope I don't have to kill this man.*

SIX

It has been my experience that immediately after certain traumatic sep-
arations – leaving one's family to go to war, for instance, or upon the death
of a family member, or after parting from one's beloved with no assurances
of reunion – there is a strange calmness, almost a sense of relief, as if
the worst has happened and nothing else need be dreaded. So it was with
the rainy, predawn morning on which I left Aenea on Old Earth.

The kayak that I paddled was small and the Mississippi River was large. At
first, in the darkness, I paddled with an intense alertness that was close to
fear, adrenaline-driven, eyes straining to make out snags and sandbars and
drifting flotsam on the raging current. The river was very wide there, the
better part of a mile, I guessed – the Old Architect had used the archaic
English units of length and distance, feet, yards, miles, and most of us at
Taliesin had fallen into the habit of imitating him – and the banks of the
river looked flooded, with dead trees showing where the waters had risen
hundreds of meters from the original banks, pushing the river to high bluffs
on both sides.

An hour or so after I had parted from my friend, the light came up slowly,
first showing the separation of gray cloud and black-gray bluff to my left,
then casting a flat, cold light on the surface of the river itself. I had been
right to be afraid in the dark: the river was snarled with snags and long
fingers of sandbars; large waterlogged trees with hydra heads of roots raged
past me on the center currents, smashing anything in their way with the
force of giant battering rams. I selected what I hoped was the most forgiving
current, paddled strongly to stay out of the way of floating debris, and tried
to enjoy the sunrise.

All that morning I paddled south, seeing no sign of human habitation on
either bank except for a single parting glimpse of ancient, once-white
buildings drowned amid the dead trees and brackish waters in what had
once been the western bank and was now a swamp at the base of the bluffs
there. Twice I put ashore on islands: once to relieve myself, and the second
time to store away the small backpack that was my only luggage. During this
second stop – late in the morning with the sun warming the river and me – I
sat on a log on the sandy bank and ate one of the cold meat and mustard
sandwiches that Aenea had made for me during the night. I had brought
two water bottles – one to fit on my belt, the other to stay in my pack – and I
drank with moderation, not knowing if the water of the Mississippi was fit to
drink and also not knowing when I would find a safe supply.

It was afternoon when I saw the city and the arch ahead of me.

Sometime before, a second river had joined the Mississippi on my right, widening the channel significantly. I was sure that it must be the Missouri, and when I queried the comlog, the ship's memory confirmed my hunch. It was not long after that when I saw the arch.

This farcaster portal looked different than the ones we had transited during our trip out to Old Earth: larger, older, duller, more rust-streaked. It may have once been high and dry on the west bank of the river, but now the metal of the arch rose out of waters hundreds of meters from shore. Skeletal remnants of drowned buildings – low 'skyscrapers' from pre-Hegira days according to my newly informed architectural sensibilities – also rose from the sluggish waters.

'St Louis,' said the comlog bracelet when I queried the ship's AI. 'Destroyed even before the Tribulations. Abandoned before the Big Mistake of '08.'

'Destroyed?' I said, aiming the kayak toward the giant hoop of the arch and seeing for the first time how the west bank behind it curved around in a perfect semicircle, forming a shallow lake. Ancient trees lined the sharp arc of the shore. An impact crater, I thought, although meteor crater or bomb crater or power-source meltdown or some other variety of violent event, I could not tell. 'How destroyed?' I said to the comlog.

'No information,' said the bracelet. 'However I do have a data entry which correlates with the arch ahead of us.'

'It's a farcaster portal, isn't it?' I said, fighting the strong current here on the west side of the main channel to aim the kayak at the east-facing arch.

'Not originally,' said the soft voice on my wrist. 'The size and orientation of the artifact coincide with position and dimensions of the so-called Gateway Arch, an architectural oddity built in the city of St Louis during the time of the United States of America nation-state in the mid-twentieth century AD. It was meant to symbolize western expansion of the hegemonic, Euro-descended proto-nationalist pioneers who migrated through here in their effort to displace the original, pre-Preserve, NorthAm indigenies.'

'The Indians,' I said, panting as I paddled the bobbing kayak through the last conflicting current and got us lined up with the huge arch. There had been an hour or two of rich sunlight, but now the cold wind and gray clouds had returned. Raindrops pattered on the fiberglass of the kayak and rippled the wavetops on either side. The current now carried the kayak toward the center of the arch, and I rested the paddle a moment, making sure not to hit the mysterious red button by accident. 'So this farcaster portal was built to honor the people who killed the Indians,' I said, leaning forward on my elbows.

'The original Gateway Arch had no farcaster function,' the ship's voice said primly.

'Did it survive the disaster that . . . did this?' I said, pointing the paddle at the impact-crater lake and its assortment of flooded buildings.

'No information,' said the comlog.

'And you don't know if it's a farcaster?' I said, panting again as I paddled hard. The arch loomed high above us now, at least a hundred meters to its apex. The winterish sunlight glinted dully on its rusted sides.

'No,' said the ship's memory. 'There is no record of any farcaster on Old Earth.'

Of course there would be no such record. Old Earth had collapsed into the Big Mistake black hole – or been kidnapped by the Lions and Tigers and Bears – at least a century and a half before the TechnoCore had given the old Hegemony farcaster technology. But there had been a small but very functional farcaster arch over that river – creek, actually – in western Pennsylvania where Aenea and I had 'cast from God's Grove four years earlier. And I had seen others in my travels.

'Well,' I said, more to myself than to the idiot comlog AI, 'if this isn't it, we'll just continue on downriver. Aenea had a reason for launching us where she did.'

Having said that, I was not so sure. There was no telltale farcaster shimmer under this arch – no glimpse of sunlight or starlight beyond. Just the darkening sky and the black band of forest on the shoreline beyond the lake.

I leaned back and looked up at the arch, shocked to see panels missing, steel ribs showing. The kayak had already passed beneath it and there was no transition, no sudden shift of light and gravity and alien scents. This thing was nothing more than a broken-down old architectural freak that just happened to resemble a . . .

Everything changed.

One second the kayak and I were bobbing on the windswept Mississippi, heading into the shallow crater lake that had been the city of St Louis, and the next instant it was night and the little fiberglass boat and I were sliding along a narrow canal between canyons of lighted buildings under a dark skylight half a kilometer or more above my head.

'Jesus,' I whispered.

'An ancient messiah figure,' said the comlog. 'Religions based on his purported teachings include Christianity, Zen-Christianity, ancient and modern Catholicism, and such Protestant sects as . . .'

'Shut up,' I said. 'Good child mode.' This command had the comlog speak only when spoken to.

There were other people boating on this canal, if canal it was. Scores of rowboats and tiny sailboats and other kayaks moved upriver and down. Close by, on riverwalks and esplanades, on skyways crisscrossing above the well-lighted waters, hundreds more walked in pairs and small groups. Stocky individuals in bright garments jogged alone.

I felt the gravity weigh my arms as I tried to lift the kayak paddle – at least half-again Earth's was my immediate impression – and I slowly lifted my face to the view of those hundreds – thousands – of lighted windows and turrets, walkways and balconies and landing pads, of more lights as chrome-silver trains hummed softly through clear tubes above the river, as EMVs sliced through the air overhead, as levitation platforms and sky ferries carried people back and forth across this incredible canyon . . . and I knew.

Lusus. This had to be Lusus.

I had met Lusians before: rich hunters come to Hyperion to shoot ducks or demi-gyres, richer offworld gamblers slumming in the Nine Tails casinos where I had worked as a bouncer, even a few expatriates in our Home Guard unit, felons fleeing Pax justice most likely. They all had the high-g, low-profile look of these short, stocky, prominently muscled joggers who chugged by on the riverwalks and esplanades like some primitive but powerful steam machines.

No one seemed to be paying any attention to my kayak or me. This surprised me: from these natives' perspectives, I must have appeared from nowhere, materializing under the farcaster portal behind me.

I looked back and understood why my appearance might have gone unnoticed. The farcaster portal was old, of course, part of the fallen Hegemony and of the former River Tethys, and the arch had been built into the Hive city walls – platforms and walkways studding and overhanging the slender portal – so that the segment of canal or river directly under the arch was the only visible section of this indoor city that lay in deep shadow. Even as I glanced back, a small motorboat glided out of that shadow, caught the glow of the sodium-vapor lights that overhung the river walkway, and seemed to pop into existence just as I had half a moment earlier.

Bulked up as I was in sweater and jacket, tightly tucked into the nylon skirt of my little kayak cockpit, I probably looked as stocky as the Lusians I saw on either side of me. A man and woman on jet skis waved as they hissed past.

I waved back.

'Jesus,' I whispered again, more in prayer than blasphemy.

This time the comlog made no comment. I will interrupt myself here.

My temptation at this point in the telling, despite the hurry-up incentive of cyanide gas hissing into the Schrödinger cat box at any moment, was to describe my interworld odyssey in great detail. It was, in truth, as close as I had come to true adventure since Aenea and I had arrived at the safety of Old Earth four standard years earlier.

In the thirty-some standard hours since Aenea had peremptorily announced my imminent departure by farcaster, I had naturally assumed that the voyage would be similar to our former trip – from Renaissance Vector to Old Earth, our voyage had been through empty or abandoned landscapes via worlds such as Hebron, New Mecca, God's Grove, and unnamed worlds such as the jungle planet on which we had left the Consul's ship in hiding. On one of the few planets where we had encountered inhabitants – ironically on Mare Infinitus, the sparsely settled ocean world – the contact had been catastrophic for everyone involved: I had blown up most of their floating platform; they had captured me, stabbed me, shot me, and almost drowned me. In the process, I had lost some of the most valuable things we had taken on the trip, including the ancient hawking mat that had been handed down since the days of the Siri and Merin legend and the equally ancient .45-caliber handgun that I had wanted to believe once belonged to Aenea's mother, Brawne Lamia.

But for the majority of our voyage, the River Tethys had carried Aenea, A. Bettik, and me through empty landscapes – ominously empty on Hebron and New Mecca, as if some terror had carried away the populations – and we had been left alone.

Not here. Lusus was alive and seething. For the first time, I understood why these planetary honeycombs were called Hives.

Traveling together through unpopulated regions, the girl, the android, and I had been left to our own devices. Now, alone and essentially unarmed in my little kayak, I found myself waving to Pax police and born-again Lusian priests who strolled by. The canal was no more than thirty meters wide here, concrete- and plastic-lined, with no tributaries or hiding places. There were shadows under the bridges and overpasses, just as under the farcaster portal upriver, but river traffic moved through these shadowy places in a constant flow. No place to hide.

For the first time I considered the insanity of farcaster travel. My clothes would be out of place, drawing immediate attention as soon as I stepped out of the kayak. My body type was wrong. My Hyperion-bred dialect would be strange. I had no money, no identity chip, no EMV license or credit cards, no Pax parish papers or place of residence. Stopping the kayak for a minute by a riverside bar – the smell of grilled steak or similar fare wafting out on fens and making me salivate with hunger, the yeast tang hinting of brewery vats and cold beer on the same breeze – I realized that I would almost certainly be arrested two minutes after going into such a place.

People traveled between worlds in the Pax – millionaires mostly, business-people and adventurers willing to spend months in cryogenic sleep and years of time-debt traveling by Mercantilus transport between the stars, smug in their cruciform certainty that job and home and family would be waiting in their steady-state Christian universe when they returned – but it was rare, and no one traveled between worlds without money and Pax permission. Two minutes after I sauntered into this café or bar or restaurant or whatever it was, someone would probably call the local police or the Pax military. Their first search would show me crossless – a heathen in a born-again Christian universe.

Licking my lips, my stomach growling, arms weary from fatigue and the extra gravity there, eyes tearing from lack of sleep and deep frustration, I paddled away from the riverside café and continued downriver, hoping that the next farcaster would be nearer rather than far.

And here I resist the temptation to tell of all the marvelous sights and sounds, the strange people glimpsed, and close encounters chanced. I had never been on a world as settled, as crowded, as *interior* as Lusus, and I could have easily spent a month exploring the bustling Hive I glimpsed from the concrete-channeled river.

After six hours' traveling downstream in the canal on Lusus, I paddled under the welcomed arch and emerged on Freude, a bustling, heavily populated world that I knew little about and could not even have identified if it had not been for the comlog's navigational files. Here I finally slept, the kayak hidden in a five-meter-high sewer pipe, me curled up under tendrils of industrial fiberplastic caught in a wire fence.

I slept a full standard day and night around on Freude, but there the days were thirty-nine standard hours long and it was only evening of the day I arrived when I found the next arch, less than five klicks downriver, and translated again.

From sunny Freude, populated by Pax citizens in elaborate harlequin fabrics and bright capes, the river took me to Nevermore with its brooding villages carved into rock and its stone castles perched on canyon sides under perpetually gloomy skies. At night on Nevermore, comets streaked the heavens and crowlike flying creatures – more giant bats than birds – flapped leathery wings low above the river and blotted out the comets' glow with their black bodies.

I was hailed by commercial rafters there, and hailed them back, all the while paddling away toward a stretch of white water that almost flipped my kayak and certainly taxed all of my fledgling kayaker's skills. Sirens were hooting from the gimlet-eyed castles on Nevermore when I paddled furiously under the next farcaster portal and found myself sweltering in the desert sunshine of a busy little world the comlog told me was called Vitus-Gray-Balianus B. I had never heard of it, not even in the old Hegemony-era atlases that Grandam had kept in her travel caravan, and which I had crept in to study by glow wand whenever I could.

The River Tethys had taken Aenea, A. Bettik, and me through desert planets on the way out to Old Earth, but these had been the oddly empty worlds of Hebron and New Mecca – their deserts devoid of life, their cities abandoned. But here on Vitus-Gray-Balianus B, adobe-style houses huddled by the river's edge, and every klick or so I would encounter a levee or lock where most of the water was being siphoned away for irrigation to the green fields that followed the river's course. Luckily the river served as the main street and central highway here, and I had emerged from the ancient farcaster arch's shadow in the lee of a massive barge, so I continued paddling blandly on in the midst of bustling river traffic – skiffs, rafts, barges, tugs, electric powerboats, houseboats, and even the occasional EM levitation barge moving three or four meters above the river's surface.

The gravity was light here, probably less than two-thirds of Old Earth's or Hyperion's, and at times I thought that my paddle strokes were going to lift the kayak and me right out of the water. But if the gravity was light, the light – sunlight – was as heavy on me as a giant, sweaty palm. Within half an hour of paddling, I had depleted the last of my second water bottle and knew that I would have to set in to find a drink.

One would think on a world of lesser gravity that the denizens would be beanpoles – the vertical antithesis of the Lusian barrel shape – but most of the men, women, and children I saw in the busy lanes and towpaths along the river were almost as short and stocky as Lusians. Their clothing was as bright as the harlequin motley on the residents of Freude, but here each person wore a single brilliant hue – tight bodysuits of head-to-toe crimson, cloaks and capes of intense cerulean, gowns and suits of eye-piercing emerald with elaborate emerald hats and scarves, flowing trains of yellow chiffon and bright amber turbans. I realized that the doors and shutters of the adobe homes, shops, and inns were also painted in these distinctive colors and wondered what the significance might be – caste? Political preference? Social or economic status? Some sort of kinship signal? Whatever it was, I would not blend in when I went ashore to find a drink, dressed as I was all in dull khaki and weathered cotton.

But it was either put ashore or die of thirst. Just past one of the many self-serve locks, I paddled to a pier, tied my bobbing kayak in place as a heavy barge exited the lock behind me, and walked toward a circular wood-and-adobe structure that I hoped was an artesian well. I had seen several of the women in saffron robes carrying what may have been water jugs from the thing, so I felt fairly safe in my guess as to function. What I had no confidence in was the odds that I could draw water there myself without violating some law, code, caste rule, religious commandment, or local custom. I had seen no visible Pax presence on the towpath or lanes – neither the black of priest nor the red and black of the standardized Pax police uniform – but that meant little. There were very few worlds, even in the Outback where the comlog informed me that Vitus-Gray-Balianus B lay, where the Pax did not have some definitive presence. I had covertly slipped the scabbard with my hunting knife from pack to back pocket under my vest, and my only plan was to use the blade to bluster an exit back to my boat if a mob formed. If Pax police arrived, with stunners or flechette pistols, my journey would be over.

It would soon be over – at least for a while – for vastly different reasons, but I had no warning – except for a backache that had been with me since before leaving Lusus – of that as I diffidently approached the well, if well it was.

It was a well.

No one reacted to my tall build or drab colors. No one – not even the children dressed in brilliant red and bright blue who paused in their game to give me a glance and then look away – interfered or seemed to notice the obvious stranger in their midst. As I drank deeply and then refilled both water bottles, I had the impression – from what source I do not know – that the inhabitants of Vitus-Gray-Balianus B, or at least of this village along this stretch of the long-abandoned River Tethys farcaster-way, were simply too polite to point and stare or ask me my business. My feeling at that moment, as I capped the second bottle and turned to return to my kayak, was that a three-headed mutant alien or – to speak in the realm of the more real bizarre – that the Shrike itself could have drunk from that artesian well on that pleasant desert afternoon and not have been accosted or questioned by the citizens.

I had taken three steps on the dusty lane when the pain struck. First I doubled over, gasping in pain, unable to take a breath, and then I went to one knee, then onto my side. I curled up in agony. I would have screamed if the terrible pain had allowed me the breath and energy. It did not. Gasping like a river fish tossed to this dusty bank, I curled tighter in a fetal position and rode waves of agony.

I should say here that I was not a total stranger to pain and discomfort. When I was in the Home Guard, a study by the Hyperion military showed that most of the conscripts sent south to fight the Ice Claw rebels had little stomach for pain. The city folks of the northern Aquila cities and the fancier Nine Tails towns had rarely, if ever, experienced any pain that they couldn't banish by popping a pill or dialing up an autosurgeon or driving to their nearest doc-in-the-box.

As a shepherd and country boy, I had a bit more experience with tolerating pain: accidental knife cuts, a broken foot from a pakbrid stepping on me, bruises and contusions from falls far out in rock country, a concussion once while wrestling in the caravan rendezvous, boils from riding, even the fat lips and black eyes from campfire brawls during the Men's Convocation. And on the Iceshelf I had been hurt three times – twice cut from shrapnel after white mines had killed buddies, once lanced from a long-range sniper – that final wound serious enough to bring in a priest who all but demanded that I accept the cruciform before it was too late.

But I had never experienced pain like this.

Moaning, gasping, the polite citizenry finally falling back from this flopping apparition and being forced to take notice of the stranger, I lifted my wrist and demanded that the comlog tell me what was happening to me. It did not answer. Between waves of unbearable pain, I asked again. Still no answer. Then I remembered that I had the damn thing in good child mode. I called it by name and repeated the query.

'May I activate the dormant biosensor function, M. Endymion?' asked the idiot AI.

I had not known that the device had a biosensor function, dormant or otherwise. I made a rude noise of assent and doubled into a tighter fetal curl. It felt as if someone had stabbed me in the upper back and was twisting the hooked blade. Pain poured through me like current through a hot wire. I vomited into the dust. A beautiful woman in pure white robes took another step back and lifted one white sandal.

'What is it?' I gasped again in the briefest of intervals between the stabbing pains. 'What's happening?' I demanded of the comlog. With my other hand, I felt my back, seeking out blood or an entrance wound. I expected to find an arrow or spear, but there was nothing.

'You are going into shock, M. Endymion,' said the lobotomized bit of the Consul ship's AI. 'Blood pressure, skin resistance, heart rate, and atropin count all support this.'

'Why?' I said again and drew the single syllable out into a long moan as the pain rolled from my back out and through my entire body. I retched again. My stomach was empty but the vomiting continued. The brightly clad citizens stayed their distance, never drawing into a curious crowd, never showing the bad manners of staring or murmuring, but obviously tarrying in their rounds.

'What's wrong?' I gasped again, trying to whisper to the comlog bracelet. 'What would cause this?'

'Gunshot,' returned the tiny, tinny voice. 'Stab wound. Spear, knife, arrow, throwing dart. Energy-weapon wound. Lance, laser, omega knife, pulse blade. Concentrated flechette strike. Perhaps a long, thin needle inserted through the upper kidney, liver, and spleen.'

Writhing in pain, I felt my back again, pulling my own knife scabbard out and casting it away. The outer vest and shirt under it felt unburned or blasted. No sharp objects protruded from my flesh.

The pain burned its way through me again and I moaned aloud. I had not done that when the sniper had lanced me on the Iceshelf or when Uncle Vanya's 'brid had broken my foot.

I found it difficult to form complete thoughts, but the direction of my thinking was . . . *the Vitus-Gray-Balianus B natives . . . somehow . . . mind power. . . poison . . . the water . . . invisible rays . . . punishing me . . . for . . .*

I gave up the effort and moaned again. Someone in a bright-blue skirt or toga and immaculate sandals, toenails painted blue, stepped closer.

'Excuse me, sir,' said a soft voice in thickly accented old Web English. 'But are you in difficulty?' *Er ye en defficoolte?*

'Aaarrrgghhhggghuhh,' I said in response, punctuating the noise with more dry retching.

'May I then be of assistance?' said the same soft voice from above the blue toga. *Ez-sest-ance?*

'Oh . . . ahhrrgghah . . . nnnrrehhakk,' I said and half swooned from the agony. Black dots danced in my vision until I could no longer see the sandals or blue toenails, but the terrible pain would not let go of me . . . I could not escape into unconsciousness.

Robes and togas rustled around me. I smelled perfume, cologne, soap . . . felt strong hands on my arms and legs and sides. Their attempt to lift me made the heated wire rip through my back and into the base of my skull.

SEVEN

The Grand Inquisitor had been ordered to appear with his aide for a papal audience at oh-eight-hundred hours Vatican time. At oh-seven-fifty-two hours, his black EMV arrived at the Via del Belvedere checkpoint entrance to the papal apartments. The Inquisitor and his aide, Father Farrell, were passed through detector portals and handheld sensors – first at the Swiss Guard checkpoint, then at the Palatine Guard station, and finally at the new Noble Guard post.

John Domenico Cardinal Mustafa, the Grand Inquisitor, gave the most subtle of looks to his aide as they were passed by this final checkpoint. The Noble Guard at this point seemed to consist of cloned twins – all thin men and women with lank hair, sallow complexions, and dead gazes. A millennium ago, Mustafa knew, the Swiss Guard had been the paid mercenary force for the Pope, the Palatine Guard had consisted of trusted locals, always of Roman birth, who provided an honor guard for His Holiness's public appearances, and the Noble Guard had been chosen from aristocracy as a form of papal reward for loyalty. Today the Swiss Guard was the most elite of Pax Fleet's regular forces, the Palatines had been reinstated only a year earlier by Pope Julius XIV, and now Pope Urban appeared to be relying upon this strange brotherhood of the new Noble Guard for his personal safety.

The Grand Inquisitor knew that the Noble Guard twins were indeed clones, early prototypes of the secret Legion in building, and vanguards of a new fighting force requested by the Pope and his Secretary of State and designed by the Core. The Inquisitor had paid dearly for this information, and he knew that his position – if not his life – might be forfeit if Lourdusamy or His Holiness discovered that he knew of it.

Past the lower guard posts, with Father Farrell straightening his cassock after the search, Cardinal Mustafa waved away the papal assistant who offered to guide them upstairs. The Cardinal personally opened the door to the ancient lift that would take them to the papal apartments.

This private way to the Pope's quarters actually began in the basement, since the reconstructed Vatican was built on a hill with the Via del Belvedere entrance beneath the usual ground floor. Rising in the creaking cage, Father Farrell nervously fidgeting with his 'scriber and folder of papers, the Grand Inquisitor relaxed as they passed the ground-floor courtyard of San Damaso. They passed the first floor with the fantastic Borgia Apartments and the Sistine Chapel. They creaked and groaned their way past the second floor with the papal state apartments, the Consistorial Hall, the library, the audience suite, and the beautiful Raphael Rooms. On the third floor they stopped and the cage doors slammed open.

Cardinal Lourdusamy and his aide, Monsignor Lucas Oddi, nodded and smiled.

'Domenico,' said Lourdusamy, taking the Grand Inquisitor's hand and squeezing it tightly.

'Simon Augustino,' said the Grand Inquisitor with a bow. So the Secretary of State was to be in this meeting. Mustafa had suspected and feared as much. Stepping out of the lift and walking with the others toward the papal private apartments, the Grand Inquisitor glanced down the hallway toward the offices of the Secretariat of State and – for the ten-thousandth time – envied this man's access to the Pope.

The Pope met the party in the wide, brilliantly lit gallery that connected the Secretariat of State offices with the two stories of rooms that were the private domain of His Holiness. The usually serious Pontiff was smiling. This day he was dressed in a white-caped cassock with a white *zucchetto* on his head and a white fascia tied around his waist. His white shoes made only the slightest of whispering noises on the tiled floors.

'Ah, Domenico,' said Pope Urban XVI as he extended his ring hand to be kissed. 'Simon. How good of you to come.'

Father Farrell and Monsignor Oddi waited on one knee for the Holy Father to turn to them so that they could kiss the Ring of St Peter.

His Holiness looked well, thought the Grand Inquisitor, definitely younger and more rested than before his most recent death. The high forehead and burning eyes were the same, but Mustafa thought that there was something simultaneously more urgent and satisfied-looking about the resurrected Pope's appearance this morning.

'We were just about to take our morning stroll in the garden,' said His Holiness. 'Would you care to join us?'

The four men nodded and fell in with the Pope's quick pace as he walked the length of the gallery and then climbed smooth, broad stairs to the roof. His Holiness's personal aides kept their distance, the Swiss Guard troopers at the entrance to the garden stood at rigid attention while staring straight ahead, Lourdusamy and the Grand Inquisitor walked only a pace behind the Holy Father, while Monsignor Oddi and Father Farrell kept pace two steps back.

The papal gardens consisted of a maze of flowered trellises, trickling fountains, perfectly trimmed hedges and topiaried trees from three hundred Pax worlds, stone walkways, and fantastic flowering shrubs. Above all this, a force-ten containment field – transparent from this side, opaqued to outside observers – provided both privacy and protection. Pacem's sky was a brilliant, unclouded blue this morning.

'Do either of you remember,' began His Holiness, his cassock rustling as they walked briskly down the garden path, 'when our sky here was yellow?'

Cardinal Lourdusamy produced the deep rumble that passed for a chuckle with him. 'Oh, yes,' he said, 'I remember when the sky was a sick yellow, the air was all but unbreathable, it was cold all the time, and the rain never ended. A marginal world then, Pacem. The only reason the old Hegemony ever allowed the Church to settle here.'

Pope Urban XVI smiled thinly and gestured toward the blue sky and warm sunlight. 'So there has been some improvement during our time of service here, eh, Simon Augustino?'

Both cardinals laughed softly. They had made a quick circuit of the rooftop, and now His Holiness took another route through the center of the garden. Stepping from stone to stone on the narrow path, the two cardinals and their aides followed the white-cassocked Pontiff in single file. Suddenly His Holiness stopped and turned. A fountain burbled softly behind him.

'You have heard,' he said, all jesting gone from his tone, 'that Admiral Aldikacti's task force has translated beyond the Great Wall?'

Both cardinals nodded.

'It is but the first of what will be many such incursions,' said the Holy Father. 'We do not hope this . . . we do not predict this . . . we *know* this.'

The head of the Holy Office and the Secretary of State and their aides waited.

The Pope looked at each man in turn. 'This afternoon, my friends, we plan to travel to Castel Gandolfo . . .'

The Grand Inquisitor stopped himself from glancing upward, knowing that the papal asteroid could not be seen during the daytime. He knew that the Pontiff was speaking in the royal 'we' and not inviting Lourdusamy and him to come along.

'. . . where we will pray and meditate for several days while composing our next encyclical,' continued the Pope. 'It will be entitled *Redemptor Hominis* and it will be the most important document of our tenure as shepherd of our Holy Mother Church.'

The Grand Inquisitor bowed his head. *The Redeemer of Mankind*, he thought. *It could be about anything.*

When Cardinal Mustafa looked up, His Holiness was smiling as if reading his thoughts. 'It will be about our sacred obligation to keep humanity human, Domenico,' said the Pope. 'It will extend, clarify, and broaden what has become known as our Crusade Encyclical. It will define Our Lord's wish . . . nay, commandment. . . that mankind remain in the form and visage of mankind, and not be denied by deliberate mutation and mutilation.'

'The final solution to the Ouster problem,' murmured Cardinal Lourdusamy.

His Holiness nodded impatiently. 'That and more. *Redemptor Hominis* will look at the Church's role in defining the future, dear friends. In a sense, it will lay out a blueprint for the next thousand years.'

Mother of Mercy, thought the Grand Inquisitor.

'The Pax has been a useful instrument,' continued the Holy Father, 'but in the days and months and years ahead, we will be laying the groundwork for the way in which the Church shall become more active in the daily lives of all Christians.'

Bringing the Pax worlds more closely under control, interpreted the Grand Inquisitor, his eyes still lowered in thoughtful attention to the Pope's words. *But how . . . with what mechanism?*

Pope Urban XVI smiled again. Cardinal Mustafa noticed, not for the first time, that the Holy Father's smiles never reached his pained and wary eyes. 'Upon the release of the encyclical,' said His Holiness, 'you may more clearly perceive the role we see for the Holy Office, for our diplomatic service, and for such underused entities and institutions as *Opus Dei,* the Pontifical Commission for Justice and Peace, and *Cor Unum.*'

The Grand Inquisitor tried to conceal his surprise. *Cor Unum?* The Pontifical Commission, officially known as *Pontifucum Consilium 'Cor Unum' de Humana et Christiana Progressione Fovenda,* had been little more than a powerless committee for centuries. Mustafa had to think to remember its president . . . Cardinal Du Noyer, he believed. A minor Vatican bureaucrat. An old woman who had never figured in Vatican politics before. *What in hell is going on here?*

'It is an interesting time,' said Cardinal Lourdusamy.

'Indeed,' said the Grand Inquisitor, recalling the ancient Chinese curse to that effect.

The Pope began walking again and the four hurried to keep up. A breeze came through the containment field and fluttered the golden blossoms on a sculpted holyoak.

'Our new encyclical shall also deal with the growing problem of usury in our new age,' said His Holiness.

The Grand Inquisitor almost stopped in his tracks. As it was, he had to take a quick half-step to keep pace. It was a greater effort to keep his expression neutral. He could all but feel the shock of Father Farrell behind him.

Usury? thought the Grand Inquisitor. *The Church has been strict in regulating Pax and Pax Mercantilus trade for three centuries . . . no return to the days of pure capitalism was desired or allowed . . . but the hand of control has been light. Is this a move to consolidate all political and economic life directly under Church control? Would Julius . . . Urban . . . make the move to abolish Pax civil autonomy and Mercantilus trade freedoms at this late date? And where does the military stand in all this?*

His Holiness paused by a beautiful shrub of white blossoms and bright blue leaves. 'Our Illyrian gentian is doing well here,' he said softly. 'It was a present from Archbishop Poske on Galabia Pescassus.'

Usury! thought the Grand Inquisitor in wild confusion. *A penalty of excommunication . . . losing the cruciform . . . upon violation of strict trade and profit controls. Direct intervention from the Vatican, Mother of Christ . . .*

'But that is not why we asked you here,' said Pope Urban XVI. 'Simon Augustino, would you be so kind as to share with Cardinal Mustafa the disturbing intelligence you received yesterday?'

They know about our biospies, thought Mustafa in panic. His heart was pounding. *They know about the agents in place . . . about the Holy Office's attempt to contact the Core directly . . . about sounding out the cardinals before the election . . . everything!* He kept his expression appropriate – alert, interested, alarmed only in a professional sense at the Holy Father's use of the word 'disturbing'.

The great mass of Cardinal Lourdusamy seemed to draw itself up. The heavy rumble of words seemed to come from the man's chest or belly more than from his mouth. Behind him, the figure of Monsignor Oddi reminded Mustafa of the scarecrows in the fields of his youth on the agricultural world of Renaissance Minor.

'The Shrike has reappeared,' began the Cardinal.

The Shrike? What does that have to do with . . . Mustafa's usually sharp mind was reeling, unable to catch up with all of the shifts and revelations. He still suspected a trap. Realizing that the Secretary of State had paused for response, the Grand Inquisitor said softly, 'Can the military authorities on Hyperion deal with it, Simon Augustino?'

Cardinal Lourdusamy's jowls vibrated as the great head moved back and forth. 'It is not on Hyperion that the demon has reappeared, Domenico.'

Mustafa registered appropriate shock. *I know through the interrogation of Corporal Kee that the monster appeared on God's Grove four standard years ago, apparently in an attempt to foil the murder of the child named Aenea. To get that, I had to arrange for the false death and kidnapping of Kee after his reassignment to Pax Fleet. Do they know? And why tell me now?* The Grand Inquisitor was still waiting for the metaphorical blade to drop on his very real neck.

'Eight standard days ago,' continued Lourdusamy, 'a monstrous creature which could only be the Shrike appeared on Mars. The death toll . . . true death, for the creature takes the cruciforms from its victims' bodies . . . has been very high.'

'Mars,' Cardinal Mustafa repeated stupidly. He looked to the Holy Father for an explanation, guidance, even the condemnation he feared, but the Pontiff was examining buds on a rosebush. Behind him, Father Farrell took a step forward, but the Grand Inquisitor waved his aide back. 'Mars?' he said again. He had not felt so stupid and ill-informed for decades, perhaps centuries.

Lourdusamy smiled. 'Yes . . . one of the terraformed worlds in Old Earth's system. FORCE used to have its command center there before the Fall, but the world is of little use or importance in the Pax. Too far away. There is no reason for you to know about it, Domenico.'

'I know *where* Mars is,' said the Grand Inquisitor, his tone more sharp than he had meant it to be. 'I simply do not understand how the Shrike creature could be there.' *And what in Dante's hell does it have to do with me?* he mentally added.

Lourdusamy was nodding. 'It is true that to our knowledge the Shrike demon has never left the world of Hyperion before this. But there can be no doubt. This terror on Mars . . . the Governor has declared a state of emergency and Archbishop Robeson has personally petitioned His Holiness for help.'

The Grand Inquisitor rubbed his cheek and nodded in concern. 'Pax, Fleet . . .'

'Elements of the Fleet already positioned in the Old Neighborhood have been dispatched, of course,' said the Secretary of State. The Supreme Pontiff was bent over a bonsai tree, his hand over the tiny, twisted branch as if he were bestowing a blessing. He seemed not to be listening.

'The ships will have a complement of Marines and Swiss Guard,' continued Lourdusamy. 'We hope that they will subdue and/or destroy the creature . . .'

My mother taught me never to trust anyone who uses the expression 'and/or', thought Mustafa. 'Of course,' he said aloud. 'I shall say a Mass with that prayer in mind.'

Lourdusamy smiled. The Holy Father glanced up from where he was bent over the stunted little tree.

'Precisely,' said Lourdusamy, and in those three syllables, Mustafa heard the sound of the overfed cat pouncing on the hapless mouse of the Grand Inquisitor. 'We agree that it is more a matter of faith than of the Fleet. The Shrike – as it was revealed to the Holy Father more than two centuries ago – is truly a demon, perhaps the principal agent of the Dark One.'

Mustafa could only nod.

'We feel that only the Holy Office is properly trained, equipped, and prepared – both spiritually and materially – to investigate this appearance properly . . . and to save the hapless men, women, and children of Mars.'

Well fuck me, thought John Domenico Cardinal Mustafa, Grand Inquisitor and Prefect for the Sacred Congregation for the Doctrine of the Faith, otherwise known as the Supreme Congregation for the Holy Inquisition of Heretical Error. He automatically offered up a mental Act of Contrition for his obscenity.

'I see,' the Grand Inquisitor said aloud, not seeing at all but almost smiling at the ingenuity of his enemies. 'I will immediately appoint a commission . . .'

'No, no, Domenico,' said His Holiness, moving close to touch the Grand Inquisitor's arm. 'You must go at once. This . . . materialization . . . of the demon threatens the entire Body of Christ.'

'Go . . .' said Mustafa stupidly.

'An archangel-class starship, one of our newest, has been requisitioned from Pax Fleet,' Lourdusamy said briskly. 'It will have a crew of twenty-eight, but you may still bring up to twenty-one members of your own staff and security service . . . twenty-one and yourself, of course.'

'Of course,' said Cardinal Mustafa and he did smile. 'Of course.'

'Pax Fleet is doing battle with the corporeal agents of Satan . . . the Ousters . . . even as we speak,' rumbled Lourdusamy. 'But this demonic threat must be confronted – and defeated – by the sacred power of the Church itself.'

'Of course,' said the Grand Inquisitor. *Mars,* he thought. *The most distant pimple on the ass-end of the civilized universe. Three centuries ago, I could have called on the fatline, but now I will be out of touch as long as they keep me there. No intelligence. No way to direct my people. And the Shrike . . . if the monster is still controlled by the Core's blasphemous Ultimate Intelligence, it may well be programmed to kill me as soon as I arrive. Brilliant.* 'Of course,' he said again. 'Holy Father, when do I leave? If there could be a few days or weeks to set the current affairs of the Holy Office in proper . . .'

The Pope smiled and squeezed Mustafa's upper arm. 'The archangel is waiting to transport you and your chosen contingent within the day, Domenico. Six hours from now would be optimum, they tell us.'

'Of course,' said Cardinal Mustafa a final time. He went to one knee to kiss the papal ring.

'God go with you and protect you always,' said the Holy Father, touching the Cardinal's bowed head as he pronounced the more formal benediction in Latin.

Kissing the ring, tasting the sour cold of stone and metal in his mouth, the Grand Inquisitor mentally smiled again at the cleverness of those whom he had thought to outsmart and outmaneuver.

Father Captain de Soya did not get a chance to talk to Sergeant Gregorius until the last minutes of *Raphael*'s first beyond-the-Outback jump.

This first jump was a practice hop to an uncharted system twenty light-years beyond the Great Wall. Like Epsilon Eridani, the star in this system was a K-type sun; unlike the Eridani orange-dwarf, this K-type was an Arcturus-like giant.

Task Force GIDEON translated without incident, the new two-day auto-mated resurrection creches functioned without glitch, and the third day found the seven archangels decelerating into the giant's system, playing tactical cat-and-mouse with the nine Hawking-class torchships that had preceded them after months of time-debt travel. The torchships had been ordered to hide within the system. The archangels' task was to sniff them out and destroy them.

Three of the torchships were far out in the Oört cloud, floating amid the proto-comets there, their drives off, their corns silenced, their internal systems at lowest ebb. The *Uriel* picked them up at a distance of point-eight-six light-years and launched three virtual Hawking hyperkinetics. De Soya stood with the other six captains in tactical space, the system's sun at their belt level, the two-hundred-kilometer flame tails of seven archangel fusion drives like chest-high diamond scratches on black glass, and he watched as holos misted, formed, and dematerialized in the Oört cloud, tracking the theoretical hyperkinetic seeker missiles as they shifted out of Hawking space, sought out the dormant torchships, and registered two virtual kills and one 'severe damage certain – high probability of a kill' on the tactical tote board.

This system had no planets as such, but four of the remaining torchships were found lurking in ambush within the planetary accretion disc along the plane of the ecliptic. The *Remiel*, the *Gabriel*, and the *Raphael* engaged at long distance and registered kills before the torchships' sensors could regis-ter the presence of the archangel intruders.

The final two torchships were hiding in the heliosphere of the giant K-type star, shielding themselves with class-ten containment fields and venting heat via trailing monofilaments half a million kilometers long. Pax Fleet more than frowned on this sort of maneuver during simulated engagements, but de Soya had to smile at the audacity of the two ships' commanders: it was the sort of thing he might have done a standard decade earlier.

These final torchships came ripping out of the K-star at high boost, their fields venting heat on the visible spectrum, two blazing, white-hot protostars spat out from their massive parent, both ships trying to close on the task force that even now was ripping through the system at three-quarters light-speed. The closest archangel – *Sariel* – killed them both without diverting an erg of power from the class-thirty bussfield the archangel had to maintain a hundred klicks beyond its bow just to clear a path through the molecule-cluttered system. Such terrible velocities demanded a terrible price if the fields failed for an instant.

Then, with Admiral Aldikacti grumbling about the 'probable' in the Oört cloud, the task force decelerated hard in one great arc around the K-type giant so that all of the commanders and execs could meet in tactical space to discuss the simulation before the GIDEON ships translated into Ouster space.

De Soya always found these conferences hubris-making: thirty-some men and women in Pax uniforms standing like giants – or in this case sitting like giants, since they used the plane of the ecliptic as a virtual tabletop – discussing kills and strategies and equipment failures and acquisition rates while the K-type sun burned brightly in the center of the space and the magnified ships moved in their slow, Newtonian ellipses like embers burning through black velvet.

During the three-hour conference, it was decided that the 'probable kill' was unacceptable and that they should have fired a spread of at least five AI-piloted hyper-ks at such difficult targets, retrieving any unused missiles after all three kills were certain. There followed a discussion of expendables, fire-rates, and the kill/conserve/reserve equations on a mission such as this where there could be no resupply. A strategy was decided whereupon one of the archangels would enter each system thirty light-minutes ahead of the others, serving as 'point' to draw all sensor and ECM queries, while another would trail half a light-hour behind, mopping up any 'probables'.

After a twenty-two-hour day spent mostly at battle stations, and with all hands fighting post-resurrection emotional jags, jump coordinates for a system known to be Ouster-infested came over the tightbeam from the *Uriel*, the seven archangels accelerated toward their translation point, and Father Captain de Soya made the rounds to chat with his new crew and to 'tuck everyone in'. He saved Sergeant Gregorius and his five Swiss Guard troopers for last.

Once, during their long chase across the spiral arm after the girl-child named Aenea and after spending months together on the old *Raphael*, Father Captain de Soya had decided that he was tired of calling Sergeant Gregorius 'Sergeant Gregorius' and called up the man's records to discover his first name. To his surprise, de Soya discovered that the sergeant had no first name. The huge noncom had come of age on the northern continent of the swamp world of Patawpha in a warrior culture where everyone was born with eight names – seven of them 'weakness names' – and where only survivors of the 'seven trials' were privileged to discard the weakness names and be known by only their strength name. The ship's AI had told the father-captain that only one warrior out of approximately three thousand attempting the 'seven trials' survived and succeeded in discarding all weakness names. The computer had no information as to the nature of the trials. In addition, the records had shown, Gregorius had been the first Patawphan Scot-Maori to become a decorated Marine and then be chosen to join the elite Swiss Guard. De Soya had always meant to ask the sergeant what the 'seven trials' were, but had never worked up the nerve.

This day, when de Soya kicked down the dropshaft in zero-g and passed through the irising wardroom soft spot, Sergeant Gregorius appeared so happy to see him that he looked as if he were about to give the father-captain a bear hug. Instead, the sergeant hooked his bare feet under a bar, snapped to attention, and shouted, 'TEN-hut in the wardroom!' His five troopers dropped what they were doing – reading, cleaning, or field-stripping – and tried to put bulkhead under their toes. For a moment the wardroom was littered with floating 'scribers, magazines, pulse knives, impact armor, and stripped-down energy lances.

Father Captain de Soya nodded to the sergeant and inspected the five commandos – three men, two women, all terribly, terribly young. They were also lean, muscular, perfectly adapted to zero-g, and obviously honed for battle. All of them were combat veterans. Each of them had distinguished himself or herself adequately to be chosen for this mission. De Soya saw their eagerness for combat and was saddened by it.

After a few minutes of inspection, introductions, and commander-to-commando chatting, de Soya beckoned for Gregorius to follow and kicked off through the aft soft spot into the launch-tube room. When they were alone, Father Captain de Soya extended his hand. 'Damned good to see you, Sergeant.'

Gregorius shook hands and grinned. The big man's square, scarred face and short-cropped hair were the same, and his grin was as broad and bright as de Soya remembered. 'Damned good t'see you, Father Captain. And when did the priesty side o' ya begin usin' profanity, sir?'

'When I was promoted to commanding this ship, Sergeant,' said de Soya. 'How have you been?'

'Fair, sir. Fair an' better.'

'You saw action in the St Anthony Incursion and the Sagittarius Salient,' said de Soya. 'Were you with Corporal Kee before he died?'

Sergeant Gregorius rubbed his chin. 'Negative, sir. I was at the Salient two years ago, but I never saw Kee. Heard about his transport bein' slagged, but never saw him. Had a couple of other friends aboard it, too, sir.'

'I'm sorry,' said de Soya. The two were floating awkwardly near one of the hyper-k storage nacelles. The father-captain grabbed a holdtite and oriented himself so that he could look Gregorius in the eye. 'Did you get through the interrogation all right, Sergeant?'

Gregorius shrugged. 'They kept me on Pacem a few weeks, sir. Kept askin' the same questions in different ways. Didn't seem to believe me about what happened on God's Grove – the woman devil, the Shrike-thingee. Eventually they seemed t' get tired o' askin' me things and busted me back down to corporal and shipped me out.'

De Soya sighed. 'I'm sorry, Sergeant. I had recommended you for a promotion and commendation.' He chuckled ruefully. 'A lot of good that did you. We're lucky we weren't both excommunicated and then executed.'

'Aye, sir,' said Gregorius, glancing out the port at the shifting starfield. 'They weren't happy with us, that's a' sure.' He looked at de Soya. 'And you, sir. I heard they took away your commission and all.'

Father Captain de Soya smiled. 'Busted me back to parish priest.'

'On a dirty, desert, no-water world, I heard tell, sir. A place where piss sells for ten marks a bootful.'

'That was true,' said de Soya, still smiling. 'MadredeDios. It was my homeworld.'

'Aw, shit, sir,' said Sergeant Gregorius, his huge hands clenching in embarrassment. 'No disrespect meant, sir. I mean . . . I didn't . . . I wouldn't . . .'

De Soya touched the big man's shoulder. 'No disrespect taken, Sergeant. You're right. Piss does sell there . . . only for fifteen marks a bootful, not ten.'

'Aye, sir,' said Gregorius, his dark skin darker with flush.

'And, Sergeant . . .'

'Aye, sir?'

'That will be fifteen Hail Marys and ten Our Fathers for the scatological outburst. I'm still your confessor, you know.'

'Aye, sir.'

De Soya's implant tingled at the same instant chimes came over the ship's communicators. 'Thirty minutes until translation,' said the father-captain. 'Get your chicks tucked in their creches, Sergeant. This next jump is for real.'

'Aye, aye, sir.' The sergeant kicked for the soft spot but stopped just as the circle irised open. 'Father Captain?'

'Yes, Sergeant.'

'It's just a feelin', sir,' said the Swiss Guardsman, his brow furrowed. 'But I've learned to trust my feelin's, sir.'

'I've learned to trust your feelings as well, Sergeant. What is it?'

'Watch your back, sir,' said Gregorius. 'I mean . . . nothin' definite, sir. But watch your back.'

'Aye, aye,' said Father Captain de Soya. He waited until Gregorius was back in his wardroom and the soft spot sealed before he kicked off for the main dropshaft and his own death couch and resurrection creche.

Pacem System was crowded with Mercantilus traffic, Pax Fleet warships, large-array habitats such as the Torus Mercantilus, Pax military bases and listening posts, herded and terraformed asteroids such as Castel Gandolfo, low-rent orbital-can cities for the millions eager to be close to humanity's center of power but too poor to pay Pacem's exorbitant rates, and the highest concentration of private in-system spacecraft in the known universe. Thus it was that when M. Kenzo Isozaki, CEO and Chairman of the Executive Council of the Pancapitalist League of Independent Catholic Transstellar Trade Organizations, wished to be absolutely alone, he had to commandeer a private ship and burn high-g for thirty-two hours into the outer ring of darkness far from Pacem's star.

Even choosing a ship had been a problem. The Pax Mercantilus maintained a small fleet of expensive in-system executive shuttles, but Isozaki had to assume that despite their best attempts to debug the ships, they were all compromised. For this rendezvous, he had considered rerouting one of the Mercantilus freighters that plied the trade lanes between orbital clusters, but he did not put it past his enemies – the Vatican, the Holy Office, Pax Fleet Intelligence Services, *Opus Dei*, rivals within the Mercantilus, countless others – to bug every ship in the Mercantilus's vast trade fleet.

In the end, Kenzo Isozaki had disguised himself, gone to the Torus public docks, bought an ancient asteroid hopper on the spot, and ordered his illegal comlog AI to pilot the thing out beyond the campfire zone of the ecliptic. On the trip out, his ship was challenged six times by Pax security patrols and stations, but the hopper was licensed, there were rocks where he was headed – mined and remined, to be sure, but still legitimate destinations for a desperate prospector – and he was passed on without personal interrogation.

Isozaki found all this melodramatic and a waste of his valuable time. He would have met his contact in his office on the Torus if the contact had agreed. The contact had not agreed, and Isozaki had to admit that he would have crawled to Aldebaran for this meeting.

Thirty-two hours after leaving the Torus, the hopper dropped his internal containment field, drained his high-g tank, and brought him up out of sleep. The ship's computer was too stupid to do anything but give him coordinates and readouts on the local rocks, but the illicit AI comlog interface scanned the entire region for ships – powered down or active – and pronounced this sphere of Pacem System space empty.

'So how does he get here if there is no ship?' muttered Isozaki.

'There is no way other than by ship, sir,' said the AI. 'Unless he is here already, which seems unlikely since . . .'

'Silence,' ordered Kenzo Isozaki. He sat in the lubricant-smelling dimness of the hopper command blister and watched the asteroid half a klick distant. Hopper and rock had matched tumble rates, so it was the familiar Pacem System starfield beyond the heavily mined and cratered stone that seemed to be spinning. Other than the asteroid, there was nothing out there except hard vacuum, hard radiation, and cold silence.

Suddenly there was a knock on the outer air-lock door.

EIGHT

At the time that all these troop movements were underway, at the same time as great armadas of matte-black starships were tearing holes in the time and space continuum of the cosmos, at the precise moment when the Church's Grand Inquisitor was sent packing to Shrike-ridden Mars and the CEO of the Pax Mercantilus was traveling alone to a secret rendezvous in deep space with a nonhuman interlocutor, I was lying helpless in bed with a tremendous pain in my back and belly.

Pain is an interesting and off-putting thing. Few if any things in life concentrate our attention so completely and terribly, and few things are more boring to listen to or read about.

This pain was all-absorbing. I was amazed by the relentless, mind-controlling quality of it. During the hours of agony that I had already endured and was yet to endure, I attempted to concentrate on my surroundings, to think of other things, to interact with the people around me, even to do simple multiplication tables in my head, but the pain flowed into all the compartments of my consciousness like molten steel into the fissures on a cracked crucible.

These things I was dimly aware of at the time: that I had been on a world my comlog had identified as Vitus-Gray-Balianus B and in the process of dipping water from a well when the pain had felled me; that a woman swathed in a blue robe, her toenails visibly blue in her open sandals as I lay writhing in the dust, had called others in blue robes and gowns and these people had carried me to the adobe house where I continued battling the pain in a soft bed; that there were several other people in the house – another woman in a blue gown and head scarf, a younger man who wore a blue robe and turban, at least two children, also dressed in blue; and that these generous people not only put up with my moaned apologies and less articulate moans as I curled and uncurled in pain, but constantly spoke to me, patted me, placed wet compresses on my forehead, removed my boots and socks and vest, and generally continued whispering reassurances in their soft dialect as I tried to fight to keep my dignity against the onslaught of agony in my back and abdomen.

It was several hours after they brought me to their home – the blue sky had faded to rose evening outside the window – when the woman who had found me near the well said, 'Citizen, we have asked the local missionary priest for help and he has gone for the doctor at the Pax base at Bombasino. For some reason, the Pax skimmers and other aricraft are all busy now, so

530

the priest and the doctor . . . if the doctor comes . . . must travel fifty pulls down the river, but with luck they should be here before sunrise.'

I did not know how long a pull was or how much time it would take to travel fifty, or even how long the night was on this world, but the thought that there might be an end point to my agony was enough to bring tears to my eyes. Nonetheless, I whispered, 'Please, ma'am, no Pax doctor.'

The woman set cool fingers against my brow. 'We must. There is no longer a medic here in Lock Lamonde. We are afraid you might die without medical help.'

I moaned and rolled away. The pain roiled through me like a hot wire being pulled through too-narrow capillaries. I realized that a Pax doctor would know immediately that I was from offworld, would report me to the Pax police or military – if the 'missionary priest' had not already done so – and that I was all but certain to be interrogated and detained. My mission for Aenea was ending early and in failure. When the old poet, Martin Silenus, had sent me on this odyssey four and a half standard years earlier, he had drunk a champagne toast to me – 'To heroes.' If only he had known how far from reality that toast had been. Perhaps he had.

The night passed with glacial slowness. Several times the two women looked in on me and at other times the children, in blue gowns that may have been sleeping apparel, peered in from the darkened hallway. They wore no headdress then and I saw that the girl had blonde hair worn much the way Aenea hàd when we first met, when she was almost twelve and I twenty-eight standard. The little boy – younger than the girl I assumed to be his sister – looked especially pale; his head was shaved quite bald. Each time he looked in, his fingers fluttered at me in a shy wave. Between rolls of pain, I would feebly wave back, but each time I opened my eyes to look again, the child would be gone.

Sunrise came and went without a doctor. Hopelessness surged in me like an outgoing tide. I could not resist this terrible pain another hour. I knew instinctively that if the kind people in this household had any painkiller, they would have long since given it to me. I had spent the night trying to think of anything I had brought with me in the kayak, but the only medicine in my stowed kit was disinfectant and some aspirin. I knew that the latter would do nothing against this tidal wave of pain.

I decided that I could hold out another ten minutes. They had removed my comlog bracelet and set it within sight on an adobe ledge near the bed, but I had not thought to measure the hours of the night with it. Now I struggled to reach it, the pain twisting in me like a hot wire, and slipped the bracelet back on my wrist. I whispered to the ship's AI in it, 'Is the biomonitor function still activated?'

'Yes,' said the bracelet.

'Am I dying?'

'Life signs are not critical,' said the ship in its usual flat tones. 'But you appear to be in shock. Blood pressure is . . .' It continued to rattle off technical information until I told it to shut up.

'Have you figured out what's doing this to me?' I gasped. Waves of nausea followed the pain. I had long since vomited anything in my stomach, but the retching doubled me over.

'It is not inconsistent with an appendicitis attack,' said the comlog.

'Appendicitis . . .' Those useless artifacts had long since been genetailored out of humanity. 'Do I have an appendix?' I whispered to the bracelet. With the sunrise had come the rustle of robes in the quiet house and several visits from the women.

'Negative,' said the comlog. 'It would be very unlikely, unless you are a genetic sport. The odds against that would be . . .'

'Silence,' I hissed. The two women in blue robes bustled in with another woman, taller, thinner, obviously offworld-born. She wore a dark jumpsuit with the cross-and-caduceus patch of the Pax Fleet Medical Corps on her left shoulder.

'I'm Dr Molina,' said the woman, unpacking a small black valise. 'All the base skimmers are on war-game maneuvers and I had to come by fitzboat with the young man who fetched me.' She set one sticky diagnostic patch on my bare chest and another on my belly. 'And don't flatter yourself that I came all this way for you . . . one of the base skimmers crashed near Keroa Tambat, eighty klicks south of here, and I have to tend to the injured Pax crew while they wait for medevac. Nothing serious, just bruises and a broken leg. They didn't want to pull a skimmer out of the games just for that.' She removed a palm-sized device from the valise and checked to see that it was receiving from the patches. 'And if you're one of those Mercantilus spacers who jumped ship at the port a few weeks ago,' she continued, 'don't get any ideas about robbing me for drugs or money. I'm traveling with two security guards and they're right outside.' She slipped earphones on. 'Now, what's wrong with you, young man?'

I shook my head, gritting my teeth against the surge of pain that was ripping through my back at that second. When I could, I said, 'I don't know, Doctor . . . my back . . . and nausea . . .'

She ignored me while checking the palm device. Suddenly she leaned over and probed my abdomen on the left side. 'Does that hurt?'

I almost screamed. 'Yes,' I said when I could speak.

She nodded and turned to the woman in blue who had saved me. 'Tell the priest who fetched me to bring in the larger bag. This man is completely dehydrated. We need to set up an IV. I'll administer the ultramorph after I get that going.'

I realized then what I had known since I was a child watching my mother die of cancer – namely, that beyond ideology and ambition, beyond thought and emotion, there was only pain. And salvation from it. I would have done anything for that rough-edged, talkative Pax Fleet doctor right then.

'What is it?' I asked her as she was setting up a bottle and tubes. 'Where is this pain coming from?' She had an old-fashioned needle syringe in her hand and was filling it from a small vial of ultramorph. If she told me that I had contracted a fatal disease and would be dead before nightfall, it would be all right as long as she gave me that shot of painkiller first.

'Kidney stone,' said Dr Molina.

I must have shown my incomprehension, because she went on, 'A little rock in your kidney . . . too large to pass . . . probably made of calcium. Have you had trouble urinating in recent days?'

I thought back to the beginning of the trip and before. I had not been drinking enough water and had attributed the occasional pain and difficulty to that fact. 'Yes, but . . .'

'Kidney stone,' she said, swabbing my left wrist. 'Little sting here.' She inserted the intravenous needle and dermplasted it in place. The sting of the needle was totally lost in the cacophony of pain from my back. There was a moment of fiddling with the intravenous tube and attaching the syringe to an offshoot of it. 'This will take about a minute to act,' she said. 'But it should eliminate the discomfort.'

Discomfort. I closed my eyes so that no one would see the tears of relief there. The woman who had found me by the well took my hand in hers.

A minute later the pain began to ebb. Nothing had ever been so welcome by its absence. It was as if a great and terrible noise had finally been turned down so that I could think. I became me again as the agony dropped to the levels I had known from knife wounds and broken bones. This I could handle and still retain my dignity and sense of self. The woman in blue was touching my wrist as the ultramorph took effect.

'Thank you,' I said through parched, cracked lips, squeezing the hand of the woman in blue. 'And thank you, Dr Molina,' I said to the Pax medic.

Dr Molina leaned over me, tapping my cheeks softly. 'You're going to sleep for a while, but I need some answers first. Don't sleep until you talk to me.'

I nodded groggily.

'What's your name?'

'Raul Endymion.' I realized that I could not lie to her. She must have put Truthtell or another drug in the IV drip.

'Where are you from, Raul Endymion?' She was holding the palmsized diagnostic device like a recorder.

'Hyperion. The continent of Aquila. My clan was . . .'

'How did you get to Lock Childe Lamonde on Vitus-Gray-Balianus B, Raul? Are you one of the spacers who jumped ship from the Mercantilus freighter last month?'

'Kayak,' I heard myself say as everything began to feel distant. A great warmth filled me, almost indistinguishable from the sense of relief that surged within me. 'Paddled downriver in the kayak,' I babbled. 'Through the farcaster. No, I'm not one of the spacers . . .'

'Farcaster?' I heard the doctor repeat, her voice puzzled. 'What do you mean you came through the farcaster, Raul Endymion? Do you mean you paddled under it the way we did? Just passed by it on your trip downriver?'

'No,' I said. 'I came *through* it. From offworld.'

The doctor glanced at the woman in blue and then turned back to me. 'You came *through* the farcaster from offworld? You mean it . . . functioned? Farcast you here?'

'Yeah.'

'From where?' said the doctor, checking my pulse with her left hand.

'Old Earth,' I said. 'I came from Earth.'

For a moment I floated, blissfully free from pain, while the doctor stepped out into the hall to talk to the ladies. I heard snatches of conversation.

'. . . obviously mentally unbalanced,' the doctor's voice was saying. 'Could not have possibly come through the . . . delusions of Old Earth . . . possibly one of the spacers on drugs . . .'

'Happy to have him stay . . .' the woman in the blue robe was saying. 'Take care of him until . . .'

'The priest and one of the guards will stay here . . .' the doctor's voice said. 'When the medevac skimmer comes to Keroa Tambat we'll stop by here to fetch him on the way back to the base . . . tomorrow or the day after tomorrow. . . don't let him leave . . . military police will probably want to . . .'

Buoyed up on the rising crest of bliss at the absence of pain, I quit fighting the current and allowed myself to drift downstream to the waiting arms of morphia.

I dreamed of a conversation Aenea and I had shared a few months earlier. It was a cool, high-desert summer night and we were sitting in the vestibule of her shelter, drinking mugs of tea and watching the stars come out. We had been discussing the Pax, but for everything negative I had said about it, Aenea had responded with something positive. Finally I got angry.

'Look,' I said, 'you're talking about the Pax as if it hadn't tried to capture you and kill you. As if Pax ships hadn't chased us halfway across the spiral arm and shot us down on Renaissance Vector. If it hadn't been for the farcaster there . . .'

'The Pax didn't chase us and shoot at us and try to kill us,' the girl said softly. 'Just elements of it. Men and women following orders from the Vatican or elsewhere.'

'Well,' I said, still exasperated and irritated, 'it only takes *elements of it* to shoot us and kill . . .' I paused a second. 'What do you mean – "from the Vatican or elsewhere"? Do you think there are others giving orders? Other than the Vatican, I mean?'

Aenea shrugged. It was a graceful motion, but irritating in the extreme. One of the least endearing of her less-than-endearing teenaged traits.

'Are there others?' I demanded, more sharply than I was used to speaking to my young friend.

'There are always others,' Aenea said quietly. 'They were right to try to capture me, Raul. Or kill me.'

In my dream as in reality, I set my mug of tea on the stone foundation of the vestibule and stared at her. 'You're saying that you . . . and I . . . should be captured or killed . . . like animals. That they have that right?'

'Of course not,' said the girl, crossing her arms in front of her chest, the tea steaming into the cool night air. 'I'm saying that the Pax is correct – from its perspective – in using extraordinary measures to try to stop me.'

I shook my head. 'I haven't heard you say anything so subversive that they should send squadrons of starships after you, kiddo. In fact, the most subversive and heretical thing I've heard you say is that love is a basic force of the universe, like gravity or electromagnetism. But that's just . . .'

'Bullshit?' said Aenea.

'Double talk,' I said.

Aenea smiled and ran her fingers through her short hair. 'Raul, my friend, it's not what I *say* that's a danger to them. It's what I *do*. What I teach by doing . . . by touching.'

I looked at her. I had almost forgotten all that One Who Teaches stuff that her Uncle Martin Silenus had woven into his *Cantos* epic. Aenea was to be the messiah that the old poet had prophesied in his long, confused poem some two centuries earlier . . . or so he had told me. So far I had seen very little from the girl that suggested messiahhood, unless one counted her trip forward through the Sphinx Time Tomb and the obsession of the Pax to capture or kill her . . . and me, since I was her guardian during the rough trip out to Old Earth.

'I haven't heard you teach much that's heretical or dangerous,' I said again, my tone almost sullen. 'Or seen you *do* anything that's a threat to the Pax, either.' I gestured to the night, the desert, and to the distant, lighted buildings of the Taliesin Fellowship, and now – in my ultramorph dream that was more memory than dream – I watched myself make that gesture as if I were observing from the darkness outside the lighted shelter.

Aenea shook her head and sipped her tea. 'You don't see, Raul, but *they* do. Already they've referred to me as a virus. They're right . . . that's exactly what I could be to the Church. A virus, like the ancient HIV strain on Old Earth or the Red Death that raked through the Outback after the Fall . . . a virus that invades every cell of the organism and reprograms the DNA in those cells . . . or at least infects enough cells that the organism breaks down, fails . . . dies.'

In my dream, I swooped above Aenea's canvas-and-stone shelter like a hawk in the night, whirling high among the alien stars above Old Earth, seeing us – the girl and the man – sitting in the kerosene lantern light of the vestibule like lost souls on a lost world. Which is precisely what we were.

For the next two days I drifted in and out of pain and consciousness the way a skiff cut loose on the ocean would float through rain squalls and patches of sunlight. I drank great volumes of water that the women in blue brought me in glass goblets. I hobbled to the toilet cubby and urinated through a filter, trying to catch the stone that was causing my intermittent agony. No stone. Each time I would hobble back to the bed and wait for the pain to start up again. It never failed to do so. Even at the time, I was aware that this was not the stuff of heroic adventure.

Before the doctor left to continue downriver to the site of the skimmer crash, I was made to understand that both the Pax guard and the local priest had com units and would radio the base if I caused any trouble whatsoever. Dr Molina let me know exactly how bad it would be for me if the Pax Fleet commander had to pull a skimmer out of the war games just to fetch a prisoner prematurely. Meanwhile, she said, keep drinking lots of water and peeing every time I could. If the stone didn't pass, she would get me into the jail infirmary at the base and break it up with sound waves. She left four more shots of ultramorph with the woman in blue and left without a good-bye. The guard – a middle-aged Lusian twice my weight with a flechette pistol in his holster and a come-along neural prod on his belt – peered in, glowered at me, and went back outside to stand by the front door.

I will stop referring to the head of the household as 'the woman in blue'. For the first few hours of agony, that had been all she had been to me – other than my savior, of course – but by the afternoon of the first full day in her home, I knew that she was named Dem Ria; that her primary marriage partner was the other woman, Dem Loa; that the third member of their tripartite marriage was the much younger man, Alem Mikail Dem Alem; that the teenaged girl in the house was Ces Ambre, Alem's daughter by a previous triune; that the pale boy with no hair – who looked to be about eight standard years old – was named Bin Ria Dem Loa Alem, was the child of the current partnership – although the biological child of which woman, I never discovered – and that he was dying of cancer.

'Our village medic elder . . . he died last month and has not been replaced . . . sent Bin to our own hospital in Keroa Tambat last winter, but they could only administer radiation and chemotherapy and hope for the best,' said Dem Ria as she sat by my bedside that afternoon. Dem Loa sat nearby on another straight-backed chair. I had asked about the boy to shift the subject of conversation away from my own problems. The women's elaborate robes glowed a deep cobalt blue even as the sunlight behind them lay as thick and red as blood on the interior adobe walls. Lace curtains cut the light and shadows into complex negative spaces. We were chatting in the intervals between the pain. My back hurt then as if someone had struck me there with a heavy club, but this was a dull ache compared to the hot agony when the stone moved. The doctor had said that the pain was a good sign – that the stone was moving when it hurt the most. And the agony did seem to be centered lower in my abdomen. But the doctor had also said that it might take months to pass the stone, if it *was* small enough to be passed naturally. Many stones, she said, had to be pulverized or removed surgically. I brought my mind back to the health of the child we were discussing.

'Radiation and chemotherapy,' I repeated, mouthing the words with distaste. It was as if Dem Ria had said that the medic had prescribed leeches and drafts of mercury for the boy. The Hegemony had known how to treat cancer, but most of the gene-tailoring knowledge and technology had been lost after the Fall. And what had not been lost had been made too expensive to share with the masses after the WorldWeb went away forever: the Pax Mercantilus carried goods and commodities between the stars, but the process was slow, expensive, and limited. Medicine had slipped back several centuries. My own mother had died of cancer – after refusing radiation and chemotherapy after the diagnosis at the Pax Moors Clinic.

But why *cure* a fatal disease when one could recover from it by dying and being resurrected by the cruciform? Even some genetically derived diseases were 'cured' by the cruciform during its restructuring of the body during resurrection. And death, as the Church was constantly pointing out, was as much a sacrament as resurrection itself. It could be offered up like a prayer. The average person could now transform the pain and hopelessness of disease and death into the glory of Christ's redemptive sacrifice. As long as the average person carried a cruciform.

I cleared my throat. 'Ah . . . Bin hasn't . . . I mean . . .' When the boy had waved at me in the night, his loose robe had shown a pale and crossless chest.

Dem Loa shook her head. The blue cowl of her robe was made of a translucent, silklike fabric. 'None of us have yet accepted the cross. But Father Clifton has been . . . convincing us.'

I could only nod. The pain in my back and groin was returning like an electric current through my nerves.

I should explain the different colored robes worn by the citizens of Lock Childe Lamonde on the world of Vitus-Gray-Balianus B. Dem Ria had explained in her melodic whisper that a little over a century ago, most of the people now living along the long river had migrated here from the nearby star system Lacaille 9352. The world there, originally called Sibiatu's Bitterness, had been recolonized by Pax religious zealots who had renamed it Inevitable Grace and begun proselytizing the indigenie cultures that had survived the Fall. Dem Ria's culture – a gentle, philosophical one stressing cooperation – decided to migrate again rather than convert. Twenty-seven thousand of her people had expended their fortunes and risked their lives to refit an ancient Hegira seedship and transport everyone – men, women, children, pets, livestock – in a forty-nine-year cold-sleep voyage to nearby Vitus-Gray-Balianus B, where the WorldWeb-era inhabitants had died out after the Fall.

Dem Ria's people called themselves the Amoiete Spectrum Helix, after the epic philosophical symphony-holo-poem by Halpul Amoiete. In his poem, Amoiete had used colors of the spectrum as a metaphor for the positive human values and shown the helical juxtapositions, interactions, synergies, and collisions created by these values. The Amoiete Spectrum Helix Symphony was meant to be performed, with the symphony, the poetry, and the holoshow all representing the philosophical interplay. Dem Ria and Dem Loa explained how their culture had borrowed the color meanings from Amoiete – white for the purity of intellectual honesty and physical love; red for the passion of art, political conviction, and physical courage; blue for the introspective revelations of music, mathematics, personal therapy to help others, and for the design of fabrics and textures; emerald green for resonance with nature, comfort with technology, and the preservation of threatened life-forms; ebony for the creation of human mysteries; and so forth. The triune marriages, nonviolence, and other cultural peculiarities grew partially from Amoiete's philosophies and largely from the rich cooperative culture the Spectrum people had created on Sibiatu's Bitterness.

'So Father Clifton is convincing you to join the Church?' I said as the pain subsided into a lull where I could think and speak once again.

'Yes,' said Dem Loa. Their tripartner, Alem Mikail Dem Alem, had come in to sit on the adobe windowsill. He listened to the conversation but rarely spoke.

'How do you feel about that?' I asked, shifting slightly to distribute the ache in my back. I had not asked for ultramorph for several hours. I was very aware of the desire to ask for it now.

Dem Ria lifted her hand in a complex motion that reminded me of Aenea's favorite gesture. 'If all of us accept the cross, little Bin Ria Dem Loa Alem will be entitled to full medical care at the Pax base at Bombasino. Even if they do not cure the cancer, Bin will . . . return to us . . . after.' She lowered her gaze and hid her expressive hands in the folds of her robe.

'They won't allow just Bin to accept the cross,' I said.

'Oh, no,' said Dem Loa. 'It is always their position that the entire family must convert. We see their point. Father Clifton is very sad about that, but very hopeful that we will accept Jesus Christ's sacraments before it is too late for Bin.'

'How does your girl – Ces Ambre – feel about becoming a born-again Christian?' I asked, realizing how personal these questions were. But I was intrigued, and the thought of the painful decision they faced took my mind off my very real but much less important pain.

'Ces Ambre loves the idea of joining the Church and becoming a full citizen of the Pax,' said Dem Loa, raising her face under the cowl of her soft blue hood. 'She would then be allowed to attend the Church academy in Bombasino or Keroa Tambat, and she thinks that the girls and boys there would make much more interesting marriage prospects.'

I started to speak, stopped myself, and then spoke anyway. 'But the triune marriage wouldn't be . . . I mean, would the Pax allow . . .'

'No,' said Alem from his place by the window. He frowned and I could see the sadness behind his gray eyes. 'The Church does not allow same-sex or multiple-partner marriages. Our family would be destroyed.'

I noticed the three exchange glances for a second and the love and sense of loss I saw in those looks would stay with me for years.

Dem Ria sighed. 'But this is inevitable anyway. I think that Father Clifton is right . . . that we must do this now, for Bin, rather than wait until he dies the true death and is lost to us forever . . . and *then* join the Church. I would rather take our boy to Mass on Sunday and laugh with him in the sunlight after, than go to the cathedral to light a candle in his memory.'

'Why is it inevitable?' I asked softly.

Dem Loa made the graceful gesture once again. 'Our Spectrum Helix society depends upon all members of it . . . all steps and components of the Helix must be in place for the interplay to work toward human progress and moral good. More and more of the Spectrum people are abandoning their colors and joining the Pax. The center will not hold.'

Dem Ria touched my forearm as if to emphasize her next words. 'The Pax has not coerced us in any way,' she said softly, her lovely dialect rising and falling like the sound of the wind through the lace curtains behind her. 'We respect the fact that they reserve their medicines and their miracle of resurrection for those who join them . . .' She stopped.

'But it is hard,' said Dem Loa, her smooth voice suddenly ragged.

Alem Mikail Dem Alem got up from the window ledge and came over to kneel between the two women. He touched Dem Loa's wrist with infinite gentleness. He put his arm around Dem Ria. For a moment, the three were lost to the world and me, encircled by their own love and sorrow.

And then the pain came back like a fiery lance in my back and lower groin, searing through me like a laser. I moaned despite myself.

The three separated with graceful, purposeful movements. Dem Ria went to get the next ultramorph syringe.

The dream began the same as before – I was flying at night above the Arizona desert, looking down at Aenea and me as we drank tea and chatted in the vestibule of her shelter – but this time the talk went far beyond the memory of our real conversation that night.

'How are you a virus?' I was asking the teenager next to me. 'How could anything you teach be a threat to something as large and powerful as the Pax?'

Aenea was looking out into the desert night, breathing in the fragrance of night-blooming blossoms. She did not look at me when she spoke. 'Do you know the major error in Uncle Martin's *Cantos*, Raul?'

'No,' I said. She had shown me several mistakes, omissions, or wrong-headed guesses in the past few years, and together we had discovered a few during our voyage to Old Earth.

'It was twofold,' she said softly. Somewhere in the desert night, a hawk called. 'First, he believed what the TechnoCore told my father.'

'About how they were the ones who had hijacked Earth?' I said.

'About everything,' said Aenea. 'Ummon was lying to the John Keats cybrid.'

'Why?' I said. 'They were just planning to destroy it.'

The girl looked at me. 'But my mother was there to record the conversation,' she said. 'And the Core knew that she would tell the old poet.'

I nodded slowly. 'And that he would put it as a fact in the epic poem he was writing,' I said. 'But why would they want to lie about . . .'

'His second mistake was more subtle and serious,' she said, interrupting me without raising her voice. A pale glow still hung behind the mountains to the north and west. 'Uncle Martin believed that the TechnoCore was humanity's enemy,' she continued.

I set my mug of tea down on stone. 'Why is that a mistake?' I said. *'Aren't they our enemy?'*

When the girl did not answer I held up my hand, five fingers splayed. 'One, according to the *Cantos*, the Core was the real force behind the attack on the Hegemony that led to the Fall of the Farcasters. Not the Ousters . . . the Core. The Church has denied that, made the Ousters responsible. Are you saying that the Church is right and the old poet was wrong?'

'No,' said Aenea. 'It was the Core that orchestrated the attack.'

'Billions dead,' I said, almost spluttering in outrage. 'The Hegemony toppled. The Web destroyed. The fatline cut . . .'

'The TechnoCore did not cut the fatline,' she said softly.

'All right,' I said, taking a breath, 'That was some mysterious entity . . . your Lions and Tigers and Bears, say. But it was still the Core behind the attack.'

Aenea nodded and poured more tea for herself.

I folded my thumb against my palm and touched the first finger with my other hand. 'Second, did or did not the TechnoCore use the farcasters as a sort of cosmic leech to suck up human neural networks for their damned Ultimate Intelligence project? Every time someone farcast, they were being . . . *used* . . . by those damned autonomous intelligences. Right or wrong?'

'Correct,' said Aenea.

'Three,' I said, folding the first finger away and tapping the next one in line, 'the poem has Rachel – the pilgrim Sol Weintraub's child who has come backward with the Time Tombs from the future – tell about a time to come when,' I shifted the tone of my voice as I quoted, ' ". . . the final war raged between the Core-spawned UI and the human spirit". Was this a mistake?'

'No,' said Aenea.

'Four,' I said, beginning to feel foolish with my little finger exercise, but angry enough to continue, 'didn't the Core admit to your father that it created him . . . created the John Keats cybrid of him . . . just as a trap for the – what did they call it? – the empathy component of the human Ultimate Intelligence that's supposed to come into existence sometime in the future?'

'That's what they said,' agreed Aenea, sipping her tea. She looked almost amused. This made me angrier.

'Five,' I said, folding the last finger back so that my right hand was a fist. 'Wasn't it the Core as well as the Pax – hell, the Core *ordering* the Pax – that tried to have you caught and killed on Hyperion, on Renaissance Vector, on God's Grove . . . halfway across the spiral arm?'

'Yes,' she said softly.

'And wasn't it the Core,' I continued angrily, forgetting my fingered checklist and the fact that we were talking about the old poet's errors, 'that created that female . . . *thing* . . . that arranged to have poor A. Bettik's arm sliced off on God's Grove and would have had your head in a bag if it hadn't been for the Shrike's intervention.' I actually shook my fist I was so angry. 'Wasn't it the fucking Core that's been trying to kill *me* as well as you, and probably *will* kill us if we're ever stupid enough to go back into Pax space?'

Aenea nodded.

I was close to panting, feeling as if I had run a fifty-meter dash. 'So?' I said lamely, unclenching my fist.

Aenea touched my knee. As contact with her always did, I felt a thrill of electric shock run through me. 'Raul, I didn't say that the Core hadn't been up to no good. I simply said that Uncle Martin had made a mistake in portraying them as humanity's enemy.'

'But if all those facts are true . . .' I shook my head, befuddled.

'*Elements* of the Core attacked the Web before the Fall,' said Aenea. 'We know from my father's visit with Ummon that the Core was not in agreement about many of its decisions.'

'But . . .' I began.

Aenea held her hand up, palm out. I fell silent.

'They used our neural networks for their UI project,' she said, 'but there's no evidence that it did humans any harm.'

My jaw almost dropped open at that comment. The thought of those damned AIs using human brains like neural bubbles in their fucking project made me want to throw up. 'They had no right!' I began.

'Of course not,' said Aenea. 'They should have asked permission. What would you have said?'

'I would have told them to go fuck themselves,' I said, realizing the absurdity of the phrase as applied to autonomous intelligences even as I uttered it.

Aenea smiled again. 'And you might remember that we've been using *their* mental power for our own purposes for more than a thousand years. I don't think that we asked permission of their ancestors when we created the first silicon AIs . . . or the first magnetic bubble and DNA entities, for that matter.'

I made an angry gesture. 'That's different.'

'Of course,' said Aenea. 'The group of AIs called the Ultimates have created problems for humanity in the past and will in the future – including trying to kill you and me – but they're only one part of the Core.'

I shook my head. 'I don't understand, kiddo,' I said, my voice softer now. 'Are you really saying that there are good AIs and bad AIs? Don't you remember that they actually considered *destroying the human race*? And that they may do it yet if we get in their way? That would make them an enemy of humanity in my book.'

Aenea touched my knee again. Her dark eyes were serious. 'Don't forget, Raul, that humanity has also come close to destroying the human race. Capitalists and communists were ready to blow up Earth when that was the only planet we lived on. And for what?'

'Yeah,' I said lamely, 'but . . .'

'And the Church is ready to destroy the Ousters even as we speak. Genocide . . . on a scale our race has never seen before.'

'The Church . . . and a lot of others . . . don't consider the Ousters human beings,' I said.

'Nonsense,' snapped Aenea. 'Of course they are. They evolved from common Earth-human origins, just as the AI TechnoCore did. All three races are orphans in the storm.'

'All three races . . .' I repeated. 'Jesus Christ, Aenea, are you including the Core in your definition of humanity?'

'We created them,' she said softly. 'Early on, we used human DNA to increase their computing power . . . their intelligence. We used to have robots. They created cybrids out of human DNA and AI personae. Right now, we have a human institution in power which gives all glory and demands all power because of its allegiance to and connection with God . . . the human Ultimate Intelligence. Perhaps the Core has a similar situation with the Ultimates in control.'

I could only stare at the girl. I did not understand.

Aenea set her other hand on my knee. I could feel her strong fingers through the whipcord of my trousers. 'Raul, do you remember what the AI Ummon said to the second Keats cybrid? That was recorded accurately in the *Cantos*. Ummon talked in sort-of Zen koans . . . or at least that's the way Uncle Martin translated the conversation.'

I closed my eyes to remember that part of the epic poem. It had been a long time since Grandam and I took turns reciting the tale around the caravan campfire.

Aenea spoke the words even as they began to form in my memory. 'Ummon said to the second Keats cybrid—

> '*[You must understand/*
> *Keats/*
> *our only chance*
> *was to create a hybrid/*
> *Son of Man/*
> *Son of Machine*
> *And make that refuge so attractive*
> *that the fleeing Empathy*
> *would consider no other home/*
> *A consciousness already as near divine*
> *as humankind has offered in thirty*
> *generations*
> *an imagination which can span*
> *space and time*
> *And in so offering/*
> *and joining/*
> *form a bond between worlds*
> *which might allow,*
> *that world to exist*
> *for both]*'

I rubbed my cheek and thought. The night wind stirred the canvas folds of Aenea's shelter entrance and brought sweet scents from the desert. Strange stars hung above Earth's old mountains on the horizon.

'Empathy was supposedly the fleeing component of the human UI,' I said slowly as if working out a word puzzle. 'Part of our evolved human consciousness in the future, come back in time.'

Aenea looked at me.

'The hybrid was the John Keats cybrid,' I continued. 'Son of Man and Machine.'

'No,' said Aenea softly. 'That was Uncle Martin's second misunderstanding. The Keats cybrids were not created to be the refuge for Empathy in this age. They were created to be the instrument of that fusion between the Core and humankind. To have a child, in other words.'

I looked at the teenaged girl's hands on my leg. 'So you're the consciousness ". . . as near divine as humankind has offered in thirty generations"?'

Aenea shrugged.

'And you have ". . . an imagination which can span space and time"?'

'All human beings have that,' said Aenea. 'It's just that when I dream and imagine, I can see things that truly will be. Remember when I told you that I remember the future?'

'Yeah.'

'Well, right now I'm remembering that you will dream this conversation some months hence, while you're lying in bed – in terrible pain, I'm afraid – on a world with a complicated name, in a home where people dress all in blue.'

'What?'

'Never mind. It will make sense when it comes about. All improbabilities do when probability waves collapse into event.'

'Aenea,' I heard myself say as I flew in ever higher circles above the desert shelter, watching myself and the girl dwindle below, 'tell me what your secret is . . . the secret that makes you this messiah, this "bond between two worlds".'

'All right, Raul, my love,' she said, suddenly appearing as a grown woman in the instant before I circled too high to make out details or hear distinct words above the rush of the air on my dream wings, 'I will tell you. Listen.'

NINE

By the time they translated into their fifth Ouster system, Task Force GIDEON had slaughter down to a science.

Father Captain de Soya knew from his courses in military history at Pax Fleet Command School that almost all space engagements fought more than half an AU from a planet, moon, asteroid, or strategic point-source in space were entered into by mutual agreement. He remembered that the same had been true of primitive ocean navies on pre-Hegira Old Earth, where most great naval battles had been fought in sight of land in the same aquatic killing grounds, with only the technology of the surface ships changing slowly – Greek trireme to steel-hulled battleship. Aircraft carriers with their long-range attack planes had changed that forever – allowing armadas to strike at each other far out to sea and at great distances – but these battles were far different from the legendary naval engagements where capital ships had slugged it out within visible range of one another. Even before cruise missiles, tactical nuclear warheads, and crude charged particle weapons had forever ended the era of the ocean-going surface combatant, the sea navies of Old Earth had grown nostalgic for the days of blazing broadsides and 'crossing the T'.

Space war had brought a return to such mutually agreed-upon engagements. The great battles of the Hegemony days – whether the ancient internecine wars with General Horace Glennon-Height and his ilk, or the centuries of warfare between Web worlds and Ouster Swarms – had usually been waged close to a planet or spaceborne farcaster portal. And distances between the combatants were absurdly short – hundreds of thousands of klicks, often tens of thousands, frequently less than that – given the light-years and parsecs traveled by the warring parties. But this closing on the enemy was necessary given the time it took a fusion-powered laser lance, a CPB, or ordinary attack missiles to cross even one AU – seven minutes for light to crawl the distance between would-be killer and target, much longer for even the highest-boost missile, where the hunt, chase, and kill could take days of seek and countermeasure, attack and parry. Ships with C-plus capability had no incentive to hang around in enemy space waiting for these seeker missiles, and the Church-sponsored restriction on AIs in warheads made the effectiveness of these weapons problematic at best. So the shape of space battles over the centuries of the Hegemony had been simple – fleets translating into disputed space and finding other translating fleets or more static in-system defenses, a quick closing to more lethal distances, a brief but terrible exchange of energies, and the inevitable retreat of the more savaged forces – or total destruction if the defending forces had nowhere to retreat – followed by consolidation of gains by the winning fleet.

Technically, the slower ships de Soya had served in previously had a powerful tactical advantage over the instantaneous-drive archangel cruisers. Revival from cryogenic fugue state took only hours at worst, minutes at best, so the captain and crew of a Hawking-drive ship could be ready to fight shortly after translating from C-plus. With the archangels, and even with papal dispensation for the accelerated and risky two-day resurrection cycles, it was fifty standard hours or more before the human elements of the ships were ready to do battle. Theoretically, this gave a great advantage to the defenders. Theoretically, the Pax could have optimized the use of Gideon-drive ships by having uncrewed craft piloted by AIs flick into enemy space, wreak havoc, and flick out again before the defenders knew that they were under attack.

But such theory did not apply here. Autonomous intelligences capable of such advanced fuzzy logic would never be allowed by the Church. More importantly, Pax Fleet had designed attack strategies to meet the requirements of resurrection so that no advantage would be surrendered to defenders. Simply put, no battles were to be fought by mutual agreement. The seven archangels had been designed to descend upon the enemy like the mailed fist of God, and that was precisely what they were doing now.

In the first three Task Force GIDEON incursions into Ouster space, Mother Captain Stone's ship, the *Gabriel*, translated first and decelerated hard in-system, drawing all long-range electromagnetic, neutrino, and other sensor probes. The restricted AIs aboard *Gabriel* were sufficient to catalogue the position and identity of all defensive positions and population centers in the system, while simultaneously monitoring the sluggish in-system movement of all Ouster attack and merchant vehicles.

Thirty minutes later, the *Uriel, Raphael, Remiel, Sariel, Michael,* and *Raguel* would translate in-system. Dropping to only three-quarters light-speed, the task force would be moving like bullets compared to the tortoise velocities of the accelerating Ouster torchships. Receiving *Gabriel*'s intelligence and targeting data via tightbeam burst, the task force would open fire with weaponry that held no respect for the limitations of light-speed. The improved Hawking-drive hyper-k missiles would wink into existence among enemy ships and above population centers, some using velocity and precise aiming to destroy targets, others detonating in carefully shaped but promiscuous plasma or thermonuclear blasts. At the same instant, recoverable Hawking-drive high-velocity probes would jump to target points and translate into real space, radiating conventional lance beams and CPBs like so many lethal sea urchins, destroying anything and everything within a hundred-thousand-klick radius.

Most terribly, the shipborne deathbeams would slice outward from the task-force archangels like invisible scythes, propagating along the Hawking-drive wakes of probes and missiles and translating into real space as surely as the terrible swift sword of God. Countless trillions of synapses were fried and scrambled in an instant. Tens of thousands of Ousters died without knowing that they were under attack.

And then the GIDEON Task Force would come back in-system on thousand-kilometer tails of flame, closing in for the final kill.

Each of the seven star systems to be attacked had been probed by instantaneous-drive drones, the presence of Ousters confirmed, preliminary targets assigned. Each of the seven star systems had a name – usually just a New Revised General Catalogue alpha-numerical designation – but the command team aboard HHS *Uriel* had given the seven systems target names coded after the seven archdemons mentioned in the Old Testament.

Father Captain de Soya thought it a bit much, all this cabalistic numerology – seven archangels, seven target systems, seven archdemons, seven deadly sins. But he soon fell into the habit of talking about the targets in this shorthand.

The target systems were – Belphegor (sloth), Leviathan (envy), Beelzebub (gluttony), Satan (anger), Asmodeus (lechery). Mammon (avarice), and Lucifer (pride).

Belphegor had been a red-dwarf system that reminded de Soya of Barnard's Star System, but instead of the lovely, fully terraformed Barnard's World floating close to the sun, Belphegor's only planet was a gas giant resembling Barnard's Star's forgotten child, Whirl. There were true military targets around this unnamed gas giant: refueling stations for the Ouster Swarm torchships en route to attack the Pax's Great Wall, gigantic dipships that shuttled the gases from the world to orbit, repair docks, and orbital shipyards by the dozen. De Soya had *Raphael* attack these without hesitation, slagging them to orbital lava.

GIDEON found most of the true Ouster population centers floating in the Trojan points beyond the gas giant, scores of small orbital forests filled with tens of thousands of space-adapted 'angels', most opening their forcefield wings to the weak, red sunlight in panic at the task force's approach. The seven archangels laid waste to these delicate ecostructures, destroying all of the forests and shepherd asteroids and watering comets, burning the fleeing space-adapted Ouster angels like putting so many moths to a flame, and all without slowing significantly between entrance and exit translation points.

The second system, Leviathan, despite its impressive name, had been a Sirius B-type white dwarf with only a dozen or so Ouster asteroids huddled close to its pale fire. Here there were none of the obvious military targets that de Soya had attacked so willingly in the Belphegor System: the asteroids were undefended, probably birthing rocks and hollowed-out pressurized environments for Ousters who had not chosen to adapt to vacuum and hard radiation. Task Force GIDEON swept them with deathbeams and passed on.

The third system, Beelzebub, was an Alpha Centauri C-like red dwarf, devoid of worlds or colonies, with only a single Ouster military base swinging in the darkness some thirty AUs out and fifty-seven Swarm ships caught in the act of refueling or refitting. Thirty-nine of these warships, ranging in size and armament from tiny ramscouts to an Orion-class attack carrier, were fit to fight and flung themselves at Task Force GIDEON. The battle lasted two minutes and eighteen seconds. All fifty-seven Ouster ships and the base complex were turned to gas molecules or lifeless sarcophagi. No archangels were damaged in the exchange. The task force moved on.

The fourth system, Satan, held no ships, only breeding colonies scattered as far out as the Oört cloud. GIDEON spent eleven days in this system, putting Lucifer's angels to the torch.

The fifth system, Asmodeus, centered by a pleasant little K-type orange dwarf not unlike Epsilon Eridani, sent waves of in-system torchships to the defense of its populated asteroid belt. The waves were burned and blasted away with an economy born of practice. The *Gabriel* reported eighty-two inhabited rocks in the belt, harboring a population estimated at a million and a half adapted and unadapted Ousters. Eighty-one of the asteroids were destroyed or deathbeamed from a great distance. Then Admiral Aldikacti ordered prisoners taken. Task Force GIDEON decelerated in a long, four-day ellipse that brought them back to the belt and its sole remaining inhabited rock – a potato-shaped asteroid less than four klicks long and a klick across at its widest, cratered point. Doppler radar showed that it was orbiting and tumbling in random patterns understood only by the gods of chaos, but that it was turning on its axis in a carefully orchestrated one-tenth-g rotisserie mode. Deep radar showed that it was hollow. Probes told that it was inhabited by as many as ten thousand Ousters. Analysis suggested that it was a birthing rock.

Six unarmed rock hoppers flung themselves at the task force. *Uriel* turned them into plasma at a distance of eighty-six thousand klicks. A thousand Ouster angels, some of them armed with low-yield energy weapons or recoilless rifles, opened forcefield wings and flew toward the distant Pax ships in long, tacking ellipses along the crest of the solar wind. Their velocity was so slow that it would have taken days to cover the distance. The *Gabriel* was given the task of burning them away with a thousand winks of coherent light.

Tightbeams flicked on between the archangels. *Raphael* and *Gabriel* acknowledged orders and closed to within a thousand klicks of the silent asteroid. Sally ports opened and twelve tiny figures – six from each ship – caught the light from the orange-dwarf star as Swiss Guard commandos, Marines, and troopers jetted toward the rock. There was no resistance. The troopers found two shielded air-lock portals. With precise timing, they blasted the outer doors open and entered in teams of three.

'Bless me, Father, for I have sinned. It's been two standard months since my last confession.'

'Go ahead.'

'Father, today's action . . . it bothers me, Father.'

'Yes?'

'It feels . . . wrong.'

Father Captain de Soya was silent. He had watched Sergeant Gregorius's attack on the virtual tactical channels. He had debriefed the men after the mission. Now he knew he was going to hear it again in the darkness of the confessional. 'Go ahead, Sergeant,' he said softly.

'Aye, sir,' said the sergeant on the other side of the partition. 'I mean, aye, Father.'

Father Captain de Soya heard the big man take a breath.

'We came onto the rock with no opposition,' began Sergeant Gregorius. 'Me an' the five young ones, I mean. We were in tightbeam contact with Sergeant Kluge's squad from the *Gabriel*. And of course, with Commanders Barnes-Avne and Uchikawa.'

De Soya remained silent in his part of the confessional booth. The booth was sectional, meant to be stored away when the *Raphael* was under boost or combat stations, which was most of the time, but now it smelled of wood and sweat and velvet and sin, as all real confessionals did. The father-captain had found this half-hour during the last stage of their climb toward translation point for the sixth Ouster system, Mammon, and offered the crew time for confession, but only Sergeant Gregorius had come forward.

'So when we landed, sir . . . Father, I had the laddies in my squad take the south polar air lock, just like in the sims. We blew the doors as easily as you please, Father, and then activated our own fields for the tunnel fighting.'

De Soya nodded. Swiss Guard fighting suits had always been the best in the human universe – capable of surviving, moving, and fighting in air, water, hard vacuum, hard radiation, slug assault, energy-lance assault, and high-explosive environment up to the kiloton-yield range, but the new commando suits carried their own class-four containment fields and were able to piggyback on the ships' more formidable fields.

'The Ousters hit us in there, Father, fighting in the dark maze of the access tunnels. Some o' them were space-adapted creatures, sir . . . angels without their wings extended. But most of them were just low-g adepts in skinsuits . . . hardly any armor to speak of a'tall, Father. They tried using lance and rifle and ray on us, but they were using basic night goggles to amplify the dim glow from the rocks, sir, and we saw 'em first with our filters. Saw 'em first and shot 'em first.' Sergeant Gregorius took another breath. 'It only took us a few minutes to fight our way to the inner locks, Father. All the Ousters who tried to stop us in the tunnels ended up floatin' there . . .'

Father Captain de Soya waited.

'Inside, Father . . . well . . .' Gregorius cleared his throat. 'Both squads blew the inner doors at the same instant, sir . . . north and south poles at once. The repeater globes we left behind in the tunnels relayed the tight-beam transmissions just fine, so we were never out of touch with Kluge's squad . . . nor with the ships, as ye know, Father. There were fail-safes on the inner doors, just as we figured, but those we blew as well, and the emergency membranes a second later. The inside of the rock was all hollow, Father . . . well, we knew that, of course . . . but I'd never been inside a birthin' asteroid before, Father. Many a military rock, aye, but never a pregnancy one . . .'

De Soya waited.

'It was about one klick across with lots o' their spidery low-g bamboo towers takin' up much of the center space, Father. The inner shell wasn't spherical or smooth, but more or less followed the shape of the outside of the rock, you know.'

'Potato,' said Father Captain de Soya.

'Yessir. And all pitted and cratered on the inside, too, Father. Lots of caves and grottoes everywhere . . . like dens for the pregnant Ousters, I suppose.'

De Soya nodded in the darkness and glanced at his chronometer, wondering if the usually concise sergeant was going to get to the perceived sins in this account before they had to stow the confessional for C-plus translation.

'It must've been pure chaos for the Ousters, Father . . . what with the cyclone howlin' as the place depressurized, all the atmosphere flowin' out o' the two blasted air locks like water out of a bathtub drain, the air all full of dirt and debris and Ousters blowin' away like so many leaves in the storm. We had our external suit phones on, Father, and the noise was unbelievable till the air got too thin to carry it – wind roarin', Ousters screamin', their lances and our lances cracklin' like so many lightning rods, plasma grenades goin' off and the sound bouncin' back at us in that big rock cavern, the echoes goin' on for minutes – it was *loud*, Father.'

'Yes,' said Father Captain de Soya in the darkness.

Sergeant Gregorius took another breath. 'Anyway, Father, the orders'd been to bring in two samples of everything . . . adult males, space-adapted, unadapted; adult females, pregnant, and not pregnant; a couple of Ouster kids, pre-puberty, and infants . . . both sexes. So Kluge's team and ours got busy, stunning and bagging 'em. There was just enough gravity on the inner surface of the rock . . . one-tenth-g . . . to keep the bags in place where we left 'em.'

There was a moment of silence. Father Captain de Soya was just about to speak, to bring this confession to a close, when Sergeant Gregorius whispered through the screen and darkness separating them.

'Sorry, Father, I know you know all this. I just . . . it's hard to . . . anyway, this was the bad part, Father. Most of the Ousters who weren't modified . . . space-adapted . . . were dead or dying at this point. From decompression or lance fire or grenades. We didn't use the deathbeam wands issued to us. Neither Kluge nor I said anything to the lads . . . just none of us used the things.

'Now those adapted Ousters went angel, their bodies turnin' all shiny as they activated their personal forcefields. They couldn't fully extend their wings in there, of course, and it wouldn't have done any good if they had . . . no sunlight to catch, and the one-tenth-g was too much for them to overcome if there had been any solar wind . . . but they went angel anyway. Some of them tried to use their wings as weapons against us.'

Sergeant Gregorius made a rough sound that might have been a parody of a chuckle. 'We had class-four fields, Father, and they were batting at us with those gossamer wings . . . Anyway, we burned them away, sent three from each squad out with the bagged specimens, and Kluge and I each took our remainin' two lads to clear out the caverns as ordered . . .'

De Soya waited. There was less than a minute before he would have to end confession.

'We knew it was a birthin' rock, Father. We knew . . . everybody knows . . . that the Ousters, even the ones who've turned the machines loose in their cells and blood and who don't look anythin' like human . . . they haven't learned how to have their females carry and bear children in pure zero-g and hard radiation, Father. We *knew* it was a birthin' rock when we went in the goddamned asteroid . . . I'm sorry, Father . . .'

De Soya stayed silent.

'But even so, Father . . . those caverns were like homes . . . beds and cubbies and flatscreen vid sets and kitchens . . . not things we're used to thinkin' Ousters have, Father. But most of those caves were . . .'

'Nurseries,' said Father Captain de Soya.

'Aye, sir. Nurseries. Wee beds with wee babies in 'em . . . not Ouster monsters, Father, not those pale, shiny things we fight against, not those damned Lucifer's angels with wings a hundred klicks across in the starlight . . . just . . . babies. By the hundreds, Father. By the thousands. Cavern after cavern. Most o' the rooms there had depressurized already, killing the little ones where they lay. Some o' the little bodies had been blown out in the depressurization, but most o' them were tucked in tight. Some o' the rooms were still airtight, though, Father. We blew our way in. Mothers . . . women in robes, pregnant women with wild hair flying in the one-tenth-g . . . they attacked us with their fingernails and teeth, Father. We ignored them until the windstorms blew them out or they died a-choking, but some of the infants . . . scores of them, Father . . . were in those little plastic respirator cases . . .'

'Incubators,' said Father Captain de Soya.

'Aye,' whispered Sergeant Gregorius, his voice tiring at last. 'And we tightbeamed back, what did they want us to do with 'em? With all the scores and scores of baby Ousters in these incubators. And Commander Barnes-Avne beamed back . . .'

'To continue on,' whispered Father Captain de Soya.

'Aye, Father . . . so we . . .'

'Followed orders, Sergeant.'

'So we used the last of our grenades in those nurseries, Father. And when the plasma grenades were gone, we lanced those incubators. Room after room, cavern after cavern. The plastic melted around the babes, covered 'em. Blankets ignited. The boxes must've been fed with pure O_2, Father, because a lot o' them went up like grenades themselves . . . we had to activate our suit fields, Father, and even so . . . it took me two hours to clean my combat armor . . . but most of the incubators didn't explode, Father, they just burned like dry tinder, burned like torches, everythin' in 'em burnin' bright like little furnaces. And by now all the rooms and caverns were in vacuum, but the boxes . . . the little incubators . . . they still had atmosphere while they burned . . . and we turned off our outside phones, sir. All of us did. But somehow we could still hear the crying and the screams through the containment fields and our helmets. I can still hear them, Father . . .'

'Sergeant,' said de Soya, his voice hard and flat with command.

'Aye, sir?'

'You were following orders, Sergeant. We were all following orders. His Holiness has long since decreed that Ousters have surrendered their humanity to nanodevices they release in their blood, to the changes they have made with their chromosomes . . .'

'But the screams, Father . . .'

'*Sergeant* . . . the Vatican Council and the Holy Father have decreed that this Crusade is necessary if the human family is to be saved from the Ouster threat. You were given orders. You obeyed them. We are soldiers.'

'Aye, sir,' whispered the sergeant in the darkness.

'We have no more time, Sergeant. We will talk about this at a later time. For now, I want you to do penance . . . not for being a soldier and following orders, but for doubting those orders. Fifty Hail Marys, Sergeant, and a hundred Our Fathers. And I want you to pray about this . . . pray very hard for understanding.'

'Aye, Father.'

'Now say a sincere Act of Contrition . . . quickly now . . .'

When the whispered words began to come through the screen, Father Captain de Soya lifted his hand in benediction as he gave absolution. '*Ego te absolvo* . . .'

Eight minutes later, the father-captain and his crew all lay back in their acceleration couches/resurrection creches as *Raphael*'s Gideon drive activated, carrying them instantaneously to Target System Mammon by way of terrible death and slow, painful rebirth.

The Grand Inquisitor had died and gone to Hell.

It was only his second death and resurrection and he had enjoyed neither experience. And Mars *was* Hell.

John Domenico Cardinal Mustafa and his contingent of twenty-one Holy Office administrators and security people – including his indispensable aide Father Farrell – had traveled to Old Earth System in the new archangel starship *Jibril* and had been given a generous four days after resurrection to recover and regroup mentally before beginning their work on the surface of Mars itself. The Grand Inquisitor had read and been briefed enough on the red planet to form an unassailable opinion – Mars was Hell.

'Actually,' Father Farrell responded the first time the Grand Inquisitor had mentioned his conclusion aloud about Mars being Hell, 'one of the other planets in this system . . . Venus . . . better fits that description, Your Excellency. Boiling temperatures, crushing pressures, lakes of liquid metal, winds like rocket exhausts . . .'

'Shut up,' the Grand Inquisitor said with a tired turn of his hand.

Mars: the first world ever colonized by the human race despite its low rating of two-point-five on the old Solmev Scale, the first attempted terraforming, the first failed terraforming – a world bypassed after the black-hole death of Old Earth because of the Hawking drive, because of the imperatives of the Hegira, because no one wanted to live on the rusty sphere of permafrost when the galaxy offered a near-infinite number of prettier, healthier, more viable worlds.

For centuries after the death of Old Earth, Mars had been such a backwater planet that the WorldWeb had not established farcaster portals there – a desert planet of interest only to the orphans of New Palestine (the legendary Colonel Fedmahn Kassad had been born in the Palestinian relocation camps there, Mustafa was surprised to learn) and to Zen Christians returning to Hellas Basin to reenact Master Schrauder's enlightenment at the Zen Massif. For a century or so it had looked as if the huge terraforming project would work – seas filled giant impact basins and cycladferns proliferated along River Marineris – but then the setbacks came, there were no funds to fight the entropy, and the next sixty-thousand-year-long ice age arrived.

At the height of the WorldWeb civilization, the Hegemony's military wing, FORCE, had brought Farcasters to the red world and honeycombed habitats into much of the huge volcano, Mons Olympus, for their Olympic Command School. Mars's isolation from Web trade and culture served FORCE well and the planet had remained a military base until the Fall of the Farcasters. In the century after the Fall, remnants of FORCE had formed a vicious military dictatorship – the so-called Martian War Machine – which extended its rule as far as the Centauri and Tau Ceti systems and might well have become the seed crystal for a second interstellar empire if the Pax had not arrived, quickly subduing the Martian fleets, driving the War Machine back to Old Earth System, sending the dispossessed warlords into hiding among the ruins of FORCE orbital bases and in the old tunnels under Mons Olympus, replacing the War Machine's presence in Old Earth System with Pax Fleet bases in the asteroid belt and among the Jovian moons, and finally sending missionaries and Pax governors to pacified Mars.

There was little left on the rust world for the missionaries to convert or the Pax administrators to govern. The air had grown thin and cold; the large cities had been plundered and abandoned; the great *simoom* pole-to-pole dust storms had reappeared; plague and pestilence stalked the icy deserts, decimating – or worse – the last bands of nomads descended from the once noble race of Martians; and little more than spindly brandy cactus now grew where the great apple orchards and fields of bradberries had long ago flourished.

Oddly, it was the downtrodden and much-abused Palestinians on the frozen Tharsis Plateau whose society had survived and thrived. The orphans of the ancient Nuclear Diaspora of AD 2038 had adapted to Mars's rough ways and extended their Islamic culture to many of the planet's surviving nomad tribes and free city-states by the time the Pax missionaries arrived. Refusing to submit to the ruthless Martian War Machine for more than a century, the New Palestinians showed no interest now in surrendering autonomy to the Church.

It was precisely in the Palestinian capital of Arafat-kaffiyeh that the Shrike had appeared and slaughtered hundreds . . . perhaps thousands . . . of people.

The Grand Inquisitor conferred with his aides, met with Pax Fleet commanders in orbit, and landed in force. The main spaceport in the capital of St Malachy was shut down to all but military traffic – no great loss, since no merchant or passenger dropships were scheduled in for a Martian week. Six assault boats preceded the Grand Inquisitor's dropship, and by the time Cardinal Mustafa set foot to Martian soil – or Pax tarmac, to be precise – a hundred Swiss Guard and Holy Office commandos had ringed the spaceport. The official Martian welcoming delegation, including Archbishop Robeson and Governor Clare Palo, were searched and sonic-probed before being allowed clearance.

From the spaceport, the Holy Office group was whisked via groundcar shuttles through decaying streets to the new Pax-built Governor's Palace on the outskirts of St Malachy. Security was heavy. Besides the Grand Inquisitor's personal security force, the Pax Fleet Marines, the Governor's troopers, and the Archbishop's contingent of Swiss Guards, there was a battle regiment of Home Guard armored infantry encamped around the palace. There the Grand Inquisitor was shown evidence of the Shrike's presence two standard weeks earlier on the Tharsis Plateau.

'This is absurd,' said the Grand Inquisitor on the night before flying to the scene of the Shrike attack. 'All these holos and vid images are two standard weeks old or taken from high altitude. I see these few holos of what must be the Shrike and some blurred scenes of carnage. I see photos of the Pax bodies the militia men found when first entering the town. But where are the local people? Where are the eyewitnesses? Where are the twenty-seven hundred citizens of Arafat-kaffiyeh?'

'We don't know,' said Governor Clare Palo.

'We reported to the Vatican via archangel drone and when the drone returned, we were told not to tamper with the evidence,' said Archbishop Robeson. 'We were told to await your arrival.'

The Grand Inquisitor shook his head and held up a flat photo image. 'And what is this?' he said. 'A Pax Fleet base on the outskirts of Arafat-kaffiyeh? This spaceport is newer than St Malachy's.'

'It is not Pax Fleet,' said Captain Wolmak, captain of the *Jibril* and new commander of the Old Earth System task force. 'Although we estimate that thirty to fifty dropships a day were using this facility during the week previous to the Shrike's appearance.'

'Thirty to fifty dropships a day,' repeated the Grand Inquisitor. 'And *not* Pax Fleet. Who then?' He scowled at Archbishop Robeson and the Governor.

'Mercantilus?' pressed the Grand Inquisitor when no one spoke.

'No,' said the Archbishop after another moment. 'Not Mercantilus.'

The Grand Inquisitor folded his arms and waited.

'The dropships were chartered by *Opus Dei*,' said Governor Palo in a tiny voice.

'For what purpose?' demanded the Grand Inquisitor. Only Holy Office guards were allowed in this suite of the palace, and they stood at six-meter intervals along the stone wall.

The Governor opened her hands. 'We do not know, Your Excellency.'

'Domenico,' said the Archbishop, his voice quavering slightly, 'we were told not to inquire.'

The Grand Inquisitor took an angry step forward. '*Told* not to . . . by whom? Who has the authority to order the presiding Archbishop and the Pax Governor of a world "*not to interfere*"?' His anger boiled through. 'In the name of Christ! Who has such power?'

The Archbishop raised pained but defiant eyes toward Cardinal Mustafa. 'In the name of Christ . . . precisely, Your Excellency. Those representing *Opus Dei* held official diskeys from the Pontifical Commission for Justice and Peace,' he said. 'We were told that it was a security matter in Arafat-kaffiyeh. We were told that it was not our business. We were told not to interfere.'

The Grand Inquisitor felt his face flushing with barely subdued rage. 'Security matters on Mars or anywhere else in the Pax are the responsibility of the Holy Office!' he said flatly. 'The Pontifical Commission for Justice and Peace has no charter here! Where are the representatives of the Commission? Why aren't they here for this meeting?'

Governor Clare Palo raised a thin hand and pointed at the flat photo in the Grand Inquisitor's hand. 'There, Your Excellency. There are the Commission authorities.'

Cardinal Mustafa looked down at the glossy photograph. Forms of white-clad bodies could be seen in the dusty red streets of Arafat-kaffiyeh. Even through the grain of the images, it was obvious that the bodies were mauled into grotesque forms and swollen from decomposition. The Grand Inquisitor spoke softly, fighting the urge to scream and then order these imbeciles tortured and shot. 'Why,' he asked softly, 'haven't these people been resurrected and questioned?'

Archbishop Robeson actually attempted a smile. 'You will see that tomorrow, Your Excellency. It will be abundantly clear tomorrow.'

EMVs were useless on Mars. They used armored Pax Security skimmers for their flight to Tharsis Plateau. Torchships and the *Jibril* monitored their progress. Scorpion fighters flew space/air combat patrol. Two hundred klicks from the plateau, five squads of Marines dropped from the skimmers and flew ahead at low altitude, raking the area with acoustic probes and setting up firing positions.

Nothing but the shifting sand moved in Arafat-kaffiyeh.

The Holy Office security skimmers set down first, their landing legs settling into sand where grass had once grown on the oval city commons, the outer ships establishing and linking a class-six containment field that made the buildings around the plaza seem to shimmer in heat haze. The

Marines had dropped into a defensive circle with the commons as their locus. Now the Governor's Pax and Home Guard troops moved out to establish a second perimeter in the streets and alleys around the plaza. The Archbishop's eight Swiss Guardsmen secured the circle just outside the containment field. Finally the Grand Inquisitor's Holy Office security force exploded down the skimmer ramps and established the inner perimeter of kneeling figures in black combat armor.

'Clear,' came the leading Marine sergeant's voice on the tactical channel.

'Nothing moving or alive within a kilometer of Site One,' rasped the lieutenant of the Home Guard. 'Bodies in the street.'

'Clear here,' said the captain of the Swiss Guard.

'Confirm nothing moving in Arafat-kaffiyeh except your people,' came the voice of the captain of the *Jibril*.

'Affirmative,' said Holy Office Security Commander Browning.

Feeling foolish and disgruntled, the Grand Inquisitor swept down the ramp and across the sandy commons. His mood was not lifted by the silly osmosis mask he had to wear, its circular boostirator slung over his shoulder like a loose medallion.

Father Farrell, Archbishop Robeson, Governor Palo, and a host of functionaries ran to keep up as Cardinal Mustafa strode by the kneeling security forms and, with an imperious wave of his hand, ordered a portal cut in the containment field. He passed through over the protests of Commander Browning and the other forms in black armor who were scuttling to catch up.

'Where is the first of . . .' began the Grand Inquisitor as he bounced down the narrow alley opposite the commons. He still was not used to the light gravity here.

'Right around this corner . . .' panted the Archbishop.

'We should really wait for the outer fields to be . . .' said Governor Palo.

'Here,' said Father Farrell, pointing down the street on to which they had emerged.

The group of fifteen stopped so quickly that those aides and security people in the rear had to catch themselves before bumping into the VIPs in front.

'Dear Lord,' whispered Archbishop Robeson and crossed himself. Through the clear osmosis mask, his face was visibly white.

'Christ!' muttered Governor Clare Palo. 'I've seen the holos and photos for two weeks, but . . . Christ.'

'Ahh,' said Father Farrell, taking a step closer to the first body.

The Grand Inquisitor joined him. He went to one knee in the red sand. The contorted form in the dirt looked as if someone had fashioned an abstract sculpture out of flesh, bone, and gristle. It would not have been recognizably human had it not been for the teeth gleaming in the wide-stretched mouth and one hand lying nearby in the shifting Martian dust.

After a moment the Grand Inquisitor said, 'Did scavengers do some or most of this? Carrion birds, perhaps? Rats?'

'Negative,' said Major Piet, the Governor's Pax Fleet groundforce commander. 'No birds on the Tharsis Plateau since the atmosphere started thinning two centuries ago. No rats . . . or any other moving thing . . . have been picked up by motion detectors since this happened.'

'The Shrike did this,' said the Grand Inquisitor. He did not sound convinced. He stood and moved to the second body. It might have been a woman. It looked as if it had been turned inside out and shredded. 'And this?'

'We think so,' said Governor Palo. 'The militia that found all this brought out the security camera which had that thirty-eight-second holo we've shown you.'

'That looked like a dozen Shrikes killing a dozen people,' said Father Farrell. 'It was hazy.'

'There was a sandstorm,' said Major Piet. 'And there was only one Shrike . . . we've studied the individual images. It simply moved through the crowd so quickly that it appeared to be multiple creatures.'

'Moved through the crowd,' murmured the Grand Inquisitor. He stepped over a third body that might have been a child or small female. 'Doing this.'

'Doing this,' said Governor Palo. She glanced at Archbishop Robeson, who had moved to a wall for support.

There were twenty to thirty bodies in this section of the street.

Father Farrell knelt and ran his gloved hand across the chest and into the chest cavity of the first cadaver. The flesh was frozen, as was the blood that fell in a black icefall. 'And there was no sign of the cruciform?' he said softly.

Governor Palo shook her head. 'Not in the two bodies the militia returned for resurrection. No sign of the cruciform whatsoever. If there had been any remnant at all . . . even a millimeter of node or bit of fiber in the brainstem or . . .'

'We *know* that,' snapped the Grand Inquisitor, ending the explanation.

'Very strange,' said Bishop Erdle, the Holy Office's expert on resurrection technique. 'To my knowledge there has never been an instance where the body was left so intact where we could not find remnant of the cruciform in the corpse. Governor Palo is correct, of course. Even the slightest bit of cruciform is all that is necessary for the Sacrament of Resurrection.'

The Grand Inquisitor stopped to inspect a body that had been thrown against an iron railing hard enough to impale it at a dozen points. 'It looks as if the Shrike was after the cruciforms. It tore every shred of them out of the bodies.'

'Not possible,' said Bishop Erdle. 'Simply not possible. There are over five hundred meters of microfiber in the cellular node extensions of . . .'

'Not possible,' agreed the Grand Inquisitor. 'But when we ship these bodies back, I'll wager that none are recoverable. The Shrike may have torn their hearts and lungs and throats out, but it was after their cruciforms.'

Security Commander Browning came around the corner with five troopers in black armor. 'Your Excellency,' he said on the tactical channel only the Grand Inquisitor could hear. 'The worst is a block over . . . this way.'

The entourage followed the man in black armor, but slowly, reluctantly.

*

They catalogued three hundred and sixty-two bodies. Many were in the streets, but the majority were in buildings in the city or inside the sheds, hangars, and spacecraft at the new spaceport on the edge of Arafat-kaffiyeh. Holos were taken and the Holy Office forensic teams took over, recording each site before taking the bodies back to the Pax base morgue outside of St Malachy. It was determined that all of the bodies were offworlders – i.e. there were no local Palestinians or native Martians among them.

The spaceport intrigued the Pax Fleet experts the most.

'Eight dropships serving the field itself,' said Major Piet. 'That's a serious number. St Malachy's spaceport uses only two.' He glanced up at the purple Martian sky. 'Assuming that the ships they were shuttling to and from had their own dropships – at least two each, if they were freighters – then we're talking about serious logistics here.'

The Grand Inquisitor looked at Mars's archbishop, but Robeson merely held his hands up. 'We knew nothing of these operations,' said the little man. 'As I explained before, it was an *Opus Dei* project.'

'Well,' said the Grand Inquisitor, 'as far as we can tell, all of the *Opus Dei* personnel are dead . . . truly, irrecoverably dead . . . so now it's a responsibility of the Holy Office. You don't have any idea what they built this port for? Heavy metals, perhaps? Some sort of mineral-mining operation?'

Governor Palo shook her head. 'This world has been mined for over a thousand years. There are no heavy metals left worth shipping. No minerals worth a local salvage operation's time, much less *Opus Dei*'s.'

Major Piet slipped his visor up and rubbed the stubble on his chin. '*Something* was being shipped in quantity here, Your Excellencies. Eight dropships . . . a sophisticated grid system . . . automated security.'

'If the Shrike . . . or whatever it was . . . had not destroyed the computers and record systems . . .' began Commander Browning.

Major Piet shook his head. 'It wasn't the Shrike. The computers had already been destroyed by shaped charges and tailored DNA viruses.' He looked around the empty administrative building. Red sand had already found its way in through portals and seams. 'It's my guess that these people destroyed their own records before the Shrike arrived. I think they were on the verge of clearing out. That's why the dropships were all in prelaunch mode . . . their onboard computers set to go.'

Father Farrell nodded. 'But all we have are the orbital coordinates. No records of who or what they were going to rendezvous with there.'

Major Piet looked out the window at the dust storm blowing there. 'There are twenty groundcar buses in that lot,' he murmured as if speaking to himself. 'Each one can transport up to eighty people. A bit of logistical overkill if the *Opus Dei* contingent here amounted to just the three hundred sixty-some people whose bodies we've found.'

Governor Palo frowned and crossed her arms. 'We don't know how many *Opus Dei* personnel were here, Major. As you pointed out, the records were destroyed. Perhaps there were thousands . . .'

Commander Browning stepped into the circle of VIPs. 'Begging your pardon, Governor, but the barracks within the field perimeter here could house about four hundred people. I think that the Major may be right . . . all of the *Opus Dei* personnel may be accounted for in the bodies we've found.'

'You can't be sure of that, Commander,' said Governor Palo, her voice sounding displeased.

'No, ma'am.'

She gestured toward the dust storm that had all but obscured the parked buses. 'And we have evidence that they needed transport for many more people.'

'Perhaps they were an advance contingent,' said Commander Browning. 'Preparing the way for a much larger population.'

'Then why destroy the records and limited AIs?' said Major Piet. 'Why does it look like they were preparing to move out for good?'

The Grand Inquisitor stepped into the circle and held up one black-gloved hand. 'We'll end the speculation for now. The Holy Office will begin taking depositions and carrying out interrogations tomorrow. Governor, may we use your office at the palace?'

'Of course, Your Excellency.' Palo lowered her face, either to show deference or to hide her eyes, or both.

'Very good,' said the Grand Inquisitor. 'Commander, Major, call the skimmers. We'll leave the forensic teams and the morgue workers out here.' Cardinal Mustafa peered out at the worsening storm. Its howl could be heard through the ten layers of window plastic now. 'What's the local word for this dust storm?'

'*Simoom*,' said Governor Palo. 'The storms used to cover the entire world. They're growing in intensity every Martian year.'

'The locals say that it's the old Martian gods,' whispered Archbishop Robeson. 'They're reclaiming their own.'

Less than fourteen light-years out from Old Earth System, above the world called Vitus-Gray-Balianus B, a starship that had once been named *Raphael* but which now held no name finished its braking run into geosynchronous orbit. The four living things on board floated in zero-g, their gazes fixed on the image of the desert world on the plotboard.

'How reliable is our reading on perturbations in the farcaster field these days?' said the female called Scylla.

'More reliable than most other clues,' said her seeming twin, Rhadamanth Nemes. 'We'll check it out.'

'Shall we start with one of the Pax bases?' said the male named Gyges.

'The largest,' said Nemes.

'That would be Pax Base Bombasino,' said Briareus, checking the code on the plotboard. 'Northern hemisphere. Along the central canal route. Population of . . .'

'It doesn't matter what the population is,' interrupted Rhadamanth Nemes. 'It just matters whether the child Aenea and the android and that bastard Endymion have come that way.'

'Dropship's prepped,' said Scylla.

They screeched into atmosphere, extended wings just as they crossed the terminator, used the Vatican diskey code via transponder to clear the way for their landing, and set down amid Scorpions, troopship skimmers, and armored EMVs. A flustered lieutenant greeted them and escorted them to the Base Commander's office.

'You say that you're members of the Noble Guard?' said Commander Solznykov, studying their faces and the readout on the diskey interphase at the same time.

'We have said it,' Rhadamanth Nemes replied tonelessly. 'Our papers, order chips, and diskey have said it. How many repetitions do you require, Commander?'

Solznykov's face and neck reddened above the high collar of his tunic. He looked down at the interphase holo instead of replying. Technically, these Noble Guard officers – members of one of the Pope's exotic new units – could pull rank on him. Technically, they could have him shot or excommunicated, since their ranks of Cohort Leaders in the Noble Guard combined the powers of both Pax Fleet and the Vatican. Technically – according to the wording and priority encryption of the diskey – they could pull rank on a planetary governor or dictate Church policy to a world's presiding archbishop. Technically, Solznykov wished these pale freaks had never shown up on his backwater world.

The Commander forced a smile. 'Our forces here are at your disposal. What can I do for you?'

The thin, pale woman named Nemes held a holocard over the Commander's desk and activated it. Suddenly the life-size heads of three people floated in the space between them – or, rather, two people, since the third face was obviously that of a blue-skinned android.

'I didn't think that there were any androids left in the Pax,' said Solznykov.

'Have you had reports of any of these three in your territory, Commander?' said Nemes, ignoring his question. 'It is probable they would have been reported along the major river which runs from your north pole to the equator.'

'It's actually a canal . . .' began Solznykov and stopped. None of the four looked as if they had any interest in small talk or extraneous information. He called his aide, Colonel Vinara, into the office.

'Their names?' said Solznykov as Vinara stood poised with his comlog ready.

Nemes gave three names that meant nothing to the Commander. 'Those aren't local names,' he said as Colonel Vinara checked records. 'Members of the indigenous culture – it's called the Amoiete Spectrum Helix – tend to accumulate names the way my hunting dog back on Patawpha collected ticks. You see, they have this triune marriage arrangement where . . .'

'These are not locals,' interrupted Nemes. Her thin lips looked as bloodless as the rest of her pale face above the red uniform collar. 'They're offworlders.'

'Ahh, well,' said Solznykov, relieved that he would not be dealing with these Noble Guard freaks for more than a minute or two more, 'then we can't help you. You see, Bombasino's the only working spaceport on Vitus-Gray-Balianus B now that we closed down the indigenie operation at Keroa Tambat, and except for a few spacers who end up in our brig, there's no immigration at all here. The locals are all Spectrum Helix . . . and, well . . . they like colors, they surely do, but an android would stand out like a . . . well, Colonel?'

Colonel Vinara looked up from his database search. 'Neither the images nor names match anything in our records except for an all-points bulletin sent through via Pax Fleet about four and a half standard years ago.' He looked questioningly at the Noble Guardsmen.

Nemes and her siblings stared back without comment.

Commander Solznykov spread his hands. 'I'm sorry. We've been busy for the last local two weeks on a major training exercise I had running here, but if anyone'd come through here who matched these descriptions . . .'

'Sir,' said Colonel Vinara, 'there were those four runaway spacers.'

Goddammit! thought Solznykov. To the Noble Guardsmen he said, 'Four Mercantilus spacers who jumped ship rather than face charges for use of illegal drugs. As I remember it, they were all men, all in their sixties, and' – he turned significantly to Colonel Vinara, trying to tell him to shut the fuck up with his gaze and tone – 'and we found their bodies in the Big Greasy, didn't we, Colonel?'

'Three bodies, sir,' said Colonel Vinara, oblivious to his commander's signals. He was checking the database again. 'One of our skimmers went down near Keroa Tambat and Med dispatched . . . ah . . . Dr Abne Molina . . . to go down-canal with a missionary to care for the injured crew.'

'What the hell does this have to do with anything, Colonel?' snapped Solznykov. 'These officers are searching for a teenager, a man in his thirties, and an android.'

'Yes, sir,' said Vinara, looking up, startled, from his comlog. 'But Dr Molina radioed in that she had treated a sick offworlder in Lock Childe Lamonde. We assumed that it was the fourth spacer . . .'

Rhadamanth Nemes took a step forward so quickly that Commander Solznykov flinched involuntarily. There was something about the slim woman's movements that was not quite human.

'Where is Lock Childe Lamonde?' demanded Nemes.

'It's just a village along the canal about eighty klicks south of here,' said Solznykov. He turned to Colonel Vinara as if all this commotion were his aide's fault. 'When are they flying the prisoner back?'

'Tomorrow morning, sir. We have a med-skimmer scheduled to pick up the crew in Keroa Tambat at oh-six-hundred hours and they'll stop in . . .' The Colonel stopped speaking as the four Noble Guard officers spun on their heels and made for the door.

Nemes paused just long enough to say, 'Commander, clear our flight path between here and this Lock Childe Lamonde. We'll be taking the dropship.'

'Ah, that's not necessary!' said the Commander, checking the screen on his desk. 'This spacer is under arrest and will be delivered . . . hey!'

The four Noble Guard officers had clattered down the steps outside his office and were crossing the tarmac. Solznykov rushed out onto the landing and shouted after them. 'Dropships aren't allowed to operate in atmosphere here except to land at Bombasino. Hey! We'll send a skimmer. Hey! This spacer's almost certainly not one of your . . . he's under guard . . . hey!'

The four did not look back as they reached their ship, ordered an escalator to morph down to them, and disappeared through the dropship hull. Sirens went off across the base and personnel ran for shelter as the heavy dropship lifted on thrusters, shifted to EM, and accelerated south across the port perimeter.

'Jesus fucking Christ,' whispered Commander Solznykov.

'Pardon me, sir?' said Colonel Vinara.

Solznykov gave him a glare that would have melted lead. 'Dispatch two combat skimmers immediately . . . no, make that three. I want a squad of Marines aboard each skimmer. This is our turf, and I don't want these anemic Noble Guard pissants doing so much as littering without our say-so. I want the skimmers there first and that fucking spacer taken into custody . . . *our* custody . . . if it means harelipping every Spectrum Helix indigenie between here and Lock Childe Lamonde. Savvy, Colonel?'

Vinara could only stare at his commander.

'*Move!*' shouted Commander Solznykov.

Colonel Vinara moved.

TEN

I was awake all that long night and the next day, writhing in pain, shuttling to the bathroom while carrying my IV-drip apparatus, trying painfully to urinate, and then checking the absurd filter I had to urinate through for any sign of the kidney stone that was killing me. Sometime in late morning I passed the thing.

For a minute I couldn't believe it. The pain had been less for the past half-hour or so, just the echo of pain in my back and groin, actually, but as I stared at the tiny, reddish thing in the filter cone – something larger than a grain of sand but much smaller than a pebble – I couldn't believe that *it* could have caused such agony for so many hours.

'Believe it,' Aenea said as she sat on the edge of the counter and watched me pull my pajama shirt back in place. 'It's often the smallest things in life that cause us the greatest pain.'

'Yeah,' I said. I knew, vaguely, that Aenea was not there – that I would never have urinated in front of anyone like that, much less in front of this girl. I had been hallucinating her presence ever since the first ultramorph injection.

'Congratulations,' said the Aenea hallucination. Her smile seemed real enough – that slightly mischievous, slightly teasing turning up of the right side of her mouth that I'd grown accustomed to – and I could see that she was wearing the green denim slacks and white cotton shirt she often wore when working in the desert heat. But I could also see the sink basin and soft towels through her.

'Thanks,' I said and shuffled back to collapse in the bed. I could not believe that the pain would not return. In fact, Dr Molina had said that there might be several stones.

Aenea was gone when Dem Ria, Dem Loa, and the trooper on guard came into the room.

'Oh, it's wonderful!' said Dem Ria.

'We're so glad,' said Dem Loa. 'We hoped that you would not have to go to the Pax infirmary for surgery.'

'Put your right hand up here,' said the trooper. He handcuffed me to the brass headboard.

'I'm a prisoner?' I said groggily.

'You always have been,' grunted the trooper. His dark skin was sweaty under his helmet visor. 'The skimmer'll be by tomorrow morning to pick you up. Wouldn't want you missing the ride.' He went back out to the shade of the barrel tree out front.

'Ah,' said Dem Loa, touching my handcuffed wrist with her cool fingers. 'We are sorry, Raul Endymion.'

'It's not your fault,' I said, feeling so tired and drugged that my tongue did not want to work right. 'You've been nothing but kind. So kind.' The fading pain kept me from sleeping.

'Father Clifton would like to come in and speak with you. Would that be all right?'

At that moment I would have welcomed spider-rats nibbling on my toes about as much as the idea of chatting with a missionary priest. I said, 'Sure. Why not?'

Father Clifton was younger than I, short – but not as short as Dem Ria or Dem Loa or her race – and pudgy, with thinning, sandy hair receding from his friendly, flushed face. I thought that I knew his type. There had been a chaplain in the Home Guard a bit like Father Clifton – earnest, mostly inoffensive, a bit of a momma's boy who may have gone into the priesthood so that he would never have to grow up and become really responsible for himself. It was Grandam who had pointed out to me how the parish priests in the various moor-end villages on Hyperion tended to remain somewhat childlike: treated with deference by their parishioners, fussed over by housekeepers and women of all ages, never in real competition with other adult males. I don't think that Grandam was actively anticlerical in spite of her refusal to accept the cross, just amused by this tendency of parish priests in the great and powerful Pax empire.

Father Clifton wanted to discuss theology.

I think that I moaned then, but it must have been taken for a reaction to the kidney stone, for the good priest merely leaned closer, patted my arm, and murmured, 'There, there, my son.'

Did I mention that he was at least five or six years younger than me?

'Raul . . . may I call you Raul?'

'Sure, Father.' I closed my eyes as if falling asleep.

'What is your opinion of the Church, Raul?'

Under my eyelids, I rolled my eyes. 'The Church, Father?'

Father Clifton waited.

I shrugged. Or to be more precise, I *tried* to shrug – it's not that easy when one wrist is handcuffed above your head and the other arm is on the receiving end of an intravenous drip.

Father Clifton must have understood my awkward motion. 'You're indifferent to it, then?' he asked softly.

As indifferent as one can be to an organization that's tried to capture or kill me, I thought. 'Not indifferent, Father,' I said. 'It's just that the Church . . . well, it hasn't been relevant to my life in most ways.'

One of the missionary's sandy eyebrows rose slightly. 'Gosh, Raul . . . the Church is a lot of things . . . not all of them spotlessly good, I'm sure . . . but I hardly think that it could be accused of being irrelevant.'

I considered shrugging again, but decided one awkward spasm of that sort was enough. 'I see what you mean,' I said, hoping that the conversation was over.

Father Clifton leaned even closer, his elbows on his knees, his hands set together in front of him – but more in the aspect of persuasion and reason than prayer. 'Raul, you know that they're taking you back to Base Bombasino in the morning.'

I nodded. My head was still free to move.

'You know that the Pax Fleet and Mercantilus punishment for desertion is death.'

'Yeah,' I said, 'but only after a fair trial.'

Father Clifton ignored my sarcasm. His brow was wrinkled with what could only be worry – although for my fate or for my eternal soul, I was not sure which. Perhaps for both. 'For Christians,' he began and paused a moment. 'For Christians, such an execution is punishment, some discomfort, perhaps even momentary terror, but then they mend their ways and go on with their lives. For you . . .'

'Nothingness,' I said, helping him end his sentence. 'The Big Gulp. Eternal darkness. Nada-ness. I become a worm's casserole.'

Father Clifton was not amused. 'This does not have to be the case, my son.'

I sighed and looked out the window. It was early afternoon on Vitus-Gray-Balianus B. The sunlight was different here than on worlds that I had known well – Hyperion, Old Earth, even Mare Infinitus, and other places I had visited briefly but intensely – but the difference was so subtle that I would have found it hard to describe. But it was beautiful. There was no arguing that. I looked at the cobalt sky, streaked with violet clouds, at the butter-rich light falling on pink adobe and the wooden sill; I listened to the sound of children playing in the alley, to the soft conversation of Ces Ambre and her sick brother, Bin, to the sudden, soft laughter as something in the game they were playing amused them, and I thought, *To lose all this forever?*

And I hallucinated Aenea's voice saying, *To lose all this forever is the essence of being human, my love.*

Father Clifton cleared his throat. 'Have you ever heard of Pascal's Wager, Raul?'

'Yes.'

'You have?' Father Clifton sounded surprised. I had the feeling that I had thrown him off stride in his prepared line of argument. 'Then you know why it makes sense,' he said rather lamely.

I sighed again. The pain was steady now, not coming and going in the tidal surges that had overwhelmed me the past few days. I remembered first encountering Blaise Pascal in conversations with Grandam when I was a kid, then discussing him with Aenea in the Arizona twilight, and finally looking up his *Pensées* in the excellent library at Taliesin West.

'Pascal was a mathematician,' Father Clifton was saying, 'pre-Hegira . . . mid-eighteenth century, I think . . .'

'Actually, he lived in the mid-1600s,' I said, '1623 to 1662, I think.' Actually, I was bluffing a bit on the dates. The numbers seemed right, but I would not have bet my life on them. I remembered the era because Aenea and I had spent a couple of weeks one winter discussing the Enlightenment and its effect on people and institutions pre-Hegira, pre-Pax.

'Yes,' said Father Clifton, 'but the *time* he lived isn't as important as his so-called wager. Consider it, Raul – on one side, the chance of resurrection, immortality, an eternity in heaven and benefiting from Christ's light. On the other side . . . how did you put it?'

'The Big Gulp,' I said. 'Nada-ness.'

'Worse than that,' said the young priest, his voice thick with earnest conviction. 'Nada means nothingness. Sleep without dreams. But Pascal realized that the absence of Christ's redemption is worse than that. It's eternal regret . . . longing . . . infinite sadness.'

'And hell?' I said. 'Eternal punishment?'

Father Clifton squeezed his hands together, obviously uncomfortable at that side of the equation. 'Perhaps,' he said. 'But even if hell were just eternal recognition of the chances one has lost . . . why risk that? Pascal realized that if the Church was wrong, nothing would be lost by embracing its hope. And if it was right . . .'

I smiled. 'A bit cynical, isn't it, Father?'

The priest's pale eyes looked directly into mine. 'Not as cynical as going to your death for no reason, Raul. Not when you can accept Christ as your Lord, do good works among other human beings, serve your community and your brothers and sisters in Christ, and save your physical life and your immortal soul in the process.'

I nodded. After a minute, I said, 'Maybe the time he lived *was* important.'

Father Clifton blinked, not following me.

'Blaise Pascal, I mean,' I said. 'He lived through an intellectual revolution the likes of which humanity has rarely seen. On top of that, Copernicus and Kepler and their ilk were opening up the universe a thousandfold. The Sun was becoming . . . well . . . just a sun, Father. Everything was being displaced, moved aside, shoved from the center. Pascal once said, "I am terrified by the eternal silence of these infinite spaces." '

Father Clifton leaned closer. I could smell the soap and shaving cream scent on his smooth skin. 'All the more reason to consider the wisdom of his wager, Raul.'

I blinked, wanting to move away from the pink and freshly scrubbed moon of a face. I was afraid that I smelled of sweat and pain and fear. I had not brushed my teeth in twenty-four hours. 'I don't think that I want to make any wager if it means dealing with a Church that has grown so corrupt that it makes obedience and submission the price of its saving the life of someone's child,' I said.

Father Chiton pulled away as if slapped. His fair skin flushed a deeper red. Then he stood and patted my arm. 'You get some sleep. We'll speak again before you leave tomorrow.'

But I did not have until tomorrow. If I had been outside at that moment, looking at just the precise quadrant of the late-afternoon sky, I would have seen the scratch of flame across the dome of cobalt as Nemes's dropship entered the landing pattern for Pax Base Bombasino.

When Father Clifton left, I fell asleep.

I watched as Aenea and I sat in the vestibule of her shelter in the desert night and continued our conversation.

'I've had this dream before,' I said, looking around and touching the stone beneath the canvas of her shelter. The rock still held some of the day's heat.

'Yes,' said Aenea. She was sipping from a fresh cup of tea.

'You were going to tell me the secret that makes you the messiah,' I heard myself say. 'The secret which makes you the "bond between two worlds" that the AI Ummon spoke of.'

'Yes,' said my young friend and nodded again, 'but first tell me if you think that your reply to Father Clifton was adequate.'

'Adequate?' I shrugged. 'I was angry.'

Aenea sipped tea. Steam rose from the cup and touched her lashes. 'But you didn't really respond to his question about Pascal's Wager.'

'That was all the response I needed to give,' I said, somewhat irritated. 'Little Bin Ria Dem Loa Alem is dying of cancer. The Church uses their cruciform as leverage. That's corrupt . . . foul. I'll have none of it.'

Aenea looked at me over the steaming cup. 'But if the Church were not corrupt, Raul . . . if it offered the cruciform without price or reservation. Would you accept it?'

'No.' The immediacy of my answer surprised me.

The girl smiled. 'So it is not the corruption of the Church that is at the heart of your objection. You reject resurrection itself.'

I started to speak, hesitated, frowned, and then rephrased what I was thinking. '*This* kind of resurrection, I reject. Yes.'

Still smiling, Aenea said, 'Is there another kind?'

'The Church used to think so,' I said. 'For almost three thousand years, the resurrection it offered was of the soul, not the body.'

'And do you believe in that other kind of resurrection?'

'No,' I said again, as quickly as I had before. I shook my head. 'Pascal's Wager never appealed to me. It seems logically . . . shallow.'

'Perhaps because it posits only two choices,' said Aenea. Somewhere in the desert night, an owl made a short, sharp sound. 'Spiritual resurrection and immortality or death and damnation,' she said.

'Those last two aren't the same thing,' I said.

'No, but perhaps to someone like Blaise Pascal they were. Someone terrified of "the eternal silence of these infinite spaces".'

'A spiritual agoraphobic,' I said.

Aenea laughed. The sound was so sincere and spontaneous that I could not help loving it. *Her.*

'Religion seems to have always offered us that false duality,' she said, setting her cup of tea on a flat stone. 'The silences of infinite space or the cozy comfort of inner certainty.'

I made a rude noise. 'The Pax Church offers a more pragmatic certainty.'

Aenea nodded. 'That may be its only recourse these days. Perhaps our reservoir of spiritual faith has run out.'

'Perhaps it should have run out a long time ago,' I said sternly. 'Superstition has taken a terrible toll on our species. Wars . . . pogroms . . . resistance to logic and science and medicine . . . not to mention gathering power in the hands of people like those who run the Pax.'

'Is all religion superstition, then, Raul? All faith then folly?'

I squinted at her. The dim light from inside the shelter and the dimmer starlight outside played on her sharp cheekbones and the gentle curve of her chin. 'What do you mean?' I said, correctly expecting a trap.

'If you had faith in me, would that be folly?'

'Faith in you . . . how?' I said, hearing my voice sounding suspicious, almost sullen. 'As a friend? Or as a messiah?'

'What's the difference?' asked Aenea, smiling again in that way that usually meant a challenge was in the offing.

'Faith in a friend is . . . friendship,' I said. 'Loyalty.' I hesitated. 'Love.'

'And faith in a messiah?' said Aenea, her eyes catching the light.

I made a brusque, throwing-away gesture. 'That's religion.'

'But what if your friend is the messiah?' she said, smiling openly now.

'You mean, "What if your friend *thinks* she's the messiah?"' I said. I shrugged again. 'I guess you stay loyal to her and try to keep her out of the asylum.'

Aenea's smile faded, but I sensed that it was not because of my harsh comment. Her gaze had turned inward. 'I wish it were that simple, my dear friend.'

Touched, filled with a wave of anxiety as real as surging nausea, I said, 'You were going to tell me why you were chosen as this messiah, kiddo. What makes you the bond between two worlds.'

The girl – young woman, I realized – nodded solemnly. 'I was chosen simply because I was that first child of the Core and humankind.'

She had said that earlier. I nodded this time. 'So those are the two worlds which you connect . . . the Core and us?'

'Two of the worlds, yes,' said Aenea, looking up at me again. 'Not the only two. That's precisely what messiahs *do*, Raul . . . bridge different worlds. Different eras. Provide the bond between two irreconcilable concepts.'

'And your connection to both these worlds makes you the messiah?' I said again.

Aenea shook her head quickly, almost impatiently. Something like anger glinted in her eyes. 'No,' she said sharply. 'I'm the messiah because of what I can *do*.'

I blinked at her vehemence. 'What can you do, kiddo?'

Aenea held out her hand and gently touched me with it. 'Remember when I said that the Church and Pax were right about me, Raul? That I was a virus?'

'Uh-huh.'

She squeezed my wrist. 'I can *pass* that virus, Raul. I can infect others. Geometric progression. A plague of carriers.'

'Carriers of what?' I said. 'Messiahhood?'

She shook her head. Her expression was so sad that it made me want to console her, put my arms around her. Her grip remained firm on my wrist. 'No,' she said. 'Just the next step in what we are. What we can be.'

I took a breath. 'You talked about teaching the physics of love,' I said. 'Of understanding love as a basic force of the universe. Is that the virus?'

Still holding my wrist, she looked at me a long moment. 'That's the source of the virus,' she said softly. 'What I teach is how to *use* that energy.'

'How?' I whispered.

Aenea blinked slowly, as if she were the one dreaming and about to awaken. 'Let's say there are four steps,' she said. 'Four stages. Four levels.'

I waited. Her fingers made a loop around my captured wrist.

'The first is learning the language of the dead,' she said.

'What does that . . .'

'Shhh!' Aenea had raised the first finger of her free hand to her lips to shush me.

'The second is learning the language of the living,' she said.

I nodded, not understanding either phrase.

'The third is hearing the music of the spheres,' she whispered.

In my reading at Taliesin West, I had run across this ancient phrase: it was all mixed up with astrology, the pre-Scientific Age on Old Earth, Kepler's little wooden models of a solar system predicated on perfect shapes, shells of stars and planets being moved by angels . . . volumes of double talk. I had no idea what my friend was talking about and how it could apply to an age when humanity moved faster than light through the spiral arm of the galaxy.

'The fourth step,' she said, her gaze turned inward again, 'is learning to take the first step.'

'The first step,' I repeated, confused. 'You mean the first step you mentioned . . . what was it? Learning the language of the dead?'

Aenea shook her head, slowly bringing me into focus. It was as if she had been elsewhere for a moment. 'No,' she said, 'I mean *taking the first step*.'

Almost holding my breath, I said, 'All right. I'm ready, kiddo. Teach me.'

Aenea smiled again. 'That's the irony, Raul, my love. If I choose to do this, I'll always be known as the One Who Teaches. But the silly thing is, I don't have to teach it, I only have to share this virus to impart each of these stages to those who wish to learn.'

I looked down at where her slim fingers encircled a part of my wrist. 'So you've already given me this . . . virus?' I said. I felt nothing except the usual electric tingle that her touch always created in me.

My friend laughed. 'No, Raul. You're not ready. And it takes communion to share the virus, not just contact. And I haven't decided what to do . . . if I *should* do this.'

'To share with me?' I said, thinking, *Communion?*

'To share with everyone,' she whispered, serious again. 'With everyone ready to learn.' She looked directly at me again. Somewhere in the desert, a coyote was yipping. 'These . . . levels, stages . . . can't coexist with a cruciform, Raul.'

'So the born-again can't learn?' I said. This would rule out the vast majority of human beings.

She shook her head. 'They can learn . . . they just can't stay born-again. The cruciform has to go.'

I let out my breath. I did not understand most of this, but that's because it seemed to be double talk. *Don't all would-be messiahs speak double talk?* asked the cynical part of me in Grandam's level voice. Aloud, I said, 'There's no way to remove a cruciform without killing the person wearing it. The true death.' I had always wondered if this fact had been the main reason I had been unwilling to go under the cross. Or perhaps it was just my youthful belief in my own immortality.

Aenea did not respond directly. She said, 'You like the Amoiete Spectrum Helix people, don't you?'

Blinking, I tried to understand this. Had I dreamed that phrase, those people, that pain? Wasn't I dreaming now? Or was this a memory of a real conversation? But Aenea knew nothing of Dem Ria, Dem Loa, and the others. The night and stone-and-canvas shelter seemed to ripple like a shredding dreamscape.

'I like them,' I said, feeling my friend remove her fingers from my wrist. *Wasn't my wrist shackled to the headboard?*

Aenea nodded and sipped her cooling tea. 'There's hope for the Spectrum Helix people. And for all the thousands of other cultures which have reverted or sprung up since the Fall. The Hegemony meant homogeneity, Raul. The Pax means even more. The human genome . . . the human soul . . . distrusts homogeneity, Raul. It – they – are always ready to take a chance, to risk change and diversity.'

'Aenea,' I said, reaching for her. 'I don't . . . we can't . . .' There was a terrible sense of falling and the dreamscape came apart like thin cardboard in a hard rain. I could not see my friend.

'Wake up, Raul. They are coming for you. The Pax is coming.'

I tried to awaken, groping toward consciousness like a sluggish machine crawling uphill, but the weight of fatigue and the painkillers kept dragging me down. I did not understand why Aenea wanted me awake. We were conversing so well in the dream.

'Wake up, Raul Endymion.' *Wek op, Rool Endmyun.* It was not Aenea. Even before I was fully awake and focused I recognized the soft voice and thick dialect of Dem Ria.

I sat straight up. The woman was undressing me! I realized that she had pulled the loose nightshirt off and was tugging my undershirt on – cleaned and smelling of fresh breezes now, but unmistakably my undershirt. My undershorts were already on. My twill pants, overshirt, and vest were laid across the bottom of the bed. How had she done this with the handcuff on my . . .

I stared at my wrist. The handcuffs were lying open on the bedclothes. My arm tingled painfully as circulation returned. I licked my lips and tried to speak without slurring. 'The Pax? Coming?'

Dem Ria pulled my shirt on as if I were her child, Bin . . . or younger. I motioned her hands away and tried to close the buttons with suddenly awkward fingers. They had used buttons rather than sealtabs at Taliesin West on Old Earth. I thought I had grown used to them, but this was taking forever.

'. . . and we heard on the radio that a dropship had landed at Bombasino. There are four people in unknown uniforms – two men, two women. They were asking the Commandant about you. They just lifted off – the dropship and three skimmers. They will be here in four minutes. Perhaps less.'

'Radio?' I said stupidly. 'I thought you said that the radio didn't work. Isn't that why the priest went to the base to get the doctor?'

'Father *Clifton*'s radio was not working,' whispered Dem Ria, pulling me to my feet. She held me steady as I stepped into my trousers. 'We have radios . . . tightbeam transmitters . . . satellite relays . . . all of which the Pax knows nothing about. And spies in place. One has warned us . . . hurry, Raul Endymion. The ships will be here in a minute.'

I came fully awake then, literally flushed with a surge of anger and hopelessness that threatened to wash me away. *Why won't these bastards leave me alone?* Four people in unknown uniforms. Pax, obviously. Evidently their search for Aenea, A. Bettik, and me had not ended when the priest-captain – de Soya – had let us escape the trap on God's Grove more than four years earlier.

I looked at the chronometer readout on my comlog. The ships would be landing in a minute or so. There was nowhere I could run in that time where Pax troopers would not find me. 'Let me go,' I said, pulling away from the short woman in the blue robe. The window was open, the afternoon breeze coming through the curtains. I imagined that I could hear the near-ultrasonic hum of skimmers. 'I have to get away from your house . . .' I had images of the Pax torching the home with young Ces Ambre and Bin still in it.

Dem Ria pulled me back from the window. At that moment, the man of the household – young Alem Mikail Dem Alem – came in with Dem Loa. They were carrying the Lusian bulk of the Pax trooper who had been left to guard me. Ces Ambre, her dark eyes bright, was lifting the guard's feet while Bin struggled to pull one of the man's huge boots off. The Lusian was fast asleep, mouth open, drool moistening the high collar of his combat fatigues.

I looked at Dem Ria.

'Dem Loa brought him some tea about fifteen minutes ago,' she said softly. She made a graceful gesture that caused the blue sleeve of her robe to billow. 'I am afraid that we used the rest of your ultramorph prescription, Raul Endymion.'

'I have to go . . .' I began. The ache in my back was bearable, but my legs were shaky.

'No,' said Dem Ria. 'They will catch you within minutes.' She pointed to the window. From outside there came the unmistakable subsonic rumble of a dropship on EM drive, followed by the thud and bark of its thrusters. The thing must be hovering right above the village, seeking a landing site. A second later the window vibrated to a triple sonic boom and two black skimmers banked above the adobe buildings next door.

Alem Mikail had stripped the Lusian to his thermal-weave underwear and had laid him out on the bed. Now he snapped the man's massive right wrist into the handcuffs and snicked the other cuff around the headboard bar. Dem Loa and Ces Ambre were sweeping up the layers of fatigue clothing, body armor, and huge boots and stuffing them in a laundry bag. Little Bin Ria Dem Loa Alem tossed the guard's helmet in the bag. The thin boy was carrying the heavy flechette pistol. I started at the sight – children and weapons was a mix I learned to avoid even when I was a child myself, learning to handle power weapons while our caravan rumbled its way across the Hyperion moors – but Alem smiled and took the pistol from the boy, patting him on the back. It was obvious from the way Bin had held the weapon – fingers away from the trigger guard, pointing the muzzle away from himself and his father, checking the safety indicator even as he gave the pistol up – that he had handled such a device before.

Bin smiled at me, took the heavy bag with the guard's clothing in it, and ran out of the room. The noise outside rose in a crescendo and I turned to look out the window.

A black skimmer kicked up dust less than thirty meters down the street that ran along the canal. I could see it through a gap between the houses. The larger dropship lowered itself out of sight to the south, probably landing in the grassy open area near the well where I had collapsed in pain from the kidney stone.

I had just finished wiggling into my boots and securing my vest when Alem handed me the flechette pistol. I checked the safety and propellant-charge indicators out of habit, but then shook my head. 'No,' I said. 'It would be suicide to attack Pax troopers with just this. Their armor . . .' I was not actually thinking about their armor at that moment, but, rather, about the return fire from assault weapons that would level this house in an instant. I thought of the boy outside with the laundry bag of trooper's armor. 'Bin . . .' I said. 'If they catch him . . .'

'We know, we know,' said Dem Ria, pulling me away from the bed and into the narrow hallway. I did not remember this part of the house. My universe for the past forty-some hours had been the bedroom and adjoining lavatory. 'Come, come,' she said.

I pulled away again, handing the pistol to Alem. 'Just let me run,' I said, my heart pounding. I gestured toward the snoring Lusian. 'They won't think that's me for a second. They can tightbeam the doctor – if she's not already in one of those skimmers – to ID me. Just tell them' – I looked at the friendly faces in their blue robes – 'tell them that I overpowered the guard and held you at gunpoint . . .' I stopped then, realizing that the guard would destroy that cover story as soon as he awoke. The family's complicity in my escape would be self-evident. I looked at the flechette pistol again, half-ready to reach for it. One burst of steel needles and the sleeping trooper would never awaken to destroy the cover-up and endanger these good people.

Only I could never do it. I might shoot a Pax trooper in a fair fight – indeed, the adrenaline rush of anger that was burning through my weakness and terror told me that it would be a welcome relief to have that opportunity – but I could never shoot this sleeping man.

But there would be no fair fight. Pax troopers in combat armor, much less these mysterious four in the dropship – Swiss Guard? – would be immune to flechettes and anything else short of Pax assault weapons. And the Swiss Guard would be immune to those. I was screwed. These good people who had shown me such kindness were screwed.

A rear door slammed open and Bin slid into the hallway, his robe hiked up to show spindly legs covered with dust. I stared at him, thinking that the boy would not get his cruciform and would die of cancer. The adults might well spend the next standard decade in a Pax prison.

'I'm sorry . . .' I said, hunting for words. I could hear the commotion in the street as troopers hurried through the evening rush of pedestrians.

'Raul Endymion,' said Dem Loa in her soft voice, handing me the rucksack they had brought from my kayak, 'please shut up and follow us. *At once.*'

There was a tunnel entrance beneath the floor of the hallway. I had always thought that hidden passages were the stuff of holodramas, but I followed Dem Ria into this one willingly enough. We were a strange procession – Dem Ria and Dem Loa sweeping down the steep staircase ahead of me, then me carrying the flechette pistol and fumbling the rucksack on my back, then little Bin followed by his sister, Ces Ambre, then, carefully locking the trapdoor behind him, Alem Mikail Dem Alem. No one stayed behind. The house was empty except for the snoring Lusian trooper.

The stairway went deeper than a normal basement level, and at first I thought that the walls were adobe like the ones above. Then I realized that the passage was cut from a soft stone, perhaps sandstone. Twenty-seven steps and we reached the bottom of the vertical shaft and Dem Ria led the way down a narrow passage illuminated by pale chemical glowglobes. I wondered why this average working-class home would have an underground passage.

As if reading my mind, Dem Loa's blue cowl turned and she whispered, 'The Amoiete Spectrum Helix demands . . . ah . . . discreet entrances to one another's homes. Especially during the Twice Darkness.'

'Twice Darkness?' I whispered back, ducking under one of the globes. We had already gone twenty or twenty-five meters – away from the canal-river, I thought – and the passage still curved out of sight to the right.

'The slow, dual eclipse of the sun by this world's two moons,' whispered

Dem Loa. 'It lasts precisely nineteen minutes. It is the primary reason that we chose this world . . . please excuse the pun.'

'Ahh,' I said. I did not understand, but it didn't seem to matter at that moment. Pax troops have sensors to find spider-holes like this,' I whispered to the women in front of me. 'They have deep radar to search through rock. They have . . .'

'Yes, yes,' said Alem from behind me, 'but they will be held up a few minutes by the Mayor and the others.'

'The Mayor?' I repeated rather stupidly. My legs were still weak from the two days in bed and pain. My back and groin ached, but it was a minor pain – inconsequential – compared to what I had passed through (and what had passed through me) during the last couple of days.

'The Mayor is challenging the Pax's right to search,' whispered Dem Ria. The passage widened and went straight for at least a hundred meters. We passed two branching tunnels. This wasn't a bolt-hole; it was a bloody catacombs. 'The Pax recognizes the Mayor's authority in Lock Childe Lamonde,' she whispered. The silken robes of the five family members in blue were also whispering against the sandstone as we hurried down the passage. 'We still have law and courts on Vitus-Gray-Balianus B, so they are not allowed unlimited search and seizure rights.'

'But they'll download permission from whatever authority they need,' I said, hurrying to keep up with the women. We came to another juncture and they turned right.

'Eventually,' said Dem Loa, 'but the streets are now filled with all of the colors of the Lock Childe Lamonde strand of the Helix – reds, whites, greens, ebonies, yellows – thousands of people from our village. And many more are coming from nearby Locks. No one will volunteer which house is the one where you were kept. Father Clifton has been lured out of town on a ruse, so he can be of no help to the Pax troopers. Dr Molina has been detained in Keroa Tambat by some of our people and is currently out of touch with her Pax superiors. And your guard will be sleeping for at least another hour. This way.'

We turned left into a wider passage, stopped at the first door we had seen, waited for Dem Ria to palmlock it open, and then stepped into a large, echoing space carved into the stone. We were standing on a metal stairway looking down on what appeared to be a subterranean garage: half a dozen long, slim vehicles with oversized wheels, stern wings, sails, and pedals clustered by primary colors. These things were like buckboards set on spidery suspensions, obviously powered by wind and muscle power, and covered over with wood, bright, silky polymer fabrics, and Perspex.

'Windcycles,' said Ces Ambre.

Several men and women in emerald-green robes and high boots were preparing three of the wagons for departure. Lashed in the back of one of the long wagonbeds was my kayak.

Everyone was moving down the clattering staircase, but I stopped at the head of the stairs. My balking was so sudden that poor Bin and Ces Ambre almost crashed into me.

'What is it?' said Alem Mikail.

I had tucked the flechette pistol in my belt and now I opened my hands. 'Why are you doing this? Why is everyone helping? What's going on?'

Dem Ria took a step back up the metal staircase and leaned on the railing. Her eyes were as bright as her daughter's had been. 'If they take you, Raul Endymion, they will kill you.'

'How do you know?' I said. My voice was soft but the acoustics of the underground garage were such that the men and women in green looked up from where they were working below.

'You spoke in your sleep,' said Dem Loa.

I cocked my head, not understanding. I had been dreaming of Aenea and our conversation. What would that have told these people?

Dem Ria took another step upward and touched my wrist with her cool hand. 'The Amoiete Spectrum Helix has foretold this woman, Raul Endymion. This one named Aenea. We call her the One Who Teaches.'

I felt goose bumps at that moment, in the chill glowglobe light of this buried place. The old poet – Uncle Martin – had spoken of my young friend as a messiah, but his cynicism leaked into everything he said or did. The people of Taliesin West had respected Aenea . . . but to believe that the energetic sixteen-year-old was actually a World Historical Figure? It seemed unlikely. And the girl and I had spoken of it in real life and in my ultra-morph dreams, but . . . my God, I was on a world scores of light-years away from Hyperion and an eternal distance from the Lesser Magellanic Cloud where Old Earth was hidden. How had these people . . .

'Halpul Amoiete knew of the One Who Teaches when he composed the Helix Symphony,' said Dem Loa. 'All of the people of the Spectrum were descended from empath stock. The Helix was and is a way to refine that empathic ability.'

I shook my head. 'I'm sorry, I don't understand . . .'

'Please understand this, Raul Endymion,' said Dem Ria, her fingers squeezing my wrist almost painfully. 'If you do not escape this place, the Pax will have your soul and body. And the One Who Teaches needs both these things.'

I squinted at the woman, thinking that she was jesting. But her pleasant, unlined face was set and serious.

'Please,' said little Bin, setting his little hand in my free one and pulling. 'Please hurry, Raul.'

I hurried down the stairs. One of the men in green handed me a red robe. Alem Mikail helped me fold and wrap it over my own clothes. He wrapped the red burnoose and cowl in a dozen quick strokes. I would never have been able to arrange it properly. I realized with a shock that the entire family – the two older women, teenaged Ces Ambre, and little Bin – had stripped naked from their blue robes and were arranging red ones around them. I saw then that I had been wrong thinking that they were like Lusians – for although their bodies were shorter than Pax-space average and heavily muscled, they were perfectly proportioned. None of the adults had any hair, either on their heads or elsewhere. Somehow this made their compact, perfectly toned bodies more attractive.

I looked away, realizing that I was blushing. Ces Ambre laughed and jostled my arm. We were all in red robes now, Alem Mikail being the last to pull his on. One glance at his heavily muscled upper torso told me that I would not last fifteen seconds in a fight with the shorter man. But then, I realized, I probably would not last more than thirty seconds with Dem Loa or Dem Ria either.

I offered the flechette pistol to Alem but he gestured for me to keep it and showed me how to tuck it in one of the multiple sashes of the long, crimson robe. I thought of my lack of weapons in the little backpack – a Navajo hunting knife and the little flashlight laser – and nodded my gratitude.

The women and children and I were hurried into the back of the wind-cycle wagon that held my kayak, and red fabric was pulled tight over the stays above us. We had to crouch low as a second layer of fabric, some wooden planks, and various crates and barrels were set in around and above us. I could just make out a glimpse of light between the tailgate and the wagon cover. I listened to footsteps on stone as Alem went up front and crawled onto one of the two pedaling saddles. I listened as one of the other men – also now in a red robe – joined him on the cycling seat on the other side of the central yoke.

With the masts still lowered above us, fabric sails reefed, we began rolling up a long ramp out of the garage.

'Where are we going?' I whispered to Dem Ria, who was lying almost next to me. The wood smelled like cedar.

'The downstream farcaster arch,' she whispered back.

I blinked. 'You know about that?'

'They gave you Truthtell,' whispered Dem Loa from the other side of a crate. 'And you did speak in your sleep.'

Bin was lying right next to me in the darkness. 'We know the One Who Teaches has sent you on a mission,' he said almost happily. 'We know you have to get to the next arch.' He patted the kayak that curved next to us. 'I wish I could go with you.'

'This is too dangerous,' I hissed, feeling the wagon roll out of the tunnel and into open air. Low sunlight illuminated the fabric above us. The windcycle wagon stopped for a second as the two men cranked the mast erect and unfurled the sail. 'Too dangerous.' I meant their taking me to the farcaster, of course, not the mission that Aenea had sent me on.

'If they know who I am,' I whispered to Dem Ria, 'they'll be watching the arch.'

I could see the silhouette of her cowl as she nodded. 'They will be watching, Raul Endymion. And it is dangerous. But darkness is almost here. In fourteen minutes.'

I glanced at my comlog. It would be another ninety minutes or more until twilight according to what I had observed the previous two days. And then almost another full hour until true nightfall.

'It is only six kilometers to the downstream arch,' whispered Ces Ambre from her place on the other side of the kayak. 'The villages will be filled with the Spectrum celebrating.'

I understood then. 'The Twice Darkness?' I whispered.

'Yes,' said Dem Ria. She patted my hand. 'We must be silent now. We will be moving into traffic along the saltway.'

'Too dangerous,' I whispered one last time as the wagon began creaking and groaning its way into traffic. I could hear the chain drive rumbling beneath the buckboard floor and feel the wind catch the sail. *Too dangerous*, I said only to myself.

If I had known what was happening a few hundred meters away, I would have realized how truly dangerous this moment was.

I peered out through the gap between wagon wood and fabric as we rumbled along the saltway. This vehicle thoroughfare appeared to be a strip of rock-hard salt between the villages clustered along the raised canal and the reticulated desert stretching as far north as I could see. 'Waste Wahhabi,' whispered Dem Ria as we picked up speed and headed south along the saltway. Other windcycle wagons roared past heading south, their sails fully engaged, their two pedalers working madly. Even more brightly canvased wagons tacked north, their sails set differently, the pedalers leaning far out for balance as the creaking wagons teetered on two wheels, the other two spinning uselessly in the air.

We covered the six kilometers in ten minutes and turned off the saltway onto a paved ramp that led through a cluster of homes – white stone this time, not adobe – and then Alem and the other man furled the sail and pedaled the windcycle slowly along the cobblestone street that ran between the homes and the canal-river. High, wispy ferns grew along the canal banks there between elaborately fashioned piers, gazebos, and multitiered docks to which were tied ornate houseboats. The city seemed to end here where the canal widened into a waterway much more riverlike than artificial, and I raised my head enough to see the huge farcaster arch a few hundred meters downstream. Through and beyond the rusted arch, I could see only fern forest on the riverbanks and desert waste to the east and west. Alem guided the windcycle onto a brick loading ramp and pulled under the cover of a copse of tall ferns.

I glanced at my comlog. Less than two minutes until the Twice Darkness.

At that instant there was a rush of warm air and a shadow passed over us. We all crouched lower as the black Pax skimmer flew out over the river at an altitude of less than a hundred meters; the aerodynamic, figure-eight shape of the thing clearly visible as it banked more steeply and then swooped low above the ships headed north and south through the arch. River traffic was brisk here where the river widened: sleek racing sculls with rowing teams of four to twelve, gleaming powerboats throwing up glistening wakes, sailboats ranging from single-person jitabouts to wallowing, square-sailed junks, canoes and rowboats, some stately houseboats churning against the current, a handful of silent electric hovercraft moving within their haloes of spray, and even some rafts that reminded me of my earlier voyage with Aenea and A. Bettik.

The skimmer flew low over these ships, passed over the farcaster arch headed south, flew back under it headed north, and disappeared in the direction of Lock Childe Lamonde.

'Come,' said Alem Mikail, folding back the fabric tarp above us and pulling at the kayak. 'We must hurry.'

Suddenly there was a rush of warm air, followed by a cooler breeze that kicked dust off the riverbank, the fernheads rustled and shook above us, and the sky grew purple and then black. Stars came out. I glanced upward just long enough to see a beaded corona around one of the moons and the burning disc of the second, lower satellite as it moved into place behind the first.

From north along the river, back in the direction of the linear city that included Lock Childe Lamonde, there came the most haunting and mournful sound I had ever heard: a long wailing, more human-throated than siren-caused, followed by a sustained note that grew deeper and deeper until it fell into the subsonic. I realized that I had heard hundreds – perhaps thousands – of horns played at the same instant as thousands, perhaps tens of thousands, of human voices had joined in chorus.

The darkness around us grew deeper. The stars blazed. The disc of the lower moon was like some great backlit dome that threatened to drop on the darkened world at any moment. Suddenly the many ships on the river to the south and the canal-river to the north began wailing with their own sirens and horns – a cacophonous howl, this, nothing like the descending harmony of the opening chorus – and then began firing off flares and fireworks: multicolored starshells, roaring St Catherine's Wheels, red parachute flares, braided strands of yellow, blue, green, red, and white fire – the Spectrum Helix? – and countless aerial bombs. The noise and light were all but overwhelming.

'Hurry,' repeated Alem, pulling the kayak from the wagon-bed. I jumped out to help him and pulled off my concealing robe, tossing it into the back of the wagon. The next minute was a flurry of coordinated motion as Dem Ria, Dem Loa, Ces Ambre, Bin, and I helped Alem and the unnamed man carry the kayak down to the river's edge and set it afloat. I went into the warm water up to my knees, stowed my backpack and the flechette pistol inside the little cockpit, held the kayak steady against the current, and looked at the two women, two young people, and two men in their billowing robes.

'What is to happen to you?' I asked. My back ached from the aftermath of the kidney stone, but at the moment the tightening of my throat was the more painful distraction.

Dem Ria shook her head. 'Nothing bad will happen to us, Raul Endymion. If the Pax authorities attempt to make trouble, we will simply disappear into the tunnels beneath Waste Wahhabi until it is time to rejoin the Spectrum elsewhere.' She smiled and adjusted her robe on her shoulder. 'But make us one promise, Raul Endymion.'

'Anything,' I said. 'If I can do it, I will.'

'If it is possible, ask the One Who Teaches to return with you to Vitus-Gray-Balianus B and the people of the Amoiete Spectrum Helix. We shall try not to convert to the Pax's Christianity until she comes to speak to us.'

I nodded, looking at Bin Ria Dem Loa Alem's shaven skull, his red cowl flapping around him in the breeze, his cheeks gaunt with chemotherapy, his eyes gleaming more with excitement than reflected fireworks. 'Yes,' I said. 'If it is at all possible, I will do that.'

They all touched me then – not to shake hands, but merely to touch, fingers against my vest or arm or face or back. I touched them back, turned the bow of the kayak into the current, and stepped into the cockpit. The paddle was in the hullclamp where I had left it. I tightened the cockpit skirt around me as if there were white water ahead, bumped my hand against the clear plastic cover over the red 'panic button' that Aenea had shown me as I set the pistol on the cockpit skirt – if this interlude had not caused me to panic, I was not sure what could – held the paddle in my left hand, and waved farewell with my right. The six robed figures blended into the shadows beneath the ferns as the kayak swept out into the middle current.

The farcaster arch grew larger. Overhead, the first moon began to move beyond the disc of the sun but the second, larger moon moved to cover both with its bulk. The fireworks and siren sounds continued, even grew in ferocity. I paddled closer to the right bank as I came close to the farcaster, trying to stay in the small-boat traffic headed downstream but not too close to anyone.

If they are going to intercept me, I thought, *they will do it here.* Without thinking, I raised the flechette pistol onto the curve of hull in front of me. The swift current had me now, and I set the paddle in its bracket and waited to pass under the farcaster. No other ships or small boats would be under the farcaster when it activated. Above me, the arch was a curve of blackness against the starry sky.

Suddenly there was violent commotion on the riverbank not twenty meters to my right.

I raised the pistol and stared, not understanding what I was seeing and hearing.

Two explosions like sonic booms. Strobe flashes of white light.

More fireworks? No, these flashes were much brighter. *Energy weapons fire?* Too bright. Too unfocused. It was more like small plasma explosives going off.

Then I saw something in a blink of an eye, more a retinal echo than a true vision: two figures locked in a violent embrace, images reversed like a negative of an ancient photograph, sudden, violent motion, another sonic boom, a flash of white that blinded me even before the image had registered in my brain – spikes, thorns, two heads butting together, six arms flailing, sparks flying, a human form and something larger, the sound of metal rending, the sound of something or someone screaming with a voice louder than the sirens wailing on the river behind me. The shock wave from whatever was happening on the bank rippled out across the river, almost tumbled my kayak, and proceeded across the water like a curtain of white spray.

Then I was under the farcaster arch, there was the flash and instant of vertigo I had known before, a bright light surrounded me through the flashbulb blindness, and the kayak and I were falling.

Truly falling. Tumbling into space. A section of water that had been farcast under me fell away into a brief waterfall, but then the kayak was falling free from the water, spinning as it fell, and in my panic I dropped the flechette pistol into the cockpit and grabbed the hull of the kayak, setting it spinning more wildly as it fell.

I blinked through the flash echoes and tried to see how far I had to fall, even as the kayak went bow down and picked up speed.

Blue sky above. Clouds all around – huge clouds, stratocumulus rising thousands of meters above and falling more thousands of meters below, cirrus many kilometers above me, black thunderstorms many more kilometers below.

There was nothing but sky and I was falling into it. Beneath me, the brief waterfall from the river had separated into giant teardrops of moisture, as if someone had taken a hundred buckets of water and hurled them into a bottomless chasm.

The kayak spun and threatened to go stern over bow. I shifted forward in the little kayak and almost tumbled out, with only my crossed legs and the lashing of the little moisture skirt holding me in.

I grabbed the rim of the cockpit in a white-knuckled, hopeless grip. Cold air whipped and roared around me as the kayak and I picked up speed, hurtling toward terminal velocity. Thousands and thousands of meters of empty, open air lay between me and the lightning-darted clouds so far below. The two-bladed paddle ripped from its bracket and tumbled away in freefall.

I did the only thing I could do under the circumstances. I opened my mouth and screamed.

ELEVEN

Kenzo Isozaki could say honestly that he had never been afraid before in his life. Raised as a business-samurai in the fern islands of Fuji, he had been taught and trained since infancy to be disdainful of fear and contemptuous of anyone who felt it. Caution he allowed – it had become an indispensable business tool for him – but fear was alien to his nature and his carefully constructed personality.

Until this moment.

M. Isozaki stood back while the inner door of the air lock cycled open. Whatever awaited within had been on the surface of an airless, tumbling asteroid a minute earlier. And it was not wearing a spacesuit.

Isozaki had chosen not to bring a weapon on the little asteroid hopper: neither he nor the ship was armed. At this moment, as ice crystals billowed like fog from the opening air lock and a humanoid figure stepped through, Kenzo Isozaki wondered if that had been a wise choice.

The humanoid figure was human . . . or at least human in appearance. Tan skin, neatly cut gray hair, a perfectly tailored gray suit, gray eyes under lashes still rimmed with frost, and a white smile.

'M. Isozaki,' said Councillor Albedo.

Isozaki bowed. He had brought his heart rate and breathing under his control, and now he concentrated on keeping his voice flat, level, and emotionless. 'It is kind of you to respond to my invitation.'

Albedo crossed his arms. The smile remained on the tanned, handsome face, but Isozaki was not fooled by it. The seas around the fern islands of Fuji were thick with sharks descended from the DNA recipes and frozen embryos of the early Bussard seedships.

'Invitation?' said Councillor Albedo in a rich voice. 'Or summons?'

Isozaki's head remained slightly bowed. His hands hung loosely at his sides. 'Never a summons, M . . .'

'You know my name, I think,' said Albedo.

'The rumors say that you are the same Councillor Albedo who advised Meina Gladstone almost three centuries ago, sir,' said the CEO of the Pax Mercantilus.

'I was more hologram than substance then,' said Albedo, uncrossing his arms. 'But the . . . personality . . . is the same. And you need not call me sir.'

Isozaki bowed slightly.

Councillor Albedo stepped deeper into the little hopper. He ran his powerful fingers over consoles and the single pilot's couch and the rim of its empty high-g tank. 'A modest ship for such a powerful person, M. Isozaki.'

'I thought it best to exercise discretion, Councillor. May I call you that?'

Instead of answering, Albedo took an aggressive step closer to the CEO. Isozaki did not flinch.

'Did you feel it an act of discretion to release an AI viral telotaxis into Pacem's crude datasphere so that it could go looking for TechnoCore nodes?' Albedo's voice filled the hopper cabin.

Kenzo Isozaki raised his eyes to meet the gray glare of the taller man. 'Yes, Councillor. If the Core still existed, it was imperative that I . . . that the Mercantilus . . . make personal contact. The telotaxis was programmed to self-destruct if detected by Pax antiviral programs, and to inoculate only if it received an unmistakable Core response.'

Councillor Albedo laughed. 'Your AI telotaxis was about as subtle as the metaphorical turd in the proverbial punchbowl, Isozaki-san.'

The Mercantilus CEO blinked in surprise at the crudity.

Albedo dropped into the acceleration couch, stretched, and said, 'Sit down, my friend. You went to all that trouble to find us. You risked torture, excommunication, real execution, and the loss of your parking privileges in the Vatican skimmer park. You want to talk . . . talk.'

Temporarily off balance, Isozaki looked for another surface on which to sit. He settled on a clear section of the plotting board. He disliked zero-g, so the crude internal containment field kept up a differential simulating one-gravity, but the effect was inconsistent enough to keep Isozaki teetering on the edge of vertigo. He took a breath and gathered his thoughts.

'You are serving the Vatican . . .' he began.

Albedo interrupted at once. 'The Core serves no one, Mercantilus man.'

Isozaki took another breath and began again. 'Your interests and the Vatican's have overlapped to the point that the TechnoCore provides counsel and technology vital to the survival of the Pax . . .'

Councillor Albedo smiled and waited.

Thinking, *For what I will say next, His Holiness will feed me to the Grand Inquisitor. I will be on the pain machine for a hundred lifetimes*, Isozaki said, 'Some of us within the Executive Council of the Pancapitalist League of Independent Catholic Transstellar Trade Organizations feel that the inter-ests of the League and the interests of the TechnoCore may well hold more in common than those of the Core and the Vatican. We feel that an . . . ah . . . investigation of those common goals and interests would be beneficial to both parties.'

Councillor Albedo showed more of his perfect teeth. He said nothing.

Feeling the hemplike texture of the noose he was placing around his own neck, Isozaki said, 'For two and three-quarter centuries, the Church and the Pax civil authorities have held as official policy that the TechnoCore was destroyed in the Fall of the Farcasters. Millions of those close to power on worlds across Pax space know the rumors of the Core's survival . . .'

'The rumors of our death are greatly exaggerated,' said Councillor Albedo. 'So?'

'So,' continued Isozaki, 'with the full understanding that this alliance between Core personalities and the Vatican has been beneficial to both parties, Councillor, the League would like to suggest ways in which a similar direct alliance with our trading organization would bring more immediate and tangible benefits to your . . . ah . . . society.'

'Suggest away, Isozaki-san,' said Councillor Albedo, leaning farther back in the pilot's chair.

'One,' said Isozaki, his voice growing firmer, 'the Pax Mercantilus is expanding in ways which no religious organization can hope to do, however hierarchical or universally accepted it might be. Capitalism is regaining power throughout the Pax. It is the true glue that holds the hundreds of worlds together.

'Two, the Church continues to carry on its endless war with the Ousters and with rebellious elements within the Pax sphere of influence. The Pax Mercantilus views all such conflicts as a waste of energy and precious human and material resources. More importantly, it involves the Techno-Core in human squabbles that can neither further Core interests nor advance Core goals.

'Three, while the Church and the Pax utilize such obviously Core-derived technologies as the instantaneous Gideon drive and the resurrection creches, the Church gives the TechnoCore no credit for these inventions. Indeed, the Church still holds the Core up as an enemy to its billions of faithful, portraying the Core entities as having been destroyed because they were in league with the Devil. The Pax Mercantilus has no need for such prejudice and artifice. If the Core were to choose continued concealment when allied with us, we should honor that policy, always willing to present the Core as visible and appreciated partners when and if you should so decide. In the meantime, however, the League would move to end, for now and forever, the demonization of the TechnoCore in history, lore, and the minds of human beings everywhere.'

Councillor Albedo looked thoughtful. After a moment of gazing out the port at the tumbling asteroid beyond, he said, 'So you will make us rich *and* respectable?'

Kenzo Isozaki said nothing. He felt that his future and the balance of power in human space was teetering on a knife's edge. He could not read Albedo: the cybrid's sarcasm could well be a prelude to negotiation.

'What would we do with the Church?' asked Albedo. 'More than two and a half human centuries of silent partnership?'

Isozaki willed his heart rate to slow again. 'We do not wish to interrupt any relationship which the Core has found useful or profitable,' he said softly. 'As businesspeople, we in the League are trained to see the limitations of any religion-based interstellar society. Dogma and hierarchy are endemic to such structures . . . indeed, such *are* the structures of any theocracy. As businesspeople dedicated to the mutual profit of ourselves and our business associates, we see ways in which a second level of Core-human cooperation, however secretive or limited, should and would be beneficial to both parties.'

Councillor Albedo nodded again. 'Isozaki-san, do you remember in your private office in the Torus when you had your associate, Anna Pelli Cognani, remove her clothes?'

Isozaki retained a neutral expression but only by the utmost effort of will. The fact that the Core was looking into his private office, recording every transaction, made his blood literally chill.

'You asked then,' continued Albedo, 'why we had helped the Church refine the cruciform. "To what ends?" I believe you said. "Where is the benefit to the Core?"'

Isozaki watched the man in gray, but more than ever he felt that he was locked in the little asteroid hopper with a cobra that had reared up and opened its hood.

'Have you ever owned a dog, Isozaki-san?' asked Albedo.

Still thinking about cobras, the Mercantilus CEO could only stare. 'A dog?' he said after a moment. 'No. Not personally. Dogs were not common on my homeworld.'

'Ah, that's right,' said Albedo, showing his white teeth again. 'Sharks were the pet of choice on your island. I believe that you had a baby shark which you tried to tame when you were about six standard years old. You named it Keigo, if I am not mistaken.'

Isozaki could not have spoken if his life had depended upon it at that second.

'And how did you keep your growing baby shark from eating you when you swam together in the Shioko Lagoon, Isozaki-san?'

After a moment of trying, Isozaki managed, 'Collar.'

'I beg your pardon?' Councillor Albedo leaned closer.

'Collar,' said the CEO. Small, perfectly black spots were dancing in the periphery of his vision. 'Shock collar. We had to carry the transmitter palmkeys. The same devices our fishermen used.'

'Ah, yes,' said Albedo, still smiling. 'If your pet did something naughty, you brought it back into line. With just a touch of your finger.' He held his hand out, cupping it as if he were cradling an invisible palmkey. His tanned finger came down on an invisible button.

It was not so much like an electrical shock passing through Kenzo Isozaki's body, more like radiating waves of pure, unadultered agony – beginning in his chest, beginning in the cruciform embedded under his skin and flesh and bone – and radiating out like telegraph signals of pain flowing through the hundreds of meters of fibers and nematodes and clustered nodes of cruciform tissue metastasized through his body like rooted tumors.

Isozaki screamed and doubled over in pain. He collapsed to the floor of the hopper.

'I believe that your palmkeys could give old Keigo increasing jolts if he got aggressive,' mused Councillor Albedo. 'Wasn't that the case, Isozaki-san?' His fingers tapped at empty air again, as if cueing a palmkey.

The pain grew worse, Isozaki urinated in his shipsuit and would have voided his bowels if they had not been already empty. He tried to scream again but his jaws clamped tight, as if from violent tetanus. Enamel on his teeth cracked and chipped away. He tasted blood as he bit through a corner of his tongue.

'On a scale of ten, that would have been about a two for old Keigo, I think,' said Councillor Albedo. He stood and walked to the air lock, tapping the cycling combination in.

Writhing on the floor, his body and brain useless appendages to a cruciform of horrific pain radiating through his body, Isozaki tried to scream through his locked jaws. His eyes were swelling out of their sockets. Blood ran from his nose and ears.

Finished with cycling the air-lock combination, Councillor Albedo tapped at the invisible key in his palm once again.

The pain vanished. Isozaki vomited across the deckplates. Every muscle in his body twitched randomly while his nerves seemed to misfire.

'I will bring your proposal to the Three Elements of the TechnoCore,' Councillor Albedo said formally. 'The proposition will be discussed and considered most seriously. In the meantime, my friend, your discretion will be counted upon.'

Isozaki tried to make an intelligible noise, but he could only curl up and retch on the metal floor. To his horror, his spasming bowels were passing wind in a ripple of flatulence.

'And there will be no more AI viral telotaxes released in anyone's datasphere, will there, Isozaki-san?' Albedo stepped into the air lock and cycled the door shut.

Outside the port, the slashed rock of the unnamed asteroid tumbled and spun in dynamics known only to the gods of chaos mathematics.

It took Rhadamanth Nemes and her three siblings only a few minutes to fly the dropship from Pax Base Bombasino to the village of Lock Childe Lamonde on the slate-dry world of Vitus-Gray-Balianus B, but the trip was complicated by the presence of three military skimmers that that meddling fool Commander Solznykov had sent along in escort. Nemes knew from the 'secure' tightbeam traffic between the base and the skimmers that the Base Commander had sent his aide, the bumbling Colonel Vinara, to take personal charge of the expedition. More than that, Nemes knew that the Colonel would be in charge of nothing – that is, Vinara would be so wired with real-time holosim pickups and tightbeam squirters that Solznykov would be in actual command of the Pax troopers without showing his jowled face again.

By the time they were hovering over the proper village – although 'village' seemed too formal a term for the four-tiered strip of adobe houses that ran along the west side of the river just as hundreds of other homes had for almost the entire way between the base and here – the skimmers had caught up and were spiraling in for a landing while Nemes looked for a site large enough and firm enough to hold the dropship.

The doors of the adobe homes were painted bright primary colors. People on the street wore robes of the same hue. Nemes knew the reason for this display of color: she had accessed both their ship's memory and the encrypted Bombasino files on the Spectrum Helix people. The data was interesting only in that it suggested that these human oddities were slow to convert to the cross, slower still to submit to Pax control. Likely, in other words, to help a rebellious child, man, and one-armed android hide from the authorities.

The skimmers landed on the dike road bordering the canal. Nemes brought the dropship down in a park, partially destroying an artesian well.

Gyges shifted in his copilot's seat and raised an eyebrow.

'Scylla and Briareus will go out to make the formal search,' Nemes said aloud. 'You stay here with me.' She had noted with no pride or vanity that her clone-siblings had long since submitted to her authority, despite the death threat they had brought from the Three Elements and the certainty of its being carried out if she were to fail again.

The other female and male went down the ramp and through the crowd of brightly robed people. Troopers in combat armor, visors sealed, jogged to meet them. Watching on the common optic channel, not via tightbeam or vid pickup, Nemes recognized Colonel Vinara's voice through his helmet speaker. 'The Mayor – a woman named Ses Gia – refuses permission for us to search the houses.'

Nemes could see Briareus's contemptuous smile reflected on the Colonel's polished visor. It was like looking at a reflection of herself with slightly stronger bone structure.

'And you allow this . . . Mayor . . . to dictate to you?' said Briareus.

Colonel Vinara raised a gauntleted hand. 'The Pax recognizes the indigenous authorities until they have become . . . part of the Pax Protectorate.'

Scylla said, 'You said that Dr Molina left a Pax trooper as guard . . .'

Vinara nodded. His breathing was amplified through the morphic, amber helmet. 'There is no sign of that trooper. We have attempted to establish communication since we left Bombasino.'

'Doesn't this trooper have a trace chip surgically implanted?' said Scylla.

'No, it is woven into his impact armor.'

'And?'

'We found the armor in a well several streets over,' said Colonel Vinara.

Scylla's voice remained level. 'I presume the trooper was not in the armor.'

'No,' said the Colonel, 'just the armor and helmet. There was no body in the well.'

'Pity,' said Scylla. She started to turn away but then looked back at the Pax Colonel. 'Just armor, you say. No weapon?'

'No.' Vinara's voice was gloomy. 'I've ordered a search of the streets and we will question the citizens until someone volunteers the location of the house where the missing spacer was put under arrest by Dr Molina. Then we will surround it and demand the surrender of all inside. I have . . . ah . . . requested the civil courts in Bombasino consider our request for a search warrant.'

Briareus said, 'Good plan, Colonel. If the glaciers don't arrive first and cover the village before the warrant is issued.'

'Glaciers?' said Colonel Vinara.

'Never mind,' said Scylla. 'If it is acceptable to you, we shall help you search the adjoining streets and await proper authorization for a house-to-house search.' To Nemes, she broadcast on the internal band, *Now what?*

Stay with him and do just what you offered, sent Nemes. *Be courteous and law-abiding. We don't want to find Endymion or the girl with these idiots around. Gyges and I will go to fast time.*

Good hunting, sent Briareus.

Gyges was already waiting at the dropship lock. Nemes said, 'I'll take the town, you move downriver to the farcaster arch and make sure that nothing gets through – going upriver or down – without your checking it out. Phase down to send a squirt message and I'll shift periodically to check the band. If you find him or the girl, ping me.' It was possible to communicate via common band while phase-shifted, but the energy expenditure was so horribly high – above and beyond the unimaginable energy needed just for the phase-shift – that it was infinitely more economical to shift down at intervals to check the common band. Even a ping alarm would use the equivalent of this world's entire energy budget for a year.

Gyges nodded and the two phase-shifted in unison, becoming chrome sculptures of a naked male and female. Outside the lock, the air seemed to thicken and the light deepen. Sound ceased. Movement stopped. Human figures became slightly out-of-focus statues with their wind-rippled robes stiff and frozen like the trappings on bronze sculptures.

Nemes did not understand the physics of phase shifting. She did not have to understand it in order to use it. She knew that it was neither the anti-entropic nor hyperentropic manipulation of time – although the future UI had both of those seemingly magical technologies at its command – nor some sort of 'speeding up' that would have had sonic booms crashing and the air temperature boiling in their wake, but that phase shifting was a sort of sidestepping into the hollowed-out boundaries of space/time. 'You will become – in the nicest sense – rats scurrying in the walls of the rooms of time,' had said the Core entity most responsible for her creation.

Nemes was not offended by the comparison. She knew the unimaginable amounts of energy that had to be transferred from the Core via the Void Which Binds to her or her siblings when they phase-shifted. The Elements had to respect even their own instruments to divert so much energy in their direction.

The two reflective figures jogged down the ramp and went opposite directions – Gyges south toward the farcaster, Nemes past her frozen siblings and the sculptures of Pax troopers and Spectrum citizens, into the adobe city.

It took her literally no time at all to find the house with the handcuffed Pax trooper asleep in the corner bedroom facing the canal. She rummaged through the downloaded Pax Base Bombasino files to identify the sleeping trooper – a Lusian named Gerrin Pawtz, thirty-eight standard years old, a lazy, initiative-free alcohol addict, two years away from retirement, six demotions and three sentences to brigtime in his file, assignments relegated to garrison duty and the most mundane base tasks – and then she deleted the file. The trooper was of no interest to her.

Checking once to make sure that the house was empty, Rhadamanth Nemes dropped out of phase shift and stood a moment in the bedroom. Sound and movement returned: the snoring of the handcuffed trooper, movement of pedestrians along the canal walk, a soft breeze stirring white curtains, the rumble of distant traffic, and even the samurai-armor rustles of the Pax troopers jogging through adjoining streets and alleys in their useless search.

Standing over the Pax trooper, Nemes extended her hand and first finger as if pointing at the man's neck. A needle emerged from under her fingernail and extended the ten centimeters to the sleeping man's neck, sliding under the skin and flesh with only the slightest speck of blood to show the intrusion. The trooper did not wake.

Nemes withdrew the needle and examined the blood within: dangerous levels of $C_{27}H_{45}OH$ – Lusians frequently were at risk from high cholesterol – as well as a low platelet count suggesting the presence of incipient immune thrombocytopenic purpura, probably brought about by the trooper's early years in hard-radiation environments on any of several garrison worlds, a blood alcohol level of 122 mg/100 ml – the trooper was drunk, although his alcoholic past probably allowed him to hide most of the effects – and – voila! – the presence of the artificial opiate called ultramorph mixed with heightened levels of caffeine. Nemes smiled. Someone had drugged the trooper with sleep-inducing amounts of ultramorph mixed with tea or coffee – but had done so while taking care to keep the levels below a dangerous overdose.

She sniffed the air. Nemes's ability to detect and identify distinct airborne organic molecules – that is, her sense of smell – was about three times more sensitive than a typical gas chromatograph mass spectrometer's: in other words, somewhere above that of the Old Earth canine called a bloodhound. The room was filled with the distinctive scents of many people. Some of the smells were old; a few were very recent. She identified the Lusian trooper's alcoholic stink, several subtle, musky female scents, the molecular imprint of at least two children – one deeply into puberty and the other younger but afflicted with some cancer requiring chemotherapy – and two adult males, one bearing the distinct sweat impressions of the diet of this planet, the other being at once familiar and alien. Alien because the man still carried the scent of a world Nemes had never visited, familiar because it was the distinctive human smell she had filed away: Raul Endymion still carrying the scent of Old Earth with him.

Nemes walked from room to room, but there was no hint of the peculiar scent she had encountered four years earlier of the girl named Aenea, nor the antiseptic android smell of the servant called A. Bettik. Only Raul Endymion had been here. But he had been here only moments before.

Nemes followed the scent trail to the trapdoor beneath the hall flooring.

Ripping the door open despite its multiple locks, she paused before descending the ladder. She squirted the information on the common band, not receiving a responding ping from Gyges, who was probably phase-shifted. It had been only ninety seconds since they had left the ship. Nemes smiled. She could ping Gyges, and he would be here before Raul Endymion and the others in the tunnel below had taken another ten heartbeats.

But Rhadamanth Nemes would like to settle this score alone. Still smiling, she jumped into the hole and dropped eight meters to the tunnel floor below.

The tunnel was lighted. Nemes sniffed the cool air, separating the adrenaline-rich scent of Raul Endymion from the other human odors. The Hyperion-born fugitive was nervous. And he had been ill or injured – Nemes picked up the underlying smell of sweat tinged with ultramorph. Endymion had certainly been the offworlder treated by Dr Molina and someone had used painkillers prescribed for him on the hapless Lusian trooper.

Nemes phase-shifted and began jogging down a tunnel now filled with thickened light. No matter how much of a head start Endymion and his allies had on her, she would catch them now. It would have pleased Nemes to slice the troublemaker's head off while she was still phase-shifted – the decapitation seeming supernatural to the real-time onlookers, performed by an invisible executioner – but she needed information from Raul Endymion. She did not need him conscious, however. The simplest plan would be to pluck him away from his Spectrum Helix friends, surrounding him with the same phased field that protected Nemes, drive a needle into his brain to immobilize him, return him to the dropship, stow him in the resurrection creche there, and then go through the charade of thanking Colonel Vinara and Commander Solznykov for their help. They could 'interrogate' Raul Endymion once their ship had left orbit: Nemes would run microfibers into the man's extracting RNA and memories at will. Endymion would never regain consciousness: when she and her siblings had learned what they needed from his memories, she would terminate him and dump the body into space. The goal was to find the child named Aenea.

Suddenly the lights went out.

While I am phase-shifted, thought Nemes. *Impossible*. Nothing could happen that quickly.

She skidded to a halt. There was no light at all in the tunnel, nothing she could amplify. She switched to infrared, scanning the passageway ahead and behind her. Empty. She opened her mouth and emitted a sonar scream, turning quickly to do the same behind her. Emptiness, the ultrasound shriek echoing back off the ends of the tunnel. She modified the field around her to blast a deep-radar pulse in both directions. The tunnel was empty, but the deep radar recorded mazes of similar tunnels for kilometers in all directions. Thirty meters ahead, beyond a thick metal door, there was an underground garage with an assortment of vehicles and human forms in it.

Still suspicious, Nemes dropped out of phase shift for an instant to see how the lights could have gone out in a microsecond.

The form was directly in front of her. Nemes had less than a ten thousandth of a second to phase-shift again as four bladed fists struck her with the force of a hundred thousand pile drivers. She was driven back the length of the tunnel, through the splintering ladder, through the tunnel wall of solid rock, and deep into the stone itself.

The lights stayed out.

In the twenty standard days during which the Grand Inquisitor stayed on Mars, he learned to hate it far more than he thought he could ever hate Hell itself.

The *simoom* planetary dust storm blew every day he was there. Despite the fact that he and his twenty-one-person team had taken over the Governor's Palace on the outskirts of the city of St Malachy, and despite the fact that the palace was theoretically as hermetically sealed as a Pax spaceship, its air filtered and boosted and refiltered, its windows consisting of fifty-two layers of high-impact plastic, its entrances more air-lock seals than doors, the Martian dust got in.

When John Domenico Cardinal Mustafa took his needle shower in the morning, the dust he had accumulated in the night ran in red rivulets of mud into the shower drain. When the Grand Inquisitor's valet helped him pull on his cassock and robes in the morning – all of the clothing fresh-cleaned during the night – there were already traces of red grit in the silken folds. As Mustafa ate breakfast – alone in the Governor's dining room – grit ground between his molars. During the Holy Office interviews and inter-rogations held in the echoing great ballroom of the palace, the Grand Inquisitor could feel the dust building up in his ankle hose and collar and hair and under his perfectly manicured fingernails.

Outside, it was ridiculous. Skimmers and Scorpions were grounded. The spaceport operated only a few hours of the day, during the rare lulls in the *simoom*. Parked ground vehicles soon became humps and drifts of red sand, and even Pax-quality filters could not keep the red particles out of the engines and motors and solid-state modules. A few ancient crawlers and rovers and fusion rocket shuttles kept food and information flowing to and from the capital, but to all intents and purposes, the Pax government and military on Mars had come to a standstill.

It was on the fifth day of the *simoom* that reports came in of Palestinian attacks on Pax bases on the Tharsis Plateau. Major Piet, the Governor's laconic groundforce commander, took a company of mixed Pax and Home Guard troopers and set out in crawlers and tracked APCs. They were ambushed a hundred klicks short of the plateau approach and only Piet and half his command returned to St Malachy.

By the second week, reports came in of Palestinian attacks on a dozen garrison posts in both hemispheres. All contact was lost with the Hellas contingent and the south polar station radioed the *Jibril* that it was pre-paring to surrender to the attacking forces.

Governor Clare Palo – working out of a small office that had belonged to one of her aides – conferred with Archbishop Robeson and the Grand

Inquisitor and released tactical fusion and plasma weapons to the beleaguered garrisons. Cardinal Mustafa agreed to the use of the *Jibril* as a
weapons platform in the struggle against the Palestinians, and South Polar
One was slagged from orbit. The Home Guard, Pax, Fleet Marines, Swiss
Guard, and Holy Office commands concentrated on making sure that the
capital of St Malachy, its cathedral, and the Governor's Palace were secure
from attack. In the relentless dust storm, any indigenie that approached
within eight klicks of the city perimeter and who was not wearing a Pax-
issued transponder was lanced and the bodies recovered later. A few were
Palestinian guerrillas.

'The *simoom* can't last forever,' grumbled Commander Browning, the
head of the Holy Office security forces.

'It can last another three to four standard months,' said Major Piet, his
upper torso bulky in a burncast. 'Perhaps longer.'

The work of the Holy Office Inquisition was going nowhere: the milita
troopers who had first discovered the massacre in Arafat-kaffiyeh were interviewed again under Truthtell and neuroprobe, but their stories remained the
same; the Holy Office forensic experts worked with the coroners at St
Malachy's Infirmary only to confirm that none of the three hundred and
sixty-two corpses could be resurrected – the Shrike had ripped out every node
and millifiber of their cruciforms; queries were sent back to Pacem via
instantaneous-drive drone regarding the identities of the victims and – more
importantly – the nature of the *Opus Dei* operations on Mars and the reasons
for the advanced spaceport, but when a drone returned after fourteen local
days, it brought only the IDs of the murdered and no explanation of their
connection to *Opus Dei* or the motives for that organization's efforts on Mars.

After fifteen days of dust storm, more reports of continued Palestinian
attacks on convoys and garrisons, and long days of interrogation and evidence sifting that led nowhere, the Grand Inquisitor was happy to hear
Captain Wolmak call on secure tightbeam from the *Jibril* to announce that
there was an emergency that would require the Grand Inquisitor and his
entourage to return to orbit as soon as possible.

The *Jibril* was one of the newest archangel-class starships, and it looked
functional and deadly to Cardinal Mustafa as their dropships closed the last
few kilometers to rendezvous. The Grand Inquisitor knew little about Pax
warships, but even he could see that Captain Wolmak had morphed the
starship to battle readiness: the various booms and sensor arrays had been
drawn in beneath the starship's skin, the bulge of the Gideon drive had
sprouted laser-reflective armor, and the various weapons portals were
cleared for action. Behind the archangel, Mars turned – a dust-shrouded
disc the color of dried blood. Cardinal Mustafa hoped that this would be his
last view of the place.

Father Farrell pointed out that all eight of the Mars System Task Force's
torchships were within five hundred klicks of the *Jibril* – a tight, defensive
grouping by space-going standards and the Grand Inquisitor realized that
something serious was in the offing.

Mustafa's dropship was the first to dock and Wolmak met them in the airlock antechamber. The interior containment field gave them gravity.

'My apologies for interrupting your Inquisition, Your Excellency . . .' began the captain.

'Never mind that,' said Cardinal Mustafa, shaking sand from the folds of his robe. 'What is so important, Captain?' Wolmak blinked at the entourage emerging from the air lock behind the Grand Inquisitor: Father Farrell, of course, followed by Security Commander Browning, three Holy Office aides, Marine Sergeant Nell Kasner, the resurrection chaplain Bishop Erdle, and Major Piet, the former groundforce commander whom Cardinal Mustafa had liberated from Governor Palo's service.

The Grand Inquisitor saw the captain's hesitation. 'You can speak freely, Captain. All in this group have been cleared by the Holy Office.'

Wolmak nodded. 'Your Excellency, we have found the ship.'

Cardinal Mustafa must have stared his incomprehension.

'The heavy-duty freighter that must have left Mars orbit the day of the massacre, Your Excellency,' continued the captain. 'We knew that their dropships had rendezvoused with *some* ship that day.'

'Yes,' said the Grand Inquisitor, 'but we assumed that it would be long gone – translated to whatever star system it was bound for.'

'Yes, sir,' said Wolmak, 'but on the off chance that the ship had never spun up to C-plus, I had the dropships do an in-system search. We found the freighter in the system's asteroid belt.'

'Was that its destination?' asked Mustafa.

The captain was shaking his head. 'I think not, Excellency. The freighter is cold and dead. It's tumbling. Our instruments show no life on board, no systems powered up . . . not even the fusion drive.'

'But it *is* a starship freighter?' questioned Father Farrell.

Captain Wolmak turned toward the tall, thin man. 'Yes, Father. The HHMS *Saigon Maru*. A three-million-ton ore and bulk freighter that's seen service since the days of the Hegemony.'

'Mercantilus,' the Grand Inquisitor said softly.

Wolmak looked grim. 'Originally, Your Excellency. But our records show that the *Saigon Maru* was decommissioned from the Mercantilus fleet and rendered into scrap metal eight standard years ago.'

Cardinal Mustafa and Father Farrell exchanged glances.

'Have you boarded the ship yet, Captain?' asked Commander Browning.

'No,' said Wolmak. 'Because of the political implications, I thought it best if His Excellency were aboard and authorized such a search.'

'Very good,' said the Grand Inquisitor.

'Also,' said Captain Wolmak, 'I wanted the full complement of Marines and Swiss Guard troopers aboard first.'

'Why is that, sir?' asked Major Piet. His uniform looked bulky over his burncast.

'Something's not right,' said the captain, looking at the major and then at the Grand Inquisitor. 'Something's very much not right.'

*

More than two hundred light-years from Mars System, Task Force GIDEON was completing its task of destroying Lucifer.

The seventh and final Ouster System in their punitive expedition was the hardest to finish off. A yellow G-type star with six worlds, two of them inhabitable without terraforming, the system was crawling with Ousters: military bases out beyond the asteroids, birthing rocks in the asteroid belt, angel environments around the innermost water world, refueling depots in low orbit around the gas giant, and an orbital forest being grown between what would have been the orbits of Venus and Old Earth in the Old Sol System. It took GIDEON ten standard days to search out and kill a majority of these nodes of Ouster life.

When they were done, Admiral Aldikacti called for a physical conference of the seven captains aboard His Holiness's Ship *Uriel* and revealed that the plans had been changed: the expedition had been so successful that they would seek out new targets and continue the attack. Aldikacti had dispatched a Gideon-drive drone to Pacem System and received permission to extend the mission. The seven archangels would translate to the nearest Pax base, Tau Ceti System, where they would be rearmed, refitted, refueled, and joined by five new archangels. Probes had already targeted a dozen new Ouster Systems, none of which had yet received news of the massacre along Task Force GIDEON's swath of destruction. Counting resurrection time, they would be attacking again within ten standard days.

The seven captains returned to their seven ships and prepared for the translation from Target System Lucifer to Tau Ceti Center Base.

Aboard HHS *Raphael*, Commander Hoagan 'Hoag' Liebler was uneasy. Besides his official capacity as executive officer of the starship, second in command to Father Captain de Soya, Liebler was paid to spy on the father-captain and to report any suspicious behavior – first to the chief of Holy Office Security aboard Admiral Aldikacti's flagship, the *Uriel*, and then – as far as the Executive Officer could tell – all the way up the chain of command to the legendary Cardinal Lourdusamy. Liebler's problem at the moment was that he was suspicious but could not articulate the cause for his suspicions.

The spy could hardly tightbeam the *Uriel* with the dangerous news that the crew of Father Captain de Soya's *Raphael* had been going to confession too frequently, but that was precisely one of the causes of Liebler's concern. Of course, Hoag Liebler was not a spy by training or inclination: he was a gentleman of reduced circumstances, forced first by financial constraints to exercise a Renaissance Minor gentleman's option of joining the military, and then constrained further – by loyalty to his Pax and Church, he convinced himself, more than by the constant need for money to reclaim and restore his estates – into spying on his captain.

The confessions were not all that out of the ordinary – the crew was made up of faithful, Church- and confession-going born-again Christian soldiers, of course, and the circumstances in which they found themselves, the possibility of a true and eternal death if one of the Ouster fusion weapons or k-beams made it through defensive containment fields, certainly added to the urgency of that faith – but Liebler sensed some extra factor at work in all these confessions since Target System Mammon. During the lulls in the vicious fighting here in Target System Lucifer, the entire crew and Swiss Guard complement of the *Raphael* – some twenty-seven hands in all, not counting the bewildered Executive Officer – had been cycling through the confessional like spacers at an Outback port whorehouse.

And the confessional was the one place at which even the ship's Executive Officer could not linger and eavesdrop.

Liebler could not imagine what conspiracy could possibly be afoot. Mutiny made no sense. First, it was unthinkable – no crew in the nearly three centuries of Pax Fleet had ever mutinied or come close to mutiny. Second, it was absurd – mutineers did not flock to the confessional to discuss the sin of a planned mutiny with the captain of the ship.

Perhaps Father Captain de Soya was recruiting these men and women for some nefarious deed, but Hoag Liebler could not imagine anything the priest-captain could offer that would suborn these loyal Pax spacers and Swiss Guard troopers. The crew did not like Hoag Liebler – he was used to being disliked by classmates and shipmates, it was the curse of his natural-born aristocracy, he knew – but he could not imagine them banding together to plan some evil deed directed his way. If Father Captain de Soya had somehow seduced this crew into treason, the worst they could do was attempt to steal the archangel – Liebler suspected that this remote possibility was the reason he had been placed aboard as a spy – but to what end? *Raphael* was never out of touch with the other archangels in the GIDEON Task Force, except for the instant of C-plus translation and the two days of hurried resurrection, so if the crew turned traitor and attempted to steal the ship, the other six archangels would cut them down in an instant.

The thought made Hoag Liebler physically queasy. He disliked dying, and did not wish to do so more than necessary. Moreover, it would not help his career as a restored Lord of the Manor on Renaissance Minor if his service duty was remembered as being a part of the Crew That Turned Treasonous. It was possible, he realized, that Cardinal Lourdusamy – or whoever was at the apex of his espionage food chain – might have him tortured, excommunicated, and executed to the true death along with the rest of the crew just to conceal the fact that the Vatican had put a spy aboard.

This thought made Hoag Liebler more than queasy.

He consoled himself with the thought that such act of treason was not just unlikely, it was insane. It was not like the old days on Old Earth or some other water world that Liebler had read about where an ocean-going war-ship goes rogue and turns pirate, preying on merchant ships and terrorizing ports. There was nowhere for a stolen archangel to run to, nowhere to hide, and nowhere to rearm and refit the ship. Pax Fleet would have their guts for garters.

Commander Hoag Liebler continued to feel queasy and uneasy despite all this forced logic.

He was on the flight deck four hours into their spinup to the translation point to Tau Ceti System when the priority squirt came in from *Uriel*: five

Ouster torchship-class destroyers had been hiding in the charged-particle dust torus of the inner moon of the outer gas giant and were now making a run toward their own translation points, using the G-type sun as a shield between them and the GIDEON Task Force. The *Gabriel* and the *Raphael* were to deviate from their translation arcs enough to find a firing trajectory for their remaining C-plus hyperkinetic missiles, destroy the torchships, and then to resume their exits from Lucifer System. *Uriel* estimated that the two archangels could spin up to translation about eight hours after the other five ships had departed.

Father Captain de Soya acknowledged the squirt and ordered a change of course, and Commander Liebler monitored the tightbeam traffic as Mother Captain Stone aboard *Gabriel* did likewise. *The Admiral isn't leaving* Raphael *behind alone*, thought the Executive Officer. *My masters aren't the only ones that don't trust de Soya.*

It was not an exciting chase – not actually a chase at all, when it came down to it. Given the gravitational dynamics of this system, it would take the old Hawking-drive Ouster torchships about fourteen hours to reach relativistic velocities prior to spinup. The two archangels would be in firing position within four hours. The Ousters had no weapons that could reach all the way across this system to hurt the archangels: both *Gabriel* and *Raphael* had enough weaponry in their depleted stock to destroy the torch-ships a dozen times over. If all else failed, they would use the hated deathbeams.

Commander Liebler had the con – the priest-captain had gone to his cubby to catch a few hours of sleep – when the two archangels cleared the sun for a firing solution. The rest of Task Force GIDEON had long since translated. Liebler turned in his acceleration chair to buzz the captain when suddenly the blast portal irised and Father Captain de Soya and several others stepped in. For a moment Liebler forgot his suspicions – forgot even that he had been paid to *be* suspicious – as he goggled at the unlikely group. Besides the captain, there was that Swiss Guard sergeant – Gregorius – and two of his troopers. Also in attendance were Weapons Systems Officer (WHIZZO) Commander Carel Shan, Energy Systems Officer (ESSO) Lieutenant Pol Denish, Environmental Systems Officer (VIRO) Commander Bettz Argyle, and Propulsion Systems Engineer (GOPRO) Lieutenant Elijah Hussein Meier.

'What in the hell . . .' began Executive Officer (XO) Liebler and then stopped. The Swiss Guard sergeant was holding a neural stunner and it was aimed at Liebler's face.

Hoag Liebler had been carrying a concealed flechette pistol in his boot for weeks, but he forgot about it completely at this moment. He had never had a weapon aimed at him before – not even a stunner – and the effect of it made him want to urinate down his own pant leg. He concentrated on not doing that. This left little room to concentrate on anything else.

One of the female troopers came over and lifted the pistol out of his boot. Liebler stared at it as if he had never seen it before.

'Hoag,' said Father Captain de Soya, 'I'm sorry about this. We took a vote and decided that there was no time to try to convince you to join us. You're going to have to go away for a while.'

Summoning up all the dialogue he had ever heard from holodramas, Liebler began blustering. 'You'll never get away with this. The *Gabriel* will destroy you. You'll all be tortured and hanged. They'll rip your cruciforms right out of your . . .'

The stunner in the giant sergeant's hand hummed. Hoag Liebler would have gone face down onto the deck if the female trooper had not caught him and lowered him carefully to the deckplates.

Father Captain de Soya took his place in the command chair. 'Break away from this course,' he said to Lieutenant Meier at the helm. 'Set in our translation coordinates. Full emergency acceleration. Go to full combat readiness.' The priest-captain glanced down at Liebler. 'Put him in his resurrection creche and set it to "store".'

The troopers carried out the sleeping man.

Even before Father Captain de Soya ordered the ship's internal containment field set to zero-g for battle stations, the priest-captain had that brief but exhilarating sense of flying one feels in the instant after having jumped off a cliff before gravity reasserts its absolute imperatives. In truth, their ship was now groaning under more than six hundred gravities of fusion acceleration, almost a hundred and eighty percent of normal high boost. Any interruption in the containment field would kill them in less than an instant. But the translation point was now less than forty minutes away.

De Soya was not sure what he was doing was right. The thought of being a traitor to his Church and Pax Fleet was the most terrible thing in the world to him. But he knew that if he did indeed have an immortal soul, he had no other choice in the matter.

Actually, what made Father Captain de Soya think that a miracle might be involved – or at least that a very improbable stroke of luck had occurred – was the fact that seven others had agreed to come along with him in this doomed mutiny. Eight, including himself, out of a crew of twenty-eight. The other twenty were sleeping off neural stuns in their resurrection creches. De Soya knew that the eight of them could handle *Raphael*'s systems and tasks under most circumstances: he was lucky – or blessed – that several of the essential flight officers had come along. In the beginning, he thought it was going to be Gregorius, his two young troopers, and himself.

The first suggestion of mutiny had come from the three Swiss Guard soldiers after their 'cleansing' of the second birthing asteroid in Lucifer System. Despite their oaths to the Pax, the Church, and the Swiss Guard, the slaughter of infants had been too much like murder for them. Lancers Dona Foo and Enos Delrino had first gone to their sergeant, and then come with Gregorius to Father Captain de Soya's confessional with their plan to defect. Originally, they had asked for absolution if they decided to jump ship in the Ouster System. De Soya had asked them to consider an alternate plan.

The Propulsion Systems Engineer Lieutenant Meier had come to confession with the same concerns. The wholesale slaughter of the beautiful forcefield angels – which he had watched in tactical space – had sickened the young man and made him want to return to his ancestral religions of Judaism and Islam. Instead, he had gone to confession to admit his spiritual weakening. Father Captain de Soya had amazed Meier by telling him that his concerns were not in conflict with true Christianity.

In the days that followed, Environmental Systems Officer Commander Bettz Argyle and Energy Systems Officer Lieutenant Pol Denish followed their consciences to the confessional. Denish was among the hardest to convince, but long, whispered conversations with his cubby-mate, Lieutenant Meier, brought him along.

WHIZZO Commander Carel Shan was the last to join: the Weapons Systems Officer could no longer authorize deathbeam attacks. He had not slept in three weeks.

De Soya had realized during their last day in Lucifer System that none of the other officers was about to defect. They saw their work as distasteful but necessary. When push came to shove, he realized, the majority of flight officers and the remaining three Swiss Guard troopers would have sided with XO Hoag Liebler. Father Captain de Soya and Sergeant Gregorius decided not to give them the chance.

'The *Gabriel* is hailing us, Father Captain,' said Lieutenant Denish. The ESSO was plugged into comtact as well as into his energy systems' console.

De Soya nodded. 'Everyone make sure your couch creches are active.' It was an unnecessary order, he knew. Every crew member went into battle stations or C-plus translation in his or her acceleration couch, each rigged as an automated resurrection creche.

Before jacking into tactical, de Soya checked their trajectory on the center pit display. They were pulling away from *Gabriel*, although the other archangel had gone to three-hundred-gravities of boost and had altered course to parallel *Raphael*'s. Across Lucifer's solar system, the five Ouster torchships were still crawling toward their own translation points. De Soya wished them well, knowing all the while that the only reason the ships still existed was the momentary distraction *Raphael*'s puzzling course change had caused for *Gabriel*. He plugged into command tactsim.

Instantly he was a giant standing in space. The six worlds and countless moons and nascent, burning orbital forests of Lucifer spread out at his belt level. Far beyond the burning sun, the six Ouster motes balanced on tiny fusion tails. *Gabriel*'s tail was much longer; *Raphael*'s the longest yet, its brilliance rivaling the central star's. Mother Captain Stone stood waiting a few giant's paces from de Soya.

'Federico,' she said, 'what in Christ's name are you doing?'

De Soya had considered not answering *Gabriel*'s hail. If it would have offered them a few more minutes, he would have stayed silent. But he knew Stone. She would not hesitate. On a separate tactical channel, he glanced at the translation plot. Thirty-six minutes to shift point.

Captain! Four missile launches detected! Translating . . . now! It was WHIZZO Commander Shan on the secure conduction line.

Father Captain de Soya felt sure that he had not visibly jumped or reacted in front of Mother Captain Stone in tactical. On his own bone line, he subvocalized, *It's all right, Carel. I can see them on tac. They've translated toward the Ouster ships.* To Stone, he said on tactical, 'You've launched against the Ousters.'

Stone's face was tight even in simlight. 'Of course. Why haven't you, Federico?'

Rather than answer, de Soya stepped closer to the central sun and watched the missiles emerge from Hawking drive immediately in front of the six Ouster torchships. They detonated within seconds: two fusion, followed by two broader plasma. All of the Ousters had their defensive containment fields to maximum – an orange glow in tactical sim – but the close-range bursts overloaded all of them. The images went from orange to red to white and then three of the ships simply ceased to exist as material objects. Two became scattered fragments tumbling toward the now infinitely distant translation points. One torchship remained intact, but its containment field dropped away and its fusion tail disappeared. If anyone aboard had survived the blast effects, they were now dead of the sleet storm of undeflected radiation that was tearing through the ship.

'What are you doing, Federico?' repeated Mother Captain Stone.

De Soya knew that Stone's first name was Halen. He chose not to make his part of the conversation personal. 'Following orders, Mother Captain.'

Even in tactsim, Stone's expression was dubious. 'What are you talking about, Father Captain de Soya?' Both knew that the conversation was being recorded. Whoever survived the next few minutes would have a record of the exchange.

De Soya kept his voice steady. 'Admiral Aldikacti's flagship tightbeamed us with a change of orders ten minutes before the flagship translated. We are carrying out those orders.'

Stone's expression was impassive, but de Soya knew that she was subvocalizing her XO to confirm that there had been a tightbeam transmission between *Uriel* and *Raphael* at that time. There had been. But the substance of it had been trivial: updating rendezvous coordinates for the Tau Ceti System.

'What were the orders, Father Captain de Soya?'

'They were eyes-only, Mother Captain Stone. They do not concern the *Gabriel*.' On the bone circuit, he said to WHIZZO Shan, *Lock on deathbeam coordinates and give me the actuator as discussed.* A second later he felt the tactsim weight of an energy weapon in his right hand. The gun was invisible to Stone, but perfectly tactile to de Soya. He tried to make his hand on the butt of the weapon look relaxed as his finger curled around the invisible trigger. De Soya could tell from the casual way that Mother Captain Stone's arm hung free from her body that she was also carrying a virtual weapon. They stood about three meters apart in tactsim space. Between them,

Raphael's long fusion tail and *Gabriel's* shorter pillar of flame climbed toward chest height from the plane of the ecliptic.

'Father Captain de Soya, your new translation point will not take you to Tau Ceti System as ordered.'

'Those orders were superseded, Mother Captain.' De Soya was watching his former first officer's eyes. Halen was always good at concealing her emotions and intentions. He had lost to her in poker on more than one occasion on their old torchship, *Balthasar.*

'What is your new destination, Father Captain?'

Thirty-three minutes to shift point.

'Classified, Mother Captain. I can tell you this – *Raphael* will be rejoining the task force in Tau Ceti System after our mission is completed.'

With her left hand, Stone rubbed her cheek. De Soya watched the curled finger of her right hand. She would not have to raise the invisible handgun to trigger the deathbeam, but it was human instinct to aim the firearm at one's opponent.

De Soya hated deathbeams and he knew that Stone did as well. They were cowardly weapons: banned by Pax Fleet and the Church until this expeditionary force incursion. Unlike the old Hegemony-era deathwands that actually cast a scythe-like beam of neural disruption, no coherent projection was involved in the ship-to-target deathbeam. Essentially, the powerful Gideon-drive accumulators extended a C-plus distortion of space/time within a finite cone. The result was a subtle twisting of the real-time matrix – similar to a failed translation into the old Hawking-drive space – but more than enough to destroy the delicate energy dance that was a human brain.

But however much Stone held the Pax Fleet officer's hatred of deathbeams, it made sense for her to use it now. The *Raphael* represented a staggering investment of Pax funds: her first goal would be to stop the crew from stealing it without damaging the ship. Her problem, however, was that killing the crew with deathbeams probably would not stop *Raphael* from translating, depending upon how much of the spinup had been preprogrammed by her crew. It was traditional for a captain to make the actual translation manually – or at least to be ready to override the ship's computer with a dead-man switch – but Stone had no assurance that de Soya would follow tradition.

'Please let me speak to Commander Liebler,' said Mother Captain Stone.

De Soya smiled. 'My executive officer is attending to duties.' He thought, *So Hoag was the spy. This is the confirmation we needed.*

Gabriel could not catch them now, not even by accelerating to six hundred gravities herself. *Raphael* would have reached translation requirements before the other ship could get within tow range. No, to stop them, Stone would have to kill the crew and then disable the ship by using the last of her physical arsenal to overload *Raphael's* external containment fields. If she was wrong – if de Soya *was* acting under last-minute orders – she would almost certainly be court-martialed and expelled from Pax Fleet. If she did nothing, and de Soya was stealing one of the Pax's archangels. Stone would be court-martialed, expelled, excommunicated, and almost certainly executed.

'Federico,' she said softly, 'please reduce thrust so that we can match velocities. You can still follow orders and spin up to your secret coordinates. I ask only that I board the *Raphael*, and confirm that everything is all right before you translate.'

De Soya hesitated. He could not use the guise of orders for his precipitous departure under six-hundred-gravities, since wherever *Raphael* ended up, there would be two days of slow resurrection for the crew before the mission could continue. He watched Stone's eyes while also checking the tiny image of *Gabriel* on its three-hundred-gravity pillar of white fire. She might try overloading his fields with a salvo of her remaining conventional weaponry. De Soya had no wish to return missile or lance fire: a vaporized *Gabriel* was not acceptable. He was now a traitor to Church and state, but he had no intention of becoming a true-death murderer.

The deathbeams it had to be then.

'All right, Halen,' he said easily. 'I'll tell Hoag to drop to two-hundred-gs long enough for you to come alongside.' He turned his head as if concentrating on issuing bone-channel orders.

His hand must have twitched. Stone's did as well, the invisible handgun rising a bit as her finger tightened on the trigger.

In the split second before the disruption struck, Father Captain de Soya saw the eight sparks leaving the simtact *Gabriel*: Stone was taking no chances – she would vaporize *Raphael* rather than have it escape.

The mother-captain's virtual image flew backward and evaporated as the deathbeam tore into her ship, severing all com connections as the humans aboard died.

Less than a second later, Father Captain de Soya felt himself jerked out of simspace as the neurons in his brain literally fried. Blood flew from his eyes, mouth, and ears, but the priest-captain was already dead, as was every conscious entity on the *Raphael* – Sergeant Gregorius and his two troopers on C deck, GOPRO Meier, VIRO Argyle, ESSO Denish, and WHIZZO Shan on the flight deck.

Sixteen seconds later, the eight Hawking-drive missiles flashed into real space and detonated on every side of the silent *Raphael*.

Gyges watched in real-time as Raul Endymion said good-bye to the family in red robes and paddled his kayak toward the farcaster arch. The world was in dual lunar eclipse. Fireworks exploded above the canal-river and strange ululations came from thousands of throats back in the linear city. Gyges stood and prepared to walk out across the water to pluck the man from his kayak. It had been agreed that if Raul Endymion was alone, that he needed to be kept alive for interrogation in the starship waiting above – finding the girl Aenea's whereabouts was the goal of this mission – but no one said anything about not making it more difficult for the man to fight or escape. While still phase-shifted, Gyges planned to hamstring Endymion and sever the tendons in his forearms. He could do that instantly, surgically, so that there would be no danger of the human bleeding to death before being stored in the ship's doc-in-the-box before interrogation.

Gyges had jogged the six klicks to the farcaster arch in no time, checking out pedestrians and the strange windcarts as he passed the frozen forms and figures. Once at the arch and concealed in a patch of willows on the canal's high bank, he shifted back to slow time. His job was to guard the back door. Nemes would ping him when she found the missing spacer.

During the twenty minutes of waiting, Gyges communicated with Scylla and Briareus on the internal common band but heard nothing from Nemes. This was surprising. They had all assumed that she would find the missing man within the first few seconds of real-time after she had shifted up. Gyges was not worried – he was not actually capable of worry in the true sense of the word – but he assumed that Nemes had been searching in widening arcs, using up real-time by frequently shifting down and then back up. He assumed that his common-band queries had been made while she was phase-shifted. Added to that was his understanding that while Nemes was a clone-sibling, she had been the first to be devatted. She was less used to common-band sharing than Scylla, Briareus, and he. To be truthful, Gyges would not have minded if their orders had been simply to pull Nemes out of the rock on God's Grove and terminate her then and there.

The river was busy. Each time a ship approached the farcaster arch from either the east or west, Gyges shifted up and walked across the spongy surface of the river to search it and check on its passengers. Some he had to disrobe to ascertain that it was not Endymion or the android, A. Bettik, or the girl, Aenea, in disguise. To be sure, he sniffed them and took needle biopsies of the robed ones' DNA to make sure that they were natives of Vitus-Gray-Balianus B. All were.

After each inspection, he would walk back to the bank and resume his watch. Eighteen minutes after he had left the ship, a Pax skimmer flew around and through the farcaster arch. It would have been tiring for Gyges to have to board it in fast time, but Scylla was already aboard with the searching Pax troopers so he was spared the effort.

This is tiresome, she said on the common band.

Yes, agreed Gyges.

Where is Nemes? It was Briareus back in the city. The clumsy troopers had received their radioed search warrant and were going from house to house.

Haven't heard from her, said Gyges.

It was during the eclipse and the accompanying ceremonial nonsense that he watched the windcycle wagon pull to a halt and Raul Endymion emerge. Gyges was sure that it was Endymion. Not only did the visuals match perfectly, but he picked up the personal scent that Nemes had downloaded to them. Gyges could have phase-shifted immediately, walked over to the frozen tableau, and taken a DNA needle biopsy, but he did not have to. This was their man.

Instead of broadcasting on the common band or pinging Nemes, Gyges waited another minute. This anticipation was pleasurable to him. He did not want to dilute it by sharing it. Besides, he reasoned, it would be better to abduct Endymion after he had separated from the Spectrum Helix family who even now were waving good-bye to the man in the kayak.

Gyges watched while Raul Endymion paddled the absurd little boat out into the current of the widening canal-river. He realized that it would be best to take the kayak as well as Endymion: the watching Spectrum Helix people would be expecting him to disappear if they knew that he was trying to escape via farcaster. From their point of view, there would be a flash and Endymion would have farcast out of sight. In reality, Gyges would still be phase-shifted, now carrying the man and kayak within the expanded phase-shift field. The kayak might also be useful in revealing where the girl, Aenea, was hiding: telltale planetary scents, methods of manufacture.

Along the riverbanks to the north, people cheered and sang. The lunar eclipse was complete. Fireworks exploded above the river and cast baroque shadows on the rusted farcaster arch. Endymion turned his attention away from the waving Spectrum Helix family and concentrated on staying in the strongest current as he paddled toward the farcaster.

Gyges stood, stretched languidly, and prepared to phase-shift.

Suddenly the thing was next to him, centimeters away, at least three meters tall, towering over him.

Impossible, thought Gyges. *I would have sensed the phase-shift distortions.*

Exploding skyrockets spilled blood-red light on the chrome carapace. Metal teeth and chrome spikes twisted the expanding flowers of yellow, white, and red across quicksilver planes. Gyges caught an instant's look at his own reflection, distorted and startled, and then he phase-shifted.

It took less than a microsecond for the shift. Somehow one of the creature's four clawed hands made it into the field before it completely formed. Bladed fingers dug through synflesh and muscle, seeking one of Gyges's hearts.

Gyges paid no heed to the attack but attacked in return, swinging his silvered, phase-shifted arm like a horizontal guillotine. It could have cut through whiskered carbon alloy as if it were wet cardboard. It did not cut through the tall form in front of him. Sparks and thunder exploded as his arm bounced away, fingers numbed, metal radius and ulna shattered.

The clawed hand within him pulled out ropes of intestine, kilometers of microfiber optics. Gyges realized that he had been opened from navel to breastbone. It did not matter. He could still function.

Gyges clenched his right hand into a sharpened bludgeon and thrust it forward into gleaming red eyes. It was a killing blow. But the great steam-shovel jaws opened, closed, faster than phase-shifting, and Gyges's right arm suddenly ended above the wrist.

Gyges threw himself at the apparition, trying to merge fields, attempting to get his own teeth within tearing distance. Two huge hands seized him, the bladed fingers sinking through shift field and flesh to hold him tight. The chrome skull in front of him slashed forward: needle-spikes pierced Gyges's right eye and penetrated the right frontal lobe of his brain.

Gyges screamed then – not out of pain, although he felt something similar for the first time in his short life – but out of pure, relentless rage.

His teeth snapped and clacked like steel rendering blades as he sought the creature's throat, but he continued being held at three-arms' length.

Then the monster ripped out both of Gyges's hearts and threw them far out over the water. A nanosecond later, it lunged forward, biting through Gyges's throat and severing his carbon-alloy spinal cord with a single snap of long teeth. Gyges's head was severed from his body. He tried to shift to telemetric control of the still-fighting body, peering through blood and fluid out of his remaining eye and broadcasting over the common band, but the transmitter in his skull had been pierced and the receiver in his spleen had been ripped away.

The world spun – first the corona of the emerging sun around the second moon, then skyrockets, then the color-dappled surface of the river, then the sky again, then darkness. With fading coherence, Gyges realized that his head had been thrown far out into the river. His last retinal image before being submerged in darkness was of his own headless and uselessly spasming body being hugged to the carapace of the creature and being impaled there on spikes and thorns. Then, with a flash, the Shrike phase-shifted out of even fast-time existence and Gyges's head struck the water and sank beneath the dark waves.

Rhadamanth Nemes arrived five minutes later. She shifted down. The riverbank was empty except for the headless corpse of her sibling. The windcycle wagon and its red-robed family were gone. No boats were visible on this section of river. The sun was beginning to emerge from behind the second moon.

Gyges is here, she sent on the common band. Briareus and Scylla were still with the troops in the city. The sleeping Pax trooper had been found and released from his handcuffs. None of the citizens queried would say whose home it was. Scylla was urging Colonel Vinara to drop the matter.

Nemes felt the discomfort as she left the shift field. All of her ribs – bone and permasteel – were either fractured or bent. Several of her internal organs had been pulped. Her left hand would not function. She had been unconscious for almost twenty standard minutes. Unconscious! She had not lost consciousness for one second in the four years she had lain in the solidified rock of God's Grove. And all this damage had been done *through* the impenetrable shift field.

It did not matter. She would allow her body to repair itself during the days of inactivity after leaving this Core-forsaken world. Nemes knelt next to her sibling's corpse. It had been clawed, decapitated, and eviscerated – almost deboned. It was still twitching, the broken fingers struggling to get a grip on an absent enemy.

Nemes shuddered – not out of sympathy for Gyges or revulsion at the damage done, she was professionally evaluating the Shrike's attack pattern and felt admiration if anything – but out of sheer frustration that she had missed this confrontation. The attack in the tunnel had been too fast for her to react – she had been in mid-phase shift – which she would have thought impossible.

I'll find him, she sent and shifted up. The air grew thick and sludge-like. Nemes went down the bank, forced her way through the thick resistance of the water's surface, and walked out along the riverbed, calling on the common band and probing with deep radar.

She found Gyges's head almost a klick downstream. The current was strong here. Freshwater crustaceans had already eaten the lips and the remaining eye and were probing in the eye sockets. Nemes brushed them away and took the head back to the bank of the canal-river.

Gyges's common-band transmitter was smashed and his vocal cords were gone. Nemes extruded a fiber-optic filament and made the connection directly to his memory center. His skull had been smashed on the left side and brain matter and bits of DNA-processing gel were spilling out.

She did not ask him questions. She phased down and downloaded the memory, squirting it to her remaining two siblings as she received it.

Shrike, sent Scylla.

No shit, Sherlock, sent Briareus.

Silence, ordered Nemes. *Finish up with those idiots. I'll clean things up here and be waiting in the dropship.*

The Gyges head – blind, leaking – was trying to speak, using what remained of its tongue to shape sibilant and glottal syllables. Nemes held it close to her ear.

'Ss-t-pp-le-ssss.' *Please.* 'Ss – he – puh.' *Help.* 'Ssss-ttp – m-eh.' *Me.*

Nemes lowered the head and studied the body on the splattered bank. Many organs were missing. Scores of meters of microfiber were spilled in the weeds and mud, some trailing away in the current. Gray intestines and neural gelpaks were split and scattered. Bits of bone caught the growing light as the sun emerged from Twice Darkness. Neither the dropship nor the old archangel's doc-in-the-boxes could help the vatborn. And Gyges might take standard months to heal himself.

Nemes set the head down while she wrapped the body in its own micro-filaments, weighting it outside and in with stones. Making sure that the river was still free of ships, she tossed the headless corpse far out into the current. She had seen that the river was alive with tough and indiscriminate scavengers. Even so, there were parts of her sibling that they would not find appetizing.

She lifted Gyges's head. The tongue was still clucking. Using the eye sockets as grips for her thumb and forefinger, she threw the head far out over the river in an easy underhand toss. It went under with barely a ripple.

Nemes jogged to the farcaster arch, ripped a hidden access plate free from the rusting and supposedly impenetrable exterior, and extruded a filament from her wrist. She jacked in.

I don't understand, came Briareus's code on the common band. *It opened to nowhere.*

Not to nowhere, sent Nemes, reeling in the filament. *Just to nowhere in the old Web. Nowhere the Core has built a farcaster.*

That's impossible, sent Scylla. *There are no farcasters except for those the Core has built.*

Nemes sighed. Her siblings were idiots. *Shut up and return to the dropship,* she sent. *We have to report this in person. Councillor Albedo will want to download personally.*

Nemes phase-shifted and jogged back to the dropship through air gone thick and sepia with slow-stirred time.

TWELVE

I did not forget that there was a panic button. The problem is simple – when there is real panic, one does not immediately think of buttons.

The kayak was falling into an endless depth of air broken only by clouds that rose tens of thousands of meters from the bruise-purple depths to the milky ceiling of more clouds thousands of meters above me. I had dropped my paddle and watched it tumble away in freefall. The kayak and I were dropping faster than the paddle for reasons of aerodynamics and terminal velocity that were beyond my powers to calculate at that particular moment. Great oval surges of water from the river I had left behind were falling ahead and behind me, separating and shaping themselves into ovoid spheres I had seen in zero-g, but then being whipped apart by the wind. It was as if I were falling in my own localized rainstorm. The flechette pistol I had liberated from the sleeping trooper in Dem Loa's bedroom was wedged between the outside of my thigh and the curved inner seal of the cockpit skirt. My arms were raised as if I were a bird preparing to take flight. My fists were clenched in terror. After my original scream, I found my jaws locked shut, my molars grinding. The fall went on and on.

I had caught a glimpse of the farcaster arch above and behind me, although 'arch' was no longer the proper word: the huge device floating unsupported was a metal ring, a torus, a rusty doughnut. For a fleeting second I saw the sky of Vitus-Gray-Balianus B through the glowing ring, and then the image faded and only clouds showed through the receding hoop. It was the only substantial thing in the entire skyscape of clouds and I had already fallen more than a thousand meters below it. In a giddy, panicked moment of fantasy, I imagined that if I were a bird I could fly back up to the farcaster ring, perch on its broad lower arc, and wait for . . .

Wait for what? I gripped the sides of the kayak as it rotated, turning me almost upside down as it plummeted bow first toward the purple depths klicks and klicks below.

That is when I remembered the panic button. *Don't touch it, whatever you do,* Aenea had said when we floated the kayak in Hannibal. *I mean, don't touch it until you absolutely have to.*

The kayak spun on its longitudinal axis again, almost shaking me out. My butt was no longer touching the padded cushion on the bottom of the hull. I was floating free inside the cramped cockpit, within a freefalling constellation of water, tumbling paddle, and plunging kayak. I decided that this qualified as an 'absolutely have to' time. I flipped up the plastic cover and depressed the red button with my thumb.

Panels popped open in front of the cockpit, near the bow, and behind me. I ducked as lines and masses of fabric billowed out. The kayak righted itself and then braked so hard that I was almost thrown out. I clung fiercely to the sides of the fiberglass boat as it rocked wildly. The shapeless mass over my head seemed to be forming itself into something more complicated than a parachute. Even in the middle of my adrenaline rush and molar-grinding panic, I recognized the fabric: memory cloth that A. Bettik and I had bought at the Indian Market near Taliesin West. The solar-powered, piezoelectric material was almost transparent, ultralight, ultrastrong, and could remember up to a dozen pre-set configurations; we had considered buying more and using it to replace the canvas over the main architects' studio since the old cover sagged, rotted, and had to be repaired and replaced regularly. But Mr Wright had insisted on keeping the old canvas. He preferred the buttery light. A. Bettik had taken the dozen or so meters of memory cloth down to his workshop and I had thought no more of it.

Until now.

The fall was stopped. Now the kayak hung under a delta-shaped parasail, supported by a dozen nylon-10 risers that rose from strategic positions along the upper hull. The boat and I were still descending, but in a gradual swoop now rather than a headlong fall. I looked up – the memory cloth was clear enough to see through – but the farcaster ring was too far behind me and hidden by clouds. The winds and air currents were carrying me away from the farcaster.

I suppose that I should have been grateful to my friends, the girl and the android, for somehow foreseeing this and preparing the kayak appropriately, but my first thought was an overwhelming *Goddamn you!* This was too much. Being dropped into a world of clouds and air, with no ground, was too damned much. If Aenea had known that I was being 'cast here, why didn't she . . .

No ground? I leaned over the edge of the kayak and looked below. Perhaps the plan was for me to float gently down to some unseen surface.

No. There were kilometers of empty air beneath me, and below that, the lower layers were purple and black, a darkness relieved only by fierce slashes of lightning. The pressure down there must be terrible. Which brought up another point: if this was a Jovian world – Whirl or Jupiter or one of the others – how was it that I was breathing oxygen? As far as I knew, all of the gas giants that humanity had encountered were made up of unfriendly gases – methane, ammonia, helium, carbon monoxide, phosphine, hydrogen cyanide, other nasties, with trace amounts of water. I had never heard of a gas giant with breathable oxygen-nitrogen mix, but I was breathing. The air was thinner here than on the other worlds I had traveled through, and it stank a bit of ammonia, but I was definitely breathing air. Then it must not be a gas giant. Where the hell was I?

I lifted my wrist and spoke to the comlog, 'Where the hell am I?'

There was a hesitation and for a moment I thought the thing had been broken on Vitus-Gray-Balianus B. Then it spoke in the ship's supercilious voice, 'Unknown, M. Endymion. I have some data, but it is incomplete.'

'Tell me.'

There followed a rapid-fire listing of temperatures in Kelvin, atmospheric pressure in millibars, estimated mean density in grams per centimeter cubed, probable escape velocity in kilometers per second, and perceived magnetic field in gauss, followed by a long list of atmospheric gases and element ratios.

'Escape velocity of fifty-four point two klicks per second,' I said. 'That's gas-giant territory, isn't it?'

'Most assuredly,' said the ship's voice. 'Jovian baseline is fifty-nine point five kilometers per second.'

'But the atmosphere isn't like a gas giant's?' I could see the stratocumulus ahead of me building, like a nature holo run at accelerated speeds. The towering cloud must have reached ten klicks above me, its base disappearing in the purple depths below. Lightning flickered at its base. The sunlight on its far side seemed rich and low: evening light.

'The atmosphere is unlike anything in my records,' said the comlog. 'Carbon monoxide, ethane, acetylene, and other hydrocarbons violating Solmev equilibrium values can be easily explained by Jovian-style molecular kinetic energy and solar radiation breaking down methane, and the presence of carbon monoxide is a standard result of methane and water vapor mixing at deep layers where the temperature exceeds twelve hundred degrees Kelvin, but the oxygen and nitrogen levels . . .'

'Yes?' I prompted.

'Indicate life,' said the comlog.

I turned completely around, inspecting the clouds, and sky as if something were sneaking up on me. 'Life on the surface?' I said.

'Doubtful,' came the flat voice. 'If this world follows Jovian-Whirl norms, the pressure at the so-called surface would be under seventy million Old Earth atmospheres with a temperature of some twenty-five thousand degrees Kelvin.'

'How high are we?' I said.

'Uncertain,' said the instrument, 'but with the current atmospheric pressure of point seven six Old Earth standard, on a standard Jovian world I would estimate that we were above the troposphere and tropopause, actually in the lower reaches of the stratosphere.'

'Wouldn't it be colder that high? That's almost outer space.'

'Not on a gas giant,' said the comlog in its insufferable professorial voice. 'The greenhouse effect creates a thermal inversion layer, heating layers of the stratosphere to almost human-optimum temperatures. Although the difference of a few thousand meters may show pronounced temperature increases or drops.'

'A few thousand meters,' I said softly. 'How much air is above and below us?'

'Unknown,' said the comlog again, 'but extrapolation would suggest that equatorial radius from the center of this world to its upper atmosphere would be approximately seventy thousand kilometers with this oxygen-nitrogen-carbon-dioxide layer extending for some three to eight thousand kilometers approximately two-thirds of the distance from the planet's hypothetical center.'

'A three- to eight-thousand-klick layer,' I repeated stupidly. 'Some fifty thousand klicks above the surface . . .'

'Approximately,' said the comlog, 'although it should be noted that at near-core pressures, molecular hydrogen becomes a metal . . .'

'Yeah,' I said. 'That's enough for now.' I felt like I was going to be sick over the side of the kayak.

'I should point out the anomaly that the interesting coloration in the nearby stratocumulus suggests the presence of ammonium monosulfide or polysulfides, although at apotropospheric altitudes, one would assume only the presence of ammonia cirrus clouds with true water clouds not forming until depths reach some ten standard atmospheres because of . . .'

'Enough,' I said.

'I only point this out because of the interesting atmospheric paradox involving . . .'

'Shut up,' I said.

It got cold after the sun went down. The sunset itself I shall remember until I die.

High, high above me, glimpses of what might be blue sky had darkened to a Hyperion-like deep lapis and then deepened further to dark purple. The clouds all around me grew brighter as the sky far above and the depths far below both grew darker. I say clouds, but the generic term is laughably unequal to conveying the power and grandeur of what I watched. I grew up in a nomadic shepherd caravan on the treeless moors between Hyperion's Great South Sea and the Pinion Plateau: I know clouds.

Far above me, feathered cirrus and rippled cirrocumulus caught the twilight in a pastel riot of soft pinks, rose glows, violet tinges, and golden backlighting. It was as if I were in a temple with a high, rosy ceiling supported by thousands of irregular columns and pillars. The columns and pillars were towering mountains of cumulus and cumulonimbus, their anvil-shaped bases disappearing in the darkening depths hundreds or thousands of kilometers below my floating kayak, their rounded summits billowing high into the halo-tinged cirrostratus hundreds or thousands of kilometers above me. Each column of cloud caught the low, rich light passing through openings in the cloud many thousands of klicks to the west, and the light seemed to ignite the clouds as if their surfaces were made of wildly flammable material.

'Monosulfide or polysulfides,' the comlog had said: well, whatever constituted these tawny cumulus in the diffuse daylight, sunset set them afire with rust-red light, brilliant crimson streaks, bloody tractus streaming away from the main cloud masses like crimson pennants, rose-colored fibratus weaving together the cirrus ceiling like muscle strands under the flesh of a living body, billowing masses of cumulus so white that they made me blink as if snowblinded, golden, striated cirroform spilling out from the boiling cumulonimbus towers like masses of blond hair blowing back from pale, upturned faces. The light deepened, richened, became so intense that it brought tears to my eyes, and then it became even more brilliant. Great, nearly horizontal shafts of Godlight burned between the columns, illuminating some here, casting others into shadow there, passing through ice clouds and bands of vertical rain on their way, spilling hundreds of simple rainbows and a thousand multiple rainbows. Then shadows moved up from the bruise-black depths, shading more and more of the still-writhing billows of cumulus and nimbus, finally climbing into the high cirrus and pond-rippled altocumulus, but at first the shadows brought not grayness or darkness, but an infinite palette of subtleties: gleaming gold dimming to bronze, pure white becoming cream and then dimming to sepia and shade, crimson with the boldness of spilled blood slowly darkening to the rust-red of dried blood, then fading to an autumnal tawny russet. The hull of my kayak lost its glint and the parasail above me quit catching the light as this vertical terminator moved past and above me. Slowly these shadows crept higher – it must have taken at least thirty minutes, although I was too absorbed in watching to check my comlog – and when they reached the cirrus ceiling, it was as if someone had dimmed all the lights in the temple.

It was one hell of a sunset.

I remember blinking then, overwhelmed by the interplay of light and cloud shadow and the oddly disturbing kinetic restlessness of all those broiling cloud masses, ready to rest my eyes while true darkness fell and to gather my thoughts. And that is when the lightning and aurora began playing.

There had been no aurora borealis on Hyperion – or if there had been, I had never seen it. But I had seen an example of Old Earth's northern lights on a peninsula that had once been the Scandinavian Republic while on my round-the-world dropship tour of that planet: they had been shimmering and gooseflesh-producing, rippling and dancing along the northern horizon like the filmy gown of a ghost dancer.

This world's aurora held none of that subtlety. Bands of light, solid striations of light – as discrete and discernible as the keys of a vertical piano – began dancing high in the sky in the direction I thought of as south. Other curtains of green, gold, red, and cobalt began shimmering against the dark world of air beneath me. These grew longer, broader, taller, stretching to meet and blend with other curtains of leaping electrons. It was as if the planet were cutting paper dolls out of shimmering light. Within minutes, every part of the sky was alive and dancing with vertical, slanted, and near-horizontal ribbons of banded color. The cloud towers became visible again, billows and pennants reflecting the strobe of thousands of these cold lights. I could almost hear the hiss and rasp of solar particles being driven along the terrifying lines of magnetic force banding this giant world.

I *could* hear them: crashes, rumbles, snappings, loud pops, long chains of cracking sounds. I swiveled in my little cockpit and leaned over the hull to look straight down. The lightning and thunder had begun.

I had seen enough lightning storms as a child on the moors. On Old Earth, Aenea, A. Bettik, and I regularly used to sit outside her shelter in the evening and watch the great electrical storms move over the mountains to the north. Nothing had prepared me for this.

The depths, as I had called them, had been little more than a dark floor so far below me as to be laughable, a broiling promise of terrible pressures and more terrible heat. But now those depths were alive with light, leaping with lightning storms that moved from one visible horizon to the rest like a chain of nuclear bombs going off. I could imagine entire hemispheres of cities being destroyed in one of those rumbling chain reactions of light. I gripped the side of the kayak and reassured myself that the storms were hundreds of klicks below me.

The lightning moved up the towers of cumulonimbus. Flashes of internal white light vied with the shimmers of colored light from the connecting auroras. The thunder-noise was subsonic, then sonic, subtly terrifying at first, then not subtle, but even more terrifying. The kayak and its parasail bucked and rocked in sudden downdrafts and elevator-quick lifts of thermals. I gripped the sides with mad strength and wished to God that I were on any other world but this.

Then the lightning discharges began flashing from cloud tower to cloud tower.

The comlog and my own reasoning had evaluated the scale of this place – an atmosphere tens of thousands of klicks deep, a horizon so far away that I could have dropped scores of Old Earths or Hyperions between me and the sunset – but the lightning bolts finally convinced me that this was a world made for giants and gods, not for humankind.

The electrical discharges were wider than the Mississippi and longer than the Amazon. I had seen those rivers and I could see these bolts. I *knew*.

I hunkered down in my little cockpit as if that would help me when one of these bolts caught my little flying kayak. The hairs on my forearms were standing straight up and I realized that the crawling sensation I felt on my neck and scalp was precisely that – the hair on my head was writhing like a nest of snakes. The comlog was flashing overload alarms on its diskey plate. It was probably shouting at me as well, but I could not have heard a laser cannon firing ten centimeters from my ear in that maelstrom. The parasail rippled and tore at the risers as heated air and imploding vacuums battered us. At one point, riding the wake of a bolt that blinded me, the kayak swung above horizontal, higher than the parasail. I was sure that the risers were going to collapse, the kayak and I were going to fall into the parasail shroud, and we would fall for minutes – hours – until pressure and heat ended my screaming.

The kayak rocked back, then back again, then continued swinging like a maddened pendulum – but *under* the sail.

In addition to the storm of lightning beneath me, in addition to the rising chain of explosions in every tower of cumulus, in addition to the searing bolts that now laced the towers like a web of firing neurons in a brain gone berserk, bundles of ball lightning and chain lightning suddenly began breaking loose from the clouds and floating in the dark spaces where my kayak flew.

I watched one of these rippling, surging spheres of electricity drift not a hundred meters beneath me: it was the size of a small, round asteroid – an electric moonlet. The noise it made was beyond description, but memories surged unbidden of being caught in a forest fire in the Aquila fens, of the tornado that skipped over our caravan on the moors when I was five years old, of plasma grenades detonating against the great blue glacier on the Claw Iceshelf. No combination of these memories could match the energy violence tumbling along beneath the kayak like some runaway boulder made of blue and gold light.

The storm lasted more than eight hours. Darkness lasted another eight. I survived the first. I slept through the last. When I awoke, shaken and thirsty, filled with dreams of light and noise, still partially deafened, badly needing to urinate and worried about falling out of the cockpit while I knelt to do so, I saw that morning light was painting the opposite side of the cloud pillars that had replaced the temple columns from the night before. Sunrise was simpler than sunset: the brilliant white and gold crawled down from the cirrus ceiling, along the roiling sides of the cumulus and nimbus, down to my layer where I sat shaking from the cold. My skin and clothes and hair were wet. Sometime during that night's bedlam, it had rained on me and rained hard.

I got to my knees on the padded floor of the hull, held tight to the cockpit rim with my left hand, made sure that the kayak's swaying had steadied somewhat, and attended to business. The thin, gold stream glinted in morning light as it dropped into infinity. The depths were black, purple, and inscrutable once again. My lower back hurt and I remembered the kidney stone nightmare of the previous few days. That seemed like another life to me now, long ago and far away. *Well*, I thought, *if there's another tiny stone being passed, I'm not going to catch it today.*

I was buttoning up and settling back into the cockpit, trying to stretch my aching legs without actually falling out, thinking about the impossibility of finding another farcaster ring anywhere in this endless sky after that night of being blown off course – as if I had ever *had* a course – when I suddenly realized that I was not alone.

Living things were rising from the depths and circling around me.

At first I saw only one creature and had no scale with which to judge the size of the visitor. The thing could have been a few centimeters across and only meters from my floating kayak, or many kilometers across and far, far away. Then the organism swam between a distant cloud pillar and a more distant cumulus tower, and I realized that kilometers was a more reasonable guess of size. As it came closer, I saw the myriad of smaller forms accompanying it through the morning sky.

Before I attempt to describe the things, I have to say that little in the history of humankind's expansion in this arm of the galaxy had prepared us to describe large alien organisms. On the hundreds of worlds explored and colonized during and after the Hegira, most of the indigenous life discovered had been plants and a few very simple organisms, such as the radiant gossamers on Hyperion. The few large, evolved animal forms – the Lantern Mouths on Mare Infinitus, say, or the zeplins of Whirl – tended to be hunted to extinction. The more common result was a world filled with a few indigenous life-forms and a myriad of human-adapted species. Humanity had terraformed all these worlds, bringing its bacteria and earthworms and fish and birds and land animals in raw DNA form, defrosting embryos in the early seedships, building birthing factories in the later expansions. The result had been much as on Hyperion – vital indigenous plants such as the tesla trees and chalma and weirwood and some surviving local insects coexisting with thriving Old Earth transplants and biotailored adapts such as triaspen, everblues, oak trees, mallards, sharks, hummingbirds, and deer. We were not used to alien animals.

And these were definitely alien animals rising to meet me.

The largest one reminded me of the cuttlefish – again, one of Old Earth's adapts – that thrived in the warm shallows of the Great South Sea on Hyperion. This creature was squidlike but almost transparent, its internal organs quite visible, although I admit that it was difficult to determine its exterior from its interior as it pulsed and throbbed and changed shape from second to second, almost like a starship morphing for battle. The thing had no head as such, not even a flattened, squidlike extension that might be considered a head, but I could make out a variety of tentacles, although fronds or filaments might be better words for the constantly swaying, retracting, extending, and quivering appendages. But these filaments were inside the pale, clear body as much as outside, and I was not sure if the creature's movement through the clear air was a result of the swimming motion of the filaments or because of gases expelled as the giant cuttlefish expanded and contracted.

As far as I could recall from old books and Grandam's explanations, the zeplins on Whirl were much simpler in appearance – blimp-shaped gasbags, mere medusalike cells to hold their mix of hydrogen and methane, storing and metabolizing helium in their crude liftsacs, giant jellyfish floating in the hydrogen-ammonia-methane atmosphere of Whirl. As best I could remember, the zeplins ate a sort of atmospheric phytoplankton that floated in the noxious atmosphere like so much airborne manna. There were no predators on Whirl . . . until humans arrived in their floating bathyscaphes to harvest the rarer gases.

As the cuttlefish creature grew closer, I saw the complexity of its innards: pale, pulsing outlines of organs and intestine-looking coils and what might be feeding filaments and tubes that might be for reproduction or elimination, and there were some appendages that might be sex organs, or perhaps eyes. And all the while it folded in on itself, retracted its curling filaments, then pulsed forward, tentacles extended fully, like a squid swimming through clear water. It was five or six hundred meters long.

I began to notice the other things. Around the cuttlefish swarmed hundreds or thousands of golden, disc-shaped creatures, ranging in size from tiny ones perhaps as large as my hand to others larger than the heavy river mantas used to pull barges on Hyperion's rivers. These things were also nearly transparent, although their insides were clouded by a sort of greenish glow that might have been an inert gas excited to luminescence by the animal's own bio-electrical field. These things swarmed around the cuttlefish, at times appearing to be swallowed or absorbed by some orifice or another, only to reappear outside again. I could not swear that I saw the cuttlefish *eating* any of the swarming discs, but at one point I thought that I could see a cloud of the green-glowing things moving along the inside of the cuttlefish's gut like ghostly platelets in a clear vein.

The monster and its cloud of companions floated closer, rising until the sunlight passed through its body on its way to light my kayak and parasail. I revised its size upward – it must be at least a klick long and a third that in width when it expanded to its widest. The living discs floated to each side of me now. I could see that they were spinning as well as curling like mantas.

I tugged out the flechette pistol Alem had given me and clicked off its safety. If the monster attacked, I would fire half the magazine of slivers into its pale side, hoping that it was as thin as it was transparent. Maybe there was a chance that I could spill whatever lift gases allowed it to float in this band of oxygen atmosphere.

At that moment, the thing's hydralike filaments flashed out in all directions, some missing my parasail by mere meters, and I realized that I could never kill or sink the monster before it destroyed my sail with one thrash of one tentacle. I waited, half expecting to be pulled into the cuttlefish's maw – if it had a maw – at any second.

Nothing happened. My kayak floated in the direction I thought of as westward, the parasail rising on thermals and descending on colder downdrafts, the clouds towering around me, and the cuttlefish and its companions – I thought of them as parasites for no good reason – stood off a few hundred meters to the 'north' and a hundred meters or so above me. I wondered if the thing was following me out of curiosity or hunger. I wondered if the green platelets drifting around me might attack at any moment.

Capable of doing nothing else, I laid the useless flechette pistol on my lap, nibbled on the last of my biscuits from my pack, and sipped from my water bottle. I had less than another day's supply of water. I cursed myself for not trying to catch rainwater during the night's terrible storm, although I had no idea if this world's water was potable.

The long morning grew into a long afternoon. Several times the drifting parasail took me into a cloud tower and I raised my face to the dripping fog, licking droplets from my lips and chin. The water tasted like water. Each time I emerged from the fog, I expected the cuttlefish to have departed, but each time it remained on station to my right and above me. Once, just after the halo that was the sun above had passed the zenith, the kayak was blown into a particularly rough patch of climbing cloud, and the parasail almost folded in the violent updraft. But it stabilized itself and when I emerged from the cloud that time, I was some kilometers higher. The air was thinner and colder. The cuttlefish had followed me up.

Perhaps it's not hungry yet. Perhaps it feeds after dark. I reassured myself with a series of these thoughts.

I kept scanning the empty sky between clouds for another farcaster ring, but none appeared. It seemed folly to expect to find one – the air currents blew me generally westward but the vagaries of the jet stream sent me klicks north and south. How could I thread such a small needle after a day and night and day of blowing around like this? It did not seem likely. But still I searched the sky.

In mid-afternoon I realized that there were other living things visible far below to the south. More cuttlefish moving about the base of an immense cloud tower, the sunlight piercing the depths enough to illuminate their clear bodies against the black of the broiling depths beneath them. There must be scores – no, hundreds – of the pulsing, swimming things along the base of that one cloud. I was too far away to make out the platelet parasites around them, but a sense of diffused light there – like dust floating – suggested their presence by the thousands or millions. I wondered if the monsters usually kept to the lower atmospheric levels and this one – still keeping pace with me within feeding-filament range – had ventured up out of curiosity.

My muscles were cramping. I pulled myself out of the cockpit and tried stretching along the top of the kayak's hull, hanging on to the parasail risers to keep my balance. It was dangerous, but I had to stretch. I lay on my back and pedaled an imaginary bicycle with my raised legs. I did push-ups, clinging to the rim of the cockpit for balance. When I had worked most of the cramps out, I crawled back into the cockpit and half dozed.

Perhaps it is odd to admit, but my mind wandered all that afternoon, even while the alien cuttlefish swam alongside within swallowing range and alien platelet creatures danced and hovered within meters of the kayak and parasail. The human mind gets used to strangeness very quickly if it does not exhibit interesting behavior.

I began thinking about the past few days and the past months and the past years. I thought of Aenea – of leaving her behind – and of all the other people I had left behind: A. Bettik and the others at Taliesin West, the old poet on Hyperion, Dem Loa and Dem Ria and their family on Vitus-Gray-Balianus B, Father Glaucus in the frozen air tunnels of Sol Draconi Septem, Cuchiat and Chiaku and Cuchtu and Chichticu and the other Chitchatuk on that same world – Aenea had been sure that Father Glaucus and our Chitchatuk friends had been murdered after we left that world, although she had never explained how she could know that – and I thought about others I had left behind, working my way back to my last sight of Grandam and the Clan members waving as I left for Home Guard service many years ago. And always my thoughts returned to leaving Aenea.

I've left too many people. And let too many people do my work and fighting for me. From now on I will fight for myself. If I ever find the girl again, I will stay with

Aenea forever. The resolution burned like anger through me, fueled by the hopelessness of rinding another farcaster ring in this endless cloudscape.

YOU KNOW
THE ONE WHO TEACHES
SHE HAS TOUCHED
YOU (!?!?)

The words were not carried by sound nor heard by my ears. Rather, they were like blows to the inside of my skull. I literally reeled, gripping the sides of the kayak to keep from falling out.

HAVE YOU
BEEN TOUCHED/CHANGED
LEARNING
TO HEAR/SEE/WALK
FROM
THE ONE WHO TEACHES
(????)

Every word was a migraine blow. Each struck with the force of brain hemorrhage. The words were shouted inside my skull in my own voice. Perhaps I was going mad.

Wiping away tears, I peered at the giant cuttlefish and its swarm of green-platelet parasites. The larger organism pulsed, contracted, extended coiling filaments, and swam through the chilly air. I could not believe that these words were coming from that creature. It was too biological. And I did not believe in telepathy. I looked at the swarming discs, but their behavior showed no more sense of higher consciousness than dust motes in a shaft of light – less than the synchronized shifting of a school of fish or the flocking of bats. Feeling foolish, I shouted, 'Who are you? Who is speaking?'

I squinted in preparation for the blast of words against my brain, but there was no response from the giant organism or its companions.

'Who spoke?' I shouted into a rising wind. There was no answering sound except for the slap of the risers against the canvas of the parasail.

The kayak slewed to the right, righted itself, and slewed again. I swiveled to my left, half expecting to see another cuttlefish monster attacking me, but instead saw something infinitely more malevolent approaching.

While I had been focusing on the alien creature to the north, a billowing, black cumulus had all but surrounded me to the south. Wind-tattered streamers of black whirled out from the heat-driven storm cloud and roiled under me like ebony rivers. I could see lightning flashing in the depths below and surging spheres of ball lightning being spat from the black column of storm. Closer, much closer, hanging from the river of black cloud flowing above me, curled a dozen or more tornadoes, their funnel clouds striking toward me like scorpion tails. Each funnel was the size of the cuttlefish monster or larger – vertical kilometers of whirling madness – and each was spawning its own cluster of smaller tornadoes. There was no way

615

that my flimsy parasail could withstand even a close miss by one of these vortexes and there was no way that the funnels were going to miss me.

I stood up in the pitching, rolling cockpit, holding my place in the boat only by grasping a riser with my left hand. With my right hand I made a fist, raised it, and shook it toward the tornadoes, toward the roiling storm beyond them, and toward the invisible sky beyond. 'Well, goddamn you then!' I shouted. My words were lost in the wind howl. My vest flapped around me. A gust nearly blew me into the maelstrom. Leaning far out over the hull of the kayak, bracing myself into the wind like a ski jumper I had seen once on the Iceshelf caught in a moment of mad, poised balance before the inevitable descent, I shook my fist again and screamed, 'Do your worst, goddamn you. I defy you gods!'

As if in answer, one of the tornado funnels came sidewinding closer, the lowest tip of its whirling cone stabbing downward as if seeking a hard surface to destroy. It missed me by a distance of hundreds of meters, but the vacuum of its passing whirled the kayak and parasail around like a toy boat in a draining bathtub. Relieved of the opposition of the wind, I fell forward onto the slippery kayak hull and would have slid into oblivion if my scrabbling hands had not found a riser to grip. My feet were fully out of the cockpit at that moment.

There was a hailstorm traveling with the passing funnel. Ice pellets – some the size of my fist – smashed through the parasail, pounded the kayak with a noise like flechette clouds slamming home, and hit me in the leg, shoulder, and lower back. The pain almost made me release my grip. That mattered little, I realized as I clung to the pitching, dipping kayak, because the sail had been torn in a hundred places. Only its canopy had saved me from being shot to bits by the hail, but now the delta-shaped foil had been riddled. It lost lift as suddenly as it had first gained it and the kayak pitched forward toward the darkness so many thousands of klicks below. Tornadoes filled the sky around me. I gripped the now-useless riser where it entered the battered hull and hung on, determined to complete that one act – hanging on – until the boat, furled sail, and I were all crushed by pressure or shredded by the winds. I realized that I was screaming again, but the sound was different in my ears – almost gleeful.

I had fallen less than a kilometer, the kayak and me gaining speed far beyond Hyperion's or Old Earth's terminal velocity, when the cuttlefish – forgotten behind and above me – made its lunge. It must have moved with blinding speed, propelling itself through the air like a squid jetting after its prey. The first I knew that it was hungry and determined not to lose its dinner was when the long feeding tendrils surged around me like so many huge tentacles coiling and probing and wrapping.

If the thing had tugged me to an immediate stop at the speeds the boat and I were falling, both kayak and I would have been snapped into small pieces. But the cuttlefish fell with us, surrounding the boat, sail, risers, and me with the smallest of its tendrils – each still two to five meters thick – and then it braked itself against the fall, jetting ammonia-smelling gases like a dropship on final approach. Then it began ascending again, up toward the storm where tornadoes still raged and the central stratocumulus rotated with its own black intensity. Only half-conscious, I realized that the cuttlefish was flying into that roiling cloud even as it reeled the bashed kayak and me toward an opening in its immense transparent body.

Well, I thought groggily, *I've found its mouth.*

Risers and shreds of parasail lay around me and over me like an oversized shroud. The kayak seemed to be draped in drab bunting as the cuttlefish pulled us in closer. I tried to turn, thought of crawling back toward the cockpit and finding the flechette gun, of cutting my way out of the thing.

The flechette gun was gone, of course, shaken out of the cockpit in all the violent tumbling and the fall. Also gone were the cockpit cushions and my backpack with the clothes, food, water, and flashlight laser. Everything was gone.

I tried to chuckle, but the sound was not quite successful as the tendrils pulled the kayak and its clinging passenger the last fifty meters to the gaping orifice on the underside of the cuttlefish's body. I could see the internal organs more clearly now – pulsing and absorbing, moving in peristaltic waves, some of them filled with the green platelet creatures. As I was pulled closer, there came an almost overwhelming stench of cleaning fluid – ammonia, I realized – that made my eyes water and throat burn.

I thought of Aenea. It was not a prolonged or eloquent thought – just a mental glimpse of how she had looked on her sixteenth birthday, all short hair, sweat, and sunburn from her desert meditations – and I formed the single message, *Sorry, kiddo. I did my best to get to the ship and bring it to you. Sorry.*

Then the long feeding tendrils curled and folded and pulled the boat and me up into a lipless mouth that I realized must be thirty or forty meters across. I thought of the fiberglass and ultranylon parasail fabric and the carbon-fiber risers that were entering with me and had time for a last thought – *I hope some of this gives you a bellyache.*

And then I was pulled into the ammonia and fish smell, was vaguely aware that the air here in the creature's gut was not really breathable, decided to jump from the kayak rather than be digested, but lost consciousness before I could act or frame another coherent thought.

Without my knowledge or observation, the cuttlefish continued to rise through cloud blacker than a moonless night, its lipless mouth closing and disappearing on its seamless flesh, the kayak and sail and me nothing more than a shadow in the fluid contents of its lower tract.

THIRTEEN

Kenzo Isozaki was not surprised when the Swiss Guard came for him.

The Corps Helvetica colonel and eight troopers in full orange-and-blue dress uniforms with energy lances and deathwands arrived at the Torus Mercantilus unannounced, demanded to see CEO Isozaki in his private office, and presented him with an encrypted diskey ordering him to dress formally and appear before His Holiness, Pope Urban XVI. Immediately.

The colonel stayed in sight of Isozaki as the CEO stepped into his personal apartment, quickly showered, and dressed in his most formal white shirt, gray vest, red cravat, the double-breasted black demisuit with the gold buttons on the side, and black velvet cape.

'May I phone my associates and issue business instructions in case I should miss meetings scheduled for later today?' he asked the colonel as they stepped out of the lift into the main reception hall where the troopers made a sort of gold and blue corridor between the workstations.

'No,' said the Swiss Guard officer.

A Pax Fleet ramscout was docked where Isozaki's personal ship was usually berthed. The Pax crew gave the Mercantilus CEO the briefest of nods, instructed him to strap into his acceleration couch, and then they were boosting in-system with two torchships visible on the tactical holo display as they dropped into escort position.

They are treating me as a prisoner, not an honored guest, thought Isozaki. His face revealed nothing, of course, but a wave of something like relief followed the pulse of fear and dread in him. He had been expecting this since his illicit meeting with Councillor Albedo. And he had slept almost not at all since that painful and traumatic rendezvous. Isozaki knew that there was no reason for Albedo not to reveal the fact of the Mercantilus's attempts to contact the TechnoCore, but he hoped that they would believe that it was his attempt and his alone. Silently, Isozaki gave thanks to whatever gods that wanted to listen that his friend and associate, Anna Pelli Cognani, was out of Pacem System, visiting Renaissance Vector for a major trade fair there.

From his couch between the Swiss Guard colonel and one of the troopers, Isozaki could see the tactical holo in front of the pilot's position. The sphere of moving light and color with its solid bars of code was highly technical, but Isozaki had been a pilot before these boys were born. He could see that they were not accelerating toward the world of Pacem, but toward a destination near the trailing Trojan point, directly in the middle of the swarm of Pax Fleet asteroid bases and system-defense forts.

A Holy Office orbital prison, thought Isozaki. Worse than Castel Sant'Angelo where the virtual pain machines were said to run all hours of the day and night. In one of the orbital dungeons, no one could hear you scream. He was sure that the command to attend a papal audience was mere irony, a way to get him out of the Pax Mercantilus without protest. Isozaki would have bet anything that within days – perhaps hours – his formal suit and cape would be bloody, sweat-soaked rags.

He was wrong on all counts. The ramscout decelerated above the plane of the ecliptic and he realized their destination: Castel Gandolfo, the Pope's 'summer retreat'.

The diskey viewer in the CEO's couch worked and he called up an exterior view as the ramscout left its escorting torchships and dropped toward the massive, potato-shaped asteroid. More than forty klicks long and twenty-five across, Castel Gandolfo was a little world of its own, its sky blue, its oxygen-rich atmosphere held in by class-twenty containment fields wrapped with infinite redundancies, the hillsides and terraces green with grass and crops, the sculpted mountains forested and running with streams and small animals. Isozaki saw the ancient Italian village pass below and knew that the peaceful vision was deceptive: surrounding Pax bases could destroy any ship or fleet in existence, while the interior of asteroid Castel Gandolfo was honeycombed with garrisons holding more than ten thousand Swiss Guard and elite Pax troopers.

The ramscout morphed wings and flew the final ten kilometers on silent electric pulse jets. Isozaki saw the Swiss Guard troopers in full battle dress rise to escort the ship the final five klicks. Rich sunlight glinted off their dynamic-flow armor and transparent face shields as they encircled the ramscout and approached the castle at dead-slow speeds. Isozaki saw several of the troopers aim probes at the ship: confirming with deep radar and infrared what the encrypted manifest readouts had told them about the number and identity of passengers and crew.

A door opened in the side of one of the castle's stone towers and the ramscout floated in, pulse jets cool, the Swiss Guard troopers tugging the aircraft into place with the blue glow of their liftpacs.

The air lock cycled. The eight Swiss Guard troopers went down the ramp first, taking up their two lines as the colonel escorted Kenzo Isozaki out and down. The CEO was looking for a lift door or stairway, but the entire berthing level of the tower began to descend. The motors and gears were silent. Only the passing stone walls of the tower told of their movement downward and then sideways into the subterranean guts of Castel Gandolfo.

They stopped. A door appeared in the wall of cold stone. Lights illuminated a corridor of polished steel with floating, fiberplastic lens pods keeping watch at ten-meter intervals. The colonel gestured and Isozaki led the procession down the echoing tunnel. At the end, blue light washed over them all as other probes and sensors searched them inside and out. A chime rang and another portal appeared and irised open. This was a more formal waiting room. Three people stood when Isozaki and his escort entered.

Damn, thought the Pax Mercantilus CEO. Anna Pelli Cognani was there, dressed in her finest fresilk robes, as were CEOs Helving Aron and Kennet Hay-Modhino, Isozaki's other counterparts on the Executive Council of the Pancapitalist League of Independent Catholic Transstellar Trade Organizations.

Damn, thought Kenzo Isozaki again, his face staying absolutely impassive while he nodded silently to his associates. *They are going to hold all of us accountable for my actions. We will all be excommunicated and executed.*

'This way,' said the Swiss Guard colonel and opened an elaborately carved door. The room beyond was darker. Isozaki smelled candles, incense, and sweating stone. He realized that the Swiss Guardsmen were not going with them through that door. Whatever waited there waited for his party alone.

'Thank you, Colonel,' said CEO Isozaki in a pleasant voice. With firm strides, he led the way into the incense-filled darkness.

It was a small chapel, dark except for red votive candles flickering in a wrought-iron stand against one stone wall and two arched, stained-glass windows behind the simple altar at the far end. Six more candles burned on the bare altar while flames in braziers on the far side of the windows cast more ruddy light into the long, narrow room. There was only one chair, tall, straight-backed, velvet-cushioned, and placed to the left of the altar. In the back of the chair was embossed what at first appeared to be a cruciform, but what, upon second glance, was revealed to be the triple cross of the Pope. The altar and chair were set upon a low stone dais.

The rest of the chapel was without chairs or pews, but red velvet cushions had been set on the dark stone on either side of the aisle down which M.s Isozaki, Cognani, Hay-Modhino, and Aron walked. There were four cushions – two on either side of the aisle – that were not in use. The Mercantilus CEOs dipped fingers in the stone font holding holy water, crossed themselves, genuflected toward the altar, and went to their knees on the cushions. Before lowering his head in prayer, Kenzo Isozaki glanced around the tiny chapel.

Nearest the altar dais knelt Vatican Secretary of State Simon Augustino Cardinal Lourdusamy – a mountain of red and black in the ruddy light, his jowls and chins hiding his clerical collar as he bowed his head in prayer – and behind him knelt the scarecrow figure of his aide, Monsignor Lucas Oddi. Across the aisle from Lourdusamy, the Holy Office's Grand Inquisitor, John Domenico Cardinal Mustafa, knelt in prayer, his eyes closed. Next to him was the infamous intelligence agent and torturer, Father Farrell.

On Lourdusamy's side of the aisle, three Pax Fleet officers were on their knees: Admiral Marusyn – his silver hair glinting in the red light – and his aide, Admiral Marget Wu, and someone whose face it took Isozaki a moment to recall – Admiral Aldikacti. On the Grand Inquisitor's side of the aisle knelt Cardinal Du Noyer, prefect and president of *Cor Unum*. Du Noyer was a woman in her healthy seventies, standard, with a strong jaw and short-cropped gray hair. Her eyes were the color of flint. Isozaki did not recognize the middle-aged man in monsignoral robes who knelt behind the Cardinal.

The final four kneeling figures were the Mercantilus CEOs – Aron and Hay-Modhino on the Grand Inquisitor's side of the aisle, Isozaki and Pelli Cognani on the Secretary of State's side. Isozaki counted a total of thirteen people in the chapel. Not an auspicious number, he thought.

At that moment, a hidden door in the wall to the right of the altar opened silently and the Pope entered with four men in attendance. The thirteen people in the chapel rose quickly from their knees and stood with their heads bowed. Kenzo Isozaki had time to recognize two of the men with the Pope as aides and the third as head of papal security – faceless functionaries – but the fourth man, the man in gray, was Councillor Albedo. Only Albedo stayed with the Pope as His Holiness walked into the room, allowing the kissing of his ring and touching the heads of the gathered men and women as they knelt again. Finally His Holiness, Pope Urban XVI, took his seat in the straight-backed throne with Albedo standing behind him. The thirteen dignitaries in the room immediately stood.

Isozaki lowered his eyes, his face remaining a study in calm, but his heart pounded at his ribs. *Will Albedo expose us all? Have all these groups attempted secret contact with the Core? Are we to be confronted by His Holiness and then taken from here, our cruciforms removed, and then executed?* Isozaki thought it likely.

'Brothers and sisters in Christ,' began His Holiness, 'we are pleased that you have agreed to join us here this day. What we must say in this secret and silent place has remained a secret for centuries and must remain within this circle until formal permission to share it with others is granted from the Holy See. We so adjure and command you, upon the pain of excommunication and the loss of your souls to the light of Christ.'

The thirteen men and women murmured prayers and acquiescence.

'In the recent months and years,' continued His Holiness, 'there have occurred events both strange and terrible. We have witnessed these from afar – some of these we have foreseen with the help of Our Lord, Jesus Christ – and many we have prayed would pass from us, sparing our people, our Pax, and our Church from a test of wills, faith, and fortitude. But events occur as the Lord wills them to occur. It is not possible for even His most faithful servant to understand all events and portents, only to trust in His mercy when those events seem most threatening and perplexing.'

The thirteen dignitaries kept their eyes carefully downcast.

'Rather than relate these events from our perspective,' His Holiness said softly, 'we shall ask some of those who participated in them to report in full. Then we shall endeavor to explain the connections between such seemingly disparate occurrences. Admiral Marusyn?'

The silver-haired Admiral shifted slightly to face the others as well as His Holiness. He cleared his throat. 'Reports from a world called Vitus-Gray-Balianus B suggest that we came close to capturing the Hyperion-born man named Raul Endymion who eluded us – with our primary subject, the girl named Aenea – almost five standard years ago. Elements of a special force of the Noble Guard . . .' The Admiral nodded toward Pope Urban XVI, who lowered his gaze in agreement. 'Elements of this special force,' continued Marusyn, 'tipped our commander on Vitus-Gray-Balianus B to the possible presence of this person. Although he escaped before our search of the area was completed, we did turn up definite DNA and micron-tag evidence that this was the same Raul Endymion who had been briefly incarcerated on the world of Mare Infinitus more than four years ago.'

Cardinal Lourdusamy cleared his throat. 'It might be helpful, Admiral, if you described how the suspect, Raul Endymion, escaped from this world of Vitus-Gray-Balianus B.'

Kenzo Isozaki did not blink, but he registered the fact that Lourdusamy was speaking for His Holiness in this conference.

'Thank you, Your Excellency,' said Admiral Marusyn. 'Yes, it appears that this Endymion both appeared on and escaped the planet via one of the ancient farcasters.'

There was no audible buzz in the room, but Isozaki sensed the psychic hum of interest and shock. There had been rumors for the past four years centering on Pax Fleet forces chasing some heretic who had managed to activate the dormant farcasters.

'And was this farcaster active when your men inspected it?' questioned Lourdusamy.

'Negative, Your Excellency,' said Admiral Marusyn. 'There was no sign of activity on either farcaster . . . the one upriver which must have granted the fugitive access to Vitus-Gray-Balianus B . . . nor the one downriver from the settlements.'

'But you are certain that this . . . Endymion . . . had not arrived on planet by some more conventional means? And equally certain that he is not hiding there now?'

'Yes, Your Excellency. This Pax world has excellent traffic control and orbital defenses. Any spacecraft approaching Vitus-Gray-Balianus B would have been detected light-hours from the planet. And we have turned the world upside down searching . . . administered Truthtell to tens of thousands of the inhabitants. The man named Endymion is not there. Witnesses did describe, however, a flash of light at the downstream farcaster at the precise moment that our sensors in and above that hemisphere registered a major energy surge consistent with old records of farcaster displacement fields.'

His Holiness raised his face and made a subtle gesture to Cardinal Lourdusamy.

'And I believe you have one other bit of unsettling news, Admiral Marusyn,' rumbled Lourdusamy.

The Admiral's countenance grew grimmer as he nodded. 'Aye, Your Excellency . . . Your Holiness. This involves the first mutiny in the history of Pax Fleet.'

Isozaki again sensed the unspoken murmur of shock. He showed no emotion or reaction, but out of the corner of his eye he saw Anna Pelli Cognani glancing at him.

'I will have Admiral Aldikacti brief us on this matter,' said Marusyn. He stepped back and folded his hands in front of him.

Isozaki noted that Aldikacti was one of those stocky Lusian women who seemed almost too androgynous to label with gender. She was as solid and blocky as a brick in a dress uniform.

Aldikacti did not waste time clearing her throat. She launched into an immediate briefing involving Task Force GIDEON, its mission to attack Ouster strongholds in seven systems far in the Outback, the successful outcome of that mission in all seven systems, and then the surprise in the final system, code-named Lucifer.

'To this point, the task force had performed beyond expectations and simulations,' barked Admiral Aldikacti. 'As a result, while completing operations in Ouster System Lucifer, I authorized a Gideon-drive drone to carry a message to Pacem . . . to His Holiness and Admiral Marusyn . . . requesting permission to refuel and refit in Tau Ceti System and then extend Task Force GIDEON's mission – attacking new Ouster systems before the alarm of our attack spread through the Outback. I received Gideon-drone permission to do this, and proceeded to take the bulk of my task force to Tau Ceti System for refueling, rearming, and rendezvous with five additional archangel starships which had come on-line since our task force had left Pax space.'

'You took the *bulk* of your task force?' queried Cardinal Lourdusamy in his soft rumble.

'Yes, Your Excellency.' There was no apology or quavering in Aldikacti's flat Lusian voice. 'Five Ouster torchships had escaped our detection and were accelerating toward a Hawking-drive translation point which would have presumably brought them out in another Ouster system. They would have spread the alarm of our task force's presence and lethality. Rather than divert the entire Task Force GIDEON, which was approaching our own translation point to Tau Ceti System, I authorized HHS *Gabriel* and HHS *Raphael* to remain in Lucifer System just long enough to intercept and destroy the Ouster torchships.'

Lourdusamy folded his pudgy hands in his robe. His voice was a deep purr. 'And you then translated your flagship, the *Uriel*, and four other archangels to Tau Ceti System?'

'Yes, Your Excellency.'

'Leaving the *Gabriel* and *Raphael* in Lucifer System?'

'Yes, Your Excellency.'

'And you were aware, Admiral, that the *Raphael* was commanded by Father Captain de Soya . . . the same captain who had been reprimanded some years earlier for not succeeding in his mission of finding and detaining the child, Aenea?'

'Yes, Your Excellency.'

'And you were aware, Admiral, that Pax Fleet and the Holy See were concerned enough about Father Captain de Soya's . . . ah . . . stability, that the Holy Office had assigned an undercover agent aboard the *Raphael* to observe and transmit observations on Father Captain de Soya's behavior and reliability?'

'A spy,' said Admiral Aldikacti. 'Commander Liebler. Yes, Your Excellency. I was aware that Holy Office agents aboard my flagship were receiving encoded tightbeam broadcasts from Commander Liebler aboard the *Raphael*.'

'And did these agents share any concerns or data from these broadcasts, Admiral Aldikacti?'

'Negative, Your Excellency. I was not made aware of the nature of the Holy Office's concerns related to Father Captain de Soya's loyalty or sanity.'

Cardinal Mustafa cleared his throat and raised one finger.

Lourdusamy, who had been in charge of what Isozaki and the others had quickly recognized as an inquisition, glanced at the Pope.

His Holiness nodded in the direction of the Grand Inquisitor.

'I feel it necessary to point out to His Holiness and the other worthies in this room that observation of Father Captain de Soya had been approved . . . directed . . . from the Office of the Holy See, with verbal authorization from the Secretary of State and Pax Fleet Command . . . specifically from Admiral Marusyn.'

There was a brief silence.

Finally Lourdusamy said, 'And can you tell us, Cardinal Mustafa, what the source of this shared concern had been?'

Mustafa licked his lips. 'Yes, Your Excellency. Our . . . ah . . . intelligence reports indicated that there might have been some chance of contamination during Father Captain de Soya's chase and rare contact with the subject named Aenea.'

'Contamination?' queried Lourdusamy.

'Yes, Your Excellency. It was our assessment that the girl named Aenea had the power to affect both the physical and psychological makeup of those Pax citizens with whom she came in contact. Our concern in this instance was for the absolute loyalty and obedience of one of Pax Fleet's starship commanders.'

'And how was this intelligence assessment made, Cardinal Mustafa?' continued Lourdusamy.

The Grand Inquisitor paused. 'A variety of intelligence sources and methods were used, Your Excellency.'

Lourdusamy did not pause. 'Among these were the fact that you have detained and . . . ah . . . interrogated one of Father Captain de Soya's fellow shipmen from the aforementioned abortive chase of subject Aenea, is that not correct, Cardinal Mustafa? A . . . ah . . . Corporal Kee, I believe?'

Mustafa blinked. 'That is correct, Your Excellency.' The Grand Inquisitor turned slightly so as to speak to the others in the room as well as the Pope and the Secretary of State. 'Such detention is unusual, but called for in a situation which appears to affect the security of the Church and the Pax.'

'Of course, Your Excellency,' murmured Cardinal Lourdusamy. 'Admiral Aldikacti, you may continue with the briefing.'

'Some hours after my five archangels jumped to Tau Ceti System,' said Aldikacti, 'and before any of us had completed our two-day resurrection cycle, a Gideon drone translated into Tau Ceti space. It had been launched by Mother Captain Stone . . .'

'Captain of the HHS *Gabriel*,' said Lourdusamy.

'Affirmative, Your Excellency. The drone's encrypted message . . . encrypted in a code for my eyes only . . . said that the Ouster torchships had been destroyed, but that the *Raphael* had gone rogue, was accelerating toward an unauthorized translation point, and would not respond to Mother Captain Stone's orders to stop.'

'In other words,' purred Lourdusamy, 'one of His Holiness's Pax Fleet ships had suffered a mutiny.'

'It appeared so, Your Excellency. Although in this case, the mutiny seemed to have been led by the ship's captain.'

'Father Captain de Soya.'

'Yes, Your Excellency.'

'And were there attempts made to contact the Holy Office agent aboard the *Raphael*?'

'Yes, Your Excellency. Father Captain de Soya said that Commander Liebler was attending to duties. Mother Captain Stone thought this unlikely.'

'And when challenged about the changed translation point?' queried Lourdusamy.

'Father Captain de Soya answered that I had tightbeamed changed orders to the *Raphael* prior to our task force's translation,' said Admiral Aldikacti.

'Did Mother Captain Stone accept this explanation?'

'Negative, Your Excellency. Mother Captain Stone closed the distance between the two archangels and engaged the *Raphael*.'

'What was the outcome of that engagement, Admiral?'

Aldikacti hesitated only a heartbeat. 'Your Excellency . . . Your Holiness . . . because Mother Captain Stone had used an eyes-only encryption for her drone message, it was a full day in Tau Ceti System – the time it took for my emergency resurrection – before I read the message and authorized an immediate return to Lucifer System.'

'How many ships did you take with you, Admiral?'

'Three, Your Excellency. My own flagship, the *Uriel*, with a fresh crew, and two of the archangels that had rendezvoused with us in Tau Ceti System . . . the *Mikal* and the *Izrail*. I felt that the risk of accelerating resurrection of the Task Force GIDEON crews was too great.'

'Although you accepted that risk yourself, Admiral,' said Lourdusamy.

Aldikacti said nothing.

'What happened then, Admiral?'

'We jumped immediately to Lucifer System, Your Excellency. There we recycled under twelve-hour automated resurrection. Many of the resurrections were unsuccessful. By combining the successfully resurrected crew members from all three ships, I was able to crew the *Uriel*. I left the other two starships in passive but automated defensive trajectories while I commenced searching for the *Gabriel* and the *Raphael*. I found neither. But a final beacon drone was soon discovered on the far side of Lucifer's yellow sun.'

'And the beacon was from . . .' prompted Lourdusamy.

'Mother Captain Stone. The beacon held the downloaded history of the *Gabriel*'s combat recorder. It showed the battle that had taken place less than two days before. Stone had attempted to destroy the *Raphael* by plasma and fusion weapons. The attempts failed. The *Gabriel* then engaged Father Captain de Soya's ship by deathbeam.'

There was silence in the tiny chapel. Isozaki watched the red light of the flickering votive candles painting the pained face of His Holiness, Pope Urban XVI.

'The outcome of that engagement?' said Lourdusamy.

'Both crews died,' said Aldikacti. 'According to automated instruments aboard the *Gabriel*, the *Raphael* completed automated translation. Mother Captain Stone had ordered her crew to resurrection-creche battle stations. She had programmed the *Gabriel*'s ship computers to resurrect her and several of the essential crew members on an emergency, eight-hour cycle. Only she and one of her officers survived the resurrection. Mother Captain Stone encoded the beacon and accelerated to the *Raphael*'s former translation point. She was determined to seek out and destroy the ship, preferably before de Soya and his crew completed resurrection . . . if they were in their creches at the time of the deathbeaming.'

'Did Mother Captain Stone know which system this translation point would open upon, Admiral?'

'Negative, Your Excellency. There were too many variables involved.'

'And what was your response to the beacon's data, Admiral?'

'I waited twelve hours for a working complement of the crews on the *Mikal* and the *Izrail* to complete resurrection, Your Excellency. I then translated all three of my ships through the jump point indicated by the *Raphael* and *Gabriel*. I left a second beacon for the archangels I was sure would be following from Tau Ceti System within hours.'

'You did not find it necessary to wait for these ships?'

'No, Your Excellency. I thought it important to translate as soon as all three of my ships were combat-ready.'

'But you *did* find it expedient to wait for the crews of these two ships, Admiral. Why did you not give chase immediately with only the *Uriel*?'

Aldikacti did not hesitate. 'It was a command combat decision, Your Excellency. I felt that the probabilities were very high that Father Captain de Soya had taken the *Raphael* to an Ouster system . . . quite possibly one more heavily armed than any Task Force GIDEON had encountered. I also felt it probable that Mother Captain Stone's ship, the *Gabriel*, had been destroyed by either the *Raphael* or Ouster ships within the unknown system. I felt that three ships of the line were the minimum force I could take into this unknown situation.'

'And was it an Ouster system, Admiral?'

'Negative, Your Excellency. Or at least, no sign of Ousters was discovered in the two weeks of investigation following this incident.'

'Where *did* the translation point take you, Admiral?'

'Into the outer shell of a red giant star,' said Admiral Aldikacti. 'Our containment-fields were, of course, activated, but it was a very close thing.'

'Did all three of your ships make it, Admiral?'

'Negative, Your Excellency. The *Uriel* and *Izrail* survived exit from the star and containment field cooling procedures. The *Mikal* was lost with all hands.'

'And did you find the *Gabriel* and the *Raphael*, Admiral?'

'Only the *Gabriel*, Your Excellency. It was discovered floating free some two AUs from the red giant. All systems were inoperative. There had been a breach of the containment field and the interior of the ship had melted into a single molten mass.'

'Were Mother Captain Stone and the other crew members found and resurrected, Admiral?'

'Unfortunately, no, Your Excellency. There was not enough discrete organic material remaining to pursue resurrection.'

'Was the slagging due to emergence in the red giant or attack from the *Raphael* or Ouster unknowns, Admiral?'

'It is still being determined by our materials experts, Your Excellency, but the preliminary report suggests an overload due to both natural and combat causes. The weapons used would have been consistent with the *Raphael*'s armament.'

'So you are saying that the *Gabriel* fought an automated engagement near this red giant sun, Admiral?'

'*Within* the star, Your Excellency. It seems that the *Raphael* turned about, reentered the star, and attacked the *Gabriel* within seconds of its emergence from Hawking space.'

'And is there a chance that the *Raphael* was also destroyed in this second engagement? The ship incinerated deep in the star?'

'A chance, Your Excellency, but we are not operating upon that assumption. It is our best guess that Father Captain de Soya then translated out of system to an unknown destination in the Outback.'

Lourdusamy nodded, his heavy jowls quivering slightly. 'Admiral Marusyn,' he rumbled, 'could you give us an assessment of this threat if the *Raphael* did indeed survive?'

The older Admiral stepped forward. 'Your Excellency, we have to assume that Father Captain de Soya and the other mutineers are hostile to the Pax and that this theft of a Pax archangel-class starship was premeditated. We also have to assume the worst-case scenario that this theft of our most secret and lethal weapons system was carried out in coordination with the Ousters.' The Admiral took a breath. 'Your Excellencies . . . Your Holiness . . . with the Gideon drive, any point in this arm of the galaxy is only an instant away from any other. The *Raphael* could translate into any Pax system – even Pacem's – without the Hawking-drive wake warnings of the earlier, and current, Ouster spacecraft. The *Raphael* could ravage our

Mercantilus transport lanes, attack undefended worlds and colonies, and generally wreak havoc before a Pax task force could respond.'

The Pope raised one finger. 'Admiral Marusyn, are we to understand that this most prized of Gideon-drive technologies may fall into the hands of the Ousters . . . be duplicated . . . and thus power many of the Enemy's ships?'

Marusyn's already florid face and neck flushed more deeply. 'Your Holiness . . . that is unlikely, Your Holiness . . . extremely unlikely. The steps of manufacture of a Gideon archangel are so complex, the cost so prohibitive, the secret elements so guarded . . .'

'But it is possible,' interrupted the Pope.

'Yes, Your Holiness.'

The Pope raised his hand like a blade cutting through the air. 'We believe that we have heard all we need to hear from our friends in Pax Fleet. You are excused, Admiral Marusyn, Admiral Aldikacti, Admiral Wu.'

The three officers genuflected, bowed their heads, stood, and backed away from His Holiness. The door whispered shut behind them.

There were now ten dignitaries present, in addition to the silent papal aides and Councillor Albedo.

The Pope inclined his head toward Secretary of State Cardinal Lourdusamy. 'Disposition, Simon Augustino?'

'Admiral Marusyn is to receive a letter of rebuke and will be transferred to general staff,' said Lourdusamy softly. 'Admiral Wu will take his place as temporary Pax Fleet commander in chief until a suitable replacement is found. Admiral Aldikacti has been recommended for excommunication and execution by firing squad.'

The Pope nodded sadly. 'We shall now hear from Cardinal Mustafa, Cardinal Du Noyer, CEO Isozaki, and Councillor Albedo before concluding this business.'

'. . . And thus ended the official inquiry by the Holy Office pertaining to the events on the Pax world of Mars,' concluded Cardinal Mustafa. He glanced at Cardinal Lourdusamy. 'It was at this time that Captain Wolmak suggested that it was imperative that my entourage and I return to the archangel *Jibril* still in orbit around that planet.'

'Please continue, Excellency,' murmured Cardinal Lourdusamy. 'Can you tell us the nature of the emergency which Captain Wolmak felt required your imperative return?'

'Yes,' said Mustafa, rubbing his lower lip. 'Captain Wolmak had found the interstellar freighter that had uploaded cargo from the unlisted base near the Martian city of Arafat-kaffiyeh. The ship had been discovered floating powerless in Old Earth System's asteroid belt.'

'Can you tell us the name of that ship, Excellency?' prompted Lourdusamy.

'The HHMS *Saigon Maru*.'

CEO Kenzo Isozaki's lips twitched despite his iron control. He remembered the ship. His oldest son had crewed on it during the early years of the boy's apprenticeship. The *Saigon Maru* had been an ancient ore and bulk freighter . . . about a three-million-ton ion sledge carrier, as he recalled.

'CEO Isozaki?' snapped Lourdusamy.

'Yes, Your Excellency?' Isozaki's voice was smooth and emotionless.

'The ship's designation suggests that it is of Mercantilus registry. Is this correct, M. Isozaki?'

'Yes, Your Excellency,' said the CEO. 'But it is my recollection that the HHMS *Saigon Maru* was sold for scrap along with sixty-some other obsolete freighters about . . . eight standard years ago, if memory serves.'

'Your Excellencies?' said Anna Pelli Cognani. 'Your Holiness? If I might?' The other CEO had whispered to her wafer-thin comlog and now touched her hearring.

'CEO Pelli Cognani,' said Cardinal Lourdusamy.

'Our records show that the *Saigon Maru* was indeed sold to independent scrap contractors some eight years, three months, and two days ago, standard. Later transmissions confirmed that the ships had been scrapped and recycled at the Armaghast orbital automated foundries.'

'Thank you, CEO Pelli Cognani,' said Lourdusamy. 'Cardinal Mustafa, you may continue.'

The Grand Inquisitor nodded and continued his briefing, covering only the most necessary details. And while he spoke he thought of the images he was not describing in detail:

The *Jibril* and its accompanying torchships slowing to silent, synchronized tumbling, matching velocities with the dark freighter. Cardinal Mustafa had always imagined asteroid belts as tightly packed clusters of moonlets, but despite the multiple images on the tactical plot, there were no rocks in sight: just the matte-black freighter, as ugly and functional as a rusted mass of pipes and cylinders, half a klick long. Matched as they were in velocity and trajectory, hanging only three klicks away with the yellow sun of humankind's birth burning beyond their sterns, *Jibril* and the *Saigon Maru* appeared motionless with only the stars wheeling slowly around them.

Mustafa remembered – and regretted – his decision to inspect the ship with the troopers who were going aboard. The indignities of suiting up in Swiss Guard combat armor: a monomol-D skinsuit layer, followed by an AI neural mesh, then the spacesuit itself – bulkier than civilian skinsuits with its polymered sheath of impact armor – and finally the web belts of gear and the morphable reaction pak. The *Jibril* had deep-radared the hulk a dozen times and was certain that nothing moved or breathed on board, but the archangel still backed off to thirty klicks' attack distance as soon as the Grand Inquisitor, Security Commander Browning, Marine Sergeant Nell Kasner, former Groundforce Commander Major Piet, and ten Swiss Guard/ Marine commandos had jumped from the sally port.

Mustafa remembered his pounding pulse as they jetted closer to the dead freighter, two commandos ferrying him across the abyss as if he were another parcel to carry. He remembered the sunlight glinting off gold blast visors as the troopers communicated with tightbeam squirts and hand signals, taking up positions on either side of the open air lock. Two troopers went in first, their reaction paks throbbing silently, assault weapons raised. Then Commander Browning and Sergeant Kasner went in fast behind them. A minute later there was a coded squirt on the tactical channel and Mustafa's handlers guided him into the waiting black hole of the air lock.

Corpses floating in the beams of flashlight lasers. Meat-locker images. Frozen carcasses, red-striped ribs, gutted abdominal cavities. Jaws locked open in eternally silent screams. Frozen streamers of blood from the gaping jaws and hemorrhaged, protruding eyes. Viscera drifting in tumbling trajectories amid the stabbing beams of light.

'Crew,' tightbeamed Commander Browning.

'Shrike?' queried Cardinal Mustafa. He was mentally saying the rosary in rapid monotone, not for spiritual reassurance but to keep his mind away from the images floating in hellish light before him. He had been warned not to vomit in his helmet. Filters and scrubbers would clean the mess before he strangled on it, but they were not foolproof.

'Probably the Shrike,' answered Major Piet, extending his gauntlet into the shattered chest cavity of one of the drifting corpses. 'See how the cruciform has been ripped out. Just as in Arafat-kaffiyeh.'

'Commander!' came a tightbeamed voice of one of the troopers who had moved aft from the air lock. 'Sergeant! Here! In the first cargo hold!'

Browning and Piet had gone ahead of the Grand Inquisitor into the long, cylindrical space. Flashlight lasers were lost in this huge space.

These corpses had not been slashed and shattered. They were stacked neatly on carbon slabs extruding from the hull on each side, held in place by nylon mesh bands. The slabs came out from all sides of the hull, leaving only a zero-g corridor down the center. Mustafa and his guides and keepers floated the length of this black space, flashlight lasers stabbing left, right, down, and up. Frozen flesh, pale flesh, barcodes on the soles of their feet, pubic hair, closed eyes, hands pale against black carbon by hipbones, flaccid penises, breasts frozen in zero-g weightlessness, hair tight on pale skulls or floating in frozen nimbuses. Children with smooth, cold skin, extended bellies, and translucent eyelids. Infants with barcoded soles.

There were tens of thousands of bodies in the four long cargo holds. All were human. All were naked. All were lifeless.

'And did you complete your inspection of the HHMS *Saigon Maru*, Grand Inquisitor?' prompted Cardinal Lourdusamy.

Mustafa realized that he had fallen silent for a long moment, possessed by the demon of that terrible memory. 'We did complete it, Your Excellency,' he answered, his voice thick.

'And your conclusions?'

'There were sixty-seven thousand eight hundred and twenty-seven human beings aboard the bulk freighter HHMS *Saigon Maru*,' said the Grand Inquisitor. 'Fifty-one of them were crew members. All of the crew members' bodies were accounted for. All had been slashed and rent in the same fashion as the victims at Arafat-kaffiyeh.'

'There were no survivors? None could be resurrected?'

'None.'

'In your opinion, Cardinal Mustafa, was the demon-creature called the Shrike responsible for the death of the crew members of the HHMS *Saigon Maru*?'

'In my opinion, it was, Your Excellency.'

'And in your opinion, Cardinal Mustafa, was the Shrike responsible for the deaths of the sixty-seven thousand seven hundred and seventy-six other bodies discovered on the *Saigon Maru*?'

Mustafa hesitated only a second. 'In my opinion, Your Excellency' – he turned his head and bowed in the direction of the man in the chair – 'Your Holiness . . . the cause of death of the sixty-seven thousand-some men, women, and children found on the HHMS *Saigon Maru* was *not* consistent with the wounds discovered on Mars's victims, or consistent with prior tales of Shrike attack.'

Cardinal Lourdusamy took a rustling step forward. 'And, according to your Holy Office forensic experts, Cardinal Mustafa, what *was* the cause of death for the human beings found aboard this freighter?'

Cardinal Mustafa's eyes were lowered as he spoke. 'Your Excellency, neither the Holy Office nor Pax Fleet forensic specialists could specify any cause of death for these people. In fact . . .' Mustafa stopped.

'In fact,' Lourdusamy continued for him, 'the bodies found aboard the *Saigon Maru* . . . exclusive of the crew . . . showed neither clear cause of death nor the attributes of death, is that not correct?'

'That is correct, Your Excellency.' Mustafa's eyes roamed to the faces of the other dignitaries in the chapel. 'They were not living, but they . . . showed no signs of decomposition, postmortem lividity, brain decay . . . none of the usual signs of physical death.'

'Yet they were not alive?' prompted Lourdusamy.

Cardinal Mustafa rubbed his cheek. 'Not within our capacity to revive, Your Excellency. Nor within our ability to detect signs of brain or cellular activity. They were . . . stopped.'

'And what was the disposition of the bulk freighter, HHMS *Saigon Maru*, Cardinal Mustafa?'

'Captain Wolmak put a prize crew aboard from the *Jibril*,' said the Grand Inquisitor. 'We returned immediately to Pacem to report the matter. The *Saigon Maru* was traveling via traditional Hawking drive, escorted by four Hawking-drive torchships, and is scheduled to arrive in the nearest Pax system with a Pax Fleet base . . . Barnard's System, I believe . . . in . . . ah . . . three standard weeks.'

Lourdusamy nodded slowly. 'Thank you, Grand Inquisitor.' The Secretary of State walked to a place near the Pope's chair, genuflected toward the altar, and crossed himself as he crossed the aisle. 'Your Holiness, I would ask that we hear from Her Excellency, Cardinal Du Noyer.'

Pope Urban raised one hand as if in benediction. 'We would be pleased to listen to Cardinal Du Noyer.'

Kenzo Isozaki's mind was reeling. Why were they being told these things? What possible purpose could it serve for the CEOs of the Pax Mercantilus to hear these things? Isozaki's blood had chilled at the summary death sentence of Admiral Aldikacti. Was that to be the fate of all of them?

No, he realized. Aldikacti had received a sentence of excommunication and execution for simple incompetence. If Mustafa, Pelli Cognani, himself, and the others were to be charged with some variety of treason . . . quick, simple execution would be the furthest thing from their fates. The pain machines in Castel Sant'Angelo would be humming and grating for centuries.

Cardinal Du Noyer obviously had chosen to be resurrected as an old woman. As with most older people, she looked in perfect health – all of her teeth, wrinkles at a minimum, dark eyes clear and bright – but she also preferred to be seen with her white hair – cut almost to the scalp – and skin tight across her sharp cheekbones. She began without preliminaries.

'Your Holiness, Excellencies, other worthies . . . I appear here today as prefect and president of *Cor Unum* and de facto spokesperson for the private agency known as *Opus Dei*. For reasons which shall become apparent, the administrators of *Opus Dei* could not and should not be present here this day.'

'Continue, Your Excellency,' said Cardinal Lourdusamy.

'The bulk freighter the HHMS *Saigon Maru* was purchased by *Cor Unum* for *Opus Dei*, diverted from scrap recycling, and delivered to that agency seven years ago.'

'For what purpose, Your Excellency?' queried Lourdusamy.

Cardinal Du Noyer's gaze moved from face to face in the small chapel, ending at His Holiness and looking down in respect. 'For the purpose of transporting the lifeless bodies of millions of people such as were found on this interrupted voyage, Excellencies, Your Holiness.'

The four Mercantilus CEOs made a noise somewhere short of a gasp, but louder than a mere intake of breath.

'Lifeless bodies . . .' repeated Cardinal Lourdusamy, but with the calm tone of a prosecuting attorney who knows in advance what the answers to all questions will be. 'Lifeless bodies from where, Cardinal Du Noyer?'

'From whatever world *Opus Dei* designates, Your Excellency,' said Du Noyer. 'In the past five years, these worlds have included Hebron, Qom-Riyadh, Fuji, Nevermore, Sol Draconi Septem, Parvati, Tsingtao-Hsishuang Panna, New Mecca, Mao Four, Ixion, the Lambert Ring Territories, Sibiatu's Bitterness, Mare Infinitus North Littoral, Renaissance Minor's terraformed moon, New Harmony, New Earth, and Mars.'

All non-Pax worlds, thought Kenzo Isozaki. *Or worlds where the Pax has only a foothold.*

'And how many bodies have these *Opus Dei* and *Cor Unum* freighters transported, Cardinal Du Noyer?' Lourdusamy asked in his low rumble.

'Approximately seven billion, Your Excellency,' said the old woman.

Kenzo Isozaki concentrated on keeping his balance. Seven billion bodies. A bulk freighter like the *Saigon Maru* could haul perhaps a hundred thousand corpses if they were stacked like cordwood. It would take the *Saigon Maru* some seventy thousand trips to haul seven billion people from star system to star system. *Absurd.* Unless there were scores of bulk freighters . . . many of them the newer nova class . . . on hundreds or thousands of shuttle trips. Each of the worlds that Du Noyer had mentioned had been closed to the Pax Mercantilus for all or some of the past four years – quarantined because of trade or diplomatic disputes with the Pax.

'These are all non-Christian worlds.' Isozaki realized that he had spoken aloud. It was the greatest breach of discipline he had ever suffered. The men and women in the chapel turned their heads in his direction.

'All non-Christian worlds,' Isozaki said again, omitting even the honorifics in addressing the others. 'Or Christian worlds with large populations of non-Christians, such as Mars or Fuji or Nevermore. *Cor Unum* and *Opus Dei* have been exterminating non-Christians. But why transport their bodies? Why not just leave them to rot on their homeworlds and then bring in the Pax colonists?'

His Holiness held up one hand. Isozaki fell silent. The Pope nodded in the direction of Cardinal Lourdusamy.

'Cardinal Du Noyer,' said the Secretary of State, as if Isozaki had not spoken, 'what is the destination of these freighters?'

'I do not know, Your Excellency.'

Lourdusamy nodded. 'And who authorized this project, Cardinal Du Noyer?'

'The Peace and Justice Commission, Your Excellency.'

Isozaki's head snapped around. The Cardinal had just laid the blame for this atrocity . . . this unprecedented mass murder . . . directly at the feet of one man. The Peace and Justice Commission had one prefect and only one prefect . . . Pope Urban XVI, formerly Pope Julius XIV. Isozaki lowered his gaze to the shoes of the fisherman and contemplated rushing the fiend, attempting to get his fingers around the Pope's scrawny throat. He knew that the silent guards in the corner would cut him down halfway there. He was still tempted to try.

'And do you know, Cardinal Du Noyer,' continued Lourdusamy as if nothing terrible had been revealed, nothing unspeakable had been spoken, 'how these people . . . these non-Christians . . . are rendered . . . lifeless?'

Rendered lifeless, thought Isozaki, who had always hated euphemisms. *Murdered, you motherfucker!*

'No,' said Cardinal Du Noyer. 'My job as prefect of *Cor Unum* is merely to provide *Opus Dei* with the transport necessary to carry out their duties. The destinations of the ships and what happened before my freighters are needed is not . . . has never been . . . my concern.'

Isozaki went to one knee on the stone floor, not to pray, but just because he could no longer stand. *How many centuries, gods of my ancestors, have accomplices to mass murder answered in this way? Since Horace Glennon-Height. Since the legendary Hitler. Since . . . forever.*

'Thank you, Cardinal Du Noyer,' said Lourdusamy.

The old woman stepped back.

Incredibly, it was the Pope who was rising, moving forward, his white slippers making soft sounds on the stone. His Holiness walked between the staring people – past Cardinal Mustafa and Father Farrell, past Cardinal Lourdusamy and Monsignor Oddi, past Cardinal Du Noyer and the unnamed monsignor behind her, past the empty pillows where the Pax Fleet officers had been, past CEO Aron and CEO Hay-Modhino and CEO Anna Pelli Cognani, to where Isozaki knelt, close to vomiting, black dots dancing in his vision.

His Holiness laid a hand on the head of the man who was even at that moment contemplating killing him.

'Rise, our son,' said the mass murderer of billions. 'Stand and listen. We command you.'

Isozaki rose, legs apart, teetering. His arms and hands tingled as if someone had zapped him with a neural stunner, but he knew it was his own body betraying him. He could not have closed his fingers around anyone's throat at that moment. It was difficult enough just to stand alone.

Pope Urban XVI extended a hand, set it on the CEO's shoulder, and steadied him. 'Listen, brother in Christ. Listen.'

His Holiness turned his head and dipped his miter forward.

Councillor Albedo stepped to the edge of the low dais and began to speak.

'Your Holiness, Your Excellencies, Honorable Chief Executive Officers,' said the man in gray. Albedo's voice was as smooth as his hair, as smooth as his gray gaze, as smooth as the silk of his gray cape.

Kenzo Isozaki trembled at the sound of it. He remembered the agony and embarrassment of the moment when Albedo had turned the CEO's cruciform into a crucible of pain.

'Tell us who you are, please,' rumbled Lourdusamy in his most congenial tone.

Personal advisor to His Holiness, Pope Urban XVI, Kenzo Isozaki was prepared to hear. Albedo's gray presence had been glimpsed and rumored for decades and decades. He was never identified other than *personal advisor to His Holiness*.

'I am an artificial construct, a cybrid, created by elements of the AI TechnoCore,' said Councillor Albedo. 'I am here as a representative of those elements of the Core.'

Everyone in the room except for His Holiness and Cardinal Lourdusamy took a step away from Albedo. No one spoke, no one gasped or cried out, but the animal scent of terror and revulsion in the little chapel could not have been stronger if the Shrike had suddenly materialized among them. Kenzo Isozaki felt the Pope's fingers still tight on his shoulder. He wondered if His Holiness could feel the pounding of his pulse through flesh and bone.

'The human beings transported from the worlds listed by Cardinal Du Noyer were . . . rendered lifeless . . . by Core technology, using Core robot spacecraft, and are being stored using Core techniques,' continued Albedo.

'As Cardinal Du Noyer reported, approximately seven billion non-Christians have been processed in this manner over the past seven years. Another forty to fifty billion must be similarly processed in the next standard decade. It is time to explain the reason for this project and to enlist your direct aid in it.'

Kenzo Isozaki was thinking – *It is possible to wire the human skeletal structure with a powerful protein-based explosive so subtle that even the Swiss Guard sniffers would not have detected it. Would to the gods I had done that before coming here.*

The Pope released Isozaki's shoulder and walked softly to the dais, touching the sleeve of Councillor Albedo's robe as he passed. His Holiness sat in his straight-backed chair. His thin face was peaceful. 'We wish you all to listen carefully,' said His Holiness. 'Councillor Albedo speaks with our authorization and approval. Continue, please.'

Albedo bowed his head slightly and turned back toward the staring dignitaries. Even the Pope's security guards had moved back to the wall.

'You have been told, largely through myth and legend, but also through Church history,' began Albedo, 'that the TechnoCore was destroyed in the Fall of the Farcasters. That is not true.

'You have been told – primarily through the banned Hyperion *Cantos* – that the Core consisted of Three Elements – the Stables, who wished to preserve the status quo between, humanity and the Core, the Volatiles, who viewed humanity as a threat and plotted to destroy it – primarily through the destruction of the Earth via the Big Mistake of '08, and the Ultimates, who thought only of creating an AI-based Ultimate Intelligence, a sort of silicon God which could predict and rule over the universe . . . or at least this galaxy.

'All these truths are lies.'

Isozaki realized that Anna Pelli Cognani had gripped his wrist with her cool fingers and was squeezing very hard.

'The TechnoCore was never grouped into three warring elements,' said Albedo, pacing in front of the altar and dais. 'From its evolution into consciousness a thousand years ago, the Core was made up of thousands of distinct elements and factions – often warring, more often cooperating, but always struggling to achieve a synthesis of agreement toward the direction autonomous intelligence and artificial life should evolve. That agreement has never crystallized.

'Almost at the same time that the TechnoCore was evolving into true autonomy, while most of humankind lived on the surface of and in near orbit around one world – Old Earth – humanity had developed the capacity to change its own genetic programming . . . that is, to determine its own evolution. This breakthrough came partially through developments in the early twenty-first century AD in genetic manipulation, but was made possible most directly through the refinement of advanced nanotechnology. At first under the direction and control of early Core AIs working in conjunction with human researchers, nanotech life-forms . . . autonomous beings, some intelligent, much smaller than a cell, some molecular in size . . . soon developed their own *raison d'être* and *raison d'état*. Nano-machines, many in the form of viruses, invaded and reshaped humanity like a terrible viral plague. Luckily for both the human race and the race of autonomous intelligences now known as the Core, the primary vector for that plague was in the early seedships and other slower-than-light colony ships launched in the years just preceding the human Hegira.

'At that time, early elements of what would become the human Hege-mony and the forecasting elements of the TechnoCore realized that the goal of the evolving nanotech communities developed on those seedships was nothing less than the destruction of humankind and the creation of a new race of nanotech-controlled biologic adapts in a thousand distant star systems. The Hegemony and the Core responded by banning advanced nanotech research and by declaring war on the nanotech seedship colonies – the groups now known as the Ousters.

'But other events overshadowed this struggle.

'Elements of the emergent Core which favored alliance with the nanotech universes – and this was more than a small faction – discovered something that terrified *all* elements of the Core.

'As you know, our early research into Hawking-drive physics and faster-than-light communication led to the discovery of the Planck-space medium, what some have called the Void Which Binds. Evolving know-ledge about this underlying and unifying substructure to the universe led to our creation of the FTL communication – the so-called fatline – as well as to the refined Hawking drive, the farcasters that united the Hegemonic WorldWeb, the planetary datspheres evolving into megaspheres of Core-directed data, today's instantaneous Gideon drive, and even experiments into antientropic bubbles within this universe – what we believe will become the Time Tombs on Hyperion.

'But these gifts to humanity were not without price. It is true that certain Ultimate factions within the Core used the farcasters as a way to tap into human brains so as to create a neural net for their own purposes. This use was harmless . . . the neural nets were created in the nontime and nonspace of farcaster Planck-space transit, and humans need never have learned of the experiments if other elements of the Core had not revealed this fact to the first John Keats cybrid persona four centuries ago – but I agree with those humans and those Core elements who consider this act as unethical, a violation of privacy.

'But those earliest neural net experiments revealed an amazing fact. There were other Cores in the universe . . . perhaps in our home galaxy. The discovery of this fact led to a civil war within our TechnoCore which still rages. Certain elements – not merely the Volatiles – decided that it was time to end the biological experiment that was the human race. Plans were made to "accidentally" drop the '08 Kiev black hole into the center of Old Earth before Hawking drives allowed for a general exodus. Other elements of the Core delayed these plans until the mechanisms for escape were given to the human race.

'In the end, neither extreme faction triumphed . . . Old Earth was not destroyed. It was kidnapped – by means which our TechnoCore cannot understand to this day – by one or more of these alien Ultimate Intelligences.'

The CEOs began babbling among themselves. Cardinal Mustafa went to both knees on his cushion and began praying. Cardinal Du Noyer looked so ill that her aide, the monsignor, whispered concerned entreaties. Even Monsignor Lucas Oddi looked as if he might faint.

His Holiness, Pope Urban XVI, held up three fingers. The chapel became silent.

'This is, of course, only background,' continued Councillor Albedo. 'What we wish to share with you today is the urgent reason for shared action.

'Three centuries ago, extreme factions of the Core – a society of autonomous intelligences ravaged and torn by eight centuries of violent debate and conflict – tried a new tack. They devised the cybrid creature known as John Keats – a human personality imbedded in an AI persona carried in a human body connected to the Core via Planck-space interface. The Keats persona had many purposes – as a sort of trap for what the UIs considered the "empathy" element of an emerging human species UI, as a prime mover to set the events in motion which eventually led to the last Hyperion pilgrimage and the opening of the Time Tombs there, to flush the Shrike out of hiding, and as a catalyst to the Fall of the Farcasters. To serve this final purpose, elements of the Core – elements to which I owe my creation and allegiance – leaked the information to CEO Meina Gladstone and others in the Hegemony that other Core elements were using the Farcasters to prey upon human neurons like some sort of neural vampires.

'Those elements of the Core, under the guise of an Ouster attack, launched a final, physical assault on the WorldWeb. Despairing of destroying the scattered human race in one stroke, these elements hoped to destroy the advanced WorldWeb society. By attacking the Core directly via destroying the farcaster medium, Gladstone and the other Hegemony leaders ended the neural-net experiments and caused a great setback to the so-called Volatiles and Ultimates in the Core civil war.

'Our elements of the Core – elements devoted to preserving not only the human race but some sort of alliance with your species – destroyed one iteration of the John Keats cybrid, but a second was created and succeeded in its primary mission.

'And that mission was to reproduce with a specific human female and create a "messiah" with connections to both the Core and humanity.

'That "messiah" lives now in the form of the child named Aenea.

'Born on Hyperion more than three centuries ago, that child fled through the Time Tombs to our age. She did so not out of fear – we would not have harmed her – but *because her mission is to destroy the Church, destroy the Pax civilization, and to end the human race as you have known it.*

'We believe that she is not aware of her true purpose or function.

'Three centuries ago, remnants of my element of the Core – a group you might think of as the Humanists – made contact with human survivors of the Fall of the Farcasters and the chaos which followed this fall.' Albedo nodded in the direction of His Holiness. The Pope lowered his head in acknowledgment.

'Father Lenar Hoyt was a survivor of the last Shrike Pilgrimage,' continued Councillor Albedo, pacing back and forth in front of the altar once again. Candle flames flickered slightly at his passing. 'He had seen firsthand the manipulations of the Ultimate Intelligence Core elements and the depredations of their monster sent back through time, the Shrike. When we first made contact – the Humanists and Father Hoyt and a few other members of a dying Church – we resolved to protect the human race from further assaults while restoring civilization. The cruciform was our instrument of salvation – literally.

'You all know that the cruciform had been a failure. Prior to the Fall, humans resurrected by this symbiote's actions were retarded and sexual neuters. The cruciform – a sort of organic computer in which is stored the neurological and physiological data of a living human being – restored the body but not the full intellect or personality. It resurrected the corpse but stole the soul.

'The origins of the cruciform lie shrouded in mystery, but we Humanist elements of the Core believe that it was developed in our future and brought back through time via the Hyperion Time Tombs. In a sense, it was sent to be discovered by young Father Lenar Hoyt.

'The failure of the symbiote was due to the simple demands of information storage and retrieval. In a human mind, there are neurons. In a human body, there are approximately 10^{28} atoms. The cruciform, in order to restore the mind and body of a human being, must not only keep track of these atoms and neurons, but remember the precise configuration of the standing holistic wave front which comprises the human memory and personality. It also must provide the energy to restructure these atoms, molecules, cells, bones, muscles, and memories so that the organism is reborn as the individual who lived in that shell before. The cruciform alone cannot do that successfully. At best, the biomachine can reproduce a crude copy of the original.

'But the Core had the computing capacity to store, retrieve, reshape, and re-form this information into a resurrected human being. And we have done so for three centuries.'

Here Kenzo Isozaki saw the panic in the exchanged glances between Cardinal Du Noyer and Cardinal Mustafa, between Father Farrell and the monsignor who was Du Noyer's aide. This was heresy. It was blasphemy. It was the end of the Sacrament of Resurrection and the beginning of the reign of the physical and mechanical once again. Isozaki himself felt sick. He glanced at Hay-Modhino and Pelli Cognani and saw that the CEOs were praying. CEO Aron looked as if he were in shock.

'Beloved,' said His Holiness. 'Do not doubt. Do not surrender faith. Your thoughts now are a betrayal of Our Lord Jesus Christ, and of His Church. The miracle of resurrection is no less a miracle because these friends in what was once known as the TechnoCore help us realize the miracle. It was the work of Jesus Christ Almighty who led these other children of God – these creations of Our Lord through His most unworthy instruments, the human race – to find their own souls and salvation. Continue, M. Albedo.'

Albedo looked mildly amused at the expressions of shock in the room. But his smooth features settled into quiet amiability as he began speaking again.

'We have given the human race immortality. In exchange, we have asked for nothing but a silent alliance with humanity. We want only peace with our creators.

'In the past three centuries, our quiet alliance has benefited both AI and humanity. We have, as His Holiness said, found our souls. Humanity has found a peace and stability missing from history for millennia . . . perhaps forever. And I admit, the alliance has been good for my element of the Core, the group known as the Humanists. We have gone from being one of the smaller, more despised factions to becoming the – not ruling party, for no element rules in the Core – the major element of consensus. Our philosophy is accepted by almost all former warring groups.

'But not by all.'

Here Councillor Albedo quit pacing and stood directly in front of the altar. He looked from face to face and his gray eyes were grim.

'The Core element which had hoped to dispose of humanity . . . the element composed of some former Ultimates and some pro-nanotech evolutionists . . . has played its trump card in the child named Aenea. She is, literally, the virus released into the body of humanity.'

Cardinal Lourdusamy stepped forward. The huge man's face was flushed and serious. His small eyes gleamed. His voice was sharp.

'Tell us, Councillor Albedo, what is the purpose of the child Aenea?'

'Her purpose,' said the man in gray, 'is threefold.'

'What is the first purpose?'

'To destroy humanity's chance at physical immortality.'

'And how can one child do that?' asked Lourdusamy.

'She is not a child, nor even human,' said Albedo. 'She is the spawn of a tailored cybrid. The persona of her cybrid father interfaced with her when she was in her mother's womb. Her mind and body have been interwoven with rogue elements of the Core since before birth.'

'But how can she steal humanity's gift of immortality?' insisted Lourdusamy.

'Her blood,' said Albedo. 'She can spread a virus that destroys the cruciform.'

'A literal virus?'

'Yes. But not a natural one. It was tailored by the rogue elements of the Core. The virus is a form of nanotech pestilence.'

'But there are hundreds of billions of born-again Christians in the Pax,' said Lourdusamy, his tone that of a lawyer leading his witness. 'How could one child pose a threat to so many? Does the virus spread from victim to victim?'

Albedo sighed. 'As far as we can tell, the virus becomes contagious once the cruciform has died. Those who have been denied resurrection through contact with Aenea will spread the virus to others. Also, those who have never carried a cruciform can be vectors for this virus.'

'Is there any cure? Any immunization?' queried Lourdusamy.

'None,' said Albedo. 'The Humanists have attempted for three centuries to create countermeasures. But because the Aenea virus is a form of autonomous nanotech, it designs its own optimum mutation vector. Our defenses can never catch up to it. Perhaps with our own legions of nanotech colonies released within humanity we could someday catch up with the Aenea virus and defeat it, but we Humanists abhor nanotechnology. And the sad fact is that all nanotech life is out of our control – out of anyone's control. The essence of nanotech life's evolution is autonomy, self-will, and goals which have nothing to do with those of the harboring life-form.'

'Humanity, you mean,' said Lourdusamy.

'Precisely.'

'Aenea's first goal,' said Cardinal Lourdusamy, 'or to be more precise the first goal of her Core rogue element creators, is to destroy all cruciforms and thus destroy human resurrection.'

'Yes.'

'You mentioned three goals. What are the other two?'

'The second goal is to destroy the Church and the Pax . . . that is, all current human civilization,' said Albedo. 'When the Aenea virus spreads, when resurrection is denied . . . with farcasters still not functional and the Gideon drive impractical for single-life-span humans . . . that second goal will be accomplished. Humanity will return to the balkanized tribalism which followed the Fall.'

'And the third goal?' said Lourdusamy.

'The final goal is actually this Core element's original goal,' said Councillor Albedo. 'The destruction of the human species.'

It was CEO Anna Pelli Cognani who shouted. 'That's impossible! Even the destruction . . . kidnapping . . . of Old Earth or the Fall of the Farcasters did not wipe out humanity. Our species is too far-flung for such extinction. Too many worlds. Too many cultures.'

Albedo was nodding, but sadly. 'That was true. *Was*. But the Aenea Plague will spread almost everywhere. The cruciform-killing viruses will have mutated to new stages. Human DNA will have been invaded everywhere. With the fall of the Pax, the Ousters will invade again . . . this time successfully. They have long since succumbed to nanotech mutation. They are no longer human. With no Church or Pax or Pax Fleet to protect humanity, the Ousters will seek out those pockets of surviving human DNA and infect them with the nanotech plague. The human species . . . as we have known it and as the Church has sought to protect it . . . will cease to exist within a few standard years.'

'And what will succeed it?' asked Cardinal Lourdusamy in a low rumble.

'No one knows,' said Albedo softly. 'Not even Aenea or the Ousters or the rogue elements of the Core who have released this final plague. The nanotech life-form colonies will evolve according to their own agenda, fashioning the human form to their own whims, and only they will be in control of their destiny. But that destiny will no longer be human.'

'My God, my God,' said Kenzo Isozaki, amazed that he was speaking aloud. 'What can we do? What can *I* do?'

Amazingly, it was His Holiness who answered.

'We have dreaded and fought this threatened plague for three hundred years,' His Holiness said softly, his sad eyes expressing more pain than his own. 'Our first effort was to capture the child, Aenea, before she could spread the infection. We knew that she fled her era to ours not out of fear – we wished her no harm – but so that she could spread the virus across the Pax.

'Actually,' amended His Holiness, 'we suspect that the child, Aenea, does not truly know the full effect her contagion will have on humanity. In some ways, she is the unknowing pawn of these rogue elements of the Core.'

It was CEO Hay-Modhino who suddenly spoke with vehemence. 'We should have plasma-bombed Hyperion to cinders on the day she was scheduled to emerge from the Time Tombs. Sterilized the entire planet. Taken no chances.'

His Holiness took no umbrage at the unpardonable interruption. 'Yes, our son, there are those who urged that. But the Church could no more be the cause of taking so many innocent lives than we could have authorized the death of the single girl. We conferred with the predictive elements of the Core . . . they saw that a Jesuit named Father Captain de Soya would be instrumental in her final capture . . . but none of our peaceful attempts to seize the child succeeded. Pax Fleet could have vaporized her ship four years ago, but it was under orders not to unless all else failed. So we continue to strive for containment of her viral invasion. What you must do, M. Isozaki – what you must all do – is continue to support the Church's efforts, even as we intensify those efforts. M. Albedo?'

The gray man spoke again.

'Imagine the coming plague as a forest fire on an oxygen-rich world. It will sweep everything before it unless we can contain it and then extinguish it. Our first effort is to remove the dead wood and brush – the inflammable elements – not necessary to the living forest.'

'The non-Christians,' murmured CEO Pelli Cognani.

'Precisely,' said Councillor Albedo.

'That is why they had to be terminated,' said the Grand Inquisitor. 'All those thousands on the *Saigon Maru*. All those millions. All those billions.'

Pope Urban XVI raised his hand, in a command to silence rather than benediction this time. '*Not* terminated!' he said sternly. 'Not a single life, not Christian, not non-Christian, has been taken.'

The dignitaries looked at one another in confusion.

'This is true,' said Councillor Albedo.

'But they were lifeless . . .' began the Grand Inquisitor and then stopped abruptly. 'My profound apologies, Holy Father,' he said to the Pope.

His Holiness shook his mitered head. 'No apology is required, John Domenico. These are emotional topics. Please explain, M. Albedo.'

'Yes, Your Holiness,' said the man in gray. 'Those aboard the *Saigon Maru* were lifeless, Your Excellency, but not dead. The Core . . . the Humanist elements in the Core . . . have perfected a method of putting human beings in temporary stasis, neither alive nor dead . . .'

'Like cryogenic fugue?' said CEO Aron, who had traveled much by Hawking drive before his conversion.

Albedo shook his head. 'Much more sophisticated. And less harmful.' He gestured with well-manicured fingers. 'During the past seven years, we have processed seven billion human beings. In the next standard decade – or sooner – we must process more than forty-two billion more. There are many worlds in the Outback, and many even within Pax space, where non-Christians are in the majority.'

'Processed?' said CEO Pelli Cognani.

Albedo smiled grimly. 'Pax Fleet declares a world quarantined without knowing the real reason for their actions. Core robot ships arrive in orbit and sweep the inhabited sections with our stasis equipment. *Cor Unum* provides the ships and funding and training. *Opus Dei* uses freighters to remove the bodies in stasis . . .'

'Why remove them?' asked the Grand Inquisitor. 'Why not leave them on their homeworlds?'

His Holiness answered. 'They must be hidden in a place where the Aenea Plague cannot find them, John Domenico. They must be carefully . . . lovingly . . . put out of harm's way until the danger is past.'

The Grand Inquisitor bowed his head in understanding and compliance.

'There is more,' said Councillor Albedo. 'My element of the Core has created a . . . breed of soldier . . . whose sole job is to find and capture this Aenea before she can spread the deadly contamination. The first one was activated four years ago and was called Rhadamanth Nemes. There are only a few others of these hunter/seekers, but they are equipped to deal with whatever obstacles the rogue elements of the Core throw at them . . . even the Shrike.'

'The Shrike is controlled by the Ultimates and other rogue elements of the Core?' asked Father Farrell. It was the first time the man had spoken.

'We think so,' answered Cardinal Lourdusamy. 'The demon seems to be in league with Aenea . . . helping her spread the contagion. In the same way, the Ultimates appear to have found a way to open certain farcaster portals for her. The Devil has found a name . . . and allies . . . in our age, I fear.'

Albedo held up one finger. 'I should stress that even Nemes and our other hunter/seekers are dangerous . . . as are any constructs so terribly single-minded. Once the child is captured, these cybrid beings will be terminated. Only the terrible danger posed by the Aenea Plague justifies their existence.'

'Holy Father,' said Kenzo Isozaki, his hands pressed together in prayer, 'what else can we do?'

Pray,' said His Holiness. His dark eyes were wells of pain and responsibility. 'Pray and support our Holy Mother Church in her effort to save humankind.'

'The Crusade against the Ousters will continue,' said Cardinal Lourdusamy. We will hold them at bay as long as we can.'

'To that end,' said Councillor Albedo, 'the Core has developed the Gideon drive and is working on new technologies for humanity's defense.'

'We shall continue our search for the girl . . . young woman, now, I believe,' added Lourdusamy. 'And if she is apprehended, she will be isolated.'

'And if she is not apprehended, Your Excellency?' asked Grand Inquisitor Cardinal Mustafa.

Lourdusamy did not answer.

'We must pray,' said His Holiness. 'We must ask for Christ's help at this time of maximum danger for our Church and our human race. We must each do everything we can and then ask more of ourselves. And we must pray for the souls of all of our brothers and sisters in Christ – even for, *especially* for, the soul of the child, Aenea, who unwittingly leads her species into such peril.'

'Amen,' said Monsignor Lucas Oddi.

Then, while all the others in the small chapel knelt and bowed their heads, His Holiness, Pope Urban XVI, stood, moved to the altar, and began to say a Mass of Thanksgiving.

FOURTEEN

Aenea. Her name came before any other conscious thought. I thought of her before I thought to think of myself.

Aenea.

And then came the pain and noise and onslaught of wetness and buffeting. Mostly it was the pain that roused me.

I opened one eye. The other appeared to be gummed shut with caked blood or other matter. Before I remembered who or where I was, I felt the pain from innumerable bruises and cuts, but also from something far worse in my right leg. Then I remembered who I was. And then I remembered where I had been.

I laughed. Or more precisely, I *tried* to laugh. My lips were split and swollen and there was more blood or goo sealing one corner of my mouth. The laugh emerged as a sort of demented moan.

I had been swallowed by some sort of aerial squid on a world all atmosphere and clouds and lightning. Even now I was being digested in the noisy belly of the beast.

It *was* noisy. Explosively so. Rumbles, blasts, and a pounding, slapping noise. Like rain on a tropical forest canopy. I squinted through my one eye. Darkness . . . then a strobe of white light . . . darkness with red retinal echoes . . . more white strobes.

I remembered the tornadoes and planet-sized storm that had been coming toward me as I floated along in my kayak under the parasail before the beast swallowed me. But this was not that storm. This was rain on a jungle canopy. The material batting at my face and chest was tattered nylon, the remains of the parasail, wet palm fronds, and pieces of shattered fiberglass. I squinted downward and waited for the next lightning flash. The kayak was there, but splintered and shattered. My legs were there . . . still partially ensconced in the kayak shell . . . the left leg intact and movable, but the right . . . I cried out in pain. The right leg was definitely broken. I could see no bone breaking through the flesh, but I was sure that there was a fracture in the lower thigh.

Otherwise I seemed intact. I was bruised and scratched. There was dried blood on my face and hands. My trousers were little more than rags. My shirt and vest were in tatters. But as I turned and arched my back, stretched my arms and flexed my fingers, wiggled the toes on my left foot and tried to wiggle those on my right, I thought that I was more or less in one piece . . . no broken back, no shattered ribs, no nerve damage except for possibly in my right leg where the agony was like barbed wire dragged through veins.

644

When the next flashes of lightning exploded, I tried to assess my surroundings. The broken kayak and I seemed to be stuck in a jungle canopy, wedged between splintered limbs, wrapped around with the tattered parasail and clinging shroud lines, being battered with palm fronds in a tropical storm, in a darkness broken only by lightning flashes, hanging some indeterminate distance above solid ground.

Trees? Solid ground?

The world I had been flying on had no solid ground . . . or at least none reachable without being compressed by pressure to something the size of my fist. And it seemed unlikely that there would be trees in the core of that Jovian world where hydrogen was squeezed to metal form. So I was not on that world. Nor was I still in the belly of the beast. Where was I?

Thunder blasted around me like plasma grenades. The wind came up, tossing the kayak in its precarious perch and making me scream aloud from the pain. I may have lost consciousness for a few moments, for when I opened my eyes again, the wind had died down and the rain was pummeling me like a thousand cold fists. I wiped the rain and matted blood from my eyes and realized that I was feverish, that my skin was burning even in that cold rain. *How long have I been here? What vicious microbes have found my open wounds? What bacteria shared the gut of that airborne squid-thing with me?*

Logic would have dictated that the entire memory of flying on the Jovian cloud world and being taken in by a tentacled squid-thing had been a fever dream – that I had farcast here . . . wherever here was . . . after escaping Vitus-Gray-Balianus B and all the rest was dreamscape. But there were the remnants of the deployed parasail all around me in the wet night. And there was the vividness of my memories. And there was the logical fact that logic did not work on this odyssey.

The wind shook the tree. The broken kayak slid along the precarious nest of shattered fronds and branches. My broken leg sent stabs of agony through me.

I realized that I had better apply some logic to this situation. At any moment the kayak was going to slide, or the branches would break, and the entire mass of shattered fiberglass, clinging nylon-10 risers, and wet memory-canvas parasail tatters was going to crash down into the darkness, dragging me and my broken leg with it. Despite the flashes of lightning . . . which came with less regularity now, leaving me in the pitching, wet darkness . . . I could see nothing below me except more branches, gaps of darkness, and the thick, gray-green trunks of trees that wound around themselves in a tight spiral. I did not recognize that sort of tree.

Where am I? Aenea . . . where have you sent me now?

I stopped that sort of thing. It was almost a form of prayer, and I was not going to get into the habit of praying to the girl I had traveled with and protected and eaten dinner with and argued with for four years. *Still and all,* I thought, *you might have sent me to some less difficult places, kiddo. If you had a choice in the matter, I mean.*

Thunder rumbled but no lightning flashed to light the scene. The kayak shifted and sagged, the broken bow tilting suddenly. I reached behind me and flailed around for the thick branch I had seen there during the earlier flashes of lightning. There were broken branches galore, razor-sharp splintered frond stems, and the sawtooth edges of the fronds themselves. I grabbed and pulled, trying to leverage my broken leg out of the broken cockpit of the kayak, but the branches were loose and I came only halfway out, reeling in nausea from the pain. I imagined that black dots were dancing in my vision, but the night was so dark that it made no difference. I retched over the side of the rocking kayak and tried again to find a firm handhold in the maze of splintered branches.

How the hell did I get in these treetops, anyway?

It did not matter. Nothing mattered at the moment except getting out of this mess of broken fiberglass and tangled shroud lines.

Get my knife, cut my way out of this clinging tangle.

My knife was gone. My *belt* was gone. The pockets of my vest had been ripped away and then the vest torn to a few tatters. My shirt was mostly gone. The flechette pistol I'd held like a talisman against the airborne cuttlefish-squid-thing was gone . . . I dimly remembered it and my backpack dropping out when the passing tornado had ripped the parasail to shreds. Clothes, flashlight laser, ration pak . . . everything gone.

Lightning flashed, although the thunder-rumble had moved farther away. My wrist glinted in the downpour.

Comlog. That goddamn band must be indestructible.

What good would the comlog do me? I wasn't sure, but it was better than nothing. Raising my left wrist close to my mouth in the drumming rain, I shouted, 'Ship! Comlog on . . . Ship! Hey!'

No response. I remembered the device flashing overload warnings during the electrical storm on the Jovian world. Inexplicably, I felt a sense of loss. The ship's memory in the comlog had been an idiot savant, at best, but it had been with me for a long time. I had grown used to its presence. And it had helped me fly the dropship that had carried us from Fallingwater to Taliesin West. And . . .

I shook away the nostalgia and thrashed around for a handhold again, finally clinging to the shroud lines that hung around me like thin vines. This worked. The parasail streamers must have caught firmly in the upper branches, and some of the shroud lines bore my weight as I scrabbled with my left foot on slick fiberglass to pull my dead leg from the wreckage.

The pain made me black out again for a few moments . . . this was as bad as the kidney stone at its worst, only coming at me in jagged waves . . . but when my mind came back into focus, I was clinging to the spiral-wrapped trunk of the palm tree rather than lying in the wreckage. A few minutes later a microburst of wind bulled through the jungle canopy and the kayak fell away in pieces, some being arrested by the still-intact shroud lines, others tumbling and crashing into darkness.

What now?

Wait for dawn, I guess.

What if there's no dawn on this world?

Wait for the pain to die down then.

Why would it die down? The fractured femur is obviously tearing at nerve and muscle. You have a wild fever. God knows how long you were lying here in the rain and torn plant material, unconscious, wounds open to every killer microbe that wants to get in. Gangrene could be settlng in. That rotting vegetation stink you smell could be you.

Gangrene doesn't happen that quickly, does it?

No answer.

I tried hanging on to the tree trunk with my left arm and feeling along my injured thigh with my right hand, but the slightest touch made me moan and sway. If I passed out again, I could easily pitch off this branch. I settled on testing my lower right leg: it was numb in most places, but felt intact. Perhaps just a simple break in the lower thighbone.

Just a simple break, Raul? On a jungle world in a storm that might be permanent for all we know. With no medkit, no way to make a fire, no tools, no weapons. Just a shattered leg and a high fever. Oh, well . . . as long as it's just a simple *fracture.*

Shut the fuck up.

I weighed alternatives as the rain pounded on me. I could cling here for the rest of the night . . . which might be ten minutes or another thirty hours . . . or I could try to lower myself to the jungle floor.

Where the predators are waiting? Good plan.

I said shut up. The jungle floor might give me a place to shelter from the rain, find a soft place to rest my leg, offer branches and vines to make a splint.

'All right,' I said aloud, and groped around in the dark to find a shroud line or vine or branch so that I could start my descent.

My guess is that it took me between two and three hours to lower myself. It might have been twice that or half that. The lightning part of the storm had passed and it would have been almost impossible to find handholds in the near absolute darkness, but a strange, faint, almost invisible reddish glow began above the thick jungle canopy and allowed my eyes to adapt enough to find a line here, a vine there, a solid branch here.

Sunrise? I thought not. The glow seemed too diffuse, too faint, almost chemical.

I guessed that I had been about twenty-five meters up in the canopy. The thick branches continued all the way down, but the density of razor-edged palm fronds diminished as I neared the bottom. There was no ground. Resting in the crotch of two branches, recovering from the pain and dizziness, I began lowering myself again only to find surging water beneath me. I pulled my left leg up quickly. The reddish glow was just bright enough to show me water all around, torrents of water flowing between the spiraled tree trunks, eddies of black water washing by like a torrent of oil.

'Shit,' I said. I wasn't going any farther this night. I had held vague notions of building a raft. I was on a different world, so there must be a farcaster upstream and another downstream. I'd gotten here somehow. I had built a raft before.

Yeah, when you were healthy, well fed, with two legs and tools . . . like an axe and a flashlight laser. Now you don't even have two legs.

Please shut up. Please.

I closed my eyes and tried to sleep. The fever was making me shake from chills now. I ignored it all and tried to think of the stories I would tell Aenea when we saw each other next.

You don't really believe that you'll ever see her again, do you?

'Shut the fuck up,' I said again, my voice lost in the sound of rain on jungle foliage and against the swirl of raging water half a meter beneath me. I realized that I should climb a couple of meters up the branches I had just lowered myself on through such pain and effort. The water might rise. Probably would rise again. Ironic to go to all that trouble just to make it easier to be swept away. Three or four meters up would be better. Would start in a minute. Just catch my breath first and let the waves of pain steady a bit. Two minutes at the most.

I awoke to a thin gruel of sunlight. I was sprawled across several sagging branches, just centimeters above the swirling, gray surface of a flood that moved between the spiraled trunks with a visible current. It was still as dim as a deep twilight. For all I knew I had slept away the day and was ready to enter another endless night. It was still raining, but this was little more than a drizzle. The temperature was tropical warm, although my fever made it hard to judge, and the humidity was near absolute.

I ached everywhere. It was hard to separate the dull agony of the shattered leg from the ache in my head and my back and my guts. My skull felt as if there were a ball of mercury in it that shifted ponderously long seconds after my head itself turned. The vertigo made me sick again, but I had nothing left to vomit. I hung on the tangle of branches and contemplated the glories of adventure.

Next time you need an errand run, kiddo, send A. Bettik.

The light did not fade, but neither did it grow brighter. I shifted position and studied the water moving by: gray, ripped by eddies, carrying detritus of palm fronds and dead vegetation. I looked up, but could see no sign of the kayak or parasail. Any fiberglass or fabric that had dropped down here during the long night had long since been swept away.

It looked like a flood, like the spring runoff through the Fens above Toschahi Bay on Hyperion where the silt was deposited for another full year, a temporary inundation, but I knew that this drowned forest, this endless everglades of a watery jungle, could just as easily be the permanent state of affairs here. *Wherever here is.*

I studied the water. It was opaque, murky as gray milk, and could have been a few centimeters or many meters deep. The drowned trunks gave no clue. The current was quick, but not so quick as to carry me away if I kept a good grip on the branches that hung low above the roiling surface of the water. With luck, with no local equivalent of the Fens' mud cysts or dracula ticks or biting garr, I might be able to wade toward . . . something.

Wading takes two legs, Raul, m'boy. Hopping through the mud is more like it for you.

All right then, hopping through the mud. I gripped the branch above me with both hands and lowered my left leg into the current while keeping my injured leg propped on the wide branch where I lay. This led to new agonies, but I persisted, lowering my foot in the clotted water, then my ankle and calf, then my knee, then shifting to see if I could stand . . . my forearms and biceps straining, my injured leg sliding off the branch with a rending surge of agony that made me gasp.

The water was less than a meter and a half deep. I could stand on my good leg while water surged about my waist and splashed my chest. It was warm and seemed to lessen the pain in my broken leg.

All those nice, juicy microbes in this warm broth, many of them mutated from seedship days. They're licking their chops, Raul, old boy.

'Shut up,' I said dully, looking around. My left eye was swollen and crusted with scab, but I could see out of it. My head hurt.

Endless trunks of trees rising from the gray water to the gray drizzle on all sides, the dripping fronds and branches so dark a gray-green that they appeared almost black. It seemed a slight bit brighter to my left. And the mud underfoot seemed a little firmer in that direction.

I began moving that way, shifting my left foot forward as I changed handholds from branch to branch, sometimes ducking beneath hanging fronds, sometimes shifting aside like a slow-motion toreador to allow floating branches or other debris to swirl past. The move toward brightness took hours more. But I had nothing better to do.

The flooded jungle ended in a river. I clung to the last branch, felt the current trying to pull my good leg out from under me, and stared out at the endless expanse of gray water. I could not see the other side, not because the water was endless – I could see from the current and eddies moving from right to left that it was a river and not some lake or ocean – but because the fog or low clouds roiled almost to the surface, blotting out everything more than a hundred meters away. Gray water, gray-green dripping trees, dark gray clouds. It seemed to be getting dimmer. Night was coming on.

I had gone as far as I could on this leg. Fever raged. Despite the jungle heat of the place, my teeth were chattering and my hands were shaking almost uncontrollably. Somewhere in my awkward progress through the flooded jungle, I had aggravated the fracture to the point where I wanted to scream. No, I admit, I *had* been screaming. Softly at first, but as the hours went by and the pain deepened and the situation worsened, I screamed out lyrics to old Home Guard marching songs, then bawdy limericks I had learned as a bargeman on the Kans River, then merely screams.

So much for the building-the-raft scenario.

I was getting used to the caustic voice in my head. It and I had made a peace when I realized that it wasn't urging me to lie down and die, just critiquing my inadequate efforts to stay alive.

There goes your best chance for a raft, Raul, old boy.

The river was carrying by an entire tree, its braided trunk rolling over and over again in the deep water. I was standing shoulder-deep here, and I was ten meters from the edge of the real current.

'Yeah,' I said aloud. My fingers slipped on the smooth bark of the branch to which I was clinging. I shifted position and pulled myself up a bit. Something grated in my leg and this time I was sure that black spots dulled my vision. 'Yeah,' I said again. *What are the odds that I'll stay conscious, or that it will stay light, or that I'll stay alive, long enough to catch one of those commuter trees?* Swimming for one was out of the question. My right leg was useless and my other three limbs were shaking as if palsied. I had just enough strength to cling to this branch for another few minutes. 'Yeah,' I said again. 'Shit.'

'Excuse me, M. Endymion. Were you speaking to me?'

The voice almost made me lose my grip on the branch. Still clinging with my right hand, I lowered my left wrist and studied it in the dimming light. The comlog had a slight glow that had not been there the last time I had looked.

'Well, I'll be damned. I thought that you were broken, Ship.'

'This instrument is damaged, sir. The memory has been wiped. The neural circuits are quite dead. Only the com chips function under emergency power.'

I frowned at my wrist. 'I don't understand. If your memory has been wiped and your neural circuits are . . .'

The river pulled at my torn leg, seducing me into releasing my grip. For a moment I could not speak.

'Ship?' I said at last.

'Yes, M. Endymion?'

'You're here.'

'Of course, M. Endymion. Just as you and M. Aenea instructed me to stay. I am pleased to say that all necessary repairs have been . . .'

'Show yourself,' I commanded. It was almost dark. Tendrils of fog curled toward me across the black river.

The starship rose dripping, horizontal, its bow only twenty meters from me in the central current, blocking the current like a sudden boulder, hovering still half in the water, a black leviathan shedding river water in noisy rivulets. Navigation lights blinked on its bow and on the dripping black shark's fin far behind it in the fog.

I laughed. Or wept. Or perhaps just moaned.

'Do you wish to swim to me, sir? Or should I come in to you?'

My fingers were slipping. 'Come in to me,' I said, and gripped the branch with both hands.

There was a doc-in-the-box on the cryogenic fugue cubby-deck where Aenea used to sleep on the voyage out from Hyperion. The doc-in-the-box was ancient – hell, the whole ship was ancient – but its autorepair worked, it was well stocked, and – according to the garrulous ship on the way out four years earlier – the Ousters had tinkered with it back in the Consul's day. It worked.

I lay in the ultraviolet warmth as soft appendages probed my skin, salved my bruises, sutured my deeper cuts, administered painkiller via IV drip, and finished diagnosing me.

'It is a compound fracture, M. Endymion,' said the ship. 'Would you care to see the X rays and ultrasound?'

'No, thanks,' I said. 'How do we fix it?'

'We've already begun,' said the ship. 'The bone is being set as we speak. The bondplast and ultrasonic grafting will commence while you sleep. Because of the repair to damaged nerves and muscle tissue, the surgeon recommends at least ten hours' sleep while it begins the procedure.'

'Soon enough,' I said.

'The diagnostic's greatest concern is your fever, M. Endymion.'

'It's a result of the break, isn't it?'

'Negative,' said the ship. 'It seems that you have a rather virulent kidney infection. Left untreated, it would have killed you before the ancillary effects of the broken femur.'

'Cheery thought,' I said.

'How so, sir?'

'Never mind,' I said. 'You say that you're totally repaired?'

'Totally, M. Endymion. Better than before the accident, if you don't mind me bragging a bit. You see, because of the loss of some material, I was afraid that I would have to synthesize carbon-carbon templates from the rather dross rock substrata of this river, but I soon found that by recycling some of the unused components of the compression dampers made superfluous by the Ouster modifications I could evince a thirty-two percent increase in autorepair efficiency if I . . .'

'Never mind, Ship,' I said. The absence of pain made me almost giddy. 'How long did it take you to finish the repairs?'

'Five standard months,' said the ship. 'Eight and one-half local months. This world has an odd lunar cycle with two highly irregular moons, which I have postulated must be captured asteroids because of the . . .'

'Five months,' I said. 'And you've just been waiting the other three and a half years?'

'Yes,' said the ship. 'As instructed. I trust that all is well with A. Bettik and M. Aenea.'

'I trust that too, Ship. But we'll find out soon enough. Are you ready to leave this place?'

'All ship's systems are functional, M. Endymion. Awaiting your command.'

'Command is given,' I said. 'Let's go.'

The ship piped in the holo showing us rising above the river. It was dark out, but the night-vision lenses showed the swollen river and the farcaster arch only a few hundred meters upstream. I had not seen it in the fog. We rose above the river, above the swirling clouds.

'River's up from the last time I was here,' I said.

'Yes,' said the ship. The curve of the planet became visible, the sun rising again above fleecy clouds. 'It floods for a period of some three standard months every local orbital cycle, which equals approximately eleven standard months.'

'So you know what world this is now?' I said. 'You weren't sure when we left you.'

'I am quite confident that this planet was not among the two thousand eight hundred and sixty-seven worlds in the General Catalogue Index,' said the ship. 'My astronomical observations have shown that it is neither in Pax space nor in the realm of the former WorldWeb or Outback.'

'Not in the old WorldWeb or Outback,' I repeated. 'Where is it then?'

'Approximately two hundred and eighty light-years galactic northwest of the Outback system known as NNGC 4645 Delta,' said the ship.

Feeling slightly groggy from the painkiller, I said, 'A new world. Beyond the Outback. Why did it have farcasters then? Why was the river part of the Tethys?'

'I do not know, M. Endymion. But I should mention that there is a multitude of interesting life-forms which I observed by remotes while resting on the river bottom. Besides the river manta-ish creature which you and M. Aenea and A. Bettik observed downriver, there are more than three hundred observed species of avian variety and at least two species of humanoids.'

'Two species of humanoids? You mean humans.'

'Negative,' said the ship. 'Humanoids. Definitely not Old Earth human. One variety is quite small – little more than a meter in height – with bilateral symmetry but quite variant skeletal structure and a definite reddish hue.'

A memory flitted by of a red-rock monolith Aenea and I had scouted on the lost hawking mat during our short stay here. Tiny steps carved in the smooth stone. I shook my head to clear it. 'That's interesting, Ship. But let's set our destination.' The curve of the world had become pronounced and stars were gleaming unblinkingly. The ship continued to rise. We passed a potato-shaped moon and moved farther from orbit. The unnamed world became a blinding sphere of sunlit clouds. 'Do you know the world known as T'ien Shan, or the "Mountains of Heaven"?'

'T'ien Shan,' repeated the ship. 'Yes. As far as my memory serves, I have never been there, but I have the coordinates. A small world in the Outback, settled by refugees of the Third Chinese Civil War late in the Hegira.'

'You won't have any trouble getting there?'

'None would be anticipated,' said the ship. 'A simple Hawking-drive jump. Although I recommend that you use the autosurgeon as your cryogenic fugue cubby during the jump.'

I shook my head again. 'I'll stay awake, Ship. At least after the doc heals my leg.'

'I would recommend against that, M. Endymion.'

I frowned. 'Why? Aenea and I stayed awake during the other jumps.'

'Yes, but those were relatively short voyages within the old WorldWeb,' said the ship. 'What you now call Pax space. This will be a bit more extensive.'

'How extensive?' I said. My naked body felt a sudden chill. Our longest jump – to Renaissance Vector System – had taken ten days of ship travel time and five months of time-debt for the Pax Fleet waiting for us. 'How extensive a trip?' I said again.

'Three standard months, eighteen days, six hours, and some minutes,' said the ship.

'That's not too bad a time-debt,' I said. I last saw Aenea just after her sixteenth birthday. She would gain a few months on me. Her hair might be longer. 'We had a greater time-debt jumping to Renaissance System.'

'That is not time-debt, M. Endymion,' said the ship. 'That is shiptime.'

This time the chill along the length of my body was real. My tongue seemed thick. 'Three months' shiptime . . . how much time-debt?'

'For someone waiting on T'ien Shan?' said the ship. The jungle world was a speck behind us now as we accelerated toward a translation point. 'Five years, two months, and one day,' said the ship. 'As you are aware, the time-debt algorithm is not a linear function of C-plus duration, but includes such factors as . . .'

'Ah, Jesus,' I said, raising my wrist to my clammy forehead in the auto-surgeon coffin. 'Ah, damn.'

'Are you in pain, M. Endymion? The dolorometer suggests you are not, but your pulse has become erratic. We can increase the level of painkiller . . .'

'No!' I snapped. 'No, it's all right. I just . . . five years . . . damn.'

Did Aenea know this? Had she known that our separation would cover years of her life? Perhaps I should have brought the ship through the downriver farcaster. No, Aenea had said to fetch the ship and fly it to T'ien Shan. The farcaster had brought us to Mare Infinitus last time. Who knows where it would have taken me this time?

'Five years,' I muttered. 'Ah, damn. She'll be . . . damn, Ship . . . she'll be twenty-one years old. A grown woman. I'll have missed . . . I won't see . . . she won't remember . . .'

'Are you sure you are not in pain, M. Endymion? Your vital signs are turbulent.'

'Ignore that, Ship.'

'Shall I prepare the autosurgeon for cryogenic fugue?'

'Soon enough, Ship. Tell it to put me under while it heals my leg tonight and deals with the fever. I want at least ten hours' sleep. How long until translation point?'

'Only seventeen hours. It is well inside this system.'

'Good,' I said. 'Wake me in ten hours. Have a full breakfast ready. What I used to have when we celebrated "Sunday" on our voyage out.'

'Very good. Anything else?'

'Yeah, do you have any record holos of . . . of Aenea . . . on our last trip?'

'I have stored several hours of such records, M. Endymion. The time you were swimming in the zero-g bubble on the outer balcony. The discussion you had about religion versus rationality. The flying lessons down the central dropshaft when . . .'

'Good,' I said. 'Cue those up. I'll look through them over breakfast.'

'I will prepare the autosurgeon for three months of cryogenic sleep after your seven-hour interlude tomorrow,' said the ship.

I took a breath. 'All right.'

'The surgeon wishes to commence repairing nerve damage and injecting antibiotics now, M. Endymion. Do you wish to sleep?'

'Yes.'

'With dreams or without? The medication may be tailored for either neurological state.'

'No dreams,' I said. 'No dreams now. There'll be time enough for those later.'

'Very good, M. Endymion. Sleep well.'

PART TWO

FIFTEEN

I am on the Phari Marketplace shelf with A. Bettik, Jigme Norbu, and George Tsarong when I hear the news that Pax ships and troops have finally come to T'ien Shan, the 'Mountains of Heaven'.

'We should tell Aenea,' I say. Around us, above us, and under us, thousands of tons of scaffolding rock and creak with the weight of crowded humanity buying, selling, trading, arguing, and laughing. Very few have heard the news of the Pax's arrival. Very few will understand the implications when they do hear it. The word comes from a monk named Chim Din who has just returned from the capital of Potala, where he works as a teacher in the Dalai Lama's Winter Palace. Luckily, Chim Din also works alternate weeks as a bamboo rigger at Hsuan-k'ung Ssu, the 'Temple Hanging in Air', Aenea's project, and he hails us in Phari Marketplace as he is on his way to the Temple. Thus we are among the first people outside the court at Potala to hear of the Pax arrival.

'Five ships,' Chim Din had said. 'Several score of Christian people. About half of them warriors in red and black. About half of the remaining half are missionaries, all in black. They have rented the old Red Hat Sect gompa near Rhan Tso, the Otter Lake, near the Phallus of Shiva. They have sanctified part of the gompa as a chapel to their triune God. The Dalai Lama will not allow them to use their flying machines or go beyond the south ridge of the Middle Kingdom, but he has allowed them free travel within this region.'

'We should tell Aenea,' I say again to A. Bettik, leaning close so that I can be heard over the marketplace babble.

'We should tell everyone at Jo-kung,' says the android. He turns and tells George and Jigme to complete the shopping – not to forget arranging porters to carry the orders of cable and extra bonsai bamboo for the construction – and then he hoists his massive rucksack, tightens his climbing hardware on his harness, and nods to me.

I heft my own heavy pack and lead the way out of the marketplace and down the scaffolding ladders to the cable level. 'I think the High Way will be faster than the Walk Way, don't you?'

The blue man nods. I had hesitated at suggesting the High Way for the return trip, since it has to be difficult for A. Bettik to handle the cables and slideways with just one hand. Upon our reunion, I had been surprised that he had not fashioned a metal hook for himself – his left arm still ends in a smooth stump halfway between his wrist and elbow – but I soon saw how he used a leather band and various leather attachments to make up for his missing digits. 'Yes, M. Endymion,' he says. 'The High Way. It is much faster. I agree. Unless you want to use one of the flyers as courier.'

I look at him, assuming that he is kidding. The flyers are a breed apart and insane. They launch their paragliders from the high structures, catching ridge lift from the great rock walls, crossing the wide spaces between the ridges and peaks where there are no cables or bridges, watching the birds, looking for thermals as if their lives depended on it . . . because their lives do depend on it. There are no flat areas on which a flyer can set down if the treacherous winds shift, or if their lift fails, or if their hang gliders develop a problem. A forced landing on a ridge wall almost always means death. Descent to the clouds below always means death. The slightest mis-calculation in gauging the winds, the updrafts, the downdrafts, the jet stream . . . any mistake means death for a flyer. That is why they live alone, worship in a secret cult, and charge a fortune to do the Dalai Lama's bidding by delivering messages from the capital at Potala, or to fly prayer streamers during a Buddhist celebration, or to carry urgent notes from a trader to his home office to beat competitors, or – so the legend goes – to visit the eastern peak of T'ai Shan, separated for months each local year from the rest of T'ien Shan by more than a hundred klicks of air and deadly cloud.

'I don't think we want to entrust this news to a flyer,' I say.

A. Bettik nods. 'Yes, M. Endymion, but the paragliders can be purchased here at the marketplace. At the Flyer's Guild stall. We could buy two and take the shortest route back. They are very expensive, but we could sell some of the pack zygoats.'

I never know when my android friend is joking. I remember the last time I was under a parasail canopy and have to resist the urge to shiver. 'Have you ever paraglided on this world?' I say.

'No, M. Endymion.'

'On any world?'

'No, M. Endymion.'

'What would you think our chances would be if we tried?' I say.

'One in ten,' he says without a second's hesitation.

'And what are our chances on the cables and slideway this late in the day?' I say.

'About nine in ten before dark,' he says. 'Less if sunset catches us short of the slideway.'

'Let's take the cables and slideway,' I say.

We wait in the short queue of market-goers leaving by cable, and then it is our turn to walk onto the step-off platform. The bamboo shelf is about twenty meters beneath the lowest marketplace scaffolding and it extends about five meters farther out over the abyss than does the rest of Phari. Beneath us there is nothing but air for thousands of meters and at the bottom of that emptiness only the ubiquitous sea of clouds that rolls against the ridges of upthrust rock like a white tide spilling against stone pilings. More kilometers beneath those clouds, I know, are poisonous gases and the surging, acidic sea that covers all of this world except its mountains.

The cablemaster gestures us forward and A. Bettik and I step onto the jump platform together. From this nexus, a score or more of cables slant out and down across the abyss, creating a black spiderweb that disappears at the edge of vision. The nearest cable terminus is more than a kilometer and a half to the north – on a little rock fang that stands out against the white glory of Chomo Lori, 'Queen of Snow' – but we are going east across the great gap between the ridges, our terminal point is more than twenty kilometers away, and the cable dropping away in that direction appears to end in midair as it blends into the evening glow of the distant rock wall. And our final destination is more than thirty-five klicks beyond that to the north and east. Walking, it would take us about six hours to make the long trip north along Phari Ridge and then east across the system of bridges and catwalks. Traveling by cable and slideway should take less than half that time, but it is late in the day and the slideway is especially dangerous. I glance at the low sun again and wonder again about the wisdom of this plan.

'Ready,' growls the cablemaster, a brown little man in a stained patch-work *chuba*. He is chewing besil root and turns to spit over the edge as we step up to the clip-on line.

'Ready,' A. Bettik and I say in unison.

'Keep'ur distance,' growls the cablemaster and gestures for me to go first.

I shake my traveling risers loose from my full-body harness, slide my hands over the crowded gear sling that we call a rack, find the two-bearing pulley by feel, clip it on to the riser ring with a carabiner, run a Munter hitch into a second carabiner as a friction-brake backup to the pulley brake, find my best offset-D carabiner and use it to clip the pulley flanges together around the cable, and then run my safety line through the first two carabiners while tying a short prusik sling on to the rope, finally clipping that on to my chest harness below the risers. All of this takes less than a minute. I raise both hands, grab the D-ring controls to the pulley, and jump up and down, testing both the pulley connection and my clip-ons. Everything holds.

The cablemaster leans over to inspect the double-D-ring attachment and the pulley clamp with expert eyes. He runs the pulley up and back a meter, making sure that the near-frictionless bearings are sliding smoothly in their compact housing. Finally he puts all of his weight on my shoulders and harness, hanging on me like a second rucksack, and then releases me to make sure that the rings and brakelines hold. I am sure that he cares nothing if I fall to my death, but if the pulley was to stick somewhere on the twenty klicks of braided monofilament cable running out there to invisibility, it will be this cablemaster who will have to clear the mess, hanging from his etriers or belay seat over kilometers of air while waiting commuters seethe. He seems satisfied with the equipment.

'Go,' he says and slaps me on the shoulder.

I jump into space, shifting my bulging rucksack high on my back as I do so. The harness webbing stretches, the cable sags, the pulley bearings hum ever so slightly, and I begin to slide faster as I release the brake with both thumbs on the D-ring controls. Within seconds I am hurtling down the cable. I lift my legs and sit back up into the harness seat in the way that has become second nature to me in the past three months. K'un Lun Ridge, our destination, glows brightly as sunset shadow begins to fill the abyss beneath me and evening shade moves down the wall of Phari Ridge behind me.

I feel a slight change in the cable tension and hear the cable humming as A. Bettik begins his descent behind me. Glancing back, I can see him leaving the jump-off platform, his legs straight ahead of him in the approved form, his body bobbing beneath the elastic risers. I can just make out the tether connecting the leather band on his left arm to the pulley brakeline. A. Bettik waves and I wave back, swiveling in my harness to pay attention to the cable screaming past me as I continue hurtling out over the gorge. Sometimes birds land on the cable to rest. Sometimes there is a sudden ice buildup or braid spurs. Very rarely there is a snagged pulley of someone who has met with an accident or cut away from their harness for reasons known only to themselves. Even more rarely, but enough to fix it in the mind, someone with a grudge or vague psychopathic tendencies will pause on the cable to loop a chock sling or spring-loaded cam around it, leaving a little surprise for the next person to come flying along the line. The penalty for that crime is death by flinging from the highest platform of Potala or Jo-kung, but this is of little solace to the person who first encounters the chock or cam.

None of these eventualities materialize as I slide across the emptiness under the ultralight cable. The only sound is the slight hum from the pulley brake as I moderate my speed and the soft rush of air. We are still in sunlight and it is late spring on this world, but the air is always chilly above eight thousand meters. Breathing is no problem. Every day since I arrived on T'ien Shan, I thank the gods of planetary evolution that even with the slightly lighter gravity here – zero-point-nine-five-four standard – the oxygen is richer at this altitude. Glancing down at the clouds some klicks below my boots, I think of the seething ocean in that blind pressure, stirred by winds of phosgene and thick CO_2. There is no real surface land on T'ien Shan, merely that thick soup of a planetary ocean and the countless sharp peaks and ridges rising thousands of meters to the O_2 layer and the bright, Hyperion-like sunlight.

Memory nudges me. I think of another cloudscape world from a few months back. I think of my first day out in the ship, before reaching the translation point and while my fever and broken leg were healing, when I said idly to the ship, 'I wonder how I got through the farcaster here. My last memory was of a giant . . .'

The ship had answered by running a holo taken from one of its buoy cameras as it sat at the bottom of the river where we had left it. It was a starlight-enhanced image – it was raining – and showed the green-glowing arch of the farcaster and tossing treetops. Suddenly a tentacle longer than the ship came through the farcaster opening, carrying what looked to be a toy kayak draped about with a mass of riddled parasail fabric. The tentacle made a single, graceful, slow-motion twist and parasail, kayak, and slumped figure in the cockpit glided – fluttered, actually – a hundred meters or so to disappear in the thrashing treetops.

'Why didn't you come get me then?' I asked, not hiding the irritation in my voice. My leg still hurt. 'Why wait all night while I hung there in the rain? I could have died.'

'I had no instructions to retrieve you upon your return,' said the arrogant, idiot-savant ship's voice. 'You might have been carrying out some important business that would brook no interruption. If I had not heard from you in several days, I would have sent a crawler drone into the jungle to inquire as to your well-being.'

I explained my opinion of the ship's logic.

'That is a strange designation,' said the ship. 'While I have certain organic elements incorporated into my substructure and decentralized DNA computing components, I am not – in the strictest sense of the term – a biological organism. I have no digestive system. No need for elimination, other than the occasional waste gas and passenger effluvium. Therefore, I have no anus in either real or figurative terms. Therefore, I hardly believe I could qualify to be called an . . .'

'Shut up,' I said.

The slide takes less than fifteen minutes. I brake cautiously as the great wall of the K'un Lun Ridge approaches. For the last few hundred meters, my shadow – and A. Bettik's – is thrown ahead of us against the orange-glowing vertical expanse of rock and we become shadow puppets – two strange stick figures with flailing appendages as we work the riser rings to brake our descent and swing our legs to brace for landing. Then the pulley brake sound grows from a low hum to a loud groan as I slow for the final approach to the landing ledge – a six-meter slab of stone with the back wall lined with padded zygoat fleece made brown and rotten by the weather.

I slide and bounce to a stop three meters from the wall, find my footing on the rock, and unclip my pulley and safety line with a speed born of practice. A. Bettik slides to a stop a moment later. Even with one hand, the android is infinitely more graceful than I on the cables; he uses up less than a meter of landing run-out.

We stand there a minute, watching the sun balance on the edge of Phari Ridge, the low light painting the ice-cone summit rising above the jet stream to the south of it. When we finish adjusting our harnesses and equipment racks to our liking, I say, 'It's going to be dark by the time we get into the Middle Kingdom.'

A. Bettik nods. 'I would prefer to have the slideway behind us before full darkness falls, M. Endymion, but I think that this will not be the case.'

Even the thought of doing the slideway in the dark makes my scrotum tighten. I wonder idly if a male android has any similar physiological reaction. 'Let's get moving,' I say, setting off down the slab ledge at a trot.

We lost several hundred meters of altitude on the cableway, and we will have to make it up now. The ledge soon runs out – there are very few flat places on the peaks of the Mountains of Heaven – and our boots clatter as we jog down a bonsai-bamboo scaffold walkway that hangs from the cliff wall and juts out over nothing. There is no railing here. The evening winds are rising and I seal my therm jacket and zygoat-fleece *chuba* as we jog along. The heavy pack bounces on my back.

The jumar point is less than a klick north of the landing ledge. We pass no one on the walkway, but far across the cloud-stirred valley we can see the torches being lit on the Walk Way between Phari and Jo-kung. The scaffold way and maze of suspension bridges on that side of the Great Abyss is coming alive with people heading north – some undoubtedly headed for the Temple Hanging in Air to hear Aenea's evening public session. I want to get there before them.

The jumar point consists of four fixed lines running up the vertical rock wall for almost seven hundred meters above us. These red lines are for ascension. A few meters away dangle the blue lines for rappelling from the ridge summit. Evening shadow covers us by now and the rising winds are chill. 'Side by side?' I say to A. Bettik, gesturing toward one of the middle ropes.

The android nods. His blue countenance looks precisely as I had remembered it from our trip out from Hyperion, almost ten of his years ago. What did I expect – an android to age?

We remove our powered ascenders from our web racks and clip on to adjoining lines, shaking the hanging microfiber lines as if that will tell us if they are still anchored properly. The fixed ropes here are checked only occasionally by the cablemasters; they could have been torn by someone's jumar clips, or abraided by hidden rock spurs, or coated with ice. We will soon know.

We each clip a daisy chain and etriers to our powered ascenders. A. Bettik unloops eight meters of climbing line and we attach this to our harnesses with locking carabiners. Now, if one of the fixed lines fails, the other person can arrest the first climber's fall. Or so goes the theory.

The powered ascenders are the most technology owned by most citizens on T'ien Shan: powered by a sealed solar battery, little larger than our hands that fit in the molded grips, the ascenders are elegant pieces of climbing equipment. A. Bettik checks his attachments and nods. I thumb both of my ascenders to life. The telltales glow green. I jumar the right ascender up a meter, clamp it, step up in the looped etrier foothold, check that I am clear, slide the left ascender up a bit farther, clamp it tight, swing my left foot up two loops, and so on. And so on for seven hundred meters, the two of us pausing occasionally to hang from our etriers and look out across the valley where the Walk Way is ablaze with torches. The sun has set now and the sky has darkened immediately to violets and purples, the brightest stars already making an appearance. I estimate that we have about twenty minutes of real twilight left. We will be doing the slideway in the dark.

I shiver as the wind howls around us.

The fixed lines hang over vertical ice for the last two hundred meters. We both carry collapsible crampons in our rack bags, but we do not need them as we continue the tiring ritual – jumar – clamp – step – pull etriers free – rest a second – jumar – clamp – step – pull – rest – jumar. It takes us almost forty minutes to do the seven hundred meters. It is quite dark as we step onto the ice-ridge platform.

T'ien Shan has five moons: four of them captured asteroids but in orbits low enough to reflect quite a bit of light, the fifth almost as large as Old Earth's moon, but fractured on its upper right quadrant by a single, huge impact crater whose rays spread like a glowing spiderweb to every visible edge of the sphere. This large moon – the Oracle – is rising in the northeast as A. Bettik and I walk slowly north along the narrow ice ridge, clipping on to fixed cables to keep from being blown away by the sub-zero winds that hurtle down from the jet stream now.

I have pulled up my thermal hood and dropped my face mask into place, but the freezing wind still burns at my eyes and any bits of exposed flesh. We cannot tarry here long. But the urge to stand and gaze is strong in me, as it always is when I stand at the cableway terminus of K'un Lun Ridge and look out over the Middle Kingdom and the world of the Mountains of Heaven.

Pausing at the flat, open icefield at the head of the slideway, I pivot in all directions, taking in the view. To the south and west across the moonlit churn of cloudtops so far below, the Phari Ridge glows in the light of the Oracle. Torches high along the ridge north of Phari clearly mark the Walk Way, and I can see the lighted suspension bridges much farther north. Beyond Phari Marketplace, there is a glow in the sky and I fancy that this is the torchlit brilliance of Potala, Winter Palace for His Holiness the Dalai Lama and home to the most magnificent stone architecture on the planet. It is just a few klicks north of there, I know, that the Pax has just been granted an enclave at Rhan Tso, in the evening shadow of Shivling – the 'Phallus of Shiva'. I smile beneath my therm mask as I imagine the Christian missionaries brooding about this heathen indignity.

Beyond Potala, hundreds of klicks to the west, is the ridge realm of Koko Nor with its countless hanging villages and dangerous bridges. Far south along the great ridge spine called the Lob-sang Gyatso lies the land of the Yellow Hat Sect, ending at the terminal peak of Nanda Devi, where the Hindu goddess of bliss is said to dwell. Southwest of them, so far around the curve of the world that the sunset still burns there, is Muztagh Alta with its tens of thousands of Islamic dwellers guarding the tombs of Ali and the other saints of Islam. North of Muztagh Alta, the ridges run into territory I have not seen – not even from orbit during my approach – harboring the high homes of the Wandering Jews along the approaches to Mt Zion and Mt Moriah, where the twin cities of Abraham and Isaak boast the finest libraries on T'ien Shan. North and west of them rise Mt Sumeru – the center of the universe – and Harney Peak, also the center of the universe, oddly enough – both some six hundred klicks southeast of the four San Francisco Peaks where the Hopi-Eskimo culture there ekes out a living on the cold ridges and fern clefts, also certain that their peaks bound the center of the universe.

As I turn and look due north, I can see the greatest mountain in our hemisphere and the northern boundary of our world since the ridge disappears beneath phosgene clouds a few klicks north of there – Chomo Lori, 'Queen of Snow'. Incredibly, the sunset still lights Chomo Lori's frozen summit even as the Oracle bathes its eastern ridges with a softer light.

From Chomo Lori, the K'un Lun and Phari ridges both run south, the gap between them widening to unbridgeable distances south of the cableway we have just crossed. I turn my back to the north wind and look to the south and east, tracing the looping K'un Lun ridgeline, imagining that I can see the torches some two hundred klicks south where the city of Hsi wang-mu, 'Queen Mother of the West' ('west' being south and west of the Middle Kingdom), shelters some thirty-five thousand people in the safety of its notches and fissures.

South of Hsi wang-mu, with only its high summit visible above the jet stream, rises the great peak of Mt Koya, where – according to the faithful who live in ice-tunnel cities on its lower reaches – Kobo Daishi, the founder of Shingon Buddhism, lies interred in his airless ice tomb, waiting for conditions to be right before emerging from his meditative trance.

East of Mt Koya, out of sight over that curve of the world, is Mt Kalais, home to Kubera, the Hindu god of wealth, as well as to Shiva, who evidently does not mind being separated from his phallus by more than a thousand kilometers of cloud space. Parvati, Shiva's wife, is also reputed to live on Mt Kalais, although no one has heard her opinion of the separation.

A. Bettik had traveled to Mt Kalais during his first full year on the planet, and he told me that the peak was beautiful, one of the tallest peaks on the planet – more than nineteen thousand meters above sea level – and he described it as looking like a marble sculpture rising from a pedestal of striated rock. The android also said that on the summit of Mt Kalais, high on the icefields where the wind is too thin to blow or breathe, sits a carboned-alloy temple to the Buddhist deity of the mountain, Demchog, the 'One of Supreme Bliss', a giant at least ten meters tall, as blue as the sky, draped with garlands of skulls and happily embracing his female consort as he dances. A. Bettik said that the blue-skinned deity looks a bit like him. The palace itself is in the precise center of the rounded summit, which lies in the center of a mandala made up of lesser snow peaks, all of it embracing the sacred circle – the physical mandala – of the divine space of Demchog, where those who meditate will discover the wisdom to set them free from the cycle of suffering.

In sight of the Mt Kalais Demchog mandala, said A. Bettik, and so far to the south that the peak is buried beneath kilometer-deep glaciers of gleaming ice, rises Helgafell – the 'Mead Hall of the Dead' – where a few hundred Hegira-transplanted Icelanders have reverted to Viking ways.

I look to the southwest. If I could someday travel the arc of the Antarctic Circle there, I know, I would come across such peaks as Gunung Agung, the navel of the world (one of dozens on T'ien Shan), where the Eka Dasa Rudra Festival is now twenty-seven years into its sixth hundred-year cycle, and where the Balinese women are said to dance with unsurpassed beauty and grace. Northwest more than a thousand klicks along the high ridge from Gunung Agung is Kilimachaggo, where the denizens of the lower terraces disinter their dead from the loamy fissures after a decent interval and carry the bones high above breathable atmosphere – climbing in handsewn skin-suits and pressure masks – to rebury their relatives in rock-hard ice near the eighteen-thousand-meter level, with the skulls staring through ice toward the summit in eternal hopefulness.

Beyond Kilimachaggo, the only peak I know by name is Croagh Patrick, which reputedly has no snakes. But as far as I know, there are no snakes anywhere else on the Mountains of Heaven.

I turn back to the northeast. The cold and wind buffet me head-on, urging me to hurry, but I take this final minute to look out toward our destination. A. Bettik also appears to be in no rush, although it might be anxiety about the coming slideway that causes him to pause here a moment with me.

To the north and east here, beyond the sheer wall of the K'un Lun Ridge, lies the Middle Kingdom with its five peaks glowing in the lantern light of the Oracle.

To the north of us, the Walk Way and a dozen suspension bridges cross the space to the town of Jo-kung and the central peak of Sung Shan, the 'Lofty', although this is by far the lowest of the five summits of the Middle Kingdom.

Ahead of us, connected from the southwest only by a sheer ice ridge branded by the looping route of the slideway, rises Hua Shan, 'Flower Mountain', the westernmost summit in the Middle Kingdom and arguably the most beautiful of the five peaks. From Hua Shan, the final klicks of cableway connect the Flower Mountain to the spur ridges north of Jo-kung where Aenea works on Hsuan-k'ung Ssu, the Temple Hanging in Air, set into a sheer cliff face looking north across the abyss to Heng Shan, the Sacred Mountain of the North.

There is a second Heng Shan some two hundred klicks to the south, marking the Middle Kingdom's boundary there, but it is an unimpressive mound compared to the sheer walls, great ridges, and sweeping profile of its northern counterpart. Looking north through the raging winds and sheets of spindrift, I remember being in the Consul's ship and floating between the noble Heng Shan and the Temple on that first hour on the planet.

Glancing to the east and north again, beyond Hua Shan and the short central peak of Sung Shan, I can easily see the incredible summit of T'ai Shan silhouetted against the rising Oracle more than three hundred klicks away. This is the Great Peak of the Middle Kingdom, eighteen thousand, two hundred meters tall, with its town of Tai'an – the City of Peace – hunkered down at the nine thousand-meter level, and its legendary twenty-seven thousand-step staircase rising from Tai'an, through the snow-fields and rock walls, all the way to the mythical Temple of the Jade Emperor on the summit.

Beyond our Sacred Mountain of the North, I know, rise the Four Mountains of Pilgrimage for the Buddhist faithful – O-mei Shan to the west;

Chiu-hua Shan, 'Nine Flower Mountain', to the south; Wu-t'ai Shan, the 'Five Terrace Mountain' with its welcoming Purple Palace to the north; and lowly but subtly beautiful P'u-t'o Shan in the far east.

I take a few final seconds on this wind-battered ice ridge, glancing toward Jo-kung, hoping to see the torchlights lining the fissure pass over to Hsuan-k'ung Ssu, but high clouds or sheets of spindrift haze the view so that only an Oracle-lighted blur is to be seen.

Turning to A. Bettik, I point toward the slideway and give the thumbs-up gesture. The wind is blowing too hard now to carry words.

A. Bettik nods and reaches back to unfurl the folding sledfoil from an outside pocket on his pack. I realize that my heart is pounding from more than exertion as I find my own sledfoil and carry it to the slideway launch platform.

The slideway is fast. That has always been its appeal. And that is its greatest danger.

There are still places in the Pax, I am sure, where the ancient custom of tobogganing still exists. In that sport, one sits on a flat-bottomed sled and hurtles down a prepared ice course. This pretty much describes the slide-way, except that instead of a flat-bottomed sled, A. Bettik and I each have a sledfoil, which is less than a meter long and curves up around us like a spoon. The sledfoil is more foil than sled, as limp as so much aluminum wrap until we each divert a bit of power from our ascenders, sending the piezoelectric message to the stiffeners in the foil structure until our little sleds seem to inflate, taking form in a few seconds.

Aenea once told me that there used to be fixed carbon-carbon lines running the length of the slideway, and the sledders had clipped on to them much as we would a cableway or rappel line, using a special low-friction clip ring similar to the cable pulley to keep from losing speed. That way, one could brake using the cable or, if the sled were to fly off into space, use the clip line as a self-arrest harness. There would be bruises and broken bones with such a safety line, but at least the body would not fly out into space with the sled.

But the cables had not worked, Aenea said. They took too much main-tenance to keep clear and functioning. Sudden ice storms would freeze them to the side of the slideway and someone traveling a hundred and fifty klicks an hour would suddenly have their clip ring encounter im-movable ice. It is hard enough these days keeping the cableway clear: the fixed lines of the slideway had been unmanageable.

So the slideways were abandoned. At least until teenagers looking for a thrill and adults in a serious hurry found that nine times out of ten, one could keep the sledfoils in the groove just by glissading – that is, by using one or more ice axes in the self-arrest position and keeping the speed low enough to stay in the trough. 'Low enough' meaning beneath a hundred and fifty klicks per hour. Nine times out of ten it would work. If one was very skillful. And if the conditions were perfect. And if it was daylight.

A. Bettik and I had taken the slideway three other times, once returning from Phari with some medicine needed to save a young girl's life and twice just to learn the turns and straightaways. The voyage had been exhilarating and terrifying those times, but we had made it safely. But each time had been in daylight . . . with no wind . . . and with other glissaders ahead of us, showing the way.

Now it is dark; the long run gleams wickedly in the moonlight ahead of us. The surface looks iced and rough as stone. I have no idea if anyone has made the run this day . . . or this week . . . if anyone has checked for fissures, ice heaves, fractures, cave-ins, crevasses, ice spikes, or other obstacles. I do not know how long the ancient toboggan runs had been, but this slideway is more than twenty klicks long, running along the side of the sheer Abruzzi Spur connecting K'un Lun Ridge to the slopes of Hua Shan, flattening out on the gradual icefields on the west side of the Flower Mountain, kilometers south of the safer and slower Walk Way looping down from the north. From Hua Shan, it is only nine klicks and three easy cable runs to the scaffolding of Jo-kung and then a brisk walk through the fissure pass and down onto the sheer-face walkways to Hsuan-k'ung Ssu.

A. Bettik and I are sitting side by side like children on sleds, waiting for a push from Mommy or Daddy. I lean over, grab my friend's shoulder, and pull him closer so that I can shout through the thermal material of his hood and face mask. The wind is stinging me with ice now. 'All right if I lead?' I yell.

A. Bettik turns his face so that our cloth-covered cheeks are touching. 'M. Endymion, I feel that I should lead. I have done this slideway two more times than you, sir.'

'In the dark?' I shout.

A. Bettik shakes his hooded head. 'Few try it in the dark these days, M. Endymion. But I have a very good memory of every curve and straight. I believe I can be helpful in showing you the proper braking points.'

I hesitate only a second. 'All right,' I say. I squeeze his hand through our gloves.

With night-vision goggles, this would be as easy as a daylight slideway glissade – which does not qualify as easy in my book. But I had lost the goggles that I had taken on my farcaster odyssey, and although the ship carried replacement pairs, I had left them in the ship. 'Bring two skinsuits and rebreathers,' Rachel had relayed from Aenea. She might have mentioned night-vision goggles.

Today's jaunt was supposed to have been an easy hike to Phari Marketplace, a night spent in the hostelry there, and then a pack trip back with George Tsarong, Jigme Norbu, and a long line of porters, hauling the heavy material for the building site.

Perhaps, I think, I'm overreacting to the news of the Pax landing. Too late now. Even if we turn around, the rappel down the fixed lines on K'un Lun Ridge would be as much trouble as this glissade. Or so I lie to myself.

I watch as A. Bettik rigs his short, thirty-eight-centimeter ice-climbing hammer in the loop of the wristband on his left arm, then readies his regular seventy-five-centimeter ice axe. Sitting cross-legged on my sled, I slip my own ice hammer into my left hand and trail my longer ice axe in my right hand like a tiller. I give the android the thumbs-up signal again and watch as he pushes off in the moonlight, spinning once, then steadying the sled expertly with his short ice hammer, chips flying, and then hurtling over the brink and out of sight for a minute. I wait until there is an interval of ten meters or so – far enough to avoid the ice spray of his passing, close enough to see him in the orange light of the Oracle – and then I push over myself.

Twenty kilometers. At an average speed of a hundred and twenty klicks per hour, we should cover the distance in ten minutes. Ten freezing, adrenaline-pumping, gorge-rising, terror-beating-against-the-ribs, react-in-a-microsecond-or-die minutes.

A. Bettik is brilliant. He sets up each turn perfectly, coming in low for the high-banked curves so that his apogee – and mine a few seconds later – will be teetering right at the lip of the icy bank, careering out of the banked turn at just the right speed for the next descending straight, then banging and skipping down the long icy ramp so fast that vision blurs, the pounding comes up through my tailbone and spine so that vision is doubled, trebled, and my head pounds with the pain of it, then blurs again with the spray of ice chips flying, creating halos in the moonlight, bright as the unblinking stars spill and reel above us – the brilliant stars competing even with the Oracle's glow and the asteroid moons' quick, tumbling light – and then we are braking low and bouncing hard and riding high again, arresting into a sharp left that takes my breath away, then skidding into a sharper right, then pounding and flying down a straight so steep that the sled and I seem to be screaming into freefall. For a minute I am looking straight down at the moonlit phosgene clouds – green as mustard gas in the lying moonlight – then we are both racketing around a series of spirals, DNA-helix switch-backs, our sleds teetering on the edge of each bank so that twice my ice-axe blade bites into nothing but freezing air, but both times we drop back down and emerge – not exiting the turns so much as being spat out of them, two rifle bullets fired just above the ice – and then we bank high again, come out accelerating onto a straight, and shoot across eight kilometers of sheer ice wall on the Abruzzi Spur, the right banked wall of the slideway now serving as the floor of our passage, my ice axe spinning chips into vertical space as our speed increases, then increases more, then becomes something more than speed as the cold, thin air slices through my mask and thermal garments and gloves and heated boots to freeze flesh and to tear at muscle. I feel the frozen skin of my cheeks stretching under my thermal mask as I grin idiotically, a rictal grimace of terror and the sheer joy of mindless speed, my arms and hands adjusting constantly, automatically, instantly to changes in the ice-axe tiller and the ice-hammer brake.

Suddenly A. Bettik swerves to the left, chips flying as he bites deep with the curved blades of both long and short axes – it makes no sense, such a move will send him – both of us! – bouncing off the inner wall, the vertical ice wall, and then screaming out into black air – but I trust him, making the decision in less than a second, and slam the blade of my large axe down, pounding hard with my ice hammer, feeling my heart in my throat as I skid sideways and threaten to slide right instead of left, on the verge of spinning and spiraling off the narrow ice ledge at a hundred and forty kilometers per hour – but I correct and stabilize and flash past a hole in the ice floor where we would have been sliding except for this wild detour, hurtling onto a broken-away ledge six or eight meters wide, a trapdoor to death – and then A. Bettik rackets down off the inner wall, catches his slide with a flash of ice-axe blades in the moonlight, and then continues hurtling down the Abruzzi Spur toward the final series of turns onto the Hua Shan ice slopes.

And I follow.

On the Flower Mountain, we are both too frozen and shaken to rise from our sleds for several cold minutes. Then, together, we get to our feet, ground the piezoelectric charges in our sleds, collapse them, and fold them away in our packs. We walk the ice path around the shoulder of Hua Shan in silence – me in awe of A. Bettik's reactions and courage, him in silence I cannot interpret but fervently hope is not anger at my hasty decision to return via this route.

The final three cableway flights are anticlimax, noted only for the beauty of the moonlight on the peaks and ridges around us, and for the difficulty I have in closing my frozen fingers on the D-ring brakes.

Jo-kung is ablaze with torches after the moonlit emptiness of the upper slopes, but we avoid the main scaffolds and take the ladders to the fissure pass. Then we are surrounded by the shadowed darkness of the north face, broken by sputtering torches along the high walkway to Hsuan-k'ung Ssu. We jog the last kilometer.

We arrive just as Aenea is beginning her early-evening discussion session. There are about a hundred people crowded into the little platform pagoda. She looks across the heads of the wailing people, sees my face, asks Rachel to begin the discussion, and comes immediately to where A. Bettik and I stand in the windy doorway.

SIXTEEN

I admit that I was confused and a bit depressed when I first arrived on the Mountains of Heaven.

I slept in cryogenic fugue for three months and two weeks. I had thought that cryogenic fugue was dreamless, but I was wrong. I had nightmares for most of the way and awoke disoriented and apprehensive.

The translation point in our outbound system had been only seventeen hours away, but in the T'ien Shan System we had to translate from C-plus out beyond the last icy planet and decelerate in-system for three full days. I jogged the various decks, up and down the spiral staircase, and even out onto the little balcony I'd had the ship extrude. I told myself that I was trying to get my leg back into shape – it still hurt despite the ship's pronouncement that the doc-in-the-box had healed it and that there should be no pain – but in truth, I knew, I was trying to work off nervous energy. I'm not sure that I remembered ever being so anxious before.

The ship wanted to tell me all about this star system in excruciating detail – G-type yellow star, blah, blah, blah – well, I could *see* that . . . eleven worlds, three gas giants, two asteroid belts, a high percentage of comets in the inner system, blah, blah, blah. I was interested only in T'ien Shan, and I sat in the carpeted holopit and watched it grow. The world was amazingly bright. Blindingly bright. A brilliant pearl set against the black of space.

'What you are seeing is the lower, permanent cloud layer,' droned the ship. 'The albedo is impressive. There are higher clouds – see those storm swirls in the lower right of the illuminated hemisphere? Those high cirrus causing shadows near the north polar cap? Those are the clouds that would bring weather to the human inhabitants.'

'Where are the mountains?' I asked.

'There,' said the ship, circling a gray shadow in the northern hemisphere. 'According to my old charts, this is a great peak in the northern reaches of the eastern hemisphere – Chomo Lori, "Queen of Snow" – and you see these striations running south from it? See how they stay close together until they pass the equator and then spread farther and farther apart until they disappear into the south polar cloud masses? These are the two great spine ridges, Phari Ridge and K'un Lun Ridge. They were the first inhabited rock lines on the planet and are excellent examples of the equivalent early Cretaceous Dakotan violent upthrust resulting in . . .'

Blah, blah, blah. And all I could think of was Aenea, and Aenea, and Aenea.

It was strange entering a system with no Pax Fleet ships to challenge us, no orbital defenses, no lunar bases . . . not even a base on the giant bull's-eye of a moon that looked as if someone had fired a single bullet into a smooth orange sphere – no register of Hawking-drive wakes or neutrino emissions or gravitational lenses or cleared swaths of Bussard-jet drones – no sign of any higher technologies. The ship said that there was a trickle of microwave broadcasting emanating from certain areas of the planet, but when I had them piped in, they turned out to be in pre-Hegira Chinese. This was a shock. I had never been on a world where the majority of humans spoke anything but a version of Web English.

The ship entered geosynchronous orbit above the eastern hemisphere. 'Your directions were to find the peak called Heng Shan, which should be approximately six hundred and fifty kilometers southeast of Chomo Lori . . . there!' The telescopic view in the holopit zoomed in on a beautiful fang of snow and ice leaping through at least three layers of cloud until the summit gleamed clear and bright above most of the atmosphere.

'Jesus,' I whispered. 'And where is Hsuan-k'ung Ssu? The Temple Hanging in Air?'

'It should be . . . *there*,' said the ship triumphantly.

We were looking straight down at a vertical ridge of ice, snow, and gray rock. Clouds broiled at the base of this incredible slab. Even looking at this through the holo viewer made me grab couch cushions and reel in vertigo.

'Where?' I said. There were no structures in sight.

'That dark triangle,' said the ship, circling what I thought was a shadow on one gray slab of rock. 'And this line . . . here.'

'What's the magnification?' I asked.

'The triangle is approximately one-point-two meters along the longest edge,' came the voice I'd grown to know so well from my comlog.

'Pretty small building for people to live in,' I pointed out.

'No, no,' said the ship. 'This is just a bit of a human-made structure protuding from under what must be a rock overhang. I would surmise that the entire so-called Temple Hanging in Air is under this overhang. The rock is more than vertical at this point . . . it pitches back some sixty or eighty meters.'

'Can you get us a side view? So that I can see the Temple?'

'I could,' said the ship. 'It would require repositioning us in a more northerly orbit so that I can use the telescope to look south over the peak of Heng Shan, and go to infrared to look through the cloud mass at eight thousand meters which is passing between the peak and the ridge spur on which the Temple is built. I would also have to . . .'

'Skip it,' I said. 'Just tightbeam that temple area . . . hell, the whole ridge . . . and see if Aenea is waiting for us.'

'Which frequency?' said the ship.

Aenea had not mentioned any frequency. She had just said something about not being able to land in a true sense, but to come down to Hsuan-k'ung Ssu anyway. Looking at this vertical and worse-than-vertical wall of snow and ice, I began to understand what she meant.

'Broadcast on whatever common frequency we would have used if you were calling a comlog extension,' I said. 'If there's no answer, dial through all the frequencies you have. You might try the frequencies that you picked up earlier.'

'They were coming from the southernmost quadrant of the western hemisphere,' said the ship in a patient voice. 'I picked up no microwave emanations from this hemisphere.'

'Just do it, please,' I said.

We hung there for half an hour, sweeping the ridge with tightbeam, then broadcasting general radio signals toward all the peaks in the area, then flooding the hemisphere with short queries. There was no response.

'Can there actually be an inhabited world where no one uses radio?' I said.

'Of course,' said the ship. 'On Ixion, it is against local law and custom to use microwave communication of any sort. On New Earth there was a group which . . .'

'Okay, okay,' I said. For the thousandth time, I wondered if there were a way to reprogram this autonomous intelligence so that it wasn't such a pain in the ass. 'Take us down,' I said.

'To which location?' said the ship. 'There are extensive inhabited areas on the high peak to the east – T'ai Shan it is called on my map – and another city south on the K'un Lun Ridge, it is called Hsi wang-mu, I believe, and other habitations along the Phari Ridge and west of there in an area marked as Koko Nor. Also . . .'

'Take us down to the Temple Hanging in Air,' I said.

Luckily, the planet's magnetic field was completely adequate for the ship's EM repulsors, so we floated down through the sky rather than having to descend on a tail of fusion flame. I went out to the balcony to watch, although the – holopit or screens in the top bedroom would have been more practical.

It seemed to take hours, but actually within minutes we were floating gently at eight thousand-some meters, drifting between the fantastic peak to the north – Heng Shan – and the ridge holding Hsuan-k'ung Ssu. I had seen the terminator rushing from the east as we descended, and according to the ship, it was late afternoon here now. I carried a pair of binoculars out to the balcony and stared. I could see the Temple clearly. I could see it, but I could not quite believe it.

What had seemed a mere play of light and shadow beneath the huge, striated, overhanging slabs of gray granite was a series of structures extending east and west for many hundreds of meters. I could see the Asian influence at once: pagoda-shaped buildings with pitched tile roofs and curling eaves, their elaborately tiled surfaces gilded and glowing in the bright sunlight; round windows and moon gates in the lower brick sections of the superstructure, airy wooden porches with elaborately carved railings; delicate wooden pillars painted the color of dried blood; red and yellow banners draped from eaves and doorways and railings; complicated carvings on the roof beams and tower ridges; and suspension bridges and stairways festooned with what I would later learn were prayer wheels and prayer flags, each offering a prayer to Buddha every time a human hand spun it or the wind fluttered it.

The Temple was still being built. I could see raw wood being carried up to high platforms, saw human figures chiseling away at the stone face of the ridge, could see scaffolding, rude ladders, crude bridges consisting of little more than some sort of woven plant material with climbing ropes for handrails, and upright figures hauling empty baskets up these ladders and bridges and more stooped figures carrying the baskets full of stone back down to a broad slab where most of the baskets were dumped into space. We were close enough that I could see that many of these human figures wore colorful robes hanging almost to their ankles – some blowing in the stiff wind that blew across the rockface here – and that these robes looked thick and lined against the cold. I would later learn that these were the ubiquitous *chuba*, and that they could be made of thick, waterproof zygoat wool or of ceremonial silk or even of cotton, although this last material was rare and much prized.

I had been nervous about showing our ship to the locals – afraid it might cause a panic or a laser-lance attack or something – but did not know what else to do. We were still several kilometers away, so at most we would be an unusual glint of sunlight on dark metal floating against the white backdrop of the northern peak. I had hoped that they would think us just another bird – the ship and I had seen many birds through the viewer, many of them with wingspans several meters across – but that hope was dashed as I saw first a few of the workers at the Temple pause in their labors and stare out in our direction, then more, and more. No one panicked. There was no rush for shelter or to retrieve weapons – I saw no weapons in sight anywhere – but we had obviously been seen. I watched two women in robes run up through the ascending series of temple buildings, hanging bridges, stairways, steep ladders, and penultimate construction scaffolding to the easternmost platform where the work seemed to consist of cutting holes in the rock wall. There was some sort of construction shack there, and one of the women disappeared into it, coming out a moment later with several taller forms in robes.

I increased the magnification of my binoculars, my heart pounding against my ribs, but there was drifting smoke from the construction work and I could not make out for sure if the tallest person there was Aenea. But through the veils of swirling smoke, I did catch a glimpse of blonde-brown hair – just shorter than shoulder length – and for a moment I lowered the binoculars and just stared out at the distant wall, grinning like an idiot.

'They are signaling,' said the ship.

I looked through the glasses again. Another person – female, I think, but with much darker hair – was flashing two handheld semaphore flags.

'It is an ancient signal code,' said the ship. 'It is called Morse. The first words are . . .'

'Quiet,' I said. We had learned Morse Code in the Home Guard and I had used it once with two bloody bandages to call in medevac skimmers on the Iceshelf.

GO . . . TO . . . THE . . . FISSURE . . . TEN KLICKS . . . TO . . . THE . . . NORTH . . . EAST.

HOVER . . . THERE.

AWAIT . . . INSTRUCTIONS.

'Got that, Ship?' I said.

'Yes.' The ship's voice always sounded cold after I was rude to it.

'Let's go,' I said. 'I think I see a gap about ten klicks to the northeast. Let's stay as far out as we can and come in from the east. I don't think they'll be able to see us from the Temple, and I don't see any other structures along the cliff face in that direction.'

Without further comment, the ship brought us out and around and back along the sheer rock wall until we came to the fissure – a vertical cleft dropping several thousand meters from the ice and snow far above to a point where it converged about four hundred meters above the level of the Temple, which now was out of sight around the curve of rockface to the west.

The ship floated vertically until we were just fifty meters above the bottom of the fissure. I was surprised to see streams running down the steep rock walls of the sides of this gap, tumbling into the center of the fissure before pouring off into thin air as a waterfall. There were trees and mosses and lichens and flowering plants everywhere along this cleft, fields of them rising many hundreds of meters alongside the streams until finally becoming mere streaks of multicolored lichen rising toward the ice levels above. At first I was sure that there was no sign of human intrusion here, but then I saw the chiseled ledges along the north wall – barely wide enough to stand on, I thought – and then the paths through the bright-green moss, and the artfully placed stepping stones in the stream, and then I noticed the tiny, weathered little structure – too small to be a cabin, more like a gazebo with windows – which sat under wind-sculpted evergreens along the stream and near the high point of the fissure's verdant pass.

I pointed and the ship moved up in that direction, hovering near the gazebo. I understood why it would be difficult, if not impossible, to land here. The Consul's ship was not that large – it had been hidden in the stone tower in the old poet's city of Endymion for centuries – but even if it landed vertically on its fins or extendable legs here, some trees, grass, moss, and flowering plants would be crushed. They seemed too rare in this vertical rock world to destroy that way.

So we hovered. And waited. And about thirty minutes after we arrived, a young woman came around the path from the direction of the rock ledges and waved heartily at us.

It was not Aenea.

I admit that I was disappointed. My desire to see my young friend again had reached the point of obsession, and I guess that I was having absurd fantasies of reunion – Aenea and I running toward one another across a flowered field, she the child of eleven again, I her protector, both of us laughing with the pleasure of seeing one another and me lifting her and swinging her around, tossing her up . . .

Well, we had the grassy field. The ship continued hovering and morphed a stairway to the flower-bedecked lawn next to the gazebo. The young woman crossed the stream, hopping from stepping stone to stepping stone with perfect balance, and came grinning toward me up the grassy knoll.

She was in her early twenties. She had the physical grace and sense of presence I remembered from a thousand images of my young friend. But I had never seen this woman before in my life.

Could Aenea have changed this much in five years? Could she have disguised herself to hide from the Pax? Had I simply forgotten what she looked like? The latter seemed improbable. No, impossible. The ship had assured me that it had been five years and some months for Aenea if she was waiting on this world for me, but my entire trip – including the cryogenic fugue part – had taken only about four months. I had aged only a few weeks. I could not have forgotten her. I would never forget her.

'Hello, Raul,' said the young woman with dark hair.

'Hello?' I said.

She stepped closer and extended her hand. She had a firm handshake. 'I'm Rachel. Aenea's described you perfectly.' She laughed. 'Of course, we haven't been expecting anyone else to come calling in a starship looking like this . . .' She waved her hand in the general direction of the ship hanging there like a vertical balloon bobbing softly in the wind.

'How is Aenea?' I said, my voice sounding strange to me. '*Where* is she?'

'Oh, she is back at the Temple. She's working. It's the middle of the busiest work shift. She couldn't get away. She asked me to come over and help you dispose of your ship.'

She couldn't get away. What the hell was this? I'd come through literal hell – suffered kidney stones and broken legs, been chased by Pax troopers, dumped into a world with no land, eaten and regurgitated by an alien – and she couldn't goddamn get away? I bit my lip, resisting the impulse to say what I was thinking. I admit that emotion was surging rather high at that moment.

'What do you mean – dispose of my ship?' I said. I looked around. 'There has to be someplace for it to land.'

'There isn't really,' said the young woman named Rachel. Looking at her now in the bright sunlight, I realized that she was probably a little older than Aenea would be – mid-twenties perhaps. Her eyes were brown and intelligent, her brown hair was chopped off as carelessly as Aenea used to cut hers, her skin was tanned from long hours in the sun, her hands were callused with work, and there were laugh lines at the corners of her eyes.

'Why don't we do this?' said Rachel. 'Why don't you get what you need from the ship, take a comlog or communicator so you can call the ship back when you need it, get two skinsuits and two rebreathers out of the storage locker, and then tell the ship to hop back up to the third moon – the second smallest captured asteroid? There's a deep crater there for it to hide in, but that moon's in a near geosynchronous orbit and it keeps one face toward this hemisphere all the time. You could tightbeam it and it could be back here in a few minutes.'

I looked suspiciously at her. 'Why the skinsuits and rebreathers?' The ship had them. They were designed for benign hard-vacuum environments where true space armor was not required. 'The air seems thick enough here,' I said.

'It is,' said Rachel. 'There's a surprisingly rich oxygen atmosphere at this altitude. But Aenea told me to ask you to bring the skinsuits and rebreathers.'

'Why?' I said.

'I don't know, Raul,' said Rachel. Her eyes were placid, seemingly clear of deceit or guile.

'Why does the ship have to hide?' I said. 'Is the Pax here?'

'Not yet,' said Rachel. 'But we've been expecting them for the last six months or so. Right now, there are no spacecraft on or around T'ien Shan . . . with the exception now of your ship. No aircraft either. No skimmers, no EMVs, no thopters or copters . . . only paragliders . . . the flyers . . . and they would never be out that far.'

I nodded but hesitated.

'The Dugpas saw something they couldn't explain today,' continued Rachel. 'The speck of your ship against Chomo Lori, I mean. But eventually they explain everything in terms of *tendrel*, so that won't be a problem.'

'What are *tendrel*?' I said. 'And who are the Dugpas?'

'*Tendrel* are signs,' said Rachel. 'Divinations within the shamanistic Buddhist tradition prevalent in this region of the Mountains of Heaven. Dugpas are the . . . well, the word translates literally as "highest". The people who dwell at the upper altitudes. There are also the Drukpas, the valley people . . . that is, the lower fissures . . . and the Drungpas, the wooded valley people . . . mostly those who live in the great fern forests and bonsai-bamboo stands on the western reaches of Phari Ridge and beyond.'

'So Aenea's at the Temple?' I said stubbornly, resisting following the young woman's 'suggestion' for hiding the ship.

'Yes.'

'When can I see her?'

'As soon as we walk over there.' Rachel smiled.

'How long have you known Aenea?'

'About four years, Raul.'

'Do you come from this world?'

She smiled again, patient with my interrogation. 'No. When you meet the Dugpas and the others, you'll see that I'm not native. Most of the people in this region are from Chinese, Tibetan, and other Central Asian stock.'

'Where are you from?' I asked flatly, sounding rude in my own ears.

'I was born on Barnard's World,' she said. 'A backwater farming planet. Cornfields and woods and long evenings and a few good universities, but not much else.'

'I've heard of it,' I said. It made me more suspicious. The 'good universities' that had been Barnard's World's claim to fame during the Hegemony had long since been converted to Church academies and seminaries. I had the sudden wish that I could see the flesh of this young woman's chest – see if there were a cruciform there, I mean. It would be all too easy for me to send the ship away and walk into a Pax trap. 'Where did you meet Aenea?' I said. 'Here?'

'No, not here. On Amritsar.'

'Amritsar?' I said. 'I've never heard of it.'

'That's not unusual. Amritsar is a Solmev-marginal world way out back of the Outback. It was only settled about a century ago – refugees from a civil war on Parvati. A few thousand Sikhs and a few thousand Sufi eke out a living there. Aenea was hired to design a desert community center there and I hired on to do the survey and ramrod the construction crew. I've been with her ever since.'

I nodded, still hesitating. I was filled with something not quite disappointment, surging like anger but not quite as clear, bordering on jealousy. But that was absurd. 'A. Bettik?' I said, feeling a sudden intuition that the android had died in the past five years. 'Is he . . .'

'He headed out yesterday for our biweekly provision trek to Phari Marketplace,' said the woman named Rachel. She touched my upper arm. 'A. Bettik's fine. He should be back by moonrise tonight. Come on. Get your stuff. Tell the ship about hiding on the third moon. You'd rather hear all this stuff from Aenea.'

I ended up taking little more than a change of clothes, good boots, my small binoculars, a small sheath knife, the skinsuits and rebreathers, and a palm-sized com unit/journal from the ship. I stuffed all this into a rucksack, hopped down the steps to the meadow, and told the ship what it should do. My anthropomorphizing had reached the point where I expected the ship to sulk at the idea of going back into hibernation mode – on an airless moon this time – but the ship acknowledged the order, suggested that it check in via tightbeam once daily to make sure that the com unit was functioning, and then it floated up and away, dwindling to a speck and then disappearing, like nothing so much as a balloon that has had its string cut.

Rachel gave me a wool *chuba* to pull on over my therm jacket. I noticed the nylon harness she wore over her jacket and trousers, the metal climbing equipment hanging on straps, and asked about it.

'Aenea has a harness for you at the temple site,' she said, rattling the hardware on the sling. 'This is the most advanced technology on this world. The metalworkers at Potala demand and receive a king's ransom for this stuff – crampons, cable pulleys, folding ice axes and ice hammers, chocks, 'biners, lost arrows, bongs, birdbeaks, you name it.'

'Will I need it?' I said dubiously. We had learned some basic ice-climbing techniques in the Home Guard – rappelling, crevasse work, that sort of thing – and I had done some roped-up quarry climbing when I worked with Avrol Hume on the Beak, but I wasn't sure about real mountaineering. I didn't like heights.

'You'll need it but you'll get used to it quickly,' assured Rachel and set off, hopping across the stepping stones and running lightly up the path toward the cliff's edge. The gear jangled softly on her harness, like steel chimes or the bells around some mountain goat's neck.

The ten-klick walk south along the sheer rockface was easy enough once I got used to the narrow ledge, the dizzy-making sheer drop to our right, the bright glare from the incredible mountain to the north and from the churning clouds far below, and the heady surge of energy from the rich atmosphere.

'Yes,' said Rachel when I mentioned the air. 'The oxygen-rich atmosphere here would be a problem if there were forests or savannahs to burn. You should see the monsoon lightning storms. But the bonsai forest back there at the fissure and the fern forests over on the rainy side of Phari is about all we have in terms of combustible materials. They're all fire species. And the bonsai wood that we use in the building is almost too dense to burn.'

For a while we walked in single file and in silence. My attention was on the ledge. We had just come around a sharp corner that required me to duck my head under the overhang when the ledge widened, the view opened up, and there was Hsuan-k'ung Ssu, the 'Temple Hanging in Air'.

From this closer view, a bit below and to the east of the Temple, it still looked to be magically suspended in midair above nothing. Some of the lower, older buildings had stone or brick bases, but the majority were built out over air. These pagoda-style buildings were sheltered by the great rock overhang some seventy-five meters above the main structures, but ladders and platforms zigged and zagged up almost to the underside of that overhang.

We came in among people. The many-hued *chubas* and ubiquitous climbing slings were not the only common denominators here: most of the faces that peered at me with polite curiosity seemed to be of Old Earth Asian stock; the people were relatively short for a roughly standard-g world; they nodded and stepped aside respectfully as Rachel led the way through the crowds, up the ladders, through the incense-and-sandalwood-smelling interior halls of some of the buildings, out and across porches and swinging bridges and up delicate staircases. Soon we were in the upper levels of the Temple where construction proceeded at a rapid pace. The small figures I had seen through binoculars were now living, breathing human beings grunting under heavy baskets of stone, individual people smelling of sweat and honest labor. The silent efficiency I had watched from the ship's terrace now became a clamorous mixture of hammers pounding, chisels ringing, pick-axes echoing, and workers shouting and gesturing amid the controlled chaos common to any construction site.

After several staircases and three long ladders rising to the highest platform, I paused to catch my breath before climbing the last ladder. Rich oxygen atmosphere or no, this climbing was hard work. I noticed Rachel watching me with the equanimity that could easily be mistaken for indifference.

I looked up to see a young woman stepping over the edge of the high platform and descending gracefully. For the briefest of seconds I felt my heart pound with nervousness – Aenea! – but then I saw how the woman moved, saw the short-cropped dark hair from the back, and knew that it was not my friend.

Rachel and I stepped back from the base of the ladder as the woman jumped down the last few rungs. She was large and solid – as tall as I was – with strong features and amazing violet eyes. She looked to be in her forties or early fifties, standard, was deeply tanned and very fit, and from the white wrinkles at the corners of her eyes and mouth, it seemed that she also enjoyed laughing. 'Raul Endymion,' she said, thrusting out her hand. 'I'm Theo Bernard. I help build things.'

I nodded. Her handshake was as firm as Rachel's.

'Aenea's just finishin' up.' Theo Bernard gestured toward the ladder.

I glanced at Rachel.

'You go on up,' she said. 'We've got things to do.'

I went up hand over hand. There were probably sixty rungs on the bamboo ladder, and I was aware as I climbed that the platform below was very narrow if one fell, the drop beyond it endless.

Stepping onto the platform, I saw the rough construction shacks and areas of chiseled stone where the last temple building would be. I was aware of the countless tons of stone starting just ten meters above me where the overhang angled up and out like a granite ceiling. Small birds with v-shaped tails darted and swooped among the cracks and fissures there.

Then all my attention became fixed on the figure emerging from the larger of the two construction shacks.

It was Aenea. The bold, dark eyes, the unselfconscious grin, the sharp cheekbones and delicate hands, the blonde-brown hair cut carelessly and blowing now in the strong wind along the cliff face. She was not that much taller than when I had seen her last – I could still not have kissed her forehead without bending – but she was *changed*.

I took in a sudden breath. I had watched people grow and come of age, of course, but most of these had been my friends when I was also growing and coming of age. Obviously I had never had children, and my careful observation of someone maturing had only been during the four years and some months of my friendship with this child. In most ways, I realized, Aenea still looked much as she had on her sixteenth birthday, five of her years earlier, minus now the last of her baby fat, with sharper cheekbones and firmer features, wider hips and slightly more prominent breasts. She wore whip trousers, high boots, a green shirt I remembered from Taliesin West, and a khaki jacket that was blowing in the wind. I could see that her arms and legs were stronger, more muscled, than I remembered from Old Earth – but not that much was changed about her.

Everything was changed about her. The child I had known was gone. A woman stood in her place; a strange woman walking quickly toward me across the rough platform. It was not just strong features and perhaps a bit more firm flesh on her still-lean form, it was . . . a solidity. A presence. Aenea had always been the most alive, animated, and *complete* person I had ever known, even as a child. Now that the child was gone, or at least submerged in the adult, I could see the solidity within that animated aura.

'Raul!' She crossed the last few steps to me, stood close, and grasped my forearms in her strong hands.

For a second I thought that she was going to kiss me on the mouth the way she had . . . the way the child of sixteen had . . . during the last minutes we had been together on Old Earth. Instead, she raised one long-fingered hand and set it against my face, running fingers down the line of my cheek to my chin. Her dark eyes were alive with . . . what? Not amusement. Vitality, perhaps. Happiness, I hoped.

I felt tongue-tied. I started to speak, stopped, raised my right hand as if to touch her cheek, dropped it.

'Raul . . . damn . . . it is *so* good to see you!' She took her hand away from my face and hugged me with an intensity bordering on violence.

'It's good to see you too, kiddo.' I patted her back, feeling the rough material of her jacket under my palm.

She stepped back, grinning very broadly now, and grabbed my upper arms. 'Was the trip to get the ship terrible? Tell me.'

'Five years!' I said. 'Why didn't you tell me . . .'

'I did. I shouted it.'

'When? At Hannibal? When I was . . .'

'Yes. Then I shouted "I love you." Remember?'

'I remember that, but . . . if you knew . . . five years, I mean . . .'

We were both talking at once, almost babbling. I found myself trying to tell her all about the farcasters, the kidney stone on Vitus-Gray-Balianus B, the Amoiete Spectrum Helix people, the cloud world, the cuttlefish-squid thing – all while I was asking her questions and babbling on again before she could answer.

Aenea kept grinning. 'You look the same, Raul. You look the same. But then, hell, I guess you *should*. It's only been . . . what . . . a week or two of travel and a cold sleep on the ship for you.'

I felt a wash of anger amid the happy giddiness. 'Goddammit, Aenea. You should have *told* me about the time-debt. And maybe about the farcast to a world with no river or solid ground too. I could have died.'

Aenea was nodding. 'But I didn't know for *sure*, Raul. There was no certainty, only the usual . . . possibilities. That's why A. Bettik and I built the parasail into the kayak.' She grinned again. 'I guess it worked.'

'But you knew it would be a long separation. Years for you.' I did not phrase it as a question.

'Yes.'

I started to speak, felt the anger wash away as quickly as it had surged, and took her by the arms. 'It's good to see you, kiddo.' She hugged me again, kissing me on the cheek this time the way she had as a kid when I had delighted her with some joke or comment.

'Come on,' she said. 'The afternoon shift is over. I'll show you our platform and introduce you to some of the people here.'

Our platform? I followed her down ladders and across bridges that I had not noticed while walking with Rachel.

'Have you been all right, Aenea? I mean . . . is everything all right?'

'Yes.' She looked back over her shoulder and smiled at me again. 'Everything is good, Raul.' We crossed a terrace on the side of the topmost of three pagodas stacked one atop the other. I could feel the platform shaking a bit as we walked the narrow terrace, and when we stepped out onto the narrow platform between pagodas, the entire structure vibrated. I noticed that people were leaving the westernmost pagoda and following the narrow ledge trail back along the cliff face.

'This part feels shaky, but it's sturdy enough,' said Aenea, noticing my apprehension. 'Beams of tougher bonsai pine are driven into holes drilled into the rock. That supports the whole infrastructure.'

'They must rot away,' I said as I followed her onto a short suspension bridge. We swayed in the wind.

'They do,' said Aenea. 'They've been replaced several times in the eight hundred-some years the Temple's been here. No one is sure exactly how many times. Their records are shakier than the floors.'

'And you've been hired to add on to the place?' I said. We had come out onto a terrace of wine-colored wood. A ladder at the end rose to another platform and a narrower bridge running from it.

'Yeah,' said Aenea. 'I'm sort of part architect, part construction boss. I'd supervised the construction of a Taoist temple over near Potala when I first arrived, and the Dalai Lama thought that I might be able to finish work on the Temple Hanging in Air. It's frustrated a few would-be renovators over the past few decades.'

'When you arrived,' I repeated. We had come onto a high platform at the center of the structure. It was bound about with beautifully carved railings and held two small pagodas perched right at the edge. Aenea stopped at the door of the first pagoda.

'A temple?' I said.

'My place.' She grinned, gesturing toward the interior. I peeked in. The square room was only three meters by three meters, its floor of polished wood with two small tatami mats. The most striking thing about it was the far wall – which simply was not there. Shoji screens had folded back and the far end of the room ended in open air. One could sleepwalk into oblivion there. The breeze up the cliff face rustled the leaves on three willow-type branches set in a beautiful mustard-yellow vase that sat on a low wood dais against the west wall. It was the only ornamentation in the room.

'We kick off our shoes in the buildings – except for the transit corridors you came through earlier,' she said. She led the way to the other pagoda. It was almost identical to the first, except for the shoji screens being latched closed here and a futon on the floor near them. 'A. Bettik's stuff,' she said, pointing to a small, red-painted locker near the futon. This is where we've set you up to bunk. Come on in.' She slipped her boots off, crossed to the tatami mat, slid the shoji back, and sat cross-legged on the mat.

I removed my boots, set the pack against the south wall, and went over to sit next to her.

'Well,' she said and gripped my forearms again. 'Gosh.'

For a minute I could not speak. I wondered if the altitude or the rich atmosphere was making me so emotional. I concentrated on watching lines of people in bright *chubas* leaving the Temple and walking the narrow ledges and bridges west along the cliff face. Directly across from our open door here was the gleaming massif of Heng Shan, its icefields glowing in the late-afternoon light. 'Jesus,' I said softly. 'It's beautiful here, kiddo.'

'Yes. And deadly if one is not careful. Tomorrow A. Bettik and I will take you up on the face and give you a refresher course on climbing gear and protocol.'

'Primer course is more like it,' I said. I could not stop looking at her face, her eyes. I was afraid that if I touched her bare skin again, visible voltage would leap between us. I remembered that electric shock whenever we had touched when she was a kid. I took a breath. 'Okay,' I said. 'When you got here, the Dalai Lama – whoever that is – said that you could work on the Temple here. So when did you get here? *How* did you get here? When did you meet Rachel and Theo? Who else do you know well here? What happened after we said good-bye in Hannibal? What happened to everyone else at Taliesin? Have the Pax troops been after you? Where did you learn all the architectural stuff? Do you still talk with the Lions and Tigers and Bears? How did you . . .'

Aenea held up one hand. She was laughing. 'One thing at a time, Raul. I need to hear all about your trip too, you know.'

I looked into her eyes. 'I dreamed that we were talking,' I said. 'You told me about the four steps . . . learning the language of the dead . . . learning . . .'

'The language of the living,' she finished for me. 'Yes. I had that dream too.'

My eyebrows must have arched.

Aenea smiled and set both her hands on mine. Her hands were larger, covering my oversized fist. I remembered when both her hands would have disappeared in one of mine. 'I do remember the dream, Raul. And I dreamed that you were in pain . . . your back . . .'

'Kidney stone,' I said, wincing at the memory.

'Yes. Well, I guess it shows that we're still friends if we can share dreams while light-years apart.'

'Light-years,' I repeated. 'All right, how did you get across them, Aenea? How did you get here? Where else have you been?'

She nodded and began speaking. The wind through the open wall screens rustled her hair. While she spoke, the evening light grew richer and higher on the great mountain to the north and across the cliff face to the east and west.

*

Aenea had been the last to leave Taliesin West, but that was only four days after I had paddled down the Mississippi. The other apprentices had left by different farcasters, she said, and the dropship had used the last of its power to ferry them to the various portals – near the Golden Gate Bridge, at the edge of the Grand Canyon, atop the stone faces at Mount Rushmore, beneath the rusted girders of launch gantries at the Kennedy Spaceport Historical Park – all over the western hemisphere of Old Earth, it seemed. Aenea's farcaster had been built into an adobe house in a pueblo north of the empty city called Santa Fe. A. Bettik had farcast with her. I blinked in jealousy at this, but said nothing.

Her first farcast had brought her to a high-gravity world called Ixion. The Pax had a presence there, but it was concentrated primarily in the opposite hemisphere. Ixion had never recovered properly from the Fall, and the high, jungle plateau where Aenea and A. Bettik had emerged was a maze of overgrown ruins populated primarily by warring tribes of neo-Marxists and Native American resurgencists, this volatile mixture further destabilized by bands of renegade and roving ARNists who were attempting to bring back all recorded species of Old Earth dinosaur.

Aenea made the tale funny – hiding A. Bettik's blue skin and obvious android status with great daubs of the decorative face paint the locals used, the audacity of a sixteen-year-old girl demanding money – or in this case, food and furs in barter – for heading up the reconstruction efforts in the old Ixion cities of Canbar, Iliumut, and Maoville. But it had worked. Not only had Aenea helped in the redesign and rebuilding of three of the old city centers and countless small homes, but she had started a series of 'discussion circles' that brought listeners in from a dozen of the warring tribes.

Here Aenea was being circumspect, I knew, but I wanted to know what these 'discussion circles' were all about.

'Just things,' she said. 'They would raise the topic, I would suggest some things to think about, and people would talk.'

'Did you teach them?' I asked, thinking of the prophecy that the child of the John Keats cybrid would be the One Who Teaches.

'In the Socratic sense, I guess,' said Aenea.

'What's that . . . oh, yeah.' I remembered the Plato she had steered me toward in the Taliesin library. Plato's teacher, Socrates, had taught by questioning, drawing out truths that people already held within themselves. I had thought that technique highly dubious, at best.

She went on. Some of the members of her discussion group had become devoted listeners, returning every evening and following her when she moved from ruined city to ruined city on Ixion.

'You mean disciples,' I said.

Aenea frowned. 'I don't like that word much, Raul.'

I folded my arms and looked out at the alpenglow illuminating the cloudtops many kilometers below and the brilliant evening light on the northern peak. 'You may not like it, but it sounds like the correct word to me, kiddo. Disciples follow their teacher wherever she travels, trying to glean one last bit of knowledge from her.'

'Students follow their teacher,' said Aenea.

'All right,' I said, not willing to derail the story by arguing. 'Go on.'

There was not much more to tell about Ixion, she said. She and A. Bettik were on the world about one local year, five months standard. Most of the building had been with stone blocks and her design had been ancient-classical, almost Greek.

'What about the Pax?' I said. 'Did they ever come sniffing around?'

'Some of the missionaries took part in the discussions,' said Aenea. 'One of them . . . a Father Clifford . . . became good friends with A. Bettik.'

'Didn't he – they – turn you in? They must still be hunting for us.'

'I am sure that Father Clifford didn't,' said Aenea. 'But eventually some of the Pax troopers began looking for us in the western hemisphere where we were working. The tribes hid us for another month. Father Clifford was coming to evening discussions even when the skimmers were flying back and forth over the jungle looking for us.'

'What happened?' I felt like a two-year-old who would ask questions just to keep the other person talking. It had only been a few months of separation – including the dream-ridden cold sleep – but I had forgotten exactly how much I loved the sound of my young friend's voice.

'Nothing, really,' she said. 'I finished the last job – an old amphitheater for plays and town meetings, fittingly enough – and A. Bettik and I left. Some of the . . . students . . . left as well.'

I blinked. 'With you?' Rachel had said that she had met Aenea on a world called Amritsar and traveled here with her. Perhaps Theo had come from Ixion.

'No, no one came with me from Ixion,' Aenea said softly. 'They had other places to go. Things to teach to others.'

I looked at her for a moment. 'You mean the Lions and Tigers and Bears are allowing others to farcast now? Or are all the old portals opening?'

'No,' answered Aenea, although to which question I was not sure. 'No, the farcasters are as dead as ever. It's just . . . well . . . a few special cases.'

Again I did not press the issue. She went on.

After Ixion, she had 'cast to the world of Maui-Covenant.

'Siri's world!' I said, remembering Grandam's voice teaching me the cadences of the Hyperion *Cantos*. That had been the locale for one of the pilgrims' tales.

Aenea nodded and continued. Maui-Covenant had been battered by revolution and Hegemony attacks way back during the Web, had recovered during the Fall interregnum, had been recolonized during the Pax expansion without the help of the locals who, in the best Siri tradition, had fought from their motile isles and alongside their dolphin companions until Pax Fleet and Swiss Guard had put their boots down hard. Now Maui-Covenant was being Christianized with a vengeance, the residents of the one large continent, the Equatorial Archipelago, and the thousands of migrating motile isles being sent to 'Christian academies' for reeducation.

But Aenea and A. Bettik had stepped through to a motile isle still belonging to the rebels – groups of neo-pagans called Sirists who sailed at night, floated among the traveling archipelagoes of empty isles during the daylight, and who fought the Pax at every turn.

'What did you build?' I asked. I thought that I remembered from the *Cantos* that the motile isles carried little except treehouses under their sailtrees.

'Treehouses,' said Aenea, grinning. 'Lots of treehouses. Also some underwater domes. That's where the pagans were spending most of their time.'

'So you designed treehouses.'

She shook her head. 'Are you kidding? These are – next to the missing God's Grove Templars – the best treehouse builders in human space. I *studied* how to build treehouses. They were gracious enough to let A. Bettik and me help.'

'Slave labor,' I said.

'Exactly.'

She had spent only some three standard months on Maui-Covenant. That is where she had met Theo Bernard.

'A pagan rebel?' I said.

'A runaway Christian,' corrected Aenea. 'She had come to Maui-Covenant as a colonist. She fled the colonies and joined the Sirists.'

I was frowning without realizing it. 'She carries a cruciform?' I said. Born-again Christians still made me nervous.

'Not anymore,' said Aenea.

'But how . . .' I knew of no way that a Christian with the cross could rid herself of a cruciform, short of the secret ritual of excommunication, which only the Church could perform.

'I'll explain later,' said Aenea. Before her tale was done, this phrase would be used more than a few times.

After Maui-Covenant, she and A. Bettik and Theo Bernard had farcast to Renaissance Vector.

'Renaissance Vector!' I almost shouted. That was a Pax stronghold. We had almost been shot down on Renaissance Vector. It was a hyperindustrialized world, all cities and robot factories and Pax centers.

'Renaissance Vector.' Aenea smiled. It had not been easy. They had been forced to disguise A. Bettik as a burn victim with a synflesh mask. It had been uncomfortable for him for the six months they were there.

'What jobs did you do there?' I asked, finding it hard to imagine my friend and her friends staying hidden in the thronging world-city that was Renaissance Vector.

'Just one job,' said Aenea. 'We worked on the new cathedral in Da Vinci – St Matthew's.'

It took me a minute of staring before I could speak. 'You worked on a *cathedral*? A Pax cathedral? A Christian church?'

'Of course,' said Aenea calmly. 'I labored alongside some of the best stonemasons, glass workers, builders, and craftsmen in the business. I was an apprentice at first, but before we left I was assistant to the chief designer working on the nave.'

I could only shake my head. 'And did you . . . have discussion circles?'

'Yes,' said Aenea. 'More came on Renaissance Vector than on any of the other worlds. Thousands of students, before it was over.'

'I'm amazed that you weren't betrayed.'

'I was,' she said. 'But not by one of the students. One of me glass workers turned us in to the local Pax garrison. A. Bettik, Theo, and I barely made it out.'

'Via farcaster,' I said.

'By . . . 'casting, yes,' said Aenea. It was only much later that I realized that there had been a slight hesitation in her voice there, an unspoken qualification.

'And did others leave with you?'

'Not with me,' she said again. 'But hundreds 'cast elsewhere.'

'Where?' I said, mystified.

Aenea sighed. 'Do you remember our discussion, Raul, where I said that the Pax thought that I was a virus? And that they were right?'

'Yeah.'

'Well, these students of mine are also carrying the virus,' she said. 'They had places to go. People to infect.'

Her litany of worlds and jobs went on. Patawpha for three – months, where she had used her treehouse experience to build mansions in the interwoven branches and trunks growing from the endless swamps there.

Amritsar, where she had worked for four standard months in the desert building tent homes and meeting places for the nomad bands of Sikhs and Sufis who wandered the green sands there.

'That's where you met Rachel,' I said.

'Correct.'

'What is Rachel's last name?' I said. 'She didn't mention it to me.'

'She has never mentioned it to me, either,' said Aenea and went on with her tale.

From Amritsar, she and A. Bettik and her two female friends had 'cast to Groombridge Dyson D. This world had been a Hegemony terraforming failure, abandoned to its encroaching methane-ammonia glaciers and ice-crystal hurricanes, its dwindling number of colonists retreating to its biodomes and orbital construction shacks. But its people – mostly Suni Muslim engineers from the failed Trans-African Genetic Reclamation Project – stubbornly refused to die during the Fall, and ended up terraforming Groombridge Dyson D into a Laplandic tundra world with breathable air and adapted-Old Earth flora and fauna, including wooly mammoths wandering the equatorial highlands. The millions of hectares of grasslands were perfect for horses – Old Earth horses of the kind that had disappeared during the Tribulations before the homeworld fell into itself – so the gene-designers took their original seedship stock and bred horses by the thousands, then by the tens of thousands. Nomad bands wandered the greenways of the southern continent, living in a kind of symbiosis with the great herds, while the farmers and city folk moved into the high foot-hills along the equator. There were violent predators there, evolved and unleashed during the centuries of accelerated and self-directed ARNying experimentation: mutant carrion-breed packs and burrowing night terrors, thirty-meter-long grass serpents descended from those from Hyperion's Sea of Grass and Fuji rock tigers, smart wolves, and IQ-enhanced grizzlies.

The humans had the technology to hunt the adapted killers to extinction in a year or less, but the residents of the world chose a different path: the nomads would take their chances, one-on-one with the predators, protecting the great horse herds as long as the grass grows and the water flows, while the city types would begin work on a wall – a single wall eventually to be more than five thousand kilometers long that would separate the wilder sections of the savage highlands from the horse-herd savannahs and evolving cyclad forests to the south. And the wall was to be more than a wall, it was to become the great linear city of Groombridge Dyson D, thirty meters tall at its lowest, its ramparts resplendent with mosques and minarets, the travelway on top wide enough that three chariots could pass without rubbing wheels.

The colonists were too few and too busy with other projects to work fulltime on such a wall, but they programmed robots and decanted androids from their seedship vaults to carry out the labor. Aenea and her friends joined in this project, working for six standard months as the wall took shape and began its relentless march along the base of the highlands and the edge of the grasslands.

'A. Bettik found two of his siblings there,' said Aenea softly.

'My God,' I whispered. I had almost forgotten. When we were on Sol Draconi Septem some years ago, sitting by the warmth of a heating cube in Father Glaucus's book-lined study inside a skyscraper that, in turn, was frozen within the eternal glacier of that world's frozen atmosphere, A. Bettik had talked about one of his reasons for coming on the odyssey with the child, Aenea, and me: he was hoping against logic to find his four siblings – three brothers and a sister. They had been separated shortly after their training period as children – if an android's accelerated early years could be called 'childhood'.

'So he found them?' I said, marveling.

'Two of them,' repeated Aenea. 'One of the other males in his growth creche – A. Anttibe – and his sister, A. Darria.'

'Were they like him?' I asked. The old poet had used androids in his empty city of Endymion, but I had not paid much attention to any of them except A. Bettik. Too much had been happening too fast.

'Much like him,' said Aenea. 'But very different, as well. Perhaps he will tell you more.'

She wrapped up her story. After six standard months working on the linear city wall on Groombridge Dyson D, they had had to leave.

'Had to leave?' I said. 'The Pax?'

'The Commission for Justice and Peace, to be precise,' said Aenea. 'We did not want to leave, but we had no choice.'

'What is the Commission for Justice and Peace?' I said. Something about the way she had pronounced the words made the hairs on my arm stand up.

'I'll explain later,' she said.

'All right,' I said, 'but explain something else now.'

Aenea nodded and waited.

'You say you spent five standard months on Ixion,' I said. 'Three months on Maui-Covenant, six months on Renaissance Vector, three months on Patawpha, four standard months on Amritsar, about six standard months on – what was it? – Groombridge Dyson D?'

Aenea nodded.

'And you've been here about a standard year you say?'

'Yes.'

'That's only thirty-nine standard months,' I said. 'Three standard years and three months.'

She waited. The corners of her mouth twitched slightly, but I realized that she was not going to smile . . . it looked more as if she was trying to avoid crying. Finally, she said, 'You were always good at math, Raul.'

'My trip here took five years' time-debt,' I said softly. 'So that's about sixty standard months for you, but you've only accounted for thirty-nine. Where are the missing twenty-one standard months, kiddo?'

I saw the tears in her eyes. Her mouth was quavering slightly, but she tried to speak in a light tone. 'It was sixty-two standard months, one week, and six days for me,' she said. 'Five years, two months, and one day time-debt on the ship, about four days accelerating and decelerating, and eight days' travel time. You forgot your travel time.'

'All right, kiddo,' I said, seeing the emotion well in her. Her hands were shaking. 'Do you want to talk about the missing . . . what was it?'

'Twenty-three months, one week, and six hours,' she said.

Almost two standard years, I thought. *And she doesn't want to tell me what happened to her during that time.* I had never seen her exercise such rigid control before; it was as if she were trying to hold herself together physically against some terrible centrifugal force.

'We'll talk about it later,' she said, pointing out the open doorway at the cliff face to the west of the Temple. 'Look.'

I could just make out figures – two-legged and four-legged – on the narrow ledge. They were still several klicks away – along the cliff face. I walked over to my pack, retrieved my binoculars, and studied the forms.

'The pack animals are zygoats,' said Aenea. 'The porters are hired in Phari Marketplace and will be returning in the morning. See anyone familiar?'

I did. The blue face in the hooded *chuba* looked much the way it had five of his years earlier. I turned back to Aenea, but she was obviously finished talking about her missing two years. I allowed her to change the subject again.

Aenea began asking me questions then and we were still talking when A. Bettik arrived. The women – Rachel and Theo – wandered in a few minutes later. One of the tatami mats folded back to reveal a cooking brazier in the floor near the open wall, and Aenea and A. Bettik began cooking for everyone. Others wandered in and were introduced – the foremen George Tsarong and Jigme Norbu, two sisters who were in charge of much of the decorative railing work – Kuku and Kay Se, Gyalo Thondup in his formal silken robes and Jigme Taring in soldier's garb, the teaching monk Chim Din and his master, Kempo Ngha Wang Tashi, abbot of the gompa at the Temple Hanging in Air, a female monk named Donka Nyapso, a traveling trade agent named Tromo Trochi of Dhomu, Tsipon Shakabpa who was the Dalai Lama's overseer of construction here at the Temple, and the famed climber and paraglide flyer Lhomo Dondrub, who was perhaps the most striking man I had ever seen and – I later discovered – one of the few flyers who would drink beer or break bread with Dugpas, Drukpas, or Drungpas.

The food was tsampa and momo – a roasted barley mixed into zygoat-buttered tea, forming a paste that one rolled into balls and ate with other balls of steamed dough holding mushrooms, cold zygoat tongue, sugared bacon, and bits of pears that A. Bettik told me were from the fabled gardens of Hsi wang-mu. More people came in as the bowls were being handed out – Labsang Samten – who, A. Bettik whispered, was the oldest brother of the current Dalai Lama and was now in his third year of monkhood here at the Temple, and various Drungpas from the wooded clefts – including master carpenter Changchi Kenchung with his long, waxed mustaches, Perri Samdup, an interpreter, and Rimsi Kyipup, a brooding and unhappy young scaffold-rigger. Not all of the monks who dropped in that night were descended from the Chinese/Tibetan Old Earth seedship colonists. Laughing and lifting their rough mugs of beer with us were the fearless high riggers Haruyuki Otaki and Kenshiro Endo, the master bamboo workers Voytek Majer and Janusz Kurtyka, and the brickmakers Kim Byung-Soon and Viki Groselj. The mayor of Jo-kung, the nearest cliff city, was there – Charles Chi-kyap Kempo – who also served as Lord Chamberlain of all the Temple's priest officials and was an appointed member of both the Tsongdu, the regional assembly of elders, and advisor to Yik-Tshang, literally the 'Nest of Letters', the secret four-person body that reviewed the monks' progress and appointed all priests. Charles Chi-kyap Kempo was the first member of our party to drink enough to pass out. Chim Din and several of the other monks dragged the snoring man away from the edge of the platform and left him sleeping in the corner.

There were others – at least forty people must have filled the little pagoda as the last of the sunlight ebbed away and the moonlight from the Oracle and three of her siblings lit the cloudtops below – but I forgot their names that night as we ate tsampa and momo, drank beer in great quantities, and made the torches burn bright in Hsuan-k'ung Ssu.

Some hours later that evening, I went out to relieve myself. A. Bettik showed me the way to the toilets. I had assumed that one would just use the edge of platforms, but he assured me that on a world where dwelling structures had many levels – most of them above or below others – this was considered bad form. The toilets were built into the side of the cliff, enclosed by bamboo partitions, and the sanitary arrangements consisted of cleverly engineered pipes and sluices leading into fissures running deep into the cliff as well as washbasins cut in stone counters. There was even a shower area and solar-heated water for washing.

When I had rinsed my hands and face and stepped back out onto the platform – the chill breeze helping to sober me a bit – I stood next to A. Bettik in the moonlight and looked into the glowing pagoda where the crowd had arranged itself in concentric circles with my young friend as the locus. The laughter and chaos had disappeared. One by one, the monks and holy men and riggers and carpenters and stonemasons and gompa abbots and mayors and bricklayers were asking soft questions of the young woman, and she was answering.

The scene reminded me of something – some recent image – and it took me only a minute to recall it: the forty-AU deceleration into this star system, with the ship offering up holo representations of the G-type sun with its eleven orbiting planets, two asteroid belts, and countless comets. Aenea was definitely the sun in this system, and all of the men and women in that room were orbiting around her as surely as had the worlds, asteroids, and comets in the ship's projection.

I leaned on a bamboo post and looked at A. Bettik in the moonlight. 'She'd better be careful,' I said softly to the android, enunciating each word carefully, 'or they'll begin treating her like a god.'

A. Bettik nodded ever so slightly. 'They do not think that M. Aenea is a god, M. Endymion,' he murmured.

'Good.' I put my arm around the android's shoulder. 'Good.'

'However,' he said, 'many of them are becoming convinced, despite her best efforts to assure them otherwise, that she is God.'

SEVENTEEN

The evening A. Bettik and I bring the news of the Pax's arrival, Aenea leaves her discussion group, comes to where we are standing at the door, and listens intently.

'Chim Din says that the Dalai Lama has allowed them to occupy the old gompa at Otter Lake,' I say, 'in the shadow of the Shivling.'

Aenea says nothing.

'They won't be allowed to use their flying machines,' I say, 'but they're free to walk anywhere in the province. *Anywhere*.'

Aenea nods.

I want to grab her and shake her. 'That means they'll hear about you soon, kiddo,' I say sharply. 'There'll be missionaries here within weeks – maybe days – spying around and sending word back to the Pax Enclave.' I let out a breath. 'Shit, we'll be lucky if it's just missionaries and not troopers.'

Aenea is silent another minute. Then she says, 'We're already lucky that it's not the Commission for Justice and Peace.'

'What's that?' I say. She had mentioned them before.

She shakes her head. 'Nothing that's immediately relevant, Raul. They must have some business here other than . . . than stamping out unorthodoxy.'

During my first days here, Aenea had told me about the fighting going on in and around Pax space – a Palestinian revolt on Mars that had resulted in the Pax evacuating the planet and nuking it from orbit, free trader rebellions in the Lambert Ring Territories and on Mare Infinitus, continued fighting on Ixion and dozens of other worlds. Renaissance Vector, with its huge Pax Fleet bases and countless bars and bordellos, had been a hornets' nest of rumors and inside intelligence. And because most of the ships of the line in Pax Fleet were now the Gideon-drive archangels, the news was usually only a few days old.

One of the most intriguing rumors that Aenea had heard before coming to T'ien Shan was that at least one of those archangel-class ships had gone rogue, escaped to Ouster space, and was now flashing into Pax space to attack convoys of Pax Mercantilus ships – disabling rather than destroying the crewed freighters – and to disrupt Pax Fleet task forces preparing to attack Ousters out beyond the Great Wall. There had been a rumor during Aenea's and A. Bettik's last weeks on Renaissance Vector that the fleet bases there were in danger. Other rumors suggested that large elements of the fleet were now being kept in Pacem System to defend the Vatican. Whatever else was true about the tales of the rogue ship *Raphael*, it was uncontestable that His Holiness's Crusade against the Ousters had been set back years by the hit-and-run attacks.

But none of that seems important now as I stand waiting for Aenea's response to this news of the Pax's arrival on T'ien Shan. What do we do now, I wonder, farcast to her next world?

Instead of discussing flight, Aenea says, 'The Dalai Lama will have a formal ceremony to welcome the Pax officials.'

'So?' I say after a moment.

'So we have to make sure that we get an invitation,' she says.

I doubt if my jaw is literally hanging slack, but it feels as if it is.

Aenea touches my shoulder. 'I'll take care of it,' she says. 'I'll talk to Charles Chi-kyap Kempo and Kempo Ngha Wang Tashi and make sure that they include us in any party invited to the ceremony.'

I am literally speechless as she goes back to her discussion group and the silent throng, their faces expectant and placid in the soft lantern light.

I read these words on microvellum, remember writing them in my last days in the Schrödinger cat box in orbit around Armaghast, remember writing them in the haste of certainty that the laws of probability and quantum mechanics would soon be releasing cyanide into my closed-cycle universe, and I marvel at the present tense of the narrative. Then I remember the reason for this choice.

When I was sentenced to death in the Schrödinger box – egg-shaped, actually – I was allowed to bring very few of my own things into terminal exile. My clothes were my own. On a whim, they had given me a small rug for the floor of my Schrödinger cell – it was an ancient rug, a bit less than two meters long and a meter wide, frayed, with a small cut missing at one end. It was a replica of the Consul's hawking mat. I had lost the real mat on Mare Infinitus many years before and the details of how it came back to me still lie ahead in my tale. I had given the actual hawking mat to A. Bettik, but it must have amused my torturers to furnish my final cell with this useless copy of a flying carpet.

So they had allowed me my clothes, the fake hawking mat and the palm-sized diskey journal I had taken from the ship on T'ien Shan. The com-unit element of the journal had been disabled – not that it would broadcast through the energy shell of the Schrödinger box or that there was anyone for me to call – but the journal memory – after their careful study of it during my inquisition trial – had been left intact. It was on T'ien Shan that I had begun making notes and daily journal entries.

It was these notes that I had brought up on to the 'scriber screen in the Schrödinger cat box, reviewing them before writing this most personal of sections, and it was the immediacy in the notes, I believe, that led me to use the present-tense narrative. All of my memories of Aenea are vivid, but some of the memories brought back by these hurried entries at the end of a long day of work or adventure on T'ien Shan were so vital as to make me weep with renewed loss. I relived those moments as I wrote those words.

And some of her discussion groups were recorded verbatim on the diskey journal. I played those during my last days just to hear Aenea's soft voice once again.

'Tell us about the TechnoCore,' one of the monks requests during the discussion hour this night of the Pax's arrival. 'Please tell us about the Core.'

Aenea hesitates only an instant, bowing her head slightly as if ordering her thoughts.

'Once upon a time,' she begins. She always begins her long explanations this way.

'Once upon a time,' says Aenea, 'more than a thousand standard years ago, before the Hegira . . . before the Big Mistake of '08 . . . the only autonomous intelligences we humans knew of were us humans. We thought that if humankind ever devised another intelligence that it would be the result of a huge project . . . a great mass of silicon and ancient amplification, switching, and detection devices called transistors and chips and circuit boards . . . a machine with lots of networking circuits, in other words, aping – if you will pardon the expression – the human brain in form and function.

'Of course, AIs did not evolve that way. They sort of slipped into existence when we humans were looking the other way.

'You have to imagine now, an Old Earth before humankind had offworld colonies. No Hawking drive. No interplanetary flight to speak of. All of our eggs were literally in one carton, and that carton was the lovely blue and white water world of Old Earth.

'By the end of the twentieth century, Christian era, this little world had a crude datasphere. Basic planetary telecommunication had evolved into a decentralized swarm system of old silicon-based computers demanding no organization or hierarchy, demanding nothing beyond a common communications protocol. Creation of a distributed-memory hive mind was then inevitable.

'The earliest lineal ancestors to today's Core personalities were not projects to create artificial intelligence, but incidental efforts to simulate artificial life. In the 1940s the great-grandfather of the TechnoCore – a mathematician named John von Neumann – had done all the proofs of artificial self-replication. As soon as the early silicon-based computers became small enough for individuals to play with, curious amateurs began practicing synthetic biology within the confines of these machines' CPU cycles. Hyperlife – self-reproducing, information-storing, interacting, metabolizing, evolving – came into existence in the 1960s. It escaped the tide pools of the individual machines in the last decade of that century, moving into the embryonic planetary datasphere that they called the Internet or the web.

'The earliest AIs were dumb as dirt. Or perhaps the better metaphor would be that they were as dumb as early cellular life that was in the dirt. Some of the earliest hypercritters floating in the warm medium of the datasphere – which was also evolving – were 80-byte organisms inserted into a block of RAM in a virtual computer – a computer simulated by a computer. One of the first humans to release such creatures into the datasphere ocean was named Tom Ray and he was not an AI expert or computer programmer or cyberpuke, which they called hackers then, but was a biologist, an insect collector, botanist, and bird-watcher, and someone who had spent years collecting ants in the jungle for a pre-Hegira scientist named E. O. Wilson. Watching ants, Tom Ray became interested in evolution, and wondered if he could not just simulate evolution in one of the early computers but create *real* evolution there. None of the cyberpukes he spoke with were interested in the idea, so he taught himself computer programming. The cyberpukes said that evolving and mutating code sequences happened all the time in computers – they were called bugs and screwed up programs. They said that if his code sequences evolved into something else they would almost certainly be nonfunctional, nonviable, as most mutations are, and would just foul up the operation of the computer software. So Tom Ray created a virtual computer – a simulated computer within his real computer – for his code-sequenced creations. And then he created an actual 80-byte code-sequence creature that could reproduce, die, and evolve in his computer-within-a-computer.

'The 80-byte copied itself into more 80-bytes. These 80-byte proto-AI cell-things would have quickly filled their virtual universe, like pond scum on top of pond scum in an Elysium early Earth, but Tom Ray gave each 80-byte a date tag, gave them age in other words, and programmed in an executioner that he called the Reaper. The Reaper wandered through this virtual universe and harvested old 80-byte critters and nonviable mutants.

'But evolution, as it is wont to do, tried to outsmart the Reaper. A mutant 79-byte creature proved not only to be viable, but soon outbred and outpaced the 80-bytes. The hyperlifes, ancestors to our Core AIs, were just born but already they were optimizing their genomes. Soon a 45-byte organism had evolved and all but eliminated the earlier artificial life-forms. As their creator, Tom Ray found this odd. Forty-five-bytes did not include enough code to allow for reproduction. More than that, the 45s were dying off as the 80s disappeared. He did an autopsy on one of the 45-creatures.

'It turned out that all of the 45-bytes were parasites. They needed reproductive code from the 80s to copy themselves. The 79s, it turned out, were immune to the 45-parasite. But as the 80s and 45s moved toward extinction in their coevolutionary downward spiral, a mutant of the 45s appeared. It was a 51-byte parasite and it *could* prey on the vital 79s. And so it went.

'I mention all this, because it is important to understand that from the very first appearance of human-created artificial life and intelligence, such life was parasitic. It was more than parasitic – it was hyperparasitic. Each new mutation led to parasites which could prey on earlier parasites. Within a few billion generations – that is to say, CPU cycles – this artificial life had become hyper-hyper-hyperparasitic. Within standard months of his creation of hyperlife, Tom Ray discovered 22-byte creatures flourishing in his virtual medium . . . creatures so algorithmically efficient that when challenged by Tom Ray, human programmers could create nothing closer than a 31-byte version. Only months after their creation, hyperlife creatures had evolved an efficiency that their creators could not match!

'By the early twenty-first century, there was a thriving biosphere of artificial life on Old Earth, both in the quickly evolving datasphere and in the macrosphere of human life. Although the breakthroughs of DNA-computing, bubble memories, standing wave-front parallel processing, and hypernetworking were just being explored, human designers had created silicon-based entities of remarkable ingenuity. And they had created them by the billions. Microchips were in everything from chairs to cans of beans on store shelves to groundcars to artificial human body parts. The machines had grown smaller and smaller until the average human home or office was filled with tens of thousands of them. A worker's chair would recognize her as soon as she sat, bring up the file she had been working on in her crude silicon computer, chat with another chip in a coffeemaker to heat up the coffee, enable the telecommunications grid to deal with calls and faxes and crude electronic mail arrivals so that the worker would not be disturbed, interact with the main house or office computer so that the temperature was optimal, and so forth. In their stores, microchips in the cans of beans on the shelves noted their own price and price changes, ordered more of themselves when they were running short, kept track of the consumers' buying habits, and interacted with the store and the other commodities in it. This web of interaction became as complex and busy as the bubble and froth of Old Earth's organic stew in its early oceans.

'Within forty years of Tom Ray's 80-byte a-cell, humans were accustomed to talking to and otherwise interacting with the countless artificial life-forms in their cars, their offices, their elevators . . . even in their bodies, as medical monitors and proto-shunts moved toward true nanotechnology.

'The TechnoCore came into autonomous being sometime during this period. Humanity had understood – quite correctly as it turned out – that for artificial life and artificial intelligence to be effective, it must be autonomous. It must evolve and diversify much as organic life had on the planet. And it did so. As well as the biosphere surrounding the planet, hyperlife now wrapped the world in a living datasphere. The Core evolved not just as an abstract entity within the information flow of the web datasphere, but among the interactions of a billion tiny, autonomous, chip-driven micromachines carrying out their mundane tasks in the human macroworld.

'Humanity and the billion-faceted, evolving Core entity soon became as symbiotic as acacia plants and the marauding ants that protect, prune, and propagate the acacia as their sole food source. This is known as coevolution, and humans understand the concept on a truly cellular level, since so much of organic life on Old Earth had been created and optimized by the reciprocal revolutionary dance. But where human beings saw a comfortable symbiosis, the early AI entities saw – were capable of seeing – only new opportunities for parasitism.

'Computers might be turned off, software programs might be terminated, but the hive mind of the proto-Core had already moved into the emerging datasphere, and that could be turned off only by planetary catastrophe.

'The Core eventually provided that catastrophe in the Big Mistake of '08, but not before it had diversified its own medium and moved beyond a mere planetary scale.

'Early experiments in the Hawking drive, conducted and understood only by advanced Core elements, had revealed the existence of the underlying Planck-space reality of the Void Which Binds. Core AIs of the day – DNA-based, wave-form in structure, driven by genetic algorithms, parallel in function – completed the construction of the early Hawking-drive ships and began design of the farcaster network.

'Human beings always saw the Hawking drive as a shortcut through time and space – a realization of their old hyperdrive dreams. They conceptualized farcaster portals as convenient holes punched through space/time. This was the human preconception, borne out by their own mathematical models, and confirmed by the most powerful Core computing AIs. It was all a lie.

'Planck space, the Void Which Binds, is a multidimensional medium with its own reality and – as the Core was soon to learn – its own topography. The Hawking drive was not and is not a drive at all, in the classic sense, but an entry device which touches on Planck-space topography just long enough to change coordinates in the four-dimensional space/time continuum. Farcaster portals, on the other hand, allow actual entry to the Void Which Binds medium.

To humans, the reality was obvious – step through a hole in space/time here, exit instantaneously via another farcaster hole there. My Uncle Martin had a farcaster home with adjoining rooms on dozens of different worlds. Farcasters created the Hegemony's WorldWeb. Another invention, the fatline – a faster-than-light communications medium – allowed for instantaneous communication between star systems. All the prerequisites for an interstellar society had been met.

'But the Core did not perfect the Hawking drive, the farcaster, and the fatline for human convenience. Indeed, the Core never perfected anything in their dealings with the Void Which Binds.

'The Core knew from the beginning that the Hawking drive was little more than a failed attempt to enter Planck space. Driving spacecraft via Hawking drive was comparable, they knew, to moving an ocean-going vessel by setting off a series of explosions at its stern and riding the waves. Crudely effective, but wildly inefficient. They knew that despite all appearances to the contrary and despite their claims of having created them, there were not millions of farcaster portals during the height of the WorldWeb . . . only one. All farcaster portals were actually a single entry door to Planck space, manipulated across space/time to provide the functioning illusion of so many doors. If the Core had attempted to explain the truth to humanity, they might have used the analogy of a flashlight beam being rapidly flashed around a closed room. There were not many sources of light, only one in rapid transition. But they never bothered to explain this . . . in truth, they have kept the secret to this day.

'And the Core knew that the topography of the Void Which Binds could be modulated to transmit information instantaneously – via the fatline – but that this was a clumsy and destructive use of the medium of Planck space, rather like communicating across a continent by means of artificially produced earthquakes. But it offered this fatline service to humanity without ever explaining it because it served their purpose to do so. They had their own plans for the Planck-space medium.

'What the Core realized in their earliest experiments was that the Void Which Binds was the perfect medium for their own existence. No longer would they have to depend upon electromagnetic communication or tightbeam or even modulated neutrino broadcast for their datasphere networks. No longer would they need human beings or robot probes to travel to the stars to expand the physical parameters of that network. By simply moving the primary elements of the Core into the Void Which Binds, the AIs would have a safe hiding place from their organic rivals . . . a hiding place which was at once nowhere and everywhere.

'It was during this migration of the Core personae from human-based dataspheres to the Void Which Binds megasphere that the Core discovered that Planck space was not an empty universe. Behind its metadimensional hills and deep in its folded quantum-space arroyos lurked . . . something different. *Someone* different. There were intelligences there. The Core probed and then recoiled in awe and terror at the potential power of these Others. These were the Lions and Tigers and Bears spoken of by Ummon, the Core persona who claimed to have created and killed my father.

'The Core's retreat had been so hasty, its reconnaissance into the Planck-space universe so incomplete, that it had no idea where in real space/time these Lions and Tigers and Bears dwelt . . . or if they existed in real-time at all. Nor could the Core AIs identify the Others as having evolved from organic life as humanity had done or from artificial life as they had. But the briefest glimpse had shown them that these Others could manipulate time and space with the ease that human beings had once manipulated steel and iron. Such power was beyond comprehension. The Core's reaction was pure panic and immediate retreat.

'This discovery and panic happened just as the Core had initiated the action of destroying Old Earth. My Uncle Martin's poem sings of how it was the Core that arranged the Big Mistake of '08, the Kiev Group's "accidental" dropping of a black hole into the guts of Old Earth, but his poem does not tell – because he did not know – of the Core's panic at the discovery of the Lions and Tigers and Bears and how they rushed to stop their planned destruction of Old Earth. It was not easy to scoop a growing black hole out of the core of the collapsing planet, but the Core designed a means and set about doing it in haste.

'Then, the home planet disappeared . . . not destroyed as it seemed to the humans, not saved as the Core had hoped . . . just *gone*. The Core knew that the Lions and Tigers and Bears had to be the ones who took the Earth, but as to how . . . and to where . . . and for what reason . . . they had no·clue. They computed the amount of energy necessary to farcast an entire planet away, and again they began quaking in their hyperlife boots. Such intelligences could explode the core of an entire galaxy to use as an energy source as easily as humans could light a campfire on a cold night. The Core entities shit hyperlife bricks in their fear.

'I should back up here to explain the reasons for the Core's decision to destroy Earth and their subsequent attempt to save it. The reasons go back to Tom Ray's 80-byte RAM creatures. As I explained, the life and intelligence which evolved in the datasphere medium knew no other form of evolution than parasitism, hyperparasitism, and hyper-hyper-hyper-hyperparasitism. But the Core was aware of the shortcomings of absolute parasitism and knew that the only way it could grow beyond parasite status and parasite psychology was to evolve in response to the physical universe – that is, to have physical bodies as well as abstract Core personae. The Core had multiple sensory inputs and could create neural networks, but what it required for nonparasitic evolution was a constant and coordinated system of neural feedback circuits – that is, eyes, ears, tongues, limbs, fingers, toes . . . bodies.

'The Core created cybrids for that purpose – bodies grown from human DNA but connected to their Core-based personae via fatline – but cybrids were difficult to monitor and became aliens when put down in a human landscape. Cybrids would never be comfortable on worlds inhabited by billions of organically evolved human beings. So the Core made its early plans to destroy Old Earth and thin out the human race by a factor of ninety percent.

'The Core did have plans for incorporating the surviving elements of the human race into their cybrid-inhabited universe after the death of Old Earth – using them as spare DNA stock and slave labor, much as we used androids – but the discovery of Lions and Tigers and Bears and the panicked retreat from Planck space complicated those plans. Until the threat of these Others was assessed and eliminated, the Core would have to continue its parasitic relationship with humanity. It devised the farcasters in the old WorldWeb just for that purpose. To humans, the trip through the farcaster medium was instantaneous. But in the timeless topography of Planck space, the subjective dwell-time there could be as long as the Core wished. The Core tapped into billions of human brains during that period, using human minds millions of times each standard day, to create a huge neural network for their own computing purposes. Every time a human stepped through a farcaster portal, it was as if the Core cut open that person's skull, removed the gray matter, laid the brain out on a workbench, and hooked it up to billions of other brains in their giant, parallel-processing, organic computer. The humans completed their step from Planck space in a subjective instant of their time and never noticed the inconvenience.

'Ummon told my father, the John Keats cybrid, that the Core consisted of three warring camps – the Ultimates, obsessed with creating their own god, the Ultimate Intelligence; the Volatiles, who wished to eliminate humanity and get on with their own goals; and the Stables, who wished to maintain the status quo vis-à-vis humankind. This explanation was an absolute lie.

'There were not and are not three camps in the TechnoCore . . . there are billions. The Core is the ultimate exercise in anarchy – hyperparasitism carried to its highest power. Core elements vie for power in alliances which might last centuries or microseconds. Billions of the parasitic personae ebb and flow in unholy alliances built to control or predict events. You see, Core personae refuse to die unless they are forced to – Meina Gladstone's death-bomb attack on the farcaster medium not only caused the Fall of the Farcasters, it killed billions of would-be immortal Core personae – but the individuals refuse to make way for others without a fight. Yet at the same time, the Core hyperlife needs death for its own evolution. But death, in the Core universe, has its own agenda.

'The Reaper program which Tom Ray created more than a thousand years ago still exists in the Core medium, mutated to a million alternate forms. Ummon never mentioned the Reapers as a Core faction, but they represent a far greater bloc than the Ultimates. It was the Reapers who created and first controlled the physical construct known as the Shrike.

'It's an interesting footnote that those Core personae which survive the Reapers do so not just through parasitism, but through a necrophilic para-sitism. This is the technique by which the original 22-byte artificial life-forms managed to evolve and survive in Tom Ray's virtual evolution machine so many centuries ago – by stealing the scattered copy code of other byte creatures who were "reaped" in the midst of reproducing. The Core parasites not only have sex, they have sex with the dead! This is how millions of the mutated Core personae survive today . . . by necrophilic hyperparasitism.

'What does the Core want from humankind now? Why has it revitalized the Catholic Church and allowed the Pax to come into existence? How do the cruciforms work and how do they serve the Core? How do the so-called Gideon-drive archangel ships really work and what is their effect on the Void Which Binds? And how is the Core dealing with the threat of the Lions and Tigers and Bears?

'These things we shall discuss another time.'

It is the day after we learn of the coming of the Pax and I am working stone on the highest scaffolds.

During the first days after my arrival, I think that Rachel, Theo, Jigme Norbu, George Tsarong, and the others were doubtful if I could earn my keep on the construction site at Hsuan-k'ung Ssu. I admit that I had doubts of my own as I watched the hard work and skill on view here. But after a few days of literally learning the ropes of gear and climbing protocols on the rockfaces, ledges, cables, scaffolds, and slideways in the area, I volunteered for work duty and was given a chance to fail. I did not fail.

Aenea knew of my apprenticeship with Avrol Hume, not only land-scaping the huge Beak estates but working stone and wood for follies and bridges, gazebos, and towers. That work served me well here, and within two weeks I had graduated from the basic scaffolding crew to the select group of high riggers and stone workers laboring on the highest platforms. Aenea's design allowed for the highest structures to rise to the great rock overhang and for various walkways and parapets actually to be incorporated into that stone. This is what we are working on now, chiseling stone and laying brick for the walkway along the edge of nothing, our scaffolds perilously cantilevered far out over the drop. In the past three months my body has grown leaner and stronger, my reaction time quicker, and my judgment more careful as I work on sheer rock walls and slippery bonsai bamboo.

Lhomo Dondrub, the skilled flyer and climber, has volunteered to free-climb the end of the overhang here to set anchor points for the final meters of scaffolding and for the last hour Viki Groselj, Kim Byung-Soon, Haruyuki Otaki, Kenshiro Endo, Changchi Kenchung, Labsang Samten, a few of the other brickworkers, masons, high riggers, and I have been watching as Lhomo moves across the rock above the overhang without protection, moving like the proverbial Old Earth fly, his powerful arms and legs flexing under the thin material of his climbing garb, three points in touch with the slick, more-than-vertical stone at all times while his free hand or foot feels for the slightest rough spot on which to rest, the smallest fissure or crack in which to work a bolt for our anchor. It is terrifying to watch him, but also a privilege – as if we were able to go back in a time machine to watch Picasso paint or George Wu read poetry or Meina Gladstone give a speech. A dozen times I am sure that Lhomo is going to peel off and fall – it would take minutes for him to freefall into the poison clouds below – but each time he magically holds his place, or finds a friction point, or miraculously discovers a crack into which he can wedge a hand or finger to support his entire body.

Finally he is done, the lines are anchored and dangling, the cable points are secured, and Lhomo slides down to his early fixed point, traverses five meters laterally, drops into the stirrups of the overhang gear, and swings onto our work platform like some legendary superhero coming in for a landing. Labsang Samten hands him an icy mug of rice beer. Kenshiro and Viki pound him on the back. Changchi Kenchung, our master carpenter with the waxed mustaches, breaks into a bawdy song of praise. I shake my head and grin like an idiot. The day is exhilarating – a dome of blue sky, the Sacred Mountain of the North – Heng Shan – gleaming brightly across the cloud gap, and the winds moderate. Aenea tells me that the rainy season will descend on us within days – a monsoon from the south bringing months of rain, slick rock, and eventual snow – but that seems unlikely and distant on such a perfect day as this.

There is a touch at my elbow and Aenea is there. She has been out on the scaffolding most of the morning, or hanging from her harness on the worked rockface, supervising the stone and brick work on the walkway and parapets.

I am still grinning from the vicarious adrenaline rush of watching Lhomo. 'Cables are ready to be rigged,' I say. 'Three or four more good days and the wooden walkway will be done here. Then your final platform there' –

I point to the ultimate edge of the overhang – 'and voilà! Your project's done except for the painting and polishing, kiddo.'

Aenea nods, but it is obvious that her mind is not on the celebration around Lhomo or the imminent completion of her year of work. 'Can you come walk with me a minute, Raul?'

I follow her down the scaffolding ladders, onto one of the permanent levels, and out onto a stone ledge. Small green birds take wing from a fissure as we pass.

From this angle, the Temple Hanging in Air is a work of art. The painted woodwork gleams rather than glows its dark red. The staircases and railings and fretwork are elegant and complex. Many of the pagodas have their shoji walls slid open and prayer flags and bedclothes flutter in the warm breeze. There are eight lovely shrines in the Temple, in ascending order along the rising walkways, each pagoda shrine representing a step in the Noble Eightfold Path as identified by the Buddha: the shrines line up on three axes relating to the three sections of the Path: Wisdom, Morality, and Meditation. On the ascending Wisdom axis of staircases and platforms are the meditation shrines for 'Right Understanding' and 'Right Thought'.

On the Morality axis are 'Right Speech', 'Right Action', 'Right Livelihood', and 'Right Effort'. These last meditation shrines can be reached only by hard climbing on a ladder rather than staircase because – as Aenea and Kempo Ngha Wang Tashi explained to me one evening early in my stay – the Buddha had meant for his path to be one of strenuous and unremitting commitment.

The highest meditation pagodas are given over to contemplation of the last two steps on the Noble Eightfold Path – 'Right Mindfulness' and 'Right Meditation'. This final pagoda, I had noticed immediately, looks out only on to the stone wall of the cliff face.

I also had noticed that there were no statues of Buddha in the Temple. The little that Grandam had explained to me about Buddhism when I'd asked as a child – having run across a reference in an old book from the Moors End library – was that Buddhists revered and prayed to statues in the likeness of the Buddha. Where were they? I had asked Aenea.

She had explained that on Old Earth Buddhist thought had been grouped into two major categories – Hinayana, an older school of thought given the pejorative term meaning 'Lesser Vehicle' – as in salvation – by the more popular schools of the Mahayana, or the self-proclaimed 'Greater Vehicle'. There had once been eighteen schools of Hinayana teaching – all of which had dealt with Buddha as a teacher and urged contemplation and study of his teachings rather than worship of him – but by the time of the Big Mistake, only one of those schools survived, the Theravada, and that only in remote sections of disease- and famine-ravaged Sri Lanka and Thailand, two political provinces of Old Earth. All the other Buddhist schools carried away on the Hegira had belonged to the Mahayana category, which focused on veneration of Buddhist statuary, meditation for salvation, saffron robes, and the other trappings that Grandam had described to me.

But, Aenea had explained, on T'ien Shan, the most Buddhist-influenced world in the Outback or old Hegemony, Buddhism had evolved backward toward rationality, contemplation, study, and careful, open-minded analysis of Buddha's teaching. Thus there were no statues to the Buddha at Hsuan-k'ung Ssu.

We stop walking at the end of this stone ledge. Birds soar and circle below us, waiting for us to leave so that they can return to their fissure nests.

'What is it, kiddo?'

'The reception at the Winter Palace in Potala is tomorrow night,' she says. Her face is flushed and dusty from her morning's work on the high scaffolds. I notice that she has scraped a rough line above her brow and that there are a few tiny crimson drops of blood. 'Charles Chi-kyap Kempo is putting together an official party numbering no more than ten to attend,' she continues. 'Kempo Ngha Wang Tashi will be in it, of course, as will Overseer Tsipon Shakabpa, the Dalai Lama's cousin Gyalo, his brother Labsang, Lhomo Dondrub because the Dalai Lama's heard of his feats and would like to meet him, Tromo Trochi of Dhomu as trade agent, and one of the foremen to represent the workers . . . either George or Jigme . . .'

'I can't imagine one going without the other,' I say.

'I can't either,' says Aenea. 'But I think it will have to be George. He talks. Perhaps Jigme will walk there with us and wait outside the palace.'

'That's eight,' I say.

Aenea takes my hand. Her fingers are roughened by work and abrasion, but are still, I think, the softest and most elegant human digits in the known universe. 'I'm nine,' she says. 'There's going to be a huge crowd there – parties from all the towns and provinces in the hemisphere. The odds are that we won't get within twenty meters of anyone from the Pax.'

'Or that we'll be the first to be introduced,' I say. 'Murphy's Law and all that.'

'Yeah,' says Aenea and the smile I see is exactly the one I had seen on the face of my eleven-year-old friend when something mischievous and perhaps a bit dangerous was afoot. 'Want to go as my date?'

I let out a breath. 'I wouldn't miss it for the world,' I say.

EIGHTEEN

On the night before the Dalai Lama's reception I am tired but I cannot sleep. A. Bettik is away, staying at Jo-kung with George and Jigme and the thirty loads of construction material that should have come in yesterday but that were held up in the fissure city by a porters' strike. A. Bettik will hire new porters in the morning and lead the procession the last few kilometers to the Temple.

Restless, I roll off my futon and slip into whipcord trousers, a faded shirt, my boots, and the light therm jacket. When I step out of my sleeping pagoda, I notice lantern light warming the opaque windows and shoji door of Aenea's pagoda. She is working late again. Walking softly so as not to disturb her by rocking the platform, I clamber down a ladder to the main level of the Temple Hanging in Air.

It always amazes me how empty this place is at night. At first I thought it was the result of the construction workers – most of whom live in the cliffside crates around Jo-kung – being gone, but I've come to realize how few people spend their nights in the temple complex. George and Jigme usually sleep in their foreman's shack but are in Jo-kung with A. Bettik tonight. The abbot Kempo Ngha Wang Tashi stays with the monks some nights, but this night he has returned to his formal home in Jo-kung. A handful of monks prefer their austere quarters here to the formal monastery in Jo-kung, including Chim Din, Labsang Samten, and the woman, Donka Nyapso. Occasionally the flyer, Lhomo, stays at the monks' quarters or in an empty shrine here, but not tonight. Lhomo has left early for the Winter Palace, having mentioned his thought of climbing Nanda Devi south of Potala.

So while I can see a soft lantern glow coming from the monks' quarters hundreds of meters away on the lowest level of the eastern edge of the complex – a glow that is extinguished even as I watch it – the rest of the temple complex is dark and quiet in the starlight. Neither the Oracle nor the other bright moons have risen yet, although the eastern horizon is beginning to glow a bit with their coming. The stars are incredibly bright, almost as brilliant and unwavering as when seen from space. There are thousands visible this night – more than I remembered from Hyperion's or Old Earth's night sky – and I crane my neck until I can see the slowly moving star that is the tiny moon where the ship is presumably hiding. I am carrying the com unit/diskey journal and all it would take is a whisper to query the ship, but Aenea and I have decided that with the Pax so near, even tightbeam transmissions to or from the ship should be reserved for emergency situations.

I sincerely hope that no emergency situations will arise soon.

Taking the ladders, staircases, and short bridges down the west side of the temple complex, I walk back along the brick-and-stone ledge beneath the lowest structures. The night wind has come up and I can hear the creak and groan of the wooden timbers as entire platform levels adjust themselves to the wind and chill. Prayer flags flap above me and I see starlight on the cloudtops where they curl against the ridge rock so far below. The wind is not quite strong enough to make the distinctive wolf's howl that woke me my first few nights here, but its passage through the fissures and timbers and cracks sets the world muttering and whispering around me.

I reach the Wisdom staircase and climb up through the Right Under-standing meditation pavilion, standing a moment at the balcony to look out at the dark and silent monks' quarters perched by itself on a boulder to the east. I recognize the infinite woodcarving skill and care of the sisters, Kuku and Kay Se, in the elaborate carvings just under my fingertips here. Wrapping my jacket tighter in the rising wind, I climb the spiral staircase to the platform pagoda for Right Thought. On the east wall of this restored pagoda, Aenea has designed a large, perfectly round window looking east toward the dip in the ridgeline there where the Oracle makes its first appearance and the moon is rising now, its bright rays illuminating first the ceiling of this pagoda and then the rear wall, where these words from the *Sutta Nipata* scripture are set into the plaster wall:

As a flame blown out by the wind
Goes to rest and cannot be defined
So the wise man freed from individuality
Goes to rest and cannot be defined.
Gone beyond all images –
Gone beyond the power of words.

I know that this passage deals with the enigmatic death of Buddha, but I read it in the moonlight with the thought of how it might apply to Aenea or myself, or the two of us. It does not seem to apply. Unlike the monks who labor here for enlightenment, I have no urge whatsoever to go beyond individuality. The world itself – *all* of the myriad worlds I have been privileged to see and walk upon – are what fascinate and delight me. I have no wish to put the world and my sense images of the world behind me. And I know that Aenea feels the same about life – that involvement with it is like the Catholic Communion, only the World is the Host, and it must be chewed.

Still, the thought of the essence of things – of people – of life going beyond all images and the power of words, this resonates with me. I have been trying – and failing – to put even the essence of this place, these days, into words and discovering the futility of it.

Leaving the Wisdom axis, I cross the long platform for cooking and common meals, and begin up the Morality axis of stairways, bridges, and platforms. The Oracle is free of the ridgeline now and the light from it and its two attendants paint the rock and red wood around me in thick moon paint.

I pass through the pavilions for Right Speech and Right Action, pausing to catch my breath in the circular pagoda for Right Livelihood. There is a bamboo barrel of drinking water just outside the pagoda for Right Effort, and I drink deeply there. Prayer flags flutter and snap along the terraces and eaves as I move softly across the long connecting platform to the highest structures.

The meditation pavilion for Right Mindfulness is part of Aenea's recent work and still smells of fresh bonsai cedar. Ten meters higher along the steep ladder, the Right Meditation pavilion perches out over the bulk of the Temple, its window looking out on the ridge wall. I stand there for several minutes, realizing for the first time that the shadow of the pagoda itself falls upon that slab of rock when the moon is rising as it is now, and that Aenea has designed the roof of the pavilion so that its shadow connects with natural clefts and discolorations in the rock to create a shadow character that I recognize as the Chinese character for Buddha.

At this moment I am taken by a chill, although the wind is not blowing any harder than it has been. Goosebumps rise along my forearms and the back of my neck feels cold. I realize – no, *see* – in that instant, that Aenea's mission, whatever it is, is doomed to failure. She and I are both going to be captured, interrogated, probably tortured, and executed. My promises to the old poet on Hyperion were so much wasted breath. Bring down the Pax, I had said. The Pax with its billions of faithful, millions of men and women in arms, thousands of warships . . . Bring back Old Earth, I had agreed. Well, I had *visited* it.

I look out the window to see the sky, but there is only the rock wall in the moonlight and the slowly cohering shadow character of the Buddha's name, the three vertical strokes like ink on slate-colored vellum, the three horizontal strokes flowing around and together, making three white faces in the negative spaces, three faces staring at me in the dark.

I had promised to protect Aenea. I vow that I will die doing that.

Shaking off the chill and the premonition, I go out onto the meditation platform, clip to a cable, and hum thirty meters across the void to the platform below the top terrace where Aenea and I have sleeping pagodas. As I climb the last ladder to the highest level, I am thinking – perhaps I will sleep now.

I made no notes on this in the diskey journal. I remember it now as I write it.

Aenea's light was out. I was pleased – she stayed up too late, worked too hard. The high work scaffolds and cliff cables were no place for an exhausted architect.

I stepped into my own shack, slid shut the shoji door, and kicked off my boots. Things were as I had left them – the outer screen wall slid back a bit, moonlight bright across my sleeping mat, the wind rattling the walls in its soft conversation with the mountains. Neither of my lanterns was lit, but I had the light from the moon and my memory of the small room in the dark. The floor was bare tatami except for my sleeping futon and a single chest near the door that held my rucksack, few food items, beer mug, the rebreathers I'd brought from the ship, and my climbing gear: there was nothing to trip over.

I hung my jacket on the hook near the door, splashed water on my face from the basin on the chest, and stripped off my shirt, socks, trousers, and underwear, stuffing them into the ditty bag in the chest. Tomorrow was laundry day. Sighing, feeling the premonition of doom I'd felt in the meditation pavilion now fading into simple fatigue, I walked over to the sleeping mat. I have always slept naked except for when in the Home Guard and during my trip in the Consul's ship with my two friends.

There was the slightest of movements in the darkness beyond the bright stripe of moonlight and, startled, I dropped into a fighting crouch. Nakedness makes one feel more vulnerable than usual. Then I realized – *A. Bettik must have returned early.* I unclenched my right fist.

'Raul?' said Aenea. She leaned forward into the moonlight. She had wrapped my sleeping blanket around the lower part of her body, but her shoulders and breasts and abdomen were bare. The Oracle touched her hair and cheekbones with soft light.

I opened my mouth to speak, started to turn back toward my clothes or jacket, decided not to walk that far, and dropped on one knee to the sleeping mat, pulling up the futon's sheet to cover myself. I was not a prude, but this was Aenea. What was she . . .

'Raul,' she said again, and this time there was no question in her voice. She moved closer to me on her knees. The blanket fell away from her.

'Aenea,' I said stupidly. 'Aenea, I . . . you . . . I don't . . . you don't really . . .'

She set her finger on my lips and removed it a second later, but before I could speak she leaned closer and pressed her lips where her finger had been.

Every time I had ever touched my young friend, the contact had been electric. I have described this before and always felt foolish discussing it, but I ascribed it to her . . . an aura . . . a charge of personality. It was real, not a metaphor. But never had I felt the surge of electricity between us as in this instant.

For a second I was passive, receiving the kiss rather than sharing in it. But then the warmth and insistence of it overcame thought, overcame doubt, overcame all of my other senses in every nuance of the word, and then I was returning her kiss, putting my arms around her to pull her closer even as she slid her arms under mine and ran strong fingers up my back. More than five years ago for her, when she had kissed me farewell at the river on Old Earth, her kiss had been urgent, electric, filled with questions and messages – but still a sixteen-year-old girl's kiss. This kiss was the warm, moist, open touch of a woman, and I responded to it in an instant.

We kissed for an eternity. I was vaguely aware of my own nudity and excitement as something I should be concerned about, embarrassed about, but it was a distant thing, secondary to the expanding warmth and urgency of the kisses that would not stop. When finally our lips came apart, feeling swollen, almost bruised, wanting to be kissed again, we kissed each other's cheeks, eyelids, forehead, ears. I lowered my face and kissed the hollow of her throat, feeling the pulse against my lips there and inhaling the perfumed scent of her skin.

She moved forward on her knees, arching her back slightly so that her breasts touched my cheek. I cupped one and kissed the nipple almost reverently; Aenea cupped the back of my head in her palm. I could feel her breath on me, quickening, as she bowed her face toward me.

'Wait, wait,' I said, pulling my face up and leaning back. 'No, Aenea, are you . . . I mean . . . I don't think . . .'

'Shhh,' she said, leaning over me again, kissing me again, pulling back so that her dark eyes seemed to fill the world. 'Shhh, Raul. Yes.' She kissed me again, leaning to her right so that we both reclined on the sleeping mat, still kissing, the rising breeze rattling the rice-paper walls, the entire platform rocking to the depth of our kiss and the motion of our bodies.

It is a problem. To tell of such things. To share the most private and sacred of moments. It feels like a violation to put such things into words. And a lie not to.

To see and feel one's beloved naked for the first time is one of life's pure, irreducible epiphanies. If there is a true religion in the universe, it must include that truth of contact or be forever hollow. To make love to the one true person who deserves that love is one of the few absolute rewards of being a human being, balancing all of the pain, loss, awkwardness, loneliness, idiocy, compromise, and clumsiness that go with the human condition. To make love to the right person makes up for a lot of mistakes.

I had never made love to the right person before. I knew that even as Aenea and I first kissed and lay against each other, even before we began moving slowly, then quickly, then slowly again. I realized that I had never really made love to anyone before – that the young-soldier-on-leave sex with friendly women or the bargeman-and-bargewoman-we-have-the-opportunity-so-why-not? sex that I had thought had explored and discovered everything to do with the subject was not even the beginning.

This was the beginning. I remember Aenea rising above me at one point, her hand hard on my chest, her own chest slick with sweat, but she was still looking at me – looking at me so intensely and so warmly that it was as if we were connected intimately by our gaze as surely as by our thighs and genitals – and I was to remember that instant every time we made love in the future, even as I seemed to be remembering forward to all those future times even during these first few moments of our intimacy.

Lying together in the moonlight, the sheets and blankets and the futon curled and thrown around us, the cool wind from the north drying the sweat on our bodies, her cheek on my chest and my thigh across her hip, we kept touching each other – her fingers playing with the hair on my chest, my fingers tracing the line of her cheek, the sole of my foot sliding up and down the back of her leg, curling around her strong calf muscles.

'Was this a mistake?' I whispered.

'No,' she whispered back. 'Unless . . .'

My heart pounded. 'Unless what?'

'Unless you didn't get those shots in the Home Guard that I'm sure you got,' she whispered. I was so anxious that I did not hear the teasing quality in her voice.

'What? Shots? What?' I said, rolling onto my elbow. 'Oh . . . shots . . . shit. You know I did. Jesus.'

'I know you did,' whispered Aenea and I could hear the smile now.

When we Hyperion lads had joined the Home Guard, the authorities had given us the usual battery of Pax-approved injections – antimalaria, anticancer, antivirus, and birth control. In a Pax universe where the vast majority of individuals chose the cruciform – chose to attempt to be immortal – birth control was a given. One could apply to Pax authorities for the antidote after marriage or simply buy it on the black market when it was time to start a family. Or, if one chose neither the way of the cross nor a family, it would last until old age or death made the issue moot. I had not thought of that shot for years. Actually, I think A. Bettik had asked me about those shots on the Consul's ship a decade ago when we were discussing preventative medicine and I had mentioned the Home Guard induction battery, our young friend of eleven or twelve curled on a couch there on the holopit level, reading a book from the ship's library, seemingly not paying attention at all . . .

'No,' I said, still on my elbow, 'I mean a *mistake*. You're . . .'

'Me,' she whispered.

'Twenty-one standard years old,' I finished. 'I'm . . .'

'You,' she whispered.

'. . . eleven standard years older than that.'

'Incredible,' said Aenea. Her whole face was in the moonlight as she looked up at me. 'You can do math. At such a moment.'

I sighed and rolled over on my stomach. The sheets smelled of us. The wind was still rising and now it rattled the walls.

'I'm cold,' whispered Aenea.

In the days and months to come, I would have held her in my arms if she said such a thing, but that night I responded literally and stood to slide shut the shoji screen. The wind was colder than usual.

'No,' she said.

'What?'

'Don't close it all the way.' She was sitting up with the sheet raised to just below her breasts.

'But it's . . .'

'The moonlight on you,' Aenea whispered.

Her voice may have caused my physical response. Or the sight of her, waiting for me in the blankets. Besides holding in our own scents, the room smelled like fresh straw because of the new tatami and the ryokan in the ceiling. And of the fresh, cool air of the mountains. But the cold breeze did not slow my reaction to her.

'Come here,' she whispered, and opened the blanket like a cape to fold me in.

The next morning and I am working on setting the overhang walkway in place and it is as if I am sleepwalking. Part of the problem is lack of sleep – the Oracle had set and the east was paling with morning when Aenea slipped back to her own pavilion – but the major reason is sheer, simple stupefaction. Life has taken a turn that I had never anticipated, never imagined.

I am setting supports into the cliff for the high walk with the high riggers Haruyuki, Kenshiro, and Voytek Majer moving ahead, drilling holes in the stone, while Kim Byung-Soon and Viki Groselj lay brick behind and beneath us and carpenter Changchi Kenchung begins work behind me on the laying of the wood floor of the terrace itself. There would be nothing to catch the high riggers and me if we fall from the wooden beams if Lhomo had not done his free-climbing exhibition yesterday and set fixed ropes and cables in place. Now as we jump from beam to beam, we just clip one of our harness carabiners into place on the next rope. I have fallen before and had the fall arrested by this sort of fixed rope: each can hold five times my weight.

Now I leap from set beam to set beam, pulling along the next beam as it dangles from one of the cables. The wind is coming up and threatens to hurl me off into space, but I balance myself with one hand touching the hanging beam and three fingers on the rockface itself. I reach the end of the third fixed rope, unclip, and prepare to clip on to the fourth of seven lines Lhomo has rigged.

I do not know what to think about last night. That is, I know how I feel – exhilarated, confused, ecstatic, in love – but I don't know how to think about it. I tried to intercept Aenea before breakfast in the communal dining pavilion near the monks' quarters, but she had already eaten and headed far out to where the terrace carvers had run into trouble on the new eastern walkway. Then A. Bettik, George Tsarong, and Jigme Norbu had shown up with the porters and an hour or two was consumed sorting materials and transporting the beams, chisels, lumber, and other items to the new high scaffolds. I had headed out onto the eastern ledge before the beam work began, but A. Bettik and Tsipon Shakabpa were conferring with Aenea, so I jogged back to the scaffolds and got busy.

Now I was jumping to the last beam set in place this morning, ready to install the next one in the hole Haruyuki and Kenshiro have chiseled and blasted into the rock with tiny, shaped charges. Then Voytek and Viki will cement the post in place. Within thirty minutes, it will be firm enough for Changchi to set a work platform on. I've become accustomed to leaping from beam to beam, catching my balance and squatting to set the next beam in place, and I do so now on the last beam, pinwheeling my left arm to keep my balance while my fingers stay in contact with the beam balancing from the cable. Suddenly the beam swings out too far ahead of me and I am off balance, leaning into nothing. I know that the safety line will catch me, but I hate to fall and be dangling here between the last beam and the newly drilled hole. If I don't have enough momentum to kick back to the beam, I'll have to wait for Kenshiro or one of the other riggers to kick out and rescue me.

In a fraction of a second, I make up my mind and jump, catching the swinging beam and kicking out hard. Because the safety rope has several meters of slack before it will catch me, all of my weight is on my fingers now. The beam is too thick for me to get a good grip on it and I can feel my fingers sliding on the iron-hard wood. But rather than go dropping to the elastic end of my fixed line, I struggle to hang on, succeed in swinging the heavy post back toward the last beam in place, and jump the last two meters, landing on the slippery beam and flailing my arms for balance. Laughing at my own foolishness, I catch my balance and stand panting for a moment, watching the clouds broiling against the rock several thousand meters below my feet.

Changchi Kenchung is leaping from beam to beam toward me, clipping on to the fixed ropes with a rapid urgency. There is something like horror in his eyes, and for a second I am sure that something has happened to Aenea. My heart begins beating so hard and anxiety washes over me so swiftly that I almost lose my balance. But I catch it again and stand balancing on the last fixed beam, waiting for Changchi with a sense of dread.

When he leaps to the last beam with me, Changchi is too winded to speak. He gestures toward me urgently, but I do not understand the motion. Perhaps he had seen my comical swing and dance and leap with the dangling beam and was concerned. To show him that it was all right, I reach up to my harness line to show him that the carabiner is locked tight to the safety line.

There is no carabiner there. I never tied on to the last fixed rope. I have been doing all this leaping, balancing, hanging, and jumping with no safety line. There has been nothing between me and . . .

Feeling a sudden stab of vertigo and nausea, I stagger three steps to the cliff wall and lean against the cold stone. The overhang tries to push me away and it is as if the entire mountain is tilting outward, pushing me off the beam.

Changchi tugs Lhomo's fixed line around, lifts a 'biner from my harness rack, and clips me on. I nod my appreciation and try not to lose my breakfast while he is here with me.

Ten meters around the bend in the cliff, Haruyuki and Kenshiro are gesturing. They have blasted another perfect hole. They want me to catch up with setting the beams in place.

The party departing for the Dalai Lama's evening reception for the Pax at Potala leaves just after the noon meal in the common dining hall. I see Aenea there, but except for a meaningful exchange of glances and a smile from her that makes my knees weak, we have no private communication.

We assemble on the lowest level with hundreds of workers, monks, cooks, scholars, and porters waving and cheering from the platforms above. Rain clouds are beginning to curl and spill between the low gaps in the eastern ridgeline, but the sky above Hsuan-k'ung Ssu is still blue and the red prayer flags flapping from the high terraces stand out with almost shocking clarity.

We are all dressed in travel clothes, our formal reception clothing carried in waterproof shoulder-strap satchels or – in my case – my rucksack. The Dalai Lama's receptions are traditionally held late at night and we have more than ten hours until our presence is required, but it is a six-hour trip on the High Way, and couriers and one flyer coming into Jo-kung earlier that day have told of bad weather beyond the K'un Lun Ridge, so we step off lively enough.

The order of march is set by protocol. Charles Chi-kyap Kempo, Mayor of Jo-kung and Lord Chamberlain of the Temple Hanging in Air, walks a few paces ahead of his near-peer, Kempo Ngha Wang Tashi, abbot of the Temple. Both men's 'traveling clothes' are more resplendent than my shot at formal wear, and they are surrounded by small hornet clusters of aides, monks, and security people.

Behind the priest politicians walk Gyalo Thondup, the young monk and cousin to the current Dalai Lama, and Labsang Samten, the third-year monk who is the Dalai Lama's brother. They have the easy stride and easier laugh of young men at the peak of physical health and mental clarity. Their white teeth gleam in their brown faces. Labsang is wearing a brilliant red climbing *chuba* that gives the appearance of his being an ambulatory prayer flag in our procession as we head west along the narrow walkway to the Jo-kung fissure.

Tsipon Shakabpa, the official overseer of Aenea's project, walks with George Tsarong, our chubby construction foreman. George's inseparable companion, Jigme Norbu, is absent now: his feelings hurt by not being invited, Jigme has stayed behind at the Temple. I believe that this is the first time that I have seen George where he is not smiling. Tsipon makes up for George's silence, however, telling stories with waving arms and extravagant gestures. Several of their workers hike with them – at least as far as Jo-kung.

Tromo Trochi of Dhomu, the flamboyant trade agent from the south, walks with his only companion for so many months on the highways – an oversized zygoat packbrid laden with the trader's goods. The zygoat has three bells hung from its shaggy neck and they chime like the Temple's prayer bells as we walk along. Lhomo Dondrub is to meet us in Potala, but his presence in the party is represented symbolically on the zygoat's topmost pack duffel by a swatch of new flight fabric for his paraglider.

Aenea and I bring up the rear of the procession. Several times I try to talk about last night, but she silences me with a finger to her lips and a nod in the direction of the nearby trader and other members of the procession. I settle for small talk about the last days of work on the Temple overhang pavilion and walkways, but my mind continues to jostle with questions.

711

Soon we are in Jo-kung, where the ramps and walkways are lined with crowds waving pennants and prayer flags. From the fissure terraces and cliff shacks, citizens of the city cheer their mayor and the rest of us.

Just beyond the fissure city of Jo-kung, near the jump-off platforms of the only cableway we will be using on this trip to Potala, we encounter another party headed to the Dalai Lama's reception: the Dorje Phamo and her nine female priests. The Dorje Phamo travels in a palanquin carried by four heavily muscled males because she is the abbess of Samden Gompa, an all-male monastery some thirty klicks out along the south wall of the same ridge that holds the Temple Hanging in Air along its north wall. The Dorje Phamo is ninety-four standard years old and was discovered to be the incarnation of the original Dorje Phamo, the Thunderbolt Sow, when she was three standard years old. She is a woman of immense importance and a separate monastery for women – the Oracle Gompa at Yamdrok Tso, some sixty klicks farther along the dangerous ridge wall – has held her as its prefect and avatar for more than seventy standard years. Now the Thunderbolt Sow, her nine female priest companions, and about thirty male carriers and guards are waiting at the cableway to attach the palanquin's massive carabiner clamps.

The Dorje Phamo peers through her curtains, spies our party, and beckons Aenea over. I know from Aenea's offhand comments that she has traveled to the Oracle Gompa at Yamdrok Tso several times to meet with the Sow and that the two are fast friends. I also know from A. Bettik's comments to me in confidence that the Dorje Phamo has recently told her female priests and monks at the Oracle Gompa and the male monks at Samden Gompa that it is Aenea, not His Holiness the current Dalai Lama, who is the incarnation of the living Buddha of Mercy. Word of this heresy has spread, according to A. Bettik, but because of the Thunderbolt Sow's popularity across the world of T'ien Shan, the Dalai Lama has not yet responded to the impertinence.

Now I watch as the two women – my young Aenea and the ancient form in the palanquin – chat and laugh easily as both parties wait to cross the cableway across the Langma Abyss. The Dorje Phamo must have insisted that we precede her group, for the carriers move the palanquin back out of the way and the nine female priests bow deeply as Aenea motions our group forward on the platform. Charles Chi-kyap Kempo and Kempo Ngha Wang Tashi look discomfited as they allow their aides to clip them on to the cable – not out of concern for their safety, I know, but out of some breach of protocol that I missed and am not particularly interested in. At that moment I am interested in getting Aenea alone and talking with her. Or perhaps just kissing her again.

It rains hard during the walk to Potala. During my three months here I've experienced more than a few summer showers, but this is a serious pre-monsoon rain, chilling, icy, with curling tendrils of fog that close around us. We clear the one cableway transit before the clouds close in, but by the time we are approaching the east side of the K'un Lun Ridge, the High Way is slick with ice.

The High Way consists of rock ledges, bricked pathways on the sheer cliffside, high wooden walkways along the northwest ridge of Hua Shan, the Flower Mountain, and a long series of platform walkways and suspension bridges connecting those icy ridgelines with K'un Lun. Then there is the second-longest suspension bridge on the planet connecting K'un Lun Ridge with Phari Ridge, followed by another series of walkways, bridges, and ledges heading southwest along the east face of Phari Ridge to Phari Marketplace. There we pass through the fissure and follow the ledge road almost due west to Potala.

Normally this is a six-hour walk in the sunshine, but this afternoon it is a dreary, dangerous trudge through the curling fog and icy rain. The aides traveling with Mayor/Lord Chamberlain Charles Chi-kyap Kempo and Abbot Kempo Ngha Wang Tashi attempt to shelter their worthies under bright red and yellow umbrellas, but the icy ledge is often narrow and the worthies frequently must get wet as they go ahead in single file. The suspension bridges are nightmares to cross – the 'floor' of each is just a single, heavily braided hemp cable with hemp ropes rising vertically, horizontal side ropes for railings, and a second thick cable above one's head – and although it is usually child's play to balance on the lower cable while keeping contact with the side ropes, it takes complete concentration in this driving rain. But all of the locals have done this through dozens of monsoons and they move along quickly; it is only Aenea and I who hesitate as the bridges flex and toss under the party's weight, the icy ropes threatening to slip out of our hands.

Despite the storm – or perhaps because of it – someone has lighted the High Way torches all along the east face of Phari Ridge, and the braziers burning through the thick fog help us find our way as the wooden walkways turn, bend, rise, descend icy staircases, and lead out to more bridges. We arrive in Phari Marketplace just at dusk, although it seems much later because of the gloom. Other groups bound for the Winter Palace join us there and there are at least seventy people headed west together past the fissure. The Dorje Phamo's palanquin still bobs along with us and I suspect that others besides myself are a bit envious of her dry perch in there.

I confess that I am disappointed: we had planned to arrive at Potala in the twilight, while there was still alpenglow lighting the north-south ridges and the higher peaks to the north and west of the palace. I have never glimpsed the palace before, and I had been looking forward to seeing this region. As it is, the broad High Way between Phari and Potala is just a series of torchlit ledges and walkways. I have brought the flashlight laser in my pack, although whether as a futile gesture for defense should things turn bad at the palace, or for finding our way in the dark, I am not sure. Ice coats the rocks, the platforms, the hemp-cable railings along this most well traveled of walkways, as well as the stairs. I cannot imagine being on the cableway this night, but rumor has it that several of the more adventurous guests are traveling that way.

We arrive at the Forbidden City some two hours before the reception is scheduled to begin. The clouds have lifted a bit, the rain relents, and our first glimpse of the Winter Palace takes my breath away and makes me forget my disappointment of not having approached it in the twilight.

The Winter Palace is built on a great peak rising from the Yellow Hat Ridge, with the higher peaks of Koko Nor behind it, and our first glimpse through the clouds is of Drepung, the surrounding monastery that houses thirty-five thousand monks, tier upon tier of tall stone buildings rising up the vertical slopes, its thousands of windows glowing with lantern light, torches at balconies, terraces, and entrances, while behind the Drepung and above it, with gold roofs touching the ceiling of boiling clouds, rises Potala – the Winter Palace of the Dalai Lama – ablaze with light, and back-lighted – even in the stormy darkness – by the lightning-lit peaks of the Koko Nor.

The aides and fellow travelers turn back here, and only we invited pilgrims press on into the Forbidden City.

The High Way now flattens and broadens to a true highway, an avenue fifty meters wide, paved with gold stones, lined with torches, and surrounded by countless temples, chortens, lesser gompas, outbuildings for the imposing monastery, and military guard posts. The rain has stopped, but the avenue glistens goldly while hundreds upon hundreds of brightly garbed pilgrims and residents of the Forbidden City bustle to and fro in front of the huge walls and gates of the Drepung and the Potala. Monks in saffron robes move in small, silent groups; palace officials in brilliant red and rich purple gowns and yellow hats looking like inverted saucers walk purposefully past soldiers in blue uniforms with black-and-white-striped pikes; official messengers jog by in skintight outfits of orange and red or gold and blue; women of the court glide across the gold stones in long silk dresses of sky blue, deep lapis lazuli, and daring cobalt, their trains making soft slithering sounds on the wet pavement; priests from the Red Hat Sect are instantly recognizable with their inverted saucer hats of crimson silk and crimson fringe, while the Drungpas – the wooded valley people – stride by with wooly hats of zygoat fur, their costumes adorned with brilliant white, red, tan, and gold feathers, carrying their great gold ceremonial swords tucked into their sashes; finally the common folk of the Forbidden City are little less colorful than the high officials, the cooks and gardeners and servants and tutors and masons and personal valets all bedecked in silk *chubas* of green and blue or gold and orange, those who work in the Dalai Lama's quarters of the Winter Palace – several thousand strong – glimpsed in the crimson and gold, everyone wearing the zygoat-banded silk hats with stiff brims some fifty centimeters broad, to preserve their pale palace complexions on sunny days and to ward off the rain during monsoon season.

Our wet band of pilgrims seems dull and shabby in these surroundings, but I have little thought of our own appearance as we pass through a sixty-meter-tall gate in one of the outer walls of the Drepung Monastery and begin to cross the Kyi Chu Bridge.

This bridge is twenty meters wide, a hundred and fifteen meters long, and made of the most modern carbon-plasteel. It shines like black chrome. Beneath it is . . . nothing. The bridge spans a terminal fissure in the ridgeline and drops thousands of meters to the phosgene clouds below. On the east side – the side from which we approach – the structures of the Drepung rise two or three kilometers above us, flat walls and glowing windows and the air above us laced with spiderweb upon spiderweb of official cable shortcuts between the monastery and the palace proper. On the west side – ahead of us – the Potala rises more than six kilometers on the cliff faces, its thousands of stone facets and hundreds of gold roofs reflecting the flickering lightning from the low clouds above it. In case of attack, the Kyi Chu Bridge can retract into the western cliff in less than thirty seconds, leaving no stairway, foothold, ledge, or window for half a kilometer of vertical stone to the first ramparts above.

The bridge does not retract as we cross it. The sides are lined with troopers in ceremonial garb, each carrying a deadly serious pike or energy rifle. At the far end of the Kyi Chu, we pause at the Pargo Kaling – the Western Gate – an ornate arch eighty-five meters tall. Light glows from within the giant arch, breaking out through a thousand intricate designs, the brightest glow coming from the two great eyes – each more than ten meters across – that stare unblinkingly across the Kyi Chu and the Drepung to the east.

We each pause as we pass under the Pargo Kaling. Our first step beyond it will bring us onto the grounds of the Winter Palace itself, although the actual doorway is still some thirty paces ahead of us. Inside that doorway are the thousand steps that will take us up to the palace proper. Aenea has told me that pilgrims have come from all over T'ien Shan by walking on their knees, or in some cases by prostrating themselves at every step – literally measuring the hundreds or thousands of kilometers with their bodies – just to be allowed to pass under the Western Gate and to touch this last section of Kyi Chu Bridge with their foreheads out of homage to the Dalai Lama.

Aenea and I step across together, glancing at one another.

After presenting our invitations to the guards and officials within the main entrance portal, we ascend the thousand stairs. I am amazed to find that the stairway is an escalator, although Tromo Trochi of Dhomu whispers that it is often left unactivated to allow the faithful a final exertion before being allowed into the upper reaches of the palace.

Above, on the first public levels, there is another flurry of invitation checking, servants divesting us of our wet outer robes, and other servants escorting us to rooms in which we might bathe and change. Lord Chamberlain Charles Chi-kyap Kempo is entitled to a small suite of rooms on the seventy-eighth level of the palace, and after what seems like further kilometers of walking down outside halls – the windows to our right showing the red rooftops of the Drepung Monastery flickering and gleaming in the storm light – we are greeted by more servants given over to our bidding. Each of our party has at least a curtained alcove in which we will sleep after the formal reception, and adjoining bathrooms offer hot water, baths, and modern sonic showers. I follow Aenea and smile at her when she winks on her way out of the steamy room.

I had no truly formal clothes at the Temple Hanging in Air – nor any in the ship currently hiding on the third moon, for that matter – but Lhomo Dondrub and some of the others roughly my size have fitted me out for tonight's honor: black trousers and highly polished, high black boots, a white silk shirt under a gold vest, with a red-and-black X-shaped wool overvest, tied together at the waist with a crimson silk sash. The formal evening cape is made of the finest warrior-silk from the western reaches of Muztagh Alta and is mostly black, but with intricate border designs of red, gold, silver, and yellow. It is Lhomo's second-best cape and he made it quite clear that he would toss me from the highest platform if I stained, tore, or lost it. Lhomo is a pleasant, easygoing man – almost unheard of in a lone flyer, I am told – but I think he was not kidding about this.

A. Bettik loaned me the requisite silver bracelets for the reception, these purchased by him on a whim in the beautiful markets of Hsi wang-mu. Over my shoulders I place the feather and zygoat-wool red hood loaned to me by Jigme Norbu, who has waited his entire life in vain for an invitation to the Winter Palace. Around my neck is a jade-and-silver-link Middle Kingdom formal talisman courtesy of master carpenter and friend Changchi Kenchung, who told me this morning that he has been to three receptions at the palace and has been bored witless each time.

Servants in gold silk come to our chambers to announce that it is time for us to congregate in the Main Reception Hall next to the Throne Room. The outside corridors are filled with hundreds of guests moving along the tiled halls, silk is rustling, jewelry rattles, and the air is filled with the clash of perfume and cologne and soap and leather. Ahead of us, I get a glimpse of the ancient Dorje Phamo – the Thunderbolt Sow herself – being helped along by two of her nine female priests, all of them in elegant saffron gowns. The Sow wears no jewelry, but her white hair is tied and ribboned in elaborate mounds and beautiful braids.

Aenea's gown is simple but breathtaking – a deep-blue silk, with a cobalt hood covering her otherwise bare shoulders, one Middle Kingdom talisman of silver and jade dropping to her bosom, and a silver comb pinned in her hair, holding a thin half veil in place. Many of the women in view are veiled for modesty tonight, and I realize how cleverly this disguises my friend's appearance.

She takes my arm and we move in procession down the endless corridors, turning right and gliding up spiral escalators toward the Dalai Lama's levels.

I lean close and whisper against her veiled ear. 'Nervous?'

I see the glint of her smile beneath the veil and she squeezes my hand.

Persisting, I whisper, 'Kiddo, you sometimes see the future. I know you do. So . . . do we get out of this alive tonight?'

I bend over as she leans close to whisper back. 'Only a few things in anyone's future are set, Raul. Most things are as liquid as . . .' She gestures toward a swirling fountain that we pass and spiral above. 'But I see no reason to worry, do you? There are thousands of guests here tonight. The

Dalai Lama can greet only a few in person. His guests . . . the Pax . . . whoever they will be, have no reason to think that we are here.'

I nod, but am not convinced.

Suddenly Labsang Samten, the Dalai Lama's brother, comes racketing down the ascending escalator in violation of all protocol. The monk is grinning and bubbling over with enthusiasm. He addresses our group, but hundreds on the rising staircase lean to listen in.

'The guests from space are very important!' he says enthusiastically. 'I have been talking to our tutor who is the assistant to the second in command to the Minister of Protocol. These are not just missionaries whom we greet tonight!'

'No?' says the Lord Chamberlain Charles Chi-kyap Kempo, resplendent in his many layers of red and gold silk.

'No!' grins Labsang Samten. 'It is a cardinal of the Pax Church. A very important cardinal. With several of his top people.'

I feel my stomach churn and then drop into freefall.

'Which cardinal?' says Aenea. Her voice seems calm and interested. We are approaching the top of the spiral staircase ride, and the sound of hundreds or thousands of softly murmuring guests fills the air.

Labsang Samten straightens his formal monk's robe. 'A Cardinal Mustafa,' he says brightly. 'Someone very close to the Pax Pope, I think. The Pax honors my brother by sending him as ambassador.'

I feel Aenea's hand close on my arm, but I cannot see her expression clearly through the veil.

'And several other important Pax guests,' continues the monk, turning as we approach the reception level. 'Including some strange Pax women. Military types, I think.'

'Did you get their names?' asks Aenea.

'One of them,' says Labsang. 'General Nemes. She is very pale.' The Dalai Lama's brother turns his wide, sincere smile on Aenea. 'The Cardinal has asked to meet you specifically, M. Aenea. You and your escort, M. Endymion. The Protocol Minister was very surprised, but has arranged for a private reception for you with the Pax people and the Regent and, of course, my brother, His Holiness, the Dalai Lama.'

Our ascent ends. The staircase slides into the marble floor. With Aenea on my arm, I step out into the noise and tightly controlled chaos of the Main Reception Hall.

NINETEEN

The Dalai Lama is only eight standard years old. I had known that – Aenea and A. Bettik and Theo and Rachel have all mentioned it more than once – but I am still surprised when I see the child sitting on his high, cushioned throne.

There must be three or four thousand people in the immense reception room. Several broad escalators disgorge guests simultaneously into an antechamber the size of a spacecraft hangar – gold pillars rising to a frescoed ceiling twenty meters above us, blue-and-white tiles underfoot with elaborate, inset images from the *Bardo Thodrol*, the *Tibetan Book of the Dead*, as well as illustrations of the vast seedship migration of the Buddhist Old Earth émigrés, huge gold arches under which we pass to enter the reception room – and the reception room is larger still, its ceiling one giant skylight through which the broiling clouds and flickering lightning and lantern-lit mountainside are quite visible. The three or four thousand guests are brilliant in their finery – flowing silk, sculpted linen, draped and dyed wool, profusions of red-black-and-white feathers, elaborate hairdos, subtle but beautifully formed bracelets, necklaces, anklets, earrings, tiaras, and belts of silver, amethyst, gold, jade, lapis lazuli, and a score of other precious metals. And scattered among all this elegance and finery are scores of monks and abbots in their simple robes of orange, gold, yellow, saffron, and red, their closely shaved heads gleaming in the light from a hundred flickering tripod braziers. Yet the room is so large that these few thousand people do not come close to filling it up – the parquet floors gleam in the firelight and there is a twenty-meter space between the first fringes of the crowd and the golden throne.

Small horns blow as the lines of guests step from the escalator staircases to the anteroom tiles. The trumpets are of brass and bone and the line of monks blowing them runs from the stairs to the entrance arches – more than sixty meters of constant noise. The hundreds of horns hold one note for minutes on end and then shift to another low note without signal from trumpeter to trumpeter and as we enter the Main Reception Hall – the antechamber acting as a giant echo chamber behind us – these low notes are taken up and amplified by twenty four-meter-long horns on either side of our procession. The monks who blow these monstrous instruments stand in small alcoves in the walls, resting the giant horns on stands set on the parquet floors, the bell-horn ends curling up like meter-wide lotus blossoms. Added to this constant, low series of notes – rather like an ocean-going ship's foghorn wrapped within a glacier's rumble – are the reverberations of a huge gong, at least five meters across, being struck at precise intervals. The air smells of incense from the braziers and the slightest veil of fragrant smoke moves above the jeweled and coiffed heads of the guests and seems to shimmer and shift with the rise and fall of the notes from the trumpets and horns and gong.

All faces are turned toward the Dalai Lama, his immediate retinue, and his guests. I take Aenea's hand and we move to our right, staying far back from the throne and its surrounding dais. Constellations of important guests move nervously between us and the distant throne.

Suddenly the deep horn notes cease. The gong's final vibrations echo and fall away. All of the guests are present. The huge doors behind us are pushed shut by straining servants. Across the giant, echoing space, I can hear the crackling of flames in the countless braziers. Rain suddenly beats at the crystal skylight far above us.

The Dalai Lama is smiling slightly as he sits cross-legged on multiple silk cushions atop a platform that brings him to eye level with his standing guests. The boy's head is bare and shaven and he wears a simple red lama's robe. To his right, and lower, on a throne of his own, sits the Regent who will rule – in consultation with other high priests – until His Holiness the Dalai Lama comes of age at eighteen standard years. Aenea has told me about this Regent, a man named Reting Tokra who is said to be the literal incarnation of cunning, but all I can see from my distant vantage point now is the usual red robe and a narrow, pinched, brown face with its slitted eyes and tiny mustache.

To the left of His Holiness the Dalai Lama is the Lord Chamberlain, abbot of abbots. This man is quite old and smiling broadly at the phalanxes of guests. To his left is the State Oracle, a thin young woman with severely cropped hair and a yellow linen shirt under her red robe. Aenea has explained that it is the State Oracle's job to predict the future while in a deep trance. To the left of the State Oracle, their faces largely blocked from my view by the gilded pillars of the Dalai Lama's throne, stand five emissaries from the Pax – I can make out a short man in cardinal's red, three forms in black cassocks, and at least one military uniform.

To the right of the Regent's throne stands the Chief Crier and Head of His Holiness's Security, the legendary Carl Linga William Eiheji, Zen archer, watercolorist, karate master, philosopher, former flyer, and flower arranger. Eiheji looks to be built of coiled steel wrapped about with pure muscle as he strides forward and fills the immense hall with his voice:

'Honored guests, visitors from beyond our world, Dugpas, Drukpas, Drungpas – those from the highest ridges, the noble fissures, and the wooded valley slopes – *Dzasas*, honored officials, the Red Hats and the Yellow Hats, monks, abbots, *getsel* novices, *Ko-sas* of the Fourth Rank and higher, blessed ones who wear the *su gi*, wives and husbands of those so honored, seekers of Enlightenment, it is my pleasure to welcome you here tonight on behalf of His Holiness, Getswang Ngwang Lobsang Tengin Gyapso Sisunwangyur Tshungpa Mapai Dhepal Sangpo – the Holy One, the

Gentle Glory, Powerful in Speech, Pure in Mind, of Divine Wisdom, Holding the Faith, Ocean-Wide!'

The small brass and bone trumpets blow high, clear notes. The great horns bellow like dinosaurs. The gong sends vibrations through our bones and teeth.

Chief Crier Eiheji steps back. His Holiness the Dalai Lama speaks, his child's voice soft but clear and firm across the great space.

'Thank you all for coming this night. We shall greet our new friends from the Pax in more intimate circumstances. Many of you have requested to see me . . . you shall receive my blessing in private audience tonight. I have requested to speak with some of you. You shall meet me in private audience tonight. Our friends from the Pax will speak with many of you this evening and in the days to come. In speaking to them, please remember that these are our brothers and sisters in the Dharma, in the quest for Enlightenment. Please remember that our breath is their breath, and that all of our breath is the breath of Buddha. Thank you. Please enjoy our celebration this night.'

And with that the dais, throne and all, slides silently back through the opening wall, is hidden by a sliding curtain, then by another curtain, and then by the wall itself, and the thousands in the main reception hall let out a breath as one.

The evening was, as I remember, a nearly surreal combination of a gala ball swirling around a formal papal reception. I had never seen a papal reception, of course – the mystery cardinal on the now-curtained dais was the highest official of the Church encountered in my experience – but the excitement of those being received by the Dalai Lama must have been similar to a Christian meeting the Pope, and the pomp and circumstance surrounding their presentation was impressive. Soldier-monks in red robes and red or yellow hats escorted the lucky few through the tented curtains and then through more curtains and finally through the door in the wall to the Dalai Lama's presence while the rest of us moved and mixed across the torchlit parquet floor, or browsed the long tables of excellent food, or even danced to the music of a small band – no brass and bone trumpets or four-meter horns there. I admit that I asked Aenea if she would like to dance, but she smiled, shook her head, and led our group to the nearest banquet table. Soon we were engaged in conversation with the Dorje Phamo and some of her female priests.

Knowing that I might be committing a faux pas, I nonetheless asked the beautiful old woman why she was called the Thunderbolt Sow. As we munched on fried balls of tsampa and drank delicious tea, the Dorje Phamo laughed and told us the story.

On Old Earth, the first such abbess of an all-male Tibetan Buddhist monastery had gained the reputation of being the reincarnation of the original Thunderbolt Sow, a demigoddess of frightening power. That first Dorje Phamo abbess was said to have transformed not only herself but all of the lamas in her monastery into pigs to frighten away enemy soldiers.

When I asked this last reincarnation of the Thunderbolt Sow if she had retained the power of transforming into a sow, the elegant old woman lifted her head and said firmly, 'If that would frighten away these current invaders, I would do so in an instant.'

In the three hours or so during which Aenea and I mixed and chatted and listened to music and watched the lightning through the grand skylight, this was the only negative thing we heard spoken – aloud – about the Pax emissaries, although under the silk finery and gala gaiety, there seemed to be an undercurrent of anxiety to the evening. This seemed natural since the world of T'ien Shan had been – except for the occasional free trader's dropship – isolated from the Pax and the rest of post-Hegemonic humanity for almost three centuries.

The evening was growing late and I was becoming convinced that Labsang Samten's statement that the Dalai Lama and his Pax guests had wished to see us was erroneous, when suddenly several palace officiaries in great, curved red and yellow hats – looking rather like illustrations I had seen of ancient Greek helmets – sought us out and asked that we accompany them to the Dalai Lama's presence.

I looked at my friend, ready to bolt with her and cover our retreat if she showed even a hint of fear or reticence, but Aenea simply nodded in compliance and took my arm. The sea of partygoers made way for us as we crossed the vast space behind the officials, the two of us walking slowly, arm in arm, as if I were her father giving her away in a traditional Church wedding . . . or as if we had always been a couple ourselves. In my pocket was the flashlight laser and the diskey journal/com unit. The laser would be worth little if the Pax was determined to seize us, but I had decided to call the ship if the worst happened. Rather than allow Aenea to be captured, I would bring the ship down on blazing reaction thrusters, right through that lovely skylight.

We passed through the outer curtain and entered a canopied space where the sounds of the band and merrymaking were still quite audible. Here several red-hat officials asked us to extend our arms with our palms upward. When we did so, they set a white silk scarf in our hands, the ends hanging down. We were waved forward through the second curtain. Here the Lord Chamberlain greeted us with a bow – Aenea responding with a graceful curtsy, me with an awkward bow in return – and led us through the door into the small room where the Dalai Lama waited with his guests.

This private room was like an extension of the young Dalai Lama's throne – gold and gilt and silk brocade and wildly ornate tapestries with reversed swastikas embroidered everywhere amid images of opening flowers and curling dragons and spinning mandalas. The doors closed behind us and the sounds of the party would have been shut out completely except for the audio pickups of three video monitors set in the wall to our left. Real-time video of the party was being fed in from different locations around the Main Reception Hall and the boy on the throne and his guests were watching it raptly.

We paused until the Lord Chamberlain gestured us forward again. He whispered to us as we approached the throne and the Dalai Lama turned in our direction. 'It is not necessary to bow until His Holiness raises his hand. Then please bow forward until after he releases his touch.'

We paused three paces from the raised throne platform with its shimmering quilts and draped cushions. Carl Linga William Eiheji, the Chief Crier, said in soft but resonant tones, 'Your Holiness, the architect in charge of construction at Hsuan-k'ung Ssu and her assistant.'

Her assistant? I moved forward a step behind Aenea, confused, but grateful that the Crier had not announced our names. I could see the five Pax figures out of the corner of my eye, but protocol demanded that I keep my gaze directed toward the Dalai Lama but lowered.

Aenea stopped at the edge of the high throne platform, her arms still held in front of her, the scarf taut between her hands. The Lord Chamberlain set several objects on the scarf and the boy reached forward and whisked them off quickly, setting them to his right on the platform. When the objects were gone, a servant stepped forward and took away the white scarf. Aenea put her hands together as if in prayer and bowed forward. The boy's smile was gentle as he leaned forward and touched my friend – my beloved – on the head, setting his fingers like a crown on her brown hair. I realized that it was a blessing. When he removed his fingers, he lifted a red scarf from a stack by his side and set it in Aenea's left hand. Then he took her right hand and shook it, his smile broadening. The Lord Chamberlain gestured for Aenea to stand in front of the Regent's lower throne as I stepped forward and went through the same quick ceremony with the Dalai Lama.

I just had time to notice that the objects set on the white scarf by the Lord Chamberlain and whisked away by the Dalai Lama included a small gold relief in the shape of three mountains, representing the world of T'ien Shan, Aenea later explained, an image of a human body, a stylized book representing speech, and a *chorten*, or temple, shape representing the mind. The appearing and disappearing act was over before I had time to pay more attention to it, and then the red scarf was in one hand while the boy's tiny hand was in my large one. His handshake was surprisingly firm. My gaze was lowered, but I could still make out his broad smile. I stepped back next to Aenea.

The same ceremony was quickly performed with the Regent – white scarf, symbolic objects placed and removed, red scarf. But the Regent did not shake hands with either of us. When we had received the Regent's blessing, the Lord Chamberlain gestured for us to raise our heads and gazes.

I almost made a grab for the flashlight laser and started firing wildly. Besides the Dalai Lama, his monk servants, the Lord Chamberlain, the Regent, the State Oracle, the Crier, the short cardinal, the three men in black cassocks, there was a woman in a black-and-red Pax Fleet uniform. She had just stepped around a tall priest so we could see her face for the first time. Her dark eyes were fixed on Aenea. The woman's hair was short and hung over her pale forehead in limp bangs. Her skin was sallow. Her gaze was reptilian – simultaneously remote and rapt.

It was the thing that had tried to kill Aenea, A. Bettik, and me on God's Grove some five of my years – more than ten of Aenea's – ago. It was the inhuman killing device that had defeated the Shrike and would have carried Aenea's head away in a bag had it not been for the intervention of Father Captain de Soya in his orbiting spacecraft; he had used the full fusion power of the ship to lance the monster downward into a cauldron of bubbling, molten rock.

And here it was again, its black, inhuman eyes fixed on Aenea's face. It had obviously sought her across the years and light-years, and now it had her. It had us.

My heart was pounding and my legs felt suddenly weak, but through the shock my mind was working like an AI. The flashlight laser was tucked in a pocket in the right side of my cape. The com unit was in my left trouser pocket. With my right hand I would flash the cutting beam into the woman-thing's eyes, then flick the selector to broad and blind the Pax priests. With my left hand I would trigger the squirt command to send the prerecorded message via tightbeam to the ship.

But even if the ship responded immediately and was not intercepted by a Pax warship on its flight, it would be several minutes before it could descend through the palace skylight. We would be dead by then.

And I knew the speed of this thing – it simply had disappeared when it fought the Shrike, a chrome blur. I would never get the flashlight laser or com unit out of my pockets. We would be dead before my hand made it halfway to the weapon.

I froze, realizing that although Aenea must have recognized the woman at once, she had not reacted with the shock I felt. To outward appearances, she had not reacted at all. Her smile remained. Her gaze had passed over the Pax visitors – including the monster – and then returned to the boy on the throne.

It was Regent Reting Tokra who spoke first. 'Our guests asked for this audience. They heard from His Holiness of the reconstruction going on at the Temple Hanging in Air and wished to meet the young woman who had designed the construction.'

The Regent's voice was as pinched and ungiving as his appearance.

The Dalai Lama spoke then and his boy's voice was soft but as generous as the Regent's had been guarded. 'My friends,' he said, gesturing toward Aenea and me, 'may I introduce our distinguished visitors from the Pax. John Domenico Cardinal Mustafa of the Catholic Church's Holy Office, Archbishop Jean Daniel Breque of the Papal Diplomatic Corps, Father Martin Farrell, Father Gerard LeBlanc, and Commander Rhadamanth Nemes of the Noble Guard.'

We nodded. The Pax dignitaries – including the monster – nodded. If there was a breach of protocol by His Holiness the Dalai Lama doing the introductions, no one seemed to notice.

John Domenico Cardinal Mustafa said in a silken voice, 'Thank you, Your Holiness. But you have introduced these exceptional people only as the architect and her assistant.' The Cardinal smiled at us, showing small, sharp teeth. 'You have names, perhaps?'

My pulse was racing. The fingers of my right hand twitched at the thought of the flashlight laser. Aenea was still smiling but showed no sign of answering the Cardinal. My mind galloped to come up with aliases. But why? Certainly they knew who we were. All this was a trap. The Nemes thing would never let us leave this throne room . . . or would be waiting for us when we did.

Surprisingly, it was the boy Dalai Lama who spoke again. 'I would be pleased to complete my introductions, Your Eminence. Our esteemed architect is called Ananda and her assistant – one of many skilled assistants I am told – is called Subhadda.'

I admit that I blinked at this. Had someone told the Dalai Lama these names? Aenea had told me that Ananda had been the Buddha's foremost disciple and a teacher in his own right; Subhadda had been a wandering ascetic who had become the Buddha's last direct disciple, becoming a follower after meeting him just hours before he died. She also told me that the Dalai Lama had come up with these names for our introduction, apparently appreciating the irony in them. I failed to see the humor.

'M. Ananda,' said Cardinal Mustafa, bowing slightly. 'M. Subhadda.' He looked us over. 'You will pardon my bluntness and ignorance, M. Ananda, but you seem of a different racial stock than most of the people we have met in the Potala or the surrounding areas of T'ien Shan.'

Aenea nodded. 'One must be careful in making generalizations, Your Eminence. There are areas of this world settled by seedship colonists from many of Old Earth's regions.'

'Of course,' purred Cardinal Mustafa. 'And I must say that your Web English is very unaccented. May I inquire as to which region of T'ien Shan you and your assistant call home?'

'Of course,' responded Aenea in as smooth a voice as the Cardinal's. 'I came into the world in a region of ridges beyond Mt Moriah and Mt Zion, north and west of Muztagh Alta.'

The Cardinal nodded judiciously. I noticed then that his collar – what Aenea later said was called his *rabat* or *rabbi* in Church terminology – was of a scarlet watered silk the same color as his red cassock and skullcap.

'Are you perchance,' he continued smoothly, 'of the Hebrew or Muslim faiths which our hosts have told us prevail in those regions?'

'I am of no faith,' said Aenea. 'If one defines faith as belief in the supernatural.'

The Cardinal's eyebrows lifted slightly. The man called Father Farrell glanced at his boss. Rhadamanth Nemes's terrible gaze never wavered.

'Yet you labor to build a temple to Buddhist beliefs,' said Cardinal Mustafa pleasantly enough.

'I was hired to reconstruct a beautiful complex,' said Aenea. 'I am proud to have been chosen to this task.'

'Despite your lack of . . . ah . . . belief in the supernatural?' said Mustafa. I could hear the Inquisition in his voice. Even on the rural moors of Hyperion, we had heard of the Holy Office.

'Perhaps because of it, Your Eminence,' said Aenea. 'And because of the trust in my own human abilities and those of my coworkers.'

'So the task is its own justification?' pressed the Cardinal. 'Even if it has no deeper significance?'

'Perhaps a task well done *is* the deeper significance,' said Aenea.

Cardinal Mustafa chuckled. It was not an altogether pleasant sound. 'Well said, young lady. Well said.'

Father Farrell cleared his throat. 'The region beyond Mt Zion,' he said musingly. 'We noticed during our orbital survey that there was a single farcaster portal set on to a ridgeline in that area. We had thought that T'ien Shan had never been a part of the Web, but our records showed that the portal was completed very shortly before the Fall.'

'But never used!' exclaimed the young Dalai Lama, lifting one slim finger. 'No one ever traveled to or from the Mountains of Heaven via the Hegemony farcaster.'

'Indeed,' said Cardinal Mustafa softly. 'Well, we assumed as much, but I must tender our apologies, Your Holiness. In our ship's zeal to probe the structure of the old farcaster portal from orbit, it accidentally melted the surrounding rocks onto it. The doorway is sealed forever under rock, I am afraid.'

I glanced at Rhadamanth Nemes when this was said. She did not blink. I had not seen her blink. Her gaze was riveted to Aenea.

The Dalai Lama swept his hand in a dismissive gesture. 'It does not matter, Your Eminence. We have no use for a farcaster portal which was never used . . . unless your Pax has found a way to reactivate the farcasters?' He laughed at the idea. It was a pleasant boyish laugh, but sharp with intelligence.

'No, Your Holiness,' said Cardinal Mustafa, smiling. 'Even the Church has not found a way to reactivate the Web. And it is almost certainly best that we never do.'

My tension was quickly turning to a sort of nausea. This ugly little man in cardinal red was telling Aenea that he knew how she had arrived on T'ien Shan and that she could not escape that way. I glanced at my friend, but she seemed placid and only mildly interested in the conversation. Could there be a second farcaster portal of which the Pax knew nothing? At least this explained why we were still alive: the Pax had sealed Aenea's mousehole and had a cat, or several cats – in the form of their diplomatic ship in orbit and undoubtedly more warships hidden elsewhere in-system – waiting for her. If I had arrived a few months later, they would have seized or destroyed our ship and still had Aenea where they wanted her.

But why wait? And why this game?

'. . . we would be very interested in seeing your – what is it called? – Temple Hanging in Air? It sounds fascinating,' Archbishop Breque was saying.

Regent Tokra was frowning. 'It may be difficult to arrange, Your Excellency,' he said. 'The monsoons are approaching, the cableways will be very dangerous, and even the High Way is hazardous during the winter storms.'

'Nonsense!' cried the Dalai Lama, ignoring the scowl the thin-faced Regent had turned in his direction. 'We will be happy to help arrange such an expedition,' continued the boy. 'You must, by all means, see Hsuan-k'ung Ssu. And all of the Middle Kingdom . . . even to the T'ai Shan, the Great Peak, where the twenty-seven-thousand-step stairway rises to the Temple to the Jade Emperor and the Princess of the Azure Clouds.'

'Your Holiness,' murmured the Lord Chamberlain, his head bowed but only after exchanging a parental glance with the Regent, 'I should remind you that the Great Peak of the Middle Kingdom can be reached by cableway only in the spring months because of the high tide of the poisonous clouds. For the next seven months, T'ai Shan is inaccessible to the rest of the Middle Kingdom and the world.'

The Dalai Lama's boyish smile disappeared . . . not, I thought, out of petulance, but from displeasure at being patronized. When he spoke next, his voice had the sharp edge of command to it. I did not know many children, but I had known more than a few military officers, and if my experience was any guide, this boy would become a formidable man and commander.

'Lord Chamberlain,' said the Dalai Lama, 'I of course know of the closure of the cableway. *Everyone* knows of the closure of the cableway. But I also know that every winter season, a few intrepid flyers make the flight from Sung Shan to the Great Peak. How else would we share our formal edicts with our friends among the faithful on T'ai Shan? And some of the parawings can accommodate more than one flyer . . . passengers even, yes?'

The Lord Chamberlain was bowing so low that I was afraid that his forehead was going to scrape the formal tiles. His voice quavered. 'Yes, yes, of course. Your Holiness, of course. I knew that you knew this, My Lord, Your Holiness. I only meant . . . I only meant to say . . .'

Regent Tokra said sharply, 'I am sure that what the Lord Chamberlain meant to say, Your Holiness, is that although a few flyers make the voyage each year, many more die in the attempt. We would not want to put our honored guests in any danger.'

The Dalai Lama's smile returned, but it was something older and more cunning – almost mocking – than the boy's smile of a few minutes earlier. He spoke to Cardinal Mustafa. 'You are not afraid of dying, are you, Your Eminence? That is the entire purpose of your visit here, is it not? To show us the wonders of your Christian resurrection?'

'Not the sole purpose, Your Holiness,' murmured the Cardinal. 'We come primarily to share the joyous news of Christ with those who wish to hear it and also to discuss possible trade relations with your beautiful world.' The Cardinal returned the boy's smile. 'And although the cross and the Sacrament of Resurrection are direct gifts from God, Your Holiness, it is a sad requirement that some portion of the body or the cruciform must be recovered for that sacrament to be given. I understand that no one returns from your sea of clouds?'

'No one,' agreed the boy with his smile widening.

Cardinal Mustafa made a gesture with his hands. 'Then perhaps we will limit our visit to the Temple Hanging in Air and other accessible destinations,' he said.

There was a silence and I looked at Aenea again, thinking that we were about to be dismissed, wondering what the signal would be, thinking that the Lord Chamberlain would lead us out, feeling my arms go to goosebumps at the intensity of the Nemes-thing's hungry gaze aimed at Aenea, when suddenly Archbishop Jean Daniel Breque broke the silence. 'I have been discussing with His Highness, Regent Tokra,' he said to us as if we might settle some argument between them, 'how amazingly similar our miracle of resurrection is to the age-old Buddhist belief in reincarnation.'

'Ahhh,' said the boy on the golden throne, his face brightening as if someone had brought up a subject of interest to him, 'but not all Buddhists believe in reincarnation. Even before the migration to T'ien Shan and the great changes in philosophy which have evolved here, not all Buddhist sects accepted the concept of rebirth. We know for a fact that the Buddha refused to speculate with his disciples on whether there was such a thing as life after death. "Such questions," he said, "are not relevant to the practice of the Path and cannot be answered while bound by the restraints of human existence." Most of Buddhism, you see, gentlemen, can be explored, appreciated, and utilized as a tool toward Enlightenment without descending into the supernatural.'

The Archbishop looked nonplussed, but Cardinal Mustafa said quickly, 'Yet did not your Buddha say – and I believe that one of your scriptures holds these as his words, Your Holiness, but correct me immediately if I am wrong – "There is an unborn, an unoriginated, an unmade, an uncompounded; were there not, there would be no escape from the world of the born, the originated, the made, and the compounded."'

The boy's smile did not waver. 'Indeed, he did, Your Eminence. Very good. But are there not elements – as yet not completely understood – within our physical universe, bound by the laws of our physical universe, which might be described as unborn, unoriginated, unmade, and uncompounded?'

'None that I know of, Your Holiness,' said Cardinal Mustafa, affably enough. 'But then I am not a scientist. Only a poor priest.'

Despite this diplomatic finesse, the boy on the throne seemed intent on pursuing the subject. 'As we have previously discussed, Cardinal Mustafa, our form of Buddhism has evolved since we landed on this mountain world. Now it is very much filled with the spirit of Zen. And one of the great Zen masters of Old Earth, the poet William Blake, once said – "Eternity is in love with the productions of time."'

Cardinal Mustafa's fixed smile showed his lack of understanding.

The Dalai Lama was no longer smiling. The boy's expression was pleasant but serious. 'Do you think perhaps that M. Blake meant that time without ending is worthless time, Cardinal Mustafa? That any being freed from mortality – even God – might envy the children of slow time?'

The Cardinal nodded but showed no agreement. 'Your Holiness, I cannot see how God could envy poor mortal humankind. Certainly God is not capable of envy.'

The boy's nearly invisible eyebrows shot up. 'Yet, is not your Christian

God, by definition, omnipotent? Certainly he, she, it must be capable of envy.'

'Ah, a paradox meant for children, Your Holiness. I confess I am trained in neither logical apologetics nor metaphysics. But as a prince of Christ's Church, I know from my catechism and in my soul that God is not capable of envy . . . especially not envy of his flawed creations.'

'Flawed?' said the boy.

Cardinal Mustafa smiled condescendingly, his tone that of a learned priest speaking to a child. 'Humanity is flawed because of its propensity for sin,' he said softly. 'Our Lord could not be envious of a being capable of sin.'

The Dalai Lama nodded slowly. 'One of our Zen masters, a man named Ikkyu, once wrote a poem to that effect—

'All the sins committed
In the Three Worlds
Will fade and disappear
Together with myself.'

Cardinal Mustafa waited a moment, but when no more poem was forthcoming, he said, 'Which three worlds was he speaking of, Your Holiness?'

'This was before spaceflight,' said the boy, shifting slightly on his cushioned throne. 'The Three Worlds are the past, present, and future.'

'Very nice,' said the Cardinal from the Holy Office. Behind him, his aide, Father Farrell, was staring at the boy with something like cold distaste. 'But we Christians do not believe that sin – or the effects of sin – or the accountability for sin, for that matter – end with one's life, Your Holiness.'

'Precisely.' The boy smiled. 'It is for this reason that I am curious why you extend life so artificially through your cruciform creature,' he said. 'We feel that the slate is washed clean with death. You feel that it brings judgment. Why defer this judgment?'

'We view the cruciform as a sacrament given to us by Our Lord Jesus Christ,' Cardinal Mustafa said softly. 'This judgment was first deferred by Our Savior's sacrifice on the cross, God Himself accepting the punishment for our sins, allowing us the option of everlasting life in heaven if we so choose it. The cruciform is another gift from Our Savior, perhaps allowing us time to set our houses in order before that final judgment.'

'Ahh, yes,' sighed the boy. 'But perhaps Ikkyu meant that there are no sinners. That there is no sin. That "our" lives do not belong to us . . .'

'Precisely, Your Holiness,' interrupted Cardinal Mustafa, as if praising a slow learner. I saw the Regent, the Lord Chamberlain, and others around the throne wince at this interruption. 'Our lives do not belong to us, but to Our Lord and Savior . . . and to serve Him, to our Holy Mother Church.'

'. . . do not belong to us, but belong to the universe,' continued the boy. 'And that our deeds – good and bad – also are property of the universe.'

Cardinal Mustafa frowned. 'A pretty phrase, Your Holiness, but perhaps too abstract. Without God, the universe can only be a machine . . . unthinking, uncaring, unfeeling.'

'Why?' said the boy.

'I beg your pardon, Your Holiness?'

'Why must the universe be unthinking, uncaring, unfeeling without your definition of a God?' the child said softly. He closed his eyes.

'The morning dew
Flees away,
And is no more;
Who may remain
In this world of ours?'

Cardinal Mustafa steepled his fingers and touched his lips as if in prayer or mild frustration. 'Very nice, Your Holiness. Ikkyu again?'

The Dalai Lama grinned broadly. 'No. Me. I write a little Zen poetry when I can't sleep.'

The priests chuckled. The Nemes creature stared at Aenea.

Cardinal Mustafa turned toward my friend. 'M. Ananda,' he said, 'do you have an opinion on these weighty matters?'

For a second I did not know whom he was addressing, but then I remembered the Dalai Lama's introduction of Aenea as Ananda, foremost disciple of the Buddha.

'I know another little verse by Ikkyu which expresses my opinion,' she said.

'More frail and illusory
Than numbers written on water,
Our seeking from the Buddha
Felicity in the afterworld.'

Archbishop Breque cleared his throat and joined in the conversation. 'That seems clear enough, young lady. You do not think that God will grant our prayers.'

Aenea shook her head. 'I think that he meant two things, Your Eminence. First, that the Buddha will not help us. It isn't in his job definition, so to speak. Secondly, that planning for the afterworld is foolish because we are, by nature, timeless, eternal, unborn, undying, and omnipotent.'

The Archbishop's face and neck reddened above his collar. 'Those adjectives can be applied only to God, M. Ananda.' He felt Cardinal Mustafa's glare on him and remembered his place as a diplomat. 'Or so we believe,' he added lamely.

'For a young person and an architect, you seem to know your Zen and poetry, M. Ananda.' Cardinal Mustafa chuckled, obviously trying to lighten the tone. 'Are there any other Ikkyu poems you feel might be relevant?'

Aenea nodded.

'We come into this world alone,
We depart alone,

This also is illusion.
I will teach you the way
Not to come, not to go!'

'That would be a good trick,' said Cardinal Mustafa with false joviality.

The Dalai Lama leaned forward. 'Ikkyu taught us that it is possible to live at least part of our lives in a timeless, spaceless world where there is no birth and death, no coming and going,' he said softly. 'A place where there is no separation in time, no distance in space, no barrier barring us from the ones we love, no glass wall between experience and our hearts.'

Cardinal Mustafa stared as if speechless.

'My friend . . . M. Ananda . . . also taught me this,' said the boy.

For a second, the Cardinal's face was twisted by something like a sneer. He turned toward Aenea. 'I would be pleased if the young lady would teach me . . . teach us all . . . this clever conjuror's trick,' he said sharply.

'I hope to,' said Aenea.

Rhadamanth Nemes took a half step toward my friend. I set my hand in my cape, lightly touching the firing stud of the flashlight laser.

The Regent tapped a gong with a cloth-wrapped stick. The Lord Chamberlain hurried forward to escort us out. Aenea bowed to the Dalai Lama and I clumsily did likewise.

The audience was over.

I dance with Aenea in the great, echoing reception hall, to the music of a seventy-two-piece orchestra, with the lords and ladies, priests and plenipotentiaries of T'ien Shan, the Mountains of Heaven, all watching from the edges of the dance floor or wheeling around us in shared motion to the music. I remember dancing with Aenea, dining again before midnight at the long tables constantly restocked with food, and then dancing again. I remember holding her tight as we moved together around the dance floor. I do not remember ever having danced before – at least when I was sober – but I dance this night, holding Aenea close to me as the torchlight from the crackling braziers dims and the Oracle casts skylight shadows across the parquet floors.

It is in the wee hours of the morning and the older guests have retired, all the monks and mayors and elder statesmen – except for the Thunderbolt Sow, who has laughed and sung and clapped along with the orchestra for every raceme quadrille, tapping her slippered feet on the polished floors – and there are only four or five hundred determined celebrants remaining in the great, shadowy space, while the band play slower and slower pieces as if their musical mainspring is wearing down.

I confess that I would have gone off to bed hours earlier if it were not for Aenea: she wants to dance. So dance we do, moving slowly, her small hand in my large one, my other hand flat on her back – feeling her spine and strong muscles under my palm through the thin silk of the dress – her hair against my cheek, her breasts soft against me, the curve of her skull against my neck and chin. She seems slightly sad, but still energetic, still celebrating.

Private audiences had ended many hours ago and word had spread that the Dalai Lama had gone to bed before midnight, but we last celebrants partied on – Lhomo Dondrub, our flyer friend, laughing and pouring champagne and rice beer for everyone, Labsang Samten, the Dalai Lama's little brother, leaping over the ember-filled braziers at some point, the serious Tromo Trochi of Dhomu suddenly metamorphosing into a magician in one corner, doing tricks with fire and hoops and levitations, and then the Dorje Phamo singing one clear, slow cappella solo in a voice so sweet that it haunts my dreams to this day, and finally the scores of others joining in the Oracle Song as the orchestra prepares to wrap up the evening's celebration before the predawn begins to fade the night sky.

Suddenly the music ends in mid-bar. The dancers stop. Aenea and I lurch to a stop and look around.

There has been no sign of the Pax guests for hours, but suddenly one of them – Rhadamanth Nemes – emerges from the shadows of the Dalai Lama's curtained alcove. She has changed her uniform and is now dressed all in red. There are two others with her, and for a moment I think they are the priests, but then I see that the two figures dressed in black are near-copies of the Nemes thing: another woman and a man, both in black combat suits, both with limp, black bangs hanging down on pale foreheads, both with eyes of dead amber.

The trio moves through the frozen dancers toward Aenea and me. Instinctively I put myself between my friend and the things, but the Nemes male and its other sibling begin to move around us, flanking us. I pull Aenea close behind me, but she steps to my side.

The frozen dancers make no noise. The orchestra remains silent. Even the moonlight seems stilled to solid shafts in the dusty air.

I remove the flashlight laser and hold it at my side. The primary Nemes thing shows small teeth. Cardinal Mustafa steps from the shadows and stands behind her. All four of the Pax creatures hold their gaze on Aenea. For a moment I think that the universe has stopped, that the dancers are literally frozen in time and space, that the music hangs above us like icy stalactites ready to shatter and fall, but then I hear the murmur through the crowd – fearful whispers, a hiss of anxiety.

There is no visible threat – only four Pax guests moving out across the ballroom floor with Aenea as the locus of their closing circle – but the sense of predators closing on their prey is too strong to ignore, as is the scent of fear through the perfume and powder and cologne.

'Why wait?' says Rhadamanth Nemes, looking at Aenea but speaking to someone else – her siblings perhaps, or the Cardinal.

'I think . . .' says Cardinal Mustafa and freezes.

Everyone freezes. The great horns near the entrance arch have blown with the bass rumble of continental crusts shifting. No one is there in the alcoves to blow them. The bone and brass trumpets bracket the endless one-note rumbling of the horns. The great gong vibrates on the bone conduction level.

There is a rustle and stifled outcry across the dance floor, in the direction of the escalators, the anteroom, and the curtained entrance arch. The thinning crowds there are parting wider, moving aside like furrowed soil ahead of a steel plow.

Something is moving behind the dosed curtains of the anteroom. Now something has passed through the curtains, not so much parting them as severing them. Now something is glinting in Oracle light and gliding across the parquet floors, gliding as if floating centimeters above the floor, glinting in the dying light of the moon. Tatters of red curtain hang from an impossibly tall form – three meters at least – and there are too many arms emerging from the folds of that crimson robe. It looks as if the hands hold steel blades. The dancers move away more quickly and there is a general and audible intake of breath. Lightning silently supersedes the moonlight and strobes off polished floors, eclipsing the Oracle with retinal echoes. When the thunder arrives some long seconds later, it is indistinguishable from the low, bone-shaking rumble of the still-reverberating horns in the entrance hall.

The Shrike glides to a halt five paces from Aenea and me, five paces from the Nemes thing, ten paces from each of the Nemes siblings frozen in their act of circling us, eight paces from the Cardinal. It occurs to me that the Shrike shrouded in its dangling red curtain tatters resembles nothing so much as a chrome and bladed caricature of Cardinal Mustafa in his crimson robe. The Nemes clones in their black uniforms look like shadows of stilettos against the walls.

Somewhere in one of the shadowed corners of the great reception hall, a tall clock slowly strikes the hour . . . one . . . two . . . three . . . four. It is, of course, the number of inhuman killing machines standing before and behind us. It has been more than four years since I have seen the Shrike, but its presence is no less terrible and no more welcome despite its intercession here. The red eyes gleam like lasers under a thin film of water. The chrome-steel jaws are parted to show row upon row of razor teeth. The thing's blades, barbs, and cutting edges emerge from the enfolding red curtain robe in scores of places. It does not blink. It does not appear to breathe. Now that the gliding has stopped, it is as motionless as a nightmare sculpture.

Rhadamanth Nemes is smiling at it.

Still holding the silly flashlight laser, I remember the confrontation on God's Grove years ago. The Nemes thing had gone silver and blurry and simply disappeared, reappearing next to twelve-year-old Aenea without warning. It had planned to cut off my friend's head and carry it away in a burlap bag, and it would have done so had not the Shrike appeared then. The Nemes thing could do so now without hope of my reacting in time. These things moved outside of time. I know the agony of a parent watching its child step into the path of a speeding groundcar, unable to move in time to protect her. Superimposed on this terror is the pain of a lover unable to protect his beloved. I would die in a second to protect Aenea from any of these things – including the Shrike – indeed, may die in a second, in less than a second – but my death will not protect her. I grind my molars in frustration.

Moving only my eyes, afraid that I will precipitate the slaughter if I move a hand or head or muscle, I see that the Shrike is not staring at Aenea or the primary Nemes thing – it is staring directly at John Domenico Cardinal Mustafa. The frog-faced priest must feel the weight of this blood-red gaze, for the Cardinal's complexion has gone a pure white above the red of his robe.

Aenea moves now. Stepping to my left side, she slips her right hand in my empty left one and squeezes my fingers. It is not a child's request for reassurance, it is a signal of reassurance to me.

'You know how it will end,' she says softly to the Cardinal, ignoring the Nemes things as they coil like cats ready to pounce.

The Grand Inquisitor licks his thick lips. 'No, I do not. There are the three of . . .'

'You know how it will end,' interrupts Aenea, her voice still soft. 'You were on Mars.'

Mars? I think. *What the hell does Mars have to do with anything?* Lightning flickers again through the skylight, throwing wild shadows. The faces of the hundreds of terror-frozen revelers are like white ovals painted on black velvet around us. I realize in a flash of insight as sudden and illuminating as the lightning that the metaphysical biosphere of this world – Zen-evolved or not – is riddled with Tibetan myth-inspired demons and malevolent spirits: cancerous *nyen* earth spirits; *sadag* 'lords of the soil' who haunt builders who disturb their realms; *tsen* red spirits who live in rocks; *gyelpo* spirits of dead kings who have failed their vows, dead, deadly, dressed all in pale armor; *dud* spirits who are so malevolent that they feed only on human flesh and wear black, beetle skin; *mamo* female deities as ferocious as unseen riptides; *matrika* sorceresses of charnel grounds and cremation platforms, first sensed by a whiff of their carrion breath; *grahas* planetary deities that cause epilepsy and other violent, thrashing illnesses; *nodjin* guardians of wealth in the soil – death to diamond miners – and a score more of night things, teethed things, clawed things, and killing things. Lhomo and the others have told me the stories well and often. I look at the white faces staring in shock at the Shrike and the Nemes creatures and think – *This night will not be so strange in the telling for these people.*

'The demon cannot vanquish all three of them,' says Cardinal Mustafa, saying the word 'demon' aloud even as I think the word. I realize that he is speaking about the Shrike.

Aenea ignores the comment. 'It will harvest your cruciform first,' she says softly. 'I cannot stop it from doing that.'

Cardinal Mustafa's head jerks back as if he has been slapped. His pale countenance grows visibly paler. Taking their cue from Rhadamanth Nemes, the clone-siblings coil tighter as if building energy toward some terrible transformation. Nemes has returned her black gaze to Aenea and the creature is smiling so broadly now that her rearmost teeth are visible.

'Stop!' cries Cardinal Mustafa and his shout echoes from the skylight and floor. The great horns cease rumbling. Revelers clutch one another in a rustling of fingernails on silk. Nemes flashes the Cardinal a look of malevolent loathing and near defiance.

'Stop!' screams the Pax holy man again, and I realize that he is talking to his own creatures first and foremost. 'I invoke the command of Albedo and the Core, by the authority of the Three Elements I command thee!' This last desperate scream has the cadence of a shouted exorcism, some profound ritual, but even I can tell that it is not Catholic or Christian. It is not the Shrike being invoked under an iron grip of talismanic control here; it is his own demons.

Nemes and her siblings slide backward on the parquet floor as if pulled by invisible strings. The clone male and clone female move around us until they join Nemes in front of Mustafa.

The Cardinal smiles but it is a tremulous gesture. 'My pets will not be unleashed until we speak again. I give my word as a prince of the Church, unholy child. Do I have your word that this' – he gestures toward the bladed Shrike in its velvet tatters – 'this demon will not stalk me until then?'

Aenea appears as calm as she has through the entire incident. 'I do not control it,' she says. 'Your only safety is to leave this world in peace.'

The Cardinal is eyeing the Shrike. The man seems poised to leap away if the tall apparition flexes so much as a fingerblade. Nemes and her ilk continue standing between him and the Shrike. 'What assurance have I,' he says, 'that the thing will not follow me into space . . . or back to Pacem?'

'None,' says Aenea.

The Grand Inquisitor points a long finger at my friend. 'We have business here that has nothing to do with you,' he says sharply, 'but you will never leave this world. I swear this to you by the bowels of Christ.'

Aenea returns his gaze and says nothing.

Mustafa turns and stalks away with a swish of his red robe and a rasp of his slippers on the polished floor. The Nemes things back all the way across the floor while following him, the male and female clones holding their gazes on the Shrike, Nemes piercing Aenea with her stare. They pass through the curtain tent of the Dalai Lama's private portal and are gone.

The Shrike stays where it is, lifeless, its four arms frozen in front of it, fingerblades catching the last drops of Oracle light before the moon moves behind the mountain and is lost.

Revelers begin moving toward the exits on a wave of whispers and exclamations. The orchestra thumps, clangs, and whistles as instruments are packed in a hurry and dragged or carried away. Aenea continues holding my hand as a small circle remains around us.

'Buddha's ass!' cries Lhomo Dondrub and strides over to the Shrike, testing his finger against a metallic thorn rising from the thing's chest. I see blood on his finger in the dimming light. 'Fantastic!' cries Lhomo and swigs from a goblet of rice beer.

The Dorje Phamo moves to Aenea's side. She takes my friend's left hand, goes to one knee, and sets Aenea's palm against her wrinkled forehead.

Aenea removes her hand from mine as she takes the Thunderbolt Sow gently by the arms and helps her rise. 'No,' whispers Aenea.

'Blessed One,' whispers the Dorje Phamo. '*Amata*, Immortal One; *Arhat*, Perfected One; *Sammasambuddha*, Fully Awakened One; command us and teach us the *dhamma*.'

'No,' snaps Aenea, still gentle with the old woman as she pulls her to her feet but stern of countenance. 'I will teach you what I know and share what I have when the time arrives. I can do no more. The hour for myth has passed.'

My friend turns, takes my hand, and leads us across the dance floor, past the immobile Shrike, and toward the tattered curtains and unmoving escalator. Former revelers part for our passing as swiftly as they had for the Shrike.

We pause at the top of the steel stairs. Lanterns glow in the hallway to our sleeping rooms far below us.

'Thank you,' says Aenea, looking up at me with her brown eyes moist.

'What?' I say stupidly. 'For . . . why . . . I don't understand.'

'Thank you for the dance,' she says and reaches up to kiss me softly on the lips.

The electricity of her touch makes me blink. I gesture back toward the roiling crowd behind us, the dance floor empty of the Shrike now, at the Potala guards rushing into the echoing space, and at the curtained alcove through which Mustafa and his creatures have disappeared. 'We can't sleep here tonight, kiddo. Nemes and the other two will . . .'

'Uh-uh,' says Aenea, 'they won't. Trust me on this. They won't come creeping down the outside wall and across our ceiling tonight. In fact, they'll all be leaving their gompa and shuttling straight up to their ship in orbit. They'll be back, but not tonight.'

I sigh.

She takes my hand. 'Are you sleepy?' she says softly.

Of course I am sleepy. I am exhausted beyond words. Last night seems days and weeks away, and I had only two or three hours' light sleep then because of . . . because we had . . . because of . . .

'Not a bit,' I say.

Aenea smiles and leads the way back to our sleeping chamber.

TWENTY

Pope Urban XVI: Send forth Thy Spirit and they shall be created.

All: Thou shalt renew the memory of Earth and the face of all worlds in God's Dominion.

Pope Urban XVI: Let us pray.

O God, You have instructed the hearts of the faithful by the light of the Holy Spirit. Grant that through the same Holy Spirit we may always be truly wise and rejoice in His consolation. Through Christ our Lord.

All: Amen.

Pope Urban XVI blesses the insignia of the Knights of the Equestrian Order of the Holy Sepulchre of Jerusalem.

Pope Urban XVI: Our help is in the name of the Lord.

All: Who made Heaven and Earth and all worlds.

Pope Urban XVI: The Lord be with you.

All: And also with you.

Pope Urban XVI: Let us pray.

Hear, we pray You, O Lord, our prayers and deign through the power of Your majesty to bless the insignia of office. Protect Your servants who desire to wear them, so that they may be strong to guard the rights of the Church, and quick to defend and spread the Christian faith. Through Christ our Lord.

All: Amen.

Pope Urban XVI sprinkles the emblems with holy water.

The Master of Ceremonies, Cardinal Lourdusamy, reads the decree of the newly appointed Knights and of those promoted in rank. Each member stands as his or her name is mentioned and remains standing. There are one thousand two hundred and eight Knights in the Basilica. Cardinal Lourdusamy lists all honorees by rank, lowest to highest, Knights first, followed by Priest Knights. At the conclusion of the reading, the Knights to be invested kneel. All others are seated.

Pope Urban XVI asks the Knights: What do you ask?

The Knights answer: I ask to be invested as a Knight of the Holy Sepulchre.

Pope Urban XVI: Today, being a Knight of the Holy Sepulchre means engaging in the battle for the Kingdom of Christ and for the extension of the Church; and undertaking works of charity with the same deep spirit of faith and love with which you may give your life in battle. Are you ready to follow this ideal throughout your life?

The Knights answer: I am.

Pope Urban XVI: I remind you that if all men and women should consider themselves honored to practice virtue, so much the more should a soldier of Christ glory in being a Knight of Jesus Christ and use every means to show by his actions and virtues that he is deserving of the honor which is being conferred upon him and of the dignity with which he is invested. Are you prepared to promise to observe the Constitutions of this holy Order?

The Knights answer: With the grace of God I promise to observe, as a true soldier of Christ, the Commandments of God, the precepts of the Church, the orders of my commanders in the field, and the Constitution of this holy Order.

Pope Urban XVI: In virtue of the decree received, I appoint and declare you Soldiers and Knights of the Holy Sepulchre of Our Lord Jesus Christ. In the name of the Father, and of the Son, and of the Holy Spirit.

The Knights enter the Sanctuary and kneel while the Pope blesses the Jerusalem Cross, the emblem of the Order.

Pope Urban XVI: Receive the Cross of Our Lord Jesus Christ for your protection, in the name of the Father, and of the Son, and of the Holy Spirit.

After kneeling in front of the Jerusalem Cross, each Knight responds: Amen.

Pope Urban XVI returns to the chair placed on the platform. When His Holiness gives the signal, the Master of Ceremonies Cardinal Lourdusamy reads the decree of each newly appointed Knight. As each Knight's name is called, the newly appointed Knight approaches the altar, genuflects, and kneels in the great space before His Holiness. One Knight has been chosen to represent all of the Knights to be invested and now that Knight approaches the altar.

Pope Urban XVI: What do you request?

Knight: I desire to be invested a Knight of the Holy Sepulchre.

Pope Urban XVI: I remind you again, that if all men should consider themselves honored to practice virtue, so much the more must a soldier of Christ, who should glory in being a Knight of Jesus Christ, use every means never to sully his good name. Finally, he ought to show by his actions and virtues that he is deserving of the honor which is being conferred upon him and of the dignity with which he is invested. Are you prepared to promise by word and in truth to observe the Constitution of this holy military Order?

The Knight puts his folded hands into the hands of His Holiness.

Knight: I declare and promise by word and in truth to God Almighty, to Jesus Christ, His Son, to the Blessed Virgin Mary, to observe, as a true soldier of Christ, all that I have been charged to do.

His Holiness, Pope Urban XVI, places his right hand on the head of the Knight.

Pope Urban XVI: Be a faithful and brave soldier of Our Lord Jesus Christ, a Knight of His Holy Sepulchre, strong and courageous, so that one day you may be admitted to His heavenly court.

His Holiness hands the golden spurs to the Knight saying: Receive these spurs that are a symbol of your Order for the honor and defense of the Holy Sepulchre.

The Knight Master of Ceremonies, Cardinal Lourdusamy, hands the unsheathed sword to His Holiness who, in turn, holds it before the newly appointed Knight and returns it to the Knight Master.

Master of Ceremonies: Receive this sword that symbolizes the defense of the Holy Church of God and the overthrow of the enemies of the Cross of Christ. Be on guard never to use it to strike anyone unjustly.

After the Knight Master of Ceremonies has returned it into the scabbard, His Holiness hands the sword to the newly appointed Knight.

Pope Urban XVI: Bear well in mind that the Saints have conquered kingdoms not by the sword, but by faith.

This part of the ceremony is repeated for each candidate. His Holiness the Pope is given the unsheathed sword and touches each Knight's right shoulder three times with the sword, saying: I appoint and declare you a Soldier and Knight of the Holy Sepulchre of Our Lord Jesus Christ. In the name of the Father, and of the Son, and of the Holy Spirit.

After returning the sword to the Knight Master of Ceremonies, His Holiness places around the neck of each the Cross, the emblem of the Order, saying: Receive the Cross of Our Lord Jesus Christ for your protection, and for that purpose repeat unceasingly: 'By the sign of the Cross, deliver us, O Lord, from our enemies.'

Each newly invested Knight arises, bows to His Holiness, and goes to the dignitary highest in rank to receive the cape from him. He then receives from the Knight assistant the beret, which he puts on immediately. He then goes to his place in the pews.

All stand as His Holiness begins the following hymn, which is continued by all present.

VENI CREATOR
Come, Holy Spirit, Creator blest,
And in our souls take up Your rest;
Come with Your grace and heavenly aid,
To fill the hearts which You have made.

O Comforter, to You we cry,
You, heavenly gift of God Most High,
You, fount of life and fire of love,
And sweet anointing from above.

You, in your sevenfold gifts are unknown;
You, finger of God's hand we own;
You, promise of the Father, You
Who do the sword with flame imbue.

Kindle our senses from on high,
And calm the hearts of those to die;
With patience firm and virtue high
The weakness of our flesh supply.

Far from us drive the foe we dread,
And grant to us Your wrath instead;
So shall we not, with You for guide,
Allow the victory be denied.

Oh, may your grace on us bestow
The Father and the Son to know;
And you, through endless times confessed,
Of both the eternal Spirit blest.

Now to the Father and the Son,
Who rose from death, be glory given,
Before You, O Holy Sword and Shield,
Be all in Pax and Heaven driven.

His Holiness Pope Urban XVI: And all the foes of Christ must yield.
   All: Amen.
   Exit His Holiness and the Master of Ceremonies.

Instead of returning to his Apostolic Apartments, the Pope led his cardinal to a small room off the Sistine Chapel.

'The Room of Tears,' said Cardinal Lourdusamy. 'I've not been in here for years.' It was a small room with brown floor tiles aged to a black hue, red flock wallpaper, low, medieval-vaulted ceilings, harsh lighting from a few gold wall sconces, no windows but heavy and incongruous white drapes along one scarlet wall. The room was barely furnished – an odd red settee in one corner, a small, black table-cum-altar with a white linen cloth, and a skeletal framework in the center upon which hung an ancient, yellowed, and somewhat unsettling alb and chasuble, with two white and absurdly decorated shoes nearby, the toes curling with age.

'The vestment belonged to Pope Pius XII,' said the Pontiff. 'He donned it here in 1939 after his election. We had it taken from the Vatican Museum and set out here. We visit it upon occasion.'

'Pope Pius XII,' mused Cardinal Lourdusamy. The Secretary of State tried to recall any special significance of that long-dead Pope. All he could think of was the disturbing statue of Pius XII done almost two millennia ago – in 1964 – by Francesco Messina, now relegated to a subterranean corridor beneath the Vatican. Messina's Pius XII is shown in rough strokes, his round glasses as empty as the eye sockets in a skull, his right arm raised defensively – bony fingers splayed – as if trying to ward off the evil of his time.

'A war pope?' guessed Lourdusamy.

Pope Urban XVI wearily shook his head. There was a welt on his forehead where the heavy orphreyed miter had rested during the long investiture ceremony. 'It is not his reign during the Old Earth world war which interests us,' said the Holy Father, 'but the complex dealings he was compelled to carry out with the very heart of darkness in order to preserve the Church and the Vatican.'

Lourdusamy nodded slowly. 'The Nazis and the Fascists,' he murmured. 'Of course.' The parallel with the Core was not without merit.

The Pope's servants had set out tea on the single table and the Secretary of State now acted as personal servant to His Holiness, pouring the tea into a fragile china cup and carrying it to the other man. Pope Urban XVI nodded wearily in gratitude and sipped the steaming liquid. Lourdusamy returned to his place in the middle of the room near the ancient hanging garments and looked critically at his pontiff. *His heart has been bothering him again. Will we have to go through another resurrection and election conclave soon?*

'Did you notice who was chosen as the representative Knight?' asked the Pope, his voice stronger now. He looked up with intense, sad eyes.

Caught off balance, Lourdusamy had to think for a second. 'Oh, yes . . . the former Mercantilus CEO. Isozaki. He will be the Knight in titular leadership of the Cassiopeia 4614 Crusade.'

'Making amends.' His Holiness smiled.

Lourdusamy rubbed his jowls. 'It may be more serious penance than M. Isozaki had counted on, Your Holiness.'

The Pope looked up. 'Serious losses forecast?'

'About forty percent casualties,' rumbled Lourdusamy. 'Half of those irretrievable for resurrection. The fighting in that sector has been very, very heavy.'

'And elsewhere?' said the Pontiff.

Lourdusamy sighed. 'The unrest has spread to about sixty Pax worlds, Your Holiness. About three million suffer the Contagion and have rejected the cruciform. There is fighting, but nothing the Pax authorities cannot handle. Renaissance Vector is the worst . . . about three-quarters of a million infected, and it is spreading very quickly.'

The Pope nodded wearily and sipped his tea. 'Tell us something positive, Simon Augustino.'

'The messenger drone translated from T'ien Shan System just before the ceremony,' said the Cardinal. 'We decrypted the holo message from Cardinal Mustafa immediately.'

The Pope held his cup and saucer and waited.

'They have encountered the Devil's Child,' said Lourdusamy. 'They met her at the Dalai Lama's palace.'

'And . . .' prompted His Holiness.

'No action was taken because of the presence of the Shrike demon,' said Lourdusamy, glancing at notes on his wrist comlog diskey. 'But identification is certain. The child named Aenea . . . she is in her twenties, standard, now of course . . . her bodyguard, Raul Endymion, whom we had arrested and lost on Mare Infinitus more than nine years ago . . . and the others.'

The Pope touched his thin lips with his thin fingers. 'And the Shrike?'

'It appeared only when the girl was threatened by Albedo's Noble Guard . . . officers,' said Cardinal Lourdusamy. 'And then disappeared. There was no fighting.'

'But Cardinal Mustafa failed to consummate the moment?' said the Pope.

Lourdusamy nodded.

'And you still think that Mustafa is the right person for the job?' murmured Pope Urban XVI.

'Yes, Holy Father. Everything is going according to plan. We had hoped to make contact prior to the actual arrest.'

'And the *Raphael*?' said the Pope.

'No sign of it yet,' said the Secretary of State, 'but Mustafa and Admiral Wu feel certain that de Soya will appear in T'ien Shan System before the allotted time to collect the girl.'

'We certainly pray that this will be the case,' said the Pontiff. 'Do you know, Simon Augustino, how much damage that renegade ship has done to our Crusade?'

Lourdusamy knew that the question was rhetorical. He and the Holy Father and the squirming Pax Fleet admirals had pored over combat action reports, casualty lists, and tonnage losses for five years. The *Raphael* and its turncoat Captain de Soya had almost been captured or destroyed a score of times, but always had managed to escape to Ouster space, leaving behind scattered convoys, tumbling hulks, and shattered Pax warships. Pax Fleet's failure to catch a single renegade archangel had become the shame of the Fleet and the best-kept secret in the Pax.

And now it was going to end.

'Albedo's Elements calculate a ninety-four percent probability that de Soya will rise to our bait,' said the Cardinal.

'It's been how long since Pax Fleet and the Holy Office planted the information?' said the Pope, finishing his tea and carefully setting the cup and saucer on the edge of the settee.

'Five weeks standard,' said Lourdusamy. 'Wu arranged for it to be encrypted in the AI aboard one of the escort torchships that the *Raphael* jumped at the edge of Ophiuchi System. But not so heavily encrypted that the Ouster-enhanced systems aboard the *Raphael* could not decipher it.'

'Won't de Soya and his people scent a trap?' mused the man who had once been Father Lenar Hoyt.

'Unlikely, Your Holiness,' said the Cardinal. 'We've used that encryption pattern before to feed reliable information to de Soya and . . .'

The Pope's head snapped up. 'Cardinal Lourdusamy,' he said sharply, 'do you mean to tell us that you sacrificed innocent Pax ships and lives . . . lives beyond resurrection . . . merely to insure that the renegades will consider this information reliable?'

'Yes, Holy Father,' said Lourdusamy.

The Pope let out a breath and nodded. 'Regrettable, but understandable . . . given the stakes involved.'

'In addition,' continued the Cardinal, 'certain officers aboard the crew of the ship positioned to be captured by the *Raphael* had been . . . ah . . . conditioned . . . by the Holy Office so that they also had the information on when we plan to move on the girl Aenea and the world of T'ien Shan.'

'All this prepared months in advance?' said the Pope.

'Yes, Your Holiness. It was an advantage given us by Councillor Albedo and the Core when they registered the activation of the T'ien Shan farcaster some months ago.'

The Pontiff laid his hands flat on his robed thighs. His fingers were bluish. 'And that escape has been denied the Devil's Child?'

'Absolutely,' said the Cardinal. 'The *Jibril* slagged the entire mountain around the farcaster portal. The farcaster itself is all but impervious, Your Holiness, but at the moment it is buried under twenty meters of rock.'

'And the Core is certain that this is the only farcaster on T'ien Shan?'

'Absolutely certain, Holy Father.'

'And the preparations for the confrontation with de Soya and his renegade archangel?'

'Well, Admiral Wu should be here to discuss the tactical details, Your Holiness . . .'

'We trust you to convey the general outline, Simon Augustino.'

'Thank you, Holy Father. Pax Fleet has stationed fifty-eight planet-class archangel cruisers within the T'ien Shan System. These have been hidden for the past six standard weeks . . .'

'Excuse us, Simon Augustino,' murmured the Pope. 'But how does one hide fifty-eight archangel-class battlecruisers?'

The Cardinal smiled thinly. 'They have been powered down, floating in strategic positions within the inner-system asteroid belt and the system's outer Kuiper Belt, Your Holiness. Completely undetectable. Ready to jump at a second's notice.'

'The *Raphael* will not escape this time?'

'No, Your Holiness,' said Cardinal Lourdusamy. 'The heads of eleven Pax Fleet commanders depend upon the success of this ambush.'

'Leaving a fifth of our archangel fleet to float for weeks in this Outback system has seriously compromised the effectiveness of our Crusade against the Ousters, Cardinal Lourdusamy.'

'Yes, Your Holiness.' The Cardinal set his own palms against his robe and was surprised to realize that his palms were damp. Besides the eleven Pax Fleet heads riding on the success of this mission, Lourdusamy knew that his own future hung in the balance.

'It will be worth it when we destroy this rebel,' murmured the Pope.

Lourdusamy took a breath.

'We presume that the ship and Captain de Soya *will* be destroyed, not taken captive,' said His Holiness.

'Yes, Holy Father. Standing orders are to slag the ship to atoms.'

'But we will *not* harm the child?'

'No, Holy Father. All precautions have been taken to assure that the contagion vector named Aenea will be taken alive.'

'That is very important, Simon Augustino,' muttered the Pope. He seemed to be whispering to himself. They had gone over these details a hundred times. 'We must have the girl alive. The others with her . . . they are expendable . . . but the girl must be captured. Tell us again the procedure.'

Cardinal Lourdusamy closed his eyes. 'As soon as the *Raphael* is interdicted and destroyed, the Core ships will move into orbit around T'ien Shan and incapacitate the planet's population.'

'Deathbeam them,' murmured His Holiness.

'Not . . . technically,' said the Cardinal. 'As you know, the Core assures us that the results of this technique are reversible. It is more the induction of a permanent coma.'

'Will the millions of bodies be transported this time, Simon Augustino?'

'Not at first, Your Holiness. Our special teams will go planetside, find the girl, and remove her to an archangel convoy that shall bring her here to Pacem, where she will be revived, isolated, interrogated, and . . .'

'Executed,' sighed the Pope. 'To show those millions of rebels on sixty worlds that their putative messiah is no more.'

'Yes, Your Holiness.'

'We look forward to speaking to this person, Simon Augustino. The Devil's Child or not.'

'Yes, Your Holiness.'

'And when will Captain de Soya take the bait and appear for his destruction, do you think?'

Cardinal Lourdusamy looked at his comlog. 'Within hours, Your Holiness. Within hours.'

'Let us pray for a successful conclusion,' whispered the Pope. 'Let us pray for the salvation of our Church and our race.'

Both men bowed their heads in the Room of Tears.

In the days immediately following our return from the Dalai Lama's Potala place, I get the first hints of the full scope of Aenea's plans and power.

I am amazed at the reception upon our return. Rachel and Theo weep as they hug Aenea. A. Bettik pounds me on the back with his remaining hand and hugs me with both arms. The usually laconic Jigme Norbu first hugs George Tsarong and then comes down the line of us pilgrims, hugging all of us, tears streaming down his thin face. The entire Temple has turned out to cheer and clap and weep. I realize then that many had not expected us – or at least Aenea – to return from the reception with the Pax. I realize then what a close thing it had been that we had returned.

We set to work finishing the reconstruction of Hsuan-k'ung Ssu. I work with Lhomo, A. Bettik, and the high riggers on the last touches to the highest promenade, while Aenea, Rachel, and Theo surpervise detail work throughout the compound.

That evening, all I can think of is turning in early with my beloved, and from our hurried but passionate kisses during our few minutes alone on the high walk after the communal dinner, I guess that Aenea reciprocates the wish for immediate and intense intimacy. But it is one of her scheduled 'discussion group' evenings – her last as it turns out – and more than a hundred people are there in the central gompa platform as darkness falls. Luckily, the monsoons have held off after the first foretaste of their gray rain, and the evening is lovely as the sun sets to the west of K'un Lun Ridge. Torches crackle along the main axis stairways and prayer pennants snap.

I am amazed by some of those in attendance this night: Tromo Trochi of Dhomu has returned from Potala in spite of his declared need to move west with his wares; the Dorje Phamo is there with all nine of her favorite priests; there are numerous famous guests from the palace reception – mostly younger people – and the youngest and most famous of all, trying to appear incognito in a plain red robe and hood, is the Dalai Lama himself, minus his Regent and Lord Chamberlain, accompanied only by his personal bodyguard and Chief Crier, Carl Linga William Eiheji.

I stand at the back of the crowded room. For an hour or so, the discussion group is a discussion group, sometimes led but never dominated by Aenea. But slowly her questioning turns the conversation her way. I realize that she is a master of Tantric and Zen Buddhism, answering monks who have spent decades mastering those disciplines in koan and Dharma. To a monk who demands to know why they should not accept the Pax offer of immortality as a form of rebirth, she quotes Buddha as teaching that no individual is reborn, that all things are subject to *annicca* – the law of mutability – and she then elaborates on the doctrine of *anatta*, literally 'no-self', the Buddha's denial that there is any such thing as a personal entity known as a soul.

Responding to another query about death, Aenea quotes a Zen koan:

'A monk said to Tozan, "A monk has died; where has he gone?" Tozan answered, "After the fire, a sprout of grass." '

'M. Aenea,' says Kuku Se, her bright face flushed, 'does that mean *mu*?'

Aenea has taught me that *mu* is an elegant Zen concept that might translate as 'Unask the question.'

My friend smiles. She is sitting farthest from the door, in an open space near the opened wall of the room, and the stars are bright and visible above the Sacred Mountain of the North. The Oracle has not risen.

'It means that to some extent,' she says softly. The room is silent to hear. 'It also means that the monk is as dead as a doornail. He hasn't gone anywhere – more importantly, he has gone nowhere. But life has also gone nowhere. It continues, in a different form. Hearts are sorrowed by the monk's death, but life is not lessened. Nothing has been removed from the balance of life in the universe. Yet that whole universe – as reproduced in the monk's mind and heart – has itself died. Seppo once said to Gensha, "Monk Shinso asked me where a certain dead monk had gone, and I told him it was like ice becoming water." Gensha said, "That was all right, but I myself would not have answered like that." "What would you have said?" asked Seppo. Gensha replied, "It's like water returning to water." '

After a moment of silence, someone near the front of the room says, 'Tell us about the Void Which Binds.'

'Once upon a time,' begins Aenea as she always begins such things, 'there was the Void. And the Void was beyond time. In a real sense, the Void was an orphan of time . . . an orphan of space.

'But the Void was not of time, not of space, and certainly was not of God. Nor is the Void Which Binds God. In truth, the Void evolved long after time and space had staked out the limits to the universe, but unbound by time, untethered in space, the Void Which Binds has leaked backward and forward across the continuum to the Big Bang beginning and the Little Whimper end of things.'

Aenea pauses here and lifts her hands to her temples in a motion I have not seen her use since she was a child. She does not look to be a child this night. Her eyes are tired but vital. There are wrinkles of fatigue or worry around those eyes. I love her eyes.

'The Void Which Binds is a *minded* thing,' she says firmly. 'It comes from minded things – many of whom were, in turn, created by minded things.

'The Void Which Binds is stitched of quantum stuff, woven with Planck space, Planck time, lying under and around space/time like a quilt cover around and under cotton batting. The Void Which Binds is neither mystical nor metaphysical, it flows from and responds to the physical laws of the universe, *but it is a product of that evolving universe*. The Void is structured from thought and feeling. It is an artifact of the universe's consciousness of itself. And not merely of human thought and feeling – the Void Which Binds is a composite of a hundred thousand sentient races across billions of years of time. It is the only constant in the evolution of the universe – the only common ground for races that will evolve, grow, flower, fade, and die millions of years and hundreds of millions of light-years apart from one another. And there is only one entrance key to the Void Which Binds . . .'

Aenea pauses again. Her young friend Rachel is sitting close to her, cross-legged and attentive. I notice now for the first time that Rachel – the woman whom I have been foolishly jealous of these past few months – is indeed beautiful: copperish-brown hair short and curly, her cheeks flushed, her large green eyes flecked with tiny specks of brown. She is about Aenea's age, early twenties, standard, and hued to a golden brown by months of work in high places under T'ien Shan's yellow sun.

Aenea touches Rachel's shoulder.

'My friend here was a baby when her father discovered an interesting fact about the universe,' says Aenea. 'Her father, a scholar named Sol, had been obsessed for decades about the historical relationship between God and man. Then one day, under the most extreme of circumstances, when faced with losing his daughter for a second time, Sol was granted *satori* – he saw totally and intuitively what only a few others have been privileged to see clearly through the million years of our slow ponderings . . . Sol saw that love was a real and equal force in the universe . . . as real as electromagnetism or weak nuclear force. As real as gravity, and governed by many of the same laws. The inverse square law, for instance, often works as surely for love as it does for gravitational attraction.

'Sol realized that love was the binding force of the Void Which Binds, the thread and fabric of the garment. And in that instant of *satori*, Sol realized that humankind was not the only seamstress of that gorgeous tapestry. Sol glimpsed the Void Which Binds and the force of love behind it, but he could not gain access to that medium. Human beings, so recently evolved from our primate cousins, have not yet gained the sensory capacity to see clearly or enter the Void Which Binds.

'I say "to see clearly" because all humans with an open heart and mind have caught rare but powerful glimpses of the Void landscape. Just as Zen is not a religion, but *is* religion, so the Void Which Binds is not a state of mind, but is the state of mind. The Void is all probability as standing waves, interacting with that standing wave front which is the human mind and personality. The Void Which Binds is touched by all of us who have wept with happiness, bidden a lover good-bye, been exalted with orgasm, stood over the grave of a loved one, or watched our baby open his or her eyes for the first time.'

Aenea is looking at me as she speaks, and I feel the gooseflesh rise along my arms.

'The Void Which Binds is always under and above the surface of our thoughts and senses,' she continues, 'invisible but as present as the breathing of our beloved next to us in the night. Its actual but unaccessible presence in our universe is one of the prime causes for our species elaborating myth and religion, for our stubborn, blind belief in extrasensory powers, in telepathy and precognition, in demons and demigods and resurrection and reincarnation and ghosts and messiahs and so many other categories of almost-but-not-quite satisfying bullshit.'

The hundred-some listening monks, workers, intellectuals, politicians, and holy men and women shift slightly at this statement. The wind is rising outside and the platform rocks gently, as it was designed to do. Thunder rumbles from somewhere to the south of Jo-kung.

'The so-called "Four Statements of the Zen Sect" ascribed to Bodhidharma in the sixth century AD are an almost perfect signpost to find the Void Which Binds, at least to find its outline as an absence of otherworldly clutter,' continues Aenea. '*First, no dependence on words and letters*. Words are the light and sound of our existence, the heat lightning by which the night is illuminated. The Void Which Binds is to be found in the deepest secrets and silences of things . . . the place where childhood dwells.

'*Second, a special transmission outside the Scriptures*. Artists recognize other artists as soon as the pencil begins to move. A musician can tell another musician apart from the millions who play notes as soon as the music begins. Poets glean poets in a few syllables, especially where the ordinary meaning and forms of poetry are discarded. Chora wrote—

'*Two came here,*
Two flew off—
Butterflies.

—and in the still-warm crucible of burned-away words and images remains the gold of deeper things, what R. H. Blyth and Frederick Franck once called "the dark flame of life that burns in all things", . . . and "seeing with the belly, not with the eye; 'with bowels of compassion' ."

'The Bible lies. The Koran lies. The Talmud and Torah lie. The New Testament lies. The *Sutta-pitaka*, the *nikayas*, the *Itivuttaka*, and the *Dhammapada* lie. The Bodhisattva and the Amitabha lie. *The Book of the Dead* lies. The *Tiptaka* lies. All Scripture lies . . . just as I lie as I speak to you now.

'All these holy books lie not from intention or failure of expression, but by their very nature of being reduced to words; all the images, precepts, laws, canons, quotations, parables, commandments, koans, zazen, and sermons in these beautiful books ultimately fail by adding only more words between the human being who is seeking and the perception of the Void Which Binds.

'*Third, direct pointing to the soul of man.* Zen, which best understood the Void by finding its absence most clearly, wrestled with the problem of pointing without a finger, of creating this art without a medium, of hearing this powerful sound in a vacuum with no sounds. Shiki wrote—

'A fishing village;
Dancing under the moon,
To the smell of raw fish.

'This – and I do not mean the poem – is the essence of seeking the key to the portal of the Void Which Binds. A hundred thousand races on a million worlds in days long dead have each had their villages with no houses, their dancing under the moon in worlds with no moons, the smell of raw fish on oceans with no fish. *This* can be shared beyond time, beyond words, beyond a race's span of existence.

'*Fourth, seeing into one's nature and the attainment of Buddhahood.* It does not take decades of zazen or baptism into the Church or pondering the Koran to do this. The Buddha nature is, after all, the after-the-crucible essence of being human. Flowers all attain their flowerhood. A wild dog or blind zygoat each attain their doghood or zygoathood. A place – any place – is granted its placehood. Only humankind struggles and fails in becoming what it is. The reasons are many and complex, but all stem from the fact that we have evolved as one of the self-seeing organs of the evolving universe. Can the eye see itself?'

Aenea pauses for a moment and in the silence we can all hear thunder rumbling somewhere beyond the ridge. The monsoon is holding off a few days, but its arrival is imminent. I try to imagine these buildings, mountains, ridges, cables, bridges, walkways, and scaffolds covered with ice and shrouded by fog. The thought makes me shiver.

'The Buddha understood that we could sense the Void Which Binds by silencing the din of the everyday,' says Aenea at last. 'In that sense, *satori* is a great and satisfying silence after listening to a neighbor's blasting sound system for days or months on end. But the Void Which Binds is more than silence . . . it is the beginning of hearing. Learning the language of the dead is the first task of those who enter the Void medium.

'Jesus of Nazareth entered the Void Which Binds. We know that. His voice is among the clearest of those who speak in the language of the dead. He stayed long enough to move to the second level of responsibility and effort – of learning the language of the dead. He learned well enough to hear the music of the spheres. He was able to ride the surging probability waves far enough to see his own death and was brave enough not to avoid it when he could. And we know that – at least on one occasion while dying on the cross – he learned to take that first step – to move through and across the space/time web of the Void Which Binds, appearing to his friends and disciples several paces into the future from where he hung dying on that cross.

'And, liberated from the restrictions of his time by his glimpse of the timelessness on the Void Which Binds, Jesus realized that it was he who was the key – not his teachings, not Scriptures based on his ideas, not groveling adulation to him or the suddenly evolving Old Testament God in which he solidly believed – but *him*, Jesus, a human man whose cells carried the decryption code to unlock the portal. Jesus knew that his ability to open that door lay not in his mind or soul but in his skin and bones and cells . . . literally in his DNA.

'When, during the Last Supper, Jesus of Nazareth asked his followers to drink of his blood and eat of his body, he was not speaking in parable or asking for magical transubstantiation or setting the place for centuries of symbolic reenactment. *Jesus wanted them to drink of his blood . . . a few drops in a great tankard of wine . . . and to eat of his body . . . a few skin scrapings in a loaf of bread.* He gave of himself in the most literal terms, knowing that those who drank of his blood would share his DNA, and be able to perceive the power of the Void Which Binds the universe.

'And so it was for some of his disciples. But, confronted with perceptions and impressions far beyond their power to absorb or to set in context – all but driven mad by the unceasing voices of the dead and their own reactions to the language of the living – *and unable to transmit their own blood music to others* – these disciples turned to dogma, reducing the inexpressible into rough words and turgid sermons, tight rules and fiery rhetoric. And the vision paled, then failed. The portal closed.'

Aenea pauses again and sips water from a wooden mug. I notice for the first time that Rachel and Theo and a few others are weeping. I swivel where I am sitting on the fresh tatami and look behind me. A. Bettik is standing in the open doorway, his ageless blue face serious and intent on our young friend's words. The android is holding his shortened forearm with his good right hand. *Does it pain him?* I wonder.

Aenea speaks again. 'Strangely enough, the first children of Old Earth to rediscover the key to the Void Which Binds were the TechnoCore. The autonomous intelligences, attempting to guide their own destiny through forced evolution at a million times the rate of biological humankind, found the DNA keycode to seeing the Void . . . although "seeing" is not the correct word, of course. Perhaps "resonating" better expresses the meaning.

'But while the Core could feel and explore the outlines of the Void medium, send their probes into the multidimensional post-Hawking reality of it, *they could not understand it.* The Void Which Binds demands a level of sentient empathy which the Core had never bothered evolving. The first step toward true *satori* in the Void is learning the language of the beloved dead – *and the Core has no beloved dead.* The Void Which Binds was like a beautiful painting to a blind man who chooses to burn it like firewood, or like a Beethoven symphony to a deaf man who feels the vibration and builds a stronger floor to damp it out.

'Instead of using the Void Which Binds as the medium as it is, the TechnoCore tore bits of it loose and offered it to humankind as clever technologies. The so-called Hawking drive did not truly evolve from the ancient master Stephen Hawking's work as the Core said, but was a perversion of his findings. The Hawking-drive ships that wove the WorldWeb and allowed the Hegemony to exist functioned by tearing small holes in the nonfabric at the edge of the Void – a minor vandalism, but vandalism nonetheless. Farcasters were a different thing. Here my similes will fail us, my friends . . . for learning to step across the medium of the Void Which Binds is a bit like learning to walk on water, if you will pardon the scriptural hubris, while the TechnoCore's farcaster burrows were more like draining the oceans so as to build highways across the seabed. Their farcaster tunneling through the boundaries of the Void was harming several billion years of organic growth there. It was the equivalent of paving great swaths through a vital, green forest – although that comparison also fails, because the forest would have to be made out of the memories and voices of the millions we have loved and lost – and the paved highways thousands of kilometers wide – for you to understand even a hint of the damage done.

'The so-called fatline which allowed for instantaneous communication across the Hegemony was also a perversion of the Void Which Binds. Again, my similes are clumsy and inept, but imagine some human aborigines discovering a working electromagnetic telecommunications grid – studios, holocameras, sound equipment, generators, transmitters, relay satellites, receivers, and projectors – and then tearing down and tearing up everything they can reach so that they can use the junk as signal flags. It is worse than that. It is worse than pre-Hegira days on Old Earth when humanity's giant oil tankers and ocean-going ships deafened the world's whales by filling their seas with mechanical noise, thus drowning out their Life Songs – destroying a million years of evolving song history before human beings even knew it was being sung. The whales all decided to die out after that; it was not the hunting of them for food and oil that killed them, but the destruction of their songs.'

Aenea takes a breath. She flexes her fingers as if her hands are cramping. When she looks around the room, her gaze touches each of us.

'I'm sorry,' she says. 'I'm wandering. Suffice it to say, that with the Fall of the Farcasters, the other races using the Void decided to stop the vandalism of the fatline. These other races had long since sent observers to live among us . . .'

There is a sudden whispering and murmuring in the room. Aenea smiles and waits for it to subside.

'I know,' she says. 'The idea surprised me, as well, even though I knew this before I was born. These observers have an important function . . . to decide if humanity can be trusted to join them in the Void Which Binds medium, or if we are only vandals. It was one of these observers among us who recommended that Old Earth be transported away before the Core could destroy it. And it was one of these observers who designed the tests and simulations carried out on Old Earth during the last three centuries of its exile in the Lesser Magellanic Cloud to better explain our species to them and measure the empathy of which we are capable.

'These other races also sent their observers – spies, if you will – to dwell among the elements of the Core. They knew that it had been the Core tampering which had damaged the boundaries of the Void, but they also know *that we created the Core*. Many of the . . . residents is not quite the right word – collaborators? cocreators? – on the Void Which Binds are ex-silicon constructs, nonorganic autonomous intelligences in their own right. But not of the variety which rules the TechnoCore today. No sentient race can appreciate the Void medium without having evolved empathy.'

Aenea raises her knees a bit and sets her elbows on them, leaning forward now as she speaks.

'My father – the John Keats cybrid – was created for this reason,' she says, and although her voice is level, I can hear the subtext of emotion there. 'As I have explained before, the Core is in a constant state of civil war, with almost every entity there fighting for itself and for no one else. It is a case of hyper-hyper-hyperparasitism to the tenth degree. Their prey – other Core elements – are not so much killed as absorbed, their coded genetic materials, memories, softwares, and reproductive sequences cannibalized. The cannibalized Core element still "lives" but as a subcomponent of the victorious element, or elements, which soon enough turn on one another for parts. Alliances are temporary. There are no philosophies, creeds, or ultimate goals – only contingency arrangements to optimize survival strategies. Every action in the Core is a result of the zero-sum game that has been playing there since the Core elements evolved into sentience. Most elements of the Core are capable of dealing with humankind in only those zero-sum terms . . . optimizing their parasite strategy in relation to us. Their gain, our loss. Our gain, their loss.

'Over the centuries, however, some of these Core elements have come to understand the true potential of the Void Which Binds. They understand that their empathy-free species of intelligence can never be part of that amalgam of living and past races. They have come to understand that the Void Which Binds was not so much constructed as evolved, like a coral reef, and that they will never find shelter there unless they change some of the parameters of their own existence.

'Thus evolved some members of the Core – not altruists, but desperate survivalists who realized that the only way ultimately to win their never-ending zero-sum game was to stop the game. And to stop the game they needed to evolve into a species capable of empathy.

'The Core knows what Teilhard de Chardin and other sentimentalists refused to acknowledge: that evolution is not progress, that there is no "goal" or direction to evolution. Evolution is change. Evolution "succeeds" if that change best adapts some leaf or branch of its tree of life to conditions of the universe. For that evolution to "succeed" for these elements of the Core, they would have to abandon zero-sum parasitism and discover true symbiosis. They would have to enter into honest coevolution with our human race.

'First the renegade Core elements continued cannibalizing to evolve more empathy-prone Core elements. They rewrote their own code as far as they were able. Then they created the John Keats cybrid – a full attempt at simulating an empathic organism with the body and DNA of a human being, and the Core-stored memories and personality of a cybrid. Opposing elements destroyed the first Keats cybrid. The second one was created in the first's image. It hired my mother – a private detective – to help it unravel the mystery of the first cybrid's death.'

Aenea is smiling and for a moment she seems oblivious of us or even of her own storytelling. She seems to be reliving old memories. I remember then what she once casually mentioned during our trip from Hyperion in the Consul's old ship – 'Raul, I had my mother's and father's memories poured into me before I was born . . . before I'd become a real fetus even. Can you imagine anything more destructive to a child's personality than to be inundated with someone else's lives even before you've begun your own? No wonder I'm a screwed-up mess.'

She does not look or act like a screwed-up mess to me at this moment. But then I love her more than life.

'He hired my mother to solve the mystery of his own persona's death,' she continues softly, 'but in truth he knew what had happened to his former self. His real reason for hiring my mother was to meet my mother, to be with my mother, to become my mother's lover.' Aenea stops for a moment and smiles, her eyes seeing distant things. 'My Uncle Martin never got that part right in his muddled-up *Cantos*. My parents were married and I don't think Uncle Martin ever told of that . . . married by the Bishop at the Shrike Temple on Lusus. It was a cult, but a legal one, and my parents' marriage would have been legal on two hundred worlds of the Hegemony.' She smiles again, looking across the crowded room directly at me. 'I can be a bastard, you know, but I wasn't born one.

'So they were married, I was conceived – probably before that ceremony – and then Core-backed elements murdered my father before my mother could begin the Shrike pilgrimage to Hyperion. And that should have been the end of any contact between my father and me except for two things – his Core persona was captured in a Schrön Loop implanted behind my mother's ear. For some months she was pregnant with two of us – me in her womb and my father, the second John Keats persona, in the Schrön Loop. His persona could not communicate directly to my mother while imprisoned in its endless-cycle Schrön Loop, but it communicated with me easily enough. The hard part was defining what "me" was at that point. My father helped by entering the Void Which Binds and taking the fetal "me" with him. I saw what was to be – who I would be – even how I would die – before my fingers were fully formed.

'And there was one other detail which Uncle Martin left out of his *Cantos*. On the day that they had gunned down my father on the steps of the Shrike Temple in the Lusian Concourse Mall, my mother was covered with his blood – the reconstructed, Core-augmented DNA of John Keats. What she did not fully understand at the time was that his blood was literally the most precious resource in the human universe at that moment. His DNA had been designed to infect others with his single gift – access to the Void. Mixed with fully human DNA in the right way, it would offer the gift of blood that would open the portal to the Void Which Binds to the entire human race.

'I am that mix. I bring the genetic ability to access the Void from the TechnoCore and the too-seldom-used human ability to perceive the universe through empathy. For better or worse, those who drink of my blood shall never see the world or the universe the same again.'

So saying, Aenea rises to her knees on the tatami mat. Theo brings a white linen cloth. Rachel pours red wine from a vase into seven large goblets. Aenea takes a small packet from her sweater – I recognize it as a ship's medkit – and removes a sterile lancet and an antiseptic swab. She pauses before using the lancet and sweeps her gaze across the crowd. There is no sound – it is as if the more than hundred people there are holding their breath.

'There is no guarantee of happiness, wisdom, or long life if you drink of me this evening,' she says, very softly. 'There is no nirvana. There is no salvation. There is no afterlife. There is no rebirth. There is only immense knowledge – of the heart as well as the mind – and the potential for great discoveries, great adventures, and a guarantee of more of the pain and terror that make up so much of our short lives.'

She looks from face to face, smiling as she meets the gaze of the eight-year-old Dalai Lama. 'Some of you,' she says, 'have attended all of our discussion sessions over the past standard year. I have told you what I know about learning the language of the dead, learning the language of the living, learning to hear the music of the spheres, and learning how to take a first step.'

She looks at me. 'Some of you have heard only some of these discussions. You were not here when I discussed the real function of the Church's cruciform or the real identity of the Shrike. You have not heard the details of learning the language of the dead or the other burdens of entering the Void Which Binds. For those of you with doubts or hesitation, I urge you to wait. For the rest of you, I say again – I am not a messiah . . . but I am a teacher. If what I have taught you these months sounds like truth, and if you wish to take this chance, drink of me this night. Be warned, that the DNA which allows us to perceive the medium of the Void Which Binds cannot coexist with the cruciform. That parasite will wither and die within twenty-four hours of the time you drink of my blood. It will never grow within you again. If you seek resurrection through the cruciform cross, do not drink the blood of my body in this wine.

'And be warned that you will become, like me, the despised and sought-out enemy of the Pax. Your blood will be contagious. Those with whom you share it – those who choose to find the Void Which Binds via your shared DNA – will become despised in turn.

'And finally, be warned that, once having drunk this wine, your children will be born with the ability to enter the Void Which Binds. For better or worse, your children and their children will be born knowing the language of the dead, the language of the living, hearing the music of the spheres, and knowing that they can take a first step across the Void Which Binds.'

Aenea touches her finger with the razor edge of the lancer. A tiny drop of blood is visible in the lantern light. Rachel holds a goblet up as the tiny drop of blood is squeezed into the large volume of wine. Then again with the next goblet, and so on until each of the seven cups has been . . . contaminated? Transubstantiated? My mind is reeling. My heart is pounding in something like alarm. This seems like some wild parody of the Catholic Church's Holy Communion. Has my young friend, my dear lover, my beloved . . . has she gone insane? Does she truly believe that she is a messiah? No, she said that she is not. Do *I* believe that I will be transformed forever by drinking of wine that is one part per million my lover's blood? I do not know. I do not understand.

About half of the people there move forward to line up and sip from one of the large goblets. *Chalices? This is blasphemy. It's not right. Or is it?* One sip is all they take, then return to their places on the tatami mats. No one seems especially energized or enlightened. No horns of light shine from anyone's forehead after they partake of the wine. No one levitates or speaks in tongues. They each take a sip and sit down.

I realize that I have been holding back, trying to catch Aenea's gaze. I have so many questions . . . Belatedly, feeling like a traitor to someone I should trust without hesitation, I move toward the back of the shortening line.

Aenea sees me. She holds her hand up briefly, palm toward me. The meaning is clear – *Not now, Raul. Not yet.* I hesitate another moment, irresolute, sick at the thought of these others – these strangers – entering into an intimacy with my darling when I cannot. Then, heart pounding and face burning, I sit back on my mat.

There is no formal end to the evening. People begin to leave in twos and threes. A couple – she drank of the wine, he did not – leave together with their arms around one another as if nothing has changed. Perhaps nothing *has* changed. Perhaps the communion ritual I've just watched is all metaphor and symbolism, or autosuggestion and self-hypnosis. Perhaps those who will themselves hard enough to perceive something called the Void Which Binds will have some internal experience that convinces them that it has happened. Perhaps it's all bullshit.

I rub my forehead. I have such a headache. Good thing I didn't drink the wine, I think. Wine sometimes brings on migraines with me. I chuckle and feel ill and empty for a moment, left behind.

Rachel says, 'Don't forget, the last stone will be set in place in the walkway tomorrow at noon. There'll be a party on the upper meditation platform! Bring your own refreshments.'

And thus ends the evening. I go upstairs to our shared sleeping platform with a mixture of elation, anticipation, regret, embarrassment, excitement, and a throbbing headache. I confess to myself that I didn't understand half of Aenea's explanation of things, but I leave with a vague sense of letdown and inappropriateness . . . I'm sure, for instance, that Jesus Christ's Last Supper did not end with a shouted reminder of a BYOB party on the upper deck.

I chuckle and then swallow the laugh. Last Supper. That has a terrible ring to it. My heart begins pounding again and my head hurts worse. Hardly the way to enter one's lover's bedroom.

The chill air on the upper platform walkway clears my head a bit. The Oracle is just a sliver above towering cumulus to the east. The stars look cold tonight.

I am just about to enter our shared room and light the lantern when suddenly the skies explode.

TWENTY-ONE

They all came up from the lower levels – all of the ones who had stayed at the Temple Hanging in Air after most of the work had been finished – Aenea and A. Bettik, Rachel and Theo, George and Jigme, Kuku and Kay, Chim Din and Gyalo Thondup, Lhomo and Labsang, Kim Byung-Soon and Viki Groselj, Kenshiro and Haruyuki, Master Abbot Kempo Ngha Wang Tashi and his master, the young Dalai Lama, Voytek Majer and Janusz Kurtyka, brooding Rimsi Kyipup and grinning Changchi Kenchung, the Dorje Phamo the Thunderbolt Sow and Carl Linga William Eiheji. Aenea came to my side and slipped her hand in mine as we watched the skies in awed silence.

I am surprised that we were not all blinded by the light show going on up there where the stars had been a moment earlier: great blossoms of white light, strobes of sulfur yellow, blazing red streaks – far brighter than a comet or meteor's tail – crisscrossed with blue, green, white, and yellow slashes – each as clear and straight as a diamond scratch on glass, then sudden bursts of orange that seemed to fold into themselves in silent implosions, followed by more white strobes and a resumption of red slashes. It was all silent, but the violence of light alone made us want to cover our ears and cringe in a sheltered place.

'What in ten hells is it?' asked Lhomo Dondrub.

'Space battle,' said Aenea. Her voice sounded terribly tired.

'I do not understand,' said the Dalai Lama. He did not sound afraid, merely curious. 'The Pax authorities assured us that they would have only one of their starships in orbit – the *Jibril*, I believe is its name – and that it was on a diplomatic mission rather than a military one. Regent Reting Tokra also assured me of this.'

The Thunderbolt Sow made a rude noise. 'Your Holiness, the Regent is in the pay of the Pax bastards.'

The boy looked at her.

'I believe it to be true, Your Holiness,' said Eiheji, his bodyguard. 'I have heard things in the palace.'

The sky had faded almost to black but now it exploded again in a score of places. The rocky cliff face behind us bled reflections of red, green, and yellow.

'How can we see their laser lances if there is no dust or other colloidal particles to highlight them?' asked the Dalai Lama, his dark eyes bright. Evidently the news of his Regent's betrayal was not surprising to him . . . or at least not as interesting as the battle going on thousands of kilometers above us. I was interested to see that the supreme holy person of the Buddhist world had been tutored in basic science.

Again, it was his bodyguard who answered. 'Some ships must have been hit and destroyed already, Your Holiness,' said Eiheji. 'The coherent beams and CPBs would become visible in the expanding fields of debris, frozen oxygen, molecular dust, and other gases.'

This caused a moment of silence in our group.

'My father watched this once, on Hyperion,' whispered Rachel. She rubbed her bare arms as if there had been a sudden chill.

I blinked and looked at the young woman. I had not missed Aenea's comment about her friend's father, Sol . . . I knew my *Cantos* well enough to identify Rachel as the infant on the legendary Hyperion pilgrimage, daughter of Sol Weintraub . . . but I admit that I had not completely believed it. The infant Rachel had become the almost mythical woman, Moneta, in the *Cantos* – someone who had traveled back in time in the Time Tombs with the Shrike. How could *that* Rachel be here, now?

Aenea put her arm around Rachel's shoulders. 'My mother as well,' she said softly. 'Only then it was thought to be the Hegemony forces against the Ousters.'

'Who is this, then?' demanded the Dalai Lama. 'The Ousters against the Pax? And why have the Pax warships come unbidden to our system?'

Several white spheres of light pulsed, grew, dimmed, and died. We all blinked away the retinal echoes.

'I believe that the Pax warships were here since their first ship arrived, Your Holiness,' said Aenea. 'But I do not think that they are fighting Ousters.'

'Who then?' said the boy.

Aenea turned her face back to the sky. 'One of their own,' she said.

Suddenly there came a series of explosions quite different than the others . . . a closer, brighter series of explosions, followed by three blazing meteor trails. One exploded quickly in the upper atmosphere, trailing a score of minor debris trails that quickly died out. The second shot to the west, blazing from yellow to red to pure white, breaking up twenty degrees above the horizon and spilling a hundred lesser trails across the cloudy western horizon. The third screeched across the sky from west of the zenith to the eastern horizon – and I say 'screeched' deliberately because we could hear the noise, at first a teakettle whistle, then a howl, then a terrible tornadic roar, diminishing as quickly as it came – finally to break up into three or four large, blazing masses in the east, all but one of which died out before reaching the horizon. This last burning fragment of starship seemed to wiggle in its flight at the last moment, with yellow bursts of light preceding it, slowing it, before it was lost to sight.

We waited another half-hour on the upper platform, but except for dozens of fusion-flame streaks for the first few minutes – starships accelerating away from T'ien Shan, I knew – there was nothing left to see. Eventually the stars were once again the brightest things in the sky and everyone moved off – the Dalai Lama to sleep in the monks' quarters here, others to permanent or temporary quarters on the lower levels.

Aenea bid a few of us stay – Rachel and Theo, A. Bettik and Lhomo Dondrub, and me.

'That is the sign I've been waiting for,' she said very softly when all the others had left the platform. 'We must leave tomorrow.'

'Leave?' I said. 'To where? Why?'

Aenea touched my forearm. I interpreted this as saying, *I will explain later.* I shut up as the others spoke.

'The wings are ready, Teacher,' said Lhomo.

'I have taken the liberty of checking over the skinsuits and rebreathers in M. Endymion's quarters while you were all away,' said A. Bettik. 'They are all serviceable.'

'We'll finish up the work and organize the ceremony tomorrow,' said Theo.

'I wish I were going,' said Rachel.

'Going where?' I said again, despite my best efforts to shut up and listen.

'You're invited,' said Aenea, still touching my arm. That did not really answer my question. 'Lhomo, and A. Bettik . . . if you're both still game.'

Lhomo Dondrub gave his broad grin. The android nodded. I began to think that I was the only one in the temple compound that didn't understand what was going on.

'Good night, all,' said Aenea. 'We'll be off at first light. You don't need to see us off.'

'To hell with that,' said Rachel. Theo nodded agreement. 'We'll be there to say good-bye,' continued Rachel.

Aenea nodded and touched their arms. Everyone clambered down ladders or slid down cables.

Aenea and I were alone on the top platform. The skies seemed dark after the battle. I realized that clouds had risen above the ridgeline and were wiping the stars away like a wet towel drawn across a black slateboard. Aenea opened the door to her sleeping room, went in, lit the lantern, and returned to stand in the entrance. 'Coming, Raul?'

We did talk. But not right away.

Lovemaking seems all too absurd when described – even the timing of our lovemaking seems absurd in the telling, with the sky literally falling and my lover having carried out a sort-of Last Supper convocation that night – but lovemaking is never absurd when you are making love to the person you truly love. And I was. If I had not realized that before the Last Supper night, I did then – completely, totally, and without reservation.

It was perhaps two hours later when Aenea pulled on a kimono and I donned a yukata and we moved away from the sleeping mat to the open shoji screens. Aenea brewed tea on the small burner set in the tatami, and we took our cups and sat with our backs against the opposing shoji frames, our bare toes and legs touching, my right side and her left knee extending over the kilometers-long drop. The air was cool and smelled of rain, but the storm had moved north of us. The summit of Heng Shan was shrouded with clouds, but all the lower ridges were illuminated by a constant play of lightning.

'Is Rachel really the Rachel from the *Cantos*?' I said. It was not the question I most wanted to ask, but I was afraid to ask it.

'Yes,' said Aenea. 'She's the daughter of Sol Weintraub – the woman who caught the Merlin Sickness on Hyperion and aged backward twenty-seven years to the infant whom Sol brought on the pilgrimage.'

'And she was also known as Moneta,' I said. 'And Memnosyne . . .'

'*Admonisher*,' murmured Aenea. 'And *Memory*. Appropriate names for her role in that time.'

'That was two hundred and eighty years ago!' I said. 'And scores of light-years away . . . on Hyperion. How did she get here?'

Aenea smiled. The warm tea breathed vapors that rose to her tousled hair. 'I started life more than two hundred and eighty years ago,' she said. 'And scores of light-years away . . . on Hyperion.'

'So did she get here the same way you did? Through the Time Tombs?'

'Yes and no,' said Aenea. She held up one hand to stop my protest. 'I know that you want straight talk, Raul . . . no parables or similes or evasions. I agree. The time for plain talk is here. But the truth is that the Sphinx Time Tombs are only part of Rachel's journey.'

I waited.

'You remember the *Cantos*,' she began.

'I remember that the pilgrim named Sol took his daughter . . . after the Keats persona somehow saved her from the Shrike and after she began aging normally . . . took her into the Sphinx into the future . . .' I stopped. '*This* future?'

'No,' said Aenea. 'The infant Rachel grew into a child again, a young woman again, in a future beyond this one. Her father raised her a second time. Their story is . . . marvelous, Raul. Literally filled with marvels.'

I rubbed my forehead. The headache had gone, but now it threatened to return. 'And she got here via the Time Tombs again?' I said. 'Moving back in time with them?'

'Partially via the Time Tombs,' said Aenea. 'She is also able to move through time on her own.'

I stared. This bordered on madness.

Aenea smiled as if reading my thoughts or just reading my expression. 'I know it seems insane, Raul. Much of what we've yet to encounter is very strange.'

'That's an understatement,' I said. Another mental tumbler clicked into place. 'Theo Bernard!' I said.

'Yes?'

There was a Theo in the *Cantos*, wasn't there?' I said. 'A man . . .' There were different versions of the oral tale, the poem to be sung, and many of these minor details were dropped in the short, popular versions. Grandam had made me learn most of the full poem, but the dull parts had never held my interest.

'Theo Lane,' said Aenea. 'At one time the Consul's aide on Hyperion, later our world's first Governor-General for the Hegemony. I met him once when I was a girl. A decent man. Quiet. He wore archaic glasses . . .'

'This Theo,' I said, trying to figure it all out. *Some sort of sex change?*

Aenea shook her head. 'Close, but no cigar, as Freud would have said.'

'Who?'

'Theo Bernard is the great-great-great-etcetera-granddaughter of Theo Lane,' said Aenea. 'Her story is an adventure in itself. But she was born in this era . . . she did escape from the Pax colonies on Maui-Covenant and join the rebels . . . but she did so because of something I told the original Theo almost three hundred years ago. It had been passed down all those generations. Theo knew that I would be on Maui-Covenant when I was . . .'

'How?' I said.

'That's what I told Theo Lane,' said my friend. 'When I would be there. The knowledge was kept alive in his family . . . much as the Shrike Pilgrimage has been kept alive by the *Cantos*.'

'So you *can* see the future,' I said flatly.

'Futures,' corrected Aenea. 'I've told you I can. And you heard me tonight.'

'You've seen your own death?'

'Yes.'

'Will you tell me what you've seen?'

'Not now, Raul. Please. When it's time.'

'But if there are *futures*,' I said, hearing the growl of pain in my own voice, 'why do you have to see one death for yourself? If you can see it, why can't you avoid it?'

'I could avoid that particular death,' she said softly, 'but it would be the wrong choice.'

'How can life over death *ever* be the wrong choice?' I said. I realized that I had shouted it. My hands were balled into fists.

She touched those fists with her warm hands, surrounding them with her slender fingers. 'That's what all this is about,' she said so softly that I had to lean forward to hear her. Lightning played on the shoulders of Heng Shan. 'Death is never preferable to life, Raul, but sometimes it's necessary.'

I shook my head. I realized that I must look sullen at that moment, but I didn't care. 'Will you tell me when I'm going to die?' I said.

She met my gaze. Her dark eyes held depths. 'I don't know,' she said simply.

I blinked. I felt vaguely hurt. Didn't she care enough to look into my future?

'Of course I care,' she whispered. 'I've just chosen not to look at those probability waves. Seeing my death is . . . difficult. Seeing yours would be . . .' She made a strange noise and I realized that she was weeping. I moved around on the tatami mat until I could put my arms around her. She leaned in against my chest.

'I'm sorry, kiddo,' I said into her hair, although I could not have said exactly what I was sorry about. It was strange to feel so happy and so miserable at the same time. The thought of losing her made me want to scream, to throw rocks at the mountainside. As if echoing my feelings, thunder rumbled from the peak to the north.

I kissed her tears away. Then we just kissed, the salt of her tears mingling with the warmth of her mouth. Then we made love again, and this time it was as slow, careful, and timeless as it had been urgent earlier.

When we were lying in the cool breeze again, our cheeks touching, her hand on my chest, she said, 'You want to ask something. I can tell it. What?'

I thought of all the questions I had been filled with during her 'discussion time' earlier – all of her talks I had missed that I needed to catch up on in order to understand why the communion ceremony was necessary: *What is the cruciform really about? What is the Pax up to on those worlds with missing populations? What does the Core really hope to gain in all this? What the hell is the Shrike . . . is the thing a monster or a guardian? Where did it come from? What's going to happen to us? What does she see in our future that I need to know in order for us to survive . . . in order for her to avoid the fate she has known about since before she was born? What's the giant secret behind the Void Which Binds and why is it so important to connect with it? How are we going to get off this world if the Pax really slagged the only farcaster portal under molten rock and there are Pax warships between the Consul's ship and us? Who are these 'observers' she talked about who have been spying on humanity for centuries? What's all this about learning the language of the dead and so forth? Why haven't the Nemes thing and her clone-siblings killed us yet?*

I asked, 'You've been with someone else? Made love with someone before me?'

This was insanity. It was none of my business. She was almost twenty-two standard years old. I'd slept with women before – I could not remember any of their last names, but in the Home Guard, while working in the Nine Tails Casino – why should I care if – what difference did it make if – I had to know.

She hesitated only a second. 'Our first time together was not my . . . first,' she said.

I nodded, feeling like a swine and a voyeur for asking. There was an actual pain in my chest, much as I had imagined angina from hearing about it. I could not stop. 'Did you love . . . him?' *How did I know it was a he? Theo . . . Rachel . . . she surrounds herself with women.* My own thoughts made me sick of myself.

'I love you, Raul,' she whispered.

It was only the second time she had said this, the first being when we had said good-bye on Old Earth more than five and a half years earlier. My heart should have soared at the words. But it hurt too much. There was something important here that I did not understand.

'But there was a man,' I said, the words like pebbles in my mouth. 'You loved him . . .' *Only one? How many?* I wanted to scream at my thoughts to shut up.

Aenea put her finger on my lips. 'I love you, Raul, remember that as I tell you these things. Everything is . . . complicated. By who I am. By what I must do. But I love you . . . I have loved you since the first time I saw you in the dreams of my future. I loved you when we met in the dust storm on Hyperion, with the confusion and shooting and the Shrike and the hawking mat. Do you remember how I squeezed my arms around you when we were flying on the mat, trying to escape? I loved you then . . .'

I waited in silence. Aenea's finger moved from my lips to my cheek. She sighed as if the weight of the worlds were on her shoulders. 'All right,' she said softly. 'There was someone. I've made love before. We . . .'

'Was it serious?' I said. My voice sounded strange to me, like the ship's artificial tones.

'We were married,' said Aenea.

Once, on the River Kans on Hyperion, I'd gotten into a fist fight with an older bargeman who was half again my weight with infinitely more experience in fighting. With no warning he had clipped me under the jaw with a single blow that had blacked out my vision, buckled my knees, and sent me reeling back over the barge railing into the river. The man had held no grudge and had personally dived in to fish me out. I'd regained consciousness in a minute or two, but it was hours before I could shake the ringing out of my head and truly focus my eyes.

This was worse than that. I could only lie there and look at her, at my beloved Aenea, and feel her fingers against my cheek as strange and cold and alien as a stranger's touch. She moved her hand away.

There was something worse.

'The twenty-three months, one week, and six hours that were unaccounted for,' she said.

'With him?' I could not remember forming the two words but I heard them spoken in my voice.

'Yes.'

'Married . . .' I said and could not go on.

Aenea actually smiled, but it was the saddest smile I think I had ever seen. 'By a priest,' she said. 'The marriage will be legal in the eyes of the Pax and the Church.'

'Will be?'

'Is.'

'You are still married?' I wanted to get up then and be sick over the edge of the platform, but I could not move.

For a second Aenea seemed confused, unable to answer. 'Yes . . .' she said, her eyes gleaming with tears. 'I mean, no . . . I'm not married now . . . you . . . dammit, if I could only . . .'

'But the man's still alive?' I interrupted, my voice as flat and emotionless as a Holy Office Inquisition interrogator's.

'Yes.' She put her hand on her own cheek. Her fingers were trembling.

'Do you love him, kiddo?'

'I love *you*, Raul.'

I pulled away slightly, not consciously, not deliberately, but I could not stay in physical contact with her while we had this discussion.

'There's something else . . .' she said.

I waited.

'We had . . . I'll . . . I had a child, a baby.' She looked at me as if trying to force understanding of all this through her gaze directly into my mind. It did not work.

'A child,' I repeated stupidly. My dear friend . . . my child friend turned woman turned lover. . . my beloved had a child. 'How old is it?' I said, hearing the banality like the thunder rumbling closer.

Again she seemed confused, as if uncertain of facts. Finally she said, 'The child is . . . nowhere I can find it now.'

'Oh, kiddo,' I said, forgetting everything but her pain. I folded her against me as she wept. 'I'm so sorry, kiddo . . . I'm so sorry,' I said as I patted her head.

She pulled back, wiping away tears. 'No, Raul, you don't understand. It's all right . . . it's not . . . that part's all right . . .'

I pulled away from her and stared. She was distraught, sobbing. 'I understand,' I lied.

'Raul . . .' Her hand felt for mine.

I patted her hand but got out of the bedclothes, pulled on my clothes, and grabbed my climbing harness and pack from their place by the door.

'Raul . . .'

'I'll be back before dawn,' I said, facing in her general direction but not looking at her. 'I'm just going for a walk.'

'Let me go with you,' she said, standing with the sheet around her. Lightning flashed behind her. Another storm was coming in.

'I'll be back before dawn,' I said and went out the door before she could dress or join me.

It was raining – a cold, sleety rain. The platforms were quickly coated and made slick. I hurtled down ladders and jogged down the vibrating stair-cases, seeing my way by the occasional lightning flash, not slowing until I was several hundred meters down the east ledge walk headed toward the fissure where I had first landed in the ship. I did not want to go there.

Half a klick from the Temple were fixed lines rising to the top of the ridge. The sleet was pounding on the cliff face now, the red and black lines were coated with a layer of ice. I clipped carabiners onto the line and harness, pulling the powered ascenders from the pack and attaching them without double-checking the connections, then began jumaring up the icy ropes.

The wind came up, whipping my jacket and pushing me away from the rock wall. Sleet pounded at my face and hands. I ignored it and ascended, sometimes sliding back three or four meters as the jumar clamps failed on the icy line, then recovering and climbing again. Ten meters below the razor's-edge summit of the ridgeline, I emerged from the clouds like a swimmer coming up out of the water. The stars still burned coldly up there, but the billowing cloud masses were piling against the north wall of the ridge and rising like a white tide around me.

I slid the ascenders higher and jumared until I reached the relatively flat area where the fixed lines were attached. Only then did I notice that I had not tied on the safety line.

'Fuck it,' I said and began walking northeast along the fifteen-centimeter-wide ridgeline. The storm was rising around me to the north. The drop to the south was kilometers of empty, black air. There were patches of ice here and it was beginning to snow.

I broke into a trot, running east, jumping icy spots and fissures, not giving a good goddamn about anything.

While I was obsessed with my own misery, there were other things occurring in the human universe. On Hyperion, when I was a boy, news filtered slowly from the interstellar Pax to our moving caravans on the moors: an important event on Pacem or Renaissance Vector or wherever would, of necessity, be many weeks or months old from Hawking-drive time-debt, with additional weeks of transit from Port Romance or another major city to our provincial region. I was used to not paying attention to events elsewhere. The lag in news had lessened, of course, when I was guiding offworld hunters in the Fens and elsewhere, but it was still old news and of little importance to me. The Pax held no fascination for me, although offworld travel certainly had. Then there had been almost ten years of disconnection during our Old Earth hiatus and my five years of time-debt odyssey. I was not used to thinking of events elsewhere except where they affected me, such as the Pax's obsession with finding us.

But this would soon change.

That night on T'ien Shan, the Mountains of Heaven, as I ran foolishly through sleet and fog down the narrow ridgeline, these were some of the events happening elsewhere:

On the lovely world of Maui-Covenant, where the long chain of events culminating with my presence here with Aenea could be said to have begun with the courtship of Siri and Merin some four centuries ago, rebellion raged. The rebels on the motile isles had long since become followers of Aenea's philosophy, had drunk of her communion wine, had rejected the Pax and the cruciform forever, and were waging a war of sabotage and resistance while trying not to harm or kill the Pax soldiers occupying the world. For the Pax, Maui-Covenant offered special problems because it was primarily a vacation world – hundreds of thousands of wealthy born-again Christians traveled there via Hawking drive every standard year to enjoy the warm seas, the beautiful beaches of the Equatorial Archipelago isles, and the dolphin/motile isles migrations. The Pax also benefited from the hundreds of oil-drilling platforms around the mostly ocean world, situated out of sight of tourist areas but vulnerable to attack from motile isles or rebel submersibles. Now many of the Pax tourists themselves were – inexplicably – rejecting the cruciform and becoming followers of Aenea's teachings. Rejecting immortality. The planetary governor, the resident archbishop, and the Vatican officials called in for the crisis could not understand it.

On cold Sol Draconi Septem, where most of the atmosphere was frozen into a single giant glacier, there were no tourists, but the Pax attempt at colonization there over the past ten years had turned into a nightmare.

The gentle bands of Chitchatuk whom Aenea, A. Bettik, and I had befriended some nine and a half years ago had turned into implacable foes of the Pax. The skyscraper frozen into the atmospheric ice where Father Glaucus had welcomed all travelers still blazed with light despite that kind man's murder at the hand of Rhadamanth Nemes. The Chitchatuk kept the place alight like a shrine. Somehow they knew who had murdered the harmless blind man and Cuchiat's tribe – Cuchiat, Chiaku, Aichacut, Cuchtu, Chithticia, Chatchia – all of those whom Aenea, A. Bettik, and I had known by name. The other Chitchatuk blamed the Pax, who were attempting to colonize the temperate bands along the equator where the air was gaseous and the great glacier melted down to the ancient permafrost.

But the Chitchatuk, not having heard of Aenea's communion and tasted the empathy of it, descended on the Pax like a Biblical plague. Having preyed upon – and been preyed upon by – the terrible snow wraiths for millennia, the Chitchatuk now drove the tunneling white beasts south to the equatorial regions, unleashing them on the Pax colonists and missionaries. The toll was frightful. Pax military units brought in to kill the primitive Chitchatuk sent patrols out onto and into the planet glacier and never saw them again.

On the city-planet of Renaissance Vector, Aenea's word of the Void Which Binds had spread to millions of followers. Thousands of Pax faithful took communion from the changed ones every day, their cruciforms dying and falling off within twenty-four hours, sacrificing immortality for . . . what? The Pax and Vatican did not understand and at that time neither did I.

But the Pax knew that it had to contain the virus. Troopers kicked in doors and crashed through windows every day and night, usually in the poorer, old-industrial sections of the planet-wide city. These people who had rejected the cruciform did not strongly resist – they would fight fiercely, but refused to kill if there was any way to avoid it. The Pax troopers did not mind killing to carry out their orders. Thousands of Aenea's followers died the true death – former immortals who would never see resurrection again – and tens of thousands were taken into custody and sent to detention centers, where they were placed into cryogenic fugue lockers so that their blood and philosophy could not contaminate others. But for every one of Aenea's adherents killed or arrested, dozens – hundreds – stayed safe in hiding, passing along Aenea's teachings, offering communion of their own changed blood, and providing largely nonviolent resistance at every turn. The great industrial machine that was Renaissance Vector had not yet broken down, but it was lurching and grinding in a way not seen in all the centuries since the Hegemony established the world as the Web's industrial nexus.

The Vatican sent more troops and debated as to how to respond.

On Tau Ceti Center, once the political center of the WorldWeb but now just a heavily populated and popular garden planet, the rebellion took a different shape. While offworld visitors had brought Aenea's anticruciform contagion, the bulk of the problem there for the Vatican centered on the

Archbishop Achilla Silvaski, a scheming woman who had taken over the role of governor and autocrat on TC^2 more than two centuries earlier. It was Archbishop Silvaski who had attempted to overthrow the reelection of the permanent pope through intrigue among the cardinals and now, having failed at that, she simply staged her own planet-wide version of the pre-Hegira Reformation, announcing that the Catholic Church on Tau Ceti Center would henceforth recognize her as pontiff and be forever separated from the 'corrupt' interstellar Church of the Pax. Because she had carefully formed an alliance with the local bishops in charge of resurrection ceremonies and machineries, she could control the Sacrament of Resurrection – and thus the local Church. More importantly, the Archbishop had wooed the local Pax military authorities with land, wealth, and power until an unprecedented event occurred – a Pax Fleet, Pax military coup that overthrew most senior officers in Tau Ceti System and replaced them with New Church advocates. No archangel starships were seized this way, but eighteen cruisers and forty-one torchships committed themselves to defending the New Church on TC^2 and its new pontiff.

Tens of thousands of faithful Church members on the planet protested. They were arrested, threatened with excommunication – i.e. immediate revocation of their cruciforms – and released on probation under the watchful eye of the Archbishop's – new pope's – New Church Security Force. Several priestly orders, most notably the Jesuits on Tau Ceti Center, refused to comply. Most were quietly arrested, excommunicated, and executed. Some hundreds escaped, however, and used their network to offer resistance to the new order – at first nonviolent, then increasingly severe. Many of the Jesuits had served as priest-officers in the Pax military before returning to civilian clerical life, and they used their military skills to create havoc in and around the planet.

Pope Urban XVI and his Pax Fleet advisors looked at their options. Already the crushing blow in the great Crusade against the Ousters had been delayed and derailed by Captain de Soya's continued harassing attacks, by the need to send Fleet units to a score of worlds to quell the Aenea contagion rebellions, by the logistical requirements for the ambush in T'ien Shan System, and now by this and other unrelated rebellions. Over Admiral Marusyn's advice to ignore the Archbishop's heresy until after other political/military goals were reached, Pope Urban XVI and his Secretary of State Lourdusamy decided to divert twenty archangels, thirty-two old-style cruisers, eight transport ships, and a hundred torchships to Tau Ceti System – although it would be many weeks of time-debt before the old Hawking-drive ships could arrive. Once formed up in that system, the task force's orders were to overcome all resistance by rebellious spacecraft, establish orbit around TC^2, demand the Archbishop's immediate surrender and the surrender of all those who supported her, and – failing compliance with that order – to slag as much of the planet as it took to destroy the New Church's infrastructure. After that, tens of thousands of Marines would drop to the planet to occupy the remaining urban centers and to reestablish the rule of the Pax and the Holy Mother Church.

On Mars, in Old Earth System, the rebellion had worsened, despite years of Pax bombardment from space and constant military incursions from orbit. Two standard months earlier, Governor Clare Palo and Archbishop Robeson had both died the true death in a nuclear suicide attack on their palace-in-exile on Phobos. The Pax response had been terrifying – asteroids diverted from the nearby belt and dropped on Mars, carpet plasma bombing, and nightly lance attacks that sliced through the new planetary dust storm kicked up by the asteroid bombardment like so many deadly searchlights crisscrossing the frozen desert. Deathbeams would have been more efficient, but the Pax Fleet planners wanted to make an example of Mars, and wanted it to be a visible example.

The results were not exactly what the Pax had hoped for. The Martian terraforming environment, already precarious after years of poor maintenance, collapsed. Breathable atmosphere on the world was now restricted to Hellas Basin and a few other low pockets. The oceans were gone, boiled away as the pressure dropped or frozen back in the poles and permafrost subcrust. The last large plants and trees died off until only the original brandy cactus and bradberry orchards were left clinging to life in the near vacuum. The dust storms would last for years, making Pax Marine patrols on the Red Planet all but impossible.

But the Martians, especially the militant Palestinian Martians, were adapted to such a life and ready for this contingency. They hunkered down, killed the Pax troopers when they landed, and waited. Templar missionaries among the other Martian colonies urged the final nanotech adaptation to the original planetary conditions. Thousands and thousands took the gamble, allowing the molecular machines to alter their bodies and DNA to the planet.

More disturbingly to the Vatican, space battles broke out as ships once belonging to the presumably defunct Martian War Machine came out of hiding in the distant Kuiper Belt and began a series of hit-and-run attacks on the Pax Fleet convoys in Old Earth System. The kill ratio in these attacks was five to one in favor of Pax Fleet, but the losses were unacceptable and the cost of maintaining the Mars operation was frightful.

Admiral Marusyn and the Joint Chiefs advised His Holiness to cut his losses and leave Old Earth System to fester for the time being. The Admiral assured the Pope that nothing would be allowed out of the system. He pointed out that there was nothing of real value in Old Earth System any longer, now that Mars was untenable. The Pope listened but refused to authorize the pullout. At each conference, Cardinal Lourdusamy stressed the symbolic importance of keeping Old Earth's system within the Pax. His Holiness decided to wait to make his decision. The hemorrhage of ships, men, money, and materiel went on.

On Mare Infinitus, the rebellion was old – based around the submarine smugglers, poachers, and those hundreds of thousands of stubborn indigenies who had always refused the cross – but stirred up anew now that the Aenea contagion had arrived. The great fishing zones were now all but off-limits to unescorted Pax fishing fleets. The automated fishing ships and isolated floating platforms were attacked and sunk. More and more of the deadly Lantern Mouth monsters were seen in shallower waters and Archbishop Jane Kelley was furious at the Pax authorities for their failure to stop the problem. When Bishop Melandriano counseled moderation, Kelley had him excommunicated. In turn, Melandriano declared the Southern Seas seceded from the Pax and Church's authority and thousands of the faithful followed the charismatic leader. The Vatican sent more Pax Fleet ships, but there was little they could do to settle the four-way surface and subsurface struggles between the rebels, the Archbishop's forces, the Bishop's forces, and the Lantern Mouths.

And in the midst of all this confusion and carnage, Aenea's message traveled with the speed of speech and secret communion.

Rebellion – both violent and spiritual – flared elsewhere: the worlds where Aenea had traveled – Ixion, Patawpha, Amritsar, and Groombridge Dyson D; on Tsintao-Hsishuang Panna where word of the roundup of non-Christians elsewhere created first panic and then grim resistance to all things Pax, on Deneb Drei where the Jamnu Republic declared the wearing of a cruciform cause for beheading; on Fuji where Aenea's message had been brought by renegede members of the Pax Mercantilus and where it spread like a planetary firestorm; on the desert world of Vitus-Gray-Balianus B where Aenea's teachings came via refugees from Sibiatu's Bitterness and combined with the realization that the Pax way of life would destroy their culture forever – the Amoiete Spectrum Helix people led the fight. The city of Keroa Tambat was liberated in the first month of fighting, and Pax Base Bombasinoe soon became a fortress under siege. Base Commander Solznykov screamed for help from Pax Fleet, but the Vatican and Pax Fleet commanders – preoccupied elsewhere – ordered him to be patient and threatened excommunication if Solznykov did not end the rebellion on his own.

Solznykov did so, but not in the way Pax Fleet or His Holiness would have countenanced: he arranged for a peace treaty with the Amoiete Spectrum Helix armies in which his Pax forces would enter the countryside only with the permission of the indigenies. In return, Pax Base Bombasino was allowed to continue its existence.

Solznykov, Colonel Vinara, and the other loyal Christians settled in to wait for Vatican and Pax Fleet retribution, but the Aenea-changed civilians were among the Spectrum Helix people who came to market at Bombasino, who met and ate and drank with the troopers, who moved among the dispirited Pax men and women and told their story, and who offered their communion. Many accepted.

This, of course, was the tiniest slice of events on the hundreds of worlds of the Pax that last, sad night I would ever spend on T'ien Shan. I did not guess at any of these events, of course, but if I had – if I had already mastered the skill and discipline of learning these things via the Void Which Binds – I still would not have cared.

Aenea had loved another man. They had been married. She must still be married . . . she had not mentioned divorce or death. She had had a child.

767

I do not know why my carelessness did not send me falling to my death those wild hours on the icy ridge east of Jo-kung and Hsuan-k'ung Ssu, but it did not. Eventually I came to my senses and returned via the ridgeline and the fixed rappelling ropes so that I could be back with Aenea by first light.

I loved her. She was my dear friend. I would give my life to protect her.

An opportunity to prove that would be offered within the day, its inevitability created by the events that unfolded shortly after my return to the Temple Hanging in Air and our departure to the east.

It was not that long after first light, in the old gompa beneath the Phallus Shiva now turned into Christian enclave, where John Domenico Cardinal Mustafa, Admiral Marget Wu, Father Farrell, Archbishop Breque, Father LeBlanc, Rhadamanth Nemes, and her two remaining siblings met in conference. In truth, it was the humans who met in conference, while Nemes and her clone sister and brother sat silently by the window looking out over the billowing cloudscapes around Otter Lake below the Shivling peak.

'And you are certain that the rogue ship *Raphael* is finished?' the Grand Inquisitor was saying.

'Absolutely,' said Admiral Wu. 'Although it destroyed seven of our archangel ships of the line before we slagged it.' She shook her head. 'De Soya was a brilliant tactician. It was the true work of the Evil One when he turned apostate.'

Father Farrell leaned over the polished bonsai-wood table. 'And there is no chance that de Soya or any of the others survived?'

Admiral Wu shrugged. 'It was a near-orbit battle,' she said. 'We let *Raphael* get within cislunar distance before springing our trap. Thousands of pieces of debris – mostly from our unfortunate ships – entered the atmosphere. None of our people appear to have survived – at least no beacons have been detected. If any of de Soya's people escaped, the chances are that their pods came down in the poisonous oceans.'

'Still . . .' began Archbishop Breque. He was a quiet man, cerebral and cautious.

Wu looked exhausted and irritated. 'Your Eminence,' she said briskly, addressing Breque but looking at Mustafa, 'we can decide the issue one way or the other if you allow us to send dropships, skimmers, and EMVs into the atmosphere.'

Breque blinked. Cardinal Mustafa shook his head. 'No,' he said, 'our orders are not to show a military presence until the Vatican commands the final step in our seizure of the girl.'

Wu smiled with apparent bitterness. 'Last night's battle just above the atmosphere must have made that order somewhat obsolete,' she said softly. 'Our military presence must have been rather impressive.'

'It was,' said Father LeBlanc. 'I have never seen anything like it.'

Admiral Wu spoke to Mustafa. 'Your Excellency, the people on this world have no energy weapons, no Hawking-drive detectors, no orbital defenses, no gravitonic detectors . . . hell, they don't have radar or a communications system as far as we can tell. We can send dropships or fighter aircraft into the atmosphere to search for survivors without them ever knowing. It has to be a lot less intrusive than last night's firefight and . . .'

'No,' said Cardinal Mustafa and there was no doubting the finality of his decision. The Grand Inquisitor pushed back his robe to glance at his chronometer. 'The Vatican courier drone should arrive any moment with final orders for the arrest of the contagion vector named Aenea. Nothing must complicate that.'

Father Farrell rubbed his lean cheeks. 'Regent Tokra called me this morning on the communicator channel we allocated him. It seems that their precious and precocious little Dalai Lama has gone missing . . .'

Breque and LeBlanc looked up in surprise.

'It doesn't matter,' said Cardinal Mustafa, obviously aware of the news. 'Nothing matters right now except receiving final go-ahead on this mission and arresting Aenea.' He looked at Admiral Wu. 'And you must tell your Swiss Guard and Marine officers that no harm can come to the young woman.'

Wu nodded wearily. She had been briefed and rebriefed for months. 'When do you think that the orders will come?' she asked the Cardinal.

Rhadamanth Nemes and her two siblings stood and walked toward the door. 'The time for waiting is over,' said Nemes with a thin-lipped smile. 'We will bring Aenea's head back to you.'

Cardinal Mustafa and the others were on their feet in an instant. 'Sit down!' bellowed the Grand Inquisitor. 'You have not been ordered to move.'

Nemes smiled and turned toward the door.

All of the clerics in the room were shouting. Archbishop Jean Daniel Breque crossed himself. Admiral Wu went for the flechette pistol in her holster.

Things then happened too quickly to perceive. The air seemed to blur. One instant, Nemes, Scylla, and Briareus were at the doorway eight meters away, the next instant they were gone and three shimmering chrome shapes stood among the black-and red-robed figures at the table.

Scylla intercepted Admiral Marget Wu before the woman could raise her flechette pistol. A chrome arm blurred. Wu's head tumbled across the polished tabletop. The headless body stood a few seconds, some random nerve impulse ordered the fingers of the right hand to close, and the flechette pistol fired, blowing apart the legs of the heavy table and splintering the stone floor in ten thousand places.

Father LeBlanc leaped between Briareus and Archbishop Breque. The blurred, silver shape disemboweled LeBlanc. Breque dropped his glasses and ran into the adjoining room. Suddenly Briareus was gone – leaving nothing but a soft implosion of air where the blurred shape had stood a second before. There was a short scream from the other room, cut off almost before it began.

Cardinal Mustafa backed away from Rhadamanth Nemes. She took one step forward for every step he took backward. The blurred field around her had dropped away, but she looked no more human or less menacing.

'Damn you for the foul thing you are,' the Cardinal said softly. 'Come ahead, I'm not afraid to die.'

Nemes raised one eyebrow. 'Of course not, Your Excellency. But would it change your mind if I tell you that we're throwing these bodies . . . and that head' – she gestured to where Marget Wu's eyes had just stopped blinking and now stared blindly – 'far out into the acid ocean, so that no resurrection will be possible?'

Cardinal Mustafa reached the wall and stopped. Nemes was only two paces in front of him. 'Why are you doing this?' he said, his voice firm.

Nemes shrugged. 'Our priorities diverge for the time being,' she said, 'Are you ready, Grand Inquisitor?'

Cardinal Mustafa crossed himself and said a hurried Act of Contrition.

Nemes smiled again, her right arm and right leg became shimmering silver things, and she stepped forward.

Mustafa watched in amazement. She did not kill him. With motions too quick to detect, she broke his left arm, shattered his right arm, kicked his legs out from under him – splintering both of them – and blinded him with two fingers that stopped just short of jabbing into his brain.

The roar of pain was without precedent for the Grand Inquisitor. Through it, he could hear her voice, still flat and lifeless. 'I know your doc-in-the-box in the dropship or on the *Jibril* will fix you up,' she said. 'We've buzzed them. They'll be here in a few minutes. When you see the Pope and his parasites, tell them that those to whom I must report did not want the girl alive. Our apologies, but her death is necessary. And tell them to be careful in the future not to act without the consent of *all* elements of the Core. Good-bye, Your Excellency. I hope that the doc on the *Jibril* can grow you new eyes. What we are about to do will be worth seeing.'

Mustafa heard footsteps, the door sliding, and then silence except for the sound of someone screaming in terrible pain. It took him several minutes to realize that it was he who was screaming.

When I returned to the Temple Hanging in Air, first light was seeping through the fog but the morning remained dark, drizzly, and cold. I had finally sobered up enough from my distraught and distracted state to take greater care while rappelling down the fixed lines, and it was good that I had – several times the brakes on the rappel gear slipped on the ice-shrouded rope and I would have fallen to my death if the safety lines had not arrested me.

Aenea was awake, dressed, and ready to leave when I arrived. She had on her thermal anorak, climbing harness, and climbing boots. A. Bettik and Lhomo Dondrub were dressed similarly, and both men carried long, heavy-looking, nylon-wrapped packages over their shoulders. They were going with us. Others were there to say good-bye – Theo, Rachel, the Dorje Phamo, the Dalai Lama, George Tsarong, Jigme Norbu – and they seemed sad and anxious. Aenea looked tired; I was sure that she had not slept either.

We made a tired-looking pair of adventurers. Lhomo walked over and handed me one of the long, nylon-wrapped bundles. It was heavy, but I shouldered it without question or complaint. I grabbed the rest of my own gear, answered Lhomo's questions about the condition of the ropes to the ridgeline – everyone evidently thought that I had unselfishly reconnoitered our route – and stepped back to look at my friend and beloved. When she gave me a searching look, I answered with a nod. *It's all right. I'm all right. I'm ready to go. We'll talk about it later.*

Theo was crying. I was aware that this was an important parting that we might not see one another again despite Aenea's assurances to the other two women that everyone would be reunited before nightfall – but I was too emotionally numbed and worn out to react to it. I stepped away from the group for a moment to take deep breaths and focus my attention. It was probable that I would need all of my wits and alertness in the next few hours just to survive. *The problem with being passionately in love*, I thought, *is that it deprives you of too much sleep.*

We left by the east platform, moved in a fast trot down the icy ledge toward the fissure, passed the ropes I'd just descended, and reached the fissure without incident. The bonsai trees and fell fields looked ancient and unreal in the shifting ice fog, the dark limbs and branches dripping on our heads when they suddenly loomed out of the mist. The streams and water-falls sounded louder than I remembered as the torrent slid over the last overhang into the void to our left.

There were old, less reliable fixed ropes on the easternmost and highest folds of the fissure, and Lhomo led the way up these, followed by Aenea, then A. Bettik, and finally me. I noticed that our android friend was climb-ing as quickly and competently as he always did, despite the missing left hand. Once on the upper ridgeline, we were beyond the farthest point of my nighttime travels – the fissure acted as a barrier to ridgeline travel the way I had gone. Now the difficulty began in earnest as we followed the narrowest of paths – worn ledges, rock outcroppings, the occasional icefield, scree slopes – on the south side of the cliff face. The ridgeline above us was all serac of wet, heavy snow and icy overhang, impossible to travel on. We moved silently, not even whispering, aware that the slightest noise could trigger an avalanche that would sweep us off these ten-centimeter ledges in a second. Finally, when the going got even tougher, we roped up – running the line through carabiners and attaching a doubled line to our web-sling harnesses – so that now if one fell he or she would be caught, or we would all go over. With Lhomo leading as strongly as ever, stepping confidently over foggy voids and icy crevasses that I would hesitate to attempt, I think that we all felt better about being connected.

I still did not know our destination. I did know that the great ridge that ran east from K'un Lun past Jo-kung would run out in a few more kilo-meters, dropping suddenly and dramatically into the poisonous clouds several klicks below. During certain weeks in the spring, the tides and vagaries of the ocean and clouds dropped the poisonous vapors low enough that the ridge emerged again, allowing supply caravans, pilgrims, monks, traders, and the simply curious to make their way east from the Middle Kingdom to T'ai Shan, the Great Peak of the Middle Kingdom, and the most inaccessible habitable point on the planet. The monks who lived on T'ai Shan, it was said, never returned to the Middle Kingdom or the rest of the Mountains of Heaven – for untold generations they had dedicated their lives to the mysterious tombs, gompas, ceremonies, and temples on that most holy of peaks. Now, as the weather worsened for us, I realized that if we started descending, we would not know when we left the roiling monsoon clouds and entered the roiling vaporous clouds until the poison air killed us.

We did not descend. After several hours of all but silent travel, we reached the precipice at the eastern boundary of the Middle Kingdom. The mountain of T'ai Shan was not visible, of course – even with the clouds having cleared a bit, little was visible except for the wet cliff face ahead of us and the twisting fog and cloud patterns all around.

There was a wide ledge here at the eastern edge of the world, and we sat on it gratefully as we dug cold handmeals out of our packs and drank from our water bottles. The tiny, succulent plants that carpeted this steep fell field were becoming tumescent as they gorged themselves on the first moisture of the monsoon months.

After we ate and drank, Lhomo and A. Bettik began opening our three heavy bundles. Aenea zipped open her own pack, which looked heavier than the duffels we men had carried. It did not surprise me what was wrapped in these three parcels – nylon, alloy struts and frames, rigging, and in Aenea's packet, more of the same as well as the two skinsuits and rebreathers that I'd brought with me from the ship and all but forgotten.

I sighed and looked to the east. 'So we're going to try to make T'ai Shan,' I said.

'Yes,' said Aenea. She began stripping out of her clothes.

A. Bettik and Lhomo looked away, but I felt my heart pound with anger at the thought of other men seeing my lover naked. I controlled myself, laid out the other skinsuit and began peeling out of my own clothes, folding them into my heavy pack as I doffed each layer. The air was cold and the fog clammy on my skin.

Lhomo and A. Bettik were assembling the parawings as Aenea and I dressed – the skinsuits were just that, almost literally a second skin, but the harness and rigging for the rebreathers allowed us some modesty. The cowl went over my head tighter than a scuba headpiece, folding my ears flat against my head. Only the filters there allowed sound to be transmitted: they would pick up the comthread transmissions once we were effectively out of real air.

Lhomo and A. Bettik had assembled four parawings from the parts we had transported. As if answering my unasked question, Lhomo said, 'I can only show you the thermals and make sure you reach the jet stream. I can't survive at that altitude. And I do not want to go to T'ai Shan when there is little chance of returning.'

Aenea touched the powerful man's arm. 'We are grateful beyond words that you will guide us to the jet stream.'

The bold flyer actually blushed.

'What about A. Bettik?' I asked and then, realizing that I was talking about our friend as if he weren't there, I turned to the android and said, 'What about you? There's no skinsuit or rebreather for you.'

A. Bettik smiled. I had always thought that his rare smiles were the wisest things I had ever seen on a human countenance – even if the blue-skinned man was not technically human.

'You forget, M. Endymion,' he said, 'I was designed to suffer a bit more abuse than the average human body.'

'But the distance . . .' I began. T'ai Shan was more than a hundred kilometers east and even if we reached the jet stream, that would be almost an hour of rarified air . . . far too thin to breathe.

A. Bettik fastened the last rigging to his parawing – a pretty thing with a great blue delta wingspan almost ten meters across – and said, 'If we are lucky enough to make the distance, I will survive it.'

I nodded and made to get into the rigging of my own kite then, not asking any more questions, not looking at Aenea, not asking her why the four of us were risking our lives this way, when suddenly my friend was at my elbow.

'Thank you, Raul,' she said, loudly enough for all to hear. 'You do these things for me out of love and friendship. I thank you from the bottom of my heart.'

I made some gesture, suddenly unable to speak, embarrassed that she was thanking me when the other two were ready to leap into the void for her as well. But she was not finished speaking.

'I love you, Raul,' said Aenea, leaning on her tiptoes to kiss me on the lips. She rocked back and looked at me, her dark eyes fathomless. 'I love you, Raul Endymion. I always have. I always will.'

I stood, bewildered and overwhelmed, as we all locked in to our parawing rigs and stood at the ultimate edge of nothing. Lhomo was the last to clip on. He moved from A. Bettik to Aenea to me, checking our riggings, checking every fastened nut, bolt, tension clip, and instaweld of our kites. Satisfied, he nodded respectfully toward A. Bettik, clipped into his own red-winged rig with a speed born of infinite practice and discipline, and moved to the edge of the cliff. Even the succulents did not grow in this last meter stretch, as if terrified of the drop. I knew that I was. The last rocky ledge was steeply pitched and slick from the rain. The fog had closed in again.

'It will be hard to see each other in this soup,' said Lhomo. 'Keep circling to the left. Stay within five meters of the one in front of you. Same order as our march – Aenea after me in your yellow wing, then the blue man in blue, then you, Raul, in the green. Our greatest risk is losing one another in the clouds.'

Aenea nodded tersely. 'I'll stay close to your wing.'

Lhomo looked at me. 'You and Aenea can communicate via your skinsuit comthreads, but that will not help you find one another. A. Bettik and I will communicate via hand signals. Be careful. Do not lose sight of the blue man's kite. If you do, keep circling up counterclockwise until you clear the cloud tops and then try to regroup with us. Keep the circles tight while inside the clouds. If you loosen them – which is the tendency with parawings – you will strike the cliff.'

My mouth was dry as I nodded.

'All right,' said Lhomo. 'I will see you all above the clouds. Then I will find the thermals for you, read the ridge lift, and get you to the jet stream. I will signal like this' – he made a fist and pumped his arm twice – 'when I am leaving you. Keep climbing and circling. Get as deeply into the stream as you can. Rise into the upper atmospheric winds until you think that they will tear your wing apart from above you. Perhaps they will. But you will have no chance to reach T'ai Shan unless you get into the center of the stream. It is a hundred and eleven klicks to the first shoulder of the Great Peak where you can breathe true air.'

We all nodded.

'May the Buddha smile on our folly today,' said Lhomo. He seemed very happy.

'Amen,' said Aenea.

Lhomo turned without another word and leaped out over the cliff's edge. Aenea followed a second later. A. Bettik leaned far forward in his harness, kicked off the ledge, and was swallowed up by clouds within seconds. I scurried to catch up. Suddenly there was no stone under my feet and I leaned forward until I was prone in the harness. Already I had lost sight of A. Bettik's blue wing. The swirling clouds confused and disoriented me. I pulled on the control bar, banking the hang glider as I had been taught, peering intently through the fog for a glimpse of any of the other kites. Nothing. Belatedly I realized that I had held the turn for too long. Or had I released it too soon? I leveled off the wing, feeling thermals pushing at the fabric above me but not being able to tell if I was actually gaining altitude because I was blind. The fog was like some terrible snowblindness. Without thinking, I shouted, hoping one of the others would shout back and orient me. A man's shout hurtled back to me from just a few meters dead ahead.

It was my own voice, echoing off the vertical rock of the cliff face I was about to strike.

Nemes, Scylla, and Briareus move south on foot from the Pax Enclave at the Phallus of Shiva. The sun is high and there are thick clouds to the east. To travel from the Pax Enclave to the Winter Palace at Potala, the old High Way southwest along me Koko Nor Ridge had been repaired and widened, and a special cable platform had been built where the ten-klick wire ran from Koko Nor southwest to the palace. A palanquin specially rigged for the Pax diplomats now hangs from pulleys at the new platform. Nemes pushes to the front of the line and steps into it, ignoring the stares from the little people in thick *chubas* who mill on the stairway and platform. When her clone-siblings are in the cage, she releases the two brakes and sends the palanquin hurtling across the gap. Dark clouds rise above the palace mountain.

A squad of twenty Palace Guard carrying halberds and crude energy lances greets them at the Great Terrace Steps on the west side of Yellow Hat Ridge where the palace drops away down the east face for several vertical kilometers. The captain of the Guard is deferential. 'You must wait here until we bring an honor guard to escort you into the palace, Most Honored Guests,' he says, bowing.

'We prefer to go in alone,' says Nemes.

The twenty Guardsmen crouch with lances at port arms. They make a solid wall of iron, zygoat fur, silk, and elaborate helmets. The Guard captain bows lower. 'I apologize for my unworthiness, Most Honored Guests, but it is not possible to enter the Winter Palace without an invitation and an honor guard. Both will be here in a minute. If you will be so kind as to wait in the shade under the pagoda roof here, Honored Guests, a personage of the proper rank to greet you will arrive in only a moment.'

Nemes nods. 'Kill them,' she says to Scylla and Briareus and walks forward into the palace as her siblings phase-shift.

They shift down during the long walk through the many-leveled palace, shifting into fast time only to kill guards and servants. When they exit by the main steps and approach the Pargo Kaling, the great Western Gate on this side of the Kyi Chu Bridge, they find Regent Reting Tokra blocking the way with five hundred of his finest Palace Guard troops. A few of these elite fighters carry swords and pikes, but most hold crossbows, slug rifles, crude energy weapons, and railguns.

'Commander Nemes,' says Tokra, lowering his head slightly but not bowing so much as to lose eye contact with the woman in front of him. 'We have heard what you did at Shivling. You can go no farther.' Tokra nods at someone high up in the gleaming eyes on the Pargo Kaling tower and the black chrome bridge of Kyi Chu slides silently back into the mountain. Only the great suspension cables remain far above, ringed about with razor wire and frictionless gel.

Nemes smiles. 'What are you doing, Tokra?'

'His Holiness has gone to Hsuan-k'ung Ssu,' says the thin-faced Regent. 'I know why you travel that way. You cannot be allowed to harm His Holiness the Dalai Lama.'

Rhadamanth Nemes shows more of her small teeth. 'What are you talking about, Tokra? You sold out your dear little boy-god to the Pax secret service for thirty pieces of silver. Are we bartering here for more of your stupid six-sided coins?'

The Regent shakes his head. 'The agreement with the Pax was that His Holiness would never be hurt. But you . . .'

'We want the girl's head,' says Nemes. 'Not your boy lama's. Get your men out of our way or lose them.'

Regent Tokra turns and barks an order at his row upon row of soldiers. The men's faces are grim as they raise their weapons to their shoulders. The mass of them blocks the way to the bridge, even though the roadway of the bridge is no longer there. Dark clouds boil in the chasm.

'Kill them all,' says Nemes, phase-shifting.

Lhomo had trained us all in the hang-glider controls, but I had never had the opportunity to fly one before. Now, as the cliff rose out of the fog in front of me, I had to do the correct thing immediately or die.

The kite was controlled by manipulating the control bar that hung in front of me as I dangled in my harness, and I leaned as far left and put as much weight on it as the rigging allowed. The parawing banked, but not steeply enough, I realized at once. The kite was going to intercept the rock wall a meter or two away from the outer apex of its arc. There was another set of controls – handle grips that spilled air from the dorsal surface at the leading edge of each side of the dorsal wing – but these were dangerous and tricky and for emergency use only.

I could see the lichen on the approaching rock wall. This was an emergency.

I pulled hard on the left panic handle, the nylon on the left side of the parawing opened like a slit purse, the right wing – still catching the strong ridge lift here – banked up steeply, the parawing turned almost upside down with its useless left wing spilling air like so much empty aluminum frame, my legs were flung out sideways as the kite threatened to stall and plummet into the rocks, my boots actually brushed stone and lichen, and then the wing was falling almost straight down, I released the left handle, the active-memory fabric on the left leading surface healed itself in an instant, and I was flying again – although in a near vertical dive.

The strong thermals rising along the cliff face struck the kite like a rising elevator and I was slammed upward, the control bar swinging back against my upper chest hard enough to knock the wind out of me, and the para-wing swooped, climbed, and tried to do a lazy loop with a radius of sixty or seventy meters. I found myself hanging almost upside down again, but this time with the kite and controls beneath me and the rock wall dead ahead again.

This was no good. I would conclude the loop on the cliff wall. I yanked the right panic handle, spilled lift, tumbled sideways in a sickening drop, sealed the wing, and tugged handles and control bar while shifting my weight wildly to establish balance and control. The clouds had parted enough for me to see the cliff twenty or thirty meters to my right as I fought the thermals and the kite itself for a clean line.

Then I was leveled and flying the contraption, spiraling around to my left again, but carefully this time – ever so carefully – thankful for the break in the clouds that allowed me to judge my distance from the cliff and leaning hard left on the control bar. Suddenly a whisper in my ear said, 'Wow! That was fun to watch. Do it again!'

I jumped at the voice in my ear and then looked up and behind me. The bright yellow triangle of Aenea's parawing circled above me, the clouds close above it like a gray ceiling.

'No thanks,' I said, allowing the comthreads on the throat of my skinsuit to pick up the subvocals. 'I guess I'm through showing off.' I glanced up at her again. 'Why are you here? Where's A. Bettik?'

'We rendezvoused above the clouds, didn't see you, and I came down to find you,' Aenea said simply, her comthreaded voice soft in my ear.

I felt a surge of nausea – more from the thought of her risking everything to do that than from the violent aerobatics of a moment earlier. 'I'm all right,' I said gruffly. 'Just had to get the feel of the ridge lift.'

'Yeah,' said Aenea. 'It's tricky. Why don't you follow me up?'

I did so, not allowing my pride to get in the way of survival. It was difficult to keep her yellow wing in sight with the shifting fog, but easier than flying blind near this cliff. She seemed to sense exactly where the rock wall was, cutting our circle within five meters of it – catching the strong center of the thermals there – but never coming too close or swinging too wide.

Within minutes we came out of the clouds. I admit that the experience took my breath away – first a slow brightening, then a rush of sunlight, then rising above the cloud level like a swimmer emerging from a white sea, then squinting into the bright light within the blinding freedom of blue sky and a seemingly infinite view on all sides.

Only the highest peaks and ridgelines were visible above the ocean of clouds: T'ai Shan gleaming cold and icy white so far to our east, Heng Shan about equidistant to the north, our ridgeline from Jo-kung rising like a razor's edge just above the tides of cloud running back to the west, K'un Lun Ridge a distant wall running northwest to southeast, and far, far away near the edge of the world, the brilliant summits of Chomo Lori, Mt Parnassus, Kangchengjunga, Mt Koya, Mt Kalais, and others I could not identify from this angle. There was a glimmer of sunlight on something tall beyond distant Phari Ridge, and I thought this might be the Potala or the lesser Shivling. I quit gawking and turned my attention back to our attempt to gain altitude.

A. Bettik circled close by and gave me a thumbs-up. I returned the signal and looked up to see Lhomo gesturing fifty meters above us: *Close up. Keep your circles tight. Follow me.*

We did that, Aenea easily climbing to her wingman position behind Lhomo, A. Bettik's blue kite circling across the climb circle from her, and me bringing up the rear fifteen meters below and fifty meters across the circle from the android.

Lhomo seemed to know exactly where the thermals were – sometimes we circled farther back west, caught the lift, and opened our circles to move east again. Sometimes we seemed to circle without gaining altitude, but then I would look north to Heng Shan and sense that we had covered another several hundred meters upward. Slowly we climbed and slowly we circled east, although T'ai Shan must still have been eighty or ninety klicks away.

It grew colder and harder to breathe. I sealed the last bit of osmosis mask and inhaled pure O_2 as we climbed. The skinsuit tightened around me, acting as a pressure suit and thermsuit all in one. I could see Lhomo shivering in his zygoat *chuba* and heavy mittens. There was ice on A. Bettik's bare forearm. And still we circled and rose. The sky darkened and the view grew more unbelievable – distant Nanda Devi in the southwest, Helgafell in the even more distant southeast, and Harney Peak far beyond the Shivling all coming into sight above the curve of the planet.

Finally Lhomo had had enough. A moment earlier I had unsealed the clear osmosis mask on my hood to see how thick the air was, tried to inhale what felt like hard vacuum, and quickly resealed the membrane. I could not imagine how Lhomo managed to breathe, think, and function at this altitude. Now he signaled us to keep circling higher on the thermal he had been working, gave us the ancient 'good luck' sign of the circled thumb and forefinger, and then spilled the thin air out of his delta kite to drop away like a hurtling Thomas hawk. Within seconds, the red delta was several thousand meters below us and swooping toward the ridgeline to the west.

We continued circling and climbing, occasionally losing the lift for a moment, but then finding it again. We were being blown eastward by the lower edges of the jet stream, but we followed Lhomo's final advice and resisted the temptation to turn toward our destination; we did not have enough altitude or tailwind yet to make the eighty-kilometer voyage.

Encountering the jet stream was like suddenly entering a whitewater rapids in a kayak. Aenea's kite found the edge of it first, and I watched the yellow fabric vibrate as if in a powerful gale, then the aluminum superstructure flex wildly. Then A. Bettik and I were into it and it was everything we could do to hold ourselves horizontal in the swinging harness behind the control bar and continue circling for altitude.

'It's hard,' came Aenea's voice in my ear. 'It wants to tear loose and head east.'

'We can't,' I gasped, pulling the parawing into the headwind again and being thrown higher in one great vertical lift ride.

'I know,' came Aenea's strained voice. I was a hundred meters away and below her now, but I could see her small form wrestling with the control bar, her legs straight, her small feet pointed backward like a cliff diver's.

I peered around. The brilliant sun was haloed by ice crystals. The ridgelines were almost invisible so far below, the summits of the highest peaks now klicks beneath us. 'How is A. Bettik doing?' asked Aenea.

I twisted and strained to see. The android was circling above me. His eyes appeared to be closed, but I could see him making adjustments to the control bar. His blue flesh gleamed with frost. 'All right, I think,' I said. 'Aenea?'

'Yes?'

'Is there any chance of the Pax at Shivling or in orbit picking up our comthread broadcasts?' The com unit/diskey journal was in my pocket, but we had decided never to use it until it was time to call the ship. It would be ironic if we were captured or killed because of using these skinsuit communicators.

'No chance,' gasped Aenea. Even with the osmosis masks and the rebreather matrix woven into the skinsuits, the air was thin and cold. 'The comthreads are very short range. Half a klick at most.'

'Then stay close,' I said and concentrated on gaining a few hundred more meters before the almost silent hurricane that was buffeting me sent the kite screaming off to the east.

Another few minutes and we could no longer resist the powerful current in this river of air. The thermal did not lessen, it just seemed to die away completely, and then we were at the mercy of the jet stream.

'Let's go!' shouted Aenea, forgetting that her slightest whisper was audible in my hearpatch.

I could see A. Bettik open his eyes and give me a thumbs-up. At the same instant, my own parawing peeled off the thermal and was swept away to the east. Even with the diminished sound, we seemed to be roaring through the air at a speed so incredible that it was audible. Aenea's yellow delta streaked east like a crossbow dart. A. Bettik's blue followed. I wrestled with the controls, realized that I did not have the strength to change course one degree, and simply held on while we rifled east and down in the pounding, flowing river of air. T'ai Shan gleamed ahead of us, but we were losing altitude quickly now and the mountain was still very far away. Kilometers beneath us, beneath the monsoon sea of white cloudtops, the greenish phosgene clouds of the acid world ocean churned away unseen but waiting.

The Pax authorities in T'ien Shan System were confused.

When Captain Wolmak in the *Jibril* received the strange pulsed alarm signal from the Pax Enclave at Shivling, he tried hailing Cardinal Mustafa and the others but received no answer. Within minutes he had dispatched a combat dropship with two dozen Pax Marines, including three medics.

The tightline report uplink was confusing. The conference room at their enclave gompa was a gory mess. Human blood and viscera were splashed everywhere, but the only body remaining was that of the Grand Inquisitor, who had been crippled and blinded. They DNA-typed the largest arterial spray and found it to be that of Father Farrell. Other pools of blood reportedly belonged to Archbishop Breque and his aide, LeBlanc. But no bodies. No cruciforms. The medics reported that Cardinal Mustafa was comatose, in deep shock, and near death; they stabilized him as best they could using only their fieldkits and asked for orders. Should they let the Grand Inquisitor die and be resurrected, or get him to the dropship doc-in-the-box and try to save him, knowing that it would be several days before he could regain consciousness and describe the attack? Or the medic could get him to life support, use drugs to bring the Cardinal out of the coma, and interrogate him within minutes – all the while with the patient under exquisite pain and on the verge of death.

Wolmak ordered them to wait and tightbeamed Admiral Lempriere, the task force commander. Out in the T'ien Shan System, many AUs distant, the forty-some ships that had come through the battle with *Raphael* were rescuing survivors from the terminally damaged archangels and awaiting the arrival of the papal drone and the TechnoCore robot ship that would be putting the planet's population in suspended animation. Neither had arrived. Lempriere was closer, four light-minutes away, and the tight-beam would take that long to reach him and bring him up to speed, but Wolmak felt he had no other choice. He waited while his message burned out-system.

Aboard the flagship *Raguel*, Lempriere found himself in a ticklish situation, with only minutes to decide about Mustafa. If he allowed the Grand Inquisitor to die, it was likely that a two-day resurrection would be successful. The Cardinal would suffer little pain. But the cause of the attack – Shrike, indigenies, the Aenea monster's disciples, Ousters – might remain a mystery until then. Lempriere took ten seconds to decide, but it was a four-minute tightbeam delay out and back.

'Have the medics stabilize him,' he tightbeamed Wolmak on the *Jibril* in orbit around the mountain planet. 'Get him to dropship life support. Bring him out of it. Interrogate him. When we know enough, have the autosurgeon give a prognosis. If it's faster to resurrect him, let him die.'

'Aye-aye, sir,' said Wolmak four minutes later, and passed word along to the Marines.

Meanwhile, the Marines were widening their search, using EMV reaction paks to search the vertical cliffsides around the Phallus of Shiva. They deep-radared Khan Tso, the so-called Otter Lake, finding neither otters nor the bodies of the missing priests. There had been an honor guard of twelve Marines in the enclave with the Grand Inquisitor's party – plus the pilot of the dropship – but these men and women were also missing. Blood and viscera were found and DNA-typed – most of the missing thus accounted for – but their bodies were not found.

'Shall we spread the search to the Winter Palace?' questioned the Marine lieutenant in charge of the party. All of the Marines had specific orders not to disturb the locals – especially the Dalai Lama and his people – before the TechnoCore ship arrived to put the population asleep.

'Just a minute,' said Wolmak. He saw that Admiral Lempriere's monitor telltale was on. The com diskey on his command web was also blinking. *Jibril*'s intelligence officer down in the sensor bubble. 'Yes?'

'Captain, we've been visually monitoring the palace area. Something terrible has happened there.'

'What?' snapped Wolmak. It was not like any member of his crew to be so vague.

'We missed it, sir,' said the Intel officer. She was a young woman, but smart, Lempriere knew. 'We were using the optics to check the area around the Enclave. But look at this . . .'

Wolmak turned his head slightly to watch the holopit fill with an image, knowing that it was being tightbeamed out to the Admiral. The east side of the Winter Palace, Potala, as if seen from a few hundred meters above the Kyi Chu Bridge.

The roadway of the bridge was gone, retracted. But on the steps and terraces between the palace and the bridge, and on some of the narrow ledges in the chasm between the palace and the Drepung Monastery on the east side, were scores of bodies – hundreds of bodies – bloodied and dismembered.

'Dear Lord,' said Captain Wolmak and crossed himself.

'We've identified the head of Regent Tokra Reting there among the body parts,' came the Intel officer's calm voice.

'The *head*?' repeated Wolmak, realizing that his useless remark was being sent to Admiral Lempriere along with all the rest of this transmission. In four minutes, Admiral Lempriere would know that Wolmak made stupid comments. No matter. 'Anyone else important there?' he queried Intel.

'Negative, sir,' came the young officer's voice. 'But they're broadcasting on various radio frequencies now.'

Wolmak raised an eyebrow. So far, the Winter Palace had maintained radio and tightbeam silence. 'What are they saying?'

'It's in Mandarin and post-Hegira Tibetan, sir,' said the officer. But then, quickly, 'They're in a panic, Captain. The Dalai Lama is missing. So is the head of the boy lama's security team. General Surkhang Sewon Chempo, leader of the Palace Guard, is dead, sir . . . they've confirmed that his headless body was found there.'

Wolmak glanced at the clock. The tightbeam broadcast was halfway to the Admiral's ship. 'Who did this, Intel? The Shrike?'

'Don't know, sir. As I said, the lenses and cameras were elsewhere. We'll check the discs.'

'Do that,' said Wolmak. He could not wait any longer. He tightbeamed the Marine lieutenant. 'Get to the palace, Lieutenant. See what the hell is going on. I'm sending down five more dropships, combat EMVs, and a thopter gunship. Search for any sign of Archbishop Breque, Father Farrell, or Father LeBlanc. And the pilot and honor guard, of course.'

'Aye-aye, sir.'

The tightbeam link went green. The Admiral was receiving the latest transmission. Too late to wait for his command. Wolmak tightbeamed the two closest Pax ships – torchships just beyond the outer moon – and ordered them on battle alert and to drop into matching orbit with the *Jibril*. He might need the firepower. Wolmak had seen the Shrike's work before, and the thought of that creature suddenly appearing on his ship made his skin go cold. He tightbeamed Captain Samuels on the torchship HHS *Saint Bonaventure*. 'Carol,' he said to the startled captain's image, 'go tactical space, please.'

Wolmak jacked in and was standing in place above the gleaming cloud planet of T'ien Shan. Samuels suddenly appeared next to him in the starry darkness.

'Carol,' said Wolmak, 'something's going on down there. I think the Shrike may be loose again. If you suddenly lose transmission data from the *Jibril*, or we start screaming gibberish . . .'

'I'll launch three boats of Marines,' said Samuels.

'Negative,' said Wolmak. 'Slag the *Jibril*. Immediately.'

Captain Samuels blinked. So did the floating telltale that showed that

Admiral Lempriere's flagship was tightbeaming. Wolmak jacked out of tactical.

The message was short. 'I've spun the *Raguel* up for a jump in-system to just beyond the critical gravity well around T'ien Shan,' said Admiral Lempriere, his thin face grave.

Wolmak opened his mouth to protest to his superior, realized that a tightbeamed protest would arrive almost three minutes after the Hawking-drive jump was executed, and shut his mouth. A jump in-system like this was sickeningly dangerous – one chance in four, at least, of a disaster that would claim all hands – but he understood the Admiral's need to get to where the information was fresh and his commands could be executed immediately.

Dear Jesus, thought Wolmak, *the Grand Inquisitor crippled, the Archbishop and the others missing, the sodding Dalai Lama's palace looking like an anthill that's been kicked over. Goddamn that Shrike thing. Where's the papal courier probe with its command? Where's that Core ship we were promised? How can things get worse than this?*

'Captain?' It was the chief Marine medic on the expeditionary force, beaming from the dropship infirmary.

'Report.'

'Cardinal Mustafa is conscious, sir . . . still blind, of course . . . in terrible pain, but . . .'

'Put him on,' snapped Wolmak.

A terrible visage filled the holosphere. Captain Wolmak sensed others on the bridge shrinking back.

The Grand Inquisitor's face was still bloodied. His teeth were bright red as he screamed. His eye sockets were ragged and void, except for tendrils of torn tissue and rivulets of blood.

At first, Captain Wolmak could not discern the word from the shriek. But then he realized what the Cardinal was screaming.

'Nemes! Nemes! Nemes!'

The constructs called Nemes, Scylla, and Briareus continue eastward.

The three remain phase-shifted, oblivious to the staggering amounts of energy this consumes. The energy is sent from elsewhere. It is not their worry. All of their existence has led to this hour.

After the timeless interlude of slaughter under the Pargo Kaling Western Gate, Nemes leads the way up the tower and across the great metal cables holding the suspension bridge in place. The three jog through Drepung Marketplace, three motile figures moving through thickened, amber air, past human forms frozen in place. At Phari Marketplace, the thousands of shopping, browsing, laughing, arguing, jostling human statues make Nemes smile her thin-lipped smile. She could decapitate all of them and they would have had no warning of their destruction. But she has an objective.

At the Phari Ridge cableway juncture, the three shift down – friction on the cable would be a problem otherwise.

Scylla, the northern High Way, Nemes sends on the common band. *Briareus, the middle bridge. I will take the cableway.*

Her siblings nod, shimmer, and are gone. The cablemaster steps forward to protest Nemes's shoving in line ahead of scores of waiting cable passengers. It is a busy time of day.

Rhadamanth Nemes picks the cablemaster up and flings him off the platform. A dozen angry men and women shove toward her, shouting, bent on revenge.

Nemes leaps from the platform and grabs the cable. She has no pulley, no brakes, no climbing harness. She phase-shifts only the palms of her inhuman hands and hurtles down the cable toward K'un Lun Ridge. The angry mob behind her clip on to the cable and give chase – a dozen, two dozen, more. The cablemaster had been liked by many.

It takes Nemes half the usual transit time to cover the great abyss between Phari and K'un Lun ridges. She brakes sloppily on the approach and slams into the rock, phase-shifting at the last instant. Pulling herself out of the crumbling indentation on the cliff behind the landing ledge, she walks back to the cable.

Pulleys whine as the first of her pursuers careen down the last few hundred meters of wire. More spread out to the horizon, black beads on a thin string. Nemes smiles, phase-shifts both her hands, reaches high, and severs the cable.

She is surprised how few of the dozens of doomed men and women scream as they slide off the twisting, falling cable to their deaths.

Nemes jogs to the fixed ropes, climbs them freehand, and cuts all of them loose – ascent lines, rappel lines, safety lines, everything. Five armed members of the K'un Lun Constabulary from Hsi wang-mu confront her on the ridgeline just south of the slideway. She phase-shifts only her left forearm and swats them off into space.

Looking northwest, Nemes adjusts her infrared and telescopic vision and zooms in on the great swinging bonsai-bamboo bridge connecting the High Way promontories between Phari Ridge and K'un Lun Ridge. The bridge falls as she watches, the slats and vines and support cables writhing as they fall back to the western ridgeline, the lower reaches of the bridge dropping into phosgene clouds.

That's that, sends Briareus.

How many on it when it fell? queries Nemes.

Many. Briareus disconnects.

A second later, Scylla logs on. *Northern bridge down, I'm destroying the High Way as I go.*

Good, sends Nemes. *I'll see you in Jo-kung.*

The three shift down as they pass through the city fissure at Jo-kung. It is raining lightly, the clouds as thick as summer fog, Nemes's thin hair is plastered to her forehead and she notices that Scylla and Briareus have the same look. The crowd parts for them. The ledge road to the Temple Hanging in Air is empty.

Nemes is leading as they approach the final, short swinging bridge before the ledge below the stairway to the Temple. This had been the first artifact repaired by Aenea – a simple, twenty-meter swinging span above a narrow fissure between dolomite spires a thousand meters above the lower crags and cloudtops – and now the monsoon clouds billow beneath and around the dripping structure.

Invisible in the thick clouds, something stands on the cliff ledge at the other side of the bridge. Nemes shifts to thermal imaging and smiles when she sees that the tall shape radiates no heat whatsoever. She pings it with her forehead-generated radar and studies the image: three meters tall, thorns, bladed fingers on four oversized hands, a perfectly radar-reflective carapace, sharp blades on chest and forehead, no respiration, razor wire rising from the shoulders and spikes from the forehead.

Perfect, sends Nemes.

Perfect, agree Scylla and Briareus.

The figure at the other end of the dripping bridge makes no response.

We made it to the mountain with only a few meters to spare. Once we dropped out of the lower reaches of the jet stream, our descent was steady and irreversible. There were few thermals out above the cloud ocean and many downdrafts, and while we made the first half of the hundred-klick gap in a few minutes of thrilling acceleration, the second half was all heart-stopping descent – now certain that we would make it with room to spare, now more certain that we would drop into the clouds and never even see our deaths rising to surround us until the kite wings struck acid sea.

We did descend into the clouds, but these were the monsoon clouds, the water vapor clouds, the breathable clouds. The three of us flew as close as we could, blue delta, yellow delta, green delta, the metal and fabric of our parawings almost touching, more fearful of losing one another and dying alone than of striking one another and falling together.

Aenea and I had the comthreads, but we talked to each other just once during that suspenseful descent to the east. The fog had thickened, I caught the merest glimpses of her yellow wing to my left, and I was thinking, *She had a child . . . she married someone else . . . she* loved *someone else*, when I heard her voice on the hearpatch of my suit, 'Raul?'

'Yes, kiddo.'

'I love you, Raul.'

I hesitated a few heartbeats, but the emotional vacuum that had pulled me a moment earlier was swept away in the surge of affection for my young friend and lover. 'I love you, Aenea.' We swept lower through the murk. I thought that I could taste an acrid scent on the wind . . . the fringes of the phosgene clouds?

'Kiddo?'

'Yes, Raul.' Her voice was a whisper in my ears. We had both removed our osmosis masks, I knew . . . although they would have protected us from the phosgene. We did not know if A. Bettik could breathe the poison. If he could not, the unspoken plan between Aenea and me was to close our masks and hope that we could reach the edges of the mountain before we struck the acid sea, dragging the android up the slope and out of the poison air if we could. We both knew that it was a flimsy plan – the radar aboard the ship during my initial descent had shown me that most of the peaks and ridges dropped abruptly beneath the phosgene cloud layer and it would be only a matter of minutes between entering the poisonous clouds before we struck the sea anyway – but it was better to have a plan than to surrender to fate. In the meantime, we both had our masks up, breathing fresh air while we could.

'Kiddo,' I said, 'if you know that this isn't going to work . . . if you've seen what you think is . . .'

'My death?' she completed the sentence for me. I could not have said it aloud.

I nodded stupidly. She could not see me through the clouds between us.

'They're only possibilities, Raul,' she said softly. 'Although the one I know of with the greatest probability is not this. Don't worry, I wouldn't have asked you both to go with me if I thought this was . . . it.' I heard the humor in her voice through the tension.

'I know,' I said, glad that A. Bettik could not pick up this conversation. 'I wasn't thinking of that.' I had been thinking that perhaps she had known that the android and I would make it to the mountain, but she would not. I did not believe that now. As long as my fate was entwined with hers, I could accept about anything. 'I was just wondering why we were running again, kiddo,' I said. 'I'm sick of running away from the Pax.'

'So am I,' said Aenea. 'And trust me, Raul, that's not all we're doing here. Oh, shit!'

Hardly the quotable pronouncement from a messiah, but in a second I saw the reason for her shout. A rocky hillside had appeared twenty meters ahead of us, large boulders visible between scree slopes, sheer cliffs lower down.

A. Bettik led the way in, pulling up on his control bar at the last minute and dropping his legs from the stirrups of the rigging, using the kite like a parachute above him. He bounced twice on his boots and set the kite down quickly, snapping off his harness. Lhomo had shown us many times that it was important on dangerous and windy landing sites to separate yourself from the parawing quickly so that it did not drag you over some edge. And there was definitely an edge to be dragged over here.

Aenea landed next, me a few seconds later. I had the sloppiest of the three landings, bouncing high, dropping almost straight down, twisting my ankle on the small stones, and going to my knees while the parawing struck hard on a boulder above me, bending metal and rending fabric. The kite tried to tip over backward then, pulling me over the cliff's edge just as Lhomo had warned, but A. Bettik grabbed the left struts, Aenea seized the broken right spar a second later, and they stabilized it long enough for me to struggle out of my harness and hobble a few steps away from the wreckage, dragging my backpack with me.

Aenea knelt on the cold, wet rocks at my feet, loosening my boot and studying my ankle. 'I don't think it's sprained badly,' she said. 'It may swell a bit, but you should be able to walk on it all right.'

'Good,' I said stupidly, aware only of her bare hands on my bare ankle. Then I jumped a bit as she sprayed something cold from her medkit on the puffy flesh.

They both helped me to my feet, we gathered our gear, and the three of us started arm-in-arm up the slick slope toward where the clouds glowed more brightly.

We came up into the sunlight high on the sacred slopes of T'ai Shan. I had pulled off the skinsuit cowl and mask, but Aenea suggested that I keep the suit on. I pulled my therm jacket on over it to feel less naked, and I noticed that my friend did the same. A. Bettik was rubbing his arms and I saw that the high altitude cold had left his flesh chilled almost white.

'Are you all right?' I asked him.

'Fine, M. Endymion,' said the android. 'Although another few minutes at that altitude . . .'

I looked down at the clouds where we had folded the damaged kites and left them. 'I guess we're not getting off this hill with the parawings.'

'Correct,' said Aenea. 'Look.'

We had come out of the boulder fields and scree slopes to grassy high-lands between great cliffs, the succulent meadows crisscrossed with zygoat trails and stepping-stone paths. Glacial melt streams trickled over rocks but there were bridges made of stone slabs. A few distant herders had watched us impassively as we climbed higher. Now we had come around a switch-back below the great icefields and looked up at what could only be temples of white stone set on gray ramparts. The gleaming buildings – bright beneath the blue-white expanse of ice and snow slopes that stretched up and out of sight to the blue zenith – looked like altars. What Aenea had pointed out was a great white stone set next to the trail, with this poem carved in its smooth face:

> With what can I compare the Great Peak?
> Over the surrounding provinces, its blue-green hue never
>   dwindles from sight.
> Infused by the Shaper of Forms with the soaring power
>   of divinity,
> Shaded and sunlit, its slopes divide night from day.
> Breast heaving as I climb toward the clouds,
> Eyes straining to follow birds flying home,
> Someday I shall reach its peerless summit,
> And behold all mountains in a single glance.
> – Tu Fu, T'ang Dynasty, China, Old Earth

And so we entered Tai'an, the City of Peace. There on the slopes were the scores of temples, hundreds of shops, inns, and homes, countless small shrines, and a busy street filled with stalls, each covered by a bright canvas awning. The people here were lovely – that is a poor word, but the only proper one, I think – all with dark hair, bright eyes, gleaming teeth, healthy skin, and a pride and vigor to their carriage and step. Their clothes were silk and dyed cotton, bright but elegantly simple, and there were many, many monks in orange and red robes. The crowds would have been forgiven if they had stared – no one visits T'ai Shan during the monsoon months – but all the glances I saw were welcoming and easy. Indeed, many of the people in the street milled around, greeting Aenea by name and touching her hand or sleeve. I remembered then that she had visited the Great Peak before.

Aenea pointed out the great slab of white rock that covered a hillside above the City of Peace. On the polished face of that slab had been carved what she explained was the *Diamond Sutra* in huge Chinese characters: one of the principal works of Buddhist philosophy, she explained, it reminded the monk and passerby of the ultimate nature of reality as symbolized in the empty expanse of blue sky overhead. Aenea also pointed out the First Heavenly Gate at the edge of the city – a gigantic stone archway under a red pagoda roof with the first of the twenty-seven thousand steps starting up toward the Jade Summit.

Incredibly, we had been expected. In the great gompa at the center of the City of Peace, more than twelve hundred red-robed monks sat cross-legged in patient files, waiting for Aenea. The resident lama greeted Aenea with a low bow – she helped him to his feet and hugged the old man – and then A. Bettik and I were sitting at one side of the low, cushioned dais while Aenea briefly addressed the waiting multitude.

'I said last spring that I would return at this time,' she said softly, her voice perfectly clear in the great marble space, 'and it pleases my heart to see you all again. For those of you who took communion with me during my last visit, I know that you have discovered the truth of learning the language of the dead, of learning the language of the living, and – for some of you – of hearing the music of the spheres, and – soon, I promise you – of taking that first step.

'This day is a sad day in many ways, but our future is bright with optimism and change. I am honored that you have allowed me to be your teacher. I am honored that we have shared in our exploration of a universe that is rich beyond imagining.' She paused and looked at A. Bettik and me. 'These are my companions . . . my friend A. Bettik and my beloved, Raul Endymion. They have shared all hardships of my longest life's voyage with me, and they will share in today's pilgrimage. When we leave you, we will pass this day through the three Heavenly Gates, enter the Mouth of the Dragon, and – Buddha and the fates of chaos willing – shall visit the Princess of Azure Clouds and see the Temple of the Jade Emperor this day.'

Aenea paused again and looked at the shaven heads and bright, dark eyes. These were not religious fanatics, I saw, not mindless servants or self-punishing ascetics, but were, instead, row upon row of intelligent, questioning, alert young men and women. I say 'young', but among the fresh and youthful faces were many with gray beards and subtle wrinkles.

'My dear friend the Lama tells me that there are more now who wish to share in communion with the Void Which Binds this day,' said Aenea.

About one hundred of the monks in the front rows went to their knees.

Aenea nodded. 'So it shall be,' she said softly. The Lama brought flagons of wine and many simple bronze cups. Before filling the cups or lancing her finger for the drops of blood, Aenea said, 'But before you partake of this communion, I must remind you that this is a physical change, not a spiritual one. Your individual quest for God or Enlightenment must remain just that . . . your individual quest. This moment of change will not bring *satori* or salvation. It will bring only . . . change.'

My young friend held up one finger, the finger she was about to prick to draw blood. 'In the cells of my blood are unique DNA and RNA arrangements along with certain viral agents which will invade your body, starting through the digestive lining of your stomachs and ending in every cell of your body. These invasive viruses are somatic . . . that is, they shall be passed along to your children.

'I have taught your teachers and they have taught you that these physical changes will allow you – after some training – to touch the Void Which Binds more directly, thus learning the language of the dead and of the living. Eventually, with much more experience and training, it may be possible for you to hear the music of the spheres and take a true step elsewhere.' She raised the finger higher. 'This is not metaphysics, my dear friends. This is a mutant viral agent. Be warned that you will never be able to wear the cruciform of the Pax, nor will your children nor their children's children. This basic change in the soul of your genes and chromosomes will ban you from that form of physical longevity forever.

'This communion will not offer you immortality, my dear friends. It insures that death will be our common end. I say again – I do not offer you eternal life or instant *satori*. If these are the things you seek most dearly, you must find them in your own religious searchings. I offer you only a deepening of the human experience of life and a connection to others – human or not – who have shared that commitment to living. There is no shame if you change your mind now. But there is duty, discomfort, and great danger to those who partake of this communion and, in so doing, become teachers themselves of the Void Which Binds, as well as fellow carriers of this new virus of human choice.'

Aenea waited, but none of the hundred monks moved or left. All remained kneeling, heads slightly bowed as if in contemplation.

'So be it,' said Aenea. 'I wish you all well.' And she pricked her finger, squeezing a droplet of blood into each prepared cup of wine held out by the elderly Lama.

It took only a few minutes for the hundred monks to pass the cups down their rows, each drinking but a drop. I rose from my cushion then, determined to go to the end of the row nearest me and partake of this communion, but Aenea beckoned me to her.

'Not yet, my dear,' she whispered in my ear, touching my shoulder.

I was tempted to argue – why was I being excluded from this? – but instead returned to my place next to A. Bettik. I leaned over and whispered to the android, 'You haven't done this so-called communion, have you?'

The blue man smiled. 'No, M. Endymion. And I never shall.'

I was about to ask why, but at that moment the communion ended, the twelve hundred monks rose to their feet, Aenea walked among them – chatting and touching hands – and I saw from her glance toward me over shaven heads that it was time for us to leave.

Nemes, Scylla, and Briareus regard the Shrike across the expanse of the suspension bridge, not phase-shifting for a moment, appreciating the real-time view of their enemy.

It's absurd, sends Briareus. *A child's bogeyman. All spikes and thorns and teeth. How silly.*

Tell, that to Gyges, responds Nemes. *Ready?*

Ready, sends Scylla.

Ready, sends Briareus.

The three phase-shift in unison. Nemes sees the air around them go thick and heavy, light becoming a sepia syrup, and she knows that even if the Shrike now does the obvious – cutting the suspension-bridge supports – it will make no difference: in fast time, it will take ages for the bridge to begin to fall . . . time enough for the trio to cross it a thousand times.

In single file, Nemes leading, they cross it now.

The Shrike does not change position. Its head does not move to follow them. Its red eyes gleam dully, like crimson glass reflecting the last bit of sunset.

Something's not right here, sends Briareus.

Quiet, commands Nemes. *Stay off the common band unless I open contact.* She is less than ten meters from the Shrike now and still the thing has not reacted. Nemes continues forward through thick air until she steps onto solid stone. Her clone sister follows, taking up position on Nemes's left. Briareus steps off the bridge and stands on Nemes's right. They are three meters in front of the Hyperion legend. It remains quiescent.

'Move out of the way or be destroyed.' Nemes shifts down long enough to speak to the chrome statue. 'Your day is long past. The girl is ours today.' The Shrike does not respond.

Destroy it, Nemes commands her siblings and phase-shifts.

The Shrike disappears, shifting through time.

Nemes blinks as the temporal shock waves ripple over and through her and then surveys the frozen surroundings with the full spectrum of her vision. There are a few human beings still here at the Temple Hanging in Air, but no Shrike.

Shift down, she commands and her siblings obey immediately. The world brightens, the air moves, and sound returns.

'Find her,' says Nemes.

In a full jog, Scylla moves to the Noble Eightfold Path axis of Wisdom and lopes up the staircase to the platform of Right Understanding. Briareus moves quickly to the axis of Morality and leaps to the pagoda of Right

Speech. Nemes takes the third stairway, the highest, toward the high pavilions of Right Mindfulness and Right Meditation. Her radar shows people in the highest structure. She arrives in a few seconds, scanning the buildings and cliff wall for concealed rooms or hiding places. Nothing. There is a young woman in the pavilion for Right Meditation and for an instant Nemes thinks that the search is over, but although she is about the same age as Aenea, it is not her. There are a few others in the elegant pagoda – a very old woman – Nemes recognizes her as the Thunderbolt Sow from the Dalai Lama's reception – the Dalai Lama's Chief Crier and Head of Security, Carl Linga William Eiheji, and the boy himself – the Dalai Lama.

'Where is she?' says Nemes. 'Where is the one who calls herself Aenea?'

Before any of the others can speak, the warrior Eiheji reaches into his cloak and hurls a dagger with lightning speed.

Nemes dodges it easily. Even without phase-shifting, her reactions are faster than most humans. But when Eiheji pulls a flechette pistol, Nemes shifts up, walks to the frozen man, encloses him in her shift field, and flings him out the open floor-to-ceiling window into the abyss. Of course, as soon as Eiheji leaves her field envelope, he seems to freeze in midair like some ungainly bird thrown from the nest, unable to fly but unwilling to fall.

Nemes turns back to the boy and shifts down. Behind her, Eiheji screams and plummets out of sight.

The Dalai Lama's jaw drops and his lips form an O. To him and the two women present, Eiheji had simply disappeared from next to them and reappeared in midair out the open shoji doors of the pavilion, as if he had chosen to teleport to his death.

'You can't . . .' begins the old Thunderbolt Sow.

'You are forbidden . . .' begins the Dalai Lama.

'You won't . . .' begins the woman who Nemes guesses is either Rachel or Theo, Aenea's compatriots.

Nemes says nothing. She shifts up, walks to the boy, folds her phase field around him, lifts him, and carries him to the open door.

Nemes! It is Briareus calling from the pavilion of Right Effort.

What?

Instead of verbalizing on the common band, Briareus uses the extra energy to send the full visual image. Looking frozen in the sepia air kilometers above them, fusion flame as solid as a blue pillar, a spaceship is descending.

Shift down, commands Nemes.

The monks and the old Lama packed us a lunch in a brown bag. They also gave A. Bettik one of the old-fashioned pressure suits of the kind I had seen only in the ancient spaceflight museum at Port Romance and tried to give two more to Aenea and me, but we showed them the skinsuits under our thermal jackets. The twelve hundred monks all turned out to wave us off through the First Heavenly Gate, and there must have been two or three thousand others pressing and craning to see us leave.

The great stairway was empty except for the three of us, climbing easily now, A. Bettik with his clear helmet folded back like a cowl, Aenea and me with our osmosis masks turned up. Each of the steps was seven meters wide, but shallow, and the first section was easy enough, with a wide terrace step every hundred steps. The steps were heated from within, so even as we moved into the region of perpetual ice and snow midway up T'ai Shan, the stairway was clear.

Within an hour we had reached the Second Heavenly Gate – a huge red pagoda with a fifteen-meter archway – and then we were climbing more steeply up the near-vertical fault line known as the Mouth of the Dragon. Here the winds picked up, the temperature dropped precipitously, and the air became dangerously thin. We had redonned our harnesses at the Second Heavenly Gate, and now we clipped on to one of the buckycarbon lines that ran along each side of the staircase, adjusting the pulley grip to act like a brake if we fell or were blown off the increasingly treacherous staircase. Within minutes, A. Bettik inflated his clear helmet and gave us a thumbs-up, while Aenea and I sealed our osmosis masks.

We kept climbing toward the South Gate of Heaven still a kilometer above us, while the world fell away all around. It was the second time in a few hours that such a sight had presented itself to us, but this time we took it all in every three hundred steps as we took a break, standing and wheezing and staring out at the early afternoon light illuminating the great peaks. Tai'an, the City of Peace, was invisble now, some fifteen thousand steps and several klicks below the icefields and rock walls through which we had climbed. I realized that the skinsuit comthreads gave us privacy once again, and said, 'How you doing, kiddo?'

'Tired,' said Aenea, but she leavened the comment with a smile from behind her clear mask.

'Can you tell me where we're headed?' I said.

'The Temple of the Jade Emperor,' said my friend. 'It's on the summit.'

'I guessed that,' I said, setting a foot down on the wide step, then raising the next foot to the next step. The stairway passed up and through a rock-and-ice overhang at this point. I knew that if I turned around to look down, vertigo might overcome me. This was infinitely worse than the paragliding. 'Can you tell me *why* we're climbing to the Temple of the Jade Emperor when everything is going to hell behind us?'

'How do you mean going to hell?' she said.

'I mean Nemes and her ilk are probably after us. The Pax definitely is going to make its move. Things are falling apart. And we're on pilgrimage.'

Aenea nodded. The wind was roaring now, as thin as it was, as we actually climbed into the jet stream. Each of us was moving forward and up with our heads bowed and our bodies arched, as if carrying a heavy load. I wondered what A. Bettik was thinking about.

'Why don't we just call the ship and get the hell out of here?' I said. 'If we're going to bail out, let's get it over with.'

I could see Aenea's dark eyes behind the mask that reflected the deepening blue sky. 'When we call the ship, there'll be two dozen Pax warships descending on us like harpy crows,' said Aenea. 'We can't do it until we're ready.'

I gestured up the steep staircase. 'And climbing this will make us ready?'

'I hope so,' she said softly. I could hear the rasp of her breathing through my hearpatches.

'What's up here, kiddo?'

We had reached the next three hundredth step. All three of us stopped and panted, too tired to appreciate the view. We had climbed into the edge of space. The sky was almost black. Several of the brighter stars were visible and I could see one of the smaller moons hurtling toward the zenith. *Or was it a Pax ship?*

'I don't *know* what we'll find, Raul,' said Aenea, her voice tired. 'I glimpse things . . . dream things again and again . . . but then I dream the same thing in a different way. I hate to talk about it until I see which reality presents itself.'

I nodded understanding, but I was lying. We began climbing again. 'Aenea?' I said.

'Yes, Raul.'

'Why don't you let me take . . . you know . . . communion?'

She made a face behind the osmosis mask. 'I hate calling it that.'

'I know, but that's what everyone calls it. But tell me this, at least . . . why don't you let me drink the wine?'

'It's not time for you to, Raul.'

'Why not?' I could feel the anger and frustration just below the surface again, mixing with the roiling current of love that I felt for this woman.

'You know the four steps I talk about . . .' she began.

'Learning the language of the dead, learning the language of the living . . . yeah, yeah, I know the four steps,' I said almost dismissively, setting my very real foot on a very physical marble step and taking another tired pace up the endless stairway.

I could see Aenea smile at my tone. 'Those things tend to . . . preoccupy the person first encountering them,' she said softly. 'I need your full attention right now. I need your *help*.'

That made sense to me. I reached over and touched her back through the thermal jacket and skinsuit material. A. Bettik looked across at us and nodded, as if approving of our contact. I reminded myself that he could not have heard our skinsuit transmissions.

'Aenea,' I said softly, 'are you the new messiah?'

I could hear her sigh. 'No, Raul. I never said I was a messiah. I never wanted to be a messiah. I'm just a tired young woman right now . . . I've got a pounding headache . . . and cramps . . . it's the first day of my period . . .'

She must have seen me blink in surprise or shock. *Well, hell*, I thought, *it's not every day that you get to confront the messiah only to hear that she's suffering from what the ancients used to call PMS.*

Aenea chuckled. 'I'm not the messiah, Raul. I was just chosen to be the One Who Teaches. And I'm trying to do it while . . . while I can.'

Something about her last sentence made my stomach knot in anxiety. 'Okay,' I said. We reached the three hundredth step and paused together, wheezing more heavily now. I looked up. Still no South Gate of Heaven visible. Even though it was midday, the sky was space black. A thousand stars burned. They barely twinkled. I realized that the hiss and roar of the jet stream had gone away. T'ai Shan was the highest peak on T'ien Shan, extending into the highest fringes of the atmosphere. If it had not been for our skinsuits, our eyes, eardrums, and lungs would have exploded like overinflated balloons. Our blood would be boiling. Our . . .

I tried to shift my thoughts on to something else.

'All right,' I said, 'but if you *were* the messiah, what would your message to humanity be?'

Aenea chuckled again, but I noticed that it was a reflective chuckle, not a derisive one. 'If *you* were a messiah,' she said between breaths, 'what would *your* message be?'

I laughed out loud. A. Bettik could not have heard the sound through the near vacuum separating us, but he must have seen me throw my head back, for he looked over quizzically. I waved at him and said to Aenea, 'I have no fucking clue.'

'Exactly,' said Aenea. 'When I was a kid . . . I mean a *little* kid, before I met you . . . and I knew that I'd have to go through some of this stuff . . . I was always wondering what message I was going to give humankind. Beyond the things I knew I'd have to teach, I mean. Something profound. Sort of a Sermon on the Mount.'

I looked around. There was no ice or snow at this terrible altitude. The clear, white steps rose through shelves of steep, black rock. 'Well,' I said, 'here's the mount.'

'Yeah,' said Aenea, and I could hear the fatigue once again.

'So what message did you come up with?' I said, more to keep her talking and distracted than to hear the answer. It had been a while since she and I had just talked.

I could see her smile. 'I kept working on it,' she said at last, 'trying to get it as short and important as the Sermon on the Mount. Then I realized that was no good – like Uncle Martin in his manic-poet period trying to outwrite Shakespeare – so I decided that my message would just be *shorter*.'

'How short?'

'I got my message down to thirty-five words. Too long. Then down to twenty-seven. Still too long. After a few years I had it down to ten. Still too long. Eventually I boiled it down to two words.'

'Two words?' I said. 'Which two?'

We had reached the next resting point . . . the seventieth or eightieth three hundredth step. We stopped gratefully and panted. I bent over to rest my skinsuit-gloved hands on my skinsuit-sheathed knees and concentrated on not throwing up. It was bad form to vomit in an osmosis mask. 'Which two?' I said again when I got some wind back and could hear the answer over my pounding heart and rasping lungs.

'Choose again,' said Aenea.

I considered that for a wheezing, panting moment. 'Choose again?' I said finally.

Aenea smiled. She had caught her wind and was actually looking down at the vertical view that I was afraid even to glance toward. She seemed to be enjoying it. I had the friendly urge to toss her off the mountain right then. Youth. It's intolerable sometimes.

'Choose again,' she said firmly.

'Care to elaborate on that?'

'No,' said Aenea. 'That's the whole idea. Keep it simple. But name a category and you get the idea.'

'Religion,' I said.

'Choose again,' said Aenea.

I laughed.

'I'm not being totally facetious here, Raul,' she said. We began climbing again. A. Bettik seemed lost in thought.

'I know, kiddo,' I said, although I had not been sure. 'Categories . . . ah . . . political systems.'

'Choose again.'

'You don't think that the Pax is the ultimate evolution of human society? It's brought interstellar peace, fairly good government, and . . . oh, yeah . . . immortality to its citizens.'

'It's time to choose again,' said Aenea. 'And speaking of our views of evolution . . .'

'What?'

'Choose again.'

'Choose what again?' I said. 'The direction of evolution?'

'No,' said Aenea. 'I mean our ideas about whether evolution *has* a direction. Most of our theories about evolution, for that matter.'

'So, do you or don't you agree with Pope Teilhard . . . the Hyperion pilgrim, Father Duré . . . when he said three centuries ago that Teilhard de Chardin had been right, that the universe was evolving toward consciousness and a conjunction with the Godhead? What he called the Omega Point?'

Aenea looked at me. 'You did do a lot of reading in the Taliesin library, didn't you?'

'Yeah.'

'No, I don't agree with Teilhard . . . either the original Jesuit or the short-lived Pope. My mother knew both Father Duré and the current pretender, Father Hoyt, you know.'

I blinked. I guess I had known that, but being reminded of the reality of that . . . of my friend's connections across the last three centuries . . . set me back a bit.

'Anyway,' continued Aenea, 'evolutionary science has really taken a bite in the butt over the last millennium. First the Core actively opposed investigation into it because of their fear of rapid human-designed genetic engineering – an explosion of our species into variant forms upon which the Core could not be parasitic. Then evolution and the biosciences were ignored by the Hegemony for centuries because of the Core's influence, and now the Pax is terrified of it.'

'Why?' I said.

'Why is the Pax terrified of biological and genetic research?'

'No,' I said, 'I think I understand that. The Core wants to keep human beings in the form and shape they're comfortable with and so does the Church. They define being human largely by counting arms, legs, and so forth. But I mean why redefine evolution? Why open up the argument about direction or nondirection and so forth? Doesn't the ancient theory hold up pretty well?'

'No,' said Aenea. We climbed several minutes in silence. Then she said, 'Except for mystics such as the original Teilhard, most early evolution scientists were very careful not to think of evolution in terms of "goals" or "purposes". That was religion, not science. Even the idea of a direction was anathema to the pre-Hegira scientists. They could only speak in terms of "tendencies" in evolution, sort of statistical quirks that kept recurring.'

'So?'

'So that was their shortsighted bias, just as Teilhard de Chardin's was his faith. There *are* directions in evolution.'

'How do you know?' I said softly, wondering if she would answer.

She answered quickly. 'Some of the data I saw before I was born,' she said, 'through my cybrid father's connections to the Core. The autonomous intelligences there have understood human evolution for many centuries, even while humans stayed ignorant. As hyper-hyperparasites, the AIs evolve only toward greater parasitism. They can only look at living things and their evolutionary curve and watch it . . . or try to stop it.'

'So what are the directions in evolution?' I asked. 'Toward greater intelligence? Toward some sort of godlike hive mind?' I was curious about her perception of the Lions and Tigers and Bears.

'Hive mind,' said Aenea. 'Ugghh. Can you conceive of anything more boring or distasteful?'

I said nothing. I had rather imagined that this was the direction of her teachings about learning the language of the dead and all that. I made a note to listen better the next time she taught.

'Almost everything interesting in the human experience is the result of an individual experiencing, experimenting, explaining, and sharing,' said my young friend. 'A hive mind would be the ancient television broadcasts, or life at the height of the datasphere . . . consensual idiocy.'

'Okay,' I said, still confused. 'What direction *does* evolution take?'

'Toward more life,' said Aenea. 'Life likes life. It's pretty much that simple. But more amazingly, nonlife likes life as well . . . and wants to get into it.'

'I don't understand,' I said.

Aenea nodded. 'Back on pre-Hegira Old Earth . . . in the 1920s . . . there was a geologist from a nation-state called Russia who understood this stuff. His name was Vladimir Vernadsky and he coined the word "biosphere", which – if things happen the way I think they will – should take on new meaning for both of us soon.'

'Why?' I said.

'You'll see, my friend,' said Aenea, touching my gloved hand with hers. 'Anyway, Vernadsky wrote in 1926 – "Atoms, once drawn into the torrent of living matter, do not readily leave it." '

I thought about this for a moment. I did not know much science – what I had picked up came from Grandam and the Taliesin library – but this made sense to me.

'It was phrased more scientifically twelve hundred years ago as Dollo's Law,' said Aenea. 'The essence of it is that evolution doesn't back up . . . exceptions like the Old Earth whale trying to become a fish again after living as a land mammal are just the rare exception. Life moves on . . . it constantly finds new niches to invade.'

'Yeah,' I said. 'Such as when humanity left Old Earth in its seedships and Hawking-drive vessels.'

'Not really,' said Aenea. 'First of all, we did that prematurely because of the influence of the Core and the fact that Old Earth was dying because of a black hole in its belly . . . also the Core's work. Secondly, because of the Hawking drive, we could jump through our arm of the galaxy to find Earth-like worlds high on the Solmev Scale . . . most of which we terraformed anyway and seeded with Old Earth life-forms, starting with soil bacteria and earthworms and moving up to the ducks you used to hunt in the Hyperion fens.'

I nodded. But I was thinking, *How else should we have done it as a species moving out into space? What's wrong with going to places that looked and smelled somewhat like home . . . especially when home wasn't going to be there to go back to?*

'There's something more interesting in Vernadsky's observations and Dollo's Law,' said Aenea.

'What's that, kiddo?' I was still thinking about ducks.

'Life doesn't retreat.'

'How so?' As soon as I asked the question I understood.

'Yeah,' said my friend, seeing my understanding. 'As soon as life gets a foothold somewhere, it stays. You name it . . . arctic cold, the Old Mars frozen desert, boiling hot springs, a sheer rockface such as here on T'ien Shan, even in autonomous intelligence programs . . . once life gets its proverbial foot in the door, it stays forever.'

'So what are the implications of that?' I said.

'Simply that left to its own devices . . . which are clever devices . . . life will someday fill the universe,' said Aenea. 'It will be a green galaxy to begin with, then off to our neighboring clusters and galaxies.'

'That's a disturbing thought,' I said.

She paused to look at me. 'Why, Raul? I think it's beautiful.'

'Green planets I've seen,' I said. 'A green atmosphere is imaginable, but weird.'

She smiled. 'It doesn't have to be just plants. Life adapts . . . birds, men and women in flying machines, you and me in paragliders, people adapted to flight . . .'

'That hasn't happened yet,' I said. 'But what I meant was, well, to have a green galaxy, people and animals and . . .'

'And living machines,' said Aenea. 'And androids . . . artificial life of a thousand forms . . .'

'Yeah, people, animals, machines, androids, whatever . . . would have to adapt to space . . . I don't see how . . .'

'We have,' said Aenea. 'And more will before too long.' We reached the next three hundredth step and paused to pant.

'What other directions are there in evolution that we've ignored?' I said when we began to climb again.

'Increasing diversity and complexity,' said Aenea. 'Scientists argued back and forth about these directions for centuries, but there's no doubt that evolution favors – in the very long run – both these attributes. And of the two, diversity is the more important.'

'Why?' I said. She must have been growing tired of that syllable. I sounded like a three-year-old child even to myself.

'Scientists used to think that basic evolutionary designs kept multi-plying,' said Aenea. 'That's called disparity. But that turned out not to be the case. Variety in basic plans tends to decrease as life's antientropic potential – evolution – increases. Look at all the orphans of Old Earth, for instance – same basic DNA, of course, but also the same basic plans: evolved from forms with tubular guts, radial symmetry, eyes, feeding mouths, two sexes . . . pretty much from the same mold.'

'But I thought you said diversity was important,' I said.

'It is,' said Aenea. 'But diversity is different than basic-plan disparity. Once evolution gets a good basic design, it tends to throw away the variants and concentrate on the near-infinite diversity within that design . . . thousands of related species . . . tens of thousands.'

'Trilobites,' I said, getting the idea.

'Yes,' said Aenea, 'and when . . .'

'Beetles,' I said. 'All those goddamn species of beetles.'

Aenea grinned at me through her mask. 'Precisely. And when . . .'

'Bugs,' I said. 'Every world I've been on has the same goddamn swarms of bugs. Mosquitoes. Endless varieties of . . .'

'You've got it,' said Aenea. 'Life shifts into high gear when the basic plan for an organism is settled and new niches open up. Life settles into those new niches by tweaking the diversity within the basic shape of those organisms. New species. There are thousands of new species of plants and animals that have come into existence in just the last millennium since interstellar flight started . . . and not all bio-engineered, some just adapted at a furious rate to the new Earth-like worlds they were dumped down on.'

'Triaspens,' I said, remembering just Hyperion. 'Everblues. Woman-grove root. Tesla trees?'

'They were native,' said Aenea.

'So the diversity's good,' I said, trying to find the original threads of this discussion.

'Diversity's good,' agreed Aenea. 'As I said, it lets life shift into high gear

and get on with its mindless business of greening up the universe. But there's at least one Old Earth species that hasn't diversified much at all . . . at least not on the friendly worlds it colonized.'

'Us,' I said. 'Humans.'

Aenea nodded grimly. 'We've been stuck in one species since our Cro-Magnon ancestors helped to wipe out the smarter Neanderthals,' she said. 'Now it's our chance to diversify rapidly, and institutions like the Hegemony, the Pax, and the Core are stopping it.'

'Does the need to diversify extend to human institutions?' I said. 'Religions? Social systems?' I was thinking about the people who had helped me on Vitus-Gray-Balianus B, Dem Ria, Dem Loa, and their families. I was thinking about the Amoiete Spectrum Helix and its complicated and convoluted beliefs.

'Absolutely,' said Aenea. 'Look over there.'

A. Bettik had paused at a slab of marble upon which words were carved in Chinese and early Web English:

High rises the Eastern Peak
Soaring up to the blue sky.
Among the rocks – an empty hollow,
Secret, still, mysterious!
Uncarved and unhewn,
Screened by nature with a roof of clouds.

Time and Seasons, what things are you,
Bringing to my life ceaseless change?
I will lodge forever in this hollow
Where springs and autumns unheeded pass.
– Tao-yun, wife of General Wang Ning-chih,
AD 400

We climbed on. I thought that I could see something red at the top of this next flight of stairs. The South Gate of Heaven and entry to the summit slope? It was about time.

'Wasn't that beautiful though?' I said, speaking of the poem. 'Isn't continuity like that as important or more important in human institutions as diversity?'

'It's important,' agreed Aenea. 'But that's almost all humanity has been doing for the last millennium, Raul . . . re-creating Old Earth institutions and ideas on different worlds. Look at the Hegemony. Look at the Church and the Pax. Look at this world . . .'

'T'ien Shan?' I said. 'I think it's wonderful . . .'

'So do I,' said Aenea. 'But it's all borrowed. The Buddhism has evolved a bit . . . at least away from idolatry and ritual back to the open-mindedness that was its earliest hallmark . . . but everything else is pretty much an attempt to recapture things lost with Old Earth.'

'Such as?' I said.

'Such as the language, dress, the names of the mountains, local customs . . . hell, Raul, even this pilgrimage trail and the Temple of the Jade Emperor, if we ever get there.'

'You mean there was a T'ai Shan mountain on Old Earth?' I said.

'Absolutely,' said Aenea. 'With its own City of Peace and Heavenly Gates and Mouth of the Dragon. Confucius climbed it more than three thousand years ago. But the Old Earth stairway had just seven thousand steps.'

'I wish we'd climbed it instead,' I said, wondering if I could keep climbing. The steps were short, but there had been a hell of a lot of them. 'I see your point though.'

Aenea nodded. 'It's wonderful to preserve tradition, but a healthy organism evolves . . . culturally and physically.'

'Which brings us back to evolution,' I said. 'What are the other directions, tendencies, goals, or whatever that you said had been ignored the last few centuries?'

'There are just a few more,' said Aenea. 'One is an ever-increasing number of individuals. Life likes gazillions of species, but it absolutely loves hyper-gazillions of individuals. In a sense, the universe is tooled up for individuals. There was a book in the Taliesin library called *Evolving Hierarchical Systems* by an Old Earth guy named Stanley Salthe. Did you see it?'

'No, I must have missed it when I was reading those early twenty-first-century holoporn novels.'

'Uh-huh,' said Aenea. 'Well, Salthe put it sort of neatly – "An indefinite number of unique individuals can exist in a finite material world if they are nested within each other and that world is expanding." '

'Nested within each other,' I repeated, thinking about it. 'Yeah, I get it. Like the Old Earth bacteria in our gut, and the paramecia we've dragged into space, and the other cells in our bodies . . . more worlds, more people . . . yeah.'

'The trick is more people,' said Aenea. 'We have hundreds of billions, but between the Fall and the Pax, the actual human population in the galaxy – not counting Ousters – has leveled off in the last few hundred years.'

'Well, birth control is important,' I said, repeating what everyone on Hyperion had been taught. 'I mean, especially with the cruciform capable of keeping people alive for centuries and centuries . . .'

'Exactly,' said Aenea. 'With artificial immortality comes more stagnation . . . physical and cultural. It's a given.'

I frowned. 'But that's not a reason to deny people the chance for extended life, is it?'

Aenea's voice seemed remote, as if she were contemplating something much larger. 'No,' she said at last, 'not in itself.'

'What are the evolutionary directions?' I asked, seeing the red pagoda come closer above us and praying that the conversation would keep my mind off collapsing, rolling back down the twenty-some thousand steps we had climbed.

'Just three more worth mentioning,' said Aenea. 'Increasing specialization, increasing codependency, and increasing evolvability. All of these are really important, but the last is most so.'

'How do you mean, kiddo?'

'I mean that evolution itself evolves. It has to. Evolvability is in itself an inherited survival trait. Systems – living and otherwise – have to learn how to evolve and, to some extent, control the direction and rate of their own evolution. We . . . I mean the human species . . . were on the verge of doing that a thousand years ago, and the Core took it away from us. At least from most of us.'

'What do you mean, "most of us"?'

'I promise that you'll see in a few days, Raul.'

We reached the South Gate of Heaven and passed through its arched entry, a red arch under a golden pagoda roof. Beyond it was the Heavenly Way, a gentle slope that ran to the summit that was just visible. The Heavenly Way was nothing more than path on bare, black rock. We could have been walking on an airless moon like Old Earth's – the conditions here were about as amenable to life. I started to say something to Aenea about this being a niche that life hadn't stuck its foot into, when she led the way off the path to a small stone temple set in among the sharp crags and fissures a few hundred meters below the summit. There was an air lock that looked so ancient it appeared to have come out on one of the earliest seedships. Amazingly, it worked when she activated the press pad and the three of us stood in it until it cycled and the inner door opened. We stepped inside.

It was a small room and almost bare except for an ornate bronze pot holding fresh flowers, some sprigs of green on a low dais, and a beautiful statue – once gold – of a life-size woman in robes that appeared to be made of gold. The woman was fat-cheeked and of pleasant demeanor – a sort of female Buddha – and she looked to be wearing a gilded crown of leaves and had an oddly Christian halo of hammered gold behind her head.

A. Bettik pulled off his helmet and said, 'The air is good. Air pressure more than adequate.'

Aenea and I folded back our skinsuit cowls. It was a pleasure to breathe regularly.

There were incense tapers and a box of matches at the statue's foot. Aenea went to one knee and used a match to light one of the tapers. The smell of incense was very strong.

'This is the Princess of the Azure Clouds,' she said, smiling up at the smiling gold face. 'The goddess of the dawn. By lighting this, I've just made an offering for the birth of grandchildren.'

I started to smile and then froze. *She has a child. My beloved has already had a child.* My throat tightened and I looked away, but Aenea walked over and took my arm.

'Shall we eat lunch?' she said.

I had forgotten about our brown bag lunch. It would have been difficult to eat it through our helmets and osmosis masks.

We sat in the dim light, in the windowless room, amid the floating smoke and scent of incense, and ate the sandwiches packed by the monks.

'Where now?' I said as Aenea began recyling the inner lock.

'I have heard that there is a precipice on the eastern edge of the summit called Suicide Cliff,' said A. Bettik. 'It used to be a place for serious sacrifice. Jumping from it is said to provide instant communion with the Jade Emperor and to insure that your offering request is honored. If you really want to guarantee grandchildren, you might jump from there.'

I stared at the android. I was never sure if he had a sense of humor or simply a skewed personality.

Aenea laughed. 'Let's walk to the Temple of the Jade Emperor first,' she said. 'See if anyone's home.'

Outside, I was struck first by the isolation of the skinsuit and the airless clarity of everything. The osmosis mask had gone almost opaque because of the unfiltered ferocity of the midday sun at this altitude. Shadows were harsh.

We were about fifty meters from the summit and the temple when a form stepped out of the blackness of shadow behind a boulder and blocked our way. I thought *Shrike* and foolishly clenched my hands into fists before I saw what it was.

A very tall man stood before us, dressed in lance-slashed, vacuum combat armor. Standard Pax Fleet Marine and Swiss Guard issue. I could see his face through the impact-proof visor – his skin was black, his features strong, and his short-cropped hair was white. There were fresh and livid scars on his dark face. His eyes were not friendly. He was carrying a Marine-class, multipurpose assault rifle, and now he raised it and leveled it at us. His transmission was on the skinsuit band.

'Stop!'

We stopped.

The giant did not seem to know what to do next. *The Pax finally have us* was my first thought.

Aenea took a step forward. 'Sergeant Gregorius?' came her voice on the skinsuit band.

The man cocked his head but did not lower the weapon. I had no doubt that the rifle would work perfectly in hard vacuum – either flechette cloud, energy lance, charged particle beam, solid slug, or hyper-k. The muzzle was aimed at my beloved's face.

'How do you know my . . .' began the giant and then seemed to rock backward. 'You're her. The one. The girl we sought for so long, across so many systems. Aenea.'

'Yes,' said Aenea. 'Are there others who survived?'

'Three,' said the man she had called Gregorius. He gestured to his right and I could just make out a black scar on black rock, with blackened remnants of something that might have been a starship escape bulb.

'Is Father Captain de Soya among them?' said Aenea.

I remembered the name. I remembered de Soya's voice on the dropship radio when he had found us and saved us from Nemes and then let us go on God's Grove almost ten of his and Aenea's years ago.

'Aye,' said Sergeant Gregorius, 'the captain's alive, but just barely. He was burned bad on the poor old *Raphael*. He'd be atoms with her, if he hadn't passed out an' given me the opportunity to drag him to a lifeboat. The other two are hurt, but the father-captain's dyin'.' He lowered the rifle and leaned on it wearily. 'Dyin' the true death . . . we have no resurrection creche and the darlin' father-captain made me promise to slag him to atoms when he went, rather than let him be resurrected a mindless idiot.'

Aenea nodded. 'Can you take me to him? I need to talk to him.'

Gregorius shouldered the heavy weapon and looked suspiciously at A. Bettik and me. 'And these two . . .'

'This is my dear friend,' said Aenea, touching A. Bettik's arm. She took my hand. 'And this is my beloved.'

The giant only nodded at this, turned, and led the way up the final stretch of slope to the summit to the Temple of the Jade Emperor.

PART THREE

TWENTY-TWO

On Hyperion, several hundred light-years toward galactic center from the events and the people on T'ien Shan, a forgotten old man rose out of the dreamless sleep of long-term cryogenic fugue and slowly became aware of his surroundings. His surroundings were a no-touch suspension bed, a gaggle of life-support modules encircling him and nuzzling him like so many feeding raptors, and uncountable tubes, wires, and umbilicals finishing their work of feeding him, detoxifying his blood, stimulating his kidneys, carrying antibiotics to fight infection, monitoring his life signs, and generally invading his body and dignity in order to revive him and keep him alive.

'Ah, fuck,' rasped the old man. 'Waking up is a fucking, goddamn, dung-eating, corpse-buggering, shit storm of a nightmare for the terminally old. I'd pay a million marks if I could just get out of bed and go piss.'

'And good morning to you, M. Silenus,' said the female android monitoring the old poet's life signs on the floating biomonitor. 'You seem to be in good spirits today.'

'Bugger all blue-skinned wenches,' mumbled Martin Silenus. 'Where are my teeth?'

'You haven't grown them back yet, M. Silenus,' said the android. She was named A. Raddik and was a little over three centuries old . . . less than one-third the age of the ancient human mummy floating in the suspension bed.

'No need to,' mumbled the old man. 'Won't fucking be awake long enough. How long was I under?'

'Two years, three months, eight days,' said A. Raddik.

Martin Silenus peered up at the open sky above his tower. The canvas roof on this highest level of his stone turret had been rolled back. Deep lapis blue. The low light of early morning or late evening. The shimmer and flit of radiant gossamers not yet illuminating their fragile half-meter butterfly wings.

'What season?' managed Silenus.

'Late spring,' said the female android. Other blue-skinned servants of the old poet moved in and out of the circular room, bent on obscure errands. Only A. Raddik monitored the last stages of the poet's revival from fugue.

'How long since they left?' He did not have to specify who the 'they' were. A. Raddik knew that the old poet meant not only Raul Endymion, the last visitor to their abandoned university city, but the girl Aenea – whom Silenus had known three centuries earlier – and whom he still hoped to see again someday.

'Nine years, eight months, one week, one day,' said A. Raddik. 'All Earth standard, of course.'

'Hggrhh,' grunted the old poet. He continued peering at the sky. The sunlight was filtered through canvas rolled to the east, pouring light on to the south wall of the stone turret while not striking him directly, but the brightness still brought tears to his ancient eyes. 'I've become a thing of darkness,' he mumbled. 'Like Dracula. Rising from my fucking grave every few years to check on the world of the living.'

'Yes, M. Silenus,' agreed A. Raddik, changing several settings on the control panel.

'Shut up, wench,' said the poet.

'Yes, M. Silenus.'

The old man moaned. 'How long until I can get into my hoverchair, Raddik?'

The hairless android pursed her lips. 'Two more days, M. Silenus. Perhaps two and a half.'

'Aw, hell and damn,' muttered Martin Silenus. 'Recovery gets slower each time. One of these times, I won't wake at all . . . the fugue machinery won't bring me back.'

'Yes, M. Silenus,' agreed the android. 'Each cold sleep is harder on your system. The resuscitation and life-support equipment is quite old. It is true that you will not survive many more awakenings.'

'Oh, shut up,' growled Martin Silenus. 'You are a morbid, gloomy old bitch.'

'Yes, M. Silenus.'

'How long have you been with me, Raddik?'

'Two hundred and forty-one years, eleven months, nineteen days,' said the android. 'Standard.'

'And you still haven't learned to make a decent cup of coffee.'

'No, M. Silenus.'

'But you *have* put a pot on, correct?'

'Yes, M. Silenus. As per your standing instructions.'

'Fucking aye,' said the poet.

'But you will not be able to ingest liquids orally for at least another twelve hours, M. Silenus,' said A. Raddik.

'Arrrggghhh!' said the poet.

'Yes, M. Silenus.'

After several minutes in which it looked like the old man had drifted back to sleep, Martin Silenus said, 'Any word from the boy or child?'

'No, sir,' said A. Raddik. 'But then, of course, we only have access to the in-system Pax com network these days. And most of their new encrypting is quite good.'

'Any gossip about them?'

'None that we are sure of, M. Silenus,' said the android. 'Things are very troubled for the Pax . . . revolution in many systems, problems with their Outback Crusade against the Ousters, a constant movement of warships and troopships within the Pax boundaries . . . and there is talk of the viral contagion, highly coded and circumspect.'

'The contagion,' repeated Martin Silenus and smiled a toothless smile. 'The child, I would guess.'

'Quite possibly, M. Silenus,' said A. Raddik, 'although it is quite possible that there is a real viral plague on those worlds where . . .'

'No,' said the poet, shaking his head almost violently. 'It's Aenea. And her teachings. Spreading like the Beijing Flu. You don't remember the Beijing Flu, do you, Raddik?'

'No, sir,' said the female, finishing her check of the readouts and setting the module to auto. 'That was before my time. It was before anyone's time. Anyone but you, sir.'

Normally there would have been some obscene outburst from the poet, but now he merely nodded. 'I know. I'm a freak of nature. Pay your two bits and come into the sideshow . . . see the oldest man in the galaxy . . . see the mummy that walks and talks . . . sort of . . . see the disgusting thing that refuses to die. Bizarre, aren't I, A. Raddik?'

'Yes, M. Silenus.'

The poet grunted. 'Well, don't get your hopes up, blue thing. I'm not going to croak until I hear from Raul and Aenea. I have to finish the *Cantos* and I don't know the ending until they create it for me. How do I know what I think until I see what they do?'

'Precisely, M. Silenus.'

'Don't humor me, blue woman.'

'Yes, M. Silenus.'

'The boy . . . Raul . . . asked me what his orders were almost ten years ago. I told him . . . save the child, Aenea . . . topple the Pax . . . destroy the Church's power . . . and bring the Earth back from wherever the fuck it went. He said he'd do it. Of course, he was stinking drunk with me at the time.'

'Yes, M. Silenus.'

'Well?' said the poet.

'Well what, sir?' said A. Raddik.

'Well, any sign of him having *done* any of the things he's promised, Raddik?'

'We know from the Pax transmissions nine years and eight months ago that he and the Consul's ship escaped Hyperion,' said the android. 'We can hope that the child Aenea is still safe and well.'

'Yes, yes,' muttered Silenus, waving his hand feebly, 'but is the Pax toppled?'

'Not that we can notice, M. Silenus,' said Raddik. 'There were the mild troubles I mentioned earlier, and offworld, born-again tourism here on Hyperion is down a bit, but . . .'

'And the sodding Church is still in the zombie business?' demanded the poet, his thin voice stronger now.

'The Church remains ascendant,' said A. Raddik. 'More of the moor people and the mountain people accept the cruciform every year.'

'Bugger all,' said the poet. 'And I don't suppose that Earth has returned to its proper place.'

'We have not heard of that improbability occurring,' said A. Raddik. 'Of course, as I mentioned, our electronic eavesdropping is restricted to in-system transmissions these days, and since the Consul's ship left with M. Endymion and M. Aenea almost ten years ago, our decryption capabilities have not been . . .'

'All right, all right,' said the old man, sounding terribly tired again. 'Get me into my hoverchair.'

'Not for another two days, at least, I am afraid,' repeated the android, her voice gentle.

'Piss up a rope,' said the ancient figure floating amid tubes and sensor wires. 'Can you wheel me over to a window, Raddik? Please? I want to look at the spring chalma trees and the ruins of this old city.'

'Yes, M. Silenus,' said the android, sincerely pleased to be doing something for the old man besides keeping his body working.

Martin Silenus watched out the window for one full hour, fighting the tides of reawakening pain and the terrible sleepy urge to return to fugue state. It was morning light. His audio implants relayed the birdsong to him. The old poet thought of his adopted young niece, the child who had decided to call herself Aenea . . . he thought of his dear friend, Brawne Lamia, Aenea's mother . . . how they had been enemies for so long, had hated each other during parts of that last great Shrike Pilgrimage so long ago . . . about the stories they had told one another and the things they had seen . . . the Shrike in the Valley of the Time Tombs, its red eyes blazing . . . the scholar . . . what was his name? . . . Sol . . . Sol and his little swaddled brat aging backward to nothing . . . and the soldier . . . Kassad . . . that was it . . . Colonel Kassad. The old poet had never given a shit about the military . . . idiots, all of them . . . but Kassad had told an interesting tale, lived an interesting life . . . the other priest, Lenar Hoyt, had been a prig and an asshole, but the first one . . . the one with the sad eyes and the leather journal . . . Paul Duré . . . there had been a man worth writing about . . .

Martin Silenus drifted back to sleep with the light of morning flooding in on him, illuminating his countless wrinkles and translucent, parchment flesh, his blue veins visible and pulsing weakly in the rich light. He did not dream . . . but part of his poet's mind was already outlining the next sections of his never-finished *Cantos*.

Sergeant Gregorius had not been exaggerating. Father Captain de Soya had been terribly battered and burned in the last battle of his ship, the *Raphael*, and was near death.

The sergeant had led A. Bettik, Aenea, and me into the temple. The structure was as strange as this encounter – outside there was a large, blank stone tablet, a smooth-faced monolith – Aenea mentioned briefly that it had been brought from Old Earth, had stood outside the original Temple of the Jade Emperor, and had never been inscribed during its thousands of years on the pilgrims' trail – while inside the sealed and pressurized court-yard of the echoing temple itself, a stone railing ran around a boulder that was actually the summit of T'ai Shan, the sacred Great Peak of the Middle Kingdom. There were small sleeping and eating rooms for pilgrims in the back of the huge temple, and it was in one of these that we found Father Captain de Soya and the other two survivors. Besides Gregorius and the dying de Soya, there were two other men – Carel Shan, a Weapons Systems Officer, now terribly burned and unconscious, and Hoagan Liebler, intro-duced by Sergeant Gregorius as the 'former' Executive Officer of the *Raphael*. Liebler was the least injured of the four – his left forearm had been broken and was in a sling, but he had no burns or other impact bruises – but there was something quiet and withdrawn about the thin man, as if he were in shock or mulling something over.

Aenea's attention went immediately to Captain Federico de Soya.

The priest-captain was on one of the uncomfortable pilgrim cots, either stripped to the waist by Gregorius or he had lost all of his upper uniform in the blast and reentry. His trousers were shredded. His feet were bare. The only place on his body where he had not been terribly burned was the parasite cruciform on his chest – it was a healthy, sickening pink. De Soya's hair had been burned away and his face was splashed with liquid metal burns and radiation slashes, but I could see that he had been a striking man, mostly because of his liquid, troubled brown eyes, not dulled even by the pain that must be overwhelming him at this moment. Someone had applied burn cream, temporary dermheal, and liquid disinfectant all over the visible portions of the dying priest-captain's body – and started a stand-ard lifeboat medkit IV drip – but this would have little effect on the out-come. I had seen combat burns like this before, not all from starship encounters. Three friends of mine during the Iceshelf fighting had died within hours when we had not been able to medevac them out. Their screams had been horrible to the point of unendurable.

Father Captain de Soya was not screaming. I could see that he was straining not to cry out from the pain, but he remained silent, his eyes focused only on the terrible concentration to silence until Aenea knelt by his side.

At first he did not recognize her. 'Bettz?' he mumbled. 'VIRO Argyle? No . . . you died at your station. The others too . . . Pol Denish . . . Elijah trying to free the aft boat . . . the young troopers when the starboard hull failed . . . but you look . . . familiar.'

Aenea started to take his hand, saw that three of de Soya's fingers were missing, and set her own hand on the stained blanket next to his. 'Father Captain,' she said very softly.

'Aenea,' said de Soya, his dark eyes really looking at her for the first time. 'You're the child . . . so many months, chasing you . . . looked at you when you stepped out of the Sphinx. Incredible child. So glad you survived.' His gaze moved to me. 'You are Raul Endymion. I saw your Home Guard dossier. Almost caught up to you on Mare Infinitus.' A wave of pain rolled over him and the priest-captain closed his eyes and bit into his burned and bloodied lower lip. After a moment, he opened his eyes and said to me, 'I have something of yours. Personal gear on the *Raphael*. The Holy Office let me have it after they ended their investigation. Sergeant Gregorius will give it to you after I am dead.'

I nodded, having no idea what he was talking about.

'Father Captain de Soya,' whispered Aenea, 'Federico . . . can you hear and understand me?'

'Yes,' murmured the priest-captain. 'Painkillers . . . said no to Sergeant Gregorius . . . didn't want to slip away forever in my sleep. Not go gently.' The pain returned. I saw that much of de Soya's neck and chest had cracked and opened, like burned scales. Pus and fluid flowed down to the blankets beneath him. The man closed his eyes until the tide of agony receded; it took longer this time. I thought of how I had folded up under just the pain of a kidney stone and tried to imagine this man's torment. I could not.

'Father Captain,' said Aenea, 'there is a way for you to live . . .'

De Soya shook his head vigorously, despite the pain that must have caused. I noticed that his left ear was little more than carbon. Part of it flaked off on the pillow as I watched. 'No!' he cried. 'I told Gregorius . . . no partial resurrection . . . idiot, sexless idiot . . .' A cough that might have been a laugh from behind scorched teeth. 'Had enough of that as a priest. Anyway . . . tired . . . tired of . . .' His blackened stubs of fingers on his right hand batted at the pink double cross on his flaked and oozing chest. 'Let the thing die with me.'

Aenea nodded. 'I didn't mean be reborn, Father Captain. I meant *live*. Be healed.'

De Soya was trying to blink, but his eyelids were burned ragged. 'Not a prisoner of the Pax . . .' he managed, finding the air to speak only each time he exhaled with a racking gasp. 'Will . . . execute . . . me. I deserve . . . it. Killed many innocent . . . men . . . women . . . in defense of . . . friends.'

Aenea leaned closer so that he could focus on her eyes. 'Father Captain, the Pax is still after us as well. But we have a ship. It has an autosurgeon.'

Sergeant Gregorius stepped forward from where he had been leaning wearily against the wall. The man named Carel Shan remained unconscious. Hoag Liebler, apparently lost in some private misery, did not respond.

Aenea had to repeat it before de Soya understood.

'Ship?' said the priest-captain. 'The ancient Hegemony ship you escaped in? Not armed, was it?'

'No,' said Aenea. 'It never has been.'

De Soya shook his head again. 'There must have been . . . fifty archangel-class . . . ships . . . jumped us. Got . . . a few . . . rest . . . still there. No chance . . . get . . . to . . . any translation point . . . before . . .' He closed his torn eyelids again while the pain washed over him. This time, it seemed, it almost carried him away. He returned as if from a far place.

'It's all right,' whispered Aenea. 'I'll worry about that. You'll be in the doc-in-the-box. But there's something you would have to do.'

Father Captain de Soya seemed too tired to speak, but he shifted his head to listen.

'You have to renounce the cruciform,' said Aenea. 'You have to surrender this type of immortality.'

The priest-captain's blackened lips pulled back from his teeth. 'Gladly . . .' he rasped. 'But sorry . . . can't . . . once accepted . . . cruciform . . . can't be . . . surrendered.'

'Yes,' whispered Aenea, 'it can. If you choose that, I can make it go away. Our autosurgeon is old. It would not be able to heal you with the cruciform parasite throughout your body. We have no resurrection creche aboard the ship . . .'

De Soya reached for her then, his flaking and three-fingerless hand still gripping tightly the sleeve of her therm jacket. 'Doesn't matter . . . doesn't matter if I die . . . get it off. Get if *off*. Will die a real . . . Catholic . . . again . . . if you . . . can help me . . . get it . . . OFF!' He almost shouted the final word.

Aenea turned to the sergeant. 'Do you have a cup or glass?'

'There's the mug in the medkit,' rumbled the giant, fumbling for it. 'But we have no water . . .'

'I brought some,' said my friend and removed the insulated bottle from her belt.

I expected wine, but it was only the water we had bottled up before leaving the Temple Hanging in Air those endless hours ago. Aenea did not bother with alcohol swabs or sterile lancets; she beckoned me closer, removed the hunting knife from my belt, and drew the blade across three of her fingertips in a swift move that made me flinch. Her blood flowed red. Aenea dipped her fingers in the clear plastic drinking mug for just a second, but long enough to send currents of thick crimson spiraling and twisting in the water.

'Drink this,' she said to Father Captain de Soya, helping to lift the dying man's head.

The priest-captain drank, coughed, drank again. His eyes closed when she eased him back onto the stained pillow.

'The cruciform will be gone within twenty-four hours,' whispered my friend.

Father Captain de Soya made that rough chuckling sound again. 'I'll be dead within an hour.'

'You'll be in the autosurgeon within fifteen minutes,' said Aenea, touching his better hand. 'Sleep now . . . but don't die on me, Federico de Soya . . . don't die on me. We have much to talk about. And you have one great service to perform for me . . . for us.'

Sergeant Gregorius was standing closer. 'M. Aenea . . .' he said, halted, shuffled his feet, and tried again. 'M. Aenea, may I partake of that . . . water?'

Aenea looked at him. 'Yes, Sergeant . . . but once you drink, you can never again carry a cruciform. Never. There will be no resurrection. And there are other . . . side effects.'

Gregorius waved away any further discussion. 'I have followed my captain for ten years. I will follow him now.' The giant drank deeply of the pinkish water.

De Soya's eyes had been closed, and I had assumed that he was asleep or unconscious from the pain, but now he opened them and said to Gregorius, 'Sergeant, would you please bring M. Endymion the parcel we dragged from the lifeboat?'

'Aye, Capt'n,' said the giant and rummaged through the litter of debris in one corner of the room. He handed me a sealed tube, a little over a meter high.

I looked at the priest-captain. De Soya seemed to be floating between delirium and shock. 'I'll open it when he's better,' I said to the sergeant.

Gregorius nodded, carried the glass over to Carel Shan, and poured some water into the unconscious Weapons Officer's gaping mouth. 'Carel may die before your ship arrives,' said the sergeant. He looked up. 'Or does the ship have two doc-in-the-boxes?'

'No,' said Aenea, 'but the one we have has three compartments. You can heal your wounds as well.'

Gregorius shrugged. He went to the man named Liebler and offered the glass. The thin man with the broken arm only looked at it.

'Perhaps later,' said Aenea.

Gregorius nodded and handed the glass back to her. 'The XO was a prisoner on our ship,' said the sergeant. 'A spy. An enemy of the captain. Father-captain still risked his last life to get Liebler out of the brig . . . got his burns retrieving him. I don't think Hoag quite understands what's happened.'

Liebler looked up then. 'I understand it,' he said softly. 'I just don't *understand* it.'

Aenea stood. 'Raul, I hope you haven't lost the ship communicator.'

I fumbled in my pockets only a few seconds before coming up with the com unit/diskey journal. 'I'll go outside and tightbeam visually,' I said. 'Use the skinsuit jack. Any instructions for the ship?'

'Tell it to hurry,' said Aenea.

It was tricky getting the semiconscious de Soya and the unconscious Carel Shan to the ship. They had no spacesuits and it was still near vacuum outside. Sergeant Gregorius told us that he had used an inflatable transfer ball to drag them from the lifeboat wreckage to the Temple of the Jade Emperor, but the ball itself had been damaged. I had about fifteen minutes to think about the problem before the ship became visible, descending on its EM repellors and blue fusion-flame tail, so when it arrived I ordered it to land directly in front of the temple air lock, to morph its escalator ramp to the air-lock door, and to extend its containment field around the door and stairway. Then it was just a matter of getting the float litters from the medbay in the ship and transferring the men to them without hurting them too much. Shan remained unconscious, but some of de Soya's skin peeled away as we moved him onto the litter. The priest-captain stirred and opened his eyes but did not cry out.

After months on T'ien Shan, the interior of the Consul's ship was still familiar, but familiar like a recurring dream one has about a house one has lived in long ago. After de Soya and the Weapons Officer were tucked away in the autosurgeon, it was strange to stand on the carpeted holopit deck with its ancient Steinway piano with Aenea and A. Bettik there as always, but also with a burned giant still holding his assault weapon and the former XO brooding silently on the holopit stairs.

'Diagnostics completed on the autosurgeons,' said the ship. 'The presence of the cross-shaped parasite nodes makes treatment impossible at this time. Shall I terminate treatment or commence cryogenic fugue?'

'Cryogenic fugue,' said Aenea. 'The doc-in-the-box should be able to operate on them in twenty-four hours. Please keep them alive and in stasis until then.'

'Affirmative,' said the ship. And then, 'M. Aenea? M. Endymion?'

'Yes,' I said.

'Are you aware that I was tracked by long-range sensors from the time I left the third moon? There are at least thirty-seven Pax warships heading this way as we speak. One is already in parking orbit around this planet and another has just committed the highly unusual tactic of jumping on Hawking drive within the system's gravity well.'

'Okay,' said Aenea. 'Don't worry about it.'

'I believe they intend to intercept and destroy us,' said the ship. 'And they can do this before we clear atmosphere.'

'We know,' sighed Aenea. 'I repeat, don't worry about it.'

'Affirmative,' said the ship in the most businesslike tone I had ever heard from it. 'Destination?'

'The bonsai fissure six kilometers east of Hsuan-k'ung Ssu,' said Aenea. 'East of the Temple Hanging in Air. Quickly.' She glanced at her wrist chronometer. 'But stay low, Ship. Within the cloud layers.'

'The phosgene clouds or the water particle clouds?' inquired the ship.

'The lowest possible,' said my friend. 'Unless the phosgene clouds create a problem for you.'

'Of course not,' said the ship. 'Would you like me to plot a course that would take us through the acid seas? It would make no difference to the Pax deep radar, but it could be done with only a small addition of time and . . .'

'No,' interrupted Aenea, 'just the clouds.'

We watched on the holopit sphereview as the ship flung itself off Suicide Cliff and dived ten kilometers through gray cloud and then into green clouds. We would be at the fissure within minutes.

We all sat on the carpeted holopit steps then. I realized that I still had the sealed tube that de Soya had given me. I rotated it through my hands.

'Go ahead and open it,' said Sergeant Gregorius. The big man was slowly removing the outer layers of his scarred combat armor. Lance burns had melted the lower layers. I was afraid to see his chest and left arm.

I hesitated. I had said that I'd wait until the priest-captain had recovered.

'Go ahead,' Gregorius said again. 'The captain's been waiting to give this back to you for nine years.'

I had no idea what it could be. How could this man have known he would see me someday? I owned nothing . . . how could he have something of mine to return?

I broke the seal on the tube and looked within. Some sort of tightly rolled fabric. With a slow realization, I pulled the thing out and unrolled it on the floor.

Aenea laughed delightedly. 'My God,' she said. 'In all my various dreams about this time, I never foresaw this. How wonderful.'

It was the hawking mat . . . the flying carpet that had carried Aenea and me from the Valley of the Time Tombs almost ten years earlier. I had lost it . . . it took me a second or two to remember. I had lost it on Mare Infinitus nine years ago when the Pax lieutenant I had been fighting had pulled a knife, cut me, pushed me off the mat into the sea. What had happened next? The lieutenant's own men on the floating sea platform had mistakenly killed him with a cloud of flechette darts, the dead man had fallen into the violet sea, and the hawking mat had flown on . . . no, I remembered that someone on the platform had intercepted it.

'How did the father-captain get it?' I asked, knowing the answer as soon as I articulated the question. De Soya had been our relentless pursuer then.

Gregorius nodded. 'The father-captain used it to find your blood and DNA samples. It's how we got your Pax service record from Hyperion. If we'd had pressure suits, I would have used the damn thing to get us off that airless mountain.'

'You mean it works?' I tapped the flight threads. The hawking mat – more tattered than I remembered it – hovered ten centimeters off the floor. 'I'll be damned,' I said.

'We're rising to the fissure at the coordinates you gave me,' came the ship's voice.

The holopit view cleared and showed the Jo-Kung Ridge rushing past. We slowed and hovered a hundred meters out. We had returned to the same forested valley fissure where the ship had dropped me more than three months earlier. Only now the green valley was filled with people. I saw Theo, Lhomo, many of the others from the Temple Hanging in Air. The ship floated lower, hovered, and waited for directions.

'Lower the escalator,' said Aenea. 'Let them all aboard.'

'May I remind you,' said the ship, 'that I have fugue couches and life support for a maximum of six people for an extended interstellar jump? There are at least fifty people there on the . . .'

'Lower the escalator and let them all aboard,' commanded Aenea. 'Immediately.'

The ship did as it was told without another word. Theo led the refugees up the ramp and the circular stairs to where we waited.

Most of those who had stayed behind at the Temple Hanging in Air were there: many of the temple monks, Tromo Trochi of Dhomu, the ex-soldier Gyalo Thondup, Lhomo Dondrub – we were delighted to see that his paraglider had brought him safely back, and from his grins and hugs, the delight was reciprocated – Abbot Kempo Ngha Wang Tashi, Chim Din, Jigme Taring, Kuku and Kay, George and Jigme, the Dalai Lama's brother Labsang, the brickworkers Viki and Kim, Overseer Tsipon Shakabpa, Rimsi Kyipup – less dour than I had ever seen him – and high riggers Haruyuki and Kenshiro, as well as the bamboo experts Voytek and Janusz, even the Mayor of Jo-kung, Charles Chi-kyap Kempo. But no Dalai Lama. And the Dorje Phamo was also missing.

'Rachel went back to fetch them,' said Theo, the last to come aboard. 'The Dalai Lama insisted on being the last to leave and the Sow stayed behind to keep him company until it was time to go. But they should have been back by now. I was just ready to go back along the ledge to check . . .'

Aenea shook her head. 'We'll all go.'

There was no way to get everyone seated or situated. People milled on the stairways, stood around the library level, had wandered up to the bedroom at the apex of the ship to look outside via the viewing walls, while others were on the fugue cubby level and down in the engine room.

'Let's go, Ship,' said Aenea. 'The Temple Hanging in Air. Make a direct approach.'

For the ship, a direct approach was a burst of thruster fire, a lob fifteen klicks into the atmosphere, and then a vertical drop with repellors and main engine burning at the last second. The entire process took about thirty seconds, but while the internal containment field kept us from being smashed to jelly, the view through the clear apex walls must have been disorienting for those watching upstairs. Aenea, A. Bettik, Theo, and I were watching the holopit and even that small view almost sent me to clutching the bulkheads or clinging to the carpet. We dropped lower and hovered fifty meters above the temple complex.

'Ah, damn,' said Theo.

The view had shown us a man falling to his death in the clouds below. There was no possibility of swooping down to catch him. One second he was freefalling, the next he had been swallowed by the clouds.

'Who was it?' said Theo.

'Ship,' said Aenea. 'Playback and enhance.'

Carl Linga William Eiheji, the Dalai Lama's bodyguard.

A few seconds later several figures emerged from the Right Meditation pavilion onto the highest platform, the one I had helped build to Aenea's plans less than a month ago.

'Shit,' I said aloud. The Nemes thing was carrying the Dalai Lama in one hand, holding him over the edge of the platform. Behind her . . . behind it . . . came her male and female clone-siblings. Then Rachel and the Dorje Phamo stepped out of the shadows onto the platform.

Aenea gripped my arm. 'Raul, do you want to come outside with me?'

815

She had activated the balcony beyond the Steinway, but I knew that this was not all that she meant. 'Of course,' I said, thinking, *Is this her death? Is this what she has foreseen since before birth? Is it my death?* 'Of course I'll come,' I said.

A. Bettik and Theo started out onto the ship's balcony with us. 'No,' said Aenea. 'Please.' She took the android's hand for a second. 'You can see everything from inside, my friend.'

'I would prefer to be with you, M. Aenea,' said A. Bettik.

Aenea nodded. 'But this is for Raul and me alone.'

A. Bettik lowered his head a second and returned to the holopit image. None of the rest of the score of people in the library level and on the spiral stairs said a word. The ship was dead silent. I walked out onto the balcony with my friend.

Nemes still held the boy out over the drop. We were twenty meters above her and her siblings now. I wondered idly how high they could jump.

'Hey!' shouted Aenea.

Nemes looked up. I was reminded that the effect of her gaze was like being stared at by empty eye sockets. Nothing human lived there.

'Put him down,' said Aenea.

Nemes smiled and dropped the Dalai Lama, catching him with her left hand at the last second. 'Be careful what you ask for, child,' said the pale woman.

'Let him and the other two go and I'll come down,' said Aenea.

Nemes shrugged. 'You won't leave here anyway,' she said, her voice not raised but perfectly audible across the gap.

'Let them go and I'll come down,' repeated Aenea.

Nemes shrugged but threw the Dalai Lama across the platform like an unwanted wad of paper.

Rachel ran to the boy, saw that he was hurt and bleeding but alive, lifted him, and turned back angrily toward Nemes and her siblings.

'*NO!*' shouted Aenea. I had never heard her use that tone before. It froze both Rachel and me in our tracks.

'Rachel,' said Aenea, her voice level again, 'please bring His Holiness and the Dorje Phamo up to the ship now.' It was polite, but an imperative that I could not have resisted. Rachel did not.

Aenea gave the command and the ship dropped lower, morphing and extending a stairway from the balcony. Aenea started down. I hurried to follow her. We stepped onto the bonsai cedar platform . . . I had helped to place all of the planks . . . and Rachel led the child and old woman past us, up the stairway. Aenea touched Rachel's head as the other woman went past. The stairway flowed uphill and shaped itself back into a balcony. Theo and A. Bettik joined Rachel and the Dorje Phamo on it. Someone had taken the bleeding child into the ship.

We stood two meters from Rhadamanth Nemes. Her siblings stepped up to the creature's side.

'This is not quite complete,' said Nemes. 'Where is your . . . ah, there.'

The Shrike flowed from the shadows of the pavilion. I say 'flowed', for although it moved, I had not seen it walk.

I was clenching and unclenching my hands. Everything was wrong for this showdown. I had peeled off my therm jacket in the ship, but still wore the stupid skinsuit and climbing harness, although most of the hardware had been left in the ship. The harness and multiple layers would still slow me down.

Slow me down from what? I thought. I had seen Nemes fight. Or rather, I had *not* seen her. When she and the Shrike had struggled on God's Grove, there had been a blur, then explosions, then nothing. She could decapitate Aenea and have my guts for garters before I got my hands clenched into fists.

Fists. The ship was unarmed, but I had left it with Sergeant Gregorius's Swiss Guard assault rifle still on the library level. The first thing they had taught us in the Home Guard was never to fight with fists when you could scrounge up a weapon.

I looked around. The platform was clean and bare, not even a railing I could wrench free to use as a club. This structure was too well built to rip anything loose.

I glanced at the cliff wall to our left. No loose rocks there. There were a few pitons and climbing bolts still imbedded in the fissures there, I knew – we had clipped on to them while building this level and pavilion and we hadn't got around to clearing all of them – but they were driven in far too tight for me to pull out and use as a weapon, although Nemes could probably do so with one finger. And what good would a piton or chock nut do against this monster?

There were no weapons to find here. I would die barehanded. I hoped that I would get one blow in before she took me down . . . or at least one swing.

Aenea and Nemes were looking only at each other. Nemes did not spare more than a glance at the Shrike ten paces to her right. The female thing said, 'You know that I am not going to take you back to the Pax, don't you, bitch child?'

'Yes,' said Aenea. She returned the creature's stare with a solid intensity.

Nemes smiled. 'But you believe that your spiked creature will save you again.'

'No,' said Aenea.

'Good,' said Nemes. 'Because it will not.' She nodded to her clone-siblings.

I know their names now – Scylla and Briareus. And I know what I saw next.

I should not have been able to see it, for all three of the Nemes things phase-shifted at that instant. There should have been the briefest glimpse of a chrome blur, then chaos, then nothing . . . but Aenea reached over and touched the back of my neck, there was the usual electric tingle I received whenever her skin touched mine, and suddenly the light was different – deeper, darker – and the air was as thick as water around us. I realized that my heart did not seem to be beating and that I did not blink or take a breath. As alarming as that sounds, it seemed irrelevant then.

Aenea's voice whispered from the hearpatch on my folded-back skinsuit cowl . . . or perhaps it spoke directly through her touch on my neck. I could not tell. *We cannot phase-shift with them or use it to fight them,* she said. *It is an abuse of the energy of the Void Which Binds. But I can help us* watch *this.*

And what we watched was incredible enough.

At Nemes's command, Scylla and Briareus threw themselves at the Shrike, while the Hyperion demon raised four arms and threw itself in the direction of Nemes – only to be intercepted by the siblings. Even with our altered vision – the ship hanging frozen in midair, our friends on the balcony frozen into unblinking statues, a bird above the cliff face locked in to the thick air like an insect in amber – the sudden movement of the Shrike and the two cloned creatures was almost too fast to follow.

There was a terrible impact just a meter short of Nemes, who had turned into a silver-surfaced effigy of herself, and who did not flinch. Briareus threw a blow that I am convinced would have split our ship in two. It reverberated off the Shrike's thorned neck with a sound like an underwater earthquake played back in slow motion, and then Scylla kicked the Shrike's legs out from under it. The Shrike went down, but not before two of its arms seized Scylla and two other razor-fingered claws sank deep into Briareus.

The Nemes siblings seemed to welcome the embrace, throwing themselves onto the tumbling Shrike with clacking teeth and flying nails. I could see that the hurtling edges of their rigid hands and forearms were razor-sharp, guillotine surfaces sharper than the Shrike's blades and thorns.

The three beat and chewed on each other in a wild frenzy, rolling across the platform, throwing bonsai cedar chips three meters into the air, and slamming against the rock wall. In a second, all three were on their feet, the Shrike's great jaws clamping on Briareus's neck even as Scylla slashed at one of the creature's four arms, bent it backward, and seemed to break it at a joint. Still holding Briareus in its jaws, the huge teeth chewing and scraping at the silver form's head, the Shrike whirled to confront Scylla, but by then both clone-siblings had their hands on the blades and thorns on the Shrike's skull, bending it backward until I waited to hear the neck snap and see its head roll away.

Instead, Nemes somehow communicated, *Now! Do it!* and without an instant's hesitation, the two siblings threw themselves away from the cliff face, toward the railing at the abyss-end side of the platform. I saw what they were going to do – throw the Shrike into space, just as they had done to the Dalai Lama's bodyguard.

Perhaps the Shrike saw this as well, for the tall creature slammed the two chrome bodies against it, its chest spikes and wrist thorns sinking deep into the forcefields around the struggling, clawing siblings. The trio whirled and tumbled and bounced up like some demented, three-part wind-up toy locked into hyperfast berserk mode, until finally the Shrike with its kicking, clawing, visibly impaled forms slammed into the sturdy cedar railing, tore through it as though it were wet cardboard, and went hurtling out over and into the drop, still fighting.

Aenea and I watched as the tall silver form with flashing spikes and the shorter silver forms with flailing limbs fell, fell, grew smaller and smaller, fell into clouds, and were swallowed. I knew that those watching from the ship would have seen nothing except a sudden disappearance of three of the figures on our platform, and then a broken railing and an emptier platform with just Nemes, Aenea, and me remaining. The silver thing that was Rhadamanth Nemes turned its featureless chrome face toward us.

The light changed. The breeze blew again. The air thinned. I felt my heart suddenly beating again . . . pounding loudly . . . and I blinked rapidly.

Nemes was in her human form again. 'So,' she said to Aenea, 'shall we finish this little farce?'

'Yes,' said Aenea.

Nemes smiled and went to phase-shift.

Nothing happened. The creature frowned and seemed to concentrate. Still nothing occurred.

'I can't stop you from phase-shifting,' said Aenea. 'But others can . . . and have.'

Nemes looked irritated for a second but then laughed. 'Those who created me will attend to that in a second, but I do not wish to wait that long, and I do not need to shift up to kill you, bitch child.'

'That's true,' said Aenea. She had stood her ground through all of this violence and confusion, her legs apart, feet firmly planted, arms easy at her sides.

Nemes showed her small teeth, but I saw that these teeth were elongating, growing sharper, as if being extruded farther from her gums and jawbone. There were at least three rows of them.

Nemes held up her hands and her fingernails – already pale and long – extended another ten centimeters, flowing into gleaming spikes.

Nemes reached down with those sharpened nails and peeled back the skin and flesh of her right forearm, revealing some sort of metallic endoskeleton that was the color of steel but which looked infinitely sharper.

'Now,' said Nemes. She stepped toward Aenea.

I stepped between them.

'No,' I said, and raised my fists like a boxer ready to start.

Nemes showed all of her rows of teeth.

TWENTY-THREE

Time and motion seem to slow again, as if I can once again see in the phase-shift mode, but this time it is merely the effect of adrenaline and total concentration. My mind shifts into overdrive. My senses become preternaturally alert. I see, feel, and calculate every microsecond with uncanny clarity.

Nemes takes a step . . . more toward Aenea to my left than toward me.

This is a chess match more than a fight. I win if I kill the unfeeling bitch or fling her off the platform long enough for us to escape. She does not have to kill me to win . . . only neutralize me long enough to kill *Aenea*. Aenea is her target. Aenea has *always* been her target. This monster was created to kill Aenea.

Chess match. Nemes has just sacrificed two of her strongest pieces – her monster siblings – to neutralize our knight, the Shrike. Now all three pieces are off the board. Only Nemes – the dark queen – Aenea, humankind's queen, and Aenea's lowly pawn . . . me.

This pawn may have to sacrifice himself, but not without taking out the dark queen. Of that he is determined.

Nemes is smiling. Her teeth are sharp and redundant. Her arms are still at her sides, long nails gleaming, her right forearm exposed like some obscene surgical exhibit . . . the interior not human . . . no, not human at all. The cutting edge of her forearm endoskeleton catches the afternoon sunlight.

'Aenea,' I say softly, 'step back, please.' This highest of platforms connects to the stone walkway and staircase we had cut to climb to the overhang walkway. I want my friend off the platform.

'Raul, I . . .'

'*Do it now*,' I say, not raising my voice but putting into it every bit of command I have learned and earned in my thirty-two standard years of life.

Aenea takes four steps back onto the stone ledge. The ship continues to hover fifty meters out and above us. There are many faces peering from the balcony. I try to will Sergeant Gregorius to step out and use his assault rifle to blow this Nemes bitch thing away, but I do not see his dark face among those staring. Perhaps he has been weakened by his wounds. Perhaps he feels that this should be a fair fight.

Fuck that, I think. I do not want a fair fight. I want to kill this Nemes creature any way I can. I would gladly accept any help from anywhere right now. *Is the Shrike really dead? Can this be? Martin Silenus's* Cantos *seemed to tell of the Shrike being defeated in some far-future battle with Colonel Fedmahn*

Kassad. But how did Silenus know this? And what does the future mean *to a monster capable of traveling through time?* If the Shrike was not dead, I would appreciate its return about now.

Nemes takes another step to her right, my left. I step left to block her access to Aenea. Under phase-shift, this thing has superhuman strength and can move so fast as to be literally invisible. *She can't phase-shift now.* I hope to God. But she still may be faster and stronger than me . . . than any human. I have to assume that she is. And she has the teeth, claws, and cutting arm.

'Ready to die, Raul Endymion?' says Nemes, her lips sliding back from those rows of teeth.

Her strengths – probable speed, strength, and inhuman construction. She may be more robot or android than human. It is almost certain that she does not feel pain. She may have other built-in weapons that she has not revealed. I have no idea how to kill or disable her . . . her skeleton is metal, not bone . . . the muscles visible in her forearm look real enough, but may be made of plastic fibers or pink steel mesh. It is unlikely that normal fighting techniques will stop her.

Her weaknesses – I do not know. Perhaps overconfidence. Perhaps she has become too used to phase-shifting – to killing her enemies when they cannot fight back. But she had taken on the Shrike and fought it to a draw nine and a half years ago – beaten it, actually, since she had gotten it out of the way to get to Aenea. Only the intervention of Father Captain de Soya's ship, lancing her with every gigavolt available on the starship, had prevented her from killing all of us.

Nemes raises her arms now and crouches, clawed fingers extended. How far can the thing jump? Can it jump over me to get to Aenea?

My strengths – two years boxing for the regiment during my Home Guard tour – I hated it, lost about a third of my matches. The others in my regiment kept betting on me, though. Pain never stopped me. I certainly felt it, but it never stopped me. Blows to the face made me see red – early on, I would forget all of my training when someone hit me in the face, and when the red mist of fury cleared, if I was still standing, I tended to have won the match. But I know that blind fury will not help me now. If I lose focus for an instant, this thing will kill me.

I was fast when I boxed . . . but that was more than a decade ago. I was strong . . . but I have not formally trained or worked out in all the intervening years. I could take hard blows in the ring, which is different than giving in to pain . . . I'd never been knocked out in the ring, even when a better fighter had sent me down a dozen times before the fight was called.

Besides boxing, I'd been a bouncer at one of the bigger Nine Tails casinos on Felix. But that was mostly psychology, knowing how to avoid fighting while moving the obnoxious drunk out the door. I had made sure that the few actual fights were over in a few seconds.

I had been trained for hand-to-hand fighting in the Home Guard, taught to kill at close range, but that sort of business was about as rare as a bayonet charge.

While working as a bargeman, I had gotten into my most serious fights –

once with a man ready and willing to carve me up with a long knife. I had survived that. But that other bargeman had knocked me out. As a hunting guide, I'd survived an offworlder coming at me with a flechette gun. But I had accidentally killed him, and he had testified against me after he was resurrected. Come to think of it, that's how all this started.

Of all my weaknesses, this was the most serious – I do not really want to hurt anyone. In all of my fights – with the possible exception of the bargemaster with the knife and the Christian hunter with his flechette gun – I had held something back, not wanting to hit them as hard as I could, not wanting to hurt them too badly.

I have to change that way of thinking immediately. This is no person . . . this is a killing machine, and if I do not disable or destroy it quickly, it will kill me even more quickly.

Nemes jumps at me, claws raking, her right arm pulling back and then slashing like a scythe.

I jump back, dodge the scythe, almost dodge all the claws, see the shirt on my left upper arm shred, see blood mist the air, and then I step in quickly and hit her – fast – hard – three times to the face.

Nemes jumps back as quickly as she came in. There is blood on the long nails of her left hand. My blood. Her nose has been smashed flat so that it lies sideways on her thin face. I have broken something – bone, cartilage, metal fiber – where her left brow was. There is no blood on her face. She does not seem to notice any of the damage. She is still grinning.

I glance at my left arm. It burns ferociously. Poison? Perhaps – it makes sense – but if she uses poison, I should be dead in seconds. No reason she would use long-acting agents.

Still here. Just burns because of the slashes. Four, I think . . . deep, but not muscle deep. They don't matter. Concentrate on her eyes. Guess what she'll do next.

Never use your bare hands. Home Guard teaching. Always find a weapon for close-in fighting. If one's personal weapon is destroyed or missing, find something else, improvise – a rock, a heavy branch, a torn piece of metal – even stones wrapped in one's fist or keys between the fingers are preferable to one's bare hands. Knuckles break more quickly than jawbones, the drill instructor always reminded us. If you absolutely *have* to use only hands, use the flat of your hand to chop. Use rigid fingers to impale. Use clawed fingers to go for the eyes and Adam's apple.

No loose rocks here, no branches, no keys . . . no weapons at all. This thing has no Adam's apple. I suspect that her eyes are as cool and hard as marbles.

Nemes moves to the left again, glancing toward Aenea. 'I'm coming, sweetheart,' hisses the thing to my friend.

I catch a glimpse of Aenea out of the corner of my eye. She is standing on the ledge just beyond the platform. She is not moving. Her face is impassive. This is unlike my beloved . . . normally she would be throwing stones, leaping on an enemy's back . . . anything but allowing me to fight this thing alone.

This is your moment, Raul, my darling. Her voice is as clear as a whisper in my mind.

It *is* a whisper. Coming from the auditory pickups in my folded-back skinsuit cowl. I am still wearing the damned thing, as well as my useless climbing harness. I start to subvocalize in response, but remember that I'd jacked into the ship's communicator in my upper pocket when I called the ship from the summit of T'ien Shan and I will be broadcasting to the ship as well as Aenea if I use it now.

I move to my left, blocking the creature's way again. Less room to maneuver now.

Nemes moves faster this time, feinting left and slashing in from my right, swinging her right arm backhand toward my ribs.

I leap back, but the blade slices meat just below my lowest right rib. I duck, but her claws flash – her left claws go for my eyes – I duck again, but her fingers slice a section of my scalp away. For an instant the air is filled with atomized blood again.

I take one step and swing my own right arm backhand, chopping down as if I were swinging a sledgehammer, my fist connecting with the side of her neck just below her right jawline. Synthetic flesh pulps and tears. The metal and tubes beneath do not bend.

Nemes slashes backhand again with her scythe arm and claws with her left hand. I leap away. She misses completely.

I step in quickly and kick the back of her knees, hoping to sweep her legs out from under her. It is eight meters to the broken railing at the far edge. If I could get her rotting . . . even if we both go over . . .

It is like kicking a steel stanchion. My leg goes numb at the force of my kick, but she does not budge. Fluids and flesh collapse over her endoskeleton, but she does not lose her footing. She must weigh twice what I do.

She kicks back and breaks a left rib or two of mine. I hear them crack. The wind goes out of me suddenly, explosively.

I reel backward, half expecting a ring rope to be there, but there is only the cliff face, a wall of hard, slick, vertical rock. A piton bolt slams into my back, stunning me for an instant.

I know now what I will do.

The next breath is like breathing through fire, so I quickly take several more painful breaths, confirming that I can breathe, trying to get my wind back. I feel lucky – I don't think the broken ribs have penetrated my left lung.

Nemes opens her arms to prevent my escape and moves in closer.

I step into her foul embrace, getting inside the killing sweep of the bladed forearm, and bring my fists together as hard as I can on either side of her head. Her ears pulp – this time there is a yellow fluid filling the air – but I feel the permasteel solidity of the skull under the bruised flesh. My hands rebound. I stagger backward, hands and arms and fists temporarily useless.

Nemes leaps.

I lean back on the rock, raise both legs, catch her on the chest as she descends, and kick out with all of the strength in my body.

She slashes as she flies backward, slicing through part of my harness, most of my jacket and skinsuit, and the muscle above my chest. It is on the right side of my chest. She has not cut through the comlink. Good.

She backflips and lands on her feet, still five meters from the edge. There is no way that I am going to get her to and over the platform edge. She will not play the game under my rules.

I rush her, fists raised.

Nemes brings her left hand up, cupped and clawed, in a quick, disemboweling scoop. I have slid to a stop millimeters short of that death blow and now, as she pulls her right arm back in preparation to scythe me in two, I pivot on one foot and kick her in her flat chest with all the strength of my body.

Nemes grunts and bites at my leg, her jaws snapping forward like a large dog's. Her teeth chew off the heel and sole of my boot, but miss flesh.

Catching my balance, I lunge forward again, gripping her right wrist with my left hand to keep the scythe arm from scraping my back clear of flesh down to my spine, and stepping in close to get a handful of her hair. She is snapping at my face, her rows of teeth directly in front of my eyes, the air between us filled with her yellow saliva or blood substitute. I am bending her head back as we pivot, two violent dancers straining against one another, but her lank, short hair is slippery with my blood and her lubricant and my fingers are slipping.

Lunging against her again to keep her off balance, I shift my fingers to her eye sockets and pull back with all of the strength in my arms and upper body.

Her head tilts back, thirty degrees – fifty – sixty – I should be hearing the snap of her spinal cord – eighty degrees – ninety. Her neck is bent backward at right angles to her torso, her marble eyes cold against my straining fingers, her wide lips stretching wider as the teeth snap at my forearm.

I release her.

She comes forward as if propelled by a giant spring. Her claws sink into my back, scrape bone at the right shoulder and left shoulder blade.

I crouch and swing short, hard blows, pounding her ribs and belly. Two – four – six fast shots, pivoting inside, the top of my head against her torn and oily chest, blood from my lacerated scalp flowing over both of us. Something in her chest or diaphragm snaps with a metallic twang and Nemes vomits yellow fluid over my neck and shoulders.

I stagger back and she grins at me, sharpened teeth gleaming through the bubbling yellow bile that drips from her chin onto the already slippery boards of the platform.

She screams – steam hissing from a dying boiler – and rushes again, scythe arm slicing through the air in an invisible arc.

I leap back. Three meters to the rock wall or ledge where Aenea stands.

Nemes swings backarm, her forearm a propeller, a whizzing pendulum of steel. She can herd me anywhere she wants me now.

She wants me dead or out of the way. She wants Aenea.

I jump back again, the blade cutting through the fabric just above belt line this time. I have jumped left this time, more toward the rock wall than the ledge.

Aenea is unprotected for this second. I am no longer between her and the creature.

Nemes's weakness. I am betting everything . . . Aenea . . . on this: she is a born predator. This close to a kill, she cannot resist finishing me.

Nemes swings to her right, keeping the option open of leaping toward Aenea, but also pursuing me toward the cliff face. The scythe swings backhand at my head for a clean decapitation.

I trip and roll farther to my left, away from Aenea. I am on the boards now, legs flailing.

Nemes straddles me, yellow fluid spattering my face and chest. She raises the scythe arm, screams, and brings the arm down.

'Ship! Land on this platform. Immediately. No discussion!'

I gasp this into the comthread pickup as I roll against Nemes's legs. Her bladed forearm slams into the tough bonsai cedar where my head was a second before.

I am under her. The blade of her arm is sunk deep into the dense wood. For just a few seconds, she is bent over to claw at me and does not have the leverage to free the cutting edge. A shadow falls over both of us.

The nails of her left hand slash the right side of my head – almost severing my ear, slicing along the jawbone, and just missing my jugular. My right hand is palm up under her jaw, trying to keep those teeth from opening and closing on my neck or face. She is stronger than I am.

My life depends upon getting out from under her.

Her forearm is still stuck in the platform floor, but this serves her purpose, anchoring her to me.

The shadow deepens. Ten seconds. No more.

Nemes claws my restraining hands away and wrenches the blade from the wood, staggering to her feet. Her eyes move left to where Aenea stands unguarded.

I roll away from Nemes . . . and away from Aenea . . . leaving my friend undefended. Claw cold rock to get to my feet. My right hand is useless – some tendon slashed in these final seconds – so I raise my left hand, pull the safety line from my harness – I can only hope it is still intact – and clip the carabiner onto the piton bolt with a metallic slap, like handcuffs slamming home.

Nemes pivots to her left, dismissing me now, black marble eyes on Aenea. My friend stands her ground.

The ship lands on the platform, turning off its EM repellors as ordered, allowing its full weight to rest on the wood, crushing the pavilion of Right Meditation with a terrible splintering, the ship's archaic fins filling most of the space, just missing Nemes and me.

The creature glances once over her shoulder at the huge black ship looming above her, obviously dismisses it, and crouches to leap at Aenea.

For a second I think that the bonsai cedar will hold . . . that the platform is even stronger than Aenea's calculations and my experience suggest . . . but then there is one horrendous, tearing, splintering sound, and the entire top Right Meditation platform and much of the stairway down to the Right Mindfulness pavilion tear away from the mountain.

I see the people watching from the ship's balcony thrown back into the interior of the ship as it falls.

'Ship!' I gasp into the comthread pickup. 'Hover!' Then I turn my attention back to Nemes.

The platform falls away beneath her. She leaps toward Aenea. My friend does not step back.

Only the platform falling out from beneath her keeps Nemes from completing her leap. She falls just short, but her claws strike the stone ledge, throw sparks, find a hold.

The platform rips and tears away, disintegrating as it tumbles into the abyss, some parts striking the main platform below, tearing it away in places, piling debris at other places.

Nemes is dangling from the rock, scrambling with her claws and feet, just a meter below where Aenea stands.

I have eight meters of safety line. Using my workable left arm, my blood making the rope dangerously slippery, I let out several meters and kick away from the cliff where I dangle.

Nemes pulls herself up to where she can get her clawed fingers over the top of the ledge. She finds a ridge or fissure and pulls herself up and out, an expert climber overcoming an overhang. Her body is arched like a bow as her feet scramble on the stone, pulling her higher so that she can throw herself up and over the ledge at Aenea, who has not moved.

I swing back away from Nemes, bouncing across the rock – feeling the slick stone against my lacerated bare sole where Nemes has torn away my boot – seeing that the rope I am depending upon has been frayed in the struggle, not knowing if it will hold for another few seconds.

I put more stress on it, swinging high away from Nemes in a pendulum arc.

Nemes pulls herself up onto Aenea's ledge, to her knees, getting to her feet a meter from my darling.

I swing high, rocks scraping my right shoulder, thinking for one sickening second that I do not have enough speed and line, but then feeling that I do – just enough – just barely enough—

Nemes swivels just as I swing up behind her, my legs opening in embrace, then closing around her, ankles crossing.

She screams and raises her scythe arm. My groin and belly are unprotected.

Ignoring that – ignoring the unraveling line and the pain everywhere – I cling tight as gravity and momentum swing us back – she is heavier than I – for another terrible second I hang connected and she does not budge – but she has not found her balance yet – she teeters on the edge – I arc backward, trying to move my center of gravity toward my bleeding shoulders – and Nemes comes off the ledge.

I open my legs immediately, releasing her.

She swings her scythe arm, missing my belly by millimeters as I swing back and out, but the motion sends her hurtling forward, farther away from the ledge and rock wall, out over the hole where the platform had been.

I scrape out and back along the cliff wall, trying to arrest my momentum. The safety line breaks.

I spread-eagle across the rockface, begin sliding down. My right hand is useless. My left fingers find a narrow hold . . . lose it . . . I am sliding faster . . . my left foot finds a ledge a centimeter wide. That and friction hold me against the rock long enough for me to look over my left shoulder.

Nemes is twisting as she falls, trying to change her trajectory enough to sink claws or scythe into the remaining edges of the lowest platform.

She misses by four or five centimeters. A hundred meters farther down, she strikes a rock outcropping and is propelled farther out above the clouds. Steps, posts, beams, and platform pillars are falling into cloud a kilometer below her.

Nemes screams – a shattered calliope scream of pure rage and frustration – and the echo bounces from rock to rock around me.

I can no longer hold on. I've lost too much blood and had too many muscles torn away. I feel the rock sliding away under my chest, cheek, palm, and straining left foot.

I look to my left to say good-bye to Aenea, if only with a gaze.

Her arm catches me as I begin to slide away. She has free-climbed out above me along the sheer face as I watched Nemes fall.

My heart pounds with the terror that my weight will pull both of us off. I feel myself slipping . . . feel Aenea's strong hands slipping . . . I am covered in blood. She does not let go.

'Raul,' she says and her voice is shaking, but with emotion, not fatigue or terror.

With her foot on the ledge the only thing holding us against the cliff, she releases her left hand, sweeps it up, and clamps her safety line on to my dangling carabiner still attached to the piton.

We both slide off and away, scraping skin. Aenea instantly hugs me with both arms, wraps both legs around me. It is a repeat of my tight embrace of Nemes, but fueled by love and the passion to survive this time, not hate and the urge to destroy.

We fall eight meters to the end of her safety line. I think that my extra weight will pull the piton out or snap the line.

We rebound, bounce three times, and hang above nothing. The piton holds. The safety line holds. Aenea's grip holds.

'Raul,' she says again. 'My God, my God.' I think that she is patting my head, but realize that she is trying to pull my torn scalp back into place, trying to keep my torn ear from coming off.

'It's all right,' I try to say, but find that my lips are bleeding and swollen. I can't enunciate the words I need to say to the ship.

Aenea understands. She leans forward and whispers into the comthread pickup on my cowl. 'Ship – hover and pick us up. Quickly.'

The shadow descends, moving in as if to crush us. The crowd is on the balcony again, eyes wide, as the giant ship floats to within three meters – gray cliffs on either side of us now – and extrudes a plank from the balcony. Friendly hands pull us in to safety.

Aenea does not release her grip with arms or legs until we are carried in off the balcony, into the carpeted interior, away from the drop.

I dimly hear the ship's voice. 'There are warships hurrying in-system toward us. Another is just above the atmosphere ten thousand kilometers to the west and closing . . .'

'Get us out of here,' orders Aenea. 'Straight up and out. I'll give you the in-system coordinates in a minute. *Go!*'

I feel dizzy and close my eyes to the sound of the fusion engines roaring. I have a faint impression of Aenea kissing me, holding me, kissing my eyelids and bloody forehead and cheek. My friend is crying.

'Rachel,' comes Aenea's voice from a distance, 'can you diagnose him?'

Fingers other than my beloved's touch me briefly. There are stabs of pain, but these are increasingly remote. A coldness is descending. I try to open my eyes but find both of them sealed shut by blood or swelling or both.

'What looks worst is the least threatening,' I hear Rachel say in her soft but no-nonsense voice. 'The scalp wound, ear, broken leg, and so forth. But I think that there are internal injuries . . . not just the ribs, but internal bleeding. And the claw wounds on his back go to the spinal cord.'

Aenea is still crying, but her tone is still in command. 'Some of you . . . Lhomo . . . A. Bettik . . . help me get him to the doc-in-the-box.'

'I'm sorry,' comes the ship's voice, just at the edge of my consciousness, 'but all three receptacles in the autosurgeon are in use. Sergeant Gregorius collapsed from his internal injuries and was brought to the third niche. All three patients are currently on full life support.'

'Damn,' I hear Aenea say under her breath. 'Raul? My dear, can you hear me?'

I start to reply, to say that I'm fine, don't worry about me, but all I hear from my own swollen lips and dislocated jaw is a garbled moan.

'Raul,' continues Aenea, 'we've got to get away from these Pax ships. We're going to carry you down to one of the cryogenic fugue cubbies, my dear. We're going to let you sleep a while until there's a slot free in the doc-in-the-box. Can you hear me, Raul?'

I decide against speaking and manage to nod. I feel something loose hanging down on my forehead, like a wet, displaced cap. My scalp.

'All right,' says Aenea. She leans close and whispers in my remaining ear. 'I love you, my dear friend. You're going to be all right. I *know* that.'

Hands lift me, carry me, eventually lay me on something hard and cool. The pain rages, but it is a distant thing and does not concern me.

Before they slide the lid closed on the cryogenic fugue cubby, I can distinctly hear the ship's voice saying calmly, 'Four Pax warships hailing us. They say that if we do not cut power in ten minutes, they will destroy us. May I point out that we are at least eleven hours from any translation point? And all four Pax warships are within firing distance.'

I hear Aenea's tired voice. 'Continue on this heading toward the coordinates I gave you, Ship. No reply to Pax warships.'

I try to smile. We have done this before – trying to outrun Pax ships against great odds. But there is one thing that I am learning that I would love to explain to Aenea, if my mouth worked and if my mind would clear a bit – it's just that however long one beats those odds, they catch up to you eventually. I consider this a minor revelation, overdue *satori*.

But now the cold is creeping over me, into me, through me – chilling my heart and mind and bones and belly. I can only hope that it is the cryogenic fugue coils cycling faster than I remember from my last trip. If it is death, then . . . well, it's death. But I want to see Aenea again.

This is my last thought.

TWENTY-FOUR

Falling! Heart pounding wildly, I awoke in what seemed to be a different universe.

I was floating, not falling. At first I thought that I was in an ocean, a salt ocean with positive buoyancy, floating like a fetus in a sepia-tinged salt sea, but then I realized that there was no gravity at all, no waves or currents, and that the medium was not water but thick sepia light. *The ship?* No, I was in a large, empty, darkened but light-circled space – an empty ovoid some fifteen meters or more across, with parchment walls through which I could see both the filtered light of a blazing sun and something more complicated, a vast organic structure curving away on all sides. I weakly moved my hands from their floating position to touch my face, head, body, and arms . . .

I *was* floating, tethered by only the lightest harness straps to some sort of sticktite strip on the curved inner wall. I was barefoot and wearing only a soft cotton tunic that I did not recognize – pajamas? hospital gown?

My face was tender and I could feel new ridges that might be scars. My hair was gone, the flesh above my skull was raw and definitely scarred, and my ear was there but very tender. My arms had several faint scars that I could see in the dim light. I pulled up my trouser leg and looked at what had been a badly broken lower leg. Healed and firm. I felt my ribs – tender but intact. I had made it to the doc-in-the-box after all.

I must have spoken aloud, for a dark figure floating nearby said, 'Eventually you did, Raul Endymion. But some of the surgery was done the old-fashioned way . . . and by me.'

I started – floating up against the sticktite strips. It had not been Aenea's voice.

The dark form floated closer and I recognized the shape, the hair, and – finally – the voice. 'Rachel,' I said. My tongue was dry, my lips cracked. I croaked the word rather than spoke it.

Rachel came closer and offered me a squeeze bottle. The first few drops came out as rumbling spheres – most of which splashed me on the face – but I soon got the knack of it and squeezed drops into my open mouth. The water tasted cool and wonderful.

'You've been getting liquids and sustenance via IV for two weeks,' said Rachel, 'but it's better if you drink directly.'

'Two weeks!' I said. I looked around. 'Aenea? Is she . . . are they . . .'

'Everyone's all right,' said Rachel. 'Aenea's busy. She's spent much of the last couple of weeks in here with you . . . watching over you . . . but when she had to go out with Minmun and the others, she had me stay with you.'

'Minmun?' I said. I peered through the translucent wall. One bright star – smaller than Hyperion's sun. The incredible geometries of the structure spreading away, curving out, from this ovoid room. 'Where am I?' I said. 'How did we get here?'

Rachel chuckled. 'I'll answer the second question first, let you see the answer to the first yourself in a few minutes. Aenea had the ship jump to this place. Father Captain de Soya, his Sergeant Gregorius, and the officer, Carel Shan, knew the coordinates for this star system. They were all unconscious, but the other survivor – their former prisoner, Hoag Liebler – knew where this place was hiding.'

I looked through the wall again. The structure seemed huge – a light-and-shadow latticework stretching out in all directions from this pod. How could they hide anything this large? And *who* hid it?

'How did we get to a translation point in time?' I croaked, taking a few more globules of water. 'I thought the Pax warships were closing in.'

'They were,' said Rachel. 'They did. We could never have gotten to a Hawking-drive translation point before they destroyed us. Here – you don't need to be stuck to the wall any longer.' She ripped off the sticktite strips and I floated free. Even in zero-g, I felt very weak.

Orienting myself so that I could still see Rachel's face in the dim sepia light, I said, 'So how did we do it?'

'We didn't translate,' said the young woman. 'Aenea directed the ship to a point in space where we farcasted directly to this system.'

'*Farcast?* There was an active space farcast portal? Like one of the kinds that the Hegemony FORCE ships used to transit? I didn't think that any of those had survived the Fall.'

Rachel was shaking her head. 'There was no farcaster portal. Nothing. Just an arbitrary point a few hundred thousand klicks from the second moon. It was quite a chase . . . the Pax ships kept hailing us and threatening to fire. Finally they did . . . lance beams leaping toward us from a dozen sources – we wouldn't even have been a debris field, just gas on a widening trajectory – but then we reached the point Aenea had pointed us toward and suddenly we were . . . here.'

I did not say *Where is here?* again, but I floated to the curved wall and tried to peer through it. The wall felt warm, spongy, organic, and it was filtering most of the sunlight. The resulting interior light was soft and beautiful, but it made it difficult to see out – just the one blazing star was visible and the hint of that incredible geometric structure beyond our pod.

'Ready to see the "where"?' said Rachel.

'Yeah.'

'Pod,' said Rachel, 'transparent surface, please.'

Suddenly there was nothing separating us from the outside. I almost shouted in terror. Instead, I flailed my arms and legs trying to find a solid surface to cling to until Rachel kicked closer and steadied me with a firm hand.

We were in space. The surrounding pod had simply disappeared. We were floating in space – seemed to be floating in space, except for the presence of air to breathe – and we were far out on a branch of a . . .

Tree is not the right word. I had seen trees. This was not a tree.

I had heard much about the old Templar worldtrees, had seen the stump of *the* Worldtree on God's Grove – and I'd heard about the kilometers-long shiptrees that had traveled between the star systems back in Martin Silenus's pilgrim days.

This was not a worldtree or a shiptree.

I had heard wild legends – from Aenea actually, so they were probably not legends – of a tree-ring around a star, a fantastical braided ring of living material stretching all the way around an Old Earth System-like sun. I had once tried to calculate how much living material that would require, and decided that it had to be nonsense.

This was no tree-ring.

What stretched out on every side of me, curving inward across expanses too large for my planet-formed mind to take in, was a branched and interwoven sphere of living plant material – trunks tens or hundreds of kilometers across, branches klicks wide, leaves hundreds of meters across, trailing root systems stretching like God's synapses for hundreds, no . . . thousands of kilometers into space – trellised and wrapped branches stretching out and inward in all directions, trunks the length of Old Earth's Mississippi River looking like tiny twigs in the distance, tree shapes the size of my home continent of Aquila on Hyperion blending into thousands of other clumps and masses of greenery, all bending inward and away, on all sides, in every direction . . . there were many black gaps, holes into space, some gaps larger than the trunks and greenery lacing through them . . . but nowhere were the gaps complete . . . everywhere the trunks and branches and roots intertwined, opening uncounted billions of green leaves to the star blazing away in the locus of vacuum at the center of . . .

I closed my eyes.

'This can't be real,' I said.

'It is,' said Rachel.

'The Ousters?' I said.

'Yes,' said Aenea's friend, the child of the *Cantos*. 'And the Templars. And the ergs. And . . . others. It's alive but a construct . . . a minded thing.'

'Impossible,' I said. 'It would take millions of years to grow this . . . sphere.'

'Biosphere,' said Rachel, smiling.

I shook my head again. 'Biosphere is an old term. It's just the closed vivisystem on and around a planet.'

'This is a biosphere,' Rachel said again. 'Only there are no planets here. Comets, yes, but no planets.' She pointed.

In the far distance, perhaps hundreds of thousands of kilometers away, where the interior of this living sphere began to fade to a green blur even in the unblinking vacuum, a long, white streak moved slowly through the black gap between trunks.

'A comet,' I repeated stupidly.

'For watering,' said Rachel. 'They have to use millions of them. Luckily there are many billions in the Oört cloud. More billions in the Kuiper Belt.'

I stared. There were other white specks out there, each with a long, glowing tail. Some moved between the trunks and branches as I watched, giving me some idea of the scale of this biosphere. *The comet trajectories were routed through the gaps in the plant material. If this is truly a sphere, the comets would have to pass back through the living globe on their way out-system. What kind of confidence does it take to do such a thing?*

'What is this thing we're in?' I said.

'An environmental pod,' said Rachel. 'Life bulb. This one is tailored for medical duty. It's not only been monitoring your IV drip, vital signs, and tissue regeneration, it's been growing and manufacturing many of the medicines and other chemicals.'

I reached out and touched the nearly transparent material. 'How thick is it?'

'About a millimeter,' said Rachel. 'But very strong. It can shield us from most micrometeorite impacts.'

'Where do the Ousters get such a material?'

'They biofacture the genes and it grows itself,' said Rachel. 'Do you feel up to going out to see Aenea and meeting some people? Everyone's been waiting for your awakening.'

'Yes,' I said, and then, quickly, 'no! Rachel?'

She floated there, waiting. I saw how lustrous her dark eyes were in the amazing light. Much like my darling's.

'Rachel . . .' I began awkwardly.

She waited, floating, reaching out to touch the transparent pod wall to orient herself head-up in relation to me.

'Rachel, we haven't really talked much . . .'

'You didn't like me,' said the young woman with a slight smile.

'That's not true . . . I mean, it was true, in a way . . . but it's because I just didn't understand things at first. It had been five years for Aenea that I'd been away . . . it was difficult . . . I guess that I was jealous.'

She arched a dark eyebrow. 'Jealous, how, Raul? Did you think that Aenea and I were lovers all those standard years you were gone?'

'Well, no . . . I mean, I didn't know . . .'

Rachel held up a hand, sparing me further flummoxing. 'We aren't,' she said. 'We never were. Aenea would never have considered such a thing. *Theo* might have entertained the possibility, but she knew from the start that Aenea and I were destined to love certain men.'

I stared. *Destined?*

Rachel smiled again. I could imagine that grin on the little girl Sol Weintraub had talked about in his Hyperion *Cantos*. 'Don't worry, Raul. I happen to know for a fact that Aenea has never loved anyone but you. Even when she was a little girl. Even before she met you. You've always been her chosen one.' The young woman's smile became rueful. 'We should all be so lucky.'

I started to speak, hesitated.

Rachel's smile faded. 'Oh. She told you about the one-year eleven-month one-week six-hour interregnum?'

'Yes,' I said. 'And about her having . . .' I stopped. It would be foolish to choke up in front of this strong woman. She would never look at me the same again.

'A baby?' finished Rachel quickly.

I looked at her as if trying to find some answer in her handsome features. 'Did Aenea tell you about it?' I said, feeling like I was betraying my dear friend somewhat by trying to get this information from someone else. But I could not stop. 'Did you know at the time what . . .'

'Where she was?' said Rachel, returning my intense gaze. 'What was happening to her? That she was getting married?'

I could only nod.

'Yes,' said Rachel. 'We knew.'

'Were you there with her?'

Rachel seemed to hesitate, as if weighing her answer. 'No,' she said at last. 'A. Bettik, Theo, and I waited for almost two years for her to return. We carried on her . . . ministry? Mission? . . . Whatever it is, we carried it on while she was gone . . . sharing some of her lessons, finding people who wished to partake of communion, letting them know when she would return.'

'So you knew when she would return?'

'Yes,' said Rachel. 'To the day.'

'How?'

'That's when she *had* to return,' said the dark-haired woman. 'She had taken every possible minute that she could without jeopardizing her mission. The Pax was hunting for us the next day . . . they would have seized all of us if Aenea had not returned and farcast us away.'

I nodded, but was not thinking about close calls with the Pax. 'Did you meet . . . him?' I said, trying unsuccessfully to keep my tone neutral.

Rachel's expression remained serious. 'Father to their child, you mean? Aenea's husband?'

I felt that Rachel was not trying to be cruel, but the words tore at me far worse than had Nemes's claws. 'Yes,' I said. 'Him.'

Rachel shook her head. 'None of us had met him when she went away.'

'But you do know why she chose him to be the father of her child?' I persisted, feeling like the Grand Inquisitor we had left behind on T'ien Shan.

'Yes,' said Rachel, returning my gaze, giving me no more.

'Was it something to do with her . . . her mission?' I said, feeling my throat growing tighter and tighter, my voice more strained. 'Is it something she had to do . . . some reason the child had to be born to them? Can you tell me anything, Rachel?'

She took my wrist then, gripping it strongly. 'Raul, you know that Aenea will explain this when it's time to do so.'

I pulled away, making a rude noise. 'When it's time,' I growled. 'Jesus H. Christ, I'm sick of hearing that phrase. And I'm sick of waiting.'

Rachel shrugged. 'Confront her then. Threaten to beat her up if she doesn't tell you. You clobbered that Nemes thing . . . Aenea shouldn't be a problem.'

I glowered at the woman.

'Seriously, Raul, this is between you and Aenea. All I can tell you is that you are the only man she has ever talked about, and – as far as I can tell – the only man she has ever loved.'

'How the hell can you . . .' I began angrily and then forced myself to shut up. I patted her arm awkwardly, the motion making me begin to pivot around the center of my own axis. It was hard to stay near someone in zero-g without touching them. 'Thank you, Rachel,' I said.

'Ready to go see everyone?'

I took a breath. 'Almost,' I said. 'Can this pod surface be made reflective?'

'Pod,' said Rachel, 'ninety percent translucence. High interior reflectivity.' To me she said, 'Checking in the mirror before your big date?'

The surface had become about as reflective as a still puddle of water – not a perfect mirror, but clear enough and bright enough to show me a Raul Endymion with scars on his face and bare scalp, the skin on his skull a babyish pink, traces of bruise and swelling under and around his eyes, and thin . . . very thin. The bones and muscles of my face and upper body seemed to have been sketched in bold pencil strokes. My eyes looked different.

'Jesus H. Christ,' I said again.

Rachel made a motion with her hand. 'The autosurgeon wanted you for another week, but Aenea couldn't wait. The scars aren't permanent . . . at least most of them. The pod medicine in the IV is taking care of the regeneration. Your hair will start growing back in two or three standard weeks.'

I touched my scalp. It was like patting the scarred and especially tender butt of an ugly newborn. 'Two or three weeks,' I said. 'Great. Fucking great.'

'Don't sweat it,' said Rachel. 'I think it looks rather dashing, actually. I'd keep that look if I were you, Raul. Besides, I hear that Aenea is a pushover for older men. And right now, you certainly look older.'

'Thanks,' I said dryly.

'You're welcome,' said Rachel. 'Pod. Open iris. Access to main pressurized stem connector.'

She led the way out, kicking and floating ahead of me through the irising wall.

Aenea hugged me so hard when I came into the room . . . pod . . . that I wondered if my broken ribs might have given way again. I hugged her back just as hard.

The trip through the pressurized stem connector had been commonplace enough, if one counted being shot down a flexible, translucent, two-meter-wide pipeline at speeds up to what I estimated as sixty klicks per hour – they used currents of oxygen flowing at high speeds in opposite directions to give a boost to one's kicking and swimming through air – all the while other people, mostly very thin, hairless, and exceptionally tall other people, whizzed by silently in the opposite direction at closing speeds in excess of a hundred and twenty klicks per hour, missing us by centimeters. Then there were the hub pods, into which Rachel and I were accelerated at high speed, like corpuscles being blasted into ventricles and auricles of a huge heart, and through which we tumbled, kicked, avoided other high-speed travelers, and exited via one of a dozen other stem-connector openings. I was lost within minutes, but Rachel seemed to know her way – she pointed out that there were subtle colors embedded in the plant flesh over each exit – and soon we had entered a pod not much larger than mine, but crowded with cubbies, sticktite seating areas, and people. Some of the people – like Aenea, A. Bettik, Theo, the Dorje Phamo, and Lhomo Dondrub – I knew well; other people there – Father Captain de Soya, obviously renewed and recovered from his terrible wounds and wearing a priest's black trousers, tunic, and Roman collar, Sergeant Gregorius in his Swiss Guard combat fatigues – I had met recently and knew by sight; other people, like the long, thin, other-worldly Ousters and the hooded Templars were wondrous and strange, but well within my range of understanding; while still other individuals there – quickly introduced by Aenea as the Templar True Voice of the Tree Het Masteen and the former Hegemony FORCE Colonel Fed-mahn Kassad, I knew of but did not actually believe I was meeting. More than Rachel or the fact of Aenea's mother, Brawne Lamia, these were figures not just from the old poet's *Cantos* but archetypes from deep myth, long dead at the very least, and probably never real to begin with in the fixed, everyday, eat-sleep-and-use-the-toilet firmament of things.

And finally in this zero-gravity Ouster pod there were the other people who were not people at all, at least from my frame of reference: such as the willowy green beings who were introduced by Aenea as LLeeoonn and OOeeaall, two of the few surviving Seneschai empaths from Hebron – *alien and intelligent beings*. I looked at these strange creatures – the palest cypress-green skin and eyes; bodies so thin that I could have encircled their torso with my fingers; symmetrical like us with two arms, two legs, a head, but, of course, not really like us at all; limbs articulated more like single, unbroken, fluid lines than evolved of hinged bone and gristle; splayed digits like toads' hands; and heads more like a human fetus's than a human adult's. Their eyes were little more than shadowy spots on the green flesh of their faces.

The Seneschai had been reported to have died out during the early days of the Hegira . . . they were little more than legend, even less real than the tale of the soldier Kassad or the Templar Het Masteen.

One of these green legends brushed its three-fingered hand over my palm as we were introduced.

There were other non-human, non-Ouster, non-android entities in the pod.

Floating near the translucent wall of the pod were what looked to be large, greenish-white platelets – soft, shuddering saucers of soft material – each almost two meters across. I had seen these life-forms before . . . on the cloud world where I had been eaten by the sky squid.

Not eaten, M. Endymion, came surges of language echoing in my head, *only transported.*

Telepathy? I thought, half directing the query to the platelets. I remembered the surge of language-thought on the cloud world, and how I had wondered where it had originated.

It was Aenea who answered. 'It feels like telepathy,' she said softly, 'but there's nothing mystical about it. The Akerataeli learned our language the old-fashioned way – their zeplin symbiotes heard the sound vibrations and the Akerataeli broke it down and analyzed it. They control the zeplins by a form of long-distance, very tightly focused microwave pulses . . .'

'The zeplin was the thing that swallowed me on the cloud world,' I said.

'Yes,' said Aenea.

'Like the zeplins on Whirl?'

'Yes, and in Jupiter's atmosphere as well.'

'I thought that they were hunted to extinction during the early Hegira years.'

'They were eradicated on Whirl,' said Aenea. 'And even before the Hegira on Jupiter. But you weren't paragliding your kayak on Jupiter or Whirl . . . but on another oxygen-rich gas giant six hundred light-years into the Outback.'

I nodded. 'I'm sorry I interrupted. You were saying . . . microwave impulses . . .'

Aenea made that graceful throwing-away gesture I'd known since she was a child. 'Just that they control their zeplin symbiote partners' actions by precise microwave stimulation of certain nerve and brain centers. We've given the Akerataeli permission to stimulate our speech centers so that we "hear" their messages. I take it that it's rather like playing a complicated piano for them . . .'

I nodded but did not really understand.

'The Akerataeli are also a spacefaring race,' said Father Captain de Soya. 'Over the eons, they have colonized more than ten thousand oxygen-rich gas giant worlds.'

'Ten thousand!' I said. I think that for a moment my jaw actually hung slack. In humankind's more than twelve hundred years of traveling in space we had explored and settled on less than ten percent of that number of planets.

'The Akerataeli have been at it longer than we,' said de Soya softly.

I looked at the gently vibrating platelets. They had no eyes that I could see, certainly no ears. Were they hearing us? They must . . . one of them had responded to my thoughts. Could they *read* minds as well as stimulate language-thoughts?

While I was staring at them, the conversation between the humans and Ousters in the room resumed.

'The intelligence is reliable,' said the pale Ouster whom I later learned was named Navson Hamnim. 'There were at least three hundred archangel-class ships gathering at System Lacaille 9352. Each ship has a representative of the Order of the Knights of Jerusalem or Malta. It is definitely a major Crusade.'

'Lacaille 9352,' mused de Soya. 'Sibiatu's Bitterness. I know the place. How old is this intelligence?'

'Twenty hours,' said Navson Hamnim. 'The data was sent via the only Gideon-drive courier drone we have left . . . of the three drones captured during your raids, two have been destroyed. We are fairly sure that the scoutship which sent this drone was detected and destroyed seconds after launching the courier.'

'Three hundred archangels,' said de Soya. He rubbed his cheeks. 'If they are aware we know about them, they could make a Gideon jump this direction within days . . . hours. Assume two days' resurrection time, we may have less than three days to prepare. Have defenses been improved since I left?'

Another Ouster whom I later knew as Systenj Coredwell opened his hands in a gesture that I would discover meant 'in no way'. I noticed that there was webbing between the long fingers. 'Most of the fighting ships have had to jump to the Great Wall salient to hold off their Task Force HORSEHEAD. The fighting is very bitter there. Few of the ships are expected to return.'

'Does your intelligence say whether the Pax knows what you have here?' asked Aenea.

Navson Hamnim opened his hands in a subtle variation of Coredwell's gesture. 'We think not. But they know now that this has been a major staging area for our recent defensive battles. I would venture that they think this is just another base – perhaps with a partial orbital forest ring.'

'Is there anything we can do to break up the Crusade before it jumps this way?' said Aenea, speaking to everyone in the room.

'No.' The flat syllable came from the tall man who had been introduced as Colonel Fedmahn Kassad. His Web English had a strange accent. He was a tall man, extremely thin but muscular, with an equally thin beard along his jawline and around his mouth. In the old poet's *Cantos*, Kassad had been described as a reasonably young man, but this warrior was in his standard sixties, at least, with heavy lines around his thin mouth and small eyes, his dark complexion burned even darker by long exposure to desert-world sun or deep-space UV, the spiked hair on top of his head rising like short silver nails.

Everyone looked at Kassad and waited.

'With de Soya's ship destroyed,' said the Colonel, 'our only chance at successful hit-and-run operations is gone. The few Hawking-drive warships we have left would take a time-debt of at least two months to jump to Lacaille 9352 and back. The Crusade archangels would almost certainly be here and gone by then . . . and we would be defenseless.'

Navson Hamnim kicked away from the pod wall and oriented himself right side up in relation to Kassad. 'These few warships do not offer us a defense in any case,' he said softly, his own Web English more musical than accented. 'Should we not consider dying while on the attack?'

Aenea floated between the two men. 'I think that we should consider not dying at all,' she said. 'Nor allowing the biosphere to be destroyed.'

A positive sentiment, a voice spoke in my head. *But not all positive sentiments can be supported by updrafts of possible action.*

'True,' said Aenea, looking at the platelets, 'but perhaps in this case the updrafts will build.'

Good thermals to you all, said the voice in my head. The platelets moved toward the pod wall, which irised open for them. Then they were gone.

Aenea took a breath. 'Shall we meet on the *Yggdrasill* to share the main meal in seven hours and continue this discussion? Perhaps someone will have an idea.'

There was no dissension. People, Ousters, and Seneschai exited by a score of openings that had not been there a moment before.

Aenea floated over and hugged me again. I patted her hair.

'My friend,' she said softly. 'Come with me.'

It was her private living pod – *our* private living pod, she informed me – and it was much like the one in which I awoke, except that there were organic shelves, niches, writing surfaces, storage cubbies, and facilities for comlog interface. Some of my clothes from the ship were folded neatly in a cubby and my extra boots were in a fiberplastic drawer.

Aenea pulled food from a cold-box cubby and began making sandwiches. 'You must be hungry, my dear,' she said, tearing off pieces of rough bread. I saw zygoat cheese on the sticktite zero-g work surface, some wrapped pieces of roast beef that must have come from the ship, bulbs of mustard, and several tankards of T'ien Shan rice beer. Suddenly I was starved.

The sandwiches were large and thick. She set them on catchplates made of some strong fiber, lifted her own meal and a beer bulb, and kicked toward the outer wall. A portal appeared and began to iris open.

'Uh . . .' I said alertly, meaning *Excuse me, Aenea, but that's space out there. Aren't we both going to explosively decompress and die horribly?*

She kicked out through the organic portal and I shrugged and followed.

There were catwalks, suspension bridges, sticktite stairways, balconies, and terraces out there – made of steel-hard plant fiber and winding around the pods, stalks, branches, and trunks like so much ivy. There was also air to breathe. It smelled of a forest after a rain.

'Containment field,' I said, thinking that I should have expected this. After all, if the Consul's ancient starship could have a balcony . . .

I looked around. 'What powers it?' I said. 'Solar receptors?'

'Indirectly,' said Aenea, finding us a sticktite bench and mat. There were no railings on this tiny, intricately woven balcony. The huge branch – at least thirty meters across – ended in a profusion of leaves above us and the latticework web of the trunks and branches 'beneath' us convinced my inner ear that we were many kilometers up on a wall made of crisscrossed green girders. I resisted the urge to throw myself down on the sticktite mat and cling for dear life. A radiant gossamer fluttered by, followed by some type of small bird with a v-shaped tail.

'Indirectly?' I said, my mouth full as I took a huge bite of sandwich.

'The sunlight – for the most part – is converted to containment fields by ergs,' continued my friend, sipping her beer and looking out at the seemingly infinite expanse of leaves above us, below us, to all sides of us, their green faces all turned toward the brilliant star. There was not enough air to give us a blue sky, but the containment field polarized the view toward the sun just enough to keep us from being blinded when we glanced that direction.

I almost spat my food out, managed to swallow instead, and said, 'Ergs? As in Aldebaran energy binders? You were serious? Ergs like the one taken on the last Hyperion pilgrimage?'

'Yes,' said Aenea. Her dark eyes were focused on me now.

'I thought they were extinct.'

'Nope,' said Aenea.

I took a long drink from the beer bulb and shook my head. 'I'm confused.'

'You have a right to be, my dear friend,' Aenea said softly.

'This place . . .' I made a weak gesture toward the wall of branches and leaves trailing away so much farther than a planetary horizon, the infinitely distant curve of green and black far above us. 'It's impossible,' I said.

'Not quite,' said Aenea. 'The Templars and Ousters have been working on it – and others like it – for a thousand years.'

I began chewing again. The cheese and roast beef were delicious. 'So this is where the thousands and millions of trees went when they abandoned God's Grove during the Fall.'

'Some of them,' said Aenea. 'But the Templars had been working with the Ousters to develop orbital forest rings and biospheres long before that.'

I peered up. The distances made me dizzy. The sense of being on this small, leafy platform so many kilometers above nothing made me reel. Far below us and to our right, something that looked like a tiny, green sprig moved slowly between the latticed branches. I saw the film of energy field around it and realized that I was looking at one of the fabled Templar treeships, almost certainly kilometers long. 'Is this finished, then?' I said. 'A true Dyson sphere? A globe around a star?'

Aenea shook her head. 'Far from it, although about twenty standard years ago, they made contact with all the primary trunk tendrils. Technically it's a sphere, but most of it is comprised of holes at this point – some many millions of klicks across.'

'Fan-fucking-tastic,' I said, realizing that I could have been more eloquent. I rubbed my cheeks, feeling the heavy growth of beard there. 'I've been out of it for two weeks?' I said.

'Fifteen standard days,' said Aenea.

'Usually the doc-in-the-box works more quickly than that,' I said. I finished the sandwich, stuck the catchplate to the table surface, and concentrated on the beer.

'Usually it does,' agreed Aenea. 'Rachel must have told you that you spent a relatively short time in the autosurgeon. She did most of the initial surgery herself.'

'Why?' I said.

'The box was full,' said Aenea. 'We defrosted you from fugue as soon as we got here, but the three in the doc ahead of you were in bad shape. De Soya was near death for a full week. The sergeant . . . Gregorius . . . was much more seriously injured than he had let on when we met him on the Great Peak. And the third officer – Carel Shan – died despite the box's and the Ouster medics' best efforts.'

'Shit,' I said, lowering the beer. 'I'm sorry to hear that.' One got used to autosurgeons fixing almost anything.

Aenea looked at me with such intensity that I could feel her gaze warming my skin as surely as I could feel the powerful sunlight. 'How *are* you, Raul?'

'Great,' I said. 'I ache a bit. I can feel the healing ribs. The scars itch. And I feel like I overslept by two weeks . . . but I feel good.'

She took my hand. I realized that her eyes were moist. 'I would have been really pissed if you'd died on me,' she said after a moment, her voice thick.

'Me too.' I squeezed her hand, looked up, and suddenly leaped to my feet, sending the beer bulb spiraling off into thin air and almost launching myself. Only the sticktite velcro soles on my soft shoes kept me anchored. 'Holy *shit*!' I said, pointing.

From this distance, it looked like a squid, perhaps only a meter or two long. From experience and a growing sense of perspective here, I knew better.

'One of the zeplins,' said Aenea. 'The Akerataeli have tens of thousands working on the Biosphere. They stay inside the CO_2 and O_2 envelopes.'

'It's not going to eat me again, is it?' I said.

Aenea grinned. 'I doubt it. The one that got a taste of you has probably spread the word.'

I looked for my beer, saw the bulb tumbling away a hundred meters below us, considered leaping after it, thought better of it, and sat down on the sticktite bench.

Aenea gave me her bulb. 'Go ahead. I can never finish those things.' She watched me drink. 'Any other questions while we're talking?'

I swallowed and made a dismissive gesture. 'Well, there happens to be a bunch of extinct, mythical, and dead people around. Care to explain that?'

'By extinct you mean the zeplins, Seneschai, and Templars?' she said.

'Yeah. And the ergs . . . although I haven't seen one of those yet.'

'The Templars and Ousters have been working to preserve such hunted sentient species the way the colonists on Maui-Covenant tried to save the Old Earth dolphins,' she said. 'From the early Hegira colonists, then the Hegemony, and now the Pax.'

'And the mythical and dead people?' I said.

'By that you mean Colonel Kassad?'

'And Het Masteen,' I said. 'And, for that matter, Rachel. We seem to have the whole cast of the friggin' Hyperion *Cantos* showing up here.'

'Not quite,' said Aenea, her voice soft and a bit sad. 'The Consul is dead. Father Duré is never allowed to live. And my mother is gone.'

'Sorry, kiddo . . .'

She touched my hand again. 'That's all right. I know what you mean . . . it's disconcerting.'

'Did you know Colonel Kassad or Het Masteen before this?' I said.

Aenea shook her head. 'My mother told me about them, of course . . . and Uncle Martin had things to add to his poem's description. But they were gone before I was born.'

'Gone,' I repeated. 'Don't you mean *dead*?' I worked to remember the *Cantos* stanzas. According to the old poet's tale, Het Masteen, the tall Templar, the True Voice of the Tree, had disappeared on the windwagon trip across Hyperion's Sea of Grass shortly after his treeship, the *Yggdrasill*, had burned in orbit. Blood in the Templar's cabin suggested the Shrike. He had left behind the erg in a Mobius cube. Sometime later, they had found Masteen in the Valley of the Time Tombs. He had not been able to explain his absence – had said only that the blood in the windwagon had not been his – had cried out that it was his job to be the Voice of the Tree of Pain – and had died.

Colonel Kassad had disappeared at about that same time – shortly after entering the Valley of the Time Tombs – but the FORCE Colonel had, according to Martin Silenus's *Cantos*, followed his phantom lover, Moneta, into the far future where he was to die in combat with the Shrike. I closed my eyes and recited aloud:

'. . . *Later, in the death carnage of the valley,*
Moneta and a few of the Chosen Warriors,
Wounded all,
Torn and tossed themselves by the Shrike horde's fury,
Found the body of Fedmahn Kassad
Still wrapped in death's embrace with the
Silent Shrike.
Lifting the warrior, carrying him, touching him
With reverence born of loss and battle,
They washed and tended his ravaged body,
And bore him to the Crystal Monolith.
Here the hero was laid on a bier of white marble,
Weapons were set at his feet.
In the valley beyond, a great bonfire filled
The air with light.
Human men and women carried torches
Through the dark,
While others descended, wingsoft, through
Morning lapis lazuli,
And some others arrived in faery craft, bubbles of light,
While still others descended on wings of energy
Or wrapped in circles of green and gold.

Later, as the stars burned in place,
Moneta made her farewells to her future's
Friends and entered the Sphinx.
Multitudes sang.
Rat things poked among fallen pennants
In the field where heroes fell,
While the wind whispered among carapace
And blade, steel, and thorn.
And thus,
In the Valley,
The great Tombs shimmered,
Faded from gold to bronze,
And started their long voyage back.'

'Impressive memory,' said Aenea.

'Grandam used to cuff me if I screwed it up,' I said. 'Don't change the subject. The Templar and the Colonel sound dead to me.'

'And so they will be,' said Aenea. 'And so shall we all.'

I waited for her to shift out of her Delphic phase.

'The *Cantos* say that Het Masteen was carried away somewhere . . . some-*when* by the Shrike,' she said. 'He later died in the Valley of the Time Tombs after returning. The poem did not say if he was gone an hour or thirty years. Uncle Martin did not know.'

I squinted at her. 'What about Kassad, kiddo? The *Cantos* are fairly specific there . . . the Colonel follows Moneta into the far future, engages in a battle with the Shrike . . .'

'With legions of Shrikes, actually,' corrected my friend.

'Yeah,' I said. I had never really understood that. 'But it seems continuous enough . . . he follows her, he fights, he dies, his body is put in the Crystal Monolith, and it and Moneta begin the long trip back through time.'

Aenea nodded and smiled. 'With the Shrike,' she said.

I paused. The Shrike had emerged from the Tombs . . . Moneta had traveled with it somehow . . . so although the *Cantos* clearly said that Kassad had destroyed the Shrike in that great, final battle, the monster was somehow alive and traveling with Moneta and Kassad's body back through . . .

Damn. Did the poem ever actually say that Kassad was dead?

'Uncle Martin had to fake parts of the tale, you know,' said Aenea. 'He had some descriptions from Rachel, but he took poetic license on the parts he did not understand.'

'Uh-huh,' I said. *Rachel. Moneta. The* Cantos *had clearly suggested that the girl-child, Rachel, who went forward with her father, Sol, to the future, would return as the woman Moneta. Colonel Kassad's phantom lover. The woman he would follow into the future to his fate . . . And what had Rachel said to me a few hours earlier when I was suspicious that she and Aenea were lovers? 'I happen to be involved with a certain soldier . . . male . . . whom you'll* meet today. Well, actually, I *will* be involved with him someday. I mean . . . shit, it's complicated.'

Indeed. My head hurt. I set down the beer bulb and held my head in my hands.

'It's more complicated than that,' said Aenea.

I peered up at her through my fingers. 'Care to explain?'

'Yes, but . . .'

'I know,' I said. 'At some other time.'

'Yes,' said Aenea, her hand on mine.

'Any reason why we can't talk about it now?' I said.

Aenea nodded. 'We have to go in our pod now and opaque the walls,' she said.

'We do?' I said.

'Yes.'

'And then what?' I said.

'Then,' said Aenea, floating free of the sticktite mat and pulling me with her, 'we make love for hours.'

TWENTY-FIVE

Zero-g. Weightlessness.

I had never really appreciated those terms and that reality before.

Our living pod was opaqued to the point that the rich evening light glowed as if through thick parchment. Once again, I had the impression of being in a warm heart. Once again I realized how much Aenea was in *my* heart.

At first the encounter bordered on the clinical as Aenea carefully removed my clothes and inspected the healing surgical scars, gently touched my repaired ribs, and ran her palm down my back.

'I should shave,' I said, 'and shower.'

'Nonsense,' whispered my friend. 'I've given you sponge and sonic baths every day . . . including this morning. You're perfectly clean, my dear. And I like the whiskers.' She moved her fingers across my cheek.

We floated above the soft and rounded cubby shelves. I helped Aenea out of her shirt, trousers, and underwear. As each piece came clear, she kicked it through the air into the cubby drawer, shutting the fiber panel with her bare foot when everything was inside. We both chuckled. My own clothes were still floating in the quiet air, the sleeves of my shirt gesturing in slow motion.

'I'll get the . . .' I began.

'No you won't,' said Aenea and pulled me closer.

Even kissing demands new skills in zero-g. Aenea's hair coiled around her head in a sunlit corona as I held her face in my hands and kissed her – her lips, eyes, cheeks, forehead, and lips again. We began tumbling slowly, brushing the smooth and glowing wall. It was as warm as my dear friend's flesh. One of us pushed off and we tumbled together into the middle of the oval pod space.

Our kissing became more urgent. Each time we moved to hold the other more tightly, we would begin to pivot around an invisible center of mass, arms and legs entangled as we pressed tighter and rotated more quickly. Without disentangling or interrupting our kiss, I held out one arm, waited for the flesh-warm walls to reach us, and stopped our tumble. The contact pushed us away from the curved, warmly glowing wall and sent us spinning very slowly toward the center again.

Aenea broke our kiss and moved her head back a moment, still holding my arms, regarding me from arm's length. I had seen her smile ten thousand times in the last ten years of her life – had thought that I knew all of her smiles – but this one was deeper, older, more mysterious, and more mischievous than any I had seen before.

'Don't move,' she whispered, and, pushing softly against my arm for leverage, rotated in space.

'Aenea . . .' was all I could say and then I could say nothing. I closed my eyes, oblivious of everything except sensation. I could feel my darling's hands tight on the backs of my legs, pulling me closer to her.

After a moment, her knees came to rest against my shoulders, her thighs bumping softly against my chest. I reached out to the hollow of her back and pulled her closer, sliding my cheek along the strong muscle of her inner thigh. At Taliesin West, one of the cooks had owned a tabby cat. Many evenings, when I was sitting alone out on the western terrace watching the sunset and feeling the stones lose their day's heat, waiting for the hour when Aenea and I could sit in her shelter and talk about everything and nothing, I would watch the cat lap slowly from her bowl of cream. I visualized that cat now, but within minutes I could visualize nothing but the immediate and overpowering sense of my dear friend opening to me, of the subtle taste of the sea, of our movements like the tide rising, of all of my senses being centered in the slow but growing sensation at the core of me.

How long we floated this way, I have no idea. Such overwhelming excitement is like a fire that consumes time. Total intimacy is an exemption from the space/time demands of the universe. Only the growing prerogatives of our passion and the ineluctable need to be even closer than this penultimate closeness marked the minutes of our lovemaking.

Aenea opened her legs wider, moved away, released me with her mouth but not her hand. We pivoted again in the sepia light, her tight fingers and my excitement the center of our slow rotation. We kissed, lips moist, Aenea's grasp tightening around me. 'Now,' she whispered. I obeyed.

If there is a true secret to the universe, it is this . . . these first few seconds of warmth and entry and complete acceptance by one's beloved. We kissed again, oblivious of our slow tumbling, the rich light taking on a heart warmth around us. I opened my eyes long enough to see Aenea's hair swirling like Ophelia's cloak in the wine-dark sea of air in which we floated. It was indeed like holding my beloved in deep, salty water – buoyed up and weightless, the warmth of her around me like the rising tide, our movements as regular as the surf against warm sand.

'Oops . . .' whispered Aenea after only a moment of this perfection.

I paused in my kissing long enough to assess what was separating us. 'Newton's Law,' I whispered against her cheek.

'For every action . . .' whispered Aenea, chuckling softly, holding my shoulders like a swimmer pausing to rest.

'. . . an equal and opposite reaction . . .' I said, smiling until she kissed me again.

'Solution,' whispered Aenea. Her legs closed tight around my hips. Her breasts floated between us, the nipples teasing my chest.

Then she lay back, again the swimmer, floating this time, her arms spread but her fingers still interlaced with mine. We continued to pivot slowly around our common center of gravity, a slow tumble, my head coming over and down and around like a rider on a porpoise doing slow cartwheels in the sunlit depths, but I was no longer interested or aware of the elegant ballistics of our lovemaking, but only in the lovemaking. We moved faster in the warm sea of air.

Some minutes later, Aenea released my hands, moved upright and forward as we tumbled together, still moving, sank her short nails into my back even while she kissed me with a wild urgency, and then moved her mouth away to gasp and cry out, once, softly. At the same instant as her cry, I felt the warm universe of her close around me with that short, tight throb, that intimate, shared pulse. A second later it was my turn to gasp, to cling to her as I throbbed within her, to whisper into her salty neck and floating hair – 'Aenea . . . Aenea.' A prayer. My only prayer then. My only prayer now.

For a long time we floated together even after we had become two people again rather than one. Our legs were still intertwined, our fingers stroking and holding one another. I kissed her throat and felt her pulse like a memory echo against my lips. She ran her fingers through my sweaty hair.

I realized that for this moment, nothing in the past mattered. Nothing terrible in the future mattered. What mattered was her skin against me, her hand holding me, the perfume of her hair and skin and the warmth of her breath against my chest. *This* was *satori*. *This* was truth.

Aenea kicked away to the pod cubby just long enough to return with a small, warm, and wet towel. We took turns wiping some of the sweat and slickness from us. My shirt floated by, the empty sleeves attempting to swim in the gentle air currents. Aenea laughed and lingered in her washing and drying, the simple act quickly turning into something else.

'Oops,' said Aenea, smiling at me. 'How did that happen?'

'Newton's Law?' I said.

'That makes sense,' she whispered. 'Then what would be the reaction if I were to do . . . this?'

I think we were both surprised by the instant result of her experiment.

'We have hours until we have to meet the others on the treeship,' she said softly. She said something to the living pod and the curved wall went absolutely transparent. It was as if we were floating among these countless branches and sail-sized leaves, the sun's warmth bathing us one moment and then being submerged in night and stars when we looked out the other side of the clear pod.

'Don't worry,' said Aenea, 'we can see out, but the exterior is opaque on the outside. Reflective.'

'How can you be sure?' I whispered, kissing her neck again, seeking the soft pulse.

Aenea sighed. 'I guess we can't without going out to look in. Sort of a David Hume problem.'

I tried to remember my philosophy readings at Taliesin, recalled our discussions of Berkeley, Hume, and Kant, and chuckled. 'There's another way we can check,' I said, rubbing my bare feet along her calves and the backs of her legs.

'How's that?' murmured my friend, her eyes closed.

'If anyone can see in,' I said, floating behind her, rubbing her back without letting her float away, 'there's going to be a huge crowd of Ouster angels and Templar treeships and comet farmers hanging out there in about thirty minutes.'

'Really,' said Aenea, eyes still closed. 'And why is that?'

I began to show her.

She opened her eyes. 'Oh, my,' she said softly.

I was afraid that I was shocking her.

'Raul?' she whispered.

'Hmmm?' I said, not stopping what I was doing. I closed my eyes.

'Maybe you're right about the pod being reflective on the outside,' she whispered and then sighed again, more deeply this time.

'Mmmhmm?' I said.

She grabbed my ears and floated around, pulled herself closer, and whispered, 'Why don't we leave the outside transparent and make the *inside* wall reflective?'

My eyes snapped open.

'Just kidding,' she whispered and pushed away from the pod wall, pulling me with her into the central sphere of warm air.

The stars blazed around us.

We wore formal black outfits to the dinner party and conference on the *Yggdrasill*. I was tense with excitement to be aboard one of the legendary treeships and it was a bit of an anticlimax when I realized that I had not noticed when we had crossed from the biosphere branches to the treeship trunk. It was only when hundreds of us were gathered on a series of platforms and opened pods, when the treeship had actually cast off and moved away from the encircling city-sized leaves, province-sized branches, and continent-sized trunks that I realized that we were aboard and moving.

The *Yggdrasill* must have been a bit more than a kilometer in length, from the narrowed crown of the tree to the resplendent root system of boiling fusion energy at its base. A bit of gravity returned under drive – probably only a few percentage points of microgravity – but it was still disconcerting after so much zero-g. It did help with our orientation though, the scores of us able to sit at tables and look one another in the eyes rather than float for a polite position . . . I thought of Aenea and our last hours together and blushed at this thought. There were tables and chairs on the multitiered platforms and many who were not seated there thronged on the flimsy suspension bridges that connected platforms to more far-flung branches, or on the helixes of spiral stairways winding up through branches, leaves, and binding the central trunk like vines, or hung from swingvines and leafy bowers.

Aenea and I were seated at the round central table along with the True

Voice of the Tree Het Masteen, the Ouster leaders, and two score of other Templars, refugees from T'ien Shan, and others. I was on Aenea's immediate left. The Templar dignitaries were seated to her right. Even now I can remember the names of most of the others present at the central table.

Besides the captain of the treeship, Het Masteen, there were half a dozen other Templars there, including Ket Rosteen – introduced as the True Voice of the Startree, High Priest of the Muir, and Spokesman of the Templar Brotherhood. The dozen Ousters at the main table included Systenj Coredwell and Navson Hamnim, but there were others who looked little like these tall, thin Ouster archetypes: Am Chipeta and Kent Quinkent, two shorter, darker Ousters – a married couple, I thought – with lively eyes and no webs between their fingers; Sian Quintana Ka'an, a female who was either wearing a resplendent robe of bright feathers or who had been born with them, and her blue-feathered partners Paul Uray and Morgan Bottoms. Two others better fit the Ouster image – Driven. Nicaagat and Palou Koror – for they were vacuum-adapted and wore their silvery skinsuits through the entire banquet.

There were four of the Hebronese Seneschai Aluit present – LLeeoonn and OOeeaall, whom I had met at the earlier gathering, as well as another pair of the willowy green figures introduced by Aenea as AAllooee and NNeelloo. I could only assume that the four were related or marriage-bound in some complex way.

The alien Akerataeli appeared to be missing until Aenea pointed to a place far out among the branches where the microgravity was even less, and there – between the gossamers and glowbirds – floated the platelet beings. Even the erg binders who were controlling the treeship's containment field were present by proxy in the form of three Mobius cubes with translator discs embedded in their black matrices.

Father Captain Federico de Soya sat to my left and his aide, Sergeant Gregorius, sat to the left of him. Next to the sergeant sat Colonel Fedmahn Kassad in his formal FORCE black uniform, looking like a holo from the deep Hegemony past. Beyond Kassad sat the Thunderbolt Sow, as upright and proud as the old FORCE warrior to her right, while next to her – eyes bright and attentive – sat Getswang Ngwang Lobsang Tengin Gyapso Sisunwangyur Tshungpa Mapai Dhepal Sangpo, the boy Dalai Lama.

All of the other refugees from T'ien Shan were somewhere on the dining platform, and I saw Lhomo Dondrub, Labsang Samten, George and Jigme, Haruyuki, Kenshiro, Voytek, Viki, Kuku, Kay, and others present at the main table. Just beyond the Templars around the table from us were A. Bettik, Rachel, and Theo Bernard. Rachel never took her eyes off Colonel Kassad, except to look at Aenea when she spoke. It was as if the rest of us were not there.

Tiny Templar servants whom Aenea whisperingly described as crew clones served water and stronger drinks and for a while there was the usual murmuring and polite, predinner conversation. Then there was a silence as thick as prayer. When Ket Rosteen, the True Voice of the Startree, stood to speak, everyone else rose as well.

'My friends,' said the small, hooded figure, 'fellow Brothers in the Muir, honored Ouster allies, sentient sisters and brothers of the ultimate Lifetree, human refugees from the Pax, and' – the True Voice of the Startree bowed in Aenea's direction – 'the most revered One Who Teaches.'

'As most of us gathered here know, what the Shrike Church once called the Days of Atonement – with us now for almost three centuries – are almost done. The True Voices of the Brotherhood of the Muir have followed the path of both prophecy and conservation, awaiting events as they came to pass, planting seeds as the soil of revelation has proved fertile.

'In these coming months and years, the future of many races – not just the human race – will be determined. Although there are those among us now who have been granted the gift of being able to glimpse patterns of the future, probabilities tossed like dice on the uneven blanket of space and time, even these gifted ones know that no single future has been pre-ordained for us or our posterity. Events are fluid. The future is like smoke from a burning forest, waiting for the wind of specific events and personal courage to blow the sparks and embers of reality this way or that.

'This day, on this treeship . . . on the reborn and rechristened *Yggdrasill* . . . we shall determine our own paths to our own futures. My own prayer to the lifeforce glimpsed by the Muir is not just that the Startree Biosphere survives, not just that the Brotherhood survives, not just that our Ouster brethren survive, not just that our hunted and harried sentient cousins of the Seneschai and the Akerataeli and the erg and the zeplin survive, not just that the species known as humankind survives, but that our prophecies begin to be realized this day and that all species of beloved life – humanity no more than the soft-shelled turtle or Mare Infinitus Lantern Mouth, the jumping spider and the tesla tree, the Old Earth raccoon and the Maui-Covenant Thomas hawk – that all species beloved of life join in rebirth of respect as distinct partners in the universe's growing cycle of life.'

The True Voice of the Startree turned to Aenea and bowed. 'Revered One Who Teaches, we are gathered here today because of you. We know from our prophecies – from those in our Brotherhood and elsewhere who have touched the nexus known as the Void Which Binds – that you are the best single hope of reconciliation between humanity and Core, between humankind and otherkind. We also know that time is short and that the immediate future holds the potential for both the beginnings of this reconciliation and our liberation . . . or for near-total destruction. Before any decisions can be made, there are those among us who must ask their final questions. Will you join in discussion with us now? Is this the time to speak of those things which must be spoken of and understood before all the worlds and abodes of Ouster and Templar and Pax and disparate humankind join in the final battle for humanity's soul?'

'Yes,' said Aenea.

The True Voice of the Startree sat down. Aenea stood, waited. I slipped my 'scriber from my vest pocket.

OUSTER SYSTENJ COREDWELL: M. Aenea, Most Respected One Who

Teaches, can you tell us with any certainty whether the Biosphere, our Startree, will be spared destruction and the Pax assault?

AENEA: I cannot, Freeman Coredwell. And if I could, it would be wrong for me to speak of it. It is not my role to predict probabilities in the great epicycles of chaos which are the futures. I can say without doubt that the next few days and weeks will determine whether this amazing Biosphere shall survive or not. Our own actions will, to a great extent, determine this. But there is no single correct course of action.

And if I may ask a question . . . there are friends of mine here new to the Startree and to Ouster space. It would help in our discussion if one of our hosts were to explain the background of the Ouster race, of the Biosphere and other projects, and of the Ouster and Templar philosophy.

OUSTER SIAN QUINTANA KA'AN: I would be pleased to speak to our new guests, Friend Aenea. It is important that all present in these deliberations understand our stake in the outcome.

As all of our Ouster and Templar brethren here well know, the Ouster race was created more than eight hundred years ago in scores of star systems far-flung from one another. Human seedships with colonists trained in the genetic arts were sent out from Old Earth System in the great pre-Hegira expansions. These seedships were – for the most part – slower-than-light craft: fleets of crude Bussard ramjets, solar sailing ships, ion scoops, nuclear-pulse propulsion craft, gravity-launched Dyson spherelets, laser-driven containment sailing ships . . . only a few dozen of the later seedships were early Hawking-drive C-plus craft.

These colonists, our ancestors – most traveling in cold sleep deeper than cryogenic fugue – were among the best ARNists, nanotechs, and genetic engineers Old Earth System had to offer. Their missions were to find habitable worlds and – in the absence of terraforming technology – to bioengineer and nanotech the millions of Old Earth life-forms frozen aboard their ships into viable adaptations for those worlds.

As we know, a few of the seedships reached habitable worlds – New Earth, Tau Ceti, Barnard's World. Most, however, reached worlds in systems where no life-forms could survive. The colonists had a choice – they could continue on, hoping that their ship life-support systems would sustain them for more long decades or centuries of travel – or they could use their gene-engineering skills to adapt themselves and their ark's embryos to conditions far harsher than the original seedship planners had imagined.

And so they did. Using the most advanced methods of nanotechnology – methods quashed on Old Earth and the early Hegemony by the TechnoCore – these human beings adapted themselves to wildly inhospitable worlds and to the even less hospitable dark spaces between worlds and stars. Within centuries, the use of Hawking drive had spread to most of these far-flung Swarms of Ouster colonists, but their urge to find friendlier worlds had faded. What they now wanted was to continue to adapt – to allow all of Old Earth's orphans to adapt – to whatever conditions the place and space offered them.

And with this new mission grew their philosophy . . . our philosophy, almost religious in fervor, of spreading life throughout the galaxy . . . throughout the universe. Not just human life . . . not just Old Earth life-forms . . . but life in all of its infinite and complex variations.

A few of our visitors here tonight may not know that the end goal of both us Ousters and our Templar brethren is not just the Biosphere Startree which we can see above us even as we speak . . . but a day in which air and water and life shall fill almost all of the space between the Startree and the yellow sun we see burning above us.

The Brotherhood of the Muir and our loose confederations of Ousters want nothing less than to turn the surface, seas, and atmosphere of every world around every star green with life. *More than that*, we work to see the galaxy grow green . . . tendrils reaching to nearby galaxies . . . superstrings of life.

One by-product of this philosophy, and the reason that the Church and the Pax seek to destroy us, is that for centuries we have been tailoring human evolution to fit the demands the environment gives us. So far, there are no distinct and separate species of humankind different than *Homo sapiens* – that is, all of us here could, if both parties were willing, interbreed with any Pax human or Templar human. But the differences are growing, the genetic separation widening. Already there are forms of Ouster humanity so different that we border on new human species . . . and *those differences are passed along genetically to our offspring.*

This the Church cannot abide. And so we are engaged in this terrible war, deciding whether humankind must remain one species forever, or whether our celebration of diversity in the universe can be allowed to continue.

AENEA: Thank you, Freewoman Sian Quintana Ka'an. I am sure that this has been helpful for my friends who are new to Ouster space, as well as important for the rest of us to remember as we make these momentous decisions. Does anyone else wish to speak?

DALAI LAMA: Friend Aenea, I have a comment and a question of you. The Pax's promise of immortality seduced even me into considering – for a few moments only – converting to their Christian faith. All here love life, it is the bright thread of our commonality. Can you tell us why the cruci-form is bad for us? And I must say – the fact that it is a symbiote or parasite does not make it that unthinkable to me or many others. Our bodies have many life-forms – the bacteria in our gut, for instance – which feed off us yet allow us to live. Friend Aenea, what is the cruciform? And why should we shun it?

AENEA: (closes her eyes for only a second, sighs, and opens them to face the boy) Your Holiness, the cruciform was born out of the TechnoCore's desperation following Meina Gladstone's attack on them in the hours before the Fall of the Farcasters.

The TechnoCore, as I have discussed with all of you in different forums, lives and thinks only as a parasite. In that sense, humankind has long been a symbiotic partner of the Core. Our technology was created and limited by Core designs. Our societies have been created, altered, and destroyed by Core plans and Core fears. Our existence as human beings has largely been defined by the endless dance of fear and parasitism with the Core AI entities.

After the Fall, after the Core lost control of the Hegemony via its dataspheres and farcasters, after the Core lost its greatest computing engine – its direct parasitism on the billions of human brains as they transited the Void Which Binds via the so-called farcasters – the TechnoCore had to find a new way to exploit humankind. And it had to find it quickly.

Thus the cruciform. This is nanotechnology at its most refined and most injurious. Where our Ouster friends use advanced genetic engineering combined with nanotechnology to advance the cause of life in the universe, the TechnoCore uses it to advance the cause of Core hyperparasitism.

Each cruciform is made up of billions of Core-connected nanotech entities, each in contact with other cruciforms and the Core via a terrible misuse of the Void Which Binds medium. The TechnoCore has known of the Void for a millennium and used it – misused it – for almost as long. The so-called Hawking drive tore holes in the Void. Then farcasters ripped at the essential fabric of the Void. The Core-driven information metasphere and instantaneous fatline medium stole information from the Void Which Binds in ways that blinded entire races, destroyed millennia of memories. But it is the cruciform that is the Core's most cynical and terrible misuse of the Void medium.

What makes the cruciform seem most miraculous to most of us is not its ability to restore some form of life – technology has offered variations of that for centuries – but its ability to restore the *personality* and *memories* of the deceased person. When one realizes that this demands information-storage capabilities in excess of 6×10^{23} bytes for *each human resurrected*, the fact of cruciform seems truly miraculous. Those in the hierarchy of the Catholic Church who know the Core's secret role in all resurrections ascribe this staggering – impossible – computing power to the Core's megasphere storage potential.

But the Core has nowhere near that computing power. Indeed, even in the heyday of the Ultimates' attempt to create the perfect artificial computing entity, the Ultimate Intelligence, the analyzer of all variables, no AI or series of AIs in the Core had the ability to store sufficient bytes for even one human body/personality to be recorded and resurrected. In fact, even if the Core had such information-storage capability, it would never have the energy necessary to re-form atoms and molecules into the precise living entity that is the body of a human being, much less reproduce the intricate wave-form dance that is a human personality.

Resurrection of a single person was and remains impossible for the Core.

That is, it was impossible unless they further ravaged the Void Which Binds – that transtemporal, interstellar medium for the memory and emotions of all sentient races.

Which the Core did without a backward glance. It is the Void Which Binds that records the individual wave-front personalities of those humans wearing cruciforms . . . the cruciform itself is little more than a Core-spawned nanotech data-transfer device.

But every time a person is resurrected, parts of thousands of personalities – human and otherwise – are erased from the more permanent record that is the Void Which Binds. Those of you who have taken communion with me, who have learned the language of the dead and of the living, who have attempted to hear the music of the spheres and have pondered the potential of taking that first step through the Void Which Binds, you understand the terrible savagery this vandalism represents. It must stop. I must stop it.

(Aenea closes her eyes for a long moment, then opens them again and continues.)

But this is not the only evil of the cruciform.

I say again, the Core AI entities are parasites. They cannot stop themselves from being parasites. Besides providing control of humanity via the Church – and, if all else fails, by administering pain to individuals via the cruciforms – there is another reason the AIs have offered humanity resurrection via these cruciform parasites.

With the Fall of the Farcasters, the use of trillions of human neurons in the Core's ultimate datasphere-connected Ultimate Intelligence effort was interrupted. Without the ruse of the farcasters by which to attach themselves like leeches on human brains, to steal the very life energy of neurons and holistic wave fronts from their human hosts, to hook billions of human minds into parallel computing devices, the Ultimate Intelligence project had to stop. With the cruciforms, this parasitism on the human brain has been resumed.

But it is now more complex than mere dataspace connections of billions of human minds in parallel for the Core's purposes. Centuries ago – as far back as the twentieth century AD – human researchers dealing with similar neural networks comprised of pre-AI silicon intelligences discovered that the best way to make a neural network creative was to kill it. In those dying seconds – even in the last nanoseconds of a sentient or near-sentient conscience's existence – the linear, essentially binary processes of neural net computing jumped barriers, became wildly creative in the near-death liberation from off-on, binary-based processing.

War-game computer simulations as far back as the late twentieth century showed that dying neural nets made unexpected but highly creative decisions: a primitive, presentient AI controlling a battered seagoing fleet in a simulated war game, for instance, suddenly sank its own damaged ships so that the remnants of its fleet could escape. Such was the genius of dying, nonlinear, neural-net creativity.

The Core has always lacked such creativity. Essentially, it has the linear, serial architecture of the serial CPUs from which it evolved, coupled with the obsessive, noncreative mentality of the ultimate parasite.

But with the cruciform, that great neural-networked Core-computing device which is the Christian-cruciformed part of the human race has found a source for almost unlimited creativity. All they need for a creativity catalyst is the death of large parts of the neural net. And humans provide that in abundance.

The Core AIs hover like vampires, waiting to feed off the dying human brains, sucking the marrow of creativity from humankind's mental bones. And when the deaths fall below the needed level or when their Core-computing demand for creative solutions rises . . . they orchestrate a few million more deaths.

Odd accidents occur. Humans' health is not what it was a few centuries ago. Death from cancer, heart disease, and the like are on the rise. And there are more clever forms of arranged mortality. Even with the Pax imposition of peace within the human interstellar empire, the incidents of violent death are on the rise. New forms of death are introduced. The archangel starships are such a beginning. Death is a cheap commodity for the born-again Christian. But it is a rich source of orchestrated creativity for the Core.

And thus the cruciform. And thus . . . I believe . . . at least one reason to eliminate the things from the human body and the human soul. (*When Aenea quits speaking, there is a long silence. Leaves on the treeship whisper in the breeze of circulating air. None of the hundreds of humans or hominids on the many platforms, branches, bridges, or stairways seem to blink, so intense are their gazes as they stare at my friend. Finally a single, strong voice speaks . . .*)

FATHER CAPTAIN DE SOYA: I still wear the collar and carry the vows of a Catholic priest. Is there no hope for my Church . . . not the Church of the Pax, held under TechnoCore control and the conceit of greedy men and women . . . but the Church of Jesus Christ and the hundreds of millions who followed His word?

AENEA: Federico . . . Father de Soya . . . it is for you to answer this question. You and the faithful like you. But I can tell you that there are billions of men and women today . . . some who wear the cruciform, more who do not . . . who yearn to return to a Church which concerns itself with spiritual matters, with the teachings of Christ and the deepest matters of the heart, rather than with this obsession with false resurrection.

TEMPLAR HET MASTEEN: Revered One Who Teaches, if I may change the subject from the cosmic and theological to the most personal and petty . . .

AENEA: Nothing of which you speak could be petty, True Voice of the Tree Het Masteen.

TEMPLAR HET MASTEEN: I was on the Hyperion pilgrimage with your mother. Revered One Who Teaches . . .

AENEA: She spoke to me of you often, True Voice of the Tree Het Masteen.

TEMPLAR HET MASTEEN: Then you know that the Lord of Pain . . . the Shrike . . . came to me as the pilgrims were crossing Hyperion's Sea of Grass on the windwagon, One Who Teaches. It came to me and carried me forward in time and across space . . . to this time, to this place.

AENEA: Yes.

TEMPLAR HET MASTEEN: And in my conversations with you and with my brethren in the Brotherhood of the Muir, I have come to understand that it is my fate to serve the Muir and the cause of Life in this age, as it was prophesied centuries ago by our own seers into the Void Which Binds. But in these days, and despite the best efforts of my brothers and other kind friends among the Ousters, I have heard of Martin Silenus's epic poem and found an edition of the *Cantos* . . .

AENEA: That is unfortunate, True Voice of the Tree Het Masteen. My Uncle Martin wrote that to the best of his knowledge, but his knowledge was incomplete.

TEMPLAR HET MASTEEN: But in the *Cantos*, Revered One Who Teaches, it says that the pilgrims in their day . . . and my friend Colonel Kassad has confirmed that this was the case . . . that they find me on Hyperion, in the Valley of the Time Tombs, and that I die shortly after they find me . . .

AENEA: This is true in the context of the *Cantos*, but . . .

TEMPLAR HET MASTEEN: *(holding up one hand to silence my friend)* It is not the inevitability of my return through time to the pilgrimage on Hyperion nor my inevitable death that worries me, Revered One Who Teaches. I understand that this is just one possible future for me . . . however probable or desirable. But what I wish to clarify is the truth of my last words according to the old poet's *Cantos*. Is it true that immediately before dying I will cry out, *I am the True Chosen. I must guide the Tree of Pain during the time of Atonement*?

AENEA: This is what is written in the *Cantos*, True Voice of the Tree Het Masteen.

TEMPLAR HET MASTEEN: *(smiling under his hood)* And this time is near, Revered One Who Teaches? Will you be using this *Yggdrasill* as the Tree of Pain for our Atonement as the prophecies attest?

AENEA: I will, True Voice of the Tree Het Masteen. I will be leaving to carry out that Atonement within standard days. I formally ask that the *Yggdrasill* be the instrument of our voyage and the instrument of that Atonement. I will be inviting many among us here tonight to join me on that final voyage. And I formally ask you, True Voice of the Tree Het Masteen, if you will captain the treeship *Yggdrasill* – forever after known as the Tree of Pain – on this voyage.

TEMPLAR HET MASTEEN: I formally accept your invitation and agree to captain the treeship *Yggdrasill* on this mission of Atonement, O Revered One Who Teaches. *(There are several minutes of silence.)*

FOREMAN JIGME NORBU: Aenea, George and I have a question.

AENEA: Yes, Jigme.

FOREMAN JIGME NORBU: You have taught us about the TechnoCore's quiet genocide on such worlds as Hebron, Qom-Riyadh, and others. Well . . . not genocide, exactly, because the populations have been put in a sort of sleeping death, but a terrible kidnapping.

AENEA: Yes.

FOREMAN JIGME NORBU: Has this happened to our beloved T'ien Shan, the Mountains of Heaven, since we left, Aenea? Have our friends and families been silenced with this Core deathwand and been carried away to some Labyrinthine world?

AENEA: Yes, Jigme, I am sad to say that it has happened. The bodies are being transported offworld even as we speak.

KUKU SE: Why? For what reason are these populations being kidnapped?

The Jews, the Muslims, the Hindus, the atheists, the Marxists, and now our beautiful Buddhist world. Is the Pax intent on destroying all other faiths?

AENEA: That is the Pax and Church's motivation, Kuku. For the TechnoCore it is a much more complicated matter. Without the cruciform parasite on these non-Christian populations, the Core cannot use these humans in its dying neural net. But by storing these billions of people in their false death, the Core can utilize their minds in its huge, parallel-processing neural network. It is a mutually beneficial deal – the Church, who carries out much of the removal work, is no longer threatened by nonbelievers – the Core, who brings the sleep death and carries out the storage in the Labyrinths, gains new circuits in its Ultimate Intelligence network.

FOREMAN GEORGE TSARONG: Is there no hope, then? Can we do nothing to help our friends?

OUSTER NAVSON HAMNIM: Excuse me for interrupting, M. Tsarong, M. Aenea, but we should explain to our friends that when the time comes for our Ouster Swarms and Templar allies to take the offensive against the Pax, our first objective is to liberate the many Labyrinthine worlds where these populations are kept in silent storage and to attempt to revive them.

THE DORJE PHAMO: (loudly) Revive them? How is this to happen? How can anyone revive them?

AENEA: By striking directly at the TechnoCore.

LHOMO DONDRUB: And where *is* the TechnoCore, Aenea? Tell me and I will go there now and do battle with these AI cowards.

AENEA: The true location of the TechnoCore has been the AI's best-kept secret since the entities left Old Earth a thousand standard years ago, Lhomo. Their actual, physical location has been hidden since then . . . their secrecy is their best defense against the hosts which might turn against their parasites.

COLONEL FEDMAHN KASSAD: CEO Meina Gladstone was convinced that the Core dwelt in the interstices of the farcaster medium . . . like invisible spiders in an unseen web. It is the reason she authorized the deathbombing of the space-portal farcaster network . . . to strike at the Core. Was she wrong? Were the farcasters destroyed for nothing?

AENEA: She was wrong, Fedmahn. The physical location of the Core was not within the farcaster medium . . . which is the fabric of the Void Which Binds. But the destruction of the farcasters was not in vain . . . it deprived the Core of the parasite medium upon which they fed on human minds, while silencing part of their megasphere data network.

LHOMO DONDRUB: But, Aenea, *you* know where the Core resides?

AENEA: I believe I do.

LHOMO DONDRUB: Will you tell us so that we can attack them with our teeth and nails and bullets and plasma weapons?

AENEA: I will not say at this time, Lhomo. Not until I am certain. And the Core cannot be attacked with physical weapons, just as it cannot be entered by physical entities.

COLONEL FEDMAHN KASSAD: So once again they are impervious to our attacks? Free from confrontation?

AENEA: No, neither impervious nor free from confrontation. If the fates allow, I will personally carry the attack to the physical Core. Indeed, that attack has already begun in ways that I hope to make clear later. And I promise you that I will confront the AIs in their lair.

COLONEL FEDMAHN KASSAD: M. Aenea, Brawne's child, may I ask another question relating to my own fate and future?

AENEA: I will endeavor to answer, Colonel, while repeating my reluctance to discuss specifics of a topic as fluid as our future.

COLONEL FEDMAHN KASSAD: Reluctant or no, child, I believe I deserve an answer to this question. I, too, have read these damned *Cantos*. In them, it says that I followed the apparition Moneta into the future while fighting the Shrike . . . trying to prevent it from slaughtering the other pilgrims. This was true . . . some months ago I arrived here. Moneta disappeared, but has reappeared in the younger version of this woman who calls herself Rachel Weintraub. But the *Cantos* also state that I will soon join in terrible battle with legions of Shrikes, will die, and will be entombed in the newly built Time Tomb called the Crystal Monolith on Hyperion, where my body travels back in time with Moneta as my companion. How can this be, M. Aenea? Have I come to the wrong time? The wrong place?

AENEA: Colonel Kassad, friend and protector of my mother and the other pilgrims, be assured that all proceeds according to whatever plan there is. Uncle Martin wrote the *Cantos* given what revelation there was granted to him. Not all details of your life . . . or mine . . . were available to him. Indeed, he was told precious little of what was to transpire outside of his presence.

I can say this to you, Colonel Kassad . . . the battle with the Shrike is true, however metaphorically rendered. One possible future is for you to die in battle with the Shrike . . . with many Shrike-like warriors . . . and to be placed in the Crystal Monolith after a hero's funeral. But if this were to come to pass, it would be after many years and many other battles. There is work for you to do in the days, months, years, and decades yet to come. I ask you now to accompany me on the *Yggdrasill* when I depart in three days . . . that will be the first step toward these battles.

COLONEL FEDMAHN KASSAD: (smiling) But you deflect the question somewhat, M. Aenea. May I ask you . . . will the Shrike be on your Tree of Pain when it leaves in three standard days' time?

AENEA: I believe it will, Colonel Kassad.

COLONEL FEDMAHN KASSAD: You have not told us here tonight, M. Aenea, *what* the Shrike is . . . where it truly comes from . . . what its role in this centuries-old and centuries-to-come game is.

AENEA: That is correct, Colonel. I have not told anyone here tonight.

COLONEL FEDMAHN KASSAD: Have you ever told anyone, child?

AENEA: No.

COLONEL FEDMAHN KASSAD: But you *know* the origin of the Shrike.

AENEA: Yes.

COLONEL FEDMAHN KASSAD: Will you tell us, Brawne Lamia's child?

AENEA: I would prefer not to, Colonel.

COLONEL FEDMAHN KASSAD: But you *will* if asked again, will you not? At least you will answer my direct questions on the matter?

AENEA: (nods silently . . . I see tears in her eyes)

COLONEL FEDMAHN KASSAD: The Shrike first appears in that same far future in which I do battle with it as per the *Cantos*, is this not correct, M. Aenea? That future in which the Core is making its last-ditch stand against its enemies?

AENEA: Yes.

COLONEL FEDMAHN KASSAD: And the Shrike is . . . will be . . . a construct, is it not? A created thing. A *Core*-created thing.

AENEA: This is accurate.

COLONEL FEDMAHN KASSAD: It will be a strange amalgam of Core technological wizardry, Void Which Binds energy, and the cybrid-recycled personality of a real human being, won't it, M. Aenea?

AENEA: Yes, Colonel. It will be all those things and more.

COLONEL FEDMAHN KASSAD: And the Shrike will be created by the Core but will become a servant and Avatar of other . . . powers . . . entities, will it not?

AENEA: Yes.

COLONEL FEDMAHN KASSAD: In truth, Aenea, would you agree that the Shrike will be a pawn of both sides . . . of *all* sides . . . in this war for the soul of humankind . . . this war that leaps back and forth across time like a four-dimensional chess game?

AENEA: Yes, Colonel . . . although not a pawn. A knight, perhaps.

COLONEL FEDMAHN KASSAD: All right, a knight. And this cybrid, Void Which Binds-connected, ARNied, DNA-engineered, nanotech-enhanced, terribly mutated knight . . . it starts with the personality of a single warrior, does it not? Perhaps an opponent in this thousand-year game?

AENEA: Do you need to know this, Colonel? There is no greater hell than seeing the precise details of one's . . .

COLONEL FEDMAHN KASSAD: (softly) Of one's future? Of one's own death? Of one's fate? I know that, Aenea, daughter of my friend Brawne Lamia. I know that you have carried such terrible certitudes and visions with you since before you were born . . . since the days when your mother and I crossed the seas and mountains of Hyperion toward what we thought was our fate with the Shrike. I know that it has been very difficult for you, Aenea, my young friend . . . harder than any of us here could imagine. None of us could have borne up under such a burden.

But still I want to know this part of my own fate. And I believe that my years of service in the cause of this battle . . . years past and years yet to be given . . . have earned me the right to an answer.

Is the Shrike based on a single human warrior's personality?

AENEA: Yes.

COLONEL FEDMAHN KASSAD: Mine? After my death in battle, the Core elements . . . or some power . . . will incorporate my will, my soul, my persona into that . . . monster . . . and send it back in time through the Crystal Monolith?

AENEA: Yes, Colonel. Parts of your persona . . . but only *parts* of it . . . will be incorporated into the living construct called the Shrike.

COLONEL FEDMAHN KASSAD: (laughing) But I can also live to *beat* it in battle?

AENEA: Yes.

COLONEL FEDMAHN KASSAD: (laughing harder now, the laughter sounding sincere and unforced) By God . . . by the will of Allah . . . if the universe has any soul, it is the soul of irony. I kill mine enemy, I eat his heart, and the enemy becomes me . . . and I become him. *(There are several more minutes of silence. I see that the treeship Yggdrasill has turned around and that we are approaching the great curve of the Biosphere Startree again.)*

RACHEL WEINTRAUB: Friend Aenea, Beloved Teacher, in the years I have listened to you teach and learned from you, one great mystery has haunted me.

AENEA: What is that, Rachel?

RACHEL WEINTRAUB: Through the Void Which Binds, you have heard the voices of the Others . . . the sentient races beyond our space and time whose memories and personalities resonate in the Void medium. Through communion with your blood, some of us have learned to hear the whispers of the echoes of those voices . . . of the Lions and Tigers and Bears, as some call them.

AENEA: You are one of my best students, Rachel. You will someday hear these voices clearly. Just as you will learn to hear the music of the spheres and to take that first step.

RACHEL WEINTRAUB: (shaking her head) That is not my question, friend Aenea. The mystery to me has been the presence in human space of an Observer or Observers sent by those . . . Others . . . those Lions and Tigers and Bears . . . to study humankind and report back to these distant races. Is the presence of this Observer . . . or these Observers . . . a literal fact?

AENEA: It is.

RACHEL WEINTRAUB: And they were able to take on the form of human or Ouster or Templar?

AENEA: The Observer or Observers are not shapeshifters, Rachel. They chose to come among us in some sort of mortal form, that is true . . . much as my father was mortal but cybrid born.

RACHEL WEINTRAUB: And this Observer or these Observers have been watching us for centuries?

AENEA: Yes.

RACHEL WEINTRAUB: Is that Observer . . . or one of these Observers . . . with us here today, on this treeship, or at this table?

AENEA: (hesitates) Rachel, it is best that I say nothing more at this time. There are those who would kill such an Observer in an instant to protect the Pax or to defend what they think it means to be 'human'. Even saying that such an Observer exists puts that entity at great risk. I am sorry . . . I promise you that this . . . this mystery . . . will be solved in the not-too-distant future and the Observer or Observers' identity revealed. Not by me, but by the Observer or Observers themselves.

TEMPLAR TRUE VOICE OF THE STARTREE KET ROSTEEN: Brothers in the Muir, respected Ouster allies, honored human guests, beloved sentient friends, Revered One Who Teaches . . . we shall finish this discussion at another time and in another place. I take it as a consensus of those among us that M. Aenea's request for the treeship *Yggdrasill* to depart for Pax space in three standard days is agreed to . . . and that, with luck and courage, thus shall be fulfilled the ancient Templar prophecies of the Tree of Pain and the time of Atonement for all children of Old Earth.

Now we will finish our meal and speak of other things. This formal meeting is adjourned, and what remains of our short voyage must be friendly conversation, good food, and the sacrament of real coffee grown from beans harvested on Old Earth . . . our common home . . . the good Earth.

This meeting is adjourned. I have spoken.

Later that evening, in the warm light of our private cubby, Aenea and I made love, spoke of personal things, and had a late, second supper of wine and zygoat cheese and fresh bread.

Aenea had gone off to the kitchen cubby for a moment and returned with two crystal bulbs of wine. Offering me one, she said, 'Here, Raul, my beloved . . . take this and drink.'

'Thanks,' I said without thinking and started to raise the bulb to my lips. Then I froze. 'Is this . . . did you . . .'

'Yes,' said Aenea. 'It is the communion that I have delayed so long for you. Now it is yours if you choose to drink. But you do not have to do this, my love. It will not change the way I feel about you if you choose not to.'

Still looking into her eyes, I drained the wine in the bulb. It tasted only of wine.

Aenea was weeping. She turned her head away, but I had already seen the tears in her lovely, dark eyes. I swept her up in my arms and we floated together in the warm womb light.

'Kiddo?' I whispered. 'What's wrong?' My heart ached as I wondered if she was thinking of the other man in her past, her marriage, the child . . . The wine had made me dizzy and a bit sick. Or perhaps it was not the wine.

She shook her head. 'I love you, Raul.'

'I love you, Aenea.'

She kissed my neck and clung to me. 'For what you have just done, for me, in my name, you will be hunted and persecuted . . .'

I forced a chuckle. 'Hey, kiddo, I've been hunted and persecuted since the day we rode the hawking mat out of the Valley of the Time Tombs together. Nothing new there. I'd miss it if the Pax quit chasing us.'

She did not smile. I felt her tears against my throat and chest as she clung more tightly. 'You will be the first among all those who follow me, Raul. You will be the leader in the decades and decades of struggle to come. You will be respected and hated, obeyed and despised . . . they will want to make a god of you, my darling.'

'Bullshit,' I whispered into my friend's hair. 'You know I'm no leader, kiddo. I haven't done anything except follow in all the years we've known each other. Hell . . . I spend most of my time just trying to catch up.'

Aenea raised her face to mine. 'You were my Chosen One before I was born, Raul Endymion. When I fall, you will continue on for us. Both of us must live through you . . .'

I put my heavy finger against her lips. I kissed the tears from her cheeks and lashes. 'No talking of falling or living without the other,' I commanded her. 'My plan is simple . . . to stay with you forever . . . through every-thing . . . to share everything. What happens to you happens to me, kiddo. I love you, Aenea.' We floated in the warm air together. I was cradling her in my arms.

'Yes,' whispered my friend, hugging me fiercely, 'I love you, Raul. To-gether. Time. Yes.'

We quit talking then. I tasted wine and the salt from her tears in our kisses. We made love for more hours, then drifted off to sleep together, each floating entwined in the other's embrace like two sea creatures, like one wonderfully complex sea creature, drifting on a warm and friendly tide.

TWENTY-SIX

The next day we took the Consul's ship out toward the sun.

I had awakened expecting to be feeling some sort of enlightenment, overnight *satori* from the communion wine, a deeper understanding of the universe at the very least, omniscience and omnipotence at best. Instead, I awoke with a full bladder, a slight headache, but pleasant memories of the night before.

Aenea was awake before me and by the time I came out of the toilet cubby, she had coffee hot in the brewing bulb, fruit in its serving globe, and fresh, warm rolls ready.

'Don't expect this service every morning,' she said with a smile.

'Okay, kiddo. Tomorrow I'll make breakfast.'

'Omelet?' she said, handing me a coffee bulb.

I broke the seal, inhaled the aroma, and squeezed out a drop, taking care not to burn my lips or to let the globule of hot coffee get away. 'Sure,' I said. 'Anything you like.'

'Good luck in finding the eggs,' she said, finishing her roll in two bites. 'This Startree is neat, but short on chickens.'

'Pity,' I said, looking through the transparent pod wall. 'And so many places to roost.' I changed tones to serious. 'Kiddo, about the wine . . . I mean, it's been about eight standard hours and . . .'

'You don't feel any different,' said Aenea. 'Hmm, I guess you're one of those rare individuals on which the magic doesn't work.'

'Really?'

My voice must have sounded alarmed, or relieved, or both, because Aenea shook her head. 'Uh-uh, just kidding. About twenty-four standard hours. You'll feel something. I guarantee it.'

'What if we're . . . ah . . . busy when the time comes?' I said, wiggling my eyebrows for emphasis. The motion made me float free a bit from the sticktite table.

Aenea sighed. 'Down, boy, before I staple those eyebrows in place.'

'Mmm,' I said, grinning at her over the coffee bulb. 'I love it when you talk dirty.'

'Hurry,' said Aenea, setting her bulb in the sonic washer bin and recycling the eating mat.

I was content to munch my roll and look at the incredible view through the wall. 'Hurry? Why? Are we going somewhere?'

'Meeting on the ship,' said Aenea. '*Our* ship. Then we have to get back and see to the last provisioning of the *Yggdrasill* for departure tomorrow evening.'

'Why on our ship?' I said. 'Won't it just be crowded compared to all these other places?'

'You'll see,' said Aenea. She had slipped into soft blue zero-g trousers, pulled tight at the ankle, with a tucked-in white shirt with several sticktite-sealing pockets. She wore gray slippers. I had gotten used to going barefoot around the cubby and in the various stems and pods.

'Hurry,' she said again. 'Ship's leaving in ten minutes and it's a long vine ride to the docking pod.'

It was crowded. And although the internal containment field held the gravity to one-sixth-g, it felt like a Jovian pull after sleeping in freefall. It seemed strange to be crowded in on one dimensional plane with everyone, letting all that airspace overhead go to waste. On the library deck of the Consul's ship with us, seated at the piano, on benches, in overstuffed chairs, and along holopit ledges, were the Ousters Navson Hamnim, Systenj Coredwell, Sian Quintana Ka'an resplendent in her feathers, the two silver, vacuum-adapted Ousters Palou Koror and Drivenj Nicaagat, as well as Paul Uray, and Am Chipeta. Het Masteen was there, as was his superior, Ket Rosteen. Colonel Kassad was present – as tall as the towering Ousters – and so was the Dorje Phamo, looking ancient and regal in an ice-gray gown that billowed beautifully in the low gravity, as well as Lhomo, Rachel, Theo, A. Bettik, and the Dalai Lama. None of the other sentient beings were there.

Several of us stepped out on the balcony to watch the inner surface of the Startree fall behind as the ship climbed toward the central star on its pillar of blue fusion flame.

'Welcome back, Colonel Kassad,' the ship said as we gathered on the library level.

I raised an eyebrow at Aenea, surprised that the ship had managed to remember this passenger from the old days.

'Thank you, Ship,' said the Colonel. The tall, dark man seemed distracted to the point of brooding.

Climbing away from the inner shell of the Biosphere Startree gave me a sense of vertigo quite distinct from watching the sphere of a planet grow smaller and fall behind. Here we were *inside* the orbital structure, and while the view from within the branches of the Startree had been one of open gaps between the leaves and trunks, glimpses of starfields on the side opposite the sun and everywhere great spaces, the view from a hundred thousand klicks and climbing was of a seemingly solid surface, the huge leaves reduced to a shimmering surface – looking for all the world like a great green, concave ocean – and the sense of being *in* some huge bowl and unable to escape was almost overwhelming.

The branches were glowing blue from the trapped atmosphere within the containment fields there, giving thousands of klicks of vinous wood and flickering leaves a sort of blue, electric glow, as if the entire inner surface were charged with voltage. And everywhere was life and motion: Ouster angels with hundred-klick wings not only flitted among the branches and beyond the leaves, but were hurled deeper into space – inward toward the sun, more quickly outward past the ten-thousand-klick root systems; a myriad of smaller life-forms shimmered in the blue envelope of atmosphere – radiant gossamers, faery chains, parrots, blue arboreals, Old Earth monkeys, vast schools of tropical fish swimming along in zero-g, seeking out the comet-misted regions, blue herons, flights of geese and Martian brandy fowl, Old Earth porpoises – we passed out of range before I could categorize a fraction of what I was seeing.

Farther out, the size of the largest life-forms and swarms of life-forms became apparent. From several thousand klicks 'up', I could see the shimmering herds of blue platelets, the sentient Akerataeli traveling together. After our first meeting here with the creatures from my cloud planet, I had asked Aenea if there were any more on the Biosphere Startree than the two in the conference. 'A few more,' my friend had said. 'About six hundred million more.' Now I could see the Akerataeli moving effortlessly on the air currents from trunk to trunk – hundreds of kilometers apart – in swarms of thousands, perhaps tens of thousands.

And with them came their obedient servants: the sky squids and zeplins and transparent medusae and vast, tendriled gas bags similar to the one that had eaten me on the cloud world. But larger. I had estimated that original monster as perhaps ten klicks long – these zeplin-like work beasts must have been several hundred klicks long, perhaps longer when one factored in the countless tentacles, tendrils, flagella, whips, tails, probes, and proboscises the things sported. I realized as I watched that all of the Akerataeli's giant beasts of burden were busy with tasks – weaving branches and stems and pods into elaborate bio-designs, pruning dead branches and city-sized leaves from the Startree, wrestling Ouster-designed structures into place or hauling material from one part of the Biosphere to another.

'How many zeplin things are the Akerataeli controlling on the Startree?' I asked Aenea when she was free for a second.

'I don't know,' she said. 'Let's ask Navson.'

The Ouster said, 'We have no idea. They breed as needed for tasks. The Akerataeli themselves are a perfect example of a swarm organism, a hive mind . . . none of the disc-entities alone is sentient . . . in parallel, they are brilliant. The sky squids and other ex-Jovian-world creatures have been reproducing as needed here for more than seven hundred standard years. I would venture that there are several hundred million working around the Biosphere . . . perhaps a billion at this point.'

I stared down at the tiny forms on the dwindling Biosphere surface. A billion creatures each the size of the Pinion Plateau on my homeworld.

Farther out and the gaps between the branches a million klicks overhead and a half million klicks underfoot became apparent enough. The section from which we had come was the oldest and densest, but far along the great inner curve of the Biosphere there were gaps and divisions – some planned, others yet to be filled in with living material. But even here space was busy and filled with motion – comets arcing between roots, branches, leaves, and trunks on precise trajectories, their gift of water being volatilized from the surface by Ouster-aimed and erg-powered heat beams from the trunks and from genetically adapted reflective leaves creating mirrors hundreds of klicks across. Once turned to water vapor, the great clouds drifted across the trailing roots and misted the billion square klicks of leaf surface.

Larger than the comets were the scores of carefully placed asteroids and shepherd moons moving a few thousand or tens of thousands of kilometers above the inner and outer surface of the living sphere – correcting for orbital drift, providing tides and tugs to help the branches grow correctly, throwing shadow on the Biosphere's inner surface where shade was needed, and serving as observation bases and work shacks for the countless Ouster and Templar gardeners who watched over the project from decade to decade and century to century.

And now, a half a light-minute out and accelerating toward the sun as if the ship were searching for a Hawking-drive translation point, there appeared to be even more traffic in the vast hollow of the green sphere: Ouster warships, all obsolete by Pax standards, with Hawking-drive blisters or giant ramscoop containment fields, old-fashioned high-g destroyers and C_3 ships from a long-gone era, elegant sunjammer cargo craft with great curved sails of gleaming monofilm – and everywhere the individual Ouster angels, wings flapping and shimmering as they tacked in toward the sun or hurtled back out toward the Biosphere.

Aenea and the others stepped back inside to continue their discussion. The topic was important – still trying to find a way to stall the Pax from attacking, some sort of feint or distraction that would keep the massing fleet from hurling itself this way – but I had more important things on my mind.

As A. Bettik turned to leave the balcony, I touched the android's right sleeve. 'Can you stay and talk a minute?'

'Of course, M. Endymion.' The blue-skinned man's voice was as gentle as always.

I waited until we were alone on the balcony, the drone of conversation from within affording us privacy outside, and leaned on the railing. 'I'm sorry we haven't had more chance to talk since arriving here at the Startree,' I said.

A. Bettik's bald scalp gleamed in the rich sunlight. His blue-eyed gaze was calm and friendly. 'That's perfectly all right, M. Endymion. Events have proved quite hectic since our arrival. I do concur, however, that this artifact does cause one to find opportunities to discuss it.' He waved his remaining hand at the huge curve of the Startree to where it seemed to fade away near the central sun's brilliance.

'It's not the Startree or the Ousters I want to talk about,' I said softly, leaning a bit closer.

A. Bettik nodded and waited.

'You were with Aenea on all of the worlds between Old Earth and T'ien Shan,' I said. 'Ixion, Maui-Covenant, Renaissance Vector, and the others?'

'Yes, M. Endymion. I had the privilege to travel with her during all the time she allowed others to travel with her.'

I chewed my lip, realizing that I was about to make a fool of myself but having no choice. 'And what about the time when she did *not* allow you to travel with her?' I said.

'While M. Rachel, M. Theo, and the others remained with me on Groombridge Dyson D?' said A. Bettik. 'We carried on with M. Aenea's work, M. Endymion. I was especially busy working on the construction of . . .'

'No, no,' I interrupted, 'I mean what do you know about her absence?'

A. Bettik paused. 'Virtually nothing, M. Endymion. She had told us that she would be away for some time. She had made provisions for our employment and continued work with her . . . students. One day she was gone and she was to stay away for approximately two standard years . . .'

'One year, eleven months, one week, six hours,' I said.

'Yes, M. Endymion. That is precisely correct.'

'And after she returned, she never told you where she had been?'

'No, M. Endymion. As far as I know, she never mentioned it to any of us.'

I wanted to grab A. Bettik's shoulders, to make him understand, to explain why this was of life-and-death importance to me. Would he have understood? I didn't know. Instead, attempting to sound calm, almost disinterested – and failing miserably – I said, 'Did you notice anything different about Aenea when she returned from that sabbatical, A. Bettik?'

My android friend paused, not, it seemed, out of hesitation to speak, but as if laboring to remember nuances of human emotion. 'We left for T'ien Shan almost immediately after that, M. Endymion, but my best recollection is that M. Aenea was very emotional for some months – elated one minute, absolutely racked with despair the next. By the time you arrived on T'ien Shan, these emotional swings had seemed to have abated.'

'And she never mentioned what caused them?' I felt like a swine going behind my beloved's back like this, but I knew that she would not talk to me about these things.

'No, M. Endymion,' said the android. 'She never talked to me about the cause. I presumed it was some event or events she experienced during her absence.'

I took a deep breath. 'Before she left . . . on the other worlds . . . Amritsar, Patawpha . . . any of the worlds before she left Groombridge Dyson D . . . had she . . . was she . . . had there been anyone?'

'I don't understand, M. Endymion.'

'Was there a man in her life, A. Bettik? Someone she showed affection for? Someone who seemed especially close to her?'

'Ah,' said the android. 'No, M. Endymion, there seemed to be no male who showed any special interest in M. Aenea . . . other than as a teacher and possible messiah, of course.'

'Yeah,' I said. 'And no one came back with her after the one year, eleven months, one week, and six hours?'

'No, M. Endymion.'

I gripped A. Bettik's shoulder. 'Thank you, my friend. I'm sorry I'm asking these stupid questions. It's just that . . . I don't understand . . . somewhere there's a . . . shit, it doesn't matter. It's just stupid human emotion.' I turned to go in to join the others.

A. Bettik stopped me with a hand on my wrist. 'M. Endymion,' he said softly, 'if love is the human emotion to which you refer, I feel that I have watched humankind long enough during my existence to know that love is never a stupid emotion. I feel that M. Aenea is correct when she teaches that it may well be the mainspring energy of the universe.'

I stood and watched, gaping, as the android left the balcony and went into the crowded library level.

They were close to making a decision.

'I think we should send the Gideon-drive courier drone with a message,' Aenea was saying as I came into the lounge. 'Send it direct and within the hour.'

'They'll confiscate the drone,' said Sian Quintana Ka'an in her musical contralto. 'And it's the only ship we have left with the instantaneous drive.'

'Good,' said Aenea. 'They're an abomination. Every time they are used, part of the Void is destroyed.'

'Still,' said Paul Uray, his thick Ouster dialect sounding like someone speaking through radio static, 'there remains the option of using the drone as a delivery system.'

'To launch nuclear warheads, or plasma weapons, against the armada?' said Aenea. 'I thought that we had dismissed that possibility.'

'It's our only way of striking at them before they strike at us,' said Colonel Kassad.

'It would do no good,' said the Templar True Voice of the Startree Ket Rosteen. 'The drones are not built for precise targeting. An archangel-class warship would destroy it light-minutes away from target. I agree with the One Who Teaches. Send the message.'

'But will the message stop their attack?' said Systenj Coredwell.

Aenea made the little gesture that I knew so well. 'There are no guarantees . . . but if it puts them off balance, at least *they* will use their instantaneous drive drones to postpone the attack. It is worth a try, I think.'

'And what will the message say?' said Rachel.

'Please hand me that vellum and stylus,' said Aenea.

Theo brought the items and set them on the Steinway. Everyone – including me – crowded close as Aenea wrote:

To Pope Urban XVI and Cardinal Lourdusamy:
I am coming to Pacem, to the Vatican.
Aenea.

'There,' said my young friend, handing the vellum to Navson Hamnim. 'Please set this in the courier drone when we dock, set the transponder to "carrying hardcopy message", and launch it to Pacem System.'

The Ouster took the vellum. I had not yet developed the knack of reading the Ouster's facial expressions, but I could tell that something was giving him pause. Perhaps it was a lesser form of the same sort of panic and confusion that was filling my chest at the moment.

I am coming to Pacem. What the goddamn hell did that mean? How could Aenea go to Pacem and survive? She could not. And wherever she was going, I was certain of only one thing . . . that I would be at her side. Which meant that she was going to kill me as well, if she was as good as her word. Which she always had been. *I am coming to Pacem.* Was it just a ploy to deter their fleet? An empty threat . . . a way of stalling them? I wanted to shake my beloved until her teeth fell out or until she explained everything to me.

'Raul,' she said, gesturing me closer.

I thought that perhaps this was the explanation I wanted, that she was reading my expression from across the room and saw the turmoil within me, but all she said was, 'Palou Koror and Drivenj Nicaagat are going to show me what it means to fly like an angel, do you want to come with me? Lhomo's coming.'

Fly like an angel? For a moment I was sure that she was speaking gibberish.

'They have an extra skinsuit if you want to come,' Aenea was saying. 'But we have to go now. We're almost back to the Startree and the ship will be docking in a few minutes. Het Masteen has to get on with the loading and provisioning of the *Yggdrasill* and I have a hundred things to do before tomorrow.'

'Yeah,' I said, not knowing what I was agreeing to. 'I'll come along.' At the time I was feeling surly enough to think that this response was a wonderful metaphor for my entire ten-year odyssey: *yeah, I don't know what I'm doing or getting into, but count me in.*

One of the space-adapted Ousters, Palou Koror, handed us the skinsuits. I had used skinsuits before, of course – the last time being just a few weeks earlier when Aenea and I had climbed T'ai Shan, the Great Peak of the Middle Kingdom – although it seemed like months or years ago – but I had never seen or felt a skinsuit like these.

Skinsuits go back many centuries, the working concept being that the best way to keep from exploding in vacuum is not a bulky pressure suit as in the earliest days of spaceflight, but a covering so thin that it allows perspiration to pass even while it protects the skin from the terrible heat, cold, and vacuum of space. Skinsuits had not changed much in all those centuries, except to incorporate rebreathing filaments and osmosis panels. Of course, my last skinsuit had been a Hegemony artifact, workable enough until Rhadamanth Nemes had clawed it to shreds.

But this was no ordinary skinsuit. Silver, malleable as mercury, the thing felt like a warm but weightless blob of protoplasm when Palou Koror dropped it in my hand. It *shifted* like mercury. No, it shifted and flowed like a living, fluid thing. I almost dropped it in my shock, catching it with my other hand only to watch it flow several centimeters up my wrist and arm like some flesh-eating alien.

I must have said something out loud, because Aenea said, 'It *is* alive, Raul.

The skinsuit's an organism . . . gene-tailored and nanoteched . . . but only three molecules thick.'

'How do I put it on?' I said, watching it flow up my arm to the sleeve of my tunic, then retreat. I had the impression that the thing was more carnivore than garment. And the problem with any skinsuit was that they had to be worn next to the *skin*: one did not wear layers *under* a skinsuit. Anywhere.

'Uh-huh,' said Aenea. 'It's easy . . . none of the pulling and tugging we had to do with the old skinsuits. Just strip naked, stand very still, and drop the thing on your head. It'll flow down over you. And we have to hurry.'

This inspired something less than great enthusiasm in me.

Aenea and I excused ourselves and jogged up the spiral stairs to the bedroom level at the apex of the ship. Once there we hurried out of our clothes. I looked at my beloved – standing naked next to the Consul's ancient (and quite comfortable, as I remembered) bed – and was about to suggest a better use of our time before the treeship docked. But Aenea just waggled a finger at me, held the blob of silver protoplasm above her, and dropped it in her hair.

It was alarming watching the silver organism engulf her – flowing down over her brown-blonde hair like liquid metal, covering her eyes and mouth and chin, flowing down her neck like reflective lava, then covering her shoulders, breasts, belly, hipbones, pubis, thighs, knees . . . finally she lifted first one foot and then the other and the engulfment was complete.

'Are you all right?' I said, my voice small, my own blob of silver still pulsing in my hand, eager to get at me.

Aenea – or the chrome statue that had been Aenea – gave me a thumbs-up and gestured to her throat. I understood: as with the Hegemony skinsuits, communication from now on would be via subvocalization pickups.

I lifted the pulsing mass in both hands, held my breath, closed my eyes, and dropped it on my head.

It took less than five seconds. For a terrible instant I was sure that I could not breathe, feeling the slick mass over my nose and mouth, but then I remembered to inhale and the oxygen came cool and fresh.

Can you hear me, Raul? Her voice was much more distinct than the hearpatch pickups on the old suit.

I nodded, then subvocalized, *Yeah. Weird feeling.*

Are you ready, M. Aenea, M. Endymion? It took me a second to realize that it was the other adapted Ouster, Drivenj Nicaagat, on the suit-line. I had heard his voice before, but translated via speech synthesizer. On the direct line, his voice was even more clear and melodious than the bird-song of Sian Quintana Ka'an.

Ready, responded Aenea, and we went down the spiral stairs, through the throng, and out onto the balcony.

Good luck, M. Aenea, M. Endymion. It was A. Bettik speaking to us through one of the ship's comlinks. The android touched each of us on our respective silver shoulders as we stepped next to Koror and Nicaagat at the balcony railing.

Lhomo was also waiting, his silver skinsuit showing every ridge of delineated muscle on his arms, thighs, and flat belly. I felt awkward for a moment, wishing either that I was wearing something over this micron-thin layer of silver fluid or that I worked harder at keeping in shape. Aenea looked beautiful, the body that I loved sculpted in chrome. I was glad that no one but the android had followed the five of us onto the balcony.

The ship was within a couple thousand klicks of the Startree and decelerating hard. Palou Koror made a motion and jumped easily onto the thin balcony rail, balancing against the one-sixth-g. Drivenj Nicaagat followed suit, and then Lhomo, then Aenea, and finally – much less gracefully – I joined them. The sense of height and exposure was all but overwhelming – the great green basin of the Startree beneath us, the leafy walls rising into the unblinking distance on all sides, the bulk of the ship curving away beneath us, balancing on the slim column of fusion fire like a building teetering on a fragile blue column. I realized with a sickening feeling that we were going to jump.

Do not worry, I will open the containment field at the precise instant you pass through and go to EM repulsors until you are clear of the drive exhaust. I realized that it was the ship speaking. I had no idea of what we were doing.

The suits should give you a rough idea of our adaptation, Palou Koror was saying. *Of course, for those of us who have chosen full integration, it is not the semisentient suits and their molecular microprocessors that allow us to live and travel in space, but the adapted circuits in our skin, our blood, our vision, and brains.*

How do we . . . I began, having some trouble subvocalizing, as if the dryness in my mouth would have any effect on my throat muscles.

Do not worry, said Nicaagat. *We will not deploy our wings until proper separation is achieved. They wll not collide . . . the fields would not allow it. Controls are quite intuitive. Your suit's optical systems should interface with your nervous system and neurosensors, calling up data when required.*

Data? What data? I had only meant to think that, but the suitcom sent it out.

Aenea took my silver hand in hers. *This will be fun, Raul. The only free minutes we're going to have today, I think. Or for a while.*

At that moment, poised on the railing on the edge of a terrifying vertical drop through fusion flame and vacuum, I did not really focus on the meaning of her words. *Come,* said Palou Koror and leaped from the railing. Still holding hands, Aenea and I jumped together.

She let go of my hand and we spun away from one another. The containment field parted and ejected us a safe distance, the fusion drive paused as the five of us spun away from the ship, then it relit – the ship seeming to hurtle upward and away from us as its deceleration outpaced our own – and we continued dropping, that sensation was overwhelming, five silver, spread-eagled forms, separating farther and farther from each other, all plummeting toward the Startree lattice still several thousand klicks beneath. Then our wings opened.

For our purposes today, the lightwings need only be a kilometer or so across, came Palou Koror's voice in my ears. *Were we traveling farther or faster, they would extend much farther . . . perhaps several hundred kilometers.*

When I raised my arms, the panels of energy extruding from my skinsuit unfurled like butterfly wings. I *felt* the sudden push of sunlight.

What we feel is more the current of the primary magnetic field line we are following, said Palou Koror. *If I may slave your suits for a second . . . there.*

Vision shifted. I looked to my left to where Aenea fell, already several klicks away – a shining silver chrysalis set within expanding gold wings. The others glowed beyond her. I could *see* the solar wind, see the charged particles and currents of plasma flowing and spiraling outward along the infinitely complex geometry of the heliosphere – red lines of twisting magnetic field coiling as if painted on the inner surfaces of an ever-shifting chambered nautilus, all this convoluted, multilayered, multicolored writhing of plasma streams flowing back to a sun that no longer seemed a pale star but was the locus of millions of converging field lines, entire sheets of plasma being evicted at four hundred kilometers a second and being drawn into these shapes by the pulsing magnetic fields in its north and south equators, I could see the violet streamers of the inward-rushing magnetic lines, weaving and interlacing with the crimson red of the outward-exploding sheets of field current, I could see the blue vortices of heliospheric shock wave around the outer edges of the Startree, the moons and comets cutting through plasma medium like ocean-going ships at night plowing through a glowing, phosphorescent sea, and could see our gold wings interacting with this plasma and magnetic medium, catching photons like billions of fireflies in our nets, sail surfaces surging to the plasma currents, our silver bodies accelerating out along the great shimmering folds and spiral magnetic geometries of the heliosphere matrix.

In addition to this enhanced vision, the suit optics were overlaying trajectory information and computational data that meant nothing to me, but must have meant life or death to these space-adapted Ousters. The equations and functions flashed by, seemingly floating in the distance at critical focus, and I remember only a sampling:

$$\frac{GM_3M_c}{r^2} = \frac{M_cV^2_{cir}}{r}$$

and

$$P_r = \frac{(1+k)\,S_r}{c}$$

and

$$k = \frac{R_a}{(R_a + A)}$$

and

$$a_s \mathord{\overline{\hspace{10em}}} a_3 = \frac{(1+k)\,(6.3 \times 10^{17})\,R_s^2\ \text{m/sec}^2}{2Mr^2}$$

and

$$V_1{}^2+\Delta V^2+2\Delta V(V_i{}^2+V_e{}^2)^{1/2} > V_i{}^2+\Delta V^2+2\Delta VV_i$$

Even without understanding any of these equations, I knew that we were approaching the Startree too fast. In addition to the ship's velocity, we had picked up our own speed from the solar wind and the plasma stream. I began to see how these Ouster energy wings could move one *out* from a star – and at an impressive velocity – but how did one *stop* within what looked to be less than a thousand kilometers?

This is fantastic, came Lhomo's voice. *Amazing.*

I rotated my head far enough to see our flyer friend from T'ien Shan far to our left and many kilometers below us. He had already entered the leaf zone and was swooping and soaring just above the blue blur of the containment field that surrounded the branches and spaces between the branches like an osmotic membrane.

How the hell did he do that? I wondered.

Again, I must have subvocalized the thought, for I heard Lhomo's deep, distinctive laugh and he sent, *USE the wings, Raul. And cooperate with the tree and the ergs!*

Cooperate with the tree and the ergs? My friend must have lost his reason.

Then I saw Aenea extending her wings, manipulating them by both thought and the movement of her arms. I looked beyond her to the world of branches approaching us at horrifying velocity, and then I began to see the trick.

That's good, came Drivenj Nicaagat's voice. *Catch the repelling wind. Good.*

I watched the two adapted Ousters flutter like butterflies, saw the torrent of plasma energy rising from the Startree to surround them, and suddenly hurtled past them as if they had opened parachutes and I was still in freefall.

Panting against the skinsuit field, my heart pounding, I spread my arms and legs and willed the wings wider. The energy folds shimmered and expanded to at least two klicks. Beneath me, an expanse of leaves shifted, turned slowly and purposefully as if in a time-lapse nature holo of flowers seeking the light, folded over one another to form a smooth, parabolic dish at least five klicks across, and then went perfectly reflective.

Sunlight blazed against me. If I had been watching with unshielded eyes, I would have been instantly blinded. As it was, the suit optics polarized. I *heard* the sunlight striking my skinsuit and wings, like hard rain on a metal roof. I opened my wings wider to catch the blazing gust of light at the same instant the ergs on the Startree below folded the heliosphere matrix, bending the plasma stream back against Aenea and me, decelerating both of us rapidly but not painfully so. Wings flapping, we passed into the bowering outbranches of the Startree while the suit optics continued to flow data across my field of vision.

$$V_f = \mathbf{V}V_c{}^2 = \frac{2(\mathbf{J} - GM_{star}\,M_c)}{r_i M_c}$$

Which somehow assured me that the tree was providing the proper amount of the sun's light based on its mass and luminosity, while the erg was providing just enough heliospheric plasma and magnetic feedback to bring us to near zero delta-v before we struck one of the huge main branches or interdicted the containment field.

Aenea and I followed the Ousters, using our wings in the same way they used theirs, soaring and then flapping, braking and then expanding to catch the true sun's light to accelerate again, swooping in among the outer branches, soaring over the leafy outer layer of the Startree, then diving deep among the branches again, folding our wings to pass between pods or covered bridges out beyond the core containment fields, swooping around busily working space squids whose tentacles were ten times longer than the Consul's ship now decelerating carefully through the leaf level, then opening our wings again to surge past floating schools of thousands of blue-pulsing Akerataeli platelets, which seemed to be waving at us as we passed.

There was a huge platform branch just below the containment-field shimmer. I did not know if the wings would work through the field, but Palou Koror passed through with only a shimmer – like a graceful diver cutting through still water – followed by Drivenj Nicaagat, then by Lhomo, then Aenea, and finally I joined them, folding my wings to a dozen or so meters across as I crossed the energy barrier into air and sound and scent and cool breezes once again.

We landed on the platform.

'Very nice for a first flight,' said Palou Koror, her voice synthesized for the atmosphere. 'We wanted to share just a moment of our lives with you.'

Aenea deactivated the skinsuit around her face, allowing it to flow into a collar of fluid mercury. Her eyes were bright, as alive as I had ever seen them. Her fair skin was flushed and her hair was damp with sweat. 'Wonderful!' she cried and turned to squeeze my hand. 'Wonderful . . . thank you so much. Thank you, thank you, thank you, Freeman Nicaagat, Freewoman Koror.'

'It was our pleasure, Revered One Who Teaches,' said Nicaagat with a bow.

I looked up and realized that the *Yggdrasill* was docked with the Startree just above us, the treeship's kilometer of branches and trunk mingling perfectly with the Biosphere branches. Only the fact that the Consul's ship had slowly docked and was being pulled into a storage pod by a worker squid allowed me to see the treeship. Crew clones were visible, working feverishly, carrying provisions and Mobius cubes onto Het Masteen's treeship, and I could see scores of plantstem life-support umbilicals and connector stems running from the Startree to the treeship.

Aenea had not released my hand. When I turned my gaze from the treeship hanging above us to my friend, she leaned closer and kissed me on the lips. 'Can you imagine, Raul? Millions of the space-adapted Ousters *living* out there . . . seeing all that energy all the time . . . flying for weeks and months in the empty spaces . . . running the bowshock rapids of magnetospheres and vortexes around planets . . . riding the solar-wind plasma shock waves out ten AUs or more, and then flying farther . . . to the heliopause termination-shock boundary seventy-five to a hundred and fifty AUs from the star, out to where the solar wind ends and the interstellar medium begins. *Hearing* the hiss and whispers and surf-crash of the universe's ocean? Can you *imagine*?'

'No,' I said. I could not. I did not know what she was talking about. Not then.

A. Bettik, Rachel, Theo, Kassad, and the others descended from a transit vine. Rachel carried clothes for Aenea. A. Bettik brought my clothes.

Ousters and others surrounded my friend again, demanding answers to urgent questions, seeking clarifications of orders, reporting on the imminent launch of the Gideon-drive drone. We were swept apart by the press of other people.

Aenea looked back and waved. I raised my hand – still silver from the skinsuit – to wave back, but she was gone.

That evening several hundred of us took a transport pod pulled by a squid to a site many thousands of klicks to the northwest above the plane of the ecliptic along the inner shell of the Biosphere Startree, but the voyage lasted less than thirty minutes because the squid took a shortcut, cutting an arc through space from our section of the sphere to the new one.

The architecture of living pods and communal platforms, branch towers and connecting bridges on this section of the tree, while still so close to our region by any meaningful geography of this huge structure, looked different – larger, more baroque, *alien* – and the Ousters and Templars here spoke a slightly different dialect, while the space-adapted Ousters ornamented themselves with bands of shimmering color that I had not seen before. There were different birds and beasts in the atmosphere zones here – exotic fish swimming through misted air, great herds of something that looked like Old Earth killer whales with short arms and elegant hands. And this was only a few thousand klicks from the region I knew. I could not imagine the diversity of cultures and life-forms throughout this Biosphere. For the first time I realized what Aenea and the others had been telling me over and over . . . there was more internal surface on the sections of the completed Biosphere than the total of all the planetary surfaces discovered by humankind in the past thousand years of interstellar flight. When the Startree was completed, the internal Biosphere quickened, the volume of habitable space would exceed all the inhabitable worlds in the Milky Way galaxy.

We were met by officials, feted for a few moments on crowded one-sixth-g platforms among hundreds of Ouster and Templar dignitaries, then taken into a pod so large that it might have been a small moon.

A crowd of several hundred thousand Ousters and Templars waited, with a few hundred Seneschai Aluit and hovering crowds of Akerataeli near the central dais. Blinking, I realized that the ergs had set the internal containment field at a comfortable one-sixth-g, pulling everyone toward the surface of the sphere, but then I noticed *that the seats continued up and over and around* the full interior of the sphere. I revised my estimate of the crowd to well over a million.

Ouster Freeman Navson Hamnim and Templar True Voice of the Startree Ket Rosteen introduced Aenea, saying that she brought with her the message that their people had awaited for centuries.

My young friend walked to the podium, looking up and around and down, as if making eye contact with every person in the huge space. The sound system was so sophisticated that we could have heard her swallow or breathe. My beloved looked calm.

'Choose again,' said Aenea. And she turned, walked away from the podium, and went down to where the chalices lay on the long table.

Hundreds of us donated our blood, mere drops, as the chalices of wine were passed out to the waiting multitudes. I knew that there was no way that a million waiting Ouster and Templar communicants could be served by a few hundred of us who had already received communion from Aenea, but the aides drew a few drops with sterile lancets, the drops were transferred to the reservoir of wine, scores of helpers passed chalice bulbs under the spigots, and within the hour, those who wished communion with Aenea's wine-blood had received it. The great sphere began emptying.

After her two words, nothing else had been said through the entire evening. For the first time on that long – endless – day, there was silence in the transport pod traveling home . . . home, back to our region of the Startree under the shadow of the *Yggdrasill* destined to depart within twenty hours.

I had felt like a fraud. I had drunk the wine almost twenty-four hours earlier, but I had felt nothing this day . . . nothing except my usual love for Aenea, which is to say, my absolutely *un*usual, unique, totally without-referent-or-equal love for Aenea.

The multitudes who wanted to drink had drunk. The great sphere had emptied, with even those who had not come to the communion silent – whether with disappointment at my beloved's two-word speech, or pondering something beyond and beneath that, I did not know.

We took the transport pod back to our region of the Startree and we were silent except for the most necessary of communications. It was not an awkward or disappointed silence, more a silence of awe bordering on fear at the terminus of one part of one's life and the beginning . . . the hope for a beginning . . . of another.

Choose again. Aenea and I made love in the darkened living pod, despite our fatigue and the late hour. Our lovemaking was slow and tender and almost unbearably sweet.

Choose again. They were the last words in my mind as I finally drifted . . .

literally . . . off to sleep. *Choose again.* I understood. I chose Aenea and life with Aenea. And I believed that she had chosen me.

And I would choose her and she would choose me again tomorrow, and the tomorrow after that, and in every hour during those tomorrows.

Choose again. Yes. Yes.

TWENTY-SEVEN

My name is Jacob Schulmann. I write this letter to my friends in Lodz:

My very dear friends, I waited to write to confirm what I'd heard. Alas, to our great grief, we now know it all. I spoke to an eyewitness who escaped. He told me everything. They're exterminated in Chelmno, near Dombie, and they're all buried in Rzuszow forest. The Jews are killed in two ways: by shooting or gas. It's just happened to thousands of Lodz Jews. Do not think that this is being written by a madman. Alas, it is the tragic, horrible truth.

'Horror, horror! Man, shed thy clothes, cover thy head with ashes, run in the streets and dance in thy madness.' I am so weary that my pen can no longer write. Creator of the universe, help us!

I write the letter on January 19, AD 1942. A few weeks later, during a February thaw when there is a false scent of spring to the woods around our city of Grabow, we – the men in the camp – are loaded into vans. Some of the vans have brightly painted pictures of tropical trees and jungle animals on them. These are the children's vans from last summer when they took the children from the camp. The paint has faded over this past winter, and the Germans have not bothered to retouch the images so that the gay pictures seem to be fading like last summer's dreams.

They drive us fifteen kilometers to Chelmno, which the Germans call Kulmhof. Here they order us out of the vans and demand that we relieve ourselves in the forest. I cannot do it . . . not with the guards and the other men looking on, but I pretend that I have urinated and button my pants again.

They put us back in the big vans and drive us to an old castle. Here they order us out again and we are marched through a courtyard littered with clothes and shoes and down into a cellar. On the wall of the cellar, in Yiddish, is written 'No one leaves here alive.' There are hundreds of us in the cellar now, all men, all Poles, most of us from the nearby villages such as Grabow and Kolo, but many from Lodz. The air smells of dampness and rot and cold stone and mildew.

After several hours, as the light is waning, we do leave the cellar alive. More vans have arrived, larger vans, with double-leaf doors. These larger vans are green. They have no pictures painted on their sides. The guards open the van doors and I can see that most of these larger vans are almost full, each holding seventy to eighty men. I recognize none of the men in them.

The Germans push and beat us to hurry us into the larger vans. I hear many of the men I know crying out so I lead them in prayer as we are packed into the foul-smelling vans – *Shema Israel*, we are praying. We are still praying as the van doors are slammed shut.

Outside, the Germans are shouting at the Polish driver and his Polish helpers. I hear one of the helpers shout 'Gas!' in Polish and there comes the sound of a pipe or hose being coupled somewhere under our truck. The engine starts again with a roar.

Some of those around me continue praying with me, but most of the men begin screaming. The van starts to move, very slowly. I know that we are taking the narrow, asphalted road that the Germans built from Chelmno into the forest. All of the villagers marveled at this, because the road goes nowhere . . . it stops in the forest where the road widens so that there is room for the vans to turn around. But there is nothing there but the forest and the ovens the Germans ordered built and the pits the Germans ordered dug. The Jews in the camp who worked on that road and who dug the pits out there and who worked to build the ovens in the forest have told us this. We had not believed them when they told us, and then they were gone . . . transported.

The air thickens. The screams rise. My head hurts. It is hard to breathe. My heart is pounding wildly. I am holding the hands of a young man – a boy – on my left, and an old man to my right. Both are praying with me.

Somewhere in our van, someone is singing above the screams, singing in Yiddish, singing in a baritone that has been trained for opera:

My God, my God,
why hast Thou forsaken us?
We have been thrust into the fire before,
but we have never denied Thy Holy Law.

Aenea! My God! What?
Shhh. It's all right, my dear. I'm here.
I don't . . . what?

My name is Kaltryn Cateyen Endymion and I am the wife of Trorbe Endymion, who died five local months ago in a hunting accident. I am also the mother of the child named Raul, now three Hyperion-years old, who is playing by the campfire in the caravan circle as aunts watch him.

I climb the grassy hill above the valley where the caravan wagons have circled for the night. There are a few triaspen along the stream in the valley, but otherwise the moors are empty of any landmarks except short grass, heather, sedge, rocks, boulders, and lichen. And sheep. Hundreds of the caravan's sheep are visible and audible on the hills to the east as they mill and surge to the sheepdogs' herding.

Grandam is mending clothes on a rock outcropping with a grand view down the valley to the west. There is a haze over the western horizon that means open water, the sea, but the immediate world is bound about by the moors, the evening sky of deepening lapis, the meteor streaks silently crossing and crisscrossing that sky, and the sound of the wind in the grass.

I take a seat on a rock next to Grandam. She is my late mother's mother, and her face is our face but older, with weathered skin, short white hair, firm bones in a strong face, a blade of a nose, and brown eyes with laugh lines at the corners.

'You're back at last,' says the older woman. 'Was the voyage home smooth?'

'Aye,' I say. 'Tom took us along the coast from Port Romance and then up the Beak Highway rather than paying the ferry toll through the Fens. We stayed at the Benbroke Inn the first night, camped along the Suiss the second.'

Grandam nods. Her fingers are busy with the sewing. There is a basket of clothes next to her on the rock. 'And the doctors?'

'The clinic was large,' I say. 'The Christians have added to it since last we were in Port Romance. The sisters . . . the nurses . . . were very kind during the tests.'

Grandam waits.

I look down the valley to where the sun is breaking free from the dark clouds. Light streaks the valley tops, throws subtle shadows behind the low boulders and rocky hilltops, and sets the heather aflame. 'It is cancer,' I say. 'The new strain.'

'We knew that from the Moor's Edge doctor,' says Grandam. 'What did they say the prognosis is?'

I pick up a shirt – it is one of Trorbe's, but belongs to his brother, Raul's Uncle Ley. I pull my own needle and thread from my apron and begin to sew on the button that Trorbe had lost just before his last hunting trip north. My cheeks are hot at the thought that I gave this shirt to Ley with the button missing. 'They recommend that I accept the cross,' I say.

'There is no cure?' says Grandam. 'With all their machines and serums?'

'There used to be,' I say. 'But evidently it used the molecular technology . . .'

'Nanotech,' says Grandam.

'Yes. And the Church banned it some time ago. The more advanced worlds have other treatments.'

'But Hyperion does not,' says Grandam and sets the clothes in her lap aside.

'Correct.' As I speak, I feel very tired, still a little ill from the tests and the trip, and very calm. But also very sad. I can hear Raul and the other boys laughing on the breeze.

'And they counsel accepting their cross,' says Grandam, the last word sounding short and sharp-edged.

'Yes. A very nice young priest talked to me for hours yesterday.'

Grandam looks me in the eye. 'And will you do it, Kaltryn?'

I return her gaze. 'No.'

'You are sure?'

'Absolutely.'

'Trorbe would be alive again and with us now if he had accepted the cruciform last spring as the missionary pleaded.'

'Not *my* Trorbe,' I say and turn away. For the first time since the pain began seven weeks ago, I am crying. Not for me, I know, but at the memory of Trorbe smiling and waving that last sunrise morn when he set out with his brothers to hunt salt bison near the coast.

Grandam is holding my hand. 'You're thinking of Raul?'

I shake my head. 'Not yet. In a few weeks, I'll think of nothing else.'

'You do not have to worry about that, you know,' Grandam says softly. 'I still remember how to raise a young one. I still have tales to tell and skills to teach. And I will keep your memory alive in him.'

'He will be so young when . . .' I say and stop.

Grandam is squeezing my hand. 'The young remember most deeply,' she says softly. 'When we are old and failing, it is the memories of childhood which can be summoned most clearly.'

The sunset is brilliant but distorted by my tears. I keep my face half turned away from Grandam's gaze. 'I don't want him remembering me only when he is old. I want to *see* him . . . every day . . . see him play and grow up.'

'Do you remember the verse of Ryokan that I taught you when you were barely older than Raul?' says Grandam.

I have to laugh. 'You taught me dozens of Ryokan verses, Grandam.'

'The first one,' says the old woman.

It takes me only a moment to recall it. I say the verse, avoiding the singsong quality to my voice just as Grandam taught me when I was little older than Raul is now:

'How happy I am
As I go hand in hand
With the children,
To gather young greens
In the fields of spring!'

Grandam has closed her eyes. I can see how thin the parchment of her eyelids is. 'You used to like that verse, Kaltryn.'

'I still do.'

'And does it say anything about the need to gather greens next week or next year or ten years from now in order to be happy now?'

I smile. 'Easy for you to say, old woman,' I say, my voice soft and affectionate to temper the disrespect in the words. 'You've been gathering greens for seventy-four springs and plan to do so for another seventy.'

'Not so many to come, I think.' She squeezes my hand a final time and releases it. 'But the important thing is to walk with the children now, in this evening's spring sunlight, and to gather the greens quickly, for tonight's dinner. I am having your favorite meal.'

I actually clap my hands at this. 'The Northwind soup? But the leeks are not ripe.'

'They are in the south swards, where I sent Lee and his boys to search. And they have a pot full. Go now, get the spring greens to add to the mix. Take your child and be back before true dark.'

'I love you, Grandam.'

'I know. And Raul loves you, Little One. And I shall take care that the circle remains unbroken. Run on now.'

I come awake falling. I have been awake. The leaves of the Startree have shaded the pods for night and the stars to the out-system side are blazing. The voices do not diminish. The images do not fade. This is not like dreaming. This is a maelstrom of images and voices . . . thousands of voices in chorus, all clamoring to be heard. I had not remembered my mother's voice until this moment. When Rabbi Schulmann cried out in Old Earth Polish and prayed in Yiddish, I had understood not only his voice but his thoughts.

I am going mad.

'No, my dear, you are not going mad,' whispers Aenea. She is floating against the warm pod wall with me, holding me. The chronometer on my comlog says that the sleep period along this region of the Biosphere Startree is almost over, that the leaves will be shifting to allow the sunlight in within the hour.

The voices whisper and murmur and argue and sob. The images flit at the back of my brain like colors after a terrible blow to the head. I realize that I am holding myself stiffly, fists clenched, teeth clenched, neck veins straining, as against a terrible wind or wave of pain.

'No, no,' Aenea is saying, her soft hands stroking my cheek and temples. Sweat floats around me like a sour nimbus. 'No, Raul, relax. You are so sensitive to this, my dear, just as I thought. Relax and allow the voices to subside. You can control this, my darling. You can listen when you wish, quiet them when you must.'

'But they never go away?' I say.

'Not far away,' whispers Aenea. Ouster angels float in the sunlight beyond the leaf barrier sunward.

'And you have listened to this since you were an infant?' I say.

'Since before I was born,' says my darling.

'My God, my God,' I say, holding my fists against my eyes. 'My God.'

My name is Amnye Machen Al Ata and I am eleven standard years old when the Pax comes to my village of Qom-Riyadh. Our village is far from the cities, far from the few highways and skyways, far, even, from the caravan routes that crisscross the rock desert and the Burning Plains.

For two days the evening skies have shown the Pax ships burning like embers as they pass from east to west in what my father says is a place above the air. Yesterday the village radio carried orders from the imam at Al-Ghazali who heard over the phone lines from Omar that everyone in the High Reaches and the Burning Plains Oasis Camps are to assemble outside their yurts and wait. Father has gone to the meeting of the men inside the mud-walled mosque in our village.

The rest of my family stands outside our yurt. The other thirty families also wait. Our village poet, Farid ud-Din Attar, walks among us, trying to settle our nerves with verse, but even the adults are fearful.

My father has returned. He tells Mother that the mullah has decided that we cannot wait for the infidels to kill us. The village radio has not been able to raise the mosque at Al-Ghazali or Omar. Father thinks that the radio is broken again, but the mullah believes that the infidels have killed everyone west of the Burning Plains.

We hear the sound of shots from the front of the other yurts. Mother and my oldest sister want to run, but Father orders them to stay. There are screams. I watch the sky, waiting for the infidel Pax ships to reappear. When I look down again, the mullah's enforcers are coming around the side of our yurt, setting new magazines in their rifles. Their faces are grim.

Father has us all hold hands. 'God is great,' he says and we respond, 'God is great.' Even I know that 'Islam' means submission to the merciful will of Allah.

At the last second, I see the embers in the sky – the Pax ships floating east to west across the zenith so high above.

'God is great!' cries Father.

I hear the shots.

'Aenea, I don't know what these things mean.'

'Raul, they do not mean, they are.'

'They are real?'

'As real as any memories can be, my love.'

'But how? I can hear the voices . . . so many voices . . . as soon as I . . . touch one with my mind . . . these are stronger than my own memories, clearer.'

'They are memories, nonetheless, my love.'

'Of the dead . . .'

'These are, yes.'

'Learning their language . . .'

'In many ways we must learn their language, Raul. Their actual tongues . . . English, Yiddish, Polish, Parsi, Tamal, Greek, Mandarin . . . but also their hearts. The soul of their memory.'

'Are these ghosts speaking, Aenea?'

'There are no ghosts, my love. Death is final. The soul is that ineffable combination of memory and personality which we carry through life . . . when life departs, the soul also dies. Except for what we leave in the memory of those who loved us.'

'And these memories . . .'

'Resonate in the Void Which Binds.'

'How? All those billions of lives . . .'

'And thousands of races and billions of years, my love. Some of your mother's memories are there . . . and my mother's . . . but so are the life impressions of beings terribly far removed from us in space and time.'

'Can I touch those as well, Aenea?'

'Perhaps. With time and practice. It took me years to understand them. Even the sense impressions of life-forms so differently evolved are difficult to comprehend, much less their thoughts, memories, and emotions.'

'But you have done it?'

'*I have tried.*'

'*Alien life-forms like the Seneschai Aluit or the Akerataeli?*'

'*Much more alien than that, Raul. The Seneschai lived hidden on Hebron near the human settlers far generations. And they are empaths – emotions were their primary language. The Akerataeli are quite different from us, but not so different from the Core entities whom my father visited.*'

'*My head hurts, kiddo. Can you help me stop these voices and images?*'

'*I can help you quiet them, my love. They will never really stop as long as we live. This is the blessing and burden of the communion with my blood. But before I show you how to quiet them, listen a few more minutes. It is almost leafturn and sunrise.*'

My name was Lenar Hoyt, priest, but now I am Pope Urban XVI, and I am celebrating the Mass of Resurrection for John Domenico Cardinal Mustafa in St Peter's Basilica with more than five hundred of the Vatican's most important faithful in attendance.

Standing at the altar, my hands outstretched, I read from the *Prayer of the Faithful*:

'*Let us confidently call upon God our Almighty Father*
Who raised Christ His Son from the dead
for the salvation of all.'

Cardinal Lourdusamy, who serves as my deacon for this Mass, intones:

'*That He may return into the perpetual company of the Faithful,*
this deceased Cardinal, John Domenico Mustafa,
who once received the seed of eternal life through Baptism,
we pray to the Lord.

'*That he, who exercised the episcopal office in the Church*
and in the Holy Office while alive,
may once again serve God in his renewed life,
we pray to the Lord.

'*That He may give to the souls of our brothers, sisters, relatives,*
and benefactors
the reward of their labor,
we pray to the Lord.

'*That He may welcome into the light of His countenance*
all who sleep in the hope of the resurrection,
and grant them that resurrection,
that they may better serve Him,
we pray to the Lord.

'*That He may assist and graciously console*
our brothers and sisters who are suffering affliction
from the assaults of the godless and the
derision of the fallen away,
we pray to the Lord.

'That He may one day call into His glorious kingdom,
all who are assembled here in faith and devotion,
and award unto us that same blessing
of temporal resurrection in Christ's name,
we pray to the Lord.'

Now, as the choir sings the Offertory Antiphon and the congregation kneels in echoing silence in anticipation of the Holy Eucharist, I turn back from the altar and say—

'Receive, Lord, these gifts which we offer You on behalf of Your servant, John Domenico Mustafa, Cardinal; You gave the reward of the high priesthood in this world; may he be briefly united with the company of Your Saints in the Kingdom of Heaven and return to us via Your Sacrament of Resurrection. Through Christ our Lord.'

The congregation responds in unison—

'Amen.'

I walk to Cardinal Mustafa's coffin and resurrection creche near the communion altar and sprinkle holy water on it, while praying:

'Father, all-powerful and ever-living God,
we do well always and everywhere to give You thanks
through Jesus Christ our Lord.

'In Him, Who rose from the dead,
our hope of resurrection dawned.
The sadness of death gives way
to the bright promise of immortality.

'Lord, for your faithful people life is changed and renewed, not ended.
When the body of our earthly dwelling lies in death
we trust in Your mercy and Your miracle to renew it to us.

'And so, with all the choirs of angels in Heaven
we proclaim Your glory
and join in their unending hymn of praise.'

The great organ in the Basilica thunders while the choir immediately begins singing the *Sanctus*:

'Holy, holy, holy Lord God of power and might,
Heaven and earth are full of Your glory.
    Hosanna in the highest.
Blessed is He who comes in the name of the Lord.
    Hosanna in the highest.'

After Communion, after the Mass ends and the congregation departs, I walk slowly to the sacristy. I am sad and my heart hurts – literally. The heart disease has advanced once again, clogging my arteries and making every step and word painful. I think – *I must not tell Lourdusamy.*

That Cardinal appears as acolytes and altar boys help divest me of my garments.

'We have received a Gideon-drone courier, Your Holiness.'

'From which front?' I inquire.

'Not from the fleet, Holy Father,' says the Cardinal, frowning at a hardcopy message that he holds in his fat hands.

'From where, then?' I say, holding out my hand impatiently. The message is written on thin vellum.

I am coming to Pacem, to the Vatican.
Aenea.

I look up at my Secretary of State. 'Can you stop the fleet, Simon Augustino?'

His jowls seem to quiver. 'No, Your Holiness. They made the jump more than twenty-four hours ago. They should be almost finished with their accelerated resurrection schedule and commencing the attack within moments. We cannot outfit a drone and send it in time to recall them.'

I realize that my hand is shaking. I give the message back to Cardinal Lourdusamy. 'Call in Marusyn and the other fleet commanders,' I say. 'Tell them to bring every remaining capital fighting ship back to Pacem System. Immediately.'

'But Your Holiness,' says Lourdusamy, his voice urgent, 'there are so many important task force missions under way at the present . . .'

'Immediately!' I snap.

Lourdusamy bows. 'Immediately, Your Holiness.'

As I turn away, the pain in my chest and the shortness in my breath are like warnings from God that time is short.

'Aenea! The Pope . . .'

'Easy, my love. I'm here.'

'I was with the Pope . . . Lenar Hoyt . . . but he's not dead, is he?'

'You are also learning the language of the living, Raul. Incredible that your first contact with another living person's memories is with him. I think . . .'

'No time, Aenea! No time. His cardinal . . . Lourdusamy . . . brought your message. The Pope tried to recall the fleet, but Lourdusamy said that it was too late . . . that they jumped twenty-four hours ago and would be attacking any moment. That could be here, Aenea. It could be the fleet massing at Lacaille 9352 . . .'

'No!' Aenea's cry brings me out of the cacophony of images and voices, memories and sense overlays, not banishing them completely, but making them recede to something not unlike loud music in an adjoining room.

Aenea has summoned a comlog unit from the cubby shelf and is calling both our ship and Navson Hamnim at the same time.

I try to focus on my friend and the moment, pulling clothes on as I do so, but like a person emerging from a vivid dream, the murmur of voices and other memories is still with me.

Father Captain Federico de Soya kneeling in prayer in his private cubby pod on the treeship Yggdrasill, *only de Soya no longer thinks of himself as 'Father Captain', but simply as 'Father'. And he is unsure of even this title as he kneels and prays, prays as he has for hours this night, and longer hours in the days and nights since the cruciform was removed from his chest and body by the communion with Aenea's blood.*

Father de Soya prays for forgiveness of which – he knows beyond doubt – he is unworthy. He prays for forgiveness for his years as a Pax Fleet captain, his many battles, the lives he has taken, the beautiful works of man and God he has destroyed. Father Federico de Soya kneels in the one-sixth-g silence of his cubby and asks his Lord and Savior . . . the God of Mercy in which he had learned to believe and which he now doubts . . . to forgive him, not for his own sake, but so that his thoughts and actions in the months and years to come, or hours if his life is to be that short, might better serve his Lord . . .

I pull away from this contact with the sudden revulsion of someone realizing that he is becoming a voyeur. I understand immediately that if Aenea has known this 'language of the living' for years, for her entire life, she has almost certainly spent more energy denying it – avoiding these unsolicited entries into other people's lives – than mastering it.

Aenea has irised an opening in the pod wall and taken the comlog out to the organic tuft of balcony there. I float through and join her, floating down to the balcony's surface under the gentle one-tenth-g pull of the containment field there. There are several faces floating above the diskey of the comlog – Het Masteen's, Ket Rosteen's, and Navson Hamnim's – but all are looking away from the visual pickups, as is Aenea.

It takes me a second to look up at what she is seeing.

Blazing streaks are cutting through the Startree past beautiful rosettes of orange and red flame. For an instant I think that it is just leafturn sunrise along the inner curve of the Biosphere, squids and angels and watering comets catching the light the way Aenea and I had hours earlier when riding the heliosphere matrix, but then I realize what I am seeing.

Pax ships cutting through the Startree in a hundred places, their fusion tails slicing away branches and trunk like cold, bright knives.

Explosions of leaves and debris hundreds of thousands of kilometers away sending earthquake tremors through the branch and pod and balcony on which we stand.

Bright confusion. Energy lances leaping through space, visible because of the billions of particles of escaping atmosphere, pulverized organic matter, burning leaves, and Ouster and Templar blood. Lances cutting and burning everything they touch.

More explosions blossom outward within a few kilometers. The containment field still holds and sound pounds us back against the pod wall that ripples like the flesh of an injured beast. Aenea's comlog goes off at the same instant the Startree curve above us bursts into flame and explodes into silent space. There are shouts and screams and roars audible, but I know that within seconds the containment field must fail and Aenea and I will be sucked out into space with the other tons of debris flying past us.

I try to pull her back into the pod, which is sealing itself in a vain attempt to survive.

'No, Raul, look!'

I look to where she points. Above us, then beneath us, around us, the

Startree is burning and exploding, vines and branches snapping, Ouster angels consumed in flame, ten-klick worker squids imploding, treeships burning as they attempt to get under way.

'They're killing the ergs!' shouts Aenea above the wind roar and explosions.

I pound on the pod wall, shouting commands. The door irises open for just a second, but long enough for me to pull my beloved inside.

There is no shelter here. The plasma blasts are visible through the polarized pod walls.

Aenea has pulled her pack out of the cubby and tugged it on. I grab mine, thrust my sheath knife in my belt as if it would help fight off the marauders.

'We have to get to the *Yggdrasill*!' cries Aenea.

We kick off to the stemway wall, but the pod will not let us out. There is a roaring through the pod hull.

'Stemway's breached,' gasps Aenea. She still carries the comlog – I see that it is the ancient one from the Consul's ship – and is calling up data from the Startree grid. 'Bridges are out. We have to get to the treeship.'

I look through the wall. Orange blossoms of flame. The *Yggdrasill* is ten klicks up and inner-surface-east of us. With the swaying bridges and stemways gone, it might as well be a thousand light-years away.

'Send the ship for us,' I say. 'The Consul's ship.'

Aenea shakes her head. 'Het Masteen is getting the *Yggdrasill* under way now . . . no time to undock our ship. We have to be there in the next three or four minutes or . . . What about the Ouster skinsuits? We can fly over.'

It is my turn for headshaking. 'They're not here. When we got out of them at the landing platform, I had A. Bettik carry both of them to the treeship.'

The pod shakes wildly and Aenea turns away to look. The pod wall is a bright red, melting.

I pull open my storage cubby, throw clothes and gear aside, and pull out the one extraneous artifact I own, tugging it out of its leather storage tube. Father Captain de Soya's gift.

I tap the activator threads. The hawking mat stiffens and hovers in zero-g. The EM field around this section of the Startree is still intact.

'Come on,' I shout as the wall melts. I pull my beloved onto the hawking mat.

We are swept out through the fissure, into vacuum and madness.

TWENTY-EIGHT

The erg-folded magnetic fields were still standing but strangely scrambled. Instead of flying along and above the boulevard-wide swath of branch toward the *Yggdrasill*, the hawking mat wanted to align itself at right angles to the branch, so that our faces seemed to be pointing *down* as the mat rose like an elevator through shaking branches, dangling bridges, severed stemways, globes of flame, and hordes of Ousters leaping off into space to do battle and die. As long as we made progress toward the treeship, I let the hawking mat do what it wanted.

There were bubbles of containment-field atmosphere remaining, but most of the erg-fields had died along with the ergs who maintained them. Despite multiple redundancies, air was either leaking or explosively decompressing all along this region of the Startree. We had no suits. What I had remembered in the pod at the last moment was that the ancient hawking mat had its own low-level field for holding passengers or air in. It was never meant as a long-term pressurization device, but we had used it nine years ago on the unnamed jungle planet when we'd flown too high to breathe, and I hoped the systems were still working.

They still worked . . . at least after a fashion. As soon as we were out of the pod and rising like a parawing through the chaos, the hawking mat's low-level field kicked in. I could almost feel the thin air leaking out, but I told myself that it should last us the length of time it would take to reach the *Yggdrasill*.

We almost did not reach the *Yggdrasill*.

It was not the first space battle I had witnessed – Aenea and I had sat on the high platform of the Temple Hanging in Air not that many standard days, eons, ago and watched the light show in cislunar space as the Pax task force had destroyed Father de Soya's ship – but this was the first space battle I had seen where someone was trying to kill me.

Where there was air, the noise was deafening: explosions, implosions, shattering trunks and stemways, rupturing branches and dying squids, the howl of alarms and babble and squeal of comlogs and other communicators. Where there was vacuum, the silence was even more deafening: Ouster and Templar bodies being blown noiselessly into space – women and children, warriors unable to reach their weapons or battle stations, robed priests of the Muir tumbling toward the sun while wrapped in the ultimate indignity of violent death – flames with no crackling, screams with no sound, cyclones with no windrush warning.

Aenea was huddled over Siri's ancient comlog as we rose through the maelstrom. I saw Systenj Coredwell shouting from the tiny holo display above the diskey, and then Kent Quinkent and Sian Quintana Ka'an speaking earnestly. I was too busy guiding the hawking mat to listen to their desperate conversations.

I could no longer see the fusion tails of the Pax Fleet archangels, only their lances cutting through gas clouds and debris fields, slicing the Startree like scalpels through living flesh. The great trunks and winding branches actually bled, their sap and other vital fluids mixing with the kilometers of fiber-optic vine and Ouster blood as they exploded into space or boiled away in vacuum. A ten-klick worker squid was sliced through and then sliced through again as I watched, its delicate tentacles spasming in a destructive dance as it died. Ouster angels took flight by the thousands and died by the thousands. A treeship tried to get under way and was lanced through in seconds, its rich oxygen atmosphere igniting within the containment field, its crew dying in the time it took for the energy globe to fill with swirling smoke.

'Not the *Yggdrasill*,' shouted Aenea.

I nodded. The dying treeship had been coming from sphere north, but the *Yggdrasill* should be close now, a klick or less above us along the vibrating, splintering branch.

Unless I had taken a wrong turn. Or unless it had already been destroyed. Or unless it had left without us.

'I talked to Het Masteen,' Aenea shouted. We were in a globe of escaping air now and the din was terrible. 'Only about three hundred of the thousand are aboard.'

'All right,' I said. I had no idea what she was talking about. What thousand? No time to ask. I caught a glimpse of the deeper green of a treeship a klick or more above us and to the left – on another branch helix altogether – and swept the hawking mat in that direction. If it was not the *Yggdrasill* we would have to seek shelter there anyway. The Startree EM fields were failing, the hawking mat losing energy and inertia.

The EM field failed. The hawking mat surged a final time and then began tumbling in the blackness between shattered branches, a kilometer or more from the nearest burning stemways. Far below and behind us I could see the cluster of environment pods from which we had come: they were all shattered, leaking air and bodies, the podstems and connecting branches writhing in blind Newtonian response.

'That's it,' I said, my voice low because there was no more air or noise outside our failing bubble of energy. The hawking mat had been designed seven centuries ago to seduce a teenage niece into loving an old man, not to keep its flyers alive in outer space. 'We tried, kiddo.' I moved back from the flight threads and put my arm around Aenea.

'No,' said Aenea, rejecting not my hug but the death sentence. She gripped my arm so fiercely that her fingers sank into the flesh of my bicep. 'No, no,' she said to herself and tapped the comlog diskey.

Het Masteen's cowled face appeared against the tumbling starfield. 'Yes,' he said. 'I see you.'

The huge treeship now hung a thousand meters above us, a single great ceiling of branches and leaves green behind the flickering violet containment field, the bulk of it slowly separating from the burning Startree. There was a sudden, violent tug, and for a second I was sure that one of the archangel lances had found us.

'The ergs are pulling us in,' said Aenea, still grasping my arm.

'Ergs?' I said. 'I thought a treeship only had one erg aboard to handle the drive and fields.'

'Usually they do,' said Aenea. 'Sometimes two if it's an extraordinary voyage . . . into the outer envelope of a star, for instance, or through the shock wave of a binary's heliosphere.'

'So there are two aboard the *Yggdrasill*?' I said, watching the tree grow and fill the sky. Plasma explosions unfolded silently behind us.

'No,' said Aenea, 'there are twenty-seven.'

The extended field pulled us in. Up rearranged itself and became down. We were lowered onto a high deck, just beneath the bridge platform near the crown of the treeship. Even before I tapped the flight threads to collapse our own puny containment field, Aenea was scooping up her comlog and backpack and was racing toward the stairway.

I rolled the hawking mat neatly, shoved it into its leather carrier, flung the tube on my back, and rushed to catch up.

Only the Templar treeship captain Het Masteen and a few of his lieutenants were on the crown bridge, but the platforms and stairways beneath the bridge level were crowded with people I knew and did not know: Rachel, Theo, A. Bettik, Father de Soya, Sergeant Gregorius, Lhomo Dondrub, and the dozens of other familiar refugees from T'ien Shan, but there were also scores of other non-Ouster, non-Templar humans, men, women, and children whom I had not seen previously. 'Refugees fleeing a hundred Pax worlds, picked up by Father Captain de Soya in the *Raphael* over the past few years,' said Aenea. 'We'd expected hundreds more to arrive today before departure, but it's too late now.'

I followed her up to the bridge level. Het Masteen stood at the locus of a circle of organic control diskeys – displays from the fiber-optic nerves running throughout the ship, holo displays from onboard, astern, and ahead of the treeship, a communicator nexus to put him in touch with the Templars standing duty with the ergs, in the singularity containment core, at the drive roots, and elsewhere, and the central holo-simulacrum of the treeship itself, which he could touch with his long fingers to call up interactives or change headings. The Templar looked up as Aenea walked quickly across the sacred bridge toward him. His countenance – shaped from Old Earth Asian stock – was calm beneath his cowl.

'I am pleased that you were not left behind, One Who Teaches,' he said dryly. 'Where do you wish us to go?'

'Out-system,' said Aenea without hesitation.

Het Masteen nodded. 'We will draw fire, of course. The Pax Fleet firepower is formidable.'

Aenea only nodded. I saw the treeship simulacrum turning slowly and looked up to see the starfield rotating above us. We had moved in-system only a few hundred kilometers and were now turning back toward the battered inner surface of the Biosphere Startree. Where our meeting and environment pods had been there was now a ragged hole in the braided branches. All across the thousands of square klicks of this region were gaping wounds and denuded branches. The *Yggdrasill* moved slowly through billions of tumbling leaves – those still in containment-field atmosphere burning brightly and painting the containment-field perimeter gray with ash – as the treeship returned to the sphere wall and carefully passed through.

Emerging from the far side and picking up speed as the erg-controlled fusion drive flared, we could see even more of the battle now. Space here was a myriad of winking pinpoints of light, fiery sparks appearing as defensive containment fields came alight under lance attack, countless thermonuclear and plasma explosions, the drive tails of missiles, hyperkinetic weapons, small attack craft, and archangels. The curving-away outer surface of the Startree looked like a fibrous volcano world erupting with flames and geysers of debris. Watering comets and shepherd asteroids, knocked from their perfect balancing act by Pax weapon blasts, tore through the Startree like cannonballs through kindling. Het Masteen called up tactical holes and we stared at the image of the entire Biosphere, pocked now with ten thousand fires – many individual conflagrations as large as my homeworld of Hyperion – and a hundred thousand visible rents and tears in the sphere fabric that had taken almost a thousand years to weave. There were thousands of under-drive objects being plotted on the radar and deep-distance sensors, but fewer each second as the powerful archangels picked off Ouster ramscouts, torchships, destroyers, and treeships with their lances at distances of several AUs. Millions of space-adapted Ousters threw themselves at the attackers, but they died like moths in a flame-thrower.

Lhomo Dondrub strode onto the bridge. He was wearing an Ouster skinsuit and carrying a long, class-four assault weapon. 'Aenea, where the goddamned hell are we going?'

'Away,' said my beloved. 'We have to leave, Lhomo.'

The flyer shook his head. 'No, we don't. We have to stay and fight. We can't just abandon our friends to these Pax carrion birds.'

'Lhomo,' said Aenea, 'we can't help the Startree. I have to leave here in order to fight the Pax.'

'Run again if you have to,' said Lhomo, his handsome features contorted by rage and frustration. He molded the silvery skinsuit cowl up over his head. '*I* am going to stay and fight.'

'They'll kill you, my friend,' said Aenea. 'You can't fight archangel-class starships.'

'Watch me,' said Lhomo, the silvery suit covering everything but his face now. He shook my hand. 'Good luck, Raul.'

'And to you,' I said, feeling my throat tighten and face flush as much from my own shame at fleeing as from bidding farewell to this brave man.

Aenea touched the powerful silver arm. 'Lhomo, you can help the fight more if you come with us . . .'

Lhomo Dondrub shook his head and lowered the fluid cowl. The audio pickups sounded metallic as they spoke for him. 'Good luck to you, Aenea. May God and the Buddha help you. May God and the Buddha help us all.' He stepped to the edge of the platform and looked back at Het Masteen. The Templar nodded, touched the control simulacrum near the crown of the tree, and whispered into one of the fiberthreads.

I felt gravity lessen. The outer field shimmered and shifted. Lhomo was lifted, turned, and catapulted out into space beyond our branches and air and lights. I saw his silver wings unfold, saw the light fill his wings, and watched him form up with a score of other Ouster angels carrying their puny weapons and riding sunlight toward the nearest archangel.

Others were coming onto the bridge now – Rachel, Theo, the Dorje Phamo, Father de Soya and his sergeant, A. Bettik, the Dalai Lama – but all held back, keeping a respectful distance from the busy Templar captain.

'They've acquired us,' said Het Masteen. 'Firing.'

The containment field exploded red. I could hear the sizzling. It was as if we had fallen into the heart of a star.

Displays flickered. 'Holding,' said the True Voice of the Tree Het Masteen. 'Holding.'

He meant the defensive fields, but the Pax ships were also holding – maintaining their energy-lance fire even as we accelerated out-system. Except for the display holos, there was no sign of our movement – no stars visible – only the crackling, hissing, boiling ovoid of destructive energy bubbling and slithering a few dozen meters above and around us.

'What is our course, please?' asked Het Masteen of Aenea.

My friend touched her forehead briefly as if tired or lost. 'Just out where we can see the stars.'

'We will never reach a translation point while under this severity of attack,' said the Templar.

'I know,' said Aenea. 'Just . . . out . . . where I can see the stars.'

Het Masteen looked up at the inferno above us. 'We may never see the stars again.'

'We have to,' Aenea said simply.

There was a sudden flurry of shouts. I looked up at where the commotion was centered.

There were only a few small platforms above the control bridge – tiny structures looking like crow's nests on a holodrama pirate ship or like a treehouse I had seen once in the Hyperion fens – and it was on one of these that the figure stood. Crew clones were shouting and pointing. Het Masteen peered up toward the tiny platform fifteen meters above us and turned to Aenea. 'The Lord of Pain rides with us.'

I could see the colors from the inferno beyond the containment field reflecting on the Shrike's forehead and chest carapace.

'I thought it died on T'ien Shan,' I said.

Aenea looked more weary than I had ever seen her. 'The thing moves through time more easily than we move through space, Raul. It may have died on T'ien Shan . . . it may die a thousand years hence in a battle with Colonel Kassad . . . it may not be capable of dying . . . we will never know.'

As if her use of his name had summoned him, Colonel Fedmahn Kassad came up the stairs to the bridge platform. The Colonel was in archaic Hegemony-era battle dress and was carrying the assault rifle I had once seen in the Consul's ship armory. He stared at the Shrike like a man possessed.

'Can I get up there?' Kassed asked the Templar captain.

Still absorbed with issuing commands and monitoring displays, Het Masteen pointed to some ratlines and rope ladders that rose to the highest platform.

'No shooting on this treeship,' Het Masteen called after the Colonel. Kassad nodded and began climbing.

The rest of us turned our attention back to the simulacra displays. There were at least three archangels directing some of their fire at us from distances of less than a million klicks. They would take turns lancing us, each then directing some of its fire at other targets. But our odd refusal to die seemed to increase their anger at us and the lances would return, creeping across the four to ten light-seconds and exploding on the containment field above us. One of the ships was about to pass around the curve of the blazing Startree, but the two others were still decelerating in-system toward us with clear fields of fire.

'Missiles launched against us,' said one of the captain's Templar lieutenants in a voice no more excited than I would use to announce the arrival of dinner. 'Two . . . four . . . nine. Sublight. Presumably plasma warheads.'

'Can we survive that?' asked Theo. Rachel had walked over to watch the Colonel climb toward the Shrike.

Het Masteen was too occupied to answer, so Aenea said, 'We don't know. It depends on the binders . . . the ergs.'

'Sixty seconds to missile impact,' said the same Templar lieutenant in the same flat tones.

Het Masteen touched a comwand. His voice sounded normal, but I realized that it was being amplified all over the klick-long treeship. 'Everyone will please shield their eyes and avoid looking toward the field. The binders will polarize the flash as much as possible, but please do not look up. May the peace of the Muir be with us.'

I looked at Aenea. 'Kiddo, does this treeship carry weapons?'

'No,' she said. Her eyes looked as weary as her voice had sounded.

'So we're not going to fight . . . just run?'

'Yes, Raul.'

I ground my molars. 'Then I agree with Lhomo,' I said. 'We've run too much. It's time to help our friends here. Time to . . .'

At least three of the missiles exploded. Later, I recall the light so blinding that I could see Aenea's skull and vertebrae through her skin and flesh, but that must be impossible. There was a sense of falling . . . of the bottom falling out of everything . . . and then the one-sixth-g field was restored. A subsonic rumble made my teeth and bones hurt.

I blinked away retinal afterimages. Aenea's face was still before me – her cheeks flushed and sweaty, her hair pulled back by a hastily tied band, her eyes tired but infinitely alive, her forearms bare and sunburned – and in a thick moment of sentimentality I thought that it would not have been unthinkable to die like that, with Aenea's face seared into my soul and memory.

Two more plasma warheads made the treeship shudder. Then four more. 'Holding,' said Het Masteen's lieutenant. 'All fields holding.'

'Lhomo and Raul are right, Aenea,' said the Dorje Phamo, stepping forward with regal elegance in her simple cotton robe. 'You have run away from the Pax for years. It is time to fight them . . . time for all of us to fight them.'

I was staring at the old woman with something close to rude intensity. I had realized that there was an aura about her . . . no, wrong word, too mystical . . . but a feeling of strong color emanating from her, a deep carmine as strong as the Thunderbolt Sow's personality. I also realized that I had been noticing that with everyone on the platform that evening – the bright blue of Lhomo's courage, the golden confidence of Het Masteen's command, the shimmering violet of Colonel Kassad's shock at seeing the Shrike – and I wondered if this was some artifact of learning the language of the living. Or perhaps it was a result of the overload of light from the plasma explosions. Whatever it was, I knew that the colors were not real – I was not hallucinating and my vision was not clouded – but I also thought that I knew that my mind was making these connections, these shorthand glimpses into the true spirit of the person, on some level below and above sight.

And I knew that the colors surrounding Aenea covered the spectrum and beyond – a glow so pervasive that it filled the treeship as surely as the plasma explosions filled the world outside it.

Father de Soya spoke. 'No, ma'am,' he said to the Dorje Phamo, his voice soft and respectful. 'Lhomo and Raul are not correct. In spite of all of our anger and our wish to strike back, Aenea is correct. Lhomo may learn – if he lives – what we all will learn if we live. That is, after communion with Aenea, we share the pain of those we attack. Truly share it. Literally share it. Physically share it. Share it as part of having learned the language of the living.'

The Dorje Phamo looked down at the shorter priest. 'I know this is true, Christian. But this does not mean that we cannot strike back when others hurt *us*.' She swept one arm upward to include the slowly clearing containment field and the starfield of fusion trails and burning embers beyond it. 'These Pax . . . monsters . . . are destroying one of the greatest achievements of the human race. We must *stop* them!'

'Not now,' said Father de Soya. 'Not by fighting them here. Trust Aenea.'

The giant named Sergeant Gregorius stepped into the circle. 'Every fiber of my being, every moment of my training, every scar from my years of fighting . . . everything urges me to fight *now*,' he growled. 'But I trusted my captain. Now I trust him as my priest. And if he says we must trust the young woman . . . then we must trust her.'

Het Masteen held up a hand. The group fell into silence. 'This argument is a waste of time. As the One Who Teaches told you, the *Yggdrasill* has no weapons and the ergs are our only defense. But they cannot phaseshift the fusion drive while providing this level of shield. Effectively, we have no propulsion . . . we are drifting on our former course only a few light-minutes beyond our original position. And five of the archangels have changed course to intercept us.' The Templar turned to face us. 'Please, everyone except the Revered One Who Teaches and her tall friend Raul, please leave the bridge platform and wait below.'

The others left without another word. I saw the direction of Rachel's gaze before she turned away and I looked up. Colonel Kassad was at the top crow's nest, standing next to the Shrike, the tall man still dwarfed by the three-meter sculpture of chrome and blades and thorns. Neither the Colonel nor the killing machine moved as they regarded one another from less than a meter's distance.

I looked back at the simulacra display. The Pax ship embers were closing fast. Above us the containment field cleared.

'Take my hand, Raul,' said Aenea.

I took her hand, remembering all of the other times I had touched it in the last ten standard years.

'The stars,' she whispered. 'Look up at the stars. And listen to them.'

The treeship *Yggdrasill* hung in low orbit around an orange-red world with white polar caps, ancient volcanoes larger than my world's Pinion Plateau, and a river valley running for more than five thousand kilometers like an appendectomy scar around the world's belly.

'This is Mars,' said Aenea. 'Colonel Kassad will leave us here.'

The Colonel had come down from his close regard of the Shrike after the quantum-shift jump. There was no word or phrase for what we did: one moment the treeship was in the Biosphere System, coasting at low velocity, drives dead, under attack by a swarm of archangels, and the next instant we were in low and stable orbit around this dead world in Old Earth System.

'How did you do that?' I had asked Aenea a second after she had done it. I'd had no doubt whatsoever that she had . . . shifted . . . us there.

'I learned to hear the music of the spheres,' she said. 'And then to take a step.'

I kept staring at her. I was still holding her hand. I had no plans to release it until she spoke to me in plain language.

'One can *understand* a place, Raul,' she said, knowing that so many others were undoubtedly listening at that moment, 'and when you do, it is like hearing the music of it. Each world a different chord. Each star system a different sonata. Each specific place a clear and distinct note.'

I did not release her hand. 'And the farcasting without a farcaster?' I said.

Aenea nodded. 'A Freecasting. A quantum leap in the real sense of the term,' she said. 'Moving in the macro universe the way an electron moves in the infinitely micro. Taking a step with the help of the Void Which Binds.'

I was shaking my head. 'Energy. Where does the energy come from, kiddo? Nothing comes from nothing.'

'But everything comes from everything.'

'What does that *mean*, Aenea?'

She pulled her fingers from mine but touched my cheek. 'Remember our discussion long, long ago about the Newtonian physics of love?'

'Love is an emotion, kiddo. Not a form of energy.'

'It's both, Raul. It truly is. And it is the only key to unlocking the universe's greatest supply of energy.'

'Are you talking about religion?' I said, half furious at either her opacity or my denseness or both.

'No,' she said, 'I'm talking about quasars deliberately ignited, about pulsars tamed, about the exploding cores of galaxies tapped for energy like steam turbines. I'm talking about an engineering project two and a half billion years old and barely begun.'

I could only stare.

She shook her head. 'Later, my love. For now understand that farcasting without a farcaster really works. There were *never* any real farcasters . . . never any magical doors opening onto different worlds . . . only the TechnoCore's perversion of this form of the Void's second most wonderful gift.'

I should have said, *What is the Void's first most wonderful gift?* but I assumed then that it was the learning-the-language-of-the-dead recording of sentient races' memories . . . my mother's voice, to be more precise. But what I did say then was, 'So this is how you moved Rachel and Theo and you from world to world without time-debt.'

'Yes.'

'And took the Consul's ship from T'ien Shan System to Biosphere with no Hawking drive.'

'Yes.'

I was about to say, *And traveled to whatever world where you met your lover, were married, and had a child*, but the words would not form.

'This is Mars,' she said next, filling the silence. 'Colonel Kassad will leave us here.'

The tall warrior stepped to Aenea's side. Rachel came closer, stood on her tiptoes, and kissed him.

'Someday you will be called Moneta,' Kassad said softly. 'And we will be lovers.'

'Yes,' said Rachel and stepped back.

Aenea took the tall man's hand. He was still in quaint battle garb, the assault rifle held comfortably in the crook of his arm. Smiling slightly, the Colonel looked up at the highest platform where the Shrike still stood, the blood light of Mars on his carapace.

'Raul,' said Aenea, 'will you come as well?'

I took her other hand.

The wind was blowing sand into my eyes and I could not breathe. Aenea handed me an osmosis mask and I slipped mine on as she set hers in place.

The sand was red, the rocks were red, and the sky was a stormy pink. We were standing in a dry river valley bounded by rocky cliffs. The riverbed was strewn with boulders – some as big as the Consul's ship. Colonel Kassad pulled on the helmet cowl of his combat suit and static rasped in our comthread pickups. 'Where I started,' he said. 'In the Tharsis Relocation Slums a few hundred klicks that direction.' He gestured toward where the sun hung low and small above the cliffs. The suited figure, ominous in its size and bulk, the heavy assault weapon looking anything but obsolete here on the plain of Mars, turned toward Aenea. 'What would you have me do, woman?'

Aenea spoke in the crisp, quick, sure syllables of command. 'The Pax has retreated from Mars and Old Earth System temporarily because of the Palestinian uprising here and the resurgence of the Martian War Machine in space. There is nothing strategic enough to hold them here now while their resources are stretched so thin.'

Kassad nodded.

'But they'll be back,' said Aenea. 'Back in force. Not just to pacify Mars, but to occupy the entire system.' She paused to look around. I followed her gaze and saw the dark human figures moving down the boulder field toward us. They carried weapons.

'You must keep them out of the system, Colonel,' said my friend. 'Do whatever you must . . . sacrifice whomever you must . . . but keep them out of Old Earth System for the next five standard years.'

I had never heard Aenea sound so adamant or ruthless.

'Five *standard* years,' said Colonel Kassad. I could see his thin smile behind the cowl visor. 'No problem. If it was five *Martian* years, I might have to strain a bit.'

Aenea smiled. The figures were moving closer through the blowing sand. 'You'll have to take the leadership of the Martian resistance movement,' she said, her voice deadly serious. 'Take it any way you can.'

'I will,' said Kassad and the firmness in his voice matched Aenea's.

'Consolidate the various tribes and warrior factions,' said Aenea.

'I will.'

'Form a more permanent alliance with the War Machine spacers.'

Kassad nodded. The figures were less than a hundred meters away now. I could see weapons raised.

'*Protect Old Earth*,' said Aenea. 'Keep the Pax away at all costs.'

I was shocked. Colonel Kassad must have been surprised as well. 'You mean Old Earth *System*,' he said.

Aenea shook her head. 'Old Earth, Fedmahn. Keep the Pax away. You have approximately a year to consolidate control of the entire system. Good luck.'

The two shook hands.

'Your mother was a fine, brave woman,' said the Colonel. 'I valued her friendship.'

'And she valued yours.'

The dark figures were moving closer, keeping to the cover of boulders and dunes. Colonel Kassad walked toward them, his right hand high, the assault weapon still easy in his arm.

Aenea came closer and took my hand again. 'It's cold, isn't it, Raul?'

It was. There was a flash of light like a painless blow to the back of one's head and we were on the bridge platform of the *Yggdrasill*. Our friends backed away at the sight of our appearance; the fear of magic dies hard in a species. Mars turned red and cold beyond our branches and containment field.

'What course, Revered One Who Teaches?' said Het Masteen.

'Just turn outward to where we can clearly see the stars,' said Aenea.

TWENTY-NINE

The *Yggdrasill* continued on. The Tree of Pain, its captain, the Templar True Voice of the Tree Het Masteen, called it. I could not argue. Each jump took more energy from my Aenea, my love, my poor, tired Aenea, and each separation filled the depleting pool of energy with a growing reservoir of sadness. And through it all the Shrike stood useless and alone on its high platform, like a hideous bowsprit on a doomed ship or a macabre dark angel on the top of a mirthless Christmas tree.

After leaving Colonel Kassad on Mars, the treeship jumped to orbit around Maui-Covenant. The world was in rebellion but deep within Pax space and I expected hordes of Pax warships to rise up in challenge, but there was no attack during the few hours we were there.

'One of the benefits of the armada attack on the Biosphere Startree,' Aenea said with sad irony. 'They've stripped the inner systems of fighting ships.'

It was Theo whose hand Aenea took for the step down to Maui-Covenant. Again, I accompanied my friend and her friend.

I blinked away the white light and we were on a motile isle, its treesails filling with warm tropical wind, the sky and sea a breathtaking blue. Other isles kept pace while dolphin outriders left white wakes on either side of the convoy.

There were people on the high platform and although they were mystified by our appearance, they were not alarmed. Theo hugged the tall blond man and his dark-haired wife who came forward to greet us.

'Aenea, Raul,' she said, 'I am pleased to introduce Merin and Deneb Aspic-Coreau.'

'Merin?' I said, feeling the strength in the man's handshake.

He smiled. 'Ten generations removed from *the* Merin Aspic,' he said. 'But a direct descendant. As Deneb is of our famed lady, Siri.' He put his hand on Aenea's shoulder. 'You have come back just as promised. And brought our fiercest fighter back with you.'

'I have,' said Aenea. 'And you must keep her safe. For the next days and months, you must keep clear of contact with the Pax.'

Deneb Aspic-Coreau laughed. I noticed without a trace of desire that she might be the healthiest, most beautiful woman I had ever seen. 'We're running for our lives as it is, One Who Teaches. Thrice we've tried to destroy the oil platform complex at Three Currents, and thrice they have cut us down like Thomas hawks. Now we are just hoping to reach the Equatorial

Archipelago and hide among the isle migration, eventually to regroup at the submersible base at Lat Zero.'

'Protect her at all costs,' repeated Aenea. She turned to Theo. 'I will miss you, my friend.'

Theo Bernard visibly attempted to keep from weeping, failed, and hugged Aenea fiercely. 'All the time . . . was *good*,' Theo said and stood back. 'I pray for your success. And I pray that you fail . . . for your own good.'

Aenea shook her head. 'Pray for all of our success.' She held her hand up in farewell and walked back to the lower platform with me.

I could smell the intoxicating salt-and-fish scent of the sea. The sun was so fierce it made me squint, but the air temperature was perfect. The water on the dolphins' skin was as clear to me as the sweat on my own forearms. I could imagine staying in this place forever.

'We have to go,' said Aenea. She took my hand.

A torchship did appear on radar just as we climbed out of Maui-Covenant's gravity well, but we ignored it as Aenea stood alone on the bridge platform, staring at the stars.

I went over to stand next to her.

'Can you hear them?' she whispered.

'The stars?' I said.

'The worlds,' she said. 'The people on them. Their secrets and silences. So many heartbeats.'

I shook my head. 'When I am not concentrating on something else,' I said, 'I am still haunted by voices and images from elsewhere. Other times. My father hunting in the moors with his brothers. Father Glaucus being thrown to his death by Rhadamanth Nemes.'

She looked at me. 'You saw that?'

'Yes. It was horrible. He could not see who it was who had attacked him. The fall . . . the darkness . . . the cold . . . the moments of pain before he died. He had refused to accept the cruciform. It was why the Church sent him to Sol Draconi Septem . . . exile in the ice.'

'Yes,' said Aenea. 'I've touched those last memories of his many times in the past ten years. But there are other memories of Father Glaucus, Raul. Warm and beautiful memories . . . filled with light. I hope you find them.'

'I just want the voices to stop,' I said truthfully. 'This . . .' I gestured around at the treeship, the people we knew, Het Masteen at his bridge controls. 'This is all too important.'

Aenea smiled. 'It's all too important. That's the damned problem, isn't it?' She turned her face back to the stars. 'No, Raul, what you have to hear before you take a step is not the resonance of the language of the dead . . . or even of the living. It is . . . the essence of things.'

I hesitated, not wanting to make a fool of myself, but then said:

'. . . *So*
A million times ocean must ebb and flow,
And be oppressed. Yet he shall not die,
These things accomplished. If he utterly . . .'

Aenea broke in:

'. . . *Scans all depths of magic, and expounds*
The meanings of all motions, shapes, and sounds;
If he explores all forms and substances
Straight homeward to their symbol-essences;
He shall not die . . .'

She smiled again. 'I wonder how Uncle Martin is. Is he cold-sleeping the years away? Railing at his poor android servants? Still working on his unfinished *Cantos*? In all my dreams, I never manage to see Uncle Martin.'

'He's dying,' I said.

Aenea blinked in shock.

'I dreamed of him . . . saw him . . . this morning,' I said. 'He's defrosted himself for the last time, he's told his faithful servants. The machines are keeping him alive. The Poulsen treatments have finally worn off. He's . . .' I stopped.

'Tell me,' said Aenea.

'He's staying alive until he can see you again,' I said. 'But he's very frail.'

Aenea looked away. 'It's strange,' she said. 'My mother fought with Uncle Martin during the entire pilgrimage. At times they could have killed one another. Before she died, he was her closest friend. Now . . .' She stopped, her voice thick.

'You'll just have to stay alive, kiddo,' I said, my own voice strange. 'Stay alive, stay healthy, and go back to see the old man. You owe him that.'

'Take my hand, Raul.'

The ship farcast through light.

Around Tau Ceti Center we were immediately attacked, not only by Pax ships but by rebel torchships fighting for the planetary secession started by the ambitious female Archbishop Achilla Silvaski. The containment field flared like a nova.

'Surely you can't 'cast through this,' I said to Aenea when she offered Tromo Trochi of Dhomu and me her hands.

'One does not 'cast *through* anything,' said my friend, and took our hands, and we were on the surface of the former capital of the late and unlamented Hegemony.

Tromo Trochi had never been to TC^2, indeed, had never been off the world of T'ien Shan, but his merchant interests were aroused by the tales of this one-time capitalist capital of the human universe.

'It is a pity that I have nothing to trade,' said the clever trader. 'In six months on so fecund a world, I would have built a commercial empire.'

Aenea reached into the shoulder pack she had carried and lifted out a heavy bar of gold. 'This should get you started,' she said. 'But remember your true duties here.'

Holding the bar, the little man bowed. 'I will never forget, One Who Teaches. I have not suffered to learn the language of the dead to no avail.'

'Just stay safe for the next few months,' said Aenea. 'And then, I am confident, you will be able to afford transport to any world you choose.'

'I would come to wherever you are, M. Aenea,' said the trader with the only visible show of emotion I had ever seen from him. 'And I would pay all of my wealth – past, future, and fantasized – to do so.'

I had to blink at this. It occurred to me for the first time that many of Aenea's disciples might be – probably were – a little bit in love with her, as well as very much in awe of her. To hear it from this coin-obsessed merchant, though, was a shock.

Aenea touched his arm. 'Be safe and stay well.'

The *Yggdrasill* was still under attack when we returned. It was under attack when Aenea 'cast us away from the Tau Ceti System.

The inner city-world of Lusus was much as I remembered it from my brief sojourn there: a series of Hive towers above the vertical canyons of gray metal. George Tsarong and Jigme Norbu bade us farewell there. The stocky, heavily muscled George – weeping as he hugged Aenea – might have passed for an average Lusian in dim light, but the skeletal Jigme would stand out in the Hive-bound crowds. But Lusus was used to off-worlders and our two foremen would do well as long as they had money. But Lusus was one of the few Pax worlds to have returned to universal credit cards and Aenea did not have one of these in her backpack.

A few minutes after we stepped from the empty Dreg's Hive corridors, however, seven figures in crimson cloaks approached. I stepped between Aenea and these ominous figures, but rather than attack, the seven men went to their knees on the greasy floor, bowed their heads, and chanted:

'BLESSED BE SHE
BLESSED BE THE SOURCE OF OUR SALVATION
BLESSED BE THE INSTRUMENT OF OUR ATONEMENT
BLESSED BE THE FRUIT OF OUR RECONCILIATION
BLESSED BE SHE.'

'The Shrike Cult,' I said stupidly. 'I thought they were gone – wiped out during the Fall.'

'We prefer to be referred to as the Church of the Final Atonement,' said the first man, rising from his knees but still bowing in Aenea's direction. 'And no . . . we were not "wiped out" as you put it . . . merely driven underground. Welcome, Daughter of Light. Welcome, Bride of the Avatar.'

Aenea shook her head with visible impatience. 'I am bride of no one, Bishop Duruyen. These are the two men I have brought to entrust to your protection for the next ten months.'

The Bishop in red bowed his bald head. 'Just as your prophecies said, Daughter of Light.'

'Not prophecies,' said Aenea. 'Promises.' She turned and hugged George and Jigme a final time.

'Will we see you again, Architect?' said Jigme.

'I cannot promise that,' said Aenea. 'But I do promise that if it is in my power, we will be in contact again.'

I followed her back to the empty hall in the dripping corridors of Dreg's Hive, where our departure would not seem so miraculous as to add to the Shrike Cult's already fertile canon.

On Tsintao-Hsishuang Panna, we said good-bye to the Dalai Lama and his brother, Labsang Samten. Labsang wept. The boy Lama did not.

'The local people's Mandarin dialect is atrocious,' said the Dalai Lama.

'But they will understand you, Your Holiness,' said Aenea. 'And they will listen.'

'But you are my teacher,' said the boy, his voice near anger. 'How can I teach them without your help?'

'I will help,' said Aenea. 'I will try to help. And then it is your job. And theirs.'

'But we may share communion with them?' asked Labsang.

'If they ask for it,' said Aenea. To the boy she said, 'Would you give me your blessing, Your Holiness?'

The child smiled. 'It is I who should be asking for a blessing, Teacher.'

'Please,' said Aenea, and again I could hear the weariness in her voice.

The Dalai Lama bowed and, with his eyes closed, said, 'This is from the "Prayer of Kuntu Sangpo", as revealed to me through the vision of my *terton* in a previous life:

'Ho! The phenomenal world and all existence, samsara and nirvana,
All has one foundation, but there are two paths and two results—
Displays of both ignorance and Knowledge.
Through Kuntu Sangpo's aspiration,
In the Palace of the Primal Space of Emptiness
Let all beings attain perfect consummation and Buddhahood.

'The universal foundation is unconditioned,
Spontaneously arising, a vast immanent expanse, beyond expression,
Where neither samsara nor nirvana exist.
Knowledge of this reality is Buddhahood,
While ignorant beings wander in samsara.
Let all sentient beings of the three realms
Attain Knowledge of the nature of the ineffable foundation.'

Aenea bowed toward the boy. 'The Palace of the Primal Space of Emptiness,' she murmured. 'How much more elegant than my clumsy description of the "Void Which Binds". Thank you, Your Holiness.'

The child bowed. 'Thank *you*, Revered Teacher. May your death be more quick and less painful than we both expect.'

Aenea and I returned to the treeship. 'What did he *mean*?' I demanded, both of my hands on her shoulders. ' "Death more quick and less painful"? What the hell does that mean? Are you planning to be crucified? Does this goddamned messiah impersonation have to go to the same bizarre end? *Tell me, Aenea!*' I realized that I was shaking her . . . shaking my dear friend, my beloved girl. I dropped my hands.

Aenea put her arms around me. 'Just stay with me, Raul. Stay with me as long as you can.'

'I will,' I said, patting her back. 'I swear to you I will.'

On Fuji we said good-bye to Kenshiro Endo and Haruyuki Otaki. On Deneb Drei it was a child whom I had never met – a ten-year-old girl named Katherine – who stayed behind, alone and seemingly unafraid. On Sol Draconi Septem, that world of frozen air and deadly wraiths where Father Glaucus and our Chitchatuk friends had been foully murdered, the sad and brooding scaffold rigger, Rimsi Kyipup, volunteered almost happily to be left behind. On Nevermore it was another man I had not had the privilege of meeting – a soft-spoken, elderly gentleman who seemed like Martin Silenus's kindlier younger brother. On God's Grove, where A. Bettik had lost part of his arm ten standard years earlier, the two Templar lieutenants of Het Masteen 'cast down with Aenea and me and did not return. On Hebron, empty now of its Jewish settlers but filled instead with good Christian colonists sent there by the Pax, the Seneschai Aluit empaths, Leeoonn and Ooeeaall, 'cast down to say good-bye to us on an empty desert evening where the rocks still held the daytime's glow.

On Parvati, the usually happy sisters Kuku Se and Kay Se wept and hugged the both of us good-bye. On Asquith, a family of two parents and their five golden-haired children stayed behind. Above the white cloud-swirl and blue ocean world of Mare Infinitus – a world whose mere name haunted me with memories of pain and friendship – Aenea asked Sergeant Gregorius if he would 'cast down with her to meet the rebels and support her cause.

'And leave the captain?' asked the giant, obviously shocked by the suggestion.

De Soya stepped forward. 'There is no more captain, Sergeant. My dear friend. Only this priest without a Church. And I suspect that we would do more good now apart than together. Am I right, M. Aenea?'

My friend nodded. 'I had hoped that Lhomo would be my representative on Mare Infinitus,' she said. 'The smugglers and rebels and Lantern Mouth hunters on this world would respect a man of strength. But it will be difficult and dangerous . . . the rebellion still rages here and the Pax takes no prisoners.'

''Tis not th' danger I object to!' cried Gregorius. 'I'm willin' to die the true death a hundred times over for a good cause.'

'I know that, Sergeant,' said Aenea.

The giant looked at his former captain and then back to Aenea. 'Lass, I know ye do not like to tell the future, even though we know you spy it now and then. But tell me this . . . is there a chance of reunion with my captain?'

'Yes,' said Aenea. 'And with some you thought dead . . . such as Corporal Kee.'

'Then I'll go. I'll do your will. I may not be of the Corps Helvetica anymore, but the obedience they taught me runs deep.'

'It's not obedience we ask now,' said Father de Soya. 'It is something harder and deeper.'

Sergeant Gregorius thought a moment. 'Aye,' he said at last and turned his back on everyone a moment. 'Let's go, lass,' he said, holding out his hand for Aenea's touch.

We left him on an abandoned platform somewhere in the South Littoral, but Aenea told him that submersibles would put in there within, a day.

Above MadredeDios, Father de Soya stepped forward, but Aenea held up her hand to stop him.

'Surely this is my world,' said the priest. 'I was born here. My diocese was here. I imagine that I will die here.'

'Perhaps,' said Aenea, 'but I need you for a more difficult place and a more dangerous job, Federico.'

'Where is that?' said the sad-eyed priest.

'Pacem,' said Aenea. 'Our last stop.'

I stepped closer. 'Wait, kiddo,' I said. 'I'm going with you to Pacem if you insist on going there. You said that I could stay with you.' My voice sounded querulous and desperate even to me.

'Yes,' said Aenea, touching my wrist with her cool fingers. 'But I would like Father de Soya to come with us when it is time.'

The Jesuit looked confused and a bit disappointed, but he bowed his head. Evidently obedience ran even deeper in the Society of Jesus than it did in the Corps Helvetica.

In the end, the T'ien Shan bamboo worker Voytek Majer and his new fiancée, the brickmaker Viki Groselj, volunteered to stay on MadredeDios.

On Freeholm, we said good-bye to Janusz Kurtyka. On Kastrop-Rauxel, recently reterraformed and settled by the Pax, it was the soldier Jigme Paring who volunteered to find the rebel population. Above Parsimony, while Pax warships turned the containment field into a torrent of noise and light, a woman named Helen Dean O'Brian stepped forward and took Aenea's hand. On Esperance, Aenea and I bid farewell to the former mayor of Jo-kung, Charles Chi-kyap Kempo. On Grass, standing shoulder high in the yellow world prairie, we waved good-bye to Isher Perpet, one of the bolder rebels once rescued from a Pax prison galley and gathered in by Father de Soya. On Qom-Riyadh, where the mosques were quickly being bulldozed or converted to cathedrals by the new Pax settlers, we 'cast down in the dead of night and whispered our farewells to a former refugee from that world named Merwin Muhammed Ali and to our former interpreter on T'ien Shan, the clever Perri Samdup.

Above Renaissance Minor, with a horde of in-system warships accelerating toward us with murderous intent, it was the silent ex-prisoner, Hoagan Liebler, who stepped forward. 'I was a spy,' said the pale man. He was speaking to Aenea but looking directly at Father de Soya. 'I sold my allegiance for money, so that I could return to this world to renew my family's lost lands and wealth. I betrayed my captain and my soul.'

'My son,' said Father de Soya, 'you have long since been forgiven those sins, if sins they were . . . by both your captain and, more importantly, by God. No harm was done.'

Liebler nodded slowly. 'The voices I have been listening to since I drank the wine with M. Aenea . . .' He trailed off. 'I know many people on this world,' he said, his voice stronger. 'I wish to return home to start this new life.'

'Yes,' said Aenea and offered her hand. On Vitus-Gray-Balianus B, Aenea, the Dorje Phamo, and I 'cast down to a desert wasteland, far from the river with its farm fields and brightly painted cottages lining the way where the kind people of the Amoiete Spectrum Helix had nursed me to health and helped me escape the Pax. Here there was only a tumble of boulders and dried fissures, mazes of tunnel entrances in the rock, and dust storms blowing in from the bloody sunset on the black-cloud horizon. It reminded me of Mars with warmer, thicker air and more of a stench of death and cordite to it.

The shrouded figures surrounded us almost immediately, flechette guns and hellwhips at the ready. I tried again to step between Aenea and the danger, but the figures in the blowing red wind surrounded us and raised their weapons.

'Wait!' cried a voice familiar to me, and one of the shrouded soldiers slid down a red dune to stand in front of us. 'Wait!' she called again to those eager to shoot, and this time she unwrapped the bands of her cowl.

'Dem Loa!' I cried and stepped forward to hug the short woman in her bulky battle garb. I saw tears leaving muddy streaks on her cheeks.

'You have brought back your special one,' said the woman who had saved me. 'Just as you promised.'

I introduced her to Aenea and then to the Dorje Phamo, feeling silly and happy at the same moment. Dem Loa and Aenea regarded one another for a moment, and then hugged.

I looked around at the other figures who still hung back in the red twilight. 'Where is Dem Ria?' I asked. 'Alem Mikail Dem Alem? And your children – Bin and Ces Ambre?'

'Dead,' said Dem Loa. 'All dead, except Ces Ambre, who is missing after the last attack from the Bombasino Pax.'

I stood speechless, stunned.

'Bin Ria Dem Loa Alem died of his illness,' continued Dem Loa, 'but the rest died in our war with the Pax.'

'War with the Pax,' I repeated. 'I hope to God that I did not start it . . .'

Dem Loa raised her hand. 'No, Raul Endymion. You did not start it. Those of us in the Amoiete Spectrum Helix who prized our own ways refused the cross . . . that is what started it. The rebellion had already begun when you were with us. After you left, we thought we had it won. The cowardly troops at Pax Base Bombasino sued for peace, ignored the orders from their commanders in space, and made treaties with us. More Pax ships arrived. They bombed their own base . . . then came after our villages. It has been war since then. When they land and try to occupy the land, we kill many of them. They send more.'

'Dem Loa,' I said, 'I am so, so sorry.'

She set her hand on my chest and nodded. I saw the smile that I remembered from our hours together. She looked at Aenea again. 'You are the one he spoke of in his delirium and his pain. You are the one whom he loved. Do you love him as well, child?'

'I do,' said Aenea.

'Good,' said Dem Loa. 'It would be sad if a man who thought he was dying expressed such love for someone who did not feel the same about him.' Dem Loa looked at the Thunderbolt Sow, silent and regal. 'You are a priestess?'

'Not a priestess,' said the Thunderbolt Sow, 'but the abbess of the Samden Gompa monastery.'

Dem Loa showed her teeth. 'You rule over monks? Over men?'

'I . . . instruct them,' said the Dorje Phamo. The wind ruffled her steel-gray hair.

'Just as good as ruling them.' Dem Loa laughed. 'Welcome then, Dorje Phamo.' To Aenea, she said, 'And are you staying with us, child? Or just touching us and passing on as our prophecies predict?'

'I must go on,' said Aenea. 'But I would like to leave the Dorje Phamo here as your ally and our . . . liaison.'

Dem Loa nodded. 'It is dangerous here now,' she said to the Thunderbolt Sow.

The Dorje Phamo smiled at the shorter woman. The strength of the two was almost a palpable energy in the air around us.

'Good,' said Dem Loa. She hugged me. 'Be kind to your love, Raul Endymion. Be good to her in the hours granted to you by the cycles of life and chaos.'

'I will,' I said.

To Aenea, Dem Loa said, 'Thank you for coming, child. It was our wish. It was our hope.' The two women hugged again. I felt suddenly shy, as if I had brought Aenea home to meet my own mother or Grandam.

The Dorje Phamo touched both of us in benediction. '*Kale pe a*,' she said to Aenea.

We moved away in the twilight dust storm and 'cast through the burst of white light. On the quiet of the *Yggdrasill*'s bridge, I said to Aenea, 'What was that she said?'

'*Kale pe a*,' repeated my friend. 'It is an ancient Tibetan farewell when a caravan sets out to climb the high peaks. It means – go slowly if you wish to return.'

And so it went for a hundred other worlds, each one visited only for moments, but each farewell moving and stirring in its own way. It is hard for me to say how many days and nights were spent on this final voyage with Aenea, because there was only the 'casting down and 'casting up, the treeship entering the light one place and emerging elsewhere, and when everyone was too tired to go on, the *Yggdrasill* was allowed to drift in empty space for a few hours while the ergs rested and the rest of us tried to sleep.

I remember at least three of these sleep periods, so perhaps we traveled for only three days and nights. Or perhaps we traveled for a week or more and slept only three times. But I remember that Aenea and I slept little and loved one another tenderly, as if each time we held each other it might be our last.

It was during one of these brief interludes alone that I whispered to her, 'Why are you doing this, kiddo? Not just so we can all become like the Ousters and catch sunlight in our wings. I mean . . . it was beautiful . . . but I *like* planets. I like dirt under my boots. I like just being . . . human. Being a man.'

Aenea had chuckled and touched my cheek. I remember that the light was dim but that I could see the perspiration still beaded between her breasts. 'I like your being a man too, Raul my love.'

'I mean . . .' I began awkwardly.

'I know what you mean,' whispered Aenea. 'I like planets too. And I like being human . . . just being a woman. It's not for some Utopian evolution of humankind into Ouster angels or Seneschai empaths that I'm doing . . . what I have to do.'

'What then?' I whispered into her hair.

'Just for the chance to choose,' she said softly. 'Just for the opportunity to continue being human, whatever that means to each person who chooses.'

'To choose again?' I said.

'Yes,' said Aenea. 'Even if that means choosing what one has had before. Even if it means choosing the Pax, the cruciform, and alliance with the Core.'

I did not understand, but at that moment I was more interested in holding her than in fully understanding.

After moments of silence, Aenea said, 'Raul . . . I also love the dirt under my boots, the sound of the wind in the grass. Would you do something for me?'

'Anything,' I said fiercely.

'If I die before you,' she whispered, 'would you return my ashes to Old Earth and sprinkle them where we were happiest together?'

If she had stabbed me in the heart, it would not have hurt as much. 'You said that I could stay with you,' I said at last, my voice thick and angry and lost. 'That I could go anywhere you go.'

'And I meant it, my love,' whispered Aenea. 'But if I go ahead of you into death, will you do that for me? Wait a few years, and then set my ashes free where we had been happiest on Old Earth?'

I felt like squeezing her until she cried out then. Until she renounced her request. Instead, I whispered, 'How the goddamned hell am I supposed to get back to Old Earth? It's in the Lesser Magellanic Cloud, isn't it? Some hundred and sixty thousand light-years away, isn't it?'

'Yes,' said Aenea.

'Well, are you going to open the farcaster doors again so I can get back there?'

'No,' said Aenea. 'Those doors are closed forever.'

'Then how the hell do you expect me to . . .' I closed my eyes. 'Don't ask me to do this, Aenea.'

'I've already asked you, my love.'

'Ask me to die with you instead.'

'No,' she said. 'I'm asking you to live for me. To do this for me.'

'Shit,' I said.

'Does that mean yes, Raul?'

'It means *shit*,' I said. 'I hate martyrs. I hate predestination. I hate love stories with sad endings.'

'So do I,' whispered Aenea. 'Will you do this for me?'

I made a noise. 'Where were we happiest on Old Earth?' I said at last. 'You must mean Taliesin West, because we didn't see much else of the planet together.'

'You'll know,' whispered Aenea. 'Let's go to sleep.'

'I don't want to go to sleep,' I said roughly.

She put her arms around me. It had been delightful sleeping together in zero gravity on the Startree. It was even more delightful sleeping together in our small bed in our private cubby in the slight gravity field of the *Yggdrasill*. I could not conceive of a time when I would have to sleep without her next to me.

'Sprinkle your ashes, eh?' I whispered eventually.

'Yes,' she murmured, more asleep than awake.

'Kiddo, my dear, my love,' I said, 'you're a morbid little bitch.'

'Yes,' murmured my Aenea. 'But I'm your morbid little bitch.'

By and by, we did get to sleep.

On our last day, Aenea 'cast us to a star system with an M3-class red dwarf at its core and a sweet Earth-like world swinging in close orbit.

'No,' said Rachel as our small group stood on Het Masteen's bridge. The three hundred had left us one by one, Aenea's many disciples left sprinkled among the Pax worlds like so many bottles cast into a great ocean but without their messages. Now Father de Soya remained, Rachel, Aenea, the captain Het Masteen, A. Bettik, a few crew clones, the ergs below, and me. And the Shrike, silent and motionless on its high platform.

'No,' Rachel said again. 'I've changed my mind. I want to go on with you.'

Aenea stood with her arms folded. She had been especially quiet all this long morning of 'casting and bidding farewells to disciples. 'As you will,' she said softly. 'You know I would not demand that you do anything, Rachel.'

'Damn you,' Rachel said softly.

'Yes,' said Aenea.

Rachel clenched her fists. 'Is this ever going to fucking end?'

'What do you mean?' said Aenea.

'You know what I mean. My father . . . my mother . . . *your* mother . . . their lives filled with this. My life . . . lived twice now . . . always fighting this unseen enemy. Running and running and waiting and waiting. Backward and forward through time like some accursed, out-of-control dreidel . . . oh, damn.'

Aenea waited.

'One request,' said Rachel. She looked at me. 'No offense, Raul. I've come to like you a lot. But could Aenea bring me down to Barnard's World alone.'

I looked at Aenea. 'It's all right with me,' I said.

Rachel sighed. 'Back to this backward world again . . . cornfields and sunsets and tiny little towns with big white houses and big wide porches. It bored me when I was eight.'

'You loved it when you were eight,' said Aenea.

'Yeah,' said Rachel. 'I did.' She shook the priest's hand, then Het Masteen's, then mine.

On a whim, remembering the most obscure verses of the old poet's *Cantos*, remembering laughing about them at the edge of the campfire's light with Grandam having me repeat them line for line, wondering if people ever really said such things, I said to Rachel, 'See you later, alligator.'

The young woman looked at me strangely, her green eyes catching the light from the world hanging above us. 'After a while, crocodile.'

She took Aenea's hand and they were gone. No flash of light when one was not traveling with Aenea. Just a sudden . . . absence.

Aenea returned within five minutes. Het Masteen stepped back from the control circle and folded his hands in the sleeves of his robe. 'One Who Teaches?'

'Pacem System, please, True Voice of the Tree Het Masteen.'

The Templar did not move. 'You know, dear friend and teacher, that by now the Pax will have recalled half of their fighting ships to the Vatican's home system.'

Aenea looked up and around at the gently rustling leaves of the beautiful tree on which we rode. A kilometer behind us, the glow of the fusion drive was pushing us slowly out of Barnard's World's gravity well. No Pax ships had challenged us here. 'Will the ergs be able to hold the fields until we get close to Pacem?' she asked.

The captain's small hands came out of the sleeves of his robe and gestured palms up. 'It is doubtful. They are exhausted. The toll these attacks have taken on them . . .'

'I know,' Aenea said. 'And I am very sorry. You need only be in-system for a minute or two. Perhaps if you accelerate now and are ready for full-drive maneuvers when we appear in Pacem System, the treeship can 'cast out before the fields are overwhelmed.'

'We will try,' said Het Masteen. 'But be prepared to 'cast away immediately. The life of the treeship may be measured in seconds after we arrive.'

'First, we have to send the Consul's ship away,' said Aenea. 'We will have to do it now, here. Just a few moments, Het Masteen.'

The Templar nodded and went back to his displays and touch panels.

'Oh, no,' I said when she turned to me. 'I'm not going to Hyperion in the ship.'

Aenea looked surprised. 'You thought that I was sending you away after I said that you could accompany me?'

I folded my arms. 'We've visited most of the Pax and Outback worlds . . . except Hyperion. Whatever you're planning, I can't believe that you'll leave our homeworld out of it.'

'I'm not going to,' said Aenea. 'But I'm also not 'casting us there.'

I did not understand.

'A. Bettik,' said Aenea, 'the ship should be about ready to depart. Do you have the letter I wrote to Uncle Martin?'

'I do, M. Aenea,' said the android. The blue-skinned man did not look happy, but neither did he look distressed.

'Please give him my love,' said Aenea.

'Wait, wait,' I said. 'A. Bettik is your . . . your envoy . . . to Hyperion?'

Aenea rubbed her cheek. I sensed that she was more exhausted than I could imagine, but saving her strength for something important yet to come. 'My envoy?' she said. 'You mean like Rachel and Theo and the Dorje Phamo and George and Jigme?'

'Yeah,' I said. 'And the three hundred others.'

'No,' said Aenea, 'A. Bettik will not be my envoy to Hyperion. Not in that sense. And the Consul's ship has a deep time-debt to pay via Hawking drive. It . . . and A. Bettik . . . will not arrive for months of our time.'

'Then who is the envoy . . . the liaison on Hyperion?' I asked, certain that this world would not be exempted.

'Can't you guess?' My friend smiled. 'Dear Uncle Martin. The poet and critic once again becomes a player in this endless chess game with the Core.'

'But the others,' I said, 'all took communion with you and . . .' I stopped.

'Yes,' said Aenea. 'When I was still a child. Uncle Martin understood. He drank the wine. It was not hard for him to adapt . . . he has been hearing the language of the dead and of the living for centuries in his own poet's way. It is how he came to write the *Cantos* in the first place. Why he thought the Shrike was his muse.'

'So why is A. Bettik taking the ship back there?' I said. 'Just to bring your message?'

'More than that,' said Aenea. 'If things work out, we will see.' She hugged the android and he awkwardly patted her back with his one hand.

A moment later, welling up with more emotion than I had imagined possible, I shook that blue hand. 'I will miss you,' I said stupidly.

The android looked at me for a long moment, nodded, and turned toward the waiting ship.

'A. Bettik!' I called just as he was about to enter the ship.

He turned back and waited while I ran to my small pile of belongings on the lower platform, then jogged back up the steps. 'Will you take this?' I said, handing him the leather tube.

'The hawking mat,' said A. Bettik. 'Yes, of course, M. Endymion. I will be happy to keep this for you until I see you again.'

'And if we don't see each other again,' I said and paused. I was about to say, *Please give it to Martin Silenus*, but I knew from my own waking visions that the old poet was near death. 'If we don't happen to see each other again, A. Bettik,' I said, 'please keep the mat as a memento of our trip together. And of our friendship.'

A. Bettik looked at me for another quiet moment, nodded again, and went into the Consul's ship. I half expected the ship to say its good-byes, filled with malapropisms and misinformation, but it simply conferred with the treeship's ergs, rose silently on repellors until it cleared the containment field, and then moved away on low thrusters until it was a safe distance from us. Its fusion tail was so bright that it made my eyes water as I watched it accelerate out and away from Barnard's World and the *Yggdrasill*. I wished then with all of my heart and will that Aenea and I were going back to Hyperion with A. Bettik, ready to sleep for days on the large bed at the apex of the ship, then listen to music on the Steinway and swim in a zero-g pool above the balcony—

'We have to go,' Aenea said to Het Masteen. 'Could you please prepare the ergs for what we are about to encounter.'

'As you wish, Revered One Who Teaches,' said the True Voice of the Tree.

'And Het Masteen . . .' said Aenea.

The Templar turned and awaited further orders.

'Thank you, Het Masteen,' she said. 'On behalf of all of those who traveled with you on this voyage and all those who will tell of your voyage for generations to come, thank you, Het Masteen.'

The Templar bowed and went back to his panels. 'Full fusion drive to point nine-two. Prepare for evasive maneuvers. Prepare for Pacem System,' he said to his beloved ergs wrapped around the invisible singularity three-quarters of a kilometer below us. 'Prepare for Pacem System.'

Father de Soya had been standing quietly nearby, but now he took Aenea's right hand in his left hand. With his right hand, he gave a quiet benediction in the direction of the Templar and the crew clones – '*In nomine Patris et Filii et Spiritu Sanctus.*'

'Amen,' I said, taking Aenea's left hand.

'Amen,' said Aenea.

THIRTY

They hit us less than two seconds after we 'cast into the system, the torch-ships and archangels converging fire on us much as the rainbow sharks had once converged on me in the seas of Mare Infinitus.

'Go!' cried the True Voice of the Tree Het Masteen above the torrent of field noise around us. 'The ergs are dying! The containment field will drop in seconds. Go! May the Muir guide your thoughts. Go!'

Aenea had had only two seconds to glimpse the yellow star at the center of Pacem System and the smaller star that was Pacem proper, but it was enough. The three of us held hands as we 'cast through light and noise as if rising through the cauldron of lance fire boiling the ship's fields, spirits rising from Hell's burning lakes.

The light faded and then resumed as diffuse sunlight. It was cloudy above the Vatican, chilly, almost wintry, and a light, cool rain fell on cobblestone streets. Aenea had dressed this day in a soft tan shirt, a brown leather vest, and more formal black trousers than I was used to seeing her wear. Her hair was brushed back and held in place by two tortoiseshell barrettes. Her skin looked fresh and clean and young and her eyes – so tired in recent days – were bright and calm. She still held my hand as the three of us turned to look at the streets and people around us.

We were at the edge of an alley looking on to a wide boulevard. Small groups of people – men and women in formal black, groups of priests, flocks of nuns, a row of children in tow behind two nuns, everywhere black and red umbrellas – moved to and fro on the pedestrian walkways while low, black groundcars glided silently down the streets. I caught a glimpse of bishops and archbishops in the backseats of the groundcars, their visages distorted by beads and rivulets of rain on the cars' bubble tops. No one seemed to be taking any notice of us or our arrival.

Aenea was looking up toward the low clouds. 'The *Yggdrasill* just 'cast out of system. Did either of you feel it?'

I closed my eyes to concentrate on the dream flow of voices and images that were ever under the surface there now. There was . . . an absence. A vision of flame as the outer branches began to burn. 'The fields collapsed just as they 'cast away,' I said. 'How did they 'cast without you, Aenea?' I saw the answer as soon as I had verbalized the question. 'The Shrike,' I said.

'Yes.' Aenea was still holding my hand. The rain was cold on us and I could hear it gurgling down gutters and drainpipes behind us. She spoke very quietly. 'The Shrike will carry the *Yggdrasill* and the True Voice of the Tree away through space and time. To his . . . destiny.'

I remembered bits of the *Cantos*. The treeship burning as the pilgrims watched from the Sea of Grass shortly before Het Masteen had mysteriously disappeared with the Shrike during the windwagon crossing. Then the Templar reappearing in the presence of the Shrike some days later near the Valley of the Time Tombs, dying from his wounds shortly after that, his tale the only one of the seven pilgrims' not to be told on the voyage. The Hyperion pilgrims: Colonel Kassad; the Hegemony Consul, Sol – Rachel's father; Brawne Lamia – Aenea's mother; the Templar Het Masteen; Martin Silenus; Father Hoyt – the current Pope; all at a loss to explain events at the time. For me as a child, just old words from a myth. Verses about strangers. How they must have thought their efforts and adventures over, only to have to pick up their burdens again. How often, I realized now as an adult in my standard thirties, how often that is the case in all of our lives.

'See that church across the street?' said Father de Soya.

I had to shake my head to focus on the *now* and to ignore the thoughts and voices whispering to me. 'Yeah,' I said, wiping the rain from my brow. 'Is that St Peter's Basilica?'

'No,' said the priest. 'That is St Anne's Parish Church and the entrance to the Vatican next to it is the Porta Sant'Anna. The main entrance to St Peter's Square is down the boulevard there and around those colonnades.'

'Are we going to St Peter's Square?' I asked Aenea. 'Into the Vatican?'

'Let's see if we can,' she said.

We started down the pedestrian walkway, just a man and a younger woman walking with a priest on a cool, rainy day. Across the street from us was a sign indicating that the imposing, windowless structure there was the barracks for the Swiss Guard. Troopers from that barracks in formal, Renaissance-era black cloaks, white ruffled collars, and yellow-and-black leggings stood holding pikes at the Porta Sant'Anna and at the intersections while Pax security police in no-nonsense black impact armor manned roadblocks and floated overhead in black skimmers.

St Peter's Square was closed off to foot traffic except for several security gates where guards were carefully checking passes and chipcard IDs.

'We won't get through there,' said Father de Soya. It was dark enough that the lights had come on atop Bernini's colonnade to illuminate statuary and the stone papal coats of arms there. The priest pointed to two windows glowing above the colonnade and to the right of St Peter's facade topped by statues of Christ, John the Baptist, and the Apostles. 'Those are the Pope's private offices.'

'Just a rifle shot away,' I said, although I had no thoughts of attacking the Pope.

Father de Soya shook his head. 'Class-ten containment field.' He glanced around. Much of the pedestrian traffic had passed through the security gates into St Peter's Square and we were becoming more obvious on the street. 'We're going to get our ID checked if we don't do something,' he said.

'Is this level of security common?' asked Aenea.

'No,' said Father de Soya. 'It may be because of your message that you were coming, but it is more probable that it is the usual security when His Holiness is saying a papal Mass. Those bells we heard were a call to an afternoon Mass at which he is presiding.'

'How do you know that?' I said, amazed that he could read so much from the sound of a few bells.

Father de Soya looked surprised. 'I know that because it is Holy Thursday,' he said, looking shocked either because we did not know such an elementary fact or because he had managed to forget it until this moment. 'This is Holy Week,' he went on, talking softly as if to himself. 'All this week His Holiness must carry out both his papal and diocesan duties. Today . . . this afternoon . . . certainly at this Mass, he performs the ceremony of washing the feet of twelve priests who symbolize the twelve disciples whose feet Jesus washed at the Last Supper. The ceremony was always held at the Pope's diocese church, the Basilica of St John Lateran, which used to be beyond the Vatican walls, but ever since the Vatican was moved to Pacem it's been held in St Peter's Basilica. The Basilica of St John Lateran was left behind during the Hegira because it had been destroyed during the Seven Nation Wars in the twenty-first century and . . .' De Soya stopped what I had thought was nervous chatter. His face had gone blank in that way common to mild epileptics or deeply thoughtful people.

Aenea and I waited. I admit that I was glancing with some anxiety toward the patrol of black-armored Pax security men moving toward us down the long boulevard.

'I know how we can get into the Vatican,' said Father de Soya and turned back toward an alley opposite the Vatican Boulevard.

'Good,' said Aenea, following quickly.

The Jesuit stopped suddenly. 'I think that I can get us in,' he said. 'But I have no idea how to get us out.'

'Just get us in, please,' said Aenea.

The steel door was at the rear of a ruined, windowless stone chapel three blocks from the Vatican. It was locked with a small padlock and a large chain. The sign on the sealed door said TOURS ON ALTERNATE SATURDAYS ONLY: Closed During Holy Week: CONTACT VATICAN TOUR OFFICE 3888 SQUARE OF THE FIRST CHRISTIAN MARTYRS.

'Can you break this chain?' Father de Soya asked me.

I felt the massive chain and the solid padlock. My only tool or weapon was the small hunting knife still in my belt sheath. 'No,' I said. 'But maybe I can pick the lock. See if you can find some wire in that garbage module there . . . baling wire would do.'

We stood there in the drizzle for at least ten minutes, with the light fading around us and the sound of traffic on nearby boulevards seeming to grow louder, waiting every minute for the Swiss Guard or security people to swoop down on us. Everything I had learned about picking locks had come from an old riverboat gambler on the Kans who had turned to gambling after the Port Romance authorities had removed two of his fingers for thieving. As I worked, I thought of the ten years of odyssey for Aenea and me, of Father de Soya's long voyage to this place, of the hundreds of light-years traveled and tens of thousands of hours of tension and pain and sacrifice and terror.

And the goddamn ten-florin lock would not budge.

Finally the point of my knife broke. I cursed, threw the knife away, and slammed the stinking lousy cretinous piece-of-shit lock and chain against the grimy stone wall. The padlock clicked open.

It was dark inside. If there was a light switch, none of us could find it. If there was an idiot AI somewhere controlling the lights, it did not respond to our commands. None of us had brought a light. After carrying a flashlight laser for years, I had left mine behind in my backpack this day. When the time had come to leave the *Yggdrasill*, I had stepped forward, and taken Aenea's hand without a thought to weapons or other necessary items.

'Is this the Basilica of St John Lateran?' whispered Aenea. It was impossible to speak in anything above a whisper in the oppressive darkness.

'No, no,' whispered Father de Soya. 'Just a tiny memorial chapel built near the original basilica in the twenty-first . . .' He stopped and I could imagine his thoughtful expression returning. 'It *is* a working chapel, I believe,' he said. 'Wait here.'

Aenea and I stood with shoulders touching as we heard Father de Soya moving around the perimeter of the tiny building. Once something heavy fell with the sound of iron on stone and we all stood holding our breath. A minute later we heard the sound of his hands sliding along the inside walls again and the rustle of his cassock. There was a muffled 'Ahhh . . .' and a second later light flared.

The Jesuit was standing less than ten meters from us, holding a lighted match. A box of matches was in his left hand. 'A chapel,' he explained. 'They still had the stand for votive candles.' I could see that the candles themselves had been melted to uselessness and never replaced, but the tapers and this one box of matches had remained for God knows how long in this dark, abandoned place. We joined him in the small circle of light, waited while he lighted a second match, and followed him to a heavy wooden door set behind rotting curtains.

'Father Baggio, my resurrection chaplain, told me about this tour when I was under house arrest near here some years ago,' whispered Father de Soya. This door was not locked, but opened with a squeal of ancient, unoiled hinges. 'I believe he thought it would appeal to my sense of the macabre,' went on Father de Soya, leading us down a narrow, spiraling stone stairway not much wider than my shoulders. Aenea followed the priest. I kept close to Aenea.

The stairway continued down, then down some more, and then more. I estimated that we were at least twenty meters beneath street level when the stairway ended and we passed through a series of narrow corridors into a wider, echoing hallway. The priest had gone through a half-dozen matches by this point, dropping each only after it had burned his fingers. I did not ask him how many matches were left in the small matchbox.

'When the Church decided to move St Peter's and the Vatican during the Hegira,' said de Soya, his voice loud enough now to echo in the black space, 'they brought it en masse to Pacem using heavy field lifters and tractor-field towers. Since mass was not a problem, they brought half of Rome with them, including the huge Castel Sant'Angelo and everything under the old city down to a depth of sixty meters. This was the twentieth-century subway system.'

Father de Soya began walking down what I realized was an abandoned railway platform. At places the ceiling tiles had fallen in and everywhere except on a narrow pathway there were centuries of dust, fallen rocks, broken plastic, unreadable signs lying in the grime, and shattered benches. We went down several corroded steel stairways – escalators halted more than a millennium ago, I realized – through a narrow corridor that continued downward along an echoing ramp, and then onto another platform. At the end of this platform, I could see a fiberplastic ladder leading down to where the tracks had been . . . where the tracks still were under the layers of dust, rubble, and rust.

We had just climbed down the ladder and stepped into the subway tunnel when the next match went out. But not before Aenea and I had seen what lay ahead.

Bones. Human bones. Bones and skulls stacked neatly almost two meters high on either side of a narrow passage between the rusted tracks. Great heaps of bones, the socket ends out, skulls neatly placed at meter-intervals or arranged in geometric designs within the knobby walls of human bones.

Father de Soya lit the next match and began striding between the walls of skeletal human remains. The breeze of his motion flickered the tiny flame that he held aloft. 'After the Seven Nations War in the early twenty-first century,' he said, his voice at a normal conversational volume now, 'the cemeteries of Rome were overflowing. There had been mass graves dug all around the suburbs of the city and in the large parks. It became quite a health problem what with the global warming and constant flooding. All of the bio and chem warheads, you know. The subways had ceased to run anyway, so the powers-that-be authorized a removal of the remains and their reinterment in the old metro systems.'

This time when the match burned out, we were in a section where the bones were stacked five layers high, each layer marked by a row of skulls, their white brows reflecting the light but the sightless sockets indifferent to our passing. The neat walls of bones went back for at least six meters on either side and rose to the vaulted ceiling ten meters above us. In a few places, there had been a small avalanche of bones and skulls and we had to pick our way over them carefully. Still there was the crunching underfoot. We did not move during the interludes of darkness between matches, but waited quietly. There was no other noise . . . not the scurry of rats nor the drip of water. Only our breathing and soft words disturbed the silence here.

'Oddly enough,' said Father de Soya after we had gone another two hundred meters, 'they did not get the idea from Rome's ancient catacombs, which lie all about us here, but from the so-called catacombs of Paris . . . old quarry tunnels deep under that city. The Parisians had to move bones from their overflowing cemeteries to those tunnels between the late-eighteenth to mid-nineteenth centuries. They found that they could easily accommodate six million dead in just a few kilometers of corridors. Ahh . . . here we are . . .'

To our left, through an even narrower corridor of bones, was a path with a few boot marks in the dust, leading to another steel door, this one unlocked. It took all three of us to leverage the door open. The priest led the way down another set of rusting spiral stairs to a depth I estimated at being at least thirty-five meters beneath the street above. The match went out just as we stepped into another tunnel – much older than the subway vault, its edges and ceiling unfinished and tumbledown. I had caught a glimpse of side passages running off, of bones spilled haphazardly everywhere in these passages, of skulls upside down, of bits of rotted garments.

'According to Father Baggio,' whispered the priest, 'this is where the real catacombs begin. The Christian catacombs which go back to the first century AD.' A new match flared. I heard a rattle in the matchbox that sounded like very few matches indeed. 'This way, I would guess,' said Father de Soya and led us to his right.

'We're under the Vatican now?' whispered Aenea a few minutes later. I could feel her impatience. The match flared and died.

'Soon, soon,' said de Soya in the darkness. He lit another one. I heard no rattle in the box.

After another hundred and fifty meters or so, the corridor simply ended. There were no tumbled bones here, no skulls, only rough stone walls and a hint of masonry where the tunnel ended. The match went out. Aenea touched my hand as we waited in the darkness.

'I am sorry,' said the priest. 'There are no more matches.'

I fought back the rise of panic in my chest. I was sure that I heard noises now . . . distant rat feet scurrying at the least, boots on stairs at the worst. 'Do we backtrack?' I said, my whisper sounding far too loud in the absolute darkness.

'I was sure that Father Baggio said that these catacombs to the north had once connected to the older ones under the Vatican,' whispered Father de Soya. 'Under St Peter's Basilica, to be precise.'

'Well, it doesn't seem to . . .' I began and stopped. In the few seconds of light before the match had gone out, I had glimpsed the relative newness of the brick wall between stones . . . a few centuries old as opposed to the millennia since the stone had been cut away. I crawled forward, feeling ahead of me until my fingers found stone, brick, loose mortar.

'This was hastily done,' I said, speaking with only the authority I had gained as an assistant landscape worker on the Beak estates years and years before. 'The mortar's cracked and some of the bricks have crumbled,' I said, my fingers moving quickly. 'Give me something to dig with. Damn, I wish I hadn't thrown away my knife . . .'

Aenea handed me a sharp-edged stick or branch in the dark and I was digging away for several minutes before I realized that I was working with a thigh bone broken at one end. The two of them joined me, digging with bones, scrabbling at the cold brick with our fingernails until the nails broke and our fingers bled. After some time at this, we paused to pant and catch our breath. Our eyes had not adapted to the darkness. There was no light here.

'The Mass will be over,' whispered Aenea. The tone in her voice made it sound like a tragic event.

'It is a High Mass,' whispered the priest. 'A long ceremony.'

'Wait!' I said. My fingers had remembered a slight movement in the bricks – not in one or a few of them, but in the entire casement.

'Get back,' I said aloud. 'Crawl to the side of the tunnel.' I backed up myself, but straight back, raised my left shoulder, lowered my head, and charged forward in a crouch, half expecting to bash my head on the stone and knock myself out.

I hit the bricks with a mighty grunt and a shower of dust and small debris. The bricks had not fallen away. But I had felt them sag away from me.

Aenea and de Soya joined me and in another minute we had pushed loose the center bricks, tumbled the entire mass away from us.

There was the faintest glimmer of light on the other side of the passage, but enough to show us a ramp of debris leading to an even deeper tunnel. We crawled down on our hands and knees, found room to stand, and moved through the earth-smelling corridor. Two more turns and we came into a catacomb as roughly hewn as the one above but illuminated by a narrow strip of glowtape running along the right wall at belt height. Another fifty meters of twisting and turning, always following the main passage illuminated by glowtape, and we came into a wider tunnel with modern glowglobes set every five meters. These globes were not lit, but the ancient glowtape continued on.

'We're under St Peter's,' whispered Father de Soya. 'This area was first rediscovered in 1939, after they buried Pope Pius XI in a nearby grotto. The excavations were carried on for another twenty years or so before being abandoned. They have not been reopened to archaeologists.'

We came into an even wider corridor – wide enough for the three of us to walk side by side for the first time. Here the ancient rock and plastered walls with the occasional marble inset were covered with frescoes, early Christian mosaics, and broken statues set above grottoes in which bones and skulls were clearly visible. Someone had once placed plastic across many of these grottoes and the material had yellowed and opaqued to make the mortal remains within almost unviewable, but by bending and peering we could see empty eye sockets and pelvic ovals peering back at us.

The frescoes showed Christian images – doves carrying olive branches, women drawing water, the ubiquitous fish – but were next to older grottoes, cremation urns, and graves offering pre-Christian images of Isis and Apollo, Bacchus welcoming the dead to the afterlife with great, overflowing flagons of wine, a scene of oxen and rams cavorting, another with satyrs dancing – I immediately noticed the likeness to Martin Silenus and turned just in time to catch Aenea's knowing glance – and still more with beings Father de Soya described as maenads, some rural scenes, partridges all in a row, a preening peacock with feathers of lapis chips that still caught the light in bright blue.

Peering through the ancient, mottled plastic and plastiglass at these things made me think that we were passing through some terrestrial aquarium of death. Finally we came to a red wall at right angles to a lower wall of faded, mottled blue with the remnants of graffiti in Latin still visible. Here the sheet of plastic was newer, fresher, and the small container of bones within quite visible. The skull had been set atop the neat pile of bones and seemed to be regarding us with some interest.

Father de Soya went to his knees in the dust, crossed himself, and bent his head in prayer. Aenea and I stood back and watched with the quiet embarrassment common to the unbeliever in the presence of any true faith.

When the priest arose, his eyes were moist. 'According to Church history and Father Baggio, the workers uncovered these poor bones in AD 1949. Later analysis showed that they belong to a robust man who died sometime in his sixties. We are directly under the high altar of St Peter's Basilica, which was built here because of the legend that St Peter had been interred secretly at just this spot. In AD 1968, Pope Paul VI announced that the Vatican was convinced that these were indeed the bones of the fisherman, the same Peter who walked with Jesus and was the Rock upon which Christ built his Church.'

We looked at the silent heap of bones and then back at the priest.

'Federico, you know that I am not trying to bring down the Church,' Aenea said. 'Only this current aberration of it.'

'Yes,' said Father de Soya, wiping his eyes roughly, leaving muddy streaks there. 'I know that, Aenea.' He looked around, went to a door, opened it. A metal staircase led upward.

'There will be guards,' I whispered.

'I think not,' said Aenea. 'The Vatican has spent eight hundred years fearing attack from space . . . from above. I do not believe they give much thought to their catacombs.' She stepped in front of the priest and started quickly but quietly up the metal steps. I hurried to follow her. I saw Father de Soya glance back toward the dim grotto, cross himself a final time, and follow us up toward St Peter's Basilica.

The light in the main basilica, although softened by evening, stained glass, and candlelight, was all but blinding after the catacombs.

We had climbed up through the subterranean shrine, up past a memorial basilica marked in stone as the Trophy of Gaius, through side corridors and service entrances, through the anteroom to the sacristy, past standing priests and craning altar boys, and out into the echoing expanse at the rear of the nave of St Peter's Basilica. Here were scores of dignitaries not important enough to have been awarded a place in the pews but still honored by being allowed to stand in the rear of the Basilica to witness this important celebration. It took only a glance to see that there were Swiss Guard and security people at all the entrances to the Basilica and in all the outer rooms with exits. Here at the back of the congregation, we were inconspicuous for the moment, just another priest and two somewhat underdressed parishioners allowed to crane their necks to see the Holy Father on Holy Thursday.

Mass was still being celebrated. The air smelled of incense and candlewax. Hundreds of brightly robed bishops and VIPs lined the gleaming rows of pews. At the marble altar rail before the baroque splendor of the canopy of the Throne of St Peter, the Holy Father himself knelt to finish his menial work of washing the feet of twelve seated priests – eight men and four women. An unseen but large choir was singing—

'O Holy Ghost, through Thee alone
Know we the father and the Son;
Be this our firm unchanging creed.
That Thou dost from them both proceed.
That Thou dost from them both proceed.

'Praise be the Lord, Father and Son
And Holy Spirit with them one;
And may the Son on us bestow.
All gifts that from the Spirit flow.
All gifts that from the Spirit flow.'

I hesitated then, wondering what we were doing here, why this endless battle of Aenea's had brought us to the center of these people's faith. I believed everything she had taught us, valued everything she had shared with us, but three thousand years of tradition and faith had formed the words of this beautiful song and had built the walls of this mighty cathedral. I could not help but remember the simple wooden platforms, the firm but inelegant bridges and stairways of Aenea's rebuilt Temple Hanging in Air. What was it . . . what were we . . . compared to this splendor and humility? Aenea was an architect, largely self-trained except for her adolescent years with the cybrid Mr Wright, building stone walls out of desert rock and mixing concrete by hand. *Michelangelo* had helped to design this Basilica.

The Mass was almost over. Some of the standing crowd in the rear of the longitudinal nave were beginning to leave, walking lightly so as not to interrupt the end of the service with their footfalls, whispering only when they reached the stairs to the piazza outside. I saw that Aenea was whispering in Father de Soya's ear and I leaned against them to hear, afraid that I might miss some vital instruction.

'Will you do me one final great service, Father?' she asked.

'Anything,' whispered the sad-eyed priest.

'Please leave the Basilica now,' Aenea whispered in his ear. 'Please go now, quietly, with these others. Leave now and lose yourself in Rome until the day comes to cease being lost.'

Father de Soya pulled his head back in shock, looking at Aenea from half a meter away with an expression of someone who has been abandoned. He leaned close to her ear. 'Ask anything else of me, Teacher.'

'This is all I ask, Father. And I ask it with love and respect.'

The choir began singing another hymn. Above the heads in front of me, I could see the Holy Father completing the washing of the priests' feet and moving back to the altar under the gilded canopy. Everyone in the pews stood in anticipation of the closing litanies and final benediction.

Father de Soya gave his own benediction to my friend, turned, and left the Basilica with a group of monks whose beads rattled as they walked.

I stared at Aenea with enough intensity to set wood aflame, trying to send her the mental message *DO NOT ASK ME TO LEAVE!*

She beckoned me close and whispered in my ear, 'Do one final thing for me, Raul, my love.'

I almost shouted 'No, goddammit!' at the top of my lungs in the echoing nave of St Peter's Basilica during the holiest moments of Holy Thursday's High Mass. Instead, I waited.

Aenea fumbled in the pockets of her vest and came out with a small vial. The liquid in it was clear but somehow looked heavier than water. 'Would you drink this?' she whispered and handed me the vial.

I thought of Romeo and Juliet, Caesar and Cleopatra, Abelard and Heloise, George Wu and Howard Sung. All star-crossed lovers. Suicide and poison. I drank down the potion in one gulp, setting the empty vial in my own shirt pocket, waiting for Aenea to take out and drink a similar potion. She did not.

'What was it?' I whispered, not fearing any answer.

Aenea was watching the final moments of the Mass. She leaned very close to whisper. 'Antidote to the Pax's birth control medication that you took when you joined the Home Guard.'

What the hell!!??!! I came close to shouting over the Holy Father's closing words. *You're worried about family planning NOW?? Are you out of your goddamn MIND???*

She leaned back, her breath warm on my neck as she whispered again. 'Thank God, I've been carrying that for two days and almost forgot it. Don't worry, it'll take about three weeks to take effect. Then you'll never be shooting blanks again.'

I blinked at her. Was this blasphemy in St Peter's Basilica or just extraordinarily bad taste? Then my mind shifted into high gear – *This is wonderful news . . . whatever happens next, Aenea sees a future for us . . . for herself . . . wants to have a child with me. But what about her first child? And why do I assume she's doing this so that she and I can . . . why would she . . . perhaps it's her idea of a farewell present . . . why would she . . . why . . .*

'Kiss me, Raul,' she whispered, loud enough to make the elderly nun standing in front of us turn around with a severe expression.

I did not question her. I kissed her. Her lips were soft and slightly moist, just as they were the first time we had kissed standing on the bank of the Mississippi River at a place called Hannibal. The kiss seemed to last a long time. She touched the back of my neck with her cool fingers before our lips parted.

The Pope was moving to the front of the apse, facing each of the two arms of the transept, then the short nave, and finally the longitudinal nave as he gave his final benediction.

Aenea walked out into the main aisle, pushing people gently aside until she was in the open space and striding toward the distant altar. 'Lenar Hoyt!' she shouted, and her voice echoed the hundred meters to the dome above. It was more than a hundred and fifty meters from where we had been standing to where the Pope now paused in his benediction, and I knew Aenea had no chance of making that distance before being intercepted, but I hurried to catch up to her.

'Lenar Hoyt!' she shouted again and hundreds of heads turned in her direction. I saw movement in the arched shadows along the sides of the nave as Swiss Guard leaped into action. 'Lenar Hoyt, I am Aenea, daughter of Brawne Lamia who traveled to Hyperion with you to face the Shrike. I am the daughter of the John Keats cybrid whom your Core masters have twice killed in the flesh!'

The Pope stood as if transfixed, one bony finger raised in benediction a moment before now pointing, shaking as if palsied. His other hand clutched his vestments above his chest. His miter trembled as his head bobbed back and forth. 'You!' he cried, his voice high, thin, and weak. 'The Abomination!'

'*You* are the abomination,' shouted Aenea; she was running now, shrugging off dark-robed figures that rose from the pews to grab at her. I pulled two men from her back and she ran on. I leaped over a lunging figure and ran at her side, watching the Swiss Guard shoving through the crowd, energy pikes aimed but hesitant to fire with so many Vatican and Mercantilus dignitaries in the line of fire. I knew that they would not hesitate if she got within ten meters of the Pope. 'You are the abomination,' she shouted again, running hard now, dodging grasping hands and lunging arms. 'You are the Judas of the Catholic Church, Lenar Hoyt, selling its sacred history to the . . .'

A heavy man in a Pax Fleet admiral's uniform pulled a ceremonial sword from his scabbard and swung it at my beloved's head. She ducked. I blocked the Admiral's arm, broke it, kicked the sword aside, and threw him halfway down the length of the pew into his subordinates.

Colonel Kassad had said that after learning the language of the living, he had *felt* the pain he administered to others. I experienced that now, feeling the torn nerves and muscle and shattered bone of my forearm and the collision of my body as the Admiral struck his men. But when I looked down, my forearm was firm and the only penalty was pain. I did not care about the pain.

A cordon of priests, monks, and bishops put themselves between Aenea and the Pope. I saw the Pontiff clutch his chest more tightly and fall, but several of the deacons standing near him caught him, carried him back under the canopy of Bernini's throne. Swiss Guardsmen hurtled into the space at the end of the aisle, blocking Aenea's way with their pikes and bodies. More filled the space behind us, roughly shoving away the on-lookers with brutal swings of their pikes. Pax security in black armor and compact repulsor flying belts came hurtling in ten meters above the heads of the congregation. Laser dots danced on Aenea's face and chest.

I threw myself between her and the imminent energy bolts and flechette clouds. The laser beam blinded my right eye as the target dot swept across it. I threw my arms wide and bellowed something . . . a challenge perhaps . . . defiance certainly.

'No! Keep them alive!' It was a huge cardinal shouting in a bass rumble like the voice of God.

A Swiss Guardsman rushed at Aenea with his pike raised to stun her with a blow to the head. She threw herself down, slid across the tile, clipped him at his knees, and sent him sprawling toward me. I kicked him in the head and turned to wrestle the pike out of another Guardsman's hands, knocking him backward into the crowd and swinging the long weapon at the five Guardsmen rushing us from the rear. They gave way.

A flying security trooper fired two darts into my left shoulder. I presumed they were tranquilizers, but I ripped them away, threw them at the flying form, and felt nothing. Two guards – a large man and a larger woman – grabbed my arms. I swung them through the air until their skulls collided and dropped them onto tile. 'Aenea!'

She was on her feet again, pulling free of one Guardsman only to have two forms in black armor block her way. The congregation was screaming. The great cathedral organ suddenly screamed like a woman in labor. A security man shot her at five-meter range. Aenea spun around. A woman in black armor clubbed my darling down, straddling her and pulling her arms behind her.

I used my forearm to swat the Pax security bitch five meters backward through the air. A Guardsman clubbed me in the stomach with his pike. A flying security shape zapped me with a neural stunner. Stunners are supposed to work instantly, guaranteed to work instantly, but I had time to close my hands on the nearest Guardsman's throat before they stunned me again, and then a third time. My body spasmed and fell and I pissed my pants as all voluntary functions ceased, my last conscious sensation being the cold flow of urine down my pant leg onto the perfect tiles of St Peter's Basilica.

I was not really aware of the dozen heavy forms landing on my back, pinning my arms, pulling me away. I did not really hear or feel the crack of my forehead striking tile or the rip it opened from my brow to hairline.

In the last three or four seconds of semiconsciousness, I saw black feet, combat boots, a fallen Swiss Guardsman's cap, more feet. I knew that Aenea had fallen to my left but I could not turn my head to see her one last time.

They dragged me away, leaving a trail of blood, urine, and saliva as they did so. I was far beyond caring.

*

And so ends my tale.

I was conscious but restrained with neural locks during my 'trial', a ten-minute appearance before the black-robed judges of the Holy Office. I was condemned to death. No human being would sully his or her soul by executing me; I was to be transferred to a Schrödinger cat box in orbit around the quarantined labyrinth world of Armaghast. The immutable laws of physics and quantum chance would execute the sentence.

As soon as the trial ended they shipped me via a Hawking-drive, high-g, robot torchship to Armaghast System – a two-month time-debt. Wherever Aenea was, whatever had happened to her, I was already two months too late to help her when I awoke just as they finished sealing the fused-energy shell of my prison.

And for uncounted days . . . perhaps months, I went insane. And then for more uncounted days, certainly more months, I have been using the 'scriber they included in my tiny egg of a cell to tell this tale. They must have known that the 'scriber would be an additional punishment as I waited to die, writing my story on my few pages of recycled microvellum like the snake devouring its own tail, knowing that no one will ever access the story in the memory chip.

I said at the beginning of all this that you, my impossible reader, were reading it for the wrong reason. I said at the beginning that if you were reading this to discover her fate, or my own, you were reading the wrong document. I was not with her when her fate was played out, and my own is closer now to its final act than when I first wrote these words.

I was not with her.

I was not with her.

Oh, Jesus God, God of Moses, Allah, dear Buddha, Zeus, Muir, Elvis, Christ . . . if any of you exist or ever existed or retain a shred of power in your dead gray hands . . . please let me die now. Now. Let the particle be detected and the gas released. Now.

I was not with her.

THIRTY-ONE

I lied to you.

I said at the beginning of this narrative that I was not with her when Aenea's fate was played out – implying that I did not know what that fate might be – and I repeated it some sleep periods ago when I 'scribed what I was sure must be the last installment of that same narrative.

But I lied by omission, as some priest of the Church might say.

I lied because I did not want to discuss it, to describe it, to relive it, to believe it. But I know now that I must do all of these things. I have relived it every hour of my incarceration here in this Schrödinger cat box prison. I have believed it since the moment I shared the experience with my dear friend, my dear Aenea.

I knew before they shipped me out of Pacem System what the fate of my dear girl had been. Having believed it and relived it, I owe it to the truth of this narrative and to the memory of our love to discuss it and describe it.

All this came to me while I was drugged and docile, tethered in a high-g tank aboard the robot shuttle an hour after my ten-minute trial in front of the Inquisition on a Pax base asteroid ten light-minutes from Pacem. I knew as soon as I heard and felt and saw these things that they were real, that they were happening at the moment I shared them, and that only my closeness to Aenea and my slow progress in learning the language of the living had allowed such a powerful sharing. When the sharing was over, I began screaming in my high-g tank, ripping at life-support umbilicals and banging the bulkhead with my head and fists, until the water-filled tank was swirling with my blood. I tried tearing at the osmosis mask that covered my face like some parasite sucking away my breath; it would not tear. For a full three hours I screamed and protested, battering myself into a state of semiconsciousness at best, reliving the shared moments with Aenea a thousand times and screaming in agony a thousand times, and then the robot ship injected sleep drugs through the leech-like umbilicals, the high-g tank drained, and I drifted away into cryogenic fugue as the torchship reached the translation point for the jump to nearby Armaghast System.

I awoke in the Schrödinger cat box. The robot ship had loaded me into the fused-energy satellite and launched it without human intervention. For a few moments I was disoriented, believing that the shared moments with Aenea had all been nightmare. Then the reality of those moments flooded back and I began screaming again. I believe that I was not sane again for some months.

Here is what drove me to madness.

Aenea had also been taken bleeding and unconscious from St Peter's Basilica, but unlike me she awoke the next day neither drugged nor shunted. She came to consciousness – and I shared this awakening more clearly than I have recalled any memory of mine, as sharp and real as a second set of sense impressions – in a huge stone room, round, some thirty meters across, with a ceiling fifty meters above the stone floor. Set in the ceiling was a glowing frosted glass that gave the sense of a skylight, although Aenea guessed that this was an illusion and that the room was deep within a larger structure.

The medics had cleaned me up for my ten-minute trial while I was unconscious, but no one had touched Aenea's wounds: the left side of her face was tender, swollen with bruises, her clothes had been torn away from her body and she was naked, her lips were swollen, her left eye was almost shut – she could see out of it only with effort and the vision from her right eye was blurred from concussion – and there were cuts and bruises on her chest, thighs, forearm, and belly. Some of these cuts had caked over, but a few were deep enough to require stitches that no one had provided. They still bled.

She was strapped in what appeared to be a rusted iron skeleton of crossed metal that hung by chains from the high ceiling and that allowed her to lean back and rest her weight against it but still kept her almost standing, her arms held low along the rusted girders, a near-vertical asterisk of cold metal hanging in air with her wrists and ankles cruelly clamped and bolted to the frame. Her toes hung about ten centimeters above a grated floor. She could move her head. The round room was empty except for this and two other objects. A broad wastebasket sat to the right of the chair. There was a plastic liner in the wastebasket. Also next to the right arm of the asterisk was a rusted metal tray with various instruments on it: ancient dental picks and pliers, circular blades, scalpels, bone saws, a long forceps of some kind, pieces of wire with barbs at three-centimeter intervals, long-bladed shears, shorter, serrated shears, bottles of dark fluid, tubes of paste, needles, heavy thread, and a hammer. Even more disturbing was the round grate some two and a half meters across beneath her, through which she could see dozens of tiny, blue flames burning like pilot lights. There was the faint smell of natural gas.

Aenea tried the restraints – they gave not at all – felt her bruised wrists and ankles throb at the attempts, and put her head back against the iron girder to wait. Her hair was matted there and she could feel a huge lump high on her scalp and another near the base of her skull. She felt nauseous and concentrated on not throwing up on herself.

After a few minutes, a hidden door in the stone wall opened and Rhadamanth Nemes came in and walked to a place just beyond the grate to the right side of Aenea. A second Rhadamanth Nemes came in and took her place on Aenea's left side. Two more Nemeses came in and took up positions farther back. They did not speak. Aenea did not speak to them.

A few minutes later, John Domenico Cardinal Mustafa shimmered into existence – his life-size holographic image taking on solidity directly in front of Aenea. The illusion of his physical presence was perfect except for the fact that the Cardinal was sitting on a chair not represented in the hologram, giving the illusion that he was floating in midair. Mustafa looked younger and healthier than he had on T'ien Shan. A few seconds later, he was joined by the holo of a more massive cardinal in a red robe, and then by the holo of a thin, tubercular-looking priest. A moment after that, a tall, handsome man dressed all in gray came through the physical door in the wall of the physical dungeon and stood with the holos. Mustafa and the other cardinal continued sitting on unseen chairs while the monsignor's holo and the physically present man in gray stood behind the chairs like servants.

'M. Aenea,' said the Grand Inquisitor, 'allow me to introduce the Vatican Secretary of State His Eminence Cardinal Lourdusamy, his aide Monsignor Lucas Oddi, and our esteemed Councillor Albedo.'

'Where am I?' asked Aenea. She had to attempt the sentence a second time because of her swollen lips and bruised jaw.

The Grand Inquisitor smiled. 'We will answer all of your questions for the moment, my dear. And then you will answer all of ours. I guarantee this. To answer your first question, you are in the deepest . . . ah . . . interview room . . . in the Castel Sant'Angelo, on the right bank of the new Tiber, near the Ponte Sant'Angelo, quite near the Vatican, still on the world of Pacem.'

'Where is Raul?'

'Raul?' said the Grand Inquisitor. 'Oh, you mean your rather useless bodyguard. At the moment, I believe he has completed his own meeting with the Holy Office and is aboard a ship preparing to leave our fair system. Is he important to you, my dear? We could make arrangements to return him to Castel Sant'Angelo.'

'He's not important,' murmured Aenea, and after my first second of hurt and anguish at the words, I could *feel* her thoughts beneath them . . . concern for me, terror for me, hope that they would not threaten me as a means to coerce her.

'As you wish,' said Cardinal Mustafa. 'It is you we want to interview today. How do you feel?'

Aenea stared at them through her good eye.

'Well,' said the Grand Inquisitor, 'one should not hope to attack the Holy Father in St Peter's Basilica and come away with impunity.'

Aenea mumbled something.

'What was that, my dear? We could not make it out.' Mustafa was smiling slightly – a toad's self-satisfied leer.

'I . . . did . . . not . . . attack . . . the . . . Pope.'

Mustafa opened his hands. 'If you insist, M. Aenea . . . but your intentions did not seem friendly. What is it that you had in mind as you ran down the central aisle toward the Holy Father?'

'Warn him,' said Aenea. Part of her mind was assessing her injuries even as she listened to the Grand Inquisitor's prattle: serious bruises but nothing broken, the sword cut on her thigh needed stitching, as did the cut on her upper chest. But something was wrong in her system – internal bleeding? She did not think so. Something alien had been administered to her via injection.

'Warn him of what?' said Cardinal Mustafa with butter smoothness.

Aenea moved her head to look with her good eye at Cardinal Lourdusamy and then at Councillor Albedo. She said nothing.

'Warn him of what?' asked Cardinal Mustafa again. When Aenea did not respond, the Grand Inquisitor nodded to the nearest Nemes clone. The pale woman walked slowly to the side of Aenea's chair, took up the smaller of the two shears, seemed to think twice about it, set the instrument back on the tray, came closer, went to one knee on the grate next to Aenea's right arm, bent back my darling's little finger, and bit it off. Nemes smiled, stood, and spit the bloody finger into the wastebasket.

Aenea screamed with the shock and pain and half swooned against the headrest.

The Nemes thing took tourniquet paste from the tube and smeared it on the stump of Aenea's little finger.

The holo of Cardinal Mustafa looked sad. 'We do not desire to administer pain, my dear, but we also shall not hesitate to do so. You shall answer our questions quickly and honestly, or more parts of you will end up in the basket. Your tongue will be the last to go.'

Aenea fought back the nausea. The pain from her mutilated hand was incredible – ten light-minutes away, I screamed with the secondhand shock of it.

'I was going to warn the Pope . . . about . . . your *coup*,' gasped Aenea, still looking at Lourdusamy and Albedo. 'Heart attack.'

Cardinal Mustafa blinked in surprise. 'You *are* a witch,' he said softly.

'And you're a traitorous asshole,' Aenea said strongly and clearly. 'All of you are. You sold out your Church. Now you're selling out your puppet Lenar Hoyt.'

'Oh?' said Cardinal Lourdusamy. He looked mildly amused. 'How are we doing that, child?'

Aenea jerked her head at Councillor Albedo. 'The Core controls everyone's life and death via the cruciforms. People die when it's convenient for the Core to have them dead . . . neural networks in the process of dying are more creative than living ones. You're going to kill the Pope again, but this time his resurrection won't be successful, will it?'

'Very perceptive, my dear,' rumbled Cardinal Lourdusamy. He shrugged. 'Perhaps it *is* time for a new pontiff.' He moved his hand in the air and a fifth hologram appeared behind them in the room: Pope Urban XVI comatose in a hospital bed, nursing nuns, human doctors, and medical machines hovering around him. Lourdusamy waved his pudgy hand again and the image disappeared.

'Your turn to be pope?' said Aenea and closed her eyes. Red spots were dancing in her vision. When she opened her eyes again, Lourdusamy was making a modest shrug.

'Enough of this,' said Councillor Albedo. He walked directly through the holos of the seated cardinals and stood at the edge of the grate, directly in front of Aenea. 'How have you been manipulating the farcaster medium? How do you farcast without the portals?'

Aenea looked at the Core representative. 'It scares you, doesn't it, Councillor? In the same way that the cardinals are too frightened to be here with me in person.'

The gray man showed his perfect teeth. 'Not at all, Aenea. But you have the ability to farcast yourself – and those near you – without portals. His Eminence Cardinal Lourdusamy and Cardinal Mustafa, as well as Monsignor Oddi, have no wish to suddenly vanish from Pacem with you. As for me . . . I would be delighted if you farcast us somewhere else.' He waited. Aenea said nothing. She did not move. Councillor Albedo smiled again. 'We know that you're the only one who has learned how to do this type of farcasting,' he said softly. 'None of your so-called disciples are close to learning the technique. But what *is* the technique? The only way we've managed to use the Void for farcasting is by wedging open permanent rifts in the medium . . . and that takes far too much energy.'

'And they don't allow you to do that anymore,' muttered Aenea, blinking away the red dots so she could meet the gray man's gaze. The pain from her hand rose and fell in and around her like long swells on an uneasy sea.

Councillor Albedo's eyebrow moved up a fraction, '*They* won't allow us to? Who is *they*, child? Describe your masters to us.'

'No masters,' murmured Aenea. She had to concentrate in order to banish the dizziness. 'Lions and Tigers and Bears,' she whispered.

'No more double talk,' rumbled Lourdusamy. The fat man nodded to the second Nemes clone, who walked to the tray, removed the rusty pair of pliers, walked around to Aenea's left hand, held it steady at the wrist, and pulled out all of my darling's fingernails.

Aenea screamed, passed out briefly, awoke, tried to turn her head away in time but failed, vomited on herself, and moaned softly.

'There is no dignity in pain, my child,' said Cardinal Mustafa. 'Tell us what the Councillor wishes to know and we will end this sad charade. You will be taken from here, your wounds will be attended to, your finger regrown, you will be cleaned and dressed and reunited with your bodyguard or disciple or whatever. This ugly episode will be over.'

At that moment, reeling in agony, Aenea's body still was aware of the alien substance that had been injected into her while she was unconscious hours earlier. Her cells recognized it. Poison. A sure, slow, terminal poison with no antidote – it would activate in twenty-four hours no matter what anyone did. She knew then what they wanted her to do and why.

Aenea had always been in contact with the Core, even before she was born, via the Schrön Loop in her mother's skull linked to her father's cybrid persona. It allowed her to touch primitive dataspheres directly, and she did this now – sensing the solid array of exotic Core machinery that lined this subterranean cell: instruments within instruments, sensors beyond human understanding or description, devices working in four dimensions and more, waiting, sniffing, waiting.

The cardinals and Councillor Albedo and the Core wanted her to escape. Everything was predicated upon her 'casting out of this intolerable situation: thus the holodrama coarseness of the torture, the melodramatic absurdity of the dungeon cell in Castel Sant'Angelo, and the heavy-handed Inquisition. They would hurt her until she could not stand it any longer, and when she 'cast away, the Core instruments would measure everything to the billionth of a nanosecond, analyze her use of the Void, and come up with a way to replicate it. The Core would finally have their farcasters back – not in their crude wormhole or Gideon-drive manner, but instant and elegant and eternally theirs.

Aenea ignored the Grand Inquisitor, licked her dry, cracked lips, and said distinctly to Councillor Albedo, 'I know where you live.'

The handsome gray man's mouth twitched. 'What do you mean?'

'I know where the Core – the physical elements of the Core – are,' said Aenea.

Albedo smiled, but Aenea saw the quick glance toward the two cardinals and tall priest. 'Nonsense,' he said. 'No human being has ever known the location of the Core.'

'In the beginning,' said Aenea, her voice slurred only slightly by pain and shock, 'the Core was a transient entity floating in the crude datasphere on Old Earth known as the Internet. Then, even before the Hegira, you moved your bubble memories and servers and core storage nexus to a cluster of asteroids in long orbit around the sun, far from the Old Earth you planned to destroy . . .'

'Silence her,' snapped Albedo, turning back toward Lourdusamy, Mustafa, and Oddi. 'She is trying to distract us from our questioning. This is not important.'

The expressions of the Mustafa, Lourdusamy, and Oddi holos suggested otherwise.

'During the days of the Hegemony,' continued Aenea, her good eyelid fluttering with the effort to focus her attention and steady her voice through the long, slow swells of pain, 'the Core decided that it was prudent to diversify the physical Core components – bubble-memory matrices deep underground on the nine Labyrinthine worlds, fatline servers in the orbital industrial complexes around Tau Ceti Center, Core entity personae traveling along farcaster combands, and the megasphere connecting it all laced through the farcaster rifts in the Void Which Binds.'

Albedo folded his arms. 'You're raving.'

'But after the Fall,' continued Aenea, holding her good eyelid open and defying the gray man with her stare, 'the Core got worried. Meina Gladstone's attack on the farcaster medium gave you pause, even if the damage to your megasphere was repairable. You decided to diversify further. Multiply your personae, miniaturize essential Core memories, and make your parasitism on the human neural networks more direct . . .'

Albedo turned his back on her and gestured toward the nearest Nemes thing. 'She's raving. Sew her lips shut.'

'No!' commanded Cardinal Lourdusamy. The fat man's eyes were bright and attentive. 'Don't touch her until I command it.'

The Nemes on Aenea's right had already picked up a needle and roll of heavy thread. Now the pale-faced female paused and looked to Albedo for instructions.

'Wait,' said the Councillor.

'You wanted your neural parasitism to be more direct,' said Aenea. 'So your billions of Core entities each formed its surrounding matrix in cruciform shape and attached themselves directly to your human hosts. Every one of your Core individuals now has a human host of its own to live in and destroy at will. You remain connected via the old dataspheres and new Gideon-drive megasphere nodes, but you enjoy dwelling so close to your food source . . .'

Albedo threw his head back and laughed, showing perfect teeth. He opened his arms and turned back to the three human holos. 'This is marvelous entertainment,' he said, still chuckling. 'You've arranged all this for her interrogation' – he flicked manicured nails in the general direction of the dungeon chamber, the skylight, the iron crossbeams upon which Aenea was clamped – 'and the *girl* ends up playing with *your* minds. Pure nonsense. But wonderfully entertaining.'

Cardinal Mustafa, Cardinal Lourdusamy, and Monsignor Oddi were looking at Councillor Albedo most attentively, but their holographic fingers were touching their holographic chests.

The red-robed holo of Lourdusamy rose from its invisible chair and walked over to the edge of the grate. The holographic illusion was so perfect that Aenea could hear the slight rustling of the pectoral cross as it swung from its cord of red silk; the cord was intertwined with gold thread and ended in a large red and gold tuft. Aenea concentrated on watching the swinging cross and its clean silk cord rather than paying attention to the agony in her mutilated hands. She could feel the poison quietly spreading its way through her limbs and torso like the tumors and nematodes of a growing cruciform. She smiled. Whatever else they did to her, the cells of her body and blood would never accept the cruciform.

'This is interesting but irrelevant, my child,' murmured Cardinal Lourdusamy. 'And this' – he flicked his short, fat fingers in the direction of her wounds and nakedness as if repulsed by it – 'is most unpleasant.' The holo leaned closer and his intelligent little pig eyes bored into her. 'And most unnecessary. Tell the Councillor what he wishes to know.'

Aenea raised her head to look into the big man's eyes. 'How to 'cast without a farcaster?'

Cardinal Lourdusamy licked his thin lips. 'Yes, yes.'

Aenea smiled. 'It is simple, Your Eminence. All you have to do is come to a few classes, learn about learning . . . the language of the dead, of the living, how to hear the music of the spheres . . . and then take communion with my blood or the blood of one of my followers who has drunk the wine.'

Lourdusamy backed away as if slapped. He raised the pectoral cross and held it in front of him like a shield. 'Blasphemy!' he bellowed. *'Jesus Christus est primogenitus mortuorum; ipsi gloria et imperium in saecula saeculorum!'*

'Jesus Christ *was* the first born of the dead,' Aenea said softly, the reflected light from the cross glaring in her good eye. 'And you *should* offer him glory. And dominion, if you choose. But it was never his intention that human beings should be revived from death like laboratory mice at the whim of thinking machines . . .'

'Nemes,' snapped Councillor Albedo and this time there was no countermand. The Nemes female near the wall walked over to the grate, extended five-centimeter nails, and raked them down Aenea's cheeks from just under each eye, slicing through muscle and exposing my dear friend's cheekbones to the harsh light. Aenea let out a long, terrible sigh and slumped back against the girder. Nemes moved her face closer and showed her small, sharp teeth in a wide grin. Her breath was carrion.

'Chew off her nose and eyelids,' said Albedo. 'Slowly.'

'No!' shouted Mustafa, leaping to his feet, hurrying forward and reaching out to stop Nemes. His holographic hands passed through Nemes's all too solid flesh.

'A moment,' said Councillor Albedo, holding up one finger. Nemes paused with her mouth open above Aenea's eyes.

'This is monstrous,' said the Grand Inquisitor. 'As was your treatment of me.'

Albedo shrugged. 'It was decided that you needed a lesson, Your Eminence.'

Mustafa was quivering with outrage. 'Do you truly believe you are our masters?'

Councillor Albedo sighed. 'We have always been your masters. You are rotting flesh wrapped around chimpanzee brains . . . gibbering primates decaying toward death from the moment of your birth. Your only role in the universe was as midwives to a higher form of self-awareness. A truly immortal life-form.'

'The Core . . .' said Cardinal Mustafa with great disdain.

'Move aside,' ordered Councillor Albedo. 'Or . . .'

'Or what?' The Grand Inquisitor laughed. 'Or you will torture me as you are torturing this deluded woman? Or will you have your monster beat me unto death again?' Mustafa swung his holographic arm back and forth through Nemes's tensed torso, then through Albedo's hard form. The Grand Inquisitor laughed and turned toward Aenea. 'You are dead anyway, child. Tell this soulless creature what it needs to know and we will put you out of your misery in seconds with no . . .'

'*Silence!*' shouted Albedo and held up one hand like a curled claw.

The holo of Cardinal Mustafa screamed, clutched its chest, rolled across the grate through Aenea's bleeding feet and the iron girder, rolled through one of the Nemeses' legs, screamed again, and winked out of existence.

Cardinal Lourdusamy and Monsignor Oddi looked at Albedo. Their faces were expressionless. 'Councillor,' said the Secretary of State in a soft, respectful tone, 'could I interrogate her for a moment? If we are not successful, you can do what you wish with her.'

Albedo stared coolly at the Cardinal, but after a second he clapped Nemes on her shoulder and the killing thing stepped back three paces and closed her wide mouth.

Lourdusamy reached toward Aenea's mutilated right hand as if to hold it. His holographic fingers seemed to sink into my darling's torn flesh. '*Quod petis?*' whispered the Cardinal, and ten light-minutes away, screaming and writhing in my high-g tank, I understood him through Aenea: *What do you seek?*

'Virtutes,' whispered Aenea. '*Concede mihi virtutes, quibus indigeo, valeum impere.*'

And drowning in fury and sorrow and the sloshing fluids of my high-g tank, accelerating farther from Aenea every second, I understood – *Strength. That I be given the strength I need to carry out this, my resolve.*

'*Desiderium tuum grave est,*' whispered Cardinal Lourdusamy. *Your desire is a serious one.* '*Quod ultra quaeris?*' *What else do you seek?*

Aenea blinked blood out of her good eye so that she could see the Cardinal's face. '*Quaero togam pacem,*' she said softly, her voice firm. *I seek peace.*

Councillor Albedo laughed again. 'Your Eminence,' he said, his voice sarcastic, 'do you think that I do not understand Latin?'

Lourdusamy looked in the direction of the gray man. 'On the contrary, Councillor, I was sure that you did. She is near breaking, you know. I see it in her face. But it is the flames she fears most . . . not the animal to which you are feeding her.'

Albedo looked skeptical.

'Give me five minutes with the flames, Councillor,' said the Cardinal. 'If that fails, turn your beast loose again.'

'Three minutes,' said Albedo, stepping back next to the Nemes that had raked furrows into Aenea's face.

Lourdusamy stepped back several paces. 'Child,' he said, speaking Web English again, 'this will hurt very much, I am afraid.' He moved his holographic hands and a jet of blue flame beneath the grate spurted into a column of flame that singed the bare soles of Aenea's clamped feet. Skin burned, blackened, and curled. The stench of burning flesh filled the cell.

Aenea screamed and attempted to pull free of the clamps. They did not budge. The hanging bar of iron on which she was pinned began to glow at the bottom, sending pain up her bare calves and thighs. She felt her skin blister there as well. She screamed again.

Cardinal Lourdusamy waved his hand again and the flame dropped back beneath the grate, becoming a pilot light watching like the blue eye of a hungry carnivore.

'That is just a taste of the pain you will feel,' murmured the Cardinal. 'And, unfortunately, when one is seriously burned, the pain continues even after the flesh and nerves are irreparably burned away. They say that it is the most painful way to die.'

Aenea gritted her teeth to keep from screaming again. Blood dripped from her torn cheeks to her pale breasts . . . those breasts I had held and kissed and fallen asleep against. Imprisoned in my high-g creche, millions of kilometers away and preparing to spin up to C-plus and fugue oblivion, I screamed and raged into silence.

Albedo stepped onto the grate and said to my dear friend, "Cast away from all this. 'Cast to the ship that is taking Raul to certain death and free him. 'Cast to the Consul's ship. The autosurgeon there will heal you. You will live for years with the man you love. It is either that or a slow and terrible death here for you, and a slow and terrible death for Raul elsewhere. You will never see him again. Never hear his voice. 'Cast away, Aenea. Save yourself while there is still time. Save the one you love. In a minute, this man will bum the flesh from your legs and arms until your bones blacken. But we will not let you die. I will turn Nemes loose to feed on you. 'Cast away, Aenea. 'Cast away now.'

'Aenea,' said Cardinal Lourdusamy, *'es igitur paratus?'* Are you ready, there- fore?

'*In nomine Humanitus, ego paratus sum,*' said Aenea, looking into the Cardinal's eyes with her one good eye. *In the name of Humanitus, I am ready.*

Cardinal Lourdusamy waved his hand. All of the gas jets flamed high at once. Flame engulfed my darling and the Albedo cybrid.

Aenea stretched in agony as the heat engulfed her.

'No!' screamed Albedo from the midst of flames and walked from the burning grate, his synthetic flesh burning away from his false bones. His expensive gray clothes rose toward the distant ceiling in burning wads of cloth and his handsome features were melting onto his chest. 'No, damn you!' he screamed again and reached for Lourdusamy's throat with blazing fingers.

Albedo's hands went through the hologram. The Cardinal was staring at Aenea's face through the flames. He raised his right hand. '*Misericordiam Dei . . . in nomine Patris, et Filii, et Spiritu Sanctus.*'

These were the last words that Aenea ever heard as the flames closed on her ears and throat and face. Her hair exploded in flame. Her vision burned a bright orange and faded as her eyes were fused with flames.

But I felt her pain in the few seconds of life left to her. And I heard her thoughts like a shout – no, like a whisper in my mind.

Raul, I love you.

Then the heat expanded, the pain expanded, her sense of life and love and mission expanded and lifted through the flames like smoke rising toward the unseen ceiling skylight, and my darling Aenea died.

I felt the second of her death like an implosion of all sight and sound and symbol essence. Everything in the universe worth loving and living for disappeared at that second.

I did not scream again. I quit pounding the walls of my high-g tank. I floated in weightlessness, feeling the tank drain, feeling the drugs and umbilicals for cryogenic fugue fall into me and onto me like worms at my flesh. I did not fight. I did not care.

Aenea was dead.

The torchship translated to quantum state. When I awoke, I was in this Schrödinger cat box death cell.

It did not matter. Aenea was dead.

THIRTY-TWO

There was neither clock nor calendar in my cell. I do not know how many standard days, weeks, or months I was beyond the reach of sanity. I may have gone many days without sleeping or slept for weeks on end. It is difficult or impossible to tell.

But eventually, when the cyanide and the laws of quantum chance continued to spare me from day to day, hour to hour, minute to minute, I began this narrative. I do not know why my imprisoners provided me with a slate text 'scriber and stylus and the ability to print a few pages of recycled microvellum. Perhaps they saw the possibility of the condemned man writing his confession or using the 'scriber stylus as an impotent way to rage at his judges and jailers. Or perhaps they saw the condemned man's writing of his sins and injuries, joys and losses of joy as an additional source of punishment. And perhaps in a way it was.

But it was also my salvation. At first it saved me from the insanity and self-destruction of uncontrollable grief and remorse. Then it saved my memories of Aenea – pulling them from the quagmire of horror at her terrible death to the firmer ground of our days together, her joy of living, her mission, our travels, and her complex but terribly straightforward message to me and all humankind. Eventually it simply saved my life.

Soon after beginning the narrative, I discovered that I could share the thoughts and actions of any of the participants in our long odyssey and failed struggle. I knew that this was a function of what Aenea had taught me through discussion and communion – with learning the language of the dead and the language of the living. I still encountered the dead in my sleeping and waking dreams: my mother often spoke to me and I tasted the agony and wisdom of uncounted others who had lived and died long ago, but it was not these lost souls who obsessed me now – it was those with some parallel view of my own experiences in all my years of knowing Aenea.

Never during my time waiting for death in the Schrödinger cat box did I believe that I could hear the current thoughts of the living beyond my prison – I assumed that the fused-energy shell of the orbital egg somehow prevented that – but I soon learned how to shut out the clamor of all those countless older voices resonating in the Void Which Binds and concentrate on the memories of those – those dead as well as presumably still living – who had been part of Aenea's story. Thus I entered into at least some of the thoughts and motives of human beings so different from my own way of thinking as to be literally alien creatures: Cardinals Simon Augustine Lourdusamy and John Domenico Mustafa, Lenar Hoyt in his incarnations as Pope Julius and Pope Urban XVI, Mercantilus traders such as Kenzo Isozaki and Anna Pelli Cognani, priests and warriors such as Father de Soya, Sergeant Gregorius, Captain Marget Wu, and Executive Officer Hoagan Liebler. Some of the characters in my tale are present in the Void Which Bind largely as scars, holes, vacancies – the Nemes creatures are such vacuums, as are Councillor Albedo and the other Core entities – but I was able to track some of the movements and actions of these beings simply by the movement of that vacancy through the matrix of sentient emotion that was the Void, much as one would see the outline of an invisible man in a hard rain. Thus, in combination with listening to the soft murmurings of the human dead, I could reconstruct Rhadamanth Nemes's slaughter of the innocents on Sol Draconi Septem and hear the sibilant hissings and see the deadly actions of Scylla, Gyges, Briareus, and Nemes on Vitus-Gray-Balianus B. But as distasteful and disorienting as these descents into moral vacuum and mental nightmare were to me, they were balanced by a taste again of the warmth of such friends as Dem Loa, Dem Ria, Father Glaucus, Het Masteen, A. Bettik, and all the rest. Many of these participants in the tale I sought out only through my own memory – wonderful people such as Lhomo Dondrub, last seen flying off on his wings of pure light in his gallant and hopeless battle against the Pax warships, and Rachel, living the second of several lives she was destined to fill with adventure, and the regal Dorje Phamo and the wise young Dalai Lama. In this way, I was using the Void Which Binds to hear my own voice, to clarify memory beyond the ability and clarity of memory, and in that sense I often saw myself as a minor character in my own tale, a not-too-intelligent follower, usually reacting rather than leading, often failing to ask questions when he should or accepting answers all too inadequate. But I also saw the lumbering Raul Endymion of the tale as a man discovering love with a person he had waited for all of his life, and in that sense his willingness to follow without question was often balanced by his willingness to give his life in an instant for his dear friend.

Although I know without doubt that Aenea is dead, I never sought her voice among the chorus of those speaking the language of the dead. Rather, I felt her presence throughout the Void Which Binds, felt her touch in the minds and hearts of all the good people who wandered through our odyssey or had their lives changed forever in our long struggle with the Pax. As I learned to dim the insensate clamor and pick out specific voices among the chorus of the dead, I realized that I often visualized these human resonances in the Void as stars – some dim but visible when one knew where to look, others blazing like supernovas, still others existing in binary combinations with other former living souls, or set forever in a constellation of love and relationship with specific individuals, others – like Mustafa and Lourdusamy and Hoyt – all but burned out and imploded by the terrible gravity of their ambition or greed or lust for power, their human radiance all but lost as they collapsed into black holes of the spirit.

But Aenea was not one of these stars. She was like the sunlight that had surrounded us during a walk on a warming spring day in the meadows above Taliesin West – constant, diffuse, flowing from a single source but warming everything and everyone around us, a source of life and energy. And as when winter comes or night falls, the absence of that sunlight brings the cold and darkness and we wait for spring and morning.

But I knew that there would be no morning for Aenea now, no resurrection for her and our love affair. The great power of her message is that the Pax version of resurrection was a lie – as sterile as the required birth-control injections administered by the Pax. In a finite universe of would-be immortals, there is almost no room for children. The Pax universe was ordered and static, unchanging and sterile. Children bring chaos and clutter and an infinite potential for the future that was anathema to the Pax.

As I thought of this and pondered Aenea's last gift to me – the antidote to the Pax birth-control implant within me – I wondered if it had been a primarily metaphorical gesture. I hoped that Aenea had not been suggesting that I use it literally; that I find another love, a wife, have children with someone else. In one of our many conversations, she and I had discussed that once – I remember it was while sitting in the vestibule of her shelter near Taliesin as the evening wind blew the scent of yucca and primrose to us – that strange elasticity of the human heart in finding new relationships, new people to share one's life with, new potentials. But I hope that Aenea's gift of fertility in that last few minutes we were together in St Peter's Basilica *was* a metaphor for the wider gift she had already given humanity, the option for chaos and clutter and wonderful, unseen options. If it was a literal gift, a suggestion that I find a new love, have children with someone else, then Aenea had not known me at all. In my writing of this narrative, I had seen all too well through the eyes of too many others that Raul Endymion was a likable enough fellow, trustworthy, awkwardly valiant on occasion, but not known for his insight or intelligence. But I was smart enough and insightful enough – at least into my own soul – to know for certain that this one love had been enough for my lifetime, and while I grew to realize – as the days and weeks and then, almost certainly, months passed in my death cell with no arrival of death – that if I somehow miraculously returned to the universe of the living, I would seek out joy and laughter and friendship again, but not a pale shadow of the love I had felt. Not children. No.

For a few wonderful days while writing the text, I convinced myself that Aenea had returned from the dead . . . that some sort of miracle had been possible. I had just reached the part of my narrative where we had reached Old Earth – passing through the farcaster on God's Grove after the terrible encounter with the first Nemes thing – and had finished that section with a description of our arrival at Taliesin West.

The night after finishing that first chunk of our story, I dreamed that Aenea had come to me there – in the Schrödinger death cell – had called my name in the dark, touched my cheek, and whispered to me, 'We're leaving here, Raul, my darling. Not soon, but as soon as you finish your tale. As soon as you remember it all and understand it all.' When I awoke, I had found that the stylus 'scriber had been activated and on its pages, in Aenea's distinctive handwriting, was a long note from her including some excerpts from her father's poetry.

For days – weeks – I was convinced that this had been a real visitation, a miracle of the sort the later apostles had insisted was visited on the original disciples after Jesus's execution – and I worked on the narrative at a fever pitch, desperate to see it all, record it all, and understand it all. But the process took me more months, and in that time I came to realize that the visit from Aenea must have been something else altogether – my first experience of hearing a whisper of her among the voices of the dead in the Void, almost certainly, and possibly, somehow, an actual message from her stored in the memory of the 'scriber and set to be triggered when I wrote those pages. It was not beyond possibility. One thing that had been certain was my darling friend's ability to catch glimpses of the future – *futures*, she always said, emphasizing the plural. It might have been possible for her to store that beautiful note in a 'scriber and somehow see to it that the instrument was included in my Schrödinger cat box cell.

Or . . . and this is the explanation I have come to accept . . . I wrote that note myself while totally immersed, although 'possessed' might be a better word, in Aenea's persona as I pursued its essence through the Void and my own memories. This theory is the least pleasing to me, but it conforms with Aenea's only expressed view of the afterlife, based as it was more or less on the Judaic tradition of believing that people live on after death only in the hearts and memories of those they loved and those they served and those they saved.

At any rate, I wrote for more months, began to see the true immensity – and futility – of Aenea's brave quest and hopeless sacrifice, and then I finished the frenzied scribbling, found the courage to describe Aenea's terrible death and my own helplessness as she died, wept as I printed out the last few pages of microvellum, read them, recycled them, ordered the 'scriber to keep the complete narrative in its memory, and shut the stylus off for what I thought was the final time.

Aenea did not appear. She did not lead me out of captivity. She was dead. I *felt* her absence from the universe as clearly as I had felt any resonance from the Void Which Binds since my communion.

So I lay in my Schrödinger cat box, tried to sleep, forgot to eat, and waited for death.

Some of my explorations among the voices of the dead had led to revelations that had no direct relevance to my narrative. Some were personal and private – waking dreams of my long-dead father hunting with his brothers, for instance, and an insight into the generosity of that quiet man I had never known, or chronicles of human cruelty that, like the memories of Jacob Schulmann from the forgotten twentieth century, acted only as subtext for my deeper understanding of today's barbarisms.

But other voices . . .

So I had finished the narrative of my life with Aenea and was waiting to die, spending longer and longer sleep periods, hoping that the decisive quantum event would occur while I was asleep, aware of the text in the memory of my 'scriber and wondering vaguely if anyone would ever figure out a way through the fixed-to-explode-if-tampered-with shell of my Schrödinger box and find my narrative someday, perhaps centuries hence, when I fell asleep again and had this dream. I knew at once that this was not a regular dream – that wave-front dance of possibilities – but was a call from one of the voices of the dead.

In my dream, the Hegemony Consul was playing the Steinway on the balcony of his ebony spaceship – that spaceship that I knew so well – while great, green, saurian things surged and bellowed in the nearby swamps. He was playing Schubert. I did not recognize the world beyond the balcony, but it was a place of huge, primitive plants, towering storm clouds, and frightening animal roars.

The Consul was a smaller man than I had always imagined. When he was finished with the piece, he sat quietly for a moment in the twilight until the ship spoke in a voice I did not recognize – a smarter, more human voice.

'Very nice,' said the ship. 'Very nice indeed.'

'Thank you, John,' said the Consul, rising from the bench and bringing the balcony into the ship with him. It was beginning to rain.

'Do you still insist on going hunting in the morning?' asked the disembodied voice that was not the ship's as I knew it.

'Yes,' said the Consul. 'It is something I do here upon occasion.'

'Do you like the taste of dinosaur meat?' asked the ship's AI.

'Not at all,' said the Consul. 'Almost inedible. It is the hunt I enjoy.'

'You mean the risk,' said the ship.

'That too.' The Consul chuckled. 'Although I do take care.'

'But what if you don't come back from your hunt tomorrow?' asked the ship. His voice was of a young man with an Old Earth British accent.

The Consul shrugged. 'We've spent – what? – more than six years exploring the old Hegemony worlds. We know the pattern . . . chaos, civil war, starvation, fragmentation. We've seen the fruit of the Fall of the Farcaster System.'

'Do you think that Gladstone was wrong in ordering the attack?' asked the ship softly.

The Consul had poured himself a brandy at the sideboard and now carried it to the chess table set near the bookcase. He took a seat and looked at the game pieces already engaged in battle on the board in front of him. 'Not at all,' he said. 'She did the right thing. But the result is sad. It will be decades, perhaps centuries before the Web begins to weave itself together in a new form.' He had been warming the brandy and sloshing it gently as he spoke, now he inhaled it and sipped. Looking up, the Consul said, 'Would you like to join me for the completion of our game, John?'

The holo of a young man appeared in the seat opposite. He was a striking young man with clear hazel-colored eyes, low brow, hollow cheeks, a compact nose and stubborn jaw, and a wide mouth that suggested both a calm masculinity and a hint of pugnaciousness. The young man was dressed in a loose blouse and high-cut breeches. His hair was auburn-colored, thick, and very curly. The Consul knew that his guest had once been described as having '. . . a brisk, winning face', and he put that down to the easy mobility of expression that came with the young man's great intelligence and vitality.

'Your move,' said John.

The Consul studied his options for several moments and then moved a bishop.

John responded at once, pointing to a pawn that the Consul obediently moved one rank forward for him. The young man looked up with sincere curiosity in his eyes. 'What if you don't come back from the hunt tomorrow?' he said softly.

Startled out of his reverie, the Consul smiled. 'Then the ship is yours, which it obviously is anyway.' He moved his bishop back. 'What will you do, John, if this should be the end of our travels together?'

John gestured to have his rook moved forward at the same lightning speed with which he replied. 'Take it back to Hyperion,' he said. 'Program it to return to Brawne if all is well. Or possibly to Martin Silenus, if the old man is still alive and working on his *Cantos*.'

'Program it?' said the Consul, frowning at the board. 'You mean you'd leave the ship's AI?' He moved his bishop diagonally another square.

'Yes,' said John, pointing to have his pawn advanced again. 'I will do that in the next few days at any rate.'

His frown deepening, the Consul looked at the board, then at the hologram across from him, and then at the board again. 'Where will you go?' he said and moved his queen to protect his king.

'Back into the Core,' said John, moving the rook two spaces.

'To confront your maker again?' asked the Consul, attacking again with his bishop.

John shook his head. His bearing was very upright and he had the habit of clearing his forehead of curls with an elegant, backward toss of his head. 'No,' he said softly, 'to start raising hell with the Core entities. To accelerate their endless civil wars and internecine rivalries. To be what my template had been to the poetic community – an irritant.' He pointed to where he wanted his remaining knight moved.

The Consul considered that move, found it not a threat, and frowned at his own bishop. 'For what reason?' he said at last.

John smiled again and pointed to the square where his rook should next appear. 'My daughter will need the help in a few years,' he said. He chuckled. 'Well, in two hundred and seventy-some years, actually. Checkmate.'

'What?' said the Consul, startled, and studied the board. 'It can't be . . .'

John waited.

'Damn,' said the Hegemony Consul at last, tipping over his king. 'Goddamn and spit and hell.'

'Yes,' said John, extending his hand. 'Thank you again for a pleasant game. And I do hope that tomorrow's hunt turns out more agreeably for you.'

'Damn,' said the Consul and, without thinking, attempted to shake the hologram's thin-fingered hand. For the hundredth time, his solid fingers went through the other's insubstantial palm. 'Damn,' he said again.

That night in the Schrödinger cell, I awoke with two words echoing in my mind. 'The child!'

The knowledge that Aenea had been married before our relationship had become a full-fledged love affair, the knowledge that she had given birth to a child, had burned in my soul and gut like a painful ember, but except for my almost obsessive curiosity about *who* and *why* – curiosity unsatisfied by my questioning of A. Bettik, Rachel, and the others who had seen her leave during her odyssey with them but who had no idea themselves where she had gone or with whom – I had not considered the reality of that child alive somewhere in the same universe I inhabited. *Her child*. The thought made me want to weep for several reasons.

'The child is nowhere I can find it now,' Aenea had said.

Where might that child be now? How old? I sat on my bunk in the Schrödinger cat box and pondered this. Aenea had just turned twenty-three standard years old when she died . . . correction: when she had been brutally murdered by the Core and its Pax puppets. She had disappeared from sight for the one year, eleven months, one week, and six hours when she had just turned twenty years old. That would make the infant about three standard years old . . . plus the time I had spent here in the Schrödinger execution egg . . . eight months? Ten? I simply did not know, but if the child were still alive, he or she . . . my God, I had never asked Aenea whether her baby had been a boy or girl and she had not mentioned it the one time she had discussed the matter with me. I had been so involved with my own hurt and childish sense of injustice that I had not thought to ask her. What an idiot I had been. The child – Aenea's son or Aenea's daughter – would now be about four standard years old. Walking . . . certainly. Talking . . . yes. My God, I realized, her child would be a rational human being at this point, talking, asking questions . . . a *lot* of questions if my few experiences with young children were any indication . . . learning to hike and fish and to love nature . . .

I had never asked Aenea her child's name. My eyes burned and my throat closed with the painful recognition of this fact. Again, she had shown no inclination to talk about that period in her life and I had not asked, telling myself in the weeks we had had together afterward that I did not want to upset her with questions or probings that would make her feel guilty and make me feel murderous. But Aenea had shown no guilt when she had briefly told me about her marriage and child. To be honest, that is part of the reason I'd felt so furious and helpless at the knowledge. But somehow, incredibly, it had not stopped us from being lovers . . . how had it been phrased on the note I had found on my stylus screen months ago, the note I was sure was from Aenea? 'Lovers of whom the poets would sing.' That was it. The knowledge of her brief marriage and the child had not stopped us from feeling toward one another like lovers who had never experienced such emotion with another person.

And perhaps she had not, I realized. I had always assumed that her marriage was one of sudden passion, almost impulse, but now I looked at it in another way. Who *was* the father? Aenea's note had said that she loved me backward and forward in time, which is precisely the way I had discovered I felt about her – it was as if I had *always* loved her, had waited my entire life to discover the reality of that love. What if Aenea's marriage had not been one of love or passion or impulse but . . . convenience? No, not the right word. *Necessity?*

It had been prophesied by the Templars, the Ousters, the Shrike Cult Church of the Final Atonement and others that Aenea's mother, Brawne Lamia, would bear a child – the One Who Teaches – Aenea, as it turned out. According to the old poet's *Cantos*, on the day that the second John Keats cybrid had died a physical death and Brawne Lamia had fought her way to the Shrike Temple for refuge, the Shrike cultists had chanted – 'Blessed be the Mother of Our Salvation – Blessed be the Instrument of our Atonement' – the salvation being Aenea herself.

What if Aenea had been destined to have a child to continue this line of prophets . . . of messiahs? I had not heard any of these prophecies of another in Aenea's line, but there was one thing I had discovered beyond argument during my months writing of Aenea's life – Raul Endymion was slow and thick-witted, usually the last to understand anything. Perhaps there had been as many prophecies of another One Who Teaches as there had been preceding Aenea herself. Or perhaps this child would have completely different powers and insights that the universe and humanity had been awaiting.

Obviously I would not be the father of such a second messiah. The union of the second John Keats cybrid and Brawne Lamia had been, by Aenea's own accounts, the great reconciliation between the best elements of the TechnoCore and humanity itself. It had taken the abilities and perceptions of both AIs and human beings to create the hybrid ability to see directly into the Void Which Binds . . . for humanity finally to learn the language of the dead and of the living. Empathy was another name for that ability, and Aenea had been the Child of Empathy, if any title suited her.

Who could the father of her child be?

The answer struck me like a thunderbolt. For a second there in the Schrödinger cat box, I was so shaken by the logic of it that I was sure that the particle detector clicking away periodically in the frozen-energy wall of my prison had detected the emitted particle at exactly the right time and the cyanide had been released. What irony to figure things out and to die in the same moment.

But it was not poison in the air, only the growing strength of my certainty on this matter and the even stronger impulse to some action.

There was one other player in the cosmic chess game Aenea and the others had been playing for three hundred standard years now: that near-mythical

Observer from the alien sentient races whom Aenea had mentioned briefly in several different contexts. The Lions and Tigers and Bears, the beings so powerful that they could kidnap Old Earth to the Lesser Magellanic Cloud rather than watch it be destroyed, had – according to Aenea – sent among us one or more Observers over the past few centuries, entities who had, according to my interpretation of what Aenea had said, taken on human form and walked among us for all this time. This would have been relatively easy during the Pax era with the virtual immortality of the cruciform so widespread. And there were certainly others who, like the ancient poet Martin Silenus, had stayed alive through a combination of WorldWeb-era medicine, Poulsen treatments, and sheer determination.

Martin Silenus was old, that was certain, perhaps the oldest human being in the galaxy – but he had not been the Observer, that was equally certain. The author of the *Cantos* was too opinionated, too active, too visible to the public at large, too obscene, and generally just too damned cantankerous to be a cool observer representing alien races so powerful that they could destroy us in an eye blink. Or so I hoped.

But somewhere – probably somewhere I had never visited and could not imagine – that Observer had been waiting and watching in human form. It made sense that Aenea might have been compelled – by both prophecy and the necessity of unhindered human evolution she had taught about and believed in – to 'cast away from her odyssey to that distant world where the Observer waited, meet him, mate with him, and bring that child into the universe. Thus would be reconciled the Core, humanity, and the distant Others.

The idea was unsettling, definitely disturbing to me, but also exciting in a way that nothing had been since Aenea's death.

I knew Aenea. Her child would be a human child – filled with life and laughter and a love of everything from nature to old holodramas. I had never understood how Aenea could have left her child behind, but now I realized that she would have had no choice. She *knew* the terrible fate that awaited her in the basement cell of Castel Sant'Angelo. She *knew* that she would die by fire and torture while surrounded by inhuman enemies and the Nemes monsters. She had known this since before she was born.

The fact of this made my knees weak. How could my dear friend have laughed with me so often, gone optimistically into new days so happily, celebrated life so thoroughly, when she knew that every day passing was another day closer to such a terrible death? I shook my head at the strength of will this implied. I did not have it – this I knew. Aenea had.

But she could not have kept the child with her, knowing when and how this terrible ending would take place. Presumably then, the father was raising the child. The Other in human form. The Observer.

I found this even more upsetting than my earlier revelations. I was struck then with the additional certainty that Aenea would have wanted me to have some role in her child's life if she had thought it possible. Her own glimpses into possible futures presumably ended with her own death. Perhaps she did not know that I would not be executed at the same time. But then, she *had* asked me to scatter her ashes on Old Earth . . . which assumed my survival. Perhaps she had thought it too much of a request to make – for me to find her child and to help in any way I could as the boy or girl came of age, to help protect it in a universe of sharp edges.

I realized that I was weeping – not softly, but with great, ragged sobs. It was the first time I had wept like this since Aenea's death, and – oddly enough – it was not primarily out of grief for Aenea's absence, but at the thought of this second chance to hold a child's hand as I had once held Aenea's when she was still twelve standard, of protecting this child of my beloved's as I had tried to protect my beloved.

And failed. The indictment was my own.

Yes, I had failed to protect Aenea in the end, but she *knew* that I would fail, that she would fail in her quest to bring down the Pax. She had loved me and loved life while knowing that we would fail.

There was no reason I had to fail with this other child. Perhaps the Observer would welcome my help, my sharing of the human experience with this almost certainly more-than-human little boy or girl. I felt it safe to say that no one had known Aenea better than I had. This would be important for the child's – for the new *messiah*'s – upbringing. I would bring this narrative now sitting useless in my 'scriber and share bits and pieces of it with the boy or girl as he or she grew older, giving it all to him or her someday.

I picked up the slate and 'scriber and paced back and forth in my Schrödinger cell. There was this small matter of my unavoidable execution. No one was coming to rescue me. The explosive shell of the egg had decided that, and if there were a way around that problem, someone would have been here by now. It was the most staggering improbability and good luck that I had survived this long when every few hours there was another crap shoot with death as the detector sniffed for the particle emission. I had beaten the laws of quantum chance for this long, but the luck could not hold.

I stopped in my pacing.

There had been four steps in Aenea's teaching of our race's new relationship with the Void Which Binds. Even before coming to my cell I had experienced, if not mastered, learning the language of the dead and of the living. I had shown in my writing of the narrative that I could gain access to the Void for at least old memories of those still living, even if the shell somehow interfered with my ability to sense what was happening now with friends such as Father de Soya or Rachel or Lhomo or Martin Silenus.

Or was there interference? Perhaps I had subconsciously refused to *try* to contact the world of the living – at least for anything beyond memories of Aenea – since I knew that I now inhabited the world of the dead.

No longer. I wanted out of here.

There were two other steps that Aenea had mentioned in her teaching but never fully explained – hearing the music of the spheres and taking the first step.

I now understood both these concepts. Without seeing Aenea 'cast, and without that great rush of gestalt understanding that had come with the terrible sharing of her death, I would not have understood. But I did now.

I had thought of hearing the music of the spheres as a sort of paranormal-radio-telescope trick – actually hearing the pop and crack and whistle of the stars as radio telescopes had for eleven centuries or more. But that had not been what Aenea had meant at all, I realized. It was not the *stars* she was listening to and for, but the resonance of those people – human and otherwise – who dwelt among and around those stars. She had been using the Void as a sort of directional beacon before farcasting herself.

Much of her personal 'casting had not made sense to me. The core-controlled farcaster doors had been rough holes torn through the Void – and thus through space/time – held open by the portals that were like crude clamps holding open the raw edges of a wound in the old days of scalpel surgery. Aenea's farcasting, I now understood, was an infinitely more graceful device.

I had wondered in the busy time when Aenea and I were freecasting down to planet surfaces and from star system to star system in the *Yggdrasill* how she had avoided having us blink into existence inside a hill or fifty meters above the surface, or the treeship inside a star. It seemed to me that blind freecasting, like unplanned Hawking-drive jumps, would be haphazard and disastrous. But we had always emerged exactly where we had to be when Aenea 'cast us. Now I saw why.

Aenea heard the music of the spheres. She resonated with the Void Which Binds, which resonates in turn to sentient life and thought, and then she used the almost illimitable energy of the Void to . . . to take the first step. To travel via the Void to where those voices waited. Aenea had once said that the Void tapped into the energy of quasars, of the exploding centers of galaxies, of black holes and black matter. Enough, perhaps, to move a few organic life-forms through space/time and deposit them in the proper place.

Love was the prime mover in the universe, Aenea had once said to me. She had joked about being the Newton who someday explained the basic physics of that largely untapped energy source. She had not lived to do so.

But I saw now what she had meant and how it worked. Much of the music of the spheres was created by the elegant harmonies and chord changes of love. Freecasting to where one's loved one waits. Learning a place after having traveled there with the one or ones you love. Loving to see new places.

Suddenly I understood why our first months together had been what had seemed at the time like useless farcaster wanderings from world to world: Mare Infinitus, Qom-Riyadh, Hebron, Sol Draconi Septem, the unnamed world where we had left the ship, all of the others, even Old Earth. There had been no working farcaster portals. Aenea had swept A. Bettik and me with her to these places – touching them, sniffing their air, feeling their sunlight on her skin, seeing them all with friends – with someone she loved – learning the music of the spheres so that it could be played later.

And my own solo odyssey, I thought: the kayak farcasting from Old Earth to Lusus and the cloud planet and all the other places. Aenea had been the energy behind that 'casting. Sending me to places so that I could taste them and find them again someday on my own.

I had thought – even as I wrote the narrative in the 'scriber that I held under my arm there in the Schrödinger death cell – that I had been little more than a fellow traveler in a series of picaresque adventures. But it had all held a purpose. I had been a lover traveling with my love – or *to* my love – through a musical score of worlds. A score that I had to learn by heart so that I could play it again someday.

I closed my eyes in the Schrödinger cat box and concentrated, then went beyond concentration to the empty mind state I had learned in meditation on T'ien Shan. *Every world had its purpose. Every minute had its purpose.*

In that unhurried emptiness, I opened myself to the Void Which Binds and the universe to which it resonated. I could not do this, I realized, without communion with Aenea's blood, without the nanotech-tailored organisms that now dwelt in my cells and would dwell in my children's cells. *No*, I thought at once, *not my children. But in the cells of those in the human race who escape the cruciform. In their children's cells.* I could not do this without having learned from Aenea. I could not have heard the voices I heard then – greater choruses than I had ever heard before – without having honed my own grammar and syntax of the language of the dead and living during the months I worked on the narrative while waiting to die.

I could not do this, I realized, if I were immortal. This degree of love of life and of one another is granted, I saw for once and for ever, not to immortals, but to those who live briefly and always under the shadow of death and loss.

As I stood there, listening to the swelling chords of the music of the spheres, able now to pick out separate star-voices in the chorus – Martin Silenus's, still alive but failing on my homeworld of Hyperion, Theo's on beautiful Maui-Covenant, Rachel's on Barnard's World, Colonel Kassad's on red Mars, Father de Soya's on Pacem – and even the lovely chords of the dead, Dem Ria's on Vitus-Gray-Balianus B, dear Father Glaucus's on cold Sol Draconi Septem, my mother's voice, again on distant Hyperion – I also heard John Keats's words, in his voice, and in Martin Silenus's, and in Aenea's:

'But this is human life: the war, the deeds,
The disappointment, the anxiety,
Imagination's struggles, far and nigh,
All human; bearing in themselves this good,
That they are still the air, the subtle food,
To make us feel existence, and to show
How quiet death is. Where soil is men grow,
Whether to weeds or flowers; but for me,
There is no depth to strike in . . .'

But the opposite was true of me at that moment – there was more than enough depth to strike in. The universe deepened at that moment, the music of the spheres grew from a mere chorus to a symphony as triumphant as Beethoven's Ninth, and I knew that I would always be able to hear it when I wished or needed to, always be able to use it to take the step I needed to see the one I loved, or, failing that, step to the place where I had been with the one I loved, or, failing that, find a place to love for its own beauty and richness.

The energy of quasars and exploding stellar nuclei filled me then. I was borne up on waves of energy more lovely and more lyrical even than the Ouster angels' wings seen sliding along corridors of sunlight. The shell of deadly energy that was my prison and execution cell seemed laughable now, Schrödinger's original joke, a child's jump rope laid around me on the ground as restraining walls.

I stepped out of the Schrödinger cat box and out of Armaghast System.

For a moment, feeling the confines of the Schrödinger prison fall away and behind me forever, existing nowhere and everywhere in space but remaining physically intact in my body and stylus and 'scriber, I felt a surge of sheer exhilaration as powerful as the dizzying effect of solo-far-casting itself. *Free! I was free!* The wave of joy was so intense that it made me want to weep, to shout into the surrounding light of no-space, to join my voice with the chorus of voices of the living and dead, to sing along with the crystal-clear symphonies of the spheres rising and plunging like a solid, acoustic surf all around me. *Free at last!*

And then I remembered that the one reason to be free, the one person who would make such freedom worthwhile, was gone. Aenea was dead. The sheer joy of escape faded suddenly and absolutely, replaced by a simple but profound satisfaction at my release from so many months of imprisonment. The universe might have had the color drained out of it for me, but at least now I was free to go anywhere I wanted within that monotone realm.

But where was I going? Floating on light, freecasting into the universe with my stylus and 'scriber tucked under my arm, I still had not decided.

Hyperion? I had promised to return to Martin Silenus. I could hear his voice resonating strong in the Void, past and present, but it would not be part of the current chorus for long. His life remaining could now be counted in days or less. But not to Hyperion. Not yet.

The Biosphere Startree? I was shocked to hear that it still existed in some form, although Lhomo's voice was absent from the choral symphony there. The place had been important to Aenea and me, and I had to return someday. But not now.

Old Earth? Amazingly, I heard the music of that sphere quite clearly, in Aenea's former voice and in mine, in the song of the friends at Taliesin with whom we had tallied there. Distance meant nothing in the Void Which Binds. Time there seasons but does not destroy. But not to Old Earth. Not now.

I heard scores of possibilities, more scores of voices I wanted to hear in person, people to hug and weep with, but the music I reacted to most strongly now was from the world where Aenea had been tortured and killed. Pacem. Home of the Church and nest of our enemies – not, I saw now, the same thing. Pacem. There was, I knew, nothing of Aenea for me on Pacem but ashes of the past.

But she had asked me to take her ashes and spread them on Old Earth. Spread them where we had laughed and loved most well.

Pacem. In the vortex of Void energy, already stepping beyond the Schrödinger cell but existing nowhere else except as pure quantum probability, I made my decision and freecast for Pacem.

THIRTY-THREE

The Vatican is broken as surely as if the fist of God had smashed down from the sky in an anger beyond human understanding. The endless bureaucratic city around it is crushed. The spaceport is destroyed. The grand boulevards are slagged and melted and rimmed with ruin. The Egyptian obelisk that had stood at the center of St Peter's Square has been snapped off at the base and the scores of colonnades around the oval space are tumbled like petrified logs. The dome of St Peter's Basilica is shattered and has fallen through the central loggia and grand facade to lie in pieces on the broken steps. The Vatican wall is tumbled down in a hundred places, completely missing for long stretches. The buildings once protected within its medieval confines – the Apostolic Palace, the Secret Archives, the barracks of the Swiss Guard, St Mother Teresa's Hospice, the papal apartments, the Sistine Chapel – are all exposed and smashed, scorched and tumbled and scattered.

Castel Sant'Angelo on this side of the river has been slagged. The towering cylinder – twenty meters of towering stone rising from its huge square base – has been melted to a mound of cooled lava.

I see all this while walking along the boulevard of broken slabs on the east side of the river. Ahead of me, the bridge, the Ponte Sant'Angelo, has been cracked into three sections and dropped into the river. Into the riverbed, I should say, for it looks as if the new Tiber has been boiled away, leaving glass where the sandy river bottom and riverbanks had been. Someone has rigged a rope suspension bridge across the debris-filled gap between the banks.

This is Pacem; I do not doubt it. The thin, cool atmosphere feels and tastes the same as when Father de Soya, Aenea, and I came through here on the day before my dear girl died, although it was raining and gray then and now the sky is rich with a sunset that manages to make even the broken, fallen-away dome of St Peter's look beautiful.

It is almost overwhelming to be walking free under an open sky after my uncounted months of tight incarceration. I clutch my 'scriber to me like a shield, like some talisman, like a Bible, and walk the once-proud boulevard with shaky legs. For months my mind has been sharing memories of many places and many people, but my own eyes and lungs and legs and skin have forgotten the feeling of real freedom. Even in my sadness, there is an exultation.

Freecasting had been superficially the same as when Aenea had freecast us both, but on a deeper level it was profoundly different. The flash of white light had been the same, the ease of sudden transition, the slight shock of different air pressure or gravity or light. But this time I had *heard* the light rather than seen it. I had been carried up by the music of the stars and their myriad worlds and chosen the one to which I wanted to step. There had been no effort on my part, no great expenditure of energy, other than the need to focus and to choose carefully. And the music had not faded completely away – I guessed that it never would – but even now played in the background like musicians practicing just beyond the hill for a summer evening's concert.

I can see signs of survivors in the city-wide wreckage. In the gold distance, two oxcarts move along the horizon with human silhouettes walking behind. On this side of the river, I can see huts, simple brick homes among the tumbles of old stone, a church, another small church. From somewhere far behind me comes the smell of meat cooking on an open fire and the unmistakable sound of children laughing.

I am just turning toward that smell and sound when a man steps out from behind a mass of debris that may have once been a guard post at the entrance to Castel Sant'Angelo. He is a small man, quick of hand, his face half-hidden behind a beard and his hair combed back to a queue, but his eyes are alert. He carries a solid slug rifle of the sort once used for ceremony by the Swiss Guard.

We stare at each other for a moment – the unarmed, weakened man carrying nothing but a 'scriber and the sun-bronzed hunter with his ready weapon – and then each recognizes the other. I have never met this man, nor he me, but I have seen him through others' memories via the Void Which Binds, although he was uniformed, armored, and clean-shaven the first time I saw him – naked and in the act of being tortured the last time. I do not know how he recognizes me, but I see that recognition in his eyes an instant before he sets the weapon aside and steps forward to seize my hand and forearm in both his hands.

'Raul Endymion!' he cries. 'The day has come! Praise be. Welcome.' The bearded apparition actually hugs me before stepping back to look at me again and grin.

'You're Corporal Kee,' I say stupidly. I remember the eyes most of all, seen from Father de Soya's point of view as he and Kee and Sergeant Gregorius and Lancer Rettig chased Aenea and me across this arm of the galaxy for years.

'Formerly Corporal Kee,' says the grinning man. 'Now just Bassin Kee, citizen of New Rome, member of the diocese of St Anne's, hunter for tomorrow's meal.' He shakes his head as he stares at me. 'Raul Endymion. My God. Some thought you would never escape that cursed Schrödinger cat thing.'

'You know about the Schrödinger egg?'

'Of course,' says Kee. 'It was part of the Shared Moment. Aenea knew where they were taking you. So we all knew. And we've sensed your presence there through the Void, of course.'

I felt suddenly dizzy and a bit sick to my stomach. The light, the air, the great distance to the horizon . . . That horizon became unstable, as if I were looking at it from aboard a small ship in a rough sea, so I closed my eyes. When I opened them, Kee was holding my arm and helping me sit on a large, white stone that looked as if it had been blasted from the cathedral far across the glass river.

'My God, Raul,' he says, 'have you just freecast from there? You've been nowhere else?'

'Yes,' I say. 'No.' I take two slow breaths and say, 'What is the Shared Moment?' I had heard the formal capital letters in his voice.

The small man studies me with his bright, intelligent gaze. His voice is soft. 'Aenea's Shared Moment,' he says. 'It is what we all call it, although of course it was more than a single moment. All the moments of her torture and death.'

'You felt that too?' I say. I suddenly feel a fist closing around my heart, although whether the emotion is joy or terrible sadness remains to be discovered.

'Everyone felt it,' says Kee. 'Everyone shared it. Everyone, that is, except her torturers.'

'Everyone else on Pacem?' I ask.

'On Pacem,' says Kee. 'On Lusus and Renaissance Vector. On Mars and Qom-Riyadh and Renaissance Minor and Tau Ceti Center. On Fuji and Ixion and Deneb Drei and Sibitu's Bitterness. On Barnard's World and God's Grove and Mare Infinitus. On Tsingtao Hsishuang Panna and Patawpha and Groombridge Dyson D.' Kee pauses and smiles at the sound of his own litany. 'On almost every world, Raul. And in places in between. We know that the Startree felt the Shared Moment . . . all the startree biospheres did.'

I blink. 'There are other startrees?'

Kee nods.

'How did all these worlds . . . share that moment?' I ask, seeing the answer even as I pose the question.

'Yes,' murmurs the former Corporal Kee. 'All of the places Aenea visited, often with you. All of the worlds where she left disciples who had partaken of communion and renounced the cruciform. Her Shared Moment . . . the hour of her death . . . was like a signal broadcast and rebroadcast through all of these worlds.'

I rub my face. It feels numb. 'So only those who had already taken communion or studied with Aenea shared in that moment?' I say.

Kee is shaking his head. 'No . . . they were the transponders, the relay stations. They pulled the Shared Moment from the Void Which Binds and rebroadcast it to everyone.'

'Everyone?' I repeat stupidly. 'Even those tens and hundreds of billions in the Pax who wear the cross?'

'Who wore the cross,' amends Bassin Kee. 'Many of those faithful have since decided not to carry a Core parasite in their bodies.'

I begin to understand then. Aenea's last shared moments had been more than words and torture and pain and horror – I had sensed her thoughts, shared her understanding of the Core's motives, of the true parasitism of the cruciform, of the cynical use of human death to tweak their neural networks, of Lourdusamy's lust for power and Mustafa's confusion and Albedo's absolute inhumanity . . . If *everyone* had shared the same Shared Moment that I had screamed and fought my way through in the high-g tank on the outward-bound robot prison torchship, then it had been a bright and terrible moment for the human race. And every living human being must have heard her final *'I love you, Raul'* as the flames swept high.

The sun is setting. Rays of gold light shine through the ruins on the west side of the river and throw a maze of shadows across the east bank. The molten mass of Castel Sant'Angelo runs down toward us like a mountain of melted glass. *She asked me to spread her ashes on Old Earth. And I can't even do that for her. I fail her even in death.*

I look up at Bassin Kee. 'On Pacem?' I say. 'She had no disciples on Pacem when . . . Oh.' She had sent Father de Soya away immediately before our doomed charge up the aisle in St Peter's Basilica, asking him to leave with the monks and blend into the city he knew so well, to avoid the Pax whatever else happened. When he had argued, Aenea's words had been – *'This is all I ask, Father. And I ask it with love and respect.'* And Father de Soya had gone out into the rain. And he had been the broadcast relay, carrying my darling girl's last agony and insight to several billion people on Pacem.

'Oh,' I say, still looking at Kee. 'But the last time I saw you . . . through the Void . . . you were being kept captive in cryogenic fugue there in that . . .' I sweep my hand in disgust toward the melted heap of Castel Sant'Angelo.

Kee nods again. 'I *was* in cryogenic fugue, Raul. I *was* stored like a sleeping slab of meat in a cold locker in a basement dungeon not far from where they murdered Aenea. But I felt the Shared Moment. Every human alive did – whether sleeping or drunk or dying or lost in madness.'

I can only stare at the man, my heart breaking again in understanding. Eventually I say, 'How did you get out? Away from there?' We are both looking at the ruins of the Holy Office headquarters now.

Kee sighs. 'There was a revolution very soon after the Shared Moment. Many people – the majority here on Pacem – no longer wanted anything to do with the cruciforms and the betrayed Church which had implanted them. Some still were cynical enough to make that trade with the devil in exchange for physical resurrection, but millions . . . hundreds of millions . . . sought out communion and freedom from the Core cross just in the first week. The Pax loyalists attempted to stop them. There was fighting . . . revolution . . . civil war.'

'Again,' I say. 'Just like the Fall of the Farcasters three centuries ago.'

'No,' says Kee. 'Nothing that bad. Remember, once one has learned the language of the dead and the living, it's *painful* to hurt someone else. The Pax loyalists did not have that restraint, but then, they were in the minority everywhere.'

I gesture toward the world of ruins. 'You call this restraint? You call this not so bad?'

'The revolution against the Vatican and the Pax and the Holy Office did not do this,' says Kee grimly. 'That was relatively bloodless. The loyalists fled in archangel starships. Their New Vatican is on a world called Madhya . . . a real shithole of a planet, guarded now by half the old fleet and several million loyalists.'

'Who then?' I say, still looking at the devastation everywhere around us.

'The Core did this,' says Kee. 'The Nemes things destroyed the city and then seized four archangel ships. Slagged us from space after the loyalists left. The Core was pissed off. Probably still is. We don't care.'

I carefully set the 'scriber down on the white stone and look around. More men and women are coming out of the ruins, staying a respectful distance from us but watching with great interest. They are dressed in work clothes and hunting garb, but not in bearskins or rags. These are obviously people living in a rough place during a hard time, but not savages. A young blond boy waves at me shyly. I wave back.

'I never really answered your question,' says Kee. 'The guards released me . . . released all of the prisoners . . . during the confusion in the week after the Shared Moment. A lot of prisoners around this arm of the galaxy found doors opening that week. After communion . . . well, it's hard to imprison or torture someone else when you end up sharing half their pain through the Void Which Binds. And the Ousters have been busy since the Shared Moment reviving the billions of Jews and Muslims and others kidnapped by the Core . . . and ferrying them home from the Labyrinthine planets to their homeworlds.'

I think about this for a minute. Then I say, 'Did Father de Soya survive?'

Kee grins even more broadly. 'I guess you can say he survived. He's our priest in the parish of St Anne's. Come on, I'll take you to him. He knows you're here by now. It's only a five-minute walk.'

De Soya hugs me so fiercely that my ribs ache for an hour. The priest is wearing a plain black cassock and Roman collar. St Anne's is not the large parish church we had glimpsed in the Vatican, but a small brick and adobe chapel set in a cleared area on the east bank. It seems that the parish consists of about a hundred families who make their livelihood hunting and farming in what had been a large park on this side of the spaceport. I am introduced to most of these hundred families as we eat outside in the lighted space near the foyer of the church and it seems that they all know of me – they act as if they know me personally, and all seem sincerely grateful that I am alive and returned to the world of the living.

As night deepens, Kee, de Soya, and I adjourn to the priest's private quarters: a spartan room adjoining the back of the church. Father de Soya brings out a bottle of wine and pours a full glass for each of us.

'One of the few benefits of the fall of civilization as we know it,' he says, 'is that there are private cellars with fine vintages everywhere one digs. It is not theft. It is archaeology.'

Kee lifts his glass as if in toast and then hesitates. 'To Aenea?' he suggests.

'To Aenea,' say Father de Soya and I. We drain our glasses and the priest pours more.

'How long was I gone?' I ask. The wine makes my face flush, as it always does. Aenea used to kid me about it.

'It has been thirteen standard months since the Shared Moment,' says de Soya.

I shake my head. I must have spent the time writing the narrative and waiting to die in work sessions of thirty hours or more, interspersed with a few hours of sleep, then another thirty or forty hours straight. I had been doing what sleep scientists call free-running: losing all connection to circadian rhythm.

'Do you have any contact with the other worlds?' I ask. I look at Kee and answer my own question. 'You must. Bassin was telling me about the reaction to the Shared Moment on other worlds and the return of the kidnapped billions.'

'A few ships set in here,' says de Soya, 'but with the archangel ships gone, travel takes time. The Templars and Ousters use their treeships to ferry the refugees home, but the rest of us hate to use the Hawking drive now that we realize how harmful it is to the Void medium. And as hard as everyone works to learn it, very few have learned how to hear the music of the spheres well enough to take that first step.'

'It is not so hard,' I say and chuckle to myself as I sip the smooth wine. 'It's goddamn hard,' I add. 'Sorry, Father.'

De Soya nods his indulgence. 'It *is* goddamn hard. I feel that I've come close a hundred times, but always lose the focus at the last moment.'

I look at the little priest. 'You've stayed Catholic,' I say at last.

Father de Soya sips the wine out of an old glass. 'I haven't just stayed Catholic, Raul. I've rediscovered what it means to be Catholic. To be a Christian. To be a believer.'

'Even after Aenea's Shared Moment?' I say. I am aware of Corporal Kee watching us from the end of the table. Shadows from the oil lights dance on the warm earth walls.

De Soya nods. 'I already understood the corruption of the Church in its pact with the Core,' he says very softly. 'Aenea's shared insights only underlined what it meant for me to be human . . . and a child of Christ.'

I am thinking about this a minute later when Father de Soya adds, 'There is talk of making me a bishop, but I am quelling that. It is why I have stayed in this region of Pacem even though most of the viable communities are away from the old urban areas. One look at the ruins of our beautiful tradition across the river reminds me of the folly of staking too much on hierarchy.'

'So there's no pope?' I say. 'No holy father?'

De Soya shrugs and pours us all more wine. After thirteen standard months of recycled food and no alcohol, the wine is going straight to my head. 'Monsignor Lucas Oddi escaped both the revolution and the Core attack and has established the papacy in exile on Madhya,' the priest says with a sharp tone in his voice. 'I don't believe that anyone in the former Pax except his immediate defenders and followers in that system honor him as a real pope.' He sips his wine. 'It is not the first time that the Mother Church has had an antipope.'

'What about Pope Urban XVI?' I say. 'Did he die of his heart attack?'

'Yes,' says Kee, leaning forward and setting his strong forearms on the table.

'And was resurrected?' I say.

'Not exactly,' says Kee.

I look at the former corporal, waiting for an explanation, but none is forthcoming.

'I've sent word across the river,' says Father de Soya. 'Bassin's comment should be explained any minute.'

Indeed, a minute later the curtains at the entrance to de Soya's comfortable little alcove are pulled back and a tall man in a black cassock enters. It is not Lenar Hoyt. It is a man I have never met but whom I feel that I know well – his elegant hands, long face, large, sad eyes, broad forehead, and thinning silver hair. I stand to shake his hand, to bow, to kiss his ring . . . something.

'Raul, my boy, my boy,' says Father Paul Duré. 'What a pleasure to meet you. How thrilled we all are that you have returned.'

The older priest shakes my hand with a firm grip, hugs me for good measure, and then goes to de Soya's cupboard as if he is familiar with it, finds a jar, pumps water into the sink, washes the jar, pours wine for himself, and sits in the chair opposite Kee at the end of the table.

'We're catching Raul up on what has happened in the past year and a month of his absence,' says Father de Soya.

'It feels like a century,' I say. My eyes are focused on something far beyond the table and this room.

'It *was* a century for me,' says the older Jesuit. His accent is quaint and somehow charming – a French-speaking Outback world, perhaps? 'Almost three centuries, actually.'

'I saw what they did to you when you were resurrected,' I say with the brazenness of the wine in me. 'Lourdusamy and Albedo murdered you so that Hoyt would be reborn again from your shared cruciforms.'

Father Duré has not actually tasted his wine, but he stares down into the glass as if waiting for it to transubstantiate. 'Time and time again,' he says in a tone that seems more wistful than anything else. 'It is a strange life, being born just to be murdered.'

'Aenea would agree,' I say, knowing that these men are friends and good men but not feeling especially friendly to the Church in general.

'Yes,' says Paul Duré and holds up his glass in a silent toast. He drinks.

Bassin Kee fills the vacuum of silence. 'Most of the faithful left on Pacem would have Father Duré as our true pope.'

I look at the elderly Jesuit. I have been through enough that it does not make me all tingly to be in the presence of a legend, someone who was central to the *Cantos*. As is always the case when you are with the actual human being behind the celebrity or legend, there is something human about the man or woman that makes things less than myth. In this case, it is the soft tufts of gray hair growing in the priest's large ears.

'Teilhard the Second?' I say, remembering that the man had reportedly been a fine pope as Teilhard I 279 years ago – for a short period before he was murdered for the first time.

Duré accepts more wine from Father de Soya and shakes his head. I can see that the sadness behind those large eyes is the same as de Soya's – earned and heartfelt, not assumed for character effect. 'No more papacy for me,' he says. 'I will spend the rest of my years attempting to learn from Aenea's teachings – listening very hard for the voices of the dead and the living – while reacquainting myself with Our Lord's lessons on humility. For years I played the archaeologist and intellectual. It is time to rediscover myself as a simple parish priest.'

'Amen,' says de Soya and hunts in his cupboard for another bottle. The former Pax starship captain sounds a bit drunk.

'You don't wear the cruciform any longer?' I say, addressing myself to all three men while looking at Duré.

All three of them look shocked. Duré says, 'Only the fools and ultimately cynical still wear the parasite, Raul. Very few on Pacem. Very few on any of the worlds where Aenea's Shared Moment was heard.' He touches his thin chest as if remembering. 'It was not a choice for me, actually. I was reborn in one of the Vatican resurrection creches at the height of the fighting. I waited for Lourdusamy and Albedo to visit me as always . . . to murder me as always. Instead, this man . . .' He extends his long fingers toward Kee, who bows slightly and pours himself a bit more wine. 'This man,' continues the former Pope Teilhard, 'came crashing in with his rebels, all combat armor and ancient rifles. He brought me a chalice of wine. I knew what it was. I had shared in the Shared Moment.'

I stare at the old priest. *Even dormant in the bubble-memory matrix of the extra cruciform, even while being resurrected?* I thought.

As if reading my gaze, Father Duré nods. 'Even there,' he says. Looking directly at me, he says, 'What will you do now, Raul Endymion?'

I hesitate only a second. 'I came to Pacem to find Aenea's ashes . . . she asked me . . . she once asked . . .'

'We know, my son,' says Father de Soya quietly.

'Anyway,' I go on when I can, 'there's no chance of that in what's left of Castel Sant'Angelo, so I'll continue with my other priority.'

'Which is?' says Father Duré with infinite gentleness. Suddenly, in this dim room with the rough table and the old wine and the male smell of clean sweat all around, I can see in the old Jesuit the powerful reality behind Uncle Martin's mythic *Cantos*. I realize without doubt that *this* was indeed the man of faith who had crucified himself not once but repeated times on the lightning-filled tesla tree rather than submit to the false cross of the cruciform. This was a true defender of the faith. This was a man whom Aenea would have loved to have met and talked with and debated with. At that moment I feel her loss with such renewed pain that I have to look down into my wine to hide my eyes from Duré and the others.

'Aenea once told me that she had given birth to a child,' I manage to say and then stop. I cannot remember if this fact had been in the gestalt of memories and thoughts that was transmitted in Aenea's Shared Moment. If so, they know all about this. I glance at them, but both priests and the corporal are waiting politely. They had not known this.

'I'm going to find that child,' I say. 'Find it and help raise it, if I am allowed.'

The priests look at one another in something like wonderment. Kee is looking at me. 'We did not know this,' says Federico de Soya. 'I am amazed. I would have wagered everything I know about human nature to say that you were the only man in her life . . . the only love. I have never seen two young people so happy.'

'There was someone else,' I say, raising my glass almost violently to swig down the last of the wine only to find the glass empty. I set it carefully on the table. 'There was someone else,' I say again, less miserably and emphatically this time. 'But that's not important. The baby . . . the child . . . *is* important. I want to find it if I can.'

'Do you have any idea where the child is?' says Kee.

I sigh and shake my head. 'None. But I'll 'cast to every world in the old Pax and Outback, to every world in the galaxy if I have to. Beyond the galaxy . . .' I stop. I am drunk and this is too important to talk about when drunk. 'Anyway, that's where I'll be going in a few minutes.'

Father de Soya shakes his head. 'You're exhausted, Raul. Spend the night here. Bassin has an extra cot in his house next door. We will all sleep tonight and see you off in the morning.'

'Have to go now,' I say and start to rise, to show them my ability to think straight and act decisively. The room tilts as if the ground has subsided suddenly on the south side of Father de Soya's little house. I grab the table for support, almost miss it, and hang on.

'Perhaps the morning would be best,' says Father Duré, standing and putting a strong hand on my shoulder.

'Yes,' I say, standing again and finding the ground tremors subsiding slightly. 'T'morrow's better.' I shake all of their hands again. Twice. I am desperately close to crying again, not from grief this time, although the grief is there, always in the background like the symphony of the spheres, but out of sheer relief at their company. I have been alone for so long now.

'Come, friend,' says former Corporal Bassin Kee of the Pax Marines and the Corps Helvetica, putting his hand on my other shoulder and walking with the former Pope Teilhard and me to his little room, where I collapse onto one of the two cots there. I am drifting away when I feel someone pulling off my boots. I think it is the former Pope.

I had forgotten that Pacem has only a nineteen-standard-hour day. The nights are too short. In the morning I am still suffused with the exhilaration of my freedom, but my head hurts, my back hurts, my stomach aches, my teeth hurt, my hair hurts, and I am sure that a pack of small, fuzzy creatures has taken up residence in the back of my mouth.

The village beyond the chapel is bustling with early morning activity. All of it too loud. Cook fires simmer. Women and children go about chores while the men emerge from the simple homes with the same stubbled, red-eyed, roadkill expression that I know I am giving to the world.

The priests are in good form, however. I watch a dozen or so parishioners leave the chapel and realize that both de Soya and Duré have celebrated an early Mass while I was snoring. Bassin Kee comes by, greets me in much too loud a voice, and shows me a small structure that is the men's washhouse. Plumbing consists of cold water pumped to an overhead reservoir that one can spill onto oneself in one quick, bone-marrow-freezing second of shower. The morning is Pacem-cool, much like mornings at the eight-thousand-meter altitude on T'ien Shan, and the shower wakes me up very quickly. Kee has brought clean new clothes for me – softened corduroy work trousers, a finely spun blue wool shirt, thick belt, and sturdy shoes that are infinitely more comfortable than the boots I have stubbornly worn for more than a standard year in the Schrödinger cat box. Shaven, clean, wearing different clothes, holding a steaming mug of coffee that Kee's young bride has handed me, the 'scriber hanging from a strap over my shoulder, I feel like a new man. My first thought at this swell of well-being is *Aenea would love this fresh morning* and the clouds obscure the sunlight for me again.

Fathers Duré and de Soya join me on a large rock overlooking the absent river. The rubble of the Vatican looks like a ruin from ancient days. I see the windshields of moving groundcars glinting in the sharp morning light and catch a glimpse of the occasional EMV flying high above the wrecked city and realize again that this is not another Fall – even Pacem has not been dropped back into barbarism. Kee had explained that the morning coffee had been shipped in by transport from the largely untouched agricultural cities in the west. The Vatican and the ruins of the administrative cities here are more of a localized disaster area: rather like survivors choosing to rebuild in the wake of a regional earthquake or hurricane.

Kee joins us again with several warm breakfast rolls and the four of us eat in agreeable silence, occasionally brushing crumbs away and sipping our coffee as the sun rises higher behind us, catching the many columns of smoke from campfires and cookstoves.

'I'm trying to understand this new way of looking at things,' I say at last. 'You're isolated here on Pacem compared to the days of the Pax empire, but you're still aware of what's going on elsewhere . . . on other worlds.'

Father de Soya nods. 'Just as you can touch the Void to listen to the language of the living, so can we reach out to those we know and care for. For instance, this morning I touched the thoughts of Sergeant Gregorius on Mare Infinitus.'

I had also heard Gregorius's distinctive thoughts while listening to the music of the spheres before freecasting, but I say, 'Is he well?'

'He is well,' says de Soya. 'The poachers and smugglers and deep-sea rebels on that world quickly isolated the few Pax loyalists, although the fighting between various Pax outposts did much damage to many of the civilian platforms. Gregorius has become sort of a local mayor or governor for the mid-lattoral region. Quite in opposition to his wishes, I might add. The sergeant was never interested in command . . . he would have been an officer many years ago if he had been.'

'Speaking of command,' I say, 'who's in charge of . . . all this?' I gesture at the ruins, the distant highway with its moving vehicles, the EMV transport coming in toward the east bank.

'Actually the entire Pacem System is under the temporary governorship of a former Pax Mercantilus CEO named Kenzo Isozaki,' says Father de Soya. 'His headquarters is in the ruins of the old Torus Mercantilus, but he visits the planet frequently.'

I show my surprise at this. 'Isozaki?' I say. 'The last I saw of him in preparing my narrative, he was involved in the attack on the Startree Biosphere.'

'He was,' agrees de Soya. 'But that attack was still under way when the Shared Moment occurred. There was much confusion. Elements of the Pax Fleet rallied to Lourdusamy and his ilk, while other elements – some led by Kenzo Isozaki who held the title of Commander of the Order of the Knights of Jerusalem – fought to stop the carnage. The loyalists kept most of the archangel starships, since they could not be used without resurrection. Isozaki brought more than a hundred of the older Hawking-drive starships back to Pacem System and drove off the last of the Core attackers.'

'Is he a dictator?' I ask, not caring too much if he is. It is not my problem.

'Not at all,' says Kee. 'Isozaki is running things temporarily with the help of elected governing councils from each of the Pacem cantons. He's excellent at arranging logistics . . . which we need. In the meantime, the local areas are running things fairly well. It's the first time there has ever been a real democracy in this system. It's sloppy, but it works. I think that Isozaki is helping to shape a sort of capitalist-with-a-conscience trading system for the days when we begin moving freely through old Pax space.'

'By freecasting?' I say.

All three of the men nod.

I shake my head again. It is hard to imagine the near future: billions . . . hundreds of billions . . . of people free to move from world to world without spacecraft or farcaster. Hundreds of billions able to contact each other by touching the Void with their hearts and minds. It will be like the height of the Hegemony WorldWeb days without the Core facade of farcaster portals and fatline transmitters. No, I realize at once, it will not be like the Hegemony days at all. It will be something completely different. Something unprecedented in human experience. Aenea has changed everything forever.

'Are you leaving today, Raul?' asks Father Duré in his soft French accent.

'As soon as I finish this fine coffee.' The sun is growing warm on my bare arms and neck.

'Where will you go?' asks Father de Soya.

I start to answer and then stop. I realize that I have no idea. Where do I look for Aenea's child? What if the Observer has taken the boy or girl to some distant system that I cannot reach by 'casting? What if they have returned to Old Earth . . . can I actually freecast one hundred and sixty thousand light-years? Aenea did. But she may have had the help of the Lions and Tigers and Bears. Will I someday be able to hear *those* voices in the complex chorus of the Void? It all seems too large and vague and irrelevant to me.

'I don't know where I'm going,' I hear myself saying in the voice of a lost boy. 'I was going to Old Earth because of Aenea's wish that I . . . her ashes . . . but . . .' Embarrassed at showing emotion again, I wave at the mountain of melted stone that had been Castel Sant'Angelo. 'Maybe I'll go back to Hyperion,' I say. 'See Martin Silenus.' *Before he dies*, I add silently.

All of us stand on the boulder, pouring out the last drops of cold coffee from the mugs and brushing away the last crumbs from the delicious rolls. I am suddenly struck by an obvious thought. 'Do any of you want to come with me?' I say. 'Or go anywhere else, for that matter. I *think* that I will remember how to freecast . . . and Aenea took us with her just by holding the person's hand. No, she freecast the entire *Yggdrasill* with her just by willing it.'

'If you are going to Hyperion,' says Father de Soya, 'I may wish to accompany you. But first I have something to show you. Excuse us, Father Duré. Bassin.'

I follow the short priest back to the village and into his little church. In the tiny sacristy, barely large enough for a wooden wardrobe cupboard for vestments and the small secondary altar in which to store the sacramental hosts and wine, de Soya pushes back a curtain on a small alcove and removes a short metal cylinder, smaller than a coffee thermos. He holds it out to me and I am reaching for it, my fingers just centimeters away, when suddenly I freeze in midmotion, unable to touch it.

'Yes,' says the priest. 'Aenea's ashes. What we could recover. Not much, I am afraid.'

My fingers trembling, still unable to touch the dull metal cylinder, I stammer, 'How? When?'

'Before the final Core attack,' de Soya says softly. 'Some of us who liberated the prisoners thought it prudent to remove our young friend's cremated remains. There are actually those who wanted to find them and hold them as holy relics . . . the start of another cult. I felt strongly that Aenea would not have wished that. Was I correct, Raul?'

'Yes,' I say, my hand shaking visibly now. I am still unable to touch the cylinder and almost unable to speak. 'Yes, absolutely, completely,' I say vehemently. 'She would have hated that. She would have cursed at the thought. I can't tell you how many times she and I discussed the tragedy of Buddha's followers treating him like a god and his remains as relics. The Buddha also asked that his body be cremated and his ashes scattered so that . . .' I have to stop there.

'Yes,' says de Soya. He pulls a black canvas shoulder bag from his cupboard and sets the cylinder in it. He shoulders the bag. 'If you would like, I could bring this with us if we are to travel together.'

'Thank you,' is all I can say. I cannot reconcile the life and energy and skin and flashing eyes and clean, female scent of Aenea, her touch and laugh and voice and hair and ultimate physical presence with that small metal cylinder. I lower my hand before the priest can see how badly it is shaking.

'Are you ready to go?' I say at last.

De Soya nods. 'Please allow me to tell a few of my village friends that I will be absent for a few days. Would it be possible for you to drop me off here later on your way . . . wherever you go?'

I blink at that. Of course it will be possible. I had thought of my leave-taking today as final, an interstellar voyage. But Pacem . . . as everywhere else in the known universe . . . will never be farther than a step away for me as long as I live. *If I remember how to hear the music of the spheres and freecast again. If I can take someone with me. If it was not a onetime gift which I have lost without knowing it.* Now my entire frame is shaking. I tell myself it is just too much coffee and say raggedly, 'Yeah, no problem. I'll go chat with Father Duré and Bassin until you're ready.'

The old Jesuit and the young soldier are at the edge of a small cornfield, arguing about whether it is the optimum time to pick the ears. I can hear Paul Duré admitting that much of his opinion to pick immediately is swayed by his love of corn on the cob. They smile at me as I approach. 'Father de Soya is accompanying you?' says Duré.

I nod.

'Please give my warmest regards to Martin Silenus,' says the Jesuit. 'He and I shared some interesting experiences in a roundabout way, long ago and worlds away. I have heard of his so-called *Cantos*, but I confess that I am loath to read them.' Duré grins. 'I understand that the Hegemony libel laws have lapsed.'

'I think he's fought to stay alive this long to finish those *Cantos*,' I say softly. 'Now he never will.'

Father Duré sighs. 'No lifetime is long enough for those who wish to create, Raul. Or for those who simply wish to understand themselves and their lives. It is, perhaps, the curse of being human, but also a blessing.'

'How so?' I ask, but before Duré can answer, Father de Soya and several of the villagers come up and there is a buzz of discussion and farewells and invitations for me to return. I look at the black shoulder bag and see that the priest has filled it with other things as well as the canister holding Aenea's ashes.

'A fresh cassock,' says de Soya, seeing the direction of my glance. 'Some clean underwear. Socks. A few peaches. My Bible and missal and the essentials for saying Mass. I am not sure when I will be back.' He gestures toward the others crowding in. 'I forget exactly how this is done. Do we need more room?'

'I don't think so,' I say. 'You and I should be in physical contact, maybe. At least for this first try.' I turn and shake hands with Kee and Duré. 'Thank you,' I say.

Kee grins and steps back as if I'm going to rise on a rocket exhaust and he does not want to get burned. Father Duré clasps my shoulder a final time. 'I think that we will see each other again, Raul Endymion,' he says. 'Although perhaps not for two years or so.'

I do not understand. I've just promised to return Father de Soya within a few days. But I nod as if I do comprehend, shake the priest's hand a second time, and move away from his touch.

'Shall we hold hands?' says de Soya.

I put my hand on the smaller priest's shoulder much as Duré had gripped mine a second earlier and check to make sure that my 'scriber is secure on its strap. 'This should do it,' I say.

'Homophobia?' says de Soya with a mischievous boy's grin.

'A reluctance to look silly more often than I have to,' I say and close my eyes, quite certain that the music of the spheres will not be there this time, that I will have forgotten completely how to take that step through the Void. *Well*, I think, *at least the coffee and conversation are good here if I have to stay forever.*

The white light surrounds and subsumes us.

THIRTY-FOUR

I had assumed that the priest and I would step out of the light into the abandoned city of Endymion, probably right next to the old poet's tower, but when we blinked away the glare of the Void, it was quite dark and we were on a rolling plain with wind whistling through grass that came to my knees and to Father de Soya's cassocked thighs.

'Did we do it?' asked the Jesuit in excited tones. 'Are we on Hyperion? It doesn't look familiar, but then I saw only portions of the northern continent more than eleven standard years ago. Is this right? The gravity feels as I remember it. The air is . . . sweeter.'

I let my eyes adapt to the night for a moment. Then I said, 'This is right.' I pointed skyward. 'Those constellations? That's the Swan. Over there are the Twin Archers. That one is actually called the Water Bearer, but Grandam always used to kid that it was named Raul's Caravan after a little cart I used to pull around.' I took a breath and looked at the rolling plain again. 'This was one of our favorite camping spots,' I said. 'Our nomad caravan's. When I was a child.' I went to one knee to study the ground in the starlight. 'Still rubber tire marks. A few weeks old. The caravans still come this way, I guess.'

De Soya's cassock made rustling sounds in the grass as he strode back and forth, as restless as a penned night hunter. 'Are we close?' he asked. 'Can we walk to Martin Silenus's place from here?'

'About four hundred klicks,' I said. 'We're on the eastern expanse of the moors, south of the Beak. Uncle Martin is in the foothills of the Pinion Plateau.' I winced inwardly when I realized that I had used Aenea's pet name for the old poet.

'Whatever,' said the priest impatiently. 'In which direction shall we set out?'

The Jesuit was actually ready to start walking, but I put my hand back on his shoulder to stop him. 'I don't think we'll have to hike,' I said softly. Something was occluding the stars to the southeast and I picked up the high hum of turbofans above the wind whistle. A minute later we could see the blinking red and green navigation lights as the skimmer turned north across the grassland and obscured the Swan.

'Is this good?' asked de Soya, his shoulder tensing slightly under my palm.

I shrugged. 'When I lived here it wouldn't be,' I said. 'Most of the skimmers belonged to the Pax. To Pax Security, to be exact.'

We waited only another moment. The skimmer landed, the fans

hummed down and died, and the left bubble at the front hinged open. The interior lights came on. I saw the blue skin, the blue eyes, the missing left hand, the blue right hand raised in greeting.

'It's good,' I said.

'How is he?' I asked A. Bettik as we flew southeast at three thousand meters. From the paling above the Pinions on the horizon, I guessed that it was about an hour before dawn.

'He's dying,' said the android. For a moment then we flew in silence.

A. Bettik had seemed delighted to see me again, although he stood awkwardly when I hugged him. Androids were never comfortable with such shows of emotion between servants and the humans they had been biofactured to serve. I asked as many questions as I could in the short flight time we had.

He had immediately expressed his regrets about Aenea's death, which gave me the opportunity to ask the question uppermost in my mind. 'Did you feel the Shared Moment?'

'Not exactly, M. Endymion,' said the android, which did not serve to enlighten me at all. But then A. Bettik was catching us up with the last standard year and month on Hyperion since that Moment.

Martin Silenus had been, just as Aenea had known he would be, the beacon relay for the Shared Moment. Everyone on my homeworld had felt it. The majority of the born-again and Pax military had deserted outright, seeking out communion to rid themselves of the cruciform parasites and shunning the Pax loyalists. Uncle Martin had supplied the wine and blood, both out of his personal stock. He had been hoarding the wine for decades and drawing off blood since his communion with the ten-year-old Aenea two hundred and fifty years earlier.

The few remaining Pax loyalists had fled in the three remaining starships and their last occupied city – Port Romance – had been liberated four months after the Moment. From his continued seclusion in the old university city of Endymion, Uncle Martin had begun broadcasting old holos of Aenea – Aenea as a youngster I had never met – explaining how to use their new access to the Void Which Binds and pleading for nonviolence. The millions of indigenies and ex-Pax faithful, who were just discovering the voices of the dead and the language of the living, did not disobey her wishes.

A. Bettik also informed me that there was a single, gigantic Templar treeship in orbit now – the *Sequoia Sempervirens* – and that it was captained by the True Voice of the Startree Ket Rosteen and was carrying several of our old friends, including Rachel, Theo, the Dorje Phamo, the Dalai Lama, and the Ousters Navson Hamnim and Sian Quintana Ka'an. George Tsarong and Jigme Norbu were also aboard. Rosteen had been radioing the old poet for permission to land for two days, said A. Bettik, but Silenus had refused – saying that he did not want to see them or anyone else until I arrived.

'Me?' I said. 'Martin Silenus knew I was coming?'

'Of course,' said the android and left it at that.

'How did Rachel and the Dorje Phamo and the others get to the treeship?' I said. 'Did the *Sequoia Sempervirens* stop by Barnard's World and Vitus-Gray-Balianus B and the other systems to pick them up?'

'It is my understanding, M. Endymion, that the Ousters traveled with the treeship from what remains of the Biosphere Startree which we were fortunate enough to visit. The others, as I am given to understand from M. Rosteen's increasingly frustrated transmissions to M. Silenus, freecast to the treeship much as you have 'cast here to us.'

I sat straight up in my seat. This was shocking news. For some reason, I had assumed that I was the only person clever enough, blessed enough, or whatever enough to have learned the freecasting trick. Now I learn that Rachel and Theo and the old abbot had done so, the young Dalai Lama, and . . . well, a Dalai Lama, maybe, and Rachel and Theo had been Aenea's earliest disciples . . . but George and Jigme? I admit to feeling a bit deflated, yet also excited by the news. Thousands of others – perhaps those, at first, whom Aenea had known and touched and taught directly – must be on the verge of their first steps. And then . . . the mind again reeled at the thought of all those billions traveling freely wherever they wished.

We landed at the abandoned mountain city just as the sky was paling in earnest to the east of the peaks. I jumped out of the skimmer, holding the 'scriber against my side as I ran up the tower steps and leaving the android and the priest behind in my eagerness to see Martin Silenus. The old man had to be happy to see me and grateful that I had done so much to help meet all his impossible requests – Aenea rescued from the original Pax ambush in the Valley of the Time Tombs, now the Pax destroyed, the corrupt Church toppled, the Shrike evidently stopped from hurting Aenea or attacking humanity – just as the old poet had requested that last drunken evening we had spent together here more than a standard decade earlier. He would *have* to be happy and grateful.

'It took you goddamn fucking long enough to get your lazy ass here,' said the mummy in the web of life-support tubes and filaments. 'I thought I'd have to go out and drag you back from wherever you were lazing around like some fucking twentieth-century welfare queen.'

The emaciated thing in the hoverbed at the locus of all the machines, monitors, respirators, and android nurses did not look much like the Poulsen-rejuvenated old man I had said good-bye to less than a decade of mine and only two waking years of his ago. This was a corpse that had neglected to be buried. Even his voice was an electronic restructuring of his subvocalized gasps and rattles.

'Are you finished fucking gawking, or do you want to buy another ticket for the freak show?' asked the voice synthesizer above the mummy's head.

'Sorry,' I mumbled, feeling like a rude child caught staring.

'Sorry doesn't feed the bulldog,' said the old poet. 'Are you going to report to me or just stand there like the indigenie hick you are?'

'Report?' I said, opening my hands and setting the 'scriber on a table tray. 'I think you know the essential things.'

'*Essential* things?' roared the synthesizer, interpreting the torrent of chokes and rattles. 'What the fuck do you know about essential things, boy?' The last of the android nurses had scurried out of sight.

I felt a flush of anger. Perhaps age had rotted the old bastard's mind as well as his manners, if he ever had any manners. After a minute of silence broken only by the rasp of the mechanical bellows below the bed, bellows that moved air in and out of the dying man's useless lungs, I said, 'Report. All right. Most of the things you asked are done, M. Silenus. Aenea ended the rule of the Pax and the Church. The Shrike seems to have disappeared. The human universe has changed forever.'

'*The human universe has changed forever*,' mimicked the old poet in his synthesizer's attempt at a sarcastic falsetto. 'Did I fucking ask you . . . or the girl for that matter . . . to change the fucking universe for fucking ever?'

I thought back to our conversations here a standard decade earlier. 'No,' I said at last.

'There you go,' snarled the old man. 'Your brain cells are beginning to stir again. Jesus H. Christ, kid, I think that Schrödinger litter box made you stupider than you were.'

I stood and waited. Perhaps if I waited long enough he would just die quietly.

'What *did* I ask you to do before you left, boy wonder?' he demanded in the tone of a furious schoolmaster.

I tried to remember details other than his demand that Aenea and I destroy the Pax's iron rule and topple a Church that controlled hundreds of worlds. The Shrike . . . well, that wasn't what he meant. By touching the Void Which Binds rather than my own fallible memory, I finally retrieved his last words before I had flown off on the hawking mat to meet the girl.

'Get going,' the old poet had said. 'Give my love to Aenea. Tell her that Uncle Martin is waiting to see Old Earth before he dies. Tell her that the old fart is eager to hear her expound the meanings of all motions, shapes, and sounds.' *The essence of things.*

'Oh,' I said aloud. 'I'm sorry that Aenea is not here to talk to you.'

'So am I, boy,' whispered the old man in his own voice. 'So am I. And don't bring up that thermos of ashes the priest is carrying. That isn't what I meant when I said I wanted to see my niece again before I died.'

I could only nod, feeling the pain in my throat and chest.

'What about the rest?' he demanded. 'You goin' to carry out my final request, or just let me die while you stand there with your big disciple's thumb up your stupid ass?'

'Final request?' I repeated. My IQ seemed to drop fifty points when I was in the presence of Martin Silenus.

The voice synthesizer sighed. 'Give me your stylus 'scriber there if you want me to spell it out in big block letters for you, boy. I want to see Old Earth before I croak. I want to go back there. I want to go home.'

In the end, it was decided that we should not move him from his tower. The android medics conferred with the Ouster medics who finally were permitted to land who conferred with the autosurgeon aboard the Consul's ship . . . which was parked just beyond the tower, exactly where A. Bettik had landed it some two months earlier after paying his time-debt for translation from Pacem System – which conferred electronically with the medical monitors surrounding the poet, as it had been constantly, and the verdict remained the same. It would probably kill him to take him aboard either the Consul's ship or the treeship by removing him from his tower and submitting him to even the most subtle changes of gravity or pressure.

So we brought the tower and a large chunk of Endymion with us.

Ket Rosteen and the Ousters handled the details, bringing down half a dozen ergs from their lair on the giant treeship. I estimated later that about ten hectares actually rose into the air during that lovely Hyperion sunrise, including the tower, the Consul's parked spaceship, the pulsing Mobius cubes that had transported the ergs, the parked skimmer, the kitchen and laundry annexes next to the tower, part of the old chemistry building on the Endymion campus, several stone dwellings, precisely half of the bridge over the Pinion River, and a few million metric tons of rock and subsoil. The liftoff was undetectable – the containment fields and lift fields were handled so perfectly by the ergs and their Ouster and Templar handlers that there was no hint of movement whatsoever, except for the morning sky becoming an unblinking starfield in the circular opening of Uncle Martin's tower above our heads, and the holos in the sickroom that showed our progress. Standing in that room, the stars burning and rotating overhead, A. Bettik, Father de Soya, a few other android nurses, and I watched those direct-feed holos as I held the old man's hand.

Endymion, our world's oldest city and the source of my indigenie family's name, slid silently up through sunrise and atmosphere to be embraced by the ten kilometers of perfect treeship waiting for us in high orbit. The *Sequoia Sempervirens* had parted its branches to make a perfect berth for us, so we could walk from Hyperion soil to the great bridges and branches and walkways of the ship with no sense of transition. Then the treeship turned out toward the stars.

'You will have to do the next part, Raul,' said the Dorje Phamo. 'M. Silenus will not survive a Hawking-drive shift or the fugue or the time-debt necessary.'

'This is a damned big treeship,' I said. 'Lots of people and machines aboard. You'll help, I hope?'

'Of course,' said the tall woman with the wild, gray hair.

'Yes,' said the Dalai Lama and George and Jigme.

'We'll help,' said Rachel as she stood next to Theo. Both women looked older.

'We will also try,' said Father de Soya, speaking for Ket Rosteen and the others gathered near.

High on the bridge of the ship, while A. Bettik tended to his former master some hundred meters below, the Dorje Phamo, Rachel, Theo, the Dalai Lama, George, Jigme, Father de Soya, the Templar captain, and the others held hands. I completed the rough circle. We closed our eyes and listened to the stars.

I had expected the sky-river of stars that was the Lesser Magellanic Cloud to hang above the treeship as we emerged from light, but it was obvious that we were still in the Milky Way, still in our arm of the Milky Way, not that many light-years from Hyperion System, if the familiar constellations were to be believed. We had gone *somewhere*. But the world that burned above the branches was not the sea blue and cloud white of Old Earth, or even an Earth-like planet, but was a red and oceanless desert world with scattered pocks of volcanic or impact-crater acne and a gleaming white polar cap.

'Mars,' said A. Bettik. 'We have returned to Old Earth System near the star named Sol.'

All of us heard the Void-voice resonance of Fedmahn Kassad on that world. We freecast down, found him, explained the voyage – he did not need the explanation because he had heard us coming through his own listening – and brought him back to the *Sequoia Sempervirens* with us. Martin Silenus sent up word that he wanted to speak to his old pilgrimage partner, and I walked the stairways and bridges to the tower with the soldier.

'Old Earth System is secure, just as the One Who Teaches commanded me,' said Kassad as we stepped onto the Hyperion soil where the fragment of city nestled in the treeship's branches. 'No Pax ships have tested our defenses for ten months. No one in-system, not even our own warships, will be allowed to approach closer than twenty million kilometers to Old Earth.'

'To Old Earth?' I repeated. I stopped in my tracks. Kassad stopped and turned his thin, dark visage toward me.

'You don't know?' he said. The soldier pointed skyward, straight up toward where the treeship was accelerating under smooth, erg-managed full thrust.

It looked like a double star, as all planets with one large moon look. But I could see the pale glow of Luna, smaller, colder. And the warm blue-and-white pulse of life that was Old Earth.

A. Bettik joined us at the entrance to the tower. 'When was it . . . when did they . . . how . . . when did it return?' I said, still looking up at Old Earth as it grew into a true sphere.

'At the time of the Shared Moment,' said Kassad. He brushed red dust from his black uniform, preparing himself to see the old poet.

'Does everyone know?' I said. Poor dumb Raul Endymion. Always the last one to get the word.

'Now they do,' said Colonel Fedmahn Kassad.

The three of us went up to see the dying man.

Martin Silenus was in good humor upon meeting his old friend after almost two hundred and eighty years of separation.

'So your black killer's soul is going to become the seed crystal when they build the Shrike a millennium hence, heh?' cackled the old man through his laboring speech synthesizer. 'Well, thanks a shitload, Kassad.'

The soldier frowned down at the grinning mummy. 'Why aren't you dead, Martin?' the Colonel said at last.

'I am, I am,' said Silenus, coughing. 'I quit breathing ages and eons ago. They just haven't been smart enough to push me over and bury me yet.' The synthesizer did not try to articulate the chokes and rattles that followed.

'Did you ever finish your worthless prose poem?' asked the soldier as the old man continued to cough, sending the web of tubes and wires shaking.

'No,' I said, speaking for the coughing form in the bed. 'He couldn't.'

'Yes,' said Martin Silenus clearly through his throat mike. 'I did.'

I just stood there.

'Actually,' cackled the poet, '*he* finished it for me.' The bony arm with its wrapping of parchment flesh rose slightly from the bed. A thumb distorted by arthritis jerked in my direction.

Colonel Kassad gave me a glance. I shook my head.

'Don't be so fucking dense, boy,' said Martin Silenus with what translated as an affectionate tone over the speaker. 'See your 'scriber anywhere?'

I whirled and looked at the bedside tray where I had left it earlier. It was gone.

'All printed out. About a billion backup memories cut. Sent it out on the datasphere before we 'cast here,' rasped Silenus.

'There is no datasphere,' I said.

Martin Silenus laughed himself into a coughing fit. Eventually the synthesizer translated some of those coughs as, 'You aren't just dumb, boy. You're helpless. What do you think the Void is? It's the goddamn universe's goddamn datasphere, boy. I been listenin' to it for centuries before the kid gave me communion to do it with nanotech bugs in me. That's what writers and artists and creators *do*, boy. Listen to the Void and try to hear dead folks' thoughts. Feel their pain. The pain of living folks too. Finding a muse is just an artist or holy man's way of getting a foot in the Void Which Binds' front door. Aenea knew that. You should have too.'

'You had no right to transmit my narrative,' I said. 'It's mine. I wrote it. It's not part of your *Cantos*.' If I had known for sure which tube passing to him was his oxygen hose, I would have stepped on it till the rattling stopped.

'Bullshit, boy,' said Martin Silenus. 'Why do you think I sent you on this eleven-year vacation?'

'To rescue Aenea,' I said.

The poet cackled and coughed. 'She didn't need rescuing, Raul. Hell, the way I saw it while it was happening, she pulled *your* worthless ass out of the fire more often than not. Even when the Shrike was doing the saving, it was only because that girl-child had tamed it for a bit.' The mummy's white eyes with their video-pickup glasses turned toward Colonel Kassad. 'Tamed *you*, I mean, you once and future killing machine.'

I stepped away from the bed and touched one of the biomonitors to steady myself. Overhead, in the wide circle that was the open top of the tower, Old Earth grew large and round. Martin Silenus's voice called me back, almost taunting me. 'But you haven't finished it yet, boy. The *Cantos* aren't done.'

I stared at him across the few cold meters of distance. 'What do you mean, old man?'

'You've got to take me down there so we can finish it, Raul. Together.'

We could not freecast down to Old Earth because there was no one there for me to use as a beacon for the 'casting, so we decided to use the ergs to land the entire slab of Endymion city. This might be fatal to the old poet, but the old poet had shouted at us to for God's sake shut the fuck up and get on with it, so we were. The *Sequoia Sempervirens* had been in low orbit around Old Earth – or just plain 'Earth' as Martin Silenus demanded we call it – for several hours. The treeship's optics, radar, and other sensors had shown a world empty of human life but healthy with animals, birds, fish, plants, and an atmosphere free of pollution. I had planned to land at Taliesin West, but telescopes showed the buildings gone. Only high desert remained, probably just as it was in the final days before Earth was supposed to have fallen into the Big Mistake of '08 black hole. The Rome to which the second John Keats cybrid had returned was gone. All of the cities and structures which I thought of as the Lions' and Tigers' and Bears' experimental reconstructions apparently were gone. The Earth had been scrubbed clean of cities and highways and signs of humankind. It throbbed with life and health as if awaiting our return.

I was near the base of the Consul's ship on Hyperion soil in the city-within-the treeship, surrounded by Aenea's old friends and speaking aloud about the trip down, wondering who wanted to go and who should accompany us, thinking all the time only of the small metal canister in Father de Soya's shoulder bag, when A. Bettik stepped forward and cleared his throat.

'Excuse me, M. Endymion, I do not mean to interrupt.' My old android friend seemed apologetic to the point of blushing under his blue skin, as he always did when he had to contradict one of us. 'But M. Aenea left specific instructions with me should you return to Old Earth, as you obviously have.'

We all waited. I had not heard her give the android instructions on the *Yggdrasill*. But then, things had been very loud and confused there toward the end.

A. Bettik cleared his throat. 'M. Aenea specified that Ket Rosteen should pilot the landing, if there were a landing, with four other individuals to disembark once landed, and asked me to apologize to all of you who wish to go down to Old Earth immediately,' he said. 'Apologize especially, she said, to dear friends such as M. Rachel, M. Theo, and others who would be especially eager to see the planet. M. Aenea asked me to assure you that you would be welcome there two weeks from the landing day – on the last day before the treeship would leave orbit. And, she asked me to say, that in two standard years . . . that is, two Earth years, of course . . . anyone who could 'cast here on their own would be welcome to visit Old Earth.'

'Two years?' I said. 'Why a two-year quarantine?'

A. Bettik shook his bald head. 'M. Aenea did not specify, M. Endymion. I am sorry.'

I held up my hands, palms up. 'Well, who does get to go down now?' I asked. If my name was not on the list, I was going to go down anyway, Aenea's last wishes or not. I'd use my fists to get aboard, if need be. Or hijack the Consul's ship and land it. Or freecast alone.

'You, sir,' said A. Bettik. 'She quite specifically mentioned you, M. Endymion. And M. Silenus, of course. Father de Soya. And . . .' The android hesitated as if embarrassed again.

'Go on,' I said more sharply than I had intended.

'Me,' said A. Bettik.

'You,' I repeated. In a second it made sense to me. The android had made our long trip out with us . . . had, in fact, spent more time with Aenea than I had over the years because of the time-debt involved in my solo odyssey. More than that, A. Bettik had risked his life for her, for us, and lost his arm in Nemes's ambush on God's Grove so many years ago. He had listened to Aenea's teachings even before Rachel and Theo . . . or I . . . had signed on as disciples. Of course she would want her friend A. Bettik there when her few ashes were scattered in the breezes of Old Earth. I felt ashamed for acting surprised. 'I am sorry,' I said aloud. 'Of course you should come.'

A. Bettik nodded very slightly.

'Two weeks,' I said to the others, most of whose disappointment was visible on their faces. 'In two weeks we'll all be down there to look around, see what surprises the Lions and Tigers and Bears have left for us.'

There were good-byes as old friends, Templars, Ousters, and others left the soil of the city Endymion to watch from the treeship's stairways and platforms. Rachel was the last to leave. To my surprise, she hugged me fiercely. 'I hope to hell that you're worth it,' she said in my ear. I had no idea what the feisty brunette was talking about. She – and most women – had always been a mystery to me.

'All right,' I said after we had trooped up the stairs to Martin Silenus's bedside. I could see Old Earth . . . Earth . . . above us. The view grew hazy and then disappeared as the containment fields merged, thickened, and then separated, the drive fields flowed, and the city pulled away from the treeship. The Templar crew members and Ousters had rigged makeshift controls to the tower sickroom, which, with all of Martin Silenus's medical machines hovering around, had become a very crowded space. I also thought that this was as good a place as any to sit out the ergs' attempt to land a mass of rock and grass, a city with a tower and a parked spaceship, and a half stump of bridge leading nowhere, on a world that was three-fifths water and that had no spaceports or traffic control. At least, I thought, if we were going to crash and die, I might get a hint of the impending catastrophe from watching Ket Rosteen's impassive visage under his overhanging Templar hood in the seconds before impact.

We did not feel entry into Earth's atmosphere. Only the gradual change of the circle of sky above us from starfields to blueness let us know that we had entered successfully. We did not feel the landing. One moment we were standing in silence, waiting, and then Ket Rosteen looked up from his displays and monitors, whispered something through the comlines to his beloved ergs, and said to us, 'We're down.'

'I forgot to tell you where we should land,' I said, thinking of the desert that had been Taliesin. It must be the place where Aenea had been happiest; where she would want those ashes – which I knew but still could not believe were hers – scattered in the warm Arizona winds.

Ket Rosteen glanced toward the floating deathbed.

'I told him where to fucking land,' rasped the old poet's voice synthesizer. 'Where I was born. Where I plan to die. Now, will you all please pull your collective thumbs out and roll me out of here so that I can see the sky?'

A. Bettik unplugged all of Silenus's monitors, everything except the most essential life-support equipment, and tied everything together within the same EM repulsor field. While we were on the treeship, the androids and the Ouster crew clones and the Templars had built a long, gradual ramp from the top tower room down to the ground, then paved an exit walk to the edge of the city slab and beyond. All of this had landed intact I noticed as we accompanied the floating sickbed out into the sunlight and down. As we passed the Consul's ebony spacecraft, a speaker on the hull of the ship said, 'Good-bye, Martin Silenus. It was an honor knowing you.'

The ancient figure in the bed managed to lift one skeletal arm in a rather jaunty wave. 'See you in hell, Ship.'

We left the city slab, stepped off the paved ramp, and looked out at grasslands and distant bluffs not so different from my childhood moors except for the line of forest to our right. The gravity and air pressure was as I remembered it from our four-year sojourn on Earth, although the air was much more humid here than in the desert.

'Where are we?' I asked of no one in particular. Ket Rosteen had stayed in the tower and only the android, the dying poet, Father de Soya, and I were outside now in what seemed to be morning sunlight in an early spring day in the northern hemisphere.

'Where my mother's estate used to be,' whispered Martin Silenus's synthesizer. 'In the heart of the heart of the North American Preserve.'

A. Bettik looked up from checking the med-unit's readouts. 'I believe that this was called Illinois in the pre-Big Mistake days,' he said. 'The center of that state, I believe. The prairies have returned, I see. Those trees are elms and chestnut . . . extinct by the twenty-first century here, if I am not mistaken. That river beyond the bluffs flows south-southwest into the Mississippi River. I believe you have . . . ah . . . traversed a portion of that river, M. Endymion.'

'Yes,' I said, remembering the flimsy little kayak and the farewell at Hannibal and Aenea's first kiss.

We waited. The sun rose higher. Wind stirred the grasses. Somewhere beyond the line of trees, a bird protested something as only birds can. I looked at Martin Silenus.

'Boy,' said the old poet's synthesizer, 'if you expect me to die on cue just to save you from sunburn, fucking forget it. I'm hanging on by my finger-nails, but those nails are old and tough and long.'

I smiled and touched his bony shoulder.

'Boy?' whispered the poet.

'Yes, sir,' I said.

'You told me years ago that your old grannie – Grandam you called her – had made you memorize the *Cantos* till they were dribbling out your ears. Was that true?'

'Yes, sir.'

'Can you recollect the lines I wrote about this place . . . as it was back in my day?'

'I can try,' I said. I closed my eyes. I was tempted to touch the Void, to seek the sound of those lessons in Grandam's voice in place of this struggle to recall them from memory, but instead I did it the hard way, using the mnemonic devices she had taught me, to recall distinct passages of verse. Standing there, eyes still closed, I spoke the passages I could recall:

'Fragile twilights fading from fuchsia to purple
above the crepe-paper silhouettes of trees
beyond the southwest sweep of lawn.
Skies as delicate as translucent china,
unsecured by cloud or contrail.
The presymphony hush of first light followed
 by the cymbal crash of sunrise.
Oranges and russets igniting to gold,
the long, cool descent to green;
leaf shadow, shade, tendrils of cypress
and weeping willow, the hushed
green velvet of the glade.

'Mother's estate – our estate – a thousand acres
centered in a million more. Lawns the size
of small prairies with grass so perfect it
beckoned a body to lie on it,
to nap on its soft perfection.
Noble shade trees making sundials of
the Earth,
their shadows circling in stately procession;
now mingling, now contracting to midday,
finally stretching eastward with the dying of the day.
Royal oak.
Giant elms.
Cottonwood and cypress and redwood and bonsai.
Banyan trees lowering new trunks
like smooth-sided columns in a temple
roofed by sky.

Willows lining carefully laid canals and haphazard
streams,
their hanging branches singing ancient dirges to
the wind.'

I stopped. The next part was hazy. I'd never enjoyed those fake-lyrical bits of the *Cantos*, preferring the battle scenes instead.

I had been touching the old poet's shoulder as I recited and I had felt it relax as I spoke. I opened my eyes, expecting to see a dead man in the bed.

Martin Silenus gave me a satyr's grin. 'Not bad, not bad,' he rasped. 'Not bad for an old hack.' His video glasses turned toward the android and the priest. 'See why I chose this boy to finish my *Cantos* for me? He can't write worth shit, but he's got a memory like an elephant's.'

I was about to ask, *What is an elephant?* when I glanced over at A. Bettik for no special reason. For one instant, after all my years of knowing the gentle android, I actually *saw* him. My mouth dropped slack.

'What?' asked Father de Soya, his voice alarmed. Perhaps he thought I was having a heart attack.

'You,' I said to A. Bettik. 'You're the Observer.'

'Yes,' said the android.

'You're one of them . . . from them . . . from the Lions and Tigers and Bears.'

The priest looked from me to A. Bettik to the still-grinning man in the bed and then back at the android.

'I have never appreciated that choice of phrase of M. Aenea's,' A. Bettik said very quietly. 'I have never seen a lion or tiger or bear in the flesh, but I understand that they share a certain fierceness which is alien to . . . ah . . . the alien race to which I belong.'

'You took the form of an android centuries ago,' I said, still staring in a deepening understanding that was as sharp and painful as a blow to the head. 'You were there for all the central events . . . the rise of the Hegemony, the discovery of the Time Tombs on Hyperion, the Fall of the Farcasters . . . good Christ, you were there for most of the last Shrike Pilgrimage.'

A. Bettik bowed his bald head slightly. 'If one is to observe, M. Endymion, one must be in the proper place to observe.'

I leaned over Martin Silenus's bed, ready to shake him alive for an answer if he had already died. 'Did you know this, old man?'

'Not before he left with you, Raul,' said the poet. 'Not until I read your narrative through the Void and realized . . .'

I took two steps back in the soft, high grass. 'I was such an idiot,' I said. 'I saw nothing. I understood nothing. I was a fool.'

'No,' said Father de Soya. 'You were in love.'

I advanced on A. Bettik as if I was ready to throttle him if he did not answer immediately and honestly. Perhaps I would have. 'You're the father,' I said. 'You lied about not knowing where Aenea disappeared to for almost two years. You're the father of the child . . . of the next messiah.'

'No,' said the android calmly. The Observer. The Observer with one arm, the friend who almost died with us a score of times. 'No,' he said again. 'I am not Aenea's husband. I am not the father.'

'Please,' I said, my hands shaking, 'do not lie to me.' Knowing that he would not lie. Had never lied.

A. Bettik looked me in the eye. 'I am not the father,' he said. 'There is no father now. There was never another messiah. There is no child.'

Dead. They're both dead . . . her child, her husband – whoever, whatever he was – Aenea herself. My dear girl. My darling girl. Nothing left. Ashes. Somehow, even as I had dedicated myself to finding the child, to pleading with the Observer father to allow me to be this child's friend and bodyguard and disciple as I had been Aenea's, to using that newfound hope as a means of escaping the Schrödinger box, I had known deep in my heart that there was no child of my darling's alive in the universe . . . I would have heard that soul's music echoing across the Void like a Bach fugue . . . no child. Everything was ashes.

I turned to Father de Soya now, ready to touch the cylinder holding Aenea's remains, ready to accept the fact of her being gone forever with the first touch of cold steel against my fingertips. I would go off alone to find a place to spread her ashes. Walk from Illinois to Arizona if I had to. Or perhaps just to where Hannibal had been . . . where we first kissed. Perhaps that is where she was happiest while we were here.

'Where is the canister?' I said, my voice thick.

'I did not bring it,' said the priest.

'Where is it?' I said. I was not angry, just very, very tired. 'I'll walk back to the tower to get it.'

Father Federico de Soya took a breath and shook his head. 'I left it in the treeship, Raul. I did not forget it. I left it there on purpose.'

I stared at him, more puzzled than angry. Then I realized that he – and A. Bettik, and even the old poet in the bed – had turned their heads toward the bluffs above the river.

It was as if a cloud had passed over but then an especially bright ray of light had illuminated the grass for a moment. The two figures were motionless for long seconds, but then the shorter of the two forms began walking briskly toward us, breaking into a run.

The taller figure was more recognizable at this distance, of course – sunlight on its chrome carapace, the red eyes visibly glinting even at this distance, the gleam of thorns and spikes and razor fingers – but I had no time to waste looking at the motionless Shrike. It had done its job. It had farcast itself and the person with it forward through time as easily as I had learned to 'cast through space.

Aenea ran the last thirty meters. She looked younger – less worn by worry and events – her hair was almost blonde in the sun and had been hastily tied back. She *was* younger, I realized, frozen in my place as she ran up to our small party on the hill. She was twenty, four years older than when I had left her in Hannibal but almost three years younger than when I saw her last.

Aenea kissed A. Bettik, hugged Father de Soya, leaned into the bed to kiss the old poet with great gentleness, and then turned to me.

I was still frozen in place.

Aenea walked closer and stood on tiptoe as she always had when she wanted to kiss me on the cheek.

She kissed me gently on the lips. 'I'm sorry, Raul,' she whispered. 'I'm sorry this had to be so hard on you. On everyone.'

So hard on me. She stood there with the full foresight of the torture to come in Castel Sant'Angelo, with the Nemes things circling her naked body like carrion birds, with the images of the rising flames . . .

She touched my cheek again. 'Raul, my dear. I'm here. This is me. For the next one year, eleven months, one week, and six hours, I'll be with you. And I will never mention the amount of time again. We have infinite time. We'll *always* be together. And our child will be there with you as well.'

Our child. Not a messiah born of necessity. Not a marriage with an Observer. Our child. Our human, fallible, falling-down-and-crying child.

'Raul?' said Aenea, touching my cheek with her work-callused fingers.

'Hello, kiddo,' I said. And I took her in my arms.

THIRTY-FIVE

Martin Silenus died late on the next day, several hours after Aenea and I were wed. Father de Soya performed the wedding service, of course, just as he later performed the funeral service just before sunset. The priest said that he was glad that he had brought along his vestments and missal.

We buried the old poet on one of the grassy bluffs above the river, where the view of the prairie and distant forests seemed most lovely. As far as we could tell, his mother's house would have been set somewhere nearby. A. Bettik, Aenea, and I had dug the grave deep since there were wild animals about – we had heard wolves howl the night before – and then carried heavy stones to the site to cover the earth. On the simple headstone, Aenea marked the dates of the old poet's birth and death – four months short of a full thousand years – carved his name in deep script, and in the space below, added only – OUR POET.

The Shrike had been standing on that grassy bluff where it had arrived with Aenea, and it had not moved during our wedding service that day, nor during the beautiful evening when the old poet died, nor during the sunset funeral service when we buried Martin Silenus not twenty meters from where the thing stood like a silver-spiked and thorn-shrouded sentinel, but as we moved away from the grave, the Shrike walked slowly forward until it stood over the grave, its head bowed, its four arms hanging limply, the last of the sky's dying glow reflected in its smooth carapace and red-jeweled eyes. It did not move again.

Father de Soya and Ket Rosteen urged us to spend another night in one of the tower rooms, but Aenea and I had other plans. We had liberated some camping gear from the Consul's ship, an inflatable raft, a hunting rifle, plenty of freeze-dried food if we were unsuccessful hunting, and managed to get it all in two very heavy backpacks. Now we stood at the edge of the city slab and looked out at the twilight world of grass and woods and deepening sky. The old poet's cairn was clearly visible against the fading sunset.

'It will be dark soon,' fussed Father de Soya.

'We have a lantern.' Aenea grinned.

'There are wild animals out there,' said the priest. 'That howl we heard last night . . . God knows what predators are just waking up.'

'This is Earth,' I said. 'Anything short of a grizzly bear I can handle with the rifle.'

'What if there *are* grizzly bears?' persisted the Jesuit. 'Besides, you'll get lost out there. There are no roads or cities. No bridges. How will you cross the rivers . . .'

'Federico,' said Aenea, setting her hand firmly but gently on the priest's forearm. 'It's our wedding night.'

'Oh,' said the priest. He hugged her quickly, shook my hand, and stepped back.

'May I make a suggestion, M. Aenea, M. Endymion?' said A. Bettik diffidently.

I looked up from sliding the sheath knife onto my belt. 'Are you going to tell us what you folks on the other side of the Void Which Binds have planned for Earth in the years to come?' I said. 'Or for finally saying hello to the human race in person?'

The android looked embarrassed. 'Ah . . . no,' he said. 'The suggestion was actually more in the line of a modest wedding present.' He handed both of us the leather case.

I recognized it at once. So did Aenea. We got down on our hands and knees to take the hawking mat out and unroll it on the grass.

It activated at first tap, hovering a meter above the ground. We piled and lashed our packs on the back, set the rifle in place, and still had room for the both of us – if I sat cross-legged and Aenea sat in the cusp of my arms and legs, her back against my chest.

'This should get us across the rivers and above the beasties,' said Aenea. 'And we're not going far tonight to find a campsite. Just across the river there, just out of earshot.'

'Out of earshot?' said the Jesuit. 'But why stay so close if we can't hear you if you call? What if you cried out for help and . . . oh.' He reddened.

Aenea hugged him. She shook Ket Rosteen's hand and said, 'In two weeks, I would be obliged if you would let Rachel and the others 'cast down or take the Consul's ship down if they want to look around. We'll meet them at Uncle Martin's grave at high noon. They're welcome to stay until sunset. In two *years*, anyone who can 'cast here on his or her own is welcome to explore to their heart's content,' she said. 'But they can only stay one month, no longer. And no permanent structures allowed. No buildings. No cities. No roads. No fences. Two years . . .' She grinned at me. 'Some years down the road, the Lions and Tigers and Bears and I have made some interesting plans for this world. But for these two years, it's ours . . . Raul's and mine. So please, True Voice of the Tree, please post a big KEEP OUT sign on your way up to your treeship, would you?'

'We will do so,' said the Templar. He went back into the tower to ready his ergs for takeoff.

We settled onto the mat. My arms were around Aenea. I had no intention of letting her go for a very long time. One Earth year, eleven months, one week, and six hours can be an eternity if you allow it to be so. A day can be so. An hour.

Father de Soya gave us his benediction and said, 'Is there anything I can do for you in the coming months? Any supplies you want sent down to Old Earth?'

I shook my head. 'No thanks, Father. With our camping gear, ship's medkit, inflatable raft, and this rifle, we should be all set. I wasn't a hunting guide on Hyperion for nothing.'

'There is one thing,' Aenea said and I caught the slight twitch of muscle at the corner of her mouth that had always warned me that mischief was imminent.

'Anything,' said Father de Soya.

'If you can come back in about a year,' said Aenea, 'I may have use for a good midwife. That should give you time to read up on the subject.'

Father de Soya blanched, started to speak, thought better of it, and nodded grimly.

Aenea laughed and touched his hand. 'Just kidding,' she said. 'The Dorje Phamo and Dem Loa have already agreed to freecast here if needed.' She looked back at me. 'And they will be needed.'

Father de Soya let out a breath, set his strong hand on Aenea's head in a final benediction, and walked slowly up onto the city slab and then up the ramp to the tower. We watched him blend with the shadows.

'What's going to happen to his Church?' I said softly to Aenea.

She shook her head. 'Whatever happens, it has a chance at a fresh start . . . to rediscover its soul.' She smiled over her shoulder at me.

'And so do we.'

I felt my heart pounding with nervousness, but I spoke anyway. 'Kiddo?'

Aenea turned her cheek against my chest and looked up at me.

'Boy or girl?' I said. 'I never asked.'

'What?' said Aenea, confused.

'The reason you'll need the Thunderbolt Sow and Dem Loa in a year or so?' I said, my voice thick. 'Will it be a boy or girl?'

'Ahhh,' said Aenea, understanding me now. She turned her face away again, settled back against me, and set the curve of her skull under my jawline. I could *feel* the words through bone conduction as she spoke next. 'I don't know, Raul. I really don't. This is one part of my life I've always avoided peeking at. Everything that happens next will be new. Oh . . . I know from glimpses of things beyond this that we will have a healthy child and that leaving the baby . . . and you . . . will be the hardest thing I ever do . . . much harder than when I have to let myself be caught in St Peter's Basilica and go to the Pax inquisitors. But I also know from those glimpses of myself after this period – when I am with you again on T'ien Shan, in my future and your past, and suffering because I am unable to tell you any of this – that I also will be consoled by the fact that in this future our baby is well and that you will be raising him or her. And I know that you will never let the child forget who I was or how much I loved the two of you.'

She took a deep breath. 'But as for knowing whether it will be a boy or girl, or what we name the baby . . . I have no clue, my darling. I have chosen not to look into this time, our time, but just to live it with you day to day. I am as blind to this future as you are.'

I lifted my arms across her chest and pulled her back tightly against me.

There came an embarrassed cough and we looked up to realize that A. Bettik was still standing next to the hawking mat.

'Old friend,' said Aenea, gripping his hand while I still held her tight. 'What words are there?'

The android shook his head, but then said, 'Have you ever read your father's sonnet "To Homer", M. Aenea?'

My dear girl thought, frowned, and said, 'I think I have, but I don't remember it.'

'Perhaps part of it is relevant to M. Endymion's query about the future of Father de Soya's Church,' said the blue man. 'And to other things as well. May I?'

'Please,' said Aenea. I could feel through the strong muscles in her back against me, and through the squeezing of her hand on my right thigh, that she was as eager as I to get away and find a camping spot. I hoped that A. Bettik's recital would be short. The android quoted:

'*Aye, on the shores of darkness there is light,*
And precipices show untrodden green;
There is a budding morrow in midnight;
There is triple sight in blindness keen . . .'

'Thank you,' said Aenea. 'Thank you, dear friend.' She freed herself enough to kiss the android a final time.

'Hey,' I said, attempting the whine of an excluded child.

She kissed me a longer time. A much longer time. A very deep time.

We waved a final good-bye, I tapped the flight threads, and the centuries-old mat rose fifty meters, flew over the errant city slab and stone tower a final time, circled the Consul's ebony spaceship, and carried us away westward. Already trusting the North Star as our guide, softly discussing a likely looking campsite on high ground some kilometers west, we passed over the old poet's grave where the Shrike still stood silent guard, flew out over the river where the ripples and whirlpools caught the last glows of sunset, and gained altitude as we gazed down on the lush meadows and enticing forests of our new playground, our ancient world . . . our new world . . . our first and future and finest world.